THE JOHN STEINBECK COLLECTION

THE JOHN STEINBECK COLLECTION

THE GRAPES
OF WRATH

THE MOON
IS DOWN

CANNERY
ROW

EAST
OF EDEN

OF MICE
AND MEN

MALLARD
PRESS

MALLARD
PRESS

The Grapes of Wrath was first published in Great Britain by William Heinemann; in the United States by The Viking Press in 1939
The Moon is Down was first published in Great Britain by William Heinemann; in the United States by The Viking Press in 1942
Cannery Row was first published in Great Britain by William Heinemann; in the United States by The Viking Press in 1945
East of Eden was first published in Great Britain by William Heinemann; in the United States by The Viking Press in 1952
Of Mice and Men was first published in Great Britain by William Heinemann; in the United States by The Viking Press in 1937

This volume first published in the United States in 1989 by

The Octopus Group Limited
Michelin House
81 Fulham Road
London SW3 6RB

This edition published in the United States in 1989 by
MALLARD PRESS
An imprint of BDD Promotional Book Company, Inc.
666 Fifth Avenue
New York, NY10103

ISBN 0 792 45007 8

Printed and bound in the United Kingdom by William Clowes Ltd, Beccles.

CONTENTS

THE GRAPES OF WRATH

11

THE MOON IS DOWN

319

CANNERY ROW

383

EAST OF EDEN

475

OF MICE AND MEN

899

THE GRAPES OF WRATH

THE GRAPES OF WRATH

TO
CAROL
who willed it

TO
TOM
who lived it

I

To the red country and part of the grey country of Oklahoma the last rains came gently, and they did not cut the scarred earth. The ploughs crossed and recrossed the rivulet marks. The last rains lifted the corn quickly and scattered weed colonies and grass along the sides of the roads so that the grey country and the dark red country began to disappear under a green cover. In the last part of May the sky grew pale and the clouds that had hung in high puffs for so long in the spring were dissipated. The sun flared down on the growing corn day after day until a line of brown spread along the edge of each green bayonet. The clouds appeared, and went away, and in a while they did not try any more. The weeds grew darker green to protect themselves, and they did not spread any more. The surface of the earth crusted, a thin hard crust, and as the sky became pale, so the earth became pale, pink in the red country and white in the grey country.

In the water-cut gullies the earth dusted down in dry little streams. Gophers and ant lions started small avalanches. And as the sharp sun struck day after day, the leaves of the young corn became less stiff and erect; they bent in a curve at first, and then, as the central ribs of strength grew weak, each leaf tilted downward. Then it was June, and the sun shone more fiercely. The brown lines on the corn leaves widened and moved in on the central ribs. The weeds frayed and edged back toward their roots. The air was thin and the sky more pale; and every day the earth paled.

In the roads where the teams moved, where the wheels milled the ground and the hooves of the horses beat the ground, the dirt crust broke and the dust formed. Every moving thing lifted the dust into the air; a walking man lifted a thin layer as high as his waist, and a wagon lifted the dust as high as the fence tops, and an automobile boiled a cloud behind it. The dust was long in settling back again.

When June was half gone, the big clouds moved up out of Texas and the Gulf, high heavy clouds, rain-heads. The men in the fields looked up at the clouds and sniffed at them and held wet fingers up to sense the wind. And the horses were nervous while the clouds were up. The rain-heads dropped a little spattering, and hurried on to some other country. Behind them the sky was pale again and the sun flared. In the dust there were drop craters where the rain had fallen, and there were clean splashes on the corn, and that was all.

A gentle wind followed the rain clouds, driving them on northward, a wind that softly clashed the drying corn. A day went by and the wind increased, steady, unbroken by gusts. The dust from the roads fluffed up and spread out and fell on the weeds beside the fields, and fell into the fields a little way. Now the wind grew strong and hard and it worked at the rain crust in the cornfields. Little by little the sky was darkened by the mixing dust, and the wind felt over the earth, loosened the dust, and carried it away. The wind grew stronger. The rain crust broke and the dust lifted up out of the fields and drove grey plumes into the air like sluggish smoke. The corn threshed the wind and made a dry, rushing sound. The finest dust did not settle back to earth now, but disappeared into the darkening sky.

The wind grew stronger, whisked under stones, carried up straws and old leaves, and even little clods, marking its course as it sailed across the fields. The air and the sky darkened and through them the sun shone redly, and there was a raw sting in the air. During the night the wind raced faster over the land, dug cunningly among the rootlets of the corn, and the corn fought the wind with its weakened leaves until the roots were freed by the prying wind and then each stalk settled wearily sideways toward the earth and pointed the direction of the wind.

The dawn came, but no day. In the grey sky a red sun appeared, a dim red circle that gave a little light, like dusk; and as that day advanced, the dusk slipped back toward darkness, and the wind cried and whimpered over the fallen corn.

Men and women huddled in their houses, and they tied handkerchiefs over their noses when they went out, and wore goggles to protect their eyes.

When the night came again it was black night, for the stars could not pierce the dust to get down, and the window lights could not even spread beyond their own yards. Now the dust was evenly mixed with the air, an emulsion of dust and air. Houses were shut tight, and cloth wedged around doors and windows, but the dust came in so thinly that it could not be seen in the air, and it settled like pollen on the chairs and tables, on the dishes. The people brushed it from their shoulders. Little lines of dust lay at the door sills.

In the middle of that night the wind passed on and left the land quiet. The dust-filled air muffled sound more completely than fog does. The people, lying in their beds, heard the wind stop. They awakened when the rushing wind was gone. They lay quietly and listened deep into the stillness. Then the roosters crowed, and their voices were muffled, and the people stirred restlessly in their beds and wanted the morning. They knew it would take a long time for the dust to settle out of the air. In the morning the dust hung like fog, and the sun was as red as ripe new blood. All day the dust sifted down from the sky, and the next day it sifted down. An even blanket covered the earth. It settled on the corn, piled up on the tops of the fence posts, piled up on the wires; it settled on roofs, blanketed the weeds and trees.

The people came out of their houses and smelled the hot stinging air and covered their noses from it. And the children came out of the houses, but they did not run or shout as they would have done after a rain. Men stood by their fences and looked at the ruined corn, dying fast now, only a little green showing through the film of dust. The men were silent and they did not move often. And the women came out of the houses to stand beside their men—to feel whether this time the men would break. The women studied the men's faces secretly, for the corn could go, as long as something else remained. The children stood near by, drawing figures in the dust with bare toes, and the children sent exploring senses out to see whether men and women would break. The children peeked at the faces of the men and women, and then drew careful lines in the dust with their toes. Horses came to the watering troughs and nuzzled the water to clear the surface dust. After a while the faces of the watching men lost their bemused perplexity and became hard and angry and resistant. Then the women knew that they were safe and that there was no break. Then they asked: What'll we do? And the men replied: I don't know. But it was all right. The women knew it was all right, and the watching children knew it was all right. Women and children knew deep in themselves that no misfortune was too great to bear if their men were whole. The women went into the houses to their work, and the children began to play, but cautiously at first. As the day went forward the sun became less red. It flared down on the dust-blanketed land. The men sat in the doorways of their houses; their hands were busy with sticks and little rocks. The men sat still–thinking–figuring.

2

A huge red transport truck stood in front of the little roadside restaurant. The vertical exhaust pipe muttered softly, and an almost invisible haze of steel-blue smoke hovered over its end. It was a new truck, shining red, and in twelve-inch letters on its side–OKLAHOMA CITY TRANSPORT COMPANY. Its double tires were new, and a brass padlock stood straight out from the hasp on the big black doors. Inside the screened restaurant a radio played, quiet dance music turned low the way it is when no one is listening. A small outlet fan turned silently in its circular hole over the entrance, and flies buzzed excitedly about the doors and windows, butting the screens. Inside, one man, the truck driver, sat on a stool and rested his elbows on the counter and looked over his coffee at the lean and lonely waitress. He talked the smart listless language of the roadsides to her: 'I seen him about three months ago. He had a operation. Cut somepin out. I forget what.' And she: 'Doesn't seem no longer ago than a week I seen him myself. Looked fine then. He's a nice sort of a guy when he ain't stinko.' Now and then the flies roared softly at the screen door. The coffee machine spurted steam, and the waitress, without looking, reached behind her and shut it off.

Outside, a man walking along the edge of the highway crossed over and approached the truck. He walked slowly to the front of it, put his hand on the shiny fender, and looked at the *No Riders* sticker on the windshield. For a moment he was about to walk on down the road, but instead he sat on the running-board on the side away from the restaurant. He was not over thirty. His eyes were very dark brown and there was a hint of brown pigment in his eyeballs. His cheek-bones were high and wide, and strong deep lines cut down his cheeks, in curves beside his mouth. His upper lip was long, and since his teeth protruded, the lips stretched to cover them, for this man kept his lips closed. His hands were hard, with broad fingers and nails as thick and ridged as little clam shells. The space between thumb and forefinger and the hams of his hands were shiny with callus.

The man's clothes were new–all of them, cheap and new. His grey cap was so new that the visor was still stiff and the button still on, not shapeless and bulged as it would be when it had served for a while all the various purposes of a cap–carrying sack, towel, handkerchief. His suit was of cheap grey hardcloth and so new that there were creases in the trousers. His blue chambray shirt was stiff and smooth with filler. The coat was too big, the trousers too short, for he was a tall man. The coat shoulder-peaks hung down on his arms, and even then the sleeves were too short and the front of the coat flapped loosely over his stomach. He wore a pair of new tan shoes of the kind called 'army last', hobnailed and with half-circles like horseshoes to protect the edges of the heels from wear. This man sat on the running-board and took off his cap and mopped his face with it. Then he put on the cap, and by pulling started the future ruin of the visor. His feet caught his attention. He leaned down and loosened the shoe-laces, and did not tie the ends again. Over his head the exhaust of the diesel engine whispered in quick puffs of blue smoke. The music stopped in the restaurant and a man's voice spoke from the loudspeaker, but the waitress did not turn him off, for she didn't know the music had stopped. Her exploring fingers had found a lump under her ear. She was trying to see it in a mirror behind the counter without letting the truck driver know, and so she pretended to push a bit of hair to neatness. The truck driver said: 'They was a big dance in Shawnee. I heard somebody got killed or somepin. You hear anything?' 'No,' said the waitress, and she lovingly fingered the lump under her ear.

Outside, the seated man stood up and looked over the cowl of the truck and watched the restaurant for a moment. Then he settled back on the running-board, pulled a sack of tobacco and a book of papers from his side pocket. He rolled his cigarette slowly and perfectly, studied it, smoothed it. At last he lighted it and pushed the burning match into the dust at his feet. The sun cut into the shade of the truck as noon approached.

In the restaurant the truck driver paid his bill and put his two nickels change in a slot machine. The whirling cylinders gave him no score. 'They fix 'em so you can't win nothin',' he said to the waitress.

And she replied: 'Guy took the jackpot not two hours ago. Three-eighty he got. How soon you gonna be back by?'

He held the screen door a little open. 'Week-ten days,' he said. 'Got to make a run to Tulsa, an' I never get back soon as I think.'

She said crossly: 'Don't let the flies in. Either go out or come in.'

'So long,' he said, and pushed his way out. The screen door banged behind him. He stood in the sun, peeling the wrapper from a piece of gum. He was a heavy man, broad in the shoulders, thick in the stomach. His face was red and his blue eyes long and slitted from having squinted always at sharp light. He wore army trousers and high-laced boots. Holding the stick of gum in front of his lips he called through the screen: 'Well, don't do nothing you don't want me to hear about.' The waitress was turned toward a mirror on the back wall. She grunted a reply. The truck driver gnawed down the stick of gum slowly, opening his jaws and lips wide with each bite. He shaped the gum in his mouth, rolled it under his tongue while he walked to the big red truck.

The hitch-hiker stood up and looked across through the windows. 'Could ya give me a lift, mister?'

The driver looked quickly back at the restaurant for a second. 'Didn't you see the *No Riders* sticker on the win'shield?'

'Sure–I seen it. But sometimes a guy'll be a good guy even if some rich bastard makes him carry a sticker.'

The driver, getting slowly into the truck, considered the parts of this answer. If he refused now, not only was he not a good guy, but he was forced to carry a sticker, was not allowed to have company. If he took in the hitch-hiker he was automatically a good guy and also he was not one whom any rich bastard could kick around. He knew he was being trapped, but he couldn't see a way out. And he wanted to be a good guy. He glanced again at the restaurant. 'Scrunch down on the running-board till we get around the bend,' he said.

The hitch-hiker flopped down out of sight and clung to the door-handle. The motor roared up for a moment, the gears clicked in, and the great truck moved away, first gear, second gear, third gear, and then a high whining pick-up and fourth gear. Under the clinging man the highway blurred dizzily by. It was a mile to the first turn in the road, then the truck slowed down. The hitch-hiker stood up, eased the door open, and slipped into the seat. The driver looked over at him, slitting his eyes, and he chewed as though thoughts and impressions were being sorted and arranged by his jaws before they were finally filed away in his brain. His eyes began at the new cap, moved down the new clothes to the new shoes. The hitch-hiker squirmed his back against the seat in comfort, took off his cap, and swabbed his sweating forehead and chin with it. 'Thanks, buddy,' he said. 'My dogs was pooped out.'

'New shoes,' said the driver. His voice had the same quality of secrecy and insinuation his eyes had. 'You oughtn' to take no walk in new shoes–hot weather.'

The hiker looked down at the dusty yellow shoes. 'Didn't have no other shoes,' he said. 'Guy got to wear 'em if he got no others.'

The driver squinted judiciously ahead and built up the speed of the truck a little. 'Goin' far?'

'Uh-uh! I'd a walked her if my dogs wasn't pooped out.'

The questions of the driver had the tone of a subtle examination. He seemed to spread nets, to set traps with his questions.

'Lookin' for a job?' he asked.

'No, my old man got a place, forty acres. He's a cropper but we been there a long time.'

The driver looked significantly at the fields along the road where the corn was fallen sideways and the dust was piled on it. Little flints shoved through the dusty soil. The driver said, as though to himself: 'A forty-acre cropper and he ain't been dusted out and he ain't been tractored out?'

''Course I ain't heard lately,' said the hitch-hiker.

'Long time,' said the driver. A bee flew into the cab and buzzed in back of the windshield. The driver put out his hand and carefully drove the bee into an air stream that blew it out of the window. 'Croppers going fast now,' he said. 'One cat' takes and shoves ten families out. Cat's all over hell now. Tear in and shove the croppers out. How's your old man hold on?' His tongue and his jaws became busy with the neglected gum, turned it and chewed it. With each opening of his mouth his tongue could be seen flipping the gum over.

'Well, I ain't heard lately. I never was no hand to write, nor my old man neither.' He added quickly: 'But the both of us can, if we want.'

'Been doing a job?' Again the secret investigating casualness. He looked out over the fields, at the shimmering air, and gathering his gum into his cheek, out of the way, he spat out the window.

'Sure have,' said the hitch-hiker.

'Thought so. I seen your hands. Been swingin' a pick or an axe or a sledge. That shines up your hands. I notice all stuff like that. Take a pride in it.'

The hitch-hiker stared at him. The truck tires sang on the road. 'Like to know anything else? I'll tell you. You ain't got to guess.'

'Now don't get sore. I wasn't gettin' nosy.'

'I'll tell you anything. I ain't hidin' nothin'.'

'Now don't get sore. I just like to notice things. Makes the time pass.'

'I'll tell you anything. Name's Joad, Tom Joad. Old man is ol' Tom Joad.' His eyes rested broodingly on the driver.

'Don't get sore. I didn't mean nothin'.'

'I don't mean nothin' neither,' said Joad. 'I'm just tryin' to get along without shovin' nobody around.' He stopped and looked out at the dry fields, and the starved tree clumps hanging uneasily in the heated distance. From his side pocket he brought out his tobacco and papers. He rolled his cigarette down between his knees, where the wind could not get at it.

The driver chewed as rhythmically, as thoughtfully, as a cow. He waited to let the whole emphasis of the preceding passage disappear and be forgotten. At last, when the air seemed neutral again, he said: 'A guy that never been a truck skinner don't know nothin' what it's like. Owners don't want us to pick up nobody. So we got to set here an' just skin her along 'less we want to take a chance of gettin' fired like I just done with you.'

''Preciate it,' said Joad.

'I've knew guys that done screwy things while they're drivin' trucks. I remember a guy use' to make up poetry. It passed the time.' He looked over secretly to see whether Joad was interested or amazed. Joad was silent, looking into the distance ahead, along the road, along the white road that waved gently, like a ground swell. The driver went on at last, 'I remember a piece of poetry this here guy wrote down. It was about him an' a couple other guys goin' all over the world drinkin' and raisin' hell and screwin' around. I wisht I could remember how that piece went. This guy had words in it that Jesus H. Christ wouldn't know what they meant. Part was like this: "An' there we spied a nigger, with a trigger that was bigger than a elephant's proboscis or the whanger of a whale." That proboscis is a nose-like. With a elephant it's his trunk. Guy showed me in a dictionary. Carried that dictionary all over hell with him. He'd look in it while he's pulled up gettin' his pie an' coffee.' He stopped, feeling lonely in the long speech. His secret eyes turned on his passenger. Joad remained silent. Nervously the driver tried to force him into participation. 'Ever know a guy that said big words like that?'

'Preacher,' said Joad.

'Well, it makes you mad to hear a guy use big words. 'Course with a preacher it's all right because nobody would fool around with a preacher anyway. But this guy was funny. You didn't give a damn when he said a big word 'cause he just done it for ducks. He wasn't puttin' on no dog.' The driver was reassured. He knew at least that Joad was listening. He swung the great truck viciously around a bend and the tires shrilled. 'Like I was sayin',' he continued, 'guy that drives a truck does screwy things. He got to. He'd go nuts just settin' here an' the road sneakin' under the wheels. Fella says once that truck skinners eats all the time–all the time in hamburger joints along the road.'

'Sure seem to live there,' Joad agreed.

'Sure they stop, but it ain't to eat. They ain't hardly ever hungry. They're just goddamn sick of goin'–get sick of it. Joints is the only place you can pull up, an' when you stop you got to buy somepin so you can sling the bull with the broad behind the counter. So you get a cup of coffee and a piece pie. Kind of gives a guy a little rest.' He chewed his gum slowly and turned it with his tongue.

'Must be tough,' said Joad with no emphasis.

The driver glanced quickly at him, looking for satire. 'Well, it ain't no goddamn cinch,' he said testily. 'Looks easy, jus' settin' here till you put in your eight or maybe your ten or fourteen hours. But the road gets into a guy. He's got to do somepin. Some sings an' some whistles. Company won't let us have no radio. A few takes a pint along, but them kind don't stick long.' He said the last smugly. 'I don't never take a drink till I'm through.'

'Yeah?' Joad asked.

'Yeah! A guy got to get ahead. Why, I'm thinkin' of takin' one of them correspondence school courses. Mechanical engineering. It's easy. Just study a few easy lessons at home. I'm thinkin' of it. Then I won't drive no truck. Then I'll tell other guys to drive trucks.'

Joad took a pint of whisky from his side coat pocket. 'Sure you won't have a snort?' His voice was teasing.

'No, by God. I won't touch it. A guy can't drink liquor all the time and study like I'm goin' to.'

Joad uncorked the bottle, took two quick swallows, re-corked it, and put it back in his pocket. The spicy hot smell of the whisky filled the cab. 'You're all wound up,' said Joad. 'What's the matter–got a girl?'

'Well, sure. But I want to get ahead anyway. I been training my mind for a hell of a long time.'

The whisky seemed to loosen Joad up. He rolled another cigarette and lighted it. 'I ain't got a hell of a lot further to go,' he said.

The driver went on quickly: 'I don't need no shot,' he said. 'I train my mind all the time. I took a course in that two years ago.' He patted the steering wheel with his right hand. 'Suppose I pass a guy on the road. I look at him, an' after I'm past I try to remember ever'thing about him, kind a clothes an' shoes an' hat, an' how he walked an' maybe how tall an' what weight an' any scars. I do it pretty good. I can jus' make a whole picture in my head. Sometimes I think I ought to take a course to be a finger-print expert. You'd be su'prised how much a guy can remember.'

Joad took a quick drink from the flask. He dragged the last smoke from his ravelling cigarette and then, with calloused thumb and forefinger, crushed out the glowing end. He rubbed the butt to a pulp and put it out the window, letting the breeze suck it from his fingers. The big tires sang a high note on the pavement. Joad's dark quiet eyes became amused as he stared along the road. The driver waited and glanced uneasily over. At last Joad's long upper lip grinned up from his teeth and he chuckled silently, his chest jerked with the chuckles. 'You sure took a hell of a long time to get to it, buddy.'

The driver did not look over. 'Get to what? How do you mean?'

Joad's lips stretched tight over his long teeth for a moment, and he licked his lips like a dog, two licks, one in each direction from the middle. His voice became harsh. 'You know what I mean. You give me a goin'-over when I first got in. I seen you.' The driver looked straight ahead, gripped the wheel so tightly that the pads of his palms bulged, and the backs of his hands paled. Joad continued: 'You know where I come from.' The driver was silent. 'Don't you?' Joad insisted.

'Well–sure. That is–maybe. But it ain't none of my business. I mind my own yard. It ain't nothing to me.' The words tumbled out now. 'I don't stick my nose in nobody's business.' And suddenly he was silent and waiting. And his hands were still white on the wheel. A grasshopper flipped through the window and lighted on top of the instrument panel, where it sat and began to scrape its wings with its angled jumping legs. Joad reached forward and crushed its hard skull-like head with his fingers, and he let it into the wind stream out the window. Joad chuckled again while he brushed the bits of broken insect from his finger-tips. 'You got me wrong, mister,' he said. 'I ain't keepin' quiet about it. Sure I been in McAlester. Been there four years. Sure these is the clothes they give me when I come out. I don't give a damn who knows it. An' I'm goin' to my old man's place so I don't have to lie to get a job.'

The driver said: 'Well–that ain't none of my business. I ain't a nosy guy.'

'The hell you ain't,' said Joad. 'That big old nose of yours been stickin' out eight miles ahead of your face. You had that big nose goin' over me like a sheep in a vegetable patch.'

The driver's face tightened. 'You got me all wrong–' he began weakly.

Joad laughed at him. 'You been a good guy. You give me a lift. Well, hell! I done time. So what! You want to know what I done time for, don't you?'

'That ain't none of my affair.'

'Nothin' ain't none of your affair except skinnin' this here bull-bitch along, an' that's the least thing you work at. Now look. See that road up ahead?'

'Yeah.'

'Well, I get off there. Sure, I know you're wettin' your pants to know what I done. I ain't a guy to let you down.' The high hum of the motor dulled and the song of the tires dropped in pitch. Joad got out his pint and took another short drink. The truck drifted to a stop where a dirt road opened at right angles to the highway. Joad got out and stood beside the cab window. The vertical exhaust pipe puttered up its barely visible blue smoke. Joad leaned toward the driver. 'Homicide,' he said quickly. 'That's a big word–means I killed a guy. Seven years. I'm sprung in four for keepin' my nose clean.'

The driver's eyes slipped over Joad's face to memorize it. 'I never asked you nothin' about it,' he said. 'I mind my own yard.'

'You can tell about it in every joint from here to Texola.' He smiled. 'So long, fella. You been a good guy. But look, when you been in stir a little while, you can smell a question comin' from hell to breakfast. You telegraphed yours the first time you opened your trap.' He spatted the metal door with the palm of his hand.

'Thanks for the lift,' he said. 'So long.' He turned away and walked into the dirt road.

For a moment the driver stared after him, and then he called: 'Luck!' Joad waved his hand without looking around. Then the motor roared up and the gears clicked and the great red truck rolled heavily away.

3

The concrete highway was edged with a mat of tangled, broken, dry grass, and the grass heads were heavy with oat beards to catch on a dog's coat, and foxtails to tangle in a horse's fetlocks, and clover burrs to fasten in sheep's wool; sleeping life waiting to be spread and dispersed, every seed armed with an appliance of dispersal, twisting darts and parachutes for the wind, little spears and balls of tiny thorns, and all waiting for animals and for the wind, for a man's trouser cuff or the hem of a woman's skirt, all passive but armed with appliances of activity, still, but each possessed of the anlage of movement.

The sun lay on the grass and warmed it, and in the shade under the grass the insects moved, ants and ant lions to set traps for them, grasshoppers to jump into the air and flick their yellow wings for a second, sow bugs like little armadillos, plodding restlessly on many tender feet. And over the grass at the roadside a land turtle crawled, turning aside for nothing, dragging its high-domed shell over the grass. His hard legs and yellow-nailed feet threshed slowly through the grass, not really walking, but boosting and dragging his shell along. The barley beards slid off his shell, and the clover burrs fell on him and rolled to the ground. His horny beak was partly open, and his fierce, humorous eyes, under brows like finger-nails, stared straight ahead. He came over the grass leaving a beaten trail behind him, and the hill, which was the highway embankment, reared up ahead of him. For a moment he stopped, his head held high. He blinked and looked up and down. At last he started to climb the embankment. Front clawed feet reached forward but did not touch. The hind feet kicked his shell along, and it scraped on the grass, and on the gravel. As the embankment grew steeper and steeper, the more frantic were the efforts of the land turtle. Pushing hind legs strained and slipped, boosting the shell along, and the horny head protruded as far as the neck could stretch. Little by little the shell slid up the embankment until at last a parapet cut straight across its line of march, the shoulder of the road, a concrete wall four inches high. As though they worked independently the hind legs pushed the shell against the wall. The head upraised and peered over the wall to the broad smooth plain of cement. Now the hands, braced on top of the wall, strained and lifted, and the shell came slowly up and rested its front end on the wall. For a moment the turtle rested. A red ant ran into the shell, into the soft skin inside the shell, and suddenly head and legs snapped in, and the armoured tail clamped in sideways. The red ant was crushed between body and legs. And one head of wild oats was clamped into the shell by a front leg. For a long moment the turtle lay still, and then the neck crept out and the old humorous frowning eyes looked about and the legs and tail came out. The back legs went to work, straining like elephant legs, and the shell tipped to an angle so that the front legs could not reach the level cement plain. But higher and higher the hind legs boosted it, until at last the centre of balance was reached, the front tipped down, the front legs scratched at the pavement, and it was up. But the head of wild oats was held by its stem around the front legs.

Now the going was easy, and all the legs worked, and the shell boosted along, waggling from side to side. A sedan driven by a forty-year-old woman approached. She saw the turtle and swung to the right, off the highway, the wheels screamed and a cloud of dust boiled up. Two wheels lifted for a moment and then settled. The car skidded back on to the road, and went on, but more slowly. The turtle had jerked into its shell, but now it hurried on, for the highway was burning hot.

And now a light truck approached, and as it came near, the driver saw the turtle and swerved to hit it. His front wheel struck the edge of the shell, flipped the turtle like a tiddly-wink, spun it like a coin, and rolled it off the highway. The truck went back to its course along the right side. Lying on its back, the turtle was tight in its shell for a long time. But at last its legs waved in the air, reaching for something to pull it over. Its front foot caught a piece of quartz and little by little the shell pulled over and flopped upright. The wild oat head fell out and three of the spearhead seeds stuck in the ground. And as the turtle crawled on down the embankment, its shell dragged dirt over the seeds. The turtle entered a dust road and jerked itself along, drawing a wavy shallow trench in the dust with its shell. The old humorous eyes looked ahead, and the horny beak opened a little. His yellow toe-nails slipped a fraction in the dust.

4

When Joad heard the truck get under way, gear climbing up to gear and the ground throbbing under the rubber beating of the tires, he stopped and turned about and watched it until it disappeared. When it was out of sight he still watched the distance and the blue air-shimmer. Thoughtfully he took the pint from his pocket, unscrewed the metal cap, and sipped the whisky delicately, running his tongue inside the bottle neck, and then around his lips, to gather in any flavour that might have escaped him. He said experimentally: 'There we spied a nigger–' and that was all he could remember. At last he turned about and faced the dusty side road that cut off at right-angles through the fields. The sun was hot, and no wind stirred the sifted dust. The road was cut with furrows where dust had slid and settled back into the wheel tracks. Joad took a few steps, and the flour-like dust spurted up in front of his yellow shoes, and the yellowness was disappearing under grey dust.

He leaned down and untied the laces, slipped off first one shoe and then the other. And he worked his damp feet comfortably in the hot dry dust until little spurts of it came up between his toes, and until the skin on his feet tightened with dryness. He took off his coat and wrapped his shoes in it and slipped the bundle under his arm. And at last he moved up the road, shooting the dust ahead of him, making a cloud that hung low to the ground behind him.

The right of way was fenced, two strands of barbed wire on willow poles. The poles were crooked and badly trimmed. Whenever a crotch came to the proper height the wire lay in it, and where there was no crotch the barbed wire was lashed to the post with rusty baling wire. Beyond the fence, the corn lay beaten down by wind and heat and drought, and the cups where leaf joined stalk were filled with dust.

Joad plodded along, dragging his cloud of dust behind him. A little bit ahead he saw the high-domed shell of a land turtle, crawling slowly along through the dust, its legs working stiffly and jerkily. Joad stopped to watch it, and his shadow fell on the turtle. Instantly head and legs were withdrawn and the short tail clamped sideways into the shell. Joad picked it up and turned it over. The back was brown-grey, like the dust, but the underside of the shell was creamy yellow, clean and smooth. Joad shifted his bundle high under his arm and stroked the smooth undershell with his finger, and he pressed it. It was softer than the back. The hard old head came out and tried to look at the pressing finger, and the legs waved wildly. The turtle wetted on Joad's hand and struggled uselessly in the air. Joad turned it back upright and rolled it up in his coat with his shoes. He could feel it pressing and struggling and fussing under his arm. He moved ahead more quickly now, dragging his heels a little in the fine dust.

Ahead of him, beside the road, a scrawny, dusty willow tree cast a speckled shade. Joad could see it ahead of him, its poor branches curving over the way, its load of leaves tattered and scraggly as a moulting chicken. Joad was sweating now. His blue shirt darkened down his back and under his arms. He pulled the visor of his cap and creased it in the middle, breaking its cardboard lining so completely that it could never look new again. And his steps took on new speed and intent toward the shade of the distant willow tree. At the willow he knew there would be shade, at least one hard bar of absolute shade thrown by the trunk, since the sun had passed its zenith. The sun whipped the back of his neck now and made a little humming in his head. He could not see the base of the tree, for it grew out of a little swale that held water longer than the level places. Joad speeded his pace against the sun, and he started down the declivity. He slowed cautiously, for the bar of absolute shade was taken. A man sat on the ground, leaning against the trunk of the tree. His legs were crossed and one bare foot extended nearly as high as his head. He did not hear Joad approaching, for he was whistling solemnly the tune of 'Yes, Sir, That's My Baby'. His extended foot swung slowly up and down in the tempo. It was not dance tempo. He stopped whistling and sang in an easy thin tenor:

'Yes, sir, that's my Saviour,
Je . . . sus is my Saviour,
Je . . . sus is my Saviour now.
On the level
'S not the devil,
Jesus is my Saviour now.'

Joad had moved into the imperfect shade of the moulting leaves before the man heard him coming, stopped his song, and turned his head. It was a long head, bony, tight of skin, and set on a neck as stringy and muscular as a celery stalk. His eyeballs were heavy and protruding; the lids stretched to cover them, and the lids were raw and red. His cheeks were brown and shiny and hairless and his mouth full–humorous or sensual. The nose, beaked and hard, stretched the skin so tightly that the bridge showed white. There was no perspiration on the face, not even on the tall pale forehead. It was an abnormally high forehead, lined with delicate blue veins at the temples. Fully half of the face was above the eyes. His stiff grey hair was mussed back from his brow as though he had combed it back with his fingers. For clothes he wore overalls and a blue shirt. A denim coat with brass buttons and a spotted brown hat creased like a pork pie lay on the ground beside him. Canvas sneakers, grey with dust, lay near by where they had fallen when they were kicked off.

The man looked long at Joad. The light seemed to go far into his brown eyes, and it picked out little golden specks deep in the irises. The strained bundle of neck muscles stood out.

Joad stood still in the speckled shade. He took off his cap and mopped his wet face with it and dropped it and his rolled coat on the ground.

The man in the absolute shade uncrossed his legs and dug with his toes at the earth.

Joad said: 'Hi. It's hotter'n hell on the road.'

The seated man stared questioningly at him. 'Now ain't you young Tom Joad–ol' Tom's boy?'

'Yeah,' said Joad. 'All the way. Goin' home now.'

'You wouldn't remember me, I guess,' the man said. He smiled and his full lips revealed great horse teeth. 'Oh, no, you wouldn't remember. You was always too busy pullin' little girls' pigtails when I give you the Holy Sperit. You was all wrapped up in yankin' that pigtail out by the roots. You maybe don't recollect but I do. The two of you come to Jesus at once 'cause of that pigtail yankin'. Baptized both of you in the irrigation ditch at once. Fightin' an' yellin' like a couple a cats.'

Joad looked at him with drooped eyes, and then he laughed. 'Why, you're the preacher. You're the preacher. I jus' passed a recollection about you to a guy not an hour ago.'

'I was a preacher,' said the man seriously. 'Reverend Jim Casy–was a Burning Busher. Used to howl out the name of Jesus to glory. And used to get an irrigation ditch so squirmin' full of repented sinners half of 'em like to drownded. But not no more,' he sighed. 'Just Jim Casy now. Ain't got the call no more. Got a lot of sinful idears–but they seem kinda sensible.'

Joad said: 'You're bound to get idears if you go thinkin' about stuff. Sure I remember you. You used ta give a good meetin'. I recollect one time you give a whole sermon walkin' around on your hands, yellin' your head off. Ma favoured you more than anybody. An' Granma says you was just lousy with the spirit.' Joad dug at his rolled coat and found the pocket and brought out his pint. The turtle moved a leg but he wrapped it up tightly. He unscrewed the cap and held out the bottle. 'Have a little snort?'

Casy took the bottle and regarded it broodingly. 'I ain't preachin' no more much. The sperit ain't in the people much no more; and worse'n that, the sperit ain't in me no more. 'Course now an' again the sperit gets movin' an' I rip out a meeting', or when folks sets out food I give 'em a grace, but my heart ain't in it. I on'y do it 'cause they expect it.'

Joad mopped his face with his cap again. 'You ain't too damn holy to take a drink, are you?' he asked.

Casy seemed to see the bottle for the first time. He tilted it and took three big swallows. 'Nice drinkin' liquor,' he said.

'Ought to be,' said Joad. 'That's fact'ry liquor. Cost a buck.'

Casy took another swallow before he passed the bottle back. 'Yes, sir!' he said. 'Yes, sir!'

Joad took the bottle from him, and in politeness did not wipe the neck with his sleeve before he drank. He squatted on his hams and set the bottle upright against his coat roll. His fingers found a twig with which to draw his thoughts on the ground. He swept the leaves from a square and smoothed the dust. And he drew angles and made little circles. 'I ain't seen you in a long time,' he said.

'Nobody seen me,' said the preacher. 'I went off alone, an' I sat and figured. The sperit's strong in me, on'y it ain't the same. I ain't so sure of a lot of things.' He sat up straighter against the tree. His bony hand dug its way like a squirrel into his overall pocket, brought out a black, bitten plug of tobacco. Carefully he brushed off bits of straw and grey pocket fuzz before he bit off a corner and settled the quid into his cheek. Joad waved his stick in negation when the plug was held out to him. The turtle dug at the rolled coat. Casy looked over at the stirring garment. 'What you got there–a chicken? You'll smother it.'

Joad rolled the coat up more tightly. 'An old turtle,' he said. 'Picked him up on the road. An old bulldozer. Thought I'd take 'im to my little brother. Kids like turtles.'

The preacher nodded his head slowly. 'Every kid got a turtle some time or other. Nobody can't keep a turtle though. They work at it and work at it, and at last one day they get out and away they go–off somewheres. It's like me. I wouldn't take the good ol' gospel that was just layin' there to my hand. I got to be pickin' at it an' workin' at it until I got it all tore down. Here I got the sperit sometimes an' nothin' to preach about. I got the call to lead the people, an' no place to lead 'em.'

'Lead 'em around and around,' said Joad. 'Sling 'em in the irrigation ditch. Tell 'em they'll burn in hell if they don't think like you. What the hell you want to lead 'em someplace for? Jus' lead 'em.' The straight trunk shade had stretched out along the ground. Joad moved gratefully into it and squatted on his hams and made a new smooth place on which to draw his thoughts with a stick. A thick-furred yellow shepherd dog came trotting down the road, head low, tongue lolling and dripping. Its tail hung limply curled, and it panted loudly. Joad whistled at it, but it only dropped its head an inch and trotted fast toward some definite destination. 'Goin' someplace,' Joad explained, a little piqued. 'Goin' for home maybe.'

The preacher could not be thrown from his subject. 'Goin' someplace,' he repeated. 'That's right, he's goin' someplace. Me–I don't know where I'm goin'. Tell you what–I use ta get the people jumpin' an' talkin' in tongues, an' glory-shoutin' till they just fell down an' passed out. An' some I'd baptize to bring 'em to. An' then–you know what I'd do? I'd take one of them girls out in the grass, an' I'd lay with her. Done it ever' time. Then I'd feel bad, an' I'd pray an' pray, but it didn't do no good. Come the nex' time, them an' me was full of the sperit, I'd do it again. I figgered there just wasn't no hope for me, an' I was a damned ol' hypocrite. But I didn't mean to be.'

Joad smiled and his long teeth parted and he licked his lips. 'There ain't nothing like a good hot meetin' for pushin' 'em over,' he said. 'I done that myself.'

Casy leaned forward excitedly. 'You see,' he cried, 'I seen it was that way, an' I started thinkin'.' He waved his bony big-knuckled hand up and down in a patting gesture. 'I got to thinkin' like this–"Here's me preachin' grace. An' here's them people gettin' grace so hard they're jumpin' an' shoutin'. Now they say layin' with a girl comes from the devil. But the more grace a girl got in her, the quicker she wants to go out in the grass." An' I got to thinkin' how in hell, s'cuse me, how can the devil get in when a girl is so full of the Holy Sperit that it's spoutin' out of her nose an' ears. You'd think that'd be one time when the devil didn't stand a snowball's chance in hell. But there it was.' His eyes were shining with excitement. He worked his cheeks for a moment and then spat into the dust, and the gob of spit rolled over and over, picking up dust until it looked like a round dry little pellet. The preacher spread out his hand and looked at his palm as though he were reading a book. 'An' there's me,' he went on softly. 'There's me with all them people's souls in my han'–responsible an' feelin' my responsibility–an' ever' time, I lay with one of them girls.' He looked over at Joad and his face looked helpless. His expression asked for help.

Joad carefully drew the torso of a woman in the dirt, breasts, hips, pelvis. 'I wasn't never a preacher,' he said. 'I never let nothin' get by when I could catch it. An' I never had no idears about it except I was goddamn glad when I got one.'

'But you wasn't a preacher,' Casy insisted. 'A girl was just a girl to you.

They wasn't nothin' to you. But to me they was holy vessels. I was savin' their souls. An' here with all that responsibility on me I'd just get 'em frothin' with the Holy Sperit, an' then I'd take 'em out in the grass.'

'Maybe I should of been a preacher,' said Joad. He brought out his tobacco and papers and rolled a cigarette. He lighted it and squinted through the smoke at the preacher. 'I been a long time without a girl,' he said. 'It's gonna take some catchin' up.'

Casy continued: 'It worried me till I couldn't get no sleep. Here I'd go to preachin' and I'd say: "By God, this time I ain't gonna do it." And right while I said it, I knowed I was.'

'You should a got a wife,' said Joad. 'Preacher an' his wife stayed at our place one time. Jehovites they was. Slep' upstairs. Held meetin's in our barnyard. Us kids would listen. That preacher's missus took a godawful poundin' after ever' night meetin'.'

'I'm glad you tol' me,' said Casy. 'I use to think it was jus' me. Finally it give me such pain I quit an' went off by myself an' give her a damn good thinkin' about.' He doubled up his legs and scratched between his dry dusty toes. 'I says to myself: "What's gnawin' you? Is it the screwin'?" An' I says: "No it's the sin." An' I says: "Why is it that when a fella ought to be just about mule-ass proof against sin, an' all full up of Jesus, why is it that's the time a fella gets fingerin' his pants buttons?"' He laid two fingers down in his palm in rhythm as though he gently placed each word there side by side. 'I says: "Maybe it ain't a sin. Maybe it's just the way folks is. Maybe we been whippin' the hell out of ourselves for nothin'." An' I thought how some sisters took to beatin' theirselves with a three-foot shag of bobwire. An' I thought how maybe they liked to hurt themselves, an' maybe I liked to hurt myself. Well, I was layin' under a tree when I figured that out, and I went to sleep. And it come night, an' it was dark when I come to. They was a coyote squawkin' near by. Before I knowed it, I was sayin' out loud: "The hell with it! There ain't no sin and there ain't no virtue. There's just stuff people do. It's all part of the same thing. And some of the things folks do is nice, and some ain't nice, but that's as far as any man got a right to say."' He paused and looked up from the palm of his hand, where he had laid down the words.

Joad was grinning at him, but Joad's eyes were sharp and interested, too. 'You give her a goin'-over,' he said. 'You figured her out.'

Casy spoke again, and his voice rang with pain and confusion. 'I says: "What's this call, this sperit?" An' I says: "It's love. I love people so much I'm fit to bust, sometimes." An' I says: "Don't you love Jesus?" Well, I thought an' thought, an' finally I says: "No, I don't know nobody name' Jesus. I know a bunch of stories, but I only love people. An' sometimes I love 'em fit to bust, an' I want to make 'em happy, so I been preachin' somepin I thought would make 'em happy." An' then–I been talkin' a hell of a lot. Maybe you wonder about me using bad words. Well, they ain't bad to me no more. They're jus' words folks use, an' they don't mean nothing bad with 'em. Anyways, I'll tell you one more thing I thought out; an' from a preacher it's the most unreligious thing, and I can't be a preacher no more because I thought it an' I believe it.'

'What's that?' Joad asked.

Casy looked shyly at him. 'If it hits you wrong, don't take no offence at it, will you?'

'I don't take no offence 'cept a bust in the nose,' said Joad. 'What did you figger?'

'I figgered about the Holy Sperit and the Jesus road. I figgered: "Why do we got to hand it on God or Jesus? Maybe," I figgered, "maybe it's all men an' all women we love; maybe that's the Holy Sperit–the human sperit–the whole shebang. Maybe all men got one big soul ever'body's a part of." Now I sat there thinkin' it, an' all of a sudden–I knew it. I knew it so deep down that it was true, and I still know it.'

Joad's eyes dropped to the ground, as though he could not meet the naked honesty in the preacher's eyes. 'You can't hold no church with idears like that,' he said. 'People would drive you out of the country with idears like that. Jumpin' an' yellin'. That's what folks like. Makes 'em feel swell. When Granma got to talkin' in tongues, you couldn't tie her down. She could knock over a full-growed deacon with her fist.'

Casy regarded him broodingly. 'Somepin I like to ast you,' he said. 'Somepin that's been eatin' on me.'

'Go ahead. I'll talk, sometimes.'

'Well'–the preacher said slowly–'here's you that I baptized right when I was in the glory roof-tree. Got little hunks of Jesus jumpin' outa my mouth that day. You won't remember 'cause you was busy pullin' that pigtail.'

'I remember,' said Joad. 'That was Susy Little. She bust my finger a year later.'

'Well–did you take any good outa that baptizin'? Was your ways better?'

Joad thought about it. 'No-o-o, can't say as I felt anything.'

'Well–did you take any bad from it? Think hard.'

Joad picked up the bottle and took a swig. 'They wasn't nothing in it, good or bad. I just had fun.' He handed the flask to the preacher.

He sighed and drank and looked at the low level of the whisky and took another tiny drink. 'That's good,' he said. 'I got to worryin' about whether in messin' around maybe I done somebody a hurt.'

Joad looked over toward his coat and saw the turtle, free of the cloth and hurrying away in the direction he had been following when Joad found him. Joad watched him for a moment and then got slowly to his feet and retrieved him and wrapped him in the coat again. 'I ain't got no present for the kids,' he said. 'Nothin' but this ol' turtle.'

'It's a funny thing,' the preacher said. 'I was thinkin' about ol' Tom Joad when you come along. Thinkin' I'd call in on him. I used to think he was a godless man. How is Tom?'

'I don't know how he is. I ain't been home in four years.'

'Didn't he write to you?'

Joad was embarrassed. 'Well, Pa wasn't no hand to write for pretty, or to write for writin'. He's sign up his name as nice as anybody, an' lick his pencil. But Pa never did write no letters. He always says what he couldn' tell a fella with his mouth wasn't worth leanin' on no pencil about.'

'Been out travellin' around?' Casy asked.

Joad regarded him suspiciously. 'Didn't you hear about me? I was in all the papers.'

'No–I never. What?' He jerked one leg over the other and settled lower against the tree. The afternoon was advancing rapidly, and a richer tone was growing on the sun.

Joad said pleasantly: 'Might's well tell you now an' get it over with. But if you was still preachin' I wouldn't tell, fear you got prayin' over me.' He drained the last of the pint and flung it from him, and the flat brown bottle skidded lightly over the dust. 'I been in McAlester them four years.'

Casy swung around to him, and his brows lowered so that his tall forehead seemed even taller. 'Ain't wantin' to talk about it, huh? I won't ask you no questions, if you done something bad–'

'I'd do what I done–again,' said Joad. 'I killed a guy in a fight. We was drunk at a dance. He got a knife in me, an' I killed him with a shovel that was layin' there. Knocked his head plumb to squash.'

Casy's eyebrows resumed their normal level. 'You ain't ashamed of nothin' then?'

'No,' said Joad, 'I ain't. I got seven years, account of he had a knife in me. Got out in four–parole.'

'Then you ain't heard nothin' about your folks for four years?'

'Oh, I heard. Ma sent me a card two years ago, an' las' Christmas Granma sent a card. Jesus, the guys in the cell block laughed! Had a tree an' shiny stuff looks like snow. It says in po'try:

"Merry Christmas, purty child,
Jesus meek an' Jesus mild,
Underneath the Christmas tree
There's a gif' for you from me."

I guess Granma never read it. Prob'ly got it from a drummer an' picked out the one with the mos' shiny stuff on it. The guys in my cell block goddamn near died laughin'. Jesus Meek they called me after that. Granma never meant it funny; she jus' figgered it was so purty she wouldn't bother to read it. She lost her glasses the year I went up. Maybe she never did find 'em.'

'How they treat you in McAlester?' Casy asked.

'Oh, awright. You eat regular, an' get clean clothes, and there's places to take a bath. It's pretty nice some ways. Makes it hard not havin' no women.' Suddenly he laughed. 'They was a guy paroled,' he said. ''Bout a month he's back for breakin' parole. A guy ast him why he bust his parole. "Well, hell," he says. "They got no conveniences at my old man's place. Got no 'lectric lights, got no shower baths. There ain't no books, an' the food's lousy." Says he come back where they got a few conveniences an' he eats regular. He says it makes him feel lonesome out there in the open havin' to think what to do next. So he stole a car an' come back.' Joad got out his tobacco and blew a brown paper free of the pack and rolled a cigarette. 'The guy's right, too,' he said. 'Las' night, thinkin' where I'm gonna sleep, I got scared. An' I got thinkin' about my bunk, an' I wonder what the stir-bug I got for a cell-mate is doin'. Me an' some guys had a string band goin'. Good one. Guy said we ought to go on the radio. An' this mornin' I didn't know what time to get up. Jus' laid there waitin' for the bell to go off.'

Casy chuckled. 'Fella can get so he misses the noise of a saw mill.'

The yellowing, dusty, afternoon light put a golden colour on the land. The cornstalks looked golden. A flight of swallows swooped overhead toward some waterhole. The turtle in Joad's coat began a new campaign of escape. Joad creased the visor of his cap. It was getting the long protruding curve of a crow's beak now. 'Guess I'll mosey along,' he said. 'I hate to hit the sun, but it ain't so bad now.'

Casy pulled himself together. 'I ain't seen ol' Tom in a bug's age,' he said. 'I was gonna look in on him anyways. I brang Jesus to your folks for a long time, an' I never took up a collection nor nothin' but a bite to eat.'

'Come along,' said Joad. 'Pa'll be glad to see you. He always said you got too long a pecker for a preacher.' He picked up his coat roll and tightened it snugly about his shoes and turtle.

Casy gathered in his canvas sneakers and shoved his bare feet into them. 'I ain't got your confidence,' he said. 'I'm always scared there's wire or glass under the dust. I don't know nothin' I hate so much as a cut toe.'

They hesitated on the edge of the shade and then they plunged into the yellow sunlight like two swimmers hastening to get to shore. After a few fast steps they slowed to a gentle, thoughtful pace. The cornstalks threw grey shadows sideways now, and the raw smell of hot dust was in the air. The cornfield ended and dark green cotton took its place, dark green leaves through a film of dust, and the bolls forming. It was spotty cotton, thick in the low places where water had stood, and bare on the high places. The plants strove against the sun. And distance, toward the horizon, was tan to invisibility. The dust road stretched out ahead of them, waving up and down. The willows of a stream lined across the west, and to the north-west a fallow section was going back to sparse brush. But the smell of burned dust was in the air and the air was dry, so that mucus in the nose dried to a crust, and the eyes watered to keep the eyeballs from drying out.

Casy said: 'See how good the corn come along until the dust got up. Been a dinger of a crop.'

'Ever' year,' said Joad. 'Ever' year I can remember, we had a good crop comin', an' it never come. Grampa says she was good the first five ploughin's, while the wild grass was still in her.' The road dropped down a little hill and climbed up another rolling hill.

Casy said: 'Ol' Tom's house can't be more'n a mile from here. Ain't she over that third rise?'

'Sure,' said Joad. ''Less somebody stole it, like Pa stole it.'

'Your pa stole it?'

'Sure, got it a mile an' a half east of here an' drug it. Was a family livin' there, an' they moved away. Grampa an' Pa an' my brother Noah like to took the whole house, but she wouldn' come. They only got part of her. That's why she looks so funny on one end. They cut her in two an' drug her over with twelve head of horses and two mules. They was goin' back for the other half an' stick her together again, but before they got there Wink Manley come with his boys and stole the other half. Pa an' Grampa was pretty sore, but a little later them an' Wink got drunk together an' laughed their heads off about it. Wink, he says his house is at stud, an' if we'll bring our'n over an' breed 'em we'll maybe get a litter of crap-houses. Wink was a great ol' fella when he was drunk. After that him an' Pa an' Grampa was friends. Got drunk together ever' chance they got.'

'Tom's a great one,' Casy agreed. They plodded dustily on down to the bottom of the draw, and then slowed their steps for the rise. Casy wiped his forehead with his sleeve and put on his flat-topped hat again. 'Yes,' he repeated, 'Tom was a great one. For a godless man he was a great one. I seen him in meetin' sometimes when the sperit got into him just a little, an' I seen him take ten-twelve foot jumps. I tell you when ol' Tom got a dose of the Holy Sperit you got to move fast to keep from gettin' run down an' tromped. Jumpy as a stud horse in a box stall.'

They topped the next rise and the road dropped into an old water-cut, ugly and raw, a ragged course, and freshet scars cutting into it from both sides. A few stones were in the crossing. Joad minced across in his bare feet. 'You talk about Pa,' he said. 'Maybe you never seen Uncle John the time they baptized him over to Polk's place. Why, he got to plungin' an' jumpin'. Jumped over a feeny bush as big as a piana. Over he'd jump, an' back he'd jump, howlin' like a dog-wolf in moon time. Well, Pa seen him, an' Pa, he figgers he's the bes' Jesus-jumper in these parts. So Pa picks out a feeny bush 'bout twicet as big as Uncle John's feeny bush, and Pa lets out a squawk like a sow litterin' broken bottles, an' he takes a run at that feeny bush an' clears her an' bust his right leg. That took the sperit out of Pa. Preacher wants to pray it set, but Pa says, no, by God, he'd got his heart full of havin' a doctor. Well, they wasn't a doctor, but they was a travellin' dentist, an' he set her. Preacher give her a prayin' over anyways.'

They plodded up the little rise on the other side of the water-cut. Now that the sun was on the wane some of its impact was gone, and while the air was hot, the hammering rays were weaker. The strung wire on crooked poles still edged the road. On the right-hand side a line of wire fence strung out across the cottonfield, and the dusty green cotton was the same on both sides, dusty and dry and dark green.

Joad pointed to the boundary fence. 'That there's our line. We didn't really need no fence there, but we had the wire, an' Pa kinda liked her there. Said it give him a feelin' that forty was forty. Wouldn't of had the fence if Uncle John didn' come drivin' in one night with six spools of wire in his wagon. He give 'em to Pa for a shoat. We never did know where he got that wire.' They slowed for the rise, moving their feet in the deep soft dust, feeling the earth with their feet. Joad's eyes were inward on his memory. He seemed to be laughing inside himself. 'Uncle John was a crazy bastard,' he said. 'Like what he done with that shoat.' He chuckled and walked on.

Jim Casy waited impatiently. The story did not continue. Casy gave it a good long time to come out. 'Well, what'd he do with that shoat?' he demanded at last, with some irritation.

'Huh? Oh! Well, he killed that shoat right there, an' he got Ma to light up the stove. He cut out pork chops an' put 'em in the pan, an' he put ribs an' a leg in the oven. He et chops till the ribs was done, an' he et ribs till the leg was done. An' then he tore into that leg. Cut off big chunks of her an' shoved 'em in his mouth. Us kids hung around slaverin', an' he give us some, but he wouldn't give Pa none. By an' by he et so much he throwed up an' went to sleep. While he's asleep us kids an' Pa finished off the leg. Well, when Uncle John woke up in the mornin' he slaps another leg in the oven. Pa says: "John, you gonna eat that whole damn pig?" An' he says: "I aim to, Tom, but I'm scairt some of her'll spoil 'fore I get her et, hungry as I am for pork. Maybe you better get a plate an' gimme back a couple rolls of wire." Well, sir, Pa wasn't no fool. He jus' let Uncle John go on an' eat himself sick of pig, an' when he drove off he hadn't et much more'n half. Pa says: "Whyn't you salt her down?" But not Uncle John; when he wants pig he wants a whole pig, an' when he's through, he don't want no pig hangin' around. So off he goes, and Pa salts down what's left'.

Casy said: 'While I was still in the preachin' sperit I'd a made a lesson of that an' spoke it to you, but I don't do that no more. What you s'pose he done a thing like that for?'

'I dunno,' said Joad. 'He jus' got hungry for pork. Makes me hungry jus' to think of it. I had jus' four slices of roastin' pork in four years–one slice ever' Christmus.'

Casy suggested elaborately: 'Maybe Tom'll kill the fatted calf like for the prodigal in Scripture.'

Joad laughed scornfully. 'You don't know Pa. If he kills a chicken most of the squawkin' will come from Pa, not the chicken. He don't never learn. He's always savin' a pig for Christmus and then it dies in September of bloat or somepin so you can't eat it. When Uncle John wanted pork he et pork. He had her.'

They moved over the curving top of the hill and saw the Joad place below them. And Joad stopped. 'It ain't the same,' he said. 'Looka that house. Somepin's happened. They ain't nobody there.' The two stood and stared at the little cluster of buildings.

5

The owners of the land came on to the land, or more often a spokesman for the owners came. They came in closed cars, and they felt the dry earth with their fingers, and sometimes they drove big earth augers into the ground for soil tests. The tenants, from their sun-beaten dooryards, watched uneasily when the closed cars drove along the fields. And at last the owner men drove into the dooryards and sat in their cars to talk out of the windows. The tenant men stood beside the cars for a while, and then squatted on their hams and found sticks with which to mark the dust.

In the open doors the women stood looking out, and behind them the children–corn-headed children, with wide eyes, one bare foot on top of the other bare foot, and the toes working. The women and the children watched their men talking to the owner men. They were silent.

Some of the owner men were kind because they hated what they had to do, and some of them were angry because they hated to be cruel, and some of them were cold because they had long ago found that one could not be an owner unless one were cold. And all of them were caught in something larger than themselves. Some of them hated the mathematics that drove them, and some were afraid, and some worshipped the mathematics because it provided a refuge from thought and from feeling. If a bank or a finance company owned the land, the owner man said: The Bank–or the Company–needs–wants–insists–must have–as though the Bank or the Company were a monster, with thought and feeling, which had ensnared them. These last would take no responsibility for the banks or the companies because they were men and slaves, while the banks were machines and masters all at the same time. Some of the owner men were a little proud to be slaves to such cold and powerful masters. The owner men sat in the cars and explained. You know the land is poor. You've scrabbed at it long enough, God knows.

The squatting tenant men nodded and wondered and drew figures in the dust, and yes, they knew, God knows. If the dust only wouldn't fly. If the top would only stay on the soil, it might not be so bad.

The owner men went on leading to their point: You know the land's getting poorer. You know what cotton does to the land: robs it, sucks all the blood out of it.

The squatters nodded–they knew, God knew. If they could only rotate the crops they might pump blood back into the land.

Well, it's too late. And the owner men explained the workings and the thinkings of the monster that was stronger than they were. A man can hold land if he can just eat and pay taxes: he can do that.

Yes, he can do that until his crops fail one day and he has to borrow money from the bank.

But–you see, a bank or a company can't do that, because those creatures don't breathe air, don't eat side-meat. They breathe profits; they eat the interest on money. If they don't get it, they die the way you die without air, without side-meat. It is a sad thing, but it is so. It is just so.

The squatting men raised their eyes to understand. Can't we just hang on? Maybe the next year will be a good year. God knows how much cotton next year. And with all the wars–God knows what price cotton will bring. Don't they make explosives out of cotton? And uniforms? Get enough wars and cotton'll hit the ceiling. Next year, maybe. They looked up questioningly.

We can't depend on it. The bank–the monster has to have profits all the time. It can't wait. It'll die. No, taxes go on. When the monster stops growing, it dies. It can't stay one size.

Soft fingers began to tap the sill of the car window, and hard fingers tightened on the restless drawing sticks. In the doorways of the sun-beaten tenant houses women sighed and then shifted feet so that the one that had been down was now on top, and the toes working. Dogs came sniffing near the owner cars and wetted on all four tires one after another. And chickens lay in the sunny dust and fluffed their feathers to get the cleansing dust down to the skin. In the little sties the pigs grunted inquiringly over the muddy remnants of the slops.

The squatting men looked down again. What do you want us to do? We can't take less share of the crop–we're half-starved now. The kids are hungry all the time. We got no clothes, torn an' ragged. If all the neighbours weren't the same, we'd be ashamed to go to meeting.

And at last the owner men came to the point. The tenant system won't work any more. One man on a tractor can take the place of twelve or fourteen families. Pay him a wage and take all the crop. We have to do it. We don't like to do it. But the monster's sick. Something's happened to the monster.

But you'll kill the land with cotton.

We know. We've got to take cotton quick before the land dies. Then we'll sell the land. Lots of families in the East would like to own a piece of land.

The tenant men looked up alarmed. But what'll happen to us? How'll we eat?

You'll have to get off the land. The ploughs'll go through the dooryard.

And now the squatting men stood up angrily. Grampa took up the land, and he had to kill the Indians to drive them away. And Pa was born here, and he killed weeds and snakes. Then a bad year came and he had to borrow a little money. An' we was born here. There in the door–our children born here. And Pa had to borrow money. The bank owned the land then, but we stayed and we got a little bit of what we raised.

We know that–all that. It's not us, it's the bank. A bank isn't like a man. Or an owner with fifty thousand acres, he isn't like a man either. That's the monster.

Sure, cried the tenant men, but it's our land. We measured it and broke it up. We were born on it, and we got killed on it, died on it. Even if it's no good, it's still ours. That's what makes it ours–being born on it, working it, dying on it. That makes ownership, not a paper with numbers on it.

We're sorry. It's not us. It's the monster. The bank isn't like a man.

Yes, but the bank is only made of men.

No, you're wrong there–quite wrong there. The bank is something else than men. It happens that every man in a bank hates what the bank does, and yet the bank does it. The bank is something more than men, I tell you. It's the monster. Men made it, but they can't control it.

The tenants cried: Grampa killed Indians, Pa killed snakes for the land. Maybe we can kill banks–they're worse than Indians and snakes. Maybe we got to fight to keep our land, like Pa and Grampa did.

And now the owner men grew angry. You'll have to go.

But it's ours, the tenant men cried. We–

No. The bank, the monster owns it. You'll have to go.

We'll get our guns, like Grampa when the Indians came. What then?

Well–first the sheriff, and then the troops. You'll be stealing if you try to stay, you'll be murderers if you kill to stay. The monster isn't men, but it can make men do what it wants.

But if we go, where'll we go? How'll we go? We got no money.

We're sorry, said the owner men. The bank, the fifty-thousand-acre owner can't be responsible. You're on land that isn't yours. Once over the line maybe you can pick cotton in the fall. Maybe you can go on relief. Why don't you go on west to California? There's work there, and it never gets cold. Why, you can reach out anywhere and pick an orange. Why, there's always some kind of crop to work in. Why don't you go there? And the owner men started their cars and rolled away.

The tenant men squatted down on their hams again to mark the dust with a stick, to figure, to wonder. Their sun-burned faces were dark, and their sun-whipped eyes were light. The women moved cautiously out of the doorways toward their men, and the children crept behind the women, cautiously, ready to run. The bigger boys squatted beside their fathers, because that made them men. After a time the women asked: What did he want?

And the men looked up for a second, and the smoulder of pain was in their eyes. We got to get off. A tractor and a superintendent. Like factories.

Where'll we go? the women asked.

We don't know. We don't know.

And the women went quickly, quietly back into the houses and herded the children ahead of them. They knew that a man so hurt and so perplexed may turn in anger, even on people he loves. They left the men alone to figure and to wonder in the dust.

After a time perhaps the tenant man looked about–at the pump put in ten years ago, with a goose-neck handle and iron flowers on the spout, at the chopping block where a thousand chickens had been killed, at the hand plough lying in the shed, and the patent crib hanging in the rafters over it.

The children crowded about the women in the houses. What we going to do, Ma? Where we going to go?

The women said: We don't know, yet. Go out and play. But don't go near your father. He might whale you if you go near him. And the women went on with the work, but all the time they watched the men squatting in the dust–perplexed and figuring.

The tractors came over the roads and into the fields, great crawlers moving like insects, having the incredible strength of insects. They crawled over the ground, laying the track and rolling on it and picking it up. Diesel tractors, puttering while they stood idle; they thundered when they moved, and then settled down to a droning roar. Snub-nosed monsters, raising the dust and sticking their snouts into it, straight down the country, across the country, through fences, through dooryards, in and out of gullies in straight lines. They did not run on the ground, but on their own roadbeds. They ignored hills and gulches, water-courses, fences, houses.

The man sitting in the iron seat did not look like a man: gloved, goggled, rubber dust-mask over nose and mouth, he was a part of the monster, a robot in the seat. The thunder of the cylinders sounded through the country, became one with the air and the earth, so that earth and air muttered in sympathetic vibration. The driver could not control it–straight across country it went, cutting through a dozen farms and straight back. A twitch at the controls could swerve the cat', but the driver's hands could not twitch because the monster that built the tractor, the monster that sent the tractor out, had somehow got into the driver's hands, into his brain and muscle, had goggled him and muzzled him–goggled his mind, muzzled his speech, goggled his perception, muzzled his protest. He could not see the land as it was, he could not smell the land as it smelled: his feet did not stamp the clods or feel the warmth and power of the earth. He sat in an iron seat and stepped on iron pedals. He could not cheer or beat or curse or encourage the extension of his power, and because of this he could not cheer or whip or curse or encourage himself. He did not know or own or trust or beseech the land. If a seed dropped did not germinate, it was nothing. If the young thrusting plant withered in drought or drowned in a flood of rain, it was no more to the driver than to the tractor.

He loved the land no more than the bank loved the land. He could admire the tractor–its machined surfaces, its surge of power, the roar of its detonating cylinders; but it was not his tractor. Behind the tractor rolled the shining disks, cutting the earth with blades–not ploughing but surgery, pushing the cut earth to the right where the second row of disks cut it and pushed it to the left; slicing blades shining, polished by the cut earth. And pulled behind the disks, the harrows combing with iron teeth so that the little clods broke up and the earth lay smooth. Behind the harrows, the long seeders–twelve curbed iron penes erected in the foundry, orgasms set by gears, raping methodically, raping without passion. The driver sat in his iron seat and he was proud of the straight lines he did not will, proud of the tractor he did not own or love, proud of the power he could not control. And when that crop grew, and was harvested, no man had crumbled a hot clod in his fingers and let the earth sift past his finger-tips. No man had touched the seed, or lusted for the growth. Men ate what they had not raised, had no connexion with the bread. The land bore under iron, and under iron gradually died; for it was not loved or hated, it had no prayers or curses.

At noon the tractor driver stopped sometimes near a tenant house and opened his lunch; sandwiches wrapped in waxed paper, white bread, pickle, cheese, Spam, a piece of pie branded like an engine part. He ate without relish. And tenants not yet moved away came out to see him, looked curiously while the goggles were taken off, and the rubber dust-mask, leaving white circles around the eyes and a large white circle around nose and mouth. The exhaust of the tractor puttered on, for fuel is so cheap it is more efficient to leave the engine running than to heat the diesel nose for a new start. Curious children crowded close, ragged children who ate their fried dough as they watched. They watched hungrily the unwrapping of the sandwiches, and their hunger-sharpened noses smelled the pickle, cheese, and Spam. They didn't speak to the driver. They watched his hand as it carried food to his mouth. They did not watch him chewing; their eyes followed the hand that held the sandwich. After a while the tenant who could not leave the place came out and squatted in the shade beside the tractor.

'Why, you're Joe Davis's boy!'

'Sure,' the driver said.

'Well, what you doing this kind of work for–against your own people?'

'Three dollars a day. I got damn sick of creeping for my dinner–and not getting it. I got a wife and kids. We got to eat. Three dollars a day, and it comes every day.'

'That's right,' the tenant said. 'But for your three dollars a day fifteen or twenty families can't eat at all. Nearly a hundred people have to go out and wander on the roads for your three dollars a day. Is that right?'

And the driver said: 'Can't think of that. Got to think of my own kids. Three dollars a day, and it comes every day. Times are changing mister, don't you know? Can't make a living on the land unless you've got two, five, ten thousand acres and a tractor. Crop land isn't for little guys like us any more. You don't kick up a howl because you can't make Fords, or because you're not the telephone company. Well, crops are like that now. Nothing to do about it. You try to get three dollars a day some place. That's the only way.'

The tenant pondered. 'Funny thing how it is. If a man owns a little property, that property is him, it's part of him, and it's like him. If he owns property only so he can walk on it and handle it and be sad when it isn't doing well, and feel fine when the rain falls on it, that property is him, and some way he's bigger because he owns it. Even if he isn't successful he's big with his property. That is so.'

And the tenant pondered more. 'But let a man get property he doesn't see, or can't take time to get his fingers in, or can't be there to walk on it–why, then the property is the man. He can't do what he wants, he can't think what he wants. The property is the man, stronger than he is. And he is small, not big. Only his possessions are big–and he's the servant of his property. That is so, too.'

The driver munched the branded pie and threw the crust away. 'Times are changed, don't you know? Thinking about stuff like that don't feed the kids. Get your three dollars a day, feed your kids. You got no call to worry about anybody's kids but your own. You get a reputation for talking like that, and you'll never get three dollars a day. Big shots won't give you three dollars a day if you worry about anything but your three dollars a day.'

'Nearly a hundred people on the road for your three dollars. Where will we go?'

'And that reminds me,' the driver said, 'you better get out soon. I'm going through the door-yard after dinner.'

'You filled in the well this morning.'

'I know. Had to keep the line straight. But I'm going through the door-yard after dinner. Got to keep the lines straight. And–well, you know Joe Davis, my old man, so I'll tell you this. I got orders wherever there's a family not moved out–if I have an accident–you know, get too close and cave the house in a little–well, I might get a couple of dollars. And my youngest kid never had no shoes yet.'

'I built it with my hands. Straightened old nails to put the sheathing on. Rafters are wired to the stringers with baling wire. It's mine. I built it. You bump it down–I'll be in the window with a rifle. You even come too close and I'll pot you like a rabbit.'

'It's not me. There's nothing I can do. I'll lose my job if I don't do it. And look–suppose you kill me? They'll just hang you, but long before you're hung there'll be another guy on the tractor, and he'll bump the house down. You're not killing the right guy.'

'That's so,' the tenant said. 'Who gave you orders? I'll go after him. He's the one to kill.'

'You're wrong. He got his orders from the bank. The bank told him: "Clear those people out for it's your job."'

'Well, there's a president of the bank. There's a board of directors. I'll fill up the magazine of the rifle and go into the bank.'

The driver said: 'Fellow was telling me the bank gets orders from the east. The orders were: "Make the land show profit or we'll close you up."'

'But where does it stop? Who can we shoot? I don't aim to starve to death before I kill the man that's starving me.'

'I don't know. Maybe there's nobody to shoot. Maybe the thing isn't men at all. Maybe, like you said, the property's doing it. Anyway, I told you my orders.'

'I got to figure,' the tenant said. 'We all got to figure. There's some way to stop this. It's not like lightning or earthquakes. We've got a bad thing made by men, and by God that's something we can change.' The tenant sat in his doorway, and the driver thundered his engine and started off, tracks falling and curving, harrows combing, and the phalli of the seeder slipping into the ground. Across the door-yard the tractor cut, and the hard, foot-beaten ground was seeded field, and the tractor cut through again; the uncut space was ten feet wide. And back he came. The iron guard bit into the house-corner, crumbled the wall, and wrenched the little house from its foundation so that it fell sideways, crushed like a bug. And the driver was goggled and a rubber mask covered his nose and mouth. The tractor cut a straight line on, and the air and the ground vibrated with its thunder. The tenant man stared after it, his rifle in his hand. His wife was beside him, and the quiet children behind. And all of them stared after the tractor.

6

The Reverend Casy and young Tom stood on the hill and looked down on the Joad place. The small unpainted house was mashed at one corner, and it had been pushed off its foundations so that it slumped at an angle, its blind front windows pointing at a spot of sky well above the horizon. The fences were gone and the cotton grew in the door-yard and up against the house, and the cotton was about the shed barn. The outhouse lay on its side, and the cotton grew close against it. Where the door-yard had been pounded hard by the bare feet of children, and by stamping horses' hooves and by the broad wagon wheels, it was cultivated now, and the dark green, dusty cotton grew. Young Tom stared for a long time at the ragged willow beside the dry horse trough, at the concrete base where the pump had been. 'Jesus!' he said at last. 'Hell musta popped here. There ain't nobody livin' there.' At last he moved quickly down the hill, and Casy followed him. He looked into the barn shed, deserted, a little ground straw on the floor, and the mule stall in the corner. And as he looked in, there was a skittering on the floor and a family of mice faded in under the straw. Joad pushed at the entrance to the tool-shed lean-to, and no tools were there–a broken plough point, a mess of hay wire in the corner, an iron wheel from a hay-rake and a rat-gnawed mule collar, a flat gallon oil-can crusted with dirt and oil, and a pair of torn overalls hanging on a nail. 'There ain't nothin' left,' said Joad. 'We had pretty nice tools. There ain't nothin' left.'

Casy said: 'If I was still a preacher I'd say the arm of the Lord had struck. But now I don't know what happened. I been away. I didn't hear nothin'.' They walked toward the concrete well-cap, walked through cotton plants to get to it, and the bolls were forming on the cotton, and the land was cultivated.

'We never planted here,' Joad said. 'We always kept this clear. Why, you can't get a horse in now without he tromps the cotton.' They paused at the dry watering trough, and the proper weeds that should grow under a trough were gone and the old thick wood of the trough was dry and cracked. On the well-cap the bolts that had held the pump stuck up, their threads rusty and the nuts gone. Joad looked into the tube of the well and spat and listened. He dropped a clod down the well and listened. 'She was a good well,' he said. 'I can't hear water.' He seemed reluctant to go to the house. He dropped clod after clod down the well. 'Maybe they're all dead,' he said. 'But somebody'd a told me. I'd a got word some way.'

'Maybe they left a letter or something to tell in the house. Would they of knowed you was comin' out?'

'I don't know,' said Joad. 'No, I guess not. I didn' know myself till a week ago.'

'Le's look in the house. She's all pushed out a shape. Something knocked the hell out of her.' They walked slowly toward the sagging house. Two of the supports of the porch roof were pushed out so that the roof flopped down on one end. And the house-corner was crushed in. Through a maze of splintered wood the room at the corner was visible. The front door hung open inward, and a low strong gate across the front door hung outward on leather hinges.

Joad stopped at the step, a twelve-by-twelve timber. 'Doorstep's here,' he said. 'But they're gone–or Ma's dead.' He pointed to the low gate across the front door. 'If Ma was anywhere about, that gate'd be shut an' hooked. That's one thing she always done–see that gate was shut.' His eyes were warm. 'Ever since the pig got in over to Jacobs' an' et the baby. Milly Jacobs was jus' out in the barn. She come in while the pig was still eatin' it. Well, Mrs Jacobs was in a family way, an' she went ravin'. Never did get over it. Touched ever since. But Ma took a lesson from it. She never lef' that pig gate open 'less she was in the house herself. Never did forget. No–they're gone–or dead.' He climbed to the split porch and looked into the kitchen. The windows were broken out, and throwing rocks lay on the floor, and the floor and walls sagged steeply away from the door, and the sifted dust was on the boards. Joad pointed to the broken glass and the rocks. 'Kids,' he said. 'They'll go twenty miles to bust a window. I done it myself. They know when a house is empty, they know. That's the fust thing kids do when folks move out.' The kitchen was empty of furniture, stove gone and the round stovepipe hole in the wall showing light. On the sink shelf lay an old beer opener and a broken fork with its wooden handle gone. Joad slipped cautiously into the room, and the floor groaned under his weight. An old copy of the Philadelphia *Ledger* was on the floor against the wall, its pages yellow and curling. Joad looked into the bedroom–no bed, no chairs, nothing. On the wall a picture of an Indian girl in colour, labelled Red Wing. A bed slat leaning against the wall, and in one corner a woman's high-button shoe, curled up at the toe and broken over the instep. Joad picked it up and looked at it. 'I remember this,' he said. 'This was Ma's. It's all wore out now. Ma liked them shoes. Had 'em for years. No, they've went–an' took ever'thing.'

The sun had lowered until it came through the angled end windows now, and it flashed on the edges of the broken glass. Joad turned at last and went out and crossed the porch. He sat down on the edge of it and rested his bare feet on the twelve-by-twelve step. The evening light was on the fields, and the cotton plants threw long shadows on the ground, and the moulting willow tree threw a long shadow.

Casy sat down beside Joad. 'They never wrote you nothin'?' he asked.

'No. Like I said, they wasn't people to write. Pa could write, but he wouldn'. Didn't like to. It give him the shivers to write. He could work out a catalogue order as good as the nex' fella, but he wouldn' write no letters just for ducks.' They sat side by side, staring off into the distance. Joad laid his rolled coat on the porch beside him. His independent hands rolled a cigarette, smoothed it, and lighted it, and he inhaled deeply and blew the smoke out through his nose. 'Somepin's wrong,' he said. 'I can't put my finger on her. I got an itch that somepin's wronger'n hell. Just this house pushed aroun' an' my folks gone.'

Casy said: 'Right over there the ditch was, where I done the baptizin'. You wasn't mean, but you was tough. Hung on to that little girl's pigtail like a bulldog. We baptize' you both in the name of the Holy Ghos', and still you hung on. Ol' Tom says, "Hol' im under water." So I shove your head down 'till you start to bubblin' before you'd let go a that pigtail. You wasn't mean, but you was tough. Sometimes a tough kid grows up with a big jolt of the sperit in him.'

A lean grey cat came sneaking out of the barn and crept through the cotton plants to the end of the porch. It leaped silently up to the porch and crept low-belly toward the men. It came to a place between and behind the two, and then it sat down, and its tail stretched out straight and flat to the floor, and the last inch of it flicked. The cat sat and looked off into the distance where the men were looking.

Joad glanced around at it. 'By God! Look who's here. Somebody stayed.' He put out his hand, but the cat leaped away out of reach and sat down and licked the pads of its lifted paw. Joad looked at it, and his face was puzzled. 'I know what's the matter,' he cried. 'That cat jus' made me figger what's wrong.'

'Seems to me there's lots wrong,' said Casy.

'No, it's more'n jus' this place. Whyn't that cat jus' move in with some neighbours–with the Rances? How come nobody ripped some lumber off this house? Ain't been nobody here for three-four months, an' nobody's stole no lumber. Nice planks on the barn shed, plenty good planks on the house, winda frames an' nobody's took 'em. That ain't right. That's what was botherin' me, an' I couldn't catch hold of her.'

'Well, what's that figger out for you?' Casy reached down and slipped off his sneakers and wriggled his long toes on the step.

'I don't know. Seems like maybe there ain't any neighbours. If there was, would all of them nice planks be here? Why, Jesus Christ! Albert Rance took his family, kids an' dogs an' all, into Oklahoma City one Christmas. They was gonna visit with Albert's cousin. Well, folks aroun' here thought Albert moved away without sayin' nothin'–figgered maybe he got debts or some woman's squarin' off at him. When Albert come back a week later there wasn't a thing lef' in the house–stove was gone, beds was gone, winda frames was gone, an' eight feet of plankin' was gone off the south side of the house so you could look right through her. He come drivin' home just as Muley Graves was goin' away with the doors an' the well pump. Took Albert two weeks drivin' aroun' the neighbours 'fore he got his stuff back.'

Casy scratched his toes luxuriously. 'Didn't nobody give him an argument? All of 'em jus' give the stuff up?'

'Sure. They wasn't stealin' it. They thought he lef' it, an' they jus' took it. He got all of it back–all but a sofa pilla, velvet with a pitcher of an Injun on it. Albert claimed Grampa got it. Claimed Grampa got Injun blood, that's why he wants that pitcher. Well, Grampa did get her, but he didn't give a damn about the pitcher on it. He jus' liked her. Used to pack her aroun' an' he'd put her wherever he was gonna sit. He never would give her back to Albert. Says, "If Albert wants this pilla so bad, let him come an' get her. But he better come shootin', 'cause I'll blow his goddamn stinkin' head off if he comes messin' aroun' my pilla." So finally Albert give up an' made Grampa a present of that pilla. It give Grampa idears, though. He took to savin' chicken feathers. Says he's gonna have a whole damn bed of feathers. But he never got no feather bed. One time Pa got mad at a skunk under the house. Pa slapped that skunk with a two-by-four, and Ma burned all Grampa's feather so we could live in the house,' He laughed, 'Grampa's a tough ol' bastard. Jus' set on that Injun pilla an' says: "Let Albert come an' get her. Why," he says, "I'll take that squirt and wring 'im out like a pair of drawers."'

The cat crept close between the men again, and its tail lay flat and its whiskers jerked now and then. The sun dropped low toward the horizon and the dusty air was red and golden. The cat reached out a grey questioning paw and touched Joad's coat. He looked around. 'Hell, I forgot the turtle. I ain't gonna pack it all over hell.' He unwrapped the land turtle and pushed it under the house. But in a moment it was out, headed south-west as it had been from the first. The cat leaped at it and struck at its straining head and slashed at its moving feet. The old, hard, humorous head was pulled in, and the thick tail slapped in under the shell, and when the cat grew tired of waiting for it and walked off, the turtle headed on south-west again.

Young Tom Joad and the preacher watched the turtle go–waving its legs and boosting its heavy, high-domed shell along toward the south-west. The cat crept along behind for a while, but in a dozen yards it arched its back to a strong taut bow and yawned, and came stealthily back toward the seated men.

'Where the hell you s'pose he's goin'?' said Joad. 'I seen turtles all my life. They're always goin' some place. They always seem to want to get there.' The grey cat seated itself between and behind them again. It blinked slowly. The skin over its shoulders jerked forward under a flea, and then slipped slowly back. The cat lifted a paw and inspected it, flicked its claws out and in again experimentally, and licked its pads with a shell-pink tongue. The red sun touched the horizon and spread out like a jellyfish, and the sky above it seemed much brighter and more alive than it had been. Joad unrolled his new yellow shoes from his coat, and he brushed his dusty feet with his hand before he slipped them on.

The preacher, staring off across the fields, said: 'Somebody's comin'. Look! Down there, right through the cotton.'

Joad looked where Casy's finger pointed. 'Comin' afoot,' he said. 'Can't see 'im for the dust he raises. Who the hell's comin' here?' They watched the figure approaching in the evening light, and the dust it raised was reddened by the setting sun. 'Man,' said Joad. The man drew closer, and as he walked past the barn, Joad said: 'Why, I know him. You know him–that's Muley Graves.' And he called: 'Hey Muley! How ya?'

The approaching man stopped, startled by the call, and then he came on quickly. He was a lean man, rather short. His movements were jerky and quick. He carried a gunny sack in his hand. His blue jeans were pale at knee and seat, and he wore an old black suit coat, stained and spotted, the sleeves torn loose from the shoulders in back, and ragged holes worn through at the elbows. His black hat was as stained as his coat, and the band, torn half free, flopped up and down as he walked. Muley's face was smooth and unwrinkled, but it wore the truculent look of a bad child's, the mouth held tight and small, the little eyes half scowling, half petulant.

'You remember Muley,' Joad said softly to the preacher.

'Who's that?' the advancing man called. Joad did not answer. Muley came close, very close, before he made out the faces. 'Well, I'll be damned,' he said. 'It's Tommy Joad. When'd you get out, Tommy?'

'Two days ago,' said Joad. 'Took a little time to hitch-hike home. An' look here what I find. Where's my folks, Muley? What's the house all smashed up for, an' cotton planted in the door-yard?'

'By God, it's lucky I come by!' said Muley. ''Cause ol' Tom worried himself. When they was fixin' to move I was settin' in the kitchen there. I jus' tol' Tom I wasn't gonna move, by God! I tol' him that, an' Tom says: "I'm worryin' myself about Tommy. S'pose he comes home an' they ain't nobody here. What'll he think?" I says: "Whyn't you write down a letter?" An' Tom says: "Maybe I will. I'll think about her. But if I don't, you keep your eye out for Tommy if you're still aroun'." "I'll be aroun'," I says. "I'll be aroun' till hell freezes over. There ain't nobody can run a guy name of Graves outa this country." An' they ain't done it, neither.'

Joad said impatiently: 'Where's my folks? Tell about you standin' up to 'em later, but where's my folks?'

'Well, they was gonna stick her out when the bank come to tractorin' off the place. Your Grampa stood out here with a rifle, an' he blowed the headlights off that cat', but she come on just the same. Your Grampa didn't wanta kill the guy drivin' that cat', an' that was Willy Feeley, an' Willy knowed it, so he jus' come on, an' bumped the hell outa the house, an' give her a shake like a dog shakes a rat. Well, it took somepin outa Tom. Kinda got into 'im. He ain't been the same ever since.'

'Where is my folks?' Joad spoke angrily.

'What I'm tellin' you. Took three trips with your Uncle John's wagon. Took the stove an' the pump an' the beds. You should a seen them beds go out with all them kids an' your Granma an' Grampa settin' up against the headboard, an' your brother Noah settin' there smokin' a cigareet, an' spittin' la-de-da over the side of the wagon.' Joad opened his mouth to speak. 'They're all at your Uncle John's,' Muley said quickly.

'Oh! All at John's. Well, what they doin' there? Now stick to her for a second, Muley. Jus' stick to her. In jus' a minute you can go on your own way. What they doin' there?'

'Well, they been choppin' cotton, all of 'em, even the kids an' your Grampa. Gettin' money together so they can shove on west. Gonna buy a car and shove on west where it's easy livin'. There ain't nothin' here. Fifty cents a clean acre for choppin' cotton, an' folks beggin' for the chance to chop.'

'An' they ain't gone yet?'

'No,' said Muley. 'Not that I know. Las' I heard was four days ago when I seen your brother Noah out shootin' jack-rabbits, an' he says they're aimin' to go in about two weeks. John got his notice he got to get off. You jus' go on about eight miles to John's place. You'll find your folks piled in John's house like gophers in a winter burrow.'

'O.K.,' said Joad. 'Now you can ride on your own way. You ain't changed a bit, Muley. If you want to tell about somepin off north-west, you point your nose straight south-east.'

Muley said truculently: 'You ain't changed neither. You was a smart-aleck kid, an' you're still a smart aleck. You ain't tellin' me how to skin my life, by any chancet?'

Joad grinned. 'No, I ain't. If you wanta drive your head into a pile of broken glass, there ain't nobody can tell you different. You know this here preacher, don't you, Muley? Rev. Casy.'

'Why, sure, sure. Didn't look over. Remember him well.' Casy stood up and the two shook hands. 'Glad to see you again,' said Muley. 'You ain't been aroun' for a hell of a long time.'

'I been off a-askin' questions,' said Casy. 'What happened here? Why they kickin' folks off the lan'?'

Muley's mouth snapped shut so tightly that a little parrot's beak in the middle of his upper lip stuck down over his under-lip. He scowled. 'Them sons-a-bitches,' he said. 'Them dirty sons-a-bitches. I tell ya, men, I'm stayin'. They ain't gettin' rid a me. If they throw me off, I'll come back, an' if they figger I'll be quiet underground, why, I'll take couple-three of the sons-a-bitches along for company.' He patted a heavy weight in his side coat pocket. 'I ain't a-goin'. My pa come here fifty years ago. An' I ain't goin'.'

Joad said: 'What's the idear of kickin' the folks off?'

'Oh! They talked pretty about it. You know what kinda years we been havin'. Dust comin' up an spoilin' ever'thing so a man didn't get enough crop to plug up an ant's ass. An' ever'body got bills at the grocery. You know how it is. Well, the folks that owns the lan' says: "We can't afford to keep no tenants." An' they says: "The share a tenant gets is jus' the margin a profit we can't afford to lose." An' they says: "If we put all our lan' in one piece we can jus' hardly make her pay." So they tractored all the tenants off a the lan'. All 'cept me, an' by God I ain't goin'. Tommy, you know me. You knowed me all your life.'

'Damn right,' said Joad, 'all my life.'

'Well, you know I ain't a fool. I know this land ain't much good. Never was much good 'cept for grazin'. Never should a broke her up. An' now she's cottoned damn near to death. If on'y they didn' tell me I got to get off, why, I'd prob'y be in California right now a-eatin' grapes an' a-pickin' an orange when I wanted. But them sons-a-bitches says I got to get off–an', Jesus Christ, a man can't, when he's tol' to!'

'Sure,' said Joad. 'I wonder Pa went so easy. I wonder Grampa didn' kill nobody. Nobody never tol' Grampa where to put his feet. An' Ma ain't nobody you can push aroun', neither. I seen her beat the hell out of a tin pedlar with a live chicken one time 'cause he gave her an argument. She had the chicken in one han' an' the axe in the other, about to cut its head off. She aimed to go for that pedlar with the axe, but she forgot which hand was which, an' she takes after him with the chicken. Couldn' even eat that chicken when she got done. They wasn't nothing but a pair of legs in her han'. Grampa throwed his hip outa joint laughin'. How'd my folks go so easy?'

'Well, the guy that come aroun' talked nice as pie. "You got to get off. It ain't my fault." "Well," I says, "whose fault is it? I'll go an' I'll nut the fella." "It's the Shawnee Lan' an' Cattle Company. I jus' got orders." "Who's the Shawnee Lan' an' Cattle Company?" "It ain't nobody. It's a company." Got a fella crazy. There wasn't nobody you could lay for. Lot a the folks jus' got tired out lookin' for somepin to be mad at–but not me. I'm mad at all of it. I'm stayin'.'

A large drop of sun lingered on the horizon and then dripped over and was gone, and the sky was brilliant over the spot where it had gone, and a torn cloud, like a bloody rag, hung over the spot of its going. And dusk crept over the sky from the eastern horizon, and darkness crept over the land from the east. The evening star flashed and glittered in the dusk. The grey cat sneaked away toward the open barn shed and passed inside like a shadow.

Joad said: 'Well, we ain't gonna walk no eight miles to Uncle John's place tonight. My dogs is burned up. How's it if we go to your place, Muley? That's only about a mile.'

'Won't do no good.' Muley seemed embarrassed. 'My wife an' the kids an' her brother all took an' went to California. They wasn't nothin' to eat. They wasn't as mad as me, so they went. They wasn't nothin' to eat here.'

The preacher stirred nervously. 'You should of went too. You shouldn't of broke up the family.'

'I couldn',' said Muley Graves. 'Somepin jus' wouldn' let me.'

'Well, by God, I'm hungry,' said Joad. 'Four solemn years I been eatin' right on the minute. My guts is yellin' bloody murder. What you gonna eat, Muley? How you been gettin' your dinner?'

Muley said ashamedly: 'For a while I et frogs an' squirrels an' prairie dogs sometimes. Had to do it. But now I got some wire nooses on the tracks in the dry stream brush. Get rabbits, an' sometimes a prairie chicken. Skunks get caught, an' 'coons, too.' He reached down, picked up his sack, and emptied it on the porch. Two cottontails and a jack-rabbit fell out and rolled over limply, soft and furry.

'God Awmighty,' said Joad, 'it's more'n four years sence I've et fresh-killed meat.'

Casy picked up one of the cottontails and held it in his hand. 'You sharin' with us, Muley Graves?' he asked.

Muley fidgeted in embarrassment. 'I ain't got no choice in the matter.' He stopped on the ungracious sound of his words. 'That ain't like I mean it. That ain't. I mean'–he stumbled–'what I mean, if a fella's got somepin to eat an' another fella's hungry–why, the first fella ain't got no choice. I mean, s'pose I pick up my rabbits an' go off somewheres an' eat 'em. See?'

'I see,' said Casy. 'I can see that. Muley sees somepin there, Tom. Muley's got a-holt of somepin, an' it's too big for him, an' it's too big for me.'

Young Tom rubbed his hands together. 'Who's got a knife? Le's get at these here miserable rodents. Le's get at 'em.'

Muley reached in his pants pocket and produced a large horn-handled pocket knife. Tom Joad took it from him, opened a blade, and smelled it. He drove the blade again and again into the ground and smelled it again, wiped it on his trouser leg, and felt the edge with his thumb.

Muley took a quart bottle of water out of his hip pocket and set it on the porch. 'Go easy on that there water,' he said. 'That's all there is. This here well's filled.'

Tom took up a rabbit in his hand. 'One of you go and get some bale wire outa the barn. We'll make a fire with some a this broken plank from the house.' He looked at the dead rabbit. 'There ain't nothin' so easy to get ready as a rabbit,' he said. He lifted the skin of the back, slit it, put his fingers in the hole, and tore the skin off. It slipped off like a stocking, slipped off the body to the neck, and off the legs to the paws. Joad picked up the knife again and cut off the head and feet. He laid the skin down, slit the rabbit along the ribs, shook out the intestines on to the skin, and then threw the mess off into the cotton-field. And the clean-muscled little body was ready. Joad cut off the legs and cut the meaty back into two pieces. He was picking up the second rabbit when Casy came back with a snarl of bale wire in his hand. 'Now build up a fire and put some stakes up,' said Joad. 'Jesus Christ, I'm hungry for these here creatures!' He cleaned and cut up the rest of the rabbits and strung them on the wire. Muley and Casy tore splintered boards from the wrecked house-corner and started a fire, and they drove a stake into the ground on each side to hold the wire.

Muley came back to Joad. 'Look out for boils on that jack-rabbit,' he said. 'I don't like to eat no jack-rabbit with boils.' He took a little cloth bag from his pocket and put it on the porch.

Joad said: 'The jack was clean as a whistle–Jesus God, you got salt too? By any chance you got some plates an' a tent in your pocket?' He poured salt in his hand and sprinkled it over the pieces of rabbit strung on the wire.

The fire leaped and threw shadows on the house, and the dry wood crackled and snapped. The sky was almost dark now and the stars were out sharply. The grey cat came out of the barn shed and trotted miaowing toward the fire, but, nearly there, it turned and went directly to one of the little piles of rabbit entrails on the ground. It chewed and swallowed, and the entrails hung from its mouth.

Casy sat on the ground beside the fire, feeding it broken pieces of board, pushing the long boards in as the flame ate off their ends. The evening bats flashed into the firelight and out again. The cat crouched back and licked its lips and washed its face and whiskers.

Joad held up his rabbit-laden wire between his two hands and walked to the fire. 'Here, take one end, Muley. Wrap your end around that stake. That's good, now! Let's tighten her up. We ought to wait till the fire's burned down, but I can't wait.' He made the wire taut, then found a stick and slipped the pieces of meat along the wire until they were over the fire. And the flames licked up around the meat and hardened and glazed the surfaces. Joad sat down by the fire, but with his stick he moved and turned the rabbit so that it would not become sealed to the wire. 'This here is a party,' he said. 'Salt,

Muley's got, an' water an' rabbits. I wish he got a pot of hominy in his pocket. That's all I wish.'

Muley said over the fire: 'You fellas'd think I'm touched, the way I live.'

'Touched, nothin',' said Joad. 'If you're touched, I wisht ever'body was touched.'

Muley continued: 'Well, sir, it's a funny thing. Somepin went an' happened to me when they tol' me I had to get off the place. Fust I was gonna go in an' kill a whole flock a people. Then all my folks all went away out west. An' I got wanderin' aroun'. Jus' walkin' aroun'. Never went far. Slep' where I was. I was gonna sleep here to-night. That's why I come. I'd tell myself: "I'm lookin' after things so when all the folks come back it'll be all right." But I knowed that wa'n't true. There ain't nothin' to look after. The folks ain't never comin' back. I'm jus' wanderin' aroun' like a damn ol' graveyard ghos'.'

'Fella gets use' to a place, it's hard to go,' said Casy. 'Fella gets use' to a way a thinkin', it's hard to leave. I ain't a preacher no more, but all the time I find I'm prayin', not even thinkin' what I'm doin'.'

Joad turned the pieces of meat over on the wire. The juice was dripping now, and every drop, as it fell in the fire, shot up a spurt of flame. The smooth surface of the meat was crinkling up and turning a faint brown. 'Smell her,' said Joad. 'Jesus, look down an' jus' smell her!'

Muley went on: 'Like a damn ol' graveyard ghos'. I been goin' aroun' the places where stuff happened. Like there's a place over by our forty; in a gully they's a bush. Fust time I ever laid with a girl was there. Me fourteen an' stampin' an' jerkin' an' snortin' like a buck deer, randy as a billygoat. So I went there an' I laid down on the groun' an' I seen it all happen again. An' there's the place down by the barn where Pa got gored to death by a bull. An' his blood is right in that groun', right now. Mus' be. Nobody never washed it out. An' I put my han' on that groun' where my own pa's blood is part of it.' He paused uneasily. 'You fellas think I'm touched?'

Joad turned the meat, and his eyes were inward. Casy, feet drawn up, stared into the fire. Fifteen feet back from the men the fed cat was sitting, the long grey tail wrapped neatly around the front feet. A big owl shrieked as it went overhead, and the firelight showed its white underside and the spread of its wings.

'No,' said Casy. 'You're lonely–but you ain't touched.'

Muley's tight little face was rigid. 'I put my han' right on the groun' where the blood is still. An' I seen my pa with a hole through his ches', an' I felt him shiver up against me like he done, an' I seen him kind of settle back an' reach with his han's an' his feet. An' I seen his eyes all milky with hurt, an' then he was still an' his eyes so clear–lookin' up. An' me a little kid settin' there, not cryin' nor nothin', jus' settin' there.' He shook his head sharply. Joad turned the meat over and over. 'An' I went in the room where Joe was born. Bed wasn't there, but it was the room. An' all them things is true, an' they're right in the place they happened. Joe come to life right there. He give a big ol' gasp an' then he let out a squawk you could hear a mile, an' his granma standin' there says: "That's a daisy, that's a daisy," over an' over. An' her so proud she bust three cups that night.'

Joad cleared his throat. 'Think we better eat her now.'

'Let her get good an' done, good an' brown, awmost black,' said Muley irritably. 'I wanta talk. I ain't talked to nobody. If I'm touched, I'm touched, an' that's the end of it. Like a ol' graveyard ghos' goin' to neighbours' houses in the night. Peters', Jacobs', Rance's, Joad's; an' the houses all dark, standin' like miser'ble ratty boxes, but they was good parties an' dancin'. An' there was meetin's and shoutin' glory. They was weddin's, all in them houses. An' then I'd want to go in town an' kill folks. 'Cause what'd they take when they tractored the folks off the lan'? What'd they get so their "margin a profit" was safe? They got Pa dyin' on the groun', an' Joe yellin' his first breath, an' me jerkin' like a billygoat under a bush in the night. What'd they get? God knows the lan' ain't no good. Nobody been able to make a crop for years. But them sons-a-bitches at their desks, they jus' chopped folks in two for their margin of profit. They jus' cut 'em in two. Place where folks live is them folks. They ain't whole, out lonely on the road in a piled-up car. They ain't alive no more. Them sons-a-bitches killed 'em.' And he was silent, his thin lips still moving, his chest still panting. He sat and looked down at his hands in the firelight. 'I–I ain't talked to nobody for a long time,' he apologized softly. 'I been sneakin' aroun' like a ol' graveyard ghos'.'

Casy pushed the long boards into the fire and the flames licked up around them and leaped up toward the meat again. The house cracked loudly as the cooler night air contracted the wood. Casy said quietly: 'I gotta see them folks that's gone out on the road. I got a feelin' I got to see them. They gonna need help no preachin' can give 'em. Hope of heaven when their lives ain't lived? Holy Sperit when their own sperit is downcast an' sad? They gonna need help. They got to live before they can afford to die.'

Joad cried nervously: 'Jesus Christ, le's eat this meat 'fore it's smaller'n a cooked mouse! Look at her. Smell her.' He leaped to his feet and slid the pieces of meat along the wire until they were clear of the fire. He took Muley's knife and sawed through a piece of meat until it was free of the wire. 'Here's for the preacher,' he said.

'I tol' you I ain't no preacher.'

'Well, here's for the man, then.' He cut off another piece. 'Here, Muley, if you ain't too goddamn upset to eat. This here's jack-rabbit. Tougher'n a bull-bitch.' He sat back and clamped his long teeth on the meat and tore out a great bite and chewed it. 'Jesus Christ! Hear her crunch!' And he tore out another bite ravenously.

Muley still sat regarding his meat. 'Maybe I oughtn' to a talked like that,' he said. 'Fella should maybe keep stuff like that in his head.'

Casy looked over, his mouth full of rabbit. He chewed, and his muscled throat convulsed in swallowing. 'Yes, you should talk,' he said. 'Sometimes a sad man can talk the sadness right out through his mouth. Sometimes a killin' man can talk the murder right out of his mouth an' not do no murder. You done right. Don't you kill nobody if you can help it.' And he bit out another hunk of rabbit. Joad tossed the bones in the fire and jumped up and cut more off the wire. Muley was eating slowly now, and his nervous little eyes went from one to the other of his companions. Joad ate scowling like an animal, and a ring of grease formed around his mouth.

For a long time Muley looked at him, almost timidly. He put down the hand that held the meat. 'Tommy,' he said.

Joad looked up and did not stop gnawing the meat. 'Yeah?' he said, around a mouthful.

'Tommy, you ain't mad with me talkin' about killin' people? You ain't huffy, Tom?"

'No,' said Tom. 'I ain't huffy. It's jus' somepin that happened.'

'Ever'body knowed it was no fault of yours,' said Muley. 'Ol man Turnbull said he was gonna get you when ya come out. Says nobody can kill one a his boys. All the folks hereabouts talked him outa it, though.'

'We was drunk,' Joad said softly. 'Drunk at a dance. I don' know how she started. An' then I felt that knife go in me, an' that sobered me up. Fust thing I see is Herb comin' for me again with his knife. They was this here shovel leanin' against the schoolhouse, so I grabbed it an' smacked 'im over the head. I never had nothing against Herb. He was a nice fella. Come a-bullin' after my sister Rosasharn when he was a little fella. No, I liked Herb.'

'Well, ever'body tol' his pa that, an' finally cooled 'im down. Somebody says they's Hatfield blood on his mother's side in ol' Turnbull, an' he got to live up to it. I don't know about that. Him an' his folks went on to California six months ago.'

Joad took the last of the rabbit from the wire and passed it around. He settled back and ate more slowly now, chewed evenly, and wiped the grease from his mouth with his sleeve. And his eyes, dark and half-closed, brooded as he looked into the dying fire. 'Ever'body's goin' west,' he said. 'I got me a parole to keep. Can't leave the state.'

'Parole?' Muley asked. 'I heard about them. How do they work?'

'Well, I got out early, three years early. They's stuff I gotta do, or they send me back in. Got to report ever' so often.'

'How they treat ya there in McAlester? My woman's cousin was in McAlester an' they give him hell.'

'It ain't so bad,' said Joad. 'Like ever'place else. They give ya hell if ya raise hell. You get along O.K. 'less some guard gets it in for ya. Then you catch plenty hell. I got along O.K. Minded my own business, like any guy would. I learned to write nice as hell. Birds an' stuff like that, too; not just a word writin'. My ol' man'll be sore when he sees me whip out a bird in one stroke. Pa's gonna be mad when he sees me do that. He don't like no fancy stuff like that. He don't even like word writin'. Kinda scares 'im, I guess. Ever' time Pa seen writin', somebody took somepin away from 'im.'

'They didn't give you no beatin's or nothin' like that?'

'No, I jus' tended my own affairs. 'Course you get goddamn good an' sick a-doin' the same thing day after day for four years. If you done somepin you was ashamed of, you might think about that. But, hell, if I seen Herb Turnbull comin' for me with a knife right now, I'd squash him down with a shovel again.'

'Anybody would,' said Muley. The preacher stared into the fire, and his high forehead was white in the settling dark. The flash of little flames picked out the cords of his neck. His hands, clasped about his knees, were busy pulling knuckles.

Joad threw the last bones into the fire and licked his fingers and then wiped them on his pants. He stood up and brought the bottle of water from the porch, took a sparing drink, and passed the bottle before he sat down again. He went on: 'The thing that give me the mos' trouble was, it didn't make no sense. You don't look for no sense when lightnin' kills a cow, or it comes up a flood. That's jus' the way things is. But when a bunch of men take an' lock you up four years, it ought to have some meaning. Men is supposed to think things out. Here they put me in, an' keep me an' feed me four years. That ought to either make me so I won't do her again or else punish me so I'll be afraid to do her again'–he paused–'but if Herb or anybody else come for me, I'd do her again. Do her before I could figure her out. Specially if I was drunk. That sort of senselessness kind a worries a man.'

Muley observed: 'Judge says he give you a light sentence 'cause it wasn't all your fault.'

Joad said: 'They's a guy in McAlester–lifer. He studies all the time. He's sec'etary of the warden–writes the warden's letters an' stuff like that. Well, he's one hell of a bright guy an' reads law an' all stuff like that. Well, I talked to him one time about her, 'cause he reads so much stuff. An' he says it don't do no good to read books. Says he's read ever'thing about prisons now, an' in the old times; an' he says she makes less sense to him now than she did before he starts readin'. He says it's a thing that started way to hell an' gone back, an' nobody seems to be able to stop her, an' nobody got sense enough to change her. He says for God's sake don't read about her because he says for one thing you'll jus' get messed up worse, an' for another you won't have no respect for the guys that work the gover'ments.'

'I ain't got a hell of a lot of respec' for 'em now,' said Muley. 'On'y kind a gover'ment we got that leans on us fellas is the "safe margin a profit". There's one thing that got me stumped, an' that's Willy Feeley–drivin' that cat', an' gonna be a straw boss on lan' his own folks used to farm. That worries me. I can see how a fella might come from some other place an' not know no better, but Willy belongs. Worried me so I went up to 'im and ast 'im. Right off he got mad. "I got two little kids," he says. "I got a wife an' my wife' mother. Them people got to eat." Gets madder'n hell. "Fust an' on'y thing I got to think about is my own folk," he says. "What happens to other folks is their lookout," he says. Seems like he's 'shamed, so he gets mad.'

Jim Casy had been staring at the dying fire, and his eyes had grown wider and his neck muscles stood higher. Suddenly he cried: 'I got her! If ever a man got a dose of the sperit, I got her! Got her all of a flash!' He jumped to his feet and paced back and forth, his head swinging. 'Had a tent one time. Drawed as much as five hundred people ever' night. That's before either you fellas seen me.' He stopped and faced them. 'Ever notice I never took no collections when I was preachin' out here to folks–in barns an' in the open?'

'By God, you never,' said Muley. 'People around here got so use' to not givin' you money they got to bein' a little mad when some other preacher come along an' passed the hat. Yes, sir!'

'I took somepin to eat,' said Casy. 'I took a pair of pants when mine was wore out, an' a ol' pair a shoes when I was walkin' through to the groun', but it wasn't like when I had the tent. Some days there I'd take in ten or twenty dollars. Wasn't happy that-a-way, so I give her up, an' for a time I was happy. I think I got her now. I don' know if I can say her. I guess I won't try to say her–but maybe there's a place for a preacher. Maybe I can preach again. Folks out lonely on the road, folks with no lan', no home to go to. They got to have some kind of home. Maybe–' He stood over the fire. The hundred muscles of his neck stood out in high relief, and the firelight went deep into his eyes and ignited red embers. He stood and looked at the fire, his face tense as though he were listening, and the hands that had been active to pick, to handle, to throw ideas, grew quiet, and in a moment crept into his pockets. The bats flittered in and out of the dull firelight, and the soft watery burble of a night hawk came from across the fields.

Tom reached quietly into his pocket and brought out his tobacco, and he rolled a cigarette slowly and looked over it at the coals while he worked. He ignored the whole speech of the preacher, as though it were some private thing that should not be inspected. He said: 'Night after night in my bunk I figgered how she'd be when I come home again. I figgered maybe Grampa or Granma'd be dead, an' maybe there'd be some new kids. Maybe Pa'd not be so tough. Maybe Ma'd set back a little an' let Rosasharn do the work. I knowed it wouldn't be the same as it was. Well, we'll sleep here I guess, an' come daylight we'll get on to Uncle John's. Leastwise I will. You think you're comin' along, Casy?'

The preacher still stood looking into the coals. He said slowly: 'Yeah, I'm goin' with you. An' when your folks start out on the road I'm goin' with them. An' where folks are on the road, I'm gonna be with them.'

'You're welcome,' said Joad. 'Ma always favoured you. Said you was a preacher to trust. Rosasharn wasn't growed up then.' He turned his head. 'Muley, you gonna walk on over with us?' Muley was looking toward the road over which they had come. 'Think you'll come along, Muley?' Joad repeated.

'Huh? No. I don't go no place, an' I don't leave no place. See that glow over there, jerkin' up an' down? That prob'ly the super'ntendent of this stretch of cotton. Somebody maybe seen our fire.'

Tom looked. The glow of light was nearing over the hill. 'We ain't doin' no harm,' he said. 'We'll jus' set here. We ain't doin' nothin'.'

Muley cackled. 'Yeah! We're doin' somepin jus' bein' here. We're trespassin'. We can't stay. They been tryin' to catch me for two months. Now you look. If that's a car comin' we go out in the cotton an' lay down. Don't have to go far. Then by God let 'em try to fin' us! Have to look up an' down ever' row. Jus' keep your head down.'

Joad demanded: 'What's come over you, Muley? You wasn't never no run-an'-hide fella. You was mean.'

Muley watched the approaching lights. 'Yeah!' he said. 'I was mean like a wolf. Now I'm mean like a weasel. When you're huntin' somepin you're a hunter, an' you're strong. Can't nobody beat a hunter. But when you get hunted–that's different. Somepin happens to you. You ain't strong: maybe you're fierce, but you ain't strong. I been hunted now for a long time. I ain't a hunter no more. I'd maybe shoot a fella in the dark, but I don't maul nobody with a fence stake no more. It don't do no good to fool you or me. That's how it is.'

'Well, you go out an' hide,' said Joad. 'Leave me an' Casy tell these bastards a few things.' The beam of light was closer now, and it bounced into the sky and then disappeared, and then bounced up again. All three men watched.

Muley said: 'There's one more thing about bein' hunted. You get to thinkin' about all the dangerous things. If you're huntin' you don't think about 'em, an' you ain't scared. Like you says to me, if you get in any trouble they'll sen' you back to McAlester to finish your time.'

'That's right,' said Joad. 'That's what they tol' me, but settin' here restin' or sleepin' on the ground–that ain't gettin' in no trouble. That ain't doin' nothin' wrong. That ain't like gettin' drunk or raisin' hell.'

Muley laughed. 'You'll see. You jus' set here, an' the car'll come. Maybe it's Willy Feeley, an' Willy's a deputy sheriff now. "What you doin' trespassin' here?" Willy says. Well, you always did know Willy was full a crap, so you says, "What's it to you?" Willy gets mad an' says: "You get off or I'll take you in." An' you ain't gonna let no Feeley push you aroun' 'cause he's mad an' scared. He's made a bluff an' he's got to go on with it, an' here's you gettin' tough an' you got to go through–oh, hell, it's a lot easier to lay out in the cotton an' let 'em look. It's more fun, too, 'cause they're mad an' can't do nothin', an' you're out there a-laughin' at 'em. But you jus' talk to Willy or any boss, an' you slug hell out of 'em an' they'll take you in an' run you back to McAlester for three years.'

'You're talkin' sense,' said Joad. 'Ever' word you said is sense. But, Jesus, I hate to get pushed around! I'd lots rather take a sock at Willy.'

'He's got a gun,' said Muley. 'He'll use it 'cause he's a deputy. Then he either got to kill you or you got to get his gun away an' kill him. Come on, Tommy. You can easy tell yourself you're foolin' them lyin' out like that. An' it all just amounts to what you tell yourself.' The strong lights angled up into the sky now, and the even drone of a motor could be heard. 'Come on, Tommy. Don't have to go far, jus' fourteen-fifteen rows over, an' we can watch what they do.'

Tom got to his feet. 'By God, you're right!' he said. 'I ain't got a thing in the worl' to win, no matter how it comes out.'

'Come on, then, over this way.' Muley moved around the house and out into the cotton field about fifty yards. 'This is good,' he said. 'Now lay down. You on'y got to pull your head down if they start the spotlight goin'. It's kinda fun.' The three men stretched out at full length and propped themselves on their elbows. Muley sprang up and ran toward the house, and in a few moments he came back and threw a bundle of coats and shoes down. 'They'd of taken 'em along just to get even,' he said. The lights topped the rise and bore down on the house.

Joad asked: 'Won't they come out here with flashlights an' look aroun' for us? I wisht I had a stick.'

Muley giggled. 'No, they won't. I tol' you I'm mean like a weasel. Willy done that one night an' I clipped 'im from behint with a fence stake. Knocked him colder'n a wedge. He tol' later how five guys come at him.'

The car drew up to the house and a spotlight snapped on. 'Duck,' said Muley. The bar of cold white light swung over their heads and criss-crossed the field. The hiding men could not see any movement, but they heard a car door slam and they heard voices. 'Scairt to get in the light,' Muley whispered. 'Once-twice I've took a shot at the headlights. That keeps Will careful. He got somebody with 'im to-night.' They heard footsteps on wood, and then from inside the house they saw the glow of a flashlight. 'Shall I shoot through the house?' Muley whispered. 'They couldn't see where it come from. Give 'em somepin to think about.'

'Sure, go ahead,' said Joad.

'Don't do it,' Casy whispered. 'It won't do no good. Jus' a waste. We got to get thinkin' about doin' stuff that means somepin.'

A scratching sound came from near the house. 'Puttin' out the fire,' Muley whispered. 'Kickin' dust over it.' The car doors slammed, the headlights swung around and faced the road again. 'Now duck!' said Muley. They dropped their heads and the spotlight swept over them and crossed and recrossed the cotton field, and then the car started and slipped away and topped the rise and disappeared.

Muley sat up. 'Willy always tries that las' flash. He done it so often I can time 'im. An' he still thinks it's cute.'

Casy said: 'Maybe they left some fellas at the house. They'd catch us when we come back.'

'Maybe. You fellas wait here. I know this game.' He walked quietly away, and only a slight crunching of clods could be heard from his passage. The two waiting men tried to hear him, but he had gone. In a moment he called from the house: 'They didn't leave anybody. Come on back.' Casy and Joad struggled up and walked back toward the black bulk of the house. Muley met them near the smoking dust pile which had been their fire. 'I didn't think they'd leave anybody,' he said proudly. 'Me knockin' Willy over an' takin' a shot at the lights once-twice keeps 'em careful. They ain't sure who it is, an' I ain't gonna let 'em catch me. I don't sleep near no house. If you fellas wanta come along, I'll show you where to sleep, where there ain't nobody gonna stumble over ya.'

'Lead off,' said Joad. 'We'll folla you. I never thought I'd be hidin' out on my old man's place.'

Muley set off across the fields, and Joad and Casy followed him. They kicked the cotton plants as they went. 'You'll be hidin' from lots of stuff,' said Muley. They marched in single file across the fields. They came to a water-cut and slid easily down to the bottom of it.

'By God, I bet I know,' cried Joad. 'Is it a cave in the bank?'

'That's right. How'd you know?'

'I dug her,' said Joad. 'Me an' my brother. Noah dug her. Lookin' for gold we says we was, but we was jus' diggin' caves like kids always does.' The walls of the water-cut were above their heads now. 'Ought to be pretty close,' said Joad. 'Seems to me I remember her pretty close.'

Muley said: 'I've covered her with bresh. Nobody couldn't find her.' The bottom of the gulch levelled off, and the footing was sand.

Joad settled himself on the clean sand. 'I ain't gonna sleep in no cave,' he said. 'I'm gonna sleep right here.' He rolled his coat and put it under his head.

Muley pulled at the covering brush and crawled into his cave. 'I like it in here,' he called. 'I feel nobody can come at me.'

Jim Casy sat down on the sand beside Joad.

'Get some sleep,' said Joad. 'We'll start for Uncle John's at daybreak.'

'I ain't sleepin',' said Casy. 'I got too much to puzzle with.' He drew up his feet and clasped his legs. He threw back his head and looked at the sharp stars. Joad yawned and brought one hand back under his head. They were silent, and gradually the skittering life of the ground, of holes and burrows, of the bush, began again; the gophers moved, and the rabbits crept to green things, the mice scampered over clods, and the winged hunters moved soundlessly overhead.

7

In the towns, on the edges of the town, in fields, in vacant lots, the used-car yards, the wreckers' yards, the garages with blazoned signs–Used Cars, Good Used Cars. Cheap transportation, three trailers. '27 Ford, clean. Checked cars, guaranteed cars. Free radio. Car with 100 gallons of petrol free. Come in and look. Used Cars. No overhead.

A lot and a house large enough for a desk and chair and a blue book. Sheaf of contracts, dog-eared, held with paper clips, and a neat pile of unused contracts. Pen–keep it full, keep it working. A sale's been lost 'cause a pen didn't work.

Those sons-of-bitches over there ain't buying. Every yard gets 'em. They're lookers. Spend all their time looking. Don't want to buy no cars; take up your time. Don't give a damn for your time. Over there, them two people–no, with the kids. Get 'em in a car. Start 'em at two hundred and work down. They look good for one and a quarter. Get 'em rolling. Get 'em out in a jalopy. Sock it to 'em! They took our time.

Owners with rolled-up sleeves. Salesmen, neat, deadly, small intent eyes watching for weaknesses.

Watch the woman's face. If the woman likes it we can screw the old man. Start 'em on that Cad'. Then you can work 'em down to that '26 Buick. 'F you start on the Buick, they'll go for a Ford. Roll up your sleeves an' get to work. This ain't gonna last forever. Show 'em that Nash while I get the slow leak pumped up on that '25 Dodge. I'll give you a Hymie when I'm ready.

What you want is transportation, ain't it? No baloney for you. Sure the upholstery is shot. Seat cushions ain't turning no wheels over.

Cars lined up, noses forward, rusty noses, flat tires. Parked close together.

Like to get in to see that one? Sure, no trouble. I'll pull her out of the line.

Get 'em under obligation. Make 'em take up your time. Don't let 'em forget they're takin' your time. People are nice, mostly. They hate to put you out. Make 'em put you out, an' then sock it to 'em.

Cars lined up, Model T's, high and snotty, creaking wheel, worn bands. Buicks, Nashes, De Sotos.

Yes, sir. '22 Dodge. Best goddamn car Dodge ever made. Never wear out. Low compression. High compression got lots a sap for a while, but the metal ain't made that'll hold it for long. Plymouths, Rocknes, Stars.

Jesus, where'd that Apperson come from, the Ark? And a Chalmers and a Chandler–ain't made 'em for years. We ain't sellin' cars–rolling junk. Goddamn it, I got to get jalopies. I don't want nothing for more'n twenty-five, thirty bucks. Sell 'em for fifty, seventy-five. That's a good profit. Christ, what cut do you make on a new car? Get jalopies. I can sell 'em fast as I get 'em. Nothing over two hundred fifty. Jim, corral that old bastard on the sidewalk. Don't know his ass from a hole in the ground. Try him on that Apperson. Say, where is that Apperson? Sold? If we don't get some jalopies we got nothing to sell.

Flags, red and white, white and blue–all along the kerb. Used Cars. Good Used Cars.

To-day's bargain–up on the platform. Never sell it. Makes folks come in, though. If we sold that bargain at that price we'd hardly make a dime. Tell 'em it's jus' sold. Take out that yard battery before you make delivery. Put in that dumb cell. Christ, what they want for six bits? Roll up your sleeves–pitch in. This ain't gonna last. If I had enough jalopies I'd retire in six months.

Listen, Jim, I heard that Chevvy's rear end. Sounds like bustin' bottles. Squirt in a couple quarts of sawdust. Put some in the gears too. We got to move that lemon for thirty-five dollars. Bastard cheated me on that one. I offer ten an' he jerks me to fifteen, an' then the son-of-a-bitch took the tools out. God Almighty! I wisht I had five hundred jalopies. This ain't gonna last. He don't like the tires? Tell 'im they got ten thousand in 'em, knock off a buck an' a half.

Piles of rusty ruins against the fence, rows of wrecks in back, fenders, grease-black wrecks, blocks lying on the ground and a pig-weed growing up through the cylinders. Brake rods, exhausts, piled like snakes. Grease, gasoline.

See if you can't find a spark plug that ain't cracked. Christ, if I had fifty trailers at under a hundred I'd clean up. What the hell is he kickin' about? We sell 'em, but we don't push 'em home for him. That's good! Don't push 'em home. Get that one in the Monthly, I bet. You don't think he's a prospect? Well, kick 'im out. We got too much to do to bother with a guy that can't make up his mind. Take the right front tire off the Graham. Turn that mended side down. The rest looks swell. Got tread an' everything.

Sure! There's fifty thousan' in that ol' heap yet. Keep plenty oil in. So long. Good luck.

Lookin' for a car? What did you have in mind? See anything attracts you? I'm dry. How about a little snort a good stuff? Come on, while your wife's lookin' at that La Salle. You don't want no La Salle. Bearings shot. Uses too much oil. Got a Lincoln '24. There's a car. Run forever. Make her into a truck.

Hot sun on rusted metal. Oil on the ground. People are wandering in, bewildered, needing a car.

Wipe your feet. Don't lean on that car, it's dirty. How do you buy a car? What does it cost? Watch the children now. I wonder how much for this one? We'll ask. It don't cost money to ask. We can ask, can't we? Can't pay a nickel over seventy-five, or there won't be enough to get to California.

God, if I could only get a hundred jalopies. I don't care if they run or not.

Tires used, bruised tires, stacked in tall cylinders; tubes, red, grey, hanging like sausages.

Tire patch? Radiator cleaner? Spark intensifier? Drop this little pill in your petrol tank and get ten extra miles to the gallon. Just paint it on–you got a new surface for fifty cents. Wipers, fan belts, gaskets? Maybe it's the valve. Get a new valve stem. What can you lose for a nickel?

All right, Joe. You soften 'em up an' shoot 'em in here. I'll close 'em, I'll deal 'em or I'll kill 'em. Don't send in no bums. I want deals.

Yes, sir, step in. You got a buy there. Yes, sir! At eighty bucks you got a buy.

I can't go no higher than fifty. The fella outside says fifty.

Fifty. Fifty? He's nuts. Paid seventy-eight fifty for that little number. Joe, you crazy fool, you tryin' to bust us? Have to can that guy. I might take sixty. Now look here, mister, I ain't got all day. I'm a business man but I ain't out to stick nobody. Got anything to trade?

Got a pair of mules I'll trade.

Mules! Hey, Joe, hear this? This guy wants to trade mules. Didn't nobody tell you this is the machine age? They don't use mules for nothing but glue no more.

Fine big mules–five and seven years old. Maybe we better look around.

Look around! You come in when we're busy, an' take up our time an' then walk out! Joe, did you know you was talkin' to pikers?

I ain't a piker. I got to get a car. We're goin' to California. I got to get a car.

Well, I'm a sucker. Joe says I'm a sucker. Says if I don't quit givin' my shirt away I'll starve to death. Tell you what I'll do–I can get five bucks apiece for them mules for dog feed.

I wouldn't want them to go for dog feed.

Well, maybe I can get ten or seven maybe. Tell you what we'll do. We'll take your mules for twenty. Wagon goes with 'em, don't it? An' you put up fifty, an' you can sign a contract to send the rest at ten dollars a month.

But you said eighty.

Didn't you never hear about carrying charges and insurance? That just boosts her a little. You'll get her all paid up in four-five months. Sign your name right here. We'll take care of ever'thing.

Well, I don't know.

Now, look here. I'm givin' you my shirt, an' you took all this time. I might a made three sales while I been talkin' to you. I'm disgusted. Yeah, sign right here. All right, sir. Joe, fill up the tank for this gentleman. We'll give him petrol.

Jesus, Joe, that was a hot one! What'd we give for that jalopy? Thirty bucks–thirty-five wasn't it? I got that team, an' if I can't get seventy-five for that team, I ain't a business man. An' I got fifty cash an' a contract for forty more. Oh, I know they're not all honest, but it'll surprise you how many kick through with the rest. One guy come through with a hundred two years after I wrote him off. I bet you this guy sends the money. Christ, if I could only get five hundred jalopies! Roll up your sleeves, Joe. Go out an' soften 'em an' send 'em in to me. You get twenty on that last deal. You ain't doing bad.

Limp flags in the afternoon sun. To-day's Bargain. '29 Ford pickup, runs good.

What do you want for fifty bucks–a Zephyr?

Horsehair curling out of seat cushions, fenders battered and hammered back. Bumpers torn loose and hanging. Fancy Ford roadster with little coloured lights at fender guide, at radiator cap, and three behind. Mud aprons, and a big die on the gear-shift lever. Pretty girl on tire cover, painted in colour and named Cora. Afternoon sun on the dusty windshields.

Christ, I ain't had time to go out an' eat! Joe, send a kid for a hamburger.

Spattering roar of ancient engines.

There's a dumb bunny lookin' at that Chrysler. Find out if he got any jack in his jeans. Some of these farm boys is sneaky. Soften 'em up an' roll 'em in to me, Joe. You're doin' good.

Sure, we sold it. Guarantee? We guarantee it to be an automobile. We didn't guarantee to wet-nurse it. Now listen here, you–you brought a car, an' now you're squawkin'. I don't give a damn if you don't make payments. We ain't got your paper. We turn that over to the finance company. They'll get after you, not us. We don't hold no paper. Yeah? Well you jus' get tough an' I'll call a cop. No, we did not switch the tires. Run 'im outa here, Joe. He bought a car, an' now he ain't satisfied. How'd you think if I bought a steak an' et half an' try to bring it back? We're runnin' a business, not a charity ward. Can ya imagine that guy, Joe? Say–looka there! Got a Elk's tooth! Run over there. Let 'em glance over that '36 Pontiac. Yeah.

Square noses, round noses, rusty noses, shovel noses, and the long curves of streamlines, and the flat surfaces before streamlining. Bargains To-day. Old monsters with deep upholstery–you can cut her into a truck easy. Two-wheel trailers, axles rusty in the hard afternoon sun. Used Cars. Good Used Cars. Clean, runs good. Don't pump oil.

Christ, look at 'er! Somebody took nice care of 'er.

Cadillacs, La Salles, Buicks, Plymouths, Packards, Chevvies, Fords, Pontiacs. Row on row, headlights glinting in the afternoon sun. Good Used Cars.

Soften 'em up, Joe. Jesus, I wisht I had a thousand jalopies! Get 'em ready to deal, an' I'll close 'em.

Goin' to California? Here's jus' what you need. Looks shot, but they's thousan's of miles in her.

Lined up side by side. Good Used Cars. Bargains. Clean, runs good.

8

The sky greyed among the stars, and the pale, late quartermoon was insubstantial and thin. Tom Joad and the preacher walked quickly along a road that was only wheel tracks and beaten caterpillar tracks through a cotton field. Only the unbalanced sky showed the approach of dawn, no horizon to the west, and a line to the east. The two men walked in silence and smelled the dust their feet kicked into the air.

'I hope you're dead sure of the way,' Jim Casy said. 'I'd hate to have the dawn come and us be way to hell an' gone somewhere.' The cotton field scurried with waking life, the quick flutter of morning birds feeding on the ground, the scamper over the clods of disturbed rabbits. The quiet thudding of the men's feet in the dust, the squeak of crushed clods under their shoes, sounded against the secret noises of the dawn.

Tom said: 'I could shut my eyes an' walk right there. On'y way I can go wrong is think about her. Jus' forget about her, an' I'll go right there. Hell, man, I was born right aroun' in here. I run aroun' here when I was a kid. They's a tree over there–look, you can jus' make it out. Well, once my old man hung up a dead coyote in that tree. Hung there till it was all sort of melted, an' then dropped off. Dried up, like. Jesus, I hope Ma's cookin' somepin. My belly's caved.'

'Me too,' said Casy. 'Like a little eatin' tobacca? Keeps ya from gettin' too hungry. Been better if we didn' start so damn early. Better if it was light.' He paused to gnaw off a piece of plug. 'I was sleepin' nice.'

'That crazy Muley done it,' said Tom. 'He got me clear jumpy. Wakes me up an' says: "'Bye, Tom. I'm goin' on. I got places to go." An' he says: "Better get goin' too, so's you'll be offa this lan' when the light comes." He's gettin' screwy as a gopher, livin' like he does. You'd think Injuns was after him. Think he's nuts?'

'Well, I dunno. You seen that car come las' night when we had a little fire. You seen how the house was smashed. They's somepin purty mean goin' on. 'Course Muley's crazy, all right. Creepin' aroun' like a coyote; that's boun' to make him crazy. He'll kill somebody purty soon an' they'll run him down with dogs. I can see it like a prophecy. He'll get worse an' worse. Wouldn' come along with us, you say?'

'No,' said Joad. 'I think he's scared to see people now. Wonder he come up to us. We'll be at Uncle John's place by sunrise.' They walked along in silence for a time, and the late owls flew over toward the barns, the hollow trees, the tank houses, where they hid from daylight. The eastern sky grew fairer and it was possible to see the cotton plants and the greying earth. 'Damn' if I know how they're all sleepin' at Uncle John's. He on'y got one room an' a cookin' leanto, an' a little bit of a barn. Must be a mob there now.'

The preacher said: 'I don't recollect that John had a fambly. Just a lone man, ain't he? I don't recollect much about him.'

'Lonest goddamn man in the world,' said Joad. 'Crazy kind of son-of-a-bitch, too, somepin like Muley, on'y worse in some ways. Might see 'im anywheres–at Shawnee, drunk, or visitin' a widow twenty miles away, or workin' his place with a lantern. Crazy. Ever'body thought he wouldn't live long. A lone man like that don't live long. But Uncle John's older'n Pa. Jus' gets stringier an' meaner ever' year. Meaner'n Grampa.'

'Look a the light comin',' said the preacher. 'Silvery-like. Didn' John never have no fambly?'

'Well, yes, he did, an' that'll show you the kind a fella he is–set in his ways. Pa tells about it. Uncle John, he had a young wife. Married four months. She was in a family way, too, an' one night she gets a pain in her stomick, an' she says: "You better go for a doctor." Well, John, he's settin' there, an' he says: "You just got a stomick-ache. You et too much. Take a dose a pain-killer. You crowd up ya stomick an' ya get a stomick-ache," he says. Nex' noon she's outa her head, an' she dies at about four in the afternoon.'

'What was it?' Casy asked. 'Poisoned from somepin she et?'

'No, somepin jus' bust in her. Ap–appendick or somepin. Well, Uncle John, he's always been a easy-goin' fella, an' he takes it hard. Takes it for a sin. For a long time he won't have nothin' to say to nobody. Just walks aroun' like he don't see nothin', an' he prays some. Took 'im two years to come out of it, an' then he ain't the same. Sort of wild. Made a damn nuisance of hisself. Ever' time one of us kids got worms or a gut-ache Uncle John brings a doctor out. Pa finally tol' him he got to stop. Kids all the time gettin' a gut-ache. He figures it's his fault his woman died. Funny fella. He's all the time makin' it up to somebody–givin' kids stuff, droppin' a sack of meal on somebody's porch. Give away about ever'thing he got, an' still he ain't very happy. Gets walkin' around alone at night sometimes. He's a good farmer, though. Keeps his lan' nice.'

'Poor fella,' said the preacher. 'Poor lonely fella. Did he go to church much when his woman died?'

'No, he didn'. Never wanted to get close to folks. Wanted to be off alone. I never seen a kid that wasn't crazy about him. He'd come to our house in the night sometimes, an' we knowed he come 'cause jus' as sure as he come there'd be a pack a gum in the bed right beside ever' one of us. We thought he was Jesus Christ Awmighty.'

The preacher walked along, head down. He didn't answer. And the light of the coming morning made his forehead seem to shine, and his hands, swinging beside him, flicked into the light and out again.

Tom was silent too, as though he had said too intimate a thing and was ashamed. He quickened his pace and the preacher kept step. They could see a little into grey distance ahead now. A snake wriggled slowly from the cotton rows into the road. Tom stopped short of it and peered. 'Gopher snake,' he said. 'Let him go.' They walked around the snake and went on their way. A little colour came into the eastern sky, and almost immediately the lonely dawn light crept over the land. Green appeared on the cotton plants and the earth was grey-brown. The faces of the men lost their greyish shine. Joad's face seemed to darken with the growing light. 'This is the good time,' Joad said softly. 'When I was a kid I used to get up an' walk around by myself when it was like this. What's that ahead?'

A committee of dogs had met in the road, in honour of a bitch. Five males, shepherd mongrels, collie mongrels, dogs whose breeds had been blurred by a freedom of social life, were engaged in complimenting the bitch. For each dog sniffed daintily and then stalked to a cotton plant on stiff legs, raised a hind foot ceremoniously and wetted, then went back to smell. Joad and the preacher stopped to watch, and suddenly Joad laughed joyously. 'By God!' he said. 'By God!' Now all dogs met and hackles rose, and they all growled and stood stiffly, each waiting for the others to start a fight. One dog mounted and, now that it was accomplished, the others gave way and watched with interest, and their tongues were out, and their tongues dripped. The two men walked on. 'By God!' Joad said. 'I think that up-dog is our Flash. I thought he'd be dead. Come, Flash!' He laughed again. 'What the hell, if somebody called me, I wouldn't hear him neither. 'Minds me of a story they tell about Willy Feeley when he was a young fella. Willy was bashful, awful bashful. Well, one day he takes a heifer over to Graves' bull. Ever'body was out but Elsie Graves, and Elsie wasn't bashful at all. Willy, he stood there turnin' red an' he couldn't even talk. Elsie says: "I know what you come for; the bull's out in back a the barn." Well, they took the heifer out there an' Willy an' Elsie sat on the fence to watch. Purty soon Willy got feelin' purty fly. Elsie looks over an' says, like she don't know: "What's a matter, Willy?" Willy's so randy he can't hardly set still. "By God," he says, "by God, I wisht I was a-doin' that!" Elsie says: "Why not, Willy? It's your heifer."

The preacher laughed softly. 'You know,' he said, 'it's a nice thing not bein' a preacher no more. Nobody use' ta tell stories when I was there, or if they did I couldn' laugh. An' I couldn' cuss. Now I cuss all I want, any time I want, an' it does a fella good to cuss if he wants to.'

A redness grew up out of the eastern horizon, and on the ground birds began to chirp, sharply. 'Look!' said Joad. 'Right ahead. That's Uncle John's tank. Can't see the win'mill, but there's his tank. See it against the sky?' He speeded his walk. 'I wonder if all the folks are there.' The hulk of the tank stood above a rise. Joad, hurrying, raised a cloud of dust about his knees. 'I wonder if Ma–' They saw the tank legs now, and the house, a square little box, unpainted and bare, and the barn, low-roofed and huddled. Smoke was rising from the tin chimney of the house. In the yard was a litter, piled furniture, the blades and motor of the windmill, bedsteads, chairs, tables. 'Holy Christ, they're fixin' to go!' Joad said. A truck stood in the yard, a truck with high sides, but a strange truck, for while the front of it was a sedan, the top had been cut off in the middle and the truck bed fitted on. And as they drew near, the men could hear pounding from the yard, and as the rim of the blinding sun came up over the horizon, it fell on the truck, and they saw a man and the flash of his hammer as it rose and fell. And the sun flashed on the windows of the house. The weathered boards were bright. Two red chickens on the ground flamed with reflected light.

'Don't yell,' said Tom. 'Let's creep up on 'em, like,' and he walked so fast that the dust rose as high as his waist. And then he came to the edge of the cotton field. Now they were in the yard proper, earth beaten hard, shiny hard, and a few dusty crawling weeds on the ground. And Joad slowed as though he feared to go on. The preacher, watching him, slowed to match his step. Tom sauntered forward, sidled embarrassedly toward the truck. It was a Hudson

Super-Six sedan, and the top had been ripped in two with a cold chisel. Old Tom Joad stood in the truck bed and he was nailing on the top rails of the truck sides. His grizzled, bearded face was low over his work, and a bunch of sixpenny nails stuck out of his mouth. He set a nail and his hammer thundered it in. From the house came the clash of a lid on the stove and the wail of a child. Joad sidled up to the truck bed and leaned against it. And his father looked at him and did not see him. His father set another nail and drove it in. A flock of pigeons started from the deck of the tank house and flew around and settled again and strutted to the edge to look over; white pigeons and blue pigeons and greys, with iridescent wings.

Joad hooked his fingers over the lowest bar of the truck side. He looked up at the ageing, greying man on the truck. He wet his thick lips with his tongue, and he said softy: 'Pa.'

'What do you want?' old Tom mumbled around his mouthful of nails. He wore a black, dirty slouch hat and a blue work shirt over which was a buttonless vest; his jeans were held up by a wide harness-leather belt with a big square brass buckle, leather and metal polished from years of wearing; and his shoes were cracked and the soles swollen and boat-shaped from years of sun and wet and dust. The sleeves of his shirt were tight on his forearms, held down by the bulging powerful muscles. Stomach and hips were lean, and legs short, heavy, and strong. His face, squared by a bristling pepper-and-salt beard, was all drawn down to the forceful chin, a chin thrust out and built out by the stubble beard which was not so greyed on the chin, and gave weight and force to its thrust. Over old Tom's unwhiskered cheekbones the skin was as brown as meerschaum, and wrinkled in rays around his eye-corners from squinting. His eyes were brown, black-coffee brown, and he thrust his head forward when he looked at a thing, for his bright dark eyes were failing. His lips, from which the big nails protruded, were thin and red.

He held his hammer suspended in the air, about to drive a set nail, and he looked over the truck side at Tom, looked resentful at being interrupted. And then his chin drove forward and his eyes looked at Tom's face, and then gradually his brain became aware of what he saw. The hammer dropped slowly to his side, and with his left hand he took the nails from his mouth. And he said wonderingly, as though he told himself the fact: 'It's Tommy–' And then, still informing himself: 'It's Tommy come home.' His mouth opened again, and a look of fear came into his eyes. 'Tommy,' he said softly, 'you ain't busted out? You ain't got to hide?' He listened tensely.

'Naw,' said Tom. 'I'm paroled. I'm free. I got my papers.' He gripped the lower bars of the truck side and looked up.

Old Tom laid his hammer gently on the floor and put his nails in his pocket. He swung his leg over the side and dropped lithely to the ground, but once beside his son he seemed embarrassed and strange. 'Tommy,' he said, 'we are goin' to California. But we was gonna write you a letter an' tell you.' And he said, incredulously: 'But you're back. You can go with us. You can go!' The lid of a coffee pot slammed in the house. Old Tom looked over his shoulder. 'Le's supprise 'em,' he said, and his eyes shone with excitement. 'Your ma got a bad feelin' she ain't never gonna see you no more. She got that quiet look like when somebody died. Almost she don't want to go to California, fear she'll never see you no more.' A stove lid clashed in the house again. 'Le's supprise 'em,' old Tom repeated. 'Le's go in like you never been away. Le's jus' see what your ma says.' At last he touched Tom, but touched him on the shoulder, timidly, and instantly took his hand away. He looked at Jim Casy.

Tom said: 'You remember the preacher, Pa. He come along with me.'

'He been in prison, too?'

'No, I met 'im on the road. He been away.'

Pa shook hands gravely. 'You're welcome here, sir.'

Casy said: 'Glad to be here. It's a thing to see when a boy comes home. It's a thing to see.'

'Home,' Pa said.

'To his folks,' the preacher amended quickly. 'We stayed at the other place last night.'

Pa's chin thrust out, and he looked back down the road for a moment. Then he turned to Tom. 'How'll we do her?' he began excitedly. 'S'pose I go in an' say: "Here's some fellas want some breakfast," or how'd it be if you jus' come in an' stood there till she seen you? How'd that be?' His face was alive with excitement.

'Don't le's give her no shock,' said Tom. 'Don't le's scare her none.'

Two rangy shepherd dogs trotted up pleasantly, until they caught the scent of strangers, and then they backed cautiously away, watchful, their tails moving slowly and tentatively in the air, but their eyes and noses quick for animosity or danger. One of them, stretching his neck, edged forward, ready to run, and little by little he approached Tom's legs and sniffed loudly at them. Then he backed away and watched Pa for some kind of signal. The other pup was not so brave. He looked about for something that could honourably divert his attention, saw a red chicken go mincing by, and ran at it. There was the squawk of an outraged hen, a burst of red feathers, and the hen ran off, flapping stubby wings for speed. The pup looked proudly back at the men, and then flopped down in the dust and beat its tail contentedly on the ground.

'Come on,' said Pa, 'come on in now. She got to see you. I got to see her face when she sees you. Come on. She'll yell breakfast in a minute. I heard her slap the salt pork in the pan a good time ago.' He led the way across the fine-dusted ground. There was no porch on this house, just a step and then the door, a chopping block beside the door, its surface matted and soft from years of chopping. The graining in the sheathing wood was high, for the dust had cut down the softer wood. The smell of burning willow was in the air, and, as the three men neared the door, the smell of frying side-meat and the smell of high brown biscuits and the sharp smell of coffee rolling in the pot. Pa stepped up into the open doorway and stood there blocking it with his wide short body. He said: 'Ma, there's a couple fellas jus' come along the road, an' they wonder if we could spare a bite.'

Tom heard his mother's voice, the remembered cool, calm drawl, friendly and humble. 'Let 'em come,' she said. 'We got a'plenty. Tell 'em they got to wash their han's. The bread is done. I'm jus' takin' up the side-meat now.' And the sizzle of the angry grease came from the stove.

Pa stepped inside, clearing the door, and Tom looked in at his mother. She was lifting the curling slices of pork from the frying-pan. The oven door was open, and a great pan of high brown biscuits stood waiting there. She looked out the door, but the sun was behind Tom, and she saw only a dark figure outlined by the bright yellow sunlight. She nodded pleasantly. 'Come in,' she said. 'Jus' lucky I made plenty bread this morning.'

Tom stood looking in. Ma was heavy, but not fat; thick with child-bearing and work. She wore a loose Mother Hubbard of grey cloth in which there had once been coloured flowers, but the colour was washed out now, so that the small flowered pattern was only a little lighter grey than the background. The dress came down to her ankles, and her strong, broad, bare feet moved quickly and deftly over the floor. Her thin, steel-grey hair was gathered in a sparse wispy knot at the back of her head. Strong, freckled arms were bare to the elbow, and her hands were chubby and delicate, like those of a plump little girl. She looked out into the sunshine. Her full face was not soft; it was controlled, kindly. Her hazel eyes seemed to have experienced all possible tragedy and to have mounted pain and suffering like steps into a high calm and a superhuman understanding. She seemed to know, to accept, to welcome her position, the citadel of the family, the strong place that could not be taken. And since old Tom and the children could not know hurt or fear unless she acknowledged hurt and fear, she had practised denying them in herself. And since, when a joyful thing happened, they looked to see whether joy was on her, it was her habit to build up laughter out of inadequate materials. But better than joy was calm. Imperturbability could be depended upon. And from her great and humble position in the family she had taken dignity and a clean calm beauty. From her position as healer, her hands had grown sure and cool and quiet; from her position as arbiter she had become as remote and faultless in judgement as a goddess. She seemed to know that if she swayed the family shook, and if she ever really deeply wavered or despaired the family would fall, the family will to function would be gone.

She looked out into the sunny yard, at the dark figure of a man. Pa stood near by, shaking with excitement. 'Come in,' he cried. 'Come right in, mister.' And Tom a little shamefacedly stepped over the doorsill.

She looked up pleasantly from the frying-pan. And then her hand sank slowly to her side and the fork clattered to the wooden floor. Her eyes opened wide, and the pupils dilated. She breathed heavily through her open mouth. She closed her eyes. 'Thank God,' she said. 'Oh, thank God!' And suddenly her face was worried. 'Tommy, you ain't wanted? You didn't bust loose?'

'No, Ma. Parole. I got the papers here.' He touched his breast. She moved toward him lithely, soundlessly in her bare feet, and her face was full of wonder. Her small hand felt his arm, felt the soundness of his muscles. And then her fingers went up to his cheek as a blind man's fingers might. And her joy was nearly like sorrow. Tom pulled his underlip between his teeth and bit it. Her eyes went wonderingly to his bitten lip, and she saw the little line of blood against his teeth and trickle of blood down his lip. Then she knew, and her control came back, and her hand dropped. Her breath came out explosively. 'Well!' she cried. 'We come mighty near to goin' without ya. An' we was wonderin' how in the worl' you could ever find us.' She picked up the fork and combed the boiling grease and brought out a dark curl of crisp pork. And she set the pot of tumbling coffee on the back of the stove.

Old Tom giggled: 'Fooled ya, huh, Ma? We aimed to fool ya, and we done it. Jus' stood there like a hammered sheep. Whisht Grampa'd been here to see. Looked like somebody'd beat ya between the eyes with a sledge. Grampa would a whacked 'imself so hard he'd a throwed his hip out–like he done when he seen Al take a shot at that grea' big airship the army got. Tommy, it come over one day, half a mile big, an' Al gets the thirty-thirty and blazes away at her. Grampa yells: "Don't shoot no fledglin's, Al; wait till a growed-up one goes over," an' then he whacked 'imself an' throwed his hip out.'

Ma chuckled and took down a heap of tin plates from a shelf.

Tom asked: 'Where is Grampa? I ain't seen the ol' devil.'

Ma stacked the plates on the kitchen table and piled cups beside them. She said confidentially: 'Oh, him an' Granma sleeps in the barn. They got to get up so much in the night. They was stumblin' over the little fellas.'

Pa broke in: 'Yeah, ever' night Grampa'd get mad. Tumble over Winfield, an' Winfield'd yell, an' Grampa'd get mad an' wet his drawers, an' that'd make him madder, an' purty soon ever'body in the house'd be yellin' their heads off.' His words tumbled out between chuckles. 'Oh, we had lively times. One night when ever'body was yellin' an' a-cussin', your brother Al, he's a smart aleck now, he says: "Goddamn it, Grampa, why don't you run off an' be a pirate?" Well, that made Grampa so goddamn mad he went for his gun. Al had to sleep out in the fiel' that night. But now Granma an' Grampa both sleeps in the barn.'

Ma said: 'They can jus' get up an' step outside when they feel like it. Pa, run on out an' tell 'em Tommy's home. Grampa's a favourite of him.'

'A course,' said Pa. 'I should of did it before.' He went out the door and crossed the yard, swinging his hands high.

Tom watched him go, and then his mother's voice called his attention. She was pouring coffee. She did not look at him. 'Tommy,' she said, hesitantly, timidly.

'Yeah?' His timidity was set off by hers, a curious embarrassment. Each one knew the other was shy, and became more shy in the knowledge.

'Tommy. I got to ask you–you ain't mad?'

'Mad, Ma?'

'You ain't poisoned mad? You don't hate anybody? They didn' do nothin' in that jail to rot you out with crazy mad?'

He looked sidewise at her, studied her, and his eyes seemed to ask how she could know such things. 'No-o-o,' he said. 'I was for a little while. But I ain't proud like some fellas. I let stuff run off'n me. What's a matter, Ma?'

Now she was looking at him, her mouth open, as though to hear better, her eyes digging to know better. Her face looked for the answer that is always concealed in language. She said in confusion: 'I knowed Purty Boy Floyd. I knowed his ma. They was good folks. He was full a hell, sure, like a good boy oughta be.' She paused and then her words poured out. 'I don' know all like this–but I know it. He done a little bad thing an' they hurt 'im, caught 'im an' hurt him so he was mad, an' the nex' bad thing he done was mad, an' they hurt 'im again. An' purty soon he was mean-mad. They shot at him like a varmint, an' he shot back, an' then they run him like a coyote, an' him a-snappin' an' a-snarlin', mean as a lobo. An' he was mad. He wasn't no boy or no man no more, he was jus' a walkin' chunk a mean-mad. But the folks that knowed him didn't hurt 'im. He wasn' mad at them. Finally they run him down an' killed 'im. No matter how they say it in the paper how he was bad–that's how it was.' She paused and she licked her dry lips, and her whole face was an aching question. 'I got to know, Tommy. Did they hurt you so much? Did they make you mad like that?'

Tom's heavy lips were pulled tight over his teeth. He looked down at his big fat hands. 'No,' he said. 'I ain't like that.' He paused and studied the broken nails, which were ridged like clam shells. 'All the time in stir I kep' away from stuff like that. I ain' so mad.'

She sighed, 'Thank God!' under her breath.

He looked up quickly: 'Ma, when I seen what they done to our house–'

She came near to him then, and stood close; and she said passionately: 'Tommy, don't you go fightin' 'em alone. They'll hunt you down like a coyote. Tommy, I got to thinkin' an' dreamin' an' wonderin'. They say there's a hun'erd thousand of us shoved out. If we was all mad the same way, Tommy–they wouldn't hunt nobody down–' She stopped.

Tommy, looking at her, gradually dropped his eyelids, until just a short glitter showed through his lashes. 'Many folks feel that way?' he demanded.

'I don't know. They're jus' kinda stunned. Walk aroun' like they was half asleep.'

From outside and across the yard came an ancient creaking bleat. 'Pu-raise Gawd fur vittory! Pu-raise Gawd fur vittory!'

Tom turned his head and grinned. 'Granma finally heard I'm home. Ma,' he said, 'you never was like this before!'

Her face hardened and her eyes grew cold. 'I never had my house pushed over,' she said. 'I never had my fambly stuck out on the road. I never had to sell–ever'thing–Here they come now.' She moved back to the stove and dumped the big pan of bulbous biscuits on two tin plates. She shook flour into the deep grease to make gravy, and her hand was white with flour. For a moment Tom watched her, and then he went to the door.

Across the yard came four people. Grampa was ahead, a lean, ragged, quick old man, jumping with quick steps and favouring his right leg–the side that came out of joint. He was buttoning his fly as he came, and his old hands were having trouble finding the buttons, for he had buttoned the top button into the second buttonhole, and that threw the whole sequence off. He wore dark ragged pants and a torn blue shirt, open all the way down, and showing long grey underwear, also unbuttoned. His lean white chest, fuzzed with white hair, was visible through the opening in his underwear. He gave up the fly and left it open and fumbled with the underwear buttons, then gave the whole thing up and hitched his brown suspenders. His was a lean excitable face with little bright eyes as evil as a frantic child's eyes. A cantankerous, complaining, mischievous, laughing face. He fought and argued, told dirty stories. He was as lecherous as always. Vicious and cruel and impatient, like a frantic child, and the whole structure overlaid with amusement. He drank too much when he could get it, ate too much when it was there, talked too much all the time.

Behind him hobbled Granma, who had survived only because she was as mean as her husband. She had held her own with a shrill ferocious religiosity that was as lecherous and as savage as anything Grampa could offer. Once, after a meeting, while she was still speaking in tongues, she fired both barrels of a shotgun at her husband, ripping one of his buttocks nearly off, and after that he admired her and did not try to torture her as children torture bugs. As she walked she hiked her Mother Hubbard up to her knees, and she bleated her shrill terrible war-cry: 'Pu-raise Gawd for vittory.'

Granma and Grampa raced each other to get across the broad yard. They fought over everything and loved and needed the fighting.

Behind them, moving slowly and evenly, but keeping up, came Pa and Noah–Noah, the first-born, tall and strange, walking always with a wondering look on his face, calm and puzzled. He had never been angry in his life. He looked in wonder at angry people, wonder and uneasiness, as normal people look at the insane. Noah moved slowly, spoke seldom, and then so slowly that people who did not know him often thought him stupid. He was not stupid, but he was strange. He had little pride, no sexual urges. He worked and slept in a curious rhythm that nevertheless sufficed him. He was fond of his folks, but never showed it in any way. Although an observer could not have told why, Noah left the impression of being misshapen, his head or his body or his legs or his mind; but no misshapen member could be recalled. Pa thought he knew why Noah was strange, but Pa was ashamed, and never told. For on the night when Noah was born, Pa, frightened at the spreading thighs, alone in the house, and horrified at the screaming wretch his wife had become, went mad with apprehension. Using his hands, his strong fingers for forceps, he had pulled and twisted the baby. The midwife, arriving late, had found the baby's head pulled out of shape, its neck stretched, its body warped; and she had pushed the head back and moulded the body with her hands. But Pa always remembered, and was ashamed. And he was kinder to Noah than to the others. In Noah's broad face, eyes too far apart, and long fragile jaw Pa though he saw the twisted, warped skull of the baby. Noah could do all that was required of him, could read and write, could work and figure, but he didn't seem to care; there was a listlessness in him toward things people wanted and needed. He lived in a strange silent house and looked out of it through calm eyes. He was a stranger to all the world, but he was not lonely.

The four came across the yard, and Grampa demanded: 'Where is he? Goddamn it, where is he?' And his fingers fumbled for his pants-button, and forgot and strayed into his pocket. And then he saw Tom standing in the door. Grampa stopped and he stopped the others. His little eyes glittered with malice. 'Lookut him,' he said. 'A jailbird. Ain't been no Joads in jail for a hell of a time.' His mind jumped. 'Got no right to put 'im in jail. He done just what I'd do. Sons-a-bitches got no right.' His mind jumped again. 'An' ol' Turnbull, stinkin' skunk, braggin' how he'll shoot ya when ya come out. Says he got Hatfield blood. Well, I sent word to him. I says: "Don't mess around with no Joad. Maybe I got McCoy blood for all I know." I says: "You lay your sights anywheres near Tommy an' I'll take it an' I'll ram it up your ass," I says. Scairt 'im, too.'

Granma, not following the conversation, bleated: 'Pu-raise Gawd fur vittory.'

Grampa walked up and slapped Tom on the chest, and his eyes grinned with affection and pride. 'How are ya, Tommy?'

'O.K.' said Tom. 'How ya keepin' yaself?'

'Full a piss an' vinegar,' said Grampa. His mind jumped. 'Jus' like I said, they ain't a gonna keep no Joad in jail. I says: "Tommy'll come a-bustin' outa that jail like a bull through a corral fence." An' you done it. Get outa my way, I'm hungry.' He crowded past, sat down, loaded his plate with pork and two big biscuits and poured the thick gravy over the whole mess, and before the others could get in, Grampa's mouth was full.

Tom grinned affectionately at him. 'Ain't he a heller?' he said. And Grampa's mouth was so full that he couldn't even splutter, but his mean little eyes smiled, and he nodded his head violently.

Granma said proudly: 'A wicketer, cussin'er man never lived. He's goin' to hell on a poker, praise Gawd! Wants to drive the truck!' she said spitefully. 'Well, he ain't goin' ta.'

Grampa choked, and a mouthful of paste sprayed into his lap, and he coughed weakly.

Granma smiled up at Tom. 'Messy, ain't he?' she observed brightly.

Noah stood on the step, and he faced Tom, and his wide-set eyes seemed to look around him. His face had little expression. Tom said: 'How ya, Noah?'

'Fine,' said Noah. 'How a' you?' That was all, but it was a comfortable thing.

Ma waved the flies away from the bowl of gravy. 'We ain't got room to set down,' she said. 'Jus' get yaself a plate an' set down wherever ya can. Out in the yard or someplace.'

Suddenly Tom said: 'Hey! Where's the preacher? He was right here. Where'd he go?'

Pa said: 'I seen him, but he's gone.'

And Granma raised a shrill voice: 'Preacher? You got a preacher? Go git him. We'll have a grace.' She pointed at Grampa. 'Too late for him–he's et. Go git the preacher.'

Tom stepped out on the porch. 'Hey, Jim! Jim Casy!' he called. He walked out in the yard. 'Oh, Casy!' The preacher emerged from under the tank, sat up, and then stood up and moved toward the house. Tom asked: 'What was you doin', hidin'?'

'Well, no. But a fella shouldn't butt his head in where a fambly got fambly stuff. I was jus' settin' a-thinkin'.'

'Come on in an' eat,' said Tom. 'Granma wants a grace.'

'But I ain't a preacher no more,' Casy protested.

'Aw, come on. Give her a grace. Don't do you no harm, an' she likes 'em.' They walked into the kitchen together.

Ma said quietly: 'You're welcome.'

And Pa said: 'You're welcome. Have some breakfast.'

'Grace fust,' Granma clamoured. 'Grace fust.'

Grampa focused his eyes fiercely until he recognized Casy. 'Oh, that preacher,' he said. 'Oh, he's all right. I always liked him since I seen him–' He winked so lecherously that Granma thought he had spoken and retorted: 'Shut up, you sinful ol' goat.'

Casy ran his fingers through his hair nervously. 'I got to tell you, I ain't a preacher no more. If me jus' bein' glad to be here an' bein' thankful for people that's kind and generous, if that's enough–why, I'll say that kinda grace. But I ain't a preacher no more.'

'Say her,' said Granma. 'An' get in a word about us goin' to California.' The preacher bowed his head, and the others bowed their heads. Ma folded her hands over her stomach and bowed her head. Granma bowed so low that her nose was nearly in her plate of biscuit and gravy. Tom, leaning against a wall, a plate in his hand, bowed stiffly, and Grampa bowed his head sidewise, so that he could keep one mean and merry eye on the preacher. And on the preacher's face there was a look not of prayer but of thought; and in his tone not supplication but conjecture.

'I been thinkin',' he said. 'I been in the hills, thinkin', almost you might say like Jesus went into the wilderness to think His way out of a mess of troubles.'

'Pu-raise Gawd!' Granma said, and the preacher glanced over at her in surprise.

'Seems like Jesus got all messed up with troubles, and He couldn't figure nothin' out, an' He got to feelin' what the hell good is it all, an' what's the use fightin' an' figurin'. Got tired, got good an' tired, an' His sperit all wore out. Jus' about come to the conclusion, the hell with it. An' so He went off into the wilderness.'

'A–men,' Granma bleated. So many years she had timed her responses to the pauses. And it was so many years since she had listened to or wondered at the words used.

'I ain't sayin' I'm like Jesus,' the preacher went on. 'But I got tired like Him, an' I got mixed up like Him, an' I went into the wilderness like Him, without no campin' stuff. Night-time I'd lay on my back an' look up at the stars; morning I'd set an' watch the sun come up; midday I'd look out from a hill at the rollin' dry country; evenin' I'd foller the sun down. Sometimes I'd pray like I always done. On'y I couldn' figure what I was prayin' to or for. There was the hills, an' there was me, an' we wasn't separate no more. We was one thing. An' that one thing was holy.'

'Hallelujah,' said Granma, and she rocked a little, back and forth, trying to catch hold of an ecstasy.

'An' I got thinkin', on'y it wasn't thinkin', it was deeper down than thinkin'. I got thinkin' how we was holy when we was one thing, an' mankin' was holy when it was one thing. An' it only got unholy when one mis'able little fella got the bit in his teeth an' run off his own way, kickin' an' draggin' an' fightin'. Fella like that bust the holiness. But when they're all workin' together, not one fella for another fella, but one fella kind of harnessed to the whole shebang–that's right, that's holy. An' then I got thinkin' I don't even know what I mean by holy.' He paused, but the bowed heads stayed down, for they had been trained like dogs to rise at the 'amen' signal. 'I can't say no grace like I use' to say. I'm glad of the holiness of breakfast. I'm glad there's love here. That's all.' The heads stayed down. The preacher looked around. 'I've got your breakfast cold,' he said; and then he remembered. 'Amen,' he said, and all the heads rose up.

'A–men,' said Granma, and she fell to her breakfast, and broke down the soggy biscuits with her hard old toothless gums. Tom ate quickly, and Pa crammed his mouth. There was no talk until the food was gone, the coffee drunk; only the crunch of chewed food and the slup of coffee cooled in transit to the tongue. Ma watched the preacher as he ate, and her eyes were questioning, probing, and understanding. She watched him as though he were suddenly a spirit, not human any more, a voice out of the ground.

The men finished and put down their plates, and drained the last of their coffee; and then the men went out, Pa and the preacher and Noah and Grampa and Tom, and they walked over to the truck, avoiding the litter of furniture, the wooden bedsteads, the windmill machinery, the old plough. They walked to the truck and stood beside it. They touched the new pine sideboards.

Tom opened the hood and looked at the big greasy engine. And Pa came up beside him. He said: 'Your brother Al looked her over before we bought her. He says she's all right.'

'What's he know? He's just a squirt,' said Tom.

'He worked for a company. Drove truck last year. He knows quite a little, smart aleck like he is. He knows. He can tinker an engine, Al can.'

Tom asked: 'Where's he now?'

'Well,' said Pa, 'he's a-billygoatin' aroun' the country. Tomcattin' hisself to death. Smart-aleck sixteen-year-older, an' his nuts is just a-eggin' him on. He don't think of nothin' but girls and engines. A plain smart aleck. Ain't been in nights for a week.'

Grampa, fumbling with his chest, had succeeded in buttoning the buttons of his blue shirt into the buttonholes of his underwear. His fingers felt that something was wrong, but he did not care enough to find out. His fingers went down to try to figure out the intricacies of the buttoning of his fly. 'I was worse,' he said happily. 'I was much worse. I was a heller, you might say. Why, they was a camp meetin' right in Sallisaw when I was a young fella a little bit older'n Al. He's just a squirt, an' punkin-soft. But I was older. An' we was to this here camp meetin'. Five hundred folks there, an' a proper sprinklin' of young heifers.'

'You look like a heller yet, Grampa,' said Tom.

'Well, I am, kinda. But I ain't nowheres near the fella I was. Jus' let me get out to California where I can pick me an orange when I want it. Or grapes. There's a thing I ain't never had enough of. Gonna get me a whole big bunch of grapes off a bush, or whatever, an' I'm gonna squash 'em on my face an' let 'em run offen my chin.'

Tom asked: 'Where's Uncle John? Where's Rosasharn? Where's Ruthie an' Winfield? Nobody said nothin' about them yet,'

Pa said: 'Nobody asked. John gone to Sallisaw with a load a stuff to sell: pump, tools, chickens, an' all the stuff we brung over. Took Ruthie an' Winfield with 'im. Went 'fore daylight.'

'Funny I never saw him,' said Tom.

'Well, you come down from the highway, didn't you? He took the back way, by Cowlington. An' Rosasharn, she's nestin' with Connie's folks. By God! You don't even know Rosasharn's married to Connie Rivers. You 'member Connie. Nice young fella. An' Rosasharn's due 'bout three-four-five months now. Swellin' up right now. Looks fine.'

'Jesus!' said Tom. 'Rosasharn was just a little kid. An' now she's gonna have a baby. So damn much happens in four years if you're away. When ya think to start out west. Pa?'

'Well, we got to take this stuff in an' sell it. If Al gets back from his squirtin' aroun', I figgered he could load the truck an' take all of it in, an' maybe we could start out to-morra or day after.We ain't got so much money, an' a fella says its' damn near two thousan' miles to California. Quicker we get started, surer it is we get there. Money's a-dribblin' out all the time. You got any money?'

'On'y a couple dollars. How'd you get money?'

'Well,' said Pa, 'we sol' all the stuff at our place, an' the whole bunch of us chopped cotton, even Grampa.'

'Sure did,' said Grampa.

'We put ever'thing together–two hundred dollars. We give seventy-five for this truck, an' me an' Al cut her in two an' built on this here back. Al was gonna grind the valves, but he's too busy messin' aroun' to get down to her. We'll have maybe a hundred an' fifty when we start. Damn ol' tires on this here truck ain't gonna go far. Got a couple of wore-out spares. Pick stuff up along the road, I guess.'

The sun, driving straight down, stung with its rays. The shadows of the truck bed were dark bars on the ground, and the truck smelled of hot oil and oilcloth and paint. The few chickens had left the yard to hide in the tool shed from the sun. In the sty the pigs lay panting, close to the fence where a thin shadow fell, and they complained shrilly now and then. The two dogs were stretched in the red dust under the truck, panting, their dripping tongues covered with dust. Pa pulled his hat low over his eyes and squatted down on his hams. And, as though this were his natural position of thought and observation, he surveyed Tom critically, the new but ageing cap, the suit, and the new shoes.

'Did you spen' your money for them clothes?' he asked. 'Them clothes are jus' gonna be a nuisance to ya.'

'They give 'em to me,' said Tom. 'When I come out they give 'em to me.' He took off his cap and looked at it with some admiration, then wiped his forehead with it and put it on rakishly and pulled at the visor.

Pa observed: 'Them's a nice-lookin' pair of shoes they give ya.'

'Yeah,' Joad agreed. 'Purty for nice, but they ain't no shoes to go walkin' aroun' in on a hot day.' He squatted beside his father.

Noah said slowly: 'Maybe if you got them side-boards all true on, we could load up this stuff. Load her up so maybe if Al comes in–'

'I can drive her, if that's what you want,' Tom said. 'I drove truck at McAlester.'

'Good,' said Pa, and then his eyes stared down the road. 'If I ain't mistaken, there's a young smart aleck draggin' his tail home right now,' he said. 'Looks purty wore out, too.'

Tom and the preacher looked up the road. And randy Al, seeing he was being noticed, threw back his shoulders, and he came into the yard with a swaying strut like that of a rooster about to crow. Cockily, he walked close before he recognized Tom; and when he did, his boasting face changed, and admiration and veneration shone in his eyes, and his swagger fell away. His stiff jeans, with the bottoms turned up eight inches to show his heeled boots, his three-inch belt with copper figures on it, even the red arm-bands on his blue shirt and the rakish angle of his Stetson hat could not build him up to his brother's stature; for his brother had killed a man, and no one would ever forget it. Al knew that even he had inspired some admiration among boys of his own age because his brother had killed a man. He had heard in Sallisaw how he was pointed out: 'That's Al Joad. His brother killed a fella with a shovel.'

And now Al, moving humbly near, saw that his brother was not a swaggerer as he had supposed. Al saw the dark brooding eyes of his brother, and the prison calm, the smooth hard face trained to indicate nothing to a prison guard, neither resistance nor slavishness. And instantly Al changed. Unconsciously he became like his brother, and his handsome face brooded and his shoulders relaxed. He hadn't remembered how Tom was.

Tom said: 'Hello, Al. Jesus, you're growin' like a bean! I wouldn't of knowed you.'

Al, his hand ready if Tom should want to shake it, grinned self-consciously. Tom stuck out his hand and Al's hand jerked out to meet it. And there was a liking between these two. 'They tell me you're a good hand with a truck,' said Tom.

And Al, sensing that his brother would not like a boaster, said: 'I don't know nothin' much about it.'

Pa said: 'Been smart-alecking aroun' the country. You look wore out. Well, you got to take a load of stuff into Sallisaw to sell.'

Al looked at his brother Tom. 'Care to ride in?' he said as casually as he could.

'No, I can't,' said Tom. 'I'll help aroun' here. We'll be–together on the road.'

Al tried to control his question. 'Did–you bust out? Of jail?'

'No,' said Tom. 'I got paroled.'

'Oh.' And Al was a little disappointed.

9

In the little houses the tenant people sifted their belongings and the belongings of their fathers and of their grandfathers. Picked over their possessions for the journey to the west. The men were ruthless because the past had been spoiled, but the women knew how the past would cry to them in the coming days. The men went into the barns and the sheds.

That plough, that harrow, remember in the war we planted mustard? Remember a fella wanted us to put in that rubber bush they call guayule? Get rich, he said. Bring out those tools–get a few dollars for them. Eighteen dollars for that plough, plus freight–Sears Roebuck.

Harness, carts, seeders, little bundles of hoes. Bring 'em out. Pile 'em up. Load 'em in the wagon. Take 'em to town. Sell 'em for what you can get. Sell the team and the wagon, too. No more use for anything.

Fifty cents isn't enough to get for a good plough. That seeder cost thirty-eight dollars. Two dollars isn't enough. Can't haul it all back–Well, take it, and a bitterness with it. Take the well pump and the harness. Take halters, collars, hames, and tugs. Take the little glass brow-band jewels, roses red under glass. Got those for the bay gelding. 'Member how he lifted his feet when he trotted?

Junk piled up in a yard.

Can't sell a hand plough any more. Fifty cents for the weight of the metal. Disks and tractors, that's the stuff now.

Well, take it–all junk–and give me five dollars. You're not buying only junk, you're buying junked lives. And more–you'll see–you're buying bitterness. Buying a plough to plough your own children under, buying the arms and spirits that might have saved you. Five dollars, not four. I can't haul 'em back–Well, take 'em for four. But I warn you, you're buying what will plough your own children under. And you won't see. You can't see. Take 'em for four. Now, what'll you give for the team and wagon? Those fine bays, matched they are, matched in colour, matched the way they walk, stride to stride. In the stiff pull–straining hams and buttocks, split second timed together. And in the morning, the light on them, bay light. They look over the fence sniffing for us, and the stiff ears swivel to hear us, and the black forelocks! I've got a girl. She likes to braid the manes and forelocks, put little red bows on them. Likes to do it. Not any more. I could tell you a funny story about that girl and that off bay. Would make you laugh. Off horse is eight, near is ten, but might of been twin colts the way they work together. See? The teeth. Sound all over. Deep lungs. Feet fair and clean. How much? Ten dollars? For both? And the wagon–Oh, Jesus Christ! I'd shoot 'em for dog feed first. Oh, take 'em! Take 'em quick, mister. You're buying a little girl plaiting the forelocks, taking off her hair ribbon to make bows, standing back, head cocked, rubbing the soft noses with her cheek. You're buying years of work, toil in the sun; you're buying a sorrow that can't talk. But watch it, mister. There's a premium goes with this pile of junk and the bay horses–so beautiful–a packet of bitterness to grow in your house and to flower, some day. We could have saved you, but you cut us down, and soon you will be cut down and there'll be none of us to save you.

And the tenant men came walking back, hands in their pockets, hats pulled down. Some bought a pint and drank it fast to make the impact hard and stunning. But they didn't laugh and they didn't dance. They didn't sing or pick the guitars. They walked back to the farms, hands in pockets and heads down, shoes kicking the red dust up.

Maybe we can start again, in the new rich land–in California, where the fruit grows. We'll start over.

But you can't start. Only a baby can start. You and me–why, we're all that's been. The anger of a moment, the thousand pictures, that's us. This land, this red land, is us; and the flood years and the dust years and the drought years are us. We can't start again. The bitterness we sold to the junk man–he got it all right, but we have it still. And when the owner men told us to go, that's us; and when the tractor hit the house, that's us until we're dead. To California or any place–every one a drum-major leading a parade of hurts, marching with our bitterness. And some day–the armies of bitterness will all be going the same way. And they'll all walk together, and there'll be a dead terror from it.

The tenant men scuffed home to the farms through the red dust.

When everything that could be sold was sold, stoves and bedsteads, chairs and tables, little corner cupboards, tubs and tanks, still there were piles of possessions; and the women sat among them, turning them over and looking off beyond and back, pictures, square glasses, and here's a vase.

Now you know well what we can take and what we can't take. We'll be camping out–a few pots to cook and wash in, and mattresses and comforts, lantern and buckets, and a piece of canvas. Use that for a tent. This kerosene can. Know what that is? That's the stove. And clothes–take all the clothes. And–the rifle? Wouldn't go out naked of a rifle. When shoes and clothes and food, when even hope is gone, we'll have the rifle. When Grampa came–did I tell you?–he had pepper and salt and a rifle. Nothing else. That goes. And a bottle of water. That just about fills us. Right up the sides of the trailer, and the kids can set in the trailer, and Granma on a mattress. Tools, a shovel and saw and wrench and pliers. An axe, too. We had that axe forty years. Look how she's wore down. And ropes, of course. The rest? Leave it–or burn it up.

And the children came.

If Mary takes that doll, that dirty rag doll, I got to take my Injun bow. I got to. An' this roun' stick–big as me. I might need this stick. I had this stick so long–a month, or maybe a year. I got to take it. And what's it like in California?

The women sat among the doomed things, turning them over and looking past them and back. This book. My father had it. He liked a book. *Pilgrim's Progress*. Used to read it. Got his name in it. And his pipe–still smells rank. And this picture–an angel. I looked at that before the fust three come–didn't seem to do much good. Think we could get this china dog in? Aunt Sadie brought it from the St Louis Fair. See? Wrote right on it. No, I guess not. Here's a letter my brother wrote the day before he died. Here's an old-time hat. These feathers–never got to use them. No, there isn't room.

How can we live without our lives? How will we know it's us without our past? No. Leave it. Burn it.

They sat and looked at it and burned it into their memories. How'll it be not to know what land's outside the door? How if you wake up in the night and know–and *know* the willow tree's not there? Can you live without the willow tree? Well, no, you can't. The willow tree is you. The pain on that mattress there–that dreadful pain–that's you.

And the children–if Sam takes his Injun bow an' his long roun' stick, I got to take two things. I choose the fluffy pilla. That's mine.

Suddenly they were nervous. Got to get out quick now. Can't wait. We can't wait. And they piled up the goods in the yards and set fire to them. They stood and watched them burning, and then frantically they loaded up the cars and drove away, drove in the dust. The dust hung in the air for a long time after the loaded cars had passed.

10

When the truck had gone, loaded with implements, with heavy tools, with beds and springs, with every movable thing that might be sold, Tom hung around the place. He mooned into the barn shed, into the empty stalls, and he walked into the implement lean-to and kicked the refuse that was left, turned a broken mower tooth with his foot. He visited places he remembered–the red bank where the swallows nested, the willow tree over the pig pen. Two shoats grunted and squirmed at him through the fence, black pigs, sunning and comfortable. And then his pilgrimage was over, and he went to sit on the doorstep where the shade was lately fallen. Behind him Ma moved about in the kitchen, washing children's clothes in a bucket; and her strong freckled arms dripped soapsuds from the elbows. She stopped her rubbing when he sat down. She looked at him a long time, and at the back of his head when he turned and stared out at the hot sunlight. And then she went back to her rubbing.

She said: 'Tom, I hope things is all right in California.'

He turned and looked at her. 'What makes you think they ain't?' he asked.

'Well–nothing. Seems too nice, kinda. I seen the han'bills fellas pass out, an' how much work they is, an' high wages an' all; an' I seen in the paper how they want folks to come an' pick grapes an' oranges an' peaches. That'd be nice work, Tom, pickin' peaches. Even if they wouldn't let you eat none, you could maybe snitch a little ratty one sometimes. An' it'd be nice under the trees, workin' in the shade. I'm scared of stuff so nice. I ain't got faith. I'm scared somepin ain't so nice about it.'

Tom said: 'Don't roust your faith bird-high an' you won't do no crawlin' with the worms.'

'I know that's right. That's Scripture, ain't it?'

'I guess so,' said Tom. 'I never could keep Scripture straight sence I read a book name' *The Winning of Barbara Worth*.'

Ma chuckled lightly and scrounged the clothes in and out of the bucket. And she wrung out overalls and shirts, and the muscles of her forearms corded out. 'Your Pa's pa, he quoted Scripture all the time. He got it all roiled up, too. It was the *Dr Miles' Almanac* he got mixed up. Used to read ever' word in that almanac out loud–letters from folks that couldn't sleep or had lame backs. An' later he'd give them people for a lesson, an' he'd say; "That's a par'ble from Scripture." Your Pa an' Uncle John troubled 'im some about it when they'd laugh.' She piled wrung clothes like cord wood on the table. 'They say it's two thousan' miles where we're goin'. How far ya think that is, Tom? I seen it on a map, big mountains like on a postcard, an' we're goin' right through 'em. How long ya s'pose it'll take to go that far, Tommy?'

'I dunno,' he said. 'Two weeks, maybe ten days if we got luck. Look, Ma, stop your worryin'. I'm a-gonna tell you somepin about bein' in the pen. You can't go thinkin' when you're gonna be out. You'd go nuts. You got to think about that day, an' then the nex' day, about the ball game Sat'dy. That's what you got to do. O' timers does that. A new young fella gets buttin' his head on the cell door. He's thinkin' how long it's gonna be. Whyn't you do that? Jus' take ever' day.'

'That's a good way,' she said, and she filled up her bucket with hot water from the stove, and she put in dirty clothes and began punching them down into the soapy water. 'Yes, that's a good way. But I like to think how nice it's gonna be, maybe, in California. Never cold. An' fruit ever'place, an' people just bein' in the nicest places, little white houses in among the orange trees. I wonder–that is, if we all get jobs an' all work–maybe we can get one of them little white houses. An' the little fellas go out an' pick oranges right off the tree. They ain't gonna be able to stand it, they'll get to yellin' so.'

Tom watched her working, and his eyes smiled. 'It done you good jus' thinkin' about it. I knowed a fella from California. He didn't talk like us. You'd of knowed he come from some far-off place jus' the way he talked. But he says they's too many folks lookin' for work right there now. An' he says the folks that pick the fruit live in dirty ol' camps an' don't hardly get enough to eat. He says wages is low an' hard to get any.'

A shadow crossed her face. 'Oh, that ain't so,' she said. 'Your father got a han'bill on yella paper, tellin' how they need folks to work. They wouldn't go to that trouble if they wasn't plenty work. Costs 'em good money to get them han'bills out. What'd they want ta lie for, an' costin' 'em money to lie?'

Tom shook his head. 'I don' know, Ma. It's kinda hard to think why they done it. Maybe–' He looked out at the hot sun, shining on the red earth.

'Maybe what?'

'Maybe it's nice, like you says. Where'd Grampa go? Where'd the preacher go?'

Ma was going out of the house, her arms loaded high with the clothes. Tom moved aside to let her pass. 'Preacher says he's gonna walk aroun'. Grampa's asleep here in the house. He comes in here in the day an' lays down sometimes.' She walked to the line and began to drape pale blue jeans and blue shirts and long grey underwear over the wire.

Behind him Tom heard a shuffling step, and he turned to look in. Grampa was emerging from the bedroom, and as in the morning, he fumbled with the buttons of his fly. 'I heerd talkin',' he said. 'Sons-a-bitches won't let a ol' fella sleep. When you bastards get dry behin' the ears, you'll maybe learn to let a ol' fella sleep.' His furious fingers managed to flip the only two buttons on his fly that had been buttoned. And his hand forgot what it had been trying to do. His hand reached in and contentedly scratched under his testicles. Ma came in with wet hands, and her palms puckered and bloated from hot water and soap.

'Thought you was sleepin'. Here, let me button you up.' And though he struggled, she held him and buttoned his underwear and his shirt and his fly. 'You go aroun' a sight,' she said, and let him go.

And he spluttered angrily: 'Fella's come to a nice–to a nice–when somebody buttons 'em. I want ta be let be to button my own pants.'

Ma said playfully: 'They don't let people run aroun' with their clothes unbutton' in California.'

'They don't, hey! Well, I'll show 'em. They think they're gonna show me how to act out there? Why, I'll go aroun' a-hangin' out if I wanta!'

Ma said: 'Seems like his language gets worse ever' year. Showin' off, I guess.'

The old man thrust out his bristly chin, and he regarded Ma with his shrewd, mean, merry eyes. 'Well, sir,' he said, 'we'll be a-startin' 'fore long now. An', by God, they's grapes out there, just a-hangin, over inta the road. Know what I'm a-gonna do? I'm gonna pick me a wash tub full a grapes, an' I'm gonna set in em, an' scrooge aroun,' an' let the juice run down my pants.'

Tom laughed, 'By God, if he lives to be two hundred you never will get Grampa house broke,' he said. 'You're all set on goin', ain't you, Grampa?'

The old man pulled out a box and sat down heavily on it. 'Yes, sir,' he said. 'An' goddamn near time, too. My brother went on out there forty years ago. Never did hear nothin' about him. Sneaky son-of-a-bitch, he was. Nobody loved him. Run off with a single-action Colt of mine. If I ever run across him or his kids, if he got any out in California, I'll ask 'em for that Colt. But if I know 'im, an' he got any kids, he cuckoo'd 'em, an' somebody else is a-raisin' 'em. I sure will be glad to get out there. Got a feelin' it'll make a new fella outa me. Go right to work in the fruit.'

Ma nodded. 'He means it, too,' she said. 'Worked right up to three months ago, when he throwed his hip out the last time.'

'Damn right,' said Grampa.

Tom looked outward from his seat on the doorstep. 'Here comes that preacher, walkin' aroun' from the back side a the barn.'

Ma said: 'Curiousest grace I ever heerd, that he give this mornin'. Wasn't hardly no grace at all. Jus' talkin', but the sound of it was like a grace.'

'He's a funny fella,' said Tom. 'Talks funny all the time. Seems like he's talkin' to hisself, though. He ain't tryin' to put nothin' over.'

'Watch the look in his eye,' said Ma. 'He looks baptized. Got that look they call lookin' through. He sure looks baptized. An' a-walkin' with his head down, a-starin' at nothin' on the groun'. There *is* a man that's baptized.' And she was silent, for Casy had drawn near the door.

'You gonna get sun-shook, walkin' around like that,' said Tom.

Casy said: 'Well, yeah–maybe.' He appealed to them all suddenly, to Ma and Grampa and Tom. 'I got to get goin' west. I got to go. I wonder if I kin go along with you folks.' And then he stood, embarrassed by his own speech.

Ma looked to Tom to speak, because he was a man, but Tom did not speak. She let him have the chance that was his right, and then she said: 'Why, we'd be proud to have you. 'Course I can't say right now; Pa says all the men'll talk to-night and figger when we gonna start. I guess maybe we better not say till the men come. John an' Pa an' Noah an' Tom an' Grampa an' Al an' Connie, they're gonna figger soon's they get back. But if they's room I'm pretty sure we'll be proud to have ya.'

The preacher sighed. 'I'll go anyways,' he said. 'Somepin's happening. I went up an' I looked, an' the houses is all empty, an' the lan' is empty, an' this whole country is empty. I can't stay here no more. I got to go where the folks is goin'. I'll work in the fiel's, an' maybe I'll be happy.'

'An' you ain't gonna preach?' Tom asked.

'I ain't gonna preach.'

'An' you ain't gonna baptize?' Ma asked.

'I ain't gonna baptize. I'm gonna work in the fiel's, in the green fiel's, an' I'm gonna be near to folks. I ain't gonna try to teach 'em nothin'. I'm gonna try to learn. Gonna learn why the folks walks in the grass, gonna hear 'em talk, gonna hear 'em sing. Gonna listen to kids eatin' mush. Gonna hear husban' an' wife a-poundin' the mattress in the night. Gonna eat with 'em an' learn.' His eyes were wet and shining. 'Gonna lay in the grass, open an' honest with anybody that'll have me. Gonna cuss an' swear an' hear the poetry of folks talkin'. All that's holy, all that's what I didn' understan'. All them things is the good things.'

Ma said: 'A-men.'

The preacher sat humbly down on the chopping block beside the door. 'I wonder what they is for a fella so lonely.'

Tom coughed delicately. 'For a fella that don't preach no more–' he began.

'Oh, I'm a talker!' said Casy. 'No gettin' away from that. But I ain't preachin'. Preachin' is tellin' folks stuff. I'm askin' 'em. That ain't preachin', is it?'

'I don't know,' said Tom. 'Preachin's a kinda tone a voice, an' preachin's a way a lookin' at things. Preachin's bein' good to folks when they wanna kill ya for it. Las' Christmas in McAlester, Salvation Army come an' done us good. Three solid hours a cornet music, an' we set there. They was bein' nice to us. But if one of us tried to walk out, we'd a drawed solitary. That's preachin'. Doin' good to a fella that's down an' can't smack ya in the puss for it. No, you ain't no preacher. But you don't blow cornets aroun' here.'

Ma threw some sticks into the stove. 'I'll get you a bite now, but it ain't much.'

Grampa brought his box outside and sat on it and leaned against the wall, and Tom and Casy leaned back against the house wall. And the shadow of the afternoon moved out from the house.

In the late afternoon the truck came back, bumping and rattling through the dust, and there was a layer of dust in the bed, and the hood was covered with dust, and the headlights were obscured with a red flour. The sun was setting when the truck came back, and the earth was bloody in its setting light. Al sat bent over the wheel, proud and serious and efficient, and Pa and Uncle John, as befitted the heads of the clan, had the honour seats beside the driver. Standing in the truck bed, holding on to the bars of the sides, rode the others, twelve-year-old Ruthie and ten-year-old Winfield, grime-faced and wild, their eyes tired but excited, their fingers and the edges of their mouths black and sticky from liquorice whips, whined out of their father in town. Ruthie, dressed in a real dress of pink muslin that came below her knees, was a little serious in her young-ladiness. But Winfield was still a trifle of a snot-nose, a little of a brooder back of the barn, and an inveterate collector and smoker of snipes. And whereas Ruthie felt the might, the responsibility, and the dignity of her developing breasts, Winfield was kid-wild and calfish. Beside them, clinging lightly to the bars, stood Rose of Sharon, and she balanced, swaying on the balls of her feet, and took up the road shock in her knees and hams. For Rose of Sharon was pregnant and careful. Her hair, braided and wrapped around her head, made an ash-blond crown. Her round soft face, which had been voluptuous and inviting a few months ago, had already put on the barrier of pregnancy, the self-sufficient smile, the knowing perfection-look; and the plump body–full soft breasts and stomach, hard hips and buttocks that had swung so freely and provocatively as to invite slapping and stroking–her whole body had become demure and serious. Her whole thought and action was directed inward on the baby. She balanced on her toes now, for the baby's sake. And the world was pregnant to her; she thought only in terms of reproduction and of motherhood. Connie, her nineteen-year-old husband, who had married a plump, passionate hoyden, was still frightened and bewildered at the change in her; for there were no more cat-fights in bed, biting and scratching with muffled giggles and final tears. There was a balanced, careful, wise creature who smiled shyly but very firmly at him. Connie was proud and fearful of Rose of Sharon. Whenever he could, he put a hand on her or stood close, so that his body touched her at hip and shoulder, and he felt that this kept a relation that might be departing. He was a sharp-faced, lean young man of a Texas strain, and his pale blue eyes were sometimes dangerous and sometimes kindly, and sometimes frightened. He was a good hard worker and would make a good husband. He drank enough, but not too much; fought when it was required of him; and never boasted. He sat quietly in a gathering and yet managed to be there and to be recognized.

Had he not been fifty years old, and so one of the natural rulers of the family, Uncle John would have preferred not to sit in the honour place beside the driver. He would have liked Rose of Sharon to sit there. This was impossible, because she was young and a woman. But Uncle John sat uneasily, his lonely haunted eyes were not at ease, and his thin strong body was not relaxed. Nearly all the time the barrier of loneliness cut Uncle John off from people and from appetites. He ate little, drank nothing, and was celibate. But underneath, his appetites swelled into pressure until they broke through. Then he would eat of some craved food until he was sick; or he would drink jake or whisky until he was a shaken paralytic with red wet eyes; or he would raven with lust for some whore in Sallisaw. It was told of him that once he went clear to Shawnee and hired three whores in one bed, and snorted and rutted on their unresponsive bodies for an hour. But when one of his appetites was sated, he was sad and ashamed and lonely again. He hid from people, and by gifts tried to make up to all people for himself. Then he crept into houses and left gum under pillows for children; then he cut wood and took no pay. Then he gave away any possession he might have: a saddle, a horse, a new pair of shoes. One could not talk to him then, for he ran away, or if confronted hid within himself and peeked out of frightened eyes. The death of his wife, followed by months of being alone, had marked him with guilt and shame and had left an unbreaking loneliness on him.

But there were things he could not escape. Being one of the heads of the family, he had to govern; and now he had to sit on the honour seat beside the driver.

The three men on the seat were glum as they drove toward home over the dusty road. Al, bending over the wheel, kept shifting eyes from the road to the instrument panel, watching the ammeter needle, which jerked suspiciously, watching the oil gauge and the heat indicator. And his mind was cataloguing weak points and suspicious things about the car. He listened to the whine, which might be the rear end, dry; and he listened to tappets lifting and falling.

He kept his hand on the gear lever, feeling the turning gears through it. And he had let the clutch out against the brake to test for slipping clutch plates. He might be a musking goat sometimes, but this was his responsibility, this truck, its running, and its maintenance. If something went wrong it would be his fault, and while no one would say it, everyone, and Al most of all, would know it was his fault. And so he felt it, watched it, and listened to it. And his face was serious and responsible. And everyone respected him and his responsibility. Even Pa, who was the leader, would hold a wrench and take orders from Al.

They were all tired on the truck. Ruthie and Winfield were tired from seeing too much movement, too many faces, from fighting to get liquorice whips; tired from the excitement of having Uncle John secretly slip gum into their pockets.

And the men in the seat were tired and angry and sad, for they had got eighteen dollars for every movable thing from the farm: the horses, the wagon, the implements, and all the furniture from the house. Eighteen dollars. They had assailed the buyer, argued; but they were routed when his interest seemed to flag and he had told them he didn't want the stuff at any price. Then they were beaten, believed him, and took two dollars less than he had first offered. And now they were weary and frightened because they had gone against a system they did not understand and it had beaten them. They knew the team and the wagon were worth much more. They knew the buyer men would get much more, but they didn't know how to do it. Merchandizing was a secret to them.

Al, his eyes darting from road to panel board, said: 'That fella, he ain't a local fella. Didn' talk like a local fella. Clothes was different, too.'

And Pa explained: 'When I was in the hardware store I talked to some men I know. They say there's fellas comin' in jus' to buy up the stuff us fellas got to sell when we get out. They say these new fellas is cleanin' up. But there ain't nothin' we can do about it. Maybe Tommy should of went. Maybe he could of did better.'

John said: 'But the fella wasn't gonna take it at all. We couldn't hand it back.'

'These men I know told about that,' said Pa. 'Said the buyer fellas always done that. Scairt folk that way. We jus' don' know how to go about stuff like that. Ma's gonna be disappointed. She'll be mad an' disappointed.'

Al said: 'When ya think we're gonna go, Pa?'

'I dunno. We'll talk her over to-night an' decide. I'm sure glad Tom's back. That makes me feel good. Tom's a good boy.'

Al said: 'Pa, some fellas was talkin' about Tom, an' they says he's parole'. An' they says that means he can't go outside the State, or if he goes, an' they catch him, they send 'im back for three years.'

Pa looked startled. 'They said that? Seem like fellas that knowed? Not jus' blowin' off?'

'I don' know,' said Al. 'They was just a-talkin' there, an' I didn' let on he's my brother. I jus' stood an' took it in.'

Pa said: 'Jesus Christ, I hope that ain't true! We need Tom. I'll ask 'im about that. We got trouble enough without they chase the hell out of us. I hope it ain't true. We got to talk that out in the open.'

Uncle John said: 'Tom, he'll know.'

They fell silent while the truck battered along. The engine was noisy, full of little clashings, and the brake rods banged. There was a wooden creaking from the wheels, and a thin jet of steam escaped through a hole in the top of the radiator cap. The truck pulled a high whirling column of red dust behind it. They rumbled up the last little rise while the sun was still half-face above the horizon, and they bore down on the house as it disappeared. The brakes squealed when they stopped, and the sound printed in Al's head–no lining left.

Ruthie and Winfield climbed yelling over the side walls and dropped to the ground. They shouted: 'Where is he? Where's Tom?' And then they saw him standing beside the door, and they stopped, embarrassed, and walked slowly toward him and looked shyly at him.

And when he said: 'Hello, how you kids doin'?' they replied softly: 'Hello! All right.' And they stood apart and watched him secretly, the great brother who had killed a man and been in prison. They remembered how they had played prison in the chicken coop and fought for the right to be prisoner.

Connie Rivers lifted the high tail-gate out of the truck and got down and helped Rose of Sharon to the ground; and she accepted it nobly, smiling her wise, self-satisfied smile, mouth tipped at the corners a little fatuously.

Tom said: 'Why, it's Rosasharn. I didn' know you was comin' with them.'

'We was walkin',' she said. 'The truck come by an' picked us up.' And then she said: 'This is Connie, my husband.' And she was grand, saying it.

The two shook hands, sizing each other up, looking deeply into each other; and in a moment each was satisfied, and Tom said: 'Well, I see you been busy.'

She looked down. 'You do not see, not yet.'

'Ma tol' me. When's it gonna be?'

'Oh, not for a long time! Not till nex' winter.'

Tom laughed. 'Gonna get 'im bore in a orange ranch, huh? In one a them white houses with orange trees all aroun'.'

Rose of Sharon felt her stomach with both her hands. 'You do not see,' she said, and she smiled her complacent smile and went into the house. The evening was hot, and the thrust of light still flowed up from the western horizon. And without any signal the family gathered by the truck, and the congress, the family government, went into session.

The film of evening light made the red earth lucent, so that its dimensions were deepened, so that a stone, a post, a building had greater depth and more solidity than in the daytime light; and these objects were curiously more individual–a post was more essentially a post, set off from the earth it stood in and the field of corn it stood out against. And plants were individuals, not the mass of crop; and the ragged willow tree was itself standing free of all other willow trees. The earth contributed a light to the evening. The front of the grey, paintless house, facing the west, was luminous as the moon is. The grey dusty truck, in the yard before the door, stood out magically in this light, in the overdrawn perspective of a stereopticon.

The people too were changed in the evening, quieted. They seemed to be a part of an organization of the unconscious. They obeyed impulses which registered only faintly in their thinking minds. Their eyes were inward and quiet, and their eyes, too, were lucent in the evening, lucent in dusty faces.

The family met at the most important place, near the truck. The house was dead, and the fields were dead; but this truck was the active thing, the living principle. The ancient Hudson, with bent and scarred radiator screen, with grease in dusty globules at the worn edges of every moving part, with hub caps gone and caps of red dust in their places–this was the new hearth, the living centre of the family; half passenger-car and half truck, high-sided and clumsy.

Pa walked around the truck, looking at it, and then he squatted down in the dust and found a stick to draw with. One foot was flat to the ground, the other rested on the ball and slightly back, so that one knee was higher than the other. Left forearm rested on the lower, left, knee; the right elbow on the right knee, and the right fist cupped for the chin. Pa squatted there, looking at the truck, his chin in his cupped fist. And Uncle John moved toward him and squatted down beside him. Their eyes were brooding. Grampa came out of the house and saw the two squatting together, and he jerked over and sat on the running-board of the truck, facing them. That was the nucleus. Tom and Connie and Noah strolled in and squatted, and the line was a half-circle with Grampa in the opening. And then Ma came out of the house, and Granma with her, and Rose of Sharon behind, walking daintily. They took their places behind the squatting men; they stood up and put their hands on their hips. And the children, Ruthie and Winfield, hopped from foot to foot beside the women; the children squidged their toes in the red dust, but they made no sound. Only the preacher was not there. He, out of delicacy, was sitting on the ground behind the house. He was a good preacher and knew his people.

The evening light grew softer and for a while the family sat and stood silently. Then Pa, speaking to no one, but to the group, made his report. 'Got skinned on the stuff we sold. The fella knowed we couldn't wait. Got eighteen dollars only.'

Ma stirred restively, but she held her peace.

Noah, the oldest son, asked: 'How much, all added up, we got?'

Pa drew figures in the dust and mumbled to himself for a moment. 'Hundred fifty-four,' he said. 'But Al here says we gonna need better tires. Says these here won't last.'

This was Al's first participation in the conference. Always he had stood behind with the women before. And now he made his report solemnly. 'She's old an' she's ornery,' he said gravely. 'I gave the whole thing a good goin'-over 'fore we bought her. Didn' listen to the fella talkin' what a hell of a bargain she was. Stuck my finger in the differential and they wasn't no sawdust. Opened the gear box an' they wasn't no sawdust. Test' her clutch an' rolled her wheels for line. Went under her an' her frame ain't splayed none. She never been rolled. Seen they was a cracked cell in her battery an' made the fella put in a good one. The tires ain't worth a damn, but they're a good size. Easy to get. She'll ride like a bull calf, but she ain't shootin' no oil. Reason I says buy her is she was a pop'lar car. Wreckin' yards is full a Hudson Super-Sixes, an' you can buy parts cheap. Could a got a bigger, fancier car for the same money, but parts too hard to get, an' too dear. That's how I figgered her anyways.' The last was his submission to the family. He stopped speaking and waited for their opinions.

Grampa was still the titular head, but he no longer ruled. His position was honorary and a matter of custom. But he did have the right of first comment, no matter how silly his old mind might be. And the squatting men and the standing women waited for him. 'You're all right, Al,' Grampa said. 'I was a squirt jus' like you, a-fartin' aroun' like a dog-wolf. But when they was a job, I done it. You've growed up good.' He finished in the tone of a benediction, and Al reddened a little with pleasure.

Pa said: 'Sounds right-side-up to me. If it was horses we wouldn' have to put the blame on Al. But Al's the on'y automobile fella here.'

Tom said: 'I know some. Worked some in McAlester. Al's right. He done good.' And now Al was rosy with the compliment. Tom went on: 'I'd like to say–well, that preacher–he wants to go along.' He was silent. His words lay in the group, and the group was silent. 'He's a nice fella,' Tom added. 'We've knowed him a long time. Talks a little wild sometimes, but he talks sensible.' And he relinquished the proposal to the family.

The light was going gradually. Ma left the group and went into the house, and the iron clang of the stove came from the house. In a moment she walked back to the brooding council.

Grampa said: 'They was two ways a thinkin'. Some folks use' ta figger that a preacher was poison luck.'

Tom said: 'This fella says he ain't a preacher no more.'

Grampa waved his hand back and forth. 'Once a fella's a preacher, he's always a preacher. That's somepin you can't get shut of. They was some folks figgered it was a good respectable thing to have a preacher along. Ef somebody died, preacher buried 'em. Weddin' come due, or overdue, an' there's your preacher. Baby come, an' you got a christener right under the roof. Me, I always said they was preachers *an*' preachers. Got to pick 'em. I kinda like this fella. He ain't stiff.'

Pa dug his stick into the dust and rolled it between his fingers so that it bored a little hole. 'They's more to this than is he lucky, or is he a nice fella,' Pa said. 'We got to figger close. It's a sad thing to figger close. Le's see, now. There's Grampa an' Granma–that's two. An' me an' John an' Ma–that's five. An' Noah an' Tommy an' Al–that's eight. Rosasharn an' Connie is ten, an' Ruthie an' Winfiel' is twelve. We got to take the dogs 'cause what'll we do else? Can't shoot a good dog, an' there ain't nobody to give 'em to. An' that's fourteen.'

'Not countin' what chickens is left, an' two pigs,' said Noah.

Pa said: 'I aim to get those pigs salted down to eat on the way. We gonna need meat. Carry the salt kegs right with us. But I'm wonderin' if we can all ride, an' the preacher too. An' kin we feed a extra mouth?' Without turning his head he asked: 'Kin we, Ma?'

Ma cleared her throat. 'It ain't kin we? It's will we?' she said firmly. 'As far as "kin", we can't do nothin', not go to California or nothin'; but as far as "will", why, we'll do what we will. An' as far as "will"–it's a long time our folks been here and east before, an' I never heard tell of no Joads or no Hazletts, neither, ever refusin' food an' shelter or a lift on the road to anybody that asked. They's been mean Joads, but never that mean.'

Pa broke in: 'But s'pose there just ain't room?' He had twisted his neck to look up at her, and he was ashamed. Her tone had made him ashamed. 'S'pose we jus' can't all get in the truck?'

'There ain't room now,' she said. 'There ain't room for more'n six, an' twelve is goin' sure. One more ain't gonna hurt; an' a man, strong an' healthy, ain't never no burden. An' any time when we got two pigs an' over a hundred dollars, an' we wonderin' if we kin feed a fella–' She stopped, and Pa turned back, and his spirit was raw from the whipping.

Granma said: 'A preacher is a nice thing to be with us. He give a nice grace this morning.'

Pa looked at the face of each one for dissent, and then he said: 'Want to call 'im over, Tommy? If he's goin', he ought ta be here.'

Tom got up from his hams and went toward the house, calling: 'Casy–oh, Casy!'

A muffled voice replied from behind the house. Tom walked to the corner and saw the preacher sitting back against the wall, looking at the flashing evening star in the light sky. 'Calling me?' Casy asked.

'Yeah. We think long as you're goin' with us, you ought to be over with us, helpin' to figure things out.'

Casy got to his feet. He knew the government of families, and he knew he had been taken into the family. Indeed his position was eminent, for Uncle John moved sideways, leaving space between Pa and himself for the preacher. Casy squatted down like the others, facing Grampa enthroned on the running-board.

Ma went to the house again. There was a screech of a lantern hood and the yellow light flashed up in the dark kitchen. When she lifted the lid of the big pot, the smell of boiling side-meat and beet greens came out the door. They waited for her to come back across the darkening yard, for Ma was powerful in the group.

Pa said: 'We got to figger when to start. Sooner the better. What we got to do 'fore we go is get them pigs slaughtered an' in salt, an' pack our stuff an' go. Quicker the better, now.'

Noah agreed: 'If we pitch in, we kin get ready to-morrow, an' we kin go bright the nex' day.'

Uncle John objected: 'Can't chill no meat in the heat a the day. Wrong time a year for slaughterin'. Meat'll be sof' if it don' chill.'

'Well, le's do her to-night. She'll chill to-night some. Much as she's gonna. After we eat, le's get her done. Got salt?'

Ma said: 'Yes. Got plenty salt. Got two nice kegs too.'

'Well, le's get her done, then,' said Tom.

Grampa began to scrabble about, trying to get a purchase to arise. 'Gettin' dark,' he said. 'I'm gettin' hungry. Come time we get to California I'll have a big bunch a grapes in my han' all the time, a-nibblin' off it all the time, by God!' He got up, and the men arose.

Ruthie and Winfield hopped excitedly about in the dust, like crazy things. Ruthie whispered hoarsely to Winfield: 'Killin' pigs *and* goin' to California. Killin' pigs *and* goin'–all the same time.'

And Winfield was reduced to madness. He stuck his finger against his throat, made a horrible face, and wobbled about, weakly shrilling: 'I'm a ol' pig. Look! I'm a ol' pig. Look at the blood, Ruthie!' And he staggered and sank to the ground, and waved his arms and legs weakly.

But Ruthie was older, and she knew the tremendousness of the time. '*And* goin' to California,' she said again. And she knew this was the great time in her life so far.

The adults moved toward the lighted kitchen through the deep dusk, and Ma served them greens and side-meat in tin plates. But before Ma ate, she put the big round wash tub on the stove and started the fire roaring. She carried buckets of water until the tub was full, and then around the tub she clustered the buckets, full of water. The kitchen became a swamp of heat, and the family ate hurriedly, and went out to sit on the doorstep until the water should get hot. They sat looking out at the dark, at the square of light the kitchen lantern threw on the ground outside the door, with a hunched shadow of Grampa in the middle of it. Noah picked his teeth thoroughly with a broom straw. Ma and Rose of Sharon washed up the dishes and piled them on the table.

And then, all of a sudden, the family began to function. Pa got up and lighted another lantern. Noah, from a box in the kitchen, brought out the bow-bladed butchering knife and whetted it on a worn little carborundum stone. And he laid the scraper on the chopping block, and the knife beside it. Pa brought two sturdy sticks, each three feet long, and pointed the ends with the axe, and he tied strong ropes, double half-hitched, to the middle of the sticks.

He grumbled: 'Shouldn't of sold those singletrees–all of 'em.'

The water in the pots steamed and rolled.

Noah asked: 'Gonna take the water down there or bring the pigs up here?'

'Pigs up here,' said Pa. 'You can't spill a pig and scald yourself like you can hot water. Water about ready?'

'Jis' about,' said Ma.

'Aw right. Noah, you an' Tom an' Al come along. I'll carry the light. We'll slaughter down there an' bring 'em up here.'

Noah took his knife, and Al the axe, and the four men moved down on the sty, their legs flickering in the lantern light. Ruthie and Winfield skittered along, hopping over the ground. At the sty Pa leaned over the fence, holding the lantern. The sleepy young pigs struggled to their feet, grunting suspiciously. Uncle John and the preacher walked down to help.

'All right,' said Pa. 'Stick 'em, an' we'll run 'em up and bleed an' scald at the house.' Noah and Tom stepped over the fence. They slaughtered quickly and efficiently. Tom struck twice with the blunt head of the axe; and Noah, leaning over the felled pigs, found the great artery with his curving knife and released the pulsing streams of blood. Then over the fence with the squealing pigs. The preacher and Uncle John dragged one by the hind legs, and Tom and Noah the other. Pa walked along with the lantern, and the black blood made two trails in the dust.

At the house, Noah slipped his knife between tendon and bone of the hind legs; the pointed sticks held the legs apart, and the carcasses were hung from the two-by-four rafters that stuck out from the house. Then the men carried the boiling water and poured it over the black bodies. Noah slit the bodies from end to end and dropped the entrails out on the ground. Pa sharpened two more sticks to hold the bodies open to the air, while Tom with the scrubber and Ma with a dull knife scraped the skins to take out the bristles. Al brought a bucket and shovelled the entrails into it, and dumped them on the ground away from the house, and two cats followed him, mewing loudly, and the dogs followed him growling lightly at the cats.

Pa sat on the doorstep and looked at the pigs hanging in the lantern light. The scraping was done now, and only a few drops of blood continued to fall from the carcasses into the black pool on the ground. Pa got up and went to the pigs and felt them with his hand, and then he sat down again. Granma and Grampa went toward the barn to sleep, and Grampa carried a candle lantern in his hand. The rest of the family sat quietly about the doorstep, Connie and Al and Tom on the ground, leaning their backs against the house wall, Uncle John on a box, Pa in the doorway. Only Ma and Rose of Sharon continued to move about. Ruthie and Winfield were sleepy now, but fighting it off. They quarrelled sleepily out in the darkness. Noah and the preacher squatted side by side, facing the house. Pa scratched himself nervously, and took off his hat and ran his fingers through his hair. 'To-morra we'll get that pork salted early in the morning, an' then we'll get the truck loaded, all but the beds, an' next morning off we'll go. Hardly is a day's work in all that,' he said uneasily.

Tom broke in: 'We'll be moonin' aroun' all day, lookin' for somepin to do.' The group stirred uneasily. 'We could get ready by daylight an' go,' Tom suggested. Pa rubbed his knee with his hand. And the restiveness spread to all of them.

Noah said: 'Prob'ly wouldn't hurt that meat to git her right down in salt. Cut her up, she'd cool quicker anyways.'

It was Uncle John who broke over the edge, his pressures too great. 'What we hangin' aroun' for? I want to get shut of this. Now we're goin', why don't we go?'

And the revulsion spread to the rest. 'Whyn't we go? Get sleep on the way.' And a sense of hurry crept into them.

Pa said: 'They say it's two thousan' miles. That's a hell of a long ways. We oughta go. Noah, you an' me can get that meat cut up an' we can put all the stuff in the truck.'

Ma put her head out of the door. 'How about if we forgit somepin not seein' it in the dark?'

'We could look 'round after daylight,' said Noah. They sat still then, thinking about it. But in a moment Noah got up and began to sharpen the bow-bladed knife on his little worn stone. 'Ma,' he said, 'git that table cleared.' And he stepped to a pig, cut a line down one side of the backbone, and began peeling the meat forward, off the ribs.

Pa stood up excitedly. 'We got to get the stuff together,' he said. 'Come on, you fellas.'

Now that they were committed to going, the hurry infected all of them. Noah carried the slabs of meat into the kitchen and cut it into small salting blocks, and Ma patted the coarse salt in, laid it piece by piece in the kegs, careful that no pieces touched each other. She laid the slabs like bricks, and pounded salt in the spaces. And Noah cut up the side-meat and he cut up the legs. Ma kept her fire going, and as Noah cleaned the ribs and the spines and leg bones of all the meat he could, she put them in the oven to roast for gnawing purposes.

In the yard and in the barn the circles of lantern light moved about, and the men brought together all the things to be taken, and piled them by the truck. Rose of Sharon brought out all the clothes the family possessed: the overalls, the thick-soled shoes, the rubber boots, the worn best suits, the sweaters and sheepskin coats. And she packed these tightly into a wooden box and got into the box and tramped them down. And then she brought out the print dresses and shawls, the black cotton stockings and the children's clothes–small overalls and cheap print dresses–and she put these in the box and tramped them down.

Tom went to the tool shed and brought what tools were left to go, a hand saw and a set of wrenches, a hammer and a box of assorted nails, a pair of pliers and a flat file and a set of rat-tail files.

And Rose of Sharon brought out the big piece of tarpaulin and spread it on the ground behind the truck. She struggled through the door with the mattresses, three double ones and a single. She piled them on the tarpaulin and brought arm-loads of folded ragged blankets and piled them up.

Ma and Noah worked busily at the carcasses, and the smell of roasting pork bones came from the stove. The children had fallen by the way in the late night. Winfield lay curled up in the dust outside the door; and Ruthie, sitting in a box in the kitchen where she had gone to watch the butchering, had dropped her head against the wall. She breathed easily in her sleep, and her lips were parted over her teeth.

Tom finished with the tools and came into the kitchen with his lantern, and the preacher followed him. 'God in the buckboard,' Tom said, 'smell that meat! An' listen to her crackle.'

Ma laid the bricks of meat in a keg and poured salt around and over them and covered the layer with salt and patted it down. She looked up at Tom and smiled a little at him, but her eyes were serious and tired. 'Be nice to have pork bones for breakfas',' she said.

The preacher stepped beside her. 'Leave me salt down this meat,' he said. 'I can do it. There's other stuff for you to do.'

She stopped her work then and inspected him oddly, as though he suggested a curious thing. And her hands were crusted with salt, pink with fluid from the fresh pork. 'It's women's work,' she said finally.

'It's all work,' the preacher replied. 'They's too much of it to split up to men's or women's work. You got stuff to do. Leave me salt the meat.'

Still for a moment she stared at him, and then she poured water from a bucket into the tin wash basin and she washed her hands. The preacher took up the blocks of pork and patted on the salt while she watched him. And he laid them in the kegs as she had. Only when he had finished a layer and covered it carefully and patted down the salt was she satisfied. She dried her bleached and bloated hands.

Tom said: 'Ma, what stuff we gonna take from here?'

She looked quickly about the kitchen. 'The bucket,' she said. 'All the stuff to eat with: plates an' the cups, the spoons an' knives an' forks. Put all them in that drawer, an' take the drawer. The big fry pan an' the big stew kettle, the coffee pot. When it gets cool, take the rack outa the oven. That's good over a fire. I'd like to take the wash tub, but I guess there ain't room. I'll wash clothes in the bucket. Don't do no good to take little stuff. You can cook little stuff in a big kettle, but you can't cook big stuff in a little pot. Take the bread pans, all of 'em. They fit down inside each other.' She stood and looked about the kitchen. 'You jus' take that stuff I tol' you, Tom. I'll fix up the rest, the big can a pepper an' the salt an' the nutmeg an' the grater. I'll take all that stuff jus' at the last.' She picked up a lantern and walked heavily into the bedroom, and her bare feet made no sound on the floor.

The preacher said: 'She looks tar'd.'

'Women always tar'd,' said Tom. 'That's just the way women is, 'cept at meetin' once an' again.'

'Yeah, but tar'der'n that. Real tar'd, like she's sick-tar'd.'

Ma was just through the door, and she heard his words. Slowly her relaxed face rightened, and the lines disappeared from the taut muscular face. Her eyes sharpened and her shoulders straightened. She glanced about the stripped room. Nothing was left in it except trash. The mattresses which had been on the floor were gone. The bureaus were sold. On the floor lay a broken comb, an empty talcum powder can, and a few dust mice. Ma set her lantern on the floor. She reached behind one of the boxes that had served as chairs and brought out a stationery box, old and soiled and cracked at the corners. She sat down and opened the box. Inside were letters, clippings, photographs, a pair of earrings, a little gold signet ring, and a watch chain braided of hair and tipped with gold swivels. She touched the letters with her fingers, touched them lightly, and she smoothed a newspaper clipping on which there was an account of Tom's trial. For a long time she held the box, looking over it, and her fingers disturbed the letters and then lined them up again. She bit her lower lip, thinking, remembering. And at last she made up her mind. She picked out the ring, the watch chain, the ear-rings, dug under the pile and found one gold cuff link. She took a letter from an envelope and dropped the trinkets in the envelope. She folded the envelope over and put it in her dress pocket. Then gently and tenderly she closed the box and smoothed the top carefully with her fingers. Her lips parted. And then she stood up, took her lantern, and went back into the kitchen. She lifted the stove lid and laid the box gently among the coals. Quickly the heat browned the paper. A flame licked up and over the box. She replaced the stove lid and instantly the fire sighed up and breathed over the box.

Out in the dark yard, working in the lantern light, Pa and Al loaded the truck. Tools on the bottom, but handy to reach in case of a breakdown. Boxes of clothes next, and kitchen utensils in a gunny sack; cutlery and dishes in their box. Then the gallon bucket tied on behind. They made the bottom of the load as even as possible, and filled the spaces between boxes with rolled blankets. Then over the top they laid the mattresses, filling the truck in level. And last they spread the big tarpaulin over the load and Al made holes in the edge, two feet apart, and inserted little ropes, and tied it down to the side-bars of the truck.

'Now, if it rains,' he said, 'we'll tie it to the bar above, an' the folks can get underneath, out of the wet. Up front we'll be dry enough.'

And Pa applauded. 'That's a good idear.'

'That ain't all,' Al said. 'First chance I git I'm gonna fin'a long plant an' make a ridge pole, an' put the tarp over that. An' then it'll be covered in, an' the folks'll be outa the sun, too.'

And Pa agreed: 'That's a good idear. Whyn't you think a that before?'

'I ain't had time,' said Al.

'Ain't had time? Why, Al, you had time to coyote all over the country. God knows where you been this las' two weeks.'

'Stuff a fella got to do when he's leavin' the country,' said Al. And then he lost some of his assurance. 'Pa,' he asked. 'You glad to be goin', Pa?'

'Huh? Well–sure. Leastwise–yeah. We had hard times here. 'Course it'll be all different out there–plenty work, an' ever'thing nice an' green, an' little white houses an' oranges growin' aroun'.'

'Is it all oranges ever'where?'

'Well, maybe not ever'where, but plenty places.'

The first grey of daylight began in the sky. And the work was done–the kegs of pork ready, the chicken coop ready to go on top. Ma opened the oven and took out the pile of roasted bones, crisp and brown, with plenty of gnawing meat left. Ruthie half awakened, and slipped down from the box, and slept again. But the adults stood around the door, shivering a little and gnawing at the crisp pork.

'Guess we oughta wake up Granma an' Grampa,' Tom said. 'Gettin' along on toward day.'

Ma said: 'Kinda hate to, till the las' minute. They need the sleep. Ruthie an' Winfield ain't hardly got no real rest neither.'

'Well, they kin all sleep on top a the load,' said Pa. 'It'll be nice an' comf'table there.'

Suddenly the dogs started up from the dust and listened; and then, with a roar, went barking off into the darkness. 'Now what in hell is that?' Pa demanded. In a moment they heard a voice speaking reassuringly to the barking dogs and the barking lost its fierceness. Then footsteps, and a man approached. It was Muley Graves, his hat pulled low.

He came near timidly. 'Morning, folks,' he said.

'Why, Muley,' Pa waved the ham bone he held. 'Step in an' get some pork for yourself, Muley.'

'Well, no,' said Muley. 'I ain't hungry, exactly.'

'Oh, get it, Muley, get it. Here!' And Pa stepped into the house and brought out a hand of spare-ribs.

'I wasn't aiming to eat none a your stuff,' he said. 'I was jus' walkin' aroun', an' I thought how you'd be goin', an' I'd maybe say good-bye.'

'Goin' in a little while now,' said Pa. 'You'd a missed us if you'd come an hour later. All packed up–see?'

'All packed up.' Muley looked at the loaded truck. 'Sometimes I wisht I'd go an' fin' my folks.'

Ma asked: 'Did you hear from 'em out in California?'

'No,' said Muley, 'I ain't heard. But I ain't been to look in the post office. I oughta go in sometimes.'

Pa said: 'Al, go down, wake up Granma, Grampa. Tell 'em to come an' eat. We're goin' before long.' And as Al sauntered toward the barn: 'Muley, ya wanta squeeze in with us an' go? We'd try to make room for ya.'

Muley took a bite of meat from the edge of a rib bone and chewed it. 'Sometimes I think I might. But I know I won't,' he said. 'I know perfectly well the las' minute I'd run an' hide like a damn ol' graveyard ghos'.'

Noah said: 'You gonna die out in the fiel' some day, Muley.'

'I know. I thought about that. Sometimes it seems pretty lonely, an' sometimes it seems all right, an' sometimes it seems good. It don't make no difference. But if ya come acrost my folks–that's really what I come to say–if ya come on any my folks in California, tell 'em I'm well. Tell 'em I'm doin' all right. Don't let on I'm livin' this way. Tell 'em I'll come to 'em soon's I git the money.'

Ma asked: 'An' will ya?'

'No,' Muley said softly. 'No, I won't. I can't go away. I got to stay now. Time back I might of went. But not now. Fella gits to thinkin', an' he gits to knowin'. I ain't never goin'.'

The light of the dawn was a little sharper now. It paled the lanterns a little. Al came back with Grampa struggling and limping by his side. 'He wasn't sleepin',' Al said. 'He was settin' out back of the barn. They's somepin wrong with 'im.'

Grampa's eyes had dulled, and there was none of the old meanness in them. 'Ain't nothin' the matter with me,' he said, 'I jus' ain't a-goin'.'

'Not goin'?' Pa demanded. 'What you mean you ain't a-goin'? Why, here we're all packed up, ready. We got to go. We got no place to stay.'

'I ain't sayin' for you to stay,' said Grampa. 'You go right on along. Me–I'm stayin'. I give her a goin'-over all night mos'ly. This here's my country. I b'long here. An' I don't give a goddamn if they's oranges an' grapes crowdin' a fella outa bed even. I ain't a-goin'. This country ain't no good, but it's my country. No, you all go ahead. I'll jus' stay right here where I b'long.'

They crowded near to him. Pa said: 'You can't, Grampa. This here lan' is goin' under the tractors. Who'd cook for you? How'd you live? You can't stay here. Why, with nobody to take care of you, you'd starve.'

Grampa cried: 'Goddamn it, I'm a ol' man, but I can still take care a myself. How's Muley here get along? I can get along as good as him. I tell ya I ain't goin', an' ya can lump it. Take Granma with ya if ya want, but ya ain't takin' me, an' that's the end of it.'

Pa said helplessly: 'Now listen to me, Grampa. Jus' listen to me, jus' a minute.'

'Ain't a-gonna listen. I tol' ya what I'm a-gonna do.'

Tom touched his father on the shoulder. 'Pa, come in the house. I wanta tell ya somepin.' And as they moved toward the house, he called: 'Ma–come here a minute, will ya?'

In the kitchen one lantern burned and the plate of pork bones was still piled high. Tom said: 'Listen, I know Grampa got the right to say he ain't goin', but he can't stay. We know that.'

'Sure he can't stay,' said Pa.

'Well, look. If we got to catch him an' tie him down, we li'ble to hurt him, an' he'll git so mad he'll hurt himself. Now we can't argue with him. If we could get him drunk it'd be all right. You got any whisky?'

'No,' said Pa. 'There ain't a drop a' whisky in the house. An' John got no whisky. He never has none when he ain't drinkin'.'

Ma said: 'Tom, I got a half a bottle soothin' syrup I got for Winfiel' when he had them ear-aches. Think that might work? Use ta put Winfiel' ta sleep when his ear-ache was bad.'

'Might,' said Tom. 'Get it, Ma. We'll give her a try anyways.'

'I throwed it out on the trash pile,' said Ma. She took the lantern and went out, and in a moment she came back with a bottle half full of black medicine.

Tom took it from her and tasted it. 'Don't taste bad,' he said. 'Make up a cup of black coffee, good an' strong. Le's see–says one teaspoon. Better put in a lot, coupla teaspoons.'

Ma opened the stove and put a kettle inside, down next to the coals, and she measured water and coffee into it. 'Have to give it to 'im in a can,' she said. 'We got the cups all packed.'

Tom and his father went back outside. 'Fella got a right to say what he's gonna do. Say, who's eatin' spare-ribs?' said Grampa.

'We've et,' said Tom. 'Ma's fixin' you a cup of coffee an' some pork.'

He went into the house, and he drank his coffee and ate his pork. The group outside in the growing dawn watched him quietly, through the door. They saw him yawn and sway, and they saw him put his arms on the table and rest his head on his arms and go to sleep.

'He was tar'd anyways,' said Tom. 'Leave him be.'

Now they were ready. Granma, giddy and vague, saying: 'What's all this? What you doin' now, so early?' But she was dressed and agreeable. And Ruthie and Winfield were awake, but quiet with the pressure of tiredness and still half dreaming. The light was sifting rapidly over the land. And the movement of the family stopped. They stood about, reluctant to make the first active move to go. They were afraid, now that the time had come–afraid in the same way Grampa was afraid. They saw the shed take shape against the light, and they saw the lanterns pale until they no longer cast their circles of yellow light. The stars went out, few by few, toward the west. And still the family stood about like dream-walkers, their eyes focused panoramically, seeing no detail, but the whole dawn, the whole land, the whole texture of the country once more.

Only Muley Graves prowled about restlessly, looking through the bars into the truck, thumping the spare tires hung on the back of the truck. And at last Muley approached Tom. 'You goin' over the State line?' he asked. 'You gonna break your parole?'

And Tom shook himself free of the numbness. 'Jesus Christ, it's near sunrise,' he said loudly. 'We got to get goin'.' And the others came out of their numbness and moved toward the truck.

'Come on,' Tom said. 'Let's get Grampa on.' Pa and Uncle John and Tom and Al went into the kitchen where Grampa slept, his forehead down on his arms, and a line of drying coffee on the table. They took him under the elbows and lifted him to his feet, and he grumbled and cursed thickly, like a drunken man. Out the door they boosted him, and when they came to the truck Tom and Al climbed up, and, leaning over, hooked their hands under his arms and lifted him gently up, and laid him on top of the load. Al untied the tarpaulin, and they rolled him under and put a box under the tarp beside him, so that the weight of the heavy canvas would not be upon him.

'I got to get that ridge pole fixed,' Al said. 'Do her to-night when we stop.' Grampa grunted and fought weakly against awakening, and when he finally settled he went deeply to sleep again.

Pa said: 'Ma, you an' Granma set in with Al for a while. We'll change aroun' so it's easier, but you start out that way.' They got into the cab, and then the rest swarmed up on top of the load, Connie and Rose of Sharon, Pa and Uncle John, Ruthie and Winfield, Tom and the preacher. Noah stood on the ground, looking up at the great load of them sitting on top of the truck.

Al walked around, looking underneath at the springs. 'Holy Jesus,' he said, 'them springs is flat as hell. Lucky I blocked under 'em.'

Noah said: 'How about the dogs, Pa?'

'I forgot the dogs,' Pa said. He whistled shrilly, and one bouncing dog ran in, but only one. Noah caught him and threw him up on the top, where he sat rigid and shivering at the height. 'Got to leave the other two,' Pa called. 'Muley, will you look after 'em some? See they don't starve?'

'Yeah,' said Muley. 'I'll like to have a couple dogs. Yeah! I'll take 'em.'

'Take them chickens, too.' Pa said.

Al got into the driver's seat. The starter whirred and caught and whirred again. And then the loose roar of the six cylinders and a blue smoke behind. 'So long, Muley,' Al called.

And the family called: 'Good-bye, Muley.'

Al slipped in the low gear and let in the clutch. The truck shuddered and strained across the yard. And the second gear took hold. They crawled up the little hill, and the red dust arose about them. 'Chr-ist, what a load!' said Al. 'We ain't makin' no time on this trip.'

Ma tried to look back, but the body of the load cut off her view. She straightened her head and peered straight ahead along the dirt road. And a great weariness was in her eyes.

The people on top of the load did look back. They saw the house and the barn and a little smoke still rising from the chimney. They saw the windows reddening under the first colour of the sun. They saw Muley standing forlornly in the door-yard looking after them. And then the hill cut them off. The cottonfields lined the road. And the truck crawled slowly through the dust toward the highway and the west.

II

The houses were left vacant on the land, and the land was vacant because of this. Only the tractor sheds of corrugated iron, silver and gleaming, were alive; and they were alive with metal and petrol and oil, the disks of the ploughs shining. The tractors had lights shining, for there is no day and night for a tractor and the disks turn the earth in the darkness and they glitter in the daylight. And when a horse stops work and goes into the barn there is a life and a vitality left, there is a breathing and a warmth, and the feet shift on the straw, and the jaws champ on the hay, and the ears and the eyes are alive. There is a warmth of life in the barn, and the heat and smell of life. But when the motor of a tractor stops, it is as dead as the ore it came from. The heat goes out of it like the living heat that leaves a corpse. Then the corrugated iron doors are closed and the tractor man drives home to town, perhaps twenty miles away, and he need not come back for weeks or months, for the tractor is dead. And this is easy and efficient. So easy that the wonder goes out of work, so efficient that the wonder goes out of land and the working of it, and with the wonder the deep understanding and the relation. And in the tractor man there grows the contempt that comes only to a stranger who has little understanding and no relation. For nitrates are not the land, nor phosphates; and the length of fibre in the cotton is not the land. Carbon is not a man, nor salt nor water nor calcium. He is all these, but he is much more, much more; and the land is so much more than its analysis. The man who is more than his chemistry, walking on the earth, turning his plough-point for a stone, dropping his handles to slide over an outcropping, kneeling in the earth to eat his lunch; that man who is more than his elements knows the land that is more than its analysis. But the machine man, driving a dead tractor on land he does not know and love, understands only chemistry; and he is contemptuous of the land and of himself. When the corrugated iron doors are shut, he goes home, and his home is not the land.

The doors of the empty houses swung open, and drifted back and forth in the wind. Bands of little boys came out from the towns to break the windows and to pick over the debris, looking for treasures. And here's a knife with half the blade gone. That's a good thing. And–smells like a rat died here. And look what Whitey wrote on the wall. He wrote that in the toilet in school, too, an' teacher made 'im wash it off.

When the folks first left, and the evening of the first day came, the hunting cats slouched in from the fields, and mewed on the porch. And when no one came out, the cats crept through the open doors and walked mewing through the empty rooms. And then they went back to the fields and were wild cats from then on, hunting gophers and fieldmice, and sleeping in ditches in the day-time. When the night came, the bats, which had stopped at the doors for fear of light, swooped into the houses and sailed about through the empty rooms, and in a little while they stayed in dark room corners during the day, folded their wings high, and hung head-down among the rafters, and the smell of their droppings was in the empty houses.

And the mice moved in and stored weed seeds in corners, in boxes, in the backs of drawers in the kitchens. And weasels came in to hunt the mice, and the brown owls flew shrieking in and out again.

Now there came a little shower. The weeds sprang up in front of the doorstep, where they had not been allowed, and grass grew up through the porch boards. The houses were vacant, and a vacant house falls quickly apart. Splits started up the sheathing from the rusted nails. A dust settled on the floors, and only mouse and weasel and cat tracks disturbed it.

On a night the wind loosened a shingle and flipped it to the ground. The next wind pried into the hole where the shingle had been, lifted off three, and the next, a dozen. The midday sun burned through the hole and threw a glaring spot on the floor. The wild cats crept in from the fields at night, but they did not mew at the doorstep any more. They moved like shadows of a cloud across the moon, into the rooms to hunt the mice. And on windy nights the doors banged, and the ragged curtains fluttered in the broken windows.

12

Highway 66 is the main migrant road. 66–the long concrete path across the country, waving gently up and down on the map, from Mississippi to Bakersfield–over the red lands and the grey lands, twisting up into the mountains, crossing the Divide and down into the bright and terrible desert, and across the desert to the mountains again, and into the rich California valleys.

66 is the path of a people in flight, refugees from dust and shrinking land, from the thunder of tractors and shrinking ownership, from the desert's slow northward invasion, from the twisting winds that howl up out of Texas, from the floods that bring no richness to the land and steal what little richness is there. From all of these the people are in flight, and they come into 66 from the tributary side roads, from the wagon tracks and the rutted country roads. 66 is the mother road, the road of flight.

Clarksville and Ozark and Van Buren and Fort Smith on 62, and there's an end of Arkansas. And all the roads into Oklahoma City, 66 down from Tulsa, 270 up from McAlester. 81 from Wichita Falls south, from Enid north. Edmond, McLoud, Purcell. 66 out of Oklahoma City; El Reno and Clinton, going west on 66. Hydro, Elk City, and Texola; and there's an end to Oklahoma. 66 across the Panhandle of Texas. Shamrock and McLean, Conway and Amarillo, the yellow. Wildorado and Vega and Boise, and there's an end of Texas. Tucumcari and Santa Rosa and into the New Mexican mountains to Albuquerque, where the road comes down from Sante Fe. Then down the gorged Rio Grande to Los Lunas and west again on 66 to Gallup and there's the border of New Mexico.

And now the high mountains, Holbrook and Winslow and Flagstaff in the high mountains of Arizona. Then the great plateau rolling like a ground swell. Ashfork and Kingman and stone mountains again, where water must be hauled and sold. Then out of the broken sun-rotted mountains of Arizona to the Colorado, with green reeds on its banks, and that's the end of Arizona. There's California just over the river, and a pretty town to start it. Needles, on the river. But the river is a stranger in this place. Up from Needles and over a burned range, and there's the desert. And 66 goes on over the terrible desert, where the distance shimmers and the black centre mountains hang unbearably in the distance. At last there's Barstow, and more desert until at last the mountains rise up again, the good mountains, and 66 winds through them. Then suddenly a pass, and below the beautiful valley, below orchards and vineyards and little houses, and in the distance a city. And, oh, my God, it's over.

The people in flight streamed out on 66, sometimes a single car, sometimes a little caravan. All day they rolled slowly along the road, and at night they stopped near water. In the day ancient leaky radiators sent up columns of steam, loose connecting-rods hammered and pounded. And the men driving the trucks and the overloaded cars listened apprehensively. How far between towns? It is a terror between towns. If something breaks–well, if something breaks we camp right here while Jim walks to town and gets a part and walks back–how much food we got?

Listen to the motor. Listen to the wheels. Listen with your ears and with your hands on the steering-wheel; listen with the palm of your hand on the gear-shift lever; listen with your feet on the floor-boards. Listen to the pounding old jalopy with all your senses; for a change of tone, a variation of rhythm may mean–a week here? That rattle–that's tappets. Don't hurt a bit. Tappets can rattle till Jesus comes again without no harm. But that thudding as the car moves along–can't hear that–just kind of feel it. Maybe oil isn't gettin' someplace. Maybe a bearing's startin' to go. Jesus, if it's a bearing, what'll we do? Money's goin' fast.

And why's the son-of-a-bitch heat up so hot to-day? This ain't no climb. Le's look. God Almighty, the fan belt's gone! Here, make a belt outa this little piece of rope. Le's see how long–there. I'll splice the ends. Now take her slow–slow, till we can get to a town. That rope belt won't last long.

'F we can on'y get to California where the oranges grow before this here ol' jub blows up. 'F we on'y can.

And the tires–two layers of fabric worn through. On'y a four-ply wire. Might get a hundred miles more outa her if we don't hit a rock an' blow her. Which'll we take–a hundred, maybe, miles, or maybe spoil the tube? Which? A hundred miles. Well, that's somepin you got to think about. We got tube patches. Maybe when she goes she'll only spring a leak. How about makin' a boot? Might get five hundred more miles. Le's go on till she blows.

We got to get a tire, but, Jesus, they want a lot for a ol' tire. They look a fella over. They know he got to go on. They know he can't wait. And the price goes up.

Take it or leave it. I ain't in business for my health. I'm here a-sellin' tires. I ain't givin' 'em away. I can't help what happens to you. I got to think what happens to me.

How far's the nex' town?

I seen forty-two cars a you fellas go by yesterday. Where you all come from? Where all of you goin'?

Well, California's a big State.

It ain't that big. The whole United States ain't that big. It ain't that big. It ain't big enough. There ain't room enough for you an' me, for your kind an' my kind, for rich and poor together all in one country, for thieves and honest men. For hunger and fat. Whyn't you go back where you come from?

This is a free country. Fella can go where he wants.

That's what *you* think! Ever hear of the border patrol on the California line? Police from Los Angeles–stopped you bastards, turned you back. Says, if you can't buy no real estate we don't want you. Says, got a driver's licence? Le's see it. Tore it up. Says you can't come in without no driver's licence.

It's a free country.

Well, try to get some freedom to do. Fella says you're jus' as free as you got jack to pay for it.

In California they get high wages. I got a han'bill here tells about it.

Baloney! I seen folks comin' back. Somebody's kiddin' you. You want that tire or don't ya?

Got to take it, but, Jesus, mister, it cuts into our money! We ain't got much left.

Well, I ain't no charity. Take her along.

Got to, I guess, Let's look her over. Open her up, look a' the casing–you son-of-a-bitch, you said the casing was good. She's broke damn near through.

The hell she is. Well–by George! How come I didn' see that?

You did see it, you son-of-a-bitch. You wanta charge us four bucks for a busted casing. I'd like to take a sock at you.

Now keep your shirt on. I didn' see it, I tell you. Here–tell ya what I'll do. I'll give ya this one for three-fifty.

You'll take a flying jump at the moon! We'll try to make the nex' town.

Think we can make it on that tire?

Got to. I'll go on the rim before I'd give that son-of-a-bitch a dime.

What do ya think a guy in business is? Like he says, he ain't in it for his health. That's what business is. What'd you think it was? Fella's got–See that sign 'longside the road there? Service Club. Luncheon Tuesday, Colmado Hotel? Welcome, brother. That's a Service Club. Fella had a story. Went to one of them meetings an' told the story to all them business men. Says, when I was a kid my ol' man give me a haltered heifer an' says take her down an' git her serviced. An' the fella says, I done it, an' ever' time since then when I hear a business man talkin' about service, I wonder who's gettin' screwed. Fella in business got to lie an' cheat, but he calls it somepin else. That's what's important. You go steal that tire an' you're a thief, but he tried to steal your four dollars for a busted tire. They call that sound business.

Danny in the back seat wants a cup of water.

Have to wait. Got no water here.

Listen–that the rear end?

Can't tell.

Sound telegraphs through the frame.

There goes a gasket. Got to go on. Listen to her whistle. Find a nice place to camp an' I'll jerk the head off. But, God Almighty, the food's gettin' low, the money's gettin' low. When we can't buy no more petrol–what then?

Danny in the back seat wants a cup a water. Little fella's thirsty.

Listen to that gasket whistle.

Chee-rist! There she went. Blowed tube an' casing all to hell. Have to fix her. Save that casing to make boots; cut 'em out an' stick 'em inside a weak place.

Cars pulled up beside the road, engine heads off, tires mended. Cars limping along 66 like wounded things, panting and struggling. Too hot, loose connexions, loose bearings, rattling bodies.

Danny wants a cup of water.

People in flight along 66. And the concrete road shone like a mirror under the sun, and in the distance the heat made it seem that there were pools of water in the road.

Danny wants a cup of water.

He'll have to wait, poor little fella. He's hot. Nex' service station. *Service* station, like the fella says.

Two hundred and fifty thousand people over the road. Fifty thousand old cars–wounded, steaming. Wrecks along the road abandoned. Well, what happened to them? What happened to the folks in that car? Did they walk? Where are they? Where does the courage come from? Where does the terrible faith come from?

And here's a story you can hardly believe, but it's true, and it's funny and it's beautiful. There was a family of twelve and they were forced off the land. They had no car. They built a trailer out of junk and loaded it with their possessions. They pulled it to the side of 66 and waited. And pretty soon a sedan picked them up. Five of them rode in the sedan and seven on the trailer, and a dog on the trailer. They got to California in two jumps. The man who pulled them fed them. And that's true. But how can such courage be, and such faith in their own species? Very few things would teach such faith.

The people in flight from the terror behind–strange things happen to them, some bitterly cruel and some so beautiful that the faith is refired forever.

13

The ancient overloaded Hudson creaked and grunted to the highway at Sallisaw and turned west, and the sun was blinding. But on the concrete road Al built up his speed because the flattened springs were not in danger any more. From Sallisaw to Gore is twenty-one miles and the Hudson was doing thirty-five miles an hour. From Gore to Warner thirteen miles; Warner to Checotah fourteen miles; Checotah a long jump to Henrietta–thirty-four miles, but a real town at the end of it. Henrietta to Castle nineteen miles, and the sun was overhead, and the red fields, heated by the high sun, vibrated the air.

Al, at the wheel, his face purposeful, his whole body listening to the car, his restless eyes jumping from the road to the instrument panel. Al was one with his engine, every nerve listening for weaknesses, for the thumps or squeals, hums and chattering that indicate a change that may cause a breakdown. He had become the soul of the car.

Granma, beside him on the seat, half slept, and whimpered in her sleep, opened her eyes to peer ahead, and then dozed again. And Ma sat beside

Granma, one elbow out the window, and the skin reddening under the fierce sun. Ma looked ahead too, but her eyes were flat and did not see the road or the fields, the petrol stations, the little eating-sheds. She did not glance at them as the Hudson went by.

Al shifted himself on the broken seat and changed his grip on the steering wheel. And he sighed: 'Makes a racket, but I think she's awright. God knows what she'll do if we got to climb a hill with the load we got. Got any hills 'tween here an' California, Ma?'

Ma turned her head slowly and her eyes came to life. 'Seems to me they's hills,' she said, ''Course I dunno. But seems to me I heard they's hills an' even mountains. Big ones.'

Granma drew a long whining sigh in her sleep.

Al said: 'We'll burn right up if we got climbin' to do. Have to throw out some a this stuff. Maybe we shouldn' a brang that preacher.'

'You'll be glad a that preacher 'fore we're through,' said Ma. 'That preacher'll help us.' She looked ahead at the gleaming road again.

Al steered with one hand and put the other on the vibrating gear-shift lever. He had difficulty in speaking. His mouth formed the words silently before he said them aloud. 'Ma–' She looked slowly around at him, her head swaying a little with the car's motion. 'Ma, you scared a goin'? You scared a goin' to a new place?'

Her eyes grew thoughtful and soft. 'A little,' she said. 'Only it ain't like scared so much. I'm jus' a settin' here waitin'. When somepin happens that I got to do somepin–I'll do it.'

'Ain't you thinkin' what's it gonna be like when we get there? Ain't you scared it won't be nice like we thought?'

'No,' she said quickly. 'No, I ain't. You can't do that. I can't do that. It's too much–livin' too many lives. Up ahead they's a thousan' lives we might live, but when it comes, it'll on'y be one. If I go ahead on all of 'em, it's too much. You got to live ahead 'cause you're so young, but–it's jus' the road goin' by for me. An' it's jus' how soon they gonna wanta eat some more pork bones.' Her face tightened. 'That's all I can do. I can't do no more. All the rest'd get upset if I done any more'n that. They all depen' on me jus' thinkin' about that.'

Granma yawned shrilly and opened her eyes. She looked wildly about. 'I got to get out, praise Gawd,' she said.

'First clump a brush,' said Al. 'They's one up ahead.'

'Brush or no brush, I got to git out, I tell ya,' And she began to whine, 'I got to git out. I got to git out.'

Al speeded up, and when he came to the low brush he pulled up short. Ma threw the door open and half pulled the struggling old lady out beside the road and into the bushes. And Ma held her so Granma would not fall when she squatted.

On top of the truck the others stirred to life. Their faces were shining with sunburn they could not escape. Tom and Casy and Noah and Uncle John let themselves wearily down. Ruthie and Winfield swarmed down the side-boards and went off into the bushes. Connie helped Rose of Sharon gently down. Under the canvas, Grampa was awake, his head sticking out, but his eyes were drugged and watery and still senseless. he watched the others, but there was little recognition in his watching.

Tom called to him: 'Want to come down, Grampa?'

The old eyes turned listlessly to him. 'No,' said Grampa. For a moment the fierceness came into his eyes. 'I ain't a-goin', I tell you. Gonna stay like Muley.' And then he lost interest again. Ma came back, helping Granma up the bank to the highway.

'Tom,' she said. 'Get that pan a bones, under the canvas in back. We got to eat somepin.' Tom got the pan and passed it around, and the family stood by the roadside, gnawing the crisp particles from the pork bones.

'Sure lucky we brang these along,' said Pa. 'Git so stiff up there can't hardly move. Where's the water?'

'Ain't it up with you?' Ma asked. 'I set out that gallon jug.'

Pa climbed the sides and looked under the canvas. 'It ain't here. We must a forgot it.'

Thirst set in instantly. Winfield moaned: 'I wanta drink. I wanta drink.' The men licked their lips, suddenly conscious of their thirst. And a little panic started.

Al felt the fear growing. 'We'll get water first service station we come to. We need some petrol, too.' The family swarmed up the truck sides; Ma helped Granma in and got in beside her. Al started the motor and they moved on.

Castle to Paden twenty-five miles and the sun passed the zenith and started down. And the radiator cap began to jiggle up and down and steam started to whish out. Near Paden there was a shack beside the road and two petrol pumps in front of it; and beside a fence, a water tap and a hose. Al drove in and nosed the Hudson up to the hose. As they pulled in, a stout man, red of face and arms, got up from a chair behind the petrol pumps and moved toward them. He wore brown corduroys, and suspenders and a polo shirt; and he had a cardboard sun helmet, painted silver, on his head. The sweat beaded on his nose and under his eyes and formed streams in the wrinkles of his neck. He strolled towards the truck, looking truculent and stern.

'You folks aim to buy anything? Petrol or stuff?' he asked.

Al was out already, unscrewing the steaming radiator cap with the tips of his fingers, jerking his hand away to escape the spurt when the cap should come loose. 'Need some petrol, mister.'

'Got any money?'

'Sure. Think we're beggin'?'

The truculence left the fat man's face. 'Well, that's all right, folks. He'p yourself to water.' And he hastened to explain. 'Road is full a people, come in, use water, dirty up the toilet, an' then, by God, they'll steal stuff an' don't buy nothin'. Got no money to buy with. Come beggin' a gallon petrol to move on.'

Tom dropped angrily to the ground and moved toward the fat man. 'We're payin' our way,' he said fiercely. 'You got no call to give us a goin'-over. We ain't asked you for nothin'.'

'I ain't,' the fat man said quickly. The sweat began to soak through his short-sleeved polo shirt. 'Ju' he'p yourself to water, and go use the toilet if you want.'

Winfield had got the hose. He drank from the end and then turned the stream over his head and face, and emerged dripping. 'It ain't cool,' he said.

'I don' know what the country's comin' to,' the fat man continued. His complaint had shifted now and he was no longer talking to or about the Joads. 'Fifty-sixty cars a folks go by ever' day, folks all movin' west with kids and househol' stuff. Where they goin'? What they gonna do?'

'Doin' the same as us,' said Tom. 'Goin' someplace to live. Tryin' to get along. That's all.'

'Well, I don' know what the country's comin' to. I jus' don' know. Here's me tryin' to get along, too. Think any them big new cars stops here? No, sir! They go on to them yella-painted company stations in town. They don't stop no place like this. Most folks stops here ain't got nothing'.'

Al flipped the radiator cap and it jumped into the air with a head of steam behind it, and a hollow bubbling sound came out of the radiator. On top of the truck, the suffering hound dog crawled timidly to the edge of the load and looked over, whimpering, toward the water. Uncle John climbed up and lifted him down by the scruff of the neck. For a moment the dog staggered on stiff legs, and then he went to lap the mud under the tap. In the highway the cars whizzed by, glistening in the heat, and the hot wind of their going fanned into the service-station yard. Al filled the radiator with the hose.

'It ain't that I'm tryin' to git trade outa rich folks,' the fat man went on. 'I'm jus' tryin' to git trade. Why, the folks that stops here begs petrol an' they trades for petrol. I could show you in my back room the stuff they'll trade for petrol an' oil: beds an' baby buggies an' pots an' pans. One family traded a doll their kid had for a gallon. An' what'm I gonna do with the stuff, open a junk shop? Why, one fella wanted to gimme his shoes for a gallon. An' if I was that kinda fella I bet I could git–' He glanced at Ma and stopped.

Jim Casy had wet his head, and the drops still coursed down his high forehead, and his muscled neck was wet, and his shirt was wet. He moved over beside Tom. 'It ain't the people's fault,' he said. 'How'd you like to sell the bed you sleep on for a tankful of petrol?'

'I know it ain't their fault. Ever' person I talked to is on the move for a damn good reason. But what's the country comin' to? That's what I wanta know. What's it comin' to? Fella can't make a livin' no more. Folks can't make a livin' farmin'. I ask you, what's it comin' to? I can't figure her out. Ever'body I ask, they can't figure her out. Fella wants to trade his shoes so he can git a hundred miles on. I can't figure her out.' He took off his silver hat and wiped his forehead with his palm. And Tom took off his cap and wiped his forehead with it. He went to the hose and wet the cap through and squeezed it and put it on again. Ma worked a tin cup through the side bars of the truck, and she took water to Granma and to Grampa on top of the load. She stood on the bars and handed the cup to Grampa, and he wet his lips, and then shook his head and refused more. The old eyes looked up at Ma in pain and bewilderment for a moment before the awareness receded again.

Al started the motor and backed the truck to the petrol pump. 'Fill her up. She'll take about seven,' said Al. 'We'll give her six so she don't spill none.'

The fat man put the hose in the tank. 'No, sir,' he said. 'I jus' don't know what the country's comin' to. Relief an' all.'

Casy said: 'I been walkin' aroun' in the country. Ever'body's askin' that. What we comin' to?' Seems to me we don't never come to nothin'. Always on the way. Always goin' and goin'. Why don't folks think about that? They's movement now. People moving. We know why, an' we know how. Movin' 'cause they got to. That's why folks always move. Movin' 'cause they want somepin better'n what they got. An' that's the on'y way they'll ever git it. Wantin' it an' needin' it, they'll go out an' git it. It's bein' hurt that makes folks mad to fightin'. I been walkin' aroun' the country, an' hearin' folks talk like you.'

The fat man pumped the petrol and the needle turned on the pump dial, recording the amount. 'Yeah, but what's it comin' to? That's what I want ta know.'

Tom broke in irritably: 'Well, you ain't never gonna know. Casy tries to tell ya an' you jest ast the same thing over. I seen fellas like you before. You ain't askin' nothin'; you're jus' singin' a kinda song. "What we comin' to?" You don' wanta know. Country's movin' aroun', goin' places. They's folks dyin' all aroun'. Maybe you'll die pretty soon, but you won't know nothin'. I seen too many fellas like you. You don't want to know nothin'. Just sing yourself to sleep with a song: "What we comin' to?" ' He looked at the petrol pump, rusted and old, and at the shack behind it, built of old lumber, the nail holes of its first use still showing through the paint that had been brave, the brave yellow paint that had tried to imitate the big company stations in town. But the paint couldn't cover the old nail holes and the old cracks in the lumber, and the paint could not be renewed. The imitation was a failure and the owner had known it was a failure. And inside the open door of the shack Tom saw the oil barrels, only two of them, and the candy counter with stale candies and liquorice whips turning brown with age, and cigarettes. He saw the broken chair and the fly screen with a rusted hole in it. And the littered yard that should have been gravelled, and behind, the corn-field drying and dying in the sun. Beside the house the little stock of used tires and retreaded tires. And he saw for the first time the fat man's cheap washed pants and his cheap polo shirt and his paper hat. He said: 'I didn'mean to sound off at ya, mister. It's the heat. You ain't got nothin'. Pretty soon you'll be on the road yourse'f. And it ain't tractors'll put you there. It's them pretty yella stations in towns. Folks is movin',' he said ashamedly. 'An' you'll be movin', mister.'

The fat man's hand slowed on the pump and stopped while Tom spoke. He looked worriedly at Tom. 'How'd you know?' he asked helplessly. 'How'd you know we was already talkin' about packin' up an' movin' west?'

Casy answered him. 'It's ever'body,' he said. 'Here's me that used to give all my fight against the devil 'cause I figgered the devil was the enemy. But they's somepin worse'n the devil got hold a the country, an' it ain't gonna let go till it's chopped loose. Ever see one a them Gila monsters take hold, mister? Grabs hold, an' you chop him in two an' his head hangs on. Chop him at the neck an' his head hangs on. Got to take a screwdriver an' pry his head apart to git him loose. An' while he's layin' there, poison is drippin' an' drippin' into the hole he's made with his teeth.' He stopped and looked sideways at Tom.

The fat man stared hopelessly straight ahead. His hand started turning the crank slowly. 'I dunno what we're comin' to,' he said softly.

Over by the water hose, Connie and Rose of Sharon stood together, talking secretly. Connie washed the tin cup and felt the water with his finger before he filled the cup again. Rose of Sharon watched the cars go by on the highway. Connie held out the cup to her. 'This water ain't cool, but it's wet,' he said.

She looked at him and smiled secretly. She was all secrets now she was pregnant, secrets and little silences that seemed to have meanings. She was pleased with herself, and she complained about things that didn't really matter. And she demanded services of Connie that were silly, and both of them knew they were silly. Connie was pleased with her too, and filled with wonder that she was pregnant. He liked to think he was in on the secrets she had. When she smiled slyly, he smiled slyly too, and they exchanged confidences in whispers. The world had drawn close around them, and they were in the centre of it, or rather Rose of Sharon was in the centre of it with Connie making a small orbit about her. Everything they said was a kind of secret.

She drew her eyes from the highway. 'I ain't very thirsty,' she said daintily.

'But maybe I *ought* to drink.'

And he nodded, for he knew well what she meant. She took the cup and rinsed her mouth and spat and then drank the cupful of tepid water. 'Want another?' he asked.

'Jus' a half.' And so he filled the cup just half, and gave it to her. A Lincoln Zephyr, silvery and low, whisked by. She turned to see where the others were and saw them clustered about the truck. Reassured, she said: 'How'd you like to be goin' along in that?'

Connie sighed: 'Maybe–after.' They both knew what he meant. 'An' if they's plenty work in California, we'll git our own car. But them'–he indicated the disappearing Zephyr–'them kind costs as much as a good-sized house. I ruther have the house.'

'I like to have the house *an*' one a them,' she said. 'But 'course the house would be first because–' and they both knew what she meant. They were terribly excited about the pregnancy.

'You feel awright?' he asked.

'Tar'd. Jus' tar'd ridin' in the sun.'

'We *got* to do that or we won't never get to California.'

'I know,' she said.

The dog wandered, sniffing, past the truck, trotted to the puddle under the hose again, and lapped at the muddy water. And then he moved away, nose down and ears hanging. He sniffed his way among the dusty weeds beside the road, to the edge of the pavement. He raised his head and looked across, and then started over. Rose of Sharon screamed shrilly. A big swift car whisked near, tires squealed. The dog dodged helplessly, and with a shriek, cut off in the middle, went under the wheels. The big car slowed for a moment and faces looked back, and then it gathered greater speed and disappeared. And the dog, a blot of blood and tangled, burst intestines, kicked slowly in the road.

Rose of Sharon's eyes were wide. 'D'you think it'll hurt?' she begged. 'Think it'll hurt?'

Connie put his arm around her. 'Come set down,' he said. 'It wasn't nothin'.'

'But I felt it hurt. I felt it kinda jar when I yelled.'

'Come set down. It wasn't nothin'. It won't hurt,' He led her to the side of the truck away from the dying dog and sat her down on the running-board.

Tom and Uncle John walked out to the mess. The last quiver was going out of the crushed body. Tom took it by the legs and dragged it to the side of the road. Uncle John looked embarrassed, as though it were his fault. 'I ought ta tied him up,' he said.

Pa looked down at the dog for a moment and then he turned away. 'Le's get outa here,' he said. 'I don' know how we was gonna feed 'im anyways. Just as well, maybe.'

The fat man came from behind the truck. 'I'm sorry, folks,' he said. 'A dog jus' don't last no time near a highway. I had three dogs run over in a year. Don't keep none, no more.' And he said: 'Don't you folks worry none about it. I'll take care of 'im. Bury 'im out in the cornfield.'

Ma walked over to Rose of Sharon, where she sat, still shuddering, on the running-board. 'You all right, Rosasharn?' she asked. 'You feelin' poorly?'

'I seen that, Give me a start.'

'I heard ya yip,' said Ma. 'Git yourself laced up, now.'

'You suppose it might of hurt?'

'No,' said Ma. ''F you go to greasin' yourself an' feelin' sorry, an' tuckin' yourself in a swalla's nest, it might. Rise up now, an' he'p me get Granma comf'table. Forget that baby for a minute. He'll take care of hisself.'

'Where is Granma?' Rose of Sharon asked.

'I dunno. She's aroun' here somewheres. Maybe in the outhouse.'

The girl went toward the toilet, and in a moment she came out, helping Granma along. 'She went to sleep in there,' said Rose of Sharon.

Granma grinned. 'It's nice in there,' she said. 'They got a patent toilet in there an' the water comes down. I like it in there,' she said contentedly. 'Would of took a good nap if I wasn't woke up.'

'It ain't a nice place to sleep,' said Rose of Sharon, and she helped Granma into the car. Granma settled herself happily. 'Maybe it ain't nice for purty, but it's nice for nice,' she said.

Tom said: 'Le's go. We got to make miles.'

Pa whistled shrilly. 'Now where'd them kids go?' He whistled again, putting his fingers in his mouth.

In a moment they broke from the cornfield, Ruthie ahead and Winfield trailing her. 'Eggs!' Ruthie cried. 'I got sof' eggs.' She rushed close, with Winfield close behind. 'Look!' A dozen soft, greyish-white eggs were in her grubby hand. And as she held up her hand, her eyes fell upon the dead dog beside the road. 'Oh!' she said. Ruthie and Winfield walked slowly toward the dog. They inspected him.

Pa called to them: 'Come on, you, 'less you want to git left.'

They turned solemnly and walked to the truck. Ruthie looked once more at the grey reptile eggs in her hand, and then she threw them away. They climbed up the side of the truck. 'His eyes was still open,' said Ruthie in a hushed tone.

But Winfield gloried in the scene. He said boldly: 'His gut was just strowed all over–all over'–he was silent for a moment–'strowed–all–over,' he said, and then he rolled over quickly and vomited down the side of the truck. When he sat up again his eyes were watery and his nose running. 'It ain't like killin' pigs,' he said in explanation.

Al had the hood of the Hudson up, and he checked the oil level. He brought a gallon can from the floor of the front seat and poured a quantity of cheap black oil into the pipe and checked the level again.

Tom came beside him. 'Want I should take her a piece?' he asked.

'I ain't tired,' said Al.

'Well, you didn't get no sleep las' night. I took a snooze this morning. Get up there on top. I'll take her.'

'Awright,' Al said reluctantly. 'But watch the oil gauge pretty close. Take her slow. An' I been watchin' for a short. Take a look a' the needle now an' then. 'F she jumps to discharge it's a short. An' take her slow, Tom. She's overloaded.'

Tom laughed. 'I'll watch her,' he said. 'You can res' easy.'

The family piled on top of the truck again. Ma settled herself beside Granma in the seat, and Tom took his place and started the motor. 'Sure is loose,' he said, and he put it in gear and pulled away down the highway.

The motor droned along steadily and the sun receded down the sky in front of them. Granma slept steadily, and even Ma dropped her head forward and dozed. Tom pulled his cap over his eyes to shut out the blinding sun.

Paden to Meeker is thirteen miles; Meeker to Harrah is fourteen miles; and then Oklahoma City–the big city. Tom drove straight on. Ma waked up and looked at the streets as they went through the city. And the family, on top of the truck, stared about at the stores, at the big houses, at the office buildings. And then the buildings grew smaller and the stores smaller. The wrecking yards and hot-dog stands, the out-city dance halls.

Ruthie and Winfield saw it all, and it embarrassed them with its bigness and its strangeness, and it frightened them with the fine-clothed people they saw. They did not speak of it to each other. Later–they would, but not now. They saw the oil derricks in the town, on the edge of the town; oil derricks black, and the smell of oil and petrol in the air. But they didn't exclaim. It was so big and so strange it frightened them.

In the street Rose of Sharon saw a man in a light suit. He wore white shoes and a flat straw hat. She touched Connie and indicated the man with her eyes, and then Connie and Rose of Sharon giggled softly to themselves, and the giggles got the best of them. They covered their mouths. And it felt so good that they looked for other people to giggle at. Ruthie and Winfield saw them giggling and it looked such fun that they tried to do it too–but they couldn't. The giggles wouldn't come. But Connie and Rose of Sharon were breathless and red with stifling laughter before they could stop. It got so bad that they had only to look at each other to start over again.

The outskirts were wide spread. Tom drove slowly and carefully in the traffic, and then they were on 66–the great western road, and the sun was sinking on the line of the road. The windshield was bright with dust. Tom pulled his cap lower over his eyes, so low that he had to tilt his head back to see out at all. Granma slept on, the sun on her closed eyelids, and the veins on her temples were blue, and the little bright veins on her cheeks were wine-coloured, and the old brown marks on her face turned darker.

Tom said: 'We stay on this road right straight through.'

Ma had been silent for a long time. 'Maybe we better fin' a place to stop 'fore sunset,' she said. 'I got to get some pork a-boilin' an' some bread made. That takes time.'

'Sure,' Tom agreed. 'We ain't gonna make this trip in one jump. Might's well stretch ourselves.'

Oklahoma City to Bethany is fourteen miles.

Tom said: 'I think we better stop 'fore the sun goes down. Al got to build that thing on the top. Sun'll kill the folks up there.'

Ma had been dozing again. Her head jerked upright. 'Got to get some supper a-cookin',' she said. And she said: 'Tom, your Pa tol' me about you crossin' the State line–'

He was a long time answering. 'Yeah? What about it, Ma?'

'Well, I'm scairt about it. It'll make you kinda runnin' away. Maybe they'll catch ya.'

Tom held his hand over his eyes to protect himself from the lowering sun. 'Don't you worry,' he said. 'I figgered her out. They's lots a fellas out on parole an' they's more goin' in all the time. If I get caught for anything else out west, well, then they got my pitcher an' my prints in Washington. They'll sen' me back. But if I don't do no crimes, they won't give a damn.'

'Well, I'm a-scairt about it. Sometimes you do a crime, an' you don't even know it's bad. Maybe they got crimes in California we don't even know about. Maybe you gonna do somepin an' it's all right, an' in California it ain't all right.'

'Be jus' the same if I wasn't on parole,' he said. 'On'y if I get caught I get a bigger jolt'n other folks. Now you quit a-worrying',' he said. 'We got plenty to worry about 'thout you figgerin' out things to worry about.'

'I can't he'p it,' she said. 'Minute you cross the line you done a crime.'

'Well, tha's better'n stickin' aroun' Sallisaw an' starvin' to death,' he said. 'We better look out for a place to stop.'

They went through Bethany and out on the other side. In a ditch, where a culvert went under the road, an old touring car was pulled off the highway and a little tent was pitched beside it, and smoke came out of a stove pipe through the tent. Tom pointed ahead. 'There's some folks campin'. Looks like as good a place as we seen.' He slowed his motor and pulled to a stop beside the road. The hood of the old touring car was up, and a middle-aged man stood looking down at the motor. He wore a cheap straw sombrero, a blue shirt, and a black spotted vest, and his jeans were stiff and shiny with dirt. His face was lean, the deep cheeklines great furrows down his face so that his cheek bones and chin stood out sharply. He looked up at the Joad truck and his eyes were puzzled and angry.

Tom leaned out of the window. 'Any law 'gainst folks stoppin' here for the night?'

The man had seen only the truck. His eyes focused down on Tom. 'I dunno,' he said. 'We on'y stopped here 'cause we couldn' git no further.'

'Any water here?'

The man pointed to a service-station shack about a quarter of a mile ahead. 'They's water there they'll let ya take a bucket of.'

Tom hesitated. 'Well, ya s'pose we could camp down 'longside?'

The lean man looked puzzled. 'We don't own it,' he said. 'We on'y stopped here 'cause this goddamn ol' trap wouldn't go no further.'

Tom insisted. 'Anyways you're here an' we ain't. You got a right to say if you wan' neighbours or not.'

The appeal to hospitality had an instant effect. The lean face broke into a smile. 'Why, sure, come on off the road. Proud to have ya.' And he called: 'Sairy, there's some folks goin' ta stay with us. Come on out an' say how d'ya do. Sairy ain't well,' he added. The tent flaps opened and a wizened woman came out–a face wrinkled as a dried leaf and eyes that seemed to flame in her face, black eyes that seemed to look out of a well of horror. She was small and shuddering. She held herself upright by a tent flap, and the hand holding on to the canvas was a skeleton covered with wrinkled skin.

When she spoke her voice had a beautiful low timbre, soft and modulated, and yet with ringing overtones. 'Tell 'em welcome,' she said. 'Tell 'em good and welcome.'

Tom drove off the road and brought his truck into the field and lined it up with the touring car. And people boiled down from the truck; Ruthie and Winfield too quickly, so that their legs gave way and they shrieked at the pins and needles that ran through their limbs. Ma went quickly to work. She untied the three-gallon bucket from the back of the truck and approached the squealing children. 'Now you go git water–right down there. Ask nice. Say: "Please, kin we git a bucket a water?" and say: "Thank you." An carry it back together helpin', an' don't spill none. An' if you see stick wood to burn, bring it on.' The children stamped away toward the shack.

By the tent a little embarrassment had set in, and social intercourse had paused before it started. Pa said: 'You ain't Oklahomy folks?'

And Al, who stood near the car, looked at the licence plates. 'Kansas,' he said.

The lean man said: 'Galena, or right about there. Wilson, Ivy Wilson.'

'We're Joads,' said Pa. 'We come from right near Sallisaw.'

'Well, we're proud to meet you folks.' said Ivy Wilson. 'Sairy, these is Joads.'

'I knowed you wasn't Oklahomy folks. You talk queer, kinda–that ain't no blame, you understan'.'

'Ever'body says words different,' said Ivy. 'Arkansas folks says 'em different, and Oklahomy folks says 'em different. And we seen a lady from Massachusetts, an' she said 'em differentest of all. Couldn' hardly make out what she was sayin'.'

Noah and Uncle John and the preacher began to unload the truck. They helped Grampa down and sat him on the ground and he sat limply, staring ahead of him. 'You sick, Grampa?' Noah asked.

'You goddamn right,' said Grampa weakly. 'Sicker'n hell.'

Sairy Wilson walked slowly and carefully toward him. 'How'd you like ta come in our tent?' she asked. 'You kin lay down on our mattress an' rest.'

He looked up at her, drawn by her soft voice. 'Come on now,' she said. 'You'll git some rest. We'll he'p you over.'

Without warning Grampa began to cry. His chin wavered and his old lips tightened over his mouth and he sobbed hoarsely. Ma rushed over to him and put her arms around him. She lifted him to his feet, her broad back straining, and she half lifted, half helped him into the tent.

Uncle John said: 'He must be good an' sick. He ain't never done that before. Never seen him blubberin' in my life.' He jumped up on the truck and tossed a mattress down.

Ma came out of the tent and went to Casy. 'You been aroun' sick people,' she said. 'Grampa's sick. Won't you go take a look at him?'

Casy walked quickly to the tent and went inside. A double mattress was on the ground, the blankets spread neatly; and a little tin stove stood on iron legs and the fire in it burned unevenly. A bucket of water, a wooden box of supplies, and a box for a table, that was all. The light of the setting sun came pinkly through the tent walls. Sairy Wilson knelt on the ground, beside the mattress, and Grampa lay on his back. His eyes were open, staring upward, and his cheeks were flushed. He breathed heavily.

Casy took the skinny old wrist in his fingers. 'Feeling kinda tired Grampa?' he asked. The staring eyes moved towards his voice but did not find him. The lips practised a speech but did not speak it. Casy felt the pulse and he dropped the wrist and put his hand on Grampa's forehead. A struggle began in the old man's body, his legs moved restlessly and his hands stirred. He said a whole string of blurred sounds that were not words, and his face was red under the spiky white whiskers.

Sairy Wilson spoke softly to Casy. 'Know what's wrong?'

He looked up at the wrinkled face and the burning eyes. 'Do you?'

'I–think so.'

'What?' Casy asked.

'Might be wrong. I wouldn't like to say.'

Casy looked back at the twitching face. 'Would you say–maybe–he's workin' up a stroke?'

'I'd say that,' said Sairy. 'I seen it three times before.'

From outside came the sounds of camp-making, wood-chopping, and the rattle of pans. Ma looked through the flaps. 'Granma wants to come in. Would she better?'

The preacher said: 'She'll jus' fret if she don't.'

'Think he's awright?' Ma asked.

Casy shook his head slowly. Ma looked quickly down at the struggling old face with blood pounding through it. She drew outside and her voice came through. 'He's awright, Granma. He's jus' takin' a little res'.'

And Granma answered sulkily: 'Well, I want ta see him. He's a tricky devil. He wouldn't never let you know.' And she came scurrying through the flaps. She stood over the mattresses and looked down. 'What's the matter'th you?' she demanded of Grampa. And again his eyes reached towards her voice and his lips writhed. 'He's sulkin',' said Granma. 'I tol' you he was tricky. He was gonna sneak away this mornin' so he wouldn't have to come. An' then his hip got a-hurtin',' she said disgustedly. 'He's jus' sulkin', I seen him when he wouldn't talk to nobody before.'

Casy said gently: 'He ain't sulkin', Granma. He's sick.'

'Oh!' She looked down at the old man again. 'Sick bad, you think?'

'Purty bad, Granma.'

For a moment she hesitated uncertainly. 'Well,' she said quickly, 'why ain't you prayin'? You're a preacher, ain't you?'

Casy's strong fingers blundered over to Granma's wrist and clasped around it. 'I tol' you, Granma. I ain't a preacher no more.'

'Pray anyway,' she ordered. 'You know all the stuff by heart.'

'I can't,' said Casy. 'I don't know what to pray for or who to pray to.'

Granma's eyes wandered away and came to rest on Sairy. 'He won't pray,' she said. 'D'I ever tell ya how Ruthie prayed when she was a little skinner? Says: "Now I lay me down to sleep. I pray the Lord my soul to keep. An' when she got there the cupboard was bare, an' so the poor dog got none. Amen." That's jus' what she done.' The shadow of someone walking between the tent and the sun crossed the canvas.

Grampa seemed to be struggling; all his muscles twitched. And suddenly he jarred as though under a heavy blow. He lay still and his breath was stopped. Casy looked down at the old man's face and saw that it was turning a blackish purple. Sairy touched Casy's shoulder. She whispered: 'His tongue, his tongue, his tongue.'

Casy nodded. 'Get in front a Granma.' He pried the tight jaws apart and reached into the old man's throat for the tongue. And as he lifted it clear, a rattling breath came out, and a sobbing breath was indrawn. Casy found a stick on the ground and held down the tongue with it, and the uneven breath rattled in and out.

Granma hopped about like a chicken. 'Pray,' she said. 'Pray, you. Pray, I tell ya.' Sairy tried to hold her back. 'Pray, goddamn you!' Granma cried.

Casy looked up at her for a moment. The rasping breath came louder and more evenly. 'Our Father who art in Heaven, hallowed be Thy name–'

'Glory!' shouted Grandma.

'Thy kingdom come, Thy will be done–on earth–as it is in Heaven.'

'Amen.'

A long gasping sigh came from the open mouth and then a crying release of air.

'Give us this day–our daily bread–and forgive us–' The breathing had stopped. Casy looked down into Grampa's eyes and they were clear and deep and penetrating, and there was a knowing serene look in them.

'Hallelujah!' said Granma. 'Go on.'

'Amen,' said Casy.

Granma was still then. And outside the tent all the noise had stopped. A car whished by on the highway. Casy still knelt on the floor beside the mattress. The people outside were listening, standing quietly intent on the sounds of the dying. Sairy took Granma by the arm and led her outside, and Granma moved with dignity and held her head high. She walked for the family and held her head straight for the family. Sairy took her to a mattress lying on the ground and sat her down on it. And Granma looked straight ahead, proudly, for she was on show now. The tent was still, and at last Casy spread the tent flaps with his hands and stepped out.

Pa said softly: 'What was it?'

'Stroke,' said Casy. 'A good quick stroke.'

Life began to move again. The sun touched the horizon and flattened over it. And along the highway there came a long line of huge freight trucks with red sides. They rumbled along, putting a little earthquake in the ground, and the standing exhaust pipes sputtered blue smoke from the diesel oil. One man drove each truck, and his relief man slept in a bunk high up against the ceiling. But the trucks never stopped; they thundered day and night and the ground shook under their heavy march.

The family became a unit. Pa squatted down on the ground, and Uncle John beside him. Pa was the head of the family now. Ma stood beside him. Noah and Tom and Al squatted, and the preacher sat down, and then reclined on his elbow. Connie and Rose of Sharon walked at a distance. Now Ruthie and Winfield, clattering up with a bucket of water held between them, felt the change, and they slowed up and set down the bucket and moved quietly to stand with Ma.

Granma sat proudly, coldly, until the group was formed, until no one looked at her, and then she lay down and covered her face with her arm. The red sun set and left a shining twilight on the land, so that faces were bright in the evening and eyes shone in reflection of the sky. The evening picked up light where it could.

Pa said: 'It was in Mr Wilson's tent.'

Uncle John nodded. 'He loaned his tent.'

'Fine friendly folks,' Pa said softly.

Wilson stood by his broken car, and Sairy had gone to the mattress to sit beside Granma, but Sairy was careful not to touch her.

Pa called: 'Mr Wilson?' The man scuffed near and squatted down, and Sairy came and stood beside him. Pa said: 'We're thankful to you folks.'

'We're proud to help,' said Wilson.

'We're beholden to you,' said Pa.

'There's no beholden in a time of dying,' said Wilson, and Sairy echoed him: 'Never no beholden.'

Al said: 'I'll fix your car–me an' Tom will.' And Al looked proud that he could return the family's obligation.

'We could use some help,' Wilson admitted the retiring of the obligation.

Pa said: 'We got to figger what to do. They's laws. You got to report a death, an' when you do that, they either take forty dollars for the undertaker or they take him for a pauper.'

Uncle John broke in: 'We never did have no paupers.'

Tom said: 'Maybe we got to learn. We never got booted off no land before, neither.'

'We done it clean,' said Pa. 'There can't no blame be laid on us. We never took nothin' we couldn't pay; we never suffered no man's charity. When Tom here got in trouble we could hold up our heads. He only done what any man would a done.'

'Then what'll we do?' Uncle John asked.

'We go in like the law says an' they'll come out for him. We on'y got a hundred an' fifty dollars. They take forty to bury Grampa an' we won't get to California–or else they'll bury him a pauper.' The men stirred restively, and they studied the darkening ground in front of their knees.

Pa said softly: 'Grampa buried his pa with his own hand, done it in dignity, an' shaped the grave nice with his own shovel. That was a time when a man had the right to be buried by his own son an' a son had the right to bury his own father.'

'The law says different now,' said Uncle John.

'Sometimes the law can't be foller'd no way,' said Pa. 'Not in decency, anyways. They's lots a times you can't. When Floyd was loose an' goin' wild, law said we got to give him up–an' nobody give him up. Sometimes a fella got to sift the law. I'm sayin' now I got the right to bury my own pa. Anybody got somepin to say?'

The preacher rose high on his elbow. 'Law changes,' he said, 'but "got to's" go on. You got the right to do what you got to do.'

Pa turned to Uncle John. 'It's your right too, John. You got any words against?'

'No word against,' said Uncle John. 'On'y it's like hidin' him in the night. Grampa's way was t'come out a-shootin'.'

Pa said ashamedly: 'We can't do like Grampa done. We got to get to California 'fore our money gives out.'

Tom broke in: 'Sometimes fellas workin' dig up a man an' then they raise hell an' figger he been killed. The gov'ment's got more interest in a dead man than a live one. They'll go hell-scrapin' trying to fin' out who he was and how he died. I offer we put a note of writin' in a bottle an' lay it with Grampa, tellin' who he is an' how he died, an' why he's buried here.'

Pa nodded agreement. 'Tha's good. Wrote out in a nice han'. Be not so lonesome too, knowin' his name is there with 'im, not jus' a old fella lonesome underground. Any more stuff to say?' The circle was silent.

Pa turned his head to Ma. 'You'll lay 'im out?'

'I'll lay 'im out,' said Ma. 'But who's to get supper?'

Sairy Wilson said: 'I'll get supper. You go right ahead. Me an' that big girl of yourn.'

'We sure thank you,' said Ma. 'Noah, you get into them kegs an' bring out some nice pork. Salt won't be deep in yet, but it'll be right nice eatin'.'

'We got a half sack a potatoes,' said Sairy.

Ma said: 'Gimme two half-dollars,' Pa dug in his pocket and gave her the silver. She found the basin, filled it full of water, and went into the tent. It was nearly dark in there. Sairy came in and lighted a candle and stuck it upright on a box and then she went out. For a moment Ma looked down at the dead old man. And then in pity she tore a strip from her own apron and tied up his jaw. She straightened his limbs, folded his hands over his chest. She held his eyelids down and laid a silver piece on each one. She buttoned his shirt and washed his face.

Sairy looked in, saying: 'Can I give you any help?'

Ma looked slowly up. 'Come in,' she said. 'I like to talk to ya.'

'That's a good big girl you got,' said Sairy. 'She's right in peelin' potatoes. What can I do to help?'

'I was gonna wash Grampa all over,' said Ma, 'but he got no other clo'es to put on. An' 'course your quilt's spoilt. Can't never get the smell a death from a quilt. I seen a dog growl an' shake at a mattress my ma died on, an' that was two years later. We'll wrop 'im in your quilt. We'll make it up to you. We got a quilt for you.'

Sairy said: 'You shouldn't talk like that. We're proud to help. I ain't felt so–safe in a long time. People needs–to help.'

Ma nodded. 'They do,' she said. She looked long into the old whiskery face, with its bound jaw and silver eyes shining in the candlelight. 'He ain't gonna look natural. We'll wrop him up.'

'The ol' lady took it good.'

'Why, she's so old,' said Ma, 'maybe she don't even rightly know what happened. Maybe she won't really know for quite a while. Besides, us folks takes a pride holdin' in. My pa used to say: "Anybody can break down. It takes a man not to." We always try to hold in.' She folded the quilt neatly about Grampa's legs and around his shoulders. She brought the corner of the quilt over his head like a cowl and pulled it down over his face. Sairy handed her half a dozen big safety pins, and she pinned the quilt neatly and tightly about the long package. And at last she stood up. 'It won't be a bad burying,' she said. 'We got a preacher to see him in, an' his folks is all aroun'.' Suddenly she swayed a little, and Sairy went to her and steadied her. 'It's sleep–' Ma said in a shamed tone. 'No, I'm awright. We been so busy gettin' ready, you see.'

'Come out in the air,' Sairy said.

'Yeah, I'm all done here.' Sairy blew out the candle and the two went out.

A bright fire burned in the bottom of the little gulch. And Tom, with sticks and wire, had made supports from which two kettles hung and bubbled furiously, and good steam poured out under the lids. Rose of Sharon knelt on the ground out of range of the burning heat, and she had a long spoon in her hand. She saw Ma come out of the tent, and she stood up and went to her.

'Ma,' she said. 'I got to ask.'

'Scared again?' Ma asked. 'Why, you can't get through nine months without sorrow.'

'But will it hurt–the baby?'

Ma said: 'They used to be a sayin', "A chile born outa sorrow'll be a happy chile." Isn't that so, Mis' Wilson?'

'I heard it like that,' said Sairy. 'An' I heard the other: "Born outa too much joy'll be a doleful boy".'

'I'm all jumpy inside,' said Rose of Sharon.

'Well, we ain't none of us jumpin' for fun,' said Ma. 'You jes' keep watchin' the pots.'

On the edge of the ring of firelight the men had gathered. For tools they had a shovel and a mattock. Pa marked out the ground eight feet long and three feet wide. The work went on in relays. Pa chopped the earth with the mattock and then Uncle John shovelled it out. Al chopped and Tom shovelled, Noah chopped and Connie shovelled. And the hole drove down, for the work never diminished in speed. The shovels of dirt flew out of the hole in quick spurts. When Tom was shoulder-deep in the rectangular pit, he said: 'How deep, Pa?'

'Good an' deep. A couple of feet more. You get out now, Tom, and get that paper wrote.'

Tom boosted himself out of the hole and Noah took his place. Tom went to Ma, where she tended the fire. 'We got any paper an' pen, Ma?'

Ma shook her head slowly. 'No-o. That's one thing we didn' bring.' She looked toward Sairy. And the little woman walked quickly to her tent. She brought back a Bible and a half pencil. 'Here,' she said. 'They's a clear page in front. Use that an' tear it out.' She handed book and pencil to Tom.

Tom sat down in the firelight. He squinted his eyes in concentration, and at last wrote slowly and carefully on the end-paper in big clear letters: 'This here is William James Joad, dyed of a stroke, old old man. His fokes bured him becaws they got no money to pay for funerls. Nobody kilt him. Jus a stroke and he dyed.' He stopped. 'Ma, listen to this here.' He read it slowly to her.

'Why, that soun's nice,' she said. 'Can't you stick on somepin' from Scripture so it'll be religious. Open up an' git a-sayin' somepin outa Scripture.'

'Got to be short,' said Tom. 'I ain't got much room lef' on the page.'

Sairy said: 'How 'bout "God have mercy on his soul"?'

'No,' said Tom. 'Sound too much like he was hung. I'll copy somepin.' He turned the pages and read, mumbling his lips, saying the words under his breath. 'Here's a good short one,' he said, ' "An' Lot said unto them, Oh, not so, my Lord." '

'Don't mean nothin',' said Ma. 'Long's you're gonna put one down, it might's well mean somepin.'

Sairy said: 'Turn to Psalms, over further. You kin always get somepin outa Psalms.'

Tom flipped the pages and looked down the verses. 'Now here *is* one,' he said. 'This here's a nice one, just blowed full of religion: "Blessed is he whose transgression is forgiven, whose sin is covered." How's that?'

'That's real nice,' said Ma. 'Put that one in.'

Tom wrote it carefully. Ma rinsed and wiped a fruit jar and Tom screwed the lid down tight on it. 'Maybe the preacher ought ta wrote it,' he said.

Ma said: 'No, the preacher wa'n't no kin.' She took the jar from him and went into the dark tent. She unpinned the covering and slipped the fruit jar in under the thin cold hands and pinned the comforter tight again. And then she went back to the fire.

The men came from the grave, their faces shining with perspiration. 'Awright,' said Pa. He and John and Noah and Al went into the tent, and they came out carrying the long, pinned bundle between them. They carried it to the grave. Pa leaped into the hole and received the bundle in his arms and laid it gently down. Uncle John put out a hand and helped Pa out of the hole. Pa asked: 'How about Granma?'

'I'll see,' Ma said. She walked to the mattress and looked down at the old woman for a moment. Then she went back to the grave. 'Sleepin',' she said. 'Maybe she'd hold it against me, but I ain't a-gonna wake her up. She's tar'd.'

Pa said: 'Where at's the preacher? We oughta have a prayer.'

Tom said: 'I seen him walkin' down the road. He don't like to pray no more.'

'Don't like to pray?'

'No,' said Tom. 'He ain't a preacher no more. He figgers it ain't right to fool people actin' like a preacher when he ain't a preacher. I bet he went away so nobody wouldn't ast him.'

Casy had come quietly near, and he heard Tom speaking. 'I didn' run away,' he said. 'I'll he'p you folks, but I won't fool ya.'

Pa said: 'Won't you say a few words? Ain't none of our folks ever been buried without a few words.'

'I'll say 'em,' said the preacher.

Connie led Rose of Sharon to the graveside, she reluctant. 'You got to,' Connie said. 'It ain't decent not to. It'll jus' be a little.'

The firelight fell on the grouped people, showing their faces and their eyes, dwindling on their dark clothes. All the hats were off now. The light danced, jerking over the people.

Casy said: 'It'll be a short one.' He bowed his head, and the others followed his lead. Casy said solemnly: 'This here ol' man jus' lived a life an' jus' died out of it. I don't know whether he was good or bad, but that don't matter much. He was alive, an' that's what matters. An' now he's dead, an' that don't matter. Heard a fella tell a poem one time, an' he says: "All that lives is holy." Got to thinkin', an' purty soon it means more than the words says. An' I wouldn' pray for a ol' fella that's dead. He's awright. He got a job to do, but it's all laid out for 'im an' there's on'y one way to do it. But us, we got a job to do, an' they's a thousan' ways, an' we don't know which one to take. An' if I was to pray, it'd be for the folks that don't know which way to turn. Grampa here, he got the easy straight. An' now cover 'im up and let 'im get to his work.' He raised his head.

Pa said 'Amen,' and the others muttered 'A-men.' Then Pa took the shovel, half filled it with dirt, and spread it gently into the black hole. He handed the shovel to Uncle John, and John dropped in a shovelful. Then the shovel went from hand to hand until every man had his turn. When all had taken their duty and their right, Pa attacked the mound of loose dirt and hurriedly filled the hole. The women moved back to the fire to see to supper. Ruthie and Winfield watched, absorbed.

Ruthie said solemnly: 'Grampa's down under there.' And Winfield looked at her with horrified eyes. And then he ran away to the fire and sat on the ground and sobbed to himself.

Pa half filled the hole, and then he stood panting with the effort while Uncle John finished it. And John was shaping up the mound when Tom stopped him. 'Listen,' Tom said. ''F we leave a grave they'll have it open in no time. We got to hide it. Level her off an' we'll strew dry grass. We got to do that.'

Pa said: 'I didn't think a that. It ain't right to leave a grave unmounded.'

'Can't he'p it,' said Tom. 'They'd dig 'im right up, an we'd get it for breakin' the law. You know what I get if I break the law.'

'Yeah,' Pa said. 'I forgot that.' He took the shovel from John and levelled the grave. 'She'll sink, come winter,' he said. 'Can't he'p that,' said Tom. 'We'll be a long ways off by winter. Tromp her in good, an' we'll strew stuff over her.'

When the pork and potatoes were done the families sat about on the ground and ate, and they were quiet, staring into the fire. Wilson, tearing a slab of meat with his teeth, sighed with contentment. 'Nice eatin' pig,' he said.

'Well,' Pa explained, 'we had a couple shoats, an' we thought we might's well eat 'em. Can't get nothin' for them. When we get kinda use' ta movin' an' Ma can't set up bread, why, it'll be pretty nice, seein' the country an' two kegs a pork right in the truck. How long you folks been on the road?'

Wilson cleared his teeth with his tongue and swallowed. 'We ain't been lucky,' he said. 'We been three weeks from home.'

'Why, God Awmighty, we aim to be in California in ten days or less.'

Al broke in: 'I dunno, Pa. With that load we're packin', we maybe ain't never gonna get there. Not if they's mountains to go over.'

They were silent about the fire. Their faces were turned downward and their hair and foreheads showed in the firelight. Above the little dome of the firelight the summer stars shone thinly, and the heat of the day was gradually withdrawing. On her mattress, away from the fire, Granma whimpered softly like a puppy. The heads of all turned in her direction.

Ma said: 'Rosasharn, like a good girl go lay down with Granma. She needs somebody now. She's knowin', now.'

Rose of Sharon got to her feet and walked to the mattress and lay beside the old woman, and the murmur of their soft voices drifted to the fire. Rose of Sharon and Granma whispered together on the mattress.

Noah said: 'Funny thing is–losin' Grampa ain't made me feel no different than I done before. I ain't no sadder than I was.'

'It's just the same thing,' Casy said. 'Grampa an' the old place, they was jus' the same thing.'

Al said: 'It's a goddamn shame. He been talkin' what he's gonna do, how he gonna squeeze grapes over his head an' let the juice run in his whiskers, an' all stuff like that.'

Casy said: 'He was foolin', all the time. I think he knowed it. An' Grampa didn' die to-night. He died the minute you took 'im off the place.'

'You sure a that?' Pa cried.

'Why, no. Oh, he was breathin',' Casy went on, 'but he was dead. He was that place, an' he knowed it.'

Uncle John said: 'Did you know he was a-dyin'?'

'Yeah,' said Casy, 'I knowed it.'

John gazed at him, and a horror grew in his face. 'An' you didn't tell nobody?'

'What good?' Casy asked.

'We–we might of did somepin.'

'What?'

'I don't know, but–'

'No,' Casy said, 'you couldn' a done nothin'. Your way was fixed an' Grampa didn' have no part in it. He didn' suffer none. Not after fust thing this mornin'. He's jus' stayin' with the lan'. He couldn' leave it.'

Uncle John sighed deeply.

Wilson said: 'We hadda leave my brother Will.' The heads turned toward him. 'Him an' me had forties side by side. He's older'n me. Neither one ever drove a car. Well, we went in an' we sol' ever'thing. Will, he bought a car, an' they give him a kid to show 'im how to use it. So the afternoon 'fore we're gonna start, Will an' Aunt Minnie go a-practisin'. Will, he comes to a bend in the road an' he yells "Whoa" an' yanks back an' he goes through a fence. An' he yells "Whoa, you bastard" an' tromps down on the gas an' goes over into a gulch. An' there he was. Didn't have nothin' more to sell an' didn't have no car. But it were his own damn fault, praise God. He's damn mad he won't come along with us, jus' set there a-cussin' an' a-cussin'.'

'What's he gonna do?'

'I dunno. He's too mad to figger. An' we couldn' wait. On'y had eighty-five dollars to go on. We couldn' set an' cut it up, but we et it up anyways. Didn' go a hundred mile when a tooth in the rear end bust, an' cost thirty dollars to get her fix', an' then we got to get a tire, an then a spark plug cracked, an' Sairy got sick. Had ta stop ten days. An' now the goddamn car is bust again an' money's gettin' low. I dunno when we'll ever get to California. 'F I could on'y fix a car, but I don' know nothin' about cars.'

Al asked importantly: 'What's the matter?'

'Well, she jus' won't run. Starts an' farts an' stops. In a minute she'll start again, an' then 'fore you can git her goin', she peters out again.'

'Runs a minute an' then dies?'

'Yes, sir. An' I can't keep her a-goin' no matter how much gas I give her. Got worse an' worse, an' now I cain't get her a-movin' a-tall.'

Al was very proud and very mature, then. 'I think you got a plugged gas line. I'll blow her out for ya.'

And Pa was proud too. 'He's a good hand with a car,' Pa said.

'Well, I'll sure thank ya for a han'. I sure will. Makes a fella kinda feel–like a little kid, when he can't fix nothin'. When we get to California I aim to get me a nice car. Maybe she won't break down.'

Pa said: 'When we get there. Gettin' ther's the trouble.'

'Oh, but she's worth it,' said Wilson. 'Why, I seen han'bills how they need folks to pick fruit, an' good wages. Why, jus' think how it's gonna be, under them shady trees a-pickin' fruit an' takin' a bite ever' once in a while. Why, hell, they don't care how much you eat 'cause they got so much. An' with them good wages, maybe a fella can get hisself a little piece a land an' work out for extra cash. Why, hell, in a couple years I bet a fella could have a place of his own.'

Pa said: 'We seen them han'bills. I got one right here.' He took out his purse and from it took a folded orange handbill. In black type it said: 'Pea Pickers Wanted in California. Good Wages All Season. 800 Pickers Wanted.'

Wilson looked at it curiously. 'Why, that's the one I seen. The very same one. You s'pose–maybe they got all eight hundred awready?'

Pa said: 'This is jus' one little part a California. Why, that's the secon' biggest State we got. S'pose they did get all them eight hunderd. They's plenty places else. I rather pick fruit anyways. Like you says, under them trees an' pickin' fruit–why, even the kids like to do that.'

Suddenly Al got up and walked to the Wilson's touring car. He looked in for a moment and then came back and sat down.

'You can't fix her to-night,' Wilson said.

'I know. I'll get to her in the morning.'

Tom had watched his young brother carefully. 'I was thinkin' somepin like that myself,' he said.

Noah asked: 'What you two fellas talkin' about?'

Tom and Al were silent, each waiting for the other. 'You tell 'em,' Al said finally.

'Well, maybe it's no good, an' maybe it ain't the same thing Al's thinking. Here she is, anyways. We got a overload, but Mr an' Mis' Wilson ain't. If some of us folks could ride with them an' take some a their light stuff in the truck, we wouldn't break no springs an' we could git up hills. An' me an' Al both knows about a car, so we could keep that car a-rollin'. We'd keep together on the road an' it'd be good for ever'body.'

Wilson jumped up. 'Why, sure. Why, we'd be proud. We certain'y would. You hear that Sairy?'

'It's a nice thing,' said Sairy. 'Wouldn' be a burden on you folks?'

'No, by God,' said Pa. 'Wouldn't be no burden at all. You'd be helpin' us.'

Wilson settled back uneasily. 'Well, I dunno.'

'What's a matter, don' you wanta?'

'Well, ya see–I on'y got 'bout thirty dollars lef', an' I won't be no burden.'

Ma said: 'You won't be no burden. Each'll help each, an' we'll all git to California. Sairy Wilson he'ped lay Grampa out,' and she stopped. The relationship was plain.

Al cried: 'That car'll take six easy. Say me to drive, an' Rosasharn an' Connie and Granma. Then we take the big light stuff an' pile her on the truck. An' we'll trade off ever' so often.' He spoke loudly, for a load of worry was lifted from him.

They smiled shyly and looked down at the ground. Pa fingered the dusty earth with his finger-tips. He said: 'Ma favours a white house with oranges growin' around. They's a big pitcher on a calendar she seen.'

Sairy said: 'If I get sick again, you got to go on an' get there. We ain't a-goin' to burden.'

Ma looked carefully at Sairy, and she seemed to see for the first time the pain-tormented eyes and the face that was haunted and shrinking with pain. And Ma said: 'We gonna see you get through. You said yourself, you can't let help go unwanted.'

Sairy studied her wrinkled hands in the firelight. 'We got to get some sleep to-night.' She stood up.

'Grampa–it's like he's dead a year,' Ma said.

The families moved lazily to their sleep, yawning luxuriously. Ma sloshed the tin plates off a little and rubbed the grease free with a flour sack. The fire died down and the stars descended. Few passenger cars went by on the highway now, but the transport trucks thundered by at intervals and put little earthquakes in the ground. In the ditch the cars were hardly visible under the starlight. A tied dog howled at the service station down the road. The families were quiet and sleeping, and the fieldmice grew bold and scampered about among the mattresses. Only Sairy Wilson was awake. She stared into the sky and braced her body firmly against pain.

14

The western land, nervous under the beginning change. The Western States, nervous as horses before a thunderstorm. The great owners, nervous, sensing a change, knowing nothing of the nature of the change. The great owners, striking at the immediate thing, the widening government, the growing labour unity; striking at new taxes, at plans; not knowing these things are results, not causes. Results, not causes; results, not causes. The causes lie deep and simply–the causes are a hunger in a stomach, multiplied a million times; a hunger in a single soul, hunger for joy and some security, multiplied a million times; muscles and mind aching to grow, to work, to create, multiplied a million times. The last clear definite function of man–muscles aching to work, minds aching to create beyond the single need–this is man. To build a wall, to build a house, a dam, and in the wall and house and dam to put something of Manself, and to Manself take back something of the wall, the house, the dam; to take hard muscles from the lifting, to take the clear lines and form from conceiving. For man, unlike anything organic or inorganic in the universe, grows beyond his work, walks up the stairs of his concepts, emerges ahead of his accomplishments. This you may say of man–when theories change and crash, when schools, philosophies, when narrow dark alleys of thought, national, religious, economic, grow and disintegrate, man reaches, stumbles forward, painfully mistakenly sometimes. Having stepped forward, he may slip back, but only half a step, never the full step back. This you may say and know it and know it. This you may know when the bombs plummet out of the black planes on the market-place, when prisoners are stuck like pigs, when the crushed bodies drain filthily in the dust. You may know it in this way. If the step were not being taken, if the stumbling-forward ache were not alive, the bombs would not fall, the throats would not be cut. Fear the time when the bombs stop falling while the bombers live–for every bomb is proof that the spirit has not died. And fear the time when the strikes stop while the great owners live–for every little beaten strike is proof that the step is being taken. And this you can know–fear the time when Manself will not suffer and die for a concept, for this one quality is the foundation of Manself, and this one quality is man, distinctive in the universe.

The Western States, nervous under the beginning change. Texas and Oklahoma, Kansas and Arkansas, New Mexico, Arizona, California. A single family moved from the land. Pa borrowed money from the bank, and now the bank wants the land. The land company–that's the bank when it has land–wants tractors, not families on the land. Is a tractor bad? Is the power that turns the long furrows wrong? If this tractor were ours it would be good–not mine, but ours. If our tractor turned the long furrows of our land, it would be good. Not my land, but ours. We could love that tractor then as we have loved this land when it was ours. But this tractor does two things–it turns the land and turns us off the land. There is little difference between this tractor and a tank. The people are driven, intimidated, hurt by both. We must think about this.

One man, one family driven from the land; this rusty car creaking along the highway to the west. I lost my land, a single tractor took my land. I am alone and I am bewildered. And in the night one family camps in a ditch and another family pulls in and the tents come out. The two men squat on their hams and the women and children listen. Here is the node, you who hate change and fear revolution. Keep these two squatting men apart; make them hate, fear, suspect each other. Here is the anlage of the thing you fear. This is the zygote. For here 'I lost my land' is changed; a cell is split and from the splitting grows the thing you hate–'We lost *our* land.' The danger is here, for two men are not as lonely and perplexed as one. And from this first 'we' there grows a still more dangerous thing: 'I have a little food' plus 'I have none.' If from this problem the sum is 'We have a little food,' the thing is on its way, the movement has direction. Only a little multiplication now, and this land, this tractor are ours. The two men squatting in a ditch, the little fire, the side-meat stewing in a single pot, the silent, stone-eyed women; behind, the children listening with their souls to words their minds do not understand. The night draws down. The baby has a cold. Here, take this blanket. It's wool. It was my mother's blanket–take it for the baby. This is the thing to bomb. This is the beginning–from 'I' to 'we'.

If you who own the things people must have could understand this, you might preserve yourself. If you could separate causes from results, if you could know that Paine, Marx, Jefferson, Lenin were results, not causes, you might survive. But that you cannot know. For the quality of owning freezes you for ever into 'I', and cuts you off for ever from the 'we'.

The Western States are nervous under the beginning change. Need is the stimulus to concept, concept to action. A half million people moving over the country; a million more restive, ready to move; ten million more feeling the first nervousness.

And tractors turning the multiple furrows in the vacant land.

15

Along 66 the hamburger-stands–Al & Susy's Place–Carl's Lunch–Joe & Minnie–Will's Eats. Board-and-bat shacks. Two petrol pumps in front, a screen door, a long bar, stools, and a foot-rail. Near the door three slot machines, showing through glass the wealth in nickels three bars will bring. And beside them, the nickel phonograph with records piled up like pies, ready to swing out to the turn-table and play dance music. 'Ti-pi-ti-pi-tin,' 'Thanks for the Memory,' Bing Crosby, Benny Goodman. At one end of the counter a covered case; candy cough-drops, caffeine sulphate called Sleepless, No-Doze; candy, cigarettes, razor blades, aspirin, Bromo-Seltzer, Alka-Seltzer. The walls decorated with posters, bathing girls, blondes with big breasts and slender hips and waxen faces, in white bathing suits, and holding a bottle of Coca-Cola and smiling–see what you get with a Coca-Cola. Long bar, and salts, peppers, mustard pots, and paper napkins. Beer-taps behind the counter, and in back the coffee-urns, shiny and steaming, with glass gauges showing the coffee-level. And piles of Post Toasties, corn flakes, stacked up in designs.

The signs on cards, picked out with shining mica: Pies Like Mother Used to Make. Credit Makes Enemies, Let's Be Friends. Ladies May Smoke But Be Careful Where You Lay Your Butts. Eat Here and Keep Your Wife for a Pet.

Down at one end the cooking plates, pots of stew, potatoes, pot roast, roast beef, grey roast pork waiting to be sliced.

Minnie or Susy or Mae, middle-ageing behind the counter, hair curled and rouge and powder on a sweating face. Taking orders in a soft low voice, calling them to cook with a screech like a peacock. Mopping the counter with circular strokes, polishing the big shining coffee-urns. The cook is Joe or Carl or Al, hot in a white coat and apron, beady sweat on white forehead, below the white cook's cap; moody, rarely speaking, looking up for a moment at each new entry. Wiping the griddle, slapping down the hamburger. He repeats Mae's orders gently, scrapes the griddle, wipes it down with burlap. Moody and silent.

Mae is the contact, smiling, irritated, near to outbreak; smiling while her eyes look on past–unless for truck drivers. There's the backbone of the joint. Where the trucks stop, that's where the customers come. Can't fool truck drivers, they know. They bring the custom. They know. Give 'em a stale cup a coffee an' they're off the joint. Treat 'em right an' they come back. Mae really smiles with all her might at truck drivers. She bridles a little, fixes her back hair so that her breasts will lift with her raised arms, passes the time of day and indicates great things, great times, great jokes. Al never speaks. He is no contact. Sometimes he smiles a little at a joke, but he never laughs. Sometimes he looks up at the vivaciousness in Mae's voice, and then he scrapes the griddle with a spatula, scrapes the grease into an iron trough around the plate. He presses down a hissing hamburger with his spatula. He lays the split buns on the plate to toast and heat. He gathers up stray onions from the plate and heaps them on the meat and presses them in with the spatula. He puts half a bun on top of the meat, paints the other half with melted butter, with thin pickle relish. Holding the bun on the meat, he slips the spatula under the thin pad of meat, flips it over, lays the buttered half on top, and drops the hamburger on a small plate. Quarter of a dill pickle, two black olives beside the sandwich. Al skims the plate down the counter like a quoit. And he scrapes his griddle with the spatula and looks moodily at the stew kettle.

Cars whisking by on 66. Licence plates. Mass., Tenn., R.I., N.Y., Vt., Ohio. Going west. Fine cars, cruising at sixty-five.

There goes one of them Cords. Looks like a coffin on wheels.

But, Jesus, how they travel!

See that La Salle? Me for that. I ain't a hog. I go for a La Salle.

'F ya goin' big, what's a matter with a Cad'? Jus' a little bigger, little faster.

I'd take a Zephyr myself. You ain't ridin' no fortune, but you got class an' speed. Give me a Zephyr.

Well, sir, you may get a laugh outa this–I'll take a Buick-Puick. That's good enough.

But, hell, that costs in the Zephyr class an' it ain't got the sap.

I don' care. I don' want nothin' to do with nothing of Henry Ford's. I don' like 'im. Never did. Got a brother worked in the plant. Oughta hear him tell.

Well, a Zephyr got sap.

The big cars on the highway. Languid, heat-raddled ladies, small nucleuses about whom revolve a thousand accoutrements: creams, ointments to grease themselves, colouring matter in phials–black, pink, red, white, green, silver–to change the colour of hair, eyes, lips, nails, brows, lashes, lids. Oils, seeds, and pills to make the bowels move. A bag of bottles, syringes, pills, powders, fluids, jellies to make their sexual intercourse safe, odourless, and unproductive. And this apart from clothes. What a hell of a nuisance!

Lines of weariness around the eyes, lines of discontent down from the mouth, breasts lying heavily in little hammocks, stomachs and thighs straining against cases of rubber. And the mouths panting, the eyes sullen, disliking sun and wind and earth, resenting food and weariness, hating time that rarely makes them beautiful and always makes them old.

Beside them, little pot-bellied men in light suits and panama hats; clean, pink men with puzzled worried eyes, with restless eyes. Worried because formulas do not work out; hungry for security and yet sensing its disappearance from the earth. In their lapels the insignia of lodges and service clubs, places where they can go and, by a weight of numbers of little worried men, reassure themselves that business is noble and not the curious ritualized thievery they know it is; that business men are intelligent in spite of the records of their stupidity; that they are kind and charitable in spite of the principles of sound business; that their lives are rich instead of the thin tiresome routines they know; and that a time is coming when they will not be afraid any more.

And these two, going to California; going to sit in the lobby of the Beverly-Wilshire Hotel and watch the people they envy go by to look at mountains–mountains, mind you, and great trees–he with his worried eyes and she thinking how the sun will dry her skin. Going to look at the Pacific Ocean, and I'll bet a hundred thousand dollars to nothing at all he will say, 'It isn't as big as I thought it would be.' And she will envy plump young bodies on the beach. Going to California really to go home again. To say: 'So-and-So was at the table next to us at the Trocadero. She's really a mess, but she does wear nice clothes.' And he: 'I talked to good sound business men out there. They don't see a chance till we get rid of that fellow in the White House.' And: 'I got it from a man in the know–she has syphilis, you know. She was in that Warner picture. Man said she'd slept her way into pictures. Well, she got what she was looking for.' But the worried eyes are never calm, and the pouting mouth is never glad. The big car cruising along at sixty.

I want a cold drink.

Well, there's something up ahead. Want to stop?

Do you think it would be clean?

Clean as you're going to find in this God-forsaken country.

Well, maybe the bottled soda will be all right.

The great car squeals and pulls to a stop. The fat worried man helps his wife out.

Mae looks at and past them as they enter. Al looks up from his griddle, and down again. Mae knows. They'll drink a five-cent soda and crab that it ain't cold enough. The woman will use six paper napkins and drop them on the floor. The man will choke and try to put the blame on Mae. The woman will sniff as though she smelled rotting meat and they will go out again and tell for ever afterwards that people in the West are sullen. And Mae, when she is alone with Al, has a name for them. She calls them shit-heels.

Truck drivers. That's the stuff.

Here's a big transport comin'. Hope they stop; take away the taste of them shit-heels. When I worked in that hotel in Albuquerque, Al, the way they steal–ever' darn thing. An' the bigger the car they got, the more they steal–towels, silver, soap-dishes. I can't figger it.

And Al, morosely: Where ya think they get them big cars and stuff? Born with 'em? You won't never have nothin'.

The transport truck, a driver and relief. How 'bout stoppin' for a cup a Java? I know this dump.

How's the schedule?

Oh, we're ahead!

Pull up, then. They's a ol' war horse in here that's a kick. Good Java too.

The truck pulls up. Two men in khaki riding trousers, boots, short jackets, and shiny-visored military caps. Screen door–slam.

H'ya, Mae?

Well, if it ain't Big Bill the Rat! When'd you get back on this run?

Week ago.

The other man puts a nickel in the phonograph, watches the disk slip free and the turn-table rise up under it. Bing Crosby's voice–golden. 'Thanks for the memory, of sunburn at the shore–You might have been a headache, but you never were a bore–' And the truck driver sings for Mae's ears, you might have been a haddock but you never was a whore–

Mae laughs. Who's ya frien', Bill? New on this run, ain't he?

The other puts a nickel in the slot machine, wins four slugs, and puts them back. Walks to the counter.

Well, what's it gonna be?

Oh, cup a Java. Kinda pie ya got?

Banana cream, pineapple cream, chocolate cream–an' apple.

Make it apple. Wait–Kind is that big thick one?

Mae lifts it out and sniffs it. Banana cream.

Cut off a hunk; make it a big hunk.

Man at the slot machine says: Two all around.

Two it is. Seen any new etchin's lately, Bill?

Well, here's one.

Now you be careful front of a lady.

Oh, this ain't bad. Little kid comes in late to school. Teacher says: 'Why ya late?' Kid says: 'Had a take a heifer down–get 'er bred.' Teacher says: 'Couldn't your ol' man do it?' Kid says: 'Sure he could, but not as good as the bull.'

Mae squeaks with laughter, harsh screeching laughter. Al, slicing onions carefully on a board, looks up and smiles, and then looks down again. Truck drivers, that's the stuff. Gonna leave a quarter each for Mae. Fifteen cents for pie an' coffee an' a dime for Mae. An' they ain't tryin' to make her, neither.

Sitting together on the stools, spoons sticking up out of the coffee mugs. Passing the time of day. And Al, rubbing down his griddle, listening but making no comment. Bing Crosby's voice stops. The turn-table drops down and the record swings into its place in the pile. The purple light goes off. The nickel, which has caused all the mechanism to work, has caused Crosby to sing and an orchestra to play–this nickel drops from between the contact points into the box where the profits go. This nickel, unlike most money, has actually done a job of work, has been physically responsible for a reaction.

Steam spurts from the valve of the coffee-urn. The compressor of the ice machine chugs softly for a time and then stops. The electric fan in the corner waves its head slowly back and forth, sweeping the room with a warm breeze. On the highway, on 66, the cars whizz by.

'They was a Massachusetts car stopped a while ago,' said Mae.

Big Bill grasped his cup around the top so that the spoon stuck up between his first and second fingers. He drew in a snort of air with the coffee, to cool it. 'You ought to be out on 66. Cars from all over the country. All headin' west. Never seen so many before. Sure some honeys on the road.'

'We seen a wreck this mornin',' his companion said. 'Big car. Big Cad', a special job and a honey, low, cream-colour, special job. Hit a truck. Folded the radiator right back into the driver. Must a been doin' ninety. Steerin' wheel went right on through the guy an' lef' him a-wigglin' like a frog on a hook. Peach of a car. A honey. You can have her for peanuts now. Drivin' alone, the guy was.'

Al looked up from his work. 'Hurt the truck?'

'Oh, Jesus Christ! Wasn't a truck. One of them cut-down cars full a stoves an' pans an' mattresses an' kids an' chickens. Goin' west, you know. This guy come by us doin' ninety–r'ared up on two wheels just to pass us, an' a car's comin' so he cuts in an' whangs this here truck. Drove like he's blin' drunk. Jesus, the air was full of bed-clothes an' chickens an' kids. Killed one kid. Never seen such a mess. We pulled up. Ol' man that's drivin' the truck, he jus' stan's there lookin' at that dead kid. Can't get a word out of 'im. Jus' rum-dumb. God Almighty, the road is full of them families goin' west. Never seen so many. Gets worse all a time. Wonder where the hell they come from?'

'Wonder where they all go to,' said Mae. 'Come here for petrol sometimes, but they don't hardly never buy nothin' else. People say they steal. We ain't got nothin' layin' around. They never stole nothin' from us.'

Big Bill, munching his pie, looked up the road through the screened window. 'Better tie your stuff down. I think you got some of 'em comin' now.'

A 1926 Nash sedan pulled wearily off the highway. The back seat was piled nearly to the ceiling with sacks, with pots and pans, and on the very top, right up against the ceiling, two boys rode. On the top of the car, a mattress and a folded tent; tent poles tied along the running-board. The car pulled up to the petrol pumps. A dark-haired, hatchet-faced man got slowly out. And the two boys slid down from the load and hit the ground.

Mae walked around the counter and stood in the door. The man was dressed in grey wool trousers and a blue shirt, dark blue with sweat on the back and under the arms. The boys in overalls and nothing else, ragged patched overalls. Their hair was light, and it stood up evenly all over their heads, for it had been roached. Their faces were streaked with dust. They went directly to the mud puddle under the hose and dug their toes into the mud.

The man asked: 'Can we git some water, ma'am?'

A look of annoyance crossed Mae's face. 'Sure, go ahead.' She said softly over her shoulder: 'I'll keep my eye on the hose.' She watched while the man slowly unscrewed the radiator cap and ran the hose in.

A woman in the car, a flaxen-haired woman, said: 'See if you can't git it here.'

The man turned off the hose and screwed on the cap again. The little boys took the hose from him and they upended it and drank thirstily. The man took off his dark, stained hat and stood with a curious humility in front of the screen. 'Could you see your way to sell us a loaf of bread, ma'am?'

Mae said: 'This ain't a grocery store. We got bread to make san'widges.'

'I know, ma'am.' His humility was insistent. 'We need bread and there ain't nothin' for quite a piece, they say.'

''F we sell bread we gonna run out.' Mae's tone was faltering.

'We're hungry,' the man said.

'Whyn't you buy a san'widge? We got nice san'widges, hamburgs.'

'We'd sure admire to do that, ma'am. But we can't. We got to make a dime do all of us.' And he said embarrassedly: 'We ain't got but a little.'

Mae said: 'You can't get no loaf a bread for a dime. We only got fifteen-cent loafs.'

From behind her Al growled: 'God Almighty, Mae, give 'em bread.'

'We'll run out 'fore the bread truck comes.'

'Run out, then, goddamn it,' said Al. And he looked sullenly down at the potato salad he was mixing.

Mae shrugged her plump shoulders and looked to the truck drivers to show them what she was up against.

She held the screen door open and the man came in, bringing a smell of sweat with him. The boys edged in behind him and they went immediately to the candy case and stared in–not with craving or with hope or even with desire, but just with a kind of wonder that such things could be. They were alike in size and their faces were alike. One scratched his dusty ankle with the toenails of his other foot. The other whispered some soft message and then they straightened their arms so that their clenched fists in the overall pockets showed through the thin blue cloth.

Mae opened the drawer and took out a long waxpaper-wrapped loaf. 'This here is a fifteen-cent loaf.'

The man put his hat back on his head. He answered with inflexible humility: 'Won't you–can't you see your way to cut off ten cents' worth?'

Al said snarlingly: 'Goddamn it, Mae. Give 'em the loaf.'

The man turned toward Al. 'No, we want to buy ten cents' worth of it. We got it figgered awful close, mister, to get to California.'

Mae said resignedly: 'You can have this for ten cents.'

'That'd be robbin' you, ma'am.'

'Go ahead–Al says to take it.' She pushed the waxpapered loaf across the counter. The man took a deep leather pouch from his rear pocket, untied the strings, and spread it open. It was heavy with silver and with greasy bills.

'May soun' funny to be so tight,' he apologized. 'We got a thousan' miles to go, an' we don' know if we'll make it.' He dug in the pouch with a forefinger, located a dime, and pinched in for it. When he put it down on the counter he had a penny with it. He was about to drop the penny back into the pouch when his eye fell on the boys frozen before the candy counter. He moved slowly down to them. He pointed in the case at big long sticks of striped peppermint. 'Is them penny candy, Ma'am?'

Mae moved down and looked in. 'Which ones?'

'There, them stripy ones.'

The little boys raised their eyes to her face and they stopped breathing; their mouths were partly opened, their half-naked bodies were rigid.

'Oh–them. Well, no–them's two for a penny.'

'Well, gimme two then, ma'am.' He placed the copper cent carefully on the counter. The boys expelled their held breath softly. Mae held the big sticks out.

'Take 'em,' said the man.

They reached timidly, each took a stick, and they held them down at their sides and did not look at them. But they looked at each other, and their mouth corners smiled rigidly with embarrassment.

'Thank you, ma'am.' The man picked up the bread and went out the door, and the little boys marched stiffly behind him, the red-striped sticks held tightly against their legs. They leaped like chipmunks over the front seat and on to the top of the load, and they burrowed back out of sight like chipmunks.

The man got in and started his car, and with a roaring motor and a cloud of blue oily smoke the ancient Nash climbed up on the highway and went on its way to the west.

From inside the restaurant the truck drivers and Mae and Al stared after them.

Big Bill wheeled back. 'Them wasn't two-for-a-cent candy,' he said.

'What's that to you?' Mae said fiercely.

'Them was nickel apiece candy,' said Bill.

'We got to get goin',' said the other man. 'We're droppin' time.' They reached in their pockets. Bill put a coin on the counter and the other man looked at it and reached again and put down a coin. They swung around and walked to the door.

'So long,' said Bill.

Mae called: 'Hey! Wait a minute. You got change.'

'You go to hell,' said Bill, and the screen door slammed.

Mae watched them get into the great truck, watched it lumber off in low gear and heard the shift up the whining gears to cruising ratio. 'Al–' she said softly.

He looked up from the hamburger he was patting thin and stacking between waxed papers. 'What ya want?'

'Look there.' She pointed at the coins beside the cups–two half-dollars. Al walked near and looked, and then he went back to his work.

'Truck drivers,' Mae said reverently, 'an' after them shit-heels.'

Flies struck the screen with little bumps and droned away. The compressor chugged for a time and then stopped. On 66 the traffic whizzed by, trucks and fine stream-lined cars and jalopies; and they went with a vicious whizz. Mae took down the plates and scraped the pie crusts into a bucket. She found her damp cloth and wiped the counter with circular sweeps. And her eyes were on the highway, where life whizzed by.

Al wiped his hands on his apron. He looked at a paper pinned to the wall over the griddle. Three lines of marks in columns on the paper. Al counted the longest line. He walked along the counter to the cash register, rang 'No Sale', and took a handful of nickels.

'What ya doin'?' Mae asked.

'Number three's ready to pay off', said Al. He went to the third slot machine and played his nickels in, and on the fifth spin of the wheels the three bars came up and the jack pot dumped out into the cup. Al gathered up the big handful of coins and went back to the counter. He dropped them in the drawer and slammed the cash register. Then he went back to his place and crossed out the line of dots. 'Number three gets more play'n the others,' he said. 'Maybe I ought to shift 'em around.' He lifted a lid and stirred the slowly simmering stew.

'I wonder what they'll do in California?' said Mae.

'Who?'

'Them folks that was just in.'

'Christ knows,' said Al.

'S'pose they'll get work?'

'How the hell would I know?' said Al.

She stared eastward along the highway. 'Here comes a transport, double. Wonder if they stop? Hope they do.' And as the huge truck came down heavily from the highway and parked, Mae seized her cloth and wiped the whole length of the counter. And she took a few swipes at the gleaming coffee-urn too, and turned up the bottle-gas under the urn. Al brought out a handful of little turnips and started to peel them. Mae's face was gay when the door opened and the two uniformed truck drivers entered.

'Hi sister!'

'I won't be a sister to no man,' said Mae. They laughed and Mae laughed. 'What'll it be, boys?'

'Oh, a cup a Java. What kinda pie ya got?'

'Pineapple cream an' banana cream an' chocolate cream an' apple.'

'Give me apple. No wait–what's that big thick one?'

Mae picked up the pie and smelled it. 'Pineapple cream,' she said.

'Well, chop out a hunk a that.'

The cars whizzed viciously by on 66.

16

Joads and Wilsons crawled westward as a unit: El Reno and Bridgeport, Clinton, Elk City, Sayre, and Texola. There's the border, and Oklahoma was behind. And this day the cars crawled on and on, through the Panhandle of Texas. Shamrock and Alanreed, Groom and Yarnell. They went through Amarillo in the evening, drove too long, and camped when it was dusk. They were tired and dusty and hot. Granma had convulsions from the heat, and she was weak when they stopped.

That night Al stole a fence rail and made a ridge pole on the truck, braced at both ends. That night they ate nothing but pan biscuits, cold and hard, held over from the breakfast. They flopped down on the mattress and slept in their clothes. The Wilsons didn't even put up their tent.

Joads and Wilsons were in flight across the Panhandle, the rolling grey country, lined and cut with old flood scars. They were in flight out of Oklahoma and across Texas. The land turtles crawled through the dust and the sun whipped the earth, and in the evening the heat went out of the sky and the earth sent up a wave of heat by itself.

Two days the families were in flight, but on the third the land was too huge for them and they settled into a new technique of living; the highway became their home and movement their medium of expression. Little by little they settled into the new life. Ruthie and Winfield first, then Al, then Connie and Rose of Sharon, and, last, the older ones. The land rolled like great stationary ground-swells. Wildorado and Vega and Bosie and Glenrio. That's the end of Texas. New Mexico and the mountains. In the far distance, waved up against the sky, the mountains stood. And the wheels of the cars creaked around, and the engines were hot, and the steam spurted around the radiator caps. They crawled to the Pecos river, and crossed at Santa Rosa. And they went on for twenty miles.

Al Joad drove the touring car, and his mother sat beside him, and Rose of Sharon beside her. Ahead the truck crawled. The hot air folded in waves over the land, and the mountains shivered in the heat. Al drove listlessly, hunched back in the seat, his hand hooked easily over the cross-bar of the steering-wheel; his grey hat, peaked and pulled to an incredibly cocky shape, was low over one eye; and as he drove, he turned and spat out of the side now and then.

Ma, beside him, had folded her hands in her lap, had retired into a resistance against weariness. She sat loosely, letting the movement of the car sway her body and her head. She squinted her eyes ahead at the mountains. Rose of Sharon was braced against the movement of the car, her feet pushed tight against the floor, and her right elbow hooked over the door. And her plump face was tight against the movement, and her head jiggled sharply because her neck muscles were tight. She tried to arch her whole body as a rigid container to preserve her foetus from shock. She turned her head toward her mother.

'Ma,' she said. Ma's eyes lighted up and she drew her attention towards Rose of Sharon. Her eyes went over the tight, tired, plump face, and she smiled. 'Ma,' the girl said, 'when we get there, all you gonna pick fruit an' kinda live in the country, ain't you?'

Ma smiled a little satirically. 'We ain't there yet,' she said. 'We don't know what it's like. We got to see.'

'Me an' Connie don't want to live in the country no more,' the girl said. 'We got it all planned up what we gonna do.'

For a moment a little worry came on Ma's face. 'Ain't you gonna stay with us–with the family?' she asked.

'Well, we talked all about it, me an' Connie. Ma, we wanna live in a town.' She went on excitedly: 'Connie gonna get a job in a store or maybe a fact'ry. An' he's gonna study at home, maybe radio, so he can git to be an expert an' maybe later have his own store. An' we'll go to pitchers whenever. An' Connie says I'm gonna have a *doctor* when the baby's born; an' he says we'll see how times is, an' maybe I'll go to a hospiddle. An' we'll have a car, little car. An' after he studies at night, why–it'll be nice, an' he tore a page outa *Western Love Stories*, an' he's gonna send off for a course, 'cause it don't cost nothin' to send off. Says right on that clipping. I seen it. An' why–they even get you a job when you take that course–radios, it is–nice clean work, and a future. An' we'll live in town an' go to pitchers whenever, an'–well, I'm gonna have a 'lectric iron, an' the baby'll have all new stuff. Connie says all new stuff–white an'–Well, you seen in the catalogue all the stuff they got for a baby. Maybe right at first while Connie's studyin' at home it won't be so easy, but–well, when the baby comes, maybe he'll be all done studyin' an' we'll have a place, little bit of a place. We don't want nothin' fancy, but we want it nice for the baby–' Her face glowed with excitement. 'An' I thought maybe we could all go in town, an' when Connie gets his store–maybe Al could work for him.'

Ma's eyes had never left the flushing face. Ma watched the structure grow and followed it. 'We don't want you to go 'way from us,' she said. 'It ain't good for folks to break up.'

Al snorted: 'Me work for Connie? How about Connie comes a-workin' for me? He thinks he's the on'y son-of-a-bitch can study at night?'

Ma suddenly seemed to know it was all a dream. She turned her head forward again and her body relaxed, but the little smile stayed around her eyes. 'I wonder how Granma feels to-day,' she said.

Al grew tense over the wheel. A little rattle had developed in the engine. He speeded up and the rattle increased. he retarded his spark and listened, and then he speeded up for a moment and listened. The rattle increased to a metallic pounding. Al blew his horn and pulled the car to the side of the road. Ahead the truck pulled up and then backed slowly. Three cars raced by, westward, and each one blew its horn and the last driver leaned out and yelled: 'Where the hell ya think you're stoppin'?'

Tom backed the truck close, and he got out and walked to the touring car. From the back of the loaded truck heads looked down. Al retarded his spark and listened to his idling motor. Tom asked: 'What's the matter, Al?'

Al speeded the motor. 'Listen to her.' The rattling pound was louder now.

Tom listened. 'Put up your spark an' idle,' he said. He opened the hood and put his head inside. 'Now speed her.' He listened for a moment and then closed the hood. 'Well, I guess you're right, Al,' he said.

'Con-rod bearing, ain't it?'

'Sounds like it,' said Tom.

'I kep' plenty oil in,' Al complained.

'Well, it jus' didn' get to her. Drier'n a bitch monkey now. Well, there ain't nothin' to do but tear her out. Look, I'll pull ahead an' find a flat place to stop. You come ahead slow. Don't knock the pan out of her.'

Wilson asked: 'Is it bad?'

'Purty bad,' said Tom, and walked back to the truck and moved slowly ahead.

Al explained: 'I don't know what made her go out. I give her plenty of oil.' Al knew the blame was on him. He felt his failure.

Ma said: 'It ain't your fault. You done ever'thing right.' And then she asked a little timidly: 'Is it terrible bad?'

'Well, it's hard to get at, an' we got to get a new con-rod or else some babbitt in this one.' He sighed deeply. 'I sure am glad Tom's here. I never fitted no bearing. Hope to Jesus Tom did.'

A huge red bill-board stood beside the road ahead, and it threw a great oblong shadow. Tom edged the truck off the road and across the shallow roadside ditch, and he pulled up in the shadow. He got out and waited until Al came up.

'Now go easy,' he called. 'Take her slow or you'll break a spring, too.'

Al's face went red with anger. He throttled down his motor. 'Goddamn it,' he yelled, 'I didn't burn that bearin' out! What d'ya mean, I'll bust a spring too?'

Tom grinned. 'Keep all four feet on the groun',' he said. 'I didn' mean nothin'. Jus' take her easy over this ditch.'

Al grumbled as he inched the touring car down, and up the other side. 'Don't you go givin' nobody no idear I burned out that bearin'.' The engine clattered loudly now. Al pulled into the shade and shut down the motor.

Tom lifted the hood and braced it. 'Can't even start on her before she cools off,' he said. The family piled down from the cars and clustered about the touring car.

Pa asked: 'How bad?' And he squatted on his hams.

Tom turned to Al. 'Ever fitted one?'

'No,' said Al, 'I never. 'Course I had the pans off.'

Tom said: 'Well, we got to tear the pan off an' get the rod out, an' we got to get a new part an' hone her an' shim her an' fit her. Good day's job. Got to go back to that las' place for a part, Santa Rosa. Albuquerque's about seventy-five miles on–Oh, Jesus, to-morra's Sunday! We can't get nothin' to-morra.' The family stood silently. Ruthie crept close and peered into the open hood, hoping to see the broken part. Tom went on softly: 'Tomorra's Sunday. Monday we'll get the thing an' prob'ly won't get her fitted 'fore Tuesday. We ain't got the tools to make it easy. Gonna be a job.' The shadow of a buzzard slid across the earth, and the family all looked up at the sailing black bird.

Pa said: 'What I'm scairt of is we'll run outa money so we can't git there't all. Here's all us eatin', an' got to buy petrol an' oil. 'F we run outa money, I don't know what we gonna do.'

Wilson said: 'Seems like it's my fault. This here goddamn wreck's give me trouble right along. You folks been nice to us. Now you jus' pack up an' get along. Me an' Sairy'll stay, an' we'll figger some way. We don't aim to put you folks out none.'

Pa said slowly: 'We ain't a-gonna do it. We got almost a kin bond. Grampa, he died in your tent.'

Sairy said tiredly: 'We been nothin' but trouble, nothin' but trouble.'

Tom slowly made a cigarette, and inspected it and lighted it. He took off his ruined cap and wiped his forehead. 'I got an idear,' he said. 'Maybe nobody gonna like it but here she is: The nearer to California our folks get, the quicker they's gonna be money rollin' in. Now this here car'll go twicet as fast as that truck. Now here's my idea. You take out some a that stuff in the truck, an' then all you folks but me an' the preacher get in an' move on. Me an' Casy'll stop here an' fix this here car an' then we drive on, day an' night, an' we'll catch up, or if we don't meet on the road, you'll be a-workin' anyways. An' if you break down, why, jus' camp 'longside the road till we come. You can't be no worse off an' if you get through, why, you'll be a-workin', an' stuff'll be easy. Casy can give me a lif' with this here car, an' we'll come a-sailing'.'

The gathered family considered it. Uncle John dropped to his hams beside Pa.

Al said: 'Won't ya need me to give ya a han' with that con-rod?'

'You said your own se'f you never fixed one.'

'That's right.' Al agreed. 'All ya got to have is a strong back. Maybe the preacher don't wanta stay.'

'Well–whoever–I don't care,' said Tom.

Pa scratched the dry earth with his forefinger. 'I kinda got a notion Tom's right,' he said. 'It ain't goin' ta do no good all of us stayin' here. We can get fifty, a hunderd miles on 'fore dark.'

Ma said worriedly: 'How you gonna find us?'

'We'll be on the same road,' said Tom. 'Sixty-six right on through. Come to a place name' Bakersfiel'. Seen it on the map I got. You go straight on there.'

'Yeah, but when we get to California an' spread out sideways off this road–?'

'Don't you worry,' Tom reassured her. 'We're gonna find ya. California ain't the whole world.'

'Looks like an awful big place on the map,' said Ma.

Pa appealed for advice. 'John, you see any reason why not?'

'No,' said John.

'Mr Wilson, it's your car. You got any objections if my boy fixes her an' brings her on?'

'I don' see none,' said Wilson. 'Seems like you folks done ever'thing for us awready. Don' see why I cain't give your boy a han'.'

'You can be workin', layin' in a little money, if we don' ketch up with ya,' said Tom. 'An' suppose we all jus' lay aroun' here. There ain't no water here, an' we can't move this here car. But s'pose you all git out there an' git to work. Why, you'd have money, an' maybe a house to live in. How about it, Casy? Wanna stay with me an' gimme a lif'?'

'I wanna do what's bes' for you folks,' said Casy. 'You took me in, carried me along. I'll do whatever.'

'Well, you'll lay on your back an' get grease in your face if you stay here,' Tom said.

'Suits me awright.'

Pa said: 'Well, if that's the way she's gonna go, we better get a-shovin'. We can maybe squeeze in a hundred miles 'fore we stop.'

Ma stepped in front of him. 'I ain't a-gonna go.'

'What you mean, you ain't gonna go? You got to go. You got to look after the family.' Pa was amazed at the revolt.

Ma stepped to the touring car and reached in on the floor of the back seat. She brought out a jack handle and balanced it in her hand easily. 'I ain't a-gonna go,' she said.

'I tell you, you got to go. We made up our mind.'

And now Ma's mouth set hard. She said softly: 'On'y way you gonna get me to go is whup me.' She moved the jack handle gently again. 'An' I'll shame you, Pa. I won't take no whuppin', cryin' an' a-beggin'. I'll light into you. An' you ain't so sure you can whup me anyways. An' if ya do get me, I swear to God I'll wait till you got your back turned, or you're settin' down, an' I'll knock you belly-up with a bucket. I swear to Holy Jesus' sake I will.'

Pa looked helplessly about the group. 'She sassy,' he said. 'I never seen her so sassy.' Ruthie giggled shrilly.

The jack handle flicked hungrily back and forth in Ma's hand. 'Come on,' said Ma. 'You made up your mind. Come on an' whup me. Jus' try it. But I ain't a-goin'; or if I do, you ain't never gonna get no sleep, 'cause I'll wait an' I'll wait, an' jus' the minute you take sleep in your eyes, I'll slap ya with a stick a stove wood.'

'So goddamn sassy,' Pa murmured. 'An' she ain't young, neither.'

The whole group watched the revolt. They watched Pa, waiting for him to break into fury. They watched his lax hands to see the fists form. And Pa's anger did not rise, and his hands hung limply at his sides. And in a moment the group knew that Ma had won, and Ma knew it too.

Tom said: 'Ma, what's eatin' on you? What ya wanna do this-a-way for! What's the matter'th you anyways? You gone john-rabbit on us?'

Ma's face softened, but her eyes were still fierce. 'You done this 'thout thinkin' much,' Ma said. 'What we got lef' in the worl'? Nothin' but us. Nothin' but the folks. We come out an' Grampa, he reached for the shovel-shelf right off. An' now, right off, you wanna bust up the folks–'

Tom cried: 'Ma, we was gonna catch up with ya. We wasn't gonna be gone long.'

Ma waved the jack handle. 'S'pose we was camped, and you went on by. S'pose we got on through, how'd we know where to leave the word, an' how'd you know where to ask?' She said: 'We got a bitter road. Granma's sick. She's up there on the truck a-pawin' for a shovel herself. She's jus' tar'd out. We got a long bitter road ahead.'

Uncle John said: 'But we could be makin' some money. We could have a little bit saved up, come time the other folks got there.'

The eyes of the whole family shifted back to Ma. She was the power. She had taken control. 'The money we'd make wouldn't do no good,' she said. 'All we got is the family unbroke. Like a bunch of cows, when the lobos are ranging, stick all together. I ain't scared while we're all here, all that's alive, but I ain't gonna see us bust up. The Wilsons here is with us, an' the preacher is with us. I can't say nothin' if they want to go, but I'm a-goin' cat-wild with this here piece a bar-arn if my own folks busts up.' Her tone was cold and final.

Tom said soothingly: 'Ma, we can't all camp here. Ain't no water here. Ain't even much shade here. Granma, she needs shade.'

'All right,' said Ma. 'We'll go along. We'll stop first place they's water an' shade. An'–the truck'll come back an' take you in town to get your part, an' it'll bring you back. You ain't goin' walkin' along in the sun, an' I ain't havin' you out all alone, so if you get picked up there ain't nobody of your folks to he'p ya.'

Tom drew his lips over his teeth and then snapped them open. He spread his hands helplessly and let them flop against his sides. 'Pa,' he said, 'if you was to rush her one side an' me the other an' then the res' pile on, an' Granma jump down on top, maybe we can get Ma 'thout more'n two-three of us gets killed with that there jack handle. But if you ain't willin' to get your head smashed, I guess Ma's went an' filled her flush. Jesus Christ, one person with their mind made up can shove a lot of folks aroun'! You win, Ma. Put away that jack handle 'fore you hurt somebody.'

Ma looked in astonishment at the bar of iron. Her hand trembled. She dropped her weapon on the ground, and Tom, with elaborate care, picked it up and put it back in the car. He said: 'Pa, you jus' get set back on your heels. Al, you drive the folks on an' get 'em camped, an' then you bring the truck back here. Me an' the preacher'll get the pan off. Then, if we can make it, we'll run in Santa Rosa an' try an' get a con-rod. Maybe we can, seein' it's Sat'd'y night. Get jumpin' now so we can go. Lemme have the monkey wrench an' pliers outa the truck.' He reached under the car and felt the greasy pan. 'Oh, yeah, lemme have a can, that ol'bucket, to catch the oil. Got to save that.' Al handed over the bucket and Tom set it under the car and loosened the oil cap with a pair of pliers. The black oil flowed down his arm while he unscrewed the cap with his fingers, and then the black stream ran silently into the bucket. Al had loaded the family on the truck by the time the bucket was half full. Tom, his face already smudged with oil, looked out between the wheels. 'Get back fast!' he called. And he was loosening the pan bolts as the truck moved gently across the shallow ditch and crawled away. Tom turned each bolt a single turn, loosening them evenly to spare the gasket.

The preacher knelt beside the wheels. 'What can I do?'

'Nothin', not right now. Soon's the oil's out an' I get these here bolts loose, you can he'p me drop the pan off.' He squirmed away under the car, loosening the bolts with a wrench and turning them out with his fingers. He left the bolts on each end loosely threaded to keep the pan from dropping. 'Ground's still hot under here,' Tom said. And then: 'Say, Casy, you been awful goddamn quiet the las' few days. Why, Jesus! When I first come up with you, you was makin' a speech ever' half-hour or so. An' here you ain't said ten words the las' couple days. What's a matter–gettin' sour?'

Casy was stretched out on his stomach, looking under the car. His chin, bristly with sparse whiskers, rested on the back of one hand. His hat was pushed back so that it covered the back of his neck. 'I done enough talkin' when I was a preacher to las' the rest a my life,' he said.

'Yeah, but you done some talkin' sense, too.'

'I'm all worried up,' Casy said. 'I didn' even know it when I was a-preachin' aroun', but I was doin' consid'able tom-cattin' aroun'. If I ain't gonna preach no more, I got to get married. Why, Tommy, I'm a-lustin' after the flesh.'

'Me, too,' said Tom. 'Say, the day I come outa McAlester I was smokin'. I ran me down a girl, a hoor girl, like she was a rabbit. I won't tell ya what happened. I wouldn' tell nobody what happened.'

Casy laughed. 'I know what happened. I went a-fastin' into the wilderness one time, an' when I come out the same damn thing happened to me.'

'Hell it did!' said Tom. 'Well, I saved my money anyway, an' I give that girl a run. Thought I was nuts. I should a paid her, but I on'y got five bucks to my name. She said she didn' want no money. Here, roll in under here an' grab a-holt. I'll tap her loose. Then you turn out that bolt an' I turn out my end, an' we let her down easy. Careful that gasket. See, she comes off in one piece. They's on'y four cylinders to these here ol' Dodges. I took one down one time. Got main bearings big as a cantaloupe. Now–let her down–hold it. Reach up an' pull down that gasket where it's stuck–easy now. There!' The greasy pan lay on the ground between them, and a little oil still lay in the wells. Tom reached into one of the front wells and picked out some broken pieces of babbitt. 'There she is,' he said. He turned the babbitt in his fingers. 'Shaft's up. Look in the back an' get the crank. Turn her over till I tell you.'

Casy got to his feet and found the crank and fitted it. 'Ready?'

'Reach–now easy–little more–little more–right there.'

Casy kneeled down and looked under again. Tom rattled the connecting-rod bearing against the shaft. 'There she is.'

'What ya s'pose done it?' Casy asked.

'Oh, hell, I don't know! This buggy been on the road thirteen years. Says sixty-thousand miles on the speedometer. That means a hunderd an' sixty, an' God knows how many times they turned the numbers back. Gets hot–maybe somebody let the oil get low–jus' went out.' He pulled the cotter-pins and put his wrench on a bearing bolt. He strained and the wrench slipped. A long gash appeared on the back of his hand. Tom looked at it–the blood flowed evenly from the wound and met the oil and dripped into the pan.

'That's too bad,' Casy said. 'Want I should do that an' you wrap up your han'?'

'Hell, no! I never fixed no car in my life 'thout cuttin' myself. Now it's done I don't have to worry no more.' He fitted the wrench again. 'Wisht I had a crescent wrench,' he said, and he hammered the wrench with the butt of his hand until the bolts loosened. He took them out and laid them with the pan bolts in the pan, and the cotter-pins with them. He loosened the bearing bolts and pulled out the piston. He put piston and connecting-rod in the pan. 'There, by God!' He squirmed free from under the car and pulled the pan out with him. He wiped his hand on a piece of gunny sacking and inspected the cut. 'Bleedin' like a son-of-a-bitch,' he said. 'Well, I can stop that.' He urinated on the ground, picked up a handful of the resulting mud, and plastered it over the wound. Only for a moment did the blood ooze out, and then it stopped. 'Bes' damn thing in the worl' to stop bleedin',' he said.

'Han'ful a spider web'll do it too,' said Casy.

'I know, but there ain't no spider web, an' you can always get piss.' Tom sat on the running-board and inspected the broken bearing. 'Now if we can on'y find a '25 Dodge an' get a used con-rod an' some shims, maybe we'll make her all right. Al must a gone a hell of a long ways.'

The shadow of the bill-board was sixty feet out by now. The afternoon lengthened away. Casy sat down on the running-board and looked westward. 'We gonna be in high mountains pretty soon,' he said, and he was silent for a few moments. Then 'Tom!'

'Yeah?'

'Tom, I been watchin' the cars on the road, them we passed an' them that passed us. I been keepin' track.'

'Track a what?'

'Tom, they's hunderds a families like us all a-goin' west. I watched. There ain't none of 'em goin' east–hunderds of 'em. Did you notice that?'

'Yeah, I noticed.'

'Why–it's like they was runnin' away from soldiers. It's like a whole country is movin'.'

'Yeah,' Tom said. 'They is a whole country movin'. We're movin' too.'

'Well–s'pose all these here folks an' ever'body–s'pose they can't get no jobs out there?'

'Goddamn it!' Tom cried, 'how'd I know? I'm jus' puttin' one foot in front a the other. I done it at Mac for four years, just marchin' in cell an' out cell an' in mess an' out mess. Jesus Christ, I thought it'd be somepin different when I come out! Couldn' think a nothin' in there, else you go stir happy, an' now can't think a nothin'.' He turned on Casy. 'This here bearing went out. We didn't know it was goin', so we didn' worry none. Now she's out an' we'll fix her. An' by Christ that goes for the rest of it! I ain't gonna worry. I can't do it. This here little piece of iron an' babbitt. See it? Ya see it? Well, that's the only goddamn thing in the world I got on my mind. I wonder where the hell Al is.'

Casy said: 'Now look, Tom. Oh, what the hell! So goddamn hard to say anything.'

Tom lifted the mud pack from his hand and threw it on the ground.The edge of the wound was lined with dirt. He glanced over to the preacher. 'You're fixin' to make a speech,' Tom said. 'Well, go ahead. I like speeches. Warden used to make speeches all the time. Didn't do us no harm an' he got a hell of a bang out of it. What you tryin' to roll out?'

Casy picked the backs of his long knotty fingers. 'They's stuff goin' on and they's folks doin' things. Them people layin' one foot down in front of the other, like you says, they ain't thinkin' where they're goin', like you says–but they're all layin' 'em down the same direction, jus' the same. An' if ya listen, you'll hear a movin', an' a sneakin', an' a rustlin', an'–an' a res'lessness. They's stuff goin' on that the folks doin' it don't know nothin' about–yet. They's gonna come somepin outa all these folks goin' wes'–outa all their farms lef' lonely. They's gonna come a thing that's gonna change the whole country.'

Tom said: 'I'm still layin' my dogs down one at a time.'

'Yeah, but when a fence comes up at ya, ya gonna climb that fence.'

'I climb fences when I got fences to climb,' said Tom.

Casy sighed. 'It's the bes' way. I gotta agree. But they's different kinda fences. They's folks like me that climbs fences that ain't even strang up yet–an' can't he'p it.'

'Ain't that Al a-comin'?' Tom asked.

'Yeah. Looks like.'

Tom stood up and wrapped the connecting-rod and both halves of the bearing in the piece of sack. 'Wanta make sure I get the same,' he said.

The truck pulled alongside the road and Al leaned out the window.

Tom said: 'You was a hell of a long time. How far'd you go?'

Al sighed. 'Got the rod out?'

'Yeah.' Tom held up the sack. 'Babbitt jus' broke down.'

'Well, it wasn't no fault of mine,' said Al.

'No. Where'd you take the folks?'

'We had a mess,' Al said. 'Granma got to bellerin', an' that set Rosasharn off an' she bellered some. Got her head under a mattress an' bellered. But Granma, she was just layin' back her jaw an' bayin' like a moonlight houn' dog. Seems like Granma ain't got no sense no more. Like a little baby. Don't speak to nobody, don' seem to reco'nize nobody. Jus' talks on like she's talkin' to Grampa.'

'Where'd ya leave 'em?' Tom insisted.

'Well, we come to a camp. Got shade an' got water in pipes. Cost half a dollar a day to stay there. But ever'body's so goddamn tired an' wore out an' mis'able, they stayed there. Ma says they got to 'cause Granma's so tired an' wore out. Got Wilson's tent up an' got our tarp for a tent. I think Granma gone nuts.'

Tom looked toward the lowering sun. 'Casy,' he said, 'somebody got to stay with this car of she'll get stripped. You jus' as soon?'

'Sure. I'll stay.'

Al took a paper bag from the seat. 'This here's some bread an' meat Ma sent, an' I got a jug a water here.'

'She don't forget nobody,' said Casy.

Tom got in beside Al. 'Look,' he said. 'We'll get back jus' as soon's we can. But we can't tell how long.'

'I'll be here.'

'Awright. Don't make no speeches to yourself. Get goin', Al.' The truck moved off in the late afternoon. 'He's nice fella,' Tom said. 'He thinks about stuff all the time.'

'Well, hell–if you been a preacher, I guess you got to. Pa's all mad about it costs fifty cents jus' to camp under a tree. He can't see that noways. Settin' a-cussin'. Says nex' thing they'll sell ya a little tank a air. But Ma says they gotta be near shade an' water 'cause a Granma.' The truck rattled along the highway, and now that it was unloaded, every part of it rattled and clashed. The sideboard of the bed, the cut body. It rode hard and light. Al put it up to thirty-eight miles an hour and the engine clattered heavily and a blue smoke of burning oil drifted up through the floorboards.

'Cut her down some,' Tom said. 'You gonna burn her right down to the hub caps. What's eatin' on Granma?'

'I don't know. 'Member the las' couple days she's been airynary, sayin' nothin' to nobody? Well, she's yellin' an' talkin' plenty now, on'y she's talkin' to Grampa. Yellin' at him. Kinda scary, too. You can almos' see 'im a-settin' there grinnin' at her the way he always done, a-fingerin' hisself an' grinnin'. Seems like she sees him a-settin' there, too. She's jus' givin' him hell. Say, Pa, he give me twenty dollars to hand you. He don' know how much you gonna need. Ever see Ma stand up to 'im like she done to-day?'

'Not I remember. I sure did pick a nice time to get paroled. I figgered I was gonna lay aroun' an' get up late an' eat a lot when I come home. I was goin' out an' dance, an' I was gonna go tomcattin'–an' here I ain't had time to do none of them things.'

Al said: 'I forgot. Ma give me a lot of stuff to tell you. She says don't drink nothin', an' don' get in no arguments, an' don't fight nobody. 'Cause she says she's scairt you'll get sent back.'

'She got plenty to get worked up about 'thout me givin' her no trouble,' said Tom.

'Well, we could get a couple beers, can't we? I'm jus' a-ravin' for a beer.'

'I dunno,' said Tom. 'Pa'd crap a litter of lizards if we buy beers.'

'Well, look, Tom. I got six dollars. You an' me could get a couple pints an' go down the line. Nobody don't know I got that six bucks. Christ, we could have a hell of a time for ourselves.'

'Keep ya jack,' Tom said. 'When we get out to the coast you an' me'll take her an' we'll raise hell. Maybe when we're workin'–' He turned in the seat. 'I didn't think you was a fella to go down the line. I figgered you was talkin' 'em out of it.'

'Well, hell, I don't know nobody here. If I'm gonna ride aroun' much, I'm gonna get married. I'm gonna have me a hell of a time when we get to California.'

'Hope so,' said Tom.

'You ain't sure a nothin' no more.'

'No, I ain't sure a nothin'.'

'When ya killed that fella–did–did ya ever dream about it or anything? Did it worry ya?'

'No.'

'Well, didn' ya never think about it?'

'Sure.I was sorry 'cause he was dead.'

'Ya didn't take no blame to yourself?'

'No. I done my time, an' I done my own time.'

'Was it–awful bad–there?'

Tom said nervously: 'Look, Al. I done my time, an' now it's done. I don' wanna do it over an' over. There's the river up ahead, an' there's the town. Let's jus' try an' get a con-rod an' the hell with the res' of it.'

'Ma's awful partial to you,' said Al. 'She mourned when you was gone. Done it all to herself. Kinda cryin' down inside of her throat. We could tell what she was thinkin' about, though.'

Tom pulled his cap down low over his eyes. 'Now look here, Al. S'pose we talk 'bout some other stuff.'

'I was jus' tellin' ya what Ma done.'

'I know–I know. But–I ruther not. I ruther jus'–lay one foot down in front a the other.'

Al relapsed into an insulted silence. 'I was jus' tryin' to tell ya,' he said, after a moment.

Tom looked at him, and Al kept his eyes straight ahead. The lightened truck bounced noisily along. Tom's long lips drew up from his teeth and he laughed softly. 'I know you was, Al. Maybe I'm kinda stir-nuts. I'll tell ya about it sometime maybe. Ya see, it's jus' somepin you wanta know. Kinda interestin'. But I got a kind a funny idear the bes' thing'd be if I forget about it for a while. Maybe in a little while it won't be that way. Right now when I think about it my guts gets all droopy an' nasty feelin'. Look here, Al, I'll tell ya one thing–the jail-house is jus' a kind a way a drivin' a guy slowly nuts. See? An' they go nuts, an' you see 'em an' hear 'em, an' pretty soon you don' know if you're nuts or not. When they get to screamin' in the night sometimes you think it's you doin' the screamin'–an' sometimes it is.'

Al said: 'Oh! I won't talk about it no more, Tom.'

'Thirty days is all right,' Tom said. 'An' a hunderd an' eighty days is all right. But over a year–I dunno. There's somepin about it that ain't like nothin' else in the worl'. Somepin screwy about it, somepin screwy about the whole idea a lockin' people up. Oh, the hell with it! I don' wanna talk about it. Look a the sun a-flashin' on them windas.'

The truck drove to the service-station belt, and there on the right-hand side of the road was a wrecking yard–an acre lot surrounded by a high barbed-wire fence, a corrugated iron shed in front with used tires piled up by the doors, and price-marked. Behind the shed there was a little shack built of scrap, scrap lumber and pieces of tin. The windows were windshields built into the walls. In the grassy lot the wrecks lay, cars with twisted, stove-in noses, wounded cars lying on their sides with the wheels gone. Engines rusting on the ground and against the shed. A great pile of junk; fenders and truck sides, wheels and axles; over the whole lot a spirit of decay, of mould and rust; twisted iron, half-gutted engines, a mass of derelicts.

Al drove the truck up on the oil ground in front of the shed. Tom got out and looked into the dark doorway. 'Don't see nobody,' he said, and he called: 'Anybody here?'

'Jesus, I hope they got a '25 Dodge.'

Behind the shed a door banged. A spectre of a man came through the dark shed. Thin, dirty, oily skin tight against stringy muscles. One eye was gone, and the raw, uncovered socket squirmed with eye muscles when his good eye moved. His jeans and shirt were thick and shiny with old grease, and his hands cracked and lined and cut. His heavy, pouting underlip hung out sullenly.

Tom asked: 'You the boss?'

The one eye glared. 'I work for the boss,' he said sullenly. 'Watcha want?'

'Got a wrecked '25 Dodge? We need a con-rod.'

'I don't know. If the boss was here he could tell ya–but he ain't here. He's went home.'

'Can we look an' see?'

The man blew his nose into the palm of his hand and wiped his hand on his trousers. 'You from hereabouts?'

'Come from east–goin' west.'

'Look aroun' then. Burn the goddamn place down, for all I care.'

'Looks like you don't love your boss none.'

The man shambled close, his one eye flaring. 'I hate 'im,' he said softly. 'I hate the son-of-a-bitch! Gone home now. Gone home to his house.' The words fell stumbling out. 'He got a way–he got a way a-pickin' a fella an' a-tearin' a fella. He–the son-of-a-bitch. Got a girl nineteen, purty. Says to me: "How'd ya like ta marry her?" Says that right to me. An' to-night–says: "They's a dance; how'd ya like to go?" Me, he says it to me!' Tears formed in his eyes and tears dripped from the corner of the red eye socket. 'Some day, by God–some day I'm gonna have a pipe wrench in my pocket. When he says them things he looks at me eye. An' I'm gonna. I'm gonna jus' take his head right down off his neck with that wrench, little piece at a time.' He panted with his fury. 'Little piece at a time, right down off'n his neck.'

The sun disappeared behind the mountains. Al looked into the lot at the wrecked cars. 'Over there, look, Tom! That there looks like a '25 or '26.'

Tom turned to the one-eyed man. 'Mind if we look?'

'Hell, no! Take any goddamn thing you want.'

They walked, threading their way among the dead automobiles, to a rusting sedan, resting on flat tires.

'Sure it's a '25,' Al cried. 'Can we yank off the pan, mister?'

Tom kneeled down and looked under the car. 'Pan's off awready. One rod's been took. Looks like one gone.' He wriggled under the car. 'Get a crank an' turn her over, Al.' He worked the rod against the shaft. 'Purty much froze with grease.' Al turned the crank slowly. 'Easy,' Tom called. He picked a splinter of wood from the ground and scraped the cake of grease from the bearing and the bearing bolts.

'How is she for tight?' Al asked.

'Well, she's a little loose, but not bad.'

'Well, how is she for wore?'

'Got plenty of shim. Ain't been all took up. Yeah, she's O.K. Turn her over easy now. Get her down, easy–there! Run over the truck an' get some tools.'

The one-eyed men said: 'I'll get you a box a tools.' He shuffled off among the rusty cars and in a moment he came back with a tin box of tools. Tom dug out a socket wrench and handed it to Al.

'You take her off. Don't lose no shims an' don't let the bolts get away, an' keep track a the cotter-pins. Hurry up. The light's gettin' dim.'

Al crawled under the car. 'We oughta get us a set a socket wrenches,' he called. 'Can't get in no place with a monkey wrench.'

'Yell out if you want a hand,' Tom said.

The one-eyed man stood helplessly by. 'I'll help ya if ya want,' he said. 'Know what that son-of-a-bitch done? He come by an' he got on white pants. An' he says: "Come on, le's go out to my yacht." By God, I'll whang him some day!' He breathed heavily. 'I ain't been out with a woman sence I los' my eye. An' he says stuff like that.' And big tears cut channels in the dirt beside his nose.

Tom said impatiently: 'Whyn't you roll on? Got no guards to keep ya here.'

'Yeah, that's easy to say. Ain't so easy to get a job–not for a one-eye' man.'

Tom turned on him. 'Now look-a-here, fella. You got that eye wide open. An' ya dirty, ya stink. Ya jus' askin' for it. Ya like it. Lets ya feel sorry for yaself. 'Course ya can't get no woman with that empty eye flappin' aroun'. Put somepin over it an' wash ya face. You ain't hittin' nobody with no pipe wrench.'

'I tell ya, a one-eye' fella got a hard row,' the man said. 'Can't see stuff the way other fellas can. Can't see how far off a thing is. Ever'thing's jus' flat.'

Tom said: 'Ya full a crap. Why, I knowed a one-legged whore one time. Think she was takin' two-bits in a alley? No, by God! She's gettin' half a dollar extra. She says: "How many one-legged women you slep' with? None!" she says. "O.K.," she says. "You got somepin pretty special here' an' it's gonna cos' ya half a buck extry." An' by God, she was gettin' 'em, too, an' the fellas comin' out thinkin' they're pretty lucky, She says she's good luck. An' I knowed a hump-back in–in a place I was. Make his whole livin' lettin' folks rub his hump for luck. Jesus Christ, an' all you got is one eye gone.'

The man said stumblingly: 'Well, Jesus, ya see somebody edge away from ya, an' it gets into ya.'

'Cover it up then, goddamn it. Ya stickin' it out like a cow's ass. Ya like to feel sorry for yaself. There ain't nothin' the matter with you. Buy yaself some white pants. Ya gettin' drunk an' cryin' in ya bed, I bet. Need any help, Al?'

'No,' said Al. 'I got this here bearin' loose. Jus' tryin' to work the piston down.'

'Don't bang yaself,' said Tom.

The one-eyed man said softly: 'Think–somebody'd like–me?'

'Why, sure,' said Tom. 'Tell' em ya dong's growed sence you los' your eye.'

'Where at you fellas goin'?'

'California. Whole family. Gonna get work out there.'

'Well, ya think a fella like me could get work? Black patch on my eye?'

'Why not? You ain't no cripple.'

'Well–could I catch a ride with you fellas?'

'Christ, no. We're so goddamn full now we can't move. You get out some other way. Fix up one a these here wrecks an' go out by yaself.'

'Maybe I will, by God,' said the one-eyed man.

There was a clash of metal. 'I got her,' Al called.

'Well, bring her out, let's look at her.' Al handed him the piston and connecting-rod and the lower half of the bearing.

Tom wiped the babbitt surface and sighted along it sideways. 'Looks O.K. to me,' he said. 'Say, by God, if we had a light we get this here in to-night.'

'Say, Tom,' Al said. 'I been thinkin'. We got no ring clamps. Gonna be a job gettin' them rings in, specially underneath.'

Tom said: 'Ya know, a fella tol' me one time ya wrap some fine brass wire aroun' the ring to hol' her.'

'Yeah, but how ya gonna get the wire off?'

'Ya don't get her off. She melts off an' don't hurt nothin'.'

'Copper wire'd be better.'

'It ain't strong enough,' said Tom. He turned to the one-eyed man. 'Got any fine brass wire?'

'I dunno. I think they's a spool somewheres. Where d'ya think a fella could get one a them patches one-eye' fellas wear?'

'I don't know,' said Tom. 'Le's see if you can fin' that wire.'

In the iron shed they dug through boxes until they found the spool. Tom set the rod in a vice and carefully wrapped the wire around the piston-rings, forcing them deep into their slots, and where the wire was twisted he hammered it flat; and then he turned the piston and tapped the wire all round until it cleared the piston wall. He ran his finger up and down to make sure that the rings and wire were flush with the wall. It was getting dark in the shed. The one-eyed man brought a flashlight and shone its beam on the work.

'There she is,' said Tom. 'Say–what'll ya take for that light?'

'Well, it ain't much good. Got fifteen cents' a new batteries. You can have her for–oh, thirty-five cents.'

'O.K. An' what we owe ya for this here con-rod an' piston?'

The one-eyed man rubbed his forehead with a knuckle, and a line of dirt peeled off. 'Well, sir, I jus' dunno. If the boss was here, he'd go to a parts book an' he'd find out how much is a new one, an' while you was workin', he'd be findin' out how bad you're hung up, an' how much jack ya got, an' then he'd–well, say it's eight bucks in the part book–he'd make a price a five bucks. An' if you put up a squawk, you'd get it for three. You say it's all me, but, by God, he's a son-of-a-bitch. Figgers how bad ya need it. I seen him git more for a ring gear than he give for the whole car.'

'Yeah! But how much am I gonna give you for this here?'

''Bout a buck, I guess.'

'Awright, an' I'll give ya a quarter for this here socket wrench. Make it twice as easy.' He handed over the silver. 'Thank ya. An' cover up that goddamn eye.'

Tom and Al got into the truck. It was deep dark. Al started the motor and turned on the lights. 'So long,' Tom called. 'See ya maybe in California.' They turned across the highway and started back.

The one-eyed man watched them go, and then he went through the iron shed to his shack behind. It was dark inside. He felt his way to the mattress on the floor, and he stretched out and cried in his bed, and the cars whizzing by on the highway only strengthened the walls of his loneliness.

Tom said: 'If you'd tol' me we'd get this here thing an' get her in to-night, I'd a said you was nuts.'

'We'll get her in awright,' said Al. 'You got to do her, though. I'd be scared I'd get her too tight an' she'd burn out, or too loose an' she'd hammer out.'

'I'll stick her in,' said Tom. 'If she goes out again, she goes out. I got nothin' to lose.'

Al peered into the dusk. The lights made no impression on the gloom; but ahead, the eyes of a hunting cat flashed green in reflexion of the lights. 'You sure give that fella hell,' Al said. 'Sure did tell him where to lay down his dogs.'

'Well, goddamn it, he was askin' for it! Jus' a pattin' hisself 'cause he got one eye, puttin' all the blame on his eye. He's a lazy, dirty son-of-a-bitch. Maybe he can snap out of it if he knowed people was wise to him.'

Al said: 'Tom, it wasn't nothin' I done burned out that bearin'.'

Tom was silent for a moment, then: 'I'm gonna take a fall outa you, Al. You jus' scrabblin' ass over tit, fear somebody gonna pin some blame on you. I know what's a matter. Young fella, all full a piss an' vinegar. Wanta be a hell of a guy all the time. But, goddamn it, Al, don' keep ya guard up when nobody ain't sparrin' with ya. You gonna be alright.'

Al did not answer him. He looked straight ahead. The truck rattled and banged over the road. A cat whipped out from the side of the road and Al swerved to hit it, but the wheels missed and the cat leaped into the grass.

'Nearly got him,' said Al. 'Say, Tom. You heard Connie talkin' how he's gonna study nights? I been thinkin' maybe I'd study nights, too. You know, radio or television or diesel engines. Fella might get started that-a-way.'

'Might,' said Tom. 'Find out how much they gonna sock ya for the lessons, first. An' figger out if you're gonna study 'em. There was fellas takin' them mail lessons in McAlester. I never knowed one of 'em that finished up. Got sick of it an' left 'em slide.'

'God Awmighty, we forgot to get somepin to eat.'

'Well, Ma sent down plenty; preacher couldn't eat it all. Be some lef'. I wonder how long it'll take us to get to California.'

'Christ, I don' know. Jus' plug away at her.'

They fell into silence, and the dark came and the stars were sharp and white.

Casy got out of the back seat of the Dodge and strolled to the side of the road when the truck pulled up. 'I never expected you so soon,' he said.

Tom gathered the parts in the piece of sacking on the floor. 'We was lucky,' he said. 'Got a flashlight, too. Gonna fix her right up.'

'You forgot to take your dinner,' said Casy.

'I'll get it when I finish. Here, Al, pull off the road a little more an' come hol' the light for me.' He went directly to the Dodge and crawled under on his back. Al crawled under on his belly and directed the beam of the flashlight. 'Not in my eyes. There, put her up.' Tom worked the piston up into the cylinder, twisting and turning. The brass wire caught a little on the cylinder wall. With a quick push he forced it past the rings. 'Lucky she's loose or the compression'd stop her. I think she's gonna work all right.'

'Hope that wire don't clog the rings,' said Al.

'Well, that's why I hammered her flat. She won't roll off. I think she'll jus' melt out an' maybe give the walls a brass plate.'

'Think she might score the walls?'

Tom laughed. 'Jesus Christ, them walls can take it. She's drinkin' oil like a gopher hole awready. Little more ain't gonna hurt none.' He worked the rod down over the shaft and tested the lower half. 'She'll take some shim.' He said: 'Casy!'

'Yeah.'

'I'm takin' up this here bearing now. Get out to that crank an' turn her over slow when I tell ya.' He tightened the bolts.

'Now. Over slow!' And as the angular shaft turned, he worked the bearing against it. 'Too much shim,' Tom said. 'Hold it, Casy.' He took out the bolts and removed thin shims from each side and put the bolts back. 'Try her again, Casy!' And he worked the rod again. 'She's a lit-tle bit loose yet. Wonder if she'd be too tight if I took out more shim. I'll try her.' Again he removed the bolts and took out another pair of the thin strips. 'Now try her, Casy.'

'That looks good,' said Al.

Tom called: 'She any harder to turn, Casy?'

'No, I don't think so.'

'Well, I think she's snug here. I hope to God she is. Can't hone no babbitt without tools. This here socket wrench makes her a hell of a lot easier.'

Al said: 'Boss a that yard gonna be purty mad when he looks for that size socket an' she ain't there.'

'That's his screwin',' said Tom. 'We didn't steal her.' He tapped the cotter-pins in and bent the ends out. 'I think that's good. Look, Casy, you hold the light while me an' Al get this here pan up.'

Casy knelt down and took the flashlight. He kept the beam on the working hands as they patted the gasket gently into place and lined the holes with the pan bolts. The two men strained at the weight of the pan, caught the end bolts, and then set in the others; and when they were all engaged, Tom took them up little by little until the pan settled evenly against the gasket, and he tightened hard against the nuts.

'I guess that's her,' Tom said. He tightened the oil tap, looked carefully up at the pan, and took the light and searched the ground. 'There she is. Le's get the oil back in her.'

They crawled out and poured the bucket of oil back in the crank case. Tom inspected the gasket for leaks.

'O.K., Al. Turn her over,' he said. Al got into the car and stepped on the starter. The motor caught with a roar. Blue smoke poured from the exhaust pipe. 'Throttle down!' Tom shouted. 'She'll burn oil till that wire goes. Gettin' thinner now.' And as the motor turned over, he listened carefully. 'Put up the spark an' let her idle.' He listened again. 'O.K., Al. Turn her off. I think we done her. Where's that meat now?'

'You make a darn good mechanic,' Al said.

'Why not? I worked in the shop a year. We'll take her good an' slow for a couple hundred miles. Give her a chance to work in.'

They wiped their grease-covered hands on bunches of weeds and finally rubbed them on their trousers. They fell hungrily on the boiled pork and swigged the water from the bottle.

'I like to starved,' said Al. 'What we gonna do now, go on to the camp?'

'I dunno,' said Tom. 'Maybe they'd charge us a extry half-buck. Le's go an' talk to the folks–tell 'em we're fixed. Then if they wanta sock us extry–we'll move on. The folks'll wanta know. Jesus, I'm glad Ma stopped us this afternoon. Look around with the light, Al. See we don't leave nothin'. Get that socket wrench in. We may need her again.'

Al searched the ground with the flashlight. 'Don't see nothin'.'

'All right. I'll drive her. You bring the truck, Al.' Tom started the engine. The preacher got in the car. Tom moved slowly, keeping the engine at a low speed, and Al followed in the truck. He crossed the shallow ditch, crawling in low gear. Tom said: 'These here Dodges can pull a house in low gear. She's sure ratio'd down. Good thing for us–I wanta break that bearin' in easy.'

On the highway the Dodge moved along slowly. The 12-volt headlights threw a short blob of yellowish light on the pavement.

Casy turned to Tom. 'Funny how you fellas can fix a car. Jus' light right in an' fix her. I couldn't fix no car, not even now when I seen you do it.'

'Got to grow into her when you're a little kid,' Tom said. 'It ain't jus' knowin'. It's more'n that. Kids now can tear down a car 'thout even thinkin' about it.'

A jack-rabbit got caught in the lights and he bounced along ahead, cruising easily, his great ears flopping with every jump. Now and then he tried to break off the road, but the wall of darkness thrust him back. Far ahead bright headlights appeared and bore down on them. The rabbit hesitated, faltered, then turned and bolted toward the lesser lights of the Dodge. There was a small soft jolt as he went under the wheels. The oncoming car swished by.

'We sure squashed him,' said Casy.

Tom said: 'Some fellas like to hit 'em. Gives me a little shakes ever' time. Car sounds O.K. Them rings must a broke loose by now. She ain't smokin' so bad.'

'You done a nice job,' said Casy.

A small wooden house dominated the camp ground, and on the porch of the house a petrol lantern hissed and threw its white glare in a great circle. Half a dozen tents were pitched near the house, and cars stood beside the tents. Cooking for the night was over, but the coals of the camp-fires still glowed on the ground by the camping places. A group of men had gathered to the porch where the lantern burned, and their faces were strong and muscled under the harsh white light, that threw black shadows of their hats over their foreheads and eyes and made their chins seem to jut out. They sat on the steps, and some stood on the ground, resting their elbows on the porch floor. The proprietor, a sullen lanky man, sat in a chair on the porch. He leaned back against the wall, and he drummed his fingers on his knee. Inside the house a kerosene lamp burned, but its thin light was blasted by the hissing glare of the petrol lantern. The gathering of men surrounded the proprietor.

Tom drove the Dodge to the side of the road and parked. Al drove through the gate in the truck. 'No need to take her in,' Tom said. He got out and walked through the gate to the white glare of the lantern.

The proprietor dropped his front chair-legs to the floor and leaned forward. 'You men wanta camp here?'

'No,' said Tom. 'We got folks here. Hi, Pa.'

Pa, seated on the bottom step, said: 'Thought you was gonna be all week. Get her fixed?'

'We was pig lucky,' said Tom. 'Got a part 'fore dark. We can get goin' fust thing in the mornin'.'

'That's a pretty nice thing,' said Pa. 'Ma's worried. Ya Granma's off her chump.'

'Yeah, Al tol' me. She any better now?'

'Well, anyways she's a-sleepin'.'

The proprietor said: 'If you wanta pull in here an' camp it'll cost you four bits. Get a place to camp an' water an' wood. An' nobody won't bother you.'

'What the hell,' said Tom. 'We can sleep in the ditch right beside the road, an' it won't cost nothin'.'

The owner drummed his knee with his fingers. 'Deputy sheriff comes on by in the night. Might make it tough for ya. Got a law against sleepin' out in this State. Got a law about vagrants.'

'If I pay you a half a dollar I ain't a vagrant, huh?'

'That's right.'

Tom's eyes glowed angrily. 'Deputy sheriff ain't your brother-'n-law by any chance?'

The owner leaned forward. 'No, he ain't. An' the time ain't come yet when us local folks got to take no talk from you goddamn bums, neither.'

'It don't trouble you none to take our four bits. An' when'd we get to be bums? We ain't asked ya for nothin'. All of us bums, huh? Well, we ain't askin' no nickels from you for the chance to lay down an' rest.'

The men on the porch were rigid, motionless, quiet. Expression was gone from their faces; and their eyes, in the shadows under their hats, moved secretly up to the face of the proprietor.

Pa growled: 'Come off it, Tom.'

'Sure, I'll come off it.'

The circle of men were quiet, sitting on the steps, leaning on the high porch. Their eyes glittered under the harsh light of the gas lantern. Their faces were hard in the hard light, and they were very still. Only their eyes moved from speaker to speaker, and their faces were expressionless and quiet. A lamp bug slammed into the lantern and broke itself, and fell into the darkness.

In one of the tents a child wailed in complaint, and a woman's soft voice soothed it and then broke into a low song: 'Jesus loves you in the night. Sleep good, sleep good. Jesus watches in the night. Sleep, oh, sleep, oh.'

The lantern hissed on the porch. The owner scratched in the V of his open shirt, where a tangle of white chest hair showed. He was watchful and ringed with trouble. He watched the men in the circle, watched for some expression. And they made no move.

Tom was silent for a long time. His dark eyes looked slowly up at the proprietor. 'I don't wanta make no trouble,' he said. 'It's a hard thing to be named a bum. I ain't afraid,' he said softly. 'I'll go for you an' your deputy with my mitts–here now, or jump Jesus. But there ain't no good in it.'

The men stirred, changed positions, and their glittering eyes moved slowly upward to the mouth of the proprietor, and their eyes watched for his lips to move. He was reassured. He felt that he had won, but not decisively enough to charge in. 'Ain't you got half a buck?' he asked.

'Yeah, I got it. But I'm gonna need it. I can't set it out jus' for sleepin'.'

'Well, we all got to make a livin'.'

'Yeah,' Tom said. 'On'y I wisht they was some way to make her 'thout takin' her away from somebody else.'

The men shifted again. And Pa said: 'We'll get movin' smart early. Look mister. We paid. This here fella is part a our folks. Can't he stay? We paid.'

'Half a dollar a car,' said the proprietor.

'Well, he ain't got no car. Car's out in the road.'

'He came in a car,' said the proprietor. 'Ever'body'd leave their car out there an' come in an' use my place for nothin'.'

Tom said: 'We'll drive along the road. Meet ya in the morning. We'll watch for ya. Al can stay an' Uncle John can come with us–' He looked at the proprietor. 'That awright with you?'

He made a quick decision, with a concession in it. 'If the same number stays that come an' paid–that's awright.'

Tom brought out his bag of tobacco, a limp grey rag by now, with a little damp tobacco dust in the bottom of it. He made a lean cigarette and tossed the bag away. 'We'll go along pretty soon,' he said.

Pa spoke generally to the circle. 'It's dirt hard for folks to tear up an' go. Folks like us that had our place. We ain't shif'less. Till we got tractored off, we was people with a farm.'

A young thin man, with eyebrows sunburned yellow, turned his head slowly. 'Croppin'?' he asked.

'Sure we was sharecroppin'. Use' ta own the place.'

The young man faced forward again. 'Same as us,' he said.

'Lucky for us it ain't gonna las' long,' said Pa. 'We'll get out west an' we'll get a piece a growin' land with water.'

Near the edge of the porch a ragged man stood. His black coat dripped torn streamers. The knees were gone from his dungarees. His face was black with dust, and lined where sweat had washed through. He swung his head toward Pa. 'You folks must have a nice little pot a money.'

'No, we ain't got no money,' Pa said. 'But they's plenty of us to work, an' we're all good men. Get good wages out there an' we'll put 'em together. We'll make out.'

The ragged man stared while Pa spoke, and then he laughed, and his laughter turned to a high whinnying giggle. The circle of faces turned to him. The giggling got out of control and turned into coughing. His eyes were red and watering when he finally controlled the spasms. 'You goin' out there–oh, Christ!' The giggling started again. 'You goin' out an' get–good wages–oh, Christ!' He stopped and said slyly: 'Pickin' oranges maybe? Gonna pick peaches?'

Pa's tone was dignified. 'We gonna take what they got. They got lots a stuff to work in.' The ragged man giggled under his breath.

Tom turned irritably. 'What's so goddamn funny about that?'

The ragged man shut his mouth and looked sullenly at the porch boards. 'You folks all goin' to California, I bet.'

'I tol' you that,' said Pa. 'You didn' guess nothin'.'

The ragged man said slowly: 'Me–I'm comin' back. I been there.'

The faces turned quickly toward him. The men were rigid. The hiss of the lantern dropped to a sigh and the proprietor lowered the front chair legs to the porch, stood up, and pumped the lantern until the hiss was sharp and high again. He went back to his chair, but he did not tilt back again. The ragged man turned toward the faces. 'I'm goin' back to starve. I ruther starve all over at oncet.'

Pa said: 'What the hell you talkin' about? I got a han'bill says they got good wages, an' little while ago I see a thing in the paper says they need folks to pick fruit.'

The ragged man turned to Pa. 'You got any place to go, back home?'

'No,' said Pa. 'We're out. They put a tractor past the house.'

'You wouldn' go back then?'

''Course not.'

'Then I ain't gonna fret you,' said the ragged man.

''Course you ain't gonna fret me. I got a han'bill says they need men. Don't make no sense if they don't need men. Costs money for them bills. They wouldn't put 'em out if they didn' need men.'

'I don't wanna fret you.'

Pa said angrily: 'You done some jackassin'. You ain't gonna shut up now. My han'bill says they need men. You laugh an' say they don't. Now, which one's a liar?'

The ragged man looked down into Pa's angry eyes. He looked sorry. 'Han'bill's right,' he said. 'They need men.'

'Then why the hell you stirrin' us up laughin'?'

''Cause you don't know what kind a men they need.'

'What you talkin' about?'

The ragged man reached a decision. 'Look,' he said. 'How many men they say they want on your han'bill?'

'Eight hunderd, an' that's in one little place.'

'Orange colour han'bill?'

'Why–yes.'

'Give the name a the fella–says so-and-so, labour contractor?'

Pa reached in his pocket and brought out the folded handbill. 'That's right. How'd you know?'

'Look,' said the man. 'It don't make no sense. This fella wants eight hunderd men. So he prints up five thousand of them things an' maybe twenty thousan' people sees 'em. An' maybe two-three thousan' folks gets movin' account a this here han'bill. Folks that's crazy with worry.'

'But it don't make no sense!' Pa cried.

'Not till you see the fella that put out this here bill. You'll see him, or somebody that's working for him. You'll be a-campin' by a ditch, you an' fifty other famblies. An' he'll look in your tent an' see if you got anything lef' to eat. An' if you got nothin', he says: "Wanna job?" An' you'll say: "I sure do, mister. I'll sure thank you for a chance to do some work." An' he'll say: "I can use you." An' you'll say: "When do I start?" An' he'll tell you where to go, an' what time, an' then he'll go on. Maybe he needs two hunderd men, so he talks to five hunderd, an' they tell other folks, an' when you get to the place, they's a thousan' men. This here fella says: "I'm payin' twenty cents an hour." An' maybe half a men walk off. But they's still five hunderd that's so goddamn hungry they'll work for nothin' but biscuits. Well, this here fella's got a contract to pick them peaches or–chop that cotton. You see now? The more fellas he can get, an' the hungrier, less he's gonna pay. An' he'll get a fella with kids if he can, 'cause–hell, I says I wasn't gonna fret ya.' The circle of faces looked coldly at him. The eyes tested his words. The ragged man grew self-conscious. 'I says I wasn't gonna fret ya, an' here I'm a-doin' it. You gonna go on. You ain't goin' back.' The silence hung on the porch. And the light hissed, and a halo of moths swung around and around the lantern. The ragged man went on nervously: 'Lemme tell ya what to do when ya meet that fella says he got work. Lemme tell ya. Ast him what he's gonna pay. Ast him to write down what he's gonna pay. Ast him that. I tell you men you're gonna get fooled if you don't.

The proprietor leaned forward in his chair, the better to see the ragged dirty man. He scratched among the grey hairs on his chest. He said coldly: 'You sure you ain't one of these here trouble-makers? You sure you ain't a labour faker?'

And the ragged man cried: 'I swear to God I ain't!'

'They's plenty of 'em,' the proprietor said. 'Goin' aroun' stirrin' up trouble. Gettin' folks mad. Chisellin' in. They's plenty of 'em. Time's gonna come when we string 'em all up, all them trouble-makers. We gonna run'em outa the country. Man wants to work, O.K. If he don't–the hell with him. We ain't gonna let him stir up trouble.'

The ragged man drew himself up. 'I tried to tell you folks,' he said. 'Somepin it took me a year to find out. Took two kids dead, took my wife dead to show me. But I can't tell you. I should of knew that. Nobody couldn't tell me, neither. I can't tell ya about them little fellas layin' in the tent with their bellies puffed out an' jus' skin on their bones, an' shiverin' an' whinin' like pups, an' me runnin' aroun' tryin' to get work–not for money, not for wages!' he shouted. 'Jesus Christ, jus' for a cup a flour an' a spoon a lard. An' then the coroner come. "Them children died a heart failure," he said. Put it on his paper. Shiverin', they was, an' their bellies stuck out like a pig bladder.'

The circle was quiet, and mouths were open a little. The men breathed shallowly, and watched.

The ragged man looked around at the circle, and then he turned and walked quickly away into the darkness. The dark swallowed him, but his dragging footsteps could be heard a long time after he had gone, footsteps along the road; and a car came by on the highway, and its lights showed the ragged man shuffling along the road, his head hanging down and his hands in the black coat pockets.

The men were uneasy. One said: 'Well–gettin' late. Got to get to sleep.'

The proprietor said: 'Prob'ly shif'less. They's so goddamn many shif'less fellas on the road now.' And then he was quiet. And he tipped his chair back against the wall again and fingered his throat.

Tom said: 'Guess I'll go see Ma for a minute, an' then we'll shove along a piece.' The Joad men moved away.

Pa said: 'S'pose he's tellin' the truth–that fella?'

The preacher answered: 'He's tellin' the truth, awright. The truth for him. He wasn't makin' nothin' up.'

'How about us?' Tom demanded. 'Is that the truth for us?'

'I don't know,' said Casy.

'I don't know,' said Pa.

They walked to the tent, tarpaulin spread over a rope. And it was dark inside, and quiet. When they came near, a greyish mass stirred near the door and arose to person height. Ma came out to meet them.

'All sleepin',' she said. 'Granma finally dozed off.' Then she saw it was Tom. 'How'd you get here?' she demanded anxiously. 'You ain't had no trouble?'

'Got her fixed,' said Tom. 'We're ready to go when the rest is.'

'Thank the dear God for that,' Ma said. 'I'm just a-twitterin' to go on. Wanta get where it's rich an' green. Wanta get there quick.'

Pa cleared his throat. 'Fella was jus' sayin'–'

Tom grabbed his arm and yanked it. 'Funny what he says,' Tom said. 'Says they's lots a folks on the way.'

Ma peered through the darkness at them. Inside the tent Ruthie coughed and snorted in her sleep. 'I washed 'em up,' Ma said. 'Fust water we got enough of to give 'em a goin'-over. Lef' the buckets out for you fellas to wash too. Can't keep nothin' clean on the road.'

'Ever'body in?' Pa asked.

'All but Connie an' Rosasharn. They went off to sleep in the open. Says it's too warm in under cover.'

Pa observed querulously: 'That Rosasharn is gettin' awful scary an' nimsy-mimsy.'

'It's her first,' said Ma. 'Her an' Connie sets a lot a store by it. You done the same thing.'

'We'll go now,' Tom said. 'Pull off the road a little piece ahead. Watch out for us ef we don't see you. Be off right-han' side.'

'Al's stayin'?'

'Yeah. Leave Uncle John come with us. 'Night, Ma.'

They walked away through the sleeping camp. In front of one tent a low fitful fire burned, and a woman watched a kettle that cooked early breakfast. The smell of the cooking beans was strong and fine.

'Like to have a plate a them,' Tom said politely as they went by.

The woman smiled. 'They ain't done or you'd be welcome,' she said. 'Come aroun' in the daybreak.'

'Thank you, ma'am,' Tom said. He and Casy and Uncle John walked by the porch. The proprietor still sat in his chair, and the lantern hissed and flared. He turned his head as the three went by. 'Ya runnin' outa gas,' Tom said.

'W'll, time to close up, anyways.'

'No more half-bucks rollin' down the road, I guess,' Tom said.

The chair-legs hit the floor. 'Don't you go a-sassin' me. I 'member you. You're one of these here trouble-makers.'

'Damn right,' said Tom. 'I'm bolshevisky.'

'They's too damn many of you kinda guys aroun'.'

Tom laughed as they went out the gate and climbed into the Dodge. He picked up a clod and threw it at the light. They heard it hit the house and saw the proprietor spring to his feet and peer into the darkness. Tom started the car and pulled into the road. And he listened closely to the motor as it turned over, listened for knocks. The road spread dimly under the weak lights of the car.

17

The cars of the migrant people crawled out of the side roads on to the great cross-country highway, and they took the migrant way to the West. In the daylight they scuttled like bugs to the westward; and as the dark caught them, they clustered like bugs near to shelter and to water. And because they were lonely and perplexed, because they had all come from a place of sadness and worry and defeat, and because they were all going to a new mysterious place, they huddled together; they talked together; they shared their lives, their food, and the things they hoped for in the new country. Thus it might be that one family camped near a spring, and another camped for the spring and for company, and a third because two families had pioneered the place and found it good. And when the sun went down, perhaps twenty families and twenty cars were there.

In the evening a strange thing happened: the twenty families became one family, the children were the children of all. The loss of home became one loss, and the golden time in the West was one dream. And it might be that a sick child threw despair into the hearts of twenty families, of a hundred people; that a birth there in a tent kept a hundred people quiet and awestruck through the night and filled a hundred people with the birth-joy in the morning. A family which the night before had been lost and fearful might search its goods to find a present for a new baby. In the evening, sitting about the fires, the twenty were one. They grew to the units of the camps, units of the evenings and the nights. A guitar unwrapped from a blanket and tuned–and the songs, which were all of the people, were sung in the nights. Men sang the words, and women hummed the tunes.

Every night a world created, complete with furniture–friends made, enemies established; a world complete with braggarts and with cowards, with quiet men, with humble men, with kindly men. Every night relationships that make a world, established; and every morning the world torn down like a circus.

At first the families were timid in the building and tumbling worlds, but gradually the technique of building worlds became their technique. Then leaders emerged, then laws were made, then codes came into being. And as the worlds moved westward they were more complete and better furnished, for their builders were more experienced in building them.

The families learned what rights must be observed–the right of privacy in the tent; the right to keep the past black hidden in the heart; the right to talk and to listen; the right to refuse help or to accept, to offer or to decline it; the right of son to court and daughter to be courted; the right of the hungry to be fed; the rights of the pregnant and the sick to transcend all other rights.

And the families learned, although no one told them, what rights are monstrous and must be destroyed; the right to intrude upon privacy, the right to be noisy while the camp slept, the right of seduction or rape, the right of adultery and theft and murder. These rights were crushed, because the little worlds could not exist for even a night with such rights alive.

And as the worlds moved westward, rules became laws, although no one told the families. It is unlawful to foul near the camp; it is unlawful in any way to foul the drinking water; it is unlawful to eat good rich food near one who is hungry, unless he is asked to share.

And with the laws, the punishments–and there were only two–a quick and murderous fight or ostracism; and ostracism was the worst. For if one broke the laws his name and face went with him, and he had no place in any world, no matter where created.

In the worlds, social conduct became fixed and rigid, so that a man must say 'Good morning' when asked for it, so that a man might have a willing girl if he stayed with her, if he fathered her children and protected them. But a man might not have one girl one night and another the next, for this would endanger the worlds.

The families moved westward, and the technique of building the worlds improved so that the people could be safe in their worlds; and the form was so fixed that a family acting in the rules knew it was safe in the rules.

There grew up a government in the worlds, with leaders, with elders. A man who was wise found that his wisdom was needed in every camp; a man who was a fool could not change his folly with his world. And a kind of insurance developed in these nights. A man with food fed a hungry man, and thus insured himself against hunger. And when a baby died a pile of silver coins grew at the door flap, for a baby must be well buried, since it has had nothing else of life. An old man may be left in a potter's field, but not a baby.

A certain physical pattern is needed for the building of a world–water, a river bank, a stream, a spring, or even a tap unguarded. And there is needed enough flat land to pitch the tents, a little brush or wood to build the fires. If there is a garbage dump not too far off, all the better; for there can be found equipment–stove tops, a curved fender to shelter the fire, and cans to cook in and to eat from.

And the worlds were built in the evening. The people, moving in from the highways, made them with their tents and their hearts and their brains.

In the morning the tents came down, the canvas was folded, the tent poles tied along the running-board, the beds put in place on the cars, the pots in their places. And as the families moved westward, the technique of building up a home in the evening and tearing it down with the morning light became fixed; so that the folded tent was packed in one place, the cooking pots counted in their box. And as the cars moved westward, each member of the family grew into his proper place, grew into his duties; so that each member, old and young, had his place in the car; so that in the weary, hot evenings, when the cars pulled into the camping places, each member had his duty and went to it without instruction: children to gather wood, to carry water; men to pitch the tents and bring down the beds; women to cook the supper and to watch while the family fed. And this was done without command. The families, which had been units of which the boundaries were a house at night, a farm by day, changed their boundaries. In the long hot light they were silent in the cars moving slowly westward; but at night they integrated with any group they found.

Thus they changed their social life–changed as in the whole universe only man can change. They were not farm men any more, but migrant men. And the thought, the planning, the long staring silence that had gone out to the fields, were now to the roads, to the distance, to the West. That man whose mind had been bound with acres lived with narrow concrete miles. And his thought and his worry were not any more with rainfall, with wind and dust, with the thrust of the crops. Eyes watched the tires, ears listened to the clattering motors, and minds struggled with oil, with petrol, with the thinning rubber between air and road. Then a broken gear was tragedy. The water in the evening was the yearning, and food over the fire. Then health to go on was the need and strength to go on, and spirit to go on. The wills thrust westward ahead of them, and fears that had once apprehended drought or flood now lingered with anything that might stop the westward crawling.

The camps became fixed–each a short day's journey from the last.

And on the road the panic overcame some of the families, so that they drove night and day, stopped to sleep in the cars, and drove on to the West, flying from the road, flying from movement. And these lusted so greatly to be settled that they set their faces into the West and drove toward it, forcing the clashing engines over the roads.

But most of the families changed and grew quickly into the new life. And when the sun went down–

Time to look out for a place to stop.

And–there's some tents ahead.

The car pulled off the road and stopped, and because others were there first, certain courtesies were necessary. And the man, the leader of the family, leaned from the car.

Can we pull up here an' sleep?

Why, sure, be proud to have you. What State you from?

Come all the way from Arkansas.

They's Arkansas people down that fourth tent.

That so?

And the great question, How's the water?

Well, she don't taste so good, but they's plenty.

Well, thank ya.

No thanks to me.

But the courtesies had to be. The car lumbered over the ground to the end tent, and stopped. Then down from the car the weary people climbed, and stretched stiff bodies. Then the new tent sprang up; the children went for water and the older boys cut brush or wood. The fires started and supper was put on to boil or to fry. Early comers moved over, and States were exchanged, and friends and sometimes relatives discovered.

Oklahoma, huh? What county?

Cherokee.

Why, I got folks there. Know the Allens? They's Allens all over Cherokee. Know the Willises?

Why, sure.

And a new unit was formed. The dusk came, but before the dark was down the new family was of the camp. A word had been passed with every family. They were known people–good people.

I knowed the Allens all my life. Simon Allen, ol' Simon, had trouble with his first wife. She was part Cherokee. Purty as–as a black colt.

Sure, an' young Simon, he married a Rudolph, didn' he? That's what I thought. They went to live in Enid an' done well–real well.

Only Allen that ever done well. Got a garage.

When the water was carried and the wood cut, the children walked shyly, cautiously among the tents. And they made elaborate acquaintanceship gestures. A boy stopped near another boy and studied a stone, picked it up, examined it closely, spat on it, and rubbed it clean and inspected it until he forced the other to demand, What you got there?

And casually, Nothin'. Jus' a rock.

Well, what you lookin' at it like that for?

Thought I seen gold in it.

How'd you know? Gold ain't gold, it's black in a rock.

Sure, ever'body knows that.

I bet it's fool's gold, an' you figgered it was gold.

That ain't so, 'cause Pa, he's foun' lots a gold an' he tol' me how to look.

How'd you like to pick up a big ol' piece of gold?

Sa-a-ay! I'd git the bigges' old son-a-bitchin' piece a candy you ever seen.

I ain't let to swear, but I do, anyways.

Me too. Le's go to the spring.

And young girls found each other and boasted shyly of their popularity and their prospects. The women worked over the fire, hurrying to get food to the stomachs of the family–pork if there was money in plenty, pork and potatoes and onions. Dutch-oven biscuits or cornbread, and plenty of gravy to go over it. Sidemeat or chops and a can of boiled tea, black and bitter. Fried dough in drippings if money was slim, dough fried crisp and brown and the drippings poured over it.

Those families which were very rich or very foolish with their money ate canned beans and canned peaches and packaged bread and bakery cake; but they ate secretly, in their tents, for it would not have been good to eat such fine things openly. Even so, children eating their fried dough smelled the warming beans and were unhappy about it.

When supper was over and the dishes dipped and wiped, the dark had come, and then the men squatted down to talk.

And they talked of the land behind them. I don' know what it's coming to, they said. The country's spoilt.

It'll come back though, on'y we won't be there.

Maybe, they thought, maybe we sinned some way we didn't know about.

Fella says to me, gov'ment fella, an' he says, she's gullied up on ya. Gov'ment fella. He says, if ya ploughed 'cross the contour, she won't gully. Never did have no chance to try her. An' the new super' ain't ploughin' 'cross the contour. Runnin' a furrow four miles long that ain't stoppin' or goin' aroun' Jesus Christ hisself.

And they spoke softly of their homes: They was a little coolhouse under the win'mill. Use' ta keep milk in there ta cream up, an' water-melons. Go in there midday when she was hotter'n a heifer, an' she'd be jus' as cool, as cool as you'd want. Cut open a melon in there an' she'd hurt your mouth, she was so cool. Water drippin' down from the tank.

They spoke of their tragedies: Had a brother Charley, hair yella as corn, an' him a growed man. Played the 'cordeen nice, too. He was harrowin' one day an' he went up to clear his lines. Well, a rattlesnake buzzed an' them horses bolted an' the harrow went over Charley, an' the points dug into his guts an' his stomach, an' they pulled his face off an'–God Almighty!

They spoke of the future: Wonder what it's like out there?

Well, the pitchers sure do look nice. I seen one where it's hot an' fine, an' walnut trees an' berries; an' right behind, close as a mule's ass to his withers, they's a tall up mountain covered with snow. That was a pretty thing to see.

If we can get work it'll be fine. Won't have no cold in the winter. Kids won't freeze on the way to school. I'm gonna take care my kids don't miss no more school. I can read good, but it ain't no pleasure to me like with a fella that's used to it.

And perhaps a man brought out his guitar to the front of his tent. And he sat on a box to play, and everyone in the camp moved slowly in toward him, drawn in toward him. Many men can chord a guitar, but perhaps this man was a picker. There you have something–the deep chords beating, beating, while the melody runs on the strings like little footsteps. Heavy hard fingers marching on the frets. The man played and the people moved slowly in on him until the circle was closed and tight, and then he sang 'Ten-Cent Cotton and Forty-Cent Meat'. And the circle sang softly with him. And he sang 'Why Do You Cut Your Hair, Girls?' And the circle sang. He wailed the song, 'I'm Leaving Old Texas', that eerie song that was sung before the Spaniards came, only the words were Indian then.

And now the group was welded to one thing, one unit, so that in the dark the eyes of the people were inward, and their minds played in other times, and their sadness was like rest, like sleep. He sang the 'McAlester Blues' and then, to make up for it to the older people, he sang 'Jesus Calls Me to His Side'. The children drowsed with the music and went into the tents to sleep, and the singing came into their dreams.

And after a while the man with the guitar stood up and yawned. Good night, folks, he said.

And they murmured, Good night to you.

And each wished he could pick a guitar, because it is a gracious thing. Then the people went to their beds, and the camp was quiet. And the owls coasted overhead, and the coyotes gabbled in the distance, and into the camp skunks walked, looking for bits of food–waddling, arrogant skunks, afraid of nothing.

The night passed, and with the first streak of dawn the women came out of the tents, built up the fires, and put the coffee to boil. And the men came out and talked softly in the dawn.

When you cross the Colorado river, there's the desert, they say. Look out for the desert. See you don't get hung up. Take plenty water, case you get hung up.

I'm gonna take her at night.

Me too. She'll cut the living Jesus outa you.

The families ate quickly, and the dishes were dipped and wiped. The tents came down. There was a rush to go. And when the sun arose, the camping place was vacant, only a little litter left by the people. And the camping place was ready for a new world in a new night.

But along the highway the cars of the migrant people crawled out like bugs, and the narrow concrete miles stretched ahead.

18

The Joad family moved slowly westward, up into the mountains of New Mexico, past the pinnacles and pyramids of the upland. They climbed into the high country of Arizona, and through a gap they looked down on the Painted Desert. A border guard stopped them.

'Where you going?'

'To California,' said Tom.

'How long you plan to be in Arizona?'

'No longer'n we can get acrost her.'

'Got any plants?'

'No plants.'

'I ought to look your stuff over.'

'I tell you we ain't got no plants.'

The guard put a little sticker on the windshield.

'O.K. Go ahead, but you better keep movin'.'

'Sure. We aim to.'

They crawled up the slopes, and the low twisted trees covered the slopes. Holbrook, Joseph City, Winslow. And then the tall trees began, and the cars spouted steam and laboured up the slopes. And there was Flagstaff, and that was the top of it all. Down from Flagstaff over the great plateaux, and the road disappeared in the distance ahead. The water grew scarce, water was to be bought, five cents, ten cents, fifteen cents a gallon. The sun drained the dry rocky country, and ahead were jagged broken peaks, the western wall of

Arizona. And now they were in flight from the sun and the drought. They drove all night, and came to the mountains in the night. And they crawled the jagged ramparts in the night, and their dim lights flickered on the pale stone walls of the road. They passed the summit in the dark and came slowly down in the late night, through the shattered stone debris of Oatman; and when the daylight came they saw the Colorado river below them. They drove to Topock, pulled up at the bridge while a guard washed off the windshield sticker. Then across the bridge and into the broken rock wilderness. And although they were dead weary and the morning heat was growing, they stopped.

Pa called: 'We're there–we're in California!' They looked dully at the broken rock glaring under the sun, and across the river the terrible ramparts of Arizona.

'We got the desert,' said Tom. 'We got to get to the water and rest.'

The road runs parallel to the river, and it was well into the morning when the burning motors came to Needles, where the river runs swiftly among the reeds.

The Joads and Wilsons drove to the river, and they sat in the cars looking at the lovely water flowing by, and the green reeds jerking slowly in the current. There was a little encampment by the river, eleven tents near the water, and the swamp grass on the ground. And Tom leaned out of the truck window. 'Mind if we stop here a piece?'

A stout woman, scrubbing clothes in a bucket, looked up. 'We don't own it, mister. Stop if you want. They'll be a cop down to look you over.' And she went back to her scrubbing in the sun.

The two cars pulled to a clear place on the swamp grass. The tents were passed down, the Wilson tent set up, the Joad tarpaulin stretched over its rope.

Winfield and Ruthie walked slowly down through the willows to the reedy place. Ruthie said with soft vehemence: 'California. This here's California an' we're right in it!'

Winfield broke a tule and twisted it free, and he put the white pulp in his mouth and chewed it. They walked into the water and stood quietly, the water about the calves of their legs.

'We got the desert yet,' Ruthie said.

'What's the desert like?'

'I don't know. I seen pitchers once says a desert. They was bones ever'place.'

'Man bones?'

'Some, I guess, but mos'ly cow bones.'

'We gonna get to see them bones?'

'Maybe. I don't know. Gonna go 'crost her at night. That's what Tom said. Tom says we get the livin' Jesus burned outa us if we go in daylight.'

'Feels nicet an' cool,' said Winfield, and he squidged his toes in the sand at the bottom.

They heard Ma calling, 'Ruthie! Winfiel'! You come back.' They turned and walked slowly back through the reeds and the willows.

The other tents were quiet. For a moment, when the cars came up, a few heads had stuck out between the flaps, and then were withdrawn. Now the family tents were up and the men gathered together.

Tom said: 'I'm gonna go down an' take a bath. That's what I'm gonna do–before I sleep. How's Granma sence we got her in the tent?'

'Don' know,' said Pa. 'Couldn' seem to wake her up.' He cocked his head toward the tent. A whining, babbling voice came from under the canvas. Ma went quickly inside.

'She woke up, awright,' said Noah. 'Seems like all night she was a-croakin' up on the truck. She's all outa sense.'

Tom said: 'Hell! She's wore out. If she don't get some res' pretty soon, she ain't gonna las'. She's jes' wore out. Anybody comin' with me? I'm gonna wash, an' I'm gonna sleep in the shade–all day long.' He moved away, the other men followed him. They took off their clothes in the willows and then they walked into the water and sat down. For a long time they sat, holding themselves with heels dug into the sand, and only their heads stuck out of the water.

'Jesus, I needed this,' Al said. He took a handful of sand from the bottom and scrubbed himself with it. They lay in the water and looked across at the sharp peaks called Needles, and at the white rock mountains of Arizona.

'We come through them,' Pa said in wonder.

Uncle John ducked his head under the water. 'Well, we're here. This here's California, an' she don't look so prosperous.'

'Got the desert yet,' said Tom. 'An I hear she's a son-of-a-bitch.'

Noah asked: 'Gonna try her to-night?'

'What ya think, Pa?' Tom asked.

'Well, I don't know. Do us good to get a little res', 'specially Granma. But other ways, I'd kinda like to get acrost her an' get settled into a job. On'y got 'bout forty dollars left. I'll feel better when we're all working', an' a little money comin' in.'

Each man sat in the water and felt the tug of the current. The preacher let his arms and hands float on the surface. The bodies were white to the neck and wrists, and burned dark brown on hands and faces, with V's of brown at the collar bones. They scratched themselves with sand.

And Noah said lazily: 'Like to jus' stay here. Like to lay here for ever. Never get hungry an' never get sad. Lay in the water all life long, lazy as a brood sow in the mud.'

And Tom, looking at the ragged peaks across the river and the Needles downstream: 'Never seen such tough mountains. This here's a murder country. This here's the bones of a country. Wonder if we'll ever get in a place where folks can live 'thout fightin' hard scrabble an' rocks. I seen pitchers of a country flat an' green an' with little houses like Ma says, white. Ma got her heart set on a white house. Get to thinkin' they ain't no such country. I seen pitchers like that.'

Pa said: 'Wait till we get to California. You'll see nice country then.'

'Jesus Christ, Pa! This here *is* California.'

Two men dressed in jeans and sweaty blue shirts came through the willows and looked toward the naked men. They called: 'How's the swimmin'?'

'Dunno,' said Tom. 'We ain't tried none. Sure feels good to set here, though.'

'Mind if we come in an' set?'

'She ain't our river. We'll len' you a little piece of her.'

The men shucked off their pants, peeled their shirts, and waded out. The dust coated their legs to the knee; their feet were pale and soft with sweat. They settled lazily into the water and washed listlessly at their flanks. Sun-bitten, they were, a father and a boy. They grunted and groaned with the water.

Pa asked politely: 'Goin' west?'

'Nope. We come from there. Goin' back home. We can't make no livin' out there.'

'Where's home?' Tom asked.

'Panhandle, come from near Pampa.'

Pa asked: 'Can you make a livin' there?'

'Nope. But at leas' we can starve to death with folks we know. Won't have a bunch of fellas that hates us to starve with.'

Pa said: 'Ya know, you're the second fella talked like that. What makes 'em hate you?'

'Dunno,' said the man. He cupped his hands full of water and rubbed his face, snorting and bubbling. Dusty water ran out of his hair and streaked his neck.

'I like to hear some more 'bout this,' said Pa.

'Me too,' Tom added. 'Why these folks out west hate ya?'

The man looked sharply at Tom. 'You jus' goin' wes'?'

'Jus' on our way.'

'You ain't never been in California?'

'No, we ain't.'

'Well, don' take my word. Go see for yourself.'

'Yeah,' Tom said, 'but a fella kind a likes to know what he's gettin' into.'

'Well, if you truly wanta know, I'm a fella that's asked questions an' give her some thought. She's a nice country. But she was stole a long time ago. You git acrost the desert an' come into the country aroun' Bakersfield. An' you never seen such purty country–all orchards an' grapes, purtiest country you ever seen. An' you'll pass lan' flat an' fine with water thirty feet down, and that lan's layin' fallow. But you can't have none of that lan'. That's a Lan' and Cattle Company. An' if they don't want ta work her, she ain't gonna git worked. You go in there an' plant you a little corn, an' you'll go to jail!'

'Good lan' you say? An' they ain't workin' her?'

'Yes, sir. Good lan' an' they ain't! Well, sir, that'll get you a little mad, but you ain't seen nothin'. People gonna have a look in their eye. They gonna look at you an' their face says: "I don't like you, you son-of-a-bitch." Gonna be deputy sheriffs, an' they'll push you aroun'. You camp on the roadside, an' they'll move you on. You gonna see in people's face how they hate you. An'–I'll tell you somepin. They hate you 'cause they're scairt. They know a hungry fella gonna get food even if he got to take it. They know that fallow lan's a sin an' somebody's gonna take it. What the hell! You never been called "Okie" yet.'

Tom said: 'Okie? What's that?'

'Well, Okie use' ta mean you was from Oklahoma. Now it means you're a dirty son-of-a-bitch. Okie means you're scum. Don't mean nothing itself, it's the way they say it. But I can't tell you nothin'. You got to go there. I hear there's three hunderd thousan' of our people there–an' livin' like hogs, 'cause ever'thing in California is owned. They ain't nothin' left. An' them people that owns it is gonna hang on to it if they got ta kill ever'body in the worl' to do it. An' they're scairt, an' that makes 'em mad. You got to see it. You got to hear it. Purtiest goddamn country you ever seen, but they ain't nice to you, them folks. They're so scairt an' worried they ain't even nice to each other.'

Tom looked down into the water and he dug his heels into the sand. 'S'pose a fella got work an' saved, couldn' he get a little lan'?'

The older man laughed and looked at his boy, and his silent boy grinned almost in triumph. And the man said: 'You ain't gonna get no steady work. Gonna scrabble for your dinner ever'day. An' you gonna do her with people lookin' mean at you. Pick cotton, an' you gonna be sure the scales ain't honest. Some of 'em is, an' some of 'em ain't. But you gonna think all the scales is crooked, an you don' know which ones. Ain't nothin' you can do about her anyways.'

Pa asked slowly: 'Ain't–ain't it nice out there at all?'

'Sure, nice to look at, but you can't have none of it. They's a grove of yella oranges–an' a guy with a gun that got the right to kill you if you touch one. They's a fella, newspaper fella near the coast, got a million acres–'

Casy looked up quickly. 'Million acres? What in the worl' can he do with a million acres?'

'I dunno. He jus' got it. Runs a few cattle. Got guards ever'place to keep folks out. Rides aroun' in a bullet-proof car. I seen pitchers of him. Fat, sof' fella with little mean eyes an' a mouth like a ass-hole. Scairt he's gonna die. Got a million acres an' scairt of dyin'.'

Casy demanded: 'What in hell can he do with a million acres? What's he want a million acres for?'

The man took his whitening, puckering hands out of the water and spread them, and he tightened his lower lip and bent his head down to one shoulder. 'I dunno,' he said. 'Guess he's crazy. Mus' be crazy. See a pitcher of him. He looks crazy. Crazy an' mean.'

'Say he's scairt to die?' Casy asked.

'That's what I heard.'

'Scairt God'll get him?'

'I dunno. Jus' scairt.'

'What's he care?' Pa said. 'Don't seem like he's havin' no fun.'

'Grampa wasn't scairt,' Tom said. 'When Grampa was havin' the most fun, he comes closest to gettin' kil't. Time Grampa an' another fella whanged into a bunch a Navajo in the night. They was havin' the time a their life, an' same time you wouldn't give a gopher for their chance.'

Casy said: 'Seems like that's the way. Fella havin' fun, he don't give a damn; but a fella mean an' lonely an' old an' disappointed–he's scared of dyin'!'

Pa asked: 'What's he disappointed about if he got a million acres?'

The preacher smiled, and he looked puzzled. He splashed a floating water bug away with his hand. 'If he needs a million acres to make him feel rich, seems to me he needs it 'cause he feels awful poor inside hisself, and if he's poor in hisself, there ain't no million acres gonna make him feel rich, an' maybe he's disappointed that nothin' he can do'll make him feel rich–not rich like Mis' Wilson was when she give her tent when Grampa died. I ain' tryin' to preach no sermon, but I never seen nobody that's busy as a prairie dog collectin' stuff that wasn't disappointed.' He grinned. 'Does kinda soun' like a sermon, don't it?'

The sun was flaming fiercely now. Pa said: 'Better scrunch down under water. She'll burn the living Jesus outa you.' And he reclined and let the gently moving water flow around his neck. 'If a fella's willin' to work hard, can't he cut her?' Pa asked.

The man sat up and faced him. 'Look, mister. I don't know ever'thing. You might go out there an' fall into a steady job an' I'd be a liar. An' then you might never get no work an' I didn' warn ya. I can tell ya mos' of the folks is purty mis'able.' He lay back in the water. 'A fella don' know ever'thing,' he said.

Pa turned his head and looked at Uncle John. 'You never was a fella to say much,' Pa said. 'But I'll be goddamned if you opened your mouth twicet sence we lef' home. What you think 'bout this here?'

Uncle John scowled. 'I don't think nothin' about it. We're agoin' there, ain't we? None of this here talk gonna keep us from goin' there. When we get there, we'll get there. When we get a job we'll work, an' when we don't get a job we'll set on our tail. This here talk ain't gonna do no good no way.'

Tom lay back and filled his mouth with water, and he spurted it into the air and he laughed. 'Uncle John don't talk much, but he talks sense. Yes, by God! He talks sense. We goin' on tonight, Pa?'

'Might's well. Might's well get her over.'

'Well, I'm goin' up in the brush an' get some sleep then.'

Tom stood up and waded to the sandy shore. He slipped his clothes on his wet body and winced under the heat of the cloth. The others followed him.

In the water, the man and his boy watched the Joads disappear. And the boy said: 'Like to see 'em in six months. Jesus!'

The man wiped his eye corners with his forefinger. 'I shouldn't of did that,' he said. 'Fella always wants to be a wise guy, wants to tell folks stuff.'

'Well, Jesus, Pa! They asked for it.'

'Yeah, I know. But like that fella says, they're a-goin' anyways. Nothin' won't be changed from what I tol' 'em, 'cept they'll be mis'able 'fore they hafta.'

Tom walked in among the willows, and he crawled into a cave of shade to lie down. And Noah followed him.

'Gonna sleep here,' Tom said.

'Tom!'

'Yeah?'

'Tom, I ain't a-goin' on.'

Tom sat up. 'What you mean?'

'Tom, I ain't a-gonna leave this here water. I'm a-gonna walk on down this here river.'

'You're crazy,' Tom said.

'Get myself a piece of line. I'll catch fish. Fella can't starve beside a nice river.'

Tom said: 'How 'bout the fam'ly? How 'bout Ma?'

'I can't he'p it. I can't leave this here water.' Noah's wide-set eyes were half closed. 'You know how it is, Tom. You know how the folks are nice to me. But they don't really care for me.'

'You're crazy.'

'No, I ain't. I know how I am. I know they're sorry. But–Well, I ain't a-goin'. You tell Ma–Tom.'

'Now you look-a-here,' Tom began.

'No. It ain't no use. I was in that there water. An' I ain't a-gonna leave her. I'm a-gonna go now, Tom–down the river. I'll catch fish an' stuff, but I can't leave her. I can't.' He crawled back out of the willow cave. 'You tell Ma, Tom.' He walked away.

Tom followed him to the river bank. 'Listen, you goddamn fool–'

'It ain't no use,' Noah said. 'I'm sad, but I can't he'p it. I got to go.' He turned abruptly and walked downstream along the shore. Tom started to follow, and then he stopped. He saw Noah disappear into the brush, and then appear again, following the edge of the river. And he watched Noah growing smaller on the edge of the river, until he disappeared into the willows at last. And Tom took off his cap and scratched his head. He went back to his willow cave and lay down to sleep.

Under the spread tarpaulin Granma lay on a mattress, and Ma sat beside her. The air was stiflingly hot, and the flies buzzed in the shade of the canvas. Granma was naked under a long piece of pink curtain. She turned her old head restlessly from side to side, and she muttered and choked. Ma sat on the ground beside her, and with a piece of cardboard drove the flies away and fanned a stream of moving hot air over the tight old face. Rose of Sharon sat on the other side and watched her mother.

Granma called imperiously: 'Will! Will! You come here, Will.' And her eyes opened and she looked fiercely about. 'Tol' him to come right here,' she said. 'I'll catch him. I'll take the hair off'n him.' She closed her eyes and rolled her head back and forth and muttered thickly. Ma fanned with the cardboard.

Rose of Sharon looked helplessly at the old woman. She said softly: 'She's awful sick.'

Ma raised her eyes to the girl's face. Ma's eyes were patient, but the lines of strain were on her forehead. Ma fanned and fanned the air, and her piece of cardboard warned off the flies. 'When you're young, Rosasharn, ever'thing that happens is a thing all by itself. It's a lonely thing. I know, I 'member, Rosasharn.' Her mouth loved the name of her daughter. 'You're gonna have a baby, Rosasharn, and that's somepin to you lonely and away. That's gonna hurt you, an' the hurt'll be lonely hurt, an' this here tent is alone in the worl', Rosasharn.' She whipped the air for a moment to drive a buzzing blowfly on, and the big shining fly circled the tent twice and zoomed out into the blinding sunlight. And Ma went on: 'They's a time of change, an' when that comes, dyin' is a piece of all dyin', and bearin' is a piece of all bearin', an' bearing an dying' is two pieces of the same thing. An' then things ain't lonely any more. An' then a hurt don't hurt so bad, 'cause it ain't a lonely hurt no more, Rosasharn. I wisht I could tell you so you'd know, but I can't.' And her voice was so soft, so full of love, that tears crowded into Rose of Sharon's eyes, and flowed over her eyes and blinded her.

'Take an' fan Granma,' Ma said, and she handed the cardboard to her daughter. 'That's a good thing to do. I wisht I could tell you so you'd know.'

Granma, scowling her brows down over her closed eyes, bleated: 'Will! You're dirty! You ain't never gonna get clean.' Her little wrinkled claws moved up and scratched her cheek. A red ant ran up the curtain cloth and scrambled over the folds of loose skin on the old lady's neck. Ma reached quickly and picked it off, crushed it between thumb and forefinger, and brushed her fingers on her dress.

Rose of Sharon waved the cardboard fan. She looked up at Ma. 'She–?' And the words parched in her throat.

'Wipe your feet, Will–you dirty pig!' Granma cried.

Ma said: 'I dunno. Maybe if we can get her where it ain't so hot, but I dunno. Don't worry yourself, Rosasharn. Take your breath in when you need it, an' let it go when you need to.'

A large woman in a torn black dress looked into the tent. Her eyes were bleared and indefinite, and the skin sagged to her jowls and hung down in little flaps. Her lips were loose, so that the upper lip hung like a curtain over her teeth, and her lower lip, by its weight, folded outward, showing her lower gums. ''Mornin', ma'am,' she said. ''Mornin', an' praise God for victory.'

Ma looked around. ''Mornin',' she said.

The woman stooped into the tent and bent her head over Granma. 'We heerd you got a soul here ready to join her Jesus. Praise God!'

Ma's face tightened and her eyes grew sharp. 'She's tar'd, tha's all,' Ma said. 'She's wore out with the road an' the heat. She's jus' wore out. Get a little res', an' she'll be well.'

The woman leaned down over Granma's face, and she seemed almost to sniff. Then she turned to Ma and nodded quickly, and her lips jiggled and her jowls quivered. 'A dear soul gonna join her Jesus,' she said.

Ma cried: 'That ain't so!'

The woman nodded, slowly this time, and put a puffy hand on Granma's forehead. Ma reached to snatch the hand away, and quickly restrained herself. 'Yes, it's so, sister,' the woman said. 'We got six in Holiness in our tent. I'll go git 'em, an' we'll hol' a meeting'–a prayer an' grace. Jehovites, all. Six, countin' me. I'll go git 'em out.'

Ma stiffened. 'No–no,' she said. 'No, Granma's tar'd. She couldn't stan' a meetin'.'

The woman said: 'Couldn't stan' grace? Couldn' stan' the sweet breath of Jesus? What you talkin' about, sister?'

Ma said: 'No, not here. She's too tar'd.'

The woman looked reproachfully at Ma. 'Ain't you believers, ma'am?'

'We always been Holiness,' Ma said, 'but Granma's tar'd, an' we been a-goin' all night. We won't trouble you.'

'It ain't no trouble, an' if it was, we'd want ta do it for a soul a-soarin' to the Lamb.'

Ma arose to her knees. 'We thank ya,' she said coldly. 'We ain't gonna have no meetin' in this here tent.'

The woman looked at her for a long time. 'Well, we ain't a-gonna let a sister go away 'thout a little praisin'. We'll git the meetin' goin' in our own tent, ma'am. An' we'll forgive ya for your hard heart.'

Ma settled back again and turned her face to Granma, and her face was still set and hard. 'She's tar'd,' Ma said. 'She's on'y tar'd.' Granma swung her head back and forth and muttered under her breath.

The woman walked stiffly out of the tent. Ma continued to look down at the old face.

Rose of Sharon fanned her cardboard and moved the hot air in a stream. She said: 'Ma!'

'Yeah?'

'Whyn't ya let 'em hol' a meetin'?'

'I dunno,' said Ma. 'Jehovites is good people. They're howlers an' jumpers. I dunno. Somepin jus' come over me. I didn' think I could stan' it. I'd jus' fly all apart.'

From some little distance there came the sound of the meeting beginning, a sing-song chant of exhortation. The words were not clear, only the tone. The voice rose and fell, and went higher at each rise. Now a response filled in the pause, and the exhortation went up with a tone of triumph, and a growl of power came into the voice. It swelled and paused, and a growl came into the response. And now gradually the sentences of exhortation shortened, grew sharper, like commands; and into the responses came a complaining note. The rhythm quickened. Male and female voices had been one tone, but now in the middle of a response one woman's voice went up in a wailing cry, wild and fierce, like the cry of a beast; and a deeper woman's voice rose up beside it, a baying voice, and a man's voice travelled up the scale in the howl of a wolf. The exhortation stopped, and only the feral howling came from the tent, and with it a thudding sound on the earth. Ma shivered. Rose of Sharon's breath was panting and short, and the chorus of howls went on so long it seemed that lungs must burst.

Ma said: 'Makes me nervous. Somepin happened to me.'

Now the high voice broke into hysteria, the gabbling screams of a hyena, the thudding became louder. Voices cracked and broke, and then the whole chorus fell to a sobbing, grunting undertone, and the slap of flesh and the thuddings on the earth; and the sobbing changed to a little whining, like that of a litter of puppies at a food dish.

Rose of Sharon cried softly with nervousness. Granma kicked the curtain off her legs, which lay like grey, knotted sticks. And Granma whined with the whining in the distance. Ma pulled the curtain back in place. And then Granma sighed deeply and her breathing grew steady and easy, and her closed eyelids ceased their flicking. She slept deeply, and snored through her half-open mouth. The whining from the distance was softer and softer until it could not be heard at all any more.

Rose of Sharon looked at Ma, and her eyes were blank with tears. 'It done good,' said Rose of Sharon. 'It done Granma good. She's a-sleepin'.'

Ma's head was down, and she was ashamed. 'Maybe I done them good people wrong. Granma is asleep.'

'Whyn't you ast our preacher if you done a sin?' the girl asked.

'I will–but he's a queer man. Maybe it's him made me tell them people they couldn't come here. That preacher, he's gettin' roun' to thinkin' that what people does is right to do.' Ma looked at her hands, and then she said: 'Rosasharn, we got to sleep. 'F we're gonna go to-night, we got to sleep.' She stretched out on the ground beside the mattress.

Rose of Sharon asked: 'How about fannin' Granma?'

'She's asleep now. You lay down an' rest.'

'I wonder where at Connie is?' the girl complained. 'I ain't seen him around for a long time.'

Ma said: 'Sh! Get some rest.'

'Ma, Connie gonna study nights an' get to be somepin.'

'Yea. You tol' me about that. Get some rest.'

The girl lay down on the edge of Granma's mattress. 'Connie's got a new plan. He's thinkin' all a time. When he gets all up on 'lectricity he gonna have his own store, an' then guess what we gonna have?'

'What?'

'Ice–all the ice you want. Gonna have a ice box. Keep it full. Stuff don't spoil if you got ice.'

'Connie's thinkin' all a time,' Ma chuckled. 'Better get some rest now.'

Rose of Sharon closed her eyes. Ma turned over on her back and crossed her hands under her head. She listened to Granma's breathing and to the girl's breathing. She moved a hand to start a fly from her forehead. The camp was quiet in the blinding heat, but the noises of hot grass–of crickets, the hum of flies–were a tone that was close to silence. Ma sighed deeply and then yawned and closed her eyes. In her half-sleep she heard footsteps approaching, but it was a man's voice that started her awake.

'Who's in here?'

Ma sat up quickly. A brown-faced man bent over and looked in. He wore boots and khaki pants and a khaki shirt with epaulets. On a Sam Browne belt a pistol holster hung, and a big silver star was pinned at the left breast. A loose-crowned military cap was on the back of his head. He beat on the tarpaulin with his hand, and the tight canvas vibrated like a drum.

'Who's in here?' he demanded again.

Ma asked. 'What is it you want, mister?'

'What you think I want? I want to know who's in here.'

'Why they's jus' us three in here. Me an' Granma an' my girl.'

'Where's your men?'

'Why, they went down to clean up. We was drivin' all night.'

'Where'd you come from?'

'Right near Sallisaw, Oklahoma.'

'Well, you can't stay here.'

'We aim to get out to-night an' cross the desert, mister.'

'Well, you better. If you're here to-morra this time I'll run you in. We don't want none of you settlin' down here.'

Ma's face blackened with anger. She got slowly to her feet. She stooped to the utensil box and picked out the iron skillet. 'Mister,' she said, 'you got a tin button an' a gun. Where I come from, you keep your voice down.' She advanced on him with the skillet. He loosened the gun in the holster. 'Go ahead,' said Ma. 'Scarin' women. I'm thankful the men folks ain't here. They'd tear ya to pieces. In my country you watch your tongue.'

The man took two steps backward. 'Well, you ain't in your country now. You're in California, an' we don't want you goddamn Okies settlin' down.'

Ma's advance stopped. She looked puzzled. 'Okies?' she said softly. 'Okies.'

'Yeah, Okies! An' if you're here when I come to-morra, I'll run ya in.' He turned and walked to the next tent and banged on the canvas with his hand. 'Who's in here?' he said.

Ma went slowly back under the tarpaulin. She put the skillet in the utensil box. She sat down slowly. Rose of Sharon watched her secretly. And when she saw Ma fighting with her face, Rose of Sharon closed her eyes and pretended to be asleep.

The sun sank low in the afternoon, but the heat did not seem to decrease. Tom awakened under his willow, and his mouth was parched and his body was wet with sweat, and his head was dissatisfied with his rest. He staggered to his feet and walked toward the water. He peeled off his clothes and waded into the stream. And the moment the water was about him, his thirst was gone. He lay back in the shallows and his body floated. He held himself in place with his elbows in the sand, and looked at his toes, which bobbed above the surface.

A pale skinny little boy crept like an animal through the reeds and slipped off his clothes. And he squirmed into the water like a musk-rat and pulled himself along like a musk-rat, only his eyes and nose above the surface. Then suddenly he saw Tom's head and saw that Tom was watching him. He stopped his game and sat up.

Tom said: 'Hello.'

''Lo!'

'Looks like you was playin' musk-rat.'

'Well, I was.' He edged gradually away toward the bank; he moved casually, and then he leaped out, gathered his clothes with a sweep of his arms, and was gone among the willows.

Tom laughed quietly. And then he heard his name called shrilly. 'Tom, oh, Tom!' He sat up in the water and whistled through his teeth, a piercing whistle with a loop on the end. The willows shook, and Ruthie stood looking at him.

'Ma wants you,' she said. 'Ma wants you right away.'

'Awright.' He stood up and strode through the water to the shore; and Ruthie looked with interest and amazement at his naked body.

Tom, seeing the direction of her eyes, said: 'Run on now. Git!' And Ruthie ran. Tom heard her calling excitedly for Winfield as she went. He put the hot clothes on his cool, wet body and he walked slowly up through the willows toward the tent.

Ma had started a fire of dry willow twigs, and she had a pan of water heating. She looked relieved when she saw him.

'What's a matter, Ma?' he asked.

'I was scairt,' she said. 'They was a policeman here. He says we can't stay here. I was scairt he talked to you. I was scairt you'd hit him if he talked to you.'

Tom said: 'What'd I go an' hit a policeman for?'

Ma smiled. 'Well–he talked so bad–I nearly hit him myself.'

Tom grabbed her arm and shook her roughly and loosely, and he laughed. He sat down on the ground, still laughing. 'My God, Ma. I knowed you when you was gentle. What's come over you?'

She looked serious. 'I don' know, Tom.'

'Fust you stan' us off with a jack handle, and now you try to hit a cop.' He laughed softly, and he reached out and patted her bare feet tenderly. 'A ol' hell-cat,' he said.

'Tom.'

'Yeah?'

She hesitated a long time. 'Tom, this here policeman–he called us–Okies. He says: "We don' want you goddamn Okies settlin' down".'

Tom studied her, and his hand still rested gently on her bare foot. 'Fella tol' about that,' he said. 'Fella tol' how they say it.' He considered: 'Ma, would you say I was a bad fella? Oughta be locked up–like that?'

'No,' she said. 'You been tried–No. What you ast me for?'

'Well, I dunno, I'd a took a sock at that cop.'

Ma smiled with amusement. 'Maybe I oughta ast you that, 'cause I nearly hit 'im with a skillet.'

'Ma, why'd he say we couldn' stop here?'

'Jes' says they don' want no damn Okies settlin' down. Says he's gonna run us in if we're here to-morra.'

'But we ain't use' ta gettin' shoved aroun' by no cops.'

'I tol' him that,' said Ma. 'He says we ain't home now. We're in California, and they do what they want.'

Tom said uneasily: 'Ma, I got somepin to tell ya. Noah–he went on down the river. He ain't a-goin' on.'

It took a moment for Ma to understand. 'Why?' she asked softly.

'I don' know. Says he got to. Says he got to stay. Says for me to tell you.'

'How'll he eat?' she demanded.

'I don' know. Says he'll catch fish.'

Ma was silent a long time 'Family's fallin' apart,' she said. 'I don' know. Seems I can't think no more. I jus' can't think. They's too much.'

Tom said lamely: 'He'll be awright, Ma. He's a funny kind a fella.'

Ma turned stunned eyes toward the river. 'I jus' can't seem to think no more.'

Tom looked down the line of tents and he saw Ruthie and Winfield standing in front of a tent in decorous conversation with someone inside. Ruthie was twisting her skirt in her hands, while Winfield dug a hole in the ground with his toe. Tom called: 'You, Ruthie!' She looked up and saw him and trotted toward him with Winfield behind her. When she came up, Tom said: 'You go get your folks. They're sleepin' down the willows. Get 'em. An' you, Winfiel'. You tell the Wilsons we're gonna get rollin' soon as we can.' The children spun around and charged off.

Tom said: 'Ma, how's Granma now?'

'Well, she got a sleep to-day. Maybe she's better. She's still a-sleepin'.'

'Tha's good. How much pork we got?'

'Not very much. Quarter hog.'

'Well, we got to fill that other keg with water. Got to take water along.' They could hear Ruthie's shrill cries for the men down in the willows.

Ma shoved willow sticks into the fire and made it crackle up about the black pot. She said: 'I pray God we gonna get some res'. I pray Jesus we gonna lay down in a nice place.'

The sun sank toward the baked and broken hills to the west. The pot over the fire bubbled furiously. Ma went under the tarpaulin and came out with an apronful of potatoes, and she dropped them into the boiling water. 'I pray God we gonna be let to wash some clothes. We ain't never been dirty like this. Don't even wash potatoes 'fore we boil 'em. I wonder why? Seems like the heart's took out of us.'

The men came trooping up from the willows, and their eyes were full of sleep, and their faces were red and puffed with daytime sleep.

Pa said: 'What's the matter?'

'We're goin',' said Tom. 'Cop says we got to go. Might's well get her over. Get a good start an' maybe we'll be through her. Near three hundred miles where we're goin'.'

Pa said: 'I thought we was gonna get a rest.'

'Well, we ain't. We got to go. Pa,' Tom said, 'Noah ain't a-goin'. He walked on down the river.'

'Ain't goin'? What the hell's the matter with him?' And then Pa caught himself. 'My fault,' he said miserably. 'That boy's all my fault.'

'No.'

'I don't wanta talk about it no more,' said Pa. 'I can't–my fault.'

'Well, we got to go,' said Tom.

Wilson walked near for the last words. 'We can't go, folks,' he said. 'Sairy's done up. She got to res'. She ain't gonna git acrost that desert alive.'

They were silent at his words; then Tom said: 'Cop says he'll run us in if we're here to-morra.'

Wilson shook his head. His eyes were glazed with worry, and a paleness showed through his dark skin. 'Jus' hafta do 'er, then. Sairy can't go. If they jail us, why they'll hafta jail us. She got to res' an' get strong.'

Pa said: 'Maybe we better wait an' all go together.'

'No,' Wilson said. 'You been nice to us; you bin kin', but you can't stay here.

You got to get on an' get jobs and work. We ain't gonna let you stay.'

Pa said excitedly: 'But you ain't got nothing.'

Wilson smiled. 'Never had nothin' when you took us up. This ain't none of your business. Don't you make me git mean. You got to go, or I'll get mean an' mad.'

Ma beckoned Pa into the cover of the tarpaulin and spoke softly to him.

Wilson turned to Casy. 'Sairy wants you should go see her.'

'Sure,' said the preacher. He walked to the Wilson tent, tiny and grey, and he slipped the flaps aside and entered. It was dusky and hot inside. The mattress lay on the ground, and the equipment was scattered about, as it had been unloaded in the morning. Sairy lay on the mattress, her eyes wide and bright. He stood and looked down at her, his large head bent and the stringy muscles of his neck tight along the sides. And he took off his hat and held it in his hand.

She said: 'Did my man tell ya we couldn' go on?'

'Tha's what he said.'

Her low, beautiful voice went on: 'I wanted us to go. I knowed I wouldn' live to the other side, but he'd be acrost anyways. But he won't go. He don' know. He thinks it's gonna be all right. He don' know.'

'He says he won't go.'

'I know,' she said. 'An' he's stubborn. I ast you to come to say a prayer.'

'I ain't a preacher,' he said softly. 'My prayers ain't no good.'

She moistened her lips. 'I was there when the ol' man died. You said one then.'

'It wasn't no prayer.'

'It was a prayer,' she said.

'It wasn't no preacher's prayer.'

'It was a good prayer. I want you should say one for me.'

'I don' know what to say.'

She closed her eyes for a minute and then opened them again. 'Then say one to yourself. Don't use no words to it. That'd be awright.'

'I got no God,' he said.

'You got a God. Don't make no difference if you don' know what he looks like.' The preacher bowed his head. She watched him apprehensively. And when he raised his head again she looked relieved. 'That's good,' she said. 'That's what I needed. Somebody close enough–to pray.'

He shook his head as though to awaken himself. 'I don' understan' this here,' he said.

And she replied: 'Yes–you know, don't you?'

'I know,' he said, 'I know, but I don't understan'. Maybe you'll res' a few days an' then come on.'

She shook her head slowly from side to side. 'I'm jus' pain covered with skin. I know what it is, but I won't tell him. He'd be too sad. He wouldn't know what to do anyways. Maybe in the night, when he's a-sleepin'–when he waked up, it won't be so bad.'

'You want I should stay with you an' not go on?'

'No,' she said. 'No. When I was a little girl I use' ta sing. Folks roun' about use' ta say I sung as nice as Jenny Lind. Folks use' ta come an' listen when I sung. An'–when they stood–an' me a-singin', why, me an' them was together more'n you could ever know. I was thankful. There ain't so many folks can feel so full up, so close, an' them folks standin' there an' me a-singin'. Thought maybe I'd sing in theatres, but I never done it. An' I'm glad. They wasn't nothin' got in between me an' them. An'–that's why I wanted you to pray. I wanted to feel that clostness, oncet more. It's the same thing, singin' an' prayin', jus' the same thing. I wisht you could a heerd me sing.'

He looked down at her, into her eyes. 'Good-bye,' he said.

She shook her head slowly back and forth and closed her lips tight. And the preacher went out of the dusky tent into the blinding light.

The men were loading up the truck, Uncle John on top, while the others passed equipment up to him. He stowed it carefully, keeping the surface level. Ma emptied the quarter of a keg of salt pork into a pan, and Tom and Al took both little barrels to the river and washed them. They tied them to the running-boards and carried water in buckets to fill them. Then over the tops they tied canvas to keep them from slopping water out. Only the tarpaulin and Granma's mattress were left to be put on.

Tom said: 'With the load we'll take, this ol' wagon'll boil her head off. We got to have plenty water.'

Ma passed the boiled potatoes out and brought the half sack from the tent and put it with the pan of pork. The family ate standing, shuffling their feet and tossing the hot potatoes from hand to hand until they cooled.

Ma went to the Wilson tent and stayed for ten minutes, and then she came out quietly. 'It's time to go,' she said.

The men went under the tarpaulin. Granma still slept, her mouth wide open. They lifted the whole mattress gently and passed it up on top of the truck. Granma drew up her skinny legs and frowned in her sleep, but she did not awaken.

Uncle John and Pa tied the tarpaulin over the cross-piece, making a little tight tent on top of the load. They lashed if down to the side-bars. And then they were ready. Pa took out his purse and dug two crushed bills from it. He went to Wilson and held them out. 'We want you should take this, an''–he pointed to the pork and potatoes–'an' that.'

Wilson hung his head and shook it sharply. 'I ain't a-gonna do it,' he said. 'You ain't got much.'

'Got enough to get there,' said Pa. 'We ain't left it all. We'll have work right off.'

'I ain't a-gonna do it,' Wilson said. 'I'll git mean if you try.'

Ma took the two bills from Pa's hand. She folded them neatly and put them on the ground and placed the pork pan over them. 'That's where they'll be,' she said. 'If you don' get 'em, somebody else will.' Wilson, his head still down, turned and went to his tent; he stepped inside and the flaps fell behind him.

For a few moments the family waited, and then: 'We got to go,' said Tom. 'It's near four, I bet.'

The family climbed on the truck, Ma on top, beside Granma, Tom and Al and Pa in the seat, and Winfield on Pa's lap. Connie and Rose of Sharon made a nest against the cab. The preacher and Uncle John and Ruthie were in a tangle on the load.

Pa called: 'Good-bye, Mister and Mis' Wilson.' There was no answer from the tent. Tom started the engine and the truck lumbered away. And as they crawled up the rough road toward Needles and the highway, Ma looked back. Wilson stood in front of his tent, staring after them, and his hat was in his hand. The sun fell on his face. Ma waved her hand at him, but he did not respond.

Tom kept the truck in second gear over the rough road, to protect the springs. At Needles he drove into a service station, checked the worn tires for air, checked the spares tied to the back. He had the petrol tank filled, and he bought two five-gallon cans of petrol and a two-gallon can of oil. He filled the radiator, begged a map, and studied it.

The service-station boy, in his white uniform, seemed uneasy until the bill was paid. He said: 'You people sure have got nerve.'

Tom looked up from the map. 'What you mean?'

''Well, crossin' in a jalopy like this.'

'You been acrost?'

'Sure, plenty, but not in no wreck like this.'

Tom said: 'If we broke down maybe somebody'd give us a han'.'

'Well, maybe. But folks are kind of scared to stop at night. I'd hate to be doing it. Take more nerves than I've got.'

Tom grinned. 'It don't take no nerve to do somepin when there ain't nothin' else you can do. Well, thanks. We'll drag on.' And he got in the truck and moved away.

The boy in white went into the iron building where his helper laboured over a book of bills. 'Jesus, what a hard-looking outfit!'

'Them Okies? They're all hard-looking.'

'Jesus, I'd hate to start out in a jalopy like that.'

'Well, you and me got sense. Them goddamn Okies got no sense and no feeling. They ain't human. A human being wouldn't live like they do. A human being couldn't stand it to be so dirty and miserable. They ain't a hell of a lot better than gorillas.'

'Just the same I'm glad I ain't crossing the desert in no Hudson Super-Six. She sounds like a threshing machine.'

The other boy looked down at his book of bills. And a big drop of sweat rolled down his finger and fell on the pink bills. 'You know, they don't have much trouble. They're so goddamn dumb they don't know it's dangerous. And, Christ Almighty, they don't know any better than what they got. Why worry?'

'I'm not worrying. Just thought if it was me, I wouldn't like it.'

'That's 'cause you know better. They don't know any better.' And he wiped the sweat from the pink bill with his sleeve.

The truck took the road and moved up the long hill, through the broken, rotten rock. The engine boiled very soon and Tom slowed down and took it easy. Up the long slope, winding and twisting through dead country, burned white and grey, and no hint of life in it. Once Tom stopped for a few moments to let the engine cool, and then he travelled on. They topped the pass while the sun was still up, and looked down on the desert–black cinder mountains in the distance, and the yellow sun reflected on the grey desert. The little starved bushes, sage and greasewood, threw bold shadows on the sand and bits of rock. The glaring sun was straight ahead. Tom held his hand before his eyes to see at all. They passed the crest and coasted down to cool the engine. They coasted down the long sweep to the floor of the desert, and the fan turned over to cool the water in the radiator. In the driver's seat Tom and Al and Pa, and Winfield on Pa's knee, looked into the bright descending sun, and their eyes were stony, and their brown faces were damp with perspiration. The burnt land and the black, cindery hills broke the even distance and made it terrible in the reddening light of the setting sun.

Al said: 'Jesus, what a place. How'd you like to walk acrost her?'

'People done it,' said Tom. 'Lots a people done it; an' if they could, we could.'

'Lots must a died,' said Al.

'Well, we ain't come out exac'ly clean.'

Al was silent for a while, and the reddening desert swept past. 'Think we'll ever see them Wilsons again?' Al asked.

Tom flicked his eyes down to the oil gauge. 'I got a hunch nobody ain't gonna see Mis' Wilson for long. Jus' a hunch I got.'

Winfield said: 'Pa, I wanta get out.'

Tom looked over at him. 'Might's well let ever'body out 'fore we settle down to drivin' to-night.' He slowed the car and brought it to a stop. Winfield scrambled out and urinated at the side of the road. Tom leaned out. 'Anybody else?'

'We're holdin' our water up here,' Uncle John called.

Pa said: 'Winfiel', you crawl up on top. You put my legs to sleep a-settin' on 'em.' The little boy buttoned his overalls and obediently crawled up the back board and on his hands and knees crawled over Granma's mattress and forward to Ruthie.

The truck moved on into the evening, and the edge of the sun struck the rough horizon and turned the desert red.

Ruthie said: 'Wouldn' leave you set up there, huh?'

'I didn' want to. It wasn't so nice as here. Couldn' lie down.'

'Well, don' you bother me, a-squawkin' an' a-talkin',' Ruthie said, ''cause I'm goin' to sleep, an' when I wake up, we gonna be there! 'Cause Tom said so! Gonna seem funny to see pretty country.'

The sun went down and left a great halo in the sky. And it grew very dark under the tarpaulin, a long cave with light at each end–a flat triangle of light.

Connie and Rose of Sharon leaned back against the cab, and the hot wind tumbling through the tent struck the backs of their heads, and the tarpaulin whipped and drummed above them. They spoke together in low tones, pitched to the drumming canvas so that no one could hear them. When Connie spoke he turned his head and spoke into her ear, and she did the same to him. She said: 'Seems like we wasn't never gonna do nothin' but move. I'm so tar'd.'

He turned his head to her ear. 'Maybe in the mornin'. How'd you like to be alone now?' In the dusk his hand moved out and stroked her hip.

She said: 'Don't. You'll make me crazy as a loon. Don't do that.' And she turned her head to hear his response.

'Maybe–when ever'body's asleep.'

'Maybe,' she said. 'But wait till they get to sleep. You'll make me crazy, an' maybe they won't get to sleep.'

'I can't hardly stop,' he said.

'I know. Me neither. Le's talk about when we get there; an' you move away 'fore I get crazy.'

He shifted away a little. 'Well, I'll get to studyin' nights right off,' he said. She sighed deeply. 'Gonna get one a them books that tells about it an' cut the coupon, right off.'

'How long, you think?' she asked.

'How long what?'

'How long 'fore you'll be makin' big money an' we got ice?'

'Can't tell,' he said importantly. 'Can't really rightly tell. Fella oughta be studied up pretty good 'fore Christmus.'

'Soon's you get studied up we could get ice an' stuff, I guess.'

He chuckled. 'It's this here heat,' he said. 'What you gonna need ice roun' Christmus for?'

She giggled. 'Tha's right. But I'd like ice any time. Now don't. You'll get me crazy!'

The dusk passed into dark and the desert stars came out in the soft sky, stars stabbing and sharp, with few points and rays to them, and the sky was velvet. And the heat changed. While the sun was up, it was a beating, flailing heat, but now the heat came from below, from the earth itself, and the heat was thick and muffling. The lights of the truck came on, and they illuminated a little blur of highway ahead, and a strip of desert on either side of the road. And sometimes eyes gleamed in the lights far ahead, but no animal showed in the lights. It was pitch dark under the canvas now. Uncle John and the preacher were curled in the middle of the truck, resting on their elbows, and staring out the back triangle. They could see the two bumps that were Ma and Granma against the outside. They could see Ma move occasionally, and her dark arm moving against the outside.

Uncle John talked to the preacher. 'Casy,' he said, 'you're a fella oughta know what to do.'

'What to do about what?'

'I dunno,' said Uncle John.

Casy said: 'Well, that's gonna make it easy for me!'

'Well, you been a preacher.'

'Look, John, ever'body take a crack at me 'cause I been a preacher. A preacher ain't nothin' but a man.'

'Yeah, but–he's–a *kind* of a man, else he wouldn't be a preacher. I wanna ast you–well, you think a fella could bring bad luck to folks?'

'I dunno,' said Casy. 'I dunno.'

'Well–see–I was married–fine, good girl. An' one night she got a pain in her stomach. An' she says: "You better get a doctor." An' I says: "Hell, you jus' et too much." 'Uncle John put his hand on Casy's knee and he peered through the darkness at him. 'She give me a *look*. An' she groaned all night, an' she died the next afternoon.' The preacher mumbled something. 'You see,' John went on, 'I kil't her. An' sence then I tried to make it up–mos'ly to kids. An' I tried to be good, an' I can't. I get drunk, an' I go wild.'

'Ever'body goes wild,' said Casy. 'I do, too.'

'Yeah, but you ain't got a sin on your soul like me.'

Casy said gently: 'Sure I got sins. Ever'body got sins. A sin is somepin you ain't sure about. Them people that's sure about ever'thing an' ain't got no sin–well, with that kind a son-of-a-bitch, if I was God I'd kick their ass right outa heaven! I couldn' stand 'em!'

Uncle John said: 'I got a feelin' I'm bringin' bad luck to my own folks. I got a feelin' I oughta go away an' let 'em be. I ain't comf'table bein' like this.'

Casy said quickly: 'I know this–a man got to do what he got to do. I can't tell you. I can't tell you. I don't think they's luck or bad luck. On'y one thing in this worl' I'm sure of, an' that's I'm sure nobody got a right to mess with a fella's life. He got to do it all hisself. Help him, maybe, but not tell him what to do.'

Uncle John said disappointedly: 'Then you don't know?'

'I don' know.'

'You think it was a sin to let my wife die like that?'

'Well,' said Casy, 'for anybody else it was a mistake, but if you think it was a sin–then it's a sin. A fella builds his own sins right up from the groun'.'

'I got to give that a goin'-over,' said Uncle John, and then he rolled on his back and lay with his knees pulled up.

The truck moved on over the hot earth, and the hours passed. Ruthie and Winfield went to sleep. Connie loosened a blanket from the load and covered himself and Rose of Sharon with it, and in the heat they struggled together, and held their breaths. And after a time Connie threw off the blanket and the hot tunnelling wind felt cool on their wet bodies.

On the back of the truck Ma lay on the mattress beside Granma, and she could not see with her eyes, but she could feel the struggling body and the struggling heart; and the sobbing breath was in her ear. And Ma said over and over,' 'All right. It's gonna be all right.' And she said hoarsely: 'You know the family got to get acrost. You know that.'

Uncle John called: 'You all right?'

It was a moment before she answered. 'All right. Guess I dropped off to sleep.' And after a time Granma was still, and Ma lay rigid beside her.

The night hours passed, and the dark was in against the truck. Sometimes cars passed them going west and away; and sometimes great trucks came up out of the west and rumbled eastward. And the stars flowed down in a slow cascade over the western horizon. It was near midnight when they neared Dagget, where the inspection station is. The road was floodlighted there, and a sign illuminated: 'KEEP RIGHT AND STOP'. The officers loafed in the office, but they came out and stood under the long covered shed when Tom pulled in. One officer put down the licence number and raised the hood.

Tom asked: 'What's this here?'

'Agricultural inspection. We got to look over your stuff. Got any vegetables or seeds?'

'No,' said Tom.

'Well, we got to look over your stuff. You got to unload.'

Now Ma climbed heavily down from the truck. Her face was swollen and her eyes were hard. 'Look, mister. We got a sick ol' lady. We got to get her to a doctor. We can't wait.' She seemed to fight with hysteria. 'You can't make us wait.'

'Yeah? Well, we got to look you over.'

'I swear we ain't got anything!' Ma cried. 'I swear it. An' Granma's awful sick.'

'You don't look so good yourself,' the officer said.

Ma pulled herself up the back of the truck, hoisted herself with huge strength. 'Look,' she said.

The officer shot a flashlight beam up on the old shrunken face. 'By God, she is,' he said. 'You swear you got no seeds or fruits or vegetables, no corn, no oranges?'

'No, no. I swear it!'

'Then go ahead. You can get a doctor in Barstow. That's only eight miles. Go ahead.'

Tom climbed in and drove on.

The officer turned to his companion. 'I couldn't hold 'em.'

'Maybe it was a bluff,' said the other.

'Oh, Jesus, no! You should of seen that ol' woman's face. That wasn't no bluff.'

Tom increased his speed to Barstow, and in the little town he stopped, got out, and walked around the truck. Ma leaned out. 'It's awright,' she said. 'I didn' wanta stop there, fear we wouldn' get acrost.'

'Yeah! But how's Granma?'

'She's awright–awright. Drive on. We got to get acrost.' Tom shook his head and walked back.

'Al,' he said, 'I'm gonna fill her up, an' then you drive some.' He pulled to an all-night petrol station and filled the tank and the radiator, and filled the crank case. Then Al slipped under the wheel and Tom took the outside, with Pa in the middle. They drove away into the darkness and the little hills near Barstow were behind them.

Tom said: 'I don' know what's got into Ma. She's flighty as a dog with a flea in his ear. Wouldn' a took long to look over the stuff. An' she says Granma's sick; an' now she says Granma's awright. I can't figger her out. She ain't right. S'pose she wore her brains out on the trip.'

Pa said: 'Ma's almost like she was when she was a girl. She was a wild one then. She wasn't scairt of nothin'. I thought havin' all the kids an' workin' took it out a her, but I guess it ain't. Christ! When she got that jack handle back there, I tell you I wouldn' wanna be the fella took it away from her.'

'I dunno what's got into her,' Tom said. 'Maybe she's jus' tar'd out.'

Al said: 'I won't be doin' no weepin' an' a-moanin' to get through. I got this goddamn car on my soul.'

Tom said: 'Well, you done a damn good job a pickin'. We ain't had hardly no trouble with her at all.'

All night they bored through the hot darkness, and jackrabbits scuttled into the lights and dashed away in long jolting leaps. And the dawn came up behind them when the lights of Mojave were ahead. And the dawn showed high mountains to the west. They filled with water and oil at Mojave and crawled into the mountains, and the dawn was about them.

Tom said: 'Jesus, the desert's past! Pa, Al, for Christ sakes! The desert's past!'

'I'm too goddamn tired to care,' said Al.

'Want me to drive?'

'No, wait awhile.'

They drove through Techachapi in the morning glow, and the sun came up behind them, and then–suddenly they saw the great valley below them. Al jammed on the brake and stopped in the middle of the road, and: 'Jesus Christ! Look!' he said. The vineyards, the orchards, the great flat valley, green and beautiful, the trees set in rows, and the farmhouses.

And Pa said: 'God Almighty!' The distant cities, the little towns in the orchard land, and the morning sun, golden on the valley. A car honked behind them. Al pulled to the side of the road and parked.

'I wanta look at her.' The grain-fields golden in the morning, and the willow lines, the eucalyptus trees in rows.

Pa sighed: 'I never knowed they was anything like her.' The peach trees and the walnut groves, and the dark green patches of oranges. And red roofs among the trees, and barns–rich barns. Al got out and stretched his legs.

He called: 'Ma–come look. We're there!'

Ruthie and Winfield scrambled down from the car, and then they stood, silent and awestruck, embarrassed before the great valley. The distance was thinned with haze, and the land grew softer and softer in the distance. A windmill flashed in the sun, and its turning blades were like a little heliograph, far away. Ruthie and Winfield looked at it, and Ruthie whispered: 'It's California.'

Winfield moved his lips silently over the syllables. 'There's fruit,' he said aloud.

Casy and Uncle John, Connie and Rose of Sharon climbed down. And they stood silently. Rose of Sharon had started to brush her hair back, when she caught sight of the valley and her hand dropped slowly to her side.

Tom said: 'Where's Ma? I want Ma to see it. Look Ma! Come here, Ma.' Ma was climbing slowly, stiffly, down the back board. Tom looked at her. 'My God, Ma, you sick?' Her face was stiff and putty-like, and her eyes seemed to have sunk deep into her head, and the rims were red with weariness. Her feet touched the ground and she braced herself by holding the truck-side.

Her voice was a croak. 'Ya say we're acrost?'

Tom pointed to the great valley. 'Look!'

She turned her head, and her mouth opened a little. Her fingers went to her throat and gathered a little pinch of skin and twisted gently. 'Thank God!' she said, 'the fambly's here.' Her knees buckled and she sat down on the running-board.

'You sick, Ma?'

'No, jus' tar'd.'

'Didn' you get no sleep?'

'No.'

'Was Granma bad?'

Ma looked down at her hands, lying together like tired lovers in her lap. 'I wisht I could wait an' not tell you. I wisht it could be all–nice.'

Pa said: 'Then Granma's bad.'

Ma raised her eyes and looked over the valley. 'Granma's dead.'

They looked at her, all of them, and Pa asked: 'When?'

'Before they stopped us las' night.'

'So that's why you didn' want 'em to look.'

'I was afraid we wouldn' get acrost,' she said. 'I tol' Granma we couldn' he'p her. The fambly had ta get acrost. I tol' her, tol' her when she was a-dyin'. We couldn't stop in the desert. There was the young ones–an' Rosasharn's baby. I tol' her.' She put her hands and covered her face up for a moment. 'She can get buried in a nice green place,' Ma said softly. 'Trees aroun' an' a nice place. She got to lay her head down in California.'

The family looked at Ma with a little terror at her strength.

Tom said: 'Jesus Christ! You layin' there with her all night long!'

'The fambly hadda get acrost,' Ma said miserably.

Tom moved close to put his hand on her shoulder.

'Don' touch me,' she said. 'I'll hol' up if you don' touch me. That'd get me.'

Pa said: 'We got to go on now. We got to go on down.'

Ma looked up at him. 'Can–can I set up front? I don' wanna go back there no more–I'm tar'd. I'm awful tar'd.'

They climbed back on the load, and they avoided the long stiff figure covered and tucked in a comforter, even the head covered and tucked. They moved to their places and tried to keep their eyes from it–from the hump on the comforter that would be the nose, and the steep cliff that would be the jut of the chin. They tried to keep their eyes away, and they could not. Ruthie and Winfield, crowded in a forward corner as far away from the body as they could get, stared at the tucked figure.

And Ruthie whispered: 'Tha's Granma, an' she's dead.'

Winfield nodded solemnly. 'She ain't breathin' at all. She's awful dead.'

And Rose of Sharon said softly to Connie: 'She was a-dyin' right when we–'

'How'd we know?' he reassured her.

Al climbed on the load to make room for Ma in the seat. and Al swaggered a little because he was sorry. He plumped down beside Casy and Uncle John. 'Well, she was ol'. Guess her time was up,' Al said. 'Ever'body got to die.' Casy and Uncle John turned eyes expressionlessly on him and looked at him as though he were a curious talking bush. 'Well, ain't they?' he demanded. And the eyes looked away, leaving Al sullen and shaken.

Casy said in wonder: 'All night long an' she was alone.' And he said: 'John, there's a woman so great with love–she scares me. Makes me afraid an' mean.'

John asked: 'Was it a sin? Is they any part of it you might call a sin?'

Casy turned on him in astonishment, 'A sin? No, there ain't no part of it that's a sin.'

'I ain't never done nothin' that wasn't part sin,' said John, and he looked at the long wrapped body.

Tom and Ma and Pa got into the front seat. Tom let the truck roll and started on compression. And the heavy truck moved, snorting and jerking and popping down the hill. The sun was behind them, and the valley golden and green before them. Ma shook her head slowly from side to side. 'It's purty,' she said. 'I wisht they could of saw it.'

'I wisht so too,' said Pa.

Tom patted the steering-wheel under his hand. 'They was too old,' he said. 'They wouldn' of saw nothin' that's here. Grampa would a been a-seein' the Injuns an' the prairie country when he was a young fella. An' Granma would a remembered an' seen the first home she lived in. They was too ol'. Who's really seein' it is Ruthie an' Winfiel'.'

Pa said: 'Here's Tommy talkin' like a growed-up man, talkin' like a preacher almos'.'

And Ma smiled sadly. 'He is. Tommy's growed way up–way up so I can't get aholt of 'im sometimes.'

They popped down the mountain, twisting and looping, losing the valley sometimes, and then finding it again. And the hot breath of the valley came up to them, with hot green smells on it, and with resinous sage and tarweed smells. The crickets crackled along the road. A rattlesnake crawled across the road and Tom hit it and broke it and left it squirming.

Tom said: 'I guess we got to go to the coroner, wherever he is. We got to get her buried decent. How much money might be lef', Pa?'

''Bout forty dollars,' said Pa.

Tom laughed. 'Jesus, are we gonna start clean! We sure ain't bringin' nothin' with us.' He chuckled a moment, and then his face straightened quickly. He pulled the visor of his cap down low over his eyes. And the truck rolled down the mountains into the great valley.

19

Once California belonged to Mexico and its land to Mexicans; and a horde of tattered feverish Americans poured in. And such was their hunger for land they took the land–stole Sutter's land, Guerrero's land, took the grants and broke them up and growled and quarrelled over them, those frantic hungry men; and they guarded with guns the land they had stolen. They put up houses and barns, they turned the earth and planted crops. And these things were possession, and possession was ownership.

The Mexicans were weak and fled. They could not resist, because they wanted nothing in the world as frantically as the Americans wanted land.

Then, with time, the squatters were no longer squatters, but owners; and their children grew up and had children on the land. And the hunger was gone from them, the feral hunger, the gnawing, tearing hunger for land, for water and earth and the good sky over it, for the green thrusting grass, for the swelling roots. They had these things so completely that they did not know about them any more. They had no more the stomach-tearing lust for a rich acre and a shining blade to plough it, for seed and a windmill beating its wings in the air. They arose in the dark no more to hear the sleepy birds' first chittering, and the morning wind around the house while they waited for the first light to go out to the dear acres. These things were lost, and crops were reckoned in dollars, and land was valued by principal plus interest, and crops were bought and sold before they were planted, Then crop failure, drought, and flood were no longer little deaths within life, but simple losses of money. And all their love was thinned with money, and all their fierceness dribbled away in interest until they were no longer farmers at all, but little shopkeepers of crops, little manufacturers who must sell before they can make. Then those farmers who were not good shopkeepers lost their land to good shopkeepers. No matter how clever, how loving a man might be with earth and growing things, he could not survive if he were not also a good shopkeeper. And as time went on, the business men had the farms, and the farms grew larger, but there were fewer of them.

Now farming became industry, and the owners followed Rome, although they did not know it. They imported slaves, although they did not call them slaves: Chinese, Japanese, Mexicans, Filipinos. They live on rice and beans, the business men said. They don't need much. They wouldn't know what to do with good wages. Why, look how they live. Why, look what they eat. And if they get funny–deport them.

And all the time the farms grew larger and the owners fewer. And there were pitifully few farmers on the land any more. And the imported serfs were beaten and frightened and starved until some went home again, and some grew fierce and were killed or driven from the country. And the farms grew larger and the owners fewer.

And the crops changed. Fruit trees took the place of grainfields, and vegetables to feed the world spread out on the bottoms: lettuce, cauliflower, artichokes, potatoes–stoop crops. A man may stand to use a scythe, a plough, a pitchfork; but he must crawl like a bug between the rows of lettuce, he must bend his back and pull his long bag between the cotton rows, he must go on his knees like a penitent across a cauliflower patch.

And it came about that owners no longer worked on their farms. They farmed on paper; and they forgot the land, the smell, the feel of it, and remembered only that they owned it, remembered only what they gained and lost by it. And some of the farms grew so large that one man could not even conceive of them any more, so large that it took batteries of bookkeepers to keep track of interest and gain and loss; chemists to test the soil, to replenish; straw bosses to see that the stooping men were moving along the rows as swiftly as the material of their bodies could stand. Then such a farmer really became a storekeeper, and kept a store. He paid the men, and sold them food, and took the money back. And after a while he did not pay the men at all, and saved bookkeeping. These farms gave food on credit. A man might work and feed himself; and when the work was done, he might find that he owed money to the company. And the owners not only did not work the farms any more, many of them had never seen the farms they owned.

And then the dispossessed were drawn west–from Kansas, Oklahoma, Texas, New Mexico; from Nevada and Arkansas, families, tribes, dusted out, tractored out. Car-loads, caravans, homeless and hungry; twenty thousand and fifty thousand and a hundred thousand and two hundred thousand. They streamed over the mountains, hungry and restless–restless as ants, scurrying to find work to do–to lift, to push, to pull, to pick, to cut–anything, any burden to bear, for food. The kids are hungry. We got no place to live. Like ants scurrying for work, for food, and most of all for land.

We ain't foreign. Seven generations back Americans, and beyond that Irish, Scotch, English, German. One of our folks in the Revolution, an' they was lots of our folks in the Civil War–both sides. Americans.

They were hungry, and they were fierce. And they had hoped to find a home, and they found only hatred. Okies–the owners hated them because the owners knew they were soft and the Okies strong, that they were fed and the Okies hungry; and perhaps the owners had heard from their grandfathers how easy it is to steal land from a soft man if you are fierce and hungry and armed. The owners hated them. And in the towns the storekeepers hated them because they had no money to spend. There is no shorter path to a storekeeper's contempt, and all his admirations are exactly opposite. The town men, little bankers, hated Okies because there was nothing to gain from them. They had nothing. And the labouring people hated Okies because a hungry man must work, and if he must work, if he has to work, the wage payer automatically gives him less for his work; and then no one can get more.

And the dispossessed, the migrants, flowed into California, two hundred and fifty thousand, and three hundred thousand. Behind them new tractors were going on the land and the tenants were being forced off. And new waves were on the way, new waves of the dispossessed and the homeless, hardened, intent, and dangerous.

And while the Californians wanted many things, accumulation, social success, amusement, luxury, and a curious banking security, the new barbarians wanted only two things–land and food; and to them the two were one. And whereas the wants of the Californians were nebulous and undefined, the wants of the Okies were beside the roads, lying there to be seen and coveted: the good fields with water to be dug for, the good green fields, earth to crumble experimentally in the hand, grass to smell, oaten stalks to chew until the sharp sweetness was in the throat. A man might look at a fallow field and know, and see in his mind that his own bending back and his own straining arms would bring the cabbages into the light, and the golden eating corn, the turnips and carrots.

And a homeless hungry man, driving the roads with his wife beside him and his thin children in the back seat, could look at the fallow fields which might produce food but not profit, and that man could know how a fallow field is a sin and the unused land a crime against the thin children. And such a man drove along the roads and knew temptation at every field, and knew the lust to take these fields and make them grow strength for his children and a little comfort for his wife. The temptation was before him always. The fields goaded him, and the company ditches with good water flowing were a goad to him.

And in the south he saw the golden oranges hanging on the trees, the little golden oranges on the dark green trees; and guards with shotguns patrolling the lines so a man might not pick an orange for a thin child, oranges to be dumped if the price was low.

He drove his old car into a town. He scoured the farms for work. Where can we sleep the night?

Well, there's Hooverville on the edge of the river. There's a whole raft of Okies there.

He drove his old car to Hooverville. He never asked again, for there was a Hooverville on the edge of every town.

The rag town lay close to water; and the houses were tents, and weed-thatched enclosures, paper houses, a great junk pile. The man drove his family in and became a citizen of Hooverville–always they were called Hooverville. The man put up his own tent as near to water as he could get; or if he had no tent, he went to the city dump and brought back cartons and built a house of corrugated paper. And when the rains came the house melted and washed away. He settled in Hooverville and he scoured the countryside for work, and the little money he had went for petrol to look for work. In the evening the men gathered and talked together. Squatting on their hams they talked of the land they had seen.

There's thirty thousan' acres, out west of here. Layin' there. Jesus, what I could do with that, with five acres of that! Why, hell, I'd have ever'thing to eat.

Notice one thing? They ain't no vegetables nor chicken nor pigs at the farms. They raise one thing–cotton, say, or peaches, or lettuce. 'Nother place'll be all chickens. They buy the stuff they could raise in the door-yard.

Jesus, what I could do with a couple pigs!

Well, it ain't yourn, an' it ain't gonna be yourn.

What we gonna do? The kids can't grow up this way.

In the camps the word would come whispering. There's work at Shafter. And the cars would be loaded in the night, the highways crowded–a gold-rush for work. At Shafter the people would pile up, five times too many to do the work. A gold-rush for work. They stole away in the night, frantic for work. And along the roads lay the temptations, the fields that could bear food.

That's owned. That ain't our'n.

Well, maybe we could get a little piece of her. Maybe–a little piece. Right down there–a patch. Jimson weed now. Christ, I could git enough potatoes off'n that little patch to feed my whole family!

It ain't our'n. It got to have Jimson weeds.

Now and then a man tried; crept on the land and cleared a piece, trying like a thief to steal a little richness from the earth. Secret gardens hidden in the weeds. A package of carrot seeds and a few turnips. Planted potato skins, crept out in the evening secretly to hoe in the stolen earth.

Leave the weeds around the edge–then nobody can see what we're a-doin'. Leave some weeds, big tall ones, in the middle.

Secret gardening in the evenings, and water carried in a rusty can.

And then one day a deputy sheriff: Well, what you think you're doin'?

I ain't doin' no harm.

I had my eye on you. This ain't your land. You're trespassing.

The land ain't ploughed, an' I ain't hurtin' it none.

You goddamned squatters. Pretty soon you'd think you owned it. You'd be sore as hell. Think you owned it. Get off now.

And the little green carrot tops were kicked off and the turnip greens trampled. And then Jimson weed moved back in. But the cop was right. A crop raised–why, that makes ownership. Land hoed and the carrots eaten–a man might fight for land he's taken food from. Get him off quick! He'll think he owns it. He might even die fighting for the little plot among the Jimson weeds.

Did ya see his face when we kicked them turnips out? Why, he'd killa fella soon's he'd look at him. We got to keep these here people down or they'll take the country. They'll take the country.

Outlanders, foreigners.

Sure, they talk the same language, but they ain't the same. Look how they live. Think any of us folks'd live like that? Hell, no!

In the evenings, squatting and talking. And an excited man: Whyn't twenty of us take a piece of lan'? We got guns. Take it an' say: 'Put us off if you can.' Whyn't we do that?

They'd jus' shoot us like rats.

Well, which'd you ruther be, dead or here? Under groun' or in a house all made of gunny sacks? Which'd you ruther for your kids, dead now or dead in two years with what they call malnutrition? Know what we et all week? Biled nettles an' fried dough! Know where we got the flour for the dough? Swep' the floor of a box-car.

Talking in the camps, and the deputies, fat-assed men with guns slung on fat hips, swaggering through the camps: Give 'em somepin to think about. Got to keep 'em in line or Christ only knows what they'll do! Why, Jesus, they're as dangerous as niggers in the South! If they ever get together there ain't nothin' that'll stop 'em.

Quote: In Lawrenceville a deputy sheriff evicted a squatter, and the squatter resisted, making it necessary for the officer to use force. The eleven-year-old son of the squatter shot and killed the deputy with a .22 rifle.

Rattlesnakes! Don't take chances with 'em, an' if they argue, shoot first. If a kid'll kill a cop, what'll the men do? Thing is, get tougher'n they are. Treat 'em rough. Scare 'em.

What if they won't scare? What if they stand up and take it and shoot back? These men were armed when they were children. A gun is an extension of themselves. What if they won't scare? What if some time an army of them marches on the land as the Lombards did in Italy, as the Germans did on Gaul and the Turks did on Byzantium? They were land-hungry, ill-armed hordes, too, and the legions could not stop them. Slaughter and terror did not stop them. How can you frighten a man whose hunger is not only in his own cramped stomach but in the wretched bellies of his children? You can't scare him–he has known a fear beyond every other.

In Hooverville the men talking: Grampa took his lan' from the Injuns.

Now, this ain't right. We're a-talkin' here. This here you're talkin' about is stealin'. I ain't no thief.

No? You stole a bottle of milk from a porch night before last. An' you stole some copper wire and sold it for a piece of meat.

Yeah, but the kids was hungry.

It's stealin', though.

Know how the Fairfiel' ranch was got? I'll tell ya. It was all gov'ment lan', an' could be took up. Ol' Fairfiel', he went into San Francisco to the bars, an' he got him three hunderd stew bums. Them bums took up the lan'. Fairfiel' kep' 'em in food an' whisky, an' then when they'd proved the lan', ol' Fairfiel' took if from 'em. He used to say the lan' cost him a pint of rotgut an acre. Would you say that was stealin'?

Well, it wasn't right, but he never went to jail for it.

No, he never went to jail for it. An' the fella that put a boat in a wagon an' made his report like it was all under water 'cause he went in a boat–he never went to jail neither. An' the fellas that bribed congressmen and the legislatures never went to jail neither.

All over the State, jabbering in the Hoovervilles.

And then the raids–the swoop of armed deputies on the squatters' camps. Get out. Department of Health orders. This camp is a menace to health.

Where we gonna go?

That's none of our business. We got orders to get you out of here. In half an hour we set fire to the camp.

They's typhoid down the line. You want ta spread it all over?

We got orders to get you out of here. Now get! In half an hour we burn the camp.

In half an hour the smoke of paper houses, of weed-thatched huts, rising to the sky, and the people in their cars rolling over the highways, looking for another Hooverville.

And in Kansas and Arkansas, in Oklahoma and Texas and New Mexico, the tractors moved in and pushed the tenants out.

Three hundred thousand in California and more coming. And in California the roads full of frantic people running like ants to pull, to push, to lift, to work. For every man-load to lift, five pairs of arms extended to lift it; for every stomachful of food available, five mouths open.

And the great owners, who must lose their land in an upheaval, the great owners with access to history, with eyes to read history and to know the great fact: when property accumulates in too few hands it is taken away. And that companion fact: when a majority of the people are hungry and cold they will take by force what they need. And the little screaming fact that sounds through all history: repression works only to strengthen and knit the repressed. The great owners ignored the three cries of history. The land fell into fewer hands, the number of the dispossessed increased, and every effort of the great owners was directed at repression. The money was spent for arms, for gas to protect the great holdings, and spies were sent to catch the murmurings of revolt so that it might be stamped out. The changing economy was ignored, plans for the change ignored; and only means to destroy revolt were considered, while the causes of revolt went on.

The tractors which throw men out of work, the belt lines which carry loads, the machines which produce, all were increased; and more and more families scampered on the highways, looking for crumbs from the great holdings, lusting after the land beside the roads. The great owners formed associations for protection and they met to discuss ways to intimidate, to kill, to gas. And always they were in fear of a principal–three hundred thousand–if they ever move under a leader–the end. Three hundred thousand, hungry and miserable; if they ever know themselves, the land will be theirs, and all the gas, all the rifles in the world won't stop them. And great owners, who had become through their holdings both more and less than men, ran to their destruction, and used every means that in the long run would destroy them. Every little means, every violence, every raid on a Hooverville, every deputy swaggering through a ragged camp put off the day a little and cemented the inevitability of the day.

The men squatted on their hams, sharp-faced men, lean from hunger and hard from resisting it, sullen eyes and hard jaws. And the rich land was around them.

D'ja hear about the kid in that fourth tent down?

No, I jus' come in.

Well, that kid's been a-cryin' in his sleep an' a-rollin' in his sleep. Them folks thought he got worms. So they give him a blaster, an' he died. It was what they call black-tongue the kid had. Comes from not gettin' good things to eat.

Poor little fella.

Yeah, but them folks can't bury him. Got to go to the county stone orchard.

Well, hell.

And hands went into pockets and little coins came out. In front of the tent a little heap of silver grew. And the family found it there.

Our people are good people; our people are kind people. Pray God some day kind people won't all be poor. Pray God some day a kid can eat.

And the associations of owners knew that some day the praying would stop.

And there's the end.

20

The family, on top of the load, the children and Connie and Rose of Sharon and the preacher were stiff and cramped. They had sat in the heat in front of the coroner's office in Bakersfield while Pa and Ma and Uncle John went in. Then a basket was brought out and the long bundle lifted down from the truck. And they sat in the sun while the examination went on, while the cause of death was found and the certificate signed.

Al and Tom strolled along the street and looked in store windows and watched the strange people on the sidewalks.

And at last Pa and Ma and Uncle John came out, and they were subdued and quiet. Uncle John climbed up on the load. Pa and Ma got in the seat. Tom and Al strolled back and Tom got under the steering wheel. He sat there silently, waiting for some instruction. Pa looked straight ahead, his dark hat pulled low. Ma rubbed the sides of her mouth with her fingers, and her eyes were far away and lost, dead with weariness.

Pa sighed deeply. 'They wasn't nothin' else to do,' he said.

'I know,' said Ma. 'She would a liked a nice funeral, though. She always wanted one.'

Tom looked sideways at them. 'County?' he asked.

'Yeah,' Pa shook his head quickly, as though to get back to some reality. 'We didn' have enough. We couldn' of done it.' He turned to Ma. 'You ain't to feel bad. We couldn' no matter how hard we tried, no matter what we done. We jus' didn' have it; embalming, an' a coffin an' a preacher, an' a plot in a graveyard. It would of took ten times what we got. We done the bes' we could.'

'I know,' Ma said. 'I jus' can't get it outa my head what store she set by a nice funeral. Got to forget it.' She sighed deeply and rubbed the side of her mouth. 'That was a purty nice fella in there. Awful bossy, but he was purty nice.'

'Yeah,' Pa said. 'He give us the straight talk, awright.'

Ma brushed her hair back with her hand. Her jaw tightened. 'We got to git,' she said. 'We got to find a place to stay. We got to get work an' settle down. No use a-lettin' the little fellas go hungry. That wasn't never Granma's way. She always et a good meal at a funeral.'

'Where we goin'?' Tom asked.

Pa raised his hat and scratched among his hair. 'Camp,' he said. 'We ain't gonna spen' what little's lef' till we get work. Drive out in the country.'

Tom started the car and they rolled through the streets and out toward the country. And by the bridge they saw a collection of tents and shacks. Tom said: 'Might's well stop here. Find out what's doin', an' where at the work is.' He drove down a steep dirt incline and parked on the edge of the encampment.

There was no order in the camp; little grey tents, shacks, cars were scattered about at random. The first house was nondescript. The south wall was made of three sheets of corrugated iron, the east wall a square of mouldy carpet tacked between two boards, the north wall a strip of roofing paper and a strip of tattered canvas, and the west wall six pieces of gunny sacking. Over the square frame, on untrimmed willow limbs, grass had been piled, not thatched, but heaped up in a low mound. The entrance, on the gunny-sack side, was cluttered with equipment. A five-gallon kerosene can served for a stove. It was laid on its side, with a section of rusty stove-pipe thrust in one end. A wash boiler rested on its side against the wall; and a collection of boxes lay about, boxes to sit on, to eat on. A Model T Ford sedan and a two-wheel trailer were parked beside the shack, and about the camp there hung a slovenly despair.

Next to the shack there was a little tent, grey with weathering, but neatly, properly set up; and the boxes in front of it were placed against the tent wall. A stove-pipe stuck out of the door flap, and the dirt in front of the tent had been swept and sprinkled. A bucketful of soaking clothes stood on a box. The camp was neat and sturdy. A Model A roadster and a little home-made bed trailer stood beside the tent.

And next there was a huge tent, ragged, torn in strips and the tears mended with pieces of wire. The flaps were up, and inside four wide mattresses lay on the ground. A clothes-line strung along the side bore pink cotton dresses and several pairs of overalls. There were forty tents and shacks, and beside each habitation some kind of automobile. Far down the line a few children stood and stared at the newly-arrived truck, and they moved toward it, little boys in overalls and bare feet, their hair grey with dust.

Tom stopped the truck and looked at Pa. 'She ain't very purty,' he said. 'Want to go somewheres else?'

'Can't go nowheres else till we know where we're at,' Pa said. 'We got to ast about work.'

Tom opened the door and stepped out. The family climbed down from the load and looked curiously at the camp. Ruthie and Winfield, from the habit of the road, took down the bucket and walked toward the willows, where there would be water; and the line of children parted for them and closed after them.

The flaps of the first shack parted and a woman looked out. Her grey hair was braided, and she wore a dirty, flowered Mother Hubbard. Her face was wizened and dull, deep grey pouches under blank eyes, and a mouth slack and loose.

Pa said: 'Can we jus' pull up anywheres an' camp?'

The head was withdrawn inside the shack. For a moment there was quiet and then the flaps were pushed aside and a bearded man in shirt-sleeves stepped out. The woman looked out after him, but she did not come into the open.

The bearded man said: 'Howdy, folks,' and his restless dark eyes jumped to each member of the family, and from them to the truck to the equipment.

Pa said: 'I jus' ast your woman if it's all right to set our stuff anywheres.'

The bearded man looked at Pa intently, as though he had said something very wise that needed thought. 'Set down anywheres, here in this place?' he asked.

'Sure. Anybody own this place, that we got to see 'fore we can camp?'

The bearded man squinted one eye nearly closed and studied Pa. 'You wanta camp here?'

Pa's irritation arose. The grey woman peered out of the burlap shack. 'What you think I'm a-sayin'?' Pa said.

'Well, if you wanta camp here, why don't ya? I ain't a-stoppin' you.'

Tom laughed. 'He got it.'

Pa gathered his temper. 'I jus' wanted to know does anybody own it? Do we got to pay?'

The bearded man thrust out his jaw. 'Who owns it?' he demanded.

Pa turned away. 'The hell with it,' he said. The woman's head popped back in the tent.

The bearded man stepped forward menacingly. 'Who owns it?' he demanded. 'Who's gonna kick us outa here? You tell *me*.'

Tom stepped in front of Pa. 'You better go take a good long sleep,' he said. The bearded man dropped his mouth open and put a dirty finger against his lower gums. For a moment he continued to look wisely, speculatively at Tom, and then he turned on his heel and popped into the shack after the grey woman.

Tom turned to Pa. 'What the hell was that?' he asked.

Pa shrugged his shoulders. He was looking across the camp. In front of a tent stood an old Buick, and the head was off. A young man was grinding the valves, and as he twisted back and forth, back and forth, on the tool, he looked up at the Joad truck. They could see that he was laughing to himself. When the bearded man had gone, the young man left his work and sauntered over.

'H'are ya?' he said, and his blue eyes were shiny with amusement. 'I seen you just met the Mayor.'

'What the hell's the matter with 'im?' Tom demanded.

The young man chuckled. 'He's jus' nuts like you an' me. Maybe he's a little nutser'n me, I don' know.'

Pa said: 'I jus' ast him if we could camp here.'

The young man wiped his greasy hands on his trousers. 'Sure. Why not? You folks jus' come acrost?'

'Yeah,' said Tom. 'Jus' got in this mornin'.'

'Never been in Hooverville before?'

'Where's Hooverville?'

'This here's her.'

'Oh!' said Tom. 'We jus' got in.'

Winfield and Ruthie came back, carrying a bucket of water between them.

Ma said: 'Le's get the camp up. I'm tuckered out. Maybe we can all rest.' Pa and Uncle John climbed up on the truck to unload the canvas and the beds.

Tom sauntered to the young man, and walked beside him back to the car he had been working on. The valve-grinding brace lay on the exposed block, and a little yellow can of valve-grinding compound was wedged on top of the vacuum tank. Tom asked: 'What the hell was the matter'th that ol' fella with the beard?'

The young man picked up his brace and went to work, twisting back and forth, grinding valve against valve seat. 'The Mayor? Chris' knows. I guess maybe he's bull-simple.'

'What's "bull-simple"?'

'I guess cops push 'im aroun' so much he's still spinning.'

Tom asked: 'Why would they push a fella like that aroun'?'

The young man stopped his work and looked in Tom's eyes. 'Chris' knows,' he said. 'You jus' come. Maybe you can figger her out. Some fellas says one thing, an' some says another thing. But you jus' camp in one place a little while, an' you see how quick a deputy sheriff shoves you along.' He lifted a valve and smeared compound on the seat.

'But what the hell for?'

'I tell ya I don' know. Some says they don' want us to vote; keep us movin' so we can't vote. An' some says so we can't get on relief. An' some says if we set in one place we'd get organized. I don' know why. I on'y know we get rode all the time. You wait, you'll see.'

'We ain't no bums,' Tom insisted. 'We're lookin' for work. We'll take any kind a work.'

The young man paused in fitting the brace to the valve slot. He looked in amazement at Tom. 'Lookin' for work?' he said. 'So you're lookin' for work. What ya think ever'body else is lookin' for? Di'monds? What you think I wore my ass down to a nub lookin' for?' He twisted the brace back and forth.

Tom looked about at the grimy tents, the junk equipment, at the old cars, the lumpy mattresses out in the sun, at the blackened cans on fire-blackened holes where the people cooked. He asked quietly: 'Ain't they no work?'

'I don' know. Mus' be. Ain't no crop right here now. Grapes to pick later, an' cotton to pick later. We're a-movin' on, soon's I get these here valves groun'. Me an' my wife an' my kids. We heard they was work up north, up aroun' Salinas.'

Tom saw Uncle John and Pa and the preacher hoisting the tarpaulin on the tent poles and Ma on her knees inside, brushing off the mattresses on the ground. A circle of quiet children stood to watch the new family get settled, quiet children with bare feet and dirty faces. Tom said, 'Back home some fellas come through with han'bills–orange one. Says they need lots a people out here to work the crops.'

The young man laughed. 'They say they's three hunderd thousan' us folks here, an' I bet ever' dam' family seen them han'bills.'

'Yeah, but if they don' need folks, what'd they go to the trouble puttin' them things out for?'

'Use you head, why don'cha?'

'Yeah, but I wanta know.'

'Look,' the young man said. 'S'pose you got a job a work, an' ther's jus' one fella wants the job. You got to pay 'im what he asts. But s'pose they's a hunderd men.' He put down his tool. His eyes hardened and his voice sharpened. 'S'pose theys a hunderd men wants that job. S'pose them men got kids, an' them kids is hungry. S'pose a lousy dime'll buy a box a mush for them kids. S'pose a nickel'll buy at leas' somepin for them kids. An' you got a hunderd men. Jus' offer 'em a nickel–why, they'll kill each other fightin' for that nickel. Know what they was payin', las' job I had? Fifteen cents an hour. Ten hours for a dollar an' a half, an' ya can't stay on the place. Got to burn petrol gettin' there.' He was panting with anger, and his eyes blazed with hate. 'That's why them han'bills was out. You can print a hell of a lot of han'bills with what ya save payin' fifteen cents an hour for fiel' work.'

Tom said: 'That's stinkin'.'

The young man laughed harshly. 'You stay out here a little while, an' if you smell any roses, you come let me smell, too.'

'But they is work,' Tom insisted. 'Christ Almighty, with all this stuff a-growin': orchards, grapes, vegetables–I seen it. They got to have men. I seen all that stuff.'

A child cried in the tent beside the car. The young man went into the tent and his voice came softly through the canvas. Tom picked up the brace, fitted it in the slot of the valve, and ground away, his hand whipping back and forth. The child's crying stopped. The young man came out and watched Tom. 'You can do her,' he said. 'Damn good thing. You'll need to.'

'How 'bout what I said?' Tom resumed. 'I seen all the stuff growin'.'

The young man squatted on his heels. 'I'll tell ya,' he said quietly. 'They's a big son-of-a-bitch of a peach orchard I worked in. Takes nine men all the year roun'.' He paused impressively. 'Takes three thousan' men for two weeks when them peaches is ripe. Got to have 'em or them peaches'll rot. So what do they do? They send out han'bills all over hell. They need three thousan', an' they get six thousan'. They get them men for what they wanta pay. If ya don' wanta take what they pay, goddamn it, they's a thousan' men waitin' for your job. So ya pick, an' ya pick, 'an then she's done. Whole part a the country's peaches. All ripe together. When ya get 'em picked, ever' goddamn one is picked. There ain't another damn thing in that part a the country to do. An' then them owners don' want you there no more. Three thousan' of you. The work's done. You might steal, you might get drunk, you might jus' raise hell. An' besides, you don' look nice, livin' in ol' tents; an' it's a pretty country, but you stink it up. They don' want you aroun'. So they kick you out, they move you along. That's how it is.'

Tom, looking down toward the Joad tent, saw his mother, heavy and slow with weariness, build a little trash fire and put the cooking pots over the flame. The circle of children drew closer, and the calm wide eyes of the children watched every move of Ma's hands. An old, old man with a bent back came like a badger out of a tent and snooped near, sniffing the air as he came. He laced his arms behind him and joined the children to watch Ma. Ruthie and Winfield stood near to Ma and eyed the strangers belligerently.

Tom said angrily: 'Them peaches got to be picked right now, don't they? Jus' when they're ripe?'

'' Course they do.'

'Well, s'pose them people got together an' says, "Let 'em rot." Wouldn't be long 'fore the price went up, by God!'

The young man looked up from the valves, looked sardonically at Tom. 'Well, you figgered out somepin, didn' you. Come right outa your own head.'

'I'm tar'd,' said Tom. 'Drove all night. I don't wanta start no argument. An' I'm so goddamn tar'd I'd argue easy. Don' be smart with me. I'm askin' you.'

The young man grinned. 'I didn' mean it. You ain't been here. Folks figgered that out. An' the folks with the peach orchard figgered her out too. Look if the folks get together, they's a leader–got to be–fella that does the talkin'. Well, first time this fella opens his mouth they grab 'im an' stick 'im in jail. An' if they's another leader pops up, why, they stick *'im* in jail.'

Tom said: 'Well, a fella eats in jail anyways.'

'His kids don't. How'd you like to be in an' your kids starvin' to death?'

'Yeah,' said Tom slowly. 'Yeah.'

'An' here's another thing. Ever hear a the blacklist?'

'What's that?'

'Well, you jus' open your trap about us folks gettin' together, an' you'll see. They take your pitcher an' send it all over. Then you can't get work nowhere. An' if you got kids–'

Tom took off his cap and twisted it in his hands. 'So we take what we can get, huh, or we starve; an' if we yelp we starve.'

The young man made a sweeping circle with his hand, and his hand took in the ragged tents and the rusty cars.

Tom looked down at his mother again, where she sat scraping potatoes. And the children had drawn closer. He said: 'I ain't gonna take it. Goddamn it, I an' my folks ain't no sheep. I'll kick the hell outa somebody.'

'Like a cop?'

'Like anybody.'

'You're nuts,' said the young man. 'They'll pick you right off. You got no name, no property. They'll find you in a ditch, with the blood dried on your mouth an' your nose. Be one little line in the paper–know what it'll say? "Vagrant foun' dead." An' that's all. You'll see a lot of them little lines, "Vagrant foun' dead."'

Tom said: 'They'll be somebody else foun' dead right 'longside of this here vagrant.'

'You're nuts,' said the young man. 'Won't be no good in that.'

'Well, what you doin' about it?' He looked into the grease-streaked face. And a veil drew down over the eyes of the young man.

'Nothin'. Where you from?'

'Us? Right near Sallisaw, Oklahoma.'

'Jus' get in?'

'Jus' to-day.'

'Gonna be aroun' here long?'

'Don't know. We'll stay wherever we can get work. Why?'

'Nothin'.' And the veil came down again.

'Got to sleep up,' said Tom. 'To-morra we'll go out lookin' for work.'

'You kin try.'

Tom turned away and moved toward the Joad tent.

The young man took up the can of valve compound and dug his finger into it. 'Hi!' he called.

Tom turned. 'What you want?'

'I want ta tell ya.' He motioned with his finger, on which a blob of compound stuck. 'I jus' want ta tell ya. Don' go lookin' for no trouble. 'Member how that bull-simple guy looked?'

'Fella in the tent up there?'

'Yeah–looked dumb–no sense?'

'What about him?'

'Well, when the cops come in, an' they come in all the time, that's how you want to be. Dumb–don't know nothin'. Don't understan' nothin'. That's how the cops like us. Don't hit no cops. That's jus' suicide. Be bull-simple.'

'Let them goddamn cops run over me, an' do nothin'?'

'No, looka here. I'll come for ya to-night. Maybe I'm wrong. There's stools aroun' all a time. I'm takin' a chancet, an' I got a kid, too. But I'll come for ya. An' if ya see a cop, why, you're a goddamn dumb Okie, see?'

'Tha's awright if we're doin' anythin',' said Tom.

'Don' you worry. We're doin' somepin, on'y we ain't stickin' our necks out. A kid starves quick. Two-three days for a kid.' He went back to his job, spread the compound on a valve seat, and his hand jerked rapidly back and forth on the brace, and his face was dull and dumb.

Tom strolled slowly back to his camp. 'Bull-simple,' he said under his breath.

Pa and Uncle John came toward the camp, their arms loaded with dry willow sticks, and they threw them down by the fire and squatted on their hams. 'Got her picked over pretty good,' said Pa. 'Had to go a long ways for wood.' He looked up at the circle of staring children. 'Lord God Almighty!' he said. 'Where'd you come from?' All of the children looked self-consciously at their feet.

'Guess they smelled the cookin',' said Ma. 'Winfiel', get out from under foot.' She pushed him out of her way. 'Got ta make us up a little stew,' she said. 'We ain't et nothin' cooked right sence we come from home. Pa you go up to the store there an' get me some neck meat. Make a nice stew here.' Pa stood up and sauntered away.

Al had the hood of the car up, and he looked down at the greasy engine. He looked up when Tom approached. 'You sure look happy as a buzzard,' Al said.

'I'm jus' gay as a toad in spring rain,' said Tom.

'Looka the engine,' Al pointed. 'Purty good, huh?'

Tom peered in. 'Looks awright to me.'

'Awright? Jesus, she's wonderful. She ain't shot no oil nor nothin'.' He unscrewed a spark plug and stuck his forefinger in the hole. 'Crusted up some, but she's dry.'

Tom said: 'You done a nice job a pickin'. That what ya want me to say?'

'Well, I sure was scairt the whole way, figgerin' she'd bust down an' it'd be my fault.'

'No, you done good. Better get her in shape, 'cause to-morra we're goin' out lookin' for work.'

'She'll roll,' said Al. 'Don't you worry none about that.' He took out a pocket-knife and scraped the points of the spark plug.

Tom walked around the side of the tent, and he found Casy sitting on the earth, wisely regarding one bare foot. Tom sat down heavily beside him. 'Think she's gonna work?'

'What?' asked Casy.

'Them toes of yourn.'

'Oh! Jus' settin' here a-thinkin'.'

'You always get good an' comf'table for it,' said Tom.

Casy waggled his big toe up and his second toe down, and he smiled quietly. 'Hard enough for a fella to think 'thout kinkin' hisself up to do it.'

'Ain't heard a peep outa you for days,' said Tom. 'Thinkin' all the time?'

'Yeah, thinkin' all the time.'

Tom took off his cloth cap, dirty now, and ruinous, the visor pointed as a bird's beak. He turned the sweat band out and renewed a long strip of folded newspaper. 'Sweat so much she's shrank,' he said. He looked at Casy's waving toes. 'Could ya come down from your thinkin' an' listen a minute?'

Casy turned his head on the stalk-like neck. 'Listen all the time. That's why I been thinkin'. Listen to people a-talkin', an' purty soon I hear the way folks are feelin'. Goin' on all the time. I hear 'em an' feel 'em; an' they're beating their wings like a bird in a attic. Gonna bust their wings on a dusty winda tryin' to get out.'

Tom regarded him with widened eyes, and then he turned and looked at a grey tent twenty feet away. Washed jeans and shirts and a dress hung to dry on the tent guys. He said softly: 'That was about what I was gonna tell ya. An' you seen awready.'

'I seen,' Casy agreed. 'They's a army of us without no harness.' He bowed his head and ran his extended hand slowly up his forehead and into his hair. 'All along I seen it,' he said. 'Ever' place we stopped I seen it. Folks hungry for side-meat, an' when they get it, they ain't fed. An' when they'd get so hungry they couldn' stan' it no more, why, they'd ast me to pray for 'em, an' sometimes I done it.' He clasped his hands around drawn-up knees and pulled his legs in. 'I use' ta think that'd cut 'er,' he said. 'Use ta rip off a prayer an' all the troubles'd stick to that prayer like flies on flypaper, an' the prayer'd go a-sailin' off, a-takin' them troubles along. But it don' work no more.'

Tom said: 'Prayer never bought in no side-meat. Takes a shoat to bring in pork.'

'Yeah,' Casy said. 'An' Almighty God never raises no wages. These here folks want to live decent and bring up their kids decent. An' when they're old they wanta set in the door an' watch the downing sun. An' when they're young they wanta dance an' sing an' lay together. They wanta eat an' get drunk and work. An' that's it–they wanta jus' fling their goddamn muscles aroun' an' get tired. Christ! What'm I talkin' about?'

'I dunno,' said Tom. 'Sounds kinda nice. When ya think you can get ta work an' quit thinkin' a spell? We got to get work. Money's 'bout gone. Pa give five dollars to get a painted piece of board stuck up over Granma. We ain't got much lef'.'

A lean brown mongrel dog came sniffling around the side of the tent. He was nervous and flexed to run. He sniffed close before he was aware of the two men, and then looking up he saw them, leaped sideways, and fled, ears back, bony tail clamped protectively. Casy watched him go, dodging around a tent to get out of sight. Casy sighed. 'I ain't doin' nobody no good,' he said. 'Me or nobody else. I was thinkin' I'd go off alone by myself. I'm a-eatin' your food an' a-takin' up room. An' I ain't give you nothin'. Maybe I could get a steady job an' maybe pay back some a the stuff you've give me.'

Tom opened his mouth and thrust his lower jaw forward, and he tapped his lower teeth with a dried piece of mustard stalk. His eyes stared over the camp, over the grey tents and the shacks of weed and tin and paper. 'Wisht I had a sack a Durham,' he said. 'I ain't had a smoke in a hell of a time. Use' ta get tobacco in McAlester. Almost wisht I was back.' He tapped his teeth again and suddenly turned on the preacher. 'Ever been in a jail-house?'

'No,' said Casy. 'Never been.'

'Don't go away right yet,' said Tom. 'Not right yet.'

'Quicker I get lookin' for work–quicker I'm gonna find some.'

Tom studied him with half-shut eyes and he put on his cap again. 'Look,' he said, 'this ain't no lan' of milk an' honey like the preachers say. They's a mean thing here. The folks here is scared of us people comin' west; an' so they got cops out tryin' to scare us back.'

'Yeah,' said Casy. 'I know. What you ask about me bein' in jail for?'

Tom said slowly: 'When you're in jail–you get to kinda–sensin' stuff. Guys ain't let to talk a hell of a lot together–two maybe, but not a crowd. An' so you get kinda sensy. If somepin's gonna bust–if say a fella's goin' stir-bugs an' take a crack at a guard with a mop handle–why you know it 'fore it happens. An' if they's gonna be a break or a riot, nobody don't have to tell ya. You're sensy about it. You know.'

'Yeah?'

'Stick aroun',' said Tom. 'Stick aroun' till to-morra anyways. Somepin's gonna come up. I was talkin' to a kid up the road. An' he's bein' jis' as sneaky an' wise as a dog coyote, but he's too wise. Dog coyote a-mindin' his own business an' innocent an' sweet, jus' havin' fun an' no harm–well, they's a hen roost clost by.'

Casy watched him intently, started to ask a question, and then shut his mouth tightly. He waggled his toes slowly and, releasing his knees, pushed out his foot so he could see it. 'Yeah,' he said, 'I won't go right yet.'

Tom said: 'When a bunch a folks, nice quiet folks, don't know nothin' about nothin'–somepin's goin' on.'

'I'll stay,' said Casy.

'An' to-morra we'll go out in the truck an' look for work.'

'Yeah!' said Casy, and he waved his toes up and down and studied them gravely. Tom settled back on his elbow and closed his eyes. Inside the tent he could hear the murmur of Rose of Sharon's voice and Connie's answering.

The tarpaulin made a dark shape and the wedge-shaped light at each end was hard and sharp. Rose of Sharon lay on a mattress and Connie squatted beside her. 'I oughta help Ma,' Rose of Sharon said. 'I tried, but ever' time I stirred about I throwed up.' Connie's eyes were sullen. 'If I'd knowed it would be like this I wouldn' of came. I'd a studied nights 'bout tractors back home an' got me a three-dollar job. Fella can live awful nice on three dollars a day, an' go to the pitcher show ever' night, too.'

Rose of Sharon looked apprehensive. 'You're gonna study nights 'bout radios,' she said. He was long in answering. 'Ain't you?' she demanded.

'Yeah, sure. Soon's I get on my feet. Get a little money.'

She rolled up on her elbow. 'You ain't givin' it up!'

'No–no–'course not. But–I didn' know they was places like this we got to live in.'

The girl's eyes hardened. 'You got to,' she said quietly.

'Sure. Sure, I know. Got to get on my feet. Get a little money. Would a been better maybe to stay home an' study 'bout tractors. Three dollars a day they get, an' pick up extra money, too.' Rose of Sharon's eyes were calculating. When he looked down at her he saw in her eyes a measuring of him, a calculation of him. 'But I'm gonna study,' he said. 'Soon's I get on my feet.'

She said fiercely: 'We got to have a house 'fore the baby comes. We ain't gonna have this baby in no tent.'

'Sure,' he said. 'Soon's I get on my feet.' He went out of the tent and looked down at Ma crouched over the brush fire. Rose of Sharon rolled on her back and stared at the top of the tent. And then she put her thumb in her mouth for a gag and she cried silently.

Ma knelt beside the fire, breaking twigs to keep the flame up under the stew kettle. The fire flared and dropped and flared and dropped. The children, fifteen of them, stood silently and watched. And when the smell of the cooking stew came to their noses, their noses crinkled slightly. The sunlight glistened on hair tawny with dust. The children were embarrassed to be there, but they did not go. Ma talked quietly to a little girl who stood inside the lusting circle. She was older than the rest. She stood on one foot, caressing the back of her leg with a bare instep. Her arms were clasped behind her. She watched Ma with steady small grey eyes. She suggested: 'I could break up some bresh if you want me, ma'am.'

Ma looked up from her work. 'You want ta get ast to eat, huh?'

'Yes, ma'am,' the girl said steadily.

Ma slipped the twigs under the pot and the flame made a puttering sound. 'Didn' you have no breakfast?'

'No, ma'am. They ain't no work hereabouts. Pa's in tryin' to sell some stuff to git gas so's we can git 'long.'

Ma looked up. 'Didn' none of these here have no breakfast?'

The circle of children shifted nervously and looked away from the boiling kettle. One small boy said boastfully: 'I did–me an' my brother did–an' them two did, 'cause I seen 'em. We et good. We're a-goin' south to-night.'

Ma smiled. 'Then you ain't hungry. They ain't enough here to go around.'

The small boy's lip stuck out. 'We et good,' he said, and he turned and ran and dived into a tent. Ma looked after him so long that the oldest girl reminded her.

'The fire's down, ma'am. I can keep it up if you want.'

Ruthie and Winfield stood inside the circle, comporting themselves with proper frigidity and dignity. They were aloof, and at the same time possessive. Ruthie turned cold and angry eyes on the little girl. Ruthie squatted down to break up the twigs for Ma.

Ma lifted the kettle lid and stirred the stew with a stick. 'I'm sure glad some of you ain't hungry. That little fella ain't, anyways.'

The girl sneered, 'Oh, him! he was a-braggin'. High an' mighty. If he don't have no supper–know what he done? Las' night, come out an' say they got chicken to eat. Well, sir, I looked in whilst they was a-eatin' an' it was fried dough jus' like ever'body else.

'Oh!' And Ma looked down toward the tent where the small boy had gone. She looked back at the little girl. 'How long you been in California?' she asked.

'Oh, 'bout six months. We lived in a gov'ment camp a while, an' then we went north, an when we come back it was full up. That's a nice place to live, you bet.'

'Where's that?' Ma asked. And she took the sticks from Ruthie's hand and fed the fire. Ruthie glared with hatred at the older girl.

'Over by Weedpatch. Got nice toilets an' baths, an' you kin wash clothes in a tub, an' they's water right handy, good drinkin' water; an' nights the folks plays music an' Sat'dy night they give a dance. Oh, you never seen anything so nice. Got a place for kids to play, an' them toilets with paper. Pull down a little jigger an' the water comes right in the toilet, an' they ain't no cops let to come look in your tent any time they want, an' the fella runs the camp is so polite, comes a-visitin' an' talks an' ain't high an' mighty. I wisht we could go live there again.'

Ma said: 'I never heard about it. I sure could use a wash tub, I tell you.'

The girl went on excitedly: 'Why, God Awmighty, they got hot water right in pipes, an' you get in under a shower bath an' it's warm. You never seen such a place.'

Ma said: 'All full now, ya say?'

'Yeah. Las' time we ast it was.'

'Mus' cost a lot,' said Ma.

'Well, it costs, but if you ain't got the money, they let you work it out–couple hours a week, cleanin' up, an' garbage cans. Stuff like that. An' nights they's music an' folks talks together an' hot water right in the pipes. You never seen nothin' so nice.'

Ma said: 'I sure wisht we could go there.'

Ruthie had stood all she could. She blurted fiercely: 'Granma died right on top a the truck.' The girl looked questioningly at her. 'Well, she did,' Ruthie said. 'An' the cor'ner got her,' She closed her lips tightly and broke up a little pile of sticks.

Winfield blinked at the boldness of the attack. 'Right on the truck,' he echoed. 'Cor'ner stuck her in a big basket.'

Ma said: 'You shush now, both of you, or you got to go away.' And she fed twigs into the fire.

Down the line Al had strolled to watch the valve-grinding job. 'Looks like you're 'bout through,' he said.

'Two more.'

'Is they any girls in this here camp?'

'I got a wife,' said the young man. 'I got no time for girls.'

'I always got time for girls,' said Al. 'I got no time for nothin' else.'

'You get a little hungry an' you'll change.'

Al laughed. 'Maybe. But I ain't never changed that notion yet.'

'Fella I talked to while ago, he's with you, ain't he?'

'Yeah! My brother Tom. Better not fool with him. He killed a fella.'

'Did? What for?'

'Fight. Fella got a knife in Tom. Tom busted 'im with a shovel.'

'Did, huh? What'd the law do?'

'Let 'im off 'cause it was a fight,' said Al.

'He don't look like a quarreller.'

'Oh, he ain't. But Tom don't take nothin' from nobody.' Al's voice was very proud. 'Tom, he's quiet. But–look out!'

'Well–I talked to 'im. He didn' soun' mean.'

'He ain't. Jus' as nice as pie till he's roused, an' then–look out.' The young man ground at the last valve. 'Like me to he'p you get them valves set an' the head on?'

'Sure, if you got nothin' else to do.'

'Oughta get some sleep,' said Al. 'But, hell, I can't keep my han's out of a tore-down car. Jus' got to git in.'

'Well, I'd admire to git a hand,' said the young man. 'My name's Floyd Knowles.'

'I'm Al Joad.'

'Proud to meet ya.'

'Me too,' said Al. 'Gonna use the same gasket?'

'Got to,' said Floyd.

Al took out his pocket-knife and scraped at the block. 'Jesus!' he said. 'They ain't nothin' I love like the guts of a engine.'

'How 'bout girls?'

'Yeah, girls too! Wisht I could tear down a Rolls an' put her back. I looked under the hood of a Cad' 16 one time an', God Awmighty, you never seen nothin' so sweet in your life! In Sallisaw–an' here's this 16 a-standin' in front of a restaurant, so I lifts the hood. An' a guy comes out an' says: "What the hell you doin'?" I says: "Jus' lookin'. Ain't she swell?" An' he jus' stands there. I don't think he ever looked in her before. Jus' stands there. Rich fella in a straw hat. Got a stripe' shirt on, an' eye-glasses. We don' say nothin'. Jus' look. An' purty soon he says: "How'd you like to drive her?"'

Floyd said, 'The Hell?'

'Sure–"How'd you like to drive her?" Well, hell I got on jeans–all dirty. I says: "I'd get her dirty." "Come on!" he says. "Jus' take her roun' the block." Well, sir, I set in that seat an' I took her roun' the block eight times, an', oh, my God Almighty!'

'Nice?' Floyd asked.

'Oh, Jesus!' said Al. 'If I could of tore her down why–I'd a give–anythin'.'

Floyd slowed his jerking arm. He lifted the last valve from its seat and looked at it. 'You better git use' ta a jalopy,' he said, ''cause you ain't goin' a drive no 16.' He put his brace down on the running-board and took up a chisel to scrape the crust from the block. Two stocky women, bare-headed and bare-footed, went by carrying a bucket of milky water between them. They limped against the weight of the bucket, and neither looked up from the ground. The sun was half down in afternoon.

Al said: 'You don't like nothin' much.'

Floyd scraped harder with the chisel. 'I been here six months,' he said. 'I been scrabbin' over this here State tryin' to work hard enough and move fast enough to get meat an' potatoes for me an' my wife an' my kids. I've run myself like a jack-rabbit an'–I can't quite make her. There just ain't quite enough to eat no matter what I do. I'm gettin' tired, that's all. I'm gettin' tired way past where sleep rests me. An' I jus' don' know what to do.'

'Ain't there no steady work for a fella?' Al asked.

'No, they ain't no steady work.' With his chisel he pushed the crust off the block, and he wiped the dull metal with a greasy rag.

A rusty touring car drove down into the camp and there were four men in it, men with brown hard faces. The car drove slowly through the camp. Floyd called to them: 'Any luck?'

The car stopped. The driver said: 'We covered a hell of a lot a ground. They ain't a hand's work in this here country. We gotta move.'

'Where to?' Al called.

'God knows. We worked this here place over.' He let in his clutch and moved slowly down the camp.

Al looked after them. 'Wouldn' it be better if one fella went alone? Then if they was one piece a work, a fella'd get it.'

Floyd put down the chisel and smiled sourly. 'You ain't learned,' he said. 'Takes petrol to get roun' the country. Petrol costs fifteen cents a gallon. Them four fellas can't take four cars. So each of 'em puts in a dime an' they get petrol. You got to learn.'

'Al!'

Al looked down at Winfield standing importantly beside him.

'Al, Ma's dishin' up stew. She says come git it.'

Al wiped his hands on his trousers' 'We ain't et to-day,' he said to Floyd. 'I'll come give you a han' when I et.'

'No need 'less you want ta.'

'Sure, I'll do it.' He followed Winfield toward the Joad camp. It was crowded now. The strange children stood close to the stew pot, so close that Ma brushed them with her elbows as she worked. Tom and Uncle John stood beside her.

Ma said helplessly: 'I dunno what to do. I got to feed the fambly. What'm I gonna do with these here?' The children stood stiffly and looked at her. Their faces were blank, rigid, and their eyes went mechanically from the pot to the tin plate she held. Their eyes followed the spoon from pot to plate, and when she passed the steaming plate up to Uncle John, their eyes followed it up. Uncle John dug his spoon into the stew, and the banked eyes rose up with the spoon. A piece of potato went into John's mouth and the banked eyes were on his face, watching to see how he would react. Would it be good? Would he like it?

And then Uncle John seemed to see them for the first time. He chewed slowly. 'You take this here,' he said to Tom. 'I ain't hungry.'

'You ain't et to-day,' Tom said.

'I know, but I got a stomick-ache. I ain't hungry.'

Tom said quietly: 'You take that plate inside the tent an' you eat it.'

'I ain't hungry,' John insisted. 'I'd still see 'em inside the tent.'

Tom turned on the children. 'You git,' he said. 'Go on now, git.' The bank of eyes left the stew and rested wondering on his face. 'Go on now, git. You ain't doin' no good. There ain't enough for you.'

Ma ladled stew into the tin plates, very little stew, and she laid the plates on the ground. 'I can't send 'em away,' she said. 'I don' know what to do. Take your plates an' go inside. I'll let 'em have what's lef'. Here, take a plate in to Rosasharn.' She smiled up at the children. 'Look,' she said, 'you little fellas go an' you get each a flat stick an' I'll put what's lef' for you. But they ain't to be no fightin'.' The group broke up with a deadly, silent swiftness. Children ran to find sticks, they ran to their own tents and brought spoons. Before Ma had finished with the plates they were back, silent and wolfish. Ma shook her head. 'I dunno what to do. I can't rob the fambly. I got to feed the fambly. Ruthie,

Winfiel', Al,' she cried fiercely. 'Take your plates. Hurry up. Git in the tent quick.' She looked apologetically at the waiting children. 'There ain't enough,' she said humbly. 'I'm a-gonna set this here kettle out, an' you'll all get a little tas', but it ain't gonna do you no good.' She faltered, 'I can't he'p it. Can't keep it from you.' She lifted the pot and set it down on the ground. 'Now wait. It's too hot,' she said, and she went into the tent quickly so she would not see. Her family sat on the ground, each with his plate; and outside they could hear the children digging into the pot with their sticks and their spoons and their pieces of rusty tin. A mound of children smothered the pot from sight. They did not talk, did not fight or argue; but there was a quiet intentness in all of them, a wooden fierceness. Ma turned her back so she couldn't see. 'We can't do that no more,' she said. 'We got to eat alone.' There was the sound of scraping at the kettle, and then the mound of children broke and the children walked away and left the scraped kettle on the ground. Ma looked at the empty plates. 'Did' none of you get nowhere near enough.'

Pa got up and left the tent without answering. The preacher smiled to himself and lay back on the ground, hands clasped behind his head. Al got to his feet. 'Got to help a fella with a car.'

Ma gathered the plates and took them outside to wash.

'Ruthie,' she called, 'Winfiel'. Go get me a bucket a water right off.' She handed them the bucket and they trudged off toward the river.

A strong broad woman walked near. Her dress was streaked with dust and splotched with car oil. Her chin was held high with pride. She stood a short distance away and regarded Ma belligerently. At last she approached. "'Afternoon,' she said coldly.

"'Afternoon,' said Ma, and she got up from her knees and pushed a box forward. 'Won't you set down?'

The woman walked near. 'No, I won't set down.'

Ma looked questioningly at her. 'Can I he'p you in any way?'

The woman set her hands on her hips. 'You kin he'p me by mindin' your own children an' lettin' mine alone.'

Ma's eyes opened wide. 'I ain't done nothin'–' she began.

The woman scowled at her. 'My little fella come back smellin' of stew. You give it to 'im. He tol' me. Don' you go a-boastin' an' a-braggin' 'bout havin' stew. Don' you do it. I got 'nuf troubles 'thout that. Come in ta me, he did, an' says: "Whyn't we have stew?"' Her voice shook with fury.

Ma moved close. 'Set down,' she said. 'Set down an' talk a piece.'

'No, I ain't gonna set down. I'm tryin' to feed my folks, an' you come along with your stew.'

'Set down,' Ma said. 'That was 'bout the las' stew we're gonna have till we get work. S'pose you was cookin' a stew an' a bunch a little fellas stood aroun' moonin', what'd you do? We didn't have enough, but you can't keep it when they look at ya like that.'

The woman's hands dropped from her hips. For a moment her eyes questioned Ma, and then she turned and walked quickly away, and she went into a tent and pulled the flaps down behind her. Ma stared after her, and then she dropped to her knees again beside the stack of tin dishes.

Al hurried near. 'Tom,' he called. 'Ma, is Tom inside?'

Tom stuck his head out. 'What you want?'

'Come on with me,' Al said excitedly.

They walked away together. 'What's a matter with you?' Tom asked.

'You'll find out. Jus' wait.' He led Tom to the torn-down car. 'This here's Floyd Knowles,' he said.

'Yeah, I talked to him. How ya?'

'Jus' gettin' her in shape,' Floyd said.

Tom ran his finger over the top of the block. 'What kinda bugs is crawlin' on you, Al?'

'Floyd jus' tol' me. Tell 'em, Floyd.'

Floyd said: 'Maybe I shouldn', but–yeah, I'll tell ya. Fella come through an' he says they's gonna be work up north.'

'Up north?'

'Yeah–place called Santa Clara Valley, way to hell an' gone up north.'

'Yeah? Kinda work?'

'Prune pickin', an' pears an' cannery work. Says it's purty near ready.'

'How far?' Tom demanded.

'Oh, Christ knows. Maybe two hundred miles.'

'That's a hell of a long ways,' said Tom. 'How we know they's gonna be work when we get there?'

'Well, we don' know,' said Floyd. 'But they ain't nothin' here, an' this fella says he got a letter from his brother, an' he's on his way. He says not to tell nobody, they'll be too many. We oughta get out in the night. Oughta get there an' get some work lined up.'

Tom studied him. 'Why we gotta sneak away?'

'Well, if ever'body gets there, ain't gonna be work for nobody.'

'It's hell of a long ways,' Tom said.

Floyd sounded hurt. 'I'm jus' givin' you the tip. You don' have to take it. Your brother here he'ped me, an' I'm givin' you the tip.'

'You sure there ain't no work here?'

'Look, I been scourin' aroun' for three weeks all over hell, an' I ain't had a bit a work, not a single han'-holt. 'F you wanna look aroun, an' burn up petrol lookin', why, go ahead. I ain't beggin' you. More that goes, the less chance I got.'

Tom said: 'I ain't findin' fault. It's jus' such a hell of a long ways. An' we kinda hoped we could get work here an' rent a house to live in.'

Floyd said patiently: 'I know ya jus' got here. They's stuff ya got to learn. If you'd let me tell ya, it'd save ya somepin. If ya don' let me tell ya, then ya got to learn the hard way. You ain't gonna settle down 'cause they ain't no work to settle ya. An' your belly ain't gonna let ya settle down. Now–that's straight.'

'Wisht I could look aroun' first,' Tom said uneasily.

A sedan drove through the camp and pulled up at the next tent. A man in overalls and a blue shirt climbed out. Floyd called to him: 'Any luck?'

'There ain't a han'-turn of work in the whole darn country, not till cotton pickin'.' And he went into the ragged tent.

'See?' said Floyd.

'Yeah, I see. But two hundred miles, Jesus!'

'Well, you ain't settlin' no place for a while. Might's well make up your mind to that.'

'We better go,' Al said.

Tom asked: 'When is they gonna be work aroun' here?'

'Well, in a month the cotton'll start. If you got plenty money you can wait for the cotton.'

Tom said: 'Ma ain't a-gonna wanna move. She's all tar'd out.'

Floyd shrugged his shoulders. 'I ain't a-tryin' to push ya north. Suit yaself. I jus' tol' ya what I heard.' He picked the oily gasket from the running-board and fitted it carefully on the block and pressed it down. 'Now,' he said to Al, ''f you want to give me a han' with that engine head.'

Tom watched while they set the heavy head gently down over the head bolts and dropped it evenly. 'Have to talk about it,' he said.

Floyd said: 'I don't want nobody but your folks to know about it. Jus' you. An' I wouldn't of tol' you if ya brother didn' he'p me out here.'

Tom said: 'Well, I sure thank ya for tellin' us. We got to figger it out. Maybe we'll go.'

Al said: 'By God, I think I'll go if the res' goes or not. I'll hitch there.'

'An' leave the fambly?' Tom asked.

'Sure. I'd come back with my jeans plumb fulla jack. Why not?'

'Ma ain't gonna like no such thing,' Tom said. 'An' Pa, he ain't gonna like it neither.'

Floyd set the nuts and screwed them down as far as he could with his fingers. 'Me an' my wife come out with our folks,' he said. 'Back home we wouldn' of thought of goin' away. Wouldn't of thought of it. But, hell, we was all up north a piece and I come down here, an' they moved on, an' now God knows where they are. Been lookin' an' askin' about 'em ever since.' He fitted his wrench to the engine-head bolts and turned them down evenly, one turn to each nut, around and around the series.

Tom squatted down beside the car and squinted his eyes up the line of tents. A little stubble was beating into the earth between tents. 'No, sir,' he said, 'Ma ain't gonna like you goin' off.'

'Well, seems to me a lone fella got more chance of work.'

'Maybe, but Ma ain't gonna like it at all.'

Two cars loaded with disconsolate men drove down into the camp. Floyd lifted his eyes, but he didn't ask them about their luck. Their dusty faces were sad and resistant. The sun was sinking now, and the yellow sunlight fell on the Hooverville and on the willows behind it. The children began to come out of the tents, to wander about the camp. And from the tents the women came and built their little fires. The men gathered in squatting groups and talked together.

A new Chevrolet coupé turned off the highway and headed down the camp. It pulled to the centre of the camp. Tom said: 'Who's this? They don't belong here.'

Floyd said: 'I dunno–cops, maybe.'

The car door opened and a man got out and stood beside the car. His companion remained seated. Now all the squatting men looked at the newcomers and the conversation was still. And the women building their fires looked secretly at the shining car. The children moved closer with elaborate circuitousness, edging inward in long curves.

Floyd put down his wrench. Tom stood up. Al wiped his hands on his trousers. The three strolled toward the Chevrolet. The man who had got out of the car was dressed in khaki trousers and a flannel shirt. He wore a flat-brimmed Stetson hat. A sheaf of papers was held in his shirt pocket by a little fence of fountain pens and yellow pencils; and from his hip pocket protruded a note-book with metal covers. He moved to one of the groups of squatting men, and they looked up at him, suspicious and quiet. They watched him and did not move; the whites of their eyes showed beneath the irises, for they did not raise their heads to look. Tom and Al and Floyd strolled casually near.

The man said: 'You men want to work?' Still they looked quietly, suspiciously. And men from all over the camp moved near.

One of the squatting men spoke at last. 'Sure we wanta work. Where's at's work?'

Tulare Country. Fruit's opening up. Need a lot of pickers.'

Floyd spoke up. 'You doin' the hiring?'

'Well, I'm contracting the land.'

The men were in a compact group now. An overalled man took off his black hat and combed back his long black hair with his fingers. 'What you payin'?' he asked.

'Well, can't tell exactly, yet. 'Bout thirty cents, I guess.'

'Why can't you tell? You took the contract, didn' you?'

'That's true,' the khaki man said. 'But it's keyed to the price. Might be a little more, might be a little less.'

Floyd stepped out ahead. He said quietly: 'I'll go, mister. You're a contractor, an' you got a licence. You jus' show your licence, an' then you give us an order to go to work, an' where, an' when, an' how much we'll get, an' you sign that, an' we'll all go.'

The contractor turned, scowling. 'You telling me how to run my own business?'

Floyd said: ''F we're workin' for you, it's our business too.'

'Well, you ain't telling me what to do. I told you I need men.'

Floyd said angrily: 'You didn't say how many men, an' you didn't say what you'd pay.'

'Goddamn it, I don't know yet.'

'If you don' know, you got no right to hire men.'

'I got a right to run my business my own way. If you men want to sit on your ass, O.K. I'm out getting men for Tulare Country. Going to need a lot of men.'

Floyd turned to the crowd of men. They were standing up now, looking quietly from one speaker to the other. Floyd said: 'Twicet now I've fell for that. Maybe he needs a thousan' men. He'll get five thousan' there an' he'll pay fifteen cents an hour. An' you poor bastards'll have to take it 'cause you'll be hungry. 'F he wants to hire men, let him hire 'em an' write it out an' say what he's gonna pay. Ast ta see his licence. He ain't allowed to contract men without a licence.'

The contractor turned to the Chevrolet and called: 'Joe!' His companion looked out and then swung the car door open and stepped out. He wore riding breeches and laced boots. A heavy pistol holster hung on a cartridge belt around his waist. On his brown shirt a deputy sheriff's star was pinned. He walked heavily over. His face was set to a thin smile. 'What you want?' The holster slid back and forth on his hip.

'Ever see this guy before, Joe?'

The deputy asked: 'Which one?'

'This fella.' The contractor pointed to Floyd.

'What'd he do?' The deputy smiled at Floyd.

'He's talkin' red, agitating trouble.'

'Hm-m-m.' The deputy moved slowly around to see Floyd's profile, and the colour slowly flowed up Floyd's face.

'You see?' Floyd cried. 'If this guy's on the level, would he bring a cop along?'

'Ever see 'im before?' the contractor insisted.

'Hmm, seems I have. Las' week when that used-car lot was busted into. Seems like I seen this fella hangin' aroun'. Yep! I'd swear it's the same fella.' Suddenly the smile left his face. 'Get in that car,' he said, and he unhooked the strap that covered the butt of his automatic.

Tom said: 'You got nothin' on him.'

The deputy swung around. ''F you'd like to go in too, you jus' open your trap once more. They was two fellas hangin' aroun' that lot.'

'I wasn't even in the State las' week,' Tom said.

'Well, maybe you're wanted someplace else. You keep your trap shut.'

The contractor turned back to the men. 'You fellas don't want ta listen to these goddamn reds. Trouble-makers–they'll get you in trouble. Now I can use all of you in Tulare Country.'

The men didn't answer.

The deputy turned back to them. 'Might be a good idear to go,' he said. The thin smile was back on his face. 'Board of Health says we got to clean out this camp. An' if it gets around that you got reds out here–why, somebody might git hurt. Be a good idear if all you fellas moved on to Tulare. They isn't a thing to do aroun' here. That's jus' a friendly way of telling you. Be a bunch a guys down here, maybe with pick handles, if you ain't gone.'

The contractor said: 'I told you I need men. If you don't want to work–well, that's your business.'

The deputy smiled. 'If they don't want to work, they ain't a place for 'em in this country. We'll float 'em quick.'

Floyd stood stiffly beside the deputy, and Floyd's thumbs were hooked over his belt. Tom stole a look at him, and then stared at the ground.

'That's all,' the contractor said: 'There's men needed in Tulare Country; plenty of work.'

Tom looked slowly up at Floyd's hands, and he saw the strings at the wrists standing out under the skin. Tom's own hands came up, and his thumbs hooked over his belt.

'Yeah, that's all. I don't want one of you here by tomorra morning.'

The contractor stepped into the Chevrolet.

'Now, you,' the deputy said to Floyd, 'you get in that car.' He reached a large hand up and took hold of Floyd's left arm. Floyd spun and swung with one movement. His fist splashed into the large face, and in the same motion he was away, dodging down the line of tents. The deputy staggered and Tom put out his foot for him to trip over. The deputy fell heavily and rolled, reaching for his gun. Floyd dodged in and out of sight down the line. The deputy fired from the ground. A woman in front of a tent screamed and then looked at a hand which had no knuckles. The fingers hung on strings against her palm, and the torn flesh was white and bloodless. Far down the line Floyd came in sight, sprinting for the willows. The deputy, sitting on the ground, raised his gun again and then, suddenly from the group of men, the Reverend Casy stepped. He kicked the deputy in the neck and then stood back as the heavy man crumpled into unconsciousness.

The motor of the Chevrolet roared and it streaked away, churning the dust. It mounted to the highway and shot away. In front of her tent, the woman still looked at her shattered hand. Little droplets of blood began to ooze from the wound. And a chuckling hysteria began in her throat, a whining laugh that grew louder and higher with each breath.

The deputy lay on his side, his mouth open against the dust.

Tom picked up his automatic, pulled out the magazine and threw it into the bush, and he ejected the live shell from the chamber. 'Fella like that ain't got no right to a gun,' he said; and he dropped the automatic to the ground.

A crowd had collected around the woman with the broken hand, and her hysteria increased, a screaming quality came into her laughter.

Casy moved closer to Tom. 'You got to git out,' he said. 'You go down in the willas an' wait. He didn' see me kick 'im, but he seen you kick out your foot.'

'I don' want ta go,' Tom said.

Casy put his head close. He whispered: 'They'll fingerprint you. You broke parole. They'll send you back.'

Tom drew in his breath quietly. 'Jesus! I forgot.'

'Go quick,' Casy said. ''Fore he comes to.'

'Like to have his gun,' Tom said.

'No. Leave it. If it's awright to come back, I'll give ya four high whistles.'

Tom strolled away casually, but as soon as he was away from the group he hurried his steps, and he disappeared among the willows that lined the river.

Al stepped over to the fallen deputy. 'Jesus,' he said admiringly. 'you sure flagged 'im down!'

The crowd of men had continued to stare at the unconscious man. And now in the great distance a siren screamed up the scale and dropped, and it screamed again, nearer this time. Instantly the men were nervous. They shifted their feet for a moment and then they moved away, each one to his own tent. Only Al and the preacher remained.

Casy turned to Al. 'Get out,' he said. 'Go on, get out–to the tent. You don't know nothin'.'

'Yeah? How 'bout you?'

Casy grinned at him, 'Somebody got to take the blame. I got no kids. They'll jus' put me in jail, an' I ain't doing' nothin' but set aroun'.'

Al said: 'Ain't no reason for-'

'Go on now,' Casy said sharply. 'You get outa this.'

Al bristled. 'I ain't takin' orders.'

Casy said softly: 'If you mess in this your whole fambly, all your folks, gonna get in trouble. I don't care about you. But your ma and pa, they'll get in trouble. Maybe they'll send Tom back to McAlester.'

Al considered it for a moment. 'O.K.,' he said. 'I think you're a damn fool, though.'

'Sure,' said Casy. 'Why not?'

The siren screamed again and again, and always it came closer. Casy knelt beside the deputy and turned him over. The man groaned and fluttered his eyes, and he tried to see. Casy wiped the dust off his lips. The families were in the tents now, and the flaps were down, and the setting sun made the air red and the grey tents bronze.

Tires squealed on the highway and an open car came swiftly into the camp. Four men, armed with rifles, piled out. Casy stood up and walked to them.

'What the hell's goin' on here?'

Casy said: 'I knocked out your man there.'

One of the armed men went to the deputy. He was conscious now, trying weakly to sit up.

'Now what happened here?'

'Well,' Casy said, 'he got tough an' I hit 'im, and he started shootin'–hit a woman down the line. So I hit 'im again.'

'Well, what'd you do in the first place?'

'I talked back,' said Casy.

'Get in the car.'

'Sure,' said Casy, and he climbed into the back seat and sat down. Two men helped the hurt deputy to his feet. He felt his neck gingerly. Casy said: 'They's a woman down the row like to bleed to death from his bad shootin'.'

'We'll see about that later. Mike, is this the fella that hit you?'

The dazed man stared sickly at Casy. 'Don't look like him.'

'It was me, all right.' Casy said. 'You got smart with the wrong fella.'

Mike shook his head slowly. 'You don't look like the right fella to me. By God, I'm gonna be sick!'

Casy said: 'I'll go 'thout no trouble. You better see how bad that woman's hurt.'

'Where's she?'

'That tent over there.'

The leader of the deputies walked to the tent, rifle in hand. He spoke through the tent walls, and then went inside. In a moment he came out and walked back. And he said, a little proudly: 'Jesus, what a mess a .45 does make! They got a tourniquet on. We'll send a doctor out.'

Two deputies sat on either side of Casy. The leader sounded his horn. There was no movement in the camp. The flaps were down tight, and the people in their tents. The engine started and the car swung around and pulled out of the camp. Between his guards Casy sat proudly, his head up and the stringy muscles of his neck prominent. On his lips there was a faint smile and on his face a curious look of conquest.

When the deputies had gone, the people came out of the tents. The sun was down now, and the gentle blue evening light was in the camp. To the east the mountains were still yellow with sunlight. The women went back to the fires that had died. The men collected to squat together and to talk softly.

Al crawled from under the Joad tarpaulin and walked toward the willows to whistle for Tom. Ma came out and built her little fire of twigs.

'Pa,' she said, 'we ain't goin' to have much. We et so late.'

Pa and Uncle John stuck close to the camp, watching Ma peeling potatoes and slicing them raw into a frying pan of deep grease. Pa said: 'Now what the hell made the preacher do that?'

Ruthie and Winfield crept close and crouched down to hear the talk.

Uncle John scratched the earth deeply with a long rusty nail. 'He knowed about sin. I ast him about sin, an' he tol' me; but I don' know if he's right. He says a fella's sinned if he thinks he's sinned.' Uncle John's eyes were tired and sad. 'I been secret all my days,' he said. 'I done things I never tol' about.'

Ma turned from the fire. 'Don' go tellin', John,' she said. 'Tell 'em to God. Don' go burdenin' other people with your sins. That ain't decent.'

'They're a-eatin' on me,' said John.

'Well, don' tell 'em. Go down the river an' stick your head under an' whisper 'em in the stream.'

Pa nodded his head slowly at Ma's words. 'She's right,' he said. 'It gives a fella relief to tell, but it jus' spreads out his sin.'

Uncle John looked up to the sun-gold mountains, and the mountains were reflected in his eyes. 'I wisht I could run it down,' he said, 'but I can't. She's a-bitin' in my guts.'

Behind him Rose of Sharon moved dizzily out of the tent. 'Where's Connie?' she asked irritably. 'I ain't seen Connie for a long time. Where'd he go?'

'I ain't seen him,' said Ma. 'If I see 'im, I'll tell 'im you want 'im.'

'I ain't feelin' good,' said Rose of Sharon. 'Connie shouldn' of left me.'

Ma looked up to the girl's swollen face. 'You been a-cryin',' she said.

The tears started freshly in Rose of Sharon's eyes.

Ma went on firmly: 'You git aholt on yaself. They's a lot of us here. You git aholt on yaself. Come here now an' peel some potatoes. You're feelin' sorry for yaself.'

The girl started to go back in the tent. She tried to avoid Ma's stern eyes, but they compelled her and she came slowly toward the fire. 'He shouldn' of went away,' she said, but the tears were gone.

'You got to work,' Ma said. 'Set in the tent an' you'll get feelin' sorry about yaself. I ain't had time to take you in han'. I will now. You take this here knife an' get to them potatoes.'

The girl knelt down and obeyed. She said fiercely: 'Wait'll I see 'im. I'll tell 'im.'

Ma smiled slowly. 'He might smack you. You got it comin' with whinin' aroun' an' candyin' yaself. If he smacks some sense in you I'll bless 'im.' The girl's eyes blazed with resentment, but she was silent.

Uncle John pushed his rusty nail deep into the ground with his broad thumb. 'I got to tell,' he said.

Pa said: 'Well, tell then, goddamn it! Who'd ya kill?'

Uncle John dug his thumb into the watch pocket of his blue jeans and scooped out a folded dirty bill. He spread it out and showed it. 'Fi' dollars,' he said.

'Steal her?' Pa asked.

'No, I had her. Kept her out.'

'She was yourn, wasn't she?'

'Yeah, but I didn't have no right to keep her out.'

'I don't see much sin in that,' Ma said. 'It's yourn.'

Uncle John said slowly: 'It ain't only the keepin' her out. I kep' her out to get drunk. I knowed they was gonna come a time when I got to get drunk, when I'd get to hurtin' inside so. I got to get drunk. Figgered time wasn' yet, an' then–the preacher went an' give' 'imself up to save Tom.'

Pa nodded his head up and down and cocked his head to hear. Ruthie moved closer, like a puppy, crawling on her elbows, and Winfield followed her. Rose of Sharon dug at a deep eye in a potato with the point of her knife. The evening light deepened and became more blue.

Ma said, in a sharp matter-of-fact tone: 'I don' see why him savin' Tom got to get you drunk.'

John said sadly: 'Can't say her. I feel awful. He done her so easy. Jus' stepped up there an' says: "I done her." An' they took 'im away. An' I'm a-gonna get drunk.'

Pa still nodded his head. 'I don't see why you got to tell,' he said. 'If it was me, I'd jus' go off an' get drunk if I had to.'

'Come a time when I coulda did somepin an' took the big sin off my soul,' Uncle John said sadly. 'An' I slipped up. I didn' jump on her, an'–an' she got away. Lookie!' he said. 'You got the money. Gimme two dollars.'

Pa reached reluctantly into his pocket and brought out the leather pouch. 'You ain't gonna need no seven dollars to get drunk. You don't need to drink champagny water.'

Uncle John held out his bill. 'You take this here an' gimme two dollars. I can get good an' drunk for two dollars. I don' want no sin of waste on me. I'll spend whatever I got. Always do.'

Pa took the dirty bill and gave Uncle John two silver dollars. 'There ya are,' he said. 'A fella got to do what he got to do. Nobody don' know enough to tell 'im.'

Uncle John took the coins. 'You ain't gonna be mad? You know I got to?'

'Christ, yes,' said Pa. 'You know what you got to do.'

'I wouldn' be able to get through this night no other way,' he said. He turned to Ma. 'You ain't gonna hold her over me?'

Ma didn't look up. 'No,' she said softly. 'No–you go 'long.'

He stood up and walked forlornly away in the evening. He walked up to the concrete highway and across the pavement to the grocery store. In front of the screen door he took off his hat, dropped it into the dust, and ground it with his heel in self-abasement. And he left his black hat there, broken and dirty. He entered the store and walked to the shelves where the whisky bottles stood behind wire-netting.

Pa and Ma and the children watched Uncle John move away. Rose of Sharon kept her eyes resentfully on the potatoes.

'Poor John,' Ma said. 'I wondered if it would a done any good if–no–I guess not. I never seen a man so drove.'

Ruthie turned on her side in the dust. She put her head close to Winfield's head and pulled his ear against her mouth. She whispered: 'I'm gonna get drunk.' Winfield snorted and pinched his mouth tight. The two children crawled away, holding their breath, their faces purple with the pressure of their giggles. They crawled around the tent and leaped up and ran squealing away from the tent. They ran to the willows, and once concealed, they shrieked with laughter. Ruthie crossed her eyes and loosened her joints; she staggered about, tripping loosely, with her tongue hanging out. 'I'm drunk,' she said.

'Look,' Winfield cried. 'Looka me, here's me, an' I'm Uncle John.' He flapped his arms and puffed, he whirled until he was dizzy.

'No,' said Ruthie. 'Here's the way. Here's the way. *I'm* Uncle John. I'm awful drunk.'

Al and Tom walked quietly through the willows, and they came on the children staggering crazily about. The dust was thick now. Tom stopped and peered. 'Ain't that Ruthie an' Winfiel'? What the hell's the matter with 'em?' They walked nearer. 'You crazy?' Tom asked.

The children stopped, embarrassed. 'We was–jus' playin',' Ruthie said.

'It's a crazy way to play,' said Al.

Ruthie said pertly: 'It ain't no crazier'n a lot of things.'

Al walked on. He said to Tom: 'Ruthie's workin' up a kick in the pants. She been workin' it up a long time. 'Bout due for it.'

Ruthie mushed her face at his back, pulled out her mouth with her forefingers, slobbered her tongue at him, outraged him in every way she knew, but Al did not turn to look at her. She looked at Winfield again to start the game, but it had been spoiled. They both knew it.

'Le's go down the water an' duck our heads,' Winfield suggested. They walked down through the willows, and they were angry at Al.

Al and Tom went quietly in the dusk. Tom said: 'Casy shouln' of did it. I might of knew, though. He was talkin' how he ain't done nothin' for us. He's a funny fella, Al. All the time thinkin'.'

'Comes from bein' a preacher,' Al said. 'They get all messed up with stuff.'

'Where ya s'pose Connie was a-goin'?'

'Goin' to take a crap, I guess.'

'Well, he was goin' a hell of a long way.'

They walked among the tents, keeping close to the walls. At Floyd's tent a soft hail stopped them. They came near to the tent flap and squatted down. Floyd raised the canvas a little. 'You gettin' out?'

Tom said: 'I don' know. Think we better?'

Floyd laughed sourly. 'You heard what that bull said. They'll burn ya out if ya don't. 'F you think that guy's gonna take a beatin' 'thout gettin' back, you're nuts. The pool-room boys'll be down here to-night to burn us out.'

'Guess we better git, then,' Tom said. 'Where you a-goin'?'

'Why, up north, like I said.'

Al said: 'Look, a fella tol' me 'bout a gov'ment camp near here. Where's it at?'

'Oh, I think that's full up.'

'Well, where's it at?'

'Go south on 99 'bout twelve-fourteen miles, an' turn east to Weedpatch. It's right near there. But I think she's full up.'

'Fella says it's nice,' Al said.

'Sure, she's nice. Treat ya like a man 'stead of a dog. Ain't no cops there. But she's full up.'

Tom said: 'What I can't understan's why that cop was so mean. Seemed like he was aimin' for trouble; seemed like he's pokin' a fella to make trouble.'

Floyd said: 'I don' know about here, but up north I knowed one a them fellas, an' he was a nice fella. He tol' me up there the deputies got to take guys in. Sheriff gets seventy-five cents a day for each prisoner, an' he feeds 'em for a quarter. If he ain't got prisoners, he don't make no profit. This fella says he didn' pick up nobody for a week, an' the sheriff tol' 'im he better bring in guys or give up his button. This fella to-day sure looks like he's out to make a pinch one way or another.'

'We got to get on,' said Tom. 'So long, Floyd.'

'So long. Prob'ly see you. Hope so.'

'Good-bye,' said Al. They walked through the dark grey camp to the Joad tent.

The frying-pan of potatoes was hissing and spitting over the fire. Ma moved the thick slices about with a spoon. Pa sat near by, hugging his knees. Rose of Sharon was sitting under the tarpaulin.

'It's Tom!' Ma cried. 'Thank God.'

'We got to get outa here,' said Tom.

'What's the matter now?'

'Well, Floyd says they'll burn the camp to-night.'

'What the hell for?' Pa asked. 'We ain't done nothin'.'

'Nothin' 'cept beat up a cop,' said Tom.

'Well, we never done it.'

'From what that cop said, they wanna push us along.'

Rose of Sharon demanded: 'You seen Connie?'

'Yeah,' said Al. 'Way to hell an' gone up the river. He's goin' south.'

'Was–was he goin' away?'

'I don' know.'

Ma turned on the girl. 'Rosasharn, you been talkin' an' actin' funny. What'd Connie say to you?'

Rose of Sharon said sullenly: 'Said it would a been a good thing if he stayed home an' studied up tractors.'

They were very quiet. Rose of Sharon looked at the fire and her eyes glistened in the firelight. The potatoes hissed sharply in the frying-pan. The girl sniffed and wiped her nose with the back of her hand.

Pa said: 'Connie wan' no good. I seen that a long time. Didn' have no guts, jus' too big for his overalls.'

Rose of Sharon got up and went into the tent. She lay down on the mattress and rolled over on her stomach and buried her head in her crossed arms.

'Wouldn' do no good to catch 'im, I guess,' Al said.

Pa replied: 'No. If he ain't no good, we don' want him.'

Ma looked into the tent, where Rose of Sharon lay on her mattress. Ma said: 'Sh! Don' say that.'

'Well, he ain't no good,' Pa insisted. 'All the time a-sayin' what he's a-gonna do. Never doin' nothin'. I didn' want ta say nothin' while he's here. But now he's run out–'

'Sh!' Ma said softly.

'Why, for Christ's sake? Why do I got to sh-h? He run out, didn' he?'

Ma turned over the potatoes with her spoon, and the grease boiled and spat. She fed twigs to the fire, and the flames laced up and lighted the tent. Ma said: 'Rosasharn gonna have a little fella an' that baby is half Connie. It ain't good for a baby to grow up with folks a-sayin' his pa ain't no good.'

'Better'n lyin' about it,' said Pa.

'No, it ain't.' Ma interrupted. 'Make out like he's dead. You would't say no bad things about Connie if he's dead.'

Tom broke in: 'Hey, what is this? We ain't sure Connie's gone for good. We got no time for talkin'. We got to eat an' get on our way.'

'On our way? We jus' come here.' Ma peered at him through the firelighted darkness.

He explained carefully: 'They gonna burn the camp to-night, Ma. Now you know I ain't got it in me to stan' by an' see our stuff burn up, nor Pa ain't got it in him, nor Uncle John. We'd come up a-fightin', an' I jus' can't afford to be took in an' mugged. I nearly got it to-day, if the preacher hadn' jumped in.'

Ma had been turning the frying potatoes in the hot grease. Now she took her decision. 'Come in!' she cried. 'Le's eat this stuff. We got to go quick.' She set out the tin plates.

Pa said: 'How 'bout John?'

'Where is Uncle John?' Tom asked.

Pa and Ma were silent for a moment, and then Pa said: 'He went to get drunk.'

'Jesus!' Tom said. 'What a time he picked out! Where'd he go?'

'I don' know,' said Pa.

Tom stood up. 'Look,' he said, 'you all eat an' get the stuff loaded. I'll go look for Uncle John. He'd of went to the store 'crost the road.'

Tom walked quickly away. The little cooking fires burned in front of the tents and the shacks, and the light fell on the faces of ragged men and women, on crouched children. In a few tents the light of kerosene lamps shone through the canvas and placed shadows of people hugely on the cloth.

Tom walked up the dusty road and crossed the concrete highway to the little grocery store. He stood in front of the screen door and looked in. The proprietor, a little grey man with an unkempt moustache and watery eyes, leaned on the counter reading a newspaper. His thin arms were bare and he wore a long white apron. Heaped around and at the back of him were mounds, pyramids, walls of canned goods. He looked up when Tom came in, and his eyes narrowed as though he aimed a shotgun.

'Good evening,' he said. 'Run out of something?'

'Run out of my uncle,' said Tom. 'Or he run out, or something.'

The grey man looked puzzled and worried at the same time. He touched the tip of his nose tenderly and waggled it around to stop an itch. 'Seems like you people always lost somebody,' he said. 'Ten times a day or more somebody comes in here an' says: "If you see a man named so-an'-so, an' looks like so-an'-so, will you tell 'im we went up north?" Somepin like that all the time.'

Tom laughed. 'Well, if you see a young snot-nose name' Connie, looks a little bit like a coyote, tell 'im to go to hell. We've went south. But he ain't the fella I'm lookin' for. Did a fella 'bout sixty years ol', black pants, sort of greyish hair, come in here an' get some whisky?'

The eyes of the grey man brightened. 'Now he sure did. I never seen anything like it. He stood out front an' he dropped his hat an' stepped on it. Here, I got his hat here.' He brought the dusty broken hat from under the counter.

Tom took it from him. 'That's him, all right.'

'Well, sir, he got a couple of pints of whisky an' he didn' say a thing. He pulled the cork an' tipped up the bottle. I ain't got a licence to drink here. I says: "Look, you can't drink here. You got to go outside." Well, sir! He jus' stepped outside the door, an' I bet he din't tilt up that pint more'n four times till it was empty. He throwed it away an' he leaned in the door. Eyes kinda dull. He says: "Thank you, sir," an' he went on. I never seen no drinkin' like that in my life.'

'Went on? Which way? I got to get him.'

'Well, it so happens I can tell you. I never seen such drinkin', so I looked out after him. He went north; an' then a car come along an' lighted him up, an' he went down the bank. Legs was beginnin' to buckle a little. He got the other pint open awready. He won't be far–not the way he was goin'.'

Tom said: 'Thank ya. I got to find him.'

'You want ta take his hat?'

'Yeah! Yeah! He'll need it. Well, thank ya.'

'What's the matter with him?' the grey man asked. 'He wasn't takin' pleasure in his drink.'

'Oh, he's kinda–moody. Well, good night. An' if you see that squirt Connie, tell 'im we've went south.'

'I got so many people to look out for an' tell stuff to, I can't ever remember 'em all.'

'Don't put yourself out too much,' Tom said. He went out the screen door carrying Uncle John's dusty black hat. He crossed the concrete road and walked along the edge of it. Below him in the sunken field, the Hooverville lay; and the little fires flickered and the lanterns shone through the tents. Somewhere in the camp a guitar sounded, slow chords, struck without any sequence, practice chords. Tom stopped and listened, and then he moved slowly along the side of the road, and every few steps he stopped to listen again. He had gone a quarter of a mile before he heard what he listened for. Down below the embankment the sound of a thick, tuneless voice, singing drably. Tom cocked his head, the better to hear.

And the dull voice sang: 'I've give my heart to Jesus, so Jesus take me home. I've give my soul to Jesus, so Jesus is my home.' The song trailed off to a murmur, and then stopped. Tom hurried down from the embankment, toward the song. After a while he stopped and listened again. And the voice was close this time, the same, slow tuneless singing: 'Oh, the night that Maggie died, she called me to her side, an' give to me them ol' red flannel draws that Maggie wore. They was baggy at the knees–'

Tom moved cautiously forward. He saw the black form sitting on the ground, and he stole near and sat down. Uncle John tilted the pint and the liquor gurgled out of the neck of the bottle.

Tom said quietly: 'Hey, wait! Where do I come in?'

Uncle John turned his head. 'Who you?'

'You forgot me awready? You had four drinks to my one.'

'No, Tom. Don't try fool me. I'm all alone here. You ain't been here.'

'Well, I'm sure here now. How 'bout givin' me a snort?'

Uncle John raised the pint again and the whisky gurgled. He shook the bottle. It was empty. 'No more,' he said. 'Wanta die so bad. Wanta die awful. Die a little bit. Got to. Like sleepin'. Die a little bit. So tar'd. Tar'd. Maybe–don' wake up no more.' His voice crooned off. 'Gonna wear a crown–a golden crown.'

Tom said: 'Listen here to me, Uncle John. We're gonna move on. You come along, an' you can go right to sleep up on the load.' John shook his head. 'No. Go on. Ain't goin'. Gonna res' here. No good goin' back. No good to nobody–jus' a-draggin' my sins like dirty drawers 'mongst nice folks. No. Ain't goin'.'

'Come on. We can't go 'less you go.'

'Go ri' 'long. I ain't no good. I ain't no good. Jus' a-draggin' my sins, a-dirtyin' ever'body.'

'You got no more sin'n anybody else.'

John put his head close, and he winked one eye wisely. Tom could see his face dimly in the starlight. 'Nobody don' know my sins, nobody but Jesus. He knows.'

Tom got down on his knees. He put his hand on Uncle John's forehead, and it was hot and dry. John brushed his hand away clumsily.

'Come on,' Tom pleaded. 'Come on now, Uncle John.'

'Ain't goin' go. Jus' tar'd. Gon' res' ri' here. Ri' here.'

Tom was very close. He put his fist against the point of Uncle John's chin. He made a small practice arc twice, for distance; and then, with his shoulder in the swing, he hit the chin a delicate perfect blow. John's chin snapped up and he fell backwards and tried to sit up again. But Tom was kneeling over him and as John got one elbow up Tom hit him again. Uncle John lay still on the ground.

Tom stood up and, bending, he lifted the loose sagging body and boosted it over his shoulder. He staggered under the loose weight. John's hanging hands tapped him on the back as he went, slowly, puffing up the bank to the highway. Once a car came by and lighted him with the limp man over his shoulder. The car slowed for a moment and then roared away.

Tom was panting when he came back to the Hooverville, down from the road and to the Joad truck. John was coming to; he struggled weakly. Tom set him gently down on the ground.

Camp had been broken while he was gone. Al passed the bundles up on the truck. The tarpaulin lay ready to bind the load.

Al said: 'He sure got a quick start.'

Tom apologized. 'I had to hit 'im a little to make 'im come. Poor fella.'

'Didn't hurt 'im?' Ma asked.

'Don' think so. He's a-comin' out of it.'

Uncle John was weakly sick on the ground. His spasms of vomiting came in little gasps.

Ma said: 'I lef' a plate of potatoes for you, Tom.'

Tom chuckled. 'I ain't just in the mood right now.'

Pa called: 'Awright, Al. Sling up the tarp.'

The truck was loaded and ready. Uncle John had gone to sleep. Tom and Al boosted and pulled him up on the load while Winfield made a vomiting noise behind the truck and Ruthie plugged her mouth with her hand to keep from squealing.

'Awready,' Pa said.

Tom asked: 'Where's Rosasharn?'

'Over there,' said Ma. 'Come on, Rosasharn. We're a-goin'.'

The girl sat still, her chin sunk on her breast. Tom walked over to her. 'Come on,' he said.

'I ain't a-goin'.' She did not raise her head.

'You got to go.'

'I want Connie. I ain't a-goin' till he comes back.'

Three cars pulled out of the camp, up the road to the highway, old cars loaded with the camps and the people. They clanked up to the highway and rolled away, their dim lights glancing along the road.

Tom said: 'Connie'll find us. I lef' word up at the store where we'd be. He'll find us.'

Ma came up and stood beside him. 'Come on, Rosasharn. Come on, honey,' she said gently.

'I wanta wait.'

'We can't wait.' Ma leaned down and took the girl by the arm and helped her to her feet.

'He'll find us,' Tom said. 'Don' you worry. He'll find us.' They walked on either side of the girl.

'Maybe he went to get them books to study up,' said Rose of Sharon. 'Maybe he was a-gonna surprise us.'

Ma said: 'Maybe that's jus' what he done.' They led her to the truck and helped her up on top of the load, and she crawled under the tarpaulin and disappeared into the dark cave.

Now the bearded man from the weed shack came timidly to the truck. He waited about, his hands clutched behind his back. 'You gonna leave any stuff a fella could use?' he asked at last.

Pa said: 'Can't think of nothin'. We ain't got nothin' to leave.'

Tom asked: 'Ain't ya gettin' out?'

For a long time the bearded man stared at him. 'No,' he said at last.

'But they'll burn ya out.'

The unsteady eyes dropped to the ground. 'I know. They done it before.'

'Well, why the hell don't ya get out?'

The bewildered eyes looked up for a moment, and then down again, and the dying firelight was reflected redly. 'I don' know. Takes so long to git stuff together.'

'You won't have nothin' if they burn ya out.'

'I know. You ain't leavin' nothin' a fella could use?'

'Cleaned out, slick,' said Pa. The bearded man vaguely wandered away. 'What's a matter with him?' Pa demanded.

'Cop-happy,' said Tom. 'Fella was sayin'–he's bull-simple. Been beat over the head too much.'

A second little caravan drove past the camp and climbed to the road and moved away.

'Come on, Pa. Let's go. Look here, Pa. You an' me an' Al ride in the seat. Ma can get on the load. No. Ma, you ride in the middle. Al'–Tom reached under the seat and brought out a big monkey wrench–'Al, you get up behind. Take this here. Jus' in case. If anybody tries to climb up–let 'im have it.'

Al took the wrench and climbed up the back board and he settled himself cross-legged, the wrench in his hand. Tom pulled the iron jack handle from under the seat and laid it on the floor, under the brake pedal. 'Awright,' he said. 'Get in the middle, Ma.'

Pa said: 'I ain't got nothin' in my han'.'

'You can reach over an' get the jack handle,' said Tom. 'I hope to Jesus you don' need it.' He stepped on the starter and the clanking flywheel turned over, the engine caught and died, and caught again. Tom turned on the lights and moved out of the camp in low gear. The dim lights fingered the road nervously. They climbed up to the highway and turned south. Tom said: 'They comes a time when a man gets mad.'

Ma broke in: 'Tom–you tol' me–you promised me you wasn't like that. You promised.'

'I know, Ma. I'm a-tryin'. But them deputies–Did you ever see a deputy that didn' have a fat ass? An' they waggle their ass an' flop their gun aroun'. Ma,' he said, 'if it was the law they was workin' with, why, we could take it. But it *ain't* the law. They're a-workin' away at our spirits. They're a-tryin' to make us cringe an' crawl like a whipped bitch. They tryin' to break us. Why, Jesus Christ, Ma, they comes a time when the on'y way a fella can keep his decency is by takin' a sock at a cop. They're workin' on our decency.'

Ma said: 'You promised, Tom. That's how Pretty Boy Floyd done. I knowed his ma. They hurt him.'

'I'm a-tryin', Ma. Honest to God, I am. You don' want me to crawl like a beat bitch, with my belly on the groun', do you?'

'I'm a-prayin'. You got to keep clear, Tom. The fambly's breakin' up. You got to keep clear.'

'I'll try, Ma. But when one a them fat asses gets to workin' me over, I got a big job tryin'. If it was the law, it'd be different. But burnin' the camp ain't the law.'

The car jolted along. Ahead, a little row of red lanterns stretched across the highway.

'Detour, I guess,' Tom said. He slowed the car and stopped it, and immediately a crowd of men swarmed about the truck. They were armed with pick-handles and shot-guns. They wore trench helmets and some American Legion caps. One man leaned in the window, and the warm smell of whisky preceded him.

'Where you think you're goin'?' He thrust a red face near to Tom's face.

Tom stiffened. His hand crept down to the floor and felt for the jack handle. Ma caught his arm and held it powerfully. Tom said: 'Well–' and then his voice took on a servile whine. 'We're strangers here,' he said. 'We heard about they's work in a place called Tulare.'

'Well, goddamn it, you're goin' the wrong way. We ain't gonna have no goddamn Okies in this town.'

Tom's shoulders and arms were rigid, and a shiver went through him. Ma clung to his arm. The front of the truck was surrounded by the armed men. Some of them, to make a military appearance, wore tunics and Sam Browne belts.

Tom whined: 'Which way is it at, mister?'

'You turn right around an' head north. An' don't come back till the cotton's ready.'

Tom shivered all over. 'Yes, sir,' he said. He put the car in reverse, backed around and turned. He headed back the way he had come. Ma released his arm and patted him softly. And Tom tried to restrain his hard smothered sobbing.

'Don' you mind,' Ma said. 'Don' you mind.'

Tom blew his nose out the window and wiped his eyes on his sleeve. 'The sons-of-bitches–'

'You done good,' Ma said tenderly. 'You done jus' good.'

Tom swerved into a side dirt road, ran a hundred yards, and turned off his lights and motor. He got out of the car, carrying the jack handle.

'Where you goin'?' Ma demanded.

'Jus' gonna look. We ain't goin' north.' The red lanterns moved up the highway. Tom watched them cross the entrance of the dirt road and continue on. In a few moments there came the sounds of shouts and screams, and then a flaring light arose from the direction of the Hooverville. The light grew and spread, and from the distance came a crackling sound. Tom got in the truck again. He turned around and ran up the dirt road without lights. At the highway he turned south again, and he turned on his lights.

Ma asked timidly: 'Where we goin', Tom?'

'Goin' south,' he said. 'We couldn' let them bastards push us aroun'. We couldn'. Try to get aroun' the town 'thout goin' through it.'

'Yeah, but where we goin'?' Pa spoke for the first time. 'That's what I want ta know.'

'Gonna look for that gov'ment camp,' Tom said. 'A fella said they don' let no deputies in there. Ma–I got to get away from 'em. I'm scairt I'll kill one.'

'Easy, Tom,' Ma soothed him. 'Easy, Tommy. You done good once. You can do it again.'

'Yeah, an' after a while I won't have no decency lef'.'

'Easy,' she said. 'You got to have patience. Why, Tom–us people will go on livin' when all them people is gone. Why, Tom, we're the people that live. They ain't gonna wipe us out. Why, we're the people–we go on.'

'We take a beatin' all the time.'

'I know.' Ma chuckled. 'Maybe that makes us tough. Rich fellas come up an' they die, an' their kids ain't no good, an' they die out. But, Tom, we keep 'a-comin'. Don' you fret none, Tom. A different time's comin'.'

'How do you know?'

'I don' know how.'

They entered the town and Tom turned down a side street to avoid the centre. By the street lights he looked at his mother. Her face was quiet and a curious look was in her eyes, eyes like the timeless eyes of a statue. Tom put out his right hand and touched her on the shoulder. He had to. And then he withdrew his hand. 'Never heard you talk so much in my life,' he said.

'Wasn't never so much reason,' she said.

He drove through the side streets and cleared the town, and then he crossed back. At an intersection the sign said '99'. He turned south on it.

'Well, anyways they never shoved us north,' he said. 'We still go where we want, even if we got to crawl for the right.'

The dim lights felt along the broad black highway ahead.

21

The moving, questing people were migrants now. Those families which had lived on a little piece of land, who had lived and died on forty acres, had eaten or starved on the produce of forty acres, had now the whole West to rove in. And they scampered about, looking for work; and the highways were streams of people, and the ditch banks were lines of people. Behind them more were coming. The great highways streamed with moving people. There in the Middle- and South-west had lived a simple agrarian folk who had not changed with industry, who had not farmed with machines or known the power and danger of machines in private hands. They had not grown up in the paradoxes of industry. Their senses were still sharp to the ridiculousness of the industrial life.

And then suddenly the machines pushed them out and they swarmed on the highways. The movement changed them; the highways, the camps along the road, the fear of hunger and the hunger itself, changed them. The children without dinner changed them, the endless moving changed them. They were migrants. And the hostility changed them, welded them, united them–hostility that made the little town group and arm as though to repel an invader, squads with pick-handles, clerks and storekeepers with shotguns, guarding the world against their own people.

In the West there was panic when the migrants multiplied on the highways. Men of property were terrified for their property. Men who had never been hungry saw the eyes of the hungry. Men who had never wanted anything very much saw the flare of want in the eyes of the migrants. And the men of the towns and of the soft suburban country gathered to defend themselves; and they reassured themselves that they were good and the invaders bad, as a man must do before he fights. They said: These goddamned Okies are dirty and ignorant. They're degenerate, sexual maniacs. These goddamned Okies are thieves. They'll steal anything. They've got no sense of property rights.

And the latter was true, for how can a man without property know the ache of ownership? And the defending people said: They bring disease, they're filthy. We can't have them in the schools. They're strangers. How'd you like to have your sister to out with one of 'em?

The local people whipped themselves into a mould of cruelty. Then they formed units, squads, and armed them–armed them with clubs, with gas, with guns. We own the country. We can't let these Okies get out of hand. And the men who were armed did not own the land, but they thought they did. And the clerks who drilled at night owned nothing, and the little storekeepers possessed only a drawerful of debts. But even a debt is something, even a job is something. The clerk thought: I get fifteen dollars a week. S'pose a goddamn Okie would work for twelve? And the little storekeeper thought: How could I compete with a debtless man?

And the migrants streamed in on the highways and their hunger was in their eyes, and their need was in their eyes. They had no argument, no system, nothing but their numbers and their needs. When there was work for a man, ten men fought for it–fought with a low wage. If that fella'll work for thirty cents, I'll work for twenty-five.

If he'll take twenty-five. I'll do it for twenty.

No, me, I'm hungry. I'll work for fifteen. I'll work for food. The kids. You ought to see them. Little boils, like, comin' out, an' they can't run aroun'. Give 'em some windfall fruit, an' they bloated up. Me, I'll work for a little piece of meat.

And this was good, for wages went down and prices stayed up. The great owners were glad and they sent out more handbills to bring more people in. And wages went down and prices stayed up. And pretty soon now we'll have serfs again.

And now the great owners and the companies invented a new method. A great owner bought a cannery. And when the peaches and the pears were ripe he cut the price of fruit below the cost of raising it. And as cannery owner he paid himself a low price for the fruit and kept the price of canned goods up and took his profit. And the little farmers who owned no canneries lost their farms, and they were taken by the great owners, the banks, and the companies who also owned the canneries. As time went on, there were fewer farms. The little farmers moved into town for a while and exhausted their credit, exhausted their friends, their relatives. And then they, too, went on the highways. And the roads were crowded with men ravenous for work, murderous for work.

And the companies, the banks worked at their own doom and they did not know it. The fields were fruitful, and starving men moved on the roads. The granaries were full and the children of the poor grew up rachitic, and the pustules of pellagra swelled on their sides. The great companies did not know that the line between hunger and anger is a thin line. And money that might have gone to wages went for gas, for guns, for agents and spies, for blacklists, for drilling. On the highways the people moved like ants and searched for work, for food. And the anger began to ferment.

22

It was late when Tom Joad drove along a country road looking for the Weedpatch camp. There were few lights in the countryside. Only a sky glare behind showed the direction of Bakersfield. The truck jiggled slowly along and hunting cats left the road ahead of it. At a cross-road there was a little cluster of white wooden buildings.

Ma was sleeping in the seat and Pa had been silent and withdrawn for a long time.

Tom said: 'I don't know where she is. Maybe we'll wait till daylight an' ast somebody.' He stopped at a boulevard signal and another car stopped at the crossing. Tom leaned out. 'Hey, mister. Know where the big camp is at?'

'Straight ahead.'

Tom pulled across into the opposite road. A few hundred yards, and then he stopped. A high wire fence faced the road, and a wide-gated driveway turned in. A little way inside the gate there was a small house with a light in the window. Tom turned in. The whole truck leaped into the air and crashed down again.

'Jesus!' Tom said. 'I didn' even see that hump.'

A watchman stood up from the porch and walked to the car. He leaned on the side. 'You hit her too fast,' he said. 'Next time you'll take it easy.'

'What is it, for God's sake?'

The watchman laughed. 'Well, a lot of kids play in here. You tell folks to go slow and they're liable to forget. But let 'em hit that hump once and they don't forget.'

'Oh! Yeah. Hope I didn' break nothin'. Say–you got any room here for us?'

'Got one camp. How many of you?'

Tom counted on his fingers. 'Me an' Pa an' Ma, Al an' Rosasharn an' Uncle John an' Ruthie an' Winfiel'. Them last is kids.'

'Well, I guess we can fix you. Got any camping stuff?'

'Got a big tarp an' beds.'

The watchman stepped up on the running-board. 'Drive down the end of that line an' turn right. You'll be in Number Four Sanitary Unit.'

'What's that?'

'Toilets and showers and wash-tubs.'

Ma demanded: 'You got wash-tubs–running water?'

'Sure.'

'Oh! Praise God,' said Ma.

Tom drove down the long dark row of tents. In the sanitary building a low light burned. 'Pull in here,' the watchman said. 'It's a nice place. Folks that had it just moved out.'

Tom stopped the car. 'Right there?'

'Yeah. Now you let the others unload while I sign you up. Get to sleep. The camp committee'll call on you in the morning and get you fixed up.'

Tom's eyes drew down. 'Cops?' he asked.

The watchman laughed. 'No cops. We got our own cops. Folks here elect their own cops. Come along.'

Al dropped off the truck and walked around. 'Gonna stay here?'

'Yeah,' said Tom. 'You an' Pa unload while I go to the office.'

'Be kinda quiet,' the watchman said. 'They's a lot of folks sleeping.'

Tom followed through the dark and climbed the office steps and entered a tiny room containing an old desk and a chair. The guard sat down at the desk and took out a form.

'Name?'

'Tom Joad.'

'That your father?'

'Yeah.'

'His name?'

'Tom Joad, too.'

The questions went on. Where from, how long in the State, what work done.

The watchman looked up. 'I'm not nosy. We got to have this stuff.'

'Sure,' said Tom.

'Now–got any money?'

'Little bit.'

'You ain't destitute?'

'Got a little. Why?'

'Well, the camp site costs a dollar a week, but you can work it out, carrying garbage, keeping the camp clean–stuff like that.'

'We'll work it out,' said Tom.

'You'll see the committee tomorrow. They'll show you how to use the camp and tell you the rules.'

Tom said: 'Say–what is this? What committee is this, anyways?'

The watchman settled himself back. 'Works pretty nice. There's five sanitary units. Each one elects a Central Committee man. Now that committee makes the laws. What they say goes.'

'S'pose they get tough,' Tom said.

'Well, you can vote 'em out jus' as quick as you vote 'em in. They've done a fine job. Tell you what they did–you know the Holy Roller preachers all the time follow the people around, preachin' an' taking up collections? Well, they wanted to preach in this camp. And a lot of the older folks wanted them. So it was up to the Central Committee. They went into meeting and here's how they fixed it. They say: "Any preacher can preach in this camp. Nobody can take up a collection in this camp." And it was kinda sad for the old folks, 'cause there hasn't been a preacher in since.'

Tom laughed and then he asked: 'You mean to say the fellas that runs the camp is jus' fellas–campin' here?'

'Sure. And it works.'

'You said about cops–'

'Central Committee keeps order an' makes rules. Then there's the ladies. They'll call on your ma. They keep care of kids an' look after the sanitary units. If you ma isn't working, she'll look after kids for the ones that is working, an' when she gets a job–why, there'll be others. They sew, and a nurse comes out an' teaches 'em. All kinds of things like that.'

'You mean to say they ain't no cops?'

'No, sir. No cop can come in here without a warrant.'

'Well, s'pose a fella is jus' mean, or drunk an' quarrelsome. What then?'

The watchman stabbed the blotter with a pencil. 'Well, the first time the Central Committee warns him. And the second time they really warn him. The third time they kick him out of the camp.'

'God Almighty, I can't hardly believe it! Tonight the deputies an' them fellas with the little caps, they burned the camp out by the river.'

'They don't get in here,' the watchman said. 'Some nights the boys patrol the fences, 'specially dance nights.'

'Dance nights? Jesus Christ!'

'We got the best dances in the county every Saturday night.'

'Well, for Christ's sake! Why ain't they more places like this?'

The watchman looked sullen. 'You'll have to find that out yourself. Go get some sleep.'

'Good night,' said Tom. 'Ma's gonna like this place. She ain't been treated decent for a long time.'

'Good night,' the watchman said. 'Get some sleep. This camp wakes early.'

Tom walked down the street between the rows of tents. His eyes grew used to the starlight. He saw that the rows were straight and that there was no litter about the tents. The ground of the street had been swept and sprinkled. From the tents came the snores of sleeping people. The whole camp buzzed and snorted. Tom walked slowly. He neared Number Four Sanitary Unit and he looked at it curiously, an unpainted building, low and rough. Under a roof, but open at the sides, the rows of wash trays. He saw the Joad truck standing near by, and went quietly toward it. The tarpaulin was pitched and the camp was quiet. As he drew near a figure moved from the shadow of the truck and came toward him.

Ma said softly: 'That you, Tom?'

'Yeah.'

'Sh!' she said. 'They're all asleep. They was tar'd out.'

'You ought to be asleep, too,' Tom said.

'Well, I wanted to see ya. Is it awright?'

'It's nice,' Tom said. 'I ain't gonna tell ya. They'll tell ya in the mornin'. Ya gonna like it.'

She whispered: 'I heard they got hot water.'

'Yeah. Now you get to sleep. I don' know when you slep' las'.'

She begged: 'What ain't you a-gonna tell me?'

'I ain't. You get to sleep.'

Suddenly she seemed girlish. 'How can I sleep if I got to think about what you ain't gonna tell me?'

'No, you don't,' Tom said. 'First thing in the mornin' you get on your other dress an' then–you'll find out.'

'I can't sleep with nothin' like that hangin' over me.'

'You got to,' Tom chuckled happily. 'You jus' got to.'

'Good night,' she said softly; and she bent down and slipped under the dark tarpaulin.

Tom climbed up over the tail-board of the truck. He lay down on his back on the wooden floor and he pillowed his head on his crossed hands, and his forearms pressed against his ears. The night grew cooler. Tom buttoned his coat over his chest and settled back again. The stars were clear and sharp over his head.

It was still dark when he awakened. A small clashing noise brought him up from sleep. Tom listened and heard again the squeak of iron on iron. He moved stiffly and shivered in the morning air. The camp still slept. Tom stood up and looked over the side of the truck. The eastern mountains were blue-black, and as he watched, the light stood up faintly behind them, coloured at the mountain rims with a washed red, then growing colder, greyer, darker, as it went up overhead, until at a place near the western horizon it merged with pure night. Down in the valley the earth was the lavender-grey of dawn.

The clash of iron sounded again. Tom looked down the line of tents, only a little lighter grey than the ground. Beside a tent he saw a flash of orange fire seeping from the cracks in an old iron stove. Grey smoke spurted up from a stubby smoke-pipe.

Tom climbed over the truck side and dropped to the ground. He moved slowly toward the stove. He saw a girl working about the stove, saw that she carried a baby on her crooked arm, and that the baby was nursing, its head up under the girl's shirtwaist. And the girl moved about, poking the fire, shifting the rusty stove lids to make a better draught, opening the oven door; and all the time the baby sucked, and the mother shifted it deftly from arm to arm. The baby didn't interfere with her work or with the quick gracefulness of her movements. And the orange fire licked out of the stove cracks and threw flickering reflections on the tent.

Tom moved closer. He smelled frying bacon and baking bread. From the east the light grew swiftly. Tom came near to the stove and stretched out his hands to it. The girl looked at him and nodded, so that her two braids jerked.

'Good mornin',' she said, and she turned the bacon in the pan.

The tent flap jerked up and a young man came out and an older man followed him. They were dressed in new blue dungarees and in dungaree coats, stiff with filler, the brass buttons shining. They were sharp-faced men, and they looked much alike. The younger man had a dark stubble beard and the older man a white stubble beard. Their heads and faces were wet, their hair dripped, water stood in drops on their stiff beards. Their cheeks shone with dampness. Together they stood looking quietly into the lightening east. They yawned together and watched the light on the hill rims. And then they turned and saw Tom.

''Mornin',' the older man said, and his face was neither friendly nor unfriendly.

''Mornin',' said Tom.

And ''Mornin',' said the younger man.

The water slowly dried on their faces. They came to the stove and warmed their hands at it.

The girl kept to her work. Once she set the baby down and tied her braids together at the back with a string, and the two braids jerked and swung as she worked. She set tin cups on a big packing-box, set tin plates and knives and forks out. Then she scooped bacon from the deep grease and laid it on a tin platter, and the bacon cricked and rustled as it grew crisp. She opened the rusty oven door and took out a square pan full of big high biscuits.

When the smell of the biscuits struck the air both of the men inhaled deeply. The younger said: 'Kee-rist!' softly.

Now the older man said to Tom: 'Had your breakfast?'

'Well, no, I ain't. But my folks is over there. They ain't up. Need the sleep.'

'Well, set down with us, then. We got plenty–thank God!'

'Why, thank ya,' Tom said. 'Smells so darn good I couldn' say no.'

'Don't she?' the younger man asked. 'Ever smell anything so good in ya life?' They marched to the packing-box and squatted around it.

'Workin' around here?' the young man asked.

'Aim to,' said Tom. 'We jus' got in las' night. Ain't had no chance to look aroun'.'

'We had twelve days' work,' the young man said.

The girl, working by the stove, said: 'They even got new clothes.' Both men looked down at their stiff blue clothes, and they smiled a little shyly. The girl set out the platter of bacon and the brown, high biscuits and a bowl of bacon gravy and a pot of coffee, and then she squatted down by the box too. The baby still nursed, its head up under the girl's shirtwaist.

They filled their plates, poured bacon gravy over the biscuits, and sugared their coffee.

The older man filled his mouth full, and he chewed and chewed and gulped and swallowed. 'God Almighty, it's good!' he said, and he filled his mouth again.

The younger man said: 'We been eatin' good for twelve days now. Never missed a meal in twelve days–none of us. Workin' an' gettin' our pay an' eatin'.' He fell to again, almost frantically, and refilled his plate. They drank the scalding coffee and threw the grounds to the earth and filled their cups again.

There was colour in the light now, a reddish gleam. The father and son stopped eating. They were facing to the east and their faces were lighted by the dawn. The image of the mountain and the light coming over it were reflected in their eyes. And then they threw the grounds from their cups to the earth, and they stood up together.

'Got to git goin',' the older man said.

The younger man turned to Tom. 'Lookie,' he said. 'We're layin' some pipe. 'F you want to walk over with us, maybe we could get you on.'

Tom said: 'Well, that's mighty nice of you. An' I sure thank ya for the breakfast.'

'Glad to have you,' the older man said. 'We'll try to git you workin' if you want.'

'Ya goddamn right I want,' Tom said. 'Jus' wait a minute. I'll tell my folks.' He hurried to the Joad tent and bent over and looked inside. In the gloom under the tarpaulin he saw lumps of sleeping figures. But a little movement started among the bed-clothes. Ruthie came wriggling out like a snake, her hair down over her eyes and her dress wrinkled and twisted. She crawled carefully out and stood up. Her grey eyes were clear and calm from sleep, and mischief was not in them. Tom moved off from the tent and beckoned her to follow, and when he turned, she looked up at him.

'Lord God, you're growin' up,' he said.

She looked away in sudden embarrassment. 'Listen here,' Tom said. 'Don't you wake nobody up, but when they get up, you tell 'em I got a chancet at a job, an' I'm a-goin' for it. Tell Ma I et breakfas' with some neighbours. You hear that?'

Ruthie nodded and turned her head away, and her eyes were little girl's eyes. 'Don't you wake 'em up,' Tom cautioned. He hurried back to his new friends. And Ruthie cautiously approached the sanitary unit and peeked in the doorway.

The two men were waiting when Tom came back. The young woman had dragged a mattress out and put the baby on it while she cleaned up the dishes.

Tom said: 'I wanted to tell my folks where-at I was. They wasn't awake.' The three walked down the street between the tents.

The camp had begun to come to life. At the new fires the women worked, slicing meat, kneading the dough for the morning's bread. And the men were stirring about the tents and about the automobiles. The sky was rosy now. In front of the office a lean old man raked the ground carefully. He so dragged his rake that the tiny marks were straight and deep.

'You're out early, Pa,' the young man said as they went by.

'Yep, yep. Got to make up my rent.'

'Rent, hell!' the young man said. 'He was drunk last Sat'dy night. Sung in his tent all night. Committee give him work for it.' They walked along the edge of the oiled road; a row of walnut trees grew beside the way. The sun shoved its edge over the mountains.

Tom said: 'Seems funny. I've et your food, an' I ain't tol' you my name–nor you ain't mentioned yours. I'm Tom Joad.'

The older man looked at him, and then he smiled a little. 'You ain't been out here long?'

'Hell, no! Jus' a couple days.'

'I knowed it. Funny, you git outa the habit a mentionin' your name. They's so goddamn many. Jist fella. Well, sir–I'm Timothy Wallace, an' this here's my boy, Wilkie.'

'Proud to know ya,' Tom said. 'You been out here long?'

'Ten months,' Wilkie said. 'Got here right on the tail a the floods las' year. Jesus! We had *a* time, *a* time! Goddamn near starve' to death.' Their feet rattled on the oiled road. A truckload of men went by, and each man was sunk into himself. Each man braced himself in the truck bed and scowled down.

'Goin' out for the Gas Company,' Timothy said. 'They got a nice job of it.'

'I could of took our truck,' Tom suggested.

'No.' Timothy leaned down and picked up a green walnut. He tested it with his thumb and then shied it at a blackbird sitting on a fence wire. The bird flew up, let the nut sail under it, and then settled back on the wire and smoothed its shining black feathers with its beak.

Tom asked: 'Ain't you got no car?'

Both Wallaces were silent, and Tom, looking at their faces, saw that they were ashamed.

Wilkie said: 'Place we work at is on'y a mile up the road.'

Timothy replied angrily: 'No, we ain't got no car. We sol' our car. Had to. Run outa food, run outa ever'thing. Couldn' git no job. Fellas come aroun' ever' week, buyin' cars. Come aroun' an' if you're hungry, why, they'll buy your car. An' if you're hungry enough, they don't hafta pay nothin' for it. An'–we was hungry enough. Give us ten dollars for her.' He spat into the road.

Wilkie said quietly: 'I was in Bakersfiel' las' week. I seen her–a-settin' in a use'-car lot–settin' right there, an' seventy-five dollars was the sign on her.'

'We had to,' Timothy said. 'It was either us let 'em steal our car or us steal somepin from them. We ain't had to steal yet, but, goddamn it, we been close!'

Tom said: 'You know, 'fore we lef' home, we heard they was plenty of work out here. Seen han'bills askin' folks to come out.'

'Yeah,' Timothy said. 'We seen' em too. An' they ain't much work. An' wages is comin' down all a time. I git so goddamn tired jus' figgerin' how to eat.'

'You got work now,' Tom suggested.

'Yeah, but it ain't gonna las' long. Workin' for a nice fella. Got a little place. Works 'longside of us. But, hell–it ain't gonna las' on time.'

Tom said: 'Why in hell you gonna git me on? I'll make it shorter. What you cuttin' your own throat for?'

Timothy shook his head slowly. 'I dunno. Got no sense, I guess. We figgered to get us each a hat. Can't do it, I guess. There's the place, off to the right there. Nice job, too. Gettin' thirty cents an hour. Nice frien'ly fella to work for.'

They turned off the highway and walked down a gravelled road, through a small kitchen orchard; and behind the trees they came to a small white farmhouse, a few shade trees, and a barn; behind a barn a vineyard and field of cotton. As the three men walked past the house a screen door banged, and a stocky sunburned man came down the steps. He wore a paper sun helmet, and he rolled up his sleeves as he came across the yard. His heavy sunburned eyebrows were drawn down in a scowl. His cheeks were sunburned a beef red.

''Mornin' Mr Thomas,' Timothy said.

''Morning.' The man spoke irritably.

Timothy said: 'This here's Tom Joad. We wondered if you could see your way to put him on?'

Thomas scowled at Tom. And then he laughed shortly, and his brows still scowled. 'Oh, sure! I'll put him on. I'll put everybody on. Maybe I'll get a hundred men on.'

'We jus' thought–' Timothy began apologetically.

Thomas interrupted him. 'Yes, I been thinkin' too.' He swung around and faced them. 'I've got some things to tell you. I been paying you thirty cents an hour–that right?'

'Why, sure–but, Mr Thomas–'

'And I been getting thirty cents' worth of work.' His heavy hard hands clasped each other.

'We try to give a good day of work.'

'Well, goddamn it, this morning you're getting twenty-five cents an hour, and you take it or leave it.' The redness of his face deepened with anger.

Timothy said: 'We've give you good work. You said so yourself.'

'I know it. But it seems like I ain't hiring my own men any more.' He swallowed. 'Look,' he said. 'I got sixty-five acres here. Did you ever hear of the Farmers' Association?'

'Why, sure.'

'Well, I belong to it. We had a meeting last night. Now, do you know who runs the Farmers' Association? I'll tell you. The Bank of the West. That bank owns most of this valley, and it's got paper on everything it don't own. So last night the member from the bank told me, he said: "You're paying thirty cents an hour. You'd better cut it down to twenty-five." I said: "I've got good men. They're worth thirty." And he says: "It isn't that," he says. "The wage is twenty-five now. If you pay thirty, it'll only cause unrest. And by the way," he says, "you going to need the usual amount for a crop loan next year?"' Thomas stopped. His breath was panting through his lips. 'You see? The rate is twenty-five cents–and like it.'

'We done good work,' Timothy said helplessly.

'Ain't you got it yet? Mr Bank hires two thousand men an' I hire three. I've got paper to meet. Now if you can figure some way out, by Christ, I'll take it! They got me.'

Timothy shook his head. 'I don' know what to say.'

'You wait here.' Thomas walked quickly to the house. The door slammed after him. In a moment he was back, and he carried a newspaper in his hand. 'Did you see this? Here, I'll read it: "Citizens, angered at red agitators, burn squatters' camp. Last night a band of citizens, infuriated at the agitation going on in a local squatters' camp, burned the tents to the ground and warned agitators to get out of the country."'

Tom began: 'Why, I–' and then he closed his mouth and was silent.

Thomas folded the paper carefully and put it in his pocket. He had himself in control again. He said quietly: 'Those men were sent out by the Association. Now I'm giving 'em away. And if they ever find out I told, I won't have a farm next year.'

'I jus' don't know what to say,' Timothy said. 'If they was agitators, I can see why they was mad.'

Thomas said: 'I watched it a long time. There's always red agitators just before a pay cut. Always. Goddamn it, they got me trapped. Now, what are you going to do? Twenty-five cents?'

Timothy look at the ground. 'I'll work,' he said.

'Me, too,' said Wilkie.

Tom said: 'Seems like I walked into somepin. Sure, I'll work. I got to work.'

Thomas pulled a bandana out of his hip pocket and wiped his mouth and chin. 'I don't know how long it can go on. I don't know how you men can feed a family on what you get now.'

'We can while we work,' Wilkie said. 'It's when we don't git work.'

Thomas looked at his watch. 'Well, let's go out and dig some ditch. By God,' he said, 'I'm a-gonna tell you. You fellas live in that government camp, don't you?'

Timothy stiffened. 'Yes, sir.'

'And you have dances every Saturday night?'

Wilkie smiled, 'We sure do.'

'Well, look out next Saturday night.'

Suddenly Timothy straightened. He stepped close. 'What you mean? I belong to the Central Committee. I got to know.'

Thomas looked apprehensive. 'Don't you ever tell I told.'

'What is it?' Timothy demanded.

'Well, the Association don't like the government camps. Can't get a deputy in there. The people make their own laws, I hear, and you can't arrest a man without a warrant. Now if there was a big fight and maybe shooting–a bunch of deputies could go in and clean out the camp.'

Timothy had changed. His shoulders were straight and his eyes cold. 'What you mean?'

'Don't you ever tell where you heard,' Thomas said uneasily. 'There's going to be a fight in the camp Saturday night. And there's going to be deputies ready to go in.'

Tom demanded: 'Why, for God's sake? Those folks ain't bothering nobody.'

'I'll tell you why,' Thomas said. 'Those folks in the camp are getting used to being treated like humans. When they go back to the squatters' camps they'll be hard to handle.' He wiped his face again. 'Go on out to work now. Jesus, I hope I haven't talked myself out of my farm. But I like you people.'

Timothy stepped in front of him and put out a hard lean hand, and Thomas took it. 'Nobody won't know who tol'. We thank you. They won't be no fight.'

'Go on to work,' Thomas said. 'And it's twenty-five cents an hour.'

'We'll take it,' Wilkie said, 'from you.'

Thomas walked away toward the house. 'I'll be out in a piece,' he said. 'You men get to work.' The screen door slammed behind him.

The three men walked out past the little whitewashed barn, and along a field edge. They came to a long narrow ditch with sections of concrete pipe lying beside it.

'Here's where we're workin',' Wilkie said.

His father opened the barn and passed out two picks and three shovels. And he said to Tom: 'Here's your beauty.'

Tom hefted the pick. 'Jumping Jesus! If she don't feel good!'

'Wait'll about 'leven o'clock,' Wilkie suggested. 'See how good she feels then.'

They walked to the end of the ditch. Tom took off his coat and dropped it on the dirt pile. He pushed up his cap and stepped into the ditch. Then he spat on his hands. The picks arose into the air and flashed down. Tom grunted softly. The pick rose and fell, and the grunt came at the moment it sank into the ground and loosened the soil.

Wilkie said: 'Yes, sir, Pa, we got here a first-grade muck-stick man. This here boy been married to that there little digger.'

Tom said: 'I put in time (*umph*). Yes, sir, I sure did (*umph*). Put in my years (*umph*). Kinda like the feel (*umph*).' The soil loosened ahead of him. The sun cleared the fruit trees now and the grape leaves were golden green on the vines. Six feet long and Tom stepped aside and wiped his forehead. Wilkie came behind him. The shovel rose and fell and the dirt flew out to the pile beside the lengthening ditch.

'I heard about this here Central Committee,' said Tom. 'So you're one of 'em.'

'Yes, sir,' Timothy replied. 'And it's a responsibility. All them people. We're doin' our best. An' the people in the camp a-doin' their best. I wisht them big farmers wouldn't plague us so. I wisht they wouldn'.'

Tom climbed back into the ditch and Wilkie stood aside. Tom said: 'How 'bout this fight (*umph*) at the dance, he tol' about (*umph*)? What they wanta do that for?'

Timothy followed behind Wilkie, and Timothy's shovel bevelled the bottom of the ditch and smoothed it ready for the pipe. 'Seems like they got to drive us,' Timothy said. 'They're scairt we'll organize, I guess. An' maybe they're right. This here camp is an organization. People there look out of theirselves. Got the nicest string band in these parts. Got a little charge account in the store for folks that's hungry. Fi' dollars–you can git that much food an' the camp'll stan' good. We ain't never had no trouble with the law. I guess the big farmers is scairt of that. Can't throw us in jail–why, it scares 'em. Figger maybe if we can gove'n ourselves, maybe we'll do other things.'

Tom stepped clear of the ditch and wiped the sweat out of his eyes. 'You hear what that paper said 'bout agitators up north a Bakersfiel'?'

'Sure,' said Wilkie. 'They do that all a time.'

'Well, I was there. They wasn't no agitators. What they call reds. What the hell is these reds anyways?'

Timothy scraped a little hill level in the bottom of the ditch. The sun made his white bristle beard shine. 'They's a lot of fellas wanta know what reds is.' He laughed. 'One of our boys foun' out.' He patted the piled earth gently with his shovel. 'Fella named Hines–got 'bout thirty thousan' acres, peaches and grapes–got a cannery an' a winery. Well, he's all a time talkin' about "them goddamn reds." "Goddamn reds is drivin' the country to ruin," he says, an' "We got to drive these here red bastards out." Well, they were a young fella jus' come out west here, an' he's listenin' one day. He kinda scratched his head an' he says: "Mr Hines, I ain't been here long. What is these goddamn reds?" Well, sir, Hines says: "A red is any son-of-a-bitch that wants thirty cents an hour when we're payin' twenty-five!" Well, this young fella he thinks about her, an' he scratches his head, an' he says: "Well, Jesus, Mr Hines. I ain't a son-of-a-bitch, but if that's what a red is–why, I want thirty cents an hour. Ever'body does. Hell, Mr Hines, we're all reds."' Timothy drove his shovel along the ditch bottom, and the solid earth shone where the shovel cut it.

Tom laughed. 'Me too, I guess,' His pick arced up and drove down, and the earth cracked under it. The sweat rolled down his forehead and down the sides of his nose, and it glistened on his neck. 'Damn it,' he said, 'a pick is a nice tool (*umph*), if you don' fight it (*umph*). You an' the pick (*umph*) workin' together (*umph*).'

In line, the three men worked, and the ditch inched along and the sun shone hotly down on them in the growing morning.

When Tom left her, Ruthie gazed in at the door of the sanitary unit for a while. Her courage was not strong without Winfield to boast to. She put a bare foot in on the concrete floor, and then withdrew it. Down the line a woman came out of a tent and started a fire in a tin camp-stove. Ruthie took a few steps in that direction, but she could not leave. She crept to the entrance of the Joad tent and looked in. On one side, lying on the ground, lay Uncle John, his mouth open and his snores bubbling spittily in his throat. Ma and Pa were covered with a comforter, their heads in, away from the light. Al was on the far side from Uncle John, and his arm was flung over his eyes. Near the front of the tent Rose of Sharon and Winfield lay, and there was the space where Ruthie had been, beside Winfield. She squatted down and peered in. Her eyes remained on Winfield's tow head; and as she looked, the little boy opened his eyes and stared out at her, and his eyes were solemn. Ruthie put her finger to her lips and beckoned with her other hand. Winfield rolled his eyes over to Rose of Sharon. Her pink flushed face was near to him, and her mouth was open a little. Winfield carefully loosened the blanket and slipped out. He crept out of the tent cautiously and joined Ruthie. 'How long you been up?' he whispered.

She led him away with elaborate caution and when they were safe she said: 'I never been to bed. I was up all night.'

'You was not,' Winfield said. 'You're a dirty liar.'

'Awright,' she said. 'If I'm a liar I ain't gonna tell you nothin' that happened. I ain't gonna tell how the fella got killed with a stab knife an' how they was a bear come in an' took off a little chile.'

'They wasn't no bear,' Winfield said uneasily. He brushed up his hair with his fingers and he pulled down his overalls at the crotch.

'All right–they wasn't no bear,' she said sarcastically. 'An' they ain't no white things made outa dis-stuff, like in the catalogues.'

Winfield regarded her gravely. He pointed to the sanitary unit. 'In there?' he asked.

'I'm a dirty liar,' Ruthie said. 'It ain't gonna do me no good to tell stuff to you.'

'Le's go look,' Winfield said.

'I already been,' Ruthie said. 'I already set on 'em. I even pee'd in one.'

'You never neither,' said Winfield.

They went to the unit building, and that time Ruthie was not afraid. Boldly she led the way into the building. The toilets lined one side of the large room, and each toilet had its compartment with a door in front of it. The porcelain was gleaming white. Hand basins lined another wall, while on the third wall were four shower compartments.

'There,' said Ruthie. 'Them's the toilets. I seen 'em in the catalogue.' The children drew near to one of the toilets. Ruthie, in a burst of bravado, boosted her skirt and sat down. 'I tol' you I been here,' she said. And to prove it, there was a tinkle of water in the bowl.

Winfield was embarrassed. His hand twisted the flushing lever. There was a roar of water. Ruthie leaped into the air and jumped away. She and Winfield stood in the middle of the room and looked inside the toilet. The hiss of water continued in it.

'You done it,' Ruthie said. 'You went an' broke it. I seen you.'

'I never. Honest I never.'

'I seen you,' Ruthie said. 'You jus' ain't to be trusted with no nice stuff.'

Winfield sunk his chin. He looked up at Ruthie and his eyes filled with tears. His chin quivered. And Ruthie was instantly contrite.

'Never you mind,' she said. 'I won't tell on you. We'll pretend like she was already broke. We'll pretend we ain't even been in here.' She led him out of the building.

The sun lipped over the mountain by now, shone on the corrugated-iron roofs of the five sanitary units, shone on the grey tents and on the swept ground of the streets between the tents. And the camp was waking up. The fires were burning in camp-stoves, in the stoves made of kerosene cans and of sheets of metal. The smell of smoke was in the air. Tent flaps were thrown back and people moved about in the streets. In front of the Joad tent Ma stood looking up and down the street. She saw the children and came over to them.

'I was worryin',' Ma said. 'Didn't know where you was.'

'We was jus' lookin',' Ruthie said.

'Well, where's Tom? You seen him?'

Ruthie became important. 'Yes, ma'am. Tom he got me up an' he tol' me what to tell you.' She paused to let her importance be apparent.

'Well–what?' Ma demanded.

'He said tell you–' She paused again and looked to see that Winfield appreciated her position.

Ma raised her hand, the back of it toward Ruthie. 'What?'

'He got work,' said Ruthie quickly. 'Went out to work.' She looked apprehensively at Ma's raised hand. The hand sank down again, and then it reached out for Ruthie. Ma embraced Ruthie's shoulders in a quick hug, and then released her.

Ruthie stared at the ground in embarrassment, and changed the subject. 'They got toilets over there,' she said. 'White ones.'

'You been in there?' Ma demanded.

'Me an' Winfiel',' she said; and then, treacherously, 'Winfiel', he bust a toilet.'

Winfield turned red. He glared at Ruthie. 'She pee'd in one,' he said viciously.

Ma was apprehensive. 'Now what did you do? You show me.' She forced them to the door and inside. 'Now what'd you do?'

Ruthie pointed. 'It was a-hissin' and a-swishin'. Stopped now.'

'Show me what you done,' Ma demanded.

Winfield went reluctantly to the toilet. 'I didn' push it hard,' he said. 'I jus' had aholt of this here, an'–' The swish of water came again. He leaped away.

Ma threw her head back and laughed, while Ruthie and Winfield regarded her resentfully. 'Tha's the way she works,' Ma said, 'I seen them before. When you finish, you push that.'

The shame of their ignorance was too great for the children. They went out the door, and they walked down the street to stare at a large family eating breakfast.

Ma watched them out of the door. And then she looked about the room. She went to the shower closets and looked in. She walked to the wash-basins and ran her finger over the white porcelain. She turned the water on a little and held her finger in the stream, and jerked her hand away when the water came hot. For a moment she regarded the basin, and then, setting the plug, she filled a bowl a little from the hot faucet, a little from the cold. And then she washed her hands in the warm water, and she washed her face. She was brushing water through her hair with her fingers when a step sounded on the concrete floor behind her. Ma swung around. An elderly man stood looking at her with an expression of righteous shock.

He said harshly: 'How you come in here?'

Ma gulped, and she felt the water dripping from her chin and soaking through her dress. 'I didn't know,' she said apologetically. 'I thought this here was for folks to use.'

The elderly man frowned on her. 'For men folks,' he said sternly. He walked to the door and pointed to a sign on it : MEN. 'There,' he said. 'That proves it. Didn' you see that?'

'No,' Ma said in shame, 'I never seen it. Ain't they a place where I can go?'

The man's anger departed. 'You jus' come?' he asked more kindly.

'Middle of the night,' said Ma.

'Then you ain't talked to the Committee?'

'What committee?'

'Why, the Ladies' Committee.'

'No, I ain't.'

He said proudly: 'The Committee'll call on you purty soon an' fix you up. We take care of folks that jus' come in. Now, if you want the ladies' toilet, you jus' go on the other side of the building. That side's yourn.'

Ma said uneasily: 'Ya say ladies' committee–comin' to my tent?'

He nodded his head. 'Purty soon, I guess.'

'Thank ya,' said Ma. She hurried out, and half ran to the tent.

'Pa,' she called. 'John, git up! You, Al. Git up an' git washed.' Startled sleepy eyes looked out at her. 'All of you,' Ma cried. 'You git up an' git your face washed. An' comb your hair.'

Uncle John looked pale and sick. There was a red bruised place on his chin.

Pa demanded: 'What's the matter?'

'The Committee,' Ma cried. 'They's a committee–a ladies' committee a-comin' to visit. Git up now, an' git washed. An' while we was a-sleepin' an' a-snorin', Tom's went out an' got work. Git up, now.'

They came sleepily out of the tent. Uncle John staggered a little, and his face was pained.

'Git over to that house and wash up,' Ma ordered. 'We got to get breakfas' an' be ready for the Committee.' She went to a little pile of split wood in the camp lot. She started a fire and put up her cooking irons. 'Pone,' she said to herself. 'Pone an' gravy. That's quick. Got to be quick.' She talked on to herself, and Ruthie and Winfield stood by, wondering.

The smoke of the morning fires arose all over the camp, and the mutter of talk came from all sides.

Rose of Sharon, unkempt and sleepy-eyed, crawled out of the tent. Ma turned from the cornmeal she was measuring in fistfuls. She looked at the girl's wrinkled and dirty dress, at her frizzled un-combed hair. 'You got to clean up,' she said briskly. 'Go right over and clean up. You got a clean dress. I washed it. Git you hair combed. Git the seeds out a your eyes.' Ma was excited.

Rose of Sharon said sullenly: 'I don' feel good. I wisht Connie would come. I don't feel like doin' nothin' 'thout Connie.'

Ma turned full around on her. The yellow cornmeal clung to her hands and wrists. 'Rosasharn,' she said sternly, 'you git upright. You jus' been mopin' enough. They's a ladies' committee a-comin', an' the fambly ain't gonna be frawny when they get here.'

'But I don' feel good.'

Ma advanced on her, mealy hands held out. 'Git,' Ma said. 'They's times when how you feel got to be kep' to yourself.'

'I'm a-goin' to vomit,' Rose of Sharon whined.

'Well, go an' vomit. 'Course you're gonna vomit. Ever'body does. Git it over an' then you clean up, an' you wash your legs an' put on them shoes of yourn.' She turned back to her work. 'An' braid your hair,' she said.

A frying-pan of grease sputtered over the fire, and it splashed and hissed when Ma dropped the pone in with a spoon. She mixed flour with grease in a kettle and added water and salt and stirred the gravy. The coffee began to turn over in the gallon can, and the smell of coffee rose from it.

Pa wandered back from the sanitary unit, and Ma looked critically up. Pa said: 'Ya say Tom's got work?'

'Yes, sir. Went out 'fore we was awake. Now look in that box an' get you some clean overalls an' a shirt. An', Pa, I'm awful busy. You git in Ruthie and Winfiel' ears. They's hot water. Will you do that? Scrounge aroun' in their ears good, an' their necks. Get 'em red an' shinin'.'

'Never seen you so bubbly,' Pa said.

Ma cried: 'This here's the time the fambly got to get decent. Comin' acrost they wasn't no chancet. But now we can. Th'ow your dirty overalls in the tent an' I'll wash 'em out.'

Pa went inside the tent, and in a moment he came out with pale blue, washed overalls and shirt on. And he led the sad and startled children toward the sanitary unit.

Ma called after him: 'Scrounge aroun' good in their ears.'

Uncle John came to the door of the men's side and looked out, and then he went back and sat on the toilet a long time and held his aching head in his hands.

Ma had taken up a panload of brown pone and was dropping spoons of dough in the grease for a second pan when a shadow fell on the ground beside her. She looked over her shoulder. A little man dressed all in white stood behind her–a man with a thin, brown, lined face and merry eyes. He was lean as a picket. His white clean clothes were frayed at the seams. He smiled at Ma. 'Good morning,' he said.

Ma looked at his white clothes and her face hardened with suspicion. ''Mornin',' she said.

'Are you Mrs Joad?'

'Yes.'

'Well, I'm Jim Rawley. I'm camp manager. Just dropped by to see if everything's all right. Got everything you need?'

Ma studied him suspiciously. 'Yes,' she said.

Rawley said: 'I was asleep when you came last night. Lucky we had a place for you.' His voice was warm.

Ma said simply: 'It's nice. 'Specially them wash-tubs.'

'You wait till the women get to washing. Pretty soon now. You never heard such a fuss. Like a meeting. Know what they did yesterday, Mrs Joad? They had a chorus. Singing a hymn tune and rubbing the clothes all in time. That was something to hear, I tell you.'

The suspicion was going out of Ma's face. 'Must a been nice. You're the boss?'

'No,' he said. 'The people here worked me out of a job. They keep the camp clean, they keep order, they do everything. I never saw such people. They're making clothes in the meeting hall. And they're making toys. Never saw such people.'

Ma looked down at her dirty dress. 'We ain't clean yet,' she said. 'You jus' can't keep clean a-travellin'.'

'Don't I know it,' he said. He sniffed the air. 'Say–is that your coffee smells so good?'

Ma smiled. 'Does smell nice, don't it? Outside it always smells nice.' And she said proudly: 'We'd take it in honour 'f you'd have some breakfus' with us.'

He came to the fire and squatted down on his hams, and the last of Ma's resistance went down. 'We'd be proud to have ya,' she said. 'We ain't got much that's nice, but you're welcome.'

The little man grinned at her. 'I had my breafast. But I'd sure like a cup of that coffee. Smells so good.'

'Why–why, sure.'

'Don't hurry yourself.'

Ma poured a tin cup of coffee from the gallon can. She said: 'We ain't got sugar yet. Maybe we'll get some to-day. If you need sugar, it won't taste good.'

'Never use sugar,' he said. 'Spoil the taste of good coffee.'

'Well, I like a little sugar,' said Ma. She looked at him suddenly and closely, to see how he had come so close so quickly. She looked for motive on his face, and found nothing but friendliness. Then she looked at the frayed seams on his white coat, and she was reassured.

He sipped the coffee. 'I guess the ladies'll be here to see you this morning.'

'We ain't clean,' Ma said. 'They shouldn't be comin' till we get cleaned up a little.'

'But they know how it is,' the manager said. 'They came in the same way. No, sir. The committee are good in this camp because they do know.' He finished his coffee and stood up. 'Well, I got to go on. Anything you want, why, come over to the office. I'm there all the time. Grand coffee. Thank you.' He put the cup on the box with the others, waved his hand, and walked down the line of tents. And Ma heard him speaking to the people as he went.

Ma put down her head and she fought with a desire to cry.

Pa came back leading the children, their eyes still set with pain at the ear-scrounging. They were subdued and shining. The sunburned skin on Winfield's nose was scrubbed off. 'There,' Pa said. 'Got dirt an' two layers of skin. Had to almost lick 'em to make 'em stan' still.'

Ma appraised them. 'They look nice,' she said. 'He'p yaself to pone an' gravy. We got to get stuff outa the way an' the tent in order.'

Pa served plates for the children and for himself. 'Wonder where Tom got work?'

'I dunno.'

'Well, if he can, we can.'

Al came excitedly to the tent. 'What a place!' he said. He helped himself and poured coffee. 'Know what a fella's doin'? He's buildin' a house trailer. Right over there, back a them tents. Got beds an' a stove–ever'thing. Jus' live in her. By God, that's the way to live! Right where you stop–tha's where you live.'

Ma said: 'I ruther have a little house. Soon's we can, I want a little house.'

Pa said: 'Al–after we've et, you an' me an' Uncle John'll take the truck an' go out lookin' for work.'

'Sure,' said Al. 'I like to get a job in a garage if they's any jobs. That's what I really like. An' get me a little ol' cut-down Ford. Paint her yella an' go a-kyoodlin' aroun'. Seen a purty girl down the road. Give her a big wink, too. Purty as hell, too.'

Pa said sternly: 'You better get you some work 'fore you go a-tom-cattin'.'

Uncle John came out of the toilet and moved slowly near. Ma frowned at him.

'You ain't washed–' she began, and then she saw how sick and weak and sad he looked. 'You go on in the tent an' lay down,' she said. 'You ain't well.'

He shook his head, 'No,' he said. 'I sinned, an' I got to take my punishment.' He squatted down disconsolately and poured himself a cup of coffee.

Ma took the last pones from the pan. She said casually: 'The manager of the camp come an' set an' had a cup of coffee.'

Pa looked over slowly. 'Yeah? What's he want awready?'

'Jus' come to pass the time,' Ma said daintily. 'Jus' set down an' had coffee. Said he didn't get good coffee so often, an' smelt our'n.'

'What'd he want?' Pa demanded again.

'Didn' want nothin'. Come to see how we was gettin' on.'

'I don' believe it,' Pa said. 'He's probably a-snootin' an' a-smellin' aroun'.'

'He was not!' Ma cried angrily. 'I can tell a fella that's snootin' aroun' quick as the nex' person.'

Pa tossed his coffee grounds out of his cup.

'You got to quit that,' Ma said. 'this here's a clean place.'

'You see she don't get so goddamn clean a fella can't live in her,' Pa said jealously. 'Hurry up, Al. We're goin' out lookin' for a job.'

Al wiped his mouth with his hand. 'I'm ready,' he said.

Pa turned to Uncle John. 'You a-comin'?'

'Yes. I'm a-comin'.'

'You don't look so good.'

'I ain't so good, but I'm comin'.'

Al got in the truck. 'Have to get gas,' he said. He started the engine. Pa and Uncle John climbed in beside him and the truck moved away down the street.

Ma watched them go. And then she took a bucket and went to the wash trays under the open part of the sanitary unit. She filled her bucket with hot water and carried it back to her camp. And she was washing the dishes in the bucket when Rose of Sharon came back.

'I put your stuff on a plate,' Ma said. And then she looked closely at the girl. Her hair was dripping and combed, and her skin was bright and pink. She had put on the blue dress printed with little white flowers. On her feet she wore the heeled slippers of her wedding. She blushed under Ma's gaze. 'You had a bath,' Ma said.

Rose of Sharon spoke huskily. 'I was in there when a lady come in an' done it. Know what you do? You get in a little stall-like, an' you turn handles, an' water comes a-floodin' down on you–hot water or col' water jus' like you want it–an' I done it!'

'I'm a-goin' to myself,' Ma cried. 'Jus' soon as I get finish' here. You show me how.'

'I'm a-gonna do it ever' day,' the girl said. 'An' that lady–she seen me, an' she seen about the baby, an'–know what she said? Said they's a nurse comes ever' week. An' I'm to go see that nurse an' she'll tell me jus' what to do so's the baby'll be strong. Says all the ladies here do that. An' I'm a-gonna do it.' The words bubbled out. 'An'–know what–? Last week they was a baby borned an' the whole camp give a party an' they give clothes an' they give stuff for the baby–even give a baby buggy–wicker one. Wasn't new, but they give it a coat a pink paint an' it was jus' like new. An' they give the baby a name an' had a cake. Oh, Lord!' She subsided, breathing heavily.

Ma said: 'Praise God, we come home to our own people. I'm a-gonna have a bath.'

'Oh, it's nice,' the girl said.

Ma wiped the tin dishes and stacked them. She said: 'We're Joads. We don't look up to nobody. Grampa's grampa, he fit in the Revolution. We was farm people till the debt. And then–them people. They done somepin to us. Ever' time they come seemed like they was a-whippin' me–all of us. An' in Needles, that police. He done somepin to me, made me feel mean. Made me feel ashamed. An' now I ain't ashamed. These folks is our folks–is our folks. An' that manager, he comes an' set an' drank coffee, an' he says: "Mrs Joad" this, an' "Mrs Joad" that–an' "How you gettin' on, Mrs Joad?"' She stopped and sighed. 'Why, I feel like people again.' She stacked the last dish. She went into the tent and dug through the clothes box for her shoes and a clean dress. And she found a little paper package with her earrings in it. As she went past Rose of Sharon, she said: 'If them ladies comes, you tell 'em I'll be right back.' She disappeared around the side of the sanitary unit.

Rose of Sharon sat down heavily on a box and regarded her wedding shoes, black patent leather and tailored black bows. She wiped the toes with her finger and wiped her finger on the inside of her skirt. Leaning down put a pressure on her growing abdomen. She sat up straight and touched herself with exploring fingers, and she smiled a little as she did it.

Along the road a stocky woman walked, carrying an apple box of dirty clothes toward the wash-tubs. Her face was brown with sun, and her eyes were black and intense. She wore a great apron, made from a cotton bag, over her gingham dress, and men's brown Oxfords were on her feet. She saw that Rose of Sharon caressed herself, and she saw the little smile on the girl's face.

'So!' she cried, and she laughed with pleasure. 'What you think it's gonna be?'

Rose of Sharon blushed and looked down at the ground, and then peeked up, and the little shiny black eyes of the woman took her in. 'I don' know,' she mumbled.

The woman plopped the apple box on the ground. 'Got a live tumour,' she said, and she cackled like a happy hen. 'Which'd you ruther?' she demanded.

'I dunno–boy, I guess. Sure–boy.'

'You jus' come in, didn' ya?'

'Las' night–late.'

'Gonna stay?'

'I don't know. 'F we can get work, guess we will.'

A shadow crossed the woman's face, and the little black eyes grew fierce. ''F you can git work. That's what we all say.'

'My brother got a job already this mornin'.'

'Did, huh? Maybe you're lucky. Look out for luck. You can't trus' luck.' She stepped close. 'You can only git one kind a luck. Cain't have more. You be a good girl,' she said fiercely. 'You be good. If you got sin on you–you better watch out for that there baby.' She squatted down in front of Rose of Sharon. 'They's scandalous things goes on in this here camp,' she said darkly. 'Ever' Sat'dy night they's dancin', an' not only squar' dancin', neither. They's some does clutch-an'-hug dancin'! I seen 'em.'

Rose of Sharon said guardedly: 'I like dancin,' squar' dancin'.' And she added virtuously: 'I never done that other kind.'

The brown woman nodded her head dismally. 'Well, some does. An' the Lord ain't lettin' it get by, neither; an' don' you think he is.'

'No, ma'am,' the girl said softly.

The woman put one brown wrinkled hand on Rose of Sharon's knee, and the girl flinched under the touch. 'You let me warn you now. They ain't but a few deep down Jesus-lovers lef'. Ever' Sat'dy night when that there string ban' starts up an' should be a-playin' hymnody, they're a-reelin'–yes, sir, a-reelin'. I seen 'em. Won' go near, myself, nor I don't let my kin go near. They's clutch-an'-hug, I tell ya.' She paused for emphasis and then said, in a hoarse whisper: 'They do more. They give a stage play.' She backed away and cocked her head to see how Rose of Sharon would take such a revelation.

'Actors?' the girl said in awe.

'No, sir!' the woman exploded 'Not *actors*, not them already damn' people. Our own kinda folks. Our own people. An' they was little children, didn' know no better, in it, an' they was pertendin' to be stuff they wasn't. I didn' go near. But I heard 'em talkin' what they was a-doin'. The devil was jus' a-struttin' through this here camp.'

Rose of Sharon listened, her eyes and mouth open. 'Oncet in school we give a Chris' chile play–Christmus.'

'Well–I ain' sayin' that's bad or good. They's good folks thinks a Chris' chile is awright. But–well, I wouldn' care to come right out flat an' say so. But this here wasn' no Chris' chile. This here was sin an' delusion an' devil stuff. Struttin' an' paradin' an' speakin' like they're somebody they ain't. An' dancin' an' clutchin' an' a-huggin'.'

Rose of Sharon sighed.

'An' not jus' a few, neither,' the brown woman went on. 'Gettin' so's you can almos' count the deep-down lamb-blood folks on your toes. An' don' you think them sinners is puttin' nothin' over on God, neither. No, sir, he's a-chalkin' 'em up sin by sin, an' he's drawin' his line an' addin' 'em up sin by sin. God's a-watchin', an' I'm a-watchin'. He's awready smoked two of 'em out.'

Rose of Sharon panted: 'Has?'

The brown woman's voice was rising in intensity. 'I seen it. Girl a-carryin' a little one, jes' like you. An' she play-acted, an' she hug-danced. And'–the voice grew bleak and ominous–'she thinned out and she skinnied out, an'–she dropped that baby dead.'

'Oh, my!' The girl was pale.

'Dead and bloody. 'Course nobody wouldn' speak to her no more. She had a go away. Can't tech sin 'thout catchin' it. No, sir. An' they was another, done the same thing. An' she skinnied out, an'–know what? One night she was gone. An' two days, she's back. Says she was visitin'. But–she ain't got no baby. Know what I think? I think the manager, he took her away to drop her baby.

He don' believe in sin. Tol' me hisself. Says the sin is bein' hungry. Says the sin is bein' cold. Says–I tell ya, he tol' me hisself–can't see God in them things. Says them girls skinnied out 'cause they didn't git 'nough food. Well, I fixed him up.' She rose to her feet and stepped back. Her eyes were sharp. She pointed a rigid forefinger in Rose of Sharon's face. 'I says: "Git back!" I says. I says: "I knowed the devil was rampagin' in this here camp. Now I know who the devil is. Git back, Satan," I says. An', by Chris', he got back! Tremblin' he was, an' sneaky. Says: "Please!" Says: "Please don' make the folks unhappy." I says: "Unhappy? How 'bout their soul? How 'bout them dead babies an' them poor sinners ruint 'count of play-actin'?" He jes' looked, an' he give a sick grin an' went away. He knowed when he met a real testifier to the Lord. I says: "I'm a-helpin' Jesus watch the goin's-on. An' you an' them other sinners ain't gittin' away with it."' She picked up her box of dirty clothes. 'You take heed. I warned you. You take heed a that pore chile in your belly an' keep outa sin.' And she strode away titanically, and her eyes shone with virtue.

Rose of Sharon watched her go, and then she put her head down on her hands and whimpered into her palms. A soft voice sounded beside her. She looked up, ashamed. It was the little white-clad manager. 'Don't worry,' he said. 'Don't you worry.'

Her eyes blinded with tears. 'But I done it,' she cried. 'I hug-danced. I didn' tell her. I done it in Sallisaw. Me an' Connie.'

'Don't worry,' he said.

'She says I'll drop the baby.'

'I know she does. I kind of keep my eye on her. She's a good woman, but she makes people unhappy.'

Rose of Sharon sniffled wetly. 'She knowed two girls los' their baby right in this here camp.'

The manager squatted down in front of her. 'Look!' he said. 'Listen to me. I know them too. They were too hungry and too tired. And they worked too hard. And they rode on a truck over bumps. They were sick. It wasn't their fault.'

'But she said–'

'Don't worry. That woman likes to make trouble.'

'But she says you was the devil.'

'I know she does. That's because I won't let her make people miserable.' He patted her shoulder. 'Don't you worry. She doesn't know.' And he walked quickly away.

Rose of Sharon looked after him; his lean shoulders jerked as he walked. She was still watching his slight figure when Ma came back, clean and pink, her hair combed and wet, and gathered in a knot. She wore her figured dress and the old cracked shoes; and the little earrings hung in her ears.

'I done it,' she said. 'I stood in there an' let warm water come a-floodin' an' a-flowin' down over me. An' they was a lady says you can do it ever' day if you want. An'–them ladies' committee come yet?'

'Uh-uh!' said the girl.

'An' you jus' set there an' didn' redd up the camp none!' Ma gathered up the tin dishes as she spoke. 'We got to get in shape,' she said. 'Come on, stir! Get the sack and kinda sweep along the groun'.' She picked up the equipment, put the pans in their box and the box in the tent. 'Get them beds neat,' she ordered. 'I tell ya I ain't never felt nothin' so nice as that water.'

Rose of Sharon listlessly followed orders. 'Ya think Connie'll be back to-day?'

'Maybe–maybe not. Can't tell.'

'You sure he knows where-at to come?'

'Sure.'

'Ma–ya don' think–they could a killed him when they burned–?'

'Not him,' Ma said confidently. 'He can travel when he wants–jack-rabbit-quick an' fox-sneaky.'

'I wisht he'd come.'

'He'll come when he comes.'

'Ma–'

'I wisht you'd get to work.'

'Well, do you think dancin' an' play-actin' is sins an'll make me drop the baby?'

Ma stopped her work and put her hands on her hips. 'Now what you talkin' about? You ain't done no play-actin'.'

'Well, some folks here done it, an' one girl, she dropped her baby–dead–an' bloody, like it was a judgement.'

Ma stared at her. 'Who tol' you?'

'Lady that came by. An' that little fella in white clothes, he come by an' he says that ain't what done it.'

Ma frowned. 'Rosasharn,' she said, 'you stop pickin' at yourself. You're jest a-teasin' yourself up to cry. I don' know what's come at you. Our folks ain't never did that. They took what come to 'em dry-eyed. I bet it's that Connie give you all them notions. He was jes' too big for his overhalls.' And she said sternly: 'Rosasharn, you're jest one person an' they's a lot of other folks. You git to your proper place. I knowed people built theirself up with sin till they figgered they was big mean shucks in the sight a the Lord.'

'But, Ma–'

'No. Jes' shut up an' git to work. You ain't big enough or mean enough to worry God much. An' I'm gonna give you the back a my han' if you don' stop this pickin' at yourself.' She swept the ashes into the fire hole and brushed the stones on its edge. She saw the committee coming along the road. 'Git workin',' she said. 'Here's the ladies' comin'. Git a-workin' now, so's I can be proud.' She didn't look again, but she was conscious of the approach of the committee.

There could be no doubt that it was the committee; three ladies, washed, dressed in their best clothes: a lean woman with stringy hair and steel-rimmed glasses, a small stout lady with curly grey hair and a small sweet mouth, and a mammoth lady, big of hock and buttock, big of breast, muscled like a dray-horse, powerful and sure. And the committee walked down the road with dignity.

Ma managed to have her back turned when they arrived. They stopped, wheeled, stood in line. And the great woman boomed:

''Mornin' Mis' Joad, ain't it?'

Ma whirled around as though she had been caught off guard. 'Why, yes–yes. How'd you know my name?'

'We're the committee,' the big woman said. 'Ladies' Committee of Sanitary Unit Number Four. We got your name in the office.'

Ma flustered: 'We ain't in very good shape yet. I'd be proud to have you ladies come an' set while I make up some coffee.'

The plump committee woman said: 'Give our names, Jessie. Mention our names to Mis' Joad. Jessie's the Chair,' she explained.

Jessie said formally: 'Mis' Joad, this here's Annie Littlefield and Ella Summers, an' I'm Jessie Bullitt.'

'I'm proud to make your acquaintance,' Ma said. 'Won't you set down? They ain't nothin' to set on yet,' she added. 'But I'll make up some coffee.'

'Oh, no,' said Annie formally. 'Don't put yaself out. We jes' come to call an' see how you was, an' try to make you feel at home.'

Jessie Bullitt said sternly: 'Annie, I'll thank you to remember I'm Chair.'

'Oh! Sure, sure. But next week I am.'

'Well, you wait'll next week then. We change ever' week,' she explained to Ma.

'Sure you wouldn' like a little coffee?' Ma asked helplessly.

'No, thank you.' Jessie took charge. 'We gonna show you 'bout the sanitary unit fust, an' then if you wanta, we'll sign you up in the Ladies' Club an' give you duty. 'Course you don' have to join.'

'Does–does it cost much?'

'Don't cost nothing but work. An' when you're knowed, maybe you can be 'lected to this committee,' Annie interrupted. 'Jessie, here, is on the committee for the whole camp. She's a big committee lady.'

Jessie smiled with pride. ''Lected unanimous,' she said. 'Well, Mis' Joad, I guess it's time we tol' you 'bout how the camp runs.'

Ma said: 'This here's my girl, Rosasharn.'

'How do,' they said.

'Better come 'long too.'

The huge Jessie spoke, and her manner was full of dignity and kindness, and her speech was rehearsed.

'You shouldn' think we're a-buttin' into your business, Mis' Joad. This here camp got a lot of stuff ever'body uses. An' we got rules we made ourself. Now we're a-goin' to the unit. That there, ever'body uses, an' ever'body got to take care of it.' They strolled to the unroofed section where the wash-trays were, twenty of them. Eight were in use, the women bending over, scrubbing the clothes, and the piles of wrung-out clothes were heaped on the clean concrete floor. 'Now you can use these here any time you want,' Jessie said. 'The on'y thing is, you got to leave 'em clean.'

The women who were washing looked up with interest. Jessie said loudly: 'This here's Mis' Joad an' Rosasharn, come to live.' They greeted Ma in a chorus, and Ma made a dumpy little bow at them and said: 'Proud to meet ya.'

Jessie led the committee into the toilet and shower room.

'I been here awready,' Ma said. 'I even took a bath.'

'That's what they're for,' Jessie said 'An' they's the same rule. You got to leave 'em clean. Ever' week they's a new committee to swab out oncet a day. Maybe you'll git on that committee. You got to bring your own soap.'

'We got to get some soap,' Ma said. 'We're all out.'

Jessie's voice became almost reverential. 'You ever used this here kind?' she asked, and pointed to the toilets.

'Yes, ma'am. Right this mornin'.'

Jessie sighed. 'Tha's good.'

Ella Summers said: 'Jes' las' week–'

Jessie interrupted sternly: 'Mis' Summers–I'll tell.'

Ella gave ground. 'Oh, awright.'

Jessie said: 'Las' week, when you was Chair, you done it all. I'll thank you to keep out this week.'

'Well, tell what that lady done,' Ella said.

'Well,' said Jessie, 'it ain't this committee's business to go a-blabbin', but I won't pass no names. Lady come in las' week, an' she got in here 'fore the committee got to her, an' she had her ol' man's pants in the toilet, an' she says: "It's too low, an' it ain't big enough. Bust your back over her," she says. "Why couldn' they stick her higher?"' The committee smiled superior smiles.

Ella broke in: 'Says: "Can't put 'nough in at oncet."' And Ella weathered Jessie's stern glance.

Jessie said: 'We got our troubles with toilet paper. Rule says you can't take none away from here.' She clicked her tongue sharply. 'Whole camp chips in for toilet paper.' For a moment she was silent, and then she confessed. 'Number Four is usin' more than any other. Somebody's a-stealin' it. Come up in general ladies' meetin' "Ladies' side, Unit Number Four, is usin' too much." Come right up in meetin'!'

Ma was following the conversation breathlessly. 'Stealin' it–what for?'

'Well,' said Jessie, 'we had trouble before. Las' time they was three little girls cuttin' paper dolls out of it. Well, we caught them. But this time we don't know. Hardly put a roll out 'fore it's gone. Come right up in the meetin'. One lady says we oughta have a little bell that rings ever' time the roll turns oncet. Then we could count how many ever'body takes.' She shook her head. 'I jes' don' know,' she said. 'I been worried all week. Somebody's a-stealin' toilet paper from Unit Four.'

From the doorway came a whining voice: 'Mis' Bullitt.' The committee turned. 'Mis' Bullitt, I hearn what you says.' A flushed, perspiring woman stood in the doorway. 'I couldn' git up in meetin', Mis' Bullitt. I jes' couldn'. They'd a-laughed or somepin.'

'What you talkin' about?' Jessie advanced.

'Well, we-all–maybe–it's us. But we ain't a-stealin', Mis' Bullitt.'

Jessie advanced on her, and the perspiration headed out on the flustery confessor. 'We can't he'p it, Mis' Bullitt.'

'Now you tell what you're tellin',' Jessie said. 'This here unit's suffered shame 'bout that toilet paper.'

'All week, Mis' Bullitt. We couldn't he'p it. You know I got five girls.'

'What they been a-doin' with it?' Jessie demanded ominously.

'Jes' usin' it. Hones', jes' usin' it.'

'They ain't got the right! Four-five sheets is enough. What's the matter'th 'em?'

The confessor bleated: 'Skitters. All five of 'em. We been low on money. They et green grapes. They all five got the howlin' skitters. Run out ever' ten minutes.' She defended them: 'But they ain't stealin' it.'

Jessie sighed, 'You should a tol',' she said. 'You got to tell. Here's Unit Four sufferin' shame 'cause you never tol'. Anybody can git the skitters.'

The meek voice whined: 'I jes' can't keep 'em from eatin' them green grapes. An' they're a-gettin' worse all a time.'

Ella Summers burst out: 'The Aid. She oughta git the Aid.'

'Ella Summers,' Jessie said, 'I'm a-tellin' you for the las' time, you ain't the Chair.' She turned back to the raddled little woman. 'Ain't you got no money, Mis' Joyce?'

She looked ashamedly down. 'No, but we might git work anytime.'

'Now you hol' up your head,' Jessie said. 'That ain't no crime. You jes' waltz right over t' the Weedpatch store an' git you some groceries. The camp got twenty dollars' credit there. You git yourself fi' dollars worth. An' you kin pay it back to the Central Committee when you git work. Mis' Joyce, you knowed that,' she said sternly. 'How come you let your girls git hungry?'

'We ain't never took no charity,' Mrs Joyce said.

'This ain't charity, an' you know it,' Jessie raged. 'We had all that out. They ain't no charity in this here camp. We won't have no charity. Now you waltz right over an' git you some groceries, an' you bring the slip to me.'

Mrs Joyce said timidly: 'S'pose we can't never pay? We ain't had work for a long time.'

'You'll pay if you can. If you can't, that ain't none of our business, an' it ain't your business. One fella went away, an' two months later he sent back the money. You ain't got the right to let your girls git hungry in this here camp.'

Mrs Joyce was cowed. 'Yes, ma'am,' she said.

'Git you some cheese for them girls,' Jessie ordered. 'That'll take care a them skitters.'

'Yes, ma'am.' And Mrs Joyce scuttled out of the door.

Jessie turned in anger on the committee. 'She got no right to be stiff-necked. She got no right, not with our own people.'

Annie Littlefield said: 'She ain't been here long. Maybe she don't know. Maybe she's took charity one time-another. Nor,' Annie said, 'don't you try to shut me up, Jessie. I got a right to pass speech.' She turned half to Ma. 'If a body's ever took charity, it makes a burn that don't come out. This ain't charity, but if you ever took it, you don't forget it. I bet Jessie ain't ever done it.'

'No, I ain't,' said Jessie.

'Well, I did,' Annie said. 'Las' winter; an' we was a-starvin'–me an' Pa an' the little fellas. An' it was a-rainin'. Fella tol' us to go to the Salvation Army.' Her eyes grew fierce. 'We was hungry–they made us crawl for our dinner. They took our dignity. They–I hate 'em! An'–maybe Mis' Joyce took charity. Maybe she didn' know this ain't charity. Mis' Joad, we don't allow nobody in this camp to build theirself up that-a-way. We don't allow nobody to give nothing to another person. They can give it to the camp, an' the camp can pass it out. We won't have no charity!' Her voice was fierce and hoarse. 'I hate 'em,' she said. 'I ain't never seen my man beat before, but them–them Salvation Army done it to 'im.'

Jessie nodded. 'I heard,' she said softly, 'I heard. We got to take Mis' Joad aroun'.'

Ma said: 'It sure is nice.'

'Le's go to the sewin' room,' Annie suggested. 'Got two machines. They's a-quiltin', an' they're makin' dresses. You might like ta work over there.'

When the committee called on Ma, Ruthie and Winfield faded imperceptibly back out of reach.

'Whyn't we go along an' listen?' Winfield asked.

Ruthie gripped his arm. 'No,' she said. 'We got washed for them sons-a-bitches. I ain't goin' with 'em.'

Winfield said: 'You tol' on me 'bout the toilet. I'm a-gonna tell what you called them ladies.'

A shadow of fear crossed Ruthie's face. 'Don' do it. I tol' 'cause I knowed you didn' really break it.'

'You did not,' said Winfield.

Ruthie said: 'Le's look aroun'.' They strolled down the line of tents, peering into each one, gawking self-consciously. At the end of the unit there was a level place on which a croquet court had been set up. Half a dozen children played seriously. In front of a tent an elderly lady sat on a bench and watched. Ruthie and Winfield broke into a trot. 'Leave us play,' Ruthie cried. 'Leave us get in.'

The children looked up. A pigtailed girl said: 'Nex' game you kin.'

'I wanna play now,' Ruthie cried.

'Well, you can't. Not till nex' game.'

Ruthie moved menacingly out on the court. 'I'm a-gonna play.' The pigtails gripped her mallet tightly. Ruthie sprang her, slapped her, pushed her, and wrested the mallet from her hands. 'I says I was gonna play,' she said triumphantly.

The elderly lady stood up and walked on to the court. Ruthie scowled fiercely and her hands tightened on the mallet. The lady said: 'Let her play–like you done with Ralph las' week.'

The children laid their mallets on the ground and trooped silently off the court. They stood at a distance and looked on with expressionless eyes. Ruthie watched them go. Then she hit a ball and ran after it. 'Come on, Winfiel'. Get a stick,' she called. And then she looked in amazement. Winfield had joined the watching children, and he, too, looked at her with expressionless eyes. Defiantly she hit the ball again. She kicked up a great dust. She pretended to have a good time. And the children stood and watched. Ruthie lined up two balls and hit both of them, and she turned her back on the watching eyes, and then turned back. Suddenly she advanced on them, mallet in hand. 'You come an' play,' she demanded. They moved silently back at her approach. For a moment she stared at them, and then she flung down the mallet and ran crying for home. The children walked back on the court.

Pigtails said to Winfield: 'You can git in the nex' game.'

The watching lady warned them: 'When she comes back an' wants to be decent, you let her. You was mean yourself, Amy.' The game went on, while in the Joad tent Ruthie wept miserably.

The truck moved along the beautiful roads, past orchards where the peaches were beginning to colour, past vineyards with the clusters pale and green, under lines of walnut trees whose branches spread half across the road. At each entrance-gate Al slowed; and at each gate there was a sign: 'No help wanted. No trespassing.'

Al said: 'Pa, they's boun' to be work when them fruits gets ready. Funny place–they tell ya they ain't no work 'fore you ask 'em.' He drove slowly on.

Pa said: 'Maybe we could go in anyways an' ask if they know where they's any work. Might do that.'

A man in blue overalls and a blue shirt walked along the edge of the road. Al pulled up beside him. 'Hey, mister,' Al said, 'know where they's any work?'

The man stopped and grinned, and his mouth was vacant of front teeth. 'No,' he said. 'Do you? I been walkin' all week, an' I can't tree none.'

'Live in that gov'ment camp?' Al asked.

'Yeah!'

'Come on, then. Git up back an' we'll all look.' The man climbed over the side-boards and dropped in the bed.

Pa said: 'I ain't got no hunch we'll find work. Guess we got to look, though.

We don't even know where-at to look.'

'Shoulda talked to the fella in the camp,' Al said. 'How you feelin', Uncle John?'

'I ache,' said Uncle John. 'I ache all over, an' I got it comin' I oughta go away where I won't bring down punishment on my own folks.'

Pa put his hand on John's knee. 'Look here,' he said, 'don' you go away. We're droppin' folks all the time–Grampa an' Granma dead, Noah an' Connie–run out, an' the preacher–in jail.'

'I got a hunch we'll see that preacher again,' John said.

Al fingered the ball on the gear-shift lever. 'You don't feel good enough to have no hunches,' he said. 'The hell with it. Le's go back an' talk, an' find out where they's some work. We're jus' huntin' skunks under water.' He stopped the truck and leaned out the window and called back: 'Hey! Lookie! We're a-goin' back to camp an' try an' see where they's work. They ain't no use burnin' petrol like this.'

The man leaned over the truck side. 'Suits me,' he said. 'My dogs is wore clean up to the ankle. An' I ain't even got a nibble.'

Al turned around in the middle of the road and headed back.

Pa said: 'Ma's gonna be purty hurt, 'specially when Tom got work so easy.'

'Maybe he never got none,' Al said. 'Maybe he jus' went lookin' too. I wisht I could get work in a garage. I'd learn that stuff quick, an' I'd like it.'

Pa grunted, and they drove back toward the camp in silence.

When the committee left, Ma sat down on a box in front of the Joad tent, and she looked helplessly at Rose of Sharon. 'Well–' she said, 'well–I ain't been so perked up in years. *Wasn't* them ladies nice?'

'I got to work in the nursery,' Rose of Sharon said. 'They tol' me. I can find out all how to do for babies, an' then I'll know.'

Ma nodded in wonder. 'Wouldn' it be nice if the men-folks all got work?' she asked. 'Them a-workin', an' a little money comin' in?' Her eyes wandered into space. 'Them a-workin', an' us a-workin' here, an' all them nice people. Fust thing we get a little ahead I'd get me a little stove–nice one. They don' cost much. An' then we'd get a tent, big enough, an' maybe secon'-han' springs for the beds. An' we'd use this here tent jus' to eat under. An' Sat'dy night we'll go to the dancin'. They says you can invite folks if you want. I wisht we had some frien's to invite. Maybe the men'll know somebody to invite.'

Rose of Sharon peered down the road. 'That lady says I'll lose the baby–' she began.

'Now you stop that,' Ma warned her.

Rose of Sharon said softly: 'I seen her. She's a-comin' here, I think. Yeah! Here she comes. Ma, don't let her–'

Ma turned and looked at the approaching figure.

'Howdy,' the woman said. 'I'm Mis' Sandry–Lisbeth Sandry. I seen your girl this mornin'.'

'Howdy do,' said Ma.

'Are you happy in the Lord?'

'Pretty happy,' said Ma.

'Are you saved?'

'I been saved.' Ma's face was closed and waiting.

'Well, I'm glad,' Lisbeth said. 'The sinners is awful strong aroun' here. You come to a awful place. They's wicketness all around about. Wicket people, wicket goin's-on that a lamb'-blood Christian jes' can't hardly stan'. They's sinners all around us.'

Ma coloured a little, and shut her mouth tightly. 'Seems to me they's nice people here,' she said shortly.

Mrs Sandry's eyes stared. 'Nice!' she cried. 'You think they're nice when they's dancin' an' huggin'? I tell ya, ya eternal soul ain't got a chancet in this here camp. Went out to a meetin' in Weedpatch las' night. Know what the preacher says? He says: "They's wicketness in that camp." He says: "The poor is tryin' to be rich." He says: "They's dancin' an' huggin' when they should be wailin' an' moanin' in sin." That's what he says. "Ever'body that ain't here is a black sinner," he says. I tell you it made a person feel purty good to hear 'im. An' we knowed we was safe. We ain't danced.'

Ma's face was red. She stood up slowly and faced Mrs Sandry. 'Git!' she said. 'Git out now, 'fore I git to be a sinner a-tellin' you where to go. Git to your wailin' an' moanin'.'

Mrs Sandry's mouth dropped open. She stepped back. And then she became fierce. 'I thought you was Christians.'

'So we are,' Ma said.

'No, you ain't. You're hell-burnin' sinners, all of you! An' I'll mention it in meetin', too. I can see your black soul a-burnin'. I can see that innocent child in that girl's belly a-burnin'.'

A low wailing cry escaped from Rose of Sharon's lips. Ma stooped down and picked up a stick of wood.

'Git!' she said coldly. 'Don' you never come back. I seen your kind before. You'd take the little pleasure, wouldn' you?' Ma advanced on Mrs Sandry.

For a moment the woman backed away and then suddenly she threw back her head and howled. Her eyes rolled up, her shoulders and arms flopped loosely at her side, and a string of thick ropy saliva ran from the corner of her mouth. She howled again and again, long deep animal howls. Men and women ran up from the other tents, and they stood near–frightened and quiet. Slowly the woman sank to her knees and the howls sank to a shuddering, bubbling moan. She fell sideways and her arms and legs twitched. The white eyeballs showed under the open eyelids.

A man said softly: 'The sperit. She got the sperit.' Ma stood looking down at the twitching form.

The little manager strolled up casually. 'Trouble?' he asked. The crowd parted to let him through. He looked down at the woman. 'Too bad,' he said. 'Will some of you help get her back to her tent?' The silent people shuffled their feet. Two men bent over and lifted the woman, one held her under the arms and the other took her feet. They carried her away, and the people moved slowly after them. Rose of Sharon went under the tarpaulin and lay down and covered her face with a blanket.

The manager looked at Ma, looked down at the stick in her hand. He smiled tiredly. 'Did you clout her?' he asked.

Ma continued to stare after the retreating people. She shook her head slowly. 'No–but I would a. Twicet to-day she worked my girl up.'

The manager said: 'Try not to hit her. She isn't well. She just isn't well.' And he added softly: 'I wish she'd go away, and all her family. She brings more trouble on the camp than all the rest together.'

Ma got herself in hand again. 'If she come back, I might hit her. I ain't sure. I won't let her worry my girl no more.'

'Don't worry about it, Mrs Joad,' he said. 'You won't ever see her again. She works over the newcomers. She won't ever come back. She thinks you're a sinner.'

'Well, I am,' said Ma.

'Sure. Everybody is, but not the way she means. She isn't well, Mrs Joad.'

Ma looked at him gratefully, and she called: 'You hear that, Rosasharn? She ain't well, she's crazy.' But the girl did not raise her head. Ma said: 'I'm warnin' you mister. If she comes back, I ain't to be trusted. I'll hit her.'

He smiled wryly. 'I know how you feel,' he said. 'But just try not to. That's all I ask–just try not to.' He walked slowly away toward the tent where Mrs Sandry had been carried.

Ma went into the tent and sat down beside Rose of Sharon. 'Look up,' she said. The girl lay still. Ma gently lifted the blanket from her daughter's face. 'That woman's kinda crazy,' she said. 'Don't you believe none of them things.'

Rose of Sharon whispered in terror: 'When she said about burnin', I–felt burnin'.'

'That ain't true,' said Ma.

'I'm tar'd out,' the girl whispered. 'I'm tar'd a things happenin'. I wanta sleep. I wanta sleep.'

'Well, you sleep, then. This here's a nice place. You can sleep.'

'But she might come back.'

'She won't,' said Ma. 'I'm a-gonna set right outside, an' I won't let her come back. Res' up now, 'cause you got to get to work in the nu'sery purty soon.'

Ma struggled to her feet and went to sit in the entrance to the tent. She sat on a box and put her elbows on her knees and her chin in her cupped hands. She saw the movement in the camp, heard the voices of the children, the hammering of an iron rim; but her eyes were staring ahead of her.

Pa, coming back along the road, found her there, and he squatted near her. She looked slowly over at him. 'Git work?' she aked.

'No,' he said, ashamed. 'We looked.'

'Where's Al and John and the truck?'

'Al's fixin' somepin. Had ta borry some tools. Fella says Al got to fix her there.'

Ma said sadly: 'This here's a nice place. We could be happy here awhile.'

'If we could get work.'

'Yeah! If you could get work.'

He felt her sadness, and studied her face. 'What you a-mopin' about? If it's such a nice place why have you got to mope?'

She gazed at him, and she closed her eyes slowly. 'Funny, ain't it! All the time we was a-movin' an' shovin', I never thought none. An' now these here folks been nice to me, been awful nice; an' what's the first thing I do? I go right back over the sad things–that night Grampa died an' we buried him. I was all full up of the road, and bumpin' and movin', an' it wasn't so bad. But now I come out here, an' it's worse now. An' Granma–an' Noah walkin' away like that! Walkin' away jus' down the river. Them things was part of all, an' now they come a-flockin' back. Granma a pauper, an' buried a pauper. That's sharp now. That's awful sharp. An' Noah walkin' away down the river. He don' know what's there. He jus' don' know. An' we don' know. We ain't never gonna know if he's alive or dead. Never gonna know. An' Connie sneakin' away. I didn' give 'em brain room before, but now they're a-flockin' back. An'

I oughta be glad 'cause we're in a nice place.' Pa watched her mouth while she talked. Her eyes were closed. 'I can remember how them mountains was, sharp as ol' teeth beside the river where Noah walked. I can remember how the stubble was on the groun' where Grampa lies. I can remember the choppin' block back home with a feather caught in it, all criss-crossed with cuts, an' black with chicken blood.'

Pa's voice took on her tone. 'I seen the ducks to-day,' he said. 'Wedgin' south–high up. Seems like they're awful dinky. An' I seen the blackbirds a-settin' on the wires, an' the doves on the fences.' Ma opened her eyes and looked at him. He went on: 'I seen a little whirlwin', like a man a-spinnin' acrost a fiel'. An' the ducks drivin' on down, wedgin' on down to the southward.'

Ma smiled. 'Remember?' she said. 'Remember what we'd always say at home? "Winter's a-comin' early," we said, when the ducks flew. Always said that, an' winter come when it was ready to come. But we always said: "She's a-comin' early." I wonder what we meant.'

'I seen the blackbirds on the wires,' said Pa. 'Settin' so close together. An' the doves. Nothin' sets so still as a dove–on the fence wires–maybe two side by side. An' this little whirlwin'–big as a man, an' dancin' off acrost a fiel'. Always did like the little fellas, big as a man.'

'Wisht I wouldn't think how it is home,' said Ma. 'It ain't our home no more. Wisht I'd forget it. An' Noah.'

'He wasn't ever right–I mean–well, it was my fault.'

'I tol' you never to say that. Wouldn' a lived at all, maybe.'

'But I should a knowed more.'

'Now stop,' said Ma. 'Noah was strange. Maybe he'll have a nice time by the river. Maybe it's better so. We can't do no worryin'. This here is a nice place, an' maybe you'll get work right off.'

Pa pointed at the sky. 'Look–more ducks. Big bunch. An' Ma, "Winter's a-comin' early."'

She chuckled. 'They's things you do, an' you don' know why.'

'Here's John,' said Pa. 'Come on an' set, John.'

Uncle John joined them. He squatted down in front of Ma. 'We didn' get nowheres,' he said. 'Jus' run aroun'. Say, Al wants to see ya. Says he got to git a tire. Only one layer of cloth lef', he says.'

Pa stood up. 'I hope he can git her cheap. We ain't got much lef'. Where is Al?'

'Down there, to the nex' cross-street an' turn right. Says gonna blow out an' spoil a tube if we don' get a new one.' Pa strolled away, and his eyes followed the giant V of ducks down the sky.

Uncle John picked a stone from the ground and dropped it from his palm and picked it up again. He did not look at Ma. 'They ain't no work,' he said.

'You didn' look all over,' Ma said.

'No, but they's signs out.'

'Well, Tom musta got work. He ain't been back.'

Uncle John suggested: 'Maybe he went away–like Connie, or like Noah.'

Ma glanced sharply at him, and then her eyes softened. 'They's things you know,' she said. 'They's stuff you're sure of. Tom's got work an' he'll come in this evenin'. That's true.' She smiled in satisfaction. 'Ain't he a fine boy!' she said. 'Ain't he a good boy!'

The cars and trucks began to come into the camp, and the men trooped by toward the sanitary unit. And each man carried clean overalls and shirt in his hand.

Ma pulled herself together. 'John, you go find Pa. Get to the store. I want beans an' sugar an'–a piece of fryin' meat an' carrots an'–tell Pa to get somepin nice–anything–but nice–for to-night. To-night–we'll have–somepin nice.'

23

The migrant people, scuttling for work, scrabbling to live, looked always for pleasure, dug for pleasure, manufactured pleasure, and they were hungry for amusement. Sometimes amusement lay in speech, and they climbed up their lives with jokes. And it came about in the camps along the roads, on the ditch banks beside the streams, under the sycamores, that the story-teller grew into being, so that the people gathered in the low firelight to hear the gifted ones. And they listened while the tales were told, and their participants made the stories great.

I was a recruit against Geronimo–

And the people listened, and their quiet eyes reflected the dying fire.

Them Injuns was cute–slick as snakes, an' quiet when they wanted. Could go through dry leaves, an' make no rustle. Try to do that sometime.

And the people listened and remembered the crash of dry leaves under their feet.

Come the change of season an' the clouds up. Wrong time. Ever hear of the army doing anything right? Give the army ten chances, an' they'll stumble along. Took three regiments to kill a hundred braves–always.

And the people listened, and their faces were quiet with listening. The story-tellers, gathering attention into their tales spoke in great rhythms, spoke in great words, because the tales were great, and the listeners became great through them.

They was a brave on a ridge, against the sun. Knowed he stood out. Spread his arms an' stood. Naked as morning, an' against the sun. Maybe he was crazy. I don' know. Stood there, arms spread out; like a cross he looked. Four hundred yards. An' the men–well, they raised their sights an' they felt the wind with their fingers; an' then they jus' lay there an' couldn' shoot. Mabe that Injun knowed somepin. Knowed we couldn' shoot. Jes' laid there with the rifles cocked, an' didn' even put 'em to our shoulders. Lookin' at him. Head-band, one feather. Could see it, an' naked as the sun. Long time we laid there an' looked, an' he never moved. An' then the captain got mad. 'Shoot, you crazy bastards, shoot!' he yells. An' we just laid there. 'I'll give you a five-count, an' then mark you down,' the captain says. Well, sir–we put up our rifles slow, an' ever' man hoped somebody'd shoot first. I ain't never been so sad in my life. An' I laid my sights on his belly, 'cause you can't stop a Injun no other place–an'–then. Well, he just plunked down an' rolled. An' we went up. An' he wasn' big–he'd looked so grand–up there. All tore to pieces an' little. Ever see a cock pheasant, stiff and beautiful, ever' feather drawed an' painted, an' even his eyes drawed pretty? An' bang! You pick him up–bloody an' twisted, an' you spoiled somepin better'n you; an' eatin' him don't never make it up to you, 'cause you spoiled somepin in yaself, an' you can't never fix it up.

And the people nodded, and perhaps the fire spurted a little light and showed their eyes looking in on themselves.

Against the sun, with his arms out. An' he looked big–as God.

And perhaps a man balanced twenty cents between food and pleasure, and he went to a movie in Marysville or Tulare, in Ceres or Mountain View. And he came back to the ditch camp with his memory crowded. And he told how it was:

They was this rich fella, an' he makes like he's poor, an' they's this rich girl, an' she purtends like she's poor too, an' they meet in a hamburg stan'.

Why?

I don't know why–that's how it was.

Why'd they purtend like they's poor?

Well, they're tired of bein' rich.

Horse-shit!

You want to hear this, or not?

Well, go on then. Sure, I wanta hear it, but if I was rich, if I was rich I'd git so many pork chops–I'd cord 'em up aroun' me like wood, an' I'd eat my way out. Go on.

Well, they each think the other one's poor. An' they git arrested an' they git to jail, an' they don' git out 'cause the other one'd find out the first one is rich. An' the jail-keeper, he's mean to 'em 'cause he thinks they're poor. Oughta see how he looks when he finds out. Jes' nearly faints, that's all.

What they git in jail for?

Well, they git caught at some kind a radical meetin' but they ain't radicals. They jes' happen to be there. An' they don't each one wanta marry fur money, ya see.

So the sons-of-bitches start lyin' to each other right off.

Well, in the pitcher it was like they was doin' good. They're nice to people, you see.

I was to a show oncet that was me, an' more'n me; an' my life, an' more'n my life, so ever'thing was bigger.

Well, I git enough sorrow. I like to git away from it.

Sure–if you can believe it.

So they got married, an' then they foun' out, an' all them people that's treated 'em mean. They was a fella had been uppity, an' he nearly fainted when this fella come in with a plug hat on. Jes' nearly fainted. An' they was a newsreel with them German soldiers kickin' up their feet–funny as hell.

And always, if he had a little money, a man could get drunk. The hard edges gone, and the warmth. Then there was no loneliness, for a man could people his brain with friends, and he could find his enemies and destroy them. Sitting in a ditch, the earth grew soft under him. Failures dulled and the future was no threat. And hunger did not skulk about, but the world was soft and easy, and a man could reach the place he started for. The stars came down wonderfully close and the sky was soft. Death was a friend, and sleep was death's brother. The old times came back–a girl with pretty feet, who danced one time at home–a horse–a long time ago. A horse and a saddle. And the leather was carved. When was that? Ought to find a girl to talk to. That's nice. Might lay with her, too. But warm here. And the stars down so close, and sadness and pleasure so close together, really the same thing. Like to stay drunk all the time. Who says it's bad? Who dares to say it's bad? Preachers–but they got their own kinda drunkenness. Thin, barren women, but they're too miserable to know. Reformers–but they don't bite deep enough into living to know. No–the stars are close and dear and I have joined the brotherhood of the worlds. And everything's holy–everything, even me.

A harmonica is easy to carry. Take it out of your hip pocket, knock it against your palm to shake out the dirt and pocket fuzz and bits of tobacco. Now it's ready. You can do anything with a harmonica; thin reedy single tone, or chords, or melody with rhythm cords. You can mould the music with curved hands, making it wail and cry like bagpipes, making it full and round like an organ, making it as sharp and bitter as the reed pipes of the hills. And you can play and put it back in your pocket. It is always with you, always in your pocket. And as you play, you learn new tricks, new ways to mould the tone with your hands, to pinch the tone with your lips, and no one teaches you. You feel around–sometimes alone in the shade at noon, sometimes in the tent door after supper when the women are washing up. Your foot taps gently on the ground. Your eyebrows rise and fall in rhythm. And if you lose it or break it, why, it's no great loss. You can buy another for a quarter.

A guitar is more precious. Must learn this thing. Fingers of the left hand must have callus caps. Thumb of the right hand a horn of callus. Stretch the left-hand fingers, stretch them like a spider's legs to put the hand pads on the frets.

This was my father's box. Wasn't no bigger'n a bug first time he give me C chord. An' when I learned as good as him, he hardly never played no more. Used to set in the door, an' listen an' tap his foot. I'm trying for a break, an' he'd scowl mean till I get her, an' then he'd settle back easy, an' he'd nod. 'Play,' he'd say. 'Play nice.' It's a good box. See how the head is wore. They's many a million songs wore down that wood an' scooped her out. Some day she'll cave in like an egg. But you can't patch her nor worry her no way or she'll lose tone. Play her in the evening, an' they's a harmonica player in the nex' tent. Makes it pretty nice together.

The fiddle is rare, hard to learn. No frets, no teacher.

Jes' listen to a ol' man an' try to pick it up. Won't tell how to double. Says it's a secret. But I watched. Here's how he done it.

Shrill as a wind, the fiddle, quick and nervous and shrill.

She ain't much of a fiddle. Give two dollars for her. Fella says they's fiddles four hundred years old, and they git mellow like whisky. Says they'll cost fifty-sixty thousan' dollars. I don't know. Soun's like a lie. Harsh ol' bastard, ain't she? Wanta dance? I'll rub up the bow with plenty rosin. Man! Then she'll squawk. Hear her a mile.

These three in the evening, harmonica and fiddle and guitar. Playing a reel and tapping out the tune, and the big deep strings of the guitar beating like a heart, and the harmonica's sharp chords and the skirl and squeal of the fiddle. People have to move close. They can't help it. 'Chicken Reel' now, and the feet up and a young lean buck takes three quick steps, and his arms hang limp. The square closes up and the dancing starts, feet on the bare ground, beating dull, strike with your heels. Hands 'round and swing. Hair falls down, and panting breaths. Lean to the side now.

Look at that Texan boy, long legs loose, taps four times for ever' damn step.

Never seen a boy swing aroun' like that. Look at him swing that Cherokee girl, red in her cheeks an' her toe points out. Look at her pant, look at her heave. Think she's tired? Think she's winded? Well, she ain't. Texas boy got his hair in his eyes, mouth's wide open, can't get air, but he pats four times for ever' darn step, an' he'll keep a-goin' with the Cherokee girl.

The fiddle squeaks and the guitar bongs. Mouth-organ man is red in the face. Texas boy and the Cherokee girl, pantin' like dogs an' a-beatin' the groun'. Ol' folks stan' a-pattin' their han's. Smilin' a little, tappin' their feet.

Back home–in the schoolhouse, it was. The big moon sailed off to the westward. An' we walked, him an' me–a little ways. Didn' talk 'cause our throats was choked up. Didn' talk none at all. An' purty soon they was a haycock. Went right to it and laid down there. Seein' the Texas boy an' that girl a-steppin' away into the dark–think nobody seen 'em go. Oh, God! I wisht I was a-goin' with that Texas boy. Moon'll be up 'fore long. I see that girl's ol' man move out to stop 'em, an' then he didn'. He knowed. Might as well stop the fall from comin', and might as well stop the sap from movin' in the trees. An' the moon'll be up 'for long.

Play more–play the story songs–'As I Walked through the Streets of Laredo'.

The fire's gone down. Be a shame to build her up. Little ol' moon'll be up 'fore long.

Beside an irrigation ditch a preacher laboured and the people cried. And the preacher paced like a tiger, whipping the people with his voice, and they grovelled and whined on the ground. He calculated them, gauged them, played on them, and when they were all squirming on the ground he stooped down and of his great strength he picked each one up in his arms and shouted, Take 'em, Christ! and threw each one in the water. And when they were all in, waist-deep in the water, and looking with frightened eyes at the master, he knelt down on the bank and he prayed for them; and he prayed that all men and women might grovel and whine on the ground. Men and women, dripping, clothes sticking tight, watched; then gurgling and sloshing in their shoes they walked back to the camp, to the tents, and they talked softly in wonder:

We been saved, they said. We're washed white as snow. We won't never sin again.

And the children, frightened and wet, whispered together:

We been saved. We won't sin no more.

Wisht I knowed what all the sins was, so I could do 'em.

The migrant people looked humbly for pleasure on the roads.

24

On Saturday morning the wash-tubs were crowded. The women washed dresses, pink ginghams and flowered cottons, and they hung them in the sun and stretched the cloth to smooth it. When afternoon came the whole camp quickened and the people grew excited. The children caught the fever and were more noisy than usual. About mid-afternoon child bathing began, and as each child was caught, subdued and washed, the noise on the playground gradually subsided. Before five, the children were scrubbed and warned about getting dirty again; and they walked about, stiff in clean clothes, miserable with carefulness.

At the big open-air dance platform a committee was busy. Every bit of electric wire had been requisitioned. The city dump had been visited for wire, every tool-box had contributed friction tape. And now the patched, spliced wire was strung out to the dance-floor, with bottle necks as insulators. This night the floor would be lighted for the first time. By six o'clock the men were back from work or from looking for work, and a new wave of bathing started. By seven, dinners were over, men had on their best clothes: freshly washed overalls, clean blue shirts, sometimes the decent blacks. The girls were ready in their print dresses, stretched and clean, their hair braided and ribboned. The worried women watched the families and cleaned up the evening dishes. On the platform the string band practised, surrounded by a double wall of children. The people were intent and excited.

In the tent of Ezra Huston, chairman, the Central Committee of five men went into meeting. Huston, a tall spare man, wind-blackened with eyes like little blades, spoke to his committee, one man from each sanitary unit.

'It's goddamn lucky we got the word they was gonna try to bust up the dance!' he said.

The tubby little representative from Unit Three spoke up. 'I think we oughta squash the hell out of 'em, an' show 'em.'

'No,' said Huston. 'That's what they want. No, sir. If they can git a fight goin', then they can run in the cops an' say we ain't orderly. They tried it before–other places.' He turned to the sad dark boy from Unit Two. 'Got the fellas together to go roun' the fences an' see nobody sneaks in?'

The sad boy nodded. 'Yeah! Twelve. Tol' 'em not to hit nobody. Jes' push 'em out ag'in.'

Huston said: 'Will you go out an' find Willie Eaton? He's chairman a the entertainment, ain't he?'

'Yeah.'

'Well, tell 'im we wanta see 'im.'

The boy went out, and he returned in a moment with a stringy Texas man. Willie Eaton had a long fragile jaw and dust-coloured hair. His arms and legs were long and loose and he had the grey sunburned eyes of the Panhandle. He stood in the tent, grinning, and his hands pivoted restlessly on his wrists.

Huston said: 'You heard about to-night?'

Willie grinned. 'Yeah!'

'Did anything 'bout it?'

'Yeah!'

'Tell what you done.'

Willie Eaton grinned happily. 'Well, sir, ordinary ent'tainment committee is five. I got twenty more–all good stong boys. They're a-gonna be a-dancin' an' a-keepin' their eyes open an' their ears open. First sign–any talk or argament, they close in tight. Worked her out purty nice. Can't even see nothing. Kinda move out, an' the fella will go with 'em.'

'Tell 'em they ain't to hurt the fellas.'

Willie laughed gleefully. 'I tol' 'em,' he said.

'Well, tell 'em so they know.'

'They know. Got five men out to the gate lookin' over the folks that comes in. Try to spot 'em 'fore they git started.'

Huston stood up. His steel-coloured eyes were stern. 'Now you look here, Willie. We don't want them fellas hurt. They's gonna be deputies out by the front gate. If you blood 'em up, why–them deputies'll git you.'

'Got that there figured out,' said Willie. 'Take 'em out the back way, into the fiel'. Some a the boys'll see they git on their way.'

'Well, it soun's awright,' Huston said worriedly. 'But don't you let nothing happen, Willie. You're responsible. Don' you hurt them fellas. Don' you use no stick nor no knife or arm, or nothing like that.'

'No, sir,' said Willie. 'We won't mark 'em.'

Huston was suspicious. 'I wisht I knowed I could trus' you, Willie. If you got to sock 'em, sock 'em where they won't bleed.'

'Yes, sir!' said Willie.

'You sure of the fellas you picked?'

'Yes, sir.'

'Awright. An' if she gits outa han', I'll be in the right-han' corner, this way on the dance floor.'

Willie saluted in mockery and went out.

Huston said: 'I dunno. I jes' hope Willie's boys don't kill nobody. What the hell the deputies want to hurt the camp for? Why can't they let us be?'

The sad boy from Unit Two said: 'I lived out at Sunlan' Lan' an' Cattle Company's place. Honest to God, they got a cop for ever' ten people. Got one water tap for 'bout two hundred people.'

The tubby man said: 'Jesus, God, Jeremy. You ain't got to tell me. I was there. They got a block of shacks–thirty-five of 'em in a row, an' fifteen deep. An' they got ten crappers for the whole shebang. An', Christ, you could smell 'em a mile. One of them deputies give me the low-down. He was settin' aroun', an' he says: "Them goddamn gov'ment camps," he said. "Give people hot water an' they gonna want hot water. Give 'em flush toilets an' they gonna want 'em." He says: "You give them goddamn Okies stuff like that an' they'll want 'em." An' he says: "They hol' red meetin's in them gov'ment camps. All figgerin' how to git on relief," he says.'

Huston asked: 'Didn' nobody sock him?'

'No. They was a little fella, an' he says: "What you mean, relief?"'

'"I mean relief–what us taxpayers puts in an' you goddamn Okies take out."

'"We pay sales tax an' petrol tax an' tobacco tax," this little guy says. An' he says: "Farmers get four cents a cotton poun' from the gov'ment–ain't that relief?" An' he says: "Railroads an' shippin' companies draws subsidies–ain't that relief?"

'"They're doin' stuff got to be done," this deputy says.

'"Well," the little guy says, "how'd your goddamn crops get picked if it wasn't for us?"' The tubby man looked around.

'What'd the deputy say?' Huston asked.

'Well, the deputy got mad. An' he says: "You goddamn reds is all the time stirrin' up trouble," he says. "You better come along with me." So he takes this little guy in, an' they give him sixty days in jail for vagrancy.'

'How'd they do that if he had a job?' asked Timothy Wallace.

The tubby man laughed. 'You know better'n that,' he said. 'You know a vagrant is anybody a cop don't like. An' that's why they hate this here camp. No cops can get in. This here's United States, not California.'

Huston sighed. 'Wisht we could stay here. Got to be goin' 'fore long. I like this here. Folks gits along nice; an', God Awmighty, why can't they let us do it 'stead of keepin' us miserable an' puttin' us in jail? I swear to God they gonna push us into fightin' if they don't quit a-worryin' us.' Then he calmed his voice. 'We jes' got to keep peaceful,' he reminded himself. 'The committee got no right to fly off'n the handle.'

The tubby man from Unit Three said: 'Anybody that thinks this committee got all cheese an' crackers ought to jes' try her. They was a fight in my unit to-day–women. Got to callin' names, an' then got to throwin' garbage. Ladies' Committee couldn't handle it, an' they come to me. Want me to bring the fight in this here committee. I tol' 'em they got to handle women trouble theirselves. This here committee ain't gonna mess with no garbage fights.'

Huston nodded. 'You done good,' he said.

And now the dusk was falling, and as the darkness deepened the practising of the string band seemed to grow louder. The lights flashed on and two men inspected the patched wire to the dance floor. The children crowded thickly about the musicians. A boy with a guitar sang the 'Down Home Blues', chording delicately for himself, and on his second chorus three harmonicas and a fiddle joined him. From the tents the people streamed toward the platform, men in their clean blue denim and women in their ginghams. They came near to the platform and then stood quietly waiting, their faces bright and intent under the light.

Around the reservation there was a high wire fence, and along the fence, at intervals of fifty feet, the guards sat in the grass and waited.

Now the cars of the guests began to arrive, small farmers and their families, migrants from other camps. And as each guest came through the gate he mentioned the name of the camper who had invited him.

The string band took a reel tune up and played loudly, for they were not practising any more. In front of their tents the Jesus-lovers sat and watched, their faces hard and contemptuous. They did not speak to one another, they watched for sin, and their faces condemned the whole proceeding.

At the Joad tent Ruthie and Winfield had bolted what little dinner they had, and then they started for the platform. Ma called them back, held up their faces with a hand under each chin, and looked into their nostrils, pulled their ears and looked inside, and sent them to the sanitary unit to wash their hands once more. They dodged around the back of the building and bolted for the platform, to stand among the children, close-packed about the band.

Al finished his dinner and spent half an hour shaving with Tom's razor. Al had a tight-fitting wool suit and a striped shirt, and he bathed and washed and combed his straight hair back. And when the washroom was vacant for a moment, he smiled engagingly at himself in the mirror, and he turned and tried to see himself in profile when he smiled. He slipped his purple armbands on and put on his tight coat. And he rubbed his yellow shoes with a piece of toilet paper. A late bather came in, and Al hurried out and walked recklessly toward the platform, his eye peeled for girls. Near the dance floor he saw a pretty blonde girl sitting in front of a tent. He sidled near and threw open his coat to show his shirt.

'Gonna dance to-night?' he asked.

The girl looked away and did not answer.

'Can't a fella pass a word with you? How 'bout you an' me dancin'?' And he said nonchalantly: 'I can waltz.'

The girl raised her eyes shyly, and she said: 'That ain't nothin'–anybody can waltz.'

'Not like me,' said Al: The music surged, and he tapped one foot in time. 'Come on,' he said.

A very fat woman poked her head out of the tent and scowled at him. 'You git along,' she said fiercely. 'This here girl's spoke for. She's a-gonna be married, an' her man's a-comin' for her.'

Al winked rakishly at the girl, and he tripped on, striking his feet to the music and swaying his shoulders and swinging his arms. And the girl looked after him intently.

Pa put down his plate and stood up. 'Come on, John,' he said; and he explained to Ma: 'We're a-goin' talk to some fellas about gettin' work.' An Pa and Uncle John walked toward the manager's house.

Tom worked a piece of store bread into the stew gravy on his plate and ate the bread. He handed his plate to Ma, and she put it in the bucket of hot water and washed it and handed it to Rose of Sharon to wipe. 'Ain't you goin' to the dance?' Ma asked.

'Sure,' said Tom. 'I'm on a committee. We're gonna entertain some fellas.'

'Already on a committee?' Ma said. 'I guess it's 'cause you got work.'

Rose of Sharon turned to put the dish away. Tom pointed at her. 'My God, she's a-gettin' big,' he said.

Rose of Sharon blushed and took another dish from Ma. 'Sure she is,' Ma said.

'An' she's gettin' prettier,' said Tom.

The girl blushed more deeply and hung her head. 'You stop it,' she said, softly.

''Course she is,' said Ma. 'Girl with a baby always gets prettier.'

Tom laughed. 'If she keeps a-swellin' like this, she gonna need a wheelbarrow to carry it.'

'Now you stop,' Rose of Sharon said, and she went inside the tent, out of sight.

Ma chuckled: 'You shouldn't ought to worry her.'

'She likes it,' said Tom.

'I know she likes it, but it worries her, too. And she's mournin' for Connie.'

'Well, she might's well give him up. He's prob'ly studyin' to be President of the United States by now.'

'Don't worry her,' Ma said. 'She ain't got no easy row to hoe.'

Willie Eaton moved near, and he grinned and said: 'You Tom Joad?'

'Yeah.'

'Well, I'm Chairman the Entertainment Committee. We gonna need you. Fella tol' me 'bout you.'

'Sure, I'll play with you,' said Tom. 'This here's Ma.'

'Howdy,' said Willie.

'Glad to meet ya.'

Willie said: 'Gonna put you on the gate to start, an' then on the floor. Want ya to look over the guys when they come in, an' try to spot 'em. You'll be with another fella. Then later I want ya to dance an' watch.'

'Yeah! I can do that awright,' said Tom.

Ma said apprehensively: 'They ain't no trouble?'

'No, ma'am,' Willie said. 'They ain't gonna be no trouble.'

'None at all,' said Tom. 'Well, I'll come 'long. See you at the dance, Ma.'

The two young men walked quickly away toward the main gate.

Ma piled the washed dishes on a box. 'Come on out,' she called, and when there was no answer: 'Rosasharn, you come out.'

The girl stepped from the tent, and she went on with the dish-wiping.

'Tom was on'y jollyin' ya.'

'I know. I di'n't mind; on'y I hate to have folks look at me.'

'Ain't no way to he'p that. Folks gonna look. But it makes folks happy to see a girl in the fambly way–makes folks sort of giggly an' happy. Ain't you a-goin' to the dance?'

'I was–but I don' know. I wisht Connie was here.' Her voice rose. 'Ma, I wisht he was here. I can't hardly stan' it.'

Ma looked closely at her. 'I know,' she said. 'But, Rosasharn–don' shame your folks.'

'I don' aim to, Ma.'

'Well, don't you shame us. We got too much on us now, without no shame.'

The girl's lip quivered. 'I–I ain' goin' to the dance. I couldn'–Ma–he'p me!' She sat down and buried her head in her arms.

Ma wiped her hands on the dish towel and she squatted down in front of her daughter, and she put her two hands on Rose of Sharon's hair. 'You're a good girl,' she said. 'You a'ways was a good girl. I'll take care a you. Don't you fret.' She put an interest in her tone. 'Know what you an' me's gonna do? We're a-goin' to that dance, an' we're a-gonna set there an' watch. If anybody says to come dance–why, I'll say you ain't strong enough. I'll say you're poorly. An' you can hear the music an' all like that.'

Rose of Sharon raised her head. 'You won't let me dance?'

'No, I won't.'

'An' don' let nobody touch me.'

'No, I won't.'

The girl sighed. She said desperately: 'I don't know what I'm a-gonna do, Ma. I jus' don' know. I don' know.'

Ma patted her knee. 'Look,' she said. 'Look here at me. I'm a-gonna tell ya. In a little while it ain't gonna be so bad. In a little while. An' that's true. Now come on. We'll go get washed up an' we'll put on our nice dress an' we'll set by the dance.' She led Rose of Sharon toward the sanitary unit.

Pa and Uncle John squatted with a group of men by the porch of the office. 'We nearly got work to-day,' Pa said. 'We was jus' a few minutes late. They awready got two fellas. An', well, sir, it was a funny thing. They's a straw boss there, an' he says: "We jus' got some two-bit men. 'Course we could use twenty-cent men. We can use a lot a twenty-cent men. You go to your camp an' say we'll put a lot of fellas on for twenty cents."'

The squatting men moved nervously. A broad-shouldered man, his face completely in the shadow of a black hat, patted his knee with his palm. 'I know it, goddamn it!' he cried. 'An' they'll git men. They'll git hungry men. You can't feed your fam'ly on twenty cents an hour, but you'll take anything. They got you goin' an' comin'. They jus' auction a job off. Jesus Christ, pretty soon they're gonna make us pay to work.'

'We would of took her,' Pa said. 'We ain't had no job. We sure would a took her, but they was them guys in there, an' the way they looked, we was scairt to take her.'

Black Hat said: 'Get crazy thinkin' I been workin' for a fella, an' he can't pick his crop. Cost more jes' to pick her than he can git for her, an' he don' know what to do.'

'Seems to me–' Pa stopped. The circle was silent for him. 'Well–I jus' thought, if a fella had a acre, well, my woman she could raise a little truck an' a couple pigs an' some chickens. An' us men could get out an' find work, an' then go back. Kids could maybe go to school. Never seen such schools as out here.'

'Our kids ain't happy in them schools,' Black Hat said.

'Why not? They're pretty nice, them schools.'

'Well, a raggedy kid with no shoes, an' them other kids with socks on, an' nice pants, an' them a-yellin' "Okie". My boy went to school. Had a fight ever' day. Done good, too. Tough little bastard. Ever' day he got to fight. Come home with his clothes tore an' his nose bloody. An' his ma'd whale him. Made her stop that. No need ever'body beatin' the hell outa him, poor little fella. Jesus! He give some a them kids a goin'-over, though–them nice-pants sons-a-bitches. I dunno. I dunno.'

Pa demanded: 'Well, what the hell am I gonna do? We're outa money. One of my boys got a short job, but that won't feed us. I'm a-gonna go an' take twenty cents. I got to.'

Black Hat raised his head, and his bristled chin showed in the light, and his stringy neck where the whiskers lay flat like fur. 'Yeah!' he said bitterly. 'You'll do that. An' I'm a two-bit man. You'll take my job for twenty cents. An' then I'll git hungry an' I'll take my job back for fifteen. Yeah! You go right on an' do her.'

'Well, what the hell can I do?' Pa demanded. 'I can't starve so's you can get two bits.'

Black Hat dipped his head again, and his chin went into the shadow. 'I dunno,' he said. 'I jes' dunno. It's bad enough to work twelve hours a day an' come out jes' a little bit hungry, but we got to figure all a time, too. My kid ain't gettin' enough to eat. I can't think all the time, goddamn it! It drives a man crazy.' The circle of men shifted their feet nervously.

Tom stood at the gate and watched the people coming in to the dance. A floodlight shone down into their faces. Willie Eaton said: 'Jes' keep your eyes open. I'm sendin' Jule Vitela over. He's half Cherokee. Nice fella. Keep your eyes open. An' see if you can pick out the ones.'

'O.K.,' said Tom. He watched the farm families come in, the girls with braided hair and the boys polished for the dance. Jule came and stood beside him.

'I'm with you,' he said.

Tom looked at the hawk nose and the high brown cheek-bones and the slender receding chin. 'They says you're half Injun. You look all Injun to me.'

'No,' said Jule. 'Jes' half. Wisht I was a full-blood. I'd have my lan' on the reservation. Them full-bloods got it pretty nice, some of 'em.'

'Look a them people,' Tom said.

The guests were moving in through the gateway, families from the farms, migrants from the ditch camps. Children straining to be free and quiet parents holding them back.

Jule said: 'These here dances done funny things. Our people got nothing, but jes' because they can ast their frien's to come here to the dance, sets 'em up an' makes 'em proud. An' the folks respect 'em 'count of these here dances. Fella got a little place where I was a-workin'. He come to a dance here. I ast him myself, an' he come. Says we got the only decent dance in the county, where a man can take his girls an' his wife. Hey! Look.'

Three young men were coming through the gate–young working men in jeans. They walked close together. The guard at the gate questioned them, and they answered and passed through.

'Look at 'em careful,' Jule said. He moved to the guard. 'Who ast them three?' he asked.

'Fella named Jackson, Unit Four.'

Jule came back to Tom. 'I think them's our fellas.'

'How ya know?'

'I dunno how. Jes' got a feelin'. They're kinda scared. Foller 'em an' tell Willie to look 'em over, an' tell Willie to check with Jackson, Unit Four. Get him to see if they're all right. I'll stay here.'

Tom strolled after the three young men. They moved toward the dance floor and took their positions quietly on the edge of the crowd. Tom saw Willie near the band and signalled him.

'What cha want?' Willie asked.

'Them three–see–there?'

'Yeah.'

'They say a fella name' Jackson, Unit Four, ast 'em.'

Willie craned his neck and saw Huston and called him over.

'Them three fellas,' he said. 'We better get Jackson, Unit Four an' see if he ast 'em.'

Huston turned on his heel and walked away; and in a few moments he was back with a lean and bony Kansan. 'This here's Jackson,' Huston said. 'Look, Jackson, see them three young fellas–?'

'Yeah.'

'Well, did you ast 'em?'

'No.'

'Ever see 'em before?'

Jackson peered at them. 'Sure. Worked at Gregorio's with 'em.'

'So they knowed your name.'

'Sure. I worked right beside 'em.'

'Awright,' Huston said. 'Don't you go near 'em. We ain't gonna th'ow 'em out if they're nice. Thanks, Mr Jackson.'

'Good work,' he said to Tom. 'I guess them's the fellas.'

'Jule picked 'em out,' said Tom.

'Hell, no wonder,' said Willie. 'His Injun blood smelled 'em. Well, I'll point 'em out to the boys.'

A sixteen-year-old boy came running through the crowd. He stopped, panting, in front of Huston. 'Mista Huston,' he said. 'I been like you said. They's a car with six men parked down by the euc'lyptus trees, an' they's one with four men up that north-side road. I ast 'em for a match. They got guns. I seen 'em.'

Huston's eyes grew hard and cruel. 'Willie,' he said, 'you sure you got ever'thing ready?'

Willie grinned happily. 'Sure have, Mr Huston. Ain't gonna be no trouble.'

'Well, don't hurt 'em. 'Member now. If you kin, quiet an' nice, I kinda like to see 'em. Be in my tent.'

'I'll see what we kin do,' said Willie.

Dancing had not formally started, but now Willie climbed on to the platform. 'Choose up your squares,' he called. The music stopped. Boys and girls, young men and women, ran about until eight squares were ready on the big floor, ready and waiting. The girls held their hands in front of them and squirmed their fingers. The boys tapped their feet restlessly. Around the floor the old folks sat, smiling slightly, holding the children back from the floor. And in the distance the Jesus-lovers sat with hard condemning faces and watched the sin.

Ma and Rose of Sharon sat on a bench and watched. And as each boy asked Rose of Sharon as partner, Ma said, 'No, she ain't well.' And Rose of Sharon blushed and her eyes were bright.

The caller stepped to the middle of the floor and held up his hands. 'All ready? Then let her go!'

The music snarled out 'Chicken Reel', shrill and clear, fiddle skirling, harmonicas nasal and sharp, and the guitars booming on the bass strings. The caller named the turns, the squares moved. And they danced forward and back, hands 'round, swing your lady. The caller, in a frenzy, tapped his feet, strutted back and forth, went through the figures as he called them.

'Swing your ladies an' a dol ce do. Join han's roun' an' away we go.' The music rose and fell, and the moving shoes beating in time on the platform sounded like drums. 'Swing to the right an' a swing to lef'; break, now–break–back to–back,' the caller sang the high vibrant monotone. Now the girls' hair lost the careful combing. Now perspiration stood out on the foreheads of the boys. Now the experts showed the tricky inter-steps. And the old people on the edge of the floor took up the rhythm, patted their hands softly, and tapped their feet; and they smiled gently and then caught one another's eyes and nodded.

Ma leaned her head close to Rose of Sharon's ear. 'Maybe you wouldn' think it, but your Pa was as nice a dancer as I ever seen, when he was young.' And Ma smiled. 'Makes me think of ol' times,' she said. And on the faces of the watchers the smiles were of old times.

'Up near Muskogee, twenty years ago, they was a blin' man with a fiddle–'

'I seen a fella oncet could slap his heels four times in one jump.'

'Swedes up in Dakota–know what they do sometimes? Put pepper on the floor. Gits up the ladies' skirts an' makes 'em purty lively–lively as a filly in season. Swedes do that sometimes.'

In the distance, the Jesus-lovers watched their restive children. 'Look on sin,' they said. 'Them folks is ridin' to hell on a poker. It's a shame the godly got to see it.' And their children were silent and nervous.

'One more roun' an' then a little res',' the caller chanted. 'Hit her hard, 'cause we're gonna stop soon.' And the girls were damp and flushed, and they danced with open mouths and serious reverent faces, and the boys flung back their long hair and pranced, pointed their toes, and clicked their heels. In and out the squares moved, crossing, backing, whirling, and the music thrilled.

Then suddenly it stopped. The dancers stood still, panting with fatigue. And the children broke from restraint, dashed on the floor, chased one another madly, ran, slid, stole caps, and pulled hair. The dancers sat down, fanning themselves with their hands. The members of the band got up and stretched themselves and sat down again. And the guitar players worked softly over their strings.

Now Willie called: 'Choose again for another square, if you can.' The dancers scrambled to their feet and new dancers plunged forward for partners.

Tom stood near the three young men. He saw them force their way through, out on the floor, toward one of the forming squares. He waved his hand at Willie, and Willie spoke to the fiddler. The fiddler squawked his bow across the strings. Twenty young men lounged slowly across the floor. The three reached the square. And one of them said: 'I'll dance with this here.'

A blond boy looked up in astonishment. 'She's my partner.'

'Listen, you little son-of-a-bitch–'

Off in the darkness a shrill whistle sounded. The three were walled in now. And each one felt the grip of hands. And then the wall of men moved slowly off the platform.

Willie yelped: 'Le's go!' The music shrilled out, the caller intoned the figures, the feet thudded on the platform.

A touring car drove to the entrance. The driver called: 'Open up. We hear you got a riot.'

The guard kept his position. 'We got no riot. Listen to that music. Who are you?'

'Deputy sheriffs.'

'Got a warrant?'

'We don't need a warrant if there's a riot.'

'Well, we got no riots here,' said the gate guard.

The men in the car listened to the music and the sound of the caller, and then the car pulled slowly away and parked in a crossroad and waited.

In the moving squad each of the three young men was pinioned, and a hand was over each mouth. When they reached the darkness the group opened up.

Tom said: 'That sure was did nice.' He held both arms of his victim from behind.

Willie ran over to them from the dance floor. 'Nice work,' he said. 'On'y need six now. Huston wants to see these here fellers.'

Huston himself emerged from the darkness. 'These the ones?'

'Sure,' said Jule. 'Went right up an' started it. But they didn' even swing once.'

'Let's look at 'em.' The prisoners were swung around to face him. Their heads were down. Huston put a flashlight beam in each sullen face. 'What did you wanta do it for?' he asked. There was no answer. 'Who the hell tol' you to do it?'

'Goldarn it, we didn't do nothing. We was jes' gonna dance.'

'No, you wasn't,' Jule said. 'You was gonna sock that kid.'

Tom said: 'Mr Huston, jus' when these here fellas moved in, somebody give a whistle.'

'Yeah, I know! The cops come right to the gate.' He turned back. 'We ain't gonna hurt you. Now who tol' you to come bus' up our dance?' He waited for a reply. 'You're our own folks,' Huston said sadly. 'You belong with us. How'd you happen to come? We know all about it,' he added.

'Well, goddamn it, a fella got to eat.'

'Well, who sent you? Who paid you to come?'

'We ain't been paid.'

'An' you ain't gonna be. No fight, no pay. Ain't that right?'

One of the pinioned men said: 'Do what you want. We ain't gonna tell nothing.'

Huston's head sunk down for a moment, and then he said softly: 'O.K. Don't tell. But looka here. Don't knife your own folks. We're tryin' to get along, havin' fun an' keepin' order. Don't tear all that down. Jes' think about it. You're jes' harmin' yourself.

'Awright, boys, put 'em over the back fence. An' don't hurt 'em. They don't know what they're doin'.'

The squad moved slowly toward the rear of the camp, and Huston looked after them.

Jule said: 'Le's jes' take one good kick at 'em.'

'No, you don't!' Willie cried. 'I said we wouldn'.'

'Jes' one nice little kick,' Jule pleaded. 'Jes' loft 'em over the fence.'

'No, sir,' Willie insisted.

'Listen, you,' he said, 'we're lettin' you off this time. But you take back the word. If'n ever this here happens again, we'll jes' natcherally kick the hell outa whoever comes; we'll bust ever' bone in their body. Now you tell your boys that. Huston says you're our kinda folks–maybe. I'd hate to think it.'

They neared the fence. Two of the seated guards stood up and moved over. 'Got some fellas goin' home early,' said Willie. The three men climbed over the fence and disappeared into the darkness.

And the squad moved quickly back toward the dance floor. And the music of 'Ol' Dan Tucker' skirled and whined from the string band. Over near the office the men still squatted and talked, and the shrill music came to them.

Pa said: 'They's change a-comin'. I don' know what. Maybe we won't live to see her. But she's a-comin'. They's a res'less feelin'. Fella can't figger nothin' out, he's so nervous.'

And Black Hat lifted his head up again, and the light fell on his bristly whiskers. He gathered some little rocks from the ground and shot them like marbles, with his thumb. 'I don' know. She's a-comin' awright, like you say. Fella tol' me what happened in Akron, Ohio. Rubber companies. They got mountain people in 'cause they'd work cheap. An' these here mountain people up an' joined the union. Well, sir, hell jes' popped. All them store-keepers and legioners an' people like that, they get drillin' and yellin', "Red!" An' they're gonna run the union right outa Akron. Preachers git a-preachin' about it, an' papers a-yowlin', an' they's pick-handles put out by the rubber companies, an' they're a-buyin' gas. Jesus, you'd think them mountain boys was reg'lar devils!' He stopped and found some more rocks to shoot. 'Well, sir–it was las' March, an' one Sunday five thousan' of them mountain men had a turkey shoot outside a town. Five thousan' of 'em marched through town with their rifles. An' they had their turkey shoot, an' then they marched back. An' that's all they done. Well, sir they ain't been no trouble sence then. These here citizens' committees give back the pick-handles, an' the storekeepers keep their stores, an' nobody been clubbed, nor tarred an' feathered, an' nobody been killed.' There was a long silence, and then Black Hat said: 'They're gettin' purty mean out here. Burned that camp an' beat up folks. I been thinkin'. All our folks got guns. I been thinkin' maybe we ought to git up a turkey shootin' club an' have meetin' ever' Sunday.'

The men looked up at him, and then down at the ground, and their feet moved restlessly and they shifted their weight from one leg to the other.

25

The spring is beautiful in California. Valleys in which the fruit blossoms are fragrant pink and white waters in a shallow sea. Then the first tendrils of the grapes, swelling from the old gnarled vines, cascade down to cover the trunks. The full green hills are round and soft as breasts. And on the level vegetable lands are the mile-long rows of pale green lettuce and the spindly little cauliflowers, the grey-green unearthly artichoke plants.

And then the leaves break out on the trees, and the petals drop from the fruit trees and carpet the earth with pink and white. The centres of the blossoms swell and grow and colour: cherries and apples, peaches and pears, figs which close the flowers in the fruit. All California quickens with produce, and the fruit grows heavy, and the limbs bend gradually under the fruit so that little crutches must be placed under them to support the weight.

Behind the fruitfulness are men of understanding and knowledge and skill, men who experiment with seed, endlessly developing the techniques for greater crops of plants whose roots will resist the million enemies of the earth: the moles, the insects, the rusts, the blights. These men work carefully and endlessly to perfect the seed, the roots. And there are the men of chemistry who spray the trees against pests, who sulphur the grapes, who cut out disease and rots, mildews and sicknesses. Doctors of preventive medicine, men at the borders who look for fruit flies, for Japanese beetle, men who quarantine the sick trees and root them out and burn them, men of knowledge. The men who graft the young trees, the little vines, are the cleverest of all, for theirs is a surgeon's job, as tender and delicate; and these men must have surgeon's hands and surgeon's hearts to slit the bark, to place the grafts, to bind the wounds and cover them from the air. These are great men.

Along the rows the cultivators move, tearing the spring grass and turning it under to make a fertile earth, breaking the ground to hold the water up near the surface, ridging the ground in little pools for the irrigation, destroying the weed roots that may drink the water away from the trees.

And all the time the fruit swells and the flowers break out in long clusters on the vines. And in the growing year the warmth grows and the leaves turn dark green. The prunes lengthen like little green birds' eggs, and the limbs sag down against the crutches under the weight. And the hard little pears take shape, and the beginning of the fuzz comes out on the peaches. Grape-blossoms shed their tiny petals and the hard little beads become green buttons, and the buttons grow heavy. The men who work in the fields, the owners of the little orchards, watch and calculate. The year is heavy with produce. And men are proud, for of their knowledge they can make the year heavy. They have transformed the world with their knowledge. The short, lean wheat has been made big and productive. Little sour apples have grown large and sweet, and that old grape that grew among the trees and fed the birds, its tiny fruit has mothered a thousand varieties, red, and black, green and pale pink, purple and yellow; and each variety with its own flavour. The men who work in the experimental farms have made new fruits: nectarines and forty kinds of plums, walnuts with paper shells. And always they work, selecting, grafting, changing, driving themselves, driving the earth to produce.

And first the cherries ripen. Cent and a half a pound. Hell, we can't pick 'em for that. Black cherries and red cherries, full and sweet, and the birds eat half of each cherry and the yellow-jackets buzz into the holes the birds made. And on the ground the seeds drop and dry with black shreds hanging from them.

The purple prunes soften and sweeten. My God, we can't pick them and dry and sulphur them. We can't pay wages, no matter what wages. And the purple prunes carpet the ground. And first the skins wrinkle a little and swarms of flies come to feast, and the valley is filled with the odour of sweet decay. The meat turns dark and the crop shrivels on the ground.

And the pears grow yellow and soft. Five dollars a ton. Five dollars for forty fifty-pound boxes; trees pruned and sprayed, orchards cultivated–pick the fruit, put it in boxes, load the trucks, deliver the fruit to the cannery–forty boxes for five dollars. We can't do it. And the yellow fruit falls heavily to the ground and splashes on the ground. The yellow-jackets dig into the soft meat, and there is a smell of ferment and rot.

Then the grapes–we can't make good wine. People can't buy good wine. Rip the grapes from the vines, good grapes, rotten grapes, wasp-stung grapes. Press stems, press dirt and rot.

But there's mildew and formic acid in the vats.

Add sulphur and tannic acid.

The smell from the ferment is not the rich odour of wine, but the smell of decay and chemicals.

Oh, well. It had alcohol in it, anyway. They can get drunk.

The little farmers watched debt creep up on them like the tide. They sprayed the trees and sold no crop, they pruned and grafted and could not pick the crop. And the men of knowledge have worked, have considered, and the fruit is rotting on the ground, and the decaying mash in the wine vats is poisoning the air. And taste the wine–no grape flavour at all, just sulphur and tannic acid and alcohol.

This little orchard will be a part of a great holding next year, for the debt will have choked the owner.

This vineyard will belong to the bank. Only the great owners can survive, for they own the canneries, too. And four pears peeled and cut in half, cooked and canned, still cost fifteen cents. And the canned pears do not spoil. They will last for years.

The decay spreads over the State, and the sweet smell is a great sorrow on the land. Men who can graft the trees and make the seed fertile and big can find no way to let the hungry people eat their produce. Men who have created new fruits in the world cannot create a system whereby their fruits may be eaten. And the failure hangs over the State like a great sorrow.

The works of the roots of the vines, of the trees, must be destroyed to keep up the price, and this is the saddest, bitterest thing of all. Car-loads of oranges dumped on the ground. The people came for miles to take the fruit, but this could not be. How would they buy oranges at twenty cents a dozen if they could drive out and pick them up? And men with hoses squirt kerosene on the oranges, and they are angry at the crime, angry at the people who have come to take the fruit. A million people hungry, needing the fruit–and kerosene sprayed over the golden mountains.

And the smell of rot fills the country.

Burn coffee for fuel in the ships. Burn corn to keep warm, it makes a hot fire. Dump potatoes in the rivers and place guards along the banks to keep the hungry people from fishing them out. Slaughter the pigs and bury them, and let the putrescence drip down into the earth.

There is a crime here that goes beyond denunciation. There is a sorrow here that weeping cannot symbolize. There is a failure here that topples all our success. The fertile earth, the straight tree rows, the sturdy trunks, and the ripe fruit. And children dying of pellagra must die because a profit cannot be taken from an orange. And coroners must fill in the certificates–died of malnutrition–because the food must rot, must be forced to rot.

The people come with nets to fish for potatoes in the river, and the guards hold them back; they come in rattling cars to get the dumped oranges, but the kerosene is sprayed. And they stand still and watch the potatoes float by, listen to the screaming pigs being killed in a ditch and covered with quicklime, watch the mountains of oranges slop down to a putrefying ooze; and in the eyes of the people there is the failure; and in the eyes of the hungry there is a growing wrath. In the souls of the people the grapes of wrath are filling and growing heavy, growing heavy for the vintage.

26

In the Weedpatch camp, on an evening when the long, barred clouds hung over the set sun and inflamed their edges, the Joad family lingered after their supper. Ma hesitated before she started to do the dishes.

'We got to do somepin,' she said. And she pointed at Winfield. 'Look at 'im,' she said. And when they stared at the little boy, 'He's a-jerkin' an' a-twistin' in his sleep. Lookut his colour.' The members of the family looked at the earth again in shame. 'Fried dough,' Ma said. 'One month we been here. An' Tom had five days' work. An' the rest of you scrabblin' out ever' day an' no work. An' scairt to talk. An' the money gone. You're scairt to talk it out. Ever' night you jus' eat, an' then you get wanderin' away. Can't bear to talk it out. Well, you got to. Rosasharn ain't far from due, an' lookut her colour. You got to talk it out. Now don't none of you get up till we figger somepin out. One day' more grease an' two days' flour, an' ten potatoes. You set here an' get busy!'

They looked at the ground. Pa cleaned his thick nails with his pocket-knife. Uncle John picked at a splinter on the box he sat on. Tom pinched his lower lip and pulled it away from his teeth.

He released his lip and said softly: 'We been a-lookin,' Ma. Been walkin' out sence we can't use the petrol no more. Been goin' in ever' gate, walkin' up to ever' house, even when we knowed they wasn't gonna be nothin'. Puts a weight on ya. Goin' out lookin' for somepin you know you ain't gonna find.'

Ma said fiercely: 'You ain't got the right to get discouraged. This here fambly's goin' under. You jus' ain't got the right.'

Pa inspected his scraped nail. 'We gotta go,' he said. 'We didn't wanta go. It's nice here, an' folks is nice here. We're feared we'll have to go live in one a them Hoovervilles.'

'Well, if we got to, we got to. First thing, we got to eat.'

Al broke in. 'I got a tankful a petrol in the truck. I didn't let nobody get into that.'

Tom smiled. 'This here Al got a lot of sense along with he's randy-pandy.'

'Now you figger,' Ma said. 'I ain't watchin' this here fambly starve no more. One day' more grease. That's what we got. Come time for Rosasharn to lay in, she got to be fed up. You figger!'

'This here hot water an' toilets–' Pa began.

'Well, we can't eat no toilets.'

Tom said: 'They was a fella come by to-day lookin' for men to go to Marysville. Pickin' fruit.'

'Well, why don't we go to Marysville?' Ma demanded.

'I dunno,' said Tom. 'Didn' seem right, somehow. He was so anxious. Wouldn' say how much the pay was. Said he didn't know exactly.'

Ma said: 'We're a-goin' to Marysville. I don' care what the pay is. We're a-goin'.'

'It's too far,' said Tom. 'We ain't got the money for petrol. We couldn' get there. Ma, you say we got to figger, I ain't done nothin' but figger the whole time.'

Uncle John said: 'Feller says they's cotton a-comin' in up north, near a place called Tulare. That ain't very far, the feller says.'

'Well, we got to git goin', an' goin' quick. I ain't a-settin' here no longer, no matter how nice.' Ma took up her bucket and walked toward the sanitary unit for hot water.

'Ma gets tough,' Tom said. 'I seen her a-gettin' mad quite a piece now. She jus' boils up.'

Pa said with relief: 'Well, she brang it into the open, anyways. I been layin' at night a-burnin' my brains up. Now we can talk her out, anyways.'

Ma came back with her bucket of steaming water. 'Well,' she demanded, 'figger anything out?'

'Jus' workin' her over,' said Tom. 'Now s'pose we jus' move up north where the cotton's at. We been over this here country. We know they ain't nothin' here. S'pose we pack up an' shove north. Then when the cotton's ready we'll be there. I kinda like to get my han's aroun' some cotton. You got a full tank, Al?'

'Almos'–'bout two inches down.'

'Should get us up to that place.'

Ma poised a dish over the bucket. 'Well?' she demanded.

Tom said: 'You win. We'll move on, I guess. Huh, Pa?'

'Guess we got to,' Pa said.

Ma glanced at him. 'When?'

'Well–no need waitin'. Might's well go in the mornin'.'

'We got to go in the mornin'. I tol' you what's lef'.'

'Now, Ma, don't think I don' wanta go. I ain't had a good gutful to eat in two weeks. 'Course I filled up, but I didn' take no good from it.'

Ma plunged the dish into the bucket. 'We'll go in the mornin',' she said.

Pa sniffled. 'Seems like times is changed,' he said sarcastically. 'Time was when a man said what we'd do. Seems like women is tellin' now. Seems like it's purty near time to get out a stick.'

Ma put the clean dripping tin dish out on a box. She smiled down at her work. 'You get your stick, Pa,' she said. 'Times when they's food an' a place to set, then maybe you can use your stick an' keep your skin whole. But you ain't a-doin' your job, either a-thinkin' or a-working'. If you was, why, you could use your stick, an' women folks'd sniffle their nose an' creep-mouse aroun'. But you jus' get you a stick now an' you ain't lickin' no woman; you're a-fightin', 'cause I got a stick all laid out too.'

Pa grinned with embarrassment. 'Now it ain't good to have the little fellas hear you talkin' like that,' he said.

'You get some bacon inside the little fellas 'fore you come tellin' what else is good for 'em,' said Ma.

Pa got up in disgust and moved away, and Uncle John followed him.

Ma's hands were busy in the water, but she watched them go, and she said proudly to Tom: 'He's all right. He ain't beat. He's like as not to take a smack at me.'

Tom laughed. 'You jus' a-treadin' him on?'

'Sure,' said Ma. 'Take a man, he can get worried an' worried, an' it eats out his liver, an' purty soon he'll jus' lay down and die with his heart et out. But if you can take an' make 'im mad, why, he'll be awright. Pa, he didn' say nothin', but he's mad now. He'll show me now. He's awright.'

Al got up. 'I'm gonna walk down the row,' he said.

'Better see the truck's ready to go,' Tom warned him.

'She's ready.'

'If she ain't, I'll turn Ma on ya.'

'She's ready.' Al strolled jauntily along the row of tents.

Tom sighed. 'I'm gettin' tired, Ma. How 'bout makin' me mad?'

'You got more sense, Tom. I don' need to make you mad. I got to lean on you. Them others–they're kinda strangers, all but you. You won't give up, Tom.'

The job fell on him. 'I don' like it,' he said. 'I wanta go out like Al. An' I wanta get mad like Pa, an' I wanta get drunk like Uncle John.'

Ma shook her head. 'You can't, Tom. I know. I knowed from the time you was a little fella. You can't. They's some folks that's just theirself an' nothin' more. There's Al–he's jus' a young fella after a girl. You wasn't never like that, Tom.'

'Sure I was,' said Tom. 'Still am.'

'No you ain't. Ever'thing you do is more'n you. When they sent you up to prison I knowed it. You're spoke for.'

'Now, Ma–cut it out. It ain't true. It's all in your head.'

She stacked the knives and forks on top of the plates. 'Maybe. Maybe it's in my head. Rosasharn, you wipe up these here an' put 'em away.'

The girl got breathlessly to her feet and her swollen middle hung out in front of her. She moved sluggishly to the box and picked up a washed dish.

Tom said: 'Gettin' so tightful it's a-pullin' her eyes wide.'

'Don't you go a-jollyin',' said Ma. 'She's doin' good. You go 'long an' say goo'-bye to anybody you wan'.'

'O.K.,' he said. 'I'm gonna see how far it is up there.'

Ma said to the girl: 'He ain't sayin' stuff like that to make you feel bad. Where's Ruthie an' Winfiel'?'

'They snuck off after Pa. I seen 'em.'

'Well, leave 'em go.'

Rose of Sharon moved sluggishly about her work. Ma inspected her cautiously. 'You feelin' pretty good? Your cheeks is kinda saggy.'

'I ain't had milk like they said I ought.'

'I know. We jus' didn' have no milk.'

Rose of Sharon said dully: 'Ef Connie hadn' went away, we'd a had a little house by now, with him studyin' an' all. Would a got milk like I need. Would a had a nice baby. This here baby ain't gonna be no good. I ought a had milk.' She reached in her apron pocket and put something into her mouth.

Ma said: 'I seen you nibblin' on somepin. What you eatin'?'

'Nothin'.'

'Come on, what you nibblin' on?'

'Jus' a piece a slack lime. Foun' a big hunk.'

'Why, tha's just like eatin' dirt.'

'I kinda feel like I wan' it.'

Ma was silent. She spread her knees and tightened her skirt. 'I know,' she said at last. 'I et coal oncet when I was in a fambly way. Et a big piece of coal. Granma says I shouldn'. Don' you say that about the baby. You got no right to think it.'

'Got no husban'! Got no milk!'

Ma said: 'If you was a well girl, I'd take a whang at you. Right in the face.' She got up and went inside the tent. She came out and stood in front of Rose of Sharon, and she held out her hand. 'Look!' The small gold earrings were in her hand. 'These is for you.'

The girl's eyes brightened for a moment, and then she looked aside. 'I ain't pierced.'

'Well, I'm a-gonna pierce ya.' Ma hurried back into the tent. She came back with a cardboard box. Hurriedly she threaded a needle, doubled the thread and tied a series of knots in it. She threaded a second needle and knotted the thread. In the box she found a piece of cork.

'It'll hurt. It'll hurt.'

Ma stepped to her, put the cork in back of the ear lobe and pushed the needle through the ear, into the cork.

The girl twitched. 'It sticks. It'll hurt.'

'No more'n that.'

'Yes, it will.'

'Well, then. Le's see the other ear first.' She placed the cork and pierced the other ear.

'It'll hurt.'

'Hush!' said Ma. 'It's all done.'

Rose of Sharon looked at her in wonder. Ma clipped the needles off and pulled one knot of each thread through the lobes.

'Now,' she said. 'Ever' day we'll pull one knot, and in a couple weeks it'll be all well an' you can wear 'em. Here–they're your'n now. You can keep 'em.'

Rose of Sharon touched her ears tenderly and looked at the tiny spots of blood on her fingers. 'It didn' hurt. Jus' stuck a little.'

'You oughta been pierced long ago,' said Ma. She looked at the girl's face, and she smiled in triumph. 'Now get them dishes all done up. Your baby gonna be a good baby. Very near let you have a baby without your ears was pierced. But you're safe now.'

'Does it mean somepin?'

'Why, 'course it does,' said Ma. ''Course it does.'

Al strolled down the street toward the dancing platform. Outside a neat little tent he whistled softly, and then moved along the street. He walked to the edge of the grounds and sat down in the grass.

The clouds over the west had lost the red edging now, and the cores were black. Al scratched his legs and looked toward the evening sky.

In a few moments a blonde girl walked near; she was pretty and sharp-featured. She sat down in the grass beside him and did not speak. Al put his hand on her waist and walked his fingers around.

'Don't,' she said. 'You tickle.'

'We're goin' away to-morra,' said Al.

She looked at him, startled. 'To-morra? Where?'

'Up north,' he said lightly.

'Well, we're gonna git married, ain't we?'

'Sure, sometime.'

'You said purty soon!' she cried angrily.

'Well, soon is when soon comes.'

'You promised.' He walked his fingers around farther.

'Git away,' she cried. 'You said we was.'

'Well, sure we are.'

'An' now you're goin' away.'

Al demanded: 'What's the matter with you? You in a fambly way?'

'No, I ain't.'

Al laughed. 'I jus' been wastin' my time, huh?'

Her chin shot out. She jumped to her feet. 'You git away from me, Al Joad. I don' wanta see you no more.'

'Aw, come on. What's the matter?'

'You think you're jus'–hell on wheels.'

'Now wait a minute.'

'You think I got to go out with you. Well, I don't! I got lots a chances.'

'Now wait a minute.'

'No, sir–you git away.'

Al lunged suddenly, caught her by the ankle, and tripped her. He grabbed her when she fell and held her and put his hand over her angry mouth. She tried to bite his palm, but he cupped it out over her mouth, and he held her down with his other arm. And in a moment she lay still, and in another moment they were giggling together in the dry grass.

'Why, we'll be a-comin' back purty soon,' said Al. 'An I'll have a pocketful of jack. We'll go down to Hollywood an' see the pitchers.'

She was lying on her back. Al bent over her. And he saw the bright evening star reflected in her eyes, and he saw the black cloud reflected in her eyes. 'We'll go on the train,' he said.

'How long ya think it'll be?' she asked.

'Oh, maybe a month,' he said.

The evening dark came down and Pa and Uncle John squatted with the heads of families out by the office. They studied the night and the future. The little manager, in his white clothes, frayed and clean, rested his elbows on the porch rail. His face was drawn and tired.

Huston looked up at him. 'You better get some sleep, mister.'

'I guess I ought. Baby born last night in Unit Three. I'm getting to be a good midwife.'

'Fella oughta know,' said Huston. 'Married fella got to know.'

Pa said: 'We're a-gittin' out in the mornin'.'

'Yeah? Which way you goin'?'

'Thought we'd go up north a little. Try to get in the first cotton. We ain't had work. We're outa food.'

'Know if they's any work?' Huston asked.

'No, but we're sure they ain't none here.'

'They will be, a little later,' Huston said. 'We'll hold on.'

'We hate to go,' said Pa. 'Folks been so nice here–an' the toilets an' all. But we got to eat. Got a tank of petrol. That'll get us a little piece up the road. We had a bath ever' day here. Never was so clean in my life. Funny thing–use' ta be I on'y got a bath ever' week an' I never seemed to stink. But now if I don't get one ever' day I stink. Wonder if takin' a bath so often makes that?'

'Maybe you couldn't smell yourself before,' the manager said.

'Maybe. I wisht we could stay.'

The little manager held his temples between his palms. 'I think there's going to be another baby to-night,' he said.

'We gonna have one in our fambly 'fore long,' said Pa. 'I wisht we could have it here. I sure wisht we could.'

Tom and Willie and Jule the half-breed sat on the edge of the dance floor and swung their feet.

'I got a sack of Durham,' Jule said. 'Like a smoke?'

'I sure would,' said Tom. 'Ain't had a smoke for a hell of a time.' He rolled the brown cigarette carefully, to keep down the loss of tobacco.

'Well, sir, we'll be sorry to see you go,' said Willie. 'You folks is good folks.'

Tom lighted his cigarette. 'I been thinkin' about it a lot. Jesus Christ, I wisht we could settle down.'

Jule took back his Durham. 'It ain't nice,' he said. 'I got a little girl. Thought when I come out here she'd get some schoolin'. But hell, we ain't in one place hardly long enough. Jes' gits goin' an' we got to drag on.'

'I hope we don't get in no more Hoovervilles,' said Tom. 'I was really scairt, there.'

'Depities push you aroun'?'

'I was scairt I'd kill somebody,' said Tom. 'Was on'y there a little while, but I was a-stewin' aroun' the whole time. Depity come in an' picked up a frien', jus' because he talked outa turn. I was jus' stewin' all the time.'

'Ever been in a strike?' Willie asked.

'No.'

'Well, I been a-thinkin' a lot. Why don' them depities get in here an' raise hell like ever' place else? Think that little guy in the office is a-stoppin' 'em? No, sir.'

'Well, what is?' Jule asked.

'I'll tell ya. It's 'cause we're all a-workin' together. Depity can't pick on one fella in this camp. He's pickin' on the whole darn camp. An' he don't dare. All we got to do is give a yell an' they's two hundred men out. Fella organizin' for the union was a-talkin' out on the road. He says we could do that any place. Jus' stick together. They ain't raisin' hell with no two hundred men. They're pickin' on one man.'

'Yeah,' said Jule, 'an' suppose you got a union? You got to have leaders. They'll jus' pick up your leaders, an' where's your union?'

'Well,' said Willie, 'we got to figure her out some time. I been out here a year, an' wages is going' right on down. Fella can't feed his fam'ly on his work now, an' it's gettin' worse all the time. It ain't gonna do no good to set aroun' an' starve. I don' know what to do. If a fella owns a team a horses, he don't raise no hell if he got to feed 'em when they ain't workin'. But if a fella got men workin' for him, he jus' don't give a damn. Horses is a hell of a lot more worth than men. I don't understan' it.'

'Gets so I don' wanta think about it,' said Jule. 'An' I got to think about it. I got this here little girl. You know how purty she is. One week they give her a prize in this camp 'cause she's so purty. Well, what's gonna happen to her? She's gettin' spindly. I ain't gonna stan' it. She's so purty. I'm gonna burst out.'

'How?' Willie asked. 'What you gonna do–steal some stuff an' git in jail? Kill somebody an'. git hung?'

'I don' know,' said Jule. 'Gits me nuts thinkin' about it. Gits me clear nuts.'

'I'm a-gonna miss them dances,' Tom said. 'Them was some of the nicest dances I ever seen. Well, I'm gonna turn in. So long. I'll be seein' you someplace.' He shook hands.

'Sure will,' said Jule.

'Well, so long.' Tom moved away into the darkness.

In the darkness of the Joad tent Ruthie and Winfield lay on their mattress, and Ma lay beside them. Ruthie whispered, 'Ma!'

'Yeah? Ain't you asleep yet?'

'Ma–they gonna have croquet where we're goin'?'

'I don't know. Get some sleep. We want to get an early start.'

'Well, I wisht we'd stay here where we're sure we got croquet.'

'Sh!' said Ma.

'Ma, Winfiel' hit a kid to-night.'

'He shouldn' of.'

'I know. I tol' im, but he hit the kid right in the nose an', Jesus, how the blood run down!'

'Don' talk like that. It ain't a nice way to talk.'

Winfield turned over. 'That kid says we was Okies,' he said in an outraged voice. 'He says he wasn't no Okie 'cause he come from Oregon. Says we was goddamn Okies. I socked him.'

'Sh! You shouldn'. He can't hurt you callin' names.'

'Well, I won't let 'im,' Winfield said fiercely.

'Sh! Get some sleep.'

Ruthie said: 'You oughta seen the blood run down–all over his clothes.'

Ma reached a hand from under the blanket and snapped Ruthie on the cheek with her finger. The little girl went rigid for a moment, and then dissolved into sniffling, quiet crying.

In the sanitary unit Pa and Uncle John sat in adjoining compartments. 'Might's well get in a good las' one,' said Pa. 'It's sure nice. 'Member how the little fellas was so scairt when they flushed 'em for the first time?'

'I wasn't so easy myself,' said Uncle John. He pulled his overalls neatly up around his knees. 'I'm gettin' bad,' he said. 'I feel sin.'

'You can't sin none,' said Pa. 'You ain't got no money. Jus' sit tight. Cos' you at leas' two bucks to sin, an' we ain't got two bucks amongst us.'

'Yeah! But I'm a-thinkin' sin.'

'Awright. You can think sin for nothin'.'

'It's jus' as bad,' said Uncle John.

'It's a whole hell of a lot cheaper,' said Pa.

'Don't you go makin' light of sin.'

'I ain't. You jus' go ahead. You always gets sinful jus' when hell's-a-poppin'.'

'I know it,' said Uncle John. 'Always was that way. I never tol' half the stuff I done.'

'Well, keep it to yaself.'

'These here nice toilets gets me sinful.'

'Go out in the bushes then. Come on, pull up ya pants an' le's get some sleep.' Pa pulled his overall straps in place and snapped the buckle. He flushed the toilet and watched thoughtfully while the water whirled in the bowl.

It was still dark when Ma roused her camp. The low night lights shone through the open doors of the sanitary units. From the tents along the road came the assorted snores of the campers.

Ma said: 'Come on, roll out. We got to be on our way. Day's not far off.' She raised the screechy shade of the lantern and lighted the wick. 'Come on, all of you.'

The floor of the tent squirmed into slow action. Blankets and comforters were thrown back and sleepy eyes squinted blindly at the light. Ma slipped on her dress over the underclothes she wore to bed. 'We got no coffee,' she said. 'I got a few biscuits. We can eat 'em on the road. Jus' get up now, an' we'll load the truck. Come on now. Don't make no noise. Don' wanta wake the neighbours.'

It was a few moments before they were fully aroused. 'Now don' you get away,' Ma warned the children. The family dressed. The men pulled down the tarpaulin and loaded up the truck. 'Make it nice an' flat,' Ma warned them. They piled the mattress on top of the load and bound the tarpaulin in place over its ridge pole.

'Awright, Ma,' said Tom. 'She's ready.'

Ma held a plate of cold biscuits in her hand. 'Awright. Here. Each take one. It's all we got.'

Ruthie and Winfield grabbed their biscuits and climbed up on the load. They covered themselves with a blanket and went back to sleep, still holding the cold hard biscuits in their hands. Tom got into the driver's seat and stepped on the starter. It buzzed a little, and then stopped.

'Goddamn you, Al!' Tom cried. 'You let the battery run down.'

Al blustered: 'How the hell was I gonna keep her up if I ain't got petrol to run her?'

Tom chuckled suddenly. 'Well, I don't know how, but it's your fault. You got to crank her.'

'I tell you it ain't my fault.'

Tom got out and found the crank under the seat. 'It's my fault,' he said.

'Gimme that crank.' Al seized it. 'Pull down the spark so she don't take my arm off.'

'O.K. Twist her tail.'

Al laboured at the crank, around and around. The engine caught, spluttered, and roared as Tom choked the car delicately. He raised the spark and reduced the throttle.

Ma climbed in beside him. 'We woke up ever'body in the camp,' she said.

'They'll go to sleep again.'

Al climbed in on the other side. 'Pa 'n' Uncle John got up top,' he said. 'Goin' to sleep again.'

Tom drove toward the main gate. The watchman came out of the office and played his flashlight on the truck. 'Wait a minute.'

'What ya want?'

'You checkin' out?'

'Sure.'

'Well, I got to cross you off.'

'O.K.'

'Know which way you're goin'?'

'Well, we're gonna try up north.'

'Well, good luck,' said the watchman.

'Same to you. So long.'

The truck edged slowly over the big hump and into the road. Tom retraced the road he had driven before, past Weedpatch and west until he came to 99, then north on the great paved road, toward Bakersfield. It was growing light when he came into the outskirts of the city.

Tom said: 'Ever' place you look is restaurants. An' them places all got coffee. Lookit that all-nighter there. Bet they got ten gallons a coffee in there, all hot!'

'Aw, shut up,' said Al.

Tom grinned over at him. 'Well, I see you got yaself a girl right off.'

'Well, what of it?'

'He's mean this mornin', Ma. He ain't good company.'

Al said irritably: 'I'm goin' out on my own purty soon. Fella can make his way lot easier if he ain't got a fambly.'

Tom said: 'You'd have yaself a fambly in nine months. I seen you playin' aroun'.'

'Ya crazy,' said Al. 'I'd get myself a job in a garage an' I'd eat in restaurants–'

'An' you'd have a wife an' kids in nine months.'

'I tell ya I wouldn'.'

Tom said: 'You're a wise guy, Al. You gonna take some beatin' over the head.'

'Who's gonna do it?'

'They'll always be guys to do it,' said Tom.

'You think jus' because you –'

'Now you jus' stop that,' Ma broke in.

'I done it,' said Tom. 'I was a-badgerin' him. I didn' mean no harm, Al. I didn' know you liked that girl so much.'

'I don't like no girls much.'

'Awright, then, you don't. You ain't gonna get no argument out of me.'

The truck came to the edge of the city. 'Look a them hot-dog stan's–hunderds of 'em,' said Tom.

Ma said: 'Tom! I got a dollar put away. You wan' coffee bad enough to spen' it?'

'No, Ma. I'm jus' foolin'.'

'You can have it if you wan' it bad enough.'

'I wouldn' take it.'

Al said: 'Then shut up about coffee.'

Tom was silent for a time. 'Seems like I got my foot in it all the time,' he said. 'There's the road we run up that night.'

'I hope we don't never have nothin' like that again,' said Ma. 'That was a bad night.'

'I didn' like it none either.'

The sun rose on their right, and the great shadow of the truck ran beside them, flicking over the fence-posts beside the road. They ran on past the rebuilt Hooverville.

'Look,' said Tom. 'They got new people there. Looks like the same place.'

Al came slowly out of his sullenness. 'Fella tol' me some a them people been burned out fifteen-twenty times. Says they jus' go hide down the willows an' then they come out an' build 'em another weed shack. Jus' like gophers. Got so use' to it they don't even get mad no more, this fella said. They jus' figger it's like bad weather.'

'Sure was bad weather for me that night,' said Tom. They moved up the wide highway. And the sun's warmth made them shiver. 'Gettin' snappy in the mornin',' said Tom. 'Winter's on the way. I jus' hope we can get some money 'fore it comes. Tent ain't gonna be nice in the winter.'

Ma sighed, and then she straightened her head. 'Tom,' she said, 'we gotta have a house in the winter. I tell ya we got to. Ruthie's awright, but Winfiel' ain't so strong. We got to have a house when the rains come. I heard it jus' rains cats aroun' here.'

'We'll get a house, Ma. You res' easy. You gonna have a house.'

'Jus' so's it's got a roof an' a floor. Jus' to keep the little fellas off'n the groun'.'

'We'll try, Ma.'

'I don' wanna worry ya now.'

'We'll try, Ma.'

'I jus' get panicky sometimes,' she said. 'I jus' lose my spunk.'

'I never seen you when you lost it.'

'Nights I do, sometimes.'

There came a harsh hissing from the front of the truck. Tom grabbed the wheel tight and he thrust the brake down to the floor. The truck bumped to a stop. Tom sighed. 'Well, there she is.' He leaned back in the seat. Al leaped out and ran to the right front tire.

'Great big nail,' he called.

'We got any tire patch?'

'No,' said Al. 'Used it all up. Got patch, but no glue stuff.'

Tom turned and smiled sadly at Ma. 'You shouldn' a tol' about that dollar,' he said. 'We'd a fixed her some way.' He got out of the car and went to the flat tire.

Al pointed to a big nail protruding from the flat casing. 'There she is!'

'If they's one nail in the country, we run over it.'

'Is it bad?' Ma called.

'No, not bad, but we got to fix her.'

The family piled down from the top of the truck. 'Puncture?' Pa asked and then he saw the tire and was silent.

Tom moved Ma from the seat and got the can of tire patch from underneath the cushion. He unrolled the rubber patch and took out the tube of cement squeezed it gently. 'She's almos' dry,' he said. 'Maybe they's enough Awright, Al. Block the back wheels. Le's get her jacked up.'

Tom and Al worked well together. They put stones behind the wheels, put the jack under the front axle, and lifted the weight off the limp casing. They ripped off the casing. They found the hole, dipped a rag in the petrol tank and washed the tube around the hole. And then, while Al held the tube tight over his knee, Tom tore the cement tube in two and spread the little fluid thinly on the rubber with his pocket-knife. He scraped the gum delicately. 'Now let her dry while I cut a patch.' He trimmed and bevelled the edge of the blue patch. Al held the tube tight while Tom put the patch tenderly in place. 'There! Now bring her to the running-board while I tap her with a hammer.' He pounded the patch carefully, then stretched the tube and watched the edges of the patch. 'There she is! She's gonna hold. Stick her on the rim an' we'll pump her up. Looks like you keep your buck, Ma.'

Al said: 'I wisht we had a spare. We got to get us a spare, Tom, on a rim an' all pumped up. Then we can fix a puncture at night.'

'When we get money for a spare we'll get us some coffee an' side-meat instead,' Tom said.

The light morning traffic buzzed by on the highway, and the sun grew warm and bright. A wind, gentle and sighing, blew in puffs from the southwest, and the mountains on both sides of the great valley were indistinct in a pearly mist.

Tom was pumping at the tire when a roadster, coming from the north, stopped on the other side of the road. A brown-faced man dressed in a light grey business suit got out and walked across to the truck. He was bareheaded. He smiled, and his teeth were very white against his brown skin. He wore a massive gold wedding ring on the third finger of his left hand. A little gold football hung on a slender chain across his waistcoat.

''Morning,' he said pleasantly.

Tom stopped pumping and looked up. ''Mornin'.'

The man ran his fingers through his coarse, short, greying hair. 'You people looking for work?'

'We sure are, mister. Lookin' even under boards.'

'Can you pick peaches?'

'We never done it,' Pa said.

'We can do anything.' Tom said hurriedly. 'We can pick anything there is.'

The man fingered his gold football. 'Well, there's plenty of work for you about forty miles north.'

'We'd sure admire to get it,' said Tom. 'You tell us how to get there, an' we'll go a-lopin'.'

'Well, you go north to Pixley, that's thirty-five or six miles, and you turn east. Go about six miles. Ask anybody where the Hooper ranch is. You'll find plenty of work there.'

'We sure will.'

'Know where there's other people looking for work?'

'Sure,' said Tom. 'Down at the Weedpatch camp they's plenty lookin' for work.'

'I'll take a run down there. We can use quite a few. Remember now, turn east at Pixley and keep straight east to the Hooper ranch.'

'Sure,' said Tom. 'An' we thank ya, mister. We need work awful bad.'

'All right. Get along as soon as you can.' He walked back across the road, climbed into his open roadster, and drove away south.

Tom threw his weight on the pump. 'Twenty apiece,' he called. 'One–two–three–four–' At twenty Al took the pump, and then Pa and then Uncle John. The tire filled out and grew plump and smooth. Three times around, the pump went. 'Let 'er down an' le's see,' said Tom.

Al released the jack and lowered the car. 'Got plenty,' he said. 'Maybe a little too much.'

They threw the tools into the car. 'Come on, le's go,' Tom called. 'We're gonna get some work at last.'

Ma got in the middle again. Al drove this time.

'Now take her easy. Don't burn her up, Al.'

They drove on through the sunny morning fields. The mist lifted from the hilltops and they were clear and brown, with black-purple creases. The wild doves flew up from the fences as the truck passed. Al unconsciously increased his speed.

'Easy,' Tom warned him. 'She'll blow up if you crowd her. We got to get there. Might even get in some work to-day.'

Ma said excitedly: 'With four men a-workin' maybe I can get some credit right off. Fust thing I'll get is coffee, 'cause you been wanting that, an' then some flour an' bakin' powder an' some meat. Better not get no side-meat right off. Save that for later. Maybe Sat'dy. An' soap. Got to get soap. Wonder where we'll stay.' She babbled on. 'An' milk. I'll get some milk 'cause Rosasharn, she ought to have milk. The lady nurse says that.'

A snake wriggled across the warm highway. Al zipped over and ran it down and came back to his own lane.

'Gopher snake,' said Tom. 'You oughtn't to done that.'

'I hate 'em,' said Al gaily. 'Hate all kinds. Give me the stomach-quake.'

The forenoon traffic on the highway increased, salesmen in shiny coupés with the insignia of their companies painted on the doors, red-and-white petrol trucks dragging clinking chains behind them, great square-doored vans from wholesale grocery houses, delivering produce. The country was rich along the roadside. There were orchards, heavy-leafed in their prime, and vine-yards with the long green crawlers carpeting the ground between the rows. There were melon patches and grain-fields. White houses stood in the greenery, roses growing over them. And the sun was gold and warm.

In the front seat of the truck Ma and Tom and Al were overcome with happiness. 'I ain't really felt so good for a long time,' Ma said. ''F we pick plenty peaches we might get a house, pay rent even, for a couple of months. We got to have a house.'

Al said: 'I'm a-gonna save up. I'll save up an' then I'm a-goin' in a town an' get me a job in a garage. Live in a room an' eat in restaurants. Go to the movin' pitchers ever' damn night. Don' cost much. Cowboy pitchers.' His hands tightened on the wheel.

The radiator bubbled and hissed steam. 'Did you fill her up?' Tom asked.

'Yeah. Wind's kinda behind us. That's what makes her boil.'

'It's a awful nice day,' Tom said. 'Use' ta work there in McAlester an' think all the things I'd do. I'd go in straight line way to hell an' gone an' never stop nowheres. Seems like a long time ago. Seems like it's years ago I was in. They was a guard made it tough. I was gonna lay for 'im. Guess that's what makes me mad at cops. Seems like ever' cop got his face. He use' ta get red in the face. Looked like a pig. Had a brother out west, they said. Use' ta get fellas paroled to his brother, an' then they had to work for nothin'. If they raised a stink, they'd get sent back for breakin' parole. That's what the fellers said.'

'Don' think about it,' Ma begged him. 'I'm a-gonna lay in a lot a stuff to eat. Lot a flour an' lard.'

'Might's well think about it,' said Tom. 'Try to shut it out, an' it'll whang back at me. They was a screwball. Never tol' you 'bout him. Looked like Happy Hooligan. Harmless kinda fella. Always was gonna make a break. Fellas all called him Hooligan.' Tom laughed to himself.

'Don' think about it,' Ma begged.

'Go on,' said Al. 'Tell about the fella.'

'It don't hurt nothin', Ma,' Tom said. 'This fella was always gonna break out. Make a plan, he would; but he couldn't keep it to hisself an' purty soon ever'body knowed it, even the warden. He'd make his break an' they'd take 'im by the han' an' lead 'im back. Well, one time he drawed a plan where he's goin' over. 'Course he showed it aroun', an' ever'body kep' still. An' he hid out, an' ever'body kep' still. So he's got himself a rope somewheres, an' he goes over the wall. They's six guards outside with a great big sack, an' Hooligan comes quiet down the rope an' they jus' hol' the sack out an' he goes right inside. They tie up the mouth an' take 'im back inside. Fellas laughed so hard they like to died. But it busted Hooligan's spirit. He jus' cried an' cried, an' moped aroun' an' got sick. Hurt his feelin's so bad. Cut his wrists with a pin an' bled to death 'cause his feelin's was hurt. No harm in 'im at all. They's all kinds a screwballs in stir.'

'Don't talk about it,' Ma said. 'I knowed Purty Boy Floyd's ma. He wa'n't a bad boy. Jus' got drove in a corner.'

The sun moved up toward noon and the shadows of the truck grew lean and moved in under the wheels.

'Mus' be Pixley up the road,' Al said. 'Seen a sign a little back.' They drove into the little town and turned eastward on a narrower road. And the orchards lined the way and made an aisle.

'Hope we can find her easy,' Tom said.

Ma said: 'That fella said the Hooper ranch. Said anybody'd tell us. Hope they's a store nearby. Might get some credit, with four men workin'. I could get a real nice supper if they'd gimme some credit. Make up a big stew maybe.'

'An' coffee,' said Tom. 'Might even get me a sack a Durham. I ain't had no tobacca of my own for a long time.'

Far ahead the road was blocked with cars, and a line of white motor-cycles was drawn up along the roadside. 'Mus' be a wreck,' Tom said.

As they drew near, a State policeman, in boots and Sam Browne belt, stepped around the last parked car. He held up his hand and Al pulled to a stop. The policeman leaned confidentially on the side of the car. 'Where you going?'

Al said: 'Fella said they was work pickin' peaches up this way.'

'Want to work, do you?'

'Damn right,' said Tom.

'O.K. Wait here a minute.' He moved to the side of the road and called ahead. 'One more. That's six cars already. Better take this batch through.'

Tom called: 'Hey! What's the matter?'

The patrol man lounged back 'Got a little trouble up ahead. Don't you worry. You'll get through. Just follow the line.'

There came the splattering blast of motor-cycles starting. The line of cars moved on, with the Joad truck last. Two motor-cycles led the way, and two followed.

Tom said uneasily: 'I wonder what's a matter.'

'Maybe the road's out,' Al suggested.

'Don' need four cops to lead us. I don' like it.'

The motor-cycles ahead speeded up. The line of old cars speeded up. Al hurried to keep at the back of the last car.

'These here is our own people, all of 'em,' Tom said. 'I don' like this.'

Suddenly the leading policeman turned off the road into a wide gravelled entrance. The old cars whipped after them. The motor-cycles roared their motors. Tom saw a line of men standing in the ditch beside the road, saw their mouths open as though they were yelling, saw their shaking fists and their furious faces. A stout woman ran towards the cars, but a roaring motor-cycle stood in her way. A high wire gate swung open. The six old cars moved through and the gate closed behind them. The four motor-cycles turned and sped back in the direction from which they had come. And now that the motors were gone, the distant yelling of the men in the ditch could be heard. Two men stood beside the gravelled road. Each one carried a shotgun.

One called: 'Go on, go on. What the hell are you waiting for?' The six cars moved ahead, turned a bend and came suddenly on the peach camp.

There were fifty little square, flat-roofed boxes, each with a door and a window, and the whole group in a square. A water tank stood high on one edge of the camp. And a little grocery store stood on the other side. At the end of each row of square houses stood two men armed with shotguns and wearing big silver stars pinned to their shirts.

The six cars stopped. Two book-keepers moved from car to car. 'Want to work?'

Tom answered: 'Sure, but what is this?'

'That's not your affair. Want to work?'

'Sure we do.'

'Name?'

'Joad.'

'How many men?'

'Four.'

'Women?'

'Two.'

'Kids?'

'Two.'

'Can all of you work?'

'Why–I guess so.'

'O.K. Find house sixty-three. Wages five cents a box. No bruised fruit. All right, move along now. Go to work right away.'

The cars moved on. On the door of each square red house a number was painted. 'Sixty,' Tom said. 'There's sixty. Must be down that way. There, sixty-one, sixty-two–There she is.'

Al parked the truck close to the door of the little house. The family came down from the top of the truck and looked about in bewilderment. Two deputies approached. They looked closely into each face.

'Name?'

'Joad,' Tom said impatiently. 'Say, what is this here?'

One of the deputies took out a long list. 'Not here. Ever see these here? Look at the licence. Nope. Ain't got it. Guess they're O.K.'

'Now you look here. We don't want no trouble with you. Jes' do your work and mind your own business and you'll be all right.' The two turned abruptly and walked away. At the end of the dusty street they sat down on two boxes and their position commanded the length of the street.

Tom stared after them. 'They sure do wanta make us feel at home.'

Ma opened the door of the house and stepped inside. The floor was splashed with grease. In the one room stood a rusty tin stove and nothing more. The tin stove rested on four bricks and its rusty stovepipe went up through the roof. The room smelled of sweat and grease. Rose of Sharon stood beside Ma. 'We gonna live here?'

Ma was silent for a moment. 'Why, sure,' she said at last. 'It ain't so bad once we wash it out. Get her mopped.'

'I like the tent better,' the girl said.

'This got a floor,' Ma suggested. 'This here wouldn' leak when it rains.' She turned to the door. 'Might as well unload,' she said.

The men unloaded the truck silently. A fear had fallen on them. The great square of boxes was silent. A woman went by in the street, but she did not look at them. Her head was sunk and her dirty gingham dress was frayed at the bottom in little flags.

The pall had fallen on Ruthie and Winfield. They did not dash away to inspect the place. They stayed close to the truck, close to the family. They looked forlornly up and down the dusty street. Winfield found a piece of baling wire and he bent it back and forth until it broke. He made a little crank of the shortest piece and turned it around and around in his hands.

Tom and Pa were carrying the mattresses into the house when a clerk appeared. He wore khaki trousers and a blue shirt and a black necktie. He wore silver-bound eyeglasses, and his eyes, through the thick lenses, were weak and red, and the pupils were staring little bull's-eyes. He leaned forward to look at Tom.

'I want to get you checked down,' he said. 'How many of you going to work?'

Tom said: 'They's four men. Is this here hard work?'

'Picking peaches,' the clerk said. 'Piece work. Give five cents a box.'

'Ain't no reason why the little fellas can't help?'

'Sure not, if they're careful.'

Ma stood in the doorway. 'Soon's I get settled down I'll come out an' help. We got nothin' to eat, mister. Do we get paid right off?'

'Well, no, not money right off. But you can get credit at the store for what you got coming.'

'Come on, let's hurry,' Tom said. 'I want ta get some meat an' bread in me to-night. Where do we go, mister?'

'I'm going out there now. Come with me.'

Tom and Pa and Al and Uncle John walked with him down the dusty street and into the orchard, in among the peach trees. The narrow leaves were beginning to turn a pale yellow. The peaches were little globes of gold and red on the branches. Among the trees were piles of empty boxes. The pickers scurried about, filling their buckets from the branches, putting the peaches in the boxes, carrying the boxes to the checking station; and at the stations, where the piles of filled boxes waited for the trucks, clerks waited to check against the names of the pickers.

'Here's four more,' the guide said to the clerk.

'O.K. Ever picked before?'

'Never did,' said Tom.

'Well, pick careful. No bruised fruit, no windfalls. Bruise your fruit an' we won't check 'em. There's some buckets.'

Tom picked up a three-gallon bucket and looked at it. 'Full a holes in the bottom.'

'Sure,' said the near-sighted clerk. 'That keeps people from stealing them. All right–down in that section. Get going.'

The four Joads took their buckets and went into the orchard. 'They don't waste no time,' Tom said.

'Christ Awmighty,' Al said. 'I ruther work in a garage.'

Pa had followed docilely into the field. He turned suddenly on Al. 'Now you jus' quit it,' he said. 'You been a-hankerin' an' a-complainin' an a bullblowin'.' You get to work. You ain't so big as I can't lick you yet.'

Al's face turned red with anger. He started to bluster.

Tom moved near to him. 'Come on, Al,' he said quietly. 'Bread an' meat. We got to get 'em.'

They reached for the fruit and dropped them in the buckets. Tom ran at his work. One bucket full, two buckets. He dumped them in a box. Three buckets. The box was full. 'I jus' made a nickel,' he called. He picked up the box and walked hurriedly to the station. 'Here's a nickel's worth,' he said to the checker.

The man looked into the box, turned over a peach or two. 'Put it over there. That's out,' he said. 'I told you not to bruise them. Dumped 'em outa the bucket, didn't you? Well, every damn peach is bruised. Can't check that one. Put 'em in easy or you're working for nothing.'

'Why–goddamn it–'

'Now go easy. I warned you before you started.'

Tom's eyes dropped sullenly. 'O.K.,' he said. 'O.K.' He went quickly back to the others. 'Might's well dump what you got,' he said. 'Yours is the same as mine. Won't take 'em.'

'Now, what the hell!' Al began.

'Got to pick easier. Can't drop 'em in the bucket. Got to lay 'em in.'

They started again, and this time they handled the fruit gently. The boxes filled more slowly. 'We could figger somepin out, I bet,' Tom said. 'If Ruthie an' Winfiel' or Rosasharn jus' put 'em in the boxes, we could work out a system.' He carried his newest box to the station. 'Is this here worth a nickel?'

The checker looked them over, dug down several layers. 'That's better,' he said. He checked the box in. 'Just take it easy.'

Tom hurried back. 'I got a nickel,' he called. 'I got a nickel. On'y got to do that there twenty times for a dollar.'

They worked on steadily through the afternoon. Ruthie and Winfield found them after a while. 'You got to work,' Pa told them. 'You got to put the peaches careful in the box. Here, now, one at a time.'

The children squatted down and picked the peaches out of the extra bucket, and a line of buckets stood ready for them. Tom carried the full boxes to the station. 'That's seven,' he said. 'That's eight. Forty cents we got. Get a nice piece of meat for forty cents.'

The afternoon passed. Ruthie tried to go away. 'I'm tar'd,' she whined. 'I got to rest.'

'You got to stay right where you're at,' said Pa.

Uncle John picked slowly. He filled one bucket to two of Tom's. His pace didn't change.

In mid-afternoon Ma came trudging out. 'I would a come before, but Rosasharn fainted,' she said. 'Jes' fainted away.'

'You been eatin' peaches,' she said to the children. 'Well, they'll blast you out.' Ma's stubby body moved quickly. She abandoned her bucket quickly and picked into her apron. When the sun went down they had picked twenty boxes.

Tom set the twentieth box down. 'A buck,' he said. 'How long do we work?'

'Work till dark, long as you can see.'

'Well, can we get credit now? Ma oughta go in an' buy some stuff to eat.'

'Sure. I'll give you a slip for a dollar now.' He wrote on a strip of paper and handed it to Tom.

He took it to Ma. 'Here you are. You can get a dollar's worth of stuff at the store.'

Ma put down her bucket and straightened her shoulders. 'Gets you, the first time, don't it?'

'Sure. We'll all get used to it right off. Roll on in an' get some food.'

Ma said: 'What'll you like to eat?'

'Meat,' said Tom. 'Meat an' bread an' a big pot a coffee with sugar in. Great big piece a meat.'

Ruthie wailed: 'Ma, we're tar'd.'

'Better come along in, then.'

'They was tar'd when they started,' Pa said. 'Wild as rabbits they're a-gettin'. Ain't gonna be no good at all 'less we can pin 'em down.'

'Soon's we get set down, they'll go to school,' said Ma. She trudged away, and Ruthie and Winfield timidly followed her.

'We got to work ever' day?' Winfield asked.

Ma stopped and waited. She took his hand and walked along holding it. 'It ain't hard work,' she said. 'Be good for you. An' you're helpin' us. If we all work, purty soon we'll live in a nice house. We all got to help.'

'But I got so tar'd.'

'I know. I got tar'd too. Ever'body gets wore out. Got to think about other stuff. Think about when you'll go to school.'

'I don't wanta go to no school. Ruthie don't, neither. Them kids that goes to school, we seen 'em, Ma. Snots! Calls us Okies. We seen 'em. I ain't a-goin'.'

Ma looked pityingly down on his straw hair. 'Don' give us no trouble right now,' she begged. 'Soon's we get on our feet, you can be bad. But not now. We got too much, now.'

'I et six of them peaches,' Ruthie said.

'Well, you'll have the skitters. An' it ain't close to no toilet where we are.'

The company's store was a large shed of corrugated iron. It had no display window. Ma opened the screen door and went in. A tiny man stood behind the counter. He was completely bald and his head was blue-white. Large brown eyebrows covered his eyes in such a high arch that his face seemed surprised and a little frightened. His nose was long and thin, and curved like a bird's beak, and his nostrils were blocked with light brown hair. Over the sleeves of his blue shirt he wore black sateen sleeve protectors. He was leaning on his elbows on the counter when Ma entered.

''Afternoon,' she said.

He inspected her with interest. The arch over his eyes became higher. 'Howdy.'

'I got a slip here for a dollar.'

'You can get a dollar's worth,' he said, and he giggled shrilly. 'Yes, sir. A dollar's worth. One dollar's worth.' He moved his hand at the stock. 'Any of it.' He pulled his sleeve protectors up neatly.

'Thought I'd get a piece of meat.'

'Got all kinds,' he said. 'Hamburg, like to have some hamburg? Twenty cents a pound, hamburg.'

'Ain't that awful high? Seems to me hamburg was fifteen las' time I got some.'

'Well,' he giggled softly, 'yes, it's high, an' the same time it ain't high. Time you go on in town for a couple poun's of hamburg, it'll cos' you 'bout a gallon petrol. So you see it ain't really high here, 'cause you got no gallon a petrol.'

Ma said sternly: It didn' cos' you no gallon a petrol to get it out here.'

He laughed delightedly. 'You're lookin' at it bassackwards,' he said. 'We ain't a-buyin' it, we're a-sellin' it. If we was buyin' it, why, that'd be different.'

Ma put two fingers to her mouth and frowned with thought. 'It looks all full a fat an' gristle.'

'I ain't guaranteein' she won't cook down,' the storekeeper said. 'I ain't guaranteein' I'd eat her myself; but they's lots of stuff I wouldn' do.'

Ma looked up at him fiercely for a moment. She controlled her voice. 'Ain't you got some cheaper kind a meat?'

'Soup bones,' he said. 'Ten cents a pound.'

'But them's jus' bones.'

'Them's jes' bones,' he said. 'Make nice soup. Jes' bones.'

'Got any boilin' beef?'

'Oh, yeah! Sure. That's two bits a poun'.'

'Maybe I can't get no meat,' Ma said. 'But they want meat. They said they wanted meat.'

'Ever'body wants meat–needs meat. That hamburg is purty nice stuff. Use the grease that comes out a her for gravy. Purty nice. No waste. Don't throw no bone away.'

'How–how much is side-meat?'

'Well, now you're gettin' into fancy stuff. Christmas stuff. Thanksgivin' stuff. Thirty-five cents a poun'. I could sell you turkey cheaper, if I had some turkey.'

Ma sighed. 'Give me two pounds hamburg.'

'Yes, ma'am.' He scooped the pale meat on a piece of waxed paper. 'An' what else?'

'Well, some bread.'

'Right here. Fine big loaf, fifteen cents.'

'That there's a twelve-cent loaf.'

'Sure, it is. Go right in town an' get her for twelve cents. Gallon a petrol. What else can I sell you, potatoes?'

'Yes, potatoes.'

'Five pounds for a quarter.'

Ma moved menacingly toward him. 'I heard enough from you. I know what they cost in town.'

The little man clamped his mouth tight. 'Then go git 'em in town.'

Ma looked at her knuckles. 'What is this?' she asked softly. 'You own this here store?'

'No. I jus' work here.'

'Any reason you got to make fun? That help you any?' She regarded her shiny wrinkled hands. The little man was silent. 'Who owns this here store?'

'Hooper Ranches, Incorporated, ma'am.'

'An' they set the prices?'

'Yes, ma'am.'

She looked up smiling a little. 'Ever'body comes in talks like me, is mad?'

He hesitated for a moment. 'Yes, ma'am.'

'An' that's why you make fun?'

'What cha mean?'

'Doin' a dirty thing like this. Shames ya, don't it? Got to act flip, huh?' Her voice was gentle. The clerk watched her, fascinated. He didn't answer. 'That's how it is,' Ma said finally. 'Forty cents for meat, fifteen for bread, quarter for potatoes. That's eighty cents. Coffee?'

'Twenty cents the cheapest, ma'am.'

'An' that's the dollar. Seven of us workin', an' that's supper.' She studied her hand. 'Wrap 'em up,' she said quickly.

'Yes, ma'am,' he said 'Thanks.' He put the potatoes in a bag and folded the top carefully down. His eyes slipped to Ma, and then hid in his work again. She watched him, and she smiled a little.

'How'd you get a job like this?' she asked.

'A fella got to eat,' he began; and then, belligerently: ' A fella got a right to eat.'

'What fella?' Ma asked.

He placed the four packages on the counter. 'Meat,' he said. 'Potatoes, bread, coffee. One dollar, even.' She handed him her slip of paper and watched him while he entered the name and the amount on a ledger. 'There,' he said. 'Now we're all even.'

Ma picked up her bags. 'Say,' she said. 'We got no sugar for the coffee. My boy Tom, he wants sugar. Look!' she said. 'They're a-workin' out there. You let me have some sugar an' I'll bring the slip in later.'

The little man looked away–took his eyes as far from Ma as he could. 'I can't do it,' he said softly. 'That's the rule. I can't. I'd get in trouble. I'd get canned.'

'But they're a-workin' out in the field now. They got more'n a dime comin'. Gimme ten cents' of sugar. Tom, he wanted sugar in his coffee. Spoke about it.'

'I can't do it, ma'am. That's the rule. No slip, no groceries. The manager, he talks about that all the time. No, I can't do it. No, I can't. They'd catch me. They always catch fellas. Always. I can't.'

'For a dime?'

'For anything, ma'am.' He looked pleadingly at her. And then his face lost its fear. He took ten cents from his pocket and rang it up in the cash register. 'There,' he said with relief. He pulled a little bag from under the counter, whipped it open and scooped some sugar into it, weighed the bag, and added a little more sugar. 'There you are,' he said. 'Now it's all right. You bring in your slip an' I'll get me dime back.'

Ma studied him. Her hand went blindly out and put the little bag of sugar on the pile in her arm. 'Thanks to you,' she said quietly. She started for the door, and when she reached it she turned about. 'I'm learnin' one good thing,' she said. 'Learnin' it all a time, ever'day. If you're in trouble or hurt or need–go to poor people. They're the only ones that'll help–the only ones.' The screen door slammed behind her.

The little man leaned his elbows on the counter and looked after her with surprised eyes. A plump tortoise-shell cat leaped up on the counter and stalked lazily near to him. It rubbed sideways against his arms, and he reached out his hand and pulled it against his cheek. The cat purred loudly, and the tip of its tail jerked back and forth.

Tom and Al and Pa and Uncle John walked in from the orchard when the dusk was deep. Their feet were a little heavy against the road.

'You wouldn' think jus' reachin' up an' pickin'd get you in the back,' Pa said.

'Be awright in a couple days,' said Tom. 'Say, Pa, after we eat I'm a-gonna walk out an' see what all that fuss is outside the gate. It's been a-workin' on me. Wanta come?'

'No,' said Pa. 'I like to have a little while to jus' work an' not think about nothin'. Seems like I jus' been beatin' my brains to death for a hell of a long time. No, I'm gonna set awhile, an' then go to bed.'

'How 'bout you, Al?'

Al looked away. 'Guess I'll look aroun' in here, first,' he said.

'Well, I know Uncle John won't come. Guess I'll go her alone. Got me all curious.'

Pa said: 'I'll get a hell of a lot curiouser 'fore I'll do anything about it–with all them cops out there.'

'Maybe they ain't there at night,' Tom suggested.

'Well, I ain't gonna find out. An' you better not tell Ma where you're a-goin'. She'll jus' squirt her head off worryin'.'

Tom turned to Al. 'Ain't you curious?'

'Guess I'll jes' look aroun' this here camp,' Al said.

'Lookin' for girls, huh?'

'Mindin' my own business,' Al said acidly.

'I'm still a-goin',' said Tom.

They emerged from the orchard into the dusty street between the red shacks. The low yellow light of kerosene lanterns shone from some of the doorways, and inside, in the half-gloom, the black shapes of people moved about. At the end of the street a guard still sat, his shotgun resting against his knee.

Tom paused as he passed the guard. 'Got a place where a fella can get a bath, mister?'

The guard studied him in the half-light. At last he said: 'See that water tank?'

'Yeah.'

'Well, there's a hose over there.'

'Any warm water?'

'Say, who in hell you think you are, J.P. Morgan?'

'No,' said Tom. 'No, I sure don't. Good night, mister.'

The guard grunted contemptuously. 'Hot water, for Christ's sake. Be wantin' tubs next.' He stared glumly after the four Joads.

A second guard came around the end house. 'S'matter, Mack?'

'Why, them goddamn Okies. "Is they warm water?" he says.'

The second guard rested his gun butt on the ground. 'It's them gov'ment camps,' he said. 'I bet that fella been in a gov'ment camp. We ain't gonna have no peace till we wipe them camps out. They'll be wantin' clean sheets, first thing we know.'

Mack asked: 'How is it out at the main gate–hear anything?'

'Well, they was out there yellin' all day. State police got it in hand. They're runnin' the hell outa them smart guys. I heard they's a long lean son-of-a-bitch spark-pluggin' the thing. Fella says they'll get him to-night, an then she'll go to pieces.'

'We won't have no job if it comes too easy,' Mack said.

'We'll have a job, all right. These goddamn Okies! You got to watch 'em all the time. Things get a little quiet, we can always stir 'em up a little.'

'Have trouble when they cut the rate here, I guess.'

'We sure will. No, you needn' worry about us havin' work–not while Hooper's snubbin' close.'

The fire roared in the Joad house. Hamburger patties splashed and hissed in the grease, and the potatoes bubbled. The house was full of smoke, and the yellow lantern light threw heavy black shadows on the walls. Ma worked quickly about the fire while Rose of Sharon sat on a box resting her heavy abdomen on her knees.

'Feelin' better now?' Ma asked.

'Smell a cookin' gets me. I'm hungry, too.'

'Go set in the door,' Ma said. 'I got to have that box to break up anyways.'

The men trooped in. 'Meat, by God!' said Tom. 'And coffee. I smell her. Jesus, I'm hungry! I et a lot of peaches, but they didn' do no good. Where can we wash, Ma?'

'Go down to the water tank. Wash down there. I jus' sent Ruthie and Winfiel' to wash.' The men went out again.

'Go on now, Rosasharn,' Ma ordered. 'Either you set in the door or else on the bed. I got to break that box up.'

The girl helped herself up with her hands. She moved heavily to one of the mattresses and sat down on it. Ruthie and Winfield came in quietly, trying by silence and by keeping close to the wall to remain obscure.

Ma looked over at them. 'I got a feelin' you little fellas is lucky they ain't much light,' she said. She pounced at Winfield and felt his hair. 'Well, you got wet, anyway, but I bet you ain't clean.'

'They wasn't no soap,' Winfield complained.

'No, that's right. I couldn' buy no soap. Not to-day. Maybe we can get some soap to-morra.' She went back to the stove, laid out the plates, and began to serve the supper. Two patties apiece and a big potato. She placed three slices of bread on each plate. When the meat was all out of the frying pan she poured a little of the grease on each plate. The men came in again, their faces dripping and their hair shining with water.

'Leave me at her,' Tom cried.

They took the plates. They ate silently, wolfishly, and wiped up the grease with the bread. The children retired into the corner of the room, put their plates on the floor, and knelt in front of the food like little animals.

Tom swallowed the last of his bread. 'Got any more, Ma?'

'No,' she said. 'That's all. You made a dollar, an' that's a dollar's worth.'

'That?'

'They charge extry out here. We got to go in town when we can.'

'I ain't full,' said Tom.

'Well, to-morra you'll get in a full day. To-morra night–we'll have plenty.'

Al wiped his mouth on his sleeve. 'Guess I'll take a look around,' he said.

'Wait, I'll go with you.' Tom followed him outside. In the darkness Tom went close to his brother. 'Sure you don' wanta come with me?'

'No' I'm gonna look aroun' like I said.'

'O.K.,' said Tom. He turned away and strolled down the street. The smoke from the houses hung low to the ground, and the lanterns threw their pictures of doorways and windows into the street. On the doorsteps people sat and looked out into the darkness. Tom could see their heads turn as their eyes followed him down the street. At the street end the dirt road continued across a stubble field, and the black lumps of haystacks were visible in the starlight. A thin blade of moon was low in the sky toward the west, and the long cloud of the Milky Way trailed clearly overhead. Tom's feet sounded softly on the dusty road, a dark patch against the yellow stubble. He put his hands in his pockets and trudged along toward the main gate. An embankment came close to the road. Tom could hear the whisper of water against the grasses in the irrigation ditch. He climbed up the bank and looked down on the dark water, and saw the stretched reflections of the stars. The State road was ahead. Car lights swooping past showed where it was. Tom set out again toward it. He could see the high wire gate in the starlight.

A figure stirred beside the road. A voice said: 'Hello–who is it?'

Tom stopped and stood still. 'Who are you?'

A man stood up and walked near. Tom could see the gun in his hand. Then a flashlight played on his face. 'Where you think you're going?'

'Well, I thought I'd take a walk. Any law against it?'

'You better walk some other way.'

Tom asked: 'Can't I even get out of here?'

'Not to-night you can't. Want to walk back, or shall I whistle some help an' take you?'

'Hell,' said Tom, 'it ain't nothin' to me. If it's gonna cause a mess, I don't give a darn. Sure, I'll go back.'

The dark figure relaxed. The flash went off. 'Ya see, it's for your own good. Them crazy pickets might get you.'

'What pickets?'

'Them goddamn reds.'

'Oh,' said Tom. 'I didn' know 'bout them.'

'You seen 'em when you come, didn' you?'

'Well, I seen a bunch a guys, but they was so many cops I didn' know. Thought it was a accident.'

'Well, you better git along back.'

'That's O.K. with me, mister.' He swung about and started back. He walked quietly along the road a hundred yards, and then he stopped and listened. The twittering call of a raccoon sounded near the irrigation ditch and, very far away, the angry howl of a tied dog. Tom sat down beside the road and listened. He heard the high soft laughter of a night hawk and the stealthy movement of a creeping animal in the stubble. He inspected the skyline in both directions, dark frames both ways, nothing to show against. Now he stood up and walked slowly to the right of the road, off into the stubble field, and he walked bent down, nearly as low as the haycocks. He moved slowly and stopped occasionally to listen. At last he came to the wire fence, five strands of taut barbed wire. Beside the fence he lay on his back, moved his head under the lowest strand, held the wire up with his hands and slid himself under, pushing against the ground with his feet.

He was about to get up when a group of men walked by on the edge of the highway. Tom waited until they were far ahead before he stood up and followed them. He watched the side of the road for tents. A few automobiles went by. A stream cut across the fields, and the highway crossed it on a small concrete bridge. Tom looked over the side of the bridge. In the bottom of the deep ravine he saw a tent and a lantern was burning inside. He watched it for a moment, saw the shadows of people against the canvas walls. Tom climbed a fence and moved down into the ravine through brush and dwarf willows; and in the bottom, beside a tiny stream, he found a trail. A man sat on a box in front of the tent.

''Evenin',' Tom said.

'Who are you?'

'Well–I guess, well–I'm jus' goin' past.'

'Know anybody here?'

'No. I tell you I was jus' goin' past.'

A head stuck out of the tent. A voice said: 'What's the matter?'

'Casy!' Tom cried. 'Casy! For Chris' sake, what you doin' here?'

'Why, my God, it's Tom Joad! Come on in, Tommy. Come on in.'

'Know him, do ya?' the man in front asked.

'Know him? Christ, yes. Knowed him for years. I come west with him. Come on in, Tom.' He clutched Tom's elbow and pulled him into the tent.

Three other men sat on the ground, and in the centre of the tent a lantern burned. The men looked up suspiciously. A dark-faced, scowling man held out his hand. 'Glad to meet ya,' he said. 'I heard what Casy said. This the fella you was tellin' about?'

'Sure. This is him. Well, for God's sake! Where's you folks? What you doin' here?'

'Well,' said Tom, 'we heard they was work this-a-way. An' we come, an' a bunch a State cops run us into this here ranch an' we been a-pickin' peaches all afternoon. I see a bunch a fellas yellin'. They wouldn' tell me nothin', so I come out here to see what's goin' on. How'n hell'd you get here, Casy?'

The preacher leaned forward and the yellow lantern light fell on his high pale forehead. 'Jail-house is a kinda funny place,' he said. 'Here's me, been a-goin' into the wilderness like Jesus to try find out somepin. Almost got her sometimes, too. But it's in the jail-house I really got her.' His eyes were sharp and merry. 'Great big ol' cell, an' she's full all a time. New guys come in, and guys go out. An' 'course I talked to all of 'em.'

''Course you did,' said Tom. 'Always talk. If you was up on the gallows you'd be passin' the time a day with the hangman. Never seen sech a talker.'

The men in the tent chuckled. A wizened little man with a wrinkled face slapped his knee. 'Talks all the time,' he said. ' Folks kinda likes to hear 'im though.'

'Use' ta be a preacher,' said Tom. 'Did he tell that?'

'Sure, he told.'

Casy grinned. 'Well, sir,' he went on. 'I begin gettin' at things. Some a them fellas in the tank was drunks, but mostly they was there 'cause they stole stuff; an' mostly it was stuff they needed an' couldn' get no other way. Ya see?' he asked.

'No,' said Tom.

'Well, they was nice fellas, ya see. What made 'em bad was they needed stuff. An' I begin to see, then. It's need that makes all the trouble. I ain't got it worked out. Well, one day they give us some beans that was sour. One fella started yellin', an' nothin' happened. He yelled his head off. Trusty come along an' looked in an' went on. Then another fella yelled. Well, sir, then we all got yellin'. And we all got on the same tone, an' I tell ya, it jus' seemed like that tank bulged an' give and swelled up. By God! Then somepin happened! They come a-runnin', and they give us some other stuff to eat–give it to us. Ya see?'

'No,' said Tom.

Casy put his chin down on his hands. 'Maybe I can't tell you,' he said. 'Maybe you got to find out. Where's your cap?'

'I come out without it.'

'How's your sister?'

'Hell, she's big as a cow. I bet she got twins. Gonna need wheels under her stomach. Got to holdin' it with her han's now. You ain't tol' me what's goin on.'

The wizened man said: 'We struck. This here's a strike.'

'Well, fi' cents a box ain't much, but a fella can eat.'

'Fi' cents?' the wizened man cried. 'Fi' cents! They payin' you fi' cents?'

'Sure. We made a buck an' a half.'

A heavy silence fell in the tent. Casy stared out the entrance, into the dark night. 'Lookie, Tom,' he said at last. 'We come to work there. They says it's gonna be fi' cents. They was a hell of a lot of us. We got there an' they says they're payin' two an' a half cents. A fella can't even eat on that, an' if he got kids–So we says we won't take it. So they druv us off. An' all the cops in the worl' come down on us. Now they're payin' you five. When they bust this here strike–ya think they'll pay five?'

'I dunno,' Tom said. 'Payin' five now.'

'Lookie,' said Casy. 'We tried to camp together, an' they druv us like pigs. Scattered us. Beat the hell outa fellas. Druv us like pigs. They run you in like pigs, too. We can't las' much longer. Some people ain't et for two days. You goin' back to-night?'

'Aim to,' said Tom.

'Well–tell the folks in there how it is, Tom. Tell 'em they're starvin' us an' stabbin' theirself in the back. 'Cause sure as cowflops she'll drop to two an' a half jus' as soon as they clear us out.'

'I'll tell 'em,' said Tom. 'I don' know how. Never seen so many guys with guns. Don' know if they'll even let a fella talk. An' folks don' pass no time of day. They jus' hang down their heads an' won't even give a fella a howdy.'

'Try an' tell 'em, Tom. They'll get two an' a half, jus' the minute we're gone. You know what two an' a half is–that's one ton of peaches picked an' carried for a dollar.' He dropped his head. 'No–you can't do it. You can't get your food for that. Can't eat for that.'

'I'll try to get to tell the folks.'

'How's your ma?'

'Purty good. She liked that gov'ment camp. Baths an' hot water.'

'Yeah–I heard.'

'It was pretty nice there. Couldn' find no work, though. Had a leave.'

'I'd like to go to one,' said Casy. 'Like to see it. Fella says they ain't no cops.'

'Folks is their own cops.'

Casy looked up excitedly. 'An' was they any trouble? Fightin', stealin', drinkin'?'

'No,' said Tom.

'Well if a fella went bad–what then? What'd they do?'

'Put 'im outa the camp.'

'But they wasn' many?'

'Hell, no,' said Tom. 'We was there a month, an' on'y one.'

Casy's eyes shone with excitement. He turned to the other men. 'Ya see?' he cried. 'I tol' you. Cops cause more trouble than they stop. Look, Tom. Try an' get the folks in there to come on out. They can do it in a couple days. Them peaches is ripe. Tell 'em.'

'They won't,' said Tom. 'They're a-gettin' five, an' they don' give a damn about nothing else.'

'But jus' the minute they ain't strike-breakin' they won't get no five.'

'I don' think they'll swalla that. Five they're a-gettin'. Tha's all they care about.'

'Well, tell 'em anyways.'

'Pa wouldn' do it,' Tom said. 'I know 'im. He'd say it wasn't none of his business.'

'Yes,' Casy said disconsolately. 'I guess that's right. Have to take a beatin' 'fore he'll know.'

'We was outa food,' Tom said. 'To-night we had meat. Not much, but we had it. Think Pa's gonna give up his meat on account a other fellas? An' Rosasharn oughta get milk. Think Ma's gonna wanta starve that baby jus' 'cause a bunch a fellas is yellin' outside a gate?'

Casy said sadly: 'I wisht they could see it. I wisht they could see the on'y way they depen' on their meat–Oh, the hell! Get tar'd sometimes. God-awful tar'd. I knowed a fella. Brang 'im in while I was in the jail-house. Been tryin' to start a union. Got one started. An' then them vigilantes bust it up. An' know what? Them very folks he been tryin' to help tossed him out. Wouldn' have nothin' to do with 'im. Scared they'd get saw in his comp'ny. Says: "Git out. You're a danger to us." Well, sir, it hurts his feelin's purty bad. But then he says: "It ain't so bad if you know." He says: "French Revolution–all them fellas that figgered her out got their heads chopped off. Always that way," he says. "Jus' as natural as rain. You didn' do it for fun no way. Doin' it 'cause you have to. 'Cause it's you. Look a Washington," he says. "Fit the Revolution, an' after, them sons-a-bitches turned on him. An' Lincoln the same. Same folks yellin' to kill 'em. Natural as rain." '

'Don't soun' like no fun,' said Tom.

'No, it don't. This fella in jail, he says: "Anyways, you do what you can. An'," he says, "the on'y thing you got to look at is that ever'time they's a little step fo'ward, she may slip back a little, but she never slips clear back. You can prove that," he says, "an' that makes the whole thing right. An' that means they wasn't no waste even if it seemed like they was." '

'Talkin',' said Tom. 'Always talkin'. Take my brother Al. He's out lookin' for a girl. He don't care 'bout nothin' else. Couple days he'll get him a girl. Think about it all day an' do it all night. He don't give a damn 'bout steps up or down or sideways.'

'Sure,' said Casy. 'Sure. He's jus' doin' what he's got to do. All of us like that.'

The man seated outside pulled the tent flap wide. 'Goddamn it, I don' like it,' he said.

Casy looked out at him. 'What's the matter?'

'I don' know. I jus' itch all over. Nervous as a cat.'

'Well, what's the matter?'

'I don' know. Seems like I hear somepin, an' then I listen an' they ain't nothin' to hear.'

'You're jus' jumpy,' the wizened man said. He got up and went outside. And in a second he looked into the tent. 'They's a great big ol' black cloud a-sailin' over. Bet she's got thunder. That's what's itchin' him–'lectricity.' He ducked out again. The other two men stood up from the ground and went outside.

Casy said softly: 'All of 'em's itchy. Them cops been sayin' how they're gonna beat the hell outa us an' run us outa the county. They figger I'm a leader 'cause I talk so much.'

The wizened face looked in again. 'Casy, turn out that lantern an' come outside. They's somepin.'

Casy turned the screw. The flame drew down into the slots and popped and went out. Casy groped outside and Tom followed him. 'What is it?' Casy said softly.

'I dunno. Listen!'

There was a wall of frog sounds that merged with silence. A high, shrill whistle of crickets. But through this background came other sounds–faint footsteps from the road, a crunch of clods up on the bank, a little swish of brush down the stream.

'Can't really tell if you hear it. Fools you. Get nervous,' Casy reassured them. 'We're all nervous. Can't really tell. You hear it, Tom?'

'I hear it,' said Tom. 'Yeah, I hear it. I think they's guys comin' from ever' which way. We better get outa here.'

The wizened man whispered: 'Under the bridge span–out that way. Hate to leave my tent.'

'Let's go,' said Casy.

They moved quietly along the edge of the stream. The black span was a cave before them. Casy bent over and moved through. Tom behind. Their feet slipped into the water. Thirty feet they moved, and their breathing echoed from the curved ceiling. Then they came out on the other side and straightened up.

A sharp call: 'There they are!' Two flashlight beams fell on the men, caught them, blinded them. 'Stand where you are.' The voices came out of the darkness. 'That's him. That shiny bastard. That's him.'

Casy stared blindly at the light. He breathed heavily. 'Listen,' he said. 'You fellas don' know what you're doin'. You're helpin' to starve kids.'

'Shut up, you red son-of-a-bitch.'

A short heavy man stepped into the light. He carried a new white pick-handle.

Casy went on: 'You don' know what you're a-doin'.'

The heavy man swung with the pick-handle. Casy dodged down into the swing. The heavy club crashed into the side of his head with a dull crunch of bone, and Casy fell sideways out of the light.

'Jesus, George. I think you killed him.'

'Put the light on him,' said George. 'Serve the son-of-a-bitch right.' The flashlight beam dropped, searched, and found Casy's crushed head.

Tom looked down at the preacher. The light crossed the heavy man's legs and the white new pick-handle. Tom leaped silently. He wrenched the club free. The first time he knew he had missed and struck a shoulder, but the second time his crushing blow found the head, and as the heavy man sank down, three more blows found his head. The lights danced about. There were shouts, the sound of running feet, crashing through bush. Tom stood over the prostrate man. And then a club reached his head, a glancing blow. He felt the stroke like an electric shock. And then he was running along the stream, bending low. He heard the splash of footsteps following him. Suddenly he turned and squirmed up into the brush, deep into a poison-oak thicket. And he lay still. The footsteps came near, the light beams glanced along the stream bottom. Tom wriggled up through the thicket to the top. He emerged in an orchard. And still he could hear the calls, the pursuit in the stream bottom. He bent low and ran over the cultivated earth; the clods slipped and rolled under his feet. Ahead he saw the bushes that bounded the field, bushes along the edges of an irrigation ditch. He slipped through the fence, edged in among vines and blackberry bushes. And then he lay still, panting hoarsely. He felt his numb face and nose. The nose was crushed, and a trickle of blood dropped from his chin. He lay still on his stomach until his mind came back. And then he crawled slowly over the edge of the ditch. He bathed his face in the cool water, tore off the tail of his blue shirt and dipped it and held it against his torn cheek and nose. The water stung and burned.

The black cloud had crossed the sky, a blob of dark against the stars. The night was quiet again.

Tom stepped into the water and felt the bottom drop from under his feet. He threshed the two strokes across the ditch and pulled himself heavily up the other bank. His clothes clung to him. He moved and made a slopping noise; his shoes squished. Then he sat down, took off his shoes and emptied them. He wrung the bottom of his trousers, took off his coat and squeezed the water from it.

Along the highway he saw the dancing beams of the flashlights, searching the ditches. Tom put on his shoes and moved cautiously across the stubble field. The squishing noise no longer came from his shoes. He went by instinct toward the other side of the stubble field, and at last he came to the road. Very cautiously he approached the square of houses.

Once a guard, thinking he heard a noise, called:'Who's there?'

Tom dropped and froze to the ground, and the flashlight beam passed over him. He crept silently to the door of the Joad house. The door squalled on its hinges. And Ma's voice, calm and steady and wide awake:

'What's that?'

'Me, Tom.'

'Well, you better get some sleep. Al ain't in yet.'

'He must a foun' a girl.'

'Go on to sleep,' she said softly. 'Over under the window.'

He found his place and took off his clothes to the skin. He lay shivering under his blanket. And his torn face awakened from its numbness, and his whole head throbbed.

It was an hour more before Al came in. He moved cautiously near and stepped on Tom's wet clothes.

'Sh!' said Tom.

Al whispered: 'You awake? How'd you get wet?'

'Sh!' said Tom. 'Tell you in the mornin'.'

Pa turned on his back, and his snoring filled the room with gasps and snorts.

'You're col',' Al said.

'Sh! Go to sleep.' The little square of the window showed grey against the black of the room.

Tom did not sleep. The nerves of his wounded face came back to life and throbbed, and his cheek-bone ached, and his broken nose bulged and pulsed with pain that seemed to toss him about, to shake him. He watched the little square window, saw the stars slide down over it and drop from sight. At intervals he heard the footsteps of the watchmen.

At last the roosters crowed, far away, and gradually the window lightened. Tom touched his swollen face with his finger-tips, and at his movement Al groaned and murmured in his sleep.

The dawn came finally. In the houses, packed together, there was a sound of movement, a crash of breaking sticks, a little clatter of pans. In the greying gloom Ma sat up suddenly. Tom could see her face, swollen with sleep. She looked at the window, for a long moment. And then she threw the blanket off and found her dress. Still sitting down, she put it over her head and held her arms up and let the dress slide down to her waist. She stood up and pulled the dress down around her ankles. Then, in bare feet, she stepped carefully to the window and looked out, and while she stared at the growing light, her quick fingers unbraided her hair and smoothed the strands and braided them up again. Then she clasped her hands in front of her and stood motionless for a moment. Her face was lighted sharply by the window. She turned, stepped carefully among the mattresses, and found the lantern. The shade screeched up, and she lighted the wick.

Pa rolled over and blinked at her. She said: 'Pa, you got more money?'

'Huh? Yeah. Paper wrote for sixty cents.'

'Well, git up an' go buy some flour an' lard. Quick now.'

Pa yawned. 'Maybe the store ain't open.'

'Make 'em open it. Got to get somepin in you fellas. You got to get out to work.'

Pa struggled into his overalls and put on his rusty coat. He went sluggishly out the door, yawning and stretching.

The children awakened and watched from under their blanket, like mice. Pale light filled the room now, but colourless light, before the sun. Ma glanced at the mattresses. Uncle John was awake. Al slept heavily. Her eyes moved to Tom. For a moment she peered at him, and then she moved quickly to him. His face was puffed and blue, and the blood was dried black on his lips and chin. The edges of the torn cheek were gathered and tight.

'Tom,' she whispered, 'what's the matter?'

'Sh!' he said. 'Don't talk loud. I got in a fight.'

'Tom!'

'I couldn' help it, Ma.'

She knelt down beside him. 'You in trouble?'

He was a long time answering. 'Yeah,' he said. 'In trouble. I can't go out to work. I got to hide.'

The children crawled near on their hands and knees, staring greedily. 'What's the matter'th him, Ma?'

'Hush!' Ma said. 'Go wash up.'

'We got no soap.'

'Well, use water.'

'What's the matter'th Tom?'

'Now you hush. An' don't you tell nobody.'

They backed away and squatted down against the far wall, knowing they would not be inspected.

Ma asked: 'Is it bad?'

'Nose busted.'

'I mean the trouble?'

'Yeah. Bad!'

Al opened his eyes and looked at Tom. 'Well, for Chris' sake! What was you in?'

'What's a matter?' Uncle John asked.

Pa clumped in. 'They was open all right.' He put a tiny bag of flour and his package of lard on the floor beside the stove. ''S'a matter?' he asked.

Tom braced himself on one elbow for a moment, and then he lay back. 'Jesus, I'm weak. I'm gonna tell ya once. So I'll tell all of ya. How 'bout the kids?'

Ma looked at them, huddled against the wall. 'Go wash ya face.'

'No,' Tom said. 'They got to hear. They got to know. They might blab if they don't know.'

'What the hell is this?' Pa demanded.

'I'm a-gonna tell. Las' night I went out to see what all the yellin' was about. An' I come on Casy.'

'The preacher?'

'Yeah, Pa. The preacher, on'y he was a-leadin' the strike. They come for him.'

Pa demanded: 'Who come for him?'

'I dunno. Same kinda guys that turned us back on the road that night. Had pick-handles.' He paused. 'They killed 'im. Busted his head. I was standin' there. I went nuts. Grabbed the pick-handle.' He looked bleakly back at the night, the darkness, the flashlights, as he spoke. 'I–I clubbed a guy.'

Ma's breath caught in her throat. Pa stiffened. 'Kill 'im?' he asked softly.

'I–don't know. I was nuts. Tried to.'

Ma asked: 'Was you saw?'

'I dunno. I dunno. I guess so. They had the lights on us.'

For a moment Ma stared into his eyes. 'Pa,' she said, 'break up some boxes. We got to get breakfas'. You got to go to work. Ruthie, Winfiel'. If anybody asts you–Tom is sick–you hear? If you tell–he'll–get sent to jail. You hear?'

'Yes, ma'am.'

'Keep your eye on 'em, John. Don' let 'em talk to nobody.' She built the fire as Pa broke the boxes that had held the goods. She made her dough, put a pot of coffee to boil. The light wood caught and roared its flame in the chimney.

Pa finished breaking the boxes. He came near to Tom. 'Casy–he was a good man. What'd he wanta mess with that stuff for?'

Tom said dully: 'They came to work for fi' cents a box.'

'That's what we're a-gettin'.'

'Yeah. What we was a-doin' was breakin' the strike. They give them fellas two an' a half cents.'

'You can't eat on that.'

'I know,' said Tom wearily. 'That's why they struck. Well, I think they bust that strike las' night. We'll maybe be gettin' two an' a half cents to-day.'

'Why, the sons-a-bitches–'

'Yeah! Pa. You see? Casy was still a–good man. Goddamn it, I can't get that pitcher outa my head. Him layin' there–head jus' crushed flat an' oozin'. Jesus!' He covered his eyes with his hand.

'Well, what we gonna do?' Uncle John asked.

Al was standing up now. 'Well, by God, I know what I'm gonna do. I'm gonna get out of it.'

'No, you ain't, Al,' Tom said. 'We need you now. I'm the one. I'm a danger now. Soon's I get on my feet I got to go.'

Ma worked at the stove. Her head was half turned to hear. She put grease in the frying pan, and when it whispered with heat, she spooned the dough into it.

Tom went on: 'You got to stay, Al. You got to take care a the truck.'

'Well, I don' like it.'

'Can't help it, Al. It's your folks. You can help 'em. I'm a danger to 'em.'

Al grumbled angrily. 'I don' know why I ain't let to get me a job in a garage.'

'Later, maybe.' Tom looked past him, and he saw Rose of Sharon lying on the mattress. Her eyes were huge–opened wide. 'Don't worry,' he called to her. 'Don't you worry. Gonna get you some milk to-day.' She blinked slowly, and didn't answer him.

Pa said: 'We got to know, Tom. Think ya killed this fella?'

'I don't know. It was dark. An' somebody smacked me. I don' know. I hope so. I hope I killed the bastard.'

'Tom!' Ma called. 'Don' talk like that.'

From the street came the sound of many cars moving slowly. Pa stepped to the window and looked out. 'They's a whole slew a new people comin' in,' he said.

'I guess they bust the strike awright,' said Tom. 'I guess you'll start at two an' a half cents.'

'But a fella could work at a run, an' still he couldn' eat.'

'I know,' said Tom. 'Eat win'fall peaches. That'll keep ya up.'

Ma turned the dough and stirred the coffee. 'Listen to me,' she said. 'I'm gettin' cornmeal to-day. We're a-gonna eat cornmeal mush. An' soon's we get enough for petrol, we're movin' away. This ain't a good place. An' I ain't gonna have Tom out alone. No, sir.'

'Ya can't do that, Ma. I tell you I'm jus' a danger to ya.'

Her chin was set. 'That's what we'll do. Here, come eat this here, an' then get out to work. I'll come out soon's I get washed up. We got to make some money.'

They ate the fried dough so hot that it sizzled in their mouths. And they tossed the coffee down and filled their cups and drank more coffee.

Uncle John shook his head over his plate. 'Don't look like we're a-gonna get shet of this here. I bet it's my sin.'

'Oh, shut up!' Pa cried. 'We ain't got the time for your sin now. Come on now. Le's get out to her. Kids, you come he'p. Ma's right. We got to go outa here.'

When they were gone, Ma took a plate and a cup to Tom. 'Better eat a little somepin.'

'I can't, Ma. I'm so darn sore I couldn' chew.'

'You better try.'

'No, I can't, Ma.'

She sat down on the edge of his mattress. 'You got to tell me,' she said. 'I got to figger how it was. I got to keep straight. What was Casy a-doin'? Why'd they kill 'im?'

'He was jus' standin' there with the lights on 'im.'

'What'd he say? Can ya 'member what he says?'

Tom said: 'Sure. Casy said: "You got no right to starve people." An' then this heavy fella called him a red son-of-a-bitch. An' Casy says: "You don' know what you're a-doin'." An' then this guy smashed 'im.'

Ma looked down. She twisted her hands together. 'Tha's what he said–"You don't know what you're doin' "?'

'Yeah!'

Ma said: 'I wisht Granma could a heard.'

'Ma–I didn't know what I was a-doin', no more'n when you take a breath. I didn' even know I was gonna do it.'

'It's awright. I wisht you didn't do it. I wisht you wasn't there. But you done what you had to do. I can't read no fault on you.' She went to the stove and dipped a cloth in the heating dishwater. 'Here,' she said. 'Put that there on your face.'

He laid the warm cloth over his nose and cheek, and winced at the heat. 'Ma, I'm a-gonna go away to-night. I can't go puttin' this on you folks.'

Ma said angrily: 'Tom! They's a whole lot I don' un'erstan'. But goin' away ain't gonna ease us. It's gonna bear us down.' And she went on: 'They was the time when we was on the lan'. They was a boundary to us then. Ol' folks died off an' little fellas come an' we was always one thing–we was the fambly–kinda whole and clear. An' now we ain't clear no more. I can't get straight. They ain't nothin' keeps us clear. Al–he's a-hankerin' an' a-jibbitin' to go off on his own. An' Uncle John is jus' a-draggin' along. Pa's lost his place. He ain't the head no more. We're crackin' up, Tom. There ain't no fambly now. An' Rosasharn–' She looked around and found the girl's wide eyes. 'She gonna have her baby an' they won't be no fambly. I don' know. I been a-tryin' to keep her goin'. Winfiel'–what's he gonna be, this-a-way? Gettin' wild, an' Ruthie too–like animals. Got nothin' to trus'. Don' go, Tom. Stay an' help.'

'O.K.,' he said tiredly. 'O.K. I shouldn', though. I know it.'

Ma went to her dish-pan and washed the tin plates and dried them. 'You didn' sleep.'

'No.'

'Well, you sleep. I seen your clothes was wet. I'll hang 'em by the stove to dry.' She finished her work. 'I'm goin' now. I'll pick. Rosasharn, if anybody comes, Tom's sick, you hear? Don' let nobody in. You hear?' Rose of Sharon nodded. 'We'll come back at noon. Get some sleep, Tom. Maybe we can get outa here tonight.' She moved swiftly to him. 'Tom, you ain't gonna slip out?'

'No, Ma.'

'You sure? You won't go?'

'No, Ma. I'll be here.'

'Awright. 'Member Rosasharn.' She went out and closed the door firmly behind her.

Tom lay still–and then a wave of sleep lifted him to the edge of unconsciousness and dropped him slowly back and lifted him again.

'You–Tom!'

'Huh? Yeah!' He started awake. He looked over at Rose of Sharon. Her eyes were blazing with resentment. 'What you want?'

'You killed a fella!'

'Yeah. Not so loud! You wanta rouse somebody?'

'What da I care?' she cried. 'That lady tol' me. She says what sin's gonna do. She tol' me. What chance I got to have a nice baby? Connie's gone, an' I ain't gettin' good food. I ain't gettin' milk.' Her voice rose hysterically 'An' now you kill a fella. What chance that baby got to get bore right? I know–gonna be a freak–a freak! I never done no dancin'.'

Tom got up. 'Sh!' he said. ' You're gonna get folks in here.'

'I don' care. I'll have a freak! I didn' dance no hug-dance.'

He went near to her. 'Be quiet.'

'You get away from me. It ain't the first fella you killed, neither.' Her face was growing red with hysteria. Her words blurred. 'I don' wanta look at you.' She covered her head with her blanket.

Tom heard the choked, smothered cries. He bit his lower lip and studied the floor. And then he went to Pa's bed. Under the edge of the mattress the rifle lay, a lever-action Winchester .38, long and heavy. Tom picked it up and dropped the lever to see that a cartridge was in the chamber. He tested the hammer on half-cock. And then he went back to his mattress. He laid the rifle on the floor beside him, stock up the barrel pointing down. Rose of Sharon's voice thinned to a whimper. Tom lay down again and covered himself, covered his bruised cheek with the blanket and made a little tunnel to breathe through. He sighed: 'Jesus, oh Jesus!'

Outside, a group of cars went by, and voices sounded.

'How many men?'

'Jes' us–three. Whatcha payin'?'

'You go to house twenty-five. Number's right on the door.'

'O.K., mister. Whatcha payin'?'

'Two and a half cents.'

'Why, goddamn it, a man can't make his dinner!'

'That's what we're payin'. There's two hundred men coming from the South that'll be glad to get it.'

'But Jesus, mister!'

'Go on now. Either take it or go on along. I got no time to argue.'

'But–'

'Look I didn' set the price. I'm just checking you in. If you want it, take it. If you don't, turn right around and go along.'

'Twenty-five, you say?'

'Yes, twenty-five.'

Tom dozed on his mattress. A stealthy sound in the room awakened him. His hand crept to the rifle and tightened on the grip. He drew back the covers from his face, Rose of Sharon was standing beside his mattress.

'What you want?' Tom demanded.

'You sleep,' she said. 'You jus' sleep off. I'll watch the door. They won't nobody get in.'

He studied her face for a moment. 'O.K.,' he said, and he covered his face with the blanket again.

In the beginning dusk Ma came back to the house. She paused on the doorstep and knocked and said: 'It's me,' so that Tom would not be worried. She opened the door and entered, carrying a bag. Tom awakened and sat up on his mattress. His wound had dried and tightened so that the unbroken skin was shiny. His left eye was drawn nearly shut. 'Anybody come while we was gone?' Ma asked.

'No,' he said. 'Nobody. I see they dropped the price.'

'How'd you know?'

'I heard folks talkin' outside.'

Rose of Sharon looked dully up at Ma.

Tom pointed at her with his thumb. 'She raised hell, Ma. Thinks all the trouble is aimed right smack at her. If I'm gonna get her upset like that I oughta go 'long.'

Ma turned on Rose of Sharon. 'What you doin'?'

The girl said resentfully: 'How'm I gonna have a nice baby with stuff like this?'

Ma said: 'Hush! You hush now. I know how you're a-feelin', an' I know you can't he'p it, but you jus' keep your mouth shut.'

She turned back to Tom. 'Don't pay her no mind, Tom. It's awful hard, an' I 'member how it is. Ever'thing is a-shootin' right at you when you're gonna have a baby, an' ever'thing anybody says is an insult, an' ever'thing's against you. Don't pay no mind. She can't he'p it. It's jus' the way she feels.'

'I don' wanta hurt her.'

'Hush! Jus' don' talk.' She set her bag down on the cold stove. 'Didn' hardly make nothin',' she said. 'I tol' you, we're gonna get outa here. Tom, try an' wrassle me some wood. No–you can't. Here, we got on'y this one box lef'. Break it up. I tol' the other fellas to pick up some sticks on the way back. Gonna have mush an' a little sugar on.'

Tom got up and stamped the last box to small pieces. Ma carefully built her fire in one end of the stove, conserving the flame under one stove hole. She filled the kettle with water and put it over the flame. The kettle rattled over the direct fire, rattled and wheezed.

'How was it pickin' to-day?' Tom asked.

Ma dipped a cup into her bag of cornmeal. 'I don' wanta talk about it. I was thinkin' to-day how they use' to be jokes. I don' like it, Tom. We don't joke no more. When they's a joke, it's a mean bitter joke, an' they ain't no fun in it. Fella says to-day: "Depression is over. I seen a jack-rabbit, an' they wasn't nobody after him." An' another fella says: "That ain't the reason. Can't afford to kill jack-rabbits no more. Catch 'em and milk 'em an' turn em' loose. One you seen prob'ly gone dry." That's how I mean. Ain't really funny, not funny like that time Uncle John converted an Injun an' brang him home, an' that Injun et his way clean to the bottom of the bean bin, an' then backslid with Uncle John's whisky. Tom, put a rag with col' water on your face.'

The dusk deepened. Ma lighted the lantern and hung it on a nail. She fed the fire and poured cornmeal gradually into the hot water. 'Rosasharn,' she said, 'can you stir the mush?'

Outside there was a patter of running feet. The door burst open and banged against the wall. Ruthie rushed in. 'Ma!' she cried. 'Ma. Winfiel' got a fit!'

'Where? Tell me!'

Ruthie panted: 'Got white an' fell down. Et so many peaches he skittered hisself all day. Jus' fell down. White!'

'Take me!' Ma demanded. 'Rosasharn, you watch that mush.'

She went out with Ruthie. She ran heavily up the street behind the little girl. Three men walked toward her in the dusk, and the centre man carried Winfield in his arms. Ma ran up to them. 'He's mine,' she cried. 'Give 'im to me.'

'I'll carry 'im for you, ma'am.'

'No, here, give 'im to me.' She hoisted the little boy and turned back; and then she remembered herself. 'I sure thank ya,' she said to the men.

'Welcome, ma'am. The little fella's purty weak. Looks like he got worms.'

Ma hurried back, and Winfield was limp and relaxed in her arms. Ma carried him into the house and knelt down and laid him on a mattress. 'Tell me. What's the matter?' she demanded. He opened his eyes dizzily and shook his head and closed his eyes again.

Ruthie said: 'I tol' ya, Ma. He skittered all day. Ever' little while. Et too many peaches.'

Ma felt his head. 'He ain't fevered. But he's white and drawed out.'

Tom came near and held the lantern down. 'I know,' he said. He's hungered. Got no strength. Get him a can a milk an' make him drink it. Make 'im take milk on his mush.'

'Winfiel',' Ma said. 'Tell how ya feel.'

'Dizzy,' said Winfield, 'jus' a-whirlin' dizzy.'

'You never seen such skitters,' Ruthie said importantly.

Pa and Uncle John and Al came into the house. Their arms were full of sticks and bits of brush. They dropped their loads by the stove. 'Now what?' Pa demanded.

'It's Winfiel'. He needs some milk.'

'Christ Awmighty! We all need stuff!'

Ma said: 'How much'd we make to-day?'

'Dollar forty-two.'

'Well, you go right over'n get a can a milk for Winfiel'.'

'Now why'd he have to get sick?'

'I don't know why, but he is. Now you git!' Pa went grumbling out the door. 'You stirrin' that mush?'

'Yeah,' Rose of Sharon speeded up the stirring to prove it.

Al complained: 'God Awmighty, Ma! Is mush all we get after workin' till dark?'

'Al, you know we got to git. Take all we got for petrol. You know.'

'But, God Awmighty, Ma! A fella needs meat if he's gonna work.'

'Jus' you sit quiet,' she said. 'We got to take the bigges' thing an' whup it fust. An' you know what that thing is.'

Tom asked: 'Is it about me?'

'We'll talk when we've et,' said Ma. 'Al, we got enough petrol to go a ways, ain't we?'

''Bout a quarter tank,' said Al.

'I wish you'd tell me,' Tom said.

'After. Jus' wait.'

'Keep a-stirrin' that mush, you. Here, lemme put on some coffee. You can have sugar on your mush or in your coffee. They ain't enough for both.'

Pa came back with one tall can of milk. ''Leven cents,' he said disgustedly.

'Here!' Ma took the can and stabbed it open. She let the thick stream out into a cup, and handed it to Tom. 'Give that to Winfiel'.'

Tom knelt beside the mattress. 'Here, drink this.'

'I can't. I'd sick it all up. Leave me be.'

Tom stood up. 'He can't take it now, Ma. Wait a little.'

Ma took the cup and set it on the window ledge. 'Don't none of you touch that,' she warned. 'That's for Winfiel'.'

'I ain't had no milk,' Rose of Sharon said sullenly. 'I oughta have some.'

'I know, but you're still on your feet. This here little fella's down. Is that mush good an' thick?'

'Yeah. Can't hardly stir it no more.'

'Awright, le's eat. Now here's the sugar. They's about one spoon each. Have it on ya mush or in ya coffee.'

Tom said: 'I kinda like salt an' pepper on mush.'

'Salt her if you like,' Ma said. 'The pepper's out.'

The boxes were all gone. The family sat on the mattresses to eat their mush. They served themselves again and again, until the pot was nearly empty. 'Save some for Winfiel',' Ma said.

Winfield sat up and drank his milk, and instantly he was ravenous. He put the mush pot between his legs and ate what was left and scraped at the crust on the sides. Ma poured the rest of the canned milk in a cup and sneaked it to Rose of Sharon to drink secretly in a corner. She poured the hot black coffee into the cups and passed them around.

'Now will you tell what's goin' on?' Tom asked. 'I wanta hear.'

Pa said uneasily: 'I wisht Ruthie an' Winfiel' didn' hafta hear. Can't they go outside?'

Ma said: 'No. They got to act growed up, even if they ain't. They's no help for it. Ruthie–you an' Winfiel' ain't ever to say what you hear, else you'll jus' break us to pieces.'

'We won't,' Ruthie said. 'We're growed up.'

'Well, jus' be quiet, then.' The cups of coffee were on the floor. The short thick flame of the lantern, like a stubby butterfly's wing, cast a yellow gloom on the walls.

'Now tell,' said Tom.

Ma said: 'Pa, you tell.'

Uncle John slupped his coffee. Pa said: 'Well, they dropped the price like you said. An' they was a whole slew a new pickers so goddamn hungry they'd pick for a loaf a bread. Go for a peach, an' somebody'd get it first. Gonna get the whole crop picked right off. Fellas runnin' to a new tree. I seen fights–one fella claims it's his tree, 'nother fella wants to pick off'n it. Brang these here folks from as far's El Centro. Hungrier'n hell. Work all day for a piece a bread. I says to the checker: "We can't work for two an' a half cents a box," an' he says: "Go on, then, quit. These fellas can." I says: "Soon's they get fed up they won't." An' he says: "Hell, we'll have these here peaches in 'fore they get fed up." ' Pa stopped.

'She was a devil,' said Uncle John. 'They say they's two hunderd more men comin' in to-night.'

Tom said: 'Yeah! But how about the other?'

Pa was silent for a while. 'Tom,' he said, 'looks like you done it.'

'I kinda thought so. Couldn' see. Felt like it.'

'Seems like the people ain't talkin' 'bout much else,' said Uncle John. 'They got posses out, an' they's fellas talkin' up a lynchin'–'course when they catch the fella.'

Tom looked over at the wide-eyed children. They seldom blinked their eyes. It was as though they were afraid something might happen in the split second of darkness. Tom said: 'Well–this fella that done it, he on'y done it after they killed Casy.'

Pa interrupted: 'That ain't the way they're tellin' it now. They're sayin' he done it fust.'

Tom's breath sighed out: 'Ah-h!'

'They're workin' up a feelin' against us folks. That's what I heard. All them drum-corpse fellas an' lodges an' all that. Say they're gonna get this here fella.'

'They know what he looks like?' Tom asked.

'Well–not exactly–but the way I heard it, they think he got hit. They think–he'll have–'

Tom put his hand up slowly and touched his bruised cheek.

Ma cried: 'It ain't so, what they say!'

'Easy, Ma,' Tom said. 'They got it cold. Anything them drum-corpse fellas say is right if it's against us.'

Ma peered through the ill light, and she watched Tom's face and particularly his lips. 'You promised,' she said.

'Ma, I–maybe this fella oughta go away. If–this fella done somepin wrong, maybe he'd think: "O.K. Le's get the hangin' over. I done wrong an' I got to take it." But this fella didn' do nothin' wrong. He don' feel no worse'n if he killed a skunk.'

Ruthie broke in: Ma, me an' Winfiel' knows. He don' have to go this-fella' in' for us.'

Tom chuckled. 'Well, this fella don' want no hangin', cause he'd do it again. An' same time, he don't aim to bring trouble down on his folks. Ma–I got to go.'

Ma covered her mouth with her fingers and coughed to clear her throat. 'You can't,' she said. 'They wouldn' be no way to hide out. You couldn' trus' nobody. But you can trus' us. We can hide you, an' we can see you get to eat while your face gets well.'

'But, Ma–'

She got to her feet. 'You ain't goin'. We're a-takin' you. Al, you back the truck against the door. Now, I got it figgered out. We'll put one mattress on the bottom, an' then Tom gets quick there, an' we take another mattress an' sort of fold it so it makes a cave, an' he's in the cave; and then we sort of wall it in. He can breathe out the end, ya see. Don't argue. That's what we'll do.'

Pa complained: 'Seems like the man ain't got no more say no more. She's jus' a heller. Come time we get settled down, I'm a-gonna smack her.'

'Come that time, you can,' said Ma. 'Roust up, Al. It's dark enough.'

Al went outside to the truck. He studied the matter and backed up near the steps.

Ma said: 'Quick now. Git that mattress in!'

Pa and Uncle John flung it over the end gate. 'Now that one.' They tossed the second mattress up. 'Now–Tom, you jump up there an' git under. Hurry up.'

Tom climbed quickly and dropped. He straightened one mattress and pulled the second on top of him. Pa bent it upwards, stood it sides up, so that the arch covered Tom. He could see out between the side-boards of the truck. Pa and Al and Uncle John loaded quickly, piled the blankets on top of Tom's cave, stood the buckets against the sides, spread the last mattress behind. Pots and pans, extra clothes, went in loose, for their boxes had been burned. They were nearly finished loading when a guard moved near, carrying his shot-gun across his crooked arm.

'What's goin' on here?' he asked.

'We're goin' out,' said Pa.

'What for?'

'Well–we got a job offered–good job.'

'Yeah? Where's it at?'

'Why–down by Weedpatch.'

'Let's have a look at you.' He turned a flashlight in Pa's face, in Uncle

John's, and in Al's. 'Wasn't there another fella with you?'

Al said: 'You mean that hitch-hiker? Little short fella with a pale face?'

'Yeah. I guess that's what he looked like.'

'We jus' picked him up on the way in. He went away this mornin' when the rate dropped.'

'What did he look like again?'

'Short fella. Pale face.'

'Was he bruised up this mornin'?'

'I didn' see nothin',' said Al. 'Is the petrol pump open?'

'Yeah, till eight.'

'Git in,' Al cried. 'If we're gonna get to Weedpatch 'fore mornin' we gotta ram on. Gettin' in front Ma?'

'No, I'll set in back,' she said. 'Pa, you set back here, too. Let Rosasharn set in front with Al an' Uncle John.'

'Give me the work slip, Pa,' said Al. 'I'll get petrol an' change if I can.'

The guard watched them pull along the street and turn left to the petrol pumps.

'Put in two,' said Al.

'You ain't goin' far.'

'No, not far. Can I get change on this here work slip?'

'Well–I ain't supposed too.'

'Look, mister,' Al said. 'We got a job offered if we get there to-night. If we don't we miss out. Be a good fella.'

'Well, O.K. You sign her over to me.'

Al got out and walked around the nose of the Hudson. 'Sure I will,' he said. He unscrewed the water-cap and filled the radiator.

'Two, you say?'

'Yeah, two.'

'Which way you goin'?'

'South. We got a job.'

'Yeah? Jobs is scarce–reg'lar jobs.'

'We got a frien',' Al said. 'Job's all waitin' for us. Well, so long.' The truck swung around and bumped over the dirt street into the road. The feeble headlight jiggled over the way, and the right headlight blinked on and off from a bad connexion. At every jolt the loose pots and pans in the truck-bed jangled and crashed.

Rose of Sharon moaned softly.

'Feel bad?' Uncle John asked.

'Yeah! Feel bad all a time. Wisht I could set still in a nice place. Wisht we was home an' never come. Connie wouldn' a went away if we was home. He would a studied up an' got some-place.' Neither Al nor Uncle John answered her. They were embarrassed about Connie.

At the white painted gate to the ranch a guard came to the side of the truck. 'Goin' out for good?'

'Yeah,' said Al. 'Goin' north. Got a job.'

The guard turned his flashlight on the truck, turned it up into the tent, Ma and Pa looked stonily down into the glare. 'O.K.' The guard swung the gate open. The truck turned left and moved toward 101, the great north-south highway.

'Know where we're a-goin'?' Uncle John asked.

'No,' said Al. 'Jus' goin' an' gettin' goddamn sick of it.'

'I ain't so tur'ble far from my time,' Rose of Sharon said threateningly. 'They better be a nice place for me.'

The night air was cold with the first sting of frost. Beside the road the leaves were beginning to drop from the fruit trees. On the load, Ma sat with her back against the truck side, and Pa sat opposite, facing her.

Ma called: 'You all right, Tom?'

His muffled voice came back, 'Kinda tight in here. We all through the ranch?'

'You be careful,' said Ma. 'Might git stopped.'

Tom lifted up one side of his cave. In the dimness of the truck the pots jangled. 'I can pull her down quick,' he said. ''Sides, I don' like gettin' trapped in here.' He rested upon his elbow. 'By God, she's gettin' cold, ain't she?'

'They's clouds up,' said Pa. 'Fella says it's gonna be an early winter.'

'Squirrels a-buildin' high, or grass seeds?' Tom asked. 'By God, you can tell weather from anythin'. I bet you could find a fella could tell weather from a old pair of under-drawers.'

'I dunno,' Pa said. 'Seems like it's gittin' on winter to me. Fella'd have to live here a long time to know.'

'Which way we a-goin'?' Tom asked.

'I dunno. Al, he turned off lef'. Seems like he's goin' back the way we come.'

Tom said: I can't figger what's best. Seems like if we get on the main highway they'll be more cops. With my face this-a-way, they'd pick me right up. Maybe we oughta keep to back roads.'

Ma said: 'Hammer on the back. Get Al to stop.'

Tom pounded on the front board with his fist; the truck pulled to a stop on the side of the road. Al got out and walked to the back. Ruthie and Winfield peeked out from under their blanket.

'What ya want?' Al demanded.

Ma said: 'We got to figger what to do. Maybe we better keep on the back roads. Tom says so.'

'It's my face,' Tom added. 'Anybody'd know. Any cop'd know me.'

'Well, which way you wanta go? I figgered north. We been south.'

'Yeah,' said Tom, 'but keep on back roads.'

Al asked: ' How 'bout pullin off an' catchin' some sleep, goin' on to-morra?'

Ma said quickly: 'Not yet. Le's get some distance fust.'

'O.K.' Al got back in his seat and drove on.

Ruthie and Winfield covered up their heads again. Ma called: 'Is Winfiel' all right?'

'Sure, he's awright,' Ruthie said. 'He been sleepin'.'

Ma leaned back against the truck side. 'Gives ya a funny feelin' to be hunted like. I'm gittin' mean.'

'Ever'body's gittin' mean,' said Pa. 'Ever'body. You seen that fight to-day. Fella changes. Down that gov'ment camp we wasn' mean.'

Al turned right on a gravelled road, and the yellow lights shuddered over the ground. The fruit trees were gone now, and cotton plants took their place. They drove on for twenty miles through the cotton, turning, angling on the country roads. The road paralleled a bushy creek and turned over a concrete bridge and followed the stream on the other side. And then, on the edge of the creek the lights showed a long line of red box-cars, wheelless; and a big sign on the edge of the road said, 'Cotton Pickers Wanted'. Al slowed down. Tom peered between the side-bars of the truck. A quarter of a mile past the box-cars

Tom hammered on the car again. Al stopped beside the road and got out again.

'Now what ya want?'

'Shut off the engine an' climb up here,' Tom said.

Al got into the seat, drove off into the ditch, cut lights and engine. He climbed over the tail gate. 'Awright,' he said.

Tom crawled over the pots and knelt in front of Ma. 'Look,' he said. 'It says they want cotton pickers. I seen that sign. Now I been tryin' to figger how I'm gonna stay with you, an' not make no trouble. When my face gets well, maybe it'll be awright, but not now. Ya see them cars back there. Well, the pickers live in them. Now maybe they's work there. How about if you get work there an' live in one of them cars?'

'How 'bout you?' Ma demanded.

'Well, you seen that crick, all full a brush. Well, I could hide in that brush an' keep outa sight, an' at night you could bring me out somepin to eat. I seen a culvert, little ways back. I could maybe sleep in there.'

Pa said: 'By God, I'd like to get my hands on some cotton! There's work I un'erstan'.'

'Them cars might be a purty place to stay,' said Ma. 'Nice an' dry. You think they's enough brush to hide in, Tom?'

'Sure. I been watchin'. I could fix up a little place, hide away. Soon's my face gets well, why, I'd come out.'

'You gonna scar purty bad,' said Ma.

'Hell! Ever'body got scars.'

'I picked four hunderd poun's oncet,' Pa said. ''Course it was a good heavy crop. If we all pick, we could get some money.'

'Could get some meat,' said Al. 'What'll we do right now?'

'Go back there, an' sleep in the truck till mornin',' Pa said. 'Git work in the mornin'. I can see them bolls even in the dark.'

'How 'bout Tom?' Ma asked.

'Now you jus' forget me, Ma I'll take me a blanket. You look out on the way back. They's a nice culvert. You can bring me some bread or potatoes, or mush, an' jus' leave it there. I'll get it.'

'Well!'

'Seems like good sense to me,' said Pa.

'It is good sense,' Tom insisted. 'Soon's my face gets a little better, why, I'll come out an' go to pickin'.'

'Well, awright,' Ma agreed. 'But don' you take no chancet. Don' let nobody see you for a while.'

Tom crawled to the back of the truck. 'I'll jus' take this here blanket. You look for that culvert on the way back, Ma.'

'Take care,' she begged. 'You take care.'

'Sure,' said Tom. 'Sure I will.' He climbed the tailboard, stepped down the bank. 'Good night,' he said.

Ma watched his figure blur with the night and disappear into the bushes beside the stream. 'Dear Jesus, I hope it's awright,' she said.

Al asked: 'You want I should go back now?'

'Yeah,' said Pa.

'Go slow,' said Ma. 'I wanta be sure an' see that culvert he said about. I got to see that.'

Al backed and filled on the narrow road, until he had reversed his direction. He drove slowly back to the line of box-cars. The truck lights showed the cat-walks up to the wide car doors. The doors were dark. No one moved in the night. Al shut off his lights.

'You and Uncle John climb up the back,' he said to Rose of Sharon. 'I'll sleep in the seat here.'

Uncle John helped the heavy girl to climb over the tailboard. Ma piled the pots in a small space. The family lay wedged close together in the back of the truck.

A baby cried, in long jerking cackles, in one of the box-cars. A dog trotted out, sniffing and snorting, and moved slowly around the Joad truck. The tinkle of moving water came from the stream-bed.

27

Cotton Pickers Wanted–placards on the road, handbills out, orange-coloured handbills–Cotton Pickers Wanted.

Here, up this road, it says.

The dark green plants stringy now, and the heavy bolls clutched in the pod. White cotton spilling out like popcorn.

Like to get our hands on the bolls. Tenderly, with the finger-tips.

I'm a good picker.

Here's the man, right here.

I aim to pick some cotton.

Got a bag?

Well, no, I ain't.

Cost ya a dollar, the bag. Take it out o' your first hunderd and fifty. Eighty cents a hunderd first time over the field. Ninety cents second time over. Get your bag there. One dollar. 'F you ain't got the buck, we'll take it out of your first hunderd and fifty. That's fair, and you know it.

Sure it's fair. Good cotton bag, last all season. An' when she's wore out, draggin', turn 'er aroun', use the other end. Sew up the open end. Open up the wore end. And when both ends is gone, why, that's nice cloth! Makes a nice pair a summer drawers. Makes nightshirts. and well, hell–a cotton bag's a nice thing.

Hang it around your waist. Straddle it, drag it between your legs. She drags light at first. And your finger-tips pick out the fluff, and the hands go twisting into the sack between your legs. Kids come along behind; got no bags for the kids–use a gunny sack or put it in your ol' man's bag. She hangs heavy, some, now. Lean forward, hoist 'er along. I'm a good hand with cotton. Finger-wise, boll-wise. Jes' move along talkin', an' maybe singin' till the bag gets heavy. Fingers go right to it. Fingers know. Eyes see the work–and don't see it.

Talkin' across the rows–

They was a lady back home–won't mention no names–had a nigger kid all of a sudden. Nobody knowed before. Never did hunt out the nigger. Couldn' never hold up her head no more. But I started to tell–she was a good picker.

Now the bag is heavy, boost it along. Set your hips and tow it along, like a work horse. And the kids pickin' into the old man's sack. Good crop here. Gets thin in the low places, thin and stringy. Never seen no cotton like this here California cotton. Long fibres, bes' damn cotton I ever seen. Spoil the lan' pretty soon. Like a fella wants to buy some cotton lan'–Don' buy her, rent her. Then when she's cottoned on down, move someplace new.

Lines of people moving across the fields. Finger-wise. Inquisitive fingers sink in and out and find the bolls. Hardly have to look.

Bet I could pick cotton if I was blind. Got a feelin' for a cotton boll. Pick clean, clean as a whistle.

Sack's full now. Take her to the scales. Argue. Scale man says you got rocks to make weight. How 'bout him? His scales is fixed. Sometimes he's right, you got rocks in the sack. Sometimes you're right, the scales is crooked. Sometimes both; rocks an' crooked scales. Always argue, always fight. Keeps your head up. An' his head up. What's a few rocks? Jus' one, maybe. Quarter pound? Always argue.

Back with the empty sack. Got our own book. Mark in the weight. Got to. If they know you're markin', then they don't cheat. But God he'p ya if ya don' keep your own weight.

This is good work. Kids runnin' aroun'. Heard 'bout the cotton-pickin' machine?

Yeah, I heard.

Think it'll ever come?

Well, if it comes–fella says it'll put han'-pickin' out.

Come night. All tired. Good pickin', though. Got three dollars, me an' the ol' woman an' the kids.

The cars move to the cotton-fields. The cotton camps set up. The screened high trucks and trailers are piled high with white fluff. Cotton clings to the fence wires, and cotton rolls in little balls along the road when the wind blows. And clean white cotton, going to the gin. And the big, lumpy bales standing, going to the compress. And cotton clinging to your clothes and stuck to your whiskers. Blow your nose, there's cotton in your nose.

Hunch along now, fill up the bag 'fore dark. Wise fingers seeking the bolls. Hips hunching along, dragging the bag. Kids are tired, now in the evening. They trip over their feet in the cultivated earth. And the sun is going down.

Wisht it would last. It ain't much money, God knows, but I wisht it would last.

On a highway the old cars piling in, drawn by the handbills.

Got a cotton bag?

No.

Cost ya a dollar, then.

If they was on'y fifty of us, we could stay awhile, but they's five hundred. She won't last hardly at all. I knowed a fella never did git his bag paid out. Ever' job he got a new bag, an' ever' fiel' was done 'fore he got his weight.

Try for God's sake to save a little money! Winter's comin' fast. They ain't no work at all in California in the winter. Fill up the bag 'fore it's dark. I seen that fella put two clods in.

Well, hell. Why not? I'm jus' balancin' the crooked scales.

Now here's my book, three hunderd an' twelve poun's.

Right!

Jesus, he never argued! His scales mus' be crooked. Well, that's a nice day anyways.

They say a thousan' men are on their way to this field. We'll be fightin' for a row to-morra. We'll be snatchin' cotton, quick.

Cotton Pickers Wanted. More men picking, quicker to the gin. Now into the cotton camp.

Side-meat to-night, by God! We got money for side-meat! Stick out a han' to the little fella, he's wore out. Run in ahead an' git us four poun' of side-meat. The ol' woman'll make some nice biscuits to-night, ef she ain't too tired.

28

The box-cars, twelve of them, stood end to end on a little flat beside the stream. There were two rows of six each, the wheels removed. Up to the big sliding doors slatted planks ran for cat-walks. They made good houses, water-tight and draughtless, room for twenty-four families, one family in each end of each car. No windows, but the wide doors stood open. In some of the cars a canvas hung down in the centre of the car, while in others only the position of the door made the boundary.

The Joads had one end of an end car. Some previous occupant had fitted up an oil can with a stove-pipe, had made a hole in the wall for the stove-pipe. Even with the door open, it was dark in the end of the car. Ma hung the tarpaulin across the middle of the car.

'It's nice,' she said. 'It's almost nicer than anything we had 'cept the gov'ment camp.'

Each night she unrolled the mattresses on the floor, and each morning rolled them up again. And every day they went into the fields and picked the cotton, and every night they had meat. On a Saturday they drove into Tulare, and they bought a tin stove and new overalls for Al and Pa and Winfield and Uncle John, and they bought a dress for Ma and gave Ma's best dress to Rose of Sharon.

'She's so big,' Ma said. 'Jes' a waste of good money to get her a new dress now.'

The Joads had been lucky. They got in early enough to have a place in the box-cars. Now the tents of the late-comers filled the little flat, and those who had the box-cars were old-timers, and in a way aristocrats.

The narrow stream slipped by, out of the willows, and back into the willows again. From each car a hard-beaten path went down to the stream. Between the cars the clothes lines hung, and every day the lines were covered with drying clothes.

In the evening they walked back from the fields, carrying their folded cotton bags under their arms. They went into the store which stood at the cross-roads, and there were many pickers in the store, buying their supplies.

'How much to-day?'

'We're doin' fine. We made three and a half to-day. Wisht she'd keep up. Them kids is gettin' to be good pickers. Ma's worked 'em up a little bag for each. They couldn' tow a growed-up bag. Dump into ours. Made bags outa couple old shirts. Work fine.'

And Ma went to the meat counter, her forefinger pressed against her lips, blowing on her finger, thinking deeply. 'Might get some pork chops,' she said. 'How much?'

'Thirty cents a pound, ma'am.'

'Well, lemme have three poun's. An' a nice piece a boilin' beef.

'My girl can cook it to-morra. An' a bottle a milk for my girl. She dotes on milk. Gonna have a baby. Nurse-lady tol' her to eat lots a milk. Now, le's see, we got potatoes.'

Pa came close, carrying a can of syrup in his hands. 'Might get this here,' he said. 'Might have some hot-cakes.'

Ma frowned. 'Well–well, yes. Here, we'll take this here. Now–we got plenty lard.'

Ruthie came near, in her hands two large boxes of Cracker Jack, in her eyes a brooding question, which on a nod or a shake of Ma's head might become tragedy or joyous excitement. 'Ma?' She held up the boxes, jerked them up and down to make them attractive.

'Now you put them back–'

The tragedy began to form in Ruthie's eyes. Pa said: 'They're on'y a nickel apiece. Them little fellas worked good to-day.'

'Well–' The excitement began to steal into Ruthie's eyes. 'Awright.'

Ruthie turned and fled. Halfway to the door she caught Winfield and rushed him out the door, into the evening.

Uncle John fingered a pair of canvas gloves with yellow leather palms, tried them on and took them off and laid them down. He moved gradually to the liquor shelves, and he stood studying the labels on the bottles. Ma saw him. 'Pa,' she said, and motioned with her head toward Uncle John.

Pa lounged over to him. 'Gettin' thirsty, John?'

'No, I ain't.'

'Jus' wait till cotton's done,' said Pa. 'Then you can go on a hell of a drunk.'

''Tain't sweatin' me none,' Uncle John said. 'I'm workin' hard an' sleepin' good. No dreams nor nothin'.'

'Jus' seen you sort of droolin' out at them bottles.'

'I didn' hardly see 'em. Funny thing. I wanta buy stuff. Stuff I don't need. Like to git one a them safety razors. Thought I'd like to have some a them gloves over there. Awful cheap.'

'Can't pick no cotton with gloves,' said Pa.

'I know that. An' I don't need no safety razor, neither. Stuff settin' out there, you jus' feel like buyin' it whether you need it or not.'

Ma called: 'Come on. We got ever'thing.' She carried a bag. Uncle John and Pa each took a package. Outside Ruthie and Winfield were waiting, their eyes strained, their cheeks puffed and full of Cracker Jack.

'Won't eat no supper, I bet,' Ma said.

People streamed towards the box-car camp. The tents were lighted. Smoke poured from the stove-pipes. The Joads climbed up their cat-walk and into their end of the box-car. Rose of Sharon sat on a box beside the stove. She had a fire started, and the tin stove was wine-coloured with heat. 'Did ya get milk?' she demanded.

'Yeah. Right here.'

'Give it to me. I ain't had any sence noon.'

'She thinks it's like medicine.'

'That nurse-lady says so.'

'You got potatoes ready?'

'Right there–peeled.'

'We'll fry 'em,' said Ma. 'Got pork chops. Cut up them potatoes in the new fry pan. And th'ow in a onion. You fellas go out an' wash, an' bring a bucket of water. Where's Ruthie an' Winfiel'? They oughta wash. They each got Cracker Jack,' Ma told Rose of Sharon. 'Each got a whole box.'

The men went out to wash in the stream. Rose of Sharon sliced the potatoes into the frying-pan and stirred them about with the knife point.

Suddenly the tarpaulin was thrust aside. A stout perspiring face looked in from the other end of the car. 'How'd you all make out, Mis' Joad?'

Ma swung around. 'Why, evenin', Mis' Wainwright. We done good. Three an' a half. Three fifty-seven, exact.'

'We done four dollars.'

'Well,' said Ma. ''Course they's more *of* you.'

'Yeah. Jonas is growin' up. Havin' pork chops, I see.'

Winfield crept in through the door. 'Ma!'

'Hush a minute. Yes, my men jus' loves pork chops.'

'I'm cookin' bacon,' said Mrs Wainwright. 'Can you smell it cookin'?'

'No–can't smell it over these here onions in the potatoes.'

'She's burnin'!' Mrs Wainwright cried, and her head jerked back.

'Ma,' Winfield said.

'What? You sick from Cracker Jack?'

'Ma–Ruthie tol'.'

'Tol' what?'

''Bout Tom.'

Ma stared. 'Tol'?' Then she knelt in front of him. 'Winfiel', who's she tell?'

Embarrassment seized Winfield. He backed away. 'Well, she on'y tol' a little bit.'

'Winfiel'! Now you tell what she said.'

'She–she didn' eat all her Cracker Jack. She kep' some, an' she et jus' one piece at a time, slow, like she always done, an' she says: "Bet you wisht you had some lef'." '

'Winfiel'!' Ma demanded. 'You tell now.' She looked back nervously at the curtain. 'Rosasharn, you go over talk to Mis' Wainwright so she don' listen.'

'How 'bout these here potatoes?'

'I'll watch'em. Now you go. I don' want her listenin' at that curtain.' The girl shuffled down the car and went around the side of the hung tarpaulin.

Ma said: 'Now, Winfiel', you tell.'

'Like I said, she et jus' one little piece at a time, an' she bust some in two so it'd las' longer.'

'Go on, hurry up.'

'Well some kids come aroun', an' 'course they tried to get some, but Ruthie, she jus' nibbled an' nibbled, an' wouldn' give 'em none. So they got mad. An' one kid grabbed her Cracker Jack box.'

'Winfiel', you tell quick about the other.'

'I am,' he said. 'So Ruthie got mad an' chased 'em, an' she fit one, an' then she fit another, an' then one big girl up an' licked her. Hit 'er a good one. So then Ruthie cried, an' she said she'd git her big brother, an' he'd kill that big girl. An' that big girl said: "Oh yeah?" Well, she got a big brother too.' Winfield was breathless in his telling. 'So then they fit, an' that big girl hit Ruthie a good one, an' Ruthie said her brother'd kill that big girl's brother. An' that big girl said how about if her brother kil't our brother. An' then–an' then,

Ruthie said our brother already kil't two fellas. An'–an'–that big girl said: "Oh, yeah! You're jus' a little smarty liar." An' Ruthie said: "Oh, yeah? Well, our brother's a-hidin' right now from killin' a fella, an' he can kill that big girl's brother too." An' then they call names an' Ruthie throwed a rock, an' that big girl chased her, an' I come home.'

'Oh, my!' Ma said wearily. 'Oh! My dear sweet Lord Jesus asleep in a manger! What we goin' to do now?' She put her forehead in her hand and rubbed her eyes. 'What we gonna do now?' A smell of burning potatoes came from the roaring stove. Ma moved automatically and turned them.

'Rosasharn!' Ma called. The girl appeared around the curtain. 'Come watch this here supper. Winfiel', you go out an' you fin' Ruthie an' bring her back here.'

'Gonna whup her, Ma?' he asked hopefully.

'No. This here you couldn' do nothin' about. Why, I wonder, did she haf' to do it? No. It won't do no good to whup her. Run now, an' find her an' bring her back.'

Winfield ran to the car door, and he met the three men tramping up the cat-walk, and he stood aside while they came in.

Ma said softly: 'Pa, I got to talk to you. Ruthie tol' some kids how Tom's a-hidin'.'

'What?'

'She tol'. Got in a fight an' tol'.'

'Why, the little bitch!'

'No, she didn' know what she was a-doin'. Now look, Pa. I want you to stay here. I'm goin' out an' try to fin' Tom an' tell him. I got to tell 'im to be careful. You stick here, Pa, an kinda watch out for things. I'll take 'im some dinner.'

'Awright,' Pa agreed.

'Don' you even mention to Ruthie what she done. I'll tell her.'

At that moment Ruthie came in, with Winfield behind her. The little girl was dirtied. Her mouth was sticky, and her nose still dripped a little blood from her fight. She looked shamed and frightened. Winfield triumphantly followed her. Ruthie looked fiercely about, but she went to a corner of the car and put her back in the corner. Her shame and fierceness were blended.

'I tol' her what she done,' Winfield said.

Ma was putting two chops and some fried potatoes on a tin plate. 'Hush, Winfiel,' she said. 'They ain't no need to hurt her feelings no more'n what they're hurt.'

Ruthie's body hurtled across the car. She grabbed Ma around the middle and buried her head in Ma's stomach, and her strangled sobs shook her whole body. Ma tried to loosen her, but the grubby fingers clung tight. Ma brushed the hair on the back of her head gently, and she patted her shoulders. 'Hush,' she said. 'You didn' know.'

Ruthie raised her dirty, tear-stained, bloody face. 'They stoled my Cracker Jack!' she cried. 'That big son-of-a-bitch of a girl she belted me–' She went off into hard crying again.

'Hush!' Ma said. 'Don' talk like that. Here. Let go. I'm a-goin' now.'

'Whyn't ya whup her, Ma? If she didn't git snotty with her Cracker Jack 'twouldn' a happened. Go on, give her a whup.'

'You jus' min' your business, mister,' Ma said fiercely. 'You'll git a whup yourself. Now leggo, Ruthie.'

Winfield retired to a rolled mattress, and he regarded the family cynically and dully. And he put himself in a good position of defence, for Ruthie would attack him at the first opportunity, and he knew it. Ruthie went quietly, heartbrokenly to the other side of the car.

Ma put a sheet of newspaper over the tin plate. 'I'm a-goin' now,' she said.

'Ain't you gonna eat nothin' yourself?' Uncle John demanded.

'Later. When I come back. I wouldn' want nothin' now.' Ma walked to the open door; she steadied herself down the steep, cleated cat-walk.

On the stream side of the box-cars, the tents were pitched close together, their guy ropes crossing one another, and the pegs of one at the canvas line of the next. The lights shone through the cloth, and all the chimneys belched smoke. Men and women stood in the doorways talking. Children ran feverishly about. Ma moved majestically down the line of tents. Here and there she was recognized as she went by. ''Evenin', Mis' Joad.'

''Evenin'.'

'Takin' somepin out, Mis' Joad?'

'They's a frien'. I'm takin' back some bread.'

She came at last to the end of the line of tents. She stopped and looked back. A glow of light was on the camp, and the soft overtone of a multitude of speakers. Now and then a harsher voice cut through. The smell of smoke filled the air. Someone played a harmonica softly, trying for an effect, one phrase over and over.

Ma stepped in among the willows beside the stream. She moved off the trail and waited, silently, listening to hear any possible follower. A man walked down the trail toward the camp, boosting his suspenders and buttoning his jeans as he went. Ma sat very still, and he passed on without seeing her. She waited five minutes and then she stood up and crept on up the trail beside the stream. She moved quietly, so quietly that she could hear the murmur of the water above her soft steps on the willow leaves. Trail and stream swung to the left and then to the right again until they neared the highway. In the grey starlight she could see the embankment and the black hole of the culvert where she always left Tom's food. She moved forward cautiously, thrust her package into the hole, and took the empty tin plate which was left there. She crept back among the willows, forced her way into a thicket, and sat down to wait. Through the tangle she could see the black hole of the culvert. She clasped her knees and sat silently. In a few moments the thicket crept to life again. The field-mice moved cautiously over the leaves. A skunk padded heavily and unselfconsciously down the trail, carrying a faint affluvium with him. And then a wind stirred the willows delicately, as though it tested them, and a shower of golden leaves coasted down to the ground. Suddenly a gust boiled in and racked the trees, and a cricking downpour of leaves fell. Ma could feel them on her hair and on her shoulders. Over the sky a plump black cloud moved, erasing the stars. The fat drops of rain scattered down, splashing loudly on the fallen leaves, and the cloud moved on and unveiled the stars again. Ma shivered. The wind blew past and left the thicket quiet, but the rushing of the trees went on down the stream. From back at the camp came the thin penetrating tone of a violin feeling about for a tune.

Ma heard a stealthy step among the leaves far to her left, and she grew tense. She released her knees and straightened her head, the better to hear. The movement stopped, and after a long moment began again. A vine rasped harshly on the dry leaves. Ma saw a dark figure creep into the open and draw near to the culvert. The black round hole was obscured for a moment, and then the figure moved back. She called softly: 'Tom!' The figure stood still, so still, so low to the ground that it might have been a stump. She called again, 'Tom, oh, Tom!' Then the figure moved.

'That you, Ma?'

'Right over here.' She stood up and went to meet him.

'You shouldn' have came,' he said.

'I got to see you. Tom. I got to talk to you.'

'It's near the trail,' he said. 'Somebody might come by.'

'Ain't you got a place, Tom?'

'Yeah–but if–well, s'pose somebody seen you with me–whole fambly'd be in a jam.'

'I got to, Tom.'

'Then come along. Come quiet.' He crossed the little stream, wading carelessly through the water, and Ma followed him. He moved through the brush, out into a field on the other side of the thicket, and along the ploughed ground. The blackening stems of the cotton were harsh against the ground, and a few fluffs of cotton clung to the stems. A quarter of a mile they went along the edge of the field, and then he turned into the brush again. He approached a great mound of wild blackberry bushes, leaned over and pulled a mat of vines aside. 'You got to crawl in,' he said.

Ma went down on her hands and knees. She felt sand under her, and then the black inside of the mound no longer touched her, and she felt Tom's blanket on the ground. He arranged the vines in place again. It was lightless in the cave.

'Where are you, Ma?'

'Here. Right here. Talk soft, Tom.'

'Don't worry. I been livin' like a rabbit some time.'

She heard him unwrap his tin plate.

'Pork chops,' she said. 'And fry potatoes.'

'God Awmighty, an' still warm.'

Ma could not see him at all in the blackness, but she could hear him chewing, tearing at the meat and swallowing.

'It's a pretty good hide-out,' he said.

Ma said uneasily: 'Tom–Ruthie tol' about you.' She heard him gulp.

'Ruthie? What for?'

'Well, it wasn' her fault. Got in a fight an' says her brother'll lick that other girl's brother. You know how they do. An she tol' that her brother killed a man an' was hidin'.'

Tom was chuckling. 'With me I was always gonna get Uncle John after 'em but he never would do it. That's jus' kid talk, Ma. That's awright.'

'No, it ain't,' Ma said. 'Them kids'll tell it aroun' an' then the folks'll hear, an' they'll tell aroun' an' pretty soon, well they liable to get men out to look, jus' in case. Tom, you got to go away.'

'That's what I said right along. I was always scared somebody'd see you put stuff in that culvert, an' then they'd watch.'

'I know. But I wanted you near. I was scared for you. I ain't seen you. Can't see you now. How's your face?'

'Gettin' well quick.'

'Come clost, Tom. Let me feel it. Come clost.' He crawled near. Her reaching hand found his head in the blackness and her fingers moved down to his nose, and then over his left cheek. 'You got a bad scar, Tom. An' your nose is all crooked.'

'Maybe tha's a good thing. Nobody wouldn't know me, maybe. If my prints wasn't on record, I'd be glad.' He went back to his eating.

'Hush,' she said. 'Listen!'

'It's the wind, Ma. Jus' the wind.' The gust poured down the stream, and the trees rustled under its passing.

She crawled close to his voice. 'I wanta touch ya again, Tom. It's like I'm blin', it's so dark. I wanta remember, even if it's on'y my fingers that remember. You got to go away, Tom.'

'Yeah! I knowed it from the start.'

'We made purty good,' she said. 'I been squirrelin' money away. Hol' out your han', Tom. I got seven dollars here.'

'I ain't gonna take ya money,' he said. 'I'll get 'long all right.'

'Hol' out ya han', Tom. I ain't gonna sleep none if you got no money. Maybe you got to take a bus, or somepin. I want you should go a long ways off, three-four hunderd miles.'

'I ain't gonna take it.'

'Tom,' she said sternly. 'You take this money. You hear me? You got no right to cause me pain.'

'You ain't playin' fair,' he said.

'I thought maybe you'd go to a big city. Los Angeles, maybe. They wouldn' never look for you there.'

'Hm-m,' he said. 'Lookie, Ma. I been all day an' all night hidin' alone. Guess who I been thinkin' about? Casy! He talked a lot. Used ta bother me. But now I been thinkin' what he said, an' I can remember–all of it. Says one time he went out in the wilderness to find his own soul, an' he foun' he didn' have no soul that was his'n. Says he foun' he jus' got a little piece of a great big soul. Says a wilderness ain't no good 'cause his little piece of soul wasn't no good' less it was with the rest, an' was whole. Funny how I remember. Didn' think I was even listenin'. But I know now a fella ain't no good alone.'

'He was a good man,' Ma said.

Tom went on: 'He spouted out some Scripture once, an' it didn' soun' like no hell-fire Scripture. He tol' it twicet, an' I remember it. Says it's from the Preacher.'

'How's it go, Tom?'

'Goes, "Two are better than one, because they have a good reward for their labour. For if they fall, the one will lif' up his fellow, but woe to him that is alone when he falleth, for he hath not another to help him up." That's part of her.'

'Go on,' Ma said. 'Go on, Tom.'

'Jus' a little bit more. "Again, if two lie together, then they have heat; but how can one be warm alone? And if one prevail against him, two shall withstand him, and a three-fold cord is not quickly broken." '

'An' that's Scripture?'

'Casy said it was. Called it the Preacher.'

'Hush–listen.'

'On'y the wind, Ma. I know the wind. An' I got to thinkin'. Ma–most of the preachin' is about the poor we shall have always with us, an' if you got nothin', why, jus' fol' your hands an' to hell with it, you gonna git ice cream on gol' plates when you're dead. An' then this here Preacher says two get a better reward for their work.'

'Tom,' she said. 'What you aimin' to do?'

He was quiet for a long time. 'I been thinkin' how it was in that gov'ment camp, how our folks took care a theirselves, an' if they was a fight they fixed it theirself; an' they wasn't no cops wagglin' their guns, but they was better order than them cops ever give. I been a-wonderin' why we can't do that all over. Throw out the cops that ain't our people. All work together for our own thing–all farm our own lan'.'

'Tom,' Ma repeated, 'what you gonna do?'

'What Casy done,' he said.

'But they killed him.'

'Yeah,' said Tom. 'He didn' duck quick enough. He wasn' doin' nothin' against the law, Ma. I been thinkin' a hell of a lot, thinkin' about our people livin' like pigs, an' the good rich lan' layin' fallow, or maybe one fella with a million acres, while a hunderd thousan' good farmers is starvin'. An' I been wonderin' if all our folks got together an' yelled, like them fellas yelled, only a few of 'em at the Hooper ranch–'

Ma said: 'Tom, they'll drive you, an' cut you down like they done to young Floyd.'

'They gonna drive me anyways. They drivin' all our people.'

'You don't aim to kill nobody, Tom?'

'No. I been thinkin', long as I'm a outlaw anyways, maybe I could–Hell, I ain't thought it out clear, Ma. Don' worry me now. Don' worry me.'

They sat silent in the coal-black cave of vines. Ma said: 'How'm I gonna know 'bout you? They might kill ya an' I wouldn' know. They might hurt ya. How'm I gonna know?'

Tom laughed uneasily. 'Well, maybe like Casy says, a fella ain't got a soul of his own, but on'y a piece of a big one–an' then–'

'Then what, Tom?'

'Then it don' matter. Then I'll be all aroun' in the dark. I'll be ever'where–wherever you look. Wherever they's a fight so hungry people can eat, I'll be there. Wherever they's a cop beatin' up a guy, I'll be there. If Casy knowed, why, I'll be in the way guys yell when they're mad an'–I'll be in the way kids laugh when they're hungry an' they know supper's ready. An' when our folks eat the stuff they raise an' live in the houses they build–why, I'll be there. See? God, I'm talkin' like Casy. Comes of thinkin' about him so much. Seems like I can see him sometimes.'

'I don' un'erstan',' Ma said. 'I don' really know.'

'Me neither,' said Tom. 'It's jus' stuff I been thinkin' about. Get thinkin' a lot when you ain't movin' aroun'. You got to get back, Ma.'

'You take the money then.'

He was silent for a moment. 'Awright,' he said.

'An', Tom, later–when it's blowed over, you'll come back. You'll find us?'

'Sure,' he said. 'Now you better go. Here, gimme your han'.' He guided her toward the entrance. Her fingers clutched his wrist. He swept the vines aside and followed her out. 'Go up to the field till you come to a sycamore on the edge, an' then cut acrost the stream. Good-bye.'

'Good-bye,' she said, and she walked quickly away. Her eyes were wet and burning, but she did not cry. Her footsteps were loud and careless on the leaves as she went through the brush. And as she went, out of the dim sky the rain began to fall, big drops and few, splashing on the dry leaves heavily. Ma stopped and stood still in the dripping thicket. She turned about–took three steps back toward the mound of vines; and then she turned quickly and went back toward the box-car camp. She went straight out to the culvert and climbed up on the road. The rain had passed now, but the sky was overcast. Behind her on the road she heard footsteps, and she turned nervously. The blinking of a dim flashlight played on the road. Ma turned back and started for home. In a moment a man caught up with her. Politely, he kept his light on the ground and did not play it in her face.

'Evenin',' he said.

Ma said: 'Howdy.'

'Looks like we might have a little rain.'

'I hope not. Stop the pickin'. We need the pickin'.'

'I need the pickin' too. You live at the camp there?'

'Yes, sir.' Their footsteps beat on the road together.

'I got twenty acres of cotton. Little late, but it's ready now. Thought I'd go down and try to get some pickers.'

'You'll get 'em awright. Season's near over.'

'Hope so. My place is only a mile up that way.'

'Six of us,' said Ma. 'Three men an' me an' two little fellas.'

'I'll put out a sign. Two miles–this road.'

'We'll be there in the mornin'.'

'I hope it don't rain.'

'Me too,' said Ma. 'Twenty acres won' las' long.'

'The less it lasts the gladder I'll be. My cotton's late. Didn' get it in till late.'

'What you payin', mister?'

'Ninety cents.'

'We'll pick. I hear fellas say nex' year it'll be seventy-five or even sixty.'

'That's what I hear.'

'They'll be trouble,' said Ma.

'Sure. I know. Little fella like me can't do anything. The Association sets the rate, and we got to mind. If we don't–we ain't got a farm. Little fella gets crowded all the time.'

They came to the camp. 'We'll be there,' Ma said. 'Not much pickin' lef'.' She went to the end box-car and climbed the cleated walk. The low light of the lantern made gloomy shadows in the car. Pa and Uncle John and an elderly man squatted against the car wall.

'Hello,' Ma said. ''Evenin', Mr Wainwright.'

He raised a delicately chiselled face. His eyes were deep under the ridges of his brows. His hair was blue-white and fine. A patina of silver beard covered his jaws and chin. ''Evenin', ma'am,' he said.

'We got pickin' to-morra,' Ma observed. 'Mile north. Twenty acres.'

'Better take the truck, I guess,' Pa said. 'Get in more pickin'.'

Wainwright raised his head eagerly. 'S'pose we can pick?'

'Why, sure. I walked a piece with the fella. He was comin' to get pickers.'

'Cotton's nearly gone. Purty thin, these here seconds. Gonna be hard to make a wage on the seconds. Got her pretty clean the fust time.'

'Your folks could maybe ride with us,' Ma said. 'Split the petrol.'

'Well–that's frien'ly of you, ma'am.'

'Saves us both,' said Ma.

Pa said: 'Mr Wainwright–he's got a worry he come to us about. We was a-talkin' her over.'

'What's the matter?'

Wainwright looked down at the floor. 'Our Aggie,' he said. 'She's a big girl–near sixteen, an' growed up.'

'Aggie's a pretty girl,' said Ma.

'Listen 'im out,' Pa said.

'Well, her an' your boy Al, they're a-walkin' out ever' night. An' Aggie's a good healthy girl that oughta have a husban', else she might get in trouble. We never had no trouble in our family. But what with us bein' so poor off, now, Mis' Wainwright an' me, we got to worryin'. S'pose she got in trouble?'

Ma rolled down a mattress and sat on it. 'They out now?' she asked.

'Always out,' said Wainwright. 'Ever' night.'

'Hm. Well, Al's a good boy. Kinda figgers he's a dunghill rooster these days, but he's a good steady boy. I couldn' want for a better boy.'

'Oh, we ain't complainin' about Al as a fella! We like him. But what scares Mis' Wainwright an' me–well, she's a growed-up woman-girl. An' what if we go away, or you go away, an' we find out Aggie's in trouble? We ain't had no shame in our family.'

Ma said softly: 'We'll try an' see that we don't put no shame on you.'

He stood up quickly. 'Thank you, ma'am. Aggie's a growed-up woman-girl. She's a good girl–jes' as nice an' good. We'll sure thank you, ma'am, if you'll keep shame from us. It ain't Aggie's fault. She's growed up.'

'Pa'll talk to Al,' said Ma. 'Or if Pa won't, I will.'

Wainwright said: 'Good night, then, an' we sure thank ya.' He went around the end of the curtain. They could hear him talking softly in the other end of the car, explaining the result of his embassy.

Ma listened a moment, and then: 'You fellas,' she said. 'Come over an' set here.'

Pa and Uncle John got heavily up from their squats. They sat on the mattress beside Ma.

'Where's the little fellas?'

Pa pointed to a mattress in the corner. 'Ruthie, she jumped Winfiel' an' bit 'im. Made 'em both lay down. Guess they're asleep. Rosasharn, she went to set with a lady she knows.'

Ma sighed. 'I foun' Tom,' she said softly. 'I–sent 'im away. Far off.'

Pa nodded slowly. Uncle John dropped his chin on his chest. 'Couldn' do nothin' else,' Pa said. 'Think he could, John?'

Uncle John looked up. 'I can't think nothin' out,' he said. 'Don't seem like I'm hardly awake no more.'

'Tom's a good boy,' Ma said; and then she apologized: 'I didn' mean no harm a-sayin' I'd talk to Al.'

'I know,' Pa said quietly. 'I ain't no good any more. Spen' all my time a-thinkin' how it use' ta be. Spen' all my time thinkin' of home, an' I ain't never gonna see it no more.'

'This here's purtier–better lan',' said Ma.

'I know. I never even see it, thinkin' how the willow's los' its leaves now. Sometimes figgerin' to mend that hole in the south fence. Funny! Woman takin' over the fambly. Woman sayin' we'll do this here, an' we'll go there. An' I don' even care.'

'Woman can change better'n a man,' Ma said soothingly. 'Woman got all her life in her arms. Man got it all in his head. Don' you mind. Maybe–well, maybe nex' year we can get a place.'

'We got nothin', now,' Pa said. 'Comin' a long time–no work, no crops.

What we gonna do then? How we gonna git stuff to eat? An' I tell you Rosasharn ain't so far from due. Git so I hate to think. Go diggin' back to a ol' time to keep from thinkin'. Seems like our life's over an' done.'

'No, it ain't,' Ma smiled. 'It ain't, Pa. An' that's one more thing a woman knows. I noticed that. Man, he lives in jerks–baby born an' a man dies, an' that's a jerk–gets a farm an' loses his farm, an' that's a jerk. Woman, it's all one flow, like a stream, little eddies, little waterfalls, but the river, it goes right on. Woman looks at it like that. We ain't gonna die out. People is goin' on–changin' a little, maybe, but goin' right on.'

'How can you tell?' Uncle John demanded. 'What's to keep ever'thing from stoppin'; all the folks from jus' gittin' tired an' layin' down?'

Ma considered. She rubbed the shiny back of one hand with the other, pushed the fingers of her right hand between the fingers of her left. 'Hard to say,' she said. 'Ever'thing we do–seems to me is aimed right at goin' on. Seems that way to me. Even gettin' hungry–even bein' sick; some die, but the rest is tougher. Jus' try to live the day, jus' the day.'

Uncle John said: 'If on'y she didn' die that time–'

'Jus' live the day,' Ma said. 'Don' worry yaself.'

'They might be a good year nex' year, back home,' said Pa.

Ma said: 'Listen!'

There were creeping steps on the cat-walk, and then Al came in past the curtain. 'Hullo,' he said, 'I thought you'd be sleepin' by now.'

'Al,' Ma said. 'We're a-talkin'. Come set here.'

'Sure–O.K. I wanta talk too. I'll hafta be goin' away pretty soon now.'

'You can't. We need you here. Why you got to go away?'

'Well, me an' Aggie Wainwright, we figgers to get married, an' I'm gonna git a job in a garage, an' we'll have a rent' house for a while, an'–' He looked up fiercely. 'Well, we are, an' they ain't nobody can stop us!'

They were staring at him. 'Al,' Ma said at last, 'we're glad. We're awful glad.'

'You are?'

'Why, 'course we are, You're a growed man. You need a wife. But don' go right now, Al.'

'I promised Aggie,' he said. 'We got to go. We can't stan' this no more.'

'Jus' stay till spring,' Ma begged. 'Jus' till spring. Won't you stay till spring? Who'd drive the truck?'

'Well–'

Mrs Wainwright put her head around the curtain. 'You heard yet?' she demanded.

'Yeah! Jus' heard.'

'Oh, my! I wisht–I wisht we had a cake. I wisht we had–a cake or somepin.'

'I'll set on some coffee an' make up some pancakes,' Ma said. 'We got syrup.'

'Oh, my!' Mrs Wainwright said. 'Well–well. Look, I'll bring some sugar. We'll put sugar in them pancakes.'

Ma broke twigs into the stove, and the coals from the dinner cooking started them blazing. Ruthie and Winfield came out of their bed like hermit crabs from shells. For a moment they were careful; they watched to see whether they were still criminals. When no one noticed them they grew bold. Ruthie hopped all the way to the door and back on one foot, without touching the wall.

Ma was pouring flour into a bowl when Rose of Sharon climbed the cat-walk. She steadied herself and advanced cautiously. 'What's a matter?' she asked.

'Why, it's news!' Ma cried. 'We're gonna have a little party count a Al an' Aggie Wainwright is gonna get married.'

Rose of Sharon stood perfectly still. She looked slowly at Al, who stood there flustered and embarrassed.

Mrs Wainwright shouted from the other end of the car: 'I'm puttin' a fresh dress on Aggie. I'll be right over.'

Rose of Sharon turned slowly. She went back to the wide door, and she crept down the cat-walk. Once on the ground, she moved slowly toward the stream and the trail that went beside it. She took the way Ma had gone earlier–into the willows. The wind blew more steadily now, and the bushes whished steadily. Rose of Sharon went down on her knees and crawled deep into the brush. The berry vines cut her face and pulled at her hair, but she didn't mind. Only when she felt the bushes touching her all over did she stop. She stretched out on her back. And she felt the weight of the baby inside her.

In the lightless car, Ma stirred, and then she pushed the blanket back and got up. At the open door of the car the grey starlight penetrated a little. Ma walked to the door and stood looking out. The stars were paling in the east. The wind blew softly over the willow thickets, and from the little stream came the quiet talking of the water. Most of the camp was still asleep, but in front of one tent a little fire burned, and people were standing about it, warming themselves. Ma could see them in the light of the new dancing fire as they stood facing the flames, rubbing their hands; and then they turned their backs and held their hands behind them. For a long moment Ma looked out, and she held her hands clasped in front of her. The uneven wind whisked up and passed, and a bite of frost was in the air. Ma shivered and rubbed her hands together. She crept back and fumbled for the matches, beside the lantern. The shade screeched up. She lighted the wick, watched it burn blue for a moment, and then put up its yellow, delicately curved ring of light. She carried the lantern to the stove and set it down while she broke the brittle dry willow twigs into the fire box. In a moment the fire was roaring up the chimney.

Rose of Sharon rolled heavily over and sat up. 'I'll git right up,' she said.

'Whyn't you lay a minute till it warms?' Ma asked.

'No, I'll git.'

Ma filled the coffee pot from the bucket and set it on the stove, and she put on the frying-pan, deep with fat, to get hot for the pones. 'What's over you?' she said softly.

'I'm a-goin' out,' Rose of Sharon said.

'Out where?'

'Goin' out to pick cotton.'

'You can't,' Ma said. 'You're too far along.'

'No, I ain't. An' I'm a-goin'.'

Ma measured coffee into the water. 'Rosasharn, you wasn't to the pancakes las' night.' The girl didn't answer. 'What you wanta pick cotton for?' Still no answer. 'Is it 'cause of Al an' Aggie?' This time Ma looked closely at her daughter. 'Oh. Well, you don' need to pick.'

'I'm goin'.'

'Awright, but don' you strain yourself.'

'Git up, Pa! Wake up, git up!'

Pa blinked and yawned. 'Ain't slep' out,' he moaned. 'Musta been on to eleven o'clock when we went down.'

'Come on, git up, all a you, an' wash.'

The inhabitants of the car came slowly to life, squirmed up out of the blankets, writhed into their clothes. Ma sliced salt pork into her second frying-pan. 'Git out an' wash,' she commanded.

A light sprang up in the other end of the car. And there came the sound of the breaking of twigs from the Wainwright end. 'Mis' Joad,' came the call. 'We're gettin' ready. We'll be ready.'

Al grumbled: 'What we got to be up so early for?'

'It's on'y twenty acres,' Ma said. 'Got to get there. Ain't much cotton lef'. Got to be there 'fore she's picked.' Ma rushed them dressed, rushed the breakfast into them. 'Come on, drink your coffee,' she said. 'Got to start.'

'We can't pick no cotton in the dark, Ma.'

'We can *be* there when it gets light.'

'Maybe it's wet.'

'Didn' rain enough. Come on now, drink your coffee. Al, soon's you're through, better get the engine runnin'.'

She called: 'You near ready, Mis' Wainwright?'

'Jus' eatin'. Be ready in a minute.'

Outside, the camp had come to life. Fires burned in front of the tents. The stovepipes from the box-cars spurted smoke.

Al tipped up his coffee and got a mouthful of grounds. He went down the cat-walk spitting them out.

'We're awready, Mis' Wainwright,' Ma called. She turned to Rose of Sharon. She said: 'You got to stay.'

The girl set her jaw. 'I'm a-goin',' she said. 'Ma, I got to go.'

'Well, you got no cotton sack. You can't pull no sack.'

'I'll pick into your sack.'

'I wisht you wouldn'.'

'I'm a-goin'.'

Ma sighed. 'I'll keep my eye on you. Wisht we could have a doctor.' Rose of Sharon moved nervously about the car. She put on a light coat and took it off. 'Take a blanket,' Ma said. 'Then if you wanta res', you can keep warm.' They heard the truck motor roar up behind the box-car. 'We gonna be first out,' Ma said exultantly. 'Awright, get your sacks. Ruthie, don' you forget them shirts I fixed for you to pick in.'

Wainwrights and Joads climbed into the truck in the dark. The dawn was coming, but it was slow and pale.

'Turn lef',' Ma told Al. 'They'll be a sign out where we're goin'.' They drove along the dark road. And other cars followed them, and behind, in the camp, the cars were being started, the families piling in; and the cars pulled out on the highway and turned left.

A piece of cardboard was tied to a mailbox on the right-hand side of the road, and on it, printed with blue crayon, 'Cotton Pickers Wanted'. Al turned into the entrance and drove out to the barn-yard. And the barn-yard was full of cars already. An electric globe on the end of the white barn lighted a group of men and women standing near the scales, their bags rolled under their arms. Some of the women wore the bags over their shoulders and crossed in front.

'We ain't so early as we thought,' said Al. He pulled the truck against a fence and parked. The families climbed down and went to join the waiting group, and more cars came in from the road and parked, and more families joined the group. Under the light on the barn end, the owner signed them in.

'Hawley?' he said 'H-a-w-l-e-y-? How many?'

'Four. Will–'

'Will.'

'Benton–'

'Benton.'

'Amelia–'

'Amelia.'

'Claire–'

'Claire. Who's next? Carpenter? How many?'

'Six.'

He wrote them in the book with a space left for the weights. 'Got your bags? I got a few. Cost you a dollar.' And the cars poured into the yard. The owner pulled his sheep-lined leather jacket up around his throat. He looked at the driveway apprehensively. 'This twenty isn't gonna take long to pick with all these people,' he said.

Children were climbing into the big cotton trailer, digging their toes into the chicken-wire sides. 'Git off there,' the owner cried. 'Come on down. You'll tear that wire loose.' And the children climbed slowly down, embarrassed and silent. The grey dawn came. 'I'll have to take a tare for dew,' the owner said. 'Change it when the sun comes out. All right, go out when you want. Light enough to see.'

The people moved quickly out into the cotton-field and took their rows. They tied the bags to their waists and they slapped their hands together to warm stiff fingers that had to be nimble. The dawn coloured over the eastern hills, and the wide line moved over the rows. And from the highway the cars still moved in and parked in the barn-yard until it was full, and they parked along the road on both sides. The wind blew briskly across the field. 'I don't know how you all found out,' the owner said. 'There must be a hell of a grape-vine. The twenty won't last till noon. What name? Hume? How many?'

The line of people moved out across the field, and the strong steady west wind blew their clothes. Their fingers flew to the spilling bolls, and flew to the long sack growing heavy behind them.

Pa spoke to the man in the row to his right. 'Back home we might get rain out of a wind like this. Seems a little mite frosty for rain. How long you been out here?' He kept his eyes down on his work as he spoke.

His neighbour didn't look up. 'I been here nearly a year.'

'Would you say it was gonna rain?'

'Can't tell, an' that ain't no insult, neither. Folks that lived here all their life can't tell. If the rain can git in the way of a crop, it'll rain. Tha's what they say out here.'

Pa looked quickly at the western hills. Big grey clouds were coasting over the ridge, riding the wind swiftly. 'Them looks like rain-heads,' he said.

His neighbour stole a squinting look. 'Can't tell,' he said. And all down the line of rows the people looked back at the clouds. And then they bent lower to their work, and their hands flew to the cotton. They raced at the picking, raced against time and cotton weight, raced against the rain and against each other–only so much cotton to pick, only so much money to be made. They came to the other side of the field and ran to get a new row. And now they faced into the wind, and they could see the high grey clouds moving over the sky toward the rising sun. And more cars parked along the roadside, and new pickers came to be checked in. The line of people moved frantically across the field, weighed at the end, marked their cotton, checked the weights into their own books, and ran for new rows.

At eleven o'clock the field was picked and the work was done. The wire-sided trailers were hooked on behind wire-sided trucks, and they moved out to the highway and drove away to the gin. The cotton fluffed out through the chicken wire and little clouds of cotton blew through the air, and rags of cotton caught and waved on the weeds beside the road. The pickers clustered disconsolately back to the barn-yard and stood in line to be paid off.

'Hume, James. Twenty-two cents. Ralph, thirty cents. Joad, Thomas, ninety cents. Winfield, fifteen cents.' The money lay in rolls, silver and nickels and pennies. And each man looked in his own book as he was being paid. 'Wainwright, Agnes, thirty-four cents. Tobin, sixty-three cents.' The line moved past slowly. The families went back to their cars, silently. And they drove slowly away.

Joads and Wainwrights waited in the truck for the driveway to clear. And as they waited, the first drops of rain began to fall. Al put his hands out of the cab to feel them. Rose of Sharon sat in the middle, and Ma on the outside. The girl's eyes were lustreless again.

'You shouldn' of came.' Ma said. 'You didn' pick more'n ten-fifteen pounds.' Rose of Sharon looked down at her great bulging belly, and she didn't reply. She shivered suddenly and held her head high. Ma, watching her closely, unrolled her cotton bag, spread it over Rose of Sharon's shoulders, and drew her close.

At last the way was clear. Al started his motor and drove out into the highway. The big infrequent drops of rain lanced down and splashed on the road, and as the truck moved along, the drops became smaller and closer. Rain pounded on the cab of the truck so loudly that it could be heard over the pounding of the old worn motor. On the truck bed the Wainwrights and Joads spread their cotton bags over their heads and shoulders.

Rose of Sharon shivered violently against Ma's arm, and Ma cried: 'Go faster, Al. Rosasharn got a chill. Gotta get her feet in hot water.'

Al speeded the pounding motor, and when he came to the box-car camp, he drove down close to the red cars. Ma was spouting orders before they were well stopped. 'Al,' she commanded 'you an' John an' Pa go into the willows an' collect all the dead stuff you can. We got to keep warm.'

'Wonder if the roof leaks.'

'No, I don' think so. Be nice an' dry, but we got to have wood. Got to keep warm. Take Ruthie an' Winfiel' too. They can get twigs. This here girl ain't well.' Ma got out, and Rose of Sharon tried to follow, but her knees buckled and she sat down heavily on the running-board.

Fat Mrs Wainwright saw her. 'What's a matter? Her time come?'

'No. I don' think so,' said Ma. 'Got a chill. Maybe took col'. Gimme a han', will you?' The two women supported Rose of Sharon. After a few steps her strength came back–her legs took her weight.

'I'm awright, Ma,' she said. 'It was jus' a minute there.'

The older women kept hands on her elbows. 'Feet in hot water,' Ma said wisely. They helped her up the cat-walk and into the box-car.

'You rub her,' Mrs Wainwright said. 'I'll get a far' goin'.' She used the last of the twigs and built up a blaze in the stove. The rain poured now, scoured at the roof of the car.

Ma looked up at it. 'Thank God we got a tight roof,' she said. 'Them tents leaks, no matter how good. Jus' put on a little water, Mis' Wainwright.'

Rose of Sharon lay still on a mattress. She let them take off her shoes and rub her feet. Mrs Wainwright bent over her. 'You got pain?' she demanded.

'No. Jus' don' feel good. Jus' feel bad.'

'I got pain-killer an' salts,' Mrs Wainwright said. 'You're welcome to 'em if you want 'em. Perfec'ly welcome.'

The girl shivered violently. 'Cover me up, Ma. I'm col'.' Ma brought all the blankets and piled them on top of her. The rain roared down on the roof.

Now the wood-gatherers returned, their arms piled high with sticks and their hats and coats dripping. 'Jesus, she's wet,' Pa said. 'Soaks you in a minute.'

Ma said: 'Better go back an' get more. Burns up awful quick. Be dark purty soon.' Ruthie and Winfield dripped in and threw their sticks on the pile. They turned to go again. 'You stay,' Ma ordered. 'Stan' up close to the fire an' get dry.'

The afternoon was silver with rain, the roads glittered with water. Hour by hour the cotton plants seemed to blacken and shrivel. Pa and Al and Uncle John made trip after trip into the thickets and brought back loads of dead wood. They piled it near the door, until the heap of it nearly reached the ceiling, and at last they stopped and walked toward the stove. Streams of water ran from their hats to their shoulders. The edges of their coats dripped and their shoes squished as they walked.

'Awright, now, get off them clothes,' Ma said. 'I got some nice coffee for you fellas. An' you got dry overhalls to put on. Don' stan' there.'

The evening came early. In the box-cars the families huddled together, listening to the pouring water on the roofs.

29

Over the high coast mountains and over the valleys the grey clouds marched in from the ocean. The wind blew fiercely and silently, high in the air, and it swished in the brush, and it roared in the forests. The clouds came in brokenly, in puffs, in folds, in grey crags; and they piled in together and settled low over the west. And then the wind stopped and left the clouds deep and solid. The rain began with gusty showers, pauses and downpours; and then gradually it settled to a single tempo, small drops and a steady beat, rain that was grey to see through, rain that cut midday light to evening. And at first the dry earth sucked the moisture down and blackened. For two days the earth drank the rain, until the earth was full. Then puddles formed, and in the low places little lakes formed in the fields. The muddy lakes rose higher, and the steady rain whipped the shining water. At last the mountains were full, and the hillsides spilled into the streams, built them to freshets, and sent them roaring down the canyons into the valleys. The rain beat on steadily. And the streams and the little rivers edged up to the bank sides and worked at willows and tree roots, bent the willows deep in the current, cut out the roots of cotton-woods and brought down the trees. The muddy water whirled along the bank sides and crept up the banks until at last it spilled over, into the fields, into the orchards, into the cotton patches where the black stems stood. Level fields became lakes, broad and grey, and the rain whipped up the surfaces. Then the water poured over the highways, and cars moved slowly, cutting the water ahead, and leaving a boiling muddy wake behind. The earth whispered under the beat of the rain, and the streams thundered under the churning freshets.

When the first rain started, the migrant people huddled in their tents, saying: It'll soon be over, and asking: How long's it likely to go on?

And when the puddles formed, the men went out in the rain with shovels and built little dykes around the tents. The beating rain worked at the canvas until it penetrated and sent streams down. And then the little dykes washed out and the water came inside, and the streams wet the beds and the blankets. The people sat in wet clothes. They set up boxes and put planks on the boxes. Then, day and night, they sat on the planks.

Beside the tents the old cars stood, and water fouled the ignition wires and water fouled the carburettors. The little grey tents stood in lakes. And at last the people had to move. Then the cars wouldn't start because the wires were shorted; and if the engines would run, deep mud engulfed the wheels. And the people waded away, carrying their wet blankets in their arms. They splashed along, carrying the children, carrying the very old, in their arms. And if a barn stood on high ground, it was filled with people, shivering and hopeless.

Then some went to the relief offices, and they came sadly back to their people.

They's rules–you got to be here a year before you can git relief. They say the gov'ment is gonna help. They don' know when.

And gradually the greatest terror of all came along.

They ain't gonna be no kinda work for three months.

In the barns the people sat huddled together; and the terror came over them, and their faces were grey with terror. The children cried with hunger, and there was no food.

Then the sickness came, pneumonia, and measles that went to the eyes and to the mastoids.

And the rain fell steadily, and the water flowed over the highways, for the culverts could not carry the water.

Then from the tents, from the crowded barns, groups of sodden men went out, their clothes slopping rags, their shoes muddy pulp. They splashed out through the water, to the towns, to the country stores, to the relief offices, to beg for food, to cringe and beg for food, to beg for relief, to try to steal, to lie. And under the begging, and under the cringing, a hopeless anger began to smoulder. And in the little towns pity for the sodden men changed to anger, and anger at the hungry people changed to fear of them. Then sheriffs swore in deputies in droves, and orders were rushed for rifles, for tear gas, for ammunition. Then the hungry men crowded the alleys behind the stores to beg for bread, to beg for rotting vegetables, to steal when they could.

Frantic men pounded on the doors of the doctors; and the doctors were busy. And sad men left word at country stores for the coroner to send a car. The coroners were not too busy. The coroners' wagon backed up through the mud and took out the dead.

And the rain pattered relentlessly down, and the streams broke their banks and spread out over the country.

Huddled under sheds, lying in wet hay, the hunger and the fear bred anger.

Then boys went out, not to beg, but to steal; and men went out weakly, to try to steal.

The sheriffs swore in new deputies and ordered new rifles; and the comfortable people in tight houses felt pity at first, and then distaste, and finally hatred for the migrant people.

In the wet hay of leaking barns babies were born to women who panted with pneumonia. And old people curled up in corners and died that way, so that the coroners could not straighten them. At night the frantic men walked boldly to hen roosts and carried off the squawking chickens. If they were shot at, they did not run, but splashed sullenly away; and if they were hit, they sank tiredly in the mud.

The rain stopped. On the fields the water stood, reflecting the grey sky, and the land whispered with moving water. And the men came out of the barns, out of the sheds. They squatted on their hams and looked out over the flooded land. And they were silent. And sometimes they talked very quietly.

No work till spring. No work.

And if no work–no money, no food.

Fella had a team of horses, had to use 'em to plough an' cultivate an' mow, wouldn' think a turnin' 'em out to starve when they wasn't workin'.

Them's horses–we're men.

The women watched the men, watched to see whether the break had come at last. The women stood silently and watched. And where a number of men gathered together, the fear went from their faces, and anger took its place. And the women sighed with relief, for they knew it was all right–the break had not come; and the break would never come as long as fear could turn to wrath.

Tiny points of grass came through the earth, and in a few days the hills were pale green with the beginning year.

30

In the box-car camp the water stood in puddles, and the rain splashed in the mud. Gradually the little stream crept up the bank toward the low flat where the box-cars stood.

On the second day of the rain, Al took the tarpaulin down from the middle of the car. He carried it out and spread it on the nose of the truck, and he came back into the car and sat down on his mattress. Now, without the separation, the two families in the car were one. The men sat together, and their spirits were damp. Ma kept a little fire going in the stove, kept a few twigs burning, and she conserved her wood. The rain poured down on the nearly flat roof of the box-car.

On the third day the Wainwrights grew restless. 'Maybe we better go 'long,' Mrs Wainwright said.

And Ma tried to keep them. 'Where'd you go an' be sure of a tight roof?'

'I dunno, but I got a feelin' we oughta go along.' They argued together, and Ma watched Al.

Ruthie and Winfield tried to play for a while, and then they, too, relapsed into sullen inactivity, and the rain drummed down on the roof.

On the third day the sound of the stream could be heard above the drumming rain. Pa and Uncle John stood in the open door and looked out on the rising stream. At both ends of the camp the water ran near to the highway, but at the camp it looped away so that the highway embankment surrounded the camp at the back and the stream closed it in on the front. And Pa said: 'How's it look to you, John? Seems to me if that crick comes up, she'll flood us.'

Uncle John opened his mouth and rubbed his bristling chin. 'Yeah,' he said. 'Might at that.'

Rose of Sharon was down with a heavy cold, her face flushed and her eyes shining with fever. Ma sat beside her with a cup of hot milk. 'Here,' she said. 'Take this here. Got bacon grease in it for strength. Here, drink it!'

Rose of Sharon shook her head weakly. 'I ain't hungry.'

Pa drew a curved line in the air with his finger. 'If we was all to get our shovels an' throw a bank, I bet we could keep her out. On'y have to go from up there down to there.'

'Yeah,' Uncle John agreed. 'Might. Dunno if them other fellas'd wanta. They'd maybe ruther move somewhere else.'

'But these here cars is dry,' Pa insisted. 'Couldn' find no dry place as good as this. You wait.' From the pile of brush in the car he picked a twig. He ran down the cat-walk, splashed through the mud to the stream and he set his twig upright on the edge of the swirling water. In a moment he was back in the car. 'Jesus, ya get wet through,' he said.

Both men kept their eyes on the little twig on the water's edge. They saw the water move slowly up around it and creep up the bank. Pa squatted down in the doorway. 'Comin' up fast,' he said.'I think we oughta go talk to the other fellas. See if they'll help ditch up. Got to git outa here if they won't.' Pa looked down the long car to the Wainwright end. Al was with them, sitting beside Aggie. Pa walked into their precinct. 'Water's risin',' he said. 'How about if we throwed up a bank. We could do her if ever'body helped.'

Wainwright said: 'We was jes' talkin'. Seems like we oughta be gettin' outa here.'

Pa said: 'You been aroun'. You know what chancet we got a gettin' a dry place to stay.'

'I know. But jes' the same–'

Al said: 'Pa, if they go, I'm a-goin' too.'

Pa looked startled. 'You can't, Al. The truck–We ain't fit to drive that truck.'

'I don' care. Me an' Aggie got to stick together.'

'Now you wait,' Pa said. 'Come on over here.' Wainwright and Al got to their feet and approached the door. 'See?' Pa said, pointing. 'Jus' a bank from there an' down to there.' He looked at his stick. The water swirled about it now, and crept up the bank.

'Be a lot a work, an' then she might come over anyways,' Wainwright protested.

'Well, we ain't doin' nothin', might's well be workin'. We ain't gonna find us no place to live like this. Come on, now. Le's go talk to the other fellas. We can do her if ever'body helps.'

Al said: 'If Aggie goes, I'm a-goin' too.'

Pa said: 'Look, Al, if them fellas won't dig, then we'll all hafta go. Come on, le's go talk to 'em. They hunched their shoulders and ran down the cat-walk to the next car and up the walk in to its open door.

Ma was at the stove, feeding a few sticks to the feeble flame. Ruthie crowded close beside her. 'I'm hungry,' Ruthie whined.

'No, you ain't,' Ma said. 'You had good mush.'

'Wisht I had a box a Cracker Jack. There ain't nothin' to do. Ain't no fun.'

'They'll be fun,' Ma said. 'You jus' wait. Be fun purty soon. Git a house an' a place, purty soon.'

'Wisht we had a dog,' Ruthie said.

'We'll have a dog; have a cat, too.'

'Yella cat?'

'Don't bother me,' Ma begged. 'Don't go plaguin' me now, Ruthie. Rosasharn's sick. Jus' you be a good girl a little while. They'll be fun.' Ruthie wandered complaining away.

From the mattress where Rose of Sharon lay covered up there came a quick sharp cry, cut off in the middle. Ma whirled and went to her. Rose of Sharon was holding her breath and her eyes were filled with terror.

'What is it?' Ma cried. The girl expelled her breath and caught it again. Suddenly Ma put her hand under the covers. Then she stood up. 'Mis' Wainwright,' she called. 'Oh, Mis' Wainwright!'

The fat little woman came down the car. 'Want me?'

'Look!' Ma pointed at Rose of Sharon's face. Her teeth were clamped on her lower lip and her forehead was wet with perspiration, and the shining terror was in her eyes.

'I think it's come,' Ma said. 'It's early.'

The girl heaved a great sigh and relaxed. She released her lip and closed her eyes. Mrs Wainwright bent over her.

'Did it kinda grab you all over–quick? Open up an' answer me.' Rose of Sharon nodded weakly. Mrs Wainwright turned to Ma. 'Yep,' she said. 'It's come. Early, ya say?'

'Maybe the fever brang it.'

'Well, she oughta be up on her feet. Oughta be walkin' aroun'.'

'She can't,' Ma said. 'She ain't got the strength.'

'Well, she oughta.' Mrs Wainwright grew quiet and stern with efficiency. 'I he'ped with lots,' she said. 'Come on, le's close that door, nearly. Keep out the draf'.' The two women pushed on the heavy sliding door, boosted it along until only a foot was open. 'I'll git our lamp, too,' Mrs Wainwright said. Her face was purple with excitement. 'Aggie,' she called. 'You take care of these here little fellas.'

Ma nodded: 'That's right. Ruthie! You an' Winfiel' go down with Aggie. Go on now.'

'Why?' they demanded.

''Cause you got to. Rosasharn gonna have her baby.'

'I wanta watch, Ma. Please let me.'

'Ruthie! You git now. You git quick.' There was no argument against such a tone. Ruthie and Winfield went reluctantly down the car. Ma lighted the lantern. Mrs Wainwright brought her Rochester lamp down and set it on the floor, and its big circular flame lighted the box-car brightly.

Ruthie and Winfield stood behind the brush pile and peered over. 'Gonna have a baby, an' we're a-gonna see,' Ruthie said softly. 'Don't you make no noise now. Ma won't let us watch. If she looks this-a-way, you scrunch down behin' the brush. Then we'll see.'

'There ain't many kids seen it,' Winfield said.

'There ain't no kids seen it,' Ruthie insisted proudly. 'On'y us.'

Down by the mattress, in the bright light of the lamp, Ma and Mrs Wainwright held conference. Their voices were raised a little over the hollow beating of the rain. Mrs Wainwright took a paring knife from her apron pocket and slipped it under the mattress. 'Maybe it don't do no good,' she said apologetically. 'Our folks always done it. Don't do no harm, anyways.'

Ma nodded. 'We used a plough point. I guess anything sharp'll work, long as it can cut birth pains. I hope it ain't gonna be a long one.'

'You feelin' awright now?'

Rose of Sharon nodded nervously. 'Is it a-comin'?'

'Sure,' Ma said. 'Gonna have a nice baby. You jus' got to help us. Feel like you could get up an' walk?'

'I can try.'

'That's a good girl,' Mrs Wainwright said. 'That *is* a good girl. We'll he'p you honey. We'll walk with ya.' They helped her to her feet and pinned a blanket over her shoulders. Then Ma held her arm from one side, and Mrs Wainwright from the other. They walked her to the brush pile and turned slowly and walked her back, over and over; and the rain drummed deeply on the roof.

Ruthie and Winfield watched anxiously. 'When's she goin' to have it?' he demanded.

'Sh! Don't draw 'em. We won't be let to look.'

Aggie joined them behind the brush pile. Aggie's lean face and yellow hair showed in the lamplight, and her nose was long and sharp in the shadow of her head on the wall.

Ruthie whispered: 'You ever saw a baby bore?'

'Sure,' said Aggie.

'Well, when's she gonna have it?'

'Oh, not for a long, long time.'

'Well, how long?'

'Maybe not 'fore to-morrow mornin'.'

'Shucks!' said Ruthie. 'Ain't no good watchin' now, then. Oh! Look!'

The walking women had stopped. Rose of Sharon had stiffened, and she whined with pain. They laid her down on the mattress and wiped her forehead while she grunted and clenched her fists. And Ma talked softly to her. 'Easy,' Ma said. 'Gonna be all right–all right. Jus' grip ya han's. Now, then, take your lip inta your teeth. Tha's good–tha's good.' The pain passed on. They let her rest awhile, and then helped her up again, and the three walked back and forth, back and forth between the pains.

Pa stuck his head through the narrow opening. His hat dripped with water. 'What ya shut the door for?' he asked. And then he saw the walking women.

Ma said: 'Her time's come.'

'Then–then we couldn' go 'f we wanted to.'

'No.'

'Then we got to buil' that bank.'

'You got to.'

Pa sloshed through the mud to the stream. His marking stick was four inches down. Twenty men stood in the rain. Pa cried: 'We got to build her. My girl got her pains.' The men gathered about him.

'Baby?'

'Yeah. We can't go now.'

A tall man said: 'It ain't our baby. We kin go.'

'Sure,' Pa said. 'You can go. Go on. Nobody's stoppin' you. They's only eight shovels.' He hurried to the lowest part of the bank and drove his shovel into the mud. The shovelful lifted with a sucking noise. He drove it again, and threw the mud into the low place on the stream bank. And beside him the other men ranged themselves. They heaped the mud up in a long embankment, and those who had no shovels cut live willow whips and wove them in a mat and kicked them into the bank. Over the men came a fury of work, a fury of battle. When one man dropped his shovel, another took it up. They had shed their coats and hats. Their shirts and trousers clung tightly to their bodies, their shoes were shapeless blobs of mud. A shrill scream came from the Joad car. The men stopped, listened uneasily, and then plunged to work again. And the little levee of earth extended until it connected with the highway embankment on either side. They were tired now, and the shovels moved more slowly. And the stream rose slowly. It edged above the place where the first dirt had been thrown.

Pa laughed in triumph. 'She'd come over if we hadn' a built up!' he cried.

The stream rose slowly up the side of the new wall, and tore at the willow mat. 'Higher!' Pa cried. 'We got to git her higher!'

The evening came, and the work went on. And now the men were beyond weariness. Their faces were set and dead. They worked jerkily, like machines. When it was dark the women set lanterns in the car doors, and kept pots of coffee handy. And the women ran one by one to the Joad car and wedged themselves inside.

The pains were coming close now, twenty minutes apart. And Rose of Sharon had lost her restraint. She screamed fiercely under the fierce pains. And the neighbour women looked at her and patted her gently and went back to their own cars.

Ma had a good fire going now, and all her utensils, filled with water, sat on the stove to heat. Every little while Pa looked in the car door. 'All right?' he asked.

'Yeah! I think so,' Ma assured him.

As it grew dark, someone brought a flashlight to work by. Uncle John plunged on, throwing mud on top of the wall.

'You take it easy,' Pa said. 'You'll kill yaself.'

'I can't help it. I can't stan' that yellin'. It's like–it's like when–'

'I know,' Pa said. 'But jus' take it easy.'

Uncle John blubbered: 'I'll run away. By God, I got to work or I'll run away.'

Pa turned from him. 'How's she stan' on the last marker?'

The man with the flashlight threw the beam on the stick. The rain cut whitely through the light. 'Comin' up.'

'She'll come up slower now,' Pa said. 'Got to flood purty far on the other side.'

'She's comin' up, though.'

The women filled the coffee pots and set them out again. And as the night went on, the men moved slower and slower, and they lifted their heavy feet like draught-horses. More mud on the levee, more willows interlaced. The rain fell heavily. When the flashlight turned on faces, the eyes showed staring, and the muscles on the cheeks were welted out.

For a long time the screams continued from the car, and at last they were still.

Pa said: 'Ma'd call me if it was bore.' He went on shovelling the mud sullenly.

The stream eddied and boiled against the bank. Then, from up the stream there came a ripping crash. The beam of the flashlight showed a great cottonwood toppling. The men stopped to watch. The branches of the tree sank into the water and edged around with the current while the stream dug out the little roots. Slowly the tree was freed, and slowly it edged down the stream. The weary men watched, their mouths hanging open. The tree moved slowly down. Then a branch caught on a stump, snagged and held. And very slowly the roots swung around and hooked themselves on the new embankment. The water piled up behind. The tree moved and tore the bank. A little stream slipped through. Pa threw himself forward and jammed mud in the break. The water piled against the tree. And then the bank washed quickly down, washed around ankles, around knees. The men broke and ran, and the current worked smoothly into the flat, under the cars, under the motor-cars.

Uncle John saw the water break through. In the murk he could see it. Uncontrollably his weight pulled him down. He went to his knees, and tugging water swirled about his chest.

Pa saw him go. 'Hey! What's the matter?' He lifted him to his feet. 'You sick? Come on, the cars is high.'

Uncle John gathered his strength. 'I dunno,' he said apologetically. 'Legs give out. Jus' give out.' Pa helped him along toward the cars.

When the dyke swept out, Al turned and ran. His feet moved heavily. The water was about his calves when he reached the truck. He flung the tarpaulin off the nose and jumped into the car. He stepped on the starter. The engine turned over and over, and there was no bark of the motor. He choked the engine deeply. The battery turned the sodden motor more and more slowly, and there was no cough. Over and over, slower and slower. Al set the spark high. He felt under the seat for the crank and jumped out. The water was higher than the running-board. He ran to the front end. Crank-case was under water now. Frantically he fitted the crank and twisted around and around, and his clenched hand on the crank splashed in the slowly flowing water at each turn. At last his frenzy gave out. The motor was full of water, the battery fouled by now. On slightly higher ground two cars were started and their lights on. They floundered in the mud and dug their wheels down until finally the drivers cut off the motors and sat still, looking into the headlight beams. And the rain whipped white streaks through the lights. Al went slowly around the truck, reached in, and turned off the ignition.

When Pa reached the cat-walk, he found the lower end floating. He stepped it down into the mud, under water. 'Think ya can make it awright, John?' he asked.

'I'll be awright. Jus' go on.'

Pa cautiously climbed the cat-walk and squeezed himself in the narrow opening. The two lamps were turned low. Ma sat on the mattress beside Rose of Sharon, and Ma fanned her still face with a piece of cardboard. Mrs Wainwright poked dry brush into the stove, and a dank smoke edged out around the lids and filled the car with a smell of burning tissue. Ma looked up at Pa when he entered, and then quickly down.

'How–is she?' Pa asked.

Ma did not look up at him again. 'Awright, I think. Sleepin'.'

The air was fetid and close with the smell of the birth. Uncle John clambered in and held himself upright against the side of the car. Mrs Wainwright left her work and came to Pa. She pulled him by the elbow toward the corner of the car. She picked up a lantern and held it over an apple box in the corner. On a newspaper lay a blue shrivelled little mummy.

'Never breathed,' said Mrs Wainwright softly. 'Never was alive.'

Uncle John turned and shuffled tiredly down the car to the dark end. The rain whished softly on the roof now, so softly that they could hear Uncle John's tired sniffling from the dark.

Pa looked up at Mrs Wainwright. He took the lantern from her hand and put it on the floor. Ruthie and Winfield were asleep on their own mattress, their arms over their eyes to cut out the light.

Pa walked slowly to Rose of Sharon's mattress. He tried to squat down, but his legs were too tired. He knelt instead. Ma fanned her square of cardboard back and forth. She looked at Pa for a moment, and her eyes were wide and staring, like a sleep-walker's eyes.

Pa said: 'We–done–what we could.'

'I know.'

'We worked all night. An' a tree cut out the bank.'

'I know.'

'You can hear it under the car.'

'I know. I heard it.'

'Think she's gonna be all right?'

'I dunno.'

'Well–couldn' we–of did nothin'?'

Ma's lips were stiff and white. 'No. They was on'y one thing to do–ever–an' we done it.'

'We worked till we dropped, an' a tree–Rain lettin' up some.' Ma looked at the ceiling, and then down again. Pa went on, compelled to talk. 'I dunno how high she'll rise. Might flood the car.'

'I know.'

'You know ever'thing.'

She was silent, and the cardboard moved slowly back and forth.

'Did we slip up?' he pleaded. 'Is they anything we could of did?'

Ma looked at him strangely. Her white lips smiled in a dreaming compassion. 'Don't take no blame. Hush! It'll be awright. They's changes–all over.'

'Maybe the water–maybe we'll have to go.'

'When it's time to go–we'll go. We'll do what we got to do. Now hush. You might wake her.'

Mrs Wainwright broke twigs and poked them in the sodden, smoking fire.

From outside came the sound of an angry voice. 'I'm goin' in an' see the son-of-a-bitch myself.'

And then, just outside the door, Al's voice: 'Where you think you're goin'?'

'Goin' in to see that bastard Joad.'

'No you ain't. What's the matter'th you?'

'If he didn't have that fool idear about the bank, we'd a got out. Now our car is dead.'

'You think ours is burnin' up the road?'

'I'm a-goin' in.'

Al's voice was cold. 'You're gonna fight your way in.'

Pa got slowly to his feet and went to the door. 'Awright Al, I'm a comin' out.

It's awright, Al.' Pa slid down the cat-walk. Ma heard him say: 'We got sickness. Come on down here.'

The rain scattered lightly on the roof now, and a new-risen breeze blew it along in sweeps. Mrs Wainwright came from the stove and looked down at Rose of Sharon. 'Dawn's a-comin' soon, ma'am. Whyn't you git some sleep? I'll set with her.'

'No,' Ma said. 'I ain't tar'd.'

'In a pig's eye,' said Mrs Wainwright. 'Come on, you lay down awhile.'

Ma fanned the air slowly with her cardboard. 'You been frien'ly,' she said. 'We thank you.'

The stout woman smiled. 'No need to thank. Ever'body's in the same wagon. S'pose we was down. You'd give us a han'.'

'Yes,' Ma said, 'we would.'

'Or anybody.'

'Or anybody. Use' ta be the fambly was fust. It ain't so now. It's anybody. Worse off we get, the more we got to do.'

'We couldn' a save it.'

'I know,' said Ma.

Ruthie sighed deeply and took her arm from over her eyes. She looked blindly at the lamp for a moment, and then turned her head and looked at Ma. 'Is it bore?' she demanded. 'Is the baby out?'

Mrs Wainwright picked up a sack and spread it over the apple box in the corner.

'Where's the baby?' Ruthie demanded.

Ma wet her lips. 'They ain't no baby. They never was no baby. We wus wrong.'

'Shucks!' Ruthie yawned. 'I wisht it had a been a baby.'

Mrs Wainwright sat down beside Ma and took the cardboard from her and fanned the air. Ma folded her hands in her lap, and her tired eyes never left the face of Rose of Sharon, sleeping in exhaustion. 'Come on,' Mrs Wainwright said. 'Jus' lay down. You'll be right beside her. Why, you'd wake up if she took a deep breath, even.'

'Awright, I will.' Ma stretched out on the mattress beside the sleeping girl. And Mrs Wainwright sat on the floor and kept watch.

Pa and Al and Uncle John sat in the car doorway and watched the steely dawn come. The rain had stopped, but the sky was deep and solid with cloud. As the light came, it was reflected on the water. The men could see the current of the stream, slipping swiftly down, bearing black branches of trees, boxes, boards. The water swirled into the flat where the box-cars stood. There was no sign of the embankment left. On the flat the current stopped. The edges of the flood were lined with yellow foam. Pa leaned out the door and placed a twig on the cat-walk, just above the water line. The men watched the water slowly climb to it, lift it gently, and float it away. Pa placed another twig an inch above the water and settled back to watch.

'Think it'll come inside the car?' Al asked.

'Can't tell. They's a hell of a lot of water got to come down from the hills yet. Can't tell. Might start up to rain again.'

Al said: 'I been a-thinkin'. If she come in, ever'thing'll get soaked.'

'Yeah.'

'Well, she won't come up more'n three-four feet in the car 'cause she'll go over the highway an' spread out first.'

'How you know?' Pa asked.

'I took a sight of her, off the end of the car.' He held his hand. ''Bout this far up she'll come.'

'Awright,' Pa said. 'What about it? We won't be here.'

'We got to be here. Truck's here. Take a week to get the water out of her when the flood goes down.'

'Well–what's your idear?'

'We can tear the side-boards of the truck an' build a kinda platform in here to pile our stuff an' to set up on.'

'Yeah? How'll we cook–how'll we eat?'

'Well, it'll keep our stuff dry.'

The light grew stronger outside, a grey metallic light. The second little stick floated away from the cat-walk. Pa placed another one higher up. 'Sure climbin',' he said. 'I guess we better do that.'

Ma turned restlessly in her sleep. Her eyes started wide open. She cried sharply in warning: 'Tom! Oh, Tom! Tom!'

Mrs. Wainwright spoke soothingly. The eyes flicked closed again and Ma squirmed under her dream. Mrs Wainwright got up and walked to the doorway. 'Hey!' she said softly. 'We ain't gonna git out soon.' She pointed to the corner of the car where the apple box was. 'That ain't doin' no good. Jus' cause trouble an' sorra. Couldn' you fellas kinda–take it out an' bury it?'

The men were silent. Pa said at last: 'Guess you're right. Jus cause sorra. 'Gainst the law to bury it.'

They's lots a things 'gainst the law that we can't he'p doin'.'

'Yeah.'

Al said: 'We oughta git them truck sides off 'fore the water comes up much more.'

Pa turned to Uncle John. 'Will you take an' bury it while Al an' me git that lumber in?'

Uncle John said sullenly: 'Why do I got to do it? Why don't you fellas? I don' like it.' And then: 'Sure. I'll do it. Sure, I will. Come on, give it to me.' His voice began to rise. 'Come on! Give it to me.'

'Don' wake 'em up,' Mrs Wainwright said. She brought the apple box to the doorway and straightened the sack decently over it.

'Shovel's standin' right behin' you,' Pa said.

Uncle John took the shovel in one hand. He slipped out the doorway into the slowly moving water, and it rose nearly to his waist before he struck bottom. He turned and settled the apple box under his other arm.

Pa said: 'Come on, Al. Le's git that lumber in.'

In the grey dawn light Uncle John waded around the end of the car, past the Joad truck; and he climbed the slippery bank to the highway. He walked down the highway, past the box-car flat, until he came to a place where the boiling stream ran close to the road, where the willows grew along the roadside. He put his shovel down, and holding the box in front of him, he edged through the brush until he came to the edge of the swift stream. For a time he stood watching it swirl by, leaving its yellow foam among the willow stems. He held the apple box against his chest. And then he leaned over and set the box in the stream and steadied it with his hand. He said fiercely: 'Go down an' tell 'em. Go down in the street an' rot an' tell 'em that way. That's the way you can talk. Don' even know if you was a boy or a girl. Ain't gonna find out. Go on down, an' lay in the street. Maybe they'll know then.' He guided the box gently out into the current and let it go. It settled low in the water, edged sideways, whirled around, and turned slowly over. The sack floated away, and the box, caught in the swift water, floated quickly away, out of sight, behind the brush. Uncle John grabbed the shovel and went rapidly to the box-cars. He sloshed down into the water and waded to the truck, where Pa and Al were working, taking down the one-by-six planks.

Pa looked over at him. 'Get it done?'

'Yeah.'

'Well, look,' Pa said. 'If you'll he'p Al, I'll go down the store an' get some stuff to eat.'

'Get some bacon,' Al said. 'I need some meat.'

'I will,' Pa said. He jumped down from the truck and Uncle John took his place.

When they pushed the planks into the car door, Ma awakened and sat up. 'What you doin'?'

'Gonna build a place to keep outa the wet.'

'Why?' Ma asked. 'It's dry in here.'

'Ain't gonna be. Water's comin' up.'

Ma struggled up to her feet and went to the door. 'We got to git outa here.'

'Can't,' Al said. 'All our stuff's here. Truck's here. Ever'thing we got.'

'Where's Pa?'

'Gone to get stuff for breakfas'.'

Ma looked down at the water. It was only six inches down from the floor by now. She went back to the mattress and looked at Rose of Sharon. The girl stared back at her.

'How you feel?' Ma asked.

'Tar'd. Jus' tar'd out.'

'Gonna get some breakfas' into you.'

'I ain't hungry.'

Mrs Wainwright moved beside Ma. 'She looks all right. Come through it fine.'

Rose of Sharon's eyes questioned Ma, and Ma tried to avoid the question. Mrs Wainwright walked to the stove.

'Ma.'

'Yeah? What you want?'

'Is–it–all right?'

Ma gave up the attempt. She kneeled down on the mattress. 'You can have more,' she said. 'We done ever'thing we knowed.'

Rose of Sharon struggled and pushed herself up. 'Ma!'

'You couldn' he'p it.'

The girl lay back again, and covered her eyes with her arms. Ruthie crept close and looked down in awe. She whispered harshly: 'She sick, Ma? She gonna die?'

''Course not. She's gonna be awright. Awright.'

Pa came in with his armload of packages. 'How is she?'

'Awright,' Ma said. 'She's gonna be awright.'

Ruthie reported to Winfield. 'She ain't gonna die. Ma says so.'

And Winfield, picking his teeth with a splinter in a very adult manner, said: 'I knowed it all the time.'

'How'd you know?'

'I won't tell,' said Winfield, and he spat out a piece of the splinter.

Ma built the fire up with the last twigs and cooked the bacon and made gravy. Pa had brought store bread. Ma scowled when she saw it. 'We got any money lef'?'

'Nope,' said Pa. 'But we was so hungry.'

'An' you got store bread,' Ma said accusingly.

'Well, we was awful hungry. Worked all night long.'

Ma sighed. 'Now what we gonna do?'

As they ate, the water crept up and up. Al gulped his food and he and Pa built the platform. Five feet wide, six feet long, four feet above the floor. And the water crept to the edge of the doorway, seemed to hesitate a long time, and then moved slowly inward over the floor. And outside, the rain began again, as it had before, big heavy drops splashing on the water, pounding hollowly on the roof.

Al said: 'Come on now, let's get the mattresses up. Let's put the blankets up, so they don't git wet.' They piled their possessions up on the platform, and the water crept over the floor. Pa and Ma, and Al and Uncle John, each at a corner, lifted Rose of Sharon's mattress, with the girl on it, and put it on the top of the pile.

And the girl protested: 'I can walk. I'm awright.' And the water crept over the floor, a thin film of it. Rose of Sharon whispered to Ma and Ma put her hand under the blanket and felt her breast and nodded.

In the other end of the box-car, the Wainwrights were pounding, building a platform for themselves. The rain thickened, and then passed away.

Ma looked down at her feet. The water was half an inch deep on the car floor by now. 'You, Ruthie–Winfiel'!' she called distractedly. 'Come get on top of the pile. You'll get cold.' She saw them safely up, sitting awkwardly beside Rose of Sharon. Ma said suddenly: 'We got to git out.'

'We can't,' Pa said. 'Like Al says, all our stuff's here. We'll pull off the box-car door an' make more room to set on.'

The family huddled on the platforms, silent and fretful. The water was six inches deep in the car before the flood spread evenly over the embankment and moved into the cotton-field on the other side. During that day and night the men slept soddenly, side by side on the box-car door. And Ma lay close to Rose of Sharon. Sometimes Ma whispered to her and sometimes sat up quietly, her face brooding. Under the blanket she hoarded the remains of the bread store.

The rain had become intermittent now–little wet squalls and quiet times. On the morning of the second day Pa splashed through the camp and came back with ten potatoes in his pockets. Ma watched him sullenly while he chopped out part of the inner wall of the car, built a fire, and scooped water into a pan. The family ate the steaming boiled potatoes with their fingers. And when this last food was gone, they stared at the grey water, and in the night they did not lie down for a long time.

When the morning came they awakened nervously. Rose of Sharon whispered to Ma.

Ma nodded her head. 'Yes,' she said. 'It's time for it.' And then she turned to the car door, where the men lay. 'We're a-gettin' outa here,' she said savagely, 'gettin' to higher groun'. An' you're comin' or you ain't comin', but I'm takin' Rosasharn an' the little fellas outa here.'

'We can't!' Pa said weakly.

'Awright, then. Maybe you'll pack Rosasharn to the highway, anyways, an' then come back. It ain't rainin' now, an' we're a-goin'.'

'Awright, we'll go,' Pa said.

Al said: 'Ma, I ain't goin'.'

'Why not?'

'Well–Aggie–why, her an' me–'

Ma smiled. ''Course,' she said. 'You stay here, Al. Take care of the stuff. When the water goes down–why, we'll come back. Come quick, 'fore it rains again,' she told Pa. 'Come on, Rosasharn. We're goin' to a dry place.'

'I can walk.'

'Maybe a little, on the road. Git your back bent, Pa.'

Pa slipped into the water and stood waiting. Ma helped Rose of Sharon down from the platform and steadied her across the car. Pa took her in his arms, held her as high as he could, and pushed his way carefully through the deep water, around the car, and to the highway. He set her down on her feet and held on to her. Uncle John carried Ruthie and followed. Ma slid down into the water, and for a moment her skirts billowed out around her.

'Winfiel', set on my shoulder. Al–we'll come back soon's the water's down. Al–' She paused. 'If–if Tom comes–tell him we'll be back. Tell him be careful. Winfiel'! Climb on my shoulder–there! Now, keep your feet still.' She staggered off through the breast-high water. At the highway embankment they helped her up and lifted Winfield from her shoulder.

They stood on the highway and looked back over the sheet of water, the dark red blocks of the cars, the trucks and motor-cars deep in the slowly moving water. And as they stood, a little misting rain began to fall.

'We got to git along,' Ma said. 'Rosasharn, you feel like you could walk?'

'Kinda dizzy,' the girl said. 'Feel like I been beat.'

Pa complained:'Now we're a-goin', where' we goin'?'

'I dunno. Come on, give your han' to Rosasharn.' Ma took the girl's right arm to steady her, and Pa her left. 'Goin' some-place where it's dry. Got to. You fellas ain't had dry clothes on for two days.' They moved slowly along the highway. They could hear the rushing of the water in the stream beside the road. Ruthie and Winfield marched together, splashing their feet against the road. They went slowly along the road. The sky grew darker and the rain thickened. No traffic moved along the highway.

'We got to hurry,' Ma said. 'If this here girl gits good an' wet–I don't know what'll happen to her.'

'You ain't said where-at we're a-hurryin' to,' Pa reminded her sarcastically.

The road curved along beside the stream. Ma searched the land and the flooded fields. Far off the road, on the left, on a slight rolling hill a rain-blackened barn stood. 'Look!' Ma said. 'Look there! I bet it's dry in that barn. Le's go there till the rain stops.'

Pa sighed. 'Prob'ly get run out by the fella owns it.'

Ahead, beside the road, Ruthie saw a spot of red. She raced to it. A scraggy geranium gone wild, and there was one rain-beaten blossom on it. She picked the flower. She took a petal carefully off and stuck it on her nose. Winfield ran up to see.

'Lemme have one?' he said.

'No, sir! It's all mine. I foun' it.' She stuck another red petal on her forehead, a little bright-red heart.

'Come on, Ruthie! Lemme have one. Come on, now.' He grabbed at the flower in her hand and missed it, and Ruthie banged him in the face with her open hand. He stood for a moment, surprised, and then his lips shook and his eyes welled.

The others caught up. 'Now what you done?' Ma asked. 'Now what you done?'

'He tried to grab my fl'ar.'

Winfield sobbed: 'I–on'y wanted one–to stick on my nose.'

'Give him one, Ruthie.'

'Leave him find his own. This here's mine.'

'Ruthie! You give him one.'

Ruthie heard the threat in Ma's tone and changed her tactics. 'Here,' she said with elaborate kindness. 'I'll stick on one for you.' The older people walked on. Winfield held his nose near to her. She wet a petal with her tongue and jabbed it cruelly on his nose. 'You little son-of-a-bitch,' she said softly. Winfield felt for the petal with his fingers, and pressed it down on his nose. They walked quickly after the others. Ruthie felt how the fun was gone. 'Here,' she said. 'Here's some more. Stick some on your forehead.'

From the right of the road there came a sharp swishing. Ma cried: 'Hurry up. They's a big rain. Le's go through the fence here. It's shorter. Come on, now! Bear on, Rosasharn.' They half dragged the girl across the ditch, helped her through the fence. And then the storm struck them. Sheets of rain fell on them. They ploughed through the mud and up the little incline. The black barn was nearly obscured by the rain. It hissed and splashed, and the growing wind drove it along. Rose of Sharon's feet slipped and she dragged between her supporters.

'Pa! Can you carry her?'

Pa leaned over and picked her up. 'We're wet through anyways,' he said. 'Hurry up. Winfiel'–Ruthie! Run on ahead.'

They came panting up to the rain-soaked barn and staggered into the open end. There was no door in this end. A few rusty farm tools lay about, a disk plough and a broken cultivator, an iron wheel. The rain hammered on the roof and curtained the entrance. Pa gently set Rose of Sharon down on an oily box. 'God Awmighty!' he said.

Ma said: 'Maybe they's hay inside. Look, there's a door.' She swung the door on its rusty hinges. 'They is hay,' she cried. 'Come on in, you.'

It was dark inside. A little light came through the cracks between the boards.

'Lay down, Rosasharn,' Ma said. 'Lay down an' res'. I'll try to figger some way to dry you off.'

Winfield said: 'Ma!' and the rain roaring on the roof drowned his voice. '*Ma!*'

'What is it? What you want?'

'Look! In the corner.'

Ma looked. There were two figures in the gloom; a man who lay on his back, and a boy sitting beside him, his eyes wide, staring at the newcomers. As she looked, the boy got slowly up to his feet and came toward her. His voice croaked. 'You own this here?'

'No,' Ma said. 'Jus' come in outa the wet. We got a sick girl. You got a dry blanket we could use an' get her wet clothes off?'

The boy went back to the corner and brought a dirty comforter and held it out to Ma.

'Thank ya,' she said. 'What's tha matter'th that fella?'

The boy spoke in a croaking monotone. 'Fust he was sick–but now he's starvin'.'

'What?'

'Starvin'. Got sick in the cotton. He ain't et for six days.'

Ma walked to the corner and looked down at the man. He was about fifty, his whiskery face gaunt, and his open eyes were vague and staring. The boy stood beside her. 'Your pa?' Ma asked.

'Yeah! Says he wasn' hungry, or he jus' et. Give me the food. Now he's too weak. Can't hardly move.'

The pounding of the rain decreased to a soothing swish on the roof. The gaunt man moved his lips. Ma knelt beside him and put her ear close. His lips moved again.

'Sure,' Ma said. 'You jus' be easy. He'll be awright. You jus' wait'll I get them wet clo'es off'n my girl.'

Ma went back to the girl. 'Now slip 'em off,' she said. She held the comforter up to screen her from view. And when she was naked, Ma folded the comforter about her.

The boy was at her side again explaining: 'I didn't know. He said he et, or he wasn' hungry. Las' night I went an' bust a winda an' stoled some bread. Made 'im chew 'er down. But he puked it all up, an' then he was weaker. Got to have soup or milk. You folks got money to git milk?'

Ma said: 'Hush. Don' worry. We'll figger somepin out.'

Suddenly the boy cried: 'He's dyin', I tell you! He's starvin' to death, I tell you.'

'Hush,' said Ma. She looked at Pa and Uncle John standing helplessly gazing at the sick man. She looked at Rose of Sharon huddled in the comforter. Ma's eyes passed Rose of Sharon's eyes, and then came back to them. And the two women looked deep into each other. The girl's breath came short and gasping.

She said 'Yes.'

Ma smiled. 'I knowed you would. I knowed!' She looked down at her hands, tight-locked in her lap.

Rose of Sharon whispered: 'Will–will you all–go out?' The rain whisked lightly on the roof.

Ma leaned forward and with her palm she brushed the tousled hair back from her daughter's forehead, and she kissed her on the forehead. Ma got up quickly. 'Come on, you fellas,' she called. 'You come out in the tool shed.'

Ruthie opened her mouth to speak. 'Hush,' Ma said. 'Hush and git.' She herded them through the door, drew the boy with her; and she closed the squeaking door.

For a moment Rose of Sharon sat still in the whispering barn.

Then she hoisted her tired body up and drew the comforter about her. She moved slowly to the corner and stood looking down at the wasted face, into the wide, frightened eyes. Then slowly she lay down beside him. He shook his head slowly from side to side. Rose of Sharon loosened one side of the blanket and bared her breast. 'You got to,' she said. She squirmed closer and pulled his head close. 'There!' she said. 'There.' Her hand moved behind his head and supported it. Her fingers moved gently in his hair. She looked up and across the barn, and her lips came together and smiled mysteriously.

THE MOON IS DOWN

I

By ten-forty-five it was all over. The town was occupied, the defenders defeated, and the war finished. The invader had prepared for this campaign as carefully as he had for larger ones. On this Sunday morning the postman and the policeman had gone fishing in the boat of Mr Corell, the popular storekeeper. He had lent them his trim sail-boat for the day. The postman and the policeman were several miles at sea when they saw the small dark transport, loaded with soldiers, go quietly past them. As officials of the town, this was definitely their business, and these two put about, but of course the battalion was in possession by the time they could make port. The policeman and the postman could not even get into their own offices in the Town Hall, and when they insisted on their rights they were taken prisoners of war and locked up in the town jail.

The local troops, all twelve of them, had been away, too, on this Sunday morning, for Mr Corell, the popular storekeeper, had donated lunch, targets, cartridges, and prizes for a shooting competition to take place six miles back in the hills, in a lovely glade Mr Corell owned. The local troops, big, loose-hung boys, heard the planes and in the distance saw the parachutes, and they came back to town at double-quick step. When they arrived, the invader had flanked the road with machine-guns. The loose-hung soldiers, having very little experience in war and none at all in defeat, opened fire with their rifles. The machine-guns clattered for a moment and six of the soldiers became dead riddled bundles, and three half-dead riddled bundles, and three of the soldiers escaped into the hills with their rifles.

By ten-thirty the brass band of the invaders was playing beautiful and sentimental music in the town square while the townsmen, their mouths a little open and their eyes astonished, stood about listening to the music and staring at the grey-helmeted men who carried sub-machine-guns in their arms.

By ten-thirty-eight the riddled six were buried, the parachutes were folded, and the battalion was billeted in Mr Corell's warehouse by the pier, which had on its shelves blankets and cots for a battalion.

By ten-forty-five old Mayor Orden had received the formal request that he grant an audience to Colonel Lanser of the invaders, an audience which was set for eleven sharp at the Mayor's five-room palace.

The drawing-room of the palace was very sweet and comfortable. The gilded chairs covered with their worn tapestry were set about stiffly like too many servants with nothing to do. An arched marble fire-place held its little basket of red flameless heat, and a hand-painted coal-scuttle stood on the hearth. On the mantel, flanked by fat vases, stood a large, curly porcelain clock which swarmed with tumbling cherubs. The wallpaper of the room was dark red with gold figures, and the woodwork was white, pretty and clean. The paintings on the wall were largely preoccupied with the amazing heroism of large dogs faced with imperilled children. Nor water nor fire nor earthquake could do in a child so long as a big dog was available.

Beside the fireplace old Doctor Winter sat, bearded and simple and benign, historian and physician to the town. He watched in amazement while his thumbs rolled over and over on his lap. Doctor Winter was a man so simple that only a profound man would know him as profound. He looked up at Joseph, the Mayor's serving-man, to see whether Joseph had observed the rolling wonders of his thumbs.

'Eleven o'clock?' Doctor Winter asked.

And Joseph answered abstractedly, 'Yes, sir. The note said eleven.'

'You read the note?'

'No, sir, His Excellency read the note to me.'

And Joseph went about testing each of the gilded chairs to see whether it had moved since he had last placed it. Joseph habitually scowled at furniture, expecting it to be impertinent, mischievous, or dusty. In a world where Mayor Orden was the leader of men, Joseph was the leader of furniture, silver, and dishes. Joseph was elderly and lean and serious, and his life was so complicated that only a profound man would know him to be simple. He saw nothing amazing about Doctor Winter's rolling thumbs; in fact he found them irritating. Joseph suspected that something pretty important was happening, what with foreign soldiers in the town and the local army killed or captured. Sooner or later Joseph would have to get an opinion about it all. He wanted no levity, no rolling thumbs, no nonsense from furniture. Doctor Winter moved his chair a few inches from its appointed place and Joseph waited impatiently for the moment when he could put it back again.

Doctor Winter repeated, 'Eleven o'clock, and they'll be here then, too. A time-minded people, Joseph.'

And Joseph said, without listening, 'Yes, sir.'

'A time-minded people,' the doctor repeated.

'Yes, sir,' said Joseph.

'Time and machines.'

'Yes, sir.'

'They hurry towards their destiny as though it would not wait. They push the rolling world along with their shoulders.'

And Joseph said, 'Quite right, sir,' simply because he was getting tired of saying, 'Yes, sir.'

Joseph did not approve of this line of conversation, since it did not help him to have an opinion about anything. If Joseph remarked to the cook later in the day, 'A time-minded people, Annie.' it would not make any sense. Annie would ask, 'Who?' and then 'Why?' and finally say, 'That's nonsense, Joseph.' Joseph had tried carrying Doctor Winter's remarks below-stairs before and it had always ended the same: Annie always discovered them to be nonsense.

Doctor Winter looked up from his thumbs and watched Joseph disciplining the chairs. 'What's the Mayor doing?'

'Dressing to receive the colonel, sir.'

'And you aren't helping him? He will be ill dressed by himself.'

'Madame is helping him. Madame wants him to look his best. She'–Joseph blushed a little–'Madame is trimming the hair out of his ears, sir. It tickles. He won't let me do it.'

'Of course it tickles,' said Doctor Winter.

'Madame insists,' said Joseph.

Doctor Winter laughed suddenly. He stood up and held his hands to the fire and Joseph skilfully darted behind him and replaced the chair where it should be.

'We are so wonderful,' the doctor said. 'Our country is falling, our town is conquered, the Mayor is about to receive the conqueror, and Madame is holding the struggling Mayor by the neck and trimming the hair out of his ears.'

'He was getting very shaggy,' said Joseph. 'His eyebrows too. His Excellency is even more upset about having his eyebrows trimmed than his ears. He says it hurts. I doubt if even Madame can do it.'

'She will try,' Doctor Winter said.

'She wants him to look his best, sir.'

Through the glass window of the entrance door a helmeted face looked in and there was a rapping on the door. It seemed that some warm light went out of the room and a little greyness took its place.

Doctor Winter looked up at the clock and said, 'They are early. Let them in, Joseph.'

Joseph went to the door and opened it. A soldier stepped in, dressed in a long coat. He was helmeted and he carried a sub-machine-gun over his arm. He glanced quickly about and then stepped aside. Behind him an officer stood in the doorway. The officer's uniform was common and it had rank showing only on the shoulders.

The officer stepped inside and looked at Doctor Winter. He was rather like an overdrawn picture of an English gentleman. He had a slouch, his face was red, his nose long but rather pleasing; he seemed about as unhappy in his uniform as most British general officers are. He stood in the doorway, staring at Doctor Winter, and he said, 'Are you Mayor Orden, sir?'

Doctor Winter smiled. 'No, no, I am not.'

'You are an official, then?'

'No, I am the town doctor and I am a friend of the Mayor.'

The officer said, 'Where is Mayor Orden?'

'Dressing to receive you. You are the colonel?'

'No, I am not. I am Captain Bentick.' He bowed and Doctor Winter returned the bow slightly. Captain Bentick continued, as though a little embarrassed at what he had to say: 'Our military regulations, sir, prescribe that we search for weapons before the commanding officer enters a room. We mean no disrespect, sir.' And he called over his shoulder, 'Sergeant!'

The sergeant moved quickly to Joseph, ran his hands over his pockets, and said, 'Nothing, sir.'

Captain Bentick said to Doctor Winter: 'I hope you will pardon us.' And the sergeant went to Doctor Winter and patted his pockets. His hands stopped at the inside coat pocket. He reached quickly in, brought out a little, flat, black leather case, and took it to Captain Bentick. Captain Bentick opened the case and found there a few simple surgical instruments–two scalpels, some surgical needles, some clamps, a hypodermic needle. He closed the case again and handed it back to Doctor Winter.

Doctor Winter said, 'You see, I am a country doctor. One time I had to perform an appendectomy with a kitchen knife. I have always carried these with me since then.'

Captain Bentick said, 'I believe there are some firearms here?' He opened a little leather book that he carried in his pocket.

Doctor Winter said, 'You are thorough.'

'Yes, our local man has been working here for some time.'

Doctor Winter said, 'I don't suppose you would tell who that man is?'

Bentick said, 'His work is all done now. I don't suppose there would be any harm in telling. His name is Corell.'

And Doctor Winter said in astonishment, 'George Corell? Why, that seems impossible! He's done a lot for this town. Why, he even gave prizes for the shooting-match in the hills this morning.' And as he said it his eyes began to understand what had happened and his mouth closed slowly, and he said, 'I see, that is why he gave the shooting-match. Yes, I see. But George Corell–that sounds impossible!'

The door to the left opened and Mayor Orden came in; he was digging in his right ear with his little finger. He was dressed in his official morning coat, with his chain of office about his neck. He had a large, white, spraying moustache and two smaller ones, one over each eye. His white hair was so recently brushed that only now were the hairs struggling to be free, to stand up again. He had been Mayor so long that he was the Idea-Mayor in the town. Even grown people when they saw the word 'mayor', printed or written, saw Mayor Orden in their minds. He and his office were one. It had given him dignity and he had given it warmth.

From behind him Madame emerged, small and wrinkled and fierce. She considered that she had created this man out of whole cloth, had thought him up, and she was sure that she could do a better job if she had it to do again. Only once or twice in her life had she ever understood all of him, but the part of him which she knew, she knew intricately and well. No little appetite or pain, no meaness in him escaped her; no thought or dream or longing in him ever reached her. And yet several times in her life she had seen the stars.

She stepped around the Mayor and she took his hand and pulled his finger out of his outraged ear and pushed his hand to his side, the way she would take a baby's thumb away from his mouth.

'I don't believe for a moment it hurts as much as you say,' she said, and to Doctor Winter, 'He won't let me fix his eyebrows.'

'It hurts,' said Mayor Orden.

'Very well, if you want to look like that there is nothing I can do about it.' She straightened his already straight tie. 'I'm glad you're here, Doctor,' she said. 'How many do you think will come?' And then she looked up and saw Captain Bentick. 'Oh," she said, 'the colonel!'

Captain Bentick said, 'No, ma'am, I'm only preparing for the colonel. Sergeant!'

The sergeant, who had been turning over pillows, looking behind pictures, came quickly to Mayor Orden and ran his hands over his pockets.

Captain Bentick said, 'Excuse him, sir, it's regulations.'

He glanced again at the little book in his hand. 'Your Excellency, I think you have firearms here. Two items, I believe?'

Mayor Orden said, 'Firearms? Guns, you mean, I guess. Yes, I have a shotgun and a sporting-rifle.' He said deprecatingly, 'You know, I don't hunt very much any more. I always think I'm going to, and then the season opens and I don't get out. I don't take the pleasure in it I used to.'

Captain Bentick insisted. 'Where are these guns, Your Excellency?'

The Mayor rubbed his cheek and tried to think. 'Why, I think–' He turned to Madame. 'Weren't they in the back of that cabinet in the bedroom with the walking-sticks?'

Madame said, 'Yes, and every stitch of clothing in that cabinet smells of oil. I wish you'd put them somewhere else.'

Captain Bentick said, 'Sergeant!' and the sergeant went quickly into the bedroom.

'It's an unpleasant duty. I'm sorry,' said the captain.

The sergeant came back, carrying a double-barrelled shotgun and rather nice sporting-rifle with a shoulder-strap. He leaned them against the side of the entrance door.

Captain Bentick said, 'That's all, thank you, Your Excellency. Thank you, Madame.'

He turned and bowed slightly to Doctor Winter. 'Thank you, Doctor. Colonel Lanser will be here directly. Good morning!'

And he went out to the front door, followed by the sergeant with the two guns in one hand and the sub-machine-gun over his right arm.

Madame said, 'For a moment I thought he was the colonel. He was a rather nice-looking young man.'

Doctor Winter said sardonically, 'No, he was just protecting the colonel.'

Madame was thinking, 'I wonder how many officers will come?' And she looked at Joseph and saw that he was shamelessly eavesdropping. She shook her head at him and frowned and he went back to the little things he had been doing. He began dusting all over again.

And Madame said, 'How many do you think will come?'

Doctor Winter pulled out a chair outrageously and sat down again, 'I don't know,' he said.

'Well'–she frowned at Joseph–'we've been talking it over. Should we offer them tea or a glass of wine? If we do, I don't know how many there will be, and if we don't, what are we to do?'

Doctor Winter shook his head and smiled. 'I don't know. It's been a long time since we conquered anybody or anybody conquered us. I don't know what is proper.'

Mayor Orden had his finger back in his itching ear. He said, 'Well, I don't think we should. I don't think the people would like it. I don't want to drink wine with them. I don't know why.'

Madame appealed to the doctor then. 'Didn't people in the old days–the leaders, that is–compliment each other and take a glass of wine?'

Doctor Winter nodded. 'Yes, indeed they did.' He shook his head slowly. 'Maybe that was different. Kings and princes played at war the way Englishmen play at hunting. When the fox was dead they gathered at a hunt breakfast. But Mayor Orden is probably right: the people might not like him to drink wine with the invader.'

Madame said, 'The people are down listening to the music. Annie told me. If they can do that, why shouldn't we keep civilised procedure alive?'

The Mayor looked steadily at her for a moment and his voice was sharp. 'Madame, I think with your permission we will not have wine. The people are confused now. They have lived at peace so long that they do not quite believe in war. They will learn and then they will not be confused any more. They elected me not to be confused. Six town boys were murdered this morning. I think we will have no hunt breakfast. The people do not fight wars for sport.'

Madame bowed slightly. There had been a number of times in her life when her husband had become the Mayor. She had learned not to confuse the Mayor with her husband.

Mayor Orden looked at his watch and when Joseph came in, carrying a small cup of black coffee, he took it absent-mindedly. 'Thank you,' he said, and he sipped it. 'I should be clear,' he said apologetically to Doctor Winter. 'I should be–do you know how many men the invader has?'

'Not many,' the doctor said. 'I don't think over two hundred and fifty; but all with those little machine-guns.'

The Mayor sipped his coffee again and made a new start. 'What about the rest of the country?'

The doctor raised his shoulders and dropped them again.

'Was there no resistance anywhere?' the Mayor went on hopelessly.

And again the doctor raised his shoulders. 'I don't know. The wires are cut or captured. There is no news.'

'And our boys, our soldiers?'

'I don't know,' said the doctor.

Joseph interrupted. 'I heard–that is, Annie heard–'

'What, Joseph?'

'Six men were killed, sir, by the machine-guns. Annie heard three were wounded and captured.'

'But there were twelve.'

'Annie heard that three escaped.'

The Mayor turned sharply. 'Which ones escaped?' he demanded.

'I don't know, sir. Annie didn't hear.'

Madame inspected a table for dust with her finger. She said, 'Joseph, when they come, stay close to your bell. We might want a little something. And put on your other coat, Joseph, the one with the buttons.' She thought for a moment. 'And, Joseph, when you finish what you are told to do, go out of the room. It makes a bad impression when you just stand around listening. It's provincial, that's what it is.'

'Yes, Madame,' Joseph said.

'We won't serve wine, Joseph, but you might have some cigarettes handy in that little silver conserve box. And don't strike the match to light the colonel's cigarette on your shoe. Strike it on the match-box.'

'Yes, Madame.'

Mayor Orden unbuttoned his coat and took out his watch and looked at it and put it back and buttoned his coat again, one button too high. Madame went to him and rebuttoned it correctly.

Doctor Winter asked, 'What time is it?'

'Five to eleven.'

'A time-minded people,' the doctor said. 'They will be here on time. Do you want me to go away?'

Mayor Orden looked startled. 'Go? No–no, stay.' He laughed softly. 'I'm a little afraid,' he said apologetically. 'Well, not afraid, but I'm nervous.' And he said helplessly. 'We have never been conquered, for a long time–' He stopped to listen. In the distance there was a sound of band music, a march. They all turned in its direction and listened.

Madame said, 'Here they come. I hope not too many try to crowd in here at once. It isn't a very big room.'

Doctor Winter said sardonically, 'Madame would prefer the Hall of Mirrors at Versailles?'

She pinched her lips and looked about, already placing the conquerors with her mind. 'It is a very small room,' she said.

The band music swelled a little and then grew fainter. There came a gentle tap on the door.

'Now, who can that be? Joseph, if it is anyone, tell him to come back later. We are very busy.'

The tap came again. Joseph went to the door and opened it a crack and then a little wider. A grey figure, helmeted and gauntleted, appeared.

'Colonel Lanser's compliments,' the head said. 'Colonel Lanser requests an audience with Your Excellency.'

Joseph opened the door wide. The helmeted orderly stepped inside and looked quickly about the room and then stood aside. 'Colonel Lanser!' he announced.

A second helmeted figure walked into the room, and his rank showed only on his shoulders. Behind him came a rather short man in a black business suit. The colonel was a middle-aged man, grey and hard and tired-looking. He had the square shoulders of a soldier, but his eyes lacked the blank look of the ordinary soldier. The little man beside him was bald and rosy-cheeked, with small black eyes and a sensual mouth.

Colonel Lanser took off his helmet. With a quick bow, he said, 'Your Excellency!' He bowed to Madame. 'Madame!' And he said, 'Close the door, please, Corporal.' Joseph quickly shut the door and stared in small triumph at the soldier.

Lanser looked questioningly at the doctor, and Mayor Orden said, 'This is Doctor Winter.'

'An official?' the colonel asked.

'A doctor, sir, and, I might say, the local historian.'

Lanser bowed slightly. He said, 'Doctor Winter, I do not mean to be impertinent, but there will be a page in your history, perhaps–'

And Doctor Winter smiled. 'Many pages, perhaps.'

Colonel Lanser turned slightly towards his companion. 'I think you know Mr Corell,' he said.

The Mayor said, 'George Corell? Of course I know him. How are you, George?'

Doctor Winter cut in sharply. He said, very formally, 'Your Excellency, our friend, George Corell, prepared this town for the invasion. Our benefactor, George Corell, sent our soldiers into the hills. Our dinner guest, George Corell, has made a list of every firearm in the town. Our friend, George Corell!'

Corell said angrily, 'I work for what I believe in! That is an honourable thing.'

Orden's mouth hung a little open. He was bewildered. He looked helplessly from Winter to Corell. 'This isn't true,' he said. 'George, this isn't true! You have sat at my table, you have drunk port with me. Why, you helped me plan the hospital! This isn't true!'

He was looking very steadily at Corell and Corell looked belligerently back at him. There was a long silence. Then the Mayor's face grew slowly tight and very formal and his whole body was rigid. He turned to Colonel Lanser and he said, 'I do not wish to speak in this gentleman's company.'

Corell said, 'I have a right to be here! I am a soldier like the rest. I simply do not wear a uniform.'

The Mayor repeated, 'I do not wish to speak in this gentleman's presence.'

Colonel Lanser said, 'Will you leave us now, Mr Corell?'

And Corell said, 'I have a right to be here!'

Lanser repeated sharply, 'Will you leave us now, Mr Corell? Do you outrank me?'

'Well, no, sir.'

'Please go, Mr Corell,' said Colonel Lanser.

And Corell looked at the Mayor angrily, and then he turned and went quickly out of the doorway. Doctor Winter chuckled and said, 'That's good enough for a paragraph in my history.' Colonel Lanser glanced sharply at him but he did not speak.

Now the door on the right opened, and straw-haired, red-eyed Annie put an angry face into the doorway. 'There's soldiers on the back porch, Madame,' she said. 'Just standing there.'

'They won't come in,' Colonel Lanser said. 'It's only military procedure.'

Madame said icily, 'Annie, if you have anything to say, let Joseph bring the message.'

'I didn't know but they'd try to get in,' Annie said. 'They smelled the coffee.'

'Annie!'

'Yes, Madame,' and she withdrew.

The colonel said, 'May I sit down?' And he explained, 'We have been a long time without sleep.'

The Mayor seemed to start out of a sleep himself. 'Yes,' he said, 'of course, sit down!'

The colonel looked at Madame and she seated herself and he settled tiredly into a chair. Mayor Orden stood, still half dreaming.

The colonel began, 'We want to get along as well as we can. You see, sir, this is more like a business venture than anything else. We need the coal-mine here and the fishing. We will try to get along with just as little friction as possible.'

The Mayor said, 'I have had no news. What about the rest of the country?'

'All taken,' said the colonel. 'It was well planned.'

'Was there no resistance anywhere?'

The colonel looked at him compassionately. 'I wish there had not been. Yes, there was some resistance, but it only caused bloodshed. We had planned very carefully.'

Orden stuck to his point. 'But there was resistance?'

'Yes, but it was foolish to resist. Just as here, it was destroyed instantly. It was sad and foolish to resist.'

Doctor Winter caught some of the Mayor's anxiousness about the point. 'Yes,' he said, 'foolish, but they resisted.'

And Colonel Lanser replied, 'Only a few and they are gone. The people as a whole are quiet.'

Doctor Winter said, 'The people don't know yet what has happened.'

'They are discovering,' said Lanser. 'They won't be foolish again.' He cleared his throat and his voice became brisk. 'Now, sir, I must get to business. I'm really very tired, but before I can sleep I must make my arrangements.' He sat forward in his chair. 'I am more engineer than soldier. This whole thing is more an engineering job than conquest. The coal must come out of the ground and be shipped. We have technicians, but the local people will continue to work the mine. Is that clear? We do not wish to be harsh.'

And Orden said, 'Yes, that's clear enough. But suppose the people do not want to work the mine?'

The colonel said, 'I hope they will want to, because they must. We must have the coal.'

'But if they don't?'

'They must. They are an orderly people. They don't want trouble.' He waited for the Mayor's reply and none came. 'Is that not so, sir?' the colonel asked.

Mayor Orden twisted his chain. 'I don't know, sir. They are orderly under their own government. I don't know how they would be under yours. It is untouched ground, you see. We have built our government over four hundred years.'

The colonel said quickly, 'We know that, and so we are going to keep your government. You will still be the Mayor, you will give the orders, you will penalise and reward. In that way, they will not give trouble.'

Mayor Orden looked at Doctor Winter. 'What are you thinking about?'

'I don't know,' said Doctor Winter. 'It would be interesting to see. I'd expect trouble. This might be a bitter people.'

Mayor Orden said, 'I don't know, either.' He turned to the colonel. 'Sir, I am of this people, and yet I don't know what they will do. Perhaps you know. Or maybe it would be different from anything you know or we know. Some people accept appointed leaders and obey them. But my people have elected me. They made me and they can unmake me. Perhaps they will if they think I have gone over to you. I just don't know.'

The colonel said, 'You will be doing them a service if you keep them in order.'

'A service?'

'Yes, a service. It is your duty to protect them from harm. They will be in danger if they are rebellious. We must get the coal, you see. Our leaders do not tell us how; they order us to get it. But you have your people to protect. You must make them do the work and thus keep them safe.'

Mayor Orden asked, 'But suppose they don't want to be safe?'

'Then you must think for them.'

Orden said, a little proudly, 'My people don't like to have others think for them. Maybe they are different from your people. I am confused, but that I am sure of.'

Now Joseph came in quickly and he stood leaning forward, bursting to speak. Madame said, 'What is it, Joseph? Get the silver box of cigarettes.'

'Pardon, Madame,' said Joseph. 'Pardon, Your Excellency.'

'What do you want?' the Mayor asked.

'It's Annie," he said. 'She's getting angry, sir.'

'What is the matter?' Madame demanded.

'Annie don't like the soldiers on the back porch.'

The colonel asked, 'Are they causing trouble?'

'They are looking through the door at Annie,' said Joseph. 'She hates that.'

The colonel said, 'They are carrying out orders. They are doing no harm.'

'Well, Annie hates to be stared at,' said Joseph.

Madame said, 'Joseph, tell Annie to take care.'

'Yes, Madame,' and Joseph went out.

The colonel's eyes dropped with tiredness. 'There's another thing, Your Excellency,' he said. 'Would it be possible for me and my staff to stay here?'

Mayor Orden thought a moment and he said, 'It's a small place. There are larger, more comfortable places.'

Then Joseph came back with the silver box of cigarettes and he opened it and held it in front of the colonel. When the colonel took one, Joseph ostentatiously lighted it. The colonel puffed deeply.

'It isn't that,' he said. 'We have found that when a staff lives under the roof of the local authority, there is more tranquillity.'

'You mean,' said Orden, 'the people feel there is collaboration involved?'

'Yes, I suppose that is it.'

Mayor Orden looked hopelessly at Doctor Winter, and Winter could offer him nothing but a wry smile. Orden said softly, 'Am I permitted to refuse this honour?'

'I'm sorry,' the colonel said. 'No. These are the orders of my leader.'

'The people will not like it,' Orden said.

'Always the people! The people are disarmed. The people have no say.'

Mayor Orden shook his head. 'You do not know, sir.'

From the doorway came the sound of an angry woman's voice, and a thump and a man's cry. Joseph came scuttling through the door. 'She's thrown boiling water,' Joseph said. 'She's very angry.'

There were commands through the door and the clump of feet. Colonel Lanser got up heavily. 'Have you no control over your servants, sir?' he asked.

Mayor Orden smiled. 'Very little,' he said. 'She's a very good cook when she is happy. Was anyone hurt?' he asked Joseph.

'The water was boiling, sir.'

Colonel Lanser said, 'We just want to do our job. It's an engineering job. You will have to discipline your cook.'

'I can't,' said Orden. 'She'll quit.'

'This is an emergency. She can't quit.'

'Then she'll throw water,' said Doctor Winter.

The door opened and a soldier stood in the opening. 'Shall I arrest this woman, sir?'

'Was anyone hurt?' Lanser asked.

'Yes, sir, scalded, and one man bitten. We are holding her, sir.'

Lanser looked helpless, then he said, 'Release her and go outside and off the porch.'

'Yes, sir,' and the door closed behind the soldier.

Lanser said, 'I could have her shot, I could lock her up.'

'Then we would have no cook,' said Orden.

'Look,' said the colonel. 'We are instructed to get along with your people.'

Madame said, 'Excuse me, sir, I will just go and see if the soldiers hurt Annie,' and she went out.

Now Lanser stood up. 'I told you I'm very tired, sir. I must have some sleep. Please co-operate with us for the good of all.' When Mayor Orden made no reply. 'For the good of all,' Lanser repeated. 'Will you?'

Orden said, 'This is a little town. I don't know. The people are confused and so am I.'

'But will you try to co-operate?'

Orden shook his head. 'I don't know. When the town makes up its mind what it wants to do, I'll probably do that.'

'But you are the authority.'

Orden smiled. 'You won't believe this, but it is true: authority is in the town. I don't know how or why, but it is so. This means we cannot act as quickly as you can, but when the direction is set, we all act together. I am confused. I don't know yet.'

Lanser said wearily, 'I hope we can get along together. It will be so much easier for everyone. I hope we can trust you. I don't like to think of the means the military will take to keep order.'

Mayor Orden was silent.

'I hope we can trust you,' Lanser repeated.

Orden put his finger in his ear and wriggled his hand. 'I don't know,' he said.

Madame came through the door then. 'Annie is furious,' she said. 'She is next door, talking to Christine. Christine is angry, too.'

'Christine is even a better cook than Annie,' said the Mayor.

2

Upstairs in the little palace of the Mayor the staff of Colonel Lanser made its headquarters. There were five of them besides the colonel. There was Major Hunter, a haunted little man of figures, a little man who, being a dependable unit, considered all other men either as dependable units or as unfit to live. Major Hunter was an engineer, and except in case of war no one would have thought of giving him command of men. For Major Hunter set his men in rows like figures and he added and subtracted and multiplied them. He was an arithmetician rather than a mathematician. None of the humour, the music, or the mysticism of higher mathematics ever entered his head. Men might vary in height or weight or colour, just as 6 is different from 8, but there was little other difference. He had been married several times and he did not know why his wives became very nervous before they left him.

Captain Bentick was a family man, a lover of dogs and pink children and Christmas. He was too old to be a captain, but a curious lack of ambition had kept him in that rank. Before the war he had admired the British country gentleman very much, wore English clothes, kept English dogs, smoked in an English pipe a special pipe mixture sent him from London, and subscribed to those country magazines which extol gardening and continually argue about the relative merits of English and Gordon setters. Captain Bentick spent all his holidays in Sussex and liked to be mistaken for an Englishman in Budapest or Paris. The war changed all that outwardly, but he had sucked on a pipe too long, had carried a stick too long, to give them up too suddenly. Once, five years before, he had written a letter to *The Times* about grass dying in the Midlands and had signed it Edmund Twitchell, Esq.; and, furthermore, *The Times* had printed it.

If Captain Bentick was too old to be a captain, Captain Loft was too young. Captain Loft was as much a captain as one can imagine. He lived and breathed his captaincy. He had no unmilitary moments. A driving ambition forced him up through the grades. He rose like cream to the top of milk. He clicked his heels as perfectly as a dancer does. He knew every kind of military courtesy and insisted on using it all. Generals were afraid of him because he knew more about the deportment of a soldier than they did. Captain Loft thought and believed that a soldier is the highest development of animal life. If he considered God at all he thought of Him as an old and honoured general, retired and grey, living among remembered battles and putting wreaths on the graves of his lieutenants several times a year. Captain Loft believed that all women fall in love with a uniform and he did not see how it could be otherwise. In the normal course of events he would be a brigadier-general at forty-five and have his picture in the illustrated papers, flanked by tall, pale, masculine women wearing lacy picture hats.

Lieutenants Prackle and Tonder were snot-noses, undergraduates, lieutenants, trained in the politics of the day, believing the great new system invented by a genius so great that they never bothered to verify its results. They were sentimental young men, given to tears and furies. Lieutenant Prackle carried a lock of hair in the back of his watch, wrapped in a bit of blue satin, and the hair was constantly getting loose and clogging the balance-wheel, so that he wore a wrist-watch for telling time. Prackle was a dancing-partner, a gay young man who nevertheless could scowl like the Leader, could brood like the Leader. He hated degenerate art and had destroyed several canvases with his own hands. In cabarets he sometimes made pencil sketches of his companions which were so good that he had often been told he should have been an artist. Prackle had several blonde sisters of whom he was so proud that he had on occasion caused a commotion when he thought they had been insulted. The sisters were a little disturbed about it because they were afraid someone might set out to prove the insults, which would not have been hard to do. Lieutenant Prackle spent nearly all his time off duty day-dreaming of seducing Lieutenant Tonder's blonde sister, a buxom girl who loved to be seduced by older men who did not muss her hair as Lieutenant Prackle did.

Lieutenant Tonder was a poet, a bitter poet, who dreamed of perfect, ideal love of elevated young men for poor girls. Tonder was a dark romantic with a vision as wide as his experience. He sometimes spoke blank verse under his breath to imaginary dark women. He longed for death on the battlefield, with weeping parents in the background, and the Leader, brave but sad in the presence of the dying youth. He imagined his death very often, lighted by a fair setting sun which glinted on broken military equipment, his men standing silently around him, with heads sunk low, as over a fat cloud galloped the Valkyries, big-breasted, mothers and mistresses in one, while Wagnerian thunder crashed in the background. And he even had his dying words ready.

These were the men of the staff, each one playing war as children play 'Run, Sheep, Run'. Major Hunter thought of war as an arithmetical job to be done so he could get back to his fireplace; Captain Loft as the proper career of a properly brought-up young man; and Lieutenants Prackle and Tonder as a dreamlike thing in which nothing was very real. And their war so far had been play–fine weapons and fine planning against unarmed, planless enemies. They had lost no fights and suffered little hurt. They were, under pressure, capable of cowardice or courage, as everyone is. Of them all, only Colonel Lanser knew what war really is in the long run.

Lanser had been in Belgium and France twenty years before and he tried not to think what he knew–that war is treachery and hatred, the muddling of incompetent generals, the torture and killing and sickness and tiredness, until at last it is over and nothing has changed except for new weariness and new hatreds. Lanser told himself he was a soldier, given orders to carry out. He was not expected to question or to think, but only to carry out orders; and he tried to put aside the sick memories of the other war and the certainty that this would be the same. This one will be different, he said to himself fifty times a day; this one will be very different.

In marching, in mobs, in football games, and in war, outlines become vague; real things become unreal and a fog creeps over the mind. Tension and excitement, weariness, movement–all merge in one great grey dream, so that, when it is over, it is hard to remember how it was when you killed men or ordered them to be killed. Then other people who were not there tell you what it was like and you say vaguely, 'Yes, I guess that's how it was.'

This staff had taken three rooms on the upper floor of the Mayor's palace. In the bedrooms they had put their cots and blankets and equipment, and in the room next to them and directly over the little drawing-room on the ground floor they had made a kind of club, rather an uncomfortable club. There were a few chairs and a table. Here they wrote letters and read letters. They talked and ordered coffee and planned and rested. On the walls between the windows there were pictures of cows and lakes and little farmhouses, and from the windows they could look down over the town to the waterfront, to the docks where the shipping was tied up, to the docks where the coal barges pulled up and took their loads and went out to sea. They could look down over the little town that twisted past the square to the waterfront, and they could see the fishing-boats lying at anchor in the bay, the sails furled, and they could smell the drying fish on the beach, right through the window.

There was a large table in the centre of the room and Major Hunter sat beside it. He had his drawing-board in his lap and resting on the table, and with a T-square and triangle he worked at a design for a new railroad siding. The drawing-board was unsteady and the major was growing angry with its unsteadiness. He called over his shoulder, 'Prackle!' And then, 'Lieutenant Prackle!'

The bedroom door opened and the lieutenant came out, half his face covered with shaving-cream. He held the brush in his hand. 'Yes?' he said.

Major Hunter jiggled his drawing-board. 'Hasn't that tripod for my board turned up in the baggage?'

'I don't know, sir,' said Prackle. 'I didn't look.'

'Well, look now, will you? It's bad enough to have to work in this light. I'll have to draw this again before I ink it.'

Prackle said, 'Just as soon as I finish shaving, I'll look.'

Hunter said irritably, 'This siding is more important than your looks. See if there is a canvas case like a golf bag under that pile in there.'

Prackle disappeared into the bedroom. The door to the right opened and Captain Loft came in. He wore his helmet, a pair of field-glasses, side-arm, and various little leather cases strung all over him. He began to remove his equipment as soon as he entered.

'You know, that Bentick's crazy,' he said. 'He was going out on duty in a fatigue cap, right down the street.'

Loft put his field-glasses on the table and took off his helmet, then his gas-mask bag. A little pile of equipment began to heap up on the table.

Hunter said, 'Don't leave that stuff there. I have to work here. Why shouldn't he wear a cap? There hasn't been any trouble. I get sick of these tin things. They're heavy and you can't see.'

Loft said primly, 'It's bad practice to leave it off. It's bad for the people here. We must maintain a military standard, an alertness, and never vary it. We'll just invite trouble if we don't.'

'What makes you think so?' Hunter asked.

Loft drew himself up a little. His mouth thinned with certainty. Sooner or later everyone wanted to punch Loft in the nose for his sureness about things. He said, 'I don't think it. I was paraphrasing *Manual X-12* on deportment in occupied countries. It is very carefully worked out.' He began to say, 'You–' and then changed it to, 'Everybody should read *X-12* very closely.'

Hunter said, 'I wonder whether the man who wrote it was ever in occupied country. These people are harmless enough. They seem to be good, obedient people.'

Prackle came through the door, his face still half covered with shaving-soap. He carried a brown canvas tube, and behind him came Lieutenant Tonder. 'Is this it?' Prackle asked.

'Yes. Unpack it, will you, and set it up.'

Prackle and Tonder went to work on the folding tripod and tested it and put it near Hunter. The major screwed his board to it, tilted it right and left, and finally settled gruntingly behind it.

Captain Loft said, 'Do you know you have soap on your face, Lieutenant?'

'Yes, sir,' Prackle said. 'I was shaving when the major asked me to get the tripod.'

'Well, you had better get it off,' Loft said. 'The colonel might see you.'

'Oh, he wouldn't mind. He doesn't care about things like that.'

Tonder was looking over Hunter's shoulder as he worked.

Loft said, 'Well, he may not, but it doesn't look right.'

Prackle took a handkerchief and rubbed the soap from his cheek. Tonder pointed to a little drawing on the corner of the major's board. 'That's a nice-looking bridge, Major. But where in the world are we going to build a bridge?'

Hunter looked down at the drawing-board and then over his shoulder at Tonder. 'Huh? Oh, that isn't any bridge we're going to build. Up here is the work drawing.'

'What are you doing with a bridge, then?'

Hunter seemed a little embarrassed. 'Well, you know, in my back-yard at home I've got a model railroad line. I was going to bridge a little creek for it. Brought the line right down to the creek, but I never did get the bridge built. I thought I'd kind of work it out while I was away.'

Lieutenant Prackle took from his pocket a folded rotogravure page and he unfolded it and held it up and looked at it. It was a picture of a girl, all legs and dress and eyelashes, a well-developed blonde in black open-work stockings and a low bodice, and this particular blonde peeped over a black lace fan. Lieutenant Prackle held her up and said, 'Isn't she something?' Lieutenant Tonder looked critically at the picture and said, 'I don't like her.'

'What don't you like about her?'

'I just don't like her,' said Tonder. 'What do you want her picture for?'

Prackle said, 'Because I do like her and I bet you do, too.'

'I do not,' said Tonder.

'You mean to say you wouldn't take a date with her if you could?' Prackle asked.

Tonder said, 'No.'

'Well, you're just crazy,' and Prackle went to one of the curtains. He said, 'I'm just going to stick her up here and let you brood about her for a while.' He pinned the picture to the curtain.

Captain Loft was gathering his equipment into his arms now, and he said, 'I don't think it looks very well out here, Lieutenant. You'd better take it down. It wouldn't make a good impression on the local people.'

Hunter looked up from his board. 'What wouldn't?' He followed their eyes to the picture. 'Who's that?' he asked.

'She's an actress,' said Prackle.

Hunter looked at her carefully. 'Oh, do you know her?'

Tonder said, 'She's a tramp.'

Hunter said, 'Oh, then you know her?'

Prackle was looking steadily at Tonder. He said, 'Say, how do you know she's a tramp?'

'She looks like a tramp,' said Tonder.

'Do you know her?'

'No, and I don't want to.'

Prackle began to say, 'Then how do you know?' when Loft broke in. He said, 'You'd better take the picture down. Put it up over your bed if you want to. This room's kind of official here.'

Prackle looked at him mutinously and was about to speak when Captain Loft said, 'That's an order, Lieutenant,' and poor Prackle folded his paper and put it into his pocket again. He tried cheerily to change the subject. 'There are some pretty girls in this town, all right,' he said. 'As soon as we get settled down and everything going smoothly, I'm going to get acquainted with a few.'

Loft said, 'You'd better read *X-12*. There's a section dealing with sexual matters.' And he went out, carrying his duffel, glasses, and equipment. Lieutenant Tonder, still looking over Hunter's shoulder, said, 'That's clever–the coal cars come right through the mines to the ship.'

Hunter came slowly out of his work and he said, 'We have to speed it up; we've got to get that coal moving. It's a big job. I'm awful thankful that the people here are calm and sensible.'

Loft came back into the room without his equipment. He stood by the window, looking out towards the harbour, towards the coal-mine, and he said, 'They are calm and sensible because we are calm and sensible. I think we can take credit for that. That's why I keep harping on procedure. It is very carefully worked out.'

The door opened and Colonel Lanser came in, removing his coat as he entered. His staff gave him military courtesy–not very rigid, but enough. Lanser said, 'Captain Loft, will you go down and relieve Bentick? He isn't feeling well, says he's dizzy.'

'Yes, sir,' said Loft. 'May I suggest, sir, that I only recently came off duty?'

Lanser inspected him closely. 'I hope you don't mind going, Captain.'

'Not at all, sir; I just mention it for the record.'

Lanser relaxed and chuckled. 'You like to be mentioned in the reports, don't you?'

'It does no harm, sir.'

'And when you have enough mentions,' Lanser went on, 'there will be a little dangler on your chest.'

'They are the milestones in a military career, sir.'

Lanser sighed. 'Yes, I guess they are. But they won't be the ones you'll remember, Captain.'

'Sir?' Loft asked.

'You'll know what I mean later–perhaps.'

Captain Loft put his equipment on rapidly. 'Yes, sir,' he said, and went out and his footsteps clattered down the wooden stairs, and Lanser watched him go with a little amusement. He said quietly, 'There goes a born soldier.' And Hunter looked up and poised his pencil and he said, 'A born ass.'

'No,' said Lanser, 'he's being a soldier the way a lot of men would be politicians. He'll be on the General Staff before long. He'll look down on war from above and so he'll always love it.'

Lieutenant Prackle said, 'When do you think the war will be over, sir?'

'Over? Over? What do you mean?'

Lieutenant Prackle continued, 'How soon will we win?'

Lanser shook his head. 'Oh, I don't know. The enemy is still in the world.'

'But we will lick them,' said Prackle.

Lanser said, 'Yes?'

'Won't we?'

'Yes; yes, we always do.'

Prackle said excitedly, 'Well, if it's quiet around Christmas, do you think there will be some furloughs granted?'

'I don't know,' said Lanser. 'Such orders will have to come from home. Do you want to get home for Christmas?'

'Well, I'd kind of like to.'

'Maybe you will,' said Lanser, 'maybe you will.'

Lieutenant Tonder said, 'We won't drop out of this occupation, will we, sir, after the war is over?'

'I don't know,' said the colonel. 'Why?'

'Well,' said Tonder, 'it's a nice country, nice people. Our men–some of them–might even settle here.'

Lanser said jokingly, 'You've seen some place you like, perhaps?'

'Well,' said Tonder, 'there are some beautiful farms here. If four or five of them were thrown together, it would be a nice place to settle, I think.'

'You have no family land, then?' Lanser asked.

'No, sir, not any more. Inflation took it away.'

Lanser was tired now of talking to children. He said, 'ah, well, we still have a war to fight. We still have coal to take out. Do you suppose we can wait until it is over before we build up these estates? Such orders will come from above. Captain Loft can tell you that.' His manner changed. He said, 'Hunter, your steel will be in tomorrow. You can get your tracks started this week.'

There was a knock at the door and a sentry put his head in. He said, 'Mr Corell wishes to see you, sir.'

'Send him in,' said the colonel. And he said to the others, 'This is the man who did the preliminary work here. We might have some trouble with him.'

'Did he do a good job?' Tonder asked.

'Yes, he did, and he won't be popular with the people here. I wonder whether he will be popular with us.'

'He deserves credit, certainly,' Tonder said.

'Yes,' Lanser said, 'and don't think he won't claim it.'

Corell came in, rubbing his hands. He radiated good-will and good-fellowship. He was dressed still in his black business suit, but on his head there was a patch of white bandage, stuck to his hair with a cross of adhesive tape. He advanced to the centre of the room and said, 'Good morning, Colonel. I should have called yesterday after the trouble downstairs, but I knew how busy you would be.'

The colonel said, 'Good morning.' Then with a circular gesture of his hand. 'This is my staff, Mr Corell.'

'Fine boys,' said Corell. 'They did a good job. Well, I tried to prepare for them well.'

Hunter looked down at his board and he took out an inking-pen and dipped it and began to ink in his drawing.

Lanser said, 'You did very well. I wish you hadn't killed those six men, though. I wish their soldiers hadn't come back.'

Corell spread his hands and said comfortably, 'Six men is a small loss for a town of this size, with a coal-mine, too.'

Lanser said sternly, 'I am not averse to killing people if that finishes it. But sometimes it is better not to.'

Corell had been studying the officers. He looked sideways at the lieutenants, and he said, 'Could we– perhaps–talk alone, Colonel?'

'Yes, if you wish. Lieutenant Prackle and Lieutenant Tonder, will you go to your room, please?' And the colonel said to Corell, 'Major Hunter is working. He doesn't hear anything when he's working.' Hunter looked up from his board and smiled quietly and looked down again. The young lieutenants left the room, and when they were gone Lanser said, 'Well, here we are. Won't you sit down?'

'Thank you sir,' and Corell sat down behind the table.

Lanser looked at the bandage on Corell's head. He said bluntly, 'Have they tried to kill you already?'

Corell felt the bandage with his fingers. 'This? Oh, this was a stone that fell from a cliff in the hills this morning.'

'You're sure it wasn't thrown?'

'What do you mean?' Corell said. 'These aren't fierce people. They haven't had a war for a hundred years. They've forgotten about fighting.'

'Well, you've lived among them,' said the colonel. 'You ought to know.' He stepped close to Corell. 'But if you are safe, these people are different from any in the world. I've helped to occupy countries before. I was in Belgium twenty years ago and in France.' He shook his head a little as though to clear it, and he said gruffly, 'You did a good job. We should thank you. I mentioned your work in my report.'

'Thank you, sir,' said Corell. 'I did my best.'

Lanser said, a little wearily, 'Well, sir, now what shall we do? Would you like to go back to the capital? We can put you on a coal barge if you're in a hurry, or on a destroyer if you want to wait.'

Corell said, 'But I don't want to go back. I'll stay here.'

Lanser studied this for a moment and he said, 'You know, I haven't a great many men. I can't give you a very adequate bodyguard.'

'But I don't need a bodyguard. I tell you these aren't violent people.'

Lanser looked at the bandage for a moment. Hunter glanced up from his board and remarked, 'You'd better start wearing a helmet.' He looked down at his work again.

Now Corell moved forward in his chair. 'I wanted particularly to talk to you, Colonel. I thought I might help with the civil administration.'

Lanser turned on his heel and walked to the window and looked out, and then he swung around and said quietly, 'What have you in mind?'

'Well, you must have a civil authority you can trust. I thought perhaps that Mayor Orden might step down and–well, if I were to take over his office, it and the military would work very nicely together.'

Lanser's eyes seemed to grow very large and bright. He came close to Corell and he spoke sharply. 'Have you mentioned this in your report?'

Corell said, 'Well, yes, naturally–in my analysis.'

Lanser interrupted. 'Have you talked to any of the town people since we arrived–outside of the Mayor, that is?'

'Well, no. You see, they are still a bit startled. They didn't expect it.' He chuckled. 'No, sir, they certainly didn't expect it.'

But Lanser pressed his point. 'So you don't really know what's going on in their minds?'

'Why, they're startled,' said Corell. 'They're–well, they're almost dreaming.'

'You don't know what they think of you?' Lanser asked.

'I have many friends here. I know everyone.'

'Did anyone buy anything in your store this morning?'

'Well, of course, business is at a standstill,' Corell answered. 'No one's buying anything.'

Lanser relaxed suddenly. He went to a chair and sat down and crossed his legs. He said quietly, 'Yours is a difficult and brave branch of the service. It should be greatly rewarded.'

'Thank you, sir.'

'You will have their hatred in time,' said the colonel.

'I can stand that, sir. They are the enemy.'

Now Lanser hesitated a long moment before he spoke, and then he said softly, 'You will not even have *our* respect.'

Corell jumped to his feet excitedly. 'This is contrary to the Leader's words!' he said. 'The Leader has said that all branches are equally honourable.'

Lanser went on very quietly, 'I hope the Leader knows. I hope he can read the minds of soldiers.' And then almost compassionately he said: 'You should be greatly rewarded.' For a moment he sat quietly, and then he pulled himself together and said, 'Now we must come to exactness. I am in charge here. My job is to get coal out. To do that I must maintain order and discipline, and to do that I must know what is in the minds of these people. I must anticipate revolt. Do you understand that?'

'Well, I can find out what you wish to know, sir. As Mayor here, I will be very effective,' said Corell.

Lanser shook his head. 'I have no orders about this. I must use my own judgment. I think you will never again know what is going on here. I think no one will speak to you; no one will be near to you except those people who will live on money, who can live on money. I think without a guard you will be in great danger. It will please me if you go back to the capital, there to be rewarded for your fine work.'

'But my place is here, sir,' said Corell. 'I have made my place. It is all in my report.'

Lanser went on as though he had not heard. 'Mayor Orden is more than a mayor,' he said. 'He is his people. He knows what they are doing, thinking, without asking, because he will think what they think. By watching him I will know them. He must stay. That is my judgment.'

Corell said, 'My work, sir, merits better treatment than being sent away.'

'Yes, it does,' Lanser said slowly. 'But to the larger work I think you are only a detriment now. If you are not hated yet, you will be. In any little revolt you will be the first to be killed. I think I will suggest that you go back.'

Corell said stiffly, 'You will, of course, permit me to wait for a reply to my report to the capital?'

'Yes, of course. But I shall recommend that you go back for your own safety. Frankly, Mr Corell, you have no value here. But–well, there must be other plans and other countries. Perhaps you will go now to some new town in some new country. You will win new confidence in a new field. You may be given a larger town, even a city, a greater responsibility. I think I will recommend you highly for your work here.'

Corell's eyes were shining with gratification. 'Thank you, sir,' he said. 'I've worked hard. Perhaps you are right. But you must permit me to wait for the reply from the capital.'

Lanser's voice was tight. His eyes were slitted. He said harshly, 'Wear a helmet; keep indoors, do not go out at night, and, above all, do not drink. Trust no woman nor any man. Do you understand that?'

Corell looked pityingly at the colonel. 'I don't think you understand. I have a little house. A pleasant country girl waits on me. I even think she's a little fond of me. These are simple, peaceful people. I know them.'

Lanser said, 'There are no peaceful people. When will you learn it? There are no friendly people. Can't you understand that? We have invaded this country–you, by what they call treachery, prepared for us.' His face grew red and his voice rose. 'Can't you understand that we are at war with these people?'

Corell said, a little smugly, 'We have defeated them.'

The colonel stood up and swung his arms helplessly, and Hunter looked up from his board and put his hand out to protect his board from being jiggled. Hunter said, 'Careful now, sir. I'm inking in. I wouldn't want to do it all over again.'

Lanser looked down at him and said, 'Sorry,' and went on as though he were instructing a class. He said, 'Defeat is a momentary thing. A defeat doesn't last. We were defeated and now we attack. Defeat means nothing. Can't you understand that? Do you know what they are whispering behind doors?'

Corell asked, 'Do you?'

'No, but I suspect.'

Then Corell said insinuatingly, 'Are you afraid, Colonel? Should the commander of this occupation be afraid?'

Lanser sat down heavily and said, 'Maybe that's it.' And he said disgustedly, 'I'm tired of people who have not been at war who know all about it.' He held his chin in his hand and said, 'I remember a little old woman in Brussels–sweet face, white hair; she was only four feet eleven; delicate old hands. You could see the veins almost black against her skin. And her black shawl and her blue-white hair. She used to sing our national songs to us in a quivering, sweet voice. She always knew where to find a cigarette or a virgin.' He dropped his hand from his chin, and he caught himself as though he had been asleep. 'We didn't know her son had been executed,' he said. 'When we finally shot her, she had killed twelve men with a long, black hat-pin. I have it yet at home. It has an enamel button with a bird over it, red and blue.'

Corell said, 'But you shot her?'

'Of course we shot her.'

'And the murders stopped?' asked Corell.

'No, the murders did not stop. And when we finally retreated, the people cut off stragglers and they burned some and they gouged the eyes from some, and some they even crucified.'

Corell said loudly, 'These are not good things to say, Colonel.'

'They are not good things to remember,' said Lanser.

Corell said, 'You should not be in command if you are afraid.'

And Lanser answered softly, 'I know how to fight, you see. If you know, at least you do not make silly errors.'

'Do you talk this way to the young officers?'

Lanser shook his head. 'No, they wouldn't believe me.'

'Why do you tell me, then?'

'Because, Mr Corell, your work is done. I remember one time–' and as he spoke there was a tumble of feet on the stairs and the door burst open. A sentry looked in and Captain Loft brushed past him. Loft was rigid and cold and military; he said, 'There's trouble, sir.'

'Trouble?'

'I have to report, sir, that Captain Bentick has been killed.'

Lanser said, 'Oh–yes–Bentick!'

There was the sound of a number of footsteps on the stairs and two stretcher-bearers came in, carrying a figure covered with blankets.

Lanser said, 'Are you sure he's dead?'

'Quite sure,' Loft said stiffly.

The lieutenants came in from the bedroom, their mouths a little open, and they looked frightened. Lanser said, 'Put him down there,' and he pointed to the wall beside the windows. When the bearers had gone, Lanser knelt and lifted a corner of the blanket and then quickly put it down again. And still kneeling, he looked at Loft and said, 'Who did this?'

'A miner,' said Loft.

'Why?'

'I was there, sir.'

'Well, make your report, then! Make your report, damn it, man!'

Loft drew himself up and said formally, 'I had just relieved Captain Bentick, as the colonel ordered. Captain Bentick was about to leave to come here when I had some trouble about a recalcitrant miner who wanted to quit work. He shouted something about being a free man. When I ordered him to work, he rushed at me with his pick. Captain Bentick tried to interfere.' He gestured slightly towards the body.

Lanser, still kneeling, nodded slowly. 'Bentick was a curious man,' he said. 'He loved the English. He loved everything about them. I don't think he liked to fight very much. . . . You captured the man?'

'Yes, sir,' Loft said.

Lanser stood up slowly and spoke as though to himself. 'So it starts again. We will shoot this man and make twenty new enemies. It's the only thing we know, the only thing we know.'

Prackle said, 'What do you say, sir?'

Lanser answered, 'Nothing, nothing at all. I was just thinking.' He turned to Loft and said, 'Please give my compliments to Mayor Orden and my request that he see me immediately. It is very important.'

Major Hunter looked up, dried his inking-pen carefully, and put it away in a velvet-lined box.

3

In the town the people moved sullenly through the streets. Some of the light of astonishment was gone from their eyes, but still a light of anger had not taken its place. In the coal shaft the working-men pushed the coalcars sullenly. The small tradesmen stood behind their counters and served the people, but no one communicated with them. The people spoke to one another in monosyllables, and everyone was thinking of the war, thinking of himself, thinking of the past and how it had suddenly been changed.

In the drawing-room of the palace of Mayor Orden a small fire burned and the lights were on, for it was a grey day outside and there was frost in the air. The room was itself undergoing a change. The tapestry-covered chairs were pushed back, the little tables out of the way, and through the doorway to the right Joseph and Annie were struggling to bring in a large, square dining-table. They had it on its side. Joseph was in the drawing-room and Annie's red face showed through the door. Joseph manœuvred the legs around sideways, and he cried, 'Don't push, Annie! Now!'

'I am 'now-ing',' said Annie the red-nosed, the red-eyed, the angry. Annie was always a little angry and these soldiers, this occupation, did not improve her temper. Indeed, what for years had been considered simply a bad disposition was suddenly become a patriotic emotion. Annie had gained some little reputation as an exponent of liberty by throwing hot water on the soldiers. She would have thrown it on anyone who cluttered up her porch, but it just happened that she had become a heroine; and since anger had been the beginning of her success, Annie went on to new successes by whipping herself into increased and constant anger.

'Don't scuff the bottom,' Joseph said. The table wedged in the doorway. 'Steady!' Joseph warned.

'I am steady,' said Annie.

Joseph stood off and studied the table, and Annie crossed her arms and glared at him. He tested a leg. 'Don't push,' he said. 'Don't push so hard.' And by himself he got the table through while Annie followed with crossed arms. 'Now, up she goes,' said Joseph, and at last Annie helped him settle it on four legs and move it to the centre of the room. 'There,' Annie said. 'If His Excellency hadn't told me to, I wouldn't have done it. What right have they got moving tables around?'

'What right coming at all?' said Joseph.

'None,' said Annie.

'None,' repeated Joseph. 'I see it like they have no right at all, but they do it, with their guns and their parachutes; they do it, Annie.'

'They got no right,' said Annie. 'What do they want with a table in here, anyway? This isn't a dining-room.'

Joseph moved a chair up to the table and he set it carefully at the right distance from the table, and he adjusted it. 'They're going to hold a trial,' he said. 'They're going to try Alexander Morden.'

'Molly Morden's husband?'

'Molly Morden's husband.'

'For bashing that fellow with a pick?'

'That's right,' said Joseph.

'But he's a nice man,' Annie said. 'They've got no right to try him. He gave Molly a big red dress for her birthday. What right have they got to try Alex?'

'Well,' Joseph explained, 'he killed this fellow.'

'Suppose he did; the fellow ordered Alex around. I heard about it. Alex doesn't like to be ordered. Alex's been an alderman in his time, and his father, too. And Molly Morden makes a nice cake,' Annie said charitably. 'But her frosting gets too hard. What'll they do with Alex?'

'Shoot him,' Joseph said gloomily.

'They can't do that.'

'Bring up the chairs, Annie. Yes, they can. They'll just do it.'

Annie shook a very rigid finger in his face. 'You remember my words,' she said angrily. 'People aren't going to like it if they hurt Alex. People like Alex. Did he ever hurt anybody before? Answer me that!'

'No,' said Joseph.

'Well, there, you see! If they hurt Alex, people are going to be mad and I'm going to be mad. I won't stand for it!'

'What will you do?' Joseph asked her.

'Well. I'll kill some of them myself,' said Annie.

'And then they'll shoot you,' said Joseph.

'Let them! I tell you Joseph, things can go too far–tramping in and out all hours of the night, shooting people.'

Joseph adjusted a chair at the head of the table, and he became in some curious way a conspirator. He said softly, 'Annie.'

She paused and, sensing his tone, walked nearer to him. He said, 'Can you keep a secret?'

She looked at him with a little admiration, for he had never had a secret before. 'Yes. What is it?'

'Well, William Deal and Walter Doggel got away last night.'

'Got away? Where?'

'They got away to England, in a boat.'

Annie sighed with pleasure and anticipation. 'Does everybody know it?'

'Well, not everybody,' said Joseph. 'Everybody but–' and he pointed a quick thumb towards the ceiling.

'When did they go? Why didn't I hear about it?'

'You were busy.' Joseph's voice and face were cold. 'You know that Corell?'

'Yes.'

Joseph came close to her. 'I don't think he's going to live long.'

'What do you mean?' Annie asked.

'Well, people are talking.'

Annie sighed with tension. 'Ah-h-h!'

Joseph at last had opinions. 'People are getting together,' he said. 'They don't like to be conquered. Things are going to happen. You keep your eyes peeled, Annie. There're going to be things for you to do.'

Annie asked, 'How about His Excellency? What's he going to do? How does His Excellency stand?'

'Nobody knows,' said Joseph. 'He doesn't say anything.'

'He wouldn't be against us,' Annie said.

'He doesn't say,' said Joseph.

The knob turned on the left-hand door, and Mayor Orden came in slowly. He looked tired and old. Behind him Doctor Winter walked. Orden said, 'That's good, Joseph. Thank you, Annie. It looks very well.'

They went out and Joseph looked back through the door for a moment before he closed it.

Mayor Orden walked to the fire and turned to warm his back. Doctor Winter pulled out the chair at the head of the table and sat down. 'I wonder how much longer I can hold this position?' Orden said. 'The people don't quite trust me, neither does the enemy. I wonder whether this is a good thing.'

'I don't know,' said Winter. 'You trust yourself, don't you? There's no doubt in your own mind?'

'Doubt? No. I am the Mayor. I don't understand many things.' He pointed to the table. 'I don't know why they have to hold this trial in here. They're going to try Alex Morden here for murder. You remember Alex? He has that pretty little wife, Molly.'

'I remember,' said Winter. 'She used to teach in the grammar school. Yes, I remember. She's so pretty, she hated to get glasses when she needed them. Well, I guess Alex killed an officer, all right. Nobody's questioned that.'

Mayor Orden said bitterly, 'Nobody questions it. But why do they try him? Why don't they shoot him? This is not a matter of doubt or certainty, justice or injustice. There's none of that here. Why must they try him–and in my house?'

Winter said, 'I would guess it is for the show. There's an idea about it; if you go through the form of a thing, you have it, and sometimes people are satisfied with the form of a thing. We had an army–soldiers with guns–but it wasn't an army, you see. The invaders will have a trial and hope to convince the people that there is justice involved. Alex did kill the captain, you know.'

'Yes, I see that,' Orden said.

And Winter went on, 'If it comes from your house, where the people expect justice–'

He was interrupted by the opening of the door to the right. A young woman entered. She was about thirty and quite pretty. She carried her glasses in her hand. She was dressed simply and neatly and she was very excited. She said quickly, 'Annie told me to come right in, sir.'

'Why, of course,' said the Mayor. 'You're Molly Morden.'

'Yes, sir, I am. They say that Alex is to be tried and shot.'

Orden looked down at the floor for a moment, and Molly went on, 'They say you will sentence him. It will be your words that send him out.'

Orden looked up, startled. 'What's this? Who says this?'

'The people in the town.' She held herself very straight and she asked, half pleadingly, half demandingly, 'You wouldn't do that, would you, sir?'

'How could the people know what I don't know?' he said.

'That is a great mystery,' said Doctor Winter. 'That is a mystery that has disturbed rulers all over the world–how the people know. It disturbs the invaders now, I am told, how news runs through censorships, how the truth of things fights free of control. It is a great mystery.'

The girl looked up, for the room had suddenly darkened, and she seemed to be afraid. 'It's a cloud,' she said. 'There's word snow is on the way, and it's early, too.' Doctor Winter went to the window and squinted up at the sky, and he said, 'Yes, it's a big cloud; maybe it will pass over.'

Mayor Orden switched on a lamp that made only a little circle of light. He switched it off again and said, 'A light in the daytime is a lonely thing.'

Now Molly came near to him again. 'Alex is not a murdering man,' she said. 'He's a quick-tempered man, but he's never broken a law. He's a respected man.'

Orden rested his hand on her shoulder and he said, 'I have known Alex since he was a little boy. I knew his father and his grandfather. His grandfather was a bear-hunter in the old days. Did you know that?'

Molly ignored him. 'You wouldn't sentence Alex?'

'No,' he said. 'How could I sentence him?'

'The people said you would, for the sake of order.'

Mayor Orden stood behind a chair and gripped its back with his hands. 'Do the people want order, Molly?'

'I don't know,' she said. 'They want to be free.'

'Well, do they know how to go about it? Do they know what method to use against an armed enemy?'

'No,' Molly said, 'I don't think so.'

'You are a bright girl, Molly; do you know?'

'No, sir, but I think the people feel that they are beaten if they are docile. They want to show these soldiers they're unbeaten.'

'They've had no chance to fight. It's no fight to go against machine-guns,' Doctor Winter said.

Orden said, 'When you know what they want to do, will you tell me, Molly?'

She looked at him suspiciously. 'Yes–' she said.

'You mean "no". You don't trust me.'

'But how about Alex?' she questioned.

'I'll not sentence him. He has committed no crime against our people,' said the Mayor.

Molly was hesitant now. She said, 'Will they–will they kill Alex?'

Orden stared at her and he said, 'Dear child, my dear child.'

She held herself rigid. 'Thank you.'

Orden came close to her and she said weakly, 'Don't touch me. Please don't touch me. Please don't touch me.' And his hand dropped. For a moment she stood still, then she turned stiffly and went out of the door.

She had just closed the door when Joseph entered. 'Excuse me, sir, the colonel wants to see you. I said you were busy. I knew she was here. And Madame wants to see you, too.'

Orden said, 'Ask Madame to come in.'

Joseph went out and Madame came in immediately.

'I don't know how I can run a house,' she began; 'it's more people than the house can stand. Annie's angry all the time.'

'Hush!' Orden said.

Madame looked at him in amazement. 'I don't know what–'

'Hush!' he said. 'Sarah, I want you to go to Alex Morden's house. Do you understand? I want you to stay with Molly Morden while she needs you. Don't talk, just stay with her.'

Madame said, 'I've a hundred things–'

'Sarah, I want you to stay with Molly Morden. Don't leave her alone. Go now.'

She comprehended slowly. 'Yes,' she said. 'Yes, I will. When will it be over?'

'I don't know,' he said. 'I'll sent Annie when it's time.'

She kissed him lightly on the cheek and went out. Orden walked to the door and called, 'Joseph, I'll see the colonel now.'

Lanser came in. He had on a new pressed uniform with a little ornamental dagger at the belt. He said, 'Good morning, Your Excellency. I wish to speak to you informally.' He glanced at Doctor Winter. 'I should like to speak to you alone.'

Winter went slowly to the door and as he reached it Orden said, 'Doctor!'

Winter turned. 'Yes?'

'Will you come back this evening?'

'You will have work for me?' the doctor asked.

'No–no. I just won't like to be alone.'

'I will be here,' said the doctor.

'And, Doctor, do you think Molly looked all right?'

'Oh, I think so. Close to hysteria, I guess. But she's good stock. She's good, strong stock. She is a Kenderly, you know.'

'I'd forgotten,' Orden said. 'Yes, she is a Kenderly, isn't she?'

Doctor Winter went out and shut the door gently behind him.

Lanser had waited courteously. He watched the door close. He looked at the table and the chairs about it. 'I will not tell you, sir, how sorry I am about this. I wish it had not happened.'

Mayor Orden bowed, and Lanser went on: 'I like you, sir, and I respect you, but I have a job to do. You surely recognise that.'

Orden did not answer. He looked straight into Lanser's eyes.

'We do not act alone or on our own judgement.'

Between sentences Lanser waited for an answer, but he received none.

'There are rules laid down for us, rules made in the capital. This man has killed an officer.'

At last Orden answered, 'Why didn't you shoot him then? That was the time to do it?'

Lanser shook his head. 'If I agreed with you, it would make no difference. You know as well as I that punishment is largely for the purpose of deterring the potential criminal. Thus, since punishment is for others than the punished, it must be publicised. It must even be dramatised.' He thrust a finger in back of his belt and flipped his little dagger.

Orden turned away and looked out of the window at the dark sky. 'It will snow tonight,' he said.

'Mayor Orden, you know our orders are inexorable. We must get the coal. If your people are not orderly, we will have to restore that order by force.' His voice grew stern. 'We must shoot people if necessary. If you wish to save your people from hurt, you must help us to keep order. Now, it is considered wise by my government that punishment emanate from the local authority. It makes for a more orderly situation.'

Orden said softly, 'So the people did know. That is a mystery.' And louder he said, 'You wish me to pass sentence of death on Alexander Morden after a trial here?'

'Yes, and you will prevent much bloodshed later if you will do it.'

Orden went to the table and pulled out the big chair at its head and sat down. And suddenly he seemed to be the judge, with Lanser the culprit. He drummed with his fingers on the table. He said, 'You and your government do not understand. In all the world yours is the only government and people with a record of defeat after defeat for centuries and every time because you did not understand people.' He paused. 'This principle does not work. First, I am the Mayor. I have no right to pass sentence of death. There is no one in this community with that right. If I should do it, I would be breaking the law as much as you.'

'Breaking the law?' said Lanser.

'You killed six men when you came in. Under our law you are guilty of murder, all of you. Why do you go into this nonsense of law, Colonel? There is no law between you and us. This is war. Don't you know you will have to kill all of us or we in time will kill all of you? You destroyed the law when you came in, and a new law took its place. Don't you know that?'

Lanser said, 'May I sit down?'

'Why do you ask? This is another lie. You could make me stand if you wished.'

Lanser said, 'No; it is true, whether you believe it or not: personally, I have respect for you and your office, and'–he put his forehead in his hand for a moment–'you see, what I think, sir, I, a man of a certain age and certain memories, is of no importance. I might agree with you, but that would change nothing. The military, the political, pattern I work in has certain tendencies which are invariable.'

Orden said, 'And these tendencies and practices have been proven wrong in every single case since the beginning of the world.'

Lanser said bitterly, 'I, an individual man with certain memories, might agree with you, might even add that one of the tendencies of the military mind and pattern is an inability to learn, an inability to see beyond the killing which is its job. But I am not a man subject to memories. The coal-miner must be shot publicly, because the theory is that others will then restrain themselves from killing our men.'

Orden said, 'We need not talk any more, then.'

'Yes, we must talk. We want you to help.'

Orden sat quietly for a while and then he said, 'I'll tell you what I'll do. How many men were on the machine-guns which killed our soldiers?'

'Oh, not more than twenty, I guess,' said Lanser.

'Very well. If you will shoot them, I will condemn Morden.'

'You're not serious!' said the colonel.

'But I am serious.'

'This can't be done. You know it.'

'I know it,' said Orden. 'And what you ask cannot be done.'

Lanser said, 'I suppose I knew. Corell will have to be Mayor after all.' He looked up quickly. 'You will stay for the trial?'

'Yes, I'll stay. Then Alex won't be so lonely.'

Lanser looked at him and smiled a little sadly. 'We have taken on a job, haven't we?'

'Yes,' said the Mayor, 'the one impossible job in the world, the one thing that can't be done.'

'And that is?'

'To break a man's spirit permanently.'

Orden's head sank a little towards the table, and he said, without looking up, 'It's started to snow. It didn't wait for night. I like the sweet, cool smell of snow.'

4

By eleven o'clock the snow was falling heavily in big, soft puffs and the sky was not visible at all. People were scurrying through the falling snow, and snow piled up in the doorways and it piled up on the statue in the public square and on the rails from the mine to the harbour. Snow piled up and the little cartwheels skidded as they were pushed along. And over the town there hung a blackness that was deeper than the cloud, and over the town there hung a sullenness and a dry, growing hatred. The people did not stand in the streets long, but they entered the doors and the doors closed and there seemed to be eyes looking from behind the curtains, and when the military went through the street or when the patrol walked down the main street, the eyes were on the patrol, cold and sullen. And in the shops people came to buy little things for lunch and they asked for the goods and got it and paid for it and exchanged no good-day with the seller.

In the little palace drawing-room the lights were on and the lights shone on the falling snow outside the window. The court was in session. Lanser sat at the head of the table with Hunter on his right, then Tonder, and, at the lower end, Captain Loft with a little pile of papers in front of him. On the opposite side, Mayor Orden sat on the colonel's left and Prackle was next to him–Prackle, who scribbled on his pad of paper. Beside the table two guards stood with bayonets fixed, with helmets on their heads, and they were little wooden images. Between them was Alex Morden, a big young man with a wide, low forehead, with deep-set eyes and a long, sharp nose. His chin was firm and his mouth sensual and wide. He was wide of shoulder, narrow of hip, and in front of him his manacled hands clasped and unclasped. He was dressed in black trousers, a blue shirt open at the neck, and a dark coat shiny from wear.

Captain Loft read from the paper in front of him: '"When ordered back to work, he refused to go, and when the order was repeated, the prisoner attacked Captain Loft with the pick-axe he carried. Captain Bentick interposed his body–" '

Mayor Orden coughed and, when Loft stopped reading, said, 'Sit down, Alex. One of you guards get him a chair.' The guard turned and pulled up a chair unquestioningly.

Loft said, 'It is customary for the prisoner to stand.'

'Let him sit down,' Orden said. 'Only we will know. You can report that he stood.'

'It is not customary to falsify reports,' said Loft.

'Sit down, Alex,' Orden repeated.

And the big young man sat down and his manacled hands were restless in his lap.

Loft began, 'This is contrary to all–'

The colonel said, 'Let him be seated.'

Captain Loft cleared his throat. ' "Captain Bentick interposed his body and received a blow on the head which crushed his skull." A medical report is appended. Do you wish me to read it?'

'No need,' said Lanser. 'Make it as quick as you can.'

' "These facts have been witnessed by several of our soldiers, whose statements are attached. This military court finds the prisoner is guilty of murder and recommends a death sentence." Do you wish me to read the statements of the soldiers?'

Lanser sighed. 'No.' He turned to Alex. 'You don't deny that you killed the captain, do you?'

Alex smiled sadly. 'I hit him,' he said. 'I don't know that I killed him.'

Orden said, 'Good work, Alex!' And the two looked at each other as friends.

Loft said, 'Do you mean to imply that he was killed by someone else?'

'I don't know,' said Alex. 'I only hit him, and then somebody hit me.'

Colonel Lanser said, 'Do you want to offer any explanation? I can't think of anything that will change the sentence, but we will listen.'

Loft said, 'I respectfully submit that the colonel should not have said that. It indicates that the court is not impartial.'

Orden laughed dryly. The colonel looked at him and smiled a little. 'Have you any explanation?' he repeated.

Alex lifted a hand to gesture and the other came with it. He looked embarrassed and put them in his lap again. 'I was mad,' he said. 'I have a pretty bad temper. He said I must work. I am a free man. I got mad and I hit him. I guess I hit him hard. It was the wrong man.' He pointed at Loft. 'That's the man I wanted to hit, that one.'

Lanser said, 'It doesn't matter whom you wanted to hit. Anybody would have been the same. Are you sorry you did it?' He said aside to the table, 'It would look well in the record if he were sorry.'

'Sorry?' Alex said. 'I am not sorry. He told me to go to work–me, a free man! I used to be alderman. He said I had to work.'

'But if the sentence is death, won't you be sorry then?'

Alex sank his head and really tried to think honestly. 'No,' he said. 'You mean, would I do it again?'

'That's what I mean.'

'No,' Alex said thoughtfully, 'I don't think I'm sorry.'

Lanser said, 'Put in the record that the prisoner was overcome with remorse. Sentence is automatic. Do you understand?' he said to Alex. 'The court has no leeway. The court finds you guilty and sentences you to be shot immediately. I do not see any reason to torture you with this any more. Captain Loft, is there anything I have forgotten?'

'You've forgotten me,' said Orden. He stood up and pushed back his chair and stepped over to Alex. And Alex, from long habit, stood up respectfully. 'Alexander, I am the elected Mayor.'

'I know it, sir.'

'Alex, these men are invaders. They have taken our country by surprise and treachery and force.'

Captain Loft said, 'Sir, this should not be permitted.'

Lanser said, 'Hush! Is it better to hear it, or would you rather it were whispered?'

Orden went on as though he had not been interrupted. 'When they came, the people were confused and I was confused. We did not know what to do or think. Yours was the first clear act. Your private anger was the beginning of a public anger. I know it is said in town that I am acting with these men. I can show the town, but you–you are going to die. I want you to know.'

Alex dropped his head and then raised it. 'I know, sir.'

Lanser said, 'Is the squad ready?'

'Outside, sir.'

'Who is commanding?'

'Lieutenant Tonder, sir.'

Tonder raised his head and his chin was hard and he held his breath.

Orden said softly, 'Are you afraid, Alex?'

And Alex said, 'Yes, sir.'

'I can't tell you not to be. I would be, too, and so would these young–gods of war.'

Lanser said, 'Call your squad.' Tonder got up quickly and went to the door. 'They're here, sir.' He opened the door wide and the helmeted men could be seen.

Orden said, 'Alex, go, knowing that these men will have no rest, no rest at all until they are gone, or dead. You will make the people one. It's a sad knowledge and little enough gift to you, but it is so. No rest at all.'

Alex shut his eyes tightly. Mayor Orden leaned close and kissed him on the cheek. 'Good-bye, Alex,' he said.

The guard took Alex by the arm and the young man kept his eyes tightly closed, and they guided him through the door. The squad faced about, and their feet marched away down out of the house and into the snow, and the snow muffled their footsteps.

The men about the table were silent. Orden looked towards the window and saw a little round spot being rubbed clear of snow by a quick hand. He stared at it, fascinated, and then he looked quickly away. He said to the colonel, 'I hope you know what you are doing.'

Captain Loft gathered his papers and Lanser asked, 'In the square, Captain?'

'Yes, in the square. It must be public,' Loft said.

And Orden said, 'I hope you know.'

'Man,' said the colonel, 'whether we know or not, it is what must be done.'

Silence fell on the room and each man listened. And it was not long. From the distance there came a crash of firing. Lanser sighed deeply. Orden put his hand to his forehead and filled his lungs deeply. Then there was a shout outside. The glass of the window crashed inward and Lieutenant Prackle wheeled about. He brought his hand up to his shoulder and stared at it.

Lanser leaped up, crying, 'So, it starts! Are you badly hurt, Lieutenant?'

'My shoulder,' said Prackle.

Lanser took command. 'Captain Loft, there will be tracks in the snow. Now, I want every house searched for firearms. I want every man who has one taken hostage. You, sir,' he said to the Mayor, 'are placed in protective custody. And understand this, please: we will shoot, five, ten, a hundred for one.'

Orden said quietly, 'A man of certain memories.'

Lanser stopped in the middle of an order. He looked over slowly at the Mayor and for a moment they understood each other. And then Lanser straightened his shoulders. 'A man of no memories!' he said sharply. And then:

'I want every weapon in town gathered. Bring in everyone who resists. Hurry, before their tracks are filled.'

The staff found their helmets and loosed their pistols and started out. And Orden went to the broken window. He said sadly, 'The sweet, cool smell of the snow.'

5

The days and the weeks dragged on, and the months dragged on. The snow fell and melted and fell and melted and finally fell and stuck. The dark buildings of the little town wore bells and hats and eyebrows of white and there were trenches through the snow to the doorways. In the harbour the coal barges came empty and went away loaded, but the coal did not come out of the ground easily. The good miners made mistakes. They were clumsy and slow. Machinery broke and took a long time to fix. The people of the conquered country settled in a slow, silent, waiting revenge. The men who had been traitors, who had helped the invaders–and many of them believed it was for a better state and an ideal way of life–found that the control they took was insecure, that the people they had known looked at them coldly and never spoke.

And there was death in the air, hovering and waiting. Accidents happened on the railway which clung to the mountains and connected the little town with the rest of the nation. Avalanches poured down on the tracks and rails were spread. No train could move unless the tracks were first inspected. People were shot in reprisal and it made no difference. Now and then a group of young men escaped and went to England. And the English bombed the coal-mine and did some damage and killed some of both their friends and their enemies. And it did no good. The cold hatred grew with the winter, the silent, sullen hatred, the waiting hatred. The food supply was controlled–issued to the obedient and withheld from the disobedient–so that the whole population turned coldly obedient. There was a point where food could not be withheld, for a starving man cannot mine coal, cannot lift and carry. And the hatred was deep in the eyes of the people, beneath the surface.

Now it was that the conqueror was surrounded, the men of the battalion alone among silent enemies, and no man might relax his guard for even a moment. If he did, he disappeared, and some snowdrift received his body. If he went alone to a woman, he disappeared, and some snowdrift received his body. If he drank, he disappeared. The men of the battalion could sing only together, could dance only together, and dancing gradually stopped and the singing expressed a longing for home. Their talk was of friends and relatives who loved them and their longings were for warmth and love, because a man can be a soldier for only so many hours a day and for only so many months in a year, and then he wants to be a man again, wants girls and drinks and music and laughter and ease, and when these are cut off, they become irresistibly desirable.

And the men thought always of home. The men of the battalion came to detest the place they had conquered, and they were curt with the people and the people were curt with them, and gradually a little fear began to grow in the conquerors, a fear that it would never be over, that they could never relax and go home, a fear that one day they would crack and be hunted through the mountains like rabbits, for the conquered never relaxed their hatred. The patrols, seeing lights, hearing laughter, would be drawn as to a fire, and when they came near, the laughter stopped, the warmth went out, and the people were cold and obedient. And the soldiers, smelling warm food from the little restaurants, went in and ordered the warm food and found that it was oversalted or overpeppered.

Then the soldiers read the news from home and from the other conquered countries, and the news was always good, and for a while they believed it, and then after a while they did not believe it any more. And every man carried in his heart the terror. 'If home crumbled, they would not tell us, and then it would be too late. These people will not spare us. They will kill us all.' They remembered stories of their men retreating through Belgium and retreating out of Russia. And the more literate remembered the frantic, tragic retreat from Moscow, when every peasant's pitchfork tasted blood and the snow was rotten with bodies.

And they knew when they cracked, or relaxed, or slept too long, it would be the same here, and their sleep was restless and their days were nervous. They asked questions their officers could not answer because they did not know. They were not told, either. They did not believe the reports from home, either.

Thus it came about that the conquerors grew afraid of the conquered and their nerves wore thin and they shot at shadows in the night. The cold, sullen silence was with them always. Then three soldiers went insane in a week and cried all night and all day until they were sent away home. And others might have gone insane if they had not heard that mercy deaths await the insane at home, and a mercy death is a terrible thing to think of. Fear crept in on the men in their billets and it made them sad, and it crept into the patrols and it made them cruel.

The year turned and the nights grew long. It was dark at three o'clock in the afternoon and not light again until nine in the morning. The jolly lights did not shine out on the snow, for by law every window must be black against the bombers. And yet when the English bombers came over, some light always appeared near the coal-mine. Sometimes the sentries shot a man with a lantern and once a girl with a flashlight. And it did no good. Nothing was cured by the shooting.

And the officers were a reflection of their men, more restrained because their training was more complete, more resourceful because they had more responsibility but the same fears were a little deeper buried in them, the same longings were more tightly locked in their hearts. And they were under a double strain, for the conquered people watched them for mistakes and their own men watched them for weakness, so that their spirits were taut to the breaking-point. The conquerors were under the terrible spiritual siege and everyone knew, conquered and conquerors, what would happen when the first crack appeared.

From the upstairs room of the Mayor's palace the comfort seemed to have gone. Over the windows black paper was tacked tightly and there were little piles of precious equipment about the room–the instruments and equipment that could not be jeopardised, the glasses and masks and helmets. And discipline here at least was laxer, as though these officers knew there must be some laxness somewhere or the machine would break. On the table were two petrol lanterns which threw a hard, brilliant light and they made great shadows on the walls, and their hissing was an undercurrent in the room.

Major Hunter went on with his work. His drawing-board was permanently ready now, for the bombs tore out his work nearly as fast as he put it in. And he had little sorrow, for to Major Hunter building was life and here he had more building than he could project or accomplish. He sat at his drawing-board with a light behind him and his T-square moved up and down the board and his pencil was busy.

Lieutenant Prackle, his arm still in a sling, sat in a straight chair behind the centre table, reading an illustrated paper. At the end of the table Lieutenant Tonder was writing a letter. He held his pen pinched high and occasionally he looked up from his letter and gazed at the ceiling, to find words to put in his letter.

Prackle turned a page of the illustrated paper and he said, 'I can close my eyes and see every shop on this street here.' And Hunter went on with his work and Tonder wrote a few more words. Prackle continued, 'There is a restaurant right behind here. You can see it in the picture. It's called Burden's.'

Hunter did not look up. He said, 'I know the place. They had good scallops.'

'Sure, they did,' Prackle said. 'Everything was good there. Not a single bad thing did they serve. And their coffee–'

Tonder looked up from his letter and said, 'They won't be serving coffee now–or scallops.'

'Well, I don't know about that,' said Prackle. 'They did and they will again. And there was a waitress there.' He described her figure with his hand, with the good hand. 'Blonde, so and so.' He looked down at the magazine. 'She had the strangest eyes–has, I mean–always kind of moist-looking as though she had just been laughing or crying.' He glanced at the ceiling and he spoke softly. 'I was out with her. She was lovely. I wonder why I didn't go back oftener. I wonder if she's still there.'

Tonder said gloomily, 'Probably not. Working in a factory, maybe.'

Prackle laughed. 'I hope they aren't rationing girls at home.'

'Why not?' said Tonder.

Prackle said playfully, 'You don't care much for girls, do you? Not much, you don't!'

Tonder said, 'I like them for what girls are for. I don't let them crawl around my other life.'

And Prackle said tauntingly, 'It seems to me that they crawl all over you all the time.'

Tonder tried to change the subject. He said, 'I hate these damn lanterns. Major, when are you going to get that dynamo fixed?'

Major Hunter looked up slowly from his board and said, 'It should be done by now. I've got good men working on it. I'll double the guard on it from now on, I guess.'

'Did you get the fellow that wrecked it?' Prackle said.

And Hunter said grimly, 'It might be any one of five men. I got all five.' He went on musingly. 'It's so easy to wreck a dynamo if you know how. Just short it and it wrecks itself.' He said, 'The light ought to be on any time now.'

Prackle still looked at his magazine. 'I wonder when we will be relieved. I wonder when we will go home for a while, Major; wouldn't you like to go home for a rest?'

Hunter looked up from his work and his face was hopeless for a moment. 'Yes, of course.' He recovered himself. 'I've built this siding four times. I don't know why a bomb always knocks out this particular siding. I'm getting tired of this piece of track. I have to change the route every time because of the craters. There's no time to fill them in. The ground is frozen too hard. It seems to be too much work.'

Suddenly the electric lights came on and Tonder automatically reached out and turned off the two petrol lanterns. The hissing was gone from the room.

Tonder said, 'Thank God for that! That hissing gets on my nerves. It makes me think there's whispering.' He folded the letter he had been writing and he said, 'It's strange more letters don't come through. I've only had one in two weeks.'

Prackle said, 'Maybe nobody writes to you.'

'Maybe,' said Tonder. He turned to the Major. 'If anything happened–at home, I mean–do you think they would let us know–anything bad, I mean, any deaths or anything like that?'

Hunter said, 'I don't know.'

'Well,' Tonder went on. 'I would like to get out of this god-forsaken hole!'

Prackle broke in, 'I thought you were going to live here after the war?' And he imitated Tonder's voice. 'Put four or five farms together. Make a nice place, a kind of family seat. Wasn't that it? Going to be a little lord of the valley, weren't you? Nice, pleasant people, beautiful lawns and deer and little children. Isn't that the way it was, Tonder?'

As Prackle spoke, Tonder's hand dropped. Then he clasped his temples with his hands and he spoke with emotion. 'Be still! Don't talk like that! These people! These horrible people! These cold people! They never look at you.' He shivered. 'They never speak. They answer like dead men. They obey, these horrible people. And the girls are frozen!'

There was a light tap on the door and Joseph came in with a scuttle of coal. He moved silently through the room and set the scuttle down so softly that he made no noise, and he turned without looking up at anyone and went towards the door again. Prackle said loudly, 'Joseph!' And Jospeh turned without replying, without looking up, and he bowed very slightly. And Prackle said, still loudly, 'Joseph, is there any wine or any brandy?' Joseph shook his head.

Tonder started up from the table, his face wild with anger, and he shouted, 'Answer, you swine! Answer in words!'

Joseph did not look up. He spoke tonelessly. 'No, sir; no, sir, there is no wine.'

And Tonder said furiously, 'And no brandy?'

Joseph looked down and spoke tonelessly again. 'There is no brandy, sir.' He stood perfectly still.

'What do you want?' Tonder said.

'I want to go, sir.'

'Then go, god-damn it!'

Joseph turned and went silently out of the room and Tonder took a handkerchief out of his pocket and wiped his face. Hunter looked up at him and said, 'You shouldn't let him beat you so easily.'

Tonder sat down on his chair and put his hands to his temples and he said brokenly, 'I want a girl. I want to go home. I want a girl. There's a girl in this town, a pretty girl. I see her all the time. She has blonde hair. She lives beside the old-iron store. I want that girl.

Prackle said, 'Watch yourself. Watch your nerves.'

At that moment the lights went out again and the room was in darkness. Hunter spoke while the matches were being struck and an attempt was being made to light the lanterns; he said, 'I thought I had all of them. I must have missed one. But I can't be running down there all the time. I've got good men down there.'

Tonder lighted the first lantern and then he lighted the other, and Hunter spoke sternly to Tonder. 'Lieutenant, do your talking to us if you have to talk. Don't let the enemy hear you talk this way. There's nothing these people would like better than to know your nerves are getting thin. Don't let the enemy hear you.'

Tonder sat down again. The light was sharp on his face and the hissing filled the room. He said, 'That's it! The enemy's everywhere! Every man, every woman, even children! The enemy's everywhere. Their faces look out of doorways. The white faces behind the curtains, listening. We have beaten them, we have won everywhere, and they wait and obey, and they wait. Half the world is ours. Is it the same in other places, Major?'

And Hunter said, 'I don't know.'

'That's it,' Tonder said. 'We don't know. The reports–everything in hand. Conquered countries cheer our soldiers, cheer the new order.' His voice changed and grew soft and still softer. 'What do the reports say about us? Do they say we are cheered, loved, flowers in our paths? Oh, these horrible people waiting in the snow!'

And Hunter said, 'Now that's off your chest, do you feel better?'

Prackle had been beating the table softly with his good fist, and he said, 'He shouldn't talk that way. He should keep things to himself. He's a soldier, isn't he? Then let him be a soldier.'

The door opened quietly and Captain Loft came in, and there was snow on his helmet and snow on his shoulders. His nose was pinched and red and his overcoat collar was high about his ears. He took off his helmet and the snow fell on to the floor and he brushed his shoulders. 'What a job!' he said.

'More trouble?' Hunter asked.

'Always trouble. I see they've got your dynamo again. Well, I think I fixed the mine for a while.'

'What's your trouble?' Hunter asked.

'Oh, the usual thing with me–the slow-down and a wrecked dump car. I saw the wrecker, though. I shot him. I think I have a cure for it, Major, now. I just thought it up. I'll make each man take out a certain amount of coal. I can't starve the men or they can't work, but I've really got the answer. If the coal doesn't come out, no food for the families. We'll have the men eat at the mine, so there's no dividing at home. That ought to cure it. They work or their kids don't eat. I told them just now.'

'What did they say?'

Loft's eyes narrowed fiercely. 'Say? What do they ever say? Nothing! Nothing at all! But we'll see whether the coal comes out now.' He took off his coat and shook it, and his eyes fell on the entrance door and he saw that it was open a crack. He moved silently to the door, jerked it open, then closed it. 'I thought I had closed that door tight,' he said.

'You did,' said Hunter.

Prackle still turned the pages of his illustrated paper. His voice was normal again. 'Those are monster guns we're using in the east. I never saw one of them. Did you, Captain?'

'Oh, yes,' said Captain Loft. 'I've seen them fired. They're wonderful. Nothing can stand up against them.'

Tonder said, 'Captain, do you get much news from home?'

'A certain amount,' said Loft.

'Is everything well there?'

'Wonderful!' said Loft. 'The armies move ahead everywhere.'

'The British aren't defeated yet?'

'They are defeated in every engagement.'

'But they fight on?'

'A few air-raids, no more.'

'And the Russians?'

'It's all over.'

Tonder said insistently. 'But they fight on?'

'A little skirmishing, no more.'

Then we have just about won, haven't we, Captain?' Tonder asked.

'Yes, we have.'

Tonder looked closely at him and said, 'You believe this, don't you, Captain?'

Prackle broke in, 'Don't let him start that again!'

Loft scowled at Tonder. 'I don't know what you mean.'

Tonder said, 'I mean this: we'll be going home before long, won't we?'

'Well, the reorganisation will take some time,' Hunter said. 'The new order can't be put into effect in a day, can it?'

Tonder said, 'All our lives, perhaps?'

And Prackle said, 'Don't let him start it again!'

Loft came very close to Tonder and he said, 'Lieutenant, I don't like the tone of your questions. I don't like the tone of doubt.'

Hunter looked up and said, 'Don't be hard on him, Loft. He's tired. We're all tired.'

'Well, I'm tired, too,' said Loft, 'but I don't let treasonable doubts get in.'

Hunter said, 'Don't bedevil him, I tell you! Where's the colonel, do you know?'

'He's making out his report. He's asking for reinforcements,' said Loft. 'It's a bigger job than we thought.'

Prackle asked excitedly, 'Will he get them–the reinforcements?'

'How would I know?'

Tonder smiled. 'Reinforcements!' he said softly. 'Or maybe replacements. Maybe we could go home for a while.' And he said, smiling, 'Maybe I could walk down the street and people would say "Hello", and they'd say, "There goes a soldier", and they'd be glad for me and they'd be glad of me. And there'd be friends about, and I could turn my back to a man without being afraid.'

Prackle said, 'Don't start that again! Don't let him get out of hand again!'

And Loft said disgustedly, 'We have enough trouble now without having the staff go crazy.'

But Tonder went on, 'You really think replacements will come, Captain?'

'I didn't say so.'

'But you said they might.'

'I said I didn't know. Look, Lieutenant, we've conquered half the world. We must police it for a while. You know that.'

'But the other half?' Tonder asked.

'They will fight on hopelessly for a while,' said Loft.

'Then we must spread out all over.'

'For a while,' said Loft.

Prackle said nervously, 'I wish you'd make him shut up. I wish you would shut him up. Make him stop it.'

Tonder got out his handkerchief and blew his nose, and he spoke a little like a man out of his head. He laughed embarrassedly. He said, 'I had a funny dream. I guess it was a dream. Maybe it was a thought. Maybe a thought or a dream.'

Prackle said, 'Make him stop it, Captain!'

Tonder said, 'Captain, is this place conquered?'

'Of course,' said Loft.

A little note of hysteria crept into Tonder's laughter. He said, 'Conquered and we're afraid; conquered and we're surrounded.' His laughter grew shrill. 'I had a dream–or a thought–out in the snow with the black shadows and the faces in the doorways, the cold faces behind curtains. I had a thought or a dream.'

Prackle said, 'Make him stop!'

Tonder said, 'I dreamed the Leader was crazy.'

And Loft and Hunter laughed together, and Loft said, 'The enemy have found out how crazy. I'll have to write that one home. The papers would print that one. The enemy have learned how crazy the Leader is.'

And Tonder went on laughing. 'Conquest after conquest, deeper and deeper into molasses.' His laughter choked him and he coughed into his handkerchief. 'Maybe the Leader is crazy. Flies conquer the flypaper! Flies captured two hundred miles of new flypaper!' His laughter was growing more hysterical now.

Prackle leaned over and shook him with his good hand. 'Stop it! You stop it! You have no right!'

And gradually Loft recognised that the laughter was hysterical and he stepped closer to Tonder and slapped him in the face. He said, 'Lieutenant, stop it!'

Tonder's laughter went on and Loft slapped him again in the face and he said, 'Stop it, Lieutenant! Do you hear me!'

Suddenly Tonder's laughter stopped and the room was quiet except for the hissing of the lanterns. Tonder looked in amazement at his hand and he felt his bruised face with his hand and he looked at his hand again and his head sank down towards the table. 'I want to go home,' he said.

6

There was a little street not far from the town square where small peaked roofs and little shops were mixed up together. The snow was beaten down on the walks and in the streets, but it piled up on the fences and it puffed on the roof peaks. It drifted against the shuttered windows of the little houses. And into the yards paths were shovelled. The night was dark and cold and no light showed from the windows to attract the bombers. And no one walked in the streets, for the curfew was strict. The houses were dark lumps against the snow. Every little while the patrol of six men walked down the street, peering about, and each man carried a long flashlight. The hushed tramp of their feet sounded in the street, the squeaks of their boots on the packed snow. They were muffled figures deep in thick coats; under their helmets were knitted caps which came down over their ears and covered their chins and mouths. A little snow fell, only a little, like rice.

The patrol talked as they walked, and they talked of things that they longed for–of meat and of hot soup and of the richness of butter, of the prettiness of girls and of their smiles and of their lips and their eyes. They talked of these things and sometimes they talked of their hatred of what they were doing and of their loneliness.

A small, peak-roofed house beside the iron shop was shaped like the others and wore its snow cap like the others. No light came from its shuttered windows and its storm doors were tightly closed. But inside a lamp burned in the small living-room and the door to the bedroom was open and the door to the kitchen was open. An iron stove was against the back wall with a little coal fire burning in it. It was a warm, poor, comfortable room, the floor covered with worn carpet, the walls papered in warm brown with an old-fashioned *fleur-de-lis* figure in gold. And on the back wall were two pictures, one of fish lying dead on a plate of ferns and the other of grouse lying dead on a fir bough. On the right wall there was a picture of Christ walking on the waves towards the despairing fishermen. Two straight chairs were in the room and a couch covered with a bright blanket. There was a little round table in the middle of the room, on which stood a kerosene lamp with a round flowered shade on it, and the light in the room was warm and soft.

The inner door, which led to the passage, which in turn led to the storm door, was beside the stove.

In a cushioned old rocking-chair beside the table Molly Morden sat alone. She was unravelling the wool from an old blue sweater and winding the yarn on a ball. She had quite a large ball of it. And on the table beside her was her knitting with the needles sticking in it, and a large pair of scissors. Her glasses lay on the table beside her, for she did not need them for knitting. She was pretty and young and neat. Her golden hair was done up on the top of her head and a blue bow was in her hair. Her hands worked quickly with the ravelling. As she worked, she glanced now and then at the door to the passage. The wind whistled in the chimney softly, but it was a quiet night, muffled with snow.

Suddenly she stopped her work. Her hands were still. She looked towards the door and listened. The tramping feet of the patrol went by in the street and the sound of their voices could be heard faintly. The sound faded away. Molly ripped out new yarn and wound it on the ball. And again she stopped. There was a rustle at the door and then three short knocks. Molly put down her work and went to the door.

'Yes?' she called.

She unlocked the door and opened it and a heavily cloaked figure came in. It was Annie, the cook, red-eyed and wrapped in mufflers. She slipped in quickly, as though practised at getting speedily through doors and getting them closed again behind her. She stood there red-nosed, sniffling and glancing quickly around the room.

Molly said, 'Good evening, Annie. I didn't expect you tonight. Take your things off and get warm. It's cold out.'

Annie said, 'The soldiers brought winter early. My father always said a war brought bad weather, or bad weather brought a war. I don't remember which.'

'Take off your things and come to the stove.'

'I can't,' said Annie importantly. 'They're coming.'

'Who are coming?' Molly said.

'His Excellency,' said Annie, 'and the doctor and the two Anders boys.'

'Here?' Molly asked. 'What for?'

Annie held out her hand and there was a little package in it. 'Take it,' she said. 'I stole it from the colonel's plate. It's meat.'

And Molly unwrapped the little cake of meat and put it in her mouth and she spoke around her chewing. 'Did you get some?'

Annie said, 'I cook it, don't I? I always get some.'

'When are they coming?'

Annie sniffled. 'The Anders boys are sailing for England. They've got to go. They're hiding now.'

'Are they?' Molly asked. 'What for?'

'Well, it was their brother Jack, was shot today for wrecking that little car. The soldiers are looking for the rest of the family. You know how they do.'

'Yes,' Molly said, 'I know how they do. Sit down, Annie.'

'No time,' said Annie. 'I've got to get back and tell His Excellency it's all right here.'

Molly said, 'Did anybody see you come?'

Annie smiled proudly. 'No, I'm awful good at sneaking.'

'How will the Mayor get out?'

Annie laughed, 'Joseph is going to be in his bed in case they look in, right in his night-shirt, right next to Madame!' And she laughed again. She said, 'Joseph better lie pretty quiet.'

Molly said, 'It's an awful night to be sailing.'

'It's better than being shot.'

'Yes, so it is. Why is the Mayor coming here?'

'I don't know. He wants to talk to the Anders boys. I've got to go now, but I came to tell you.'

Molly said, 'How soon are they coming?'

'Oh, maybe half, maybe three-quarters of an hour,' Annie said. 'I'll come in first. Nobody bothers with old cooks.' She started for the door and she turned midway, and as though accusing Molly of saying the last words she said truculently, 'I'm not so old!' And she slipped out of the door and closed it behind her.

Molly went on knitting for a moment and then she got up and went to the stove and lifted the lid. The glow of the fire lighted her face. She stirred the fire and added a few lumps of coal and closed the stove again. Before she could get to her chair, there was a knocking on the outer door. She crossed the room and said to herself, 'I wonder what she forgot.' She went into the passage and she said, 'What do you want?'

A man's voice answered her. She opened the door and a man's voice said, 'I don't mean any harm. I don't mean any harm.'

Molly backed into the room and Lieutenant Tonder followed her in. Molly said, 'Who are you? What do you want? You can't come in here. What do you want?'

Lieutenant Tonder was dressed in his great grey overcoat. He entered the room and took off his helmet and he spoke pleadingly. 'I don't mean any harm. Please let me come in.'

Molly said, 'What do you want?'

She shut the door behind him and he said, 'Miss, I only want to talk, that's all. I want to hear you talk. That's all I want.'

'Are you forcing yourself on me?' Molly asked.

'No, Miss, just let me stay a little while and then I'll go.'

'What is it you want?'

Tonder tried to explain. 'Can you understand this–can you believe this? Just for a little while, can't we forget this war? Just for a little while. Just for a little while, can't we talk together like people–together?'

Molly looked at him for a long time and then a smile came to her lips. 'You don't know who I am, do you?'

Tonder said, 'I've seen you in the town. I know you're lovely. I know I want to talk to you.'

And Molly still smiled. She said softly, 'You don't know who I am.' She sat in her chair and Tonder stood like a child, looking very clumsy. Molly continued, speaking quietly: 'Why, you're lonely. It's as simple as that, isn't it?'

Tonder licked his lips and he spoke eagerly. 'That's it,' he said. 'You understand. I knew you would. I knew you'd have to.' His words came tumbling out. 'I'm lonely to the point of illness. I'm lonely in the quiet and the hatred.' And he said pleadingly; 'Can't we talk, just a little bit?'

Molly picked up her knitting. She looked quickly at the front door. 'You can stay not more than fifteen minutes. Sit down a little, Lieutenant.'

She looked at the door again. The house creaked. Tonder became tense and he said, 'Is someone here?'

'No, the snow is heavy on the roof. I have no man any more to push it down.'

Tonder said gently, 'Who did it? Was it something we did?'

And Molly nodded, looking far off. 'Yes.'

He sat down. 'I'm sorry.' After a moment he said, 'I wish I could do something. I'll have the snow pushed off the roof.'

'No,' said Molly, 'no.'

'Why not?'

'Because the people would think I had joined with you. They would expel me. I don't want to be expelled.'

Tonder said, 'Yes, I see how that would be. You all hate us. But I'll take care of you if you'll let me.'

Now Molly knew she was in control, and her eyes narrowed a little cruelly and she said, 'Why do you ask? You are the conqueror. Your men don't have to ask. They take what they want.'

'That's not what I want,' Tonder said. 'That's not the way I want it.'

And Molly laughed, still a little cruelly. 'You want me to like you, don't you, Lieutenant?'

He said simply, 'Yes,' and he raised his head and he said, 'You are so beautiful, so warm. Your hair is bright. Oh, I've seen no kindness in a woman's face for so long!'

'Do you see any in mine?' she asked.

He looked closely at her. 'I want to.'

She dropped her eyes at last. 'You're making love to me, aren't you, Lieutenant?'

He said clumsily, 'I want you to like me. Surely I want you to like me. Surely

I want to see that in your eyes. I have seen you in the streets. I have watched you pass by. I've given orders that you mustn't be molested. Have you been molested?'

And Molly said quietly, 'Thank you; no, I've not been molested.'

His words rushed on. 'Why, I've even written a poem for you. Would you like to see my poem?'

And she said sardonically, 'Is it a long poem? You have to go very soon.'

He said, 'No, it's a little tiny poem. It's a little bit of a poem.' He reached inside his tunic and brought out a folded paper and handed it to her. She leaned close to the lamp and put on her glasses and she read quietly:

> Your eyes in their deep heavens
> Possess me and will not depart;
> A sea of blue thoughts rushing
> And pouring over my heart.

She folded the paper and put it in her lap. 'Did you write this, Lieutenant?'

'Yes.'

She said a little tauntingly, 'To me?'

And Tonder answered uneasily, 'Yes.'

She looked at him steadily, smiling. 'You didn't write it, Lieutenant, did you?'

He smiled back like a child caught in a lie. 'No.'

Molly asked him, 'Do you know who did?'

Tonder said, 'Yes, Heine wrote it. It's "*Mit deinen blauen Augen*". I've always loved it.' He laughed embarrassedly and Molly laughed with him, and suddenly they were laughing together. He stopped laughing just as suddenly and a bleakness came into his eyes. 'I haven't laughed like this since forever.' He said, 'They told us the people would like us, would admire us. They do not. They only hate us.' And then he changed the subject as though he worked against time. 'You are so beautiful. You are as beautiful as the laughter.'

Molly said, 'You're beginning to make love to me, Lieutenant. You must go in a moment.'

And Tonder said, 'Maybe I want to make love to you. A man needs love. A man dies without love. His insides shrivel and his chest feels like a dry chip. I'm lonely.'

Molly got up from her chair. She looked nervously at the door and she walked to the stove and, coming back, her face grew hard and her eyes grew punishing and she said, 'Do you want to go to bed with me, Lieutenant?'

'I didn't say that! Why do you talk that way?'

Molly said cruelly, 'Maybe I'm trying to disgust you. I was married once. My husband is dead now. You see, I'm not a virgin.' Her voice was bitter.

Tonder said, 'I only want you to like me.'

And Molly said, 'I know. You are a civilised man. You know that love-making is more full and whole and delightful if there is liking, too.'

Tonder said, 'Don't talk that way! Please don't talk that way!'

Molly glanced quickly at the door. She said, 'We are conquered people, Lieutenant. You have taken the food away. I'm hungry. I'll like you better if you feed me.'

Tonder said, 'What are you saying?'

'Do I disgust you, Lieutenant? Maybe I'm trying to. My price is two sausages.'

Tonder said, 'You can't talk this way!'

'What about your own girls, Lieutenant, after the last war? A man could choose among your girls for an egg or a slice of bread. Do you want me for nothing, Lieutenant? Is the price too high?'

He said, 'You fooled me for a moment. But you hate me, too, don't you? I thought maybe you wouldn't.'

'No, I don't hate you,' she said. 'I'm hungry and–I hate you!'

Tonder said, 'I'll give you anything you need, but–'

And she interrupted him. 'You want to call it something else? You don't want a whore. Is that what you mean?'

Tonder said, 'I don't know what I mean. You make it sound full of hatred.'

Molly laughed. She said, 'It's not nice to be hungry. Two sausages, two fine, fat sausages can be the most precious things in the world.'

'Don't say those things,' he said. 'Please don't!'

'Why not? They're true.'

'They aren't true! This can't be true!'

She looked at him for a moment and then she sat down and her eyes fell to her lap and she said, 'No, it's not true. I don't hate you. I'm lonely too. And the snow is heavy on the roof.'

Tonder got up and moved near to her. He took one of her hands in both of his and he said softly, 'Please don't hate me. I'm only a lieutenant. I didn't ask to come here. You didn't ask to be my enemy. I'm only a man, not a conquering man.'

Molly's fingers encircled his hands for a moment and she said softly, 'I know; yes, I know.'

And Tonder said, 'We have some right to life in all this death.'

She put her hand to his cheek for a moment and she said, 'Yes.'

'I'll take care of you,' he said. 'We have some right to life in all the killing.' His hand rested on her shoulder. Suddenly she grew rigid and her eyes were wide and staring as though she saw a vision. His hand released her and he asked, 'What's the matter? What is it?' Her eyes stared straight ahead and he repeated, 'What is it?'

Molly spoke in a haunted voice. 'I dressed him like a little boy for his first day in school. And he was afraid. I buttoned his shirt and tried to comfort him, but he was beyond comfort. And he was afraid.'

Tonder said, 'What are you saying?'

And Molly seemed to see what she described. 'I don't know why they let him come home. He was confused. He didn't know what was happening. He didn't even kiss me when he went away. He was afraid, and very brave, like a little boy on his first day of school.'

Tonder stood up. 'That was your husband.'

Molly said, 'Yes, my husband. I went to the Mayor, but he was helpless. And then he marched away–not very well, not steadily–and you took him out and you shot him. It was more strange than terrible then. I didn't quite believe it then.'

Tonder said, 'Your husband!'

'Yes; and now, in the quiet house, I believe it. Now, with the heavy snow on the roof, I believe it. And in the loneliness before daybreak, in the half-warmed bed, I know it then.'

Tonder stood in front of her. His face was full of misery. 'Good night,' he said. 'God keep you. May I come back?'

And Molly looked at the wall and at the memory; 'I don't know,' she said.

'I'll come back.'

'I don't know.'

He looked at her and then he quietly went out of the door, and Molly still stared at the wall. 'God keep me.' She stayed for a moment staring at the wall. The door opened silently and Annie came in. Molly did not even see her.

Annie said disapprovingly, 'The door was open.'

Molly looked slowly towards her, her eyes still wide open. 'Yes, oh yes, Annie.'

'The door was open. There was a man came out. I saw him. He looked like a soldier.'

And Molly said, 'Yes, Annie.'

'Was it a soldier here?'

'Yes, it was a soldier.'

And Annie asked suspiciously, 'What was he doing here?'

'He came to make love to me.'

Annie said, 'Miss, what are you doing? You haven't joined them, have you? You aren't with them, like that Corell?'

'No, I'm not with them, Annie.'

Annie said, 'If the Mayor's here and they come back, it'll be your fault if anything happens; it'll be your fault!'

'He won't come back. I won't let him come back.'

But the suspicion stayed with Annie. She said, 'Shall I tell them to come in now? Do you say it's safe?'

'Yes, it's safe. Where are they?'

'They're out behind the fence,' said Annie.

'Tell them to come in.'

And while Annie went out, Molly got up and smoothed her hair and she shook her head, trying to be alive again. There was a little sound in the passage. Two tall, blond young men entered. They were dressed in pea-jackets and dark turtle-neck sweaters. They wore stocking caps perched on their heads. They were wind-burned and strong and they looked almost like twins, Will Anders and Tom Anders, the fishermen.

'Good evening, Molly. You've heard?'

'Annie told me. It's a bad night to go.'

Tom said, 'It's better than a clear night. The planes see you on a clear night. What's the Mayor want, Molly?'

'I don't know. I heard about your brother. I'm sorry.'

The two were silent and they looked embarrassed. Tom said, 'You know how it is, better than most.'

'Yes; I know.'

Annie came in the door again and she said in a hoarse whisper, 'They're here!' And Mayor Orden and Doctor Winter came in. They took off their coats and caps and laid them on the couch. Orden went to Molly and kissed her on the forehead.

'Good evening, dear.'

He turned to Annie. 'Stand in the passage, Annie. Give us one knock for the patrol, one when it's gone, and two for danger. You can leave the outer door open a crack so that you can hear if anyone comes.'

Annie said, 'Yes, sir.' She went into the passage and shut the door behind her.

Doctor Winter was at the stove, warming his hands. 'We got word you boys were going tonight.'

'We've got to go,' Tom said.

Orden nodded. 'Yes, I know. We heard you were going to take Mr Corell with you.'

Tom laughed bitterly. 'We thought it would be only right. We're taking his boat. We can't leave him around. It isn't good to see him in the streets.'

Orden said sadly, 'I wish he had gone away. It's just a danger to you, taking him.'

'It isn't good to see him in the streets.' Will echoed his brother. 'It isn't good for the people to see him here.'

Winter asked, 'Can you take him? Isn't he cautious at all?'

'Oh, yes, he's cautious, in a way. At twelve o'clock, though, he walks to his house usually. We'll be behind the wall. I think we can get him through his lower garden to the water. His boat's tied up there. We were on her today getting her ready.'

Orden repeated, 'I wish you didn't have to. It's just an added danger. If he makes a noise, the patrol might come.'

Tom said, 'He won't make a noise, and it's better if he disappears at sea. Some of the town people might get him and then there would be too much killing. No, it's better if he goes to sea.'

Molly took up her knitting again. She said, 'Will you throw him overboard?'

Will blushed. 'He'll go to sea, ma'am.' He turned to the Mayor. 'You wanted to see us, sir?'

'Why, yes, I want to talk to you. Doctor Winter and I have tried to think–there's so much talk about justice, injustice, conquest. Our people are invaded, but I don't think they're conquered.'

There was a sharp knock on the door and the room was silent. Molly's needles stopped, and the Mayor's outstretched hand remained in the air. Tom, scratching his ear, left his hand there and stopped scratching. Everyone in the room was motionless. Every eye was turned towards the door. Then, first faintly and then growing louder, there came the tramp of the patrol, the squeak of their boots in the snow, and the sound of their talking as they went by. They passed the door and their footsteps disappeared in the distance. There was a second tap on the door. And in the room the people relaxed.

Orden said, 'It must be cold out there for Annie.' He took up his coat from the couch and opened the inner door and handed his coat through. 'Put this around your shoulders, Annie,' he said and closed the door.

'I don't know what I'd do without her,' he said. 'She gets everywhere, she sees and hears everything.'

Tom said, 'We should be going pretty soon, sir.'

And Winter said, 'I wish you'd forget about Mr Corell.'

'We can't. It isn't good to see him in the streets.' He looked inquiringly at Mayor Orden.

Orden began slowly. 'I want to speak simply. This is a little town. Justice and injustice are in terms of little things. Your brother's shot and Alex Morden's shot. Revenge against a traitor. The people are angry and they have no way to fight back. But it's all in little terms. It's people against people, not idea against idea.'

Winter said, 'It's funny for a doctor to think of destruction, but I think all invaded people want to resist. We are disarmed; our spirits and bodies aren't enough. The spirit of a disarmed man sinks.'

Will Anders asked, 'What's all this for, sir? What do you want of us?'

'We want to fight them and we can't,' Orden said. 'They're using hunger on the people now. Hunger brings weakness. You boys are sailing for England. Maybe nobody will listen to you, but tell them from us–from a small town–to give us weapons.'

Tom asked, 'You want guns?'

Again there was a quick knock on the door and the people froze where they were, and from outside there came the sound of the patrol, but at double step, running. Will moved quickly towards the door. The running steps came abreast of the house. There were muffled orders and the patrol ran by, and there was a second tap at the door.

Molly said, 'They must be after somebody. I wonder who, this time.'

'We should be going,' Tom said uneasily. 'Do you want guns, sir? Shall we ask for guns?'

'No, tell them how it is. We are watched. Any move we make calls for reprisals. If we could have simple, secret weapons, weapons of stealth, explosives, dynamite to blow up rails, grenades, if possible, even poison.' He spoke angrily. 'This is no honourable war. This is a war of treachery and murder. Let us use the methods that have been used on us! Let the British bombers drop their big bombs on the works, but let them also drop us little bombs to use, to hide, to slip under the rails, under tanks. Then we will be armed, secretly armed. Then the invader will never know which of us is armed. Let the bombers bring us simple weapons. We will know how to use them!'

Winter broke in. 'They'll never know where it will strike. The soldiers, the patrol, will never know which of us is armed.'

Tom wiped his forehead. 'If we get through, we'll tell them, sir, but–well, I've heard it said that in England there are still men in power who do not care to put weapons in the hands of common people.'

Orden stared at him. 'Oh! I hadn't thought of that. Well, we can only see. If such people still govern England and America, the world is lost, anyway. Tell them what we say, if they will listen. We must have help, but if we get it'–his face grew very hard–'if we get it, we will help ourselves.'

Winter said, 'If they will even give us dynamite to hide, to bury in the ground to be ready against need, then the invader can never rest again, never! We will blow up his supplies.'

The room grew excited. Molly said fiercely, 'Yes, we could fight his rest, then. We could fight his sleep. We could fight his nerves and his certainties.'

Will asked quietly, 'Is that all, sir?'

'Yes.' Orden nodded. 'That's the core of it.'

'What if they won't listen?'

'You can only try, as you are trying the sea tonight.'

'Is that all, sir?'

The door opened and Annie came quietly in. Orden went on, 'That's all. If you have to go now, let me send Annie out to see that the way is clear.' He looked up and saw that Annie had come in. Annie said, 'There's a soldier coming up the path. He looks like the soldier that was here before. There was a soldier here with Molly before.'

The others looked at Molly. Annie said, 'I locked the door.'

'What does he want?' Molly asked. 'Why does he come back?'

There was a gentle knocking at the outside door. Orden went to Molly.

'What is this, Molly? Are you in trouble?'

'No,' she said, 'no! Go out the back way. You can get out through the back. Hurry, hurry out!'

The knocking continued on the front door. A man's voice called softly. Molly opened the door to the kitchen. She said, 'Hurry, hurry!'

The Mayor stood in front of her. 'Are you in trouble, Molly? You haven't done anything?'

Annie said coldly, 'It looks like the same soldier. There was a soldier here before.'

'Yes,' Molly said to the Mayor. 'Yes, there was a soldier here before.'

The Mayor said, 'What did he want?'

'He wanted to make love to me.'

'But he didn't?' Orden said.

'No,' she said, 'he didn't. Go now, and I'll take care.'

Orden said, 'Molly, if you're in trouble, let us help you.'

'The trouble I'm in no one can help me with,' she said. 'Go now,' and she pushed them out of the door.

Annie remained behind. She looked at Molly. 'Miss, what does this soldier want?'

'I don't know what he wants.'

'Are you going to tell him anything?'

'No.' Wonderingly, Molly repeated, 'No.' And then sharply she said, 'No, Annie, I'm not!'

Annie scowled at her. 'Miss, you'd better not tell him anything!' And she went out and closed the door behind her.

The tapping continued on the front door and a man's voice could be heard through the door.

Molly went to the centre lamp, and her burden was heavy on her. She looked down at the lamp. She looked at the table, and she saw the big scissors lying beside her knitting. She picked them up wonderingly by the blades. The blades slipped through her fingers until she held the long shears and she was holding them like a knife, and her eyes were horrified. She looked down into the lamp and the light flooded up in her face. Slowly she raised the shears and placed them inside her dress.

The tapping continued on the door. She heard the voice calling to her. She leaned over the lamp for a moment and then suddenly she blew out the light. The room was dark except for a spot of red that came from the coal stove. She opened the door. Her voice was strained and sweet. She called, 'I'm coming, Lieutenant. I'm coming!'

7

In the dark, clear night, a white, half-withered moon brought little light. The wind was dry and singing over the snow, a quiet wind that blew steadily, evenly from the cold point of the Pole. Over the land the snow lay very deep and dry as sand. The houses snuggled down in the hollows of banked snow, and their windows were dark and shuttered against the cold, and only a little smoke rose from the banked fires.

In the town the footpaths were frozen hard and packed hard. And the streets were silent, too, except when the miserable, cold patrol came by. The houses were dark against the night, and a little lingering warmth remained in the houses against the morning. Near the mine entrance the guards watched the sky and trained their instruments on the sky and turned their listening-instruments against the sky, for it was a clear night for bombing. On nights like this the feathered steel spindles came whistling down and roared to splinters. The land would be visible from the sky tonight, even though the moon seemed to throw little light.

Down towards one end of the village, among the small houses, a dog complained about the cold and the loneliness. He raised his nose to his god and gave a long and fulsome account of the state of the world as it applied to him. He was a practised singer with a full bell throat and great versatility of range and control. The six men of the patrol slogging dejectedly up and down the streets heard the singing of the dog, and one of the muffled soldiers said, 'Seems to me he's getting worse every night. I suppose we ought to shoot him.'

And another answered, 'Why? Let him howl. He sounds good to me. I used to have a dog at home that howled. I never could break him. Yellow dog. I don't mind the howl. They took my dog when they took the others,' he said factually, in a dull voice.

And the corporal said, 'Couldn't have dogs eating up food that was needed.'

'Oh, I'm not complaining. I know it was necessary. I can't plan the way the leaders do. It seems funny to me, though, that some people here have dogs, and they don't have even as much food as we have. They're pretty gaunt, though, dogs and people.'

'They're fools,' said the corporal. 'That's why they lost so quickly. They can't plan the way we can.'

'I wonder if we'll have dogs again after it's over,' said the soldier. 'I suppose we could get them from America or some place and start the breeds again. What kind of dogs do you suppose they have in America?'

'I don't know,' said the corporal. 'Probably dogs as crazy as everything else they have.' And he went on, 'Maybe dogs are no good, anyway. It might be just as well if we never bothered with them, except for police work.'

'It might be,' said the soldier. 'I've heard the Leader doesn't like dogs. I've heard they make him itch and sneeze.'

'You hear all kinds of things,' the corporal said. 'Listen!' The patrol stopped and from a great distance came the bee hum of planes.

'There they come,' the corporal said. 'Well, there aren't any lights. It's been two weeks, hasn't it, since they came before?'

'Twelve days,' said the soldier.

The guards at the mine heard the high drone of the planes. 'They're flying high,' a sergeant said. And Captain Loft tilted his head back so that he could see under the rim of his helmet. 'I judge over 20,000 feet,' he said. 'Maybe they're going on over.'

'Aren't very many.' The sergeant listened. 'I don't think there are more than three of them. Shall I call the battery?'

'Just see they're alert, and then call Colonel Lanser–no, don't call him. Maybe they aren't coming here. They're nearly over and they haven't started to dive yet.'

'Sounds to me like they're circling. I don't think there are more than two,' the sergeant said.

In their beds the people heard the planes and they squirmed deep into their feather-beds and listened. In the palace of the Mayor the little sound awakened Colonel Lanser, and he turned over on his back and looked at the dark ceiling with wide-open eyes, and he held his breath to listen better and then his heart beat so that he could not hear as well as he could when he was breathing. Mayor Orden heard the planes in his sleep and they made a dream for him and he moved and whispered in his sleep.

High in the air the two bombers circled, mud-coloured planes. They cut their throttles and soared, circling. And from the belly of each one tiny little objects dropped, hundreds of them, one after another. They plummeted a few feet and then little parachutes opened and drifted small packages silently and slowly downward towards the earth, and the planes raised their throttles and gained altitude, and then cut their throttles and circled again, and more of the little objects plummeted down, and then the planes turned and flew back in the direction from which they had come.

The tiny parachutes floated like thistledown and the breeze spread them out and distributed them as seeds on the ends of thistledown are distributed. They drifted so slowly and landed so gently that sometimes the ten-inch packages of dynamite stood upright in the snow, and the little parachutes folded gently down around them. They looked black against the snow. They landed in the white fields and among the woods of the hills and they landed in trees and hung down from the branches. Some of them landed on the house-tops of the little town, some in the small front yards, and one landed and stood upright in the snow crown on top of the head of the village statue of St Albert the Missionary.

One of the little parachutes came down in the street ahead of the patrol and the sergeant said: 'Careful! It's a time bomb.'

'It ain't big enough,' a soldier said.

'Well, don't go near it.' The sergeant had his flashlight out and he turned it on the object, a little parachute no bigger than a handkerchief, coloured light blue, and hanging from it a package wrapped in blue paper.

'Now don't anybody touch it,' the sergeant said. 'Harry, you go down to the mine and get the captain. We'll keep an eye on this damn thing.'

The late dawn came and the people moving out of their houses in the country saw the spots of blue against the snow. They went to them and picked them up. They unwrapped the paper and read the printed words. They saw the gift and suddenly each finder grew furtive, and he concealed the long tube under his coat and went to some secret place and hid the tube.

And word got to the children about the gift and they combed the countryside in a terrible Easter-egg hunt, and when some lucky child saw the blue colour, he rushed to the prize and opened it and then he hid the tube and told his parents about it. There were some people who were frightened, who turned the tubes over to the military, but they were not very many. And the soldiers scurried about the town in another Easter-egg hunt, but they were not so good at it as the children were.

In the drawing-room of the palace of the Mayor the dining-table remained with the chairs about as it had been placed the day Alex Morden was shot. The room had not the grace it had when it was still the palace of the Mayor. The walls, bare of standing chairs, looked very blank. The table with a few papers scattered about on it made the room look like a business office. The clock on the mantel struck nine. It was a dark day now, overcast with clouds, for the dawn had brought the heavy snow-clouds.

Annie came out of the Mayor's room: she stopped by the table and glanced at the papers that lay there. Captain Loft came in. He stopped in the doorway, seeing Annie.

'What are you doing here?' he demanded.

And Annie said sullenly, 'Yes, sir.'

'I said, what are you doing here?'

'I thought to clean up, sir.'

'Let things alone, and go along.'

And Annie said, 'Yes, sir,' and she waited until he was clear of the door, and she scuttled out.

Captain Loft turned back through the doorway and he said, 'All right, bring it in.' A soldier came through the door behind him, his rifle hung over his shoulder by a strap, and in his arms he held a number of the blue packages, and from the ends of the packages there dangled the little strings and pieces of blue cloth.

Loft said, 'Put them on the table.' The soldier gingerly laid the packages down. 'Now go upstairs and report to Colonel Lanser that I'm here with the–things,' and the soldier wheeled about and left the room.

Loft went to the table and picked up one of the packages, and his face wore a look of distaste. He held up the little blue cloth parachute, held it above his head and dropped it, and the cloth opened and the package floated to the floor. He picked up the package again and examined it.

Now Colonel Lanser came quickly into the room followed by Major Hunter. Hunter was carrying a square of yellow paper in his hand. Lanser said, 'Good morning, Captain,' and he went to the head of the table and sat down. For a moment he looked at the little piles of tubes, and then he picked up one and held it in his hand. 'Sit down, Hunter,' he said. 'Have you examined these?'

Hunter pulled out a chair and sat down. He looked at the yellow paper in his hand. 'Not very carefully,' he said. 'There are three breaks in the railroad all within ten miles.'

'Well, take a look at them and see what you think,' Lanser said.

Hunter reached for a tube and stripped off the outer covering, and inside was a small package next to the tube. Hunter took out a knife and cut into the tube. Captain Loft looked over his shoulder. Then Hunter smelled the cut and rubbed his fingers together, and he said, 'It's silly. It's commercial dynamite. I don't know what per cent of nitroglycerine until I test it.' He looked at the end. 'It has a regular dynamite cap, fulminate of mercury, and a fuse–about a minute, I suppose.' He tossed the tube back on to the table. 'It's very cheap and very simple,' he said.

The colonel looked at Loft. 'How many do you think were dropped?'

'I don't know, sir,' said Loft. 'We picked up about fifty of them, and about ninety parachutes they came in. For some reason the people leave the parachutes when they take the tubes, and there are probably a lot we haven't found yet.'

Lanser waved his hand. 'It doesn't really matter,' he said. 'They can drop as many as they want. We can't stop it, and we can't use it against them, either. They haven't conquered anybody.'

Loft said fiercely, 'We can beat them off the face of the earth!'

Hunter was prising the copper cap out of the top of one of the sticks, and

Lanser said, 'Yes–we can do that. Have you looked at this wrapper, Hunter?'

'Not yet, I haven't had time.'

'It's kind of devilish, this thing,' said Colonel Lanser. 'The wrapper is blue, so that it's easy to see. Unwrap the outer paper and here'–he picked up the small package–'here is a piece of chocolate. Everybody will be looking for it. I'll bet our own soldiers steal the chocolate. Why, the kids will be looking for them, like Easter eggs.'

A soldier came in and laid a square of yellow paper in front of the colonel and retired, and Lanser glanced at it and laughed harshly. 'Here's something for you, Hunter. Two more breaks in your line.'

Hunter looked up from the copper cap he was examining, and he asked, 'How general is this? Did they drop them everywhere?'

Lanser was puzzled. 'Now, that's the funny thing. I've talked to the capital. This is the only place they've dropped them.'

'What do you make of that?' Hunter asked.

'Well, it's hard to say. I think this is a test place. I suppose if it works here they'll use it everywhere, and if it doesn't work here they won't bother.'

'What are you going to do?' Hunter asked.

'The capital orders me to stamp this out so ruthlessly that they won't drop it anywhere else.'

Hunter said plaintively, 'How am I going to mend five breaks in the railroad? I haven't rails now for five breaks.'

'You'll have to rip out some of the old sidings, I guess,' said Lanser.

Hunter said, 'That'll make a hell of a road-bed.'

'Well, anyway, it will make a road-bed.'

Major Hunter tossed the tube he had torn apart on to the pile, and Loft broke in, 'We must stop this thing at once, sir. We must arrest and punish the people who pick these things up, before they use them. We have to get busy so these people won't think we are weak.'

Lanser was smiling at him, and he said, 'Take it easy, Captain. Let's see what we have first, and then we'll think of remedies.'

He took a new package from the pile and unwrapped it. He took the little piece of chocolate, tasted it, and he said, 'This is a devilish thing. It's good chocolate, too. I can't even resist it myself. The prize in the grab-bag.' Then he picked up the dynamite. 'What do you think of this really, Hunter?'

'What I told you. It's very cheap and very effective for small jobs, dynamite with a cap and a one-minute fuse. It's good if you know how to use it. It's no good if you don't.'

Lanser studied the print on the inside of the wrapper. 'Have you read this?'

'Glanced at it,' said Hunter.

'Well, I have read it, and I want you to listen to it carefully,' said Lanser. He read from the paper: '"To the unconquered people: Hide this. Do not expose yourself. You will need this later. It is a present from your friends to you and from you to the invader of your country. Do not try to do large things with it."' He began to skip through the bill. 'Now, here, "rails in the country"; and, "work at night"; and, "tie up transportation". Now here, "Instructions: rails. Place stick under rail close to the joint, and tight against a tie. Pack mud or hard-beaten snow around it so that it is firm. When the fuse is lighted you have a slow count of sixty before it explodes."'

He looked up at Hunter, and Hunter said simply, 'It works.' Lanser looked back at his paper and he skipped through.

'"Bridges: Weaken, do not destroy." And here, "transmission poles", and here, "culverts, trucks".' He laid the blue handbill down. 'Well, there it is.'

Loft said angrily, 'We must do something! There must be a way to control this. What does headquarters say?'

Lanser pursed his lips and his fingers played with one of the tubes. 'I could have told you what they'd say before they said it. I have the orders. "Set booby-traps and poison the chocolate."' He paused for a moment and then he said, 'Hunter, I'm a good, loyal man, but sometimes when I hear the brilliant ideas of headquarters I wish I were a civilian, an old, crippled civilian. They always think they are dealing with stupid people. I don't say that this is a measure of their intelligence, do I?'

Hunter looked amused. 'Do you?'

Lanser said sharply, 'No, I don't But what will happen? One man will pick up one of these and get blown to bits by our booby-trap. One kid will eat chocolate and die of strychnine poisoning. And then?' He looked down at his hands. 'They will poke with poles, or lasso them, before they touch them. They will try the chocolate on the cat. God damn it, Major, these are intelligent people. Stupid traps won't catch them twice.'

Loft cleared his throat. 'Sir, this is defeatist talk,' he said. 'We must do something. Why do you suppose it was only dropped here, sir?'

And Lanser said, 'For one of two reasons: either this town was picked at random or else there is communication between this town and the outside. We know that some of the young men have got away.'

Loft repeated dully, 'We must do something, sir.'

Now Lanser turned on him. 'Loft, I think I'll recommend you for the General staff. You want to get to work before you even know what the problem is. This is a new kind of conquest. Always before, it was possible to disarm a people and keep them in ignorance. Now they listen to their radios and we can't stop them. We can't even find their radios.'

A soldier looked in through the doorway. 'Mr Corell to see you, sir.'

Lanser replied, 'Tell him to wait.' He continued to talk to Loft. 'They read the handbills, weapons drop from the sky for them. Now it's dynamite, Captain. Pretty soon it may be grenades, and then poison.'

Loft said anxiously, 'They haven't dropped poison yet.'

'No, but they will. Can you think what will happen to the morale of our men or even to you if the people had some of those little game darts, you know, those silly little things you throw at a target, the points coated perhaps with cyanide, silent, deadly little things that you couldn't hear coming, that would pierce the uniform and make no noise? And what if our men knew that arsenic was about. Would you or they drink or eat comfortably?'

Hunter said dryly, 'Are you writing the enemy's campaign, Colonel?'

'No, I'm trying to anticipate it.'

Loft said, 'Sir, we sit here talking when we should be searching for this dynamite. If there is organisation among these people, we have to find it, we have to stamp it out.'

'Yes,' said Lanser, 'we have to stamp it out, ferociously I suppose. You take a detail, Loft. Get Prackle to take one. I wish we had more junior officers. Tonder's getting killed didn't help us a bit. Why couldn't he let women alone?'

Loft said, 'I don't like the way Lieutenant Prackle is acting, sir.'

'What's he doing?'

'He isn't doing anything, but he's jumpy and he's gloomy.'

'Yes,' Lanser said, 'I know. It's a thing I've talked about so much. You know,' he said, 'I might be a major-general if I hadn't talked about it so much. We trained our young men for victory and you've got to admit they're glorious in victory, but they don't quite know how to act in defeat. We told them they were brighter and braver than other young men. It was a kind of shock to them to find out they aren't a bit braver or brighter than other young men.'

Loft said harshly, 'What do you mean by defeat? We are not defeated.'

And Lanser looked coldly up at him for a long moment and did not speak, and finally Loft's eyes wavered, and he said, 'Sir.'

'Thank you,' said Lanser.

'You don't demand it of the others, sir.'

'They don't think about it, so it isn't an insult. When you leave it out, it's insulting.'

'Yes, sir,' said Loft.

'Go on, now, try to keep Prackle in hand. Start your search. I don't want any shooting unless there's an overt act, do you understand?'

'Yes, sir,' said Loft, and he saluted formally and went out of the room.

Hunter regarded Colonel Lanser amusedly. 'Weren't you rough on him?'

'I had to be. He's frightened. I know his kind. He has to be disciplined when he's afraid or he'll go to pieces. He relies on discipline the way other men rely on sympathy. I suppose you'd better get to your rails. You might as well expect that tonight is the time when they'll really blow them, though.'

Hunter stood up and he said, 'Yes, I suppose the orders are coming in from the capital?'

'Yes.'

'Are they–?'

'You know what they are,' Lanser interrupted. 'You know what they'd have to be. Take the leaders, shoot the leaders, take hostages, shoot the hostages, take more hostages, shoot them'–his voice had risen but now it sank almost to a whisper–'and the hatred growing and the hurt between us deeper and deeper.'

Hunter hesitated. 'Have they condemned any from the list of names?' and he motioned slightly towards the Mayor's bedroom.

Lanser shook his head. 'No, not yet. They are just arrested, so far.'

Hunter said quietly, 'Colonel, do you want me to recommend–maybe you're overtired, Colonel? Could I–you know–could I report that you're overtired?'

For a moment Lanser covered his eyes with his hand, and then his shoulders straightened and his face grew hard. 'I'm not a civilian, Hunter. We're short enough of officers already. You know that. Get to your work, Major. I have to see Corell.'

Hunter smiled. He went to the door and opened it, and he said out of the door, 'Yes, he's here,' and over his shoulder he said to Lanser, 'It's Prackle. He wants to see you.'

'Send him in,' said Lanser.

Prackle came in, his face sullen, belligerent. 'Colonel Lanser, sir, I wish to–'

'Sit down,' said Lanser. 'Sit down and rest a moment. Be a good soldier, Lieutenant.'

The stiffness went out of Prackle quickly. He sat down beside the table and rested his elbows on it. 'I wish–'

And Lanser said, 'Don't talk for a moment. I know what it is. You didn't think it would be this way, did you? You thought it would be rather nice.'

'They hate us,' Prackle said. 'They hate us so much.'

Lanser smiled. 'I wonder if I know what it is. It takes young men to make good soldiers, and young men need young women, is that it?'

'Yes, that's it.'

'Well,' Lanser said kindly, 'does she hate you?'

Prackle looked at him in amazement. 'I don't know, sir. Sometimes I think she's only sorry.'

'And you're pretty miserable?'

'I don't like it here, sir.'

'No, you thought it would be fun, didn't you? Lieutenant Tonder went to pieces and then he went out and they got a knife in him. I could send you home. Do you want to be sent home, knowing we need you here?'

Prackle said uneasily, 'No, sir, I don't.'

'Good. Now I'll tell you, and I hope you'll understand it. You're not a man any more. You are a soldier. Your comfort is of no importance and, Lieutenant, your life isn't of much importance. If you live, you will have memories. That's about all you will have. Meanwhile you must take orders and carry them out. Most of the orders will be unpleasant, but that's not your business. I will not lie to you, Lieutenant. They should have trained you for this, and not for flower-strewn streets. They should have built your soul with truth, not led it along with lies.' His voice grew hard. 'But you took the job, Lieutenant. Will you stay with it or quit it? We can't take care of your soul.'

Prackle stood up. 'Thank you, sir.'

'And the girl,' Lanser continued, 'the girl, Lieutenant, you may rape her, or protect her, or marry her–that is of no importance so long as you shoot her when it is ordered.'

Prackle said wearily, 'Yes, sir, thank you, sir.'

'I assure you it is better to know. I assure you of that. It is better to know. Go now, Lieutenant, and if Corell is still waiting, send him in.' And he watched Lieutenant Prackle out of the doorway.

When Mr Corell came in, he was a changed man. His left arm was in a cast, and he was no longer the jovial, friendly, smiling Corell. His face was sharp and bitter, and his eyes squinted down like little dead pig's eyes.

'I should have come before, Colonel,' he said, 'but your lack of co-operation made me hesitant.'

Lanser said, 'You were waiting for a reply to your report, I remember.'

'I was waiting for much more than that. You refused me a position of authority. You said I was valueless. You did not realise that I was in this town long before you were. You left the Mayor in his office, contrary to my advice.'

Lanser said, 'Without him here we might have had more disorder than we have.'

'That is a matter of opinion,' Corell said. 'This man is a leader of a rebellious people.'

'Nonsense,' said Lanser; 'he's just a simple man.'

With his good hand Corell took a black notebook from his right pocket and opened it with his fingers. 'You forgot, Colonel, that I had my sources, that I had been here a long time before you. I have to report to you that Mayor Orden has been in constant contact with every happening in this community. On the night when Lieutenant Tonder was murdered, he was in the house where the murder was committed. When the girl escaped to the hills, she stayed with one of his relatives. I traced her there, but she was gone. Whenever men have escaped, Orden has known about it and has helped them. And I even strongly suspect that he is somewhere in the picture of these little parachutes.'

Lanser said eagerly, 'But you can't prove it.'

'No,' Corell said, 'I can't prove it. The first thing I know; the last I only suspect. Perhaps now you will be willing to listen to me.'

Lanser said quietly, 'What do you suggest?'

'These suggestions, Colonel, are a little stronger than suggestions. Orden must now be a hostage and his life must depend on the peacefulness of this community. His life must depend on the lighting of a single fuse on one single stick of dynamite.'

He reached into his pocket again and brought out a little folding book, and he flipped it open and laid it in front of the colonel. 'This, sir, was the answer to my report from headquarters. You will notice that it gives me certain authority.'

Lanser looked at the little book and he spoke quietly: 'You really did go over my head, didn't you?' He looked up at Corell with frank dislike in his eyes. 'I heard you'd been injured. How did it happen?'

Corell said, 'On the night when your lieutenant was murdered I was waylaid. The patrol saved me. Some of the townsmen escaped in my boat that night. Now, Colonel, must I express more strongly than I have that Mayor Order must be held hostage?'

Lanser said, 'He is here, he hasn't escaped. How can we hold him more hostage than we are?'

Suddenly in the distance there was a sound of an explosion, and both men looked around in the direction from which it came. Corell said, 'There it is, Colonel, and you know perfectly well that if this experiment succeeds there will be dynamite in every invaded country.'

Lanser repeated quietly, 'What do you suggest?'

'Just what I have said. Orden must be held against rebellion.'

'And if they rebel and we shoot Orden?'

'Then that little doctor is next; although he holds no position, he's next in authority in the town.'

'But he holds no office.'

'He has the confidence of the people.'

'And when we shoot him, what then?'

'Then we have authority. Then rebellion will be broken. When we have killed the leaders, the rebellion will be broken.'

Lanser asked quizzically, 'Do you really think so?'

'It must be so.'

Lanser shook his head slowly and then he called, 'Sentry!' The door opened and a soldier appeared in the doorway. 'Sergeant,' said Lanser, 'I have placed Mayor Orden under arrest, and I have placed Doctor Winter under arrest. You will see to it that Orden is guarded and you will bring Winter here immediately.'

The sentry said, 'Yes, sir.'

Lanser looked up at Corell and he said, 'You know, I hope you know what you're doing. I do hope you know what you're doing.'

8

In the little town the news ran quickly. It was communicated by whispers in doorways, by quick, meaningful looks–'The Mayor's been arrested'–and through the town a little quiet jubilance ran, a fierce little jubilance, and people talked quietly together and went apart, and people going in to buy food leaned close to the shopmen for a moment and a word passed between them.

The people went into the country, into the woods, searching for dynamite. And children playing in the snow found the dynamite, and by now even the children had their instructions. They opened the packages and ate the chocolate, and then they buried the dynamite in the snow and told their parents where it was.

Far out in the country a man picked up a tube and read the instructions and he said to himself, 'I wonder if this works.' He stood the tube up in the snow and lighted the fuse, and he ran back from it and counted, but his count was fast. It was sixty-eight before the dynamite exploded. He said, 'It does work,' and he went hurriedly about looking for more tubes.

Almost as though at a signal the people went into their houses and the doors were closed, the streets were quiet. At the mine the soldiers carefully searched every miner who went into his shaft, searched and researched, and the soldiers were nervous and rough and they spoke harshly to the miners. The miners looked coldly at them, and behind their eyes was a little fierce jubilance.

In the drawing-room of the palace of the Mayor the table had been cleaned up, and a soldier stood guard at Mayor Orden's bedroom door. Annie was on her knees in front of the coal grate, putting little pieces of coal on the fire. She looked up at the sentry standing in front of Mayor Orden's door and she said truculently, 'Well, what are you going to do to him?' The soldier did not answer.

The outside door opened and another soldier came in, holding Doctor Winter by the arm. He closed the door behind Doctor Winter and stood against the door inside the room. Doctor Winter said, 'Hello, Annie, how's His Excellency?'

And Annie pointed at the bedroom and said, 'He's in there.'

'He isn't ill?' Doctor Winter said.

'No, he didn't seem to be,' said Annie. 'I'll see if I can tell him you're here.' She went to the sentry and spoke imperiously. 'Tell His Excellency that Doctor Winter is here, do you hear me?'

The sentry did not answer and did not move, but behind him the door opened and Mayor Orden stood in the doorway. He ignored the sentry and brushed past him and stepped into the room. For a moment the sentry considered taking him back, and then he returned to his place beside the door. Orden said: 'Thank you, Annie. Don't go too far away, will you? I might need you.'

Annie said, 'No, sir, I won't. Is Madame all right?'

'She's doing her hair. Do you want to see her, Annie?'

'Yes, sir,' said Annie, and she brushed past the sentry too, and went into the bedroom and shut the door.

Orden said, 'Is there something you want, Doctor?'

Winter grinned sardonically and pointed over his shoulder to his guard. 'Well, I guess I'm under arrest. My friend here brought me.'

Orden said, 'I suppose it was bound to come. What will they do now, I wonder?' And the two men looked at each other for a long time and each one knew what the other one was thinking.

And then Orden continued as though he had been talking. 'You know, I couldn't stop it if I wanted to.'

'I know,' said Winter, 'but they don't know.' And he went on with a thought he had been having. 'A time-minded people,' he said, 'and the time is nearly up. They think that just because they have only one leader and one head, we are all like that. They know that ten heads lopped off will destroy them, but we are a free people; we have as many heads as we have people, and in a time of need leaders pop up among us like mushrooms.'

Orden put his hand on Winter's shoulder and he said, 'Thank you. I knew it, but it's good to hear you say it. The little people won't go under, will they?' He searched Winter's face anxiously.

And the doctor reassured him, 'Why, no, they won't. As a matter of fact, they will grow stronger with outside help.'

The room was silent for a moment. The sentry shifted his position a little and his rifle clinked on a button.

Orden said, 'I can talk to you, Doctor, and I probably won't be able to talk again. There are little shameful things in my mind.' He coughed and glanced at the rigid soldier, but the soldier gave no sign of having heard. 'I have been thinking of my own death. If they follow the usual course, they must kill me, and then they must kill you.' And when Winter was silent, he said, 'Mustn't they?'

'Yes, I guess so.' Winter walked to one of the gilt chairs, and as he was about to sit down he noticed that its tapestry was torn, and he petted the seat with his fingers as though that would mend it. And he sat down gently because it was torn.

And Orden went on, 'You know, I'm afraid, I have been thinking of ways to escape, to get out of it. I have been thinking of running away. I have been thinking of pleading for my life, and it makes me ashamed.'

And Winter, looking up, said, 'But you haven't done it.'

'No, I haven't.'

'And you won't do it.'

Orden hesitated. 'No, I won't. But I have thought of it.'

And Winter said, gently, 'How do you know everyone doesn't think of it? How do you know I haven't thought of it?'

'I wonder why they arrested you too,' Orden said. 'I guess they will have to kill you too.'

'I guess so,' said Winter. He rolled his thumbs and watched them tumble over and over.

'You know so.' Orden was silent for a moment and then he said, 'You know, Doctor, I am a little man and this is a little town, but there must be a spark in little men that can burst into flame. I am afraid, I am terribly afraid, and I thought of all the things I might do to save my own life, and then that went away, and sometimes now I feel a kind of exultation, as though I were bigger and better than I am, and do you know what I have been thinking, Doctor?' He smiled, remembering. 'Do you remember in school, in the *Apology*? Do you remember Socrates says: "Someone will say, 'And are you not ashamed, Socrates, of a course of life which is likely to bring you to an untimely end?' To him I may fairly answer, 'There you are mistaken: a man who is good for anything ought not to calculate the chance of living or dying; he ought only to consider whether he is doing right or wrong.'"' Orden paused, trying to remember.

Doctor Winter sat tensely forward now, and he went on with it: '"Acting the part of a good man or of a bad." I don't think you have it quite right. You never were a good scholar. You were wrong in the denunciation, too.'

Orden chuckled. 'Do you remember that?'

'Yes,' said Winter, eagerly, 'I remember it well. You forgot a line or a word. It was graduation, and you were so excited you forgot to tuck in your shirt-tail and your shirt-tail was out. You wondered why they laughed.'

Orden smiled to himself, and his hand went secretly behind him and patrolled for a loose shirt-tail. 'I was Socrates,' he said, 'and I denounced the School Board. How I denounced them! I bellowed it, and I could see them grow red.'

Winter said, 'They were holding their breaths to keep from laughing. Your shirt-tail was out.'

Mayor Orden laughed. 'How long ago? Forty years.'

'Forty-six.'

The sentry by the bedroom door moved quietly over to the sentry by the outside door. They spoke softly out of the corners of their mouths like children whispering in school. 'How long you been on duty?'

'All night. Can't hardly keep my eyes open.'

'Me too. Hear from your wife on the boat yesterday?'

'Yes! She said say hello to you. Said she heard you was wounded. She don't write much.'

'Tell her I'm all right.'

'Sure–when I write.'

The Mayor raised his head and looked at the ceiling and he muttered, 'Um–um–um. I wonder if I can remember–how does it go?'

And Winter prompted him, '"And now, O men–"'

And Orden said softly, '"And now, O men who have condemned me–"'

Colonel Lanser came quietly into the room; the sentries stiffened. Hearing the words, the colonel stopped and listened.

Orden looked at the ceiling, lost in trying to remember the old words. '"And now, O men who have condemned me,"' he said, '"I would fain prophesy to you–for I am about to die–and–in the hour of death–men are gifted with prophetic power. And I–prophesy to you who are my murderers–that immediately after my–my death–"'

And Winter stood up, saying, 'departure.'

Orden looked at him. 'What?'

And Winter said, 'The word is "departure", not "death". You made the same mistake before. You made that mistake forty-six years ago.'

'No, it is death. It is death.' Orden looked around and saw Colonel Lanser watching him. He asked, 'Isn't it "death"?'

Colonel Lanser said, '"Departure". It is "immediately after my departure".'

Doctor Winter insisted, 'You see, that's two against one. "Departure" is the word. It is the same mistake you made before.'

Then Orden looked straight ahead and his eyes were in his memory, seeing nothing outward. And he went on: '"I prophesy to you who are my murderers that immediately after my–departure punishment far heavier than you have inflicted on me will surely await you."'

Winter nodded encouragingly, and Colonel Lanser nodded, and they seemed to be trying to help him to remember. And Orden went on: '"Me you have killed because you wanted to escape the accuser, and not to give an account of your lives–"'

Lieutenant Prackle entered excitedly, crying, 'Colonel Lanser!'

Colonel Lanser said, 'Shh–' and he held out his hand to restrain him.

And Orden went on softly, '"But that will not be as you suppose; far otherwise."' His voice grew stronger. '"For I say that there will be more accusers of you than there are now"'–he made a little gesture with his hand, a speech-making gesture–'"accusers whom hitherto I have restrained; and as they are younger they will be more inconsiderate with you, and you will be more offended at them."' He frowned, trying to remember.

And Lieutenant Prackle said, 'Colonel Lanser, we have found some men with dynamite.'

And Lanser said, 'Hush.'

Orden continued, '"If you think that by killing men you can prevent someone from censuring your evil lives, you are mistaken."' He frowned and thought and he looked at the ceiling, and he smiled embarrassedly and he said, 'That's all I can remember. It is gone away from me.'

And Doctor Winter said, 'It's very good after forty-six years, and you weren't very good at it forty-six years ago.'

Lieutenant Prackle broke in, 'The men have dynamite, Colonel Lanser.'

'Did you arrest them?'

'Yes, sir. Captain Loft and–'

Lanser said, 'Tell Captain Loft to guard them.' He recaptured himself and he advanced into the room and he said, 'Orden, these things must stop.'

And the Mayor smiled helplessly at him. 'They cannot stop, sir.'

Colonel Lanser said harshly, 'I arrested you as a hostage for the good behaviour of your people. Those are my orders.'

'But that won't stop it.' Orden said simply. 'You don't understand. When I have become a hindrance to the people, they will do without me.'

Lanser said, 'Tell me truly what you think. If the people know that you will be shot if they light another fuse, what will they do?'

The Mayor looked helplessly at Doctor Winter. And then the bedroom door opened and Madame came out, carrying the Mayor's chain of office in her hand. She said, 'You forgot this.'

Orden said, 'What? Oh, yes,' and he stooped his head and Madame slipped the chain of office over his head, and he said, 'Thank you, my dear.'

Madame complained, 'You always forget it. You forget it all the time.'

The Mayor looked at the end of the chain he held in his hand–the gold medallion with the insignia of his office carved on it. Lanser pressed him: 'What will they do?'

'I don't know,' said the Mayor. 'I think they will light the fuse.'

'Suppose you ask them not to?'

Winter said, 'Colonel, this morning I saw a little boy building a snow man, while three grown soldiers watched to see that he did not caricature your leader. He made a pretty good likeness, too, before they destroyed it.'

Lanser ignored the doctor. 'Suppose you ask them not to?' he repeated.

Orden seemed half asleep; his eyes were drooped, and he tried to think. He said, 'I am not a very brave man, sir. I think they will light it, anyway.' He struggled with his speech. 'I hope they will, but if I ask them not to, they will be sorry.'

Madame said, 'What is this all about?'

'Be quiet a moment, dear,' the Mayor said.

'But you think they will light it?' Lanser insisted.

The Mayor spoke proudly, 'Yes, they will light it. I have no choice of living or dying, you see, sir, but–I do have a choice of how I do it. If I tell them not to fight, they will be sorry, but they will fight. If I tell them to fight, they will be glad, and I who am not a very brave man will have made them a little braver.' He smiled apologetically. 'You see, it is an easy thing to do, since the end for me is the same.'

Lanser said, 'If you say yes, we can tell them you said no. We can tell them you begged for your life.'

And Winter broke in angrily, 'They would know. You do not keep secrets. One of your men got out of hand one night and he said the flies had conquered the flypaper, and now the whole nation knows his words. They have made a song of it. The flies conquered the flypaper. You do not keep secrets, Colonel.'

From the direction of the mine a whistle tooted shrilly. And a quick gust of wind sifted dry snow against the windows.

Orden fingered his gold medallion. He said quietly, 'You see, sir, nothing can change it. You will be destroyed and driven out.' His voice was very soft. 'The people don't like to be conquered, sir, and so they will not be. Free men cannot start a war, but once it is started, they can fight on in defeat. Herd men, followers of a leader, cannot do that, and so it is always the herd men who win battles and the free men who win wars. You will find that is so, sir.'

Lanser was erect and stiff. 'My orders are clear. Eleven o'clock was the deadline. I have taken hostages. If there is violence, the hostages will be executed.'

And Doctor Winter said to the colonel, 'Will you carry out the orders, knowing they will fail?'

Lanser's face was tight. 'I will carry out my orders no matter what they are, but I do think, sir, a proclamation from you might save many lives.'

Madame broke in plaintively, 'I wish you would tell me what all this nonsense is.'

'It is nonsense, dear.'

'But they can't arrest the Mayor,' she explained to him.

Orden smiled at her. 'No,' he said, 'they can't arrest the Mayor. The Mayor is an idea conceived by free men. It will escape arrest.'

From the distance there was a sound of an explosion, and the echo of it rolled to the hills and back again. The whistle at the coal-mine tooted a shrill, sharp warning. Orden stood very tensely for a moment and then he smiled. A second explosion roared–nearer this time and heavier–and its echo rolled back from the mountains. Orden looked at his watch and then he took his watch and chain and put them in Doctor Winter's hand. 'How did it go about the flies?' he asked.

'The flies have conquered the flypaper,' Winter said.

Orden called, 'Annie!' The bedroom door opened instantly and the Mayor said, 'Were you listening?'

'Yes, sir.' Annie was embarrassed.

And now an explosion roared near by and there was a sound of splintering wood and breaking glass, and the door behind the sentries puffed open. And Orden said, 'Annie, I want you to stay with Madame as long as she needs you. Don't leave her alone.' He put his arm round Madame and he kissed her on the forehead and then he moved slowly towards the door where Lieutenant Prackle stood. In the doorway he turned back to Doctor Winter. 'Crito, I owe a cock to Asclepius,' he said tenderly. 'Will you remember to pay the debt?'

Winter closed his eyes for a moment before he answered, 'The debt shall be paid.'

Orden chuckled then. 'I remembered that one. I didn't forget that one.' He put his hand on Prackle's arm, and the lieutenant flinched away from him.

And Winter nodded slowly. 'Yes, you remembered. The debt shall be paid.'

CANNERY ROW

CANNERY ROW

FOR ED RICKETTS
Who knows why, or should

Cannery Row in Monterey in California is a poem, a stink, a grating noise, a quality of light, a tone, a habit, a nostalgia, a dream. Cannery Row is the gathered and scattered, tin and iron and rust and splintered wood, chipped pavement and weedy lots and junk heaps, sardine canneries of corrugated iron, honky-tonks, restaurants and whore-houses, and little crowded groceries, and laboratories and flop houses. Its inhabitants are, as the man once said, 'whores, pimps, gamblers, and sons of bitches,' by which he meant Everybody. Had the man looked through another peep-hole he might have said: 'Saints and angels and martyrs and holy men,' and he would have meant the same thing.

In the morning when the sardine fleet had made a catch, the purse-seiners waddle heavily into the bay blowing their whistles. The deep-laden boats pull in against the coast where the canneries dip their tails into the bay. The figure is advisedly chosen, for if the canneries dipped their mouths into the bay the canned sardines which emerge from the other end would be metaphorically, at least, even more horrifying. Then cannery whistles scream and all over the town men and women scramble into their clothes and come running down to the Row to go to work. Then shining cars bring the upper classes down: superintendents, accountants, owners who disappear into offices. Then from the town pour Wops and Chinamen and Polaks, men and women in trousers and rubber coats and oilcloth aprons. They come running to clean and cut and pack and cook and can the fish. The whole street rumbles and groans and screams and rattles while the silver rivers of fish pour in out of the boats and the boats rise higher and higher in the water until they are empty. The canneries rumble and rattle and squeak until the last fish is cleaned and cut and cooked and canned and then the whistles scream again and the dripping, smelly, tired Wops and Chinamen and Polaks, men and women, straggle out and droop their ways up the hill into the town and Cannery Row becomes itself again–quiet and magical. Its normal life returns. The bums who retired in disgust under the black cypress-tree come out to sit on the rusty pipes in the vacant lot. The girls from Dora's emerge for a bit of sun if there is any. Doc strolls from the Western Biological Laboratory and crosses the street to Lee Chong's grocery for two quarts of beer. Henri the painter noses like an Airedale through the junk in the grass-grown lot for some part or piece of wood or metal he needs for the boat he is building. Then the darkness edges in and the street light comes on in front of Dora's–the lamp which makes perpetual moonlight in Cannery Row. Callers arrive at Western Biological to see Doc, and he crosses the street to Lee Chong's for five quarts of beer.

How can the poem and the stink and the grating noise–the quality of light, the tone, the habit and the dream–be set down alive? When you collect marine animals there are certain flat worms so delicate that they are almost impossible to capture whole, for they break and tatter under the touch. You must let them ooze and crawl of their own will on to a knife blade and then lift them gently into your bottle of sea water. And perhaps that might be the way to write this book–to open the page and to let the stories crawl in by themselves.

I

Lee Chong's grocery, while not a model of neatness, was a miracle of supply. It was small and crowded but within its single room a man could find everything he needed or wanted to live and to be happy–clothes, food, both fresh and canned, liquor, tobacco, fishing equipment, machinery, boats, cordage, caps, pork-chops. You could buy at Lee Chong's a pair of slippers, a silk kimono, a quarter-pint of whisky, and a cigar. You could work out combinations to fit almost any mood. The one commodity Lee Chong did not keep could be had across the lot at Dora's.

The grocery opened at dawn and did not close until the last wandering vagrant dime had been spent or retired for the night. Not that Lee Chong was avaricious. He wasn't, but if one wanted to spend money, he was available. Lee's position in the community surprised him as much as he could be surprised. Over the course of the years everyone in Cannery Row owed him money. He never pressed his clients, but when the bill became too large, Lee cut off credit. Rather than walk into the town up the hill, the client usually paid or tried to.

Lee was round-faced and courteous. He spoke a stately English without ever using the letter R. When the tong wars were going on in California, it happened now and then that Lee found a price on his head. Then he would go secretly to San Francisco and enter a hospital until the trouble blew over. What he did with his money, no one ever knew. Perhaps he didn't get it. Maybe his wealth was entirely in unpaid bills. But he lived well and he had the respect of all his neighbours. He trusted his clients until further trust became ridiculous. Sometimes he made business errors, but even these he turned to advantage in good will if in no other way. It was that way with the Palace Flophouse and Grill. Anyone but Lee Chong would have considered the transaction a total loss.

Lee Chong's station in the grocery was behind the cigar counter. The cash register was then on his left and the abacus on his right. Inside the glass case were the brown cigars, the cigarettes, the Bull Durham, the Duke's mixture, the five Brothers, while behind him in racks on the wall were the pints, half-pints, and quarters of Old Green River, Old Town House, Old Colonel, and the favourite–Old Tennessee, a blended whisky guaranteed four months old, very cheap and known in the neighbourhood as Old Tennis Shoes. Lee Chong did not stand between the whisky and the customer without reason. Some very practical minds had on occasion tried to divert his attention to another part of the store. Cousins, nephews, sons, and daughters-in-law waited on the rest of the store, but Lee never left the cigar counter. The top of the glass was his desk. His fat delicate hands rested on the glass, the fingers moving like small restless sausages. A broad golden wedding-ring on the middle finger of his left hand was his only jewellery and with it he silently tapped on the rubber change mat from which the little rubber tits had long been worn. Lee's mouth was full and benevolent and the flash of gold when he smiled was rich and warm. He wore half-glasses and since he looked at everything through them, he had to tilt his head back to see the distance. Interest and discounts, addition, subtraction he worked out on the abacus with his little restless sausage fingers, and his brown friendly eyes roved over the grocery and his teeth flashed at the customers.

On an evening when he stood in his place on a pad of newspaper to keep his feet warm, he contemplated with humour and sadness a business deal that had been consummated that afternoon and reconsummated later the same afternoon. When you leave the grocery, if you walk catty-cornered across the grass-grown lot, threading your way among the great rusty pipes thrown out of the canneries, you will see a path worn in the weeds. Follow it past the cypress-tree, across the railroad track, up a chicken-walk with cleats, and you will come to a long low building which for a long time was used as a storage place for fish meal. It was just a great big roofed room and it belonged to a worried gentleman named Horace Abbeville. Horace had two wives and six children, and over a period of years he had managed through pleading and persuasion to build a grocery debt second to none in Monterey. That afternoon he had come into the grocery and his sensitive tired face had flinched at the shadow of sternness that crossed Lee's face. Lee's fat finger tapped the rubber mat. Horace laid his hands palms up on the cigar counter. 'I guess I owe you plenty dough,' he said simply.

Lee's teeth flashed up in appreciation of an approach so different from any he had ever heard. He nodded gravely, but he waited for the trick to develop.

Horace wet his lips with his tongue, a good job from corner to corner. 'I hate to have my kids with that hanging over them,' he said. 'Why, I bet you wouldn't let them have a pack of spearmint now.'

Lee Chong's face agreed with this conclusion. 'Plenty dough,' he said.

Horace continued: 'You know that place of mine across the track up there where the fish meal is.'

Lee Chong nodded. It was his fish meal.

Horace said earnestly: 'If I was to give you that place–would it clear me up with you?'

Lee Chong tilted his head back and stared at Horace through his half-glasses while his mind flicked among accounts and his right hand moved restlessly to the abacus. He considered the construction which was flimsy and the lot which might be valuable if a cannery ever wanted to expand. 'Shu,' said Lee Chong.

'Well, get out the accounts and I'll make you a bill of sale on that place.' Horace seemed in a hurry.

'No need papers,' said Lee. 'I make paid-in-full paper.'

They finished the deal with dignity and Lee Chong threw in a quarter-pint of Old Tennis Shoes. And then Horace Abbeville walking very straight went across the lot and past the cypress-tree and across the track and up the chicken-walk and into the building that had been his, and he shot himself on a heap of fish meal. And although it has nothing to do with this story, no Abbeville child, no matter who its mother was, knew the lack of a stick of spearmint ever afterward.

But to get back to the evening. Horace was on the trestles with the embalming needles in him, and his two wives were sitting on the steps of his house with their arms about each other (they were good friends until after the funeral, and then they divided up the children and never spoke to each other again). Lee Chong stood behind the cigar counter and his nice brown eyes were turned inward on a calm and eternal Chinese sorrow. He knew he could not have helped it, but he wished he might have known and perhaps tried to help. It was deeply a part of Lee's kindness and understanding that man's right to kill himself is inviolable, but sometimes a friend can make it unnecessary. Lee had already underwritten the funeral and sent a wash-basket of groceries to the stricken families.

Now Lee Chong owned the Abbeville building–a good roof, a good floor, two windows and a door. True it was piled high with fish meal and the smell of it was delicate and penetrating. Lee Chong considered it as a storehouse for groceries, as a kind of warehouse, but he gave that up on second thought. It was too far away and anyone can go in through a window. He was tapping the rubber mat with his gold ring and considering the problem when the door opened and Mack came in. Mack was the elder, leader, mentor, and to a small extent the exploiter of a little group of men who had in common no families, no money, and no ambitions beyond food, drink, and contentment. But whereas most men in their search for contentment destroy themselves and fall wearily short of their targets, Mack and his friends approached contentment casually, quietly, and absorbed it gently. Mack and Hazel, a young man of great strength, Eddie who filled in as a bar-tender at 'La Ida', Hughie and Jones who occasionally collected frogs and cats for Western Biological, were currently living in those large rusty pipes in the lot next to Lee Chong's. That is, they lived in the pipes when it was damp, but in fine weather they lived in the shadow of the black cypress-tree at the top of the lot. The limbs folded down and made a canopy under which a man could lie and look out at the flow and vitality of Cannery Row.

Lee Chong stiffened ever so slightly when Mack came in and his eyes glanced quickly about the store to make sure that Eddie or Hazel or Hughie or Jones had not come in too and drifted away among the groceries.

Mack laid out his cards with a winning honesty. 'Lee,' he said, 'I and Eddie and the rest heard you own the Abbeville place.'

Lee Chong nodded and waited.

'I and my friends thought we'd ast you if we could move in there. We'll keep up the property,' he added quickly. 'Wouldn't let anybody break in or hurt anything. Kids might knock out the windows, you know . . .' Mack suggested. 'Place might burn down if somebody don't keep an eye on it.'

Lee tilted his head back and looked into Mack's eyes through the half-glasses and Lee's tapping finger slowed its tempo as he thought deeply. In Mack's eyes there was good will and good fellowship and a desire to make everyone happy. Why then did Lee Chong feel slightly surrounded? Why did his mind pick its way as delicately as a cat through cactus? It had been sweetly done, almost in a spirit of philanthropy. Lee's mind leaped ahead at the possibilities–no, they were probabilities, and his finger tapping slowed still further. He saw himself refusing Mack's request and he saw the broken glass from the windows. Then Mack would offer a second time to watch over and preserve Lee's property and at the second refusal, Lee could smell the smoke, could see the little flames creeping up the walls. Mack and his friends would try to help to put it out. Lee's finger came to a gentle rest on the change-mat. He was beaten. He knew that. There was left to him only the possibility of saving face, and Mack was likely to be very generous about that. Lee said: 'You like pay lent my place? You like live there same hotel?'

Mack smiled broadly and he was generous. 'Say . . .' he cried. 'That's an idear. Sure. How much?'

Lee considered. He knew it didn't matter what he charged. He wasn't going to get it, anyway. He might just as well make it a really sturdy face-saving sum. 'Fi' dolla' week,' said Lee.

Mack played it through to the end. 'I'll have to talk to the boys about it,' he said dubiously. 'Couldn't you make that four dollars a week?'

'Fi' dolla,' said Lee firmly.

'Well, I'll see what the boys say,' said Mack.

And that was the way it was. Everyone was happy about it. And if it be thought that Lee Chong suffered a total loss, at least his mind did not work that way. The windows were not broken. Fire did not break out, and while no rent was ever paid, if the tenants ever had any money, and quite often they did have, it never occurred to them to spend it anywhere except at Lee Chong's grocery. What he had was a little group of active and potential customers under wraps. But it went further than that. If a drunk caused trouble in the grocery, if the kids swarmed down from New Monterey intent on plunder, Lee Chong had only to call and his tenants rushed to his aid. One further bond it established–you cannot steal from your benefactor. The saving to Lee Chong in cans of beans and tomatoes and milk and water-melons more than paid the rent. And if there was a sudden and increased leakage among the groceries in New Monterey that was none of Lee Chong's affair.

The boys moved in and the fish-meal moved out. No one knows who named the house that has been known ever after as the Palace Flophouse Grill. In the pipes and under the cypress-tree there had been no room for furniture and the little niceties which are not only the diagnoses but the boundaries of our civilization. Once in the Palace Flophouse, the boys set about furnishing it. A chair appeared and a cot and another chair. A hardware store supplied a can of red paint not reluctantly because it never knew about it, and as a new table or footstool appeared it was painted, which not only made it very pretty but also disguised it to a certain extent in case a former owner looked in. And the Palace Flophouse Grill began to function. The boys could sit in front of their door and look down across the track and across the lot and across the street right into the front windows of Western Biological. They could hear the music from the laboratory at night. And their eyes followed Doc across the street when he went to Lee Chong's for beer. And Mack said: 'That Doc is a fine fellow. We ought to do something for him.'

2

The word is a symbol and a delight which sucks up men and scenes, trees, plants, factories, and Pekinese. Then the Thing becomes the Word and back to Thing again, but warped and woven into a fantastic pattern. The Word sucks up Cannery Row, digests it, and spews it out, and the Row has taken the shimmer of the green world and the sky-reflecting seas. Lee Chong is more than a Chinese grocer. He must be. Perhaps he is evil balanced and held suspended by good–an Asiatic planet held to its orbit by the pull of Lao Tze and held away from Lao Tze by the centrifugality of abacus and cash register–Lee Chong suspended, spinning, whirling among groceries and ghosts. A hard man with a can of beans–a soft man with the bones of his grandfather. For Lee Chong dug into the grave on China Point and found the yellow bones, the skull with grey ropy hair still sticking to it. And Lee carefully packed the bones, femurs, and tibias really straight, skull in the middle, with pelvis and clavicle surrounding it and ribs curving on either side. Then Lee Chong sent his boxed and brittle grandfather over the western sea to lie at last in ground made holy by his ancestors.

Mack and the boys, too, spinning in their orbits. They are the Virtues, the Graces, the Beauties of the hurried mangled craziness of Monterey and the cosmic Monterey where men in fear and hunger destroy their stomachs in the fight to secure certain food, where men hungering for love destroy everything lovable about them. Mack and the boys are the Beauties, the Virtues, the Graces. In the world ruled by tigers with ulcers, rutted by strictured bulls, scavenged by blind jackals, Mack and the boys dine delicately with the tigers, fondle the frantic heifers, and wrap up the crumbs to feed the sea-gulls of Cannery Row. What can it profit a man to gain the whole world and to come to his property with a gastric ulcer, a blown prostate, and bifocals? Mack and the boys avoid the trap, walk around the poison, step over the noose while a generation of trapped, poisoned, and trussed-up men scream at them and call them no-goods, come-to-bad-ends, blots-on-the-town, thieves, rascals, bums. Our Father who art in nature, who has given the gift of survival to the coyote, the common brown rat, the English sparrow, the house-fly, and the moth, must have a great and overwhelming love for no-goods and blots-on-the-town and bums, and Mack and the boys. Virtues and graces and laziness and zest. Our Father who art in nature.

3

Lee Chong's is to the right of the vacant lot (although why it is called vacant when it is piled high with old boilers, with rusting pipes, with great square timbers, and stacks of five-gallon cans, no one can say). In the rear of the vacant lot is the railroad track and the Palace Flophouse. But on the left-hand boundary of the lot is the stern and stately whore-house of Dora Flood; a decent, clean, honest, old-fashioned sporting house where a man can take a glass of beer among friends. This is no fly-by-night cheap clip-joint, but a sturdy, virtuous club, built, maintained, and disciplined by Dora, who, madam and girl of fifty years, has through the exercise of special gifts of tact and honesty, charity and a certain realism, made herself respected by the intelligent, the learned, and the kind. And by the same token she is hated by the twisted and lascivious sisterhood of married spinsters whose husbands respect the home but don't like it very much.

Dora is a great woman, a great big woman with flaming orange hair and a taste for Nile-green evening dresses. She keeps an honest, one-price house, sells no hard liquor, and permits no loud or vulgar talk in her house. Of her girls some are fairly inactive, due to age and infirmities, but Dora never puts them aside, although, as she says, some of them don't turn three tricks a month, but they go right on eating three meals a day. In a moment of local love Dora named her place the Bear Flag Restaurant and the stories are many of people who have gone in for a sandwich. There are normally twelve girls in the house, counting the old ones, a Greek cook and a man who is known as a watchman, but who undertakes all manner of delicate and dangerous tasks. He stops fights, ejects drunks, soothes hysteria, cures headaches, and tends bar. He bandages cuts and bruises, passes the time of day with cops, and since a good half of the girls are Christian Scientists, reads aloud his share of *Science and Health* on a Sunday morning. His predecessor, being a less well-balanced man, came to an evil end as shall be reported, but Alfred has triumphed over his environment and has brought his environment up with him. He knows what men should be there and what men shouldn't be there. He knows more about the home life of Monterey citizens than anyone in town.

As for Dora–she leads a ticklish existence. Being against the law, at least against its letter, she must be twice as law-abiding as anyone else. There must be no drunks, no fighting, no vulgarity, or they close Dora up. Also being illegal Dora must be especially philanthropic. Everyone puts the bite on her. If the police give a dance for their pension fund and everyone else gives a dollar, Dora has to give fifty dollars. When the Chamber of Commerce improved its gardens, the merchants each gave five dollars, but Dora was asked for and gave a hundred. With everyone else it is the same, Red Cross, Community Chest, Boy Scouts, Dora's unsung, unpublicized, shameless dirty wages of sin lead the list of donations. But during the depression she was hardest hit. In addition to the usual charities, Dora saw the hungry children of Cannery Row and the jobless fathers and the worried women, and Dora paid grocery bills right and left for two years and very nearly went broke in the process. Dora's girls are well trained and pleasant. They never speak to a man on the street although he may have been in the night before.

Before Alfy, the present watchman, took over, there was a tragedy in the Bear Flag Restaurant which saddened everyone. The previous watchman was named William, and he was a dark and lonesome-looking man. In the day-time when his duties were few he would grow tired of female company. Through the windows he could see Mack and the boys sitting on the pipes in the vacant lot, dangling their feet in the mallow weeds and taking the sun while they discoursed slowly and philosophically of matters of interest but of no importance. Now and then as he watched them he saw them take out a pint of Old Tennis Shoes and wiping the neck of the bottle on a sleeve, raise the pint one after another. And William began to wish he could join that good group. He walked out one day and sat on the pipe. Conversation stopped and an uneasy and hostile silence fell on the group. After a while William went disconsolately back to the Bear Flag, and through the window he saw the conversation spring up again, and it saddened him. He had a dark and ugly face and a mouth twisted with brooding.

The next day he went again, and this time he took a pint of whisky. Mack and the boys drank the whisky, after all they weren't crazy, but all the talking they did was 'Good luck,' and 'Lookin' at you.'

After a while William went back to the Bear Flag and he watched them through the window, and he heard Mack raise his voice saying: 'But God damn it, I hate a pimp!' Now this was obviously untrue, although William didn't know that. Mack and the boys just didn't like William.

Now William's heart broke. The bums would not receive him socially. They felt that he was too far beneath them. William had always been introspective and self-accusing. He put on his hat and walked out along the sea, clear out to the Lighthouse. And he stood in the pretty little cemetery where you can hear the waves drumming always. William thought dark and broody thoughts. No one loved him. No one cared about him. They might call him a watchman, but he was a pimp–a dirty pimp, the lowest thing in the world. And then he thought how he had a right to live and be happy just like anyone else, by God he had. He walked back angrily, but his anger went away when he came to the Bear Flag and climbed the steps. It was evening and the juke-box was playing *Harvest Moon* and William remembered that the first hooker who ever gaffed for him used to like that song before she ran away and got married and disappeared. The song made him awfully sad. Dora was in the back parlour having a cup of tea when William came in. She said: 'What's the matter, you sick?'

'No,' said William. 'But what's the percentage? I feel lousy. I think I'll bump myself off.'

Dora had handled plenty of neurotics in her time. Kid 'em out of it was her motto. 'Well, do it on your own time and don't mess up the rugs,' she said.

A grey damp cloud folded over William's heart and he walked slowly out and down the hall and knocked on Eva Flanagan's door. She had red hair and went to confession every week. Eva was quite a spiritual girl with a big family of brothers and sisters, but she was an unpredictable drunk. She was painting her nails and messing them pretty badly when William went in and he knew she was bagged and Dora wouldn't let a bagged girl work. Her fingers were nail polish to the first joint and she was angry. 'What's eating you?' she said. William grew angry too. 'I'm going to bump myself off,' he said fiercely.

Eva screeched at him. 'That's a dirty, lousy, stinking sin,' she cried, and then: 'Wouldn't it be like you to get the joint pinched just when I got almost enough kick to take a trip to East St Louis. You're a no-good bastard.' She was still screaming at him when William shut her door after him and went to the kitchen. He was very tired of women. The Greek would be restful after women.

The Greek, big apron, sleeves rolled up, was frying pork-chops in two big skillets, turning them over with an ice-pick. 'Hello, Kits. How is going things?' The pork-chops hissed and swished in the pan.

'I don't know, Lou,' said William. 'Sometimes I think the best thing to do would be–kluck!' He drew his finger across his throat.

The Greek laid the ice-pick on the stove and rolled his sleeves higher. 'I tell you what I hear, Kits,' he said. 'I hear like the fella talks about it don't never do it.' William's hand went out for the ice-pick and he held it easily in his hand. His eyes looked deeply into the Greek's dark eyes, and he saw disbelief and amusement, and then as he stared the Greek's eyes grew troubled and then worried. And William saw the change, saw first how the Greek knew he could do it and then the Greek knew he would do it. As soon as he saw that in the Greek's eyes William knew he had to do it. He was sad because now it seemed silly. His hand rose and the ice-pick snapped into his heart. It was amazing how easily it went in. William was the watchman before Alfred came. Everyone liked Alfred. He could sit on the pipes with Mack and the boys any time. He could even visit up at the Palace Flophouse.

4

In the evening just at dusk, a curious thing happened on Cannery Row. It happened in the time between sunset and the lighting of the street light. There is a small quiet grey period then. Down the hill, past the Palace Flophouse, down the chicken-walk, and through the vacant lot came an old Chinaman. He wore an ancient flat straw hat, blue jeans, both coat and trousers, and heavy shoes of which one sole was loose so that it slapped the ground when he walked. In his hand he carried a covered wicker-basket. His face was lean and brown and corded as jerky and his old eyes were brown, even the whites were brown and deep-set so that they looked out of holes. He came by just at dusk and crossed the street and went through the opening between Western Biological and the Hediondo Cannery. Then he crossed the little beach and disappeared among the piles and steel posts which support the piers. No one saw him again until dawn.

But in the dawn, during that time when the street light has been turned off and the daylight has not come, the old Chinaman crept out from among the piles, crossed the beach and the street. His wicker-basket was heavy and wet and dripping now. His loose sole flap-flapped on the street. He went up the hill to the second street, went through a gate in a high board fence, and was not seen again until evening. People, sleeping, heard his flapping shoe go by and they awakened for a moment. It had been happening for years, but no one ever got used to him. Some people thought he was God and very old people thought he was Death and children thought he was a very funny old Chinaman, as children always think anything old and strange is funny. But the children did not taunt him or shout at him as they should, for he carried a little cloud of fear about with him.

Only one brave and beautiful boy of ten named Andy from Salinas ever crossed the old Chinaman. Andy was visiting in Monterey and he saw the old man and knew he must shout at him if only to keep his self-respect, but even Andy, brave as he was, felt the little cloud of fear. Andy watched him go by evening after evening, while his duty and his terror wrestled. And then one evening Andy braced himself and marched behind the old man singing in a shrill falsetto: 'Ching-Chong Chinaman sitting on a rail–'Long came a white man an' chopped off his tail.'

The old man stopped and turned. Andy stopped. The deep-brown eyes looked at Andy and the thin corded lips moved. What happened then Andy was never able either to explain or to forget. For the eyes spread out until there was no Chinaman. And then it was one eye–one huge brown eye as big as a church door. Andy looked through the shiny transparent brown door and through it he saw a lonely countryside, flat for miles but ending against a row of fantastic mountains shaped like cows' and dogs' heads and tents and mushrooms. There was low coarse grass on the plain and here and there a little mound. And a small animal like a woodchuck sat on each mound. And the loneliness–the desolate cold aloneness of the landscape made Andy whimper because there wasn't anybody at all in the world and he was left. Andy shut his eyes so he wouldn't have to see it any more and when he opened them, he was in Cannery Row and the old Chinaman was just flip-flapping between Western Biological and the Hediondo Cannery. Andy was the only boy who ever did that and he never did it again.

5

Western Biological was right across the street and facing the vacant lot. Lee Chong's grocery was on its catty-corner right and Dora's Bear Flag Restaurant was on its catty-corner left. Western Biological deals in strange and beautiful wares. It sells the lovely animals of the sea, the sponges, tunicates, anemones, the stars and buttlestars, and sun stars, the bivalves and barnacles, the worms and shells, the fabulous and multiform little brothers, the living moving flowers of the sea, nudibranchs and ectibranchs, the spiked and nobbed and needy urchins, the crabs and demi-crabs, the little dragoons, the snapping shrimps, and ghost shrimps so transparent that they hardly throw a shadow. And Western Biological sells bugs and snails and spiders, and rattlesnakes, and rats, and honey bees and gila monsters. These are all for sale. Then there are little unborn humans, some whole and others sliced thin and mounted on slides. And for students there are sharks with the blood drained out and yellow and blue colour substituted in veins and arteries, so that you may follow the systems with a scalpel. And there are cats with coloured veins and arteries, and frogs the same. You can order anything living from Western Biological and sooner or later you will get it.

It is a low building facing the street. The basement is the store-room with shelves, shelves clear to the ceiling, loaded with jars of preserved animals. And in the basement is a sink and instruments for embalming and for injecting. Then you go through the backyard to a covered shed on piles over the ocean and here are the tanks for the larger animals, the sharks and rays and octopi, each in their concrete tanks. There is a stairway up the front of the building and a door that opens into an office where there is a desk piled high with unopened mail, filing cabinets, and a safe with the door propped open. Once the safe got locked by mistake and no one knew the combination. And in the safe was an open can of sardines and a piece of Roquefort cheese. Before the combination could be sent by the maker of the lock, there was trouble in the safe. It was then that Doc devised a method for getting revenge on a bank if anyone should ever want to. 'Rent a safety-deposit box,' he said, 'then deposit in it one whole fresh salmon and go away for six months.' After the trouble with the safe, it was not permitted to keep food there any more. It is kept in the filing cabinets. Behind the office is a room where in aquaria are many living animals; there are also the microscopes and the slides and the drug cabinets, the cases of laboratory glass, the work benches and little motors, the chemicals. From this room come smells–formaline, and dry starfish, and sea water and menthol, carbolic acid and acetic acid, smell of brown wrapping-paper and straw and rope, smell of chloroform and ether, smell of ozone from the motors, smell of fine steel and thin lubricant from the microscopes, smell of banana oil and rubber tubing, smell of drying wool socks and boots, sharp pungent smell of rattlesnakes, and musty frightening smell of rats. And through the back door comes the smell of kelp and barnacles when the tide is out and the smell of salt and spray when the tide is in.

To the left the office opens into a library. The walls are bookcases to the ceiling, boxes of pamphlets and separate books of all kinds, dictionaries, encyclopaedias, poetry, plays. A great phonograph stands against the wall with hundreds of records lined up beside it. Under the window is a red-wood bed and on the walls and to the bookcases are pinned reproductions of Daumiers, and Graham, Titian, and Leonardo and Picasso, Dali and George Grosz, pinned here and there at eye level, so that you can look at them if you want to. There are chairs and benches in this little room and of course, the bed. As many as forty people have been here at one time.

Behind this library or music-room, or whatever you want to call it, is the kitchen, a narrow chamber with a gas-stove, a water-heater, and a sink. But whereas some food is kept in the filing cabinets in the office, dishes and cooking fat and vegetables are kept in glass-fronted sectional bookcases in the kitchen. No whimsy dictated this. It just happened. From the ceiling of the kitchen hang pieces of bacon, and salami, and black bêche-de-mer. Behind the kitchen is a toilet and a shower. The toilet leaked for five years until a clever and handsome guest fixed it with a piece of chewing-gum.

Doc is the owner and operator of the Western Biological Laboratory. Doc is rather small, deceptively small, for he is wiry and very strong and when passionate anger comes on him he can be very fierce. He wears a beard and his face is half Christ and half satyr and his face tells the truth. It is said that he has helped many a girl out of one trouble and into another. Doc has the hands of a brain surgeon, and a cool warm mind. Doc tips his hat to dogs as he drives by and the dogs look up and smile at him. He can kill anything for need, but he could not even hurt a feeling for pleasure. He has one great fear–that of getting his head wet, so that summer or winter he ordinarily wears a rain hat. He will wade in a tide pool up to the chest without feeling damp, but a drop of rain water on his head makes him panicky.

Over a period of years Doc dug himself into Cannery Row to an extent not even he suspected. He became the fountain of philosophy and science and art. In the laboratory the girls from Dora's heard the Plain Songs and Gregorian music for the first time. Lee Chong listened while Li Po was read to him in English. Henri the painter heard for the first time the Book of the Dead and was so moved that he changed his medium. Henri had been painting with glue, iron dust, and coloured chicken feathers, but he changed and his next four paintings were done entirely with different kinds of nutshells. Doc would listen to any kind of nonsense and change it for you to a kind of wisdom. His mind had no horizon–and his sympathy had no warp. He could talk to children, telling them very profound things so that they understood. He lived in a world of wonders, of excitement. He was concupiscent as a rabbit and gentle as hell. Everyone who knew him was indebted to him. And everyone who thought of him thought next: 'I really must do something nice for Doc.'

6

Doc was collecting marine animals in the Great Tide Pool on the tip of the Peninsula. It is a fabulous place; when the tide is in, a wave-churned basin, creamy with foam, whipped by the combers that roll in from the whistling buoy on the reef. But when the tide goes out the little water world becomes quiet and lovely. The sea is very clear and the bottom becomes fantastic with hurrying, fighting, feeding, breeding animals. Crabs rush from frond to frond of the waving algae. Starfish squat over mussels and limpets, attach their million little suckers and then slowly lift with incredible power until the prey is broken from the rock. And then the starfish stomach comes out and envelops its food. Orange and speckled and fluted nudibranchs slide gracefully over the rocks, their skirts waving like the dresses of Spanish dancers. And black eels poke their heads out of crevices and wait for prey. The snapping shrimps with their trigger claws pop loudly. The lovely, coloured world is glassed over. Hermit crabs like frantic children scamper on the bottom sand. And now one, finding an empty snail shell he likes better than his own, creeps out, exposing his soft body to the enemy for a moment, and then pops into the new shell. A wave breaks over the barrier, and churns the glassy water for a moment and mixes bubbles into the pool, and then it clears and is tranquil and lovely and murderous again. Here a crab tears a leg from his brother. The anemones expand like soft and brilliant flowers, inviting any tired and perplexed animal to lie for a moment in their arms, and when some small crab or little tide-pool Johnnie accepts the green and purple invitation, the petals whip in, the stinging cells shoot tiny narcotic needles into the prey and it grows weak and perhaps sleepy while the searing caustic digestive acids melt its body down.

Then the creeping murderer, the octopus, steals out, slowly, softly, moving like a grey mist, pretending now to be a bit of weed, now a rock, now a lump of decaying meat, while its evil goat eyes watch coldly. It oozes and flows toward a feeding crab, and as it comes close its yellow eyes burn and its body turns rosy with the pulsing colour of anticipation and rage. Then suddenly it runs lightly on the tip of its arms, as ferociously as a charging cat. It leaps savagely on the crab, there is a puff of black fluid, and the struggling mass is obscured in the sepia cloud while the octopus murders the crab. On the exposed rocks out of water, the barnacles bubble behind their closed doors and the limpets dry out. And down to the rocks come the black flies to eat anything they can find. The sharp smell of iodine from the algae, and the lime smell of calcareous bodies and the smell of powerful protean, smell of sperm and ova fill the air. On the exposed rocks the starfish emit semen and eggs from between their rays. The smells of life and richness, of death and digestion, of decay and birth, burden the air. And salt spray blows in from the barrier where the ocean waits for its rising-tide strength to permit it back into the Great Tide Pool again. And on the reef the whistling buoy bellows like a sad and patient bull.

In the pool Doc and Hazel worked together. Hazel lived in the Palace Flophouse with Mack and the boys. Hazel got his name in as haphazard a way as his life was ever afterward. His worried mother had had seven children in eight years. Hazel was the eighth, and his mother became confused about his sex when he was born. She was tired and run down anyway from trying to feed and clothe seven children and their father. She had tried every possible way of making money–paper flowers, mushrooms at home, rabbits for meat and fur–while her husband from a canvas chair gave her every help his advice and reasoning and criticism could offer. She had a great aunt named Hazel who was reputed to carry life insurance. The eighth child was named Hazel before the mother got it through her head that Hazel was a boy and by that time she was used to the name and never bothered to change it. Hazel grew up–did four years in grammar school, four years in reform school, and didn't learn anything in either place. Reform schools are supposed to teach viciousness and criminality, but Hazel didn't pay enough attention. He came out of reform school as innocent of viciousness as he was of fractions and long division. Hazel loved to hear conversation but he didn't listen to words–just to the tone of conversation. He asked questions, not to hear the answers but simply to continue the flow. He was twenty-six–dark-haired and pleasant, strong, willing and loyal. Quite often he went collecting with Doc and he was very good at it once he knew what was wanted. His fingers would creep like an octopus, could grab and hold like an anemone. He was sure-footed on the slippery rocks and he loved the hunt. Doc wore his rain hat and high rubber-boots as he worked, but Hazel sloshed about in tennis-shoes and blue jeans. They were collecting starfish. Doc had an order for three hundred.

Hazel picked a nobby purplish starfish from the bottom of the pool and popped it into his nearly-full gunny sack. 'I wonder what they do with them,' he said.

'Do with what?' Doc asked.

'The starfish,' said Hazel. 'You sell 'em. You'll send out a barrel of 'em. What do the guys do with 'em? You can't eat 'em.'

'They study them,' said Doc patiently and he remembered that he had answered this question for Hazel dozens of times before. But Doc had one mental habit he could not get over. When anyone asked a question, Doc thought he wanted to know the answer. That was the way with Doc. *He* never asked unless he wanted to know and he could not conceive of the brain that would ask without wanting to know. But Hazel, who simply wanted to hear talk, had developed a system of making the answer to one question the basis of another. It kept conversation going.

'What do they find to study?' Hazel continued. 'They're just starfish. There's millions of 'em around. I could get you a million of 'em.'

'They're complicated and interesting animals,' Doc said a little defensively. 'Besides, these are going to the Middle West to Northwestern University.'

Hazel used his trick. 'They got no starfish there?'

'They got no ocean there,' said Doc.

'Oh!' said Hazel and he cast frantically about for a peg to hang a new question on. He hated to have a conversation die out like this. He wasn't quick enough. While he was looking for a question Doc asked one. Hazel hated that, it meant casting about in his mind for an answer and casting about in Hazel's mind was like wandering alone in a deserted museum. Hazel's mind was choked with uncatalogued exhibits. He never forgot anything, but he never bothered to arrange his memories. Everything was thrown together like fishing-tackle in the bottom of a rowboat, hooks and sinkers and line and lures and gaffs all snarled up.

Doc asked: 'How are things going up at the Palace?'

Hazel ran his fingers through his dark hair and he peered into the clutter of his mind. 'Pretty good,' he said. 'That fellow Gay is moving in with us, I guess. He wife hits him pretty bad. He don't mind that when he's awake, but she waits 'til he gets to sleep and then hits him. He hates that. He has to wake up and beat her up and then when he goes back to sleep she hits him again. He don't get any rest, so he's moving in with us.'

'That's a new one,' said Doc. 'She used to swear out a warrant and put him in jail.'

'Yeah!' said Hazel. 'But that was before they built the new jail in Salinas. Used to be thirty days and Gay was pretty hot to get out, but this new jail–radio in the tank and good bunks and the sheriff's a nice fellow. Gay gets in there and he don't want to come out. He likes it so much his wife won't get him arrested any more. So she figured out this hitting him while he's asleep. It's nerve racking, he says. And you know as good as me–Gay never did take any pleasure in beating her up. He only done it to keep his self-respect. But he gets tired of it. I guess he'll be with us now.'

Doc straightened up. The waves were beginning to break over the barrier of the Great Tide Pool. The tide was coming in and little rivers from the sea had begun to flow over the rocks. The wind blew freshly in from the whistling buoy and the barking sea-lions came from round the point. Doc pushed his rain hat on the back of his head. 'We've got enough starfish,' he said and then went on: 'Look, Hazel, I know you've got six or seven undersized abalones in the bottom of your sack. If we get stopped by a game warden, you're going to say they're mine, on my permit–aren't you?'

'Well–hell,' said Hazel.

'Look,' Doc said kindly. 'Suppose I get an order for abalones and maybe the game warden thinks I'm using my collecting permit too often. Suppose he thinks I'm eating them.'

'Well–hell,' said Hazel.

'It's like the industrial alcohol board. They've got suspicious minds. They always think I'm drinking the alcohol. They think that about everyone.'

'Well, ain't you?'

'Not much of it,' said Doc. 'That stuff they put in it tastes terrible and it's a big job to re-distil it.'

'That stuff ain't so bad,' said Hazel. 'Me and Mack had a snort at it the other day. What is it they put in?'

Doc was about to answer when he saw it was Hazel's trick again. 'Let's get moving,' he said. He hoisted his sack of starfish on his shoulder. And he had forgotten the illegal abalones in the bottom of Hazel's sack.

Hazel followed him up out of the tide pool and up the slippery trail to solid ground. The little crabs scampered and skittered out of their way. Hazel felt that he had better cement the grave over the topic of the abalones.

'That painter guy came back to the Palace,' he offered.

'Yes?' said Doc.

'Yeah! You see, he done all our pictures in chicken-feathers and now he says he got to do them all over again with nut-shells. He says he changed his–his med–medium.'

Doc chuckled. 'He still building his boat?'

'Sure,' said Hazel. 'He's got it all changed around. New kind of a boat. I guess he'll take it apart and change it. Doc–is he nuts?'

Doc swung his heavy sack of starfish to the ground and stood panting a little. 'Nuts?' he asked. 'Oh, yes, I guess so. Nuts about the same amount we are, only in a different way.'

Such a thing had never occurred to Hazel. He looked upon himself as a crystal pool of clarity and on his life as a troubled glass of misunderstood virtue. Doc's last statement had outraged him a little. 'But the boat . . .' he cried. 'He's been building that boat for seven years that I know of. The blocks rotted out and he made concrete blocks. Every time he gets it nearly finished he changes it and starts over again. I think he's nuts. Seven years on a boat.'

Doc was sitting on the ground pulling off his rubber boots. 'You don't understand,' he said gently. 'Henri loves boats, but he's afraid of the ocean.'

'What's he want a boat for then?' Hazel demanded.

'He likes boats,' said Doc. 'But suppose he finishes his boat. Once it's finished people will say: "Why don't you put it in the water?" Then if he puts it in the water, he'll have to go out in it, and he hates the water. So you see, he never finishes the boat–so he doesn't ever have to launch it.'

Hazel had followed this reasoning to a certain point, but he abandoned it before it was resolved, not only abandoned it but searched for some way to change the subject. 'I think he's nuts,' he said lamely.

On the black earth on which the ice-plants bloomed hundreds of black stink bugs crawled. And many of them stuck their tails up in the air. 'Look at all them stink bugs,' Hazel remarked, grateful to the bugs for being there.

'They're interesting,' said Doc.

'Well, what they got their asses up in the air for?'

Doc rolled up his wool socks and put them in the rubber-boots and from his pocket he brought out dry socks and a pair of thin moccasins. 'I don't know why,' he said. 'I looked them up recently–they're very common animals and one of the commonest things they do is put their tails up in the air. And in all the books there isn't one mention of the fact that they put their tails up in the air or why.'

Hazel turned one of the stink bugs over with the toe of his wet tennis-shoe and the shining black beetle strove madly with floundering legs to get upright again. 'Well, why do *you* think they do it?'

'I think they're praying,' said Doc.

'What!' Hazel was shocked.

'The remarkable thing,' said Doc, 'isn't that they put their tails up in the air–the really incredibly remarkable thing is that we find it remarkable. We can only use ourselves as yardsticks. If we did something as inexplicable and strange we'd probably be praying–so maybe they're praying.'

'Let's get the hell out of here,' said Hazel.

7

The Palace Flophouse was no sudden development. Indeed when Mack and Hazel and Eddie and Hughie and Jones moved into it, they looked upon it as little more than shelter from the wind and the rain, as a place to go when everything else had closed or when their welcome was thin and sere with overuse. Then the Palace was only a long bare room, lit dimly by two small windows, walled with unpainted wood smelling strongly of fish meal. They had not loved it then. But Mack knew that some kind of organization was necessary, particularly among such a group of ravening individualists.

A training army which has not been equipped with guns and artillery and tanks uses artificial guns and masquerading trucks to simulate its destructive panoply–and its toughening soldiers get used to field-guns by handling logs on wheels.

Mack, with a piece of chalk, drew five oblongs on the floor, each seven feet long and four feet wide, and in each square he wrote a name. These were the simulated beds. Each man had property rights inviolable in his space. He could legally fight a man who encroached on his square. The rest of the room was property common to all. That was in the first days when Mack and the boys sat on the floor, played cards hunkered down, and slept on the hard boards. Perhaps, save for an accident of weather, they might always have lived that way. However, an unprecedented rainfall which went on for over a month changed all that. House-ridden, the boys grew tired of squatting on the floor. Their eyes became outraged by the bare board walls. Because it sheltered them the house grew dear to them. And it had the charm of never knowing the entrance of an outraged landlord. For Lee Chong never came near it. Then one afternoon Hughie came in with an army cot which had a torn canvas. He spent two hours sewing up the rip with fishing-line. And that night the others lying on the floor in their squares watched Hughie ooze gracefully into his cot–they heard him sigh with abysmal comfort and he was asleep and snoring before anyone else.

The next day Mack puffed up the hill carrying a rusty set of springs he had found on a scrap-iron dump. The apathy was broken then. The boys outdid one another in beautifying the Palace Flophouse until after a few months it was, if anything, over-furnished. There were old carpets on the floor, chairs with and without seats. Mack had a wicker chaise-longue painted bright red. There were tables, a grandfather clock without dial face or works. The walls were whitewashed, which made it almost light and airy. Pictures began to appear–mostly calendars showing improbably luscious blondes holding bottles of Coca-Cola. Henri had contributed two pieces from his chicken-feather period. A bundle of gilded cat-tails stood in one corner and a sheaf of peacock-feathers was nailed to the wall beside the grandfather clock.

They were some time acquiring a stove and when they did find what they wanted, a silver-scrolled monster with floriated warming ovens and a front like a nickle-plated tulip garden, they had trouble getting it. It was too big to steal and its owner refused to part with it to the sick widow with eight children whom Mack invented and patronized in the same moment. The owner wanted a dollar and a half and didn't come down to eighty cents for three days. The boys closed at eighty cents and gave him an IOU, which he probably still has. This transaction took place in Seaside and the stove weighed three hundred pounds. Mack and Hughie exhausted every possibility of haulage for ten days and only when they realized that no one was going to take this stove home for them did they begin to carry it. It took them three days to carry it to Cannery Row, a distance of five miles, and they camped beside it at night. But once installed in the Palace Flophouse it was the glory and the heart and the centre. Its nickel flowers and foliage shone with a cheery light. It was the gold tooth of the Palace. Fired up, it warmed the big room. Its oven was wonderful and you could fry an egg on its shiny black lids.

With the great stove came pride, and with pride, the Palace became home. Eddie planted morning glories to run over the door and Hazel acquired some rather rare fuchsia-bushes planted in five gallon cans which made the entrance formal and a little cluttered. Mack and the boys loved the Palace and they even cleaned it a little sometimes. In their minds they sneered at unsettled people who had no house to go to and occasionally in their pride they brought a guest home for a day or two.

Eddie was understudy bar-tender at 'La Ida'. He filled in when Whitey the regular bar-tender was sick, which was as often as Whitey could get away with it. Every time Eddie filled in, a few bottles disappeared, so he couldn't fill in too often. But Whitey liked to have Eddie take his place because he was convinced, and correctly, that Eddie was one man who wouldn't try to keep his job permanently. Almost anyone could have trusted Eddie to this extent. Eddie didn't have to remove much liquor. He kept a gallon jug under the bar and in the mouth of the jug there was a funnel. Anything left in the glasses Eddie poured into the funnel before he washed the glasses. If an argument or a song were going on at 'La Ida', or late at night when good fellowship had reached its logical conclusion, Eddie poured glasses half or two-thirds full into the funnel. The resulting punch which he took back to the Palace was always interesting and sometimes surprising. The mixture of rye, beer, bourbon, Scotch, wine, rum, and gin was fairly constant, but now and then some effete customer would order a stinger or an anisette or a curaçao and these little touches gave a distinct character to the punch. It was Eddie's habit always to shake a little Angostura into the jug before he left. On a good night Eddie got three-quarters of a gallon. It was a source of satisfaction to him that nobody was out anything. He had observed that a man got just as drunk on half a glass as on a whole one, that is, if he was in the mood to get drunk at all.

Eddie was a very desirable inhabitant of the Palace Flophouse. The others never asked him to help with the house-cleaning and once Hazel washed four pairs of Eddie's socks.

Now on the afternoon when Hazel was out collecting with Doc in the Great Tide Pool, the boys were sitting around in the Palace sipping the result of Eddie's latest contribution. Gay was there too, the latest member of the group. Eddie sipped speculatively from his glass and smacked his lips. 'It's funny how you get a run,' he said. 'Take last night. There was at least ten guys ordered Manhattans. Sometimes maybe you don't get two calls for a Manhattan in a month. It's the grenadine gives the stuff that taste.'

Mack tasted his–a big taste–and refilled his glass. 'Yes,' he said sombrely, 'it's little things make the difference.' He looked about to see how this gem had set with the others.

Only Gay got the full impact. 'Sure is,' he said. 'Does . . .'

'Where's Hazel today?' Mack asked.

Jones said: 'Hazel went out with Doc to get some starfish.'

Mack nodded his head soberly. 'That Doc is a hell of a nice fella,' he said. 'He'll give you a quarter any time. When I cut myself he put on a new bandage every day. A hell of a nice fella.'

The others nodded in profound agreement.

'I been wondering for a long time,' Mack continued, 'what we could do for him–something nice. Something he'd like.'

'He'd like a dame,' said Hughie.

'He's got three four dames,' said Jones. 'You can always tell–when he pulls them front curtains closed and when he plays that kind of church music on the phonograph.'

Mack said reprovingly to Hughie: 'Just because he doesn't run no dame naked through the streets in the daytime, you think Doc's celebrate.'

'What's celebrate?' Eddie asked.

'That's when you can't get no dame,' said Mack.

'I thought it was a kind of party,' said Jones.

A silence fell on the room. Mack shifted in his chaise-longue. Hughie let the front legs of his chair down on the floor. They looked into space and then they all looked at Mack. Mack said: 'Hum!'

Eddie said: 'What kind of a party you think Doc'd like?'

'What other kind is there?' said Jones.

Mack mused: 'Doc wouldn't like this stuff from the winin' jug.'

'How do you know?' Hughie demanded. 'You never offered him none.'

'Oh, I know,' said Mack. 'He's been to college. Once I seen a dame in a fur coat go in there. Never did see her come out. It was two o'clock the last I looked–and that church music goin'. No–you couldn't offer him none of this.' He filled his glass again.

'This tastes pretty nice after the third glass,' Hughie said loyally.

'No,' said Mack. 'Not for Doc. Have to be whisky–the real thing.'

'He likes beer,' said Jones. 'He's all the time going over to Lee's for beer–sometimes in the middle of the night.'

Mack said: 'I figure when you buy beer, you're buying too much tare. Take 8 per cent beer–why you're spending your dough for 92 per cent water and colour and hops and stuff like that. Eddie,' he added, 'you think you could get four five bottles of whisky at "La Ida" next time Whitey's sick?'

'Sure,' said Eddie. 'Sure I could get it, but that'd be the end–no more golden eggs. I think Johnnie's suspicious anyways. Other day he says: "I smell a mouse named Eddie." I was gonna lay low and only bring the jug for a while.'

'Yeah!' said Jones. 'Don't you lose that job. If something happened to Whitey, you could fall right in there for a week or so 'til they got somebody else. I guess if we're goin' to give a party for Doc, we got to buy the whisky. How much is whisky a gallon?'

'I don't know,' said Hughie. 'I never got more than a half-pint at a time myself–at one time that is. I figure you get a quart and right away you got friends. But you get a half-pint and you can drink it in the lot before–well before you got a lot of folks around.'

'It's going to take dough to give Doc a party,' said Mack. 'If we're going to give him a party at all it ought to be a good one. Should have a big cake. I wonder when is his birthday?'

'Don't need a birthday for a party,' said Jones.

'No–but it's nice,' said Mack. 'I figure it would take ten or twelve bucks to give Doc a party you wouldn't be ashamed of.'

They looked at one another speculatively. Hughie suggested: 'The Hediondo Cannery is hiring guys.'

'No,' said Mack quickly. 'We got good reputations and we don't want to spoil them. Every one of us keeps a job for a month or more when we take one. That's why we can always get a job when we need one. S'pose we take a job for a day or so–why we'll lose our reputation for sticking. Then if we needed a job there wouldn't nobody have us.' The rest nodded quick agreement.

'I figure I'm gonna work a couple of months–November and part of December,' said Jones. 'Makes it nice to have money around Christmas. We could cook a turkey this year.' 'By God, we could,' said Mack. 'I know a place up Carmel Valley where there's fifteen hundred in one flock.'

'Valley,' said Hughie. 'You know I used to collect stuff up the Valley for Doc, turtles and crayfish and frogs. Got a nickel apiece for frogs.'

'Me, too,' said Gay. 'I got five hundred frogs one time.'

'If Doc needs frogs it's a set-up,' said Mack. 'We could go up the Carmel River and have a little outing and we wouldn't tell Doc what it was for and then we'd give him one hell of a party.'

A quiet excitement grew in the Palace Flophouse. 'Gay,' said Mack, 'take a look out the door and see if Doc's car is in front of his place.'

Gay set down his glass and looked out. 'Not yet,' he said.

'Well, he ought to be back any minute,' said Mack. 'Now here's how we'll go about it . . .'

8

In April 1932, the boiler at the Hediondo Cannery blew a tube for the third time in two weeks and the board of directors, consisting of Mr Randolph and a stenographer, decided that it would be cheaper to buy a new boiler than to have to shut down so often. In time the new boiler arrived and the old one was moved into the vacant lot between Lee Chong's and the Bear Flag Restaurant, where it was set on blocks to await an inspiration on Mr Randolph's part on how to make some money out of it. Gradually, the plant engineer removed the tubing to use to patch other out-worn equipment at the Hediondo. The boiler looked like an old-fashioned locomotive without wheels. It had a big door in the centre of its nose and a low fire door. Gradually, it became red and soft with rust and gradually the mallow weeds grew up around it and the flaking rust fed the weeds. Flowering myrtle crept up its sides and the wild anise perfumed the air about it. Then someone threw out a datura root and the thick fleshy tree grew up and the great white bells hung over the boiler door and at night the flowers smelled of love and excitement, an incredibly sweet and moving odour.

In 1935 Mr and Mrs Sam Malloy moved into the boiler. The tubing was all gone now and it was a roomy, dry and safe apartment. True, if you came in through the fire door you had to get down on your hands and knees, but once in there was head room in the middle and you couldn't want a dryer, warmer place to stay. They shagged a mattress through the fire door and settled down. Mr Malloy was happy and contented there and for quite a long time so was Mrs Malloy.

Below the boiler on the hill there were numbers of large pipes also abandoned by the Hediondo. Toward the end of 1937 there was a great catch of fish and the canneries were working full time and a housing shortage occurred. Then it was that Mr Malloy took to renting the larger pipes as sleeping-quarters for single men at a very nominal fee. With a piece of tar paper over one end and a square of carpet over the other, they made comfortable bedrooms, although men used to sleeping curled up had to change their habits or move out. There were those too who claimed that their snores echoing back from the pipes woke them up. But on the whole Mr Malloy did a steady small business and was happy.

Mrs Malloy had been contented until her husband became a landlord and then she began to change. First it was a rug, then a wash-tub, then a lamp with a coloured silk shade. Finally, she came into the boiler on her hands and knees one day and she stood up and said a little breathlessly: 'Holman's are having a sale of curtains. Real lace curtains and edges of blue and pink–$1.98 a set with curtain rods thrown in.'

Mr Malloy sat up on the mattress. 'Curtains?' he demanded. 'What in God's name do you want curtains for?'

'I like things nice,' said Mrs Malloy. 'I always did like to have things nice for you,' and her lower lip began to tremble.

'But, darling,' Sam Malloy cried, 'I got nothing against curtains. I like curtains.'

'Only $1.98,' Mrs Malloy quavered, 'and you begrutch me $1.98,' and she sniffled and her chest heaved.

'I don't begrutch you,' said Mr Malloy. 'But, darling–for Christ's sake what are we going to do with curtains? We got no windows.'

Mrs Malloy cried and cried and Sam held her in his arms and comforted her.

'Men just don't understand how a woman feels,' she sobbed. 'Men just never try to put themselves in a woman's place.'

And Sam lay beside her and rubbed her back for a long time before she went to sleep.

9

When Doc's car came back to the laboratory, Mack and the boys secretly watched Hazel help to carry in the sacks of starfish. In a few minutes Hazel came damply up the chicken-walk to the Palace. His jeans were wet with sea water to the thighs and where it was drying the white salt rings were forming. He sat heavily in the patient rocker that was his and shucked off his wet tennis shoes.

Mack asked: 'How is Doc feeling?'

'Fine,' said Hazel. 'You can't understand a word he says. Know what he said about stink bugs? No–I better not tell you.'

'He seem in a nice friendly mood?' Mack asked.

'Sure,' said Hazel. 'We got two three hundred starfish. He's all right.'

'I wonder if we better all go over?' Mack asked himself and he answered himself: 'No, I guess it would be better if one went alone. It might get him mixed up if we all went.'

'What is this?' Hazel asked.

'We got plans,' said Mack. 'I'll go myself so as not to startle him. You guys stay here and wait. I'll come back in a few minutes.'

Mack went out and he teetered down the chicken-walk and across the track. Mr Malloy was sitting on a brick in front of his boiler.

'How are you, Sam?' Mack asked.

'Pretty good.'

'How's the missus?'

'Pretty good,' said Mr Malloy. 'You know any kind of glue that you can stick cloth to iron?'

Ordinarily, Mack would have thrown himself headlong into this problem, but now he was not to be deflected. 'No,' he said.

He went across the vacant lot, crossed the street, and entered the basement of the laboratory.

Doc had his hat off now, since there was practically no chance of getting his head wet unless a pipe broke. He was busy removing the starfish from the wet sacks and arranging them on the cool concrete floor. The starfish were twisted and knotted up, for a starfish loves to hang on to something and for an hour these had found only each other. Doc arranged them in long lines and very slowly they straightened out until they lay in symmetrical stars on the concrete floor. Doc's pointed brown beard was damp with perspiration as he worked. He looked up a little nervously as Mack entered. It was not that trouble always came in with Mack, but something always entered with him.

'Hiya, Doc?' said Mack.

'All right,' said Doc uneasily.

'Hear about Phyllis Mae over at the Bear Flag? She hit a drunk and got his tooth in her fist and it's infected clear to the elbow. She showed me the tooth. It was out of a plate. Is a false-tooth poison, Doc?'

'I guess everything that comes out the human mouth is poison,' said Doc warningfully. 'Has she got a doctor?'

'The bouncer fixed her up,' said Mack.

'I'll take her some sulfa,' said Doc, and he waited for the storm to break. He knew Mack had come for something and Mack knew he knew it.

Mack said: 'Doc, you got any need for any kind of animals now?'

Doc sighed with relief. 'Why?' he asked guardedly.

Mack became open and confidential. 'I'll tell you, Doc. I and the boys got to get some dough–we simply got to. It's for a good purpose, you might say a worthy cause.'

'Phyllis Mae's arm?'

Mack saw the chance, weighed it, and gave it up. 'Well–no,' he said. 'It's more important than that. You can't kill a whore. No–this is different. I and the boys thought if you needed something why we'd get it for you and that way we could make a little piece of change.'

It seemed simple and innocent. Doc laid down four more starfish in lines. 'I could use three or four hundred frogs,' he said. 'I'd get them myself, but I've got to go down to La Jolla tonight. There's a good tide tomorrow and I have to get some octopi.'

'Same price for frogs?' Mack asked. 'Five cents apiece.'

'Same price,' said Doc.

Mack was jovial. 'Don't you worry about frogs, Doc,' he said. 'We'll get you all the frogs you want. You just rest easy about frogs. Why we can get them right up Carmel River. I know a a place.'

'Good,' said Doc. 'I'll take all you get, but I need about three hundred.'

'Just you rest easy, Doc. Don't you lose no sleep about it. You'll get your frogs, maybe seven eight hundred.' He put the Doc at his ease about frogs and then a little cloud crossed Mack's face. 'Doc,' he said, 'any chance of using your car to go up the Valley?'

'No,' said Doc. 'I told you. I have to drive to La Jolla tonight to make tomorrow's tide.'

'Oh,' said Mack dispiritedly. 'Oh. Well, don't you worry about it, Doc. Maybe we can get Lee Chong's old truck.' And then his face fell a little further. 'Doc,' he said, 'on a business deal like this, would you advance two or three bucks for petrol? I know Lee Chong won't give us petrol.'

'No,' said Doc. He had fallen into this before. Once he had financed Gay to go for turtles. He financed him for two weeks and at the end of that time Gay was in jail on his wife's charge and he never did go for turtles.

'Well, maybe we can't go then,' said Mack sadly.

Now Doc really needed the frogs. He tried to work out some method which was business and not philanthropy. 'I'll tell you what I'll do,' he said. 'I'll give you a note to my petrol station so you can get ten gallons of petrol. How will that be?'

Mack smiled. 'Fine,' he said. 'That will work out just fine. I and the boys will get an early start tomorrow. Time you get back from the south, we'll have more damn frogs than you ever seen in your life.'

Doc went to the labelling desk and wrote a note to Red Williams at the petrol station, authorizing the issue of ten gallons of petrol to Mack. 'Here you are,' he said.

Mack was smiling broadly. 'Doc,' he said, 'you can get to sleep tonight and not even give frogs a thought. We'll have piss-pots full of them by the time you get back.'

Doc watched him go a little uneasily. Doc's dealings with Mack and the boys had always been interesting, but rarely had they been profitable to Doc. He remembered ruefully the time Mack sold him fifteen tom-cats and by night the owners came and got every one. 'Mack,' he had asked, 'why all tom-cats?'

Mack said: 'Doc, it's my own invention, but I'll tell you because you're a good friend. You make a big wire trap and then you don't use bait. You use–well–you use a lady cat. Catch every God-damn tom-cat in the country that way.'

From the laboratory Mack crossed the street and went through the swinging screen doors into Lee Chong's grocery. Mrs Lee was cutting bacon on the big butcher's block. A Lee cousin primped up slightly wilted heads of lettuce the way a girl primps a loose finger wave. A cat lay asleep on a big pile of oranges. Lee Chong stood in his usual place behind the cigar counter and in front of the liquor shelves. His tapping finger on the change mat speeded up a little when Mack came in.

Mack wasted no time in sparring. 'Lee,' he said, 'Doc over there's got a problem. He's got a big order for frogs from the New York Museum. Means a lot to Doc. Besides the dough there's a lot of credit getting an order like that. Doc's got to go south and I and the boys said we'd help him out. I think a guy's friends ought to help him out of a hole when they can, especially a nice guy like Doc. Why I bet he spends sixty seventy dollars a month with you.'

Lee Chong remained silent and watchful. His fat finger barely moved on the change mat, but it flicked slightly like a tense cat's tail.

Mack plunged into his thesis. 'Will you let us take your old truck to go up Carmel Valley for frogs for Doc–for good old Doc?'

Lee Chong smiled in triumph. 'Tluck no good,' he said. 'Bloke down.'

This staggered Mack for a moment, but he recovered. He spread the order for petrol on the cigar counter. 'Look!' he said 'Doc needs them frogs. He give me this order for petrol to get them. I can't let Doc down. Now Gay is a good mechanic. If he fixes your truck and puts it in good shape, will you let us take it?'

Lee put back his head so that he could see Mack through his half-glasses. There didn't seem to be anything wrong with the proposition. The truck really wouldn't run. Gay really was a good mechanic and the order for petrol was definite evidence of good faith.

'How long you be gone?' Lee asked.

'Maybe half a day, maybe a whole day. Just 'til we get the frogs.'

Lee was worried, but he couldn't see any way out. The dangers were all there and Lee knew all of them. 'Okay,' said Lee.

'Good,' said Mack. 'I knew Doc could depend on you. I'll get Gay right to work on that truck.' He turned about to leave. 'By the way,' he said. 'Doc's paying us five cents apiece for those frogs. We're going to get seven or eight hundred. How about taking a pint of Old Tennis Shoes just 'til we can get back with the frogs?'

'No!' said Lee Chong.

10

Frankie began coming to Western Biological when he was eleven years old. For a week or so he just stood outside the basement door and looked in. Then one day he stood inside the door. Ten days later he was in the basement. He had very large eyes and his hair was a dark wiry, dirty shock. His hands were filthy. He picked up a piece of excelsior and put it in a garbage can and then he looked at Doc where he worked labelling specimen bottles containing purple Velella. Finally Frankie got to the work-bench and he put his dirty fingers on the bench. It took Frankie three weeks to get that far, and he was ready to bolt every instant of the time.

Finally one day Doc spoke to him. 'What's your name, son?'

'Frankie.'

'Where do you live?'

'Up there,' a gesture up the hill.

'Why aren't you in school?'

'I don't go to school.'

'Why not?'

'They don't want me there.'

'Your hands are dirty. Don't you ever wash?'

Frankie looked stricken and then he went to the sink and scrubbed his hands, and always afterwards he scrubbed his hands almost raw every day.

And he came to the laboratory every day. It was an association without much talk. Doc by a telephone call established that what Frankie said was true. They didn't want him in school. He couldn't learn and there was something a little wrong with his co-ordination. There was no place for him. He wasn't an idiot, he wasn't dangerous, his parents, or parent, would not pay for his keep in an institution. Frankie didn't often sleep at the laboratory, but he spent his days there. And sometimes he crawled in the excelsior crate and slept. That was probably when there was a crisis at home.

Doc asked: 'Why do you come here?'

'You don't hit me or give me a nickel,' said Frankie.

'Do they hit you at home?'

'There's uncles around all the time at home. Some of them hit me and tell me to get out and some of them give me a nickel and tell me to get out.'

'Where's your father?'

'Dead,' said Frankie vaguely.

'Where's your mother?'

'With the uncles.'

Doc clipped Frankie's hair and got rid of the lice. At Lee Chong's he got him a new pair of overalls and a striped sweater and Frankie became his slave.

'I love you,' he said one afternoon. 'Oh, I love you.'

He wanted to work in the laboratory. He swept out every day, but there was something a little wrong. He couldn't get a floor quite clean. He tried to help with grading crayfish for size. There they were in a bucket, all sizes. They were to be grouped in the big pans–laid out–all the three-inch ones together and all the four-inch ones, and so forth. Frankie tried and the perspiration stood on his forehead, but he couldn't do it. Size relationships just didn't get through to him.

'No,' Doc would say. 'Look, Frankie. Put them beside your finger like this so you'll know which ones are this long. See? This one goes from the tip of your finger to the base of your thumb. Now you just pick out another one that goes from the tip of your finger down to the same place and it will be right.' Frankie tried and he couldn't do it. When Doc went upstairs Frankie crawled in the excelsior box and didn't come out all afternoon.

But Frankie was a nice, good, kind boy. He learned to light Doc's cigars and wanted Doc to smoke all the time so he could light the cigars.

Better than anything else Frankie loved it when there were parties upstairs in the laboratory. When girls and men gathered to sit and talk, when the great phonograph played music that throbbed in his stomach and made beautiful and huge pictures form vaguely in his head. Frankie loved it. Then he crouched down in a corner behind a chair where he was hidden and could watch and listen. When there was laughter at a joke he didn't understand Frankie laughed delightedly behind his chair, and when the conversation dealt with abstractions his brow furrowed and he became intent and serious.

One afternoon he did a desperate thing. There was a small party in the laboratory. Doc was in the kitchen pouring beer when Frankie appeared beside him. Frankie grabbed a glass of beer and rushed it through the door and gave it to a girl sitting in a big chair.

She took the glass and said: 'Why, thank you,' and she smiled at him.

And Doc coming through the door said: 'Yes, Frankie is a great help to me.'

Frankie couldn't forget that. He did the thing in his mind over and over, just how he had taken the glass and just how the girl sat and then her voice–'Why, thank you,' and Doc '–a great help to me–Frankie is a great help to me–sure Frankie is a great help–Frankie,' and Oh, my God!

He knew a big party was coming because Doc bought steaks and a great deal of beer and Doc let him help clean out all the upstairs. But that was nothing, for a great plan had formed in Frankie's mind and he could see just how it would be. He went over it again and again. It was beautiful. It was perfect.

Then the party started and people came and sat in the front room, girls and young women and men.

Frankie had to wait until he had the kitchen to himself, and the door closed. And it was some time before he had it so. But at last he was alone and the door was shut. He could hear the chatter of conversation and the music from the great phonograph. He worked very quietly–first the tray–then get out the glasses without breaking any. Now fill them with beer and let the foam settle a little and then fill again.

Now he was ready. He took a great breath and opened the door. The music and the talk roared around him. Frankie picked up the tray of beer and walked through the door. He knew how. He went straight toward the same young woman who had thanked him before. And then right in front of her, the thing happened, and co-ordination failed, the hands fumbled, the muscles panicked, the nerves telegraphed to a dead operator, the responses did not come back. Tray and beer collapsed forward into the young woman's lap. For a moment

Frankie stood still. And then he turned and ran.

The room was quiet. They could hear him run downstairs and go into the cellar. The heard a hollow scrabbling sound–and then silence.

Doc walked quietly down the stairs and into the cellar. Frankie was in the excelsior box burrowed down clear to the bottom, with the pile of excelsior on top of him. Doc could hear him whimpering there. Doc waited for a moment and then he went quietly back upstairs.

There wasn't a thing in the world he could do.

11

The Model T Ford truck of Lee Chong had a dignified history. In 1923 it had been a passenger car belonging to Dr W. T. Waters. He used it for five years and sold it to an insurance man named Rattle. Mr Rattle was not a careful man. The car he got in clean nice condition he drove like fury. Mr Rattle drank on Saturday nights and the car suffered. The fenders were broken and bent. He was a pedal rider too and the bands had to be changed often. When Mr Rattle embezzled a client's money and ran away to San Jose, he was caught with a high-hair blonde and sent up within ten days.

The body of the car was so battered that its next owner cut it in two and added a little truck bed.

The next owner took off the front of the cab and the windshield. He used it to haul squids and he liked a fresh breeze to blow in his face. His name was Francis Almones, and he had a sad life, for he always made just a fraction less than he needed to live. His father had left him a little money, but year by year and month by month, no matter how hard Francis worked or how careful he was, his money grew less until he just dried up and blew away.

Lee Chong got the truck in payment of a grocery bill.

By this time the truck was little more than four wheels and an engine, and the engine was so crotchety and sullen and senile that it required expert care and consideration. Lee Chong did not give it these things, with the result that the truck stood in the tall grass back of the grocery most of the time with the mallows growing between its spokes. It had solid tyres on its back wheels and blocks held its front wheels off the ground.

Probably any one of the boys from the Palace Flophouse could have made the truck run, for they were all competent practical mechanics, but Gay was an inspired mechanic. There is no term comparable to green thumbs to apply to such a mechanic, but there should be. For there are men who can look, listen, tap, make an adjustment, and a machine works. Indeed there are men near whom a car runs better. And such a one was Gay. His fingers on a timer or a carburettor adjustment screw were gentle and wise and sure. He could fix the delicate electric motors in the laboratory. He could have worked in the canneries all the time had he wished, for in that industry, which complains bitterly when it does not make back its total investment every year in profits, the machinery is much less important than the fiscal statement. Indeed, if you could can sardines with ledgers, the owners would have been very happy. As it was they used decrepit, struggling old horrors of machines that needed the constant attention of a man like Gay.

Mack got the boys up early. They had their coffee and immediately moved over to the truck where it lay among the weeds. Gay was in charge. He kicked the blocked-up front wheels. 'Go borrow a pump and get those pumped up,' he said. Then he put a stick in the petrol-tank under the board which served as a seat. By some miracle there was a half-inch of petrol in the tank. Now Gay went over the most probable difficulties. He took out the coil boxes, scraped the points, adjusted the gap, and put them back. He opened the carburettor to see that petrol came through. He pushed on the crank to see that the whole shaft wasn't frozen and the pistons rusted in their cylinders.

Meanwhile the pump arrived and Eddie and Jones spelled each other on the tyres.

Gay hummed: 'Dum tiddy–dum tiddy,' as he worked. He removed the spark-plugs and scraped the points and bored the carbon out. Then Gay drained a little petrol into a can and poured some into each cylinder before he put the spark-plugs back. He straightened up. 'We're going to need a couple of dry cells,' he said. 'See if Lee Chong will let us have a couple.'

Mack departed and returned almost immediately with a universal No which was designed by Lee Chong to cover all future requests.

Gay thought deeply. 'I know where's a couple–pretty good ones too, but I won't go get them.'

'Where?' asked Mack.

'Down cellar at my house,' said Gay. 'They run the front-door bell. If one of you fellas wants to kind of edge into my cellar without my wife seeing you, they're on top of the side stringer on the left-hand side as you go in. But for God's sake, don't let my wife catch you.'

A conference elected Eddie to go and he departed.

'If you get caught don't mention me,' Gay called out after him. Meanwhile Gay tested the bands. The low-high pedal didn't quite touch the floor, so he knew there was a little band left. The brake pedal did touch the floor, so there was no brake, but the reverse pedal had lots of band left. On a Model T Ford the reverse is your margin of safety. When your brake is gone, you can use reverse as a brake. And when the low gear band is worn too thin to pull up a steep hill, why, you can turn round and back up it. Gay found there was plenty of reverse and he knew everything was all right.

It was a good omen that Eddie came back with the dry cells without trouble. Mrs Gay had been in the kitchen. Eddie could hear her walking about, but she didn't hear Eddie. He was very good at such things.

Gay connected the dry cells and he advanced the petrol and retarded the spark-lever. 'Twist her tail,' he said.

He was such a wonder, Gay was–the little mechanic of God, the St Francis of all things that turn and twist and explode, the St Francis of coils and armatures and gears. And if at some time all the heaps of cars, cut-down Dusenbergs, Buicks, De Sotos and Plymouths, American Austins and Isotta-Fraschinis praise God in a great chorus–it will be largely due to Gay and his brotherhood.

One twist–one little twist and the engine caught and laboured and faltered and caught again. Gay advanced the spark and reduced the petrol. He switched over the magneto and the Ford of Lee Chong chuckled and jiggled and clattered happily as though it knew it was working for a man who loved and understood it.

There were two small technical legal difficulties with the truck–it had no recent licence plates and it had no lights. But the boys hung a rag permanently and accidentally on the rear plate to conceal its vintage and they dabbed the front plate with good thick mud. The equipment of the expedition was slight: some long-handled frog-nets and some gunny-sacks. City hunters going out for sport load themselves with food and liquor, but not Mack. He presumed rightly that the country was where food came from. Two loaves of bread and what was left of Eddie's wining jug was all the supply. The party clambered on the truck. Gay drove and Mack sat beside him; they bumped round the corner of Lee Chong's and down through the lot, threading among the pipes. Mr Malloy waved at them from his seat by the boiler. Gay eased across the pavement and down off the kerb gently because the front tyres showed fabric all the way around. With all their alacrity, it was afternoon when they got started.

The truck eased into Red Williams' service station. Mack got out and gave his paper to Red. He said: 'Doc was a little short of change. So if you'll put five gallons in and just give us a buck instead of the other five gallons, why, that's what Doc wants. He had to go south, you know. Had a big deal down there.'

Red smiled good-naturedly. 'You know, Mack,' he said, 'Doc got to figuring if there was some kind of loop-hole, and he put his finger on the same one you did. Doc's a pretty bright fellow. So he phoned me last night.'

'Put in the whole ten gallons,' said Mack. 'No–wait. It'll slop around and spill. Put in five and give us five in a can–one of them sealed cans.'

Red smiled happily. 'Doc kind of figured that one too,' he said.

'Put in ten gallons,' said Mack. 'And don't go leaving none in the hose.'

The little expedition did not go through the centre of Monterey. A delicacy about the licence plates and the lights made Gay choose back streets. There would be the time when they would go up Carmel Hill and down into the Valley, a good four miles on a main highway, exposed to any passing cop until they turned up the fairly unfrequented Carmel Valley road. Gay chose a back street that brought them out on the main highway at Peter's Gate just before the steep Carmel Hill starts. Gay took a good noisy clattering run at the hill and in fifty yards he put the pedal down too low. He knew it wouldn't work, the band was worn too thin. On the level it was all right, but not on a hill. He stopped, let the truck back round and aimed it down the hill. Then he gave it the petrol and the reverse pedal. And the reverse was not worn. The truck crawled steadily and slowly but backward up Carmel Hill.

And they very nearly made it. The radiator boiled, of course, but most Model T experts believed that it wasn't working well if it wasn't boiling.

Someone should write an erudite essay on the moral, physical, and aesthetic effect of the Model T Ford on the American nation. Two generations of Americans knew more about the Ford coil than the clitoris, about the planetary system of gears than the solar system of stars. With the Model T, part of the concept of private property disappeared. Pliers ceased to be privately owned and a tyre-pump belonged to the last man who had picked it up. Most of the babies of the period were conceived in Model T Fords and not a few were born in them. The theory of the Anglo-Saxon home became so warped that it never quite recovered.

The truck backed sturdily up Carmel Hill and it got past the Jack's Peak road and was just going into the last and steepest pull when the motor's breathing quicked, gulped, and strangled. It seemed very quiet when the motor was still. Gay, who was heading down-hill, anyway, ran down the hill fifty feet and turned into the Jack's Peak road entrance.

'What is it?' Mack asked.

'Carburettor, I think,' said Gay. The engine sizzled and creaked with heat and the jet of steam that blew down the overflow-pipe sounded like the hiss of an alligator.

The carburettor of a Model T is not complicated, but it needs all of its parts to function. There is a needle valve, and the point must be on the needle and must sit in its hole or the carburettor does not work.

Gay held the needle in his hand and the point was broken off. 'How in the hell you s'pose that happened?' he asked.

'Magic,' said Mack, 'just pure magic. Can you fix it?'

'Hell, no,' said Gay. 'Got to get another one.'

'How much they cost?'

'About a buck if you buy one new–quarter at a wrecker's.'

'You got a buck?' Mack asked.

'Yeah, but I won't need it.'

'Well, get back as soon as you can, will you? We'll just stay right here.'

'Anyways, you won't go running off without a needle valve,' said Gay. He stepped out to the road. He thumbed three cars before one stopped for him. The boys watched him climb in and start down the hill. They didn't see him again for one hundred and eighty days.

Oh, the infinity of possibility! How could it happen that the car that picked up Gay broke down before it got into Monterey? If Gay had not been a mechanic, he would not have fixed the car. If he had not fixed it the owner wouldn't have taken him to Jimmy Brucia's for a drink. And why was it Jimmy's birthday? Out of all the possibilities in the world–the millions of them–only events occurred that lead to the Salinas jail. Sparky Enea and Tiny Colletti had made up a quarrel and were helping Jimmy to celebrate his birthday. The blonde came in. The musical argument in front of the juke-box. Gay's new friend who knew a judo hold and tried to show it to Sparky and got his wrist broken when the hold went wrong. The policeman with a bad stomach–all unrelated, irrelevant details and yet all running in one direction. Fate just didn't intend Gay to go on that frog-hunt, and Fate took a hell of a lot of trouble and people and accidents to keep him from it. When the final climax came with the front of Holman's bootery broken out and the party trying on the shoes in the display window only Gay didn't hear the fire whistle. Only Gay didn't go to the fire, and when the police came they found him sitting all alone in Holman's window wearing one brown Oxford and one patent leather dress shoe with a grey cloth top.

Back at the truck the boys built a little fire when it got dark and the chill crept up from the ocean. The pines above them soughed in the fresh sea wind. The boys lay in the pine-needles and looked at the lonely sky through the pine branches. For a while they spoke of the difficulties Gay must be having getting a needle valve, and then gradually as the time passed they didn't mention him any more.

'Somebody should of gone with him,' said Mack.

About ten o'clock Eddie got up. 'There's a construction camp a piece up the hill,' he said. 'I think I'll go up and see if they got any Model T's.'

12

Monterey is a city with a long and brilliant literary tradition. It remembers with pleasure and some glory that Robert Louis Stevenson lived there. Treasure Island certainly has the topography and the coastal plan of Pt Lobos. More recently in Carmel there have been a great number of literary men about, but there is not the old flavour, the old dignity of the true *belles-lettres*. Once the town was greatly outraged over what the citizens considered a slight to an author. It had to do with the death of Josh Billings, the great humorist.

Where the new post office is, there used to be a deep gulch with water flowing in it and a little foot-bridge over it. On one side of the gulch was a fine old adobe and on the other the house of the doctor who handled all the sickness, birth, and death in the town. He worked with animals too and, having studied in France, he even dabbled in the new practice of embalming bodies before they were buried. Some of the old-timers considered this sentimental and some thought it wasteful, and to some it was sacrilegious since there was no provision for it in any sacred volume. But the better and richer families were coming to it, and it looked to become a fad.

One morning elderly Mr Carriaga was walking from his house on the hill down toward Alvarado Street. He was just crossing the foot-bridge when his attention was drawn to a small boy and a dog struggling up out of the gulch. The boy carried a liver while the dog dragged yards of intestine at the end of which a stomach dangled. Mr Carriaga paused and addressed the little boy politely: 'Good morning.'

In those days little boys were courteous. 'Good morning, sir.'

'Where are you going with the liver?'

'I'm going to make some chum and catch some mackerel.'

Mr Carriaga smiled. 'And the dog, will he catch mackerel too?'

'The dog found that. It's his, sir. We found them in the gulch.'

Mr Carriaga smiled and strolled on and then his mind began to work. That isn't a beef liver, it's too small. And it isn't a calf's liver, it's too red. It isn't a sheep's liver . . . Now his mind was alert. At the corner he met Mr Ryan.

'Anyone die in Monterey last night?' he asked.

'Not that I know of,' said Mr Ryan.

'Anyone killed?'

'No.'

They walked on together and Mr Carriaga told about the little boy and the dog.

At the 'Adobe Bar' a number of citizens were gathered for their morning conversation. There Mr Carriaga told his story again, and he had just finished when the constable came into the 'Adobe'. He should know if anyone had died. 'No one died in Monterey,' he said. 'But Josh Billings died out at the Hotel del Monte.'

The men in the bar were silent. And the same thought went through all their minds. Josh Billings was a great man, a great writer. He had honoured Monterey by dying there and he had been degraded. Without much discussion a committee formed made up of everyone there. The stern men walked quickly to the gulch and across the foot-bridge and they hammered on the door of the doctor who had studied in France.

He had worked late. The knocking got him out of bed and brought him tousled of hair and beard to the door in his nightgown. Mr Carriaga addressed him sternly: 'Did you embalm Josh Billings?'

'Why–yes.'

'What did you do with his "innards"?'

'Why–I threw them in the gulch where I always do.'

They made him dress quickly then and they hurried down to the beach. If the little boy had gone quickly about his business, it would have been too late. He was just getting into a boat when the committee arrived. The intestine was in the sand where the dog had abandoned it.

Then the French doctor was made to collect the parts. He was forced to wash them reverently and pick out as much sand as possible. The doctor himself had to stand the expense of the leaden box which went into the coffin of Josh Billings. For Monterey was not a town to let dishonour come to a literary man.

13

Mack and the boys slept peacefully on the pine-needles. Some time before dawn Eddie came back. He had gone a long way before he found a Model T. And then when he did, he wondered whether or not it would be a good idea to take the needle out of its seat. It might not fit. So he took the whole carburettor. The boys didn't wake up when he got back. He lay down beside them and slept under the pine-trees. There was one nice thing about Model T's. The parts were not only interchangeable, they were unidentifiable.

There is a beautiful view from the Carmel grade, the curving bay with the waves creaming on the sand, the dune country around Seaside and right at the bottom of the hill, the warm intimacy of the town.

Mack got up in the dawn and hustled his pants where they bound him and he stood looking down on the bay. He could see some of the purse-seiners coming in. A tanker stood over against Seaside, taking on oil. Behind him the rabbits stirred in the bush. Then the sun came up and shook the night chill out of the air the way you'd shake a rug. When he felt the first sun warmth, Mack shivered.

The boys ate a little bread while Eddie installed the new carburettor. And when it was ready, they didn't bother to crank it. They pushed it out to the highway and coasted in gear until it started. And then, Eddie driving, they backed up over the rise, over the top and turned and headed forward and down past Hatton Fields. In Carmel Valley the artichoke plants stood grey-green, and the willows were lush along the river. They turned left up the valley. Luck blossomed from the first. A dusty Rhode Island red rooster who had wandered too far from his own farmyard crossed the road and Eddie hit him without running too far off the road. Sitting in the back of the truck, Hazel picked him as they went and let the feathers fly from his hand, the most widely distributed evidence on record, for there was a little breeze in the morning blowing down from Jamesburg and some of the red chicken feathers were deposited on Pt Lobos and some even blew out to sea.

The Carmel is a lovely little river. It isn't very long, but in its course it has everything a river should have. It rises in the mountains, and tumbles down a while, runs through shallows, is dammed to make a lake, spills over the dam, crackles among round boulders, wanders lazily under sycamores, spills into pools where trout live, drops in against banks where crayfish live. In the winter it becomes a torrent, a mean little fierce river, and in the summer it is a place for children to wade in and for fishermen to wander in. Frogs blink from its banks and the deep ferns grow beside it. Deer and foxes come to drink from it, secretly in the morning and evening, and now and then a mountain lion crouched flat laps its water. The farms of the rich little valley back up to the river and take its water for the orchards and the vegetables. The quail call beside it and the wild doves come whistling in at dusk. Raccoons pace its edges looking for frogs. It's everything a river should be.

A few miles up the valley the river cuts in under a high cliff from which vines and ferns hang down. At the base of this cliff there is a pool, green and deep, and on the other side of the pool there is a little sandy place where it is good to sit and to cook your dinner.

Mack and the boys came down to this place happily. It was perfect. If frogs were available, they would be here. It was a place to relax, a place to be happy. On the way out they had thriven. In addition to the big red chicken there was a sack of carrots which had fallen from a vegetable truck, half a dozen onions which had not. Mack had a bag of coffee in his pocket. In the truck there was a five-gallon can with the top cut off. The wining jug was nearly half full. Such things as salt and pepper had been brought. Mack and the boys would have thought anyone who travelled without salt, pepper, and coffee very silly indeed.

Without effort, confusion, or much thought, four round stones were rolled together on the little beach. The rooster who had challenged the sunrise of this very day lay dismembered and clean in water in the five-gallon can with peeled onions about him, while a little fire of dead willow sticks sputtered between the stones, a very little fire. Only fools build big fires. It would take a long time to cook this rooster, for it had taken him a long time to achieve this size and muscularity. But as the water began to boil gently about him, he smelled good from the beginning.

Mack gave them a pep talk. 'The best time for frogs is at night,' he said, 'so I guess we'll just lay around 'til it gets dark.' They sat in the shade and gradually one by one they stretched out and slept.

Mack was right. Frogs do not move around much in the day-time; they hide under ferns and they look secretly out of holes under rocks. The way to catch frogs is with a flashlight at night. The men slept knowing they might have a very active night. Only Hazel stayed awake to replenish the little fire under the cooking chicken.

There is no golden afternoon next to the cliff. When the sun went over it at about two o'clock a whispering shade came to the beach. The sycamores rustled in the afternoon breeze. Little water-snakes slipped down to the rocks and then gently entered the water and swam along through the pool, their heads held up like little periscopes and a tiny wake spreading behind them. A big trout jumped in the pool. The gnats and mosquitoes which avoid the sun came out and buzzed over the water. All of the sun bugs, the flies, the dragonflies, the wasps, the hornets, went home. And as the shadow came to the beach, as the first quail began to call, Mack and the boys awakened. The smell of the chicken stew was heart-breaking. Hazel had picked a fresh bay-leaf from a tree by the river and he had dropped it in. The carrots were in now. Coffee in its own can was simmering on its own rock, far enough from the flame so that it did not boil too hard. Mack awakened, started up, stretched, staggered to the pool, washed his face with cupped hands, hacked, spat, washed out his mouth, broke wind, tightened his belt, scratched his legs, combed his wet hair with his fingers, drank from the jug, belched, and sat down by the fire. 'By God that smells good,' he said.

Men all do about the same things when they wake up. Mack's process was loosely the one all of them followed. And soon they had all come to the fire and complimented Hazel. Hazel stuck his pocket-knife into the muscles of the chicken.

'He ain't going to be what you'd call tender,' said Hazel. 'You'd have to cook him about two weeks to get him tender. How old about do you judge he was, Mack?'

'I'm forty-eight and I ain't as tough as he is,' said Mack.

Eddie said: 'How old can a chicken get, do you think–that's if nobody pushed him around or he don't get sick?'

'That's something nobody isn't ever going to find out,' said Jones.

It was a pleasant time. The jug went around and warmed them.

Jones said: 'Eddie, I don't mean to complain none. I was just thinkin'. S'pose you had two or three jugs back of the bar. S'pose you put all the whisky in one and all the wine in another and all the beer in another . . .'

A slightly shocked silence followed the suggestion. 'I didn't mean nothin',' said Jones quickly. 'I like it this way . . .' Jones talked too much then because he knew he had made a social blunder and he wasn't able to stop. 'What I like about it this way is you never know what kind of a drunk you're going to get out of it,' he said. 'You take whisky,' he said hurriedly. 'You more or less know what you'll do. A fightin' guy fights and a cryin' guy cries, but this'–he said magnanimously–'why, you don't know whether it'll run you up a pine-tree or start you swimming to Santa Cruz. It's more fun that way,' he said weakly.

'Speaking of swimming,' said Mack to fill in the indelicate place in the conversation and to shut Jones up. 'I wonder whatever happened to that guy McKinley Moran. Remember that deep-sea diver?'

'I remember him,' said Hughie. 'I and him used to hang around together. He just didn't get much work and then he got to drinking. It's kind of tough on you divin' and drinkin'. Got to worryin' too. Finally he sold his suit and helmet and pump and went on a hell of a drunk and then he left town. I don't know where he went. He wasn't no good after he went down after that Wop that got took down with the anchor from the *Twelve Brothers*. McKinley just dove down. Bust his ear-drums, and he wasn't no good after that. Didn't hurt the Wop a bit.'

Mack sampled the jug again. 'He used to make a lot of dough during Prohibition,' Mack said. 'Used to get twenty-five bucks a day from the government to dive lookin' for liquor on the bottom and he got three dollars a case from Louie for not findin' it. Had it worked out so he brought up one case a day to keep the government happy. Louie didn't mind that none. Made it so they didn't get in no new divers. McKinley made a lot of dough.'

'Yeah,' said Hughie. 'But he's like everybody else–gets some dough and he wants to get married. He got married three times before his dough run out. I could always tell. He'd buy a white fox piece and bang!–next thing you'd know, he's married.'

'I wonder what happened to Gay,' Eddie asked. It was the first time they had spoken of him.

'Same thing, I guess,' said Mack. 'You just can't trust a married guy. No matter how much he hates his old lady why he'll go back to her. Get to thinkin' and broodin' and back he'll go. You can't trust him no more. Take Gay,' said Mack. 'His old lady hits him. But I bet you when Gay's away from her three days, he gets it figured out that it's his fault and he goes back to make it up to her.'

They ate long and daintily, spearing out pieces of chicken, holding the dripping pieces until they cooled, and then gnawing the muscled meat from the bone. They speared the carrots on pointed willow switches and finally they passed the can and drank the juice. And around them the evening crept in as delicately as music. The quail called each other down to the water. The trout jumped in the pool. And the moths came down and fluttered about the pool as the daylight mixed into the darkness. They passed the coffee-can about and they were warm and fed and silent. At last Mack said: 'God damn it. I hate a liar.'

'Who's been lyin' to you?' Eddie asked.

'Oh, I don't mind a guy that tells a little one to get along or to hop up a conversation, but I hate a guy that lies to himself.'

'Who done that?' Eddie asked.

'Me,' said Mack. 'And maybe you guys. Here we are,' he said earnestly, 'the whole God damned shabby lot of us. We worked it out that we wanted to give Doc a party. So we come out here and have a hell of a lot of fun. Then we'll go back and get the dough from Doc. There's five of us, so we'll drink five times as much liquor as he will. And I ain't sure we're doin' it for Doc. I ain't sure we ain't doin' it for ourselves. And Doc's too nice a fella to do that to. Doc is the nicest fella I ever knew. I don't want to be the kind of a guy that would take advantage of him. You know one time I put the bee on him for a buck. I give him a hell of a story. Right in the middle I seen he knew God damn well the story was so much malarky. So right in the middle I says: "Doc, that's a fuggin' lie!" And he put his hand in his pocket and brought out a buck. "Mack," he says, "I figure a guy that needs it bad enough to make up a lie to get it, really needs it," and he give me the buck. I paid him that buck back the next day. I never did spend it. Just kept it overnight and then give it back to him.'

Hazel said: 'There ain't nobody likes a party better than Doc. We're givin' him the party. What the hell is the beef?'

'I don't know,' said Mack, 'I'd like just to give him some thing when I didn't get most of it back.'

'How about a present?' Hughie suggested. 'S'pose we just bought the whisky and give it to him and let him do what he wants.'

'Now you're talkin',' said Mack. 'That's just what we'll do. We'll just give him the whisky and fade out.'

'You know what'll happen,' said Eddie. 'Henri and them people from Carmel will smell that whisky out and then instead of only five of us there'll be twenty. Doc told me one time himself they can smell him fryin' a steak from Cannery Row clear down to Point Sur. I don't see the percentage. He'd come out better if we give him the party ourselves.'

Mack considered this reasoning. 'Maybe you're right,' he said at last. 'But s'pose we give him something except whisky, maybe cuff-links with his initials.'

'Oh, horse shit,' said Hazel. 'Doc don't want stuff like that.'

The night was in by now and the stars were white in the sky. Hazel fed the fire and it put a little room of light on the beach. Over the hill a fox was barking sharply. And now in the night the smell of sage came down from the hills. The water chuckled on the stones where it went out of the deep pool.

Mack was mulling over the last piece of reasoning when the sound of footsteps on the ground made them turn. A man dark and large stalked near and he had a shot-gun over his arm and a pointer walked shyly and delicately at his heel.

'What the hell are you doing here?' he asked.

'Nothing,' said Mack.

'The land's posted. No fishing, hunting, fires, camping. Now you just pack up and put that fire out and get off this land.'

Mack stood up humbly. 'I didn't know, Captain,' he said. 'Honest we never seen the sign, Captain.'

'There's signs all over. You couldn't have missed them.'

'Look, Captain, we made a mistake and we're sorry,' said Mack. He paused and looked closely at the slouching figure. 'You are a military man, aren't you, sir? I can always tell. Military men don't carry his shoulders the same as ordinary people. I was in the army so long, I can always tell.'

Imperceptibly the shoulders of the man straightened, nothing obvious, but he held himself differently.

'I don't allow fires on my place,' he said.

'Well, we're sorry,' said Mack. 'We'll get right out, Captain. You see, we're workin' for some scientist. We're goin' to get some frogs. They're working on cancer and we're helpin' out getting some frogs.'

The man hesitated for a moment. 'What do they do with the frogs?' he asked.

'Well, sir,' said Mack, 'they give cancer to the frogs and then they can study and experiment and they got it nearly licked if they can just get some frogs. But if you don't want us on your land, Captain, we'll get right out. Never would of come in if we knew.' Suddenly Mack seemed to see the pointer for the first time. 'By God that's a fine-lookin' bitch,' he said enthusiastically. 'She looks like Nola that win the field trials in Virginia last year. She a Virginia dog, Captain?'

The captain hesitated and then he lied. 'Yes,' he said shortly. 'She's lame. Tick got her right on her shoulder.'

Mack was instantly solicitous. 'Mind if I look, Captain? Come, girl. Come on, girl.' The pointer looked up at her master and then sidled up to Mack. 'Pile on some twigs so I can see,' he said to Hazel.

'It's up where she can't lick it,' said the captain, and he leaned over Mack's shoulder to look.

Mack pressed some pus out of the evil-looking crater on the dog's shoulder. 'I had a dog once had a thing like this and it went right in and killed him. She just had pups, didn't she?'

'Yes,' said the captain, 'six. I put iodine on that place.'

'No,' said Mack, 'that won't draw. You got any Epsom salts up at your place?'

'Yes–there's a big bottle.'

'Well, you make a hot poultice of Epsom salts and put it on there. She's weak, you know, from the pups. Be a shame if she got sick now. You'd lose the pups too.' The pointer looked deep into Mack's eyes and then she licked his hand.

'Tell you what I'll do, Captain. I'll look after her myself. Epsom salts'll do the trick. That's the best thing.'

The captain stroked the dog's head. 'You know, I've got a pond up by the house that's so full of frogs I can't sleep nights. Why don't you look up there? They bellow all night. I'd be glad to get rid of them.'

'That's mighty nice of you,' said Mack. 'I'll bet those docs would thank you for that. But I'd like to get a poultice on this dog.' He turned to the others. 'You put out this fire,' he said. 'Make sure there ain't a spark left and clean up around. You don't want to leave no mess. I and the captain will go and take care of Nola here. You fellows follow along when you get cleared up.' Mack and the captain walked away together.

Hazel kicked sand on the fire. 'I bet Mack could of been president of the US if he wanted,' he said.

'What could he do with it if he had it?' Jones asked. 'There wouldn't be no fun in that.'

14

Early morning is a time of magic in Cannery Row. In the grey time after the light has come and before the sun has risen, the Row seems to hang suspended out of time in a silvery light. The street lights go out, and the weeds are a brilliant green. The corrugated iron of the canneries glows with the pearly lucence of platinum or old pewter. No automobiles are running then. The street is silent of progress and business. And the rush and drag of the waves can be heard as they splash in among the piles of the canneries. It is a time of great peace, a deserted time, a little era of rest. Cats drip over the fences and slither like syrup over the ground to look for fish-heads. Silent early-morning dogs parade majestically, picking and choosing judiciously whereon to pee. The sea-gulls come flapping in to sit on the cannery roofs to await the day of refuse. They sit on the roof peaks shoulder to shoulder. From the rocks near the Hopkins Marine Station comes the barking of sea-lions like the baying of hounds. The air is cool and fresh. In the back gardens the gophers push up the morning mounds of fresh damp earth and they creep out and drag flowers into their holes. Very few people are about, just enough to make it seem more deserted than it is. One of Dora's girls comes home from a call on a patron too wealthy or too sick to visit the Bear Flag. Her make-up is a little sticky and her feet are tired. Lee Chong brings the garbage cans out and stands them on the kerb. The old Chinaman comes out of the sea and flap-flaps across the street and up past the Palace. The cannery watchmen look out and blink at the morning light. The bouncer at the Bear Flag steps out on the porch in his shirt-sleeves and stretches and yawns and scratches his stomach. The snores of Mr Malloy's tenants in the pipes have a deep tunnelly quality. It is the hour of the pearl–the interval between day and night when time stops and examines itself.

On such a morning and in such a light two soldiers and two girls strolled easily along the street. They had come out of 'La Ida' and they were very tired and very happy. The girls were hefty, big-breasted, and strong and their blonde hair was in slight disarray. They wore printed rayon party dresses, wrinkled now and clinging to their convexities. And each girl wore a soldier's cap, one far back on her head and the other with the visor down almost on her nose. They were full-lipped, broad-nosed, hippy girls and they were very tired.

The soldiers' tunics were unbuttoned and their belts were threaded through their epaulettes. The ties were pulled down a little so the shirt-collars could be unbuttoned. And the soldiers wore the girls' hats, one a tiny yellow straw boater with a bunch of daisies on the crown, the other a white knitted half-hat to which medallions of blue cellophane adhered. They walked holding hands, swinging their hands rhythmically. The soldier on the outside had a large brown paper bag filled with cold canned beer. They strolled softly in the pearly light. They had had a hell of a time and they felt good. They smiled delicately like weary children remembering a party. They looked at one another and smiled and they swung their hands. Past the Bear Flag they went and said 'Hiya' to the bouncer who was scratching his stomach. They listened to the snores from the pipes and laughed a little. At Lee Chong's they stopped and looked into the messy display window where tools and clothes and food crowded for attention. Swinging their hands and scuffing their feet, they came to the end of Cannery Row and turned up to the railroad track. The girls climbed on the rails and walked along on them and the soldiers put their arms around the plump waists to keep them from falling. Then they went past the boat-works and turned down into the park-like property of the Hopkins Marine Station. There is a tiny curved beach in front of the station, a miniature beach between little reefs. The gentle morning waves licked up the beach and whispered softly. The fine smell of seaweed came from the exposed rocks. As the four came to the beach a sliver of the sun broke over Tom Work's land across the head of the bay and it gilded the water and made the rocks yellow. The girls sat formally down in the sand and straightened their skirts over their knees. One of the soldiers punched holes in four cans of beer and handed them round. And then the men lay down and put their heads in the girls' laps and looked up into their faces. And they smiled at each other, a tired and peaceful and wonderful secret.

From up near the station came the barking of a dog–the watchman, a dark and surly man, had seen them and his black and surly cocker spaniel had seen them. He shouted at them, and when they did not move he came down on the beach and his dog barked monotonously. 'Don't you know you can't lay around here? You got to get off. This is private property!'

The soldiers did not even seem to hear him. They smiled on and the girls were stroking their hair over the temples. At last in slow motion one of the soldiers turned his head so that his cheek was cradled between the girl's legs. He smiled benevolently at the caretaker. 'Why don't you take a flying fuggut the moon?' he said kindly, and he turned back to look at the girl.

The sun lighted her blonde hair and she scratched him over one ear. They didn't even see the caretaker go back to his house.

15

By the time the boys got up to the farm-house Mack was in the kitchen. The pointer bitch lay on her side, and Mack held a cloth saturated with Epsom salts against her tick-bite. Among her legs the big fat wiener pups nuzzled and bumped for milk and the bitch looked patiently up into Mack's face, saying: 'You see how it is? I try to tell him, but he doesn't understand.'

The captain held a lamp and looked down on Mack.

'I'm glad to know about that,' he said.

Mack said: 'I don't want to tell you about your business, sir, but these pups ought to be weaned. She ain't got a hell of a lot of milk left and them pups are chewin' her to pieces.'

'I know,' said the captain. 'I s'pose I should have drowned them all but one. I've been so busy trying to keep the place going. People don't take the interest in bird dogs they used to. It's all poodles and boxers and Dobermans.'

'I know,' said Mack. 'And there ain't no dog like a pointer for a man. I don't know what's come over people. But you wouldn't of drowned them, would you, sir?'

'Well,' said the captain, 'since my wife went into politics, I'm just running crazy. She got elected to the Assembly for this district and when the Legislature isn't in session, she's off making speeches. And when she's home she's studying all the time and writing bills.'

'Must be lousy in–I mean it must be pretty lonely,' said Mack. 'Now if I had a pup like this'–he picked up a squirming puzz-faced pup–'why, I bet I'd have a real bird dog in three years. I'd take a bitch every time.'

'Would you like to have one?' the captain asked.

Mack looked up. 'You mean you'd let me have one? Oh! Jesus Christ yes.'

'Take your pick,' said the Captain. 'Nobody seems to understand bird dogs any more.'

The boys stood in the kitchen and gathered quick impressions. It was obvious that the wife was away–the opened cans, the frying-pan with lace from fried egg still sticking to it, the crumbs on the kitchen table, the open box of shot-gun shells on the bread-box all shrieked of the lack of a woman, while the white curtains and the papers on the dish shelves and the too small towels on the rack told them a woman had been there. And they were unconsciously glad she wasn't there. The kind of woman who put papers on shelves and had little towels like that instinctively distrusted and disliked Mack and the boys. Such women knew that they were the worst threats to a home, for they offered ease and thought and companionship as opposed to neatness, order, and properness. They were glad she was away.

Now the captain seemed to feel they were doing him a favour. He didn't want them to leave. He said hesitantly: 'S'pose you boys would like a little something to warm you up before you go out for the frogs?'

The others looked at Mack. Mack was frowning as though he was thinking it through. 'When we're out doin' scientific stuff, we make it a kind of a rule not to touch nothin',' he said, and then quickly, as though he might have gone too far: 'But seein' as how you been so nice to us–well, I wouldn't mind a short one myself. I don't know about the boys.'

The boys agreed that they wouldn't mind a short one either. The captain got a flashlight and went down in the cellar. They could hear him moving lumber and boxes about, and he came back upstairs with a five-gallon oak keg in his arms. He set it on the table. 'During Prohibition I got some corn whisky and laid it away. I just got to thinking I'd like to see how it is. It's pretty old now. I'd almost forgot it. You see–my wife . . .' he let it go at that because it was apparent that they understood. The captain knocked out the oak plug from the end of the keg and got glasses down from the shelf that had scallop-edged paper laid on it. It is a hard job to pour a small drink from a five-gallon keg. Each of them got half a water-glass of the clear brown liquor. They waited ceremoniously for the captain and then they said: 'Over the river,' and tossed it back. They swallowed, tasted their tongues, sucked their lips, and there was a far-away look in their eyes.

Mack peered into his empty glass as though some holy message was written in the bottom. And then he raised his eyes. 'You can't say nothin' about that,' he said. 'They don't put that in bottles.' He breathed in deeply and sucked his breath as it came out. 'I don't think I ever tasted nothin' as good as that,' he said.

The captain looked pleased. His glance wandered back to the keg. 'It is good,' he said. 'You think we might have another little one?'

Mack stared into his glass again. 'Maybe a short one,' he agreed. 'Wouldn't it be easier to pour out some in a pitcher? You're liable to spill it that way.'

Two hours later they recalled what they had come for.

The frog pool was square–fifty feet wide and seventy feet long and four feet deep. Lush soft grass grew about its edge and a little ditch brought the water from the river to it and from it little ditches went out to the orchards. There were frogs there all right, thousands of them. Their voices beat the night, they boomed and barked and croaked and rattled. They sang to the stars, to the waning moon, to the waving grasses. They bellowed love songs and challenges. The men crept through the darkness towards the pool. The captain carried a nearly-filled pitcher of whisky and every man had his own glass. The captain had found them flashlights that worked. Hughie and Jones carried gunny-sacks. As they drew quietly near, the frogs heard them coming. The night had been roaring with frog song and then suddenly it was silent. Mack and the boys and the captain sat down on the ground to have one last short one and to map their campaign. And the plan was bold.

During the millennia that frogs and men have lived in the same world, it is probable that men have hunted frogs. And during that time a pattern of hunt and parry has developed. The man with net or bow or lance or gun creeps noiselessly, as he thinks, toward the frog. The pattern requires that the frog sit still, sit very still and wait. The rules of the game require the frog to wait until the final flicker of a second, when the net is descending, when the lance is in the air, when the finger squeezes the trigger, then the frog jumps, plops into the water, swims to the bottom, and waits until the man goes away. That is the way it is done, the way it has always been done. Frogs have every right to expect it will always be done that way. Now and then the net is too quick, the lance pierces, the gun flicks, and that frog is gone, but it is all fair and in the framework. Frogs don't resent that. But how could they have anticipated Mack's new method? How could they have foreseen the horror that followed? The sudden flashing of lights, the shouting and squealing of men, the rush of feet. Every frog leaped, plopped into the pool, and swam frantically to the bottom. Then into the pool plunged the line of men, stamping, churning, moving in a crazy line up the pool, flinging their feet about. Hysterically the frogs, displaced from their placid spots, swam ahead of the crazy thrashing feet and the feet came on. Frogs are good swimmers, but they haven't much endurance. Down the pool they went until finally they were bunched and crowded against the ends. And the feet and wildly-plunging bodies followed them. A few frogs lost their heads and floundered among the feet and got through and these were saved. But the majority decided to leave this pool for ever, to find a new home in a new country where this kind of thing didn't happen. A wave of frantic, frustrated frogs, big ones, little ones, brown ones, green ones, men frogs and women frogs, a wave of them broke over the bank, crawled, leaped, scrambled. They clambered up the grass, they clutched at each other, little ones rode on big ones. And then–horror on horror–the flashlights found them. Two men gathered them like berries. The line came out of the water and closed in on their rear and gathered them like potatoes. Tens and fifties of them were flung into the gunny-sacks and the sacks filled with tired, frightened, and disillusioned frogs, with dripping, whimpering frogs. Some got away, of course, and some had been saved in the pool. But never in frog history had such an execution taken place. Frogs by the pound, by the fifty pounds. They weren't counted, but there must have been six or seven hundred. Then happily Mack tied up the necks of the sacks. They were soaking, dripping wet and the air was cool. They had a short one in the grass before they went back to the house, so they wouldn't catch cold.

It is doubtful whether the captain had ever had so much fun. He was indebted to Mack and the boys. Later when the curtains caught fire and were put out with the little towels, the captain told the boys not to mind it. He felt it was an honour to have them burn his house clear down, if they wanted to. 'My wife is a wonderful woman,' he said in a kind of peroration. 'Most wonderful woman. Ought to of been a man. If she was a man I wouldn' of married her.' He laughed for a long time over that and repeated it three or four times and resolved to remember it, so he could tell it to a lot of other people. He filled a jug with whisky and gave it to Mack. He wanted to go to live with them in the Palace Flophouse. He decided that his wife would like Mack and the boys if she only knew them. Finally, he went to sleep on the floor with his head among the puppies. Mack and the boys poured themselves a short one and regarded him seriously.

Mack said: 'He give me that jug of whisky, didn't he? You heard him?'

'Sure he did,' said Eddie. 'I heard him.'

'And he give me a pup?'

'Sure, pick of the litter. We all heard him. Why?'

'I never did roll a drunk and I ain't gonna start now,' said Mack. 'We got to get out of here. He's gonna wake up feelin' lousy and it's goin' to be all our fault. I just don't want to be here.' Mack glanced at the burned curtains, at the floor glistening with whisky and puppy dirt, at the bacon grease that was coagulating on the stove front. He went to the pups, looked them over carefully, felt bone and frame, looked in eyes, and regarded jaws, and he picked out a beautifully-spotted bitch with a liver-coloured nose and a fine dark-yellow eye. 'Come on, darling,' he said.

They blew out the lamp because of the danger of fire. It was just turning dawn as they left the house.

'I don't think I ever had such a fine trip,' said Mack. 'But I got to thinkin' about his wife comin' back and it gave me the shivers.' The pup whined in his arms and he put it under his coat. 'He's a real nice fella,' said Mack. 'After you get him feelin' easy, that is.' He strode on toward the place where they had parked the Ford. 'We shouldn't go forgettin' we're doin' all this for Doc,' he said. 'From the way things are pannin' out, it looks like Doc is a pretty lucky guy.'

16

Probably the busiest time the girls of the Bear Flag ever had was the March of the big sardine catch. It wasn't only that the fish ran in silvery billions and money ran almost as freely. A new regiment moved into the Presidio and a new bunch of soldiers always shop around a good deal before they settle down. Dora was short-handed just at that time too, for Eva Flanagan had gone to East St Louis on a vacation, Phyllis Mae had broken her leg getting out of the roller coaster in Santa Cruz, and Elsie Doublebottom had made a novena and wasn't much good for anything else. The men from the sardine fleet, loaded with dough, were in and out all afternoon. They sail at dark and fish all night, so they must play in the afternoon. In the evening the soldiers of the new regiment came down and stood around playing the musical-box and drinking Coca-Cola and sizing up the girls for the time when they would be paid. Dora was having trouble with her income-tax, for she was entangled in that curious enigma which said the business was illegal and then taxed her for it. In addition to everything else there were the regulars–the steady customers who had been coming down for years, the labourers from the gravel-pits, the riders from the ranches, the railroad men who came in the front door, and the city officials and prominent business men who came in the rear entrance by the tracks and who had little chintz sitting-rooms assigned to them.

All in all it was a terrific month and right in the middle of it the influenza epidemic had to break out. It came to the whole town. Mrs Talbot and her daughter of the San Carlos hotel had it. Tom Work had it. Benjamin Peabody and his wife had it. Excelentisima Maria Antonia Field had it. The whole Gross family came down with it.

The doctors of Monterey–and there were enough of them to take care of the ordinary diseases, accidents, and neuroses–were running crazy. They had more business than they could do among clients who, if they didn't pay their bills, at least had the money to pay them. Cannery Row, which produces a tougher breed than the rest of the town, was late in contracting it, but finally it got them too. The schools were closed. There wasn't a house that hadn't feverish children and sick parents. It was not a deadly disease, as it was in 1917, but with children it had a tendency to go into the mastoids. The medical profession was very busy, and besides, Cannery Row was not considered a very good financial risk.

Now Doc of the Western Biological Laboratory had no right to practise medicine. It was not his fault that everyone in the Row came to him for medical advice. Before he knew it he found himself running from shanty to shanty taking temperatures, giving physics, borrowing and delivering blankets, and even taking food from house to house where mothers looked at him with inflamed eyes from their beds, and thanked him and put the full responsibility for their children's recovery on him. When a case got really out of hand he phoned a local doctor and sometimes one came, if it seemed to be an emergency. But to the families it was all emergency. Doc didn't get much sleep. He lived on beer and canned sardines. In Lee Chong's where he went to get beer he met Dora, who was there to buy a pair of nail clippers.

'You look done in,' Dora said.

'I am,' Doc admitted. 'I haven't had any sleep for about a week.'

'I know,' said Dora, 'I hear it's bad. Comes at a bad time too.'

'Well, we haven't lost anybody yet,' said Doc. 'But there are some awful sick kids. The Ransel kids have all developed mastoiditis.'

'Is there anything I can do?' Dora asked.

Doc said: 'You know there is. People get so scared and helpless. Take the Ransels–they're scared to death and they're scared to be alone. If you, or some of the girls, could just sit with them.'

Dora, who was soft as a mouse's belly, could be as hard as carborundum. She went back to the Bear Flag and organized it for service. It was a bad time for her, but she did it. The Greek cook made a ten-gallon cauldron of strong soup and kept it full and kept it strong. The girls tried to keep up their business, but they went in shifts to sit with the families, and they carried pots of soup when they went. Doc was in almost constant demand. Dora consulted him and detailed the girls where he suggested. And all the time the business at the Bear Flag was booming. The musical-box never stopped playing. The men of the fishing fleet and the soldiers stood in line. And the girls did their work and then they took their pots of soup and went to sit with the Ransels, with the McCarthys, with the Ferrias. The girls slipped out the back door, and sometimes staying with the sleeping children the girls dropped to sleep in their chairs. They didn't use make-up for work any more. They didn't have to. Dora herself said she could have used the total membership of the old ladies' home. It was the busiest time the girls at the Bear Flag could remember. Everyone was glad when it was over.

17

In spite of his friendliness and his friends Doc was a lonely and a set-apart man. Mack probably noticed it more than anybody. In a group, Doc seemed always alone. When the lights were on and the curtains drawn, and the Gregorian music played on the great phonograph, Mack used to look down on the laboratory from the Palace Flophouse. He knew Doc had a girl in there, but Mack used to get a dreadful feeling of loneliness out of it. Even in the dear close contact with a girl Mack felt that Doc would be lonely. Doc was a night crawler. The lights were on in the lab all night and yet he seemed to be up in the daytime too. And the great shrouds of music came out of the lab at any time of the day or night. Sometimes when it was all dark and when it seemed that sleep had come at last, the diamond-true child voices of the Sistine Choir would come from the windows of the laboratory.

Doc had to keep up his collecting. He tried to get to the good tides along the coast. The sea rocks and the beaches were his stock pile. He knew where everything was when he wanted it. All the articles of his trade were filed away on the coast, sea cradles here, octopi here, tubs worms in another place, sea pansies in another. He knew where to get them, but he could not go for them exactly when he wanted. For Nature locked up the items and released them only occasionally. Doc had to know not only the tides, but when a particular low tide was good in a particular place. When such a low tide occurred, he packed his collecting tools in his car, he packed his jars, his bottles, his plates and preservatives and he went to the beach or reef or rock ledge where the animals he needed were stored.

Now he had an order for small octopi and the nearest place to get them was the boulder-strewn inter-tidal zone at La Jolla, between Los Angeles and San Diego. It meant a five-hundred-mile drive each way and his arrival had to coincide with the retreating waters.

The little octopi live among the boulders embedded in sand. Being timid and young, they prefer a bottom on which there are many caves and little crevices and lumps of mud where they hide from predators and protect themselves from the waves. But on the same flat there are millions of sea cradles. While filling a definite order for octopi, Doc could replenish his stock of the cradles.

Low tide was 5.17 a.m. on a Thursday. If Doc left Monterey on Wednesday morning he could be there easily in time for the tide on Thursday. He would have taken someone with him for company, but quite by accident everyone was away or was busy. Mack and the boys were up Carmel Valley collecting frogs. Three young women he knew and would have enjoyed as companions had jobs and couldn't get away in the middle of the week. Henri the painter was occupied, for Holman's Department Store had employed not a flag-pole sitter, but a flag-pole skater. On a tall mast on top of the store he had a little round platform and there he was on skates going round and round. He had been there three days and three nights. He was out to set a new record for being on skates on a platform. The previous record was 127 hours, so he had some time to go. Henri had taken up his post across the street at Red Williams' petrol station. Henri was fascinated. He thought of doing a huge abstraction called Substratum Dream of a Flag-pole Skater. Henri couldn't leave town while the skater was up there. He protested that there were philosophic implications in flag-pole skating that no one had touched. Henri sat in a chair, leaned back against the lattice which concealed the door of the men's toilet at Red Williams'. He kept his eye on the eyrie skating platform and obviously he couldn't go with Doc to La Jolla. Doc had to go alone because the tide would not wait.

Early in the morning he got his things together. Personal things went in a small satchel. Another satchel held instruments and syringes. Having packed, he combed and trimmed his brown beard, saw that his pencils were in his shirt pocket, and his magnifying glass attached to his lapel. He packed the trays, bottles, glass plates, preservatives, rubber-boots, and a blanket into the back of his car. He worked through the pearly time, washed three days' dishes, put the garbage into the surf. He closed the doors, but did not lock them, and by nine o'clock was on his way.

It took Doc longer to go places than other people. He didn't drive fast and he stopped and ate hamburgers very often. Driving up to Lighthouse Avenue he waved at a dog that looked round and smiled at him. In Monterey before he even started, he felt hungry and stopped at Herman's for a hamburger and beer. While he ate his sandwich and sipped his beer, a lot of conversation came back to him. Blaisedell, the poet, had said to him: 'You love beer so much. I'll bet some day you'll go in and order a beer milk-shake.' It was a simple piece of foolery, but it had bothered Doc ever since. He wondered what a beer milk-shake would taste like. The idea gagged him, but he couldn't let it alone. It cropped up every time he had a glass of beer. Would it curdle the milk? Would you add sugar? It was like a shrimp ice-cream. Once the thing got into your head you couldn't forget it. He finished his sandwich and paid Herman. He purposely didn't look at the milk-shake machines lined up so shiny against the back wall. If a man ordered a beer milk-shake, he thought, he'd better do it in a town where he wasn't known. But then, a man with a beard, ordering a beer milk-shake in a town where he wasn't known–they might call the police. A man with a beard was always a little suspect anyway. You couldn't say you wore a beard because you like a beard. People didn't like you for telling the truth. You had to say you had a scar, so you couldn't shave. Once when Doc was at the University of Chicago he had loved trouble and he had worked too hard. He thought it would be nice to take a very long walk. He put on a little knapsack and he walked through Indiana and Kentucky and North Carolina and Georgia, clear to Florida. He walked among farmers and mountain people, among the swamp people and fishermen. And everywhere people asked him why he was walking through the country.

Because he loved true things he tried to explain. He said he was nervous and besides he wanted to see the country, smell the ground and look at grass and birds and trees, to savour the country, and there was no other way to do it save on foot. And people didn't like him for telling the truth. They scowled, or shook and tapped their heads, they laughed as though they knew it was a lie and they appreciated a liar. And some, afraid for their daughters or their pigs, told him to move on, to get along, just not to stop near their place if he knew what was good for him.

And so he stopped trying to tell the truth. He said he was doing it on a bet–that he stood to win a hundred dollars. Everyone liked him then and believed him. They asked him in to dinner and gave him a bed and they put lunches up for him and wished him good luck and thought he was a hell of a fine fellow. Doc still loved true things, but he knew it was not a general love and it could be a very dangerous mistress.

Doc didn't stop in Salinas for a hamburger. But he stopped in Gonzales, in King City, and in Paso Robles. He had hamburger and beer at Santa Maria–two in Santa Maria, because it was a long pull from there to Santa Barbara. In Santa Barbara he had soup, lettuce and string-bean salad, pot roast and mashed potatoes, pineapple-pie and blue cheese and coffee, and after that he filled the petrol tank and went to the toilet. While the service station checked his oil and tyres, Doc washed his face and combed his beard and when he came back to the car a number of potential hitch-hikers were waiting.

'Going south, Mister?'

Doc travelled on the highways a good deal. He was an old hand. You have to pick your hitch-hikers very carefully. It's best to get an experienced one, for he relapses into silence. But the new ones try to pay for their ride by being interesting. Doc had had a leg talked off by some of these. Then after you have made up your mind about the one you want to take, you protect yourself by saying you aren't going far. If your man turns out too much for you, you can drop him. On the other hand, you may be just lucky and get a man very much worth knowing. Doc made a quick survey of the line and chose his company, a thin-faced salesman-like man in a blue suit. He had deep lines beside his mouth and dark brooding eyes.

He looked at Doc with dislike. 'Going south, Mister?'

'Yes,' said Doc, 'A little way.'

'Mind taking me along?'

'Get in!' said Doc.

When they got to Ventura it was pretty soon after the heavy dinner, so Doc only stopped for beer. The hitch-hiker hadn't spoken once. Doc pulled up at a roadside stand.

'Want some beer?'

'No,' said the hitch-hiker. 'And I don't mind saying I think it's not a very good idea to drive under the influence of alcohol. It's none of my business what you do with your own life, but in this case you've got an automobile, and that can be a murderous weapon in the hands of a drunken driver.'

At the beginning Doc had been slightly startled. 'Get out of the car,' he said softly.

'What?'

'I'm going to punch you on the nose,' said Doc, 'if you aren't out of this car before I count ten. One–two–three . . .'

The man fumbled at the door catch and backed hurriedly out of the car. But once outside he howled: 'I'm going to find an officer. I'm going to have you arrested.'

Doc opened the box on the dashboard and took out a monkey wrench. His guest saw the gesture and walked hurriedly away.

Doc walked angrily to the counter of the stand.

The waitress, a blonde beauty with just the hint of a goitre, smiled at him.

'What'll it be?'

'Beer milk-shake,' said Doc.

'What?'

Well here it was and what the hell. Might just as well get it over with now as some time later.

The blonde asked: 'Are you kidding?'

Doc knew wearily that he couldn't explain, couldn't tell the truth. 'I've got a bladder complaint,' he said. 'Bipalychaetsonectomy, the doctors call it. I'm supposed to drink a *beer milk-shake*. Doctor's orders.'

The blonde smiled reassuringly. 'Oh! I thought you was kidding,' she said archly. 'You tell me how to make it. I didn't know you was sick.'

'Very sick,' said Doc, 'and due to be sicker. Put in some milk, and add half a bottle of beer. Give me the other half in a glass–no sugar in the milk-shake.' When she served it, he tasted it wryly. And it wasn't so bad–it just tasted like stale beer and milk.

'It sounds awful,' said the blonde.

'It's not so bad when you get used to it,' said Doc. 'I've been drinking it for seventeen years.'

18

Doc had driven slowly. It was late afternoon when he stopped in Ventura, so late in fact that when he stopped in Carpentaria he only had a cheese sandwich and went to the toilet. Besides, he intended to get a good dinner in Los Angeles, and it was dark when he got there. He drove on through and stopped at a big Chicken-in-the-Rough place he knew about. And there he had fried chicken, julienne potatoes, hot biscuits and honey, and a piece of pineapple-pie and blue cheese. And here he filled his thermos-bottle with hot coffee, had them make up six ham sandwiches, and bought two quarts of beer for breakfast.

It was not so interesting driving at night. No dogs to see, only the highway lighted with his headlights. Doc speeded up to finish the trip. It was about two o'clock when he got to La Jolla. He drove through the town and down to the cliff below which his tidal flat lay. There he stopped the car, ate a sandwich, drank some beer, turned out the lights, and curled up in the seat to sleep.

He didn't need a clock. He had been working in a tidal pattern so long that he could feel a tide change in his sleep. In the dawn he awakened, looked out through the windshield, and saw the water was already retreating down the bouldery flat. He drank some hot coffee, ate three sandwiches, and had a quart of beer.

The tide goes out imperceptibly. The boulders show and seem to rise up and the ocean recedes, leaving little pools, leaving wet weed and moss and sponge, iridescence and brown and blue and China red. On the bottoms lie the incredible refuse of the sea, shells broken and chipped and bits of skeleton, claws, the whole sea bottom a fantastic cemetery on which the living scamper and scramble.

Doc pulled on his rubber-boots and set his rain hat fussily. He took his buckets and jars and his crowbar, and put his sandwiches in one pocket and his thermos-bottle in another pocket, and he went down the cliff to the tidal flat. Then he worked down the flat after the retreating sea. He turned over the boulders with his crowbar and now and then his hand darted quickly into the standing-water and brought out a little angry squirming octopus, which blushed with rage and spat ink on his hand. Then he dropped it into a jar of sea water with the others, and usually the newcomer was so angry that it attacked its fellows.

It was good hunting that day. He got twenty-two little octopi. And he picked off several hundred sea cradles and put them in his wooden bucket. As the tide moved out he followed it, while the morning came and the sun arose. The flat extended out two hundred yards and then there was a line of heavy weed-encrusted rocks before it stopped off to deep water. Doc worked out to the barrier edge. He had about what he wanted now and the rest of the time he looked under stones, leaned down, and peered into the tide pools, with their brilliant mosaics and their scuttling, bubbling life. And he came at last to the outer barrier, where the long leathery brown algae hung down into the water. Red starfish clustered on the rocks, and the sea pulsed up and down against the barrier, waiting to get in again. Between two weeded rocks on the barrier Doc saw a flash of white under water and then the floating weed covered it. He climbed to the place over the slippery rocks, held himself firmly, and gently reached down and parted the brown algae. Then he grew rigid. A girl's face looked up at him, a pretty, pale girl with dark hair. The eyes were open and clear and the face was firm and the hair washed gently about her head. The body was out of sight, caught in the crevice. The lips were slightly parted and the teeth showed, and on the face was only comfort and rest. Just under the water it was and the clear water made it very beautiful. It seemed to Doc that he looked at it for many minutes, and the face burned into his picture memory.

Very slowly he raised his hand and let the brown weed float back and cover the face. Doc's heart pounded deeply and his throat felt tight. He picked up his bucket and his jars and his crowbar and went slowly over the slippery rocks back toward the beach.

And the girl's face went ahead of him. He sat down on the beach in the coarse dry sand and pulled off his boots. In the jar the little octopi were huddled up, each keeping as far as possible from the others. Music sounded in Doc's ears, a high thin piercingly sweet flute carrying a melody he could never remember, and against this, a pounding surf-like woodwind section. The flute went up into regions beyond the hearing range and even there it carried its unbelievable melody. Goose pimples came out on Doc's arms. He shivered and his eyes were wet the way they get in the focus of great beauty. The girl's eyes had been grey and clear and the dark hair floated, drifted lightly over the face. The picture was set for all time. He sat there while the first little spout of water came over the reef, bringing the returning tide. He sat there hearing the music, while the sea crept in again over the bouldery flat. His hand tapped out the rhythm, and the terrifying flute played in his brain. The eyes were grey and the mouth smiled a little or seemed to catch its breath in ecstasy.

A voice seemed to awaken him. A man stood over him. 'Been fishing?'

'No, collecting.'

'Well–what are them things?'

'Baby octopi.'

'You mean devil-fish? I didn't know there was any there. I've lived here all my life.'

'You've got to look for them,' said Doc listlessly.

'Say,' said the man, 'aren't you feeling well? You look sick.'

The flute climbed again and plucked cellos sounded below and the sea crept in and in toward the beach. Doc shook off the music, shook off the face, shook the chill out of his body. 'Is there a police station near?'

'Up in town. Why, what's wrong?'

'There's a body out on the reef.'

'Where?'

'Right out there–wedged between two rocks. A girl.'

'Say . . .' said the man. 'You get a bounty for finding a body. I forget how much.'

Doc stood up and gathered his equipment. 'Will you report it? I'm not feeling well.'

'Give you a shock, did it? Is it–bad? Rotten or eat up?'

Doc turned away. 'You take the bounty,' he said. 'I don't want it.' He started toward the car. Only the tiniest piping of the flute sounded in his head.

19

Probably nothing in the way of promotion Holman's Department Store ever did attracted so much favourable comment as the engagement of the flag-pole skater. Day after day, there he was up on his little round platform skating round and round, and at night he could be seen up there too, dark against the sky, so that everybody knew he didn't come down. It was generally agreed, however, that a steel rod came up through the centre of the platform at night and he strapped himself to it. But he didn't sit down and no one minded the steel rod. People came from Jamesburg to see him and from down the coast as far as Grimes Point. Salinas people came over in droves and the Farmers Mercantile of that town put in a bid for the next appearance when the skater could attempt to break his own record and thus give the new world's record to Salinas. Since there weren't many flag-pole skaters and since this one was by far the best, he had for the last year gone about breaking his own world's record.

Holman's was delighted about the venture. They had a white sale, a remnant sale, an aluminium sale, and a crockery sale all going at the same time. Crowds of people stood in the street watching the lone man on his platform.

His second day up, he sent down word that someone was shooting at him with an air-gun. The display department used its head. it figured the angles and located the offender. It was old Doctor Merrivale, hiding behind the curtains of his office, plugging away with a Daisy air-rifle. They didn't denounce him and he promised to stop. He was very prominent in the Masonic Lodge.

Henri the painter kept his chair at Red Williams' service station. He worked out every possible philosophic approach to the situation and came to the conclusion that he would have to build a platform at home and try it himself. Everyone in the town was more or less affected by the skater. Trade fell off out of sight of him and got better the nearer you came to Holman's. Mack and the boys went up and looked for a moment and then went back to the Palace. They couldn't see that it made much sense.

Holman's set up a double bed in their windows. When the skater broke the world's record he was going to come down and sleep right in the window without taking off his skates. The trade name of the mattress was on a little card at the foot of the bed.

Now in the whole town there was interest and discussion about this sporting event, but the most interesting question of all and the one that bothered the whole town was never spoken of. No one mentioned it, and yet it was there haunting everyone. Mrs Trolat wondered about it as she came out of the Scotch bakery with a bag of sweet buns. Mr Hall in men's furnishings wondered about it. The three Willoughby girls giggled whenever they thought of it. But no one had the courage to bring it into the open.

Richard Frost, a highly-strung and brilliant young man, worried about it more than anyone else. It haunted him. Wednesday night he worried and Thursday night he fidgeted. Friday night he got drunk and had a fight with his wife. She cried for a while and then pretended to be asleep. She heard him slip from bed and go into the kitchen. He was getting another drink. And then she heard him dress quietly and go out. She cried some more then. It was very late. Mrs Frost was sure he was going down to Dora's Bear Flag.

Richard walked sturdily down the hill through the pines until he came to Lighthouse Avenue. He turned left and went up toward Holman's. He had the bottle in his pocket and just before he came to the store he took one more slug of it. The street lights were turned down low. The town was deserted. Not a soul moved. Richard stood in the middle of the street and looked up.

Dimly on top of the high mast he could see the lonely figure of the skater. He took another drink. He cupped his hands and called huskily: 'Hey!' There was no answer. 'Hey!' he called louder, and looked around to see if the cops had come out of their place beside the bank.

Down from the sky came a surly reply: 'What do you want?'

Richard cupped his hands again. 'How–how do you–go to the toilet?'

'I've got a can up here,' said the voice.

Richard turned and walked back the way he had come. He walked along Lighthouse and up through the pines and he came to his house and let himself in. As he undressed he knew his wife was awake. She bubbled a little when she was asleep. He got into bed and she made room for him.

'He's got a can up there,' Richard said.

20

In mid-morning the Model T truck rolled triumphantly home to Cannery Row and hopped the gutter and creaked up through the weeds to its place behind Lee Chong's. The boys blocked up the front wheels, drained what petrol was left into a five-gallon can, took their frogs, and went wearily home to the Palace Flophouse. Then Mack made a ceremonious visit to Lee Chong while the boys got a fire going in the big stove. Mack thanked Lee with dignity for lending the truck. He spoke of the great success of the trip, of the hundreds of frogs taken. Lee smiled shyly and waited for the inevitable.

'We're in the chips,' Mack said enthusiastically. 'Doc pays us a nickel a frog and we got about a thousand.'

Lee nodded. The price was standard. Everybody knew that.

'Doc's away,' said Mack. 'Jesus, is he gonna be happy when he sees all them frogs.'

Lee nodded again. He knew Doc was away and he also knew where the conversation was going.

'Say, by the way,' said Mack as though he had just thought of it. 'We're a little bit short right now . . .' He managed to make it sound like a very unusual situation.

'No whisky,' said Lee Chong, and he smiled.

Mack was outraged. 'What would we want whisky for? Why, we got a gallon of the finest whisky you ever laid a lip over–a whole full God-damned-running-over gallon. By the way,' he continued, 'I and the boys would like to have you just step up for a snort with us. They told me to ask you.'

In spite of himself Lee smiled with pleasure. They wouldn't offer it if they didn't have it.

'No,' said Mack, 'I'll lay it on the line. I and the boys are pretty short and we're pretty hungry. You know the price of frogs is twenty for a buck. Now Doc is away and we're hungry. So what we thought is this. We don't want to see you lose nothing, so we'll make over to you twenty-five frogs for a buck. You got a five-frog profit there and nobody loses his shirt.'

'No,' said Lee. 'No money.'

'Well, hell, Lee, all we need is a little groceries. I'll tell you what–we want to give Doc a little party when he gets back. We got plenty of liquor, but we'd like to get maybe some steaks, and stuff like that. He's such a nice guy. Hell, when your wife had that bad tooth, who give her the laudanum?'

Mack had him. Lee was indebted to Doc–deeply indebted. What Lee was having trouble comprehending was how his indebtedness to Doc made it necessary that he give credit to Mack.

'We don't want you to have like a mortgage on frogs,' Mack went on. 'We will actually deliver right into your hands twenty-five frogs for every buck of groceries you let us have and you can come to the party too.'

Lee's mind nosed over the proposition like a mouse in a cheese cupboard. He could find nothing wrong with it. The whole thing was legitimate. Frogs *were* cash as far as Doc was concerned, the price was standard, and Lee had a double profit. He had his five-frog margin and also he had the grocery mark-up. The whole thing hinged on whether they actually had any frogs.

'We go see flog,' Lee said at last.

In front of the Palace he had a drink of the whisky, inspected the damp sacks of frogs, and agreed to the transaction. He stipulated, however, that he would take no dead frogs. Now Mack counted fifty frogs into a can and walked back to the grocery with Lee and got two dollars' worth of bacon and eggs and bread.

Lee, anticipating a brisk business, brought a big packing-case out and put it into the vegetable department. He emptied the fifty frogs into it and covered it with a wet gunny-sack to keep his charges happy.

And business was brisk. Eddie sauntered down and bought two frogs' worth of Bull Durham. Jones was outraged a little later when the price of Coca-Cola went up from one to two frogs. In fact bitterness arose as the day wore on and prices went up. Steak, for instance–the very best steak shouldn't have been more than ten frogs a pound, but Lee set it at twelve and a half. Canned peaches were sky high, eight frogs for a No 2 can. Lee had a stranglehold on the consumers. He was pretty sure that the Thrift Market or Holman's would not approve of this new monetary system. If the boys wanted steak, they knew they had to pay Lee's prices. Feeling ran high when Hazel, who had coveted a pair of yellow silk arm-bands for a long time, was told that if he didn't want to pay thirty-five frogs for them he could go somewhere else. The poison of greed was already creeping into the innocent and laudable merchandising agreement. Bitterness was piling up. But in Lee's packing-case the frogs were piling up too.

Financial bitterness could not eat too deeply into Mack and the boys, for they were not mercantile men. They did not measure their joy in goods sold, their egos in bank balances, nor their loves in what they cost. While they were mildly irritated that Lee was taking them for an economic ride or perhaps hop, two dollars' worth of bacon and eggs was in their stomachs lying right on top of a fine slug of whisky and right on top of the breakfast was another slug of whisky. And they sat in their own chairs in their own house and watched Darling learning to drink canned milk out of a sardine can. Darling was and was destined to remain a very happy dog, for in the group of five men there were five distinct theories of dog training, theories which clashed so that Darling never got any training at all. From the first she was a precocious bitch. She slept on the bed of the man who had given her the last bribe. They really stole for her sometimes. They wooed her away from one another. Occasionally all five agreed that things had to change and that Darling must be disciplined, but in the discussion of method the intention invariably drifted away. They were in love with her. They found the little puddles she left on the floor charming. They bored all their acquaintances with her cuteness and they would have killed her with food if in the end she hadn't had better sense than they.

Jones made her a bed in the bottom of the grandfather clock, but Darling never used it. She slept with one or another of them as the fancy moved her. She chewed the blankets, tore the mattresses, sprayed the feathers out of the pillows. She coquetted and played her owners against one another. They thought she was wonderful. Mack intended to teach her tricks and go in vaudeville and he didn't even house-break her.

They sat in the afternoon, smoking, digesting, considering, and now and then having a delicate drink from the jug. And each time they warned that they must not take her too much, for it was to be for Doc. They must not forget that for a minute.

'What time you figure he'll be back?' Eddie asked.

'Usually gets in about eight or nine o'clock,' said Mack. 'Now we got to figure when we're going to give it. I think we ought to give it tonight.'

'Sure,' the others agreed.

'Maybe he might be tired,' Hazel suggested. 'That's a long drive.'

'Hell,' said Jones, 'nothing rests you like a good party. I've been so dog-tired my pants was draggin' and then I've went to a party and felt fine.'

'We got to do some real thinkin',' said Mack. 'Where we going to give it–here?'

'Well, Doc, he likes his music. He's always got his phonograph going at a party. Maybe he'd be more happy if we give it over at his place.'

'You got something there,' said Mack. 'But I figure it ought to be like a surprise party. And how we going to make like it's a party and not just bringin' over a jug of whisky?'

'How about decorations?' Hughie suggested. 'Like Fourth of July or Hallowe'en.'

Mack's eyes looked off into space and his lips were parted. He could see it all. 'Hughie,' he said, 'I think you got something there. I never would of thought you could do it, but by God you really rang a duck that time.' His voice grew mellow and his eyes looked into the future. 'I can just see it,' he said. 'Doc comes home. He's tired. He drives up. The place is all lit up. He thinks somebody's broke in. He goes up the stairs, and by God the place has got the hell decorated out of it. There's crêpe paper and there's favours and a big cake, Jesus, he'd know it was a party then. And it wouldn't be no little mouse fart party neither. And we're kind of hiding so for a minute he don't know who done it. And then we come out yelling. Can't you see his face? By God, Hughie, I don't know how you thought of it.'

Hughie blushed. His conception had been much more conservative, based in fact on the New Year's party at 'La Ida', but if it was going to be like that, why Hughie was willing to take credit. 'I just thought it would be nice,' he said.

'Well, it's a pretty nice thing,' said Mack, 'and I don't mind saying when the surprise kind of wears off, I'm going to tell Doc who thought it up.' They leaned back and considered the thing. And in their minds the decorated laboratory looked like the conservatory at the Hotel del Monte. They had a couple more drinks, just to savour the plan.

Lee Chong kept a very remarkable store. For instance, most stores buy yellow-and-black crêpe paper and black paper cats, masks and papier-mâché pumpkins in October. There is a brisk business for Hallowe'en and then these items disappear. Maybe they are sold or thrown out, but you can't buy them, say, in June. The same is true of Fourth of July equipment, flags and bunting and sky-rockets. Where are they in January? Gone–no one knows where. This was not Lee Chong's way. You could buy Valentines in November at Lee Chong's, shamrocks, hatchets, and paper cherry-trees in August. He had fire-crackers he had laid up in 1920. One of the mysteries was where he kept his stock since his was not a very large store. He had bathing-suits he had bought when long skirts and black stockings and head bandanas were in style. He had bicycle clips and tatting shuttles and Mah Jong sets. He had badges that said 'Remember the Maine' and felt pennants commemorating 'Fighting Bob'. He had mementos of the Panama Pacific International Exposition of 1915–little towers of jewels. And there was one other unorthodoxy in Lee's way of doing business. He never had a sale, never reduced a price, and never remaindered. An article that cost thirty cents in 1912 still was thirty cents, although mice and moths might seem to some to have reduced its value. But there was no question about it. If you wanted to decorate a laboratory in a general way, not being specific about the season but giving the impression of a cross between Saturnalia and a pageant of the Flags of all Nations, Lee Chong's was the place to go for your stuff.

Mack and the boys knew that, but Mack said: 'Where we going to get a big cake? Lee hasn't got nothing but them little bakery cakes.'

Hughie had been so successful before he tried again. 'Why'n't Eddie bake a cake?' he suggested. 'Eddie used to be fry cook at the San Carlos for a while.'

The instant enthusiasm for the idea drove from Eddie's brain the admission that he had never baked a cake.

Mack put it on a sentimental basis besides. 'It would mean more to Doc,' he said. 'It wouldn't be like no God damned old soggy bought cake. It would have some heart in it.'

As the afternoon and the whisky went down the enthusiasm rose. There were endless trips to Lee Chong's. The frogs were gone from one sack and Lee's packing-case was getting crowded. By six o'clock they had finished the gallon of whisky and were buying half-pints of Old Tennis Shoes at fifteen frogs a crack, but the pile of decorating materials was heaped on the floor of the Palace Flophouse–miles of crêpe paper commemorating every holiday in vogue and some that had been abandoned.

Eddie watched his stove like a mother hen. He was baking a cake in a wash-basin. The recipe was guaranteed not to fail by the company which made the shortening. But from the first the cake had acted strangely. When the batter was completed it writhed and panted as though animals were squirming and crawling inside it. Once in the oven it put up a bubble like a baseball which grew tight and shiny and then collapsed with a hissing sound. This left such a crater that Eddie made a new batch of batter and filled in the hole. And now the cake was behaving very curiously, for while the bottom was burning and sending out a black smoke the top was rising and falling glueyly with a series of little explosions.

When Eddie finally put it out to cool, it looked like one of Bel Geddes's miniatures of a battlefield on a lava bed.

This cake was not fortunate, for while the boys were decorating the laboratory Darling ate what she could of it, was sick on it, and finally curled up in its still warm dough and went to sleep.

But Mack and the boys had taken the crêpe paper, the masks, the broomsticks and paper pumpkins, the red, white and blue bunting, and moved over the lot and across the street to the laboratory. They disposed of the last of the frogs for a quart of Old Tennis Shoes and two gallons of 49-cent wine.

'Doc is very fond of wine,' said Mack. 'I think he likes it even better than whisky.'

Doc never locked the laboratory. He went on the theory that anyone who really wanted to break in could easily do it, that people were essentially honest, and that finally there wasn't much the average person would want to steal there, anyway. The valuable things were books and records, surgical instruments and optical glass and such things that a practical working burglar wouldn't look at twice. His theory had been sound as far as burglars, snatch thieves, and kleptomaniacs were concerned, but it had been completely ineffective regarding his friends. Books were often 'borrowed'. No can of beans ever survived his absence, and on several occasions, returning late, he had found guests in his bed.

The boys piled the decorations in the ante-room and then Mack stopped them. 'What's going to make Doc happiest?' he asked.

'The party!' said Hazel.

'No,' said Mack.

'The decorations?' Hughie suggested. He felt responsible for the decorations.

'No,' said Mack, 'the frogs. That's going to make him feel best of all. And maybe by the time he gets here, Lee Chong might be closed and he can't even see his frogs until tomorrow. No, sir,' Mack cried. 'Them frogs ought to be right here, right in the middle of the room with a piece of bunting on it and a sign that says: "Welcome Home, Doc".'

The committee which visited Lee met with stern opposition. All sorts of possibilities suggested themselves to his suspicious brain. It was explained that he was going to be at the party so he could watch his property, that no one questioned that they were his. Mack wrote out a paper transferring the frogs to Lee in case there should be any question.

When his protests weakened a little they carried the packing-case over to the laboratory, tacked red, white, and blue bunting over it, lettered the big sign with iodine on a card, and they started the decorating from there. They had finished the whisky by now and they really felt in a party mood. They criss-crossed the crêpe paper, and put the pumpkins up. Passers-by in the street joined the party and rushed over to Lee's to get more to drink. Lee Chong joined the party for a while, but his stomach was notoriously weak and he got sick and had to go home. At eleven o'clock they fried the steaks and ate them. Someone digging through the records found an album of Count Basie and the great phonograph roared out. The noise could be heard from the boat-works to 'La Ida'. A group of customers from the Bear Flag mistook Western Biological for a rival house and charged up the stairs whooping with joy. They were evicted by the outraged hosts, but only after a long, happy, and bloody battle that took out the front door and broke two windows. The crashing of jars was unpleasant. Hazel going through the kitchen to the toilet tipped the frying-pan of hot grease on himself and the floor and was badly burned.

At one-thirty a drunk wandered in and passed a remark which was considered insulting to Doc. Mack hit him a clip which is still remembered and discussed. The man rose off his feet, described a small arc, and crashed through the packing-case in among the frogs. Someone trying to change a record dropped the tone arm down and broke the crystal.

No one has studied the psychology of a dying party. It may be raging, howling, boiling, and then a fever sets in and a little silence and then quickly it is gone, the guests go home or go to sleep or wander away to some other affair and they leave a dead body.

The lights blazed in the laboratory. The front door hung sideways by one hinge. The floor was littered with broken glass. Phonograph records, some broken, some only nicked, were strewn about. The plates with pieces of steak ends and coagulating grease were on the floor, on top of the book-cases, under the bed. Whisky-glasses lay sadly on their sides. Someone trying to climb the bookcases had pulled out a whole section of books and spilled them in broken-backed confusion on the floor. And it was empty, it was over.

Through the broken end of the packing-case a frog hopped and sat feeling the air for danger, and then another joined him. They could smell the fine, damp, cool air coming in the door and in through the broken windows. One of them sat on the fallen card which said: 'Welcome Home, Doc.' And then the two hopped timidly toward the door.

For quite a while a little river of frogs hopped down the steps, a swirling, moving river. For quite a while Cannery Row crawled with frogs–was overrun with frogs. A taxi which brought a very late customer to the Bear Flag squashed five frogs in the street. But well before dawn they had all gone. Some found the sewer and some worked their way up the hill to the reservoir and some went into culverts and some only hid among the weeds in the vacant lot.

And the lights blazed in the quiet empty laboratory.

21

In the back room of the laboratory the white rats in their cages ran and skittered and squeaked. In the corner of a separate cage a mother rat lay over her litter of blind, naked children and let them suckle and the mother stared about nervously and fiercely.

In the rattlesnake cage the snakes lay with their chins resting on their own coils and they stared straight ahead out of their scowling dusty black eyes. In another cage a Gila monster with a skin like a beaded bag reared slowly up and clawed heavily and sluggishly at the wire. The anemones in the aquaria blossomed open, with green and purple tentacles and pale green stomachs. The little sea-water pump whirred softly and the needles of driven water hissed into the tanks, forcing lines of bubbles under the surface.

It was the hour of the pearl. Lee Chong brought his garbage cans out to the kerb. The bouncer stood on the porch of the Bear Flag and scratched his stomach. Sam Malloy crawled out of the boiler and sat on his wood block and looked at the lightening east. Over on the rocks near Hopkins Marine Station the sea-lions barked monotonously. The old Chinaman came up out of the sea with his dripping basket and flip-flapped up the hill.

Then a car turned into Cannery Row and Doc drove up to the front of the laboratory. His eyes were red-rimmed with fatigue. He moved slowly with tiredness. When the car had stopped, he sat still for a moment to let the road jumps get out of his nerves. Then he climbed out of the car. At his step on the stairs, the rattlesnakes ran out their tongues and listened with their waving forked tongues. The rats scampered madly about the cages. Doc climbed the stairs. He looked in wonder at the sagging door and at the broken window. The weariness seemed to go out of him. He stepped quickly inside. Then he went quickly from room to room, stepping round the broken glass. He bent down quickly and picked up a smashed phonograph record and looked at its title.

In the kitchen the spilled grease had turned white on the floor. Doc's eyes flamed red with anger. He sat down on his couch and his head settled between his shoulders and his body weaved with rage. Suddenly he jumped up and turned on the power in his great phonograph. He put on a record and put down the arm. Only a hissing roar came from the loud-speaker. He lifted the arm, stopped the turntable, and sat down on the couch again.

On the stairs there were bumbling uncertain footsteps and through the door came Mack. His face was red. He stood uncertainly in the middle of the room. 'Doc . . .' he said–'I and the boys . . .'

For the moment Doc hadn't seemed to see him. Now he leaped to his feet. Mack shuffled backward. 'Did you do this?'

'Well, I and the boys . . .' Doc's small hard fist whipped out and splashed against Mack's mouth. Doc's eyes shone with a red animal rage. Mack sat down heavily on the floor. Doc's fist was hard and sharp. Mack's lips were split against his teeth and one front tooth bent sharply inward. 'Get up!' said Doc.

Mack lumbered to his feet. His hands were at his sides. Doc hit him again, a cold, calculated, punishing punch in the mouth. The blood spurted from Mack's lips and ran down his chin. He tried to lick his lips.

'Put up your hands. Fight, you son of a bitch,' Doc cried, and he hit him again and heard the crunch of breaking teeth.

Mack's head jolted, but he was braced now so he wouldn't fall. And his hands stayed at his side. 'Go ahead, Doc,' he said thickly through his broken lips. 'I got it coming.'

Doc's shoulders sagged with defeat. 'You son of a bitch,' he said bitterly. 'Oh, you dirty son of a bitch.' He sat down on the couch and looked at his cut knuckles.

Mack sat down in a chair and looked at him. Mack's eyes were wide and full of pain. He didn't even wipe away the blood that flowed down his chin. In Doc's head the monotonal opening of Monteverdi's *Hor ch' il Ciel e la Terra* began to form, the infinitely sad and resigned mourning of Petrarch for Laura. Doc saw Mack's broken mouth through the music, the music that was in his head and in the air. Mack sat perfectly still, almost as though he could hear the music too. Doc glanced at the place where the Monteverdi album was and then he remembered that the phonograph was broken.

He got to his feet. 'Go wash your face,' he said, and he went out and down the stairs and across the street to Lee Chong's. Lee wouldn't look at him as he got two quarts of beer out of the ice-box. He took the money without saying anything. Doc walked across the street.

Mack was in the toilet cleaning his bloody face with wet paper towels. Doc opened a bottle and poured gently into a glass, holding it at an angle so that very little collar rose to the top. He filled a second tall glass and carried the two into the front room. Mack came back dabbing at his mouth with wet towelling. Doc indicated the beer with his head. Now Mack opened his throat and poured down half the glass without swallowing. He sighed explosively and stared into the beer. Doc had already finished his glass. He brought the bottle in and filled both glasses again. He sat down on his couch.

'What happened?' he asked.

Mack looked at the floor and a drop of blood fell from his lips to his beer. He mopped his split lips again. 'I and the boys wanted to give you a party. We thought you'd be home last night.'

Doc nodded his head. 'I see.'

'She got out of hand,' said Mack. 'It don't do no good to say I'm sorry. I been sorry all my life. This ain't no new thing. It's always like this.' He swallowed deeply from his glass. 'I had a wife,' Mack said. 'Same thing. Ever'thing I done turned sour. She couldn't stand it any more. If I done a good thing it got poisoned up some way. If I give her a present they was something wrong with it. She only got hurt from me. She couldn't stand it no more. Same thing ever'place 'til I just got to clowning. I don't do nothin' but clown no more. Try to make the boys laugh.'

Doc nodded again. The music was sounding in his head again, complaint and resignation all in one. 'I know,' he said.

'I was glad when you hit me,' Mack went on. 'I thought to myself: "Maybe this will teach me. Maybe I'll remember this." But, hell, I won't remember nothin'. I won't learn nothin'. Doc,' Mack cried. 'The way I seen it, we was all happy and havin' a good time. You was glad because we was givin' you a party. And we was glad. The way I seen it, it was a good party.' He waved his hand at the wreckage on the floor. 'Same thing when I was married. I'd think her out and then–but it never come off that way.'

'I know,' said Doc. He opened the second quart of beer and poured the glasses full.

'Doc,' said Mac. 'I and the boys will clean up here–and we'll pay for the stuff that's broke. If it takes us five years we'll pay for it.'

Doc shook his head slowly and wiped the beer foam from his moustache. 'No,' he said, 'I'll clean it up. I know where everything goes.'

'We'll pay for it, Doc.'

'No you won't, Mack,' said Doc. 'You'll think about it and it'll worry you for quite a long time, but you won't pay for it. There's maybe three hundred dollars in broken museum glass. Don't say you'll pay for it. That will just keep you uneasy. It might be two or three years before you forgot about it and felt entirely easy again. And you wouldn't pay it, anyway.'

'I guess you're right,' said Mack. 'God damn it, I *know* you're right. What can we do?'

'I'm over it,' said Doc. 'Those socks in the mouth got it out of my system. Let's forget it.'

Mack finished his beer and stood up. 'So long, Doc,' he said.

'So long. Say, Mack–what happened to your wife?'

'I don't know,' said Mack. 'She went away.' He walked clumsily down the stairs and crossed over and walked up the lot and up the chicken walk to the Palace Flophouse. Doc watched his progress through the window. And then wearily he got a broom from behind the water-heater. It took him all day to clean up the mess.

22

Henri the painter was not French and his name was not Henri. Also he was not really a painter. Henri had so steeped himself in stories of the Left Bank in Paris that he lived there although he had never been there. Feverishly he followed in periodicals the Dadaist movements and schisms, the strangely feminine jealousies and religiousness, the obscurantisms of the forming and breaking schools. Regularly he revolted against outworn techniques and materials. One season he threw out perspective. Another year he abandoned red, even as the mother of purple. Finally he gave up paint entirely. It is not known whether Henri was a good painter or not, for he threw himself so violently into movements that he had very little time left for painting of any kind.

About his painting there is some question. You couldn't judge very much from his productions in different coloured chicken feathers and nut-shells. But as a boat-builder he was superb. Henri was a wonderful craftsman. He had lived in a tent years ago when he started his boat and until galley and cabin were complete enough to move into. But once he was housed and dry he had taken his time on the boat. The boat was sculptured rather than built. It was thirty-five feet long and its lines were in a constant state of flux. For a while it had a clipper bow and a fan-tail like a destroyer. Another time it looked vaguely like a caravel. Since Henri had no money, it sometimes took him months to find a plank or a piece of iron or a dozen brass screws. That was the way he wanted it, for Henri never wanted to finish his boat.

It sat among the pine-trees on a lot Henri rented for five dollars a year. This paid the taxes and satisfied the owner. The boat rested in a cradle on concrete foundations. A rope ladder hung over the side except when Henri was at home. Then he pulled up the rope ladder and only put it down when guests arrived. His little cabin had a wide padded seat that ran round three sides of the room. On this he slept and on this his guests sat. A table folded down when it was needed and a brass lamp hung from the ceiling. His galley was a marvel of compactness, but every item in it had been the result of months of thought and work.

Henri was swarthy and morose. He wore a beret long after other people abandoned them, he smoked a calabash pipe and his dark hair fell about his face. Henri had many friends whom he loosely classified as those who could feed him and those whom he had to feed. His boat had no name. Henri said he would name it when it was finished.

Henri had been living and building his boat for ten years. During that time he had been married twice and had promoted a number of semi-permanent liaisons. And all of these young women had left him for the same reason. The seven-foot cabin was too small for two people. They resented bumping their heads when they stood up and they definitely felt the need for a toilet. Marine toilets obviously would not work in a shore-bound boat, and Henri refused to compromise with a spurious landsman's toilet. He and his friend of the moment had to stroll away among the pines. And one after another his loves left him.

Just after the girl he had called Alice left him, a very curious thing happened to Henri. Each time he was left alone, he mourned formally for a while, but actually he felt a sense of relief. He could stretch out in his little cabin. He could eat what he wanted. He was glad to be free of the endless female biologic functions for a while.

It had become his custom, each time he was deserted, to buy a gallon of wine, to stretch out on the comfortably hard bunk and get drunk. Sometimes he cried a little all by himself, but it was luxurious stuff and he usually had a wonderful feeling of well-being from it. He would read Rimbaud aloud with a very bad accent, marvelling the while at his fluid speech.

It was during one of his ritualistic mournings for the lost Alice that the strange thing began to happen. It was night and his lamp was burning and he had just barely begun to get drunk when suddenly he knew he was no longer alone. He let his eye wander cautiously up and across the cabin, and there on the other side sat a devilish young man, a dark, handsome young man. His eyes gleamed with cleverness and spirit and energy and his teeth flashed. There was something very dear and yet very terrible in his face. And beside him sat a golden-haired little boy, hardly more than a baby. The man looked down at the baby and the baby looked back and laughed delightedly as though something wonderful were about to happen. Then the man looked over at Henri and smiled and he glanced back at the baby. From his upper left vest pocket he took an old-fashioned straight edged razor. He opened it and indicated the child with a gesture of his head. He put a hand among the curls and the baby laughed gleefully, and then the man tilted the chin and cut the baby's throat and the baby went right on laughing. But Henri was howling with terror. It took him a long time to realize that neither the man nor the baby was still there.

Henri, when his shaking had subsided a little, rushed out of his cabin, leaped over the side of the boat and hurried away down the hill through the pines. He walked for several hours and at last he walked down to Cannery Row.

Doc was in the basement working on cats when Henri burst in. Doc went on working while Henri told about it, and when it was over Doc looked closely at him to see how much actual fear and how much theatre was there. And it was mostly fear.

'Is it a ghost, do you think?' Henri demanded. 'Is it some reflection of something that has happened or is it some Freudian horror out of me, or am I completely nuts? I saw it, I tell you. It happened right in front of me as plainly as I see you.'

'I don't know,' said Doc.

'Well, will you come up with me, and see if it comes back?'

'No,' said Doc. 'If I saw it, it might be a ghost and it would scare me badly because I don't believe in ghosts. And if you saw it again and I didn't it would be a hallucination and you would be frightened.'

'But what am I going to do?' Henri asked. 'If I see it again I'll know what's going to happen and I'm sure I'll die. You see, he doesn't look like a murderer. He looks nice and the kid looks nice and neither of them give a damn. But he cut that baby's throat. I saw it.'

'I don't know,' said Doc. 'I'm not a psychiatrist or a witch-hunter and I'm not going to start now.'

A girl's voice called into the basement. 'Hi, Doc, can I come in?'

'Come along,' said Doc.

She was a rather pretty and a very alert girl.

Doc introduced her to Henri.

'He's got a problem,' said Doc. 'He either has a ghost or a terrible conscience and he doesn't know which. Tell her about it, Henri.'

Henri went over the story again and the girl's eyes sparkled.

'But that's horrible,' she said when he finished. 'I've never in my life even caught the smell of a ghost. Let's go back up and see if he comes again.'

Doc watched them go a little sourly. After all, it had been his date.

The girl never did see the ghost, but she was fond of Henri, and it was five months before the cramped cabin and the lack of a toilet drove her out.

23

A black gloom settled over the Palace Flophouse. All the joy went out of it. Mack came back from the laboratory with his mouth torn and his teeth broken. As a kind of penance, he did not wash his face. He went to his bed and pulled his blanket over his head and he didn't get up all day. His heart was as bruised as his mouth. He went over all the bad things he had done in his life and everything he had ever done seemed bad. He was very sad.

Hughie and Jones sat for a while staring into space and then morosely they went over to the Hediondo Cannery and applied for jobs and got them.

Hazel felt so bad that he walked to Monterey and picked a fight with a soldier and lost it on purpose. That made him feel a little better to be utterly beaten by a man Hazel could have licked without half trying.

Darling was the only happy one of the whole club. She spent the day under Mack's bed happily eating up his shoes. She was a clever dog and her teeth were very sharp. Twice in his black despair, Mack reached under the bed and caught her and put her in bed with him for company, but she squirmed out and went back to eating his shoes.

Eddie mooned on down to 'La Ida' and talked to his friend the bar-tender. He got a few drinks and borrowed some nickels with which he played *Melancholy Baby* five times on the musical-box.

Mack and the boys were under a cloud and they knew it, and they knew they deserved it. They had become social outcasts. All their good intentions were forgotten now. The fact that the party was given for Doc, if it was known, was never mentioned or taken into consideration. The story ran through the Bear Flag. It was told in the canneries. At 'La Ida' drunks discussed it virtuously. Lee Chong refused to comment. He was feeling financially bruised. And the story as it grew went this way: They had stolen liquor and money. They had maliciously broken into the laboratory and systematically destroyed it out of pure malice and evil. People who really knew better took this view. Some of the drunks at 'La Ida' considered going over and beating the hell out of the whole lot of them to show them they couldn't do a thing like that to Doc.

Only a sense of the solidarity and fighting ability of Mack and the boys saved them from some kind of reprisal. There were people who felt virtuous about the affair who hadn't had the material of virtue for a long time. The fiercest of the whole lot was Tom Sheligan, who would have been at the party if he had known about it.

Socially Mack and the boys were beyond the pale. Sam Malloy didn't speak to them as they went by the boiler. They drew into themselves and no one could foresee how they would come out of the cloud. For there are two possible reactions to social ostracism–either a man emerges determined to be better, purer, and kindlier or he goes bad, challenges the world, and does even worse things. This last is by far the commonest reaction to stigma.

Mack and the boys balanced on the scales of good and evil. They were kind and sweet to Darling: they were forbearing and patient with one another. When the first reaction was over they gave the Palace Flophouse a cleaning such as it had never had. They polished the bright work on the stove and they washed all their clothes and blankets. Financially they had become dull and solvent. Hughie and Jones were working and bringing home their pay. They bought groceries up the hill at the Thrift Market because they could not stand the reproving eyes of Lee Chong.

It was during this time that Doc made an observation which may have been true, but since there was one factor missing in his reasoning it is not known whether he was correct. It was the Fourth of July. Doc was sitting in the laboratory with Richard Frost. They drank beer and listened to a new album of Scarlatti and looked out the window. In front of the Palace Flophouse there was a large log of wood where Mack and the boys were sitting in the mid-morning sun. They faced down the hill toward the laboratory.

Doc said: 'Look at them. There are your true philosophers. I think,' he went on, 'that Mack and the boys know everything that has ever happened in the world and possibly everything that will happen. I think they survive in this particular world better than other people. In a time when people tear themselves to pieces with ambition and nervousness and covetousness, they are relaxed. All of our so-called successful men are sick men, with bad stomachs, and bad souls, but Mack and the boys are healthy and curiously clean. They can do what they want. They can satisfy their appetites without calling them something else.' This speech so dried out Doc's throat that he drained his beer glass. He waved two fingers in the air and smiled. 'There's nothing like that first taste of beer,' he said.

Richard Frost said: 'I think they're just like anyone else. They just haven't any money.'

'They could get it,' Doc said. 'They could ruin their lives and get money. Mack has qualities of genius. They're all very clever if they want something. They just know the nature of things too well to be caught in that wanting.'

If Doc had known of the sadness of Mack and the boys he would not have made the next statement, but no one had told him about the social pressure that was exerted against the inmates of the Palace.

He poured beer slowly into his glass. 'I think I can show you proof,' he said. 'You see how they are sitting facing this way? Well–in about half an hour the Fourth of July Parade is going to pass on Lighthouse Avenue. By just turning their heads they can see it, by standing up they can watch it, and by walking two short blocks they can be right beside it. Now I'll bet you a quart of beer they won't even turn their heads.'

'Suppose they don't?' said Richard Frost. 'What will that prove?'

'What will it prove?' cried Doc. 'Why, just that they know what will be in the parade. They will know that the Mayor will ride first in an automobile with bunting streaming back from the hood. Next will come Long Bob on his white horse with the flag. Then the city council, then two companies of soldiers from the Presidio, next the Elks with purple umbrellas, then the Knights Templars in white ostrich feathers and carrying swords. Next the Knights of Columbus with red ostrich feathers and carrying swords. Mack and the boys know that. The band will play. They've seen it all. They don't have to look again.'

'The man doesn't live who doesn't have to look at a parade,' said Richard Frost.

'Is it a bet then?'

'It's a bet.'

'It has always seemed strange to me,' said Doc. 'The things we admire in men, kindness and generosity, openness, honesty, understanding, and feeling, are the concomitants of failure in our system. And those traits we detest, sharpness, greed, acquisitiveness, meanness, egotism, and self-interest, are the traits of success. And while men admire the quality of the first they love the produce of the second.'

'Who wants to be good if he has to be hungry too?' said Richard Frost.

'Oh, it isn't a matter of hunger. It's something quite different. The sale of souls to gain the whole world is completely voluntary and almost unanimous–but not quite. Everywhere in the world there are Mack and the boys. I've seen them in an ice-cream seller in Mexico and in an Aleut in Alaska. You know how they tried to give me a party and something went wrong. But they wanted to give me a party. That was their impulse. Listen,' said Doc.

'Isn't that the band I hear?' Quickly he filled two glasses with beer and the two of them stepped close to the window.

Mack and the boys sat dejectedly on their log and faced the laboratory. The sound of the band came from Lighthouse Avenue, the drums echoing back from the buildings. And suddenly the Mayor's car crossed and it sprayed bunting from the radiator–then Long Bob on his white horse carrying the flag, then the band, then the soldiers, the Elks, the Knights Templar, the Knights of Columbus. Richard and the Doc leaned forward tensely, but they were watching the line of men sitting on the log.

And not a head turned, not a neck straightened up. The parade filed past and they did not move. And the parade was gone. Doc drained his glass and waved two fingers gently in the air and he said: 'Hah! There's nothing in the world like that first taste of beer.'

Richard started for the door. 'What kind of beer do you want?'

'The same kind,' said Doc gently. He was smiling up the hill at Mack and the boys.

It's all fine to say: 'Time will heal everything, this too shall pass away. People will forget'–and things like that when you are not involved, but when you are there is no passage of time, people do not forget, and you are in the middle of something that does not change. Doc didn't know the pain and self-destructive criticism in the Palace Flophouse or he might have tried to do something about it. And Mack and the boys did not know how he felt or they would have held up their heads again.

It was a bad time. Evil stalked darkly in the vacant lot. Sam Malloy had a number of fights with his wife and she cried all the time. The echoes inside the boiler made it sound as though she were crying under water. Mack and the boys seemed to be the node of trouble. The nice bouncer at the Bear Flag threw out a drunk, but threw him too hard and too far and broke his back. Alfred had to go over to Salinas three times before it was cleared up, and that didn't make Alfred feel very well. Ordinarily he was too good a bouncer to hurt anyone. His A and C was a miracle of rhythm and grace.

On top of that a group of high-minded ladies in the town demanded that the dens of vice must close to protect young American manhood. This happened about once a year in the dead period between the Fourth of July and the County Fair. Dora usually closed the Bear Flag for a week when it happened. It wasn't so bad. Everyone got a vacation and little repairs to the plumbing and the walls could be made. But this year the ladies went on a real crusade. They wanted somebody's scalp. It had been a dull summer and they were restless. It got so bad that they had to be told who actually owned the property where vice was practised, what the rents were, and what little hardships might be the result of their closing. That was how close they were to being a serious menace.

Dora was closed a full two weeks and there were three conventions in Monterey while the Bear Flag was closed. Word got around and Monterey lost five conventions for the following year. Things were bad all over. Doc had to get a loan at the bank to pay for the glass that was broken at the party. Elmer Rechati went to sleep on the Southern Pacific track and lost both legs. A sudden and completely unexpected storm tore a purse-seiner and three lampara boats loose from their moorings and tossed them broken and sad on Del Monte beach.

There is no explaining a series of misfortunes like that. Every man blames himself. People in their black minds remember sins committed secretly and wonder whether they have caused the evil sequence. One man may put it down to sun-spots while another invoking the law of probabilities doesn't believe it. Not even the doctors had a good time of it, for while many people were sick none of it was good-paying sickness. It was nothing a good physic or a patent medicine wouldn't take care of.

And to cap it all, Darling got sick. She was a very fat and lively puppy when she was struck down, but five days of fever reduced her to a little skin-covered skeleton. Her liver-coloured nose was pink and her gums were white. Her eyes glazed with illness and her whole body was hot, although she trembled sometimes with cold. She wouldn't eat and she wouldn't drink and her fat little belly shrivelled up against her spine, and even her tail showed the articulations through the skin. It was obviously distemper.

Now a genuine panic came over the Palace Flophouse. Darling had come to be vastly important to them. Hughie and Jones instantly quit their jobs so they could be near to help. They sat up in shifts. They kept a cool, damp cloth on her forehead and she got weaker and weaker. Finally, although they didn't want to, Hazel and Jones were chosen to call on Doc. They found him working over a tide-chart while he ate a chicken stew of which the principal ingredient was not chicken but sea cucumber. They thought he looked at them a little coldly.

'It's Darling,' they said. 'She's sick.'

'What's the matter with her?'

'Mack says it's distemper.'

'I'm no veterinarian,' said Doc. 'I don't know how to treat these things.'

Hazel said: 'Well, couldn't you just take a look at her? She's sick as hell.'

They stood in a circle while Doc examined Darling. He looked at her eyeballs and her gums and felt in her ear for fever. He ran his finger over the ribs that stuck out like spokes and at the poor spine. 'She won't eat?' he asked.

'Not a thing,' said Mack.

'You'll have to force feed her–strong soups and eggs and cod liver oil.'

They thought he was cold and professional. He went back to his tide-charts and his stew.

But Mack and the boys had something to do now. They boiled meat until it was as strong as whisky. They put cod liver oil far back on her tongue so that some of it got down her. They held up her head and made a little funnel of her chops and poured the cool soup in. She had to swallow or drown. Every two hours they fed her and gave her water. Before they had slept in shifts–now no one slept. They sat silently and waited for Darling's crisis.

It came early in the morning. The boys sat in their chairs half asleep, but Mack was awake and his eyes were on the puppy. He saw her ears flip twice, and her chest heave. With infinite weakness she climbed slowly to her spindly legs, dragged herself to the door, took four laps of water, and collapsed on the floor.

Mack shouted the others awake. He danced heavily. All the boys shouted at one another. Lee Chong heard them and snorted to himself as he carried out the garbage cans. Alfred the bouncer heard them and thought they were having a party.

By nine o'clock Darling had eaten a raw egg and half a pint of whipped cream by herself. By noon she was visibly putting on weight. In a day she romped a little and by the end of the week she was a well dog.

At last a crack had developed in the wall of evil. There were evidences of it everywhere. The purse-seiner was hauled back into the water and floated. Word came down to Dora that it was all right to open up the Bear Flag. Earl Wakefield caught a sculpin with two heads and sold it to the museum for eight dollars. The wall of evil and of waiting was broken. It broke away in chinks. The curtains were drawn at the laboratory that night and the Gregorian music played until two o'clock and then the music stopped and no one came out. Some force wrought with Lee Chong's heart and all in an Oriental moment he forgave Mack and the boys and wrote off the frog debt, which had been a monetary headache from the beginning. And to prove to the boys that he had forgiven them he took a pint of Old Tennis Shoes up and presented it to them. Their trading at the Thrift Market had hurt his feelings, but it was all over now. Lee's visit coincided with the first destructive healthy impulse Darling had since her illness. She was completely spoiled now and no one thought of housebreaking her. When Lee Chong came in with his gift, Darling was deliberately and happily destroying Hazel's only pair of rubber-boots, while her happy masters applauded her.

Mack never visited the Bear Flag professionally. It would have seemed a little like incest to him. There was a house out by the baseball park he patronized. Thus, when he went into the front bar, everyone thought he wanted a beer. He stepped up to Alfred. 'Dora around?' he asked.

'What do you want with her?' Alfred asked.

'I got something I want to ask her.'

'What about?'

'That's none of your God damn business,' said Mack.

'Okay. Have it your way. I'll see if she wants to talk to you.'

A moment later he led Mack into the sanctum. Dora sat at a roll-top desk. Her orange hair was piled in ringlets on her head and she wore a green eyeshade. With a stub pen she was bringing her books up-to-date, a fine old double-entry ledger. She was dressed in a magnificent pink silk wrapper with lace at the wrists and throat. When Mack came in she whirled her pivot-chair about and faced him. Alfred stood in the door and waited. Mack stood until Alfred closed the door and left.

Dora scrutinized him suspiciously. 'Well–what can I do for you?' she demanded at last.

'You see, ma'am,' said Mack. 'Well I guess you heard what we done over at Doc's some time back.'

Dora pushed the eyeshade back up on her head and she put the pen in an old-fashioned coil-spring holder. 'Yeah!' she said. 'I heard.'

'Well, ma'am, we did it for Doc. You may not believe it but we wanted to give him a party. Only he didn't get home in time and–well, she got out of hand.'

'So I heard,' said Dora. 'Well, what you want me to do?'

'Well,' said Mack, 'I and the boys thought we'd ask you. You know what we think of Doc. We wanted to ask you what you thought we could do for him that would kind of show him.'

Dora said: 'Hum,' and she flopped back in her pivot-chair and crossed her legs and smoothed her wrapper over her knees. She shook out a cigarette, lighted it, and studied. 'You gave him a party he didn't get to. Why don't you give him a party he does get to?' she said.

'Jesus,' said Mack afterwards talking to the boys. 'It was just as simple as that. Now there is one hell of a woman. No wonder she got to be madam. There is one hell of a woman.'

24

Mary Talbot, Mrs Tom Talbot, that is, was lovely. She had red hair with green lights in it. Her skin was golden, with a green under-cast, and her eyes were green, with little golden spots. Her face was triangular, with wide cheek-bones, wide-set eyes, and her chin was pointed. She had long dancer's legs and dancer's feet, and she seemed never to touch the ground when she walked. When she was excited, and she was excited a good deal of the time, her face flushed with gold. Her great-great-great-great-great grandmother had been burned as a witch.

More than anything in the world Mary Talbot loved parties. She loved to give parties and she loved to go to parties. Since Tom Talbot didn't make much money Mary couldn't give parties all the time, so she tricked people into giving them. Sometimes she telephoned a friend and said bluntly: 'Isn't it about time you gave a party?'

Regularly, Mary had six birthdays a year, and she organized costume parties, surprise parties, holiday parties. Christmas Eve at her house was a very exciting thing. For Mary glowed with parties. She carried her husband along on the wave of her excitement.

In the afternoons when Tom was at work Mary sometimes gave tea-parties for the neighbourhood cats. She set a footstool with doll cups and saucers. She gathered the cats, and there were plenty of them, and then she held long and detailed conversations with them. It was a kind of play she enjoyed very much–a kind of satiric game, and it covered and concealed from Mary the fact that she didn't have very nice clothes and the Talbots didn't have any money. They were pretty near absolute bottom most of the time, and when they really scraped, Mary managed to give some kind of a party.

She could do that. She could infect a whole house with gaiety and she used her gift as a weapon against the despondency that lurked always around outside the house waiting to get in at Tom. That was Mary's job as she saw it–to keep the despondency away from Tom because everyone knew he was going to be a great success some time. Mostly she was successful in keeping the dark things out of the house, but sometimes they got in at Tom and laid him out. Then he would sit and brood for hours, while Mary frantically built up a back-fire of gaiety.

One time when it was the first of the month and there were curt notes from the water company and the rent wasn't paid and a manuscript had come back from *Collier's* and the cartoons had come back from *The New Yorker* and pleurisy was hurting Tom pretty badly, he went into the bedroom and lay down on the bed.

Mary came softly in, for the blue-grey colour of his gloom had seeped out under the door and through the keyhole. She had a little bouquet of candytuft in a collar of paper lace.

'Smell,' she said and held the bouquet to his nose. He smelled the flowers and said nothing. 'Do you know what day this is?' she asked and thought wildly for something to make it a bright day.

Tom said: 'Why don't we face it for once? We're down. We're going under. What's the good kidding ourselves?'

'No we're not,' said Mary. 'We're magic people. We always have been. Remember that ten dollars you found in a book–remember when your cousin sent you five dollars? Nothing can happen to us.'

'Well, it has happened,' said Tom. 'I'm sorry,' he said.'I just can't talk myself out of it this time. I'm sick of pretending everything. For once I'd like to have it real–just for once.'

'I thought of giving a little party tonight,' said Mary.

'On what? You're not going to cut out the baked ham picture from a magazine again and serve it on a platter, are you? I'm sick of that kind of kidding. It isn't funny any more. It's sad.'

'I could give a little party,' she insisted. 'Just a small affair. Nobody will dress. It's the anniversary of the founding of the Bloomer League–you didn't even remember that.'

'It's no use,' said Tom. 'I know it's mean, but I just can't rise to it. Why don't you just go out and shut the door and leave me alone? I'll get you down if you don't.'

She looked at him closely and saw that he meant it. Mary walked quietly out and shut the door, and Tom turned over on the bed and put his face down between his arms. He could hear her rustling about in the other room.

She decorated the door with old Christmas things, glassballs, and tinsel, and she made a placard that said: 'Welcome Tom, our Hero'. She listened at the door and she couldn't hear anything. A little disconsolately she got out the footstool and spread a napkin over it. She put her bouquet in a glass in the middle of the footstool and set out four little cups and saucers. She went into the kitchen, put the tea in the teapot and set the kettle to boil. Then she went out into the yard.

Kitty Randolph was sunning herself by the front fence. Mary said: 'Miss Randolph–I'm having a few friends in to tea if you would care to come.' Kitty Randolph rolled over languorously on her back and stretched in the warm sun. 'Don't be later than four o'clock,' said Mary. 'My husband and I are going to the Bloomer League Centennial Reception at the Hotel.'

She strolled round the house to the backyard, where the blackberry vines clambered over the fence. Kitty Casini was squatting on the ground growling to herself and flicking her tail fiercely. 'Mrs Casini,' Mary began, and then she stopped for she saw what the cat was doing. Kitty Casini had a mouse. She patted it gently with her unarmed paw and the mouse squirmed horribly away, dragging its paralysed hind legs behind it. The cat let it get nearly to the covert of the blackberry vines and then she reached delicately out and white thorns had sprouted on her paw. Daintily she stabbed the mouse through the back and drew it wriggling to her and her tail flicked with tense delight.

Tom must have been at least half asleep when he heard his name called over and over. He jumped up shouting: 'What is it? Where are you?' He could hear Mary crying. He ran out into the yard and saw what was happening. 'Turn your head,' he shouted and he killed the mouse. Kitty Casini had leaped to the top of the fence, where she watched him angrily. Tom picked up a rock and hit her in the stomach and knocked her off the fence.

In the house Mary was still crying a little. She poured the water into the teapot and brought it to the table. 'Sit there,' she told Tom and he squatted down on the floor in front of the footstool.

'Can't I have a big cup?' he asked.

'I can't blame Kitty Casini,' said Mary. 'I know how cats are. It isn't her fault. But–Oh, Tom! I'm going to have trouble inviting her again. I'm just not going to like her for a while no matter how much I want to.' She looked closely at Tom and saw that the lines were gone from his forehead and that he was not blinking badly. 'But then I'm so busy with the Bloomer League these days,' she said. 'I just don't know how I'm going to get everything done.'

Mary Talbot gave a pregnancy party that year. And everyone said: 'God! A kid of hers is going to have fun.'

25

Certainly all of Cannery Row and probably all of Monterey felt that a change had come. It's all right not to believe in luck and omens. Nobody believes in them. But it doesn't do any good to take chances with them and no one takes chances. Cannery Row, like every other place else, is not superstitious, but will not walk under a ladder or open an umbrella in the house. Doc was a pure scientist and incapable of superstition and yet when he came in late one night and found a line of white flowers across the door-sill he had a bad time of it. But most people in Cannery Row simply do not believe in such things and then live by them.

There was no doubt in Mack's mind that a dark cloud had hung on the Palace Flophouse. He had analysed the abortive party and found that a misfortune had crept into every crevice, that bad luck had come up like hives on the evening. And once you got into a routine like that the best thing to do was just go to bed until it was over. You couldn't buck it. Not that Mack was superstitious.

Now a kind of gladness began to penetrate into the Row and to spread out from there. Doc was almost supernaturally successful with a series of lady visitors. He didn't half try. The puppy at the Palace was growing like a pole bean, and, having a thousand generations of training behind her, she began to train herself. She got disgusted with wetting on the floor and took to going outside. It was obvious that Darling was going to grow up a good and charming dog. And she had developed no chorea from her distemper.

The benignant influence crept like gas through the Row. It got as far as Herman's hamburger stand, it spread to the San Carlos Hotel. Jimmy Brucia felt it and Johnny his singing bar-tender. Sparky Evea felt it and joyously joined battle with three new out-of-town cops. It even got as far as the County Jail in Salinas, where Gay, who had lived a good life by letting the sheriff beat him at draughts, suddenly grew cocky and never lost another game. He lost his privileges that way, but he felt a whole man again.

The sea-lions felt it and their barking took on a tone and a cadence that would have gladdened the heart of St Francis. Little girls studying their catechism suddenly looked up and giggled for no reason at all. Perhaps some electrical finder could have been developed so delicate that it could have located the source of all this spreading joy and fortune. And triangulation might possibly have located it in the Palace Flophouse and Grill. Certainly the Palace was lousy with it. Mack and the boys were charged. Jones was seen to leap from his chair only to do a quick tap dance and sit down again. Hazel smiled vaguely at nothing at all. The joy was so general and so suffused that Mack had a hard time keeping it centred and aimed at its objective. Eddie, who had worked at 'La Ida' pretty regularly, was accumulating a cellar of some promise. He no longer added beer to the wining jug. It gave a flat taste to the mixture, he said.

Sam Malloy had planted morning glories to grow over the boiler. He had put out a little awning and under it he and his wife often sat in the evening. She was crocheting a bedspread.

The joy even got into the Bear Flag. Business was good. Phyllis Mae's leg was knitting nicely and she was nearly ready to go to work again. Eva Flanagan got back from East St Louis very glad to be back. It had been hot in East St Louis and it hadn't been as fine as she remembered it. But then she had been younger when she had had so much fun there.

The knowledge or conviction about the party for Doc was no sudden thing. It did not burst out full blown. People knew about it, but let it grow gradually, like a pupa in the cocoons of their imaginations.

Mack was realistic about it. 'Last time we forced her,' he told the boys. 'You can't never give a good party that way. You got to let her creep up on you.'

'Well, when's it going to be?' Jones asked impatiently.

'I don't know,' said Mack.

'Is it gonna be a surprise party?' Hazel asked.

'It ought to, that's the best kind,' said Mack.

Darling brought him a tennis ball she had found and he threw it out the door into the weeds. She bounced away after it.

Hazel said: 'If we knew when was Doc's birthday, we could give him a birthday-party.'

Mack's mouth was open. Hazel constantly surprised him. 'By God, Hazel, you got something,' he cried. 'Yes, sir, if it was his birthday there'd be presents. That's just the thing. All we got to find out is when it is.'

'That ought to be easy,' said Hughie. 'Why don't we ask him?'

'Hell,' said Mack. 'Then he'd catch on. You ask a guy when is his birthday and especially if you've already give him a party like we done, and he'll know what you want to know for. Maybe I'll just go over and smell around a little and not let on.'

'I'll go with you,' said Hazel.

'No–if two of us went, he might figure we were up to something.'

'Well, hell, it was my idear,' said Hazel.

'I know,' said Mack. 'And when it comes off why I'll tell Doc it was your idear. But I think I better go over alone.'

'How is he–friendly?' Eddie asked.

'Sure, He's all right.'

Mack found Doc way back in the downstairs part of the laboratory. He was dressed in a long rubber apron and he wore rubber gloves to protect his hands from the formaldehyde. He was injecting the veins and arteries of small dogfish with colour mass. His little ball mill rolled over and over, mixing the blue mass. The red fluid was already in the pressure-gun. Doc's fine hands worked precisely, slipping the needle into place and pressing the compressed-air trigger that forced the colour into the veins. He laid the finished fish in a neat pile. He would have to go over these again to put the blue mass in the arteries. The dog-fish made good dissection specimens.

'Hi, Doc,' said Mack. 'Keepin' pretty busy?'

'Busy as I want,' said Doc. 'How's the pup?'

'Doin' just fine. She would of died if it hadn't been for you.'

For a moment a wave of caution went over Doc and then slipped off. Ordinarily a compliment made him wary. He had been dealing with Mack for a long time. But the tone had nothing but gratefulness in it. He knew how Mack felt about the pup.'How are things going up at the Palace?'

'Fine, Doc, just fine. We got two new chairs. I wish you'd come up and see us. It's pretty nice up there now.'

'I will,' said Doc. 'Eddie still bring back the jug?'

'Sure,' said Mack. 'He ain't puttin' beer in it no more and I think the stuff is better. It's got more zip.'

'It had plenty of zip before,' said Doc.

Mack waited patiently. Sooner or later Doc was going to wade into it and he was waiting. If Doc seemed to open the subject himself it would be less suspicious. This was always Mack's method.

'Haven't seen Hazel for some time. He isn't sick, is he?'

'No,' said Mack and he opened the campaign. 'Hazel is all right. Him and Hughie are havin' one hell of a battle. Been goin' on for a week,' he chuckled. 'An' the funny thing is it's about somethin' they don't neither of them know nothin' about. I stayed out of it because I don't know nothin' about it neither, but not them. They've even got a little mad at each other.'

'What's it about?' Doc asked.

'Well, sir,' said Mack, 'Hazel's all the time buyin' these here charts and lookin' up lucky days and stars and stuff like that. And Hughie says it's all a bunch of malarky. Hazel, he says if you know when a guy is born you can tell about him and Hughie says they're just sellin' Hazel them charts for two bits apiece. Me, I don't know nothin' about it. What do you think, Doc?'

'I'd kind of side with Hughie,' said Doc. He stopped the ball mill, washed out the colour-gun and filled it with blue mass.

'They got goin' hot the other night,' said Mack. 'They ask me when I'm born so I tell 'em April 12 and Hazel he goes and buys one of them charts and read all about me. Well it did seem to hit in some places. But it was nearly all good stuff and a guy will believe good stuff about himself. It said I'm brave and smart and kind to my friends. But Hazel says it's all true. When's your birthday, Doc?' At the end of the long discussion it sounded perfectly casual. You couldn't put your finger on it. But it must be remembered that Doc had known Mack a very long time. If he had not he would have said December 18, which was his birthday, instead of October 27, which was not. 'October 27,' said Doc. 'Ask Hazel what that makes me.'

'It's probably so much malarky,' said Mack, 'but Hazel he takes it serious. I'll ask him to look you up, Doc.'

When Mack left, Doc wondered casually what the build-up was. For he recognized it as a lead. He knew Mack's technique, his method. He recognized his style. And he wondered to what purpose Mack could put the information. It was only later, when rumours began to creep in, that Doc added the whole thing up. Now he felt slightly relieved, for he had expected Mack to put the bite on him.

26

The two little boys played in the boat-works yard until a cat climbed the fence. Instantly they gave chase, drove it across the tracks, and there filled their pockets with granite stones from the roadbed. The cat got away from them in the tall weeds, but they kept the stones because they were perfect in weight, shape, and size for throwing. You can't ever tell when you're going to need a stone like that. They turned down Cannery Row and whanged a stone at the corrugated-iron front of Morden's Cannery. A startled man looked out the office window and then rushed for the door, but the boys were too quick for him. They were lying behind a wooden stringer in the lot before he even got near the door. He couldn't have found them in a hundred years.

'I bet he could look all his life and he couldn't find us,' said Joey.

They got tired of hiding after a while with no one looking for them. They got up and strolled on down Cannery Row. They looked a long time in Lee's window, coveting the pliers, the hacksaws, the engineers' caps, and the bananas. Then they crossed the street and sat down on the lower step of the stairs that went to the second storey of the laboratory.

Joey said: 'You know, this guy in here got babies in bottles.'

'What kind of babies?' Willard asked.

'Regular babies, only before they're borned.'

'I don't believe it,' said Willard.

'Well, it's true. The Sprague kid seen them and he says they ain't no bigger than this and they got little hands and feet and eyes.'

'And hair?' Willard demanded.

'Well, the Sprague kid didn't say about hair.'

'You should of asked him. I think he's a liar.'

'You better not let him hear you say that,' said Joey.

'Well, you can tell him I said it. I ain't afraid of him and I ain't afraid of you. I ain't afraid of anybody. You want to make something of it?' Joey didn't answer. 'Well, do you?'

'No,' said Joey. 'I was thinkin', why don't we just go up and ask the guy if he's got babies in bottles? Maybe he'd show them to us, that is if he's got any.'

'He ain't there,' said Willard. 'When he's here, his car's here. He's away some place. I think it's a lie. I think the Sprague kid is a liar. I think you're a liar. You want to make something of that?'

It was a lazy day. Willard was going to have to work hard to get up any excitement. 'I think you're a coward too. You want to make something of that?' Joey didn't answer. Willard changed his tactics. 'Where's your old man now?' he asked in a conversational tone.

'He's dead,' said Joey.

'Oh yeah? I didn't hear. What'd he die of?'

For a moment Joey was silent. He knew Willard knew, but he couldn't let on he knew, not without fighting Willard, and Joey was afraid of Willard.

'He committed–he killed himself.'

'Yeah?' Willard put on a long face. 'How'd he do it?'

'He took rat poison.'

Willard's voice shrieked with laughter. 'What'd he think he was–a rat?'

Joey chuckled a little at the joke, just enough, that is.

'He must of thought he was a rat,' Willard cried. 'Did he go crawling around like this–look Joey–like this? Did he wrinkle up his nose like this? Did he have a big old long tail?' Willard was helpless with laughter. 'Why'n't he just get a rat-trap and put his head in it?' They laughed themselves out on that one. Willard really wore it out. Then he probed for another joke. 'What'd he look like when he took it–like this?' He crossed his eyes and opened his mouth and stuck out his tongue.

'He was sick all day,' said Joey. 'He didn't die 'til the middle of the night. It hurt him.'

Willard said: 'What'd he do it for?'

'He couldn't get a job,' said Joey. 'Nearly a year he couldn't get a job. And you know a funny thing? The next morning a guy come around to give him a job.'

Willard tried to recapture his joke. 'I guess he just figured he was a rat,' he said, but it fell through even for Willard.

Joey stood up and put his hands in his pockets. He saw a little coppery shine in the gutter and walked toward it, but just as he reached it Willard shoved him aside and picked up the penny.

'I saw it first,' Joey cried. 'It's mine.'

'You want to try and make something of it?' said Willard. 'Why'n't you go and take rat poison?'

27

Mack and the boys–the Virtues, the Beatitudes, the Beauties. They sat in the Palace Flophouse and they were the stone dropped in the pool, the impulse which sent out ripples to all of Cannery Row and beyond, to Pacific Grove, to Monterey, even over the hill to Carmel.

'This time,' said Mack, 'we got to be sure he gets to the party. If he don't get there, we don't give it.'

'Where we going to give it this time?' Jones asked.

Mack tipped his chair back against the wall and hooked his feet around the front legs. 'I've give that a lot of thought,' he said. 'Of course we could give it here, but it would be pretty hard to surprise him here. And Doc likes his own place. He's got his music there.' Mack scowled around the room. 'I don't know who broke his phonograph last time,' he said. 'But if anybody so much as lays a finger on it next time I personally will kick the hell out of him.'

'I guess we'll just have to give it at his place,' said Hughie.

People didn't get the news of the party–the knowledge of it just slowly grew up in them. And no one was invited. Everyone was going. October 27 had a mental red circle around it. And since it was to be a birthday party there were presents to be considered.

Take the girls at Dora's. All of them had at one time or another gone over to the laboratory for advice or medicine or simply for unprofessional company. And they had seen Doc's bed. It was covered with an old faded red blanket full of fox tails and burrs and sand, for he took it on all his collecting trips. If money came in he bought laboratory equipment. It never occurred to him to buy a new blanket for himself. Dora's girls were making a patchwork quilt, a beautiful thing of silk. And since most of the silks available came from underclothing and evening dresses, the quilt was glorious in strips of flesh pink and orchid and pale-yellow and cerise. They worked on it in the late mornings and in the afternoons before the boys from the sardine fleet came in. Under the community of effort, those fights and ill feelings that always are present in a whore-house completely disappeared.

Lee Chong got out and inspected a twenty-five-foot string of fire-crackers and a big bag of China lily bulbs. These to his way of thinking were the finest things you could have for a party.

Sam Malloy had long had a theory of antiques. He knew that old furniture and glass and crockery, which had not been very valuable in its day, had when time went by taken on desirability and cash value out of all proportion to its beauty or utility. He knew of one chair that had brought five hundred dollars. Sam collected pieces of historic automobiles and he was convinced that some day his collection, after making him very rich, would repose on black velvet in the best museums. Sam gave the party a good deal of thought and then he went over his treasures, which he kept in a big locked box behind the boiler. He decided to give Doc one of his finest pieces–the connecting-rod and piston from a 1916 Chalmers. He rubbed and polished this beauty until it gleamed like a piece of ancient armour. He made a little box for it and lined it with black cloth.

Mack and the boys gave the problem considerable thought and came to the conclusion that Doc always wanted cats and had some trouble getting them. Mack brought out his double cage. They borrowed a female in an interesting condition and set their trap under the cypress-tree at the top of the vacant lot. In the corner of the Palace they built a wire cage and in it their collection of angry tom-cats grew every night. Jones had to make two trips a day to the canneries for fish heads to feed their charges. Mark considered correctly that twenty-five tom-cats would be as nice a present as they could give Doc.

'No decorations this time,' said Mack. 'Just a good solid party with lots of liquor.'

Gay heard about the party clear over in the Salinas jail, and he made a deal with the sheriff to get off that night, and borrowed two dollars from him for a round-trip bus ticket. Gay had been very nice to the sheriff, who wasn't a man to forget it, particularly because election was coming up and Gay could, or said he could, swing quite a few votes. Besides, Gay could give the Salinas jail a bad name if he wanted to.

Henri had suddenly decided that the old-fashioned pin-cushion was an art form which had flowered and reached its peak in the 'Nineties and had since been neglected. He revived the form and was delighted to see what could be done with coloured pins. The picture was never completed–you could change it by re-arranging the pins. He was preparing a group of these pieces for a one-man show when he heard about the party, and he finally abandoned his own work and began a giant pin-cushion for Doc. It was to be an intricate and provocative design in green, yellow, and blue pins, all cool colours, and its title was Pre-Cambrian Memory.

Henri's friend Eric, a learned barber who collected the first editions of writers who never had a second edition or a second book, decided to give Doc a rowing-machine he had got at the bankruptcy proceedings of a client with a three-year barber bill. The rowing-machine was in fine condition. No one had rowed it much. No one ever uses a rowing-machine.

The conspiracy grew and there were endless visits back and forth, discussions of presents, of liquor, of what time will we start and nobody must tell Doc.

Doc didn't know when he first became aware that something was going on that concerned him. In Lee Chong's, conversation stopped when he entered. At first it seemed to him that people were cold to him. When at least half a dozen people asked him what he was doing October 27 he was puzzled, for he had forgotten he had given this date as his birthday. Actually he had been interested in the horoscope for a spurious birthdate but Mack had never mentioned it again and so Doc forgot it.

One evening he stopped in at the Halfway House because they had a draught beer he liked and kept it at the right temperature. He gulped his first glass and then settled down to enjoy his second when he heard a drunk talking to the bar-tender. 'You goin' to the party?'

'What party?'

'Well,' said the drunk confidentially, 'you know Doc, down in Cannery Row.'

The bar-tender looked up the bar and then back.

'Well,' said the drunk, 'they're givin' him a hell of a party on his birthday.'

'Who is?'

'Everybody.'

Doc mulled this over. He did not know the drunk at all.

His reaction to the idea was not simple. He felt a great warmth that they should want to give him a party and at the same time he quaked inwardly, remembering the last one they had given.

Now everything fell into place–Mack's question and the silences when he was about. He thought of it a lot that night sitting beside his desk. He glanced about, considering what things would have to be locked up. He knew the party was going to cost him plenty.

The next day he began making his own preparations for the party. His best records he carried into the back room, where they could be locked away. He moved every bit of equipment that was breakable back there too. He knew how it would be–his guests would be hungry and they wouldn't bring anything to eat. They would run out of liquor early, they always did. A little wearily he went up to the Thrift Market, where there was a fine and understanding butcher. They discussed meat for some time. Doc ordered fifteen pounds of steak, ten pounds of tomatoes, twelve heads of lettuces, six loaves of bread, a big jar of peanut butter, and one of strawberry jam, five gallons of wine, and four quarts of a good substantial, but not distinguished, whisky. He knew he would have trouble at the bank the first of the month. Three or four such parties, he thought, and he would lose the laboratory.

Meanwhile, on the Row, the planning reached a crescendo. Doc was right, no one thought of food, but there were odd pints and quarts put away all over.

The collection of presents was growing and the guest list, if there had been one, was a little like a census. At the Bear Flag a constant discussion went on about what to wear. Since they would not be working, the girls did not want to wear the long beautiful dresses which were their uniforms. They decided to wear street clothes. It wasn't as simple as it sounded. Dora insisted that a skeleton crew remain on duty to take care of the regulars. The girls divided up into shifts, some to stay until they were relieved by others. They had to flip for who would go to the party first. The first ones would see Doc's face when they gave him the beautiful quilt. They had it on a frame in the dining-room and it was nearly finished. Mrs Malloy had put aside her bedspread for a while. She was crocheting six doilies for Doc's beer glasses. The first excitement was gone from the Row now and its place was taken by a deadly cumulative earnestness. There were fifteen tom-cats in the cage at the Palace Flophouse and their yowling made Darling a little nervous at night.

28

Sooner or later Frankie was bound to hear about the party. For Frankie drifted about like a small cloud. He was always on the edge of groups. No one noticed him or paid any attention to him. You couldn't tell whether he was listening or not. But Frankie did hear about the party and he heard about the presents and a feeling of fullness swelled in him and a feeling of sick longing.

In the window of Jacob's Jewellery Store was the most beautiful thing in the world. It had been there a long time. It was a black onyx clock with a gold face, but on top of it was the real beauty. On top was a bronze group–St George killing the dragon. The dragon was on his back with his claws in the air and in his breast was St George's spear. The saint was in full armour, with the visor raised, and he rode a fat, big-buttocked horse. With his spear he pinned the dragon to the ground. But the wonderful thing was that he wore a pointed beard and he looked a little like Doc.

Frankie walked to Alvarado Street several times a week to stand in front of the window and look at this beauty. He dreamed about it too, dreamed of running his fingers over the rich, smooth bronze. He had known about it for months when he heard of the party and the presents.

Frankie stood on the pavement for an hour before he went inside. 'Well?' said Mr Jacobs. He had given Frankie a visual searching as he came in and he knew there wasn't seventy-five cents on him.

'How much is that?' Frankie asked huskily.

'What?'

'That.'

'You mean the clock? Fifty dollars–with the group seventy-five dollars.'

Frankie walked out without replying. He went down to the beach and crawled under an overturned rowboat and peeked out at the little waves. The bronze beauty was so strong in his head that it seemed to stand out in front of him. And a frantic trapped feeling came over him. He had to get the beauty. His eyes were fierce when he thought of it.

He stayed under the boat all day and at night he emerged and went back to Alvarado Street. While people went to the movies and came out and went to the Golden Poppy, he walked up and down the block. And he didn't get tired or sleepy, for the beauty burned in him like fire.

At last the people thinned out and gradually disappeared from the streets and the parked cars drove away and the town settled to sleep.

A policeman looked closely at Frankie. 'What you doing out?' he asked.

Frankie took to his heels and fled around the corner and hid behind a barrel in the alley. At two-thirty he crept to the door of Jacob's and tried the knob. It was locked. Frankie went back to the alley and sat behind the barrel and thought. He saw a broken piece of concrete lying beside the barrel and he picked it up.

The policeman reported that he heard the crash and ran to it. Jacob's window was broken. He saw the prisoner walking rapidly away and chased him. He didn't know how the boy could run that far and that fast carrying fifty pounds of clock and bronze, but the prisoner nearly got away. If he had not blundered into a blind street he would have got away.

The chief called Doc the next day. 'Come on down, will you? I want to talk to you.'

They brought Frankie in very dirty and frowzy. His eyes were red, but he held his mouth firm and he even smiled a little welcome when he saw Doc.

'What's the matter, Frankie?' Doc asked.

'He broke into Jacob's last night,' the chief said. 'Stole some stuff. We got in touch with his mother. She says it's not her fault, because he hangs around your place all the time.'

'Frankie–you shouldn't have done it,' said Doc. The heavy stone of inevitability was on his heart. 'Can't you parole him to me?' Doc asked.

'I don't think the judge will do it,' said the chief. 'We've got a mental report. You know what's wrong with him?'

'Yes,' said Doc. 'I know.'

'And you know what's likely to happen when he comes into puberty?'

'Yes,' said Doc, 'I know,' and the stone weighed terribly on his heart.

'The doctor thinks we better put him away. We couldn't before, but now he's got a felony on him, I think we better.'

As Frankie listened the welcome died in his eyes.

'What did he take?' Doc asked.

'A great big clock and a bronze statue.'

'I'll pay for it.'

'Oh, we got it back. I don't think the judge will hear of it. It'll just happen again. You know that.'

'Yes,' said Doc softly, 'I know. But maybe he had a reason. Frankie,' he said, 'why did you take it?'

Frankie looked a long time at him. 'I love you,' he said.

Doc ran out and got in his car and went collecting in the caves below Pt Lobos.

29

At four o'clock on October 27 Doc finished bottling the last of a lot of jellyfish. He washed out the formaline jug, cleaned his forceps, powdered and took off his rubber-gloves. He went upstairs, fed the rats, and put some of his best records and his microscopes in the back room. Then he locked it. Sometimes an illuminated guest wanted to play with the rattlesnakes. By making careful preparations, by foreseeing possibilities, Doc hoped to make this party as non-lethal as possible without making it dull.

He put on a pot of coffee, started the *Great Fugue* on the phonograph, and took a shower. He was very quick about it, for he was dressed in clean clothes and was having his cup of coffee before the music was completed.

He looked out through the window at the lot and up at the Palace, but no one was moving. Doc didn't know who or how many were coming to his party. But he knew he was watched. He had been conscious of it all day. Not that he had seen anyone, but someone or several people had kept him in sight. So it was to be a surprise party. He might as well be surprised. He would follow his usual routine, as though nothing were happening. He crossed to Lee Chong's and bought two quarts of beer. There seemed to be a suppressed Oriental excitement at Lee's. So they were coming too. Doc went back to the laboratory and poured out a glass of beer. He drank the first off for thirst and poured a second one to taste. The lot and the street were still deserted.

Mack and the boys were in the Palace and the door was closed. All the afternoon the stove had roared, heating water for baths. Even Darling had been bathed and she wore a red bow round her neck.

'What time you think we should go over?' Hazel asked.

'I don't think before eight o'clock,' said Mack. 'But I don't see nothin' against us havin' a short one to kind of get warmed up.'

'How about Doc getting warmed up?' Hughie said. 'Maybe I ought to just take him a bottle like it was just nothing.'

'No,' said Mack. 'Doc just went over to Lee's for some beer.'

'You think he suspects anything?' Jones asked.

'How could he?' asked Mack.

In the corner cage two tom-cats started an argument and the whole cageful commented with growls and arched backs. There were only twenty-one cats. They had fallen short of their mark.

'I wonder how they'll get them cats over there?' Hazel began. 'We can't carry that big cage through the door.'

'We won't,' said Mack. 'Remember how it was with the frogs. No, we'll just tell Doc about them. He can come over and get them.' Mack got up and opened one of Eddie's wining jugs. 'We might as well get warmed up,' he said.

At five-thirty the old Chinaman flap-flapped down the hill, past the Palace. He crossed the lot, crossed the street, and disappeared between Western

Biological and the Hediondo.

At the Bear Flag the girls were getting ready. A kind of anchor watch had been chosen by straws. The ones who stayed were to be relieved every hour.

Dora was splendid. Her hair freshly dyed orange was curled and piled on her head. She wore her wedding ring and a big diamond brooch on her breast. Her dress was white silk, with a black bamboo pattern. In the bedrooms the reverse of ordinary procedure was in practice.

Those who were staying wore long evening dresses, while those who were going had on short print dresses and looked very pretty. The quilt, finished and backed, was in a big cardboard box in the bar. The bouncer grumbled a little, for it had been decided that he couldn't go to the party. Someone had to look after the house. Contrary to orders, each girl had a pint hidden and each girl watched for the signal to fortify herself a little for the party.

Dora strode magnificently into her office and closed the door. She unlocked the top drawer of the roll-top desk, took out a bottle and a glass, and poured herself a snort. And the bottle clinked softly on the glass. A girl listening outside the door heard the clink and spread the word. Dora would not be able to smell breaths now. And the girls rushed for their rooms and got out their pints. Dusk had come to Cannery Row, the grey time between daylight and street light. Phyllis Mae peeked round the curtain in the front parlour.

'Can you see him?' Doris asked.

'Yeah. He's got the lights on. He's sitting there like he's reading. Jesus, how that guy does read. You'd think he'd ruin his eyes. He's got a glass of beer in his hand.'

'Well,' said Doris, 'we might as well have a little one, I guess.'

Phyllis Mae was still limping a little, but she was as good as new. She could, she said, lick her weight in City Councilmen. 'Seems kind of funny,' she said. 'There he is, sitting over there and he don't know what's going to happen.'

'He never comes in here for a trick,' Doris said a little sadly.

'Lots of guys don't want to pay,' said Phyllis Mae. 'Costs them more, but they figure it different.'

'Well, hell, maybe he likes them.'

'Likes who?'

'Them girls that go over there.'

'Oh, yeah–maybe he does. I been over there. He never made a pass at me.'

'He wouldn't,' said Doris. 'But that don't mean if you didn't work here you wouldn't have to fight your way out.'

'You mean he don't like our profession.'

'No, I don't mean that at all. He probably figures a girl that's workin' has got a different attitude.'

They had another small snort.

In her office Dora poured herself one more, swallowed it, and locked the drawer again. She fixed her perfect hair in the wall mirror, inspected her shining red nails, and went out to the bar. Alfred the bouncer was sulking. It wasn't anything he said nor was his expression unpleasant, but he was sulking just the same. Dora looked him over coldly. 'I guess you figure you're getting the blocks, don't you?'

'No,' said Alfred. 'No, it's quite all right.'

That quite threw Dora. 'Quite all right, is it? You got a job, Mister. Do you want to keep it or not?'

'It's quite all right,' Alfred said frostily. 'I ain't putting out no beef.' He put his elbows on the bar and studied himself in the mirror. 'You just go and enjoy yourself,' he said. 'I'll take care of everything here. You don't need to worry.'

Dora melted under his pain. 'Look,' she said. 'I don't like to have the place without a man. Some lush might get smart and the kids couldn't handle him. But a little later you can come over and you could kind of keep your eye on the place out of the window. How would that be? You could see if anything happened.'

'Well,' said Alfred, 'I would like to come.' He was mollified by her permission. 'Later I might drop over for just a minute or two. They was a mean drunk in last night. An' I don't know, Dora–I kind of lost my nerve since I bust that guy's back. I just ain't sure of myself no more. I'm gonna pull a punch some night and get took.'

'You need a rest,' said Dora. 'Maybe I'll get Mack to fill in and you can take a couple of weeks off.' She was a wonderful madam, Dora was.

Over at the laboratory, Doc had a little whisky after his beer. He was feeling a little mellow. It seemed a nice thing to him that they would give him a party. He played the *Pavane to a Dead Princess* and felt sentimental and a little sad. And because of his feeling he went on with *Daphnis and Chloe*. There was a passage in it that reminded him of something else. The observers in Athens before Marathon reported seeing a great line of dust crossing the Plain, and they heard the clash of arms and they heard the Eleusinian Chant. There was part of the music that reminded him of that picture.

When it was done he got another whisky and he debated in his mind about the *Brandenburg*. That would snap him out of the sweet and sickly mood he was getting into. But what was wrong with the sweet and sickly mood? It was rather pleasant. 'I can play anything I want,' he said aloud. 'I can play *Clair de Lune* or *The Maiden with Flaxen Hair*. I'm a free man.'

He poured a whisky and drunk it. And he compromised with the *Moonlight Sonata*. He could see the neon light of 'La Ida' blinking on and off. And then the street light in front of the Bear Flag came on.

A squadron of huge brown beetles hurled themselves against the light and then fell to the ground and moved their legs and felt around with their antennae. A lady cat strolled lonesomely along the gutter looking for adventure. She wondered what had happened to all the tom-cats who had made life interesting and the nights hideous.

Mr Malloy on his hands and knees peered out of the boiler door to see if anyone had gone to the party yet. In the Palace the boys sat restlessly watching the black hands of the alarm clock.

30

The nature of parties has been imperfectly studied. It is, however, generally understood that a party has a pathology, that it is a kind of an individual, and that it is likely to be a very perverse individual. And it is also generally understood that a party hardly ever goes the way it is planned or intended. This last, of course, excludes those dismal slave parties, whipped and controlled and dominated, given by ogreish professional hostesses. These are not parties at all, but acts and demonstrations, about as spontaneous as peristalsis and as interesting as its end product.

Probably everyone in Cannery Row had projected his imagination to how the party would be–the shouts of greeting, the congratulations, the noise and good feeling. And it didn't start that way at all. Promptly at eight o'clock Mack and the boys, combed and clean, picked up their jugs and marched down the chicken-walk, over the railroad track, through the lot across the street and up the steps of Western Biological. Everyone was embarrassed. Doc held the door open and Mack made a little speech. 'Being as how it's your birthday, I and the boys thought we would wish you happy birthday and we got twenty-one cats for you for a present.'

He stopped and they stood forlornly on the stairs.

'Come on in,' said Doc. 'Why–I'm–surprised. I didn't even know you knew it was my birthday.'

'All tom-cats,' said Hazel. 'We didn't bring 'em down.'

They sat down formally in the room at the left. There was a long silence. 'Well,' said Doc, 'now you're here, how about a little drink?'

Mack said: 'We brought a little snort,' and he indicated the three jugs Eddie had been accumulating. 'They ain't no beer in it,' said Eddie.

Doc covered his early evening reluctance. 'No,' he said. 'You've got to have a drink with me. It just happens I laid in some whisky.'

They were just seated formally, sipping delicately at the whisky, when Dora and the girls came in. They presented the quilt. Doc laid it over his bed and it was beautiful. And they accepted a little drink. Mr and Mrs Malloy followed with their presents.

'Lots of folks don't know what this stuff's going to be worth,' said Sam Malloy as he brought out the Chalmers 1916 piston and connecting-rod. 'There probably isn't three of these here left in the world.'

And now the people began to arrive in droves. Henri came in with a pin cushion three by four feet. He wanted to give a lecture on his new art form, but by this time the formality was broken. Mr and Mrs Gay came in. Lee Chong presented the great string of fire-crackers and the China lily bulbs. Someone ate the lily bulbs by eleven o'clock, but the fire-crackers lasted longer. A group of comparative strangers came in from 'La Ida'. The stiffness was going out of the party quickly. Dora sat in a kind of throne, her orange hair flaming. She held her whisky-glass daintily, with her little finger extended. And she kept an eye on the girls to see that they conducted themselves properly. Doc put dance music on the phonograph and he went to the kitchen and began to fry the steaks.

The first fight was not a bad one. One of the group from 'La Ida' made an immoral proposal to one of Dora's girls. She protested and Mack and the boys, outraged at this breach of propriety, threw him out quickly and without breaking anything. They felt good then, for they knew they were contributing.

Out in the kitchen Doc was frying steaks in three skillets, and he cut up tomatoes and piled sliced bread. He felt very good. Mack was personally taking care of the phonograph. He had found an album of Benny Goodman's trios. Dancing had started, indeed the party was beginning to take on depth and vigour. Eddie went into the office and did a tap-dance. Doc had taken a pint with him to the kitchen and he helped himself from the bottle. He was feeling better and better. Everyone was surprised when he served the meat. Nobody was really hungry and they cleaned it up instantly. Now the food set the party into a kind of rich digestive sadness. The whisky was gone and Doc brought out the gallons of wine.

Dora, sitting enthroned, said: 'Doc, play some of that nice music. I get Christ awful sick of that musical-box over home.'

Then Doc played *Ardo* and the *Amor* from an album of Monteverdi. And the guests sat quietly and their eyes were inward. Dora breathed beauty. two newcomers crept up the stairs and entered quietly. Doc was feeling a golden pleasant sadness. The guests were silent when the music stopped. Doc brought out a book and he read in a clear, deep voice:

Even now
If I see in my soul the citron-breasted fair one
Still gold-tinted, her face like our night stars,
Drawing unto her; her body beaten about with flame,
Wounded by the flaring spear of love,
My first of all by reason of her fresh years,
Then is my heart buried alive in snow.

Even now
If my girl with lotus eyes came to me again
Weary with the dear weight of young love,
Again I would give her to these starved twins of arms
And from her mouth drink down the heavy wine,
As a reeling pirate bee in fluttered ease
Steals up the honey from the nenuphar.

Even now
If I saw her lying all wide eyes
And with collyrium the indent of her cheek
Lengthened to the bright ear and her pale side
So suffering the fever of my distance,
Then would my love for her be ropes of flowers, and night
A black-haired lover on the breasts of day.

Even now
My eyes that hurry to see no more are painting, painting
Faces of my lost girl. O golden rings
That tap against cheeks of small magnolia-leaves,
O whitest so soft parchment where
My poor divorcèd lips have written excellent
Stanzas of kisses, and will write no more.

Even now
Death sends me the flickering of powdery lids
Over wild eyes and the pity of her slim body
All broken up with the weariness of joy;
The little red flowers of her breasts to be my comfort
Moving above scarves, and for my sorrow
Wet crimson lips that once I marked as mine.

Even now
They chatter her weakness through the two bazaars
Who was so strong to love me. And small men
That buy and sell for silver being slaves
Crinkles the fat about their eyes; and yet
No Prince of the Cities of the Sea has taken her,
Leading to his grim bed. Little lonely one,
You cling to me as a garment clings; my girl.

Even now
I love long black eyes that caress like silk,
Ever and ever sad and laughing eyes,

Whose lids make such sweet shadow when they close
It seems another beautiful look of hers.
I love a fresh mouth, ah, a scented mouth,
And curving hair, subtle as a smoke,
And light fingers, and laughter of green gems.

Even now
I remember that you made answer very softly,
We being one soul, your hand on my hair,
The burning memory rounding your near lips;
I haven't seen the priestnesses of Rati make love at moon fall
And then in a carpeted hall with a bright gold lamp
Lie down carelessly anywhere to sleep.*

Phyllis Mae was openly weeping when he stopped and Dora herself dabbed at her eyes. Hazel was so taken by the sound of the words that he had not listened to their meaning. But a little world sadness had slipped over all of them. Everyone was remembering a lost love, everyone a call.

Mack said: 'Jesus, that's pretty. Reminds me of a dame . . .' and he let it pass. They filled the wineglasses and became quiet. The party was slipping away in sweet sadness. Eddie went out in the office and did a little tap-dance and came back and sat down again. The party was about to recline and go to sleep when there was a tramp of feet on the stairs. A great voice shouted: 'Where's the girls?'

Mack got up almost happily and crossed quickly to the door. And a smile of joy illuminated the faces of Hughie and Jones. 'What girls you got in mind?' Mack asked softly.

'Ain't this a whore-house? Cab-driver said they was one down here.'

'You made a mistake, Mister.' Mack's voice was gay.

'Well, what's them dames in there?'

They joined battle then. They were the crew of a San Pedro tuna-boat, good, hard, happy, fight-wise men. With the first rush they burst through to the party. Dora's girls had each one slipped off a shoe and held it by the toe. As the fight raged by they would clip a man on the head with the spike heel. Dora leaped for the kitchen and came roaring out with a meat grinder. Even Doc was happy. He flailed about with the Chalmers 1916 piston and connecting-rod.

It was a good fight. Hazel tripped and got kicked in the face twice before he could get to his feet again. The Franklin stove went over with a crash. Driven to a corner the newcomers defended themselves with heavy books from the bookcases. But gradually they were driven back. The two front windows were broken out. Suddenly Alfred, who had heard the trouble from across the street, attacked from the rear with his favourite weapon, an indoor ball bat. The fight raged down the steps and into the street and across into the lot. The front door was hanging limply from one hinge again. Doc's shirt was torn off and his slight strong shoulder dripped blood from a scratch. The enemy was driven halfway up the lot when the sirens sounded. Doc's birthday-party had barely time to get inside the laboratory and wedge the broken door closed and turn out the lights before the police car cruised up. The cops didn't find anything. But the party was sitting in the dark giggling happily and drinking wine. The shift changed at the Bear Flag. The fresh contingent raged in full of hell. And then the party really got going. The cops came back, looked in, clicked their tongues and joined in. Mack and the boys used the squad car to go to Jimmy Brucia's for more wine and Jimmy came back with them. You could

**Black Marigolds*, translated from the Sanskrit by E. Powys Mathers.

hear the roar of the party from end to end of Cannery Row. The party had all the best qualities of a riot and a night on the barricades. The crew from the San Pedro tuna-boat crept humbly back and joined the party. They were embraced and admired. A woman five blocks away called the police to complain about the noise and couldn't get anyone. The cops reported their own car stolen and found it later on the beach. Doc sitting cross-legged on the table smiled and tapped his fingers gently on his knee. Mack and Phyllis Mae were doing Indian wrestling on the floor. And the cool bay wind blew in through the broken windows. It was then that someone lighted the twenty-five-foot string of fire-crackers.

31

A well-grown gopher took up residence in a thicket of mallow weeds in the vacant lot on Cannery Row. It was a perfect place. The deep green luscious mallows towered up crisp and rich, and as they matured their little cheeses hung down provocatively. The earth was perfect for a gopher-hole too, black and soft and yet with a little clay in it so that it didn't crumble and the tunnels didn't cave in. The gopher was fat and sleek and he had always plenty of food in his cheek pouches. His little ears were clean and well set and his eyes were as black as old-fashioned pin-heads and just about the same size. His digging hands were strong and the fur on his back was glossy brown and the fawn-coloured fur on his chest was incredibly soft and rich. He had long curving yellow teeth and a little short tail. Altogether he was a beautiful gopher and in the prime of his life.

He came to the place over-land and found it good and he began his burrow on a little eminence where he could look out among the mallow weeds and see the trucks go by on Cannery Row. He could watch the feet of Mack and the boys as they crossed the lot to the Palace Flophouse. As he dug down into the coal-black earth he found it even more perfect, for there were great rocks under the soil. When he made his great chamber for the storing of food it was under a rock so that it could never cave in, no matter how hard it rained. It was a place where he could settle down and raise any number of families and the burrow could increase in all directions.

It was beautiful in the early morning when he first poked his head out of the burrow. The mallows filtered green light down on him and the first rays of the rising sun shone into his hole and warmed it so that he lay there content and very comfortable.

When he had dug his great chamber and his four emergency exits and his waterproof deluge room, the gopher began to store food. He cut down only the perfect mallow stems and trimmed them to the exact length he needed and he took them down the hole and stacked them neatly in his great chamber, and arranged them so they wouldn't ferment or get sour. He had found the perfect place to live. There were no gardens about, so no one would think of setting a trap for him. Cats there were, many of them, but they were so bloated with fish-heads and guts from the canneries that they had long ago given up hunting. The soil was sandy enough, so that water never stood about or filled a hole for long. The gopher worked and worked until he had his great chamber crammed with food. Then he made little side chambers for the babies who would inhabit them. In a few years there might be thousands of his progeny spreading out from the original hearthstone.

But as time went on the gopher began to be a little impatient, for no female appeared. He sat in the entrance of his hole in the morning and made penetrating squeaks that are inaudible to the human ear but can be heard deep in the earth by other gophers. And still no female appeared. Finally in a sweat of impatience he went up across the track until he found another gopher-hole. He squeaked provocatively in the entrance. He heard a rustling and smelled female, and then out of the hole came an old battle-torn bull gopher who mauled and bit him so badly that he crept home and lay in his great chamber for three days recovering and he lost two toes from one front paw from that fight.

Again he waited and squeaked beside his beautiful burrow in the beautiful place, but no female ever came, and after a while he had to move away. He had to move two blocks up the hill to a dahlia garden where they put out traps every night.

32

Doc awakened very slowly and clumsily like a fat man getting out of a swimming-pool. His mind broke the surface and fell back several times. There was red lipstick on his beard. He opened one eye, saw the brilliant colours of the quilt, and closed his eye quickly. But after a while he looked again. His eye went past the quilt to the floor, to the broken plate in the corner, to the glasses standing on the table turned over on the floor, to the spilled wine and the books like heavy fallen butterflies. There were little bits of curled red paper all over the place and the sharp smell of firecrackers. He could see through the kitchen door to the steak plates stacked high and the skillets deep in grease. Hundreds of cigarette-butts were stamped out on the floor. And under the fire-cracker smell was a fine combination of wine and whisky and perfume. His eye stopped for a moment on a little pile of hairpins in the middle of the floor.

He rolled over slowly and supporting himself on one elbow he looked out the broken window. Cannery Row was quiet and sunny. The boiler door was open. The door of the Palace Flophouse was closed. A man slept peacefully among the weeds in the vacant lot. The Bear Flag was shut up tight.

Doc got up and went into the kitchen and lighted the gas water-heater on his way to the toilet. Then he came back and sat on the edge of his bed and worked his toes together while he surveyed the wreckage. From up the hill he could hear the church bells ringing. When the gas heater began rumbling he went back to the bathroom and took a shower and he put on blue jeans and a flannel shirt. Lee Chong was closed, but he saw who was at the door and opened it. He went to the refrigerator and brought out a quart of beer without being asked. Doc paid him.

'Good time?' Lee asked. His brown eyes were a little inflamed in their pouches.

'Good time!' said Doc, and he went back to the laboratory with his cold beer. He made a peanut-butter sandwich to eat with his beer. It was very quiet in the street. No one went by at all. Doc heard music in his head–violas and 'cellos, he thought. And they played cool, soft, soothing music with nothing much to distinguish it. He ate his sandwich and sipped his beer and listened to the music. When he had finished his beer, Doc went into the kitchen, and cleared the dirty dishes out of the sink. He ran hot water in it and poured soap chips under the running water so that the foam stood high and white. Then he moved about collecting all the glasses that weren't broken. He put them in the soapy hot water. The steak-plates were piled high on the stove with their brown juice and their white grease sticking them together. Doc cleared a place on the table for the clean glasses as he washed them. Then he unlocked the door of the back room and brought out one of his albums of Gregorian music and he put a Paternoster and Agnus Dei on the turntable and started it going. The angelic, disembodied voices filled the laboratory. They were incredibly pure and sweet. Doc worked carefully washing the glasses so that they would not clash together and spoil the music. The boys' voices carried the melody up and down, simply but with the richness that is no other singing. When the record had finished, Doc wiped his hands and turned it off. He saw a book lying half under his bed and picked it up and he sat down on the bed. For a moment he read to himself, but then his lips began to move and in a moment he read aloud–slowly, pausing at the end of each line.

> Even now
> I mind the coming and talking of wise men from towers
> Where they had thought away their youth. And I, listening,
> Found not the salt of the whispers of my girl,
> Murmur of confused colours, as we lay near sleep;
> Little wise words and little witty words,
> Wanton as water, honied with eagerness.

In the sink the high white foam cooled and ticked as the bubbles burst. Under the piers it was very high tide and the waves splashed on rocks they had not reached in a long time.

> Even now
> I mind that I loved cypress and roses, clear,
> The great blue mountains and the small grey hills,
> The sounding of the sea. Upon a day
> I saw strange eyes and hands like butterflies;
> For me at morning larks flew from the thyme
> And children came to bathe in little streams.

Doc closed the book. He could hear the waves beat under the piles and he could hear the scampering of white rats against the wire. He went into the kitchen and felt the cooling water in the sink. He ran hot water into it. He spoke aloud to the sink and the white rats, and to himself:

> Even now
> I know that I have savoured the hot taste of life
> Lifting green cups and gold at the great feast.
> Just for a small and a forgotten time
> I have had full in my eyes from off my girl
> The whitest pouring of eternal light . . .

He wiped his eyes with the back of his hand. And the white rats scampered and scrambled in their cages. And behind the glass the rattlesnakes lay still and stared into space with their dusty, frowning eyes.

EAST
OF EDEN

EAST OF EDEN

PASCAL COVICI

Dear Pat,

You came upon me carving some kind of little figure out of wood and you said, 'Why don't you make something for me?'

I asked you what you wanted, and you said, 'A box.'

'What for?'

'To put things in.'

'What things?'

'Whatever you have,' you said.

Well, here's your box. Nearly everything I have is in it, and it is not full. Pain and excitement are in it, and feeling good or bad and evil thoughts and good thoughts–the pleasure of design and some despair and the indescribable joy of creation.

And on top of these are all the gratitude and love I have for you.

And still the box is not full.

JOHN

PART I

CHAPTER 1

I

The Salinas Valley is in Northern California. It is a long narrow swale between two ranges of mountains, and the Salinas River winds and twists up the centre until it falls at last into Monterey Bay.

I remember my childhood names for grasses and secret flowers. I remember where a toad may live and what time the birds awaken in the summer–and what trees and seasons smelled like–how people looked and walked and smelled even. The memory of odours is very rich.

I remember that the Gabilan Mountains to the east of the valley were light gay mountains full of sun and loveliness and a kind of invitation, so that you wanted to climb into their warm foothills almost as you want to climb into the lap of a beloved mother. They were beckoning mountains with a brown grass love. The Santa Lucias stood up against the sky to the west and kept the valley from the open sea, and they were dark and brooding–unfriendly and dangerous. I always found in myself a dread of west and a love of east. Where I ever got such an idea I cannot say, unless it could be that the morning came over the peaks of the Gabilans and the night drifted back from the ridges of the Santa Lucias. It may be that the birth and death of the day had some part in my feeling about the two ranges of mountains.

From both sides of the valley little streams slipped out of the hill canyons and fell into the bed of the Salinas River. In the winter of wet years the streams ran full-freshet, and they swelled the river until sometimes it raged and boiled, bank-full, and then it was a destroyer. The river tore the edges of the farm lands and washed whole acres down; it toppled barns and houses into itself, to go floating and bobbing away. It trapped cows and pigs and sheep and drowned them in its muddy brown water and carried them to the sea. Then when the late spring came, the river drew in from its edges and the sandbanks appeared. And in the summer the river didn't run at all above ground. Some pools would be left in the deep swirl places under a high bank. The tules and grasses grew back, and willows straightened up with the flood débris in their upper branches. The Salinas was only a part-time river. The summer sun drove it underground. It was not a fine river at all, but it was the only one we had, and so we boasted about it–how dangerous it was in a wet winter and how dry it was in a dry summer. You can boast about anything if it's all you have. Maybe the less you have, the more you are required to boast.

The floor of the Salinas Valley, between the ranges and below the foothills, is level because this valley used to be the bottom of a hundred-mile inlet from the sea. The river mouth at Moss Landing was centuries ago the entrance to this long inland water. Once, fifty miles down the valley, my father bored a well. The drill came up first with topsoil and then with gravel and then with white sea sand full of shells and even pieces of whale-bone. There were twenty feet of sand and then black earth again, and even a piece of redwood, that imperishable wood that does not rot. Before the inland sea the valley must have been a forest. And those things had happened right under our feet. And it seemed to me sometimes at night that I could feel both the sea and the redwood forest before it.

On the wide level acres of the valley the topsoil lay deep and fertile. It required only a rich winter of rain to make it break forth in grass and flowers. The spring flowers in a wet year were unbelievable. The whole valley floor, and the foothills too, would be carpeted with lupins and poppies. Once a woman told me that coloured flowers would seem more bright if you added a few white flowers to give the colours definition. Every petal of blue lupin is edged with white, so that a field of lupins is more blue than you can imagine. And mixed with these were splashes of California poppies. These too are a burning colour–not orange, not gold, but if pure gold were liquid and could raise a cream, that golden cream might be like the colour of the poppies. When their season was over the yellow mustard came up and grew to a great height. When my grandfather came into the valley the mustard was so tall that a man on horseback showed only his head above the yellow flowers. On the uplands the grass would be strewn with buttercups, with hen-and-chickens, with black-centred yellow violets. And a little later in the season there would be red and yellow stands of Indian paintbrush. These were the flowers of the open spaces exposed to the sun.

Under the live oaks, shaded and dusky, the maidenhair flourished and gave a good smell, and under the mossy banks of the watercourses whole clumps of five-fingered ferns and goldy-backs hung down. Then there were harebells, tiny lanterns, cream white and almost sinful-looking, and these were so rare and magical that a child, finding one, felt singled out and special all day long.

When June came the grasses headed out and turned brown, and the hills turned a brown which was not brown but a gold and saffron and red–an indescribable colour. And from then on until the next rains the earth dried and the streams stopped. Cracks appeared on the level ground. The Salinas River sank under its sand. The wind blew down the valley, picking up dust and straws, and grew stronger and harsher as it went south. It stopped in the evening. It was a rasping nervous wind, and the dust particles cut into a man's skin and burned his eyes. Men working in the fields wore goggles and tied handkerchiefs around their noses to keep the dirt out.

The valley land was deep and rich, but the foothills wore only a skin of topsoil no deeper than the grass roots; and the farther up the hills you went, the thinner grew the soil, with flints sticking through, until at the brush line it was a kind of dry flinty gravel that reflected the hot sun blindingly.

I have spoken of the rich years when the rainfall was plentiful. But there were dry years too, and they put a terror on the valley. The water came in a thirty-year cycle. There would be five or six wet and wonderful years when there might be nineteen to twenty-five inches of rain, and the land would shout with grass. Then would come six or seven pretty good years of twelve to sixteen inches of rain. And then the dry years would come, and sometimes there would be only seven or eight inches of rain. The land dried up and the grasses headed out miserably a few inches high and great bare scabby places appeared in the valley. The live oaks got a crusty look and the sagebrush was grey. The land cracked and the springs dried up and the cattle listlessly nibbled dry twigs. Then the farmers and the ranchers would be filled with disgust for the Salinas Valley. The cows would grow thin and sometimes starve to death. People would have to haul water in barrels to their farms just for drinking. Some families would sell out for nearly nothing and move away. And it never failed that during the dry years the people forgot about the rich years, and during the wet years they lost all memory of the dry years. It was always that way.

2

And that was the long Salinas Valley. Its history was like that of the rest of the state. First there were Indians, an inferior breed without energy, inventiveness, or culture, a people that lived on grubs and grasshoppers and shellfish, too lazy to hunt or fish. They ate what they could pick up and planted nothing. They pounded bitter acorns for flour. Even their warfare was a weary pantomime.

Then the hard, dry Spaniards came exploring through, greedy and realistic, and their greed was for gold or God. They collected souls as they collected jewels. They gathered mountains and valleys, rivers and whole horizons, the way a man might now gain title to building lots. These tough, dried-up men moved restlessly up the coast and down. Some of them stayed on grants as large as principalities, given to them by Spanish kings who had not the faintest idea of the gift. These first owners lived in poor feudal settlements, and their cattle ranged freely and multiplied. Periodically the owners killed the cattle for their hides and tallow and left the meat to the vultures and coyotes.

When the Spaniards came they had to give everything they saw a name. This is the first duty of any explorer–a duty and a privilege. You must name a thing before you can note it on your hand-drawn map. Of course they were religious people, and the men who could read and write, who kept the records and drew the maps, were the tough untiring priests who travelled with the soldiers. Thus the first names of places were saints' names or religious holidays celebrated at stopping places. There are many saints, but they are not inexhaustible, so that we find repetitions in the first namings. We have San Miguel, St Michael, San Ardo, San Bernardo, San Benito, San Lorenzo, San Carlos, San Francisquito. And then the holidays–Natividad, the Nativity; Nacimiente, the Birth; Soledad, the Solitude. But places were also named from the way the expedition felt at the time: Buena Esperanza, good hope; Buena Vista because the view was beautiful; and Chualar because it was pretty. The descriptive names followed: Paso de los Robles because of the oak trees; Los Laureles for the laurels; Tularcitos because of the reeds in the swamp; and Salinas for the alkali which was white as salt.

Then places were named after animals and birds seen–Gabilanes for the hawks which flew in those mountains; Topo for the mole; Los Gatos for the wild cats. The suggestions sometimes came from the nature of the place itself: Tassajara, a cup and saucer; Laguna Seca, a dry lake; Corral de Tierra for a fence of earth; Paraiso because it was like Heaven.

Then the Americans came–more greedy because there were more of them. They took the lands, remade the laws to make their titles good. And farmholds spread over the land, first in the valleys and then up the foothill slopes, small wooden houses roofed with redwood shakes, corrals of split poles. Wherever a trickle of water came out of the ground a house sprang up and a family began to grow and multiply. Cuttings of red geraniums and rose bushes were planted in the door-yards. Wheel tracks of buckboards replaced the trails, and fields of corn and barley and wheat squared out of the yellow mustard. Every ten miles along the travelled routes a general store and blacksmith shop happened, and these became the nuclei of little towns, Bradley, King City, Greenfield.

The Americans had a greater tendency to name places after people than had the Spaniards. After the valleys were settled the names of places refer more to things which happened there, and these to me are the most fascinating of all names because each name suggests a story that has been forgotten. I think of Bolsa Neuva, a new purse; Morocojo, a lame Moor (who was he and how did he get there?); Wild Horse Canyon and Mustang Grade and Shirt Tail Canyon. The names of places carry a charge of the people who named them, reverent or irreverent, descriptive, either poetic or disparaging. You can name anything San Lorenzo, but Shirt Tail Canyon or the Lame Moor is something quite different.

The winds whistled over the settlements in the afternoon, and the farmers began to set out mile-long wind-breaks of eucalyptus to keep the ploughed topsoil from blowing away. And this is about the way the Salinas Valley was when my grandfather brought his wife and settled in the foothills to the east of King City.

CHAPTER 2

I

I must depend on hearsay, on old photographs, on stories told, and on memories which are hazy and mixed with fable in trying to tell you about the Hamiltons. They were not eminent people, and there are few records concerning them except for the usual papers on birth, marriage, land ownership, and death.

Young Samuel Hamilton came from the north of Ireland and so did his wife. He was the son of small farmers, neither rich nor poor, who had lived on the landhold and in one stone house for many hundreds of years. The Hamiltons managed to be remarkably well educated and well read; and, as is so often true in that green country, they were connected and related to very great people and very small people, so that one cousin might be a baronet and another cousin a beggar. And of course they were descended from the ancient kings of Ireland, as every Irishman is.

Why Samuel left the stone house and the green acres of his ancestors I do not know. He was never a political man, so it is not likely a charge of rebellion drove him out, and he was scrupulously honest, which eliminates the police as prime movers. There was a whisper–not even a rumour but rather an unsaid feeling–in my family that it was love drove him out, and not love of the wife he married. But whether it was too successful love or whether he left in pique at unsuccessful love, I do not know. We always preferred to think it was the former. Samuel had good looks and charm and gaiety. It is hard to imagine that any country Irish girl refused him.

He came to the Salinas Valley full-blown and hearty, full of inventions and energy. His eyes were very blue, and when he was tired one of them wandered outwards a little. He was a big man but delicate in a way. In the dusty business of ranching he seemed always immaculate. His hands were clever. He was a good blacksmith and carpenter and woodcarver, and he could improvise anything with bits of wood and metal. He was for ever inventing a new way of doing an old thing and doing it better and quicker, but he never in his whole life had any talent for making money. Other men who had the talent took Samuel's tricks and sold them and grew rich, but Samuel barely made wages all his life.

I don't know what directed his steps towards the Salinas Valley. It was an unlikely place for a man from a green country to come to, but he came about thirty years before the turn of the century and he brought with him his tiny Irish wife, a tight hard little woman humourless as a chicken. She had a dour Presbyterian mind and a code of morals that pinned down and beat the brains out of nearly everything that was pleasant to do.

I do not know where Samuel met her, how he wooed her, married. I think there must have been some other girl printed somewhere in his heart, for he was a man of love and his wife was not a woman to show her feelings. And in spite of this, in all the years from his youth to his death in the Salinas Valley, there was no hint that Samuel ever went to any other woman.

When Samuel and Liza came to the Salinas Valley all the level land was taken, the rich bottoms, the little fertile creases in the hills, the forests, but there was still marginal land to be homesteaded, and in the barren hills, to the east of what is now King City, Samuel Hamilton homesteaded.

He followed the usual practice. He took a quarter-section for himself and a quarter-section for his wife, and since she was pregnant he took a quarter-section for the child. Over the years nine children were born, four boys and five girls, and with each birth another quarter-section was added to the ranch, and that makes eleven quarter-sections, or seventeen hundred and sixty acres.

If the land had been any good the Hamiltons would have been rich people. But the acres were harsh and dry. There were no springs, and the crust of topsoil was so thin that the flinty bones stuck through. Even the sagebrush struggled to exist, and the oaks were dwarfed from lack of moisture. Even in reasonably good years there was so little feed that the cattle kept thin running about looking for enough to eat. From their barren hills the Hamiltons could look down to the west and see the richness of the bottom land and the greenness around the Salinas River.

Samuel built his house with his own hands, and he built a barn and a blacksmith shop. He found quite soon that even if he had ten thousand acres of hill country he could not make a living on the bony soil without water. His clever hands built a well-boring rig, and he bored wells on the lands of luckier men. He invented and built a threshing machine and moved through the bottom farms in harvest time, threshing the grain his own farm would not raise. And in his shop he sharpened ploughs and mended harrows and welded broken axles and shod horses. Men from all over the district brought him tools to mend and to improve. Besides, they loved to hear Samuel talk of the world and its thinking, of the poetry and philosophy that were going on outside the Salinas Valley. He had a rich deep voice, good both in song and in speech, and while he had no brogue there was a rise and lilt and a cadence to his talk that made it sound sweet in the ears of the taciturn farmers from the valley bottom. They brought whisky too, and out of sight of the kitchen window and the disapproving eye of Mrs Hamilton they took hot nips from the bottle and nibbled cuds of green wild anise to cover the whisky breath. It was a bad day when three or four men were not standing around the forge, listening to Samuel's hammer and his talk. They called him a comical genius and carried his stories carefully home, and they wondered at how the stories spilled out on the way, for they never sounded the same repeated in their own kitchens.

Samuel should have been rich from his well rig and his threshing machine and his shop, but he had no gift for business. His customers, always pressed for money, promised payment after harvest, and then after Christmas, and then after–until at last they forgot it. Samuel had no gift for reminding them. And so the Hamiltons stayed poor.

The children came along as regularly as the years. The few overworked doctors of the county did not often get to the ranches for a birth unless the joy turned nightmare and went on for several days. Samuel Hamilton delivered all his own children and tied the cords neatly, spanked the bottoms and cleaned up the mess. When his youngest was born with some small obstruction and began to turn black, Samuel put his mouth against the baby's mouth and blew air in and sucked it out until the baby could take over for himself. Samuel's hands were so good and gentle that neighbours from twenty miles away would call on him to help with a birth. And he was equally good with mare, cow, or woman.

Samuel had a great black book on an available shelf and it had gold letters on the cover–*Dr Gunn's Family Medicine*. Some pages were bent and beat up from use, and others were never opened to the light. To look through *Dr Gunn* is to know the Hamiltons' medical history. These are the used sections–broken bones, cuts, bruises, mumps, measles, back-ache, scarlet fever, diphtheria, rheumatism, female complaints, hernia, and of course everything to do with pregnancy and the birth of children. The Hamiltons must have been either lucky or moral, for the sections on gonorrhea and syphilis were never opened.

Samuel had no equal for soothing hysteria and bringing quiet to a frightened child. It was the sweetness of his tongue and the tenderness of his soul. And just as there was a cleanness about his body, so there was a cleanness in his thinking. Men coming to his blacksmith shop to talk and listen dropped their cursing for a while, not from any kind of restraint but automatically, as though this were not the place for it.

Samuel kept always a foreignness. Perhaps it was in the cadence of his speech, and this had the effect of making men, and women too, tell him things they would not tell to relatives or close friends. His slight strangeness set him apart and made him safe as a repository.

Liza Hamilton was a very different kettle of fish. Her head was small and round and it held small round convictions. She had a button nose and a hard little set-back chin, a gripping jaw set on its course even though the angels of God argued against it.

Liza was a good plain cook, and her house–it was always her house–was brushed and pummelled and washed. Bearing her children did not hold her back very much–two weeks at the most she had to be careful. She must have had a pelvic arch of whalebone, for she had big children one after the other.

Liza had a finely developed sense of sin. Idleness was a sin, and card playing, which was a kind of idleness to her. She was suspicious of fun, whether it involved dancing or singing or even laughter. She felt that people having a good time were wide open to the devil. And this was a shame, for Samuel was a laughing man, but I guess Samuel was wide open to the devil. His wife protected him whenever she could.

She wore her hair always pulled tight back and bunned behind in a hard knot. And since I can't remember how she dressed, it must have been that she wore clothes that matched herself exactly. She had no spark of humour and only occasionally a blade of cutting wit. She frightened her grandchildren because she had no weakness. She suffered bravely and uncomplainingly through life, convinced that that was the way her God wanted everyone to live. She felt that rewards came later.

2

When people first came to the West, particularly from the owned and fought-over farmlets of Europe, and saw so much land to be had for the signing of a paper and the building of a foundation, an itching land-greed seemed to come over them. They wanted more and more land–good land if possible, but land anyway. Perhaps they had filaments of memory of feudal Europe where great families became and remained great because they owned things. The early settlers took up land they didn't need and couldn't use; they took up worthless land just to own it. And all proportions changed. A man who might have been well-to-do on ten acres in Europe was rat-poor on two thousand in California.

It wasn't very long until all the land in the barren hills near King City and San Ardo was taken up, and ragged families were scattered through the hills, trying their best to scratch a living from the thin flinty soil. They and the coyotes lived clever, despairing, sub-marginal lives. They landed with no money, no equipment, no tools, no credit, and particularly with no knowledge of the new country and no technique for using it. I don't know whether it was a divine stupidity or a great faith that let them do it. Surely such venture is nearly gone from the world. And the families did survive and grow. They had a tool or a weapon that is also nearly gone, or perhaps it is only dormant for a while. It is argued that because they believed thoroughly in a just, moral God they could put their faith there and let the smaller securities take care of themselves. But I think that because they trusted themselves and respected themselves as individuals, because they knew beyond doubt that they were valuable and potentially moral units–because of this they could give God their own courage and dignity and then receive it back. Such things have disappeared perhaps because men do not trust themselves any more, and when that happens there is nothing left except perhaps to find some strong sure man, even though he may be wrong, and to dangle from his coat-tails.

While many people came to the Salinas Valley penniless, there were others who, having sold out somewhere else, arrived with money to start a new life. These usually bought land, but good land, and built their houses of planed lumber, and had carpets and coloured-glass diamond panes in their windows. There were numbers of these families and they got the good land of the valley and cleared the yellow mustard away and planted wheat.

Such a man was Adam Trask.

CHAPTER 3

I

Adam Trask was born on a farm on the outskirts of a little town which was not far from a big town in Connecticut. He was an only son, and he was born six months after his father was mustered into a Connecticut regiment in 1862. Adam's mother ran the farm, bore Adam, and still had time to embrace a primitive theosophy. She felt that her husband would surely be killed by the wild and barbarous rebels, and she prepared herself to get in touch with him in what she called the beyond. He came home six weeks after Adam was born. His right leg was off at the knee. He stumped in on a crude wooden leg he himself had carved out of beechwood. And already it was splitting. He had in his pocket and placed on the parlour table the lead bullet they had given him to bite while they cut off his frayed leg.

Adam's father Cyrus was something of a devil–had always been wild–drove a two-wheeled cart too fast, and managed to make his wooden leg seem jaunty and desirable. He had enjoyed his military career, what there was of it. Being wild by nature, he had liked his brief period of training and the drinking and gambling and whoring that went with it. Then he marched south with a group of replacements, and he enjoyed that too–seeing the country and stealing chickens and chasing rebel girls up into the haystacks. The grey, despairing weariness of protracted manœuvres and combat did not touch him. The first time he saw the enemy was at eight o'clock one spring morning, and at eight-thirty he was hit in the right leg by a heavy slug that mashed and splintered the bones beyond repair. Even then he was lucky, for the rebels retreated and the field surgeons moved up immediately. Cyrus Trask did have his five minutes of horror while they cut the shreds away and sawed the bone off square and burned the open flesh. The tooth-marks in the bullet proved that. And there was considerable pain while the wound healed under the unusually septic conditions in the hospitals of that day. But Cyrus had vitality and swagger. While he was carving his beechwood leg and hobbling about on a crutch, he contracted a particularly virulent dose of the clap from a negro girl who whistled at him from under a pile of lumber and charged him ten cents. When he had his new leg, and painfully knew his condition, he hobbled about for days, looking for the girl. He told his bunk-mates what he was going to do when he found her. He planned to cut off her ears and her nose with his pocket-knife and get his money back. Carving on his wooden leg he showed his friend how he would cut her. 'When I finish her she'll be a funny-looking bitch,' he said. 'I'll make her so a drunk Indian won't take out after her.' His light-of-love must have sensed his intentions, for he never found her. By the time Cyrus was released from the hospital and the army, his gonorrhea was dried up. When he got home to Connecticut there remained only enough of it for his wife.

Mrs Trask was a pale, inside-herself woman. No heat of sun ever reddened her cheeks, and no open laughter raised the corners of her mouth. She used religion as a therapy for the ills of the world and of herself, and she changed the religion to fit the ill. When she found that the theosophy she had developed for communication with a dead husband was not necessary, she cast about for some new unhappiness. Her search was quickly rewarded by the infection Cyrus brought home from the war. And as soon as she was aware that a condition existed, she devised a new theology. Her god of communication became a god of vengeance–to her the most satisfactory deity she had devised so far–and, as it turned out, the last. It was quite easy for her to attribute her condition to certain dreams she had experienced while her husband was away. But the disease was not punishment enough for her nocturnal philandering. Her new god was an expert in punishment. He demanded of her a sacrifice. She searched her mind for some proper egotistical humility and almost happily arrived at the sacrifice–herself. It took her two weeks to write her last letters with revisions and corrected spelling. In it she confessed to crimes she could not possibly have committed and admitted faults far beyond her capacity. And then, dressed in a secretly made shroud, she went out on a moonlight night and drowned herself in a pond so shallow that she had to get down on her knees in the mud and hold her head under water. This required great will-power. As the warm unconsciousness finally crept over her, she was thinking with some irritation of how her white lawn shroud would have mud down the front when they pulled her out in the morning. And it did.

Cyrus Trask mourned for his wife with a keg of whisky and three old army friends who had dropped in on their way home to Maine. Baby Adam cried a good deal at the beginning of the wake, for the mourners, not knowing about babies, had neglected to feed him. Cyrus soon solved the problem. He dipped a rag in whisky and gave it to the baby to suck, and after three or four dippings young Adam went to sleep. Several times during the mourning period he awakened and complained and got the dipped rag again and went to sleep. The baby was drunk for two days and a half. Whatever may have happened in his developing brain, it proved beneficial to his metabolism: from that two and half days he gained an iron health. And when at the end of three days his father finally went out and bought a goat, Adam drank the milk greedily, vomited, drank more, and was on his way. His father did not find the reaction alarming, since he was doing the same thing.

Within a month Cyrus Trask's choice fell on the seventeen-year-old daughter of a neighbouring farmer. The courtship was quick and realistic. There was no doubt in anybody's mind about his intentions. They were honourable and reasonable. Her father abetted the courtship. He had two younger daughters, and Alice, the eldest, was seventeen. This was her first proposal.

Cyrus wanted a woman to take care of Adam. He needed someone to keep house and cook, and a servant cost money. He was a vigorous man and needed the body of a woman, and that too cost money–unless you were married to it.

Within two weeks Cyrus had wooed, wedded, bedded, and impregnated her. His neighbours did not find his action hasty. It was quite normal in that day for a man to use up three or four wives in a normal lifetime.

Alice Trask had a number of admirable qualities. She was a deep scrubber and a corner-cleaner in the house. She was not very pretty, so there was no need to watch her. Her eyes were pale, her complexion sallow, and her teeth crooked, but she was extremely healthy and never complained during her pregnancy. Whether she liked children or not no one ever knew. She was not asked, and she never said anything unless she was asked. From Cyrus's point of view this was possibly the greatest of virtues. She never offered any opinion or statement, and when a man was talking she gave a vague impression of listening while she went about doing the housework.

The youth, inexperience, and taciturnity of Alice Trask all turned out to be assets for Cyrus. While he continued to operate his farm as such farms were operated in the neighbourhood, he entered a new career–that of the old soldier. And that energy which had made him wild now made him thoughtful. No one now outside the War Department knew the quality and duration of his service. His wooden leg was at once a certificate of proof of his soldiering and a guarantee that he wouldn't ever have to do it again. Timidly he began to tell Alice about his campaigns, but as his technique grew so did his battles. At the very first he knew he was lying, but it was not long before he was equally sure that every one of his stories were true. Before he had entered the service he had not been much interested in warfare; now he bought every book about war, read every report, subscribed to the New York papers, studied maps. His knowledge of geography had been shaky and his information about the fighting non-existent; now he became an authority. He knew not only the battles, movements, campaigns, but also the units involved, down to the regiments, their colonels, and where they originated. And from telling he became convinced that he had been there.

All of this was a gradual development, and it took place while Adam was growing to boyhood and his young half-brother behind him. Adam and little Charles would sit silent and respectful while their father explained how every general thought and planned and where they had made their mistakes and what they should have done. And then–he had known it at the time–he had told Grant and McClellan where they were wrong and had begged them to take his analysis of the situation. Invariably they refused his advice and only afterwards was he proved right.

There was one thing Cyrus did not do, and perhaps it was clever of him. He never once promoted himself to non-commissioned rank. Private Trask he began, and Private Trask he remained. In the total telling, it made him at once the most mobile and ubiquitous private in the history of warfare. It made it necessary for him to be in as many as four places at once. But perhaps instinctively he did not tell those stories close to each other. Alice and the boys had a complete picture of him: a private soldier, and proud of it, who not only happened to be where every spectacular and important action was taking place but who wandered freely into staff meetings and joined or dissented in the decisions of general officers.

The death of Lincoln caught Cyrus in the pit of the stomach. Always he remembered how he felt when he first heard the news. And he could never mention it or hear of it without quick tears in his eyes. And while he never actually said it, you got the indestructible impression that Private Cyrus Trask was one of Lincoln's closest, warmest, and most trusted friends. When Mr Lincoln wanted to know about the army, the real army, not those prancing dummies in gold braid, he turned to Private Trask. How Cyrus managed to make this understood without saying it was a triumph of insinuation. No one would call him a liar. And this was mainly because the lie was in his head, and any truth coming from his mouth carried the colour of the lie.

Quite early he began to write letters and then articles about the conduct of the war, and his conclusions were intelligent and convincing. Indeed, Cyrus developed an excellent military mind. His criticisms both of the war as it had been conducted and of the army organization as it persisted were irresistibly penetrating. His articles in various magazines attracted attention. His letters to the War Department, printed simultaneously in the newspapers, began to have a sharp effect on decisions in the army. Perhaps if the Grand Army of the Republic had not assumed political force and direction his voice might not have been heard so clearly in Washington, but the spokesman for a block of nearly a million men was not to be ignored. And such a voice in military matters Cyrus Trask became. It came about that he was consulted in matters of army organization, in officer relationships, in personnel and equipment. His expertness was apparent to everyone who heard him. He had a genius for the military. More than that, he was one of those responsible for the organization of the GAR as a cohesive and potent force in the national life. After several unpaid offices in that organization, he took a paid secretaryship which he kept for the rest of his life. He travelled from one end of the country to the other, attending conventions, meetings, and encampments. So much for his public life.

His private life was also laced through with his new profession. He was a man devoted. His house and farm he organized on a military basis. He demanded and got reports on the conduct of his private economy. It is probable that Alice preferred it this way. She was not a talker. A terse report was easiest for her. She was busy with the growing boys and with keeping the house clean and the clothes washed. Also, she had to conserve her energy, though she did not mention this in any of her reports. Without warning her energy would leave her, and she would have to sit down and wait until it came back. In the night she would be drenched with perspiration. She knew perfectly well that she had what was called consumption, would have known even if she was not reminded by a hard, exhausting cough. And she did not know how long she would live. Some people wasted on for quite a few years. There wasn't any rule about it. Perhaps she didn't dare to mention it to her husband. He had devised a method of dealing with sickness which resembled punishment. A stomach-ache was treated with a purge so violent that it was a wonder anyone survived it. If she had mentioned her condition, Cyrus might have started a treatment which would have killed her off before her consumption could have done it. Besides, as Cyrus became more military, his wife learned the only technique through which a soldier can survive. She never made herself noticeable, never spoke unless spoken to, performed what was expected and no more, and tried for no promotions. She became a rear rank private. It was much easier that way. Alice retired to the background until she was barely visible at all.

It was the little boys who really caught it. Cyrus had decided that even though the army was not perfect, it was still the only honourable profession for a man. He mourned the fact that he could not be a permanent soldier because of his wooden leg, but he could not imagine any career for his sons except the army. He felt a man should learn soldiering from the ranks, as he had. Then he would know what it was about from experience, not from charts and textbooks. He taught them the manual of arms when they could barely walk. By the time they were in grade school, close-order drill was as natural as breathing and as hateful as hell. He kept them hard with exercises, beating out the rhythm with a stick on his wooden leg. He made them walk for miles, carrying knapsacks loaded with stones to make their shoulders strong. He worked constantly on their marksmanship in the wood-lot behind the house.

2

When a child first catches adults out–when it first walks into his grave little head that adults do not have divine intelligence, that their judgements are not always wise, their thinking true, their sentences just–his world falls into panic desolation. The gods are fallen and all safety gone. And there is one sure thing about the fall of gods: they to not fall a little; they crash and shatter or sink deeply into green muck. It is a tedious job to build them up again; they never quite shine. And the child's world is never quite whole again. It is an aching kind of growing.

Adam found his father out. It wasn't that his father changed, but that some new quality came to Adam. He had always hated the discipline, as every normal animal does, but it was just and true and inevitable as measles, not to be denied or cursed, only to be hated. And then–it was very fast, almost a click in the brain–Adam knew that, for him at least, his father's methods had no reference to anything in the world but his father. The techniques and training were not designed for the boys at all but only to make Cyrus a great man. And the same click in the brain told Adam that his father was not a great man, that he was, indeed, a very strong-willed and concentrated little man wearing a huge busby. Who knows what causes this–a look in the eye, a lie found out, a moment of hesitation?–then god comes crashing down in a child's brain.

Young Adam was always an obedient child. Something in him shrank from violence, from contention, from the silent shrieking tensions that can rip at a house. He contributed to the quiet he wished for by offering no violence, no contention and to do this he had to retire into secretness, since there is some violence in everyone. He covered his life with a veil of vagueness, while behind his quiet eyes a rich full life went on. This did not protect him from assault but it allowed him an immunity.

His half-brother, Charles, only a little over a year younger, grew up with his father's assertiveness. Charles was a natural athlete, with instinctive timing and co-ordination and the competitor's will to win over others, which makes for success in the world.

Young Charles won all contests with Adam whether they involved skill, or strength, or quick intelligence, and won them so easily that quite early he lost interest and had to find his competition among other children. Thus it came about that a kind of affection grew between the two boys, but it was more like an association between brother and sister than between brothers. Charles fought any boy who challenged or slurred Adam and usually won. He protected Adam from his father's harshness with lies and even with blame-taking. Charles felt for his brother the affection one has for helpless things, for blind puppies and new babies.

Adam looked out of his covered brain–out of the long tunnels of his eyes–at the people of his world. His father, a one-legged natural force at first, installed justly to make little boys feel littler and stupid boys aware of their stupidity; and then–after god had crashed–he saw his father as the policeman laid on by birth, the officer who might be circumvented, or fooled, but never challenged. And out of the long tunnels of his eyes Adam saw his half-brother Charles as a bright being of another species, gifted with muscle and bone, speed and alertness, quite on a different plane, to be admired as one admires the sleek lazy danger of a black leopard, not by any chance to be compared with oneself. And it would no more have occurred to Adam to confide in his brother–to tell him the hunger, the grey dreams, the plans and silent pleasures that lay at the back of the tunnelled eyes–than to share his thoughts with a lovely tree or a pheasant in flight. Adam was glad of Charles the way a woman is glad of a fat diamond, and he depended on his brother in the way that same woman depends on the diamond's glitter and the self-security tied up in its worth; but love, affection, empathy, were beyond conception.

Towards Alice Trask, Adam concealed a feeling that was akin to a warm shame. She was not his mother–that he knew because he had been told many times. Not from things said but from the tone in which other things were said, he knew that he had once had a mother and that she had done some shameful thing, such as forgetting the chickens or missing the target on the range in the wood-lot. And as a result of her fault she was not here. Adam thought sometimes that if he could only find out what sin it was she had committed, why, he would sin it too–and not be here.

Alice treated the boys equally, washed them and fed them, and left everything else to their father, who had let it be known clearly and with finality that training the boys physically and mentally was his exclusive province. Even praise and reprimand he would not delegate. Alice never complained, quarrelled, laughed, or cried. Her mouth was trained to a line that concealed nothing and offered nothing too. But once when Adam was quite small he wandered silently into the kitchen. Alice did not see him. She was darning socks and she was smiling. Adam retired secretly and walked out of the house and into the wood-lot to a sheltered place behind a stump that he knew well. He settled deep between the protecting roots. Adam was as shocked as though he had come upon her naked. He breathed excitedly, high against his throat. For Alice had been naked–she had been smiling. He wondered how she had dared such wantonness. And he ached towards her with a longing that was passionate and hot. He did not know what it was about, but all the long lack of holding, of rocking, of caressing, the hunger for breast and nipple, and the softness of a lap, and the voice-tone of love and compassion, and the sweet feeling of anxiety–all these were in his passion, and he did not know it because he did not know that such things existed, so how could he miss them.

Of course it occurred to him that he might be wrong, that some misbegotten shadow had fallen across his face and warped his seeing. And so he cast back to the sharp picture in his head and knew that the eyes were smiling too. Twisted light could do one or the other but not both.

He stalked her then, game-wise, as he had the woodchucks on the knoll when day after day he had lain lifeless as a young stone and watched the old wary chucks bring their children out to sun. He spied on Alice, hidden, and from unsuspected eye-corner, and it was true. Sometimes when she was alone, and knew she was alone, she permitted her mind to play in a garden, and she smiled. And it was wonderful to see how quickly she could drive the smile to earth the way the woodchucks holed their children.

Adam concealed his treasure deep in his tunnels, but he was inclined to pay for his pleasure with something. Alice began to find gifts–in her sewing basket, in her worn-out purse, under her pillow–two cinnamon pinks, a bluebird's tail-feather, half a stick of green sealing wax, a stolen handkerchief. At first Alice was startled, but then that passed, and when she found some unsuspected present the garden smile flashed and disappeared the way a trout crosses a knife of sunshine in a pool. She asked no questions and made no comment.

Her coughing was very bad at night, so loud and disturbing that Cyrus had at last to put her in another room or he would have got no sleep. But he did visit her very often–hopping on his one bare foot, steadying himself with hand on wall. The boys could hear and feel the jar of his body through the house as he hopped to and from Alice's bed.

As Adam grew he feared one thing more than any other. He feared the day he would be taken and enlisted in the army. His father never let him forget that such a time would come. He spoke of it often. It was Adam who needed the army to make a man of him. Charles was pretty near a man already. And Charles was a man, and a dangerous man, even at fifteen, and when Adam was sixteen.

3

The affection between the two boys had grown with the years. It may be that part of Charles's feeling was contempt, but it was a protective contempt. It happened that one evening the boys were playing peewee, a new game to them, in the door-yard. A small pointed stick was laid on the ground, then struck near one end with a bat. The small stick flew into the air and then was batted as far as possible.

Adam was not good at games. But by some accident of eye and timing he beat his brother at peewee. Four times he drove the peewee farther than Charles did. It was a new experience to him, and a wild flush came over him, so that he did not watch and feel out his brother's mood as he usually did. The fifth time he drove the peewee it flew humming like a bee far out in the field. He turned happily to face Charles and suddenly he froze deep in his chest. The hatred in Charles's face frightened him. 'I guess it was just an accident,' he said lamely. 'I bet I couldn't do it again.'

Charles set his peewee, struck it, and, as it rose into the air, struck at it and missed. Charles moved slowly towards Adam, his eyes cold and non-committal. Adam edged away in terror. He did not dare to turn and run, for his brother could outrun him. He backed slowly away, his eyes frightened and his throat dry. Charles moved close and struck him in the face with his bat. Adam covered his bleeding nose with his hands, and Charles swung his bat and hit him in the ribs, knocked the wind out of him, swung at his head and knocked him out. And as Adam lay unconscious on the ground Charles kicked him heavily in the stomach and walked away.

After a while Adam became conscious. He breathed shallowly because his chest hurt. He tried to sit up and fell back at the wrench of the torn muscles over his stomach. He saw Alice looking out, and there was something in her face that he had never seen before. He did not know what it was, but it was not soft or weak, and it might be hatred. She saw that he was looking at her, dropped the curtains into place, and disappeared. When Adam finally got up from the ground and moved, bent over, into the kitchen, he found a basin of hot water standing ready for him and a clean towel beside it. He could hear his step-mother coughing in her room.

Charles had one great quality. He was never sorry–ever. He never mentioned the beating, apparently never thought of it again. But Adam made very sure that he didn't win again–at anything. He had always felt the danger in his brother, but now he understood that he must never win unless he was prepared to kill Charles. Charles was not sorry. He had very simply fulfilled himself.

Charles did not tell his father about the beating, and Adam did not, and surely Alice did not, and yet he seemed to know. In the months that followed he turned a gentleness on Adam. His speech became softer towards him. He did not punish him any more. Almost nightly he lectured him, but not violently. And Adam was more afraid of the gentleness than he had been at the violence, for it seemed to him that he was being trained as a sacrifice, almost as though he was being subjected to kindness before death, the way victims intended for the gods were cuddled and flattered so that they might go happily to the stone and not outrage the gods with unhappiness.

Cyrus explained softly to Adam the nature of a soldier. And though his knowledge came from research rather than experience, he knew and he was accurate. He told his son of the sad dignity that can belong to a soldier, how he is necessary in the light of all the failures of man–the penalty of our frailties. Perhaps Cyrus discovered these things in himself as he told them. It was very different from the flag-waving, shouting bellicosity of his younger days. The humilities are piled on a soldier, so Cyrus said, in order that he may, when the time comes, be not too resentful of the final humility–a meaningless and dirty death. And Cyrus talked to Adam alone and did not permit Charles to listen.

Cyrus took Adam to walk with him one late afternoon, and the black conclusions of all of his study and his thinking came out and flowed with a kind of thick terror over his son. He said, 'I'll have you know that a soldier is the most holy of all humans becaue he is the most tested–most tested of all. I'll try to tell you. Look now–in all of history men have been taught that killing of men is an evil thing not to be countenanced. Any man who kills must be destroyed because this is a great sin, maybe the worst sin we know. And then we take a soldier and put murder in his hands and we say to him, "Use it well, use it wisely." We put no checks on him. Go out and kill as many of a certain kind or classification of your brothers as you can. And we will reward you for it because it is a violation of your early training.'

Adam wet his dry lips and tried to ask and failed and tried again. 'Why do they have to do it?' he said. 'Why is it?'

Cyrus was deeply moved and he spoke as he had never spoken before. 'I don't know,' he said. 'I've studied and maybe learned how things are, but I'm not even close to why they are. And you must not expect to find that people understand what they do. So many things are done instinctively, the way a bee makes honey or a fox dips his paws in a stream to fool dogs. A fox can't say why he does it, and what bee remembers winter or expects it to come again? When I knew you had to go I thought to leave the future open so you could dig out your own findings, and then it seemed better if I could protect you with the little I know. You'll go in soon now–you've come to the age.'

I don't want to,' said Adam quickly.

'You'll go in soon,' his father went on, not hearing. 'And I want to tell you so you won't be surprised. They'll first strip off your clothes, but they'll go deeper than that. They'll shuck off any little dignity you have–you'll lose what you think of as your decent right to live and to be let alone to live. They'll make you live and eat and sleep and shit close to other men. And when they dress you up again you'll not be able to tell youself from the others. You can't even wear a scrap or pin a note on your breast to say, "This is me–separate from the rest."'

'I don't want to do it,' said Adam.

'After a while,' said Cyrus, 'you'll think no thought the others do not think. You'll know no word the others can't say. And you'll do things because the others do them. You'll feel the danger in any difference whatever–a danger to the whole crowd of like-thinking, like-acting men.'

'What if I don't?' Adam demanded.

'Yes,' said Cyrus, 'sometimes that happens. Once in a while there is a man who won't do what is demanded of him, and do you know what happens? The whole machine devotes itself coldly to the destruction of his difference. They'll beat your spirit and your nerves, your body and your mind, with iron rods until the dangerous difference goes out of you. And if you can't finally give in, they'll vomit you up and leave you stinking outside–neither part of themselves nor yet free. It's better to fall in with them. They only do it to protect themselves. A thing so triumphantly illogical, so beautifully senseless as an army can't allow a question to weaken it. Within itself, if you do not hold it up to other things for comparison and derision, you'll find slowly, surely, a reason and a logic and a kind of dreadful beauty. A man who can accept it is not a worse man always, and sometimes is a much better man. Pay good heed to me, for I have thought long about it. Some men there are who go down the dismal wrack of soldiering, surrender themselves and become faceless. But these had not much face to start with. And maybe you're like that. But there are others who go down, submerge in the common slough, and then rise more themselves than they were, because–because they have lost a littleness of vanity and have gained all the gold of the company and the regiment. If you can go down so low, you will be able to rise higher than you can conceive, and you will know a holy joy, a companionship almost like that of a heavenly company of angels. Then you will know the quality of men even if they are inarticulate. But until you have gone way down you can never know this.'

As they walked back towards the house Cyrus turned left and entered the wood-lot among the trees, and it was dusk. Suddenly Adam said, 'You see that stump there, sir? I used to hide between the roots on the far side. After you punished me I used to hide there, and sometimes I went there just because I felt bad.'

'Let's go and see the place,' his father said. Adam led him to it, and Cyrus looked down at the nest-like hole between the roots. 'I knew about it long ago,' he said. 'Once when you were gone a long time I thought you must have such a place, and I found it because I felt the kind of a place you would need. See how the earth is tamped and the little grass is torn? And while you sat in there you stripped little pieces of bark to shreds. I knew it was the place when I came upon it.'

Adam was staring at his father in wonder. 'You never came here looking for me,' he said.

'No,' Cyrus replied. 'I wouldn't do that. You can drive a human too far. I wouldn't do that. Always you must leave a man one escape before death. Remember that! I knew, I guess, how hard I was pressing you. I didn't want to push you over the edge.'

They moved restlessly off through the trees. Cyrus said, 'So many things I want to tell you. I'll forget most of them. I want to tell you that a soldier gives up so much to get something back. From the day of a child's birth he is taught by every circumstance, by every law and rule and right, to protect his own life. He starts with that great instinct, and everything confirms it. And then he is a soldier and he must learn to violate all of this–he must learn coldly to put himself in the way of losing his own life without going mad. And if you can do that–and, mind you, some can't–then you will have the greatest gift of all. Look, son,' Cyrus said earnestly, 'nearly all men are afraid, and they don't even know what causes their fear–shadows, perplexities, dangers without names or numbers, fear of a faceless death. But if you can bring yourself to face not shadows but real death, described and recognizable, by bullet or sabre, arrow or lance, then you need never be afraid again, at least not in the same way you were before. Then you will be a man set apart from other men, safe where other men may cry in terror. This is the great reward. Maybe this is the only reward. Maybe this is the final purity all ringed with filth. It's nearly dark. I'll want to talk to you again tomorrow night when both of us have thought about what I've told you.'

But Adam said, 'Why don't you talk to my brother? Charles will be going. He'll be good at it, much better than I am.'

'Charles won't be going,' Cyrus said. 'There'd be no point in it.'

'But he would be a better soldier.'

'Only outside on his skin,' said Cyrus. 'Not inside. Charles is not afraid, so he could never learn anything about courage. He does not know anything outside himself, so he could never gain the things I've tried to explain to you. To put him in an army would be to let loose things which in Charles must be chained down, not let loose. I would not dare to let him go.'

Adam complained, 'You never punished him, you let him live his own life, you praised him, you did not haze him, and now you let him stay out of the army.' He stopped, frightened at what he had said, afraid of the rage or the contempt or the violence his words might let loose.

His father did not reply. He walked on out of the wood-lot, and his head hung down so that his chin rested on his chest, and the rise and fall of his hip when his wooden leg struck the ground was monotonous. The wood leg made a side-semicircle to get ahead when its turn came.

It was completely dark by now, and the golden light of the lamps shone out from the open kitchen window. Alice came to the doorway and peered out, looking for them, and then she heard the uneven footsteps approaching and went back to the kitchen.

Cyrus walked to the kitchen stoop before he stopped and raised his head. 'Where are you?' he asked.

'Here–right behind you–right here.'

'You asked a question. I guess I'll have to answer. Maybe it's good and maybe it's bad to answer. You're not clever. You don't know what you want. You have no proper fierceness. You let other people walk over you. Sometimes I think you're a weakling who will never amount to a dog turd. Does that answer your question? I love you better. I always have. This may be a bad thing to tell you, but it's true. I love you better. Else why would I have given myself the trouble of hurting you? Now shut your mouth and go to your supper. I'll talk to you tomorrow night. My leg aches.'

4

There was no talk at supper. The quiet was disturbed only by the slup of soup and gnash of chewing, and his father waved his hand to try to drive the moths away from the chimney of the kerosene lamp. Adam thought his brother watched him secretly. And he caught an eye-flash from Alice when he looked up suddenly. After he had finished eating, Adam pushed back his chair. 'I think I'll go for a walk,' he said.

Charles stood up. 'I'll go with you.'

Alice and Cyrus watched them go out of the door, and then she asked one of her rare questions. She asked nervously, 'What did you do?'

'Nothing,' he said.

'Will you make him go?'

'Yes.'

'Does he know?'

Cyrus stared bleakly out of the open door into the darkness. 'Yes, he knows.'

'He won't like it. It's not right for him.'

'It doesn't matter,' Cyrus said, and he repeated loudly, 'It doesn't matter,' and his tone said, 'Shut your mouth. This is not your affair.' They were silent a moment, and then he said almost in a tone of apology, 'It isn't as though he were your child.'

Alice did not reply.

The boys walked down the dark rutty road. Ahead they could see a few pinched lights where the village was.

'Want to go in and see if anything's stirring at the inn?' Charles asked.

'I hadn't thought of it,' said Adam.

'Then what the hell are you walking out at night for?'

'You didn't have to come,' said Adam.

Charles moved close to him. 'What did he say to you this afternoon? I saw you walking together. What did he say?'

'He just talked about the army–like always.'

'Didn't look like that to me,' Charles said suspiciously. 'I saw him leaning close, talking the way he talks to men–not telling, talking.'

'He was telling,' Adam said patiently, and he had to control his breath, for a little fear had begun to press up against his stomach. He took as deep a gulp of air as he could and held it to push back at the fear.

'What did he tell you?' Charles demanded again.

'About the army and how it is to be a soldier.'

'I don't believe you,' said Charles. 'I think you're a goddam mealy-mouthed liar. What're you trying to get away with?'

'Nothing,' said Adam.

Charles said harshly, 'Your crazy mother drowned herself. Maybe she took a look at you. That'd do it.'

Adam let out his breath gently, pressing down the dismal fear. He was silent.

Charles cried, 'You're trying to take him away! I don't know how you're going about it. What do you think you're doing?'

'Nothing,' said Adam.

Charles jumped in front of him so that Adam had to stop, his chest almost against his brother's chest. Adam backed away, but carefully, as one backs away from a snake.

'Look at his birthday!' Charles shouted. 'I took six bits and I bought him a knife made in Germany–three blades and a corkscrew, pearl-handled. Where's that knife? Do you ever see him use it? Did he give it to you? I never even saw him hone it. Have you got that knife in your pocket? What did he do with it? "Thanks," he said, like that. And that's the last I heard of a pearl-handled German knife that cost six bits.'

Rage was in his voice and Adam felt the creeping fear; but he knew also that he had a moment left. Too many times he had seen the destructive machine that chopped down anything standing in its way. Rage came first and then a coldness, a possession; non-committal eyes and a pleased smile and no voice at all, only a whisper. When that happened murder was on the way, but cool, deft murder, and hands that worked precisely, delicately. Adam swallowed saliva to dampen his dry throat. He could think of nothing to say that would be heard, for once in rage his brother would not listen, would not even hear. He bulked darkly in front of Adam, shorter, wider, thicker, but still not crouched. In the starlight his lips shone with wetness, but there was no smile yet and his voice still raged.

'What did you do on his birthday? You think I didn't see? Did you spend six bits or even four bits. You brought him a mongrel pup you had picked up in the wood-lot. You laughed like a fool and said it would make a good bird dog. That dog sleeps in his room. He plays with it while he's reading. He's got it all trained. And where's the knife? "Thanks," he said, just "Thanks".' Charles spoke in a whisper and his shoulders dropped.

Adam made one desperate jump backwards and raised his hands to guard his face. His brother moved precisely, each foot planted firmly. One fist lanced delicately to get the range, and then the bitter-frozen work–a hard blow in the stomach, and Adam's hands dropped; then four punches to the head. Adam felt the bone and gristle of his nose crunch. He raised his hands again and Charles drove at his heart. And all this time Adam looked at his brother as the condemned look hopelessly and puzzled at the executioner.

Suddenly, to his own surprise, Adam launched a wild, overhand, harmless swing which had neither force nor direction. Charles ducked in and under it and the helpless arm went around his neck. Adam wrapped his arms around his brother and hung close to him, sobbing. He felt the square fists whipping nausea into his stomach and still he held on. Time was slowed to him. With his body he felt his brother move sideways to force his legs apart. And he felt the knee come up, past his knees, scraping his thighs, until it crashed against his testicles and flashing white pain ripped and echoed through his body. His arms let go. He bent over and vomited, while the cold killing went on.

Adam felt the punches on temples, cheeks, eyes. He felt his lip split and tatter over his teeth, but his skin seemed thickened and dull, as though he were encased in heavy rubber. Dully he wondered why his legs did not buckle, why he did not fall, why unconsciousness did not come to him. The punching continued eternally. He could hear his brother panting with the quick explosive breath of a sledge-hammer man, and in the sick starlit dark he could see his brother through the tear-watered blood that flowed from his eyes. He saw the innocent, non-committal eyes, the small smile on wet lips. And as he saw these things–a flash of light and darkness.

Charles stood over him, gulping air like a run-out dog. And then he turned and walked quickly back, towards the house, kneading his bruised knuckles as he went.

Consciousness came back quick and frightening to Adam. His mind rolled in a painful mist. His body was heavy and thick with hurt. But almost instantly he forgot his hurts. He heard quick footsteps on the road. The instinctive fear and fierceness of a rat came over him. He pushed himself up on his knees and dragged himself off the road to the ditch that kept it drained. There was a foot of water in the ditch, and the tall grass grew up from its sides. Adam crawled quietly into the water, being very careful to make no splash.

The footsteps came close, slowed, moved on a little, came back. From his hiding-place Adam could see only a darkness in the dark. And then a sulphur match was struck and burned a tiny blue until the wood caught, lighting his brother's face grotesquely from below. Charles raised the match and peered around, and Adam could see the hatchet in his right hand.

When the match went out the night was blacker than before. Charles moved slowly on and struck another match, and on and struck another. He searched the road for signs. At last he gave it up. His right hand rose and he threw the hatchet far off into the field. He walked rapidly away towards the pinched lights of the village.

For a long time Adam lay in the cool water. He wondered how his brother felt, wondered whether now that his passion was chilling he would feel panic or sorrow or sick conscience or nothing. These things Adam felt for him. His conscience bridged him to his brother and did his pain for him the way at other times he had done his homework.

Adam crept out of the water and stood up. His hurts were stiffening and the blood was dried in a crust on his face. He thought he would stay outside in the darkness until his father and Alice went to bed. He felt that he could not answer any questions, because he did not know any answers, and trying to find one was harsh to his battered mind. Dizziness edged with blue lights came fringing his forehead, and he knew that he would be fainting soon.

He shuffled slowly up the road with wide-spread legs. At the stoop he paused, looked in. The lamp hanging by its chain from the ceiling cast a yellow circle and lighted Alice and her mending-basket on the table in front of her. On the other side his father chewed a wooden pen and dipped it in an open ink bottle and made entries in his black record book.

Alice, glancing up, saw Adam's bloody face. Her hand rose to her mouth and her fingers hooked over her lower teeth.

Adam drag-footed up one step and then the other and supported himself in the doorway.

Then Cyrus raised his head. He looked with a distant curiosity. The identity of the distortion came to him slowly. He stood up, puzzled and wondering. He stuck the wooden pen in the ink bottle and wiped his fingers on his trousers. 'Why did he do it?' Cyrus asked softly.

Adam tried to answer, but his mouth was caked and dry. He licked his lips and started them bleeding again. 'I don't know,' he said.

Cyrus stumped over to him and grasped him by the arm so fiercely that he winced and tried to pull away. 'Don't lie to me! Why did he do it? Did you have an argument?'

'No.'

Cyrus wrenched at him. 'Tell me! I want to know. Tell me! You'll have to tell me. I'll make you tell me! Goddam it, you're always protecting him! Don't you think I know that? Did you think you were fooling me? Now tell me, or by God I'll keep you standing there all night!'

Adam cast about for an answer. 'He doesn't think you love him.'

Cyrus released the arm and hobbled back to his chair and sat down. He rattled the pen in the ink bottle and looked blindly at his record book. 'Alice,' he said, 'help Adam to bed. You'll have to cut his shirt off, I guess. Give him a hand.' He got up again, went to the corner of the room where the coats hung on nails and, reaching behind the garments, brought out his shotgun, broke it to verify its load, and clumped out of the door.

Alice raised her hand as though she would hold him back with a rope of air. And her rope broke and her face hid her thoughts. 'Go in your room,' she said. 'I'll bring some water in a basin.'

Adam lay on the bed, a sheet pulled up to his waist, and Alice patted the cuts with a linen handerchief dipped in warm water. She was silent for a long time and then she continued Adam's sentence as though there had never been an interval, 'He doesn't think his father loves him. But you love him–you always have.'

Adam did not answer her.

She went on quietly, 'He's a strange boy. You have to know him–all rough shell, all anger until you know.' She paused to cough, leaned down and coughed, and when the spell was over her cheeks were flushed and she was exhausted. 'You have to know him,' she repeated. 'For a long time he has given me little presents, pretty things you wouldn't think he'd even notice. But he doesn't give them right out. He hides them where he knows I'll find them. And you can look at him for hours and he won't ever give the slightest sign he did it. You have to know him.'

She smiled at Adam and he closed his eyes.

CHAPTER 4

I

Charles stood at the bar in the village inn and Charles was laughing delightedly at the funny stories the night-stranded drummers were telling. He got out his tobacco sack with its meagre jingle of silver and bought the men a drink to keep them talking. He stood and grinned and rubbed his split knuckles. And when the drummers, accepting his drink, raised their glasses and said, 'Here's to you,' Charles was delighted. He ordered another drink for his new friends, and then he joined them for some kind of deviltry in another place.

When Cyrus stumped out into the night he was filled with a kind of despairing anger at Charles. He looked on the road for his son, and he went to the inn to look for him, but Charles was gone. It is probable that if he had found him that night he would have killed him, or tried to. The direction of a big act will warp history, but probably all acts do the same in their degree, down to a stone stepped over in the path or a breath caught at sight of a pretty girl or a finger-nail nicked in the garden soil.

Naturally it was not long before Charles was told that his father was looking for him with a shotgun. He hid out for two weeks, and when he finally did return, murder had sunk back to simple anger and he paid his penalty in overwork and a false, theatrical humility.

Adam lay four days in bed, so stiff and aching that he could not move without a groan. On the third day his father gave evidence of his power with the military. He did it as a poultice to his own pride and also as a kind of prize for Adam. Into the house, into Adam's bedroom, came a captain of cavalry and two sergeants in dress uniform of blue. In the door-yard their horses were held by two privates. Lying in his bed, Adam was enlisted in the army as a private in the cavalry. He signed the Articles of war and took the oath while his father and Alice looked on. And his father's eyes glistened with tears.

After the soldiers had gone his father sat with him a long time. 'I've put you in the cavalry for a reason,' he said. 'Barrack life is not a good life for long. But the cavalry has work to do. I made sure of that. You'll like going for the Indian country. There's action coming. I can't tell you how I know. There's fighting on the way.'

'Yes, sir,' Adam said.

2

It has always seemed strange to me that it is usually men like Adam who have to do the soldiering. He did not like fighting to start with, and far from learning to love it, as some men do, he felt an increasing revulsion for violence. Several times his officers looked closely at him for malingering, but no charge was brought. During these five years of soldiering Adam did more detail work than any man in the squadron, but if he killed an enemy it was an accident of ricochet. Being a marksman and sharpshooter, he was peculiarly fitted to miss. By this time the Indian fighting had become like dangerous cattle-drives–the tribes were forced into revolt, driven and decimated, and the sad, sullen remnants settled on starvation lands. It was not nice work, but, given the pattern of the country's development, it had to be done.

To Adam, who was an instrument, who saw not the future farms but only the torn bellies of fine humans, it was revolting and useless. When he fired his carbine to miss he was committing treason against his unit, and he didn't care. The emotion of non-violence was building in him until it became a prejudice like any other thought-stultifying prejudice. To inflict any hurt on anything for any purpose became inimical to him. He became obsessed with this emotion, for such it surely was, until it blotted out any possible thinking in its area. Indeed he was commended three times and then decorated for bravery.

As he revolted more and more from violence, his impulse took the opposite direction. He ventured his life a number of times to bring in wounded men. He volunteered for work in field hospitals even when he was exhausted from his regular duties. He was regarded by his comrades with contemptuous affection and the unspoken fear men have of impulses they do not understand.

Charles wrote to his brother regularly–of the farm and the village, of sick cows and a foaling mare, of the added pasture and the lightning-struck barn, of Alice's choking death from her consumption and his father's move to a permanent paid position in the GAR in Washington. As with many people, Charles, who could not talk, wrote with fullness. He set down his loneliness and his perplexities, and he put on paper many things he did not know about himself.

During the time Adam was away he knew his brother better than ever before or afterwards. In the exchange of letters there grew a closeness neither of them could have imagined.

Adam kept one letter from his brother, not because he understood it completely but because it seemed to have a covered meaning he could not get at. 'Dear Brother Adam,' the letter said, 'I take my pen in hand to hope you are in good health'–he always started this way to ease himself gently into the task of writing. 'I have not had your answer to my last letter, but I presume you have other things to do–ha! ha! The rain came wrong and damned the apple blossoms. There won't be many to eat next winter but I will save what I can. Tonight I cleaned the house and it is wet and soapy and maybe not any cleaner. How do you suppose Mother kept it the way she did? It does not look the same. Something settles down on it. I don't know what, but it will not scrub off. But I have spread the dirt around more evenly anyways. Ha! ha!

'Did Father write you anything about his trip? He's gone clean out to San Francisco in California for an encampment of the Grand Army. The Secty. of War is going to be there, and Father is to introduce him. But this is not any great shucks to Father. He has met the President, three, four times and even been to supper to the White House. I would like to see the White House. Maybe you and me can go together when you come home. Father could put us up for a few days and he would be wanting to see you anyways.

'I think I better look around for a wife. This is a good farm, and even if I'm no bargain there's girls could do worse than this farm. What do you think? You did not say if you are going to come live home when you get out of the army. I hope so. I miss you.'

The writing stopped there. There was a scratch on the page and a splash of ink and then it went on in pencil, but the writing was different.

In pencil it said, 'Later. Well, right there the pen give out. One of the points broke off. I'll have to buy another pen-point in the village–rusted right through.'

The words began to flow more smoothly. 'I guess I should wait for a new pen-point and not write with a pencil. Only I was sitting here in the kitchen with the lamp on and I guess I got to thinking and it come on late–after twelve, I guess, but I never looked. Old Black Joe started crowing out in the hen-house. Then Mother's rocking-chair cricked for all the world like she was sitting in it. You know I don't take truck with that, but it set me minding backwards, you know how you do sometimes. I guess I'll tear this letter up maybe, because what's the good of writing stuff like this.'

The words began to race now as though they couldn't get out fast enough. 'If I'm to throw it away I'd just as well set it down,' the letter said. 'It's like the whole house was alive and had eyes everywhere, and like there was people behind the door just ready to come in if you looked away. It kind of makes my skin crawl. I want to say–I want to say–I mean, I never understood–well, why our father did it. I mean, why didn't he like that knife I bought for him on his birthday. Why didn't he? It was a good knife and he needed a good knife. If he had used it or even honed it, or took it out of his pocket and looked at it–that's all he had to do. If he'd liked it I wouldn't have took out after you. I had to take out after you. Seems like to me my mother's chair is rocking a little. It's just the light. I don't take any truck with that. Seems like to me there's something not finished. Seems like when you half finished a job and can't think what it was. Something didn't get done. I shouldn't be here. I ought to be wandering around the world instead of sitting here on a good farm looking for a wife. There is something wrong, like it didn't get finished, like it happened too soon and left something out. It's me should be where you are and you here. I never thought like this before. Maybe because it's late–it's later than that. I just looked out and it's first dawn. I don't think I fell off to sleep. How could the night go so fast? I can't go to bed now. I couldn't sleep anyways.'

The letter was not signed. Maybe Charles forgot he had intended to destroy it and sent it along. But Adam saved it for a time, and whenever he read it again it gave him a chill and he didn't know why.

CHAPTER 5

On the ranch the little Hamiltons began to grow up, and every year there was a new one. George was a tall handsome boy, gentle and sweet, who had from the first a kind of courtliness. Even as a little boy he was polite and what they used to call 'no trouble'. From his father he inherited the neatness of clothing and body and hair, and he never seemed ill-dressed even when he was. George was a sinless boy and grew to be a sinless man. No crime of commission was ever attributed to him, and his crimes of omission were only misdemeanours. In his middle life, at about the time such things were known about, it was discovered that he had pernicious anaemia. It is possible that his virtue lived on a lack of energy.

Behind George, Will grew along, dumpy and stolid. Will had little imagination but he had great energy. From childhood on he was a hard worker, if anyone would tell him what to work at, and once told he was indefatigable. He was a conservative, not only in politics but in everything. Ideas he found revolutionary, and he avoided them with suspicion and distaste. Will lived to live so that no one could find fault with him, and to do that he had to live as nearly like other people as possible.

Maybe his father had something to do with Will's distaste for either change or variation. When Will was a growing boy, his father had not been long enough in the Salinas Valley to be thought of as an 'old-timer'. He was in fact a foreigner and an Irishman. At that time the Irish were much disliked in America. They were looked upon with contempt, particularly on the East Coast, but a little of it must have seeped out to the West. And Samuel had not only variability but was a man of ideas and innovations. In small cut-off communities such a man is always regarded with suspicion until he has proved he is no danger to the others. A shining man like Samuel could, and can, cause a lot of trouble. He might, for example, prove too attractive to the wives of men who knew they were dull. Then there were his education and his reading, the books he bought and borrowed, his knowledge of things that could not be eaten or worn or co-habited with, his interest in poetry and his respect for good writing. If Samuel had been a rich man like the Thornes or the Delmars, with their big houses and wide flat lands, he would have had a great library.

The Delmars had a library–nothing but books in it and panelled in oak. Samuel, by borrowing, had read many more of the Delmars' books than the Delmars had. In that day an educated rich man was acceptable. He might send his sons to college without comment, might wear a vest and white shirt and tie in the day-time of a week-day, might wear gloves and keep his nails clean. And since the lives and practices of rich men were mysterious, who knows what they could use or not use? But a poor man–what need had he for poetry or for painting or for music not fit for singing or dancing? Such things did not help him bring in a crop or keep a scrap of cloth on his children's backs. And if in spite of this he persisted, maybe he had reasons which would not stand the light of scrutiny.

Take Samuel, for instance. He made drawings of work he intended to do with iron or wood. That was good and understandable, even enviable. But on the edges of the plans he made other drawings, sometimes trees, sometimes faces or animals or bugs, sometimes just figures that you couldn't make out at all. And these caused men to laugh with embarrassed uneasiness. Then, too, you never knew in advance what Samuel would think or say or do–it might be anything.

The first few years after Samuel came to Salinas Valley there was a vague distrust of him. And perhaps Will as a little boy heard talk in the San Lucas store. Little boys don't want their fathers to be different from other men. Will might have picked up his conservatism right then. Later, as the other children came along and grew, Samuel belonged to the valley, and it was proud of him in the way a man who owns a peacock is proud. They weren't afraid of him any more, for he did not seduce their wives or lure them out of sweet mediocrity.

The Salinas Valley grew fond of Samuel, but by that time Will was formed.

Certain individuals, not by any means always deserving, are truly beloved of the gods. Things come to them without their effort or planning. Will Hamilton was one of these. And the gifts he received were the ones he could appreciate. As a growing boy Will was lucky. Just as his father could not make money, Will could not help making it. When Will Hamilton raised chickens and his hens began to lay, the price of eggs went up. As a young man, when two of his friends who ran a little store came to the point of despondent bankruptcy, Will was asked to lend them a little money to tide them over the quarter's bills, and they gave him a one-third interest for a pittance. He was not niggardly. He gave them what they asked for. The store was on its feet within one year, expanding in two, opening branches in three, and its descendants, a great mercantile system, now dominate a large part of the area.

Will also took over a bicycle-and-tool shop for a bad debt. Then a few rich people of the valley bought automobiles, and his mechanic worked on them. Pressure was put on him by a determined poet whose dreams were brass, cast iron, and rubber. This man's name was Henry Ford, and his plans were ridiculous if not illegal. Will grumblingly accepted the southern half of the valley as his exclusive area, and within fifteen years the valley was two-deep in Fords and Will was a rich man driving a Marmon.

Tom, the third son, was most like his father. He was born in fury and he lived in lightning. Tom came headlong into life. He was a giant in joy and enthusiasms. He didn't discover the world and its people, he created them. When he read his father's books, he was the first. He lived in a world shining and fresh and as uninspected as Eden on the sixth day. His mind plunged like a colt in a happy pasture, and when later the world put up fences he plunged against the wire, and when the final stockade surrounded him, he plunged right through it and out. And as he was capable of giant joy, so did he harbour huge sorrow, so that when his dog died, the world ended.

Tom was as inventive as his father but he was bolder. He would try things his father would not dare. Also, he had a large concupiscence to put the spurs in his flanks, and this Samuel did not have. Perhaps it was his driving sexual need that made him remain a bachelor. It was a very moral family he was born into. It might be that his dreams and his longing, and his outlets, for that matter, made him feel unworthy, drove him sometimes whining into the hills. Tom was a nice mixture of savagery and gentleness. He worked inhumanly, only to lose in effort his crushing impulses.

The Irish do have a despairing quality of gaiety, but they have also a dour and brooding ghost that rides on their shoulders and peers in on their thoughts. Let them laugh too loudly, it sticks a long finger down their throats. They condemn themselves before they are charged, and this makes them defensive always.

When Tom was nine years old he worried because his pretty little sister Mollie had an impediment in her speech. He asked her to open her mouth wide and he saw that a membrane under her tongue caused the trouble. 'I can fix that,' he said. He led her to a secret place far from the house, whetted his pocket-knife on a stone, and cut the offending halter of speech. And then he ran way and was sick.

The Hamilton house grew as the family grew. It was designed to be unfinished, so that lean-tos could jut out as they were needed. The original room and kitchen soon disappeared in a welter of these lean-tos.

Meanwhile Samuel got no richer. He developed a very bad patent habit, a disease many men suffer from. He invented a part of a threshing machine, better, cheaper, and more efficient than any in existence. The patent attorney ate up his little profit for the year. Samuel sent his models to a manufacturer, who promptly rejected the plans and used the method. The next few years were kept lean by the suing, and the drain stopped only when he lost the suit. It was his first sharp experience with the rule that without money you cannot fight money. But he had caught the patent fever, and year after year the money made by threshing and by smithing was drained off in patents. The Hamilton children went barefoot, and their overalls were patched and food was sometimes scarce, to pay for the crisp blueprints with cogs and planes and elevations.

Some men think big and some think little. Samuel and his sons Tom and Joe thought big and George and Will thought little. Joseph was the fourth son—a kind of mooning boy, greatly beloved and protected by the whole family. He early discovered that a smiling helplessness was his best protection from work. His brothers were tough hard workers, all of them. It was easier to do Joe's work than to make him do it. His mother and father thought him a poet because he wasn't any good at anything else. And they so impressed him with this that he wrote glib verses to prove it. Joe was physically lazy, and probably mentally lazy too. He day-dreamed out his life, and his mother loved him more than the others because she thought he was helpless. Actually he was the least helpless, because he got exactly what he wanted with a minimum of effort. Joe was the darling of the family.

In feudal times an ineptness with sword and spear headed a young man for the Church: in the Hamilton family Joe's inability properly to function at farm and forge headed him for a higher education. He was not sickly or weak but he did not lift very well; he rode horses badly and detested them. The whole family laughed with affection when they thought of Joe trying to learn to plough; his tortuous first furrow wound about like a flatland stream, and his second furrow touched his first only once and then to cross it and wander off.

Gradually he eliminated himself from every farm duty. His mother explained that his mind was in the clouds, as though this were some singular virtue.

When Joe had failed at every job, his father in despair put him to herding sixty sheep. This was the least difficult job of all and the one classically requiring no skill. All he had to do was to stay with the sheep. And Joe lost them—lost sixty sheep and couldn't find them where they were huddled in the shade of a dry gulch. According to the family story, Samuel called the family together, girls and boys, and made them promise to take care of Joe after he was gone, for if they did not Joe would surely starve.

Interspersed with the Hamilton boys were five girls: Una the oldest, a thoughtful studious, dark girl; Lizzie—I guess Lizzie must have been the oldest since she was named after her mother—I don't know much about Lizzie. She early seemed to find a shame for her family. She married young and went away and thereafter was seen only at funerals. Lizzie had a capacity for hatred and bitterness unique among the Hamiltons. She had a son, and when he grew up and married a girl Lizzie didn't like she did not speak to him for many years.

Then there was Dessie, whose laughter was so constant that everyone near her was glad to be there because it was more fun to be with Dessie than with anyone else.

The next sister was Olive, my mother. And last was Mollie, who was a little beauty with lovely blonde hair and violet eyes.

These were the Hamiltons, and it was almost a miracle how Liza, skinny little biddy that she was, produced them year after year and fed them, baked bread, made their clothes, and clothed them with good manners and iron morals too.

It is amazing how Liza stamped her children. She was completely without experience in the world, she was unread and, except for the one long trip from Ireland, untravelled. She had no experience with men save only her husband, and that she looked upon as a tiresome and sometimes painful duty. A good part of her life was taken up with bearing and raising. Her total intellectual association was the Bible, except the talk of Samuel and her children, and to them she did not listen. In that one book she had her history and her poetry, her knowledge of people and things, her ethics, her morals, and her salvation. She never studied the Bible or inspected it; she just read it. The many places where it seems to refute itself did not confuse her in the least. And finally she came to a point where she knew it so well that she went right on reading it without listening.

Liza enjoyed universal respect because she was a good woman and raised good children. She could hold up her head anywhere. Her husband and her children and her grandchildren respected her. There was a nail-hard strength in her, a lack of any compromise, a rightness in the face of all opposing wrongness, which made you hold her in a kind of awe but not in warmth.

Liza hated alcoholic liquors with an iron zeal. Drinking alcohol in any form she regarded as a crime against a properly outraged deity. Not only would she not touch it herself, but she resisted its enjoyment by anyone else. The result naturally was that her husband Samuel and all her children had a good lusty love for a drink.

Once when he was very ill Samuel asked, 'Liza, couldn't I have a glass of whisky to ease me?'

She set her little hard chin. 'Would you go to the throne of God with liquor on your breath? You would not!' she said.

Samuel rolled over on his side and went about his illness without ease.

When Liza was about seventy her elimination slowed up and her doctor told her to take a tablespoon of port wine for medicine. She forced down the first spoonful, making a crooked face, but it was not so bad. And from that moment she never drew a completely sober breath. She always took the wine in a tablespoon, it was always medicine, but after a time she was doing over a quart a day and she was a much more relaxed and happy woman.

Samuel and Liza Hamilton got all of their children raised and well towards adulthood before the turn of the century. It was a whole clot of Hamiltons growing up on the ranch to the east of King City. And they were American children and young men and women. Samuel never went back to Ireland and gradually he forgot it entirely. He was a busy man. He had no time for nostalgia. The Salinas Valley was the world. A trip to Salinas sixty miles to the north at the head of the valley was event enough for a year, and the incessant work on the ranch, the care and feeding and clothing of his bountiful family, took most of his time–but not all. His energy was large.

His daughter Una had become a brooding student, tense and dark. He was proud of her wild, exploring mind. Olive was preparing to take county examinations after a stretch in the secondary schools in Salinas. Olive was going to be a teacher, an honour like having a priest in the family in Ireland. Joe was to be sent to college because he was no damn good at anything else. Will was well along the way to accidental fortune. Tom bruised himself on the world and licked his cuts. Dessie was studying dress-making, and Mollie, pretty Mollie, would obviously marry some well-to-do man.

There was no question of inheritance. Although the hill ranch was large it was abysmally poor. Samuel sunk well after well and could not find water on his own land. That would have made the difference. Water would have made them comparatively rich. The one poor pipe of water pumped up from deep near the house was the only source; sometimes it got dangerously low, and twice it ran dry. The cattle had to come from the far fringe of the ranch to drink and then go out again to feed.

All in all it was a good firm-grounded family, permanent, and successfully planted in the Salinas Valley, not poorer than many and not rioher than many either. It was a well-balanced family with its conservatives and its radicals, its dreamers and its realists. Samuel was well pleased with the fruit of his loins.

CHAPTER 6

I

After Adam joined the army and Cyrus moved to Washington, Charles lived alone on the farm. He boasted about getting himself a wife, but he did not go about doing it by the usual process of meeting girls, taking them to dances, testing their virtues or otherwise, and finally slipping feebly into marriage. The truth of it was that Charles was abysmally timid of girls. And, like most shy men, he satisfied his normal needs in the anonymity of the prostitute. There is great safety for a shy man with a whore. Having been paid for, and in advance, she has become a commodity, and a shy man can be gay with her and even brutal to her. Also, there is none of the horror of the possible turn-down which shrivels the guts of timid men.

The arrangement was simple and reasonably secret. The owner of the inn kept three rooms on his top floor for transients, which he rented to girls for two-week periods. At the end of two weeks a new set of girls took their place. Mr Hallam, the innkeeper, had no part in the arrangement. He could almost say with truth that he didn't know anything about it. He simply colleced five times the normal rent for his three rooms. The girls were assigned, procured, moved, disciplined, and robbed by a whore-master named Edwards, who lived in Boston. His girls moved in a slow circuit among the small towns, never staying anywhere more than two weeks. It was an extremely workable system. A girl was not in town long enough to cause remark either by citizen or town marshal. They stayed pretty much in the rooms and avoided public places. They were forbidden on pain of beating to drink or make noise or to fall in love with anyone. Meals were served in their rooms, and the clients were carefully screened. No drunken man was permitted to go up to them. Every six months each girl was given one month of vacation to get drunk and raise hell. On the job, let a girl be disobedient to the rules, and Mr Edwards personally stripped her, gagged her, and horse-whipped her within an inch of her life. If she did it again she found herself in jail, charged with vagrancy and public prostitution.

The two-week stands had another advantage. Many of the girls were diseased, and a girl had nearly always gone away by the time her gift had incubated in a client. There was no one for a man to get mad at. Mr Hallam knew nothing about it, and Mr Edwards never appeared publicly in his business capacity. He had a very good thing in his circuit.

The girls were all pretty much alike–big, healthy, lazy, and dull. A man could hardly tell there had been a change. Charles Trask made it a habit to go to the inn at least once every two weeks, to creep up to the top floor, do his quick business, and return to the bar to get mildly drunk.

The Trask house had never been gay, but lived in only by Charles it took on a gloomy, rustling decay. The lace curtains were grey, the floors, although swept, grew sticky and dank. The kitchen was lacquered–walls, windows, and ceiling–with grease from the frying-pans.

The constant scrubbing by the wives who had lived there and the bi-annual deep-seated scouring had kept the dirt down. Charles rarely did more than sweep. He gave up sheets on his bed and slept between blankets. What good to clean the house when there was no one to see it? Only on the nights he went to the inn did he wash himself and put on clean clothes.

Charles developed a restlessness that got him out at dawn. He worked the farm mightily because he was lonely. Coming in from his work, he gorged himself on fried food and went to bed and to sleep in the resulting torpor.

His dark face took on the serious expressionlessness of a man who is nearly always alone. He missed his brother more than he missed his mother and father. He remembered quite inaccurately the time before Adam went away as the happy time, and he wanted it to come again.

During the years he was never sick, except of course for the chronic indigestion which was universal, and still is, with men who live alone, cook for themselves, and eat in solitude. For this he took a powerful purge called Father George's Elixir of Life.

One accident he did have in the third year of his aloneness. He was digging out rocks and sledding them to the stone wall. One large boulder was difficult to move. Charles prised it with a long iron bar, and the rock bucked and rolled back again and again. Suddenly he lost his temper. The little smile came on his face, and he fought the stone as though it were a man, in silent fury. He drove his bar deep behind it and threw his whole weight back. The bar slipped and its upper end crashed against his forehead. For a few moments he lay unconscious in the field and then he rolled over and staggered, half-blinded, to the house. There was a long torn welt on his forehead from hairline to a point between his eyebrows. For a few weeks his head was bandaged over a draining infection, but that did not worry him. In that day pus was thought to be benign, a proof that a wound was healing properly. When the wound did heal, it left a long and crinkled scar, and while most scar tissue is lighter than the surrounding skin, Charles's scar turned dark brown. Perhaps the bar had forced iron rust under the skin and made a kind of tattoo.

The wound had not worried Charles, but the scar did. It looked like a long fingermark laid on his forehead. He inspected it often in the little mirror by the stove. He combed his hair down over his forehead to conceal as much of it as he could. He conceived a shame for his scar; he hated his scar. He became restless when anyone looked at it, and fury rose in him if any question was asked about it. In a letter to his brother he put down his feeling about it.

'It looks,' he wrote, 'like somebody marked me like a cow. The damn thing gets darker. By the time you get home it will maybe be black. All I need is one going the other way and I would look like a Papist on Ash Wednesday. I don't know why it bothers me. I got plenty other scars. It just seems like I was marked. And when I go into town, like to the inn, why, people are always looking at it. I can hear them talking about it when they don't know I can hear. I don't know why they're so damn curious about it. It gets so I don't feel like going in town at all.'

2

Adam was discharged in 1885 and started to beat his way home. In appearance he had changed little. There was no military carriage about him. The cavalry didn't act that way. Indeed some units took pride in sloppy posture.

Adam felt that he was sleep-walking. It is a hard thing to leave any deeply routined life, even if you hate it. In the morning he awakened on a split second and lay awaiting reveille. His calves missed the hub of leggings and his throat felt naked without its tight collar. He arrived in Chicago, and there, for no reason, rented a furnished room for a week, stayed in it for two days, went to Buffalo, changed his mind, and moved to Niagara Falls. He didn't want to go home and he put it off as long as possible. Home was not a pleasant place in his mind. The kind of feelings he had had there were dead in him, and he had a reluctance to bring them to life. He watched the falls by the hour. Their roar stupefied and hypnotized him.

One evening he felt a crippling loneliness for the close men in barracks and tent. His impulse was to rush into a crowd for warmth, any crowd. The first crowded public place he could find was a little bar, thronged and smoky. He sighed with pleasure, almost nestled in the human clot the way a cat nestles into a woodpile. He ordered whisky and drank it and felt warm and good. He did not see or hear. He simply absorbed the contact.

As it grew late and the men began to drift away, he became fearful of the time when he would have to go home. Soon he was alone with the bar-tender, who was rubbing and rubbing the mahogany of the bar and trying with his eyes and his manner to get Adam to go.

'I'll have one more,' Adam said.

The bar-tender set the bottle out. Adam noticed him for the first time. He had a strawberry mark on his forehead.

'I'm a stranger in these parts,' said Adam.

'That's what we mostly get at the falls,' the bar-tender said.

'I've been in the army. Cavalry.'

'Yeah!' the bar-tender said.

Adam felt suddenly that he had to impress the man, had to get under his skin some way. 'Fighting Indians,' he said. 'Had some great times.'

The man did not answer him.

'My brother has a mark on his head.'

The bar-tender touched the strawberry mark with his fingers. 'Birthmark,' he said. 'Gets bigger every year. Your brother got one?'

'His came from a cut. He wrote me about it.'

'You notice this one of mine looks like a cat?'

'Sure it does.'

'That's my nickname, Cat. Had it all my life. They say my old lady must of been scared by a cat when she was having me.'

'I'm on my way home. Been away a long time. Won't you have a drink?'

'Thanks. Where you staying?'

'Mrs May's boarding-house.'

'I know her. What they tell is she fills you up with soup so you can't eat much meat.'

'I guess there are tricks to every trade,' said Adam.

'I guess that's right. There's sure plenty in mine.'

'I bet that's true,' said Adam.

'But the one trick I need I haven't got. I wisht I knew that one.'

'What is it?'

'How the hell to get you to go home and let me close up.'

Adam stared at him, stared at him and did not speak.

'It's a joke,' the bar-tender said uneasily.

'I guess I'll go home in the morning,' said Adam. 'I mean my real home.'

'Good luck,' the bar-tender said.

Adam walked through the dark town, increasing his speed as though loneliness sniffed along behind him. The sagging front steps of his boarding-house creaked a warning as he climbed them. The hall was gloomed with the dot of yellow light from an oil-lamp turned down so low that it jerked expiringly.

The landlady stood in her open doorway and her nose made a shadow to the bottom of her chin. Her cold eyes followed Adam as do the eyes of a front-painted portrait, and she listened with her nose for the whisky that was in him.

'Good night,' said Adam.

She did not answer him.

At the top of the first flight he looked back. Her head was raised, and now her chin made a shadow on her throat and her eyes had no pupils.

His room smelled of dust dampened and dried many times. He picked a match from his block and scratched it on the side of the block. He lighted the shank of candle in the japanned candlestick and regarded the bed–as spineless as a hammock and covered with a dirty patchwork quilt, the cotton batting spilling from the edges.

The porch steps complained again, and Adam knew the woman would be standing in the doorway ready to spray inhospitality on the new arrival.

Adam sat down in a straight chair and put his elbows on his knees and supported his chin in his hands. A lodger down the hall began a patient, continuing cough against the quiet night.

And Adam knew he could not go home. He had heard old soldiers tell of doing what he was going to do.

'I just couldn't stand it. Didn't have no place to go. Didn't know nobody. Wandered around and pretty soon I got in a panic like a kid, and first thing I knowed I'm begging the sergeant to let me back in–like he was doing me a favour.'

Back in Chicago, Adam re-enlisted and asked to be assigned to his old regiment. On the train going west the men of his squadron seemed very dear and desirable.

While he waited to change trains in Kansas City, he heard his name called and a message was shoved into his hand–orders to report to Washington to the office of the Secretary of War. Adam in his five years had absorbed rather than learned never to wonder about an order. To an enlisted man the high far gods in Washington were crazy, and if a soldier wanted to keep his sanity he thought about generals as little as possible.

In due course Adam gave his name to a clerk and went to sit in an ante-room. His father found him there. It took Adam a moment to recognize Cyrus, and much longer to get used to him. Cyrus had become a great man. He dressed like a great man–black broadcloth coat and trousers, wide black hat, overcoat with a velvet collar, ebony cane which he made to seem a sword. And Cyrus conducted himself like a great man. His speech was slow and mellow, measured and unexcited, his gestures were wide, and new teeth gave him a vulpine smile out of all proportion to his emotion.

After Adam had realized that this was his father he was still puzzled. Suddenly he looked down–no wooden leg. The leg was straight, bent at the knee, and the foot was clad in a polished kid congress gaiter. When he moved there was a limp, but not a clumping wooden-legged limp.

Cyrus saw the look. 'Mechanical,' he said. 'Works on a hinge. Got a spring. Don't even limp when I set my mind to it. I'll show it to you when I take it off. Come along with me.'

Adam said, 'I'm under orders, sir. I'm to report to Colonel Wells.'

'I know you are. I told Wells to issue the orders. Come along.'

Adam said uneasily, 'If you don't mind, sir, I think I'd better report to Colonel Wells.'

His father reversed himself. 'I was testing you,' he said grandly. 'I wanted to see whether the army has any discipline these days. Good boy. I knew it would be good for you. You're a man and a soldier, my boy.'

'I'm under orders, sir,' said Adam. This man was a stranger to him. A faint distaste arose in Adam. Something was not true. And the speed with which doors opened straight to the Colonel, the obsequious respect of that officer, the words, 'The Secretary will see you now, sir,' did not remove Adam's feeling.

'This is my son, a private soldier, Mr Secretary–just as I was–a private soldier in the United States Army.'

'I was discharged a corporal, sir,' said Adam. He hardly heard the exchange of compliments. He was thinking, 'This is the Secretary of War. Can't he see that this isn't the way my father is? He's play-acting. What's happened to him? It's funny the Secretary can't see it.'

They walked to the small hotel where Cyrus lived, and on the way Cyrus pointed out the sights, the buildings, the spots of history, with the expansiveness of a lecturer. 'I live in a hotel,' he said. 'I've thought of getting a house, but I'm on the move so much it wouldn't hardly pay. I'm all over the country most of the time.'

The hotel clerk couldn't see either. He bowed to Cyrus, called him 'Senator', and indicated that he would give Adam a room if he had to throw someone out.

'Send a bottle of whisky to my room, please.'

'I can send some chipped ice if you like.'

'Ice!' said Cyrus. 'My son is a soldier.' He rapped his leg with his stick and it gave forth a hollow sound. 'I have been a soldier–a private soldier. What do we want ice for?'

Adam was amazed at Cyrus's accommodation. He had not only a bedroom but a sitting-room beside it, and the toilet was in a closet right in the bedroom.

Cyrus sat down in a deep chair and sighed. He pulled up his trouser leg and Adam saw the contraption of iron and leather and hardwood. Cyrus unlaced the leather sheath that held it on his stump and stood the travesty-on-flesh beside his chair. 'It gets to pinching pretty bad,' he said.

With his leg off, his father became himself again, the self Adam remembered. He had experienced the beginning of contempt, but now the childhood fear and respect and animosity came back to him, so that he seemed a little boy testing his father's immediate mood to escape trouble.

Cyrus made his preparations, drank his whisky, and loosened his collar. He faced Adam. 'Well?'

'Sir?'

'Why did you re-enlist?'

'I–I don't know, sir. I just wanted to.'

'You don't like the army, Adam.'

'No, sir.'

'Why did you go back?'

'I didn't want to go home.'

Cyrus sighed and rubbed the tips of his fingers on the arms of his chair. 'Are you going to stay in the army?' he asked.

'I don't know, sir.'

'I can get you into West Point. I have influence. I can get you discharged so you can enter West Point.'

'I don't want to go there.'

'Are you defying me?' Cyrus asked quietly.

Adam took a long time to answer, and his mind sought escape before he said, 'Yes, sir.'

Cyrus said, 'Pour me some whisky, son,' and when he had it he continued, 'I wonder if you know how much influence I really have. I can throw the Grand Army at any candidate like a sock. Even the President likes to know what I think about public matters. I can get senators defeated and I can pick appointments like apples. I can make men and I can destroy them. Do you know that?'

Adam knew more than that. He knew that Cyrus was defending himself with threats. 'Yes, sir. I've heard.'

'I could get you assigned to Washington–assigned to me even–teach you your way about.'

'I'd rather go back to my regiment, sir.' He saw the shadow of loss darken his father's face.

'Maybe I made a mistake. You've learned the dumb resistance of a soldier.' He sighed. 'I'll get you ordered to your regiment. You'll rot in barracks.'

'Thank you, sir.' After a pause Adam asked, 'Why didn't you bring Charles here?'

'Because I — No, Charles is better where he is–better where he is.'

Adam remembered his father's tone and how he looked. And he had plenty of time to remember, because he did rot in barracks. He remembered that Cyrus was lonely and alone–and knew it.

3

Charles had looked forward to Adam's return after five years. He had painted the house and the barn, and as the time approached he had a woman in to clean the house, to clean it to the bone.

She was a clean, mean old woman. She looked at the dust-grey rotting curtains, threw them out, and made new ones. She dug grease out of the stove that had been there since Charles's mother died. And she leached the walls of a brown shiny nastiness deposited by cooking-fat and kerosene lamps. She pickled the floors with lye, soaked the blankets in sal soda, complaining the whole time to herself, 'Men–dirty animals. Pigs is clean compared. Rot in their own juice. Don't see how no woman ever marries them. Stink like measles. Look at oven–pie juice from Methusaleh.'

Charles had moved into a shed where his nostrils would not be assailed by the immaculate but painful smells of lye and soda and ammonia and yellow soap. He did, however, get the impression that she didn't approve of his housekeeping. When finally she grumbled away from the shining house Charles remained in the shed. He wanted to keep the house clean for Adam. In the shed where he slept were the tools of the farm and the tools for their repair and maintenance. Charles found that he could cook his fried and boiled meats more quickly and efficiently on the forge than he could on the kitchen stove. The bellows forced quick flaring heat from the coke. A man didn't have to wait for a stove to heat up. He wondered why he had never thought of it before.

Charles waited for Adam, and Adam did not come. Perhaps Adam was ashamed to write. It was Cyrus who told Charles in an angry letter about Adam's re-enlistment against his wishes. And Cyrus indicated that, in some future, Charles could visit him in Washington, but he never asked him again.

Charles moved back to the house and lived in a kind of savage filth, taking a satisfaction in overcoming the work of the grumbling woman.

It was a year before Adam wrote to Charles–a letter of embarrassed newsiness building his courage to say, 'I don't know why I signed again. It was like somebody else doing it. Write soon and tell me how you are.'

Charles did not reply until he had received four anxious letters, and then he replied coolly, 'I didn't hardly expect you anyway,' and he went on with a detailed account of farm and animals.

Time had got in its work. After that Charles wrote right after New Year's Day and received a letter from Adam written right after New Years's Day. They had grown so apart that there was little mutual reference and no questions.

Charles began to keep one slovenly woman after another. When they got on his nerves he threw them out the way he would sell a pig. He didn't like them and had no interest in whether or not they liked him. He grew away from the village. His contacts were only with the inn and the postmaster. The village people might denounce his manner of life, but one thing he had which balanced his ugly life even in their eyes. The farm had never been so well run. Charles cleared land, built up his walls, improved his drainage, and added a hundred acres to the farm. More than that, he was planting tobacco, and a long new tobacco barn stood impressively behind the house. For these things he kept the respect of his neighbours. A farmer cannot think too much evil of a good farmer. Charles was spending most of his money and all of his energy on the farm.

CHAPTER 7

I

Adam spent his next five years doing the things an army uses to keep its men from going insane–endless polishing of metal and leather, parade and drill and escort, ceremony of bugle and flag, a ballet of business for men who aren't doing anything. In 1886 the big packing-house strike broke out in Chicago and Adam's regiment entrained, but the strike was settled before they were needed. In 1888 the Seminoles, who had never signed a peace treaty, stirred restlessly, and the cavalry entrained again; but the Seminoles retired into their swamps and were quiet, and the dream-like routine settled on the troops again.

Time interval is a strange and contradictory matter in the mind. It would be reasonable to suppose that a routine time or an eventless time would seem interminable. It should be so, but it is not. It is the dull eventless times that have no duration whatever. A time splashed with interest, wounded with tragedy, crevassed with joy–that's the time that seems long in the memory. And this is right when you think about it. Eventlessness has no posts to drape duration on. From nothing to nothing is no time at all.

Adam's second five years were up before he knew it. It was late in 1890, and he was discharged with sergeant's stripes in the Presidio in San Francisco. Letters between Charles and Adam had become great rarities, but Adam wrote his brother just before his discharge, 'This time I'm coming home,' and that was the last Charles heard of him for over three years.

Adam waited out the winter, wandering up the river to Sacramento, ranging in the valley of the San Joaquin, and when the spring came Adam had no money. He rolled a blanket and started slowly eastward, sometimes walking and sometimes with groups of men on the rods under slow-moving freight-cars. At night he jungled up with wandering men in the camping places on the fringes of towns. He learned to beg, not for money but for food. And before he knew it he was a bindlestiff himself.

Such men are rare now, but in the nineties there were many of them, wandering men, lonely men, who wanted it that way. Some of them ran from responsibilities and some felt driven out of society by injustice. They worked a little, but not for long. They stole a little, but only food and occasionally needed garments from a wash-line. They were all kinds of men–literate men and ignorant men, clean men and dirty men–but all of them had restlessness in common. They followed warmth and avoided great heat and great cold. As the spring advanced they tracked it eastward, and the first frost drove them west and south. They were brothers to the coyote which, being wild, lives close to man and his chicken-yards: they were near towns but not in them. Associations with other men were for a week or for a day and then they drifted apart.

Around the little fires where communal stew bubbled there was all manner of talk and only the personal was unmentionable. Adam heard of the development of the IWW with its angry angels. He listened to philosophic discussions, to metaphysics, to aesthetics, to impersonal experience. His companions for the night might be a murderer, an unfrocked priest or one who had unfrocked himself, a professor forced from his warm berth by a dull faculty, a lone driven man running from memory, a fallen archangel and a devil in training, and each contributed bits of thought to the fire as each contributed carrots and potatoes and onions and meat to the stew. He learned the technique of shaving with broken glass, of judging a house before knocking to ask for a hand-out. He learned to avoid or get along with hostile police and to evaluate a woman for her warmth of heart.

Adam took pleasure in the new life. When autumn touched the trees he had got as far as Omaha, and without question or reason or thought he hurried west and south, fled through the mountains and arrived with relief in Southern California. He wandered by the sea from the border north as far as San Luis Obispo, and he learned to pilfer the tide pools for abalones and eels and mussels and perch, to dig the sandbars for clams, and to trap a rabbit in the dunes with a noose of fish-line. And he lay in the sun-warmed sand, counting the waves.

Spring urged him east again, but more slowly than before. Summer was cool in the mountains, and the mountain people were kind as lonesome people are kind. Adam took a job on a widow'. outfit near Denver and shared her table and her bed humbly until the frost drove him south again. He followed the Rio Grande past Albuquerque and El Paso through the Big Bend, through Laredo to Brownsville. He learned Spanish words for food and pleasure, and he learned that when people are very poor they still have something to give and the impulse to give it. He developed a love for poor people he could not have conceived if he had not been poor himself. And by now he was an expert tramp, using humility as a working principle. He was lean and sun-darkened, and he could withdraw his own personality until he made no stir of anger or jealousy. His voice had grown soft, and he had merged many accents and dialects into his own speech, so that his speech did not seem foreign anywhere. This was the great safety of the tramp, a protective veil. He rode the trains very infrequently, for there was a growing anger against tramps, based on the angry violence of the IWW and aggravated by the fierce reprisals against them. Adam was picked up for vagrancy. The quick brutality of police and prisoners frightened him and drove him away from the gatherings of tramps. He travelled alone after that and made sure that he was shaven and clean.

When spring came again he started north. He felt that his time of rest and peace was over. He aimed north towards Charles and the weakening memories of his childhood.

Adam moved rapidly across interminable East Texas, through Louisiana and the butt ends of Mississippi and Alabama, and into the flank of Florida. He felt that he had to move quickly. The negroes were poor enough to be kind, but they could not trust any white man no matter how poor, and the poor white men had a fear of strangers.

Near Tallahassee he was picked up by sheriff's men, judged vagrant, and put on a road gang. That's how the roads were built. His sentence was six months. He was released and instantly picked up again for a second six months. And now he learned how men can consider other men as beasts and that the easiest way to get along with such men was to be a beast. A clean face, an open face, an eye raised to meet an eye–these drew attention and attention drawn brought punishment. Adam thought how a man doing an ugly or a brutal thing has hurt himself and must punish someone for the hurt. To be guarded at work by men with shotguns, to be shackled by the ankle at night to a chain, were simple matters of precaution, but the savage whippings for the least stir of will, for the smallest shred of dignity or resistance, these seemed to indicate that guards were afraid of prisoners, and Adam knew from his years in the army that a man afraid is a dangerous animal. And Adam, like anyone in the world, feared what whipping would do to his body and his spirit. He drew a curtain around himself. He removed expression from his face, light from his eyes, and silenced his speech. Later he was not so much astonished that it had happened to him but that he had been able to take it and with a minimum of pain. It was much more horrible afterwards than when it was happening. It is a triumph of self-control to see a man whipped until the muscles of his back show white and glistening through the cuts and to give no sign of pity or anger or interest. And Adam learned this.

People are felt rather than seen after the first few moments. During his second sentence on the roads of Florida, Adam reduced his personality to a minus. He caused no stir, put out no vibration, became as nearly invisible as it is possible to be. And when the guards could not feel him, they were not afraid of him. They gave him the jobs of cleaning the camps, of handing out the slops to the prisoners, of filling the water buckets.

Adam waited until three days before his second release. Right after noon that day he filled the water buckets and went back to the little river for more. He filled his buckets with stones and sank them, and then he eased himself into the water and swam a long way down-stream, rested and swam further down. He kept moving in the water until at dusk he found a place under a bank with bushes for cover. He did not get out of the water.

Late in the night he heard the hounds go by, covering both sides of the river. He had rubbed his hair hard with green leaves to cover human odour. He sat in the water with his nose and eyes clear. In the morning the hounds came back, disinterested, and the men were too tired to beat the banks properly. When they were gone, Adam dug a piece of water-logged fried sawbelly out of his pocket and ate it.

He had schooled himself against hurry. Most men were caught bolting. It took Adam five days to cross the short distance into Georgia. He took no chances, held back his impatience with an iron control. He was astonished at his ability.

On the edge of Valdosta, Georgia, he lay hidden until long after midnight, and he entered the town like a shadow, crept to the rear of a cheap store, forced a window slowly so that the screws of the lock were pulled from the sun-rotted wood. Then he replaced the lock but left the window open. He had to work by moonlight drifting through dirty windows. He stole a pair of cheap trousers, a white shirt, black shoes, black hat, and an oilskin raincoat, and he tried on each article for fit. He forced himself to make sure nothing looked disturbed before he climbed out of the window. He had taken nothing which was not heavily stocked. He had not even looked for the cash drawer. He lowered the window carefully and slipped from shadow to shadow in the moonlight.

He lay hidden during the day and went in search of food at night–turnips, a few ears of corn from a crib, a few windfall apples–nothing that would be missed. He broke the newness of the shoes with rubbed sand and kneaded the raincoat to destroy its newness. It was three days before he got the rain he needed, or in his extreme caution felt he needed.

The rain started late in the afternoon. Adam huddled under his oilskin, waiting for the dark to come, and when it did he walked through the dripping night into the town of Valdosta. His black hat was pulled down over his eyes and his yellow oilskin was strapped tight against his throat. He made his way to the station and peered through a rain-blurred window. The station agent, in green eyeshade and black alpaca work-sleeves, leaned through the ticket window, talking to a friend. It was twenty minutes before the friend went away. Adam watched him off the platform. He took a deep breath to calm himself and went inside.

2

Charles received very few letters. Sometimes he did not inquire at the post office for weeks. In February of 1894 when a thick letter came from a firm of attorneys in Washington the postmaster thought it might be important. He walked out to the Trask farm, found Charles cutting wood, and gave him the letter. And since he had taken so much trouble, he waited around to hear what the letter said.

Charles let him wait. Very slowly he read all five pages, went back and read them again, moving his lips over the words. Then he folded it up and turned towards the house.

The postmaster called after him, 'Anything wrong, Mr Trask?'

'My father is dead,' Charles said, and he walked into the house and closed the door.

'Took it hard,' the postmaster reported in town. 'Took it real hard. Quiet man. Don't talk much.'

In the house Charles lighted the lamp, although it was not dark yet. He laid the letter on the table, and he washed his hands before he sat down to read it again.

There hadn't been anyone to send him a telegram. The attorneys had found his address among his father's papers. They were sorry–offered their condolences. And they were pretty excited too. When they had made Trask's will they thought he might have a few hundred dollars to leave his sons. That is what he looked to be worth. When they inspected his bank-books they found that he had over ninety-three thousand dollars in the bank and ten thousand dollars in good securities. They felt very different about Mr Trask then. People with that much money were rich. They would never have to worry. It was enough to start a dynasty. The lawyers congratulated Charles and his brother Adam. Under the will, they said, it was to be shared equally. After the money they listed the personal effects left by the deceased: five ceremonial swords presented to Cyrus at various GAR conventions, an olivewood gavel with a gold plate on it, a Masonic watch charm with a diamond set in the dividers, the gold caps from the teeth he had out when he got his plates, watch (silver), gold-headed stick, and so forth.

Charles read the letter twice more and cupped his forehead in his hands. He wondered about Adam. He wanted Adam home.

Charles felt puzzled and dull. He built up the fire and put the frying-pan to heat and sliced thick slices of salt pork into it. Then he went back to stare at the letter. Suddenly he picked it up and put it in the drawer of the kitchen table. He decided not to think of the matter at all for a while.

Of course he thought of little else, but it was a dull circular thinking that came back to the starting point again and again: Where had he got it?

When two events have something in common, in their natures or in time or place, we leap happily to the conclusion that they are similar, and from this tendency we create magics and store them for re-telling. Charles had never before had a letter delivered at the farm in his life. Some weeks later a boy ran out to the farm with a telegram. Charles always connected the letter and the telegram the way we group two deaths and anticipate a third. He hurried to the village railroad station, carrying the telegram in his hand.

'Listen to this,' he said to the operator.

'I already read it.'

'You did?'

'It comes over the wire,' said the inspector. 'I wrote it down.'

'Oh! Yes, sure. "Urgent need you telegraph me one hundred dollars. Coming home. Adam."'

'Came collect,' the operator said. 'You owe me sixty cents.'

'Valdosta, Georgia–I never heard of it.'

'Neither'd I, but it's there.'

'Say, Carlton, how do you go about telegraphing money?'

'Well, you bring me a hundred and two dollars and sixty cents and I send a wire telling the Valdosta operator to pay Adam one hundred dollars. You owe me sixty cents too.'

'I'll pay–say, how do I know it's Adam? What's to stop anybody from collecting it?'

The operator permitted himself a smile of worldliness. 'Way we go about it, you give me a question couldn't nobody else know the answer. So I send both the question and the answer. Operators asks this fella that question, and if he can't answer he don't get his money.'

'Say, that's pretty cute. I better think up a good one.'

'You better get the hundred dollars while Old Breen still got the window open.'

Charles was delighted with the game. He came back with the money in his hand. 'I got the question,' he said.

'I hope it ain't your mother's middle name. Lot of people don't remember.'

'No, nothing like that. It's this. "What did you give father on his birthday just before you went in the army?"'

'It's a good question, but it's long as hell. Can't you cut it down to ten words?'

'Who's paying for it? Answer is, "A pup."'

'Wouldn't nobody guess that,' said Carlton. 'Well, it's you paying, not me.'

'Be funny if he forgot,' said Charles. 'He wouldn't ever get home.'

3

Adam came walking out from the village. His shirt was dirty and the stolen clothes were wrinkled and soiled from having been slept in for a week. Between the house and the barn he stopped and listened for his brother, and in a moment he heard him hammering at something in the big new tobacco barn. 'Oh, Charles!' Adam called.

The hammering stopped, and there was silence. Adam felt as though his brother were inspecting him through the cracks in the barn. Then Charles came out quickly and hurried to Adam and shook hands.

'How are you?'

'Fine,' said Adam.

'Good God, you're thin!'

'I guess I am. And I'm years older too.'

Charles inspected him from head to foot. 'You don't look prosperous.'

'I'm not.'

'Where's your valise?'

'I haven't got one.'

'Jesus Christ! Where've you been?'

'Mostly wandering about all over.'

'Like a hobo?'

'Like a hobo.'

After all the years and the life that had made creased leather out of Charles's skin and redness in his dark eyes, Adam knew from remembering that Charles was thinking of two things–the questions and something else.

'Why didn't you come home?'

'I just got to wandering. Couldn't stop. It gets into you. That's a real bad scar you've got there.'

'That's the one I wrote you about. Gets worse all the time. Why didn't you write? Are you hungry?' Charles's hands itched into his pockets and out and touched his chin and scratched his head.

'It may go away. I saw a man once–bar-tender–he had one that looked like a cat. It was a birthmark. His nickname was Cat.'

'Are you hungry?'

'Sure. I guess I am.'

'Plan to stay home now?'

'I–I guess so. Do you want to get to it now?'

'I–I guess so,' Charles echoed him. 'Our father is dead.'

'I know.'

'How the hell do *you* know?'

'Station agent told me. How long ago did he die?'

''Bout a month.'

'What of?'

'Pneumonia.'

'Buried here?'

'No. In Washington. I got a letter and newspapers. Carried him on a caisson with a flag over it. The Vice-President was there and the President sent a wreath. All in the papers. Pictures too–I'll show you. I've got it all.'

Adam studied his brother's face until Charles looked away. 'Are you mad at something?' Adam asked.

'What should I be mad at?'

'It just sounded–'

'I've got nothing to be mad at. Come on, I'll get you something to eat.'

'All right. Did he linger long?'

'No. It was galloping pneumonia. Went right out.'

Charles was covering up something. He wanted to tell it, but he didn't know how to go about it. He kept hiding in words. Adam fell silent. It might be a good thing to be quiet and let Charles sniff and circle until he came out with it.

'I don't take much stock in messages from the beyond,' said Charles. 'Still, how can you know? Some people claim they've had messages–old Sarah Whitburn. She swore. You just don't know what to think. You didn't get a message, did you? Say, what the hell's bit off your tongue?'

Adam said, 'Just thinking.' And he was thinking with amazement, 'Why, I'm not afraid of my brother! I used to be scared to death of him, and I'm not any more. Wonder why not. Could it be the army? Or the chain gang? Could it be Father's death? Maybe–but I don't understand it.' With the lack of fear, he knew he could say anything he wanted to, whereas before he had picked over his words to avoid trouble. It was a good feeling he had, almost as though he himself had been dead and resurrected.

They walked into the kitchen he remembered and didn't remember. It seemed smaller and dingier. Adam said almost gaily, 'Charles, I been listening. You want to tell me something and you're walking around it like a terrier around a bush. You better tell before it bites you.'

Charles's eyes sparked with anger. He raised his head. His force was gone. He thought with desolation, 'I can't lick him any more. I can't.'

Adam chuckled. 'Maybe it's wrong to feel good when our father's just died, but, you know, Charles, I never felt better in my whole life. I never felt so good. Spill it, Charles. Don't let it chew on you.'

Charles asked, 'Did you love our father?'

'I won't answer you until I know what you're getting at.'

'Did you or didn't you?'

'What's that got to do with you?'

'Tell me.'

The creative free boldness was all through Adam's bones and brain. 'All right, I'll tell you. No. I didn't. Sometimes he scared me. Sometimes–yes, sometimes I admired him, but most of the time I hated him. Now tell me why you want to know.'

Charles was looking down at his hands. 'I don't understand,' he said. 'I just can't get it through my head. He loved you more than anything in the world.'

'I don't believe that.'

'You don't have to. He liked everything you brought him. He didn't like me. He didn't like anything I gave him. Remember the present I gave him, the pocket-knife? I cut and sold a load of wood to get that knife. Well, he didn't even take it to Washington with him. It's right in his bureau right now. And you gave him that pup. It didn't cost you a thing. Well, I'll show you a picture of that pup. It was at his funeral. A colonel was holding it–it was blind, couldn't walk. They shot it after the funeral.'

Adam was puzzled by the fierceness of his brother's tone. 'I don't see,' he said. 'I don't see what you're getting at.'

'I loved him,' said Charles. And, for the first time that Adam could remember, Charles began to cry. He put his head down in his arms and cried.

Adam was about to go to him when a little of the old fear came back. No, he thought, if I touched him he would try to kill me. He went to the open doorway and stood looking out, and he could hear his brother's sniffling behind him.

It was not a pretty farm near the house–never had been. There was litter about it, an unkemptness, a run-downness, a lack of plan; no flowers, and bits of paper and scraps of wood scattered about on the ground. The house was not pretty either. It was a well-built shanty for shelter and cooking. It was a grim farm and a grim house, unloved and unloving. It was no home, no place to long for or to come back to. Suddenly Adam thought of his step-mother–as unloved as the farm, inadequate, clean in her way, but no more wife than the farm was a home.

His brother's sobbing had stopped. Adam turned. Charles was looking blankly straight ahead. Adam said, 'Tell me about Mother.'

'She died. I wrote you.'

'Tell me about her.'

'I told you. She died. It's so long ago. She wasn't your Mother.'

The smile Adam had once caught on her face flashed up in his mind. Her face was projected in front of him.

Charles's voice came through the image and exploded it. 'Will you tell me one thing–not quick–think before you tell me, and maybe don't answer unless it's true, your answer.' Charles moved his lips to form the question in advance. 'Do you think it would be possible for our father to be–dishonest?'

'What do you mean?'

'Isn't that plain enough? I said it plain. There's only one meaning to dishonest.'

'I don't know,' said Adam. 'I don't know. No one ever said it. Look what he got to be. Stayed overnight in the White House. The Vice-President came to his funeral. Does that sound like a dishonest man? Come on, Charles,' he begged, 'tell me what you've been wanting to tell me from the minute I got here.'

Charles wet his lips. The blood seemed to have gone out of him, and with it energy and all ferocity. His voice became a monotone. 'Father made a will. Left everything equal to me and you.'

Adam laughed. 'Well, we can always live on the farm. I guess we won't starve.'

'It's over a hundred thousand dollars,' the dull voice went on.

'You're crazy. More like a hundred dollars. Where would he get it?'

'It's no mistake. His salary with the GAR was a hundred and thirty-five dollars a month. He paid his own room and board. He got five-cents a mile and hotel expenses when he travelled.'

'Maybe he had it all the time and we never knew.'

'No, he didn't have it all the time.'

'Well, why don't you write to the GAR and ask? Someone there might know.'

'I wouldn't dare,' said Charles.

'Now look! Don't go off half-cocked. There's such a thing as speculation. Lots of men struck it rich. He knew big men. Maybe he got in on a good thing. Think of the men who went to the gold rush in California and came back rich.'

Charles's face was desolate. His voice dropped so that Adam had to lean close to hear. It was as toneless as a report. 'Our father went into the Union Army in June, 1862. He had three months' training here in this state. That makes it September. He marched south. October twelfth he was hit in the leg and sent to the hospital. He came home in January.'

'I don't see what you're getting at.'

Charles' words were thin and sallow. 'He was not at Chancellorsville. He was not at Gettysburg or the Wilderness or Richmond or Appomattox.'

'How do you know?'

'His discharge. It came down with his other papers.'

Adam sighed deeply. In his chest, like beating fists, was a surge of joy. He shook his head almost in disbelief.

Charles said, 'How did he get away with it? How in hell did he get away with it? Nobody ever questioned it. Did you? Did I? Did my mother? Nobody did. Not even in Washington.'

Adam stood up. 'What's in the house to eat? I'm going to warm up something.'

'I killed a chicken last night. I'll fry it if you can wait.'

'Anything quick?'

'Some salt pork and plenty of eggs.'

'I'll have that,' said Adam.

They left the question lying there, walked mentally around it, stepped over it. Their words ignored it, but their minds never left it. They wanted to talk about it and could not. Charles fried salt pork, warmed up a skillet of beans, fried eggs.

'I ploughed the pasture,' he said. 'Put in rye.'

'How did it do?'

'Just fine, once I got the rocks out.' He touched his forehead. 'I got this damn thing trying to pry out a stone.'

'You wrote about that,' Adam said. 'Don't know whether I told you your letters meant a lot to me.'

'You never wrote much what you were doing,' said Charles.

'I guess I didn't want to think about it. It was pretty bad, most of it.'

'I read about the campaigns in the papers. Did you go on those?'

'Yes. I didn't want to think about them. Still don't.'

'Did you kill Injuns?'

'Yes, we killed Injuns.'

'I guess they're real ornery.'

'I guess so.'

'You don't have to talk about it if you don't want to.'

'I don't want to.'

They ate their dinner under the paraffin lamp. 'We'd get more light if I would only get around to washing that lampshade.'

'I'll do it,' said Adam. 'It's hard to think of everything.'

'It's going to be fine having you back. How would you like to go to the inn after supper?'

'Well, we'll see. Maybe I'd like just to sit awhile.'

'I didn't write about it in a letter, but they've got girls at the inn. I didn't know but you'd like to go in with me. They change every two weeks. I didn't know but you'd like to look them over.'

'Girls?'

'Yes, they're upstairs. Makes it pretty handy. And I thought you just coming home–'

'Not tonight. Maybe later. How much do they charge?'

'A dollar. Pretty nice girls mostly.'

'Maybe later,' said Adam. 'I'm surprised they let them come in.'

'I was too at first. But they worked out a system.'

'You go often?'

'Every two or three weeks. It's pretty lonesome here, a man living alone.'

'You wrote once you were thinking of getting married.'

'Well, I was. Guess I didn't find the right girl.'

All around the main subject the brothers beat. Now and then they would almost step into it, and quickly pull away, back into crops and local gossip and politics and health. They knew they would come back to it sooner or later. Charles was more anxious to strike in deep than Adam was, but then Charles had had the time to think of it, and to Adam it was a new field of thinking and feeling. He would have preferred to put it over until another day, and at the same time he knew his brother would not permit him to.

Once he said openly, 'Let's sleep on that other thing.'

'Sure, if you want to,' said Charles.

Gradually they ran out of escape talk. Every acquaintance was covered and every local event. The talk lagged and the time went on.

'Feel like turning in?' Adam asked.

'In a little while.'

They were silent, and the night moved restlessly about the house, nudging them and urging them.

'I sure would like to've seen that funeral,' said Charles.

'Must have been pretty fancy.'

'Would you care to see the clippings from the papers? I've got them all in my room.'

'No. Not tonight.'

Charles squared his chair round and put his elbows on the table. 'We'll have to figure it out,' he said nervously. 'We can put it off all we want, but we goddam well got to figure what we're going to do.'

'I know that,' said Adam. 'I guess I just wanted some time to think about it.'

'Would that do any good? I've had time, lots of time, and I just went in circles. I tried not to think about it, and I still went in circles. You think time is going to help?'

'I guess not. I guess not. What do you want to talk about first? I guess we might as well get into it. We're not thinking about anything else.'

'There's the money,' said Charles. 'Over a hundred thousand dollars–a fortune.'

'What about the money?'

'Well, where did it come from?'

'How do I know? I told you he might have speculated. Somebody might have put him on to a good thing there in Washington.'

'Do you believe that?'

'I don't believe anything,' Adam said. 'I don't know, so what can I believe?'

'It's a lot of money,' said Charles. 'It's a fortune left to us. We can live the rest of our lives on it, or we can buy a hell of a lot of land and make it pay. Maybe you didn't think about it, but we're rich. We're richer than anybody hereabouts.'

Adam laughed. 'You say it like it was a jail sentence.'

'Where did it come from?'

'What do you care?' Adam asked. 'Maybe we should just settle back and enjoy it.'

'He wasn't at Gettysburg. He wasn't at any goddam battle in the whole war. He was hit in a skirmish. Everything he told was lies.'

'What are you getting at?' said Adam.

'I think he stole the money,' Charles said miserably. 'You asked me and that's what I think.'

'Do you know where he stole it?'

'No.'

'Then why do you think he stole it?'

'He told lies about the war.'

'What?'

'I mean, if he lied about the war–why, he could steal.'

'How?'

'He held jobs in the GAR–big jobs. He maybe could have got into the treasury, rigged the books.'

Adam sighed. 'Well, if that's what you think, why don't you write to them and tell them? Have them go over the books. If it's true we could give back the money.'

Charles's face was twisted and the scar on his forehead showed dark. 'The Vice-President came to his funeral. The President sent a wreath. There was a line of carriages half a mile long and hundreds of people on foot. And do you know who the pall-bearers were?'

'What are you digging at?'

'S'pose we found out he's a thief. Then it would come out how he never was at Gettysburg or anyplace else. Then everybody would know he was a liar too, and his whole life was a goddam lie. Then even if sometimes he did tell the truth, nobody would believe it was the truth.'

Adam sat very still. His eyes were untroubled, but he was watchful. 'I thought you loved him,' he said calmly. He felt released and free.

'I did. I do. That's why I hate this–his whole life gone–all gone. And his grave–they might even dig it up and throw him out.' His words were ragged with emotion. 'Didn't you love him at all?' he cried.

'I wasn't sure until now,' said Adam. 'I was all mixed up with how I was supposed to feel. No. I did not love him.'

'Then you don't care if his life is spoiled and his poor body rooted up and–oh, my God almighty!'

Adam's brain raced, trying to find words for his feeling. 'I don't have to care.'

'No, you don't,' Charles said bitterly. 'Not if you didn't love him, you don't. You can help kick him in the face.'

Adam knew that his brother was no longer dangerous. There was no jealousy to drive him. The whole weight of his father was on him, but it was his father and no one could take his father away from him.

'How will you feel, walking in town, after everyone knows?' Charles demanded. 'How will you face anybody?'

'I told you I don't care. I don't have to care because I don't believe it.'

'You don't believe what?'

'I don't believe he stole any money. I believe in the war he did just what he said he did and was just where he said he was.'

'But the proof–how about the discharge?'

'You haven't any proof that he stole. You just made that up because you don't know where the money came from.'

'His army papers–'

'They could be wrong,' Adam said. 'I believe they are wrong. I believe in my father.'

'I don't see how you can.'

Adam said, 'Let me tell you. The proofs that God does not exist are very strong, but in lots of people they are not as strong as the feeling that He does.'

'But you said you did not love our father. How can you have faith in him if you didn't love him?'

'Maybe that's the reason,' Adam said slowly, feeling his way. 'Maybe if I had loved him I would have been jealous of him. You were. Maybe–maybe love makes you suspicious and doubting. Is it true that when you love a woman you are never sure–never sure of her because you aren't sure of yourself? I can see it pretty clearly. I can see how you loved him and what it did to you. I did not love him. Maybe he loved me. He tested me and hurt me and punished me and finally he sent me out like a sacrifice, maybe to make up for something. But he did not love you, and so he had faith in you. Maybe–why, maybe it's a kind of reverse.

Charles stared at him. 'I don't understand,' he said.

'I'm trying to,' said Adam. 'It's a new thought to me. I feel good. I feel better maybe than I have ever felt in my whole life. I've got rid of something. Maybe sometimes I'll get what you have, but I haven't got it now.'

'I don't understand,' Charles said again.

'Can you see that I don't think our father was a thief? I don't believe he was a liar.'

'But the papers–'

'I won't look at the papers. Papers are no match at all for my faith in my father.'

Charles was breathing heavily. 'Then you would take the money?'

'Of course.'

'Even if he stole it?'

'He did not steal it. He couldn't have stolen it.'

'I don't understand,' said Charles.

'You don't? Well, it does seem that maybe this might be the secret of the whole thing. Look, I've never mentioned this–do you remember when you beat me up just before I went away?'

'Yes.'

'Do you remember later? You came back with a hatchet to kill me.'

'I don't remember very well. I must have been crazy.'

'I didn't know then, but I know now–you were fighting for your love.'

'Love?'

'Yes,' said Adam. 'We'll use the money well. Maybe we'll stay here. Maybe we'll go away–maybe to California. We'll have to see what we'll do. And of course we must set up a monument to our father–a big one.'

'I couldn't ever go away from here,' said Charles.

'Well, let's see how it goes. There's no hurry. We'll feel it out.'

CHAPTER 8

I

I believe there are monsters born in the world to human parents. Some you can see, misshapen and horrible, with huge heads or tiny bodies; some are born with no arms, no legs, some with three arms, some with tails or mouths in odd places. They are accidents and no one's fault, as used to be thought. Once they were considered the visible punishment for concealed sins.

And just as there are physical monsters, can there not be mental or psychic monsters born? The face and body may be perfect, but if a twisted gene or malformed egg can produce physical monsters, may not the same process produce a malformed soul?

Monsters are variations from the accepted normal to a greater or a less degree. As a child may be born without an arm, so one may be born without kindness or the potential of conscience. A man who loses his arms in an accident has a great struggle to adjust himself to the lack, but one born without arms suffers only from people who find him strange. Having never had arms, he cannot miss them. Sometimes when we are little we imagine how it would be to have wings, but there is no reason to suppose it is the same feeling birds have. No, to a monster the norm must seem monstrous, since everyone is normal to himself. To the inner monster it must be even more obscure, since he has no visible thing to compare with others. To a man born without conscience, a soul-stricken man must seem ridiculous. To a criminal, honesty is foolish. You must not forget that a monster is only a variation, and that to a monster the norm is monstrous.

It is my belief that Cathy Ames was born with the tendencies, or lack of them, which drove and forced her all of her life. Some balance wheel was misweighted, some gear out of ratio. She was not like other people, never was from birth. And just as a cripple may learn to utilize his lack so that he becomes more effective in a limited field than the uncrippled, so did Cathy, using her difference, make a painful and bewildering stir in her world.

There was a time when a girl like Cathy would have been called possessed by the devil. She would have been exorcised to cast out the evil spirit, and if after many trials that did not work, she would have been burned as a witch for the good of the community. The one thing that may not be forgiven a witch is her ability to distress people, to make them restless and uneasy and even envious.

As though nature concealed a trap, Cathy had from the first a face of innocence. Her hair was gold and lovely; wide-set hazel eyes with upper lids that drooped made her look mysteriously sleepy. Her nose was delicate and thin, and her cheekbones high and wide, sweeping down to a small chin so that her face was heart-shaped. Her mouth was well shaped and well lipped but abnormally small–what used to be called a rosebud. Her ears were very little, without lobes, and they pressed so close to her head that even with her hair combed up they made no silhouette. They were thin flaps sealed against her head.

Cathy always had a child's figure even after she was grown, slender, delicate arms and hands–tiny hands. Her breasts never developed very much. Before her puberty the nipples turned inward. Her mother had to manipulate them out when they became painful in Cathy's tenth year. Her body was a boy's body, narrow-hipped, straight-legged, but her ankles were thin and straight without being slender. Her feet were small and round and stubby, with fat insteps almost like little hoofs. She was a pretty child and she became a pretty woman. Her voice was huskily soft, and it could be so sweet as to be irresistible. But there must have been some steel cord in her throat, for Cathy's voice could cut like a file when she wished.

Even as a child she had some quality that made people look at her, then look away, then look back at her, troubled at something foreign. Something looked out of her eyes, and was never there when one looked again. She moved quietly and talked little, but she could enter no room without causing everyone to turn towards her.

She made people uneasy but not so that they wanted to go away from her. Men and women wanted to inspect her, to be close to her, to try to find what caused the disturbance she distributed so subtly. And since this had always been so, Cathy did not find it strange.

Cathy was different from other children in many ways, but one thing in particular set her apart. Most children abhor difference. They want to look, talk, dress, and act exactly like all of the others. If the style of dress is an absurdity, it is pain and sorrow to a child not to wear that absurdity. If necklaces of pork chops were accepted, it would be a sad child who could not wear pork chops. And this slavishness to the group normally extends into every game, every practice, social or otherwise. It is a protective coloration children utilize for their safety.

Cathy had none of this. She never conformed in dress or conduct. She wore whatever she wanted to. The result was that quite often other children imitated her.

As she grew older the group, the herd, which is any collection of children, began to sense what adults felt, that there was something foreign about Cathy. After a while only one person at a time associated with her. Groups of boys and girls avoided her as though she carried a nameless danger.

Cathy was a liar, but she did not lie the way most children do. Hers was no day-dream lying, when the thing imagined is told and, to make it seem more real, told as real. That is just ordinary deviation from external reality. I think the difference between a lie and a story is that a story utilizes the trappings and appearance of truth for the interest of the listener as well as of the teller. A story has in it neither gain nor loss. But a lie is a device for profit or escape. I suppose if that definition is strictly held to, then a writer of stories is a liar–if he is financially fortunate.

Cathy's lies were never innocent. Their purpose was to escape punishment, or work, or responsibility, and they were used for profit. Most liars are tripped up either because they forget what they have told or because the lie is suddenly faced with an incontrovertible truth. But Cathy did not forget her lies, and she developed the most effective method of lying. She stayed close enough to the truth so that one could never be sure. She knew two other methods also–either to interlard her lies with truth or to tell a truth as though it were a lie. If one is accused of a lie and it turns out to be the truth, there is a backlog that will last a long time and protect a number of untruths.

Since Cathy was an only child her mother had no close contrast in the family. She thought all children were like her own. And since all parents are worriers she was convinced that all her friends had the same problems.

Cathy's father was not so sure. He operated a small tannery in a town in Massachusetts, which made a comfortable, careful living if he worked very hard. Mr Ames came in contact with other children away from his home and he felt that Cathy was not like other children. It was a matter more felt than known. He was uneasy about his daughter but he could not have said why.

Nearly everyone in the world has appetites and impulses, trigger emotions, islands of selfishness, lusts just beneath the surface. And most people either hold such things in check or indulge them secretly. Cathy knew not only these impulses in others but how to use them for her own gain. It is quite possible that she did not believe in any other tendencies in humans, for while she was preternaturally alert in some directions she was completely blind in others.

Cathy learned when she was very young that sexuality with all its attendant yearnings and pains, jealousies and taboos, is the most disturbing impulse humans have. And in that day it was even more disturbing than it is now, because the subject was unmentionable and unmentioned. Everyone concealed that little hell in himself, while publicly pretending it did not exist–and when he was caught up in it he was completely helpless. Cathy learned that by the manipulation and use of this one part of people she could gain and keep power over nearly anyone. It was at once a weapon and a threat. It was irresistible. And since the blind helplessness seems never to have fallen on Cathy, it is probable that she had very little of the impulse herself and indeed felt a contempt for those who did. And when you think of it in one way, she was right.

What freedom men and women could have, were they not constantly tricked and trapped and enslaved and tortured by their sexuality! The only drawback in that freedom is that without it one would not be a human. One would be a monster.

At ten Cathy knew something of the power of the sex impulse and began coldly to experiment with it. She planned everything coldly, foreseeing difficulties and preparing for them.

The sex play of children has always gone on. Everyone, I guess, who is not abnormal has foregathered with little girls in some dim leafy place, in the bottom of a manger, under a willow, in a culvert under a road–or at least has dreamed of doing so. Nearly all parents are faced with the problem sooner or later, and then the child is lucky if the parent remembers his own childhood. In the time of Cathy's childhood, however, it was harder. The parents, denying it in themselves, were horrified to find it in their children.

2

On a spring morning when in the late-surviving dew the young grass bristled under the sun, when the warmth crept into the ground and pushed the yellow dandelions up, Cathy's mother finished hanging the washed clothes on the line. The Ameses lived on the edge of town, and behind their house were barn and carriage house, vegetable garden, and fenced paddock for two horses.

Mrs Ames remembered having seen Cathy stroll away towards the barn. She called for her, and when there was no answer she thought she might have been mistaken. She was about to go into the house when she heard a giggle from the carriage house. 'Cathy!' she called. There was no answer. An uneasiness came over her. She reached back in her mind for the sound of the giggle. It had not been Cathy's voice. Cathy was not a giggler.

There is no knowing how or why dread comes on a parent. Of course many times apprehension arises when there is no reason for it at all. And it comes most often to the parents of only children, parents who have indulged in black dreams of loss.

Mrs Ames stood still, listening. She heard soft secret voices and moved quietly towards the carriage house. The double doors were closed. The murmur of voices came from inside, but she could not make out Cathy's voice. She made a quick stride and pulled the doors open and the bright sun crashed inside. She froze, mouth open, at what she saw. Cathy lay on the floor, her skirts pulled up. She was naked to the waist, and beside her two boys about fourteen were kneeling. The shock of the sudden light froze them too. Cathy's eyes were blank with terror. Mrs Ames knew the boys, knew their parents.

Suddenly one of the boys leaped up, darted past Mrs Ames, and ran around the corner of the house. The other boy helplessly edged away from the woman and with a cry rushed through the doorway. Mrs Ames clutched at him, but her fingers slipped from his jacket and he was gone. She could hear his running footsteps outside.

Mrs Ames tried to speak and her voice was a croaking whisper. 'Get up!'

Cathy stared blankly up at her and made no move. Mrs Ames saw that Cathy's wrists were tied with a heavy rope. She screamed and flung herself down and fumbled with the knots. She carried Cathy into the house and put her to bed.

The family doctor, after he had examined Cathy, could find no evidence that she had been mistreated. 'You can just thank God you got there in time,' he said over and over to Mrs Ames.

Cathy did not speak for a long time. Shock, the doctor called it. And when she did come out of the shock Cathy refused to talk. When she was questioned her eyes widened until the whites showed all around the pupils and her breathing stopped and her body grew rigid and her cheeks reddened from holding her breath.

The conference with the parents of the boys was attended by Dr Williams. Mr Ames was silent most of the time. He carried the rope which had been around Cathy's wrists. His eyes were puzzled. There were things he did not understand, but he did not bring them up.

Mrs Ames settled down to a steady hysteria. She had been there. She had seen. She was the final authority. And out of her hysteria a sadistic devil peered. She wanted blood. There was a kind of pleasure in her demands for punishment. The town, the country, must be protected. She put it on that basis. She had arrived in time, thank God. But maybe the next time she would not; and how would other mothers feel? And Cathy was only ten years old.

Punishments were more savage then than they are now. A man truly believed that the whip was an instrument of virtue. First singly and then together the boys were whipped, whipped to raw cuts.

Their crime was bad enough, but the lies proved an evil that not even the whip could remove. And their defence was from the beginning ridiculous. Cathy, they said, had started the whole thing, and they had each given her five cents. They had not tied her hands. They said they remembered that she was playing with a rope.

Mrs Ames said it first and the whole town echoed it. 'Do they mean to say she tied her own hands? A ten-year-old child?'

If the boys had owned up to the crime they might have escaped some of the punishment. Their refusal brought a torturing rage not only to their fathers, who did the whipping, but to the whole community. Both boys were sent to a house of correction with the approval of their parents.

'She's haunted by it,' Mrs Ames told the neighbours. 'If she could only talk about it, maybe she would get better. But when I ask her about it–it's like it came right back to her and she goes into shock again.'

The Ameses never spoke of it to her again. The subject was closed. Mr Ames very soon forgot his haunting reservations. He would have felt bad if two boys were in the house of correction for something they did not do.

After Cathy had fully recovered from her shock, boys and girls watched her from a distance and then moved closer, fascinated by her. She had no girl crushes, as is usual at twelve and thirteen. Boys did not want to take the chance of being ragged by their friends for walking home from school with her. But she exercised a powerful effect on both boys and girls. And if any boy could come on her alone, he found himself drawn to her by a force he could neither understand nor overcome.

She was dainty and very sweet and her voice was low. She went for long walks by herself, and it was a rare walk when some boy did not blunder out of a wood-lot and come on her by accident. And while whispers went scurrying about, there is no knowing what Cathy did. If anything happened, only vague whispers followed, and this in itself was unusual at an age when there are many secrets and none of them kept long enough to raise a cream.

Cathy developed a little smile, just a hint of a smile. She had a way of looking sideways and down that hinted to a lone boy of secrets he could share.

In her father's mind another question stirred, and he shoved it down deep and felt dishonest for thinking about it at all. Cathy had remarkable luck in finding things–a gold charm, money, a little silken purse, a silver cross with red stones said to be rubies. She found many things, and when her father advertised in the weekly *Courier* about the cross no one ever claimed it.

Mr William Ames, Cathy's father, was a covert man. He rarely told the thoughts in his mind. He wouldn't have dared so far to expose himself to the gaze of his neighbours. He kept the little flame of suspicion to himself. It was better if he didn't know anything, safer, wiser, and much more comfortable. As for Cathy's mother, she was so bound and twisted in a cocoon of gauzy half-lies, warped truth, suggestions, all planted by Cathy, that she would not have known a true thing if it had come to her.

3

Cathy grew more lovely all the time. The delicate blooming skin, the golden hair, the wide-set, modest, and yet promising eyes, the little mouth full of sweetness, caught attention and held it. She finished the eight grades of grammar school with such a good record that her parents entered her in the small high school, although in that time it was not usual for a girl to go on with her studies. But Cathy said she wanted to be a teacher, which delighted her mother and father, for this was the one profession of dignity open to a girl of a good but not well-to-do family. Parents took honour from a daughter who was a teacher.

Cathy was fourteen when she entered high school. She had always been precious to her parents, but with her entrance into the rarities of algebra and Latin she climbed into clouds where her parents could not follow. They had lost her. They felt that she was transported to a higher order.

The teacher of Latin was a pale intense young man who had failed in divinity school and yet had enough education to teach the inevitable grammar, Caesar, Cicero. He was a quiet young man who warmed his sense of failure to his bosom. Deep in himself he felt that he had been rejected by God, and for cause.

For a time it was noticed that a flame leaped in James Grew and some force glowed in his eyes. He was never seen with Cathy and no relationship was even suspected.

James Grew became a man. He walked on his toes and sang to himself. He wrote letters so persuasive that the directors of his divinity school looked favourably on re-admitting him.

And then the flame went out. His shoulders, held so high and square, folded dejectedly. His eyes grew feverish and his hands twitched. He was seen in church at night, on his knees, moving his lips over prayers. He missed school and sent word that he was ill when it was known that he was walking all alone in the hills beyond the town.

One night, late, he tapped on the door of the Ames house. Mr Ames complained his way out of bed, lighted a candle, flung an overcoat over his night-gown, and went to the door. It was a wild and crazy-looking James Grew who stood before him, his eyes shining and his body one big shudder.

'I've got to see you,' he said hoarsely to Mr Ames.

'It's after midnight,' Mr Ames said sternly.

'I've got to see you alone. Put on some clothes and come outside. I've got to talk to you.'

'Young man, I think you're drunk or sick. Go home and get some sleep. It's after midnight.'

'I can't wait. I've got to talk to you.'

'Come down to the tannery in the morning,' said Mr Ames, and he closed the door firmly on the reeling caller and stood inside, listening. He heard the wailing voice, 'I can't wait. I can't wait,' and then the feet dragged slowly down the steps.

Mr Ames shielded the candlelight away from his eyes with his cupped hand and went back to bed. He thought he saw Cathy's door close very silently, but perhaps the leaping candlelight had fooled his eyes, for a portière seemed to move too.

'What in the world?' his wife demanded when he came back to the bedside.

Mr Ames didn't know why he answered as he did–perhaps to save discussion. 'A drunken man,' he said. 'Got the wrong house.'

'I don't know what the world is coming to,' said Mrs Ames.

As he lay in the darkness after the light was out he saw the green circle left in his eyes by the candle flame, and in its whirling, pulsing flame he saw the frantic, beseeching eyes of James Grew. He didn't go back to sleep for a long time.

In the morning a rumour ran through the town, distorted here and there, added to, but by afternoon the story clarified. The sexton had found James Grew stretched on the floor in front of the altar. The whole top of his head blown off. Beside him lay a shotgun, and beside it the piece of stick with which he had pushed the trigger. Near him on the floor was a candlestick from the altar. One of the three candles was still burning. The other two had not been lighted. And on the floor were two books, the hymnal and the Book of Common Prayer, one on top of the other. The way the sexton figured it, James Grew had propped the gun-barrel on the books to bring it in line with his temple. The recoil of the discharge had thrown the shotgun off the books.

A number of people remembered having heard an explosion early in the morning, before daylight. James Grew left no letter. No one could figure why he had done it.

Mr Ames's first impulse was to go to the coroner with his story of the midnight call. Then he thought, 'What good would it do? If I knew anything it would be different. But I don't know a single thing.' He had a sick feeling in his stomach. He told himself over and over that it was not his fault. 'How could I have helped it? I don't even know what he wanted.' He felt guilty and miserable.

At dinner his wife talked about the suicide and he couldn't eat. Cathy sat silent, but no more silent than usual. She ate with little dainty nips and wiped her mouth often on her napkin.

Mrs Ames went over the matter of the body and the gun in detail. 'There's one thing I meant to speak of,' she said. 'That drunken man who came to the door last night–could that have been young Grew?'

'No,' he said quickly.

'Are you sure? Could you see him in the dark?'

'I had a candle,' he said sharply. 'Didn't look anything like, had a big beard.'

'No need to snap at me,' she said. 'I just wondered.'

Cathy wiped her mouth, and when she laid her napkin on her lap she was smiling.

Mrs Ames turned to her daughter. 'You saw him every day in school, Cathy. Has he seemed sad lately? Did you notice anything that might mean–'

Cathy looked down at her plate and then up. 'I thought he was sick,' she said. 'Yes, he has looked bad. Everybody was talking in school today. And somebody–I don't remember who–said that Mr Grew was in some kind of trouble in Boston. I didn't hear what kind of trouble. We all liked Mr Grew.' She wiped her lips delicately.

That was Cathy's method. Before the next day was out everybody in town knew that James Grew had been in trouble in Boston, and no one could possibly imagine that Cathy had planted the story. Even Mrs Ames had forgotten where she heard it.

4

Soon after her sixteenth birthday a change came over Cathy. One morning she did not get up for school. Her mother went into her room and found her in bed, staring at the ceiling. 'Hurry, you'll be late. It's nearly nine.'

'I'm not going.' There was no emphasis in her voice.

'Are you sick?'

'No.'

'Then hurry, get up.'

'I'm not going.'

'You must be sick. You've never missed a day.'

'I'm not going to school,' Cathy said calmly. 'I'm never going to school again.'

Her mother's mouth fell open. 'What do you mean?'

'Not ever,' said Cathy and continued to stare at the ceiling.

'Well, we'll just see what your father has to say about that! With all our work and expense, and two years before you get your certificate!' Then she came close and said softly, 'You aren't thinking of getting married?'

'No.'

'What's that book you're hiding?'

'Here! I'm not hiding it.'

'Oh! *Alice in Wonderland*. You're too big for that.'

Cathy said, 'I can get to be *so* little you can't even see me.'

'What in the world are you talking about?'

'Nobody can find me.'

Her mother said angrily, 'Stop making jokes. I don't know what you're thinking of. What does Miss Fancy think she is going to do?'

'I don't know yet,' said Cathy. 'I think I'll go away.'

'Well, you just lie there, Miss Fancy, and when your father comes home he'll have a thing or two to say to you.'

Cathy turned her head very slowly and looked at her mother. Her eyes were expressionless and cold. And suddenly Mrs Ames was afraid of her daughter. She went out quietly and closed the door. In her kitchen she sat down and cupped her hands in her lap and stared out of the window at the weathering carriage house.

Her daughter had become a stranger to her. She felt, as most parents do at one time or another, that she was losing control, that the bridle put in her hands for the governing of Cathy was slipping through her fingers. She did not know that she had never had any power over Cathy. She had been used for Cathy's purposes always. After a while Mrs Ames put on a bonnet and went to the tannery. She wanted to talk to her husband away from the house.

In the afternoon Cathy rose listlessly from her bed and spent a long time in front of the mirror.

That evening Mr Ames, hating what he had to do, delivered a lecture to his daughter. He spoke of her duty, her obligation, her natural love for her parents. Towards the end of his speech he was aware that she was not listening to him. This made him angry and he fell into threats. He spoke of the authority God had given him over his child and of how this natural authority had been armed by the state. He had her attention now. She looked him right in the eyes. Her mouth smiled a little, and her eyes did not seem to blink. Finally he had to look away, and this enraged him further. He ordered her to stop her nonsense. Vaguely he threatened her with whipping if she did not obey him.

He ended on a note of weakness. 'I want you to promise me that you will go to school in the morning and stop your foolishness.'

Her face was expressionless. The little mouth was straight. 'All right,' she said.

Later that night Mr Ames said to his wife with an assurance he did not feel, 'You see, it just needs a little authority. Maybe we've been too lax. But she has been a good child. I guess she forgot who's boss. A little sternness never hurt anybody.' He wished he were as confident as his words.

In the morning she was gone. Her straw travelling basket was gone and the best of her clothing. Her bed was neatly made. The room was impersonal–nothing to indicate that a girl had grown up in it. There were no pictures, no mementos, none of the normal clutter of growing. Cathy had never played with dolls. The room had no Cathy imprint.

In his way Mr Ames was an intelligent man. He clapped on his derby hat and walked quickly to the railroad station. The station agent was certain. Cathy had taken the early morning train. She had bought a ticket for Boston. He helped Mr Ames write a telegram to the Boston police. Mr Ames bought a round-trip ticket and caught the nine-fifty to Boston. He was a very good man in a crisis.

That night Mrs Ames sat in the kitchen with the door closed. She was white and she gripped the table with her hands to control her shaking. The sound, first of the blows and then of the screaming, came clearly to her through the closed doors.

Mr Ames was not good at whipping because he had never done it. He lashed at Cathy's legs with the buggy whip, and when she stood quietly staring at him with calm cold eyes he lost his temper. The first blows were tentative and timid, but when she did not cry he slashed at her sides and shoulders. The whip licked and cut. In his rage he missed her several times or got too close so that the whip wrapped around her body.

Cathy learned quickly. She found him out and knew him, and once she had learned she screamed, she writhed, she cried, she begged, and she had the satisfaction of feeling the blows instantly become lighter.

Mr Ames was frightened at the noise and hurt he was creating. He stopped. Cathy dropped back on the bed, sobbing. And if he had looked, her father would have seen that there were no tears in her eyes, but rather the muscles of her neck were tight and there were lumps just under the temples where the jaw muscles knotted.

He said, 'Now will you ever do that again?'

'No, oh, no! Forgive me,' Cathy said. She turned over on the bed so that her father could not see the coldness in her face.

'See you remember who you are. And don't forget what I am.'

Cathy's voice caught. She produced a dry sob. 'I won't forget,' she said.

In the kitchen Mrs Ames wrestled her hands. Her husband put his fingers on her shoulder.

'I hated to do it,' he said. 'I had to. And I think it did her good. She seems like a changed girl to me. Maybe we haven't bent the twig enough. We've spared the rod. Maybe we were wrong.' And he knew that although his wife had insisted on the whipping, although she had forced him to whip Cathy, she hated him for doing it. Despair settled over him.

5

There seemed no doubt that it was what Cathy needed. As Mr Ames said, 'It kind of opened her up.' She had always been tractable but now she became thoughtful too. In the weeks that followed she helped her mother in the kitchen and offered to help more than was needed. She started to knit an afghan for her mother, a large project that would take months. Mrs Ames told the neighbours about it. 'She has such a fine colour sense–rust and yellow. She's finished three squares already.'

For her father Cathy kept a ready smile. She hung up his hat when he came in and turned his chair properly under the light to make it easy for him to read.

Even in school she was changed. Always she had been a good student, but now she began to make plans for the future. She talked to the principal about examinations for her teaching certificate, perhaps a year early. And the principal looked over her record and thought she might well try it with hope of success. He called on Mr Ames at the tannery to discuss it.

'She didn't tell us any of this,' Mr Ames said proudly.

'Well, maybe I shouldn't have told you. I hope I haven't ruined a surprise.'

Mr and Mrs Ames felt that they had blundered on some magic which solved all of their problems. They put it down to an unconscious wisdom which comes only to parents. 'I never saw such a change in a person in my life,' Mr Ames said.

'But she was always a good child,' said his wife. 'And have you noticed how pretty she's getting? Why, she's almost beautiful. Her cheeks have so much colour.'

'I don't think she'll be teaching school long, with her looks,' said Mr Ames.

It was true that Cathy glowed. The childlike smile was constantly on her lips while she went about her preparations. She had all the time in the world. She cleaned the cellar and stuffed papers all around the edges of the foundation to block the draught. When the kitchen door squeaked she oiled the hinges and then the lock that turned too hard, and while she had the oil-can out she oiled the front-door hinges too. She made it her duty to keep the lamps filled and their chimneys clean. She invented a way of dipping the chimneys in a big can of kerosene she had in the basement.

'You'd have to see it to believe it,' her father said.

And it wasn't only at home either. She braved the smell of the tannery to visit her father. She was just past sixteen and of course he thought of her as a baby. He was amazed at her questions about business.

'She's smarter than some men I could name,' he told his foreman. 'She might be running the business some day.'

She was interested not only in the tanning processes but in the business end too. Her father explained the loans, the payments, the billing, and the pay-roll. He showed her how to open the safe and was pleased that after the first try she remembered the combination.

'The way I look at it is this,' he told his wife. 'We've all of us got a little of the Old Nick in us. I wouldn't want a child that didn't have some gumption. The way I see it, that's just a kind of energy. If you just check it and keep it in control, why, it will go in the right direction.'

Cathy mended all of her clothes and put her things in order.

One day in May she came home from school and went directly to her knitting needles. Her mother was dressed to go out. 'I have to go to the Altar Guild,' she said. 'It's about the cake sale next week. I'm chairman. Your father wondered if you would go by the bank and pick up the money for the pay-roll and take it to the tannery. I told him about the cake sale so I can't do it.'

'I'd like to,' said Cathy.

'They'll have the money ready for you in a bag,' said Mrs Ames, and she hurried out.

Cathy worked quickly but without hurry. She put on an old apron to cover her clothes. In the basement she found a jelly jar with a top and carried it out to the carriage house, where the tools were kept. In the chicken-yard she caught a little pullet, took it to the block and chopped its head off, and held the writhing neck over the jelly jar until it was half full of blood. Then she carried the quivering pullet to the manure pile and buried it deep. Back in the kitchen she took off the apron and put it in the stove and poked the coals until a flame sprang up on the cloth. She washed her hands and inspected her shoes and stockings and wiped a dark spot from the toe of her right shoe. She looked at her face in the mirror. Her cheeks were bright with colour and her eyes shone and her mouth turned up in its small childlike smile. On her way out she hid the jelly jar under the lowest part of the kitchen steps. Her mother had not been gone even ten minutes.

Cathy walked lightly, almost dancing, round the house and into the street. The trees were breaking into leaf and a few early dandelions were in yellow flower on the lawns. Cathy walked gaily towards the centre of the town, where the bank was. And she was so fresh and pretty that people walking turned and looked after her when she had passed.

6

The fire broke out at about three o'clock in the morning. It rose, flared, roared, crashed, and crumbled in on itself almost before anyone noticed it. When the volunteers ran up, pulling their hose-cart, there was nothing for them to do but wet down the roofs of the neighbouring houses to keep them from catching fire.

The Ames house had gone up like a rocket. The volunteers and the ordinary audience fires attract looked round at the lighted faces, trying to see Mr and Mrs Ames and their daughter. It came to everyone at once that they were not there. People gazed at the broad ember-bed and saw themselves and their children in there, and hearts rose up and pumped against throats. The volunteers began to dump water on the fire almost as though they might even so late save some corporeal part of the family. The frightened talk ran through the town that the whole Ames family had burned.

By sunrise everyone in town was tight-packed about the smoking black pile. Those in front had to shield their faces against the heat. The volunteers continued to pump water to cool off the charred mess. By noon the coroner was able to throw wet planks down and probe with a crowbar among the sodden heaps of charcoal. Enough remained of Mr and Mrs Ames to make sure there were two bodies. Near neighbours pointed out the approximate place where Cathy's room had been, but although the coroner and any number of helpers worked over the débris with a garden rake they could find no tooth or bone.

The chief of the volunteers meanwhile had found the door-knobs and lock of the kitchen door. He looked at the blackened metal, puzzled, but not quite knowing what puzzled him. He borrowed the coroner's rake and worked furiously. He went to the place where the front door had been and raked until he found that lock, crooked and half melted. By now he had his own small crowd, who demanded, 'What are you looking for, George?' and 'What did you find, George?'

Finally the coroner came over to him. 'What's on your mind, George?'

'No keys in the locks,' the chief said uneasily.

'Maybe they fell out.'

'How?'

'Maybe they melted.'

'The locks didn't melt.'

'Maybe Bill Ames took them out.'

'On the inside?' He held up his trophies. Both bolts stuck out.

Since the owner's house was burned and the owner ostensibly burned with it, the employees of the tannery, out of respect, did not go to work. They hung around the burned house, offering to help in any way they could, feeling official and generally getting in the way.

It wasn't until afternoon that Joel Robinson, the foreman, went down to the tannery. He found the safe open and papers scattered all over the floor. A broken window showed how the thief had entered.

Now the whole complexion changed. So, it was not an accident. Fear took the place of excitement and sorrow, and anger, brother of fear, crept in. The crowd began to spread.

They had not far to go. In the carriage house there was what is called 'signs of a struggle'–in this case a broken box, a shattered carriage lamp, scraped marks in the dust, and straw on the floor. The onlookers might not have known these as signs of a struggle had there not been a quantity of blood on the floor.

The constable took control. This was his province. He pushed and herded everyone out of the carriage house. 'Want to gum up all these clues?' he shouted at them. 'Now you all stay clear outside the door.'

He searched the room, picked up something, and in a corner found something else. He came to the door, holding his discoveries in his hands–a blood-spattered blue hair-ribbon and a cross with red stones. 'Anybody recognize these here?' he demanded.

In a small town where everyone knows everyone it is almost impossible to believe that one of your acquaintances could murder anyone. For that reason, if the signs are not pretty strong in a particular direction, it must be some dark stranger, some wanderer from the outside world where such things happen. Then the hobo camps are raided and vagrants brought in and hotel registers scrutinized. Every man who is not known is automatically suspected. It was May, remember, and the wandering men had only recently taken to the roads, now that the warming months let them spread their blankets by any watercourse. And the gypsies were out too–a whole caravan less than five miles away. And what a turning out those poor gypsies got!

The ground for miles around was searched for new-turned earth, and likely pools were dragged for Cathy's body. 'She was so pretty,' everyone said, and they meant that in themselves they could see a reason for carrying Cathy off. At length a bumbling hairy half-wit was brought in for questioning. He was a fine candidate for hanging because not only did he have no alibis, he could not remember what he had done at any time in his life. His feeble mind sensed that these questioners wanted something of him and, being a friendly creature, he tried to give it to them. When a baited and set question was offered to him, he walked happily into the trap and was glad when the constable looked happy. He tried manfully to please these superior beings. There was something very nice about him. The only trouble with his confession was that he confessed too much in too many directions. Also, he had constantly to be reminded of what he was supposed to have done. He was really pleased when he was indicted by a stern and frightened jury. He felt that at last he amounted to something.

There were, and are, some men who become judges whose love for the law and for its attention of promoting justice has the quality of love for a woman. Such a man presided at the examination before plea–a man so pure and good that he cancelled out a lot of wickedness with his life. Without the prompting the culprit was used to, his confession was nonsense. The judge questioned him and found out that although the suspect was trying to follow instructions he simply could not remember what he did, whom he killed, how or why. The judge sighed wearily and motioned him out of the courtroom and crooked his fingers at the constable.

'Now look here, Mike,' he said, 'you shouldn't do a thing like that. If that poor fellow had been just a little smarter you might have got him hanged.'

'He said he did it.' The constable's feelings were hurt, because he was a conscientious man.

'He would have admitted climbing the golden stairs and cutting St Peter's throat with a bowling ball,' the judge said. 'Be more careful, Mike. The law was designed to save, not to destroy.'

In all such local tragedies time works like a damp brush on water-colour. The sharp edges blur, the ache goes out of it, the colours melt together, and from the many separated lines a solid grey emerges. Within a month it was not so necessary to hang someone, and within two months nearly everybody discovered that there wasn't any real evidence against anyone. If it had not been for Cathy's murder, fire and robbery might have been a coincidence. Then it occurred to people that without Cathy's body you couldn't prove anything even though you thought she was dead.

Cathy left a scent of sweetness behind her.

CHAPTER 9

I

Mr Edwards carried on his business of whoremaster in an orderly and unemotional way. He maintained his wife and his two well-mannered children in a good house in a good neighbourhood in Boston. The children, two boys, were entered on the books of Groton when they were infants.

Mrs Edwards kept a dustless house and controlled her servants. There were of course many times when Mr Edwards had to be away from home on business, but he managed to live an amazingly domestic life and to spend more evenings at home than you could imagine. He ran his business with a public accountant's neatness and accuracy. He was a large and powerful man, running a little to fat in his late forties, and yet in surprisingly good condition for a time when a man wanted to be fat if only to prove he was a success.

He had invented his business–the circuit route through the small towns, the short stay of each girl, the discipline, the percentages. He felt his way along and made few mistakes. He never sent his girls into the cities. He could handle the hungry constables of the villages, but he had respect for the experienced and voracious big-city police. His ideal stand was a small town with a mortgaged hotel and no amusements, one where his only competition came from wives and an occasional wayward girl. At this time he had ten units. Before he died at sixty-seven of strangulation on a chicken bone, he had groups of four girls in each of thirty-three small towns in New England. He was better than well fixed–he was rich; and the manner of his death was in itself symbolic of success and well-being.

At the present time the institution of the whorehouse seems to a certain extent to be dying out. Scholars have various reasons to give. Some say that the decay of morality among girls has dealt the whorehouse its death-blow. Others, perhaps more realistic, maintain that police supervision on an increased scale is driving the houses out of existence. In the late days of the last century and the early part of this one, the whorehouse was an accepted if not openly discussed institution. It was said that its existence protected decent women. An unmarried man could go to one of these houses and evacuate the sexual energy which was making him uneasy and at the same time maintain the popular attitudes about the purity and loveliness of women. It was a mystery, but then there are many mysterious things in our social thinking.

These houses ranged from palaces filled with gold and velvet to the crummiest cribs where the stench would drive a pig away. Every once in a while a story would start about how young girls were stolen and enslaved by the controllers of the industry, and perhaps many of the stories were true. But the great majority of whores drifted into their profession through laziness and stupidity. In the houses they had no responsibility. They were fed and clothed and taken care of until they were too old, and then they were kicked out. This ending was no deterrent. No one who is young is ever going to be old.

Now and then a smart girl came into the profession, but she usually moved up to better things. She got a house of her own or worked successfully at blackmail or married a rich man. There was even a special name for the smart ones. They were grandly called courtesans.

Mr Edwards had no trouble either in recruiting or in controlling his girls. If a girl was not properly stupid, he threw her out. He did not want very pretty girls either. Some local young man might fall in love with a pretty whore and there would be hell to pay. When any of his girls became pregnant they had the choice of leaving or of being aborted so brutally that a fair proportion died. In spite of this the girls usually chose abortion.

It was not always smooth sailing for Mr Edwards. He did have his problems. At the time of which I am telling you he had been subjected to a series of misfortunes. A train wreck had killed off two units of four girls each. Another of his units he lost to conversion when a small-town preacher suddenly caught fire and began igniting the townsfolk with his sermons. The swelling congregation had to move out of the church and into the fields. Then, as happens so often, the preacher turned over his hole-card, the sure-fire card. He predicted the date of the end of the world, and the whole county moved bleating in on him. Mr Edwards went to the town, took the heavy quirt from his suitcase, and whipped the girls unmercifully; instead of seeing things his way, the girls begged for more whipping to wipe out their fancied sins. He gave up in disgust, took their clothes, and went back to Boston. The girls achieved a certain prominence when they went naked to the camp meeting to confess and testify. That is how Mr Edwards happened to be interviewing and recruiting numbers of girls instead of picking one up here and there. He had three units to rebuild from the ground.

I don't know how Cathy Ames heard about Mr Edwards. Perhaps a hack driver told her. The word got around when a girl really wanted to know. Mr Edwards had not had a good morning when she came into his office. The pain in his stomach he ascribed to a halibut chowder his wife had given him for supper the night before. He had been up all night. The chowder had blown both ways and he still felt weak and crampy.

For this reason he did not take in all at once the girl who called herself Catherine Amesbury. She was far too pretty for his business. Her voice was low and throaty, she was slight, almost delicate, and her skin was lovely. In a word she was not Mr Edwards's kind of girl at all. If he had not been weak he would have rejected her instantly. But while he did not look at her very closely during the routine questioning, mostly about relatives who might cause trouble, something in Mr Edwards's body began to feel her. Mr Edwards was not a concupiscent man, and besides he never mixed his professional life with his private pleasures. His reaction startled him. He looked up, puzzled, at the girl, and her eyelids dipped sweetly and mysteriously, and there was just a suggestion of a sway on her lightly padded hips. Her little mouth wore a cat smile. Mr Edwards leaned forward at his desk, breathing heavily. He realized that he wanted this one for his own.

'I can't understand why a girl like you–' he began, and fell right into the oldest conviction in the world–that the girl you are in love with can't possibly be anything but true and honest.

'My father is dead,' Catherine said modestly. 'Before he died he had let things go to pieces. We didn't know he had borrowed money on the farm. And I can't let the bank take it away from my mother. The shock would kill her.' Catherine's eyes dimmed with tears. 'I thought maybe I could make enough to keep up the interest.'

If ever Mr Edwards had a chance it was now. And indeed a little warning buzz did sound in his brain, but it was not loud enough. About eighty per cent of the girls who came to him needed money to pay off a mortgage. And Mr Edwards made it an unvarying rule not to believe anything his girls said at any time, beyond what they had for breakfast, and they sometimes lied about that. And here he was, a big, fat, grown-up whoremaster, leaning his stomach against his desk while his cheeks darked with blood and excited chills ran up his legs and thighs.

Mr Edwards heard himself saying, 'Well now, my dear, let's talk this over. Maybe we can figure some way for you to get the interest money.' And this to a girl who had simply asked for a job as a whore–or had she?

2

Mrs Edwards was persistently if not profoundly religious. She spent a great part of her time with the mechanics of her church, which did not leave her time for either its background or its effects. To her, Mr Edwards was in the importing business, and even if she had known–which she probably did–what business he was really in, she would not have believed it. And this is another mystery. Her husband had always been to her a coldly thoughtful man who made few and dutiful physical demands on her. If he had never been warm, he had never been cruel either. Her dramas and her emotions had to do with the boys, with the vestry, and with food. She was content with her life and thankful. When her husband's disposition began to disintegrate, causing him to be restless and snappish, to sit staring and then to rush out of the house in a nervous rage, she ascribed it first to his stomach and then to business reverses. When by accident she came upon him in the bathroom, sitting on the toilet and crying softly to himself, she knew he was a sick man. He tried quickly to cover his red brimming eyes from her scrutiny. When neither herb teas nor physics cured him she was helpless.

If in all the years Mr Edwards had heard about anyone like himself he would have laughed. For Mr Edwards, as cold-blooded a whoremaster as ever lived, had fallen hopelessly, miserably in love with Catherine Amesbury. He rented a sweet little brick house for her, and then gave it to her. He bought her every imaginable luxury, over-decorated the house, kept it over-warm. The carpeting was too deep and the walls were crowded with heavy-framed pictures.

Mr Edwards had never experienced such misery. As a matter of business he had learned so much about women that he did not trust one for a second. And since he deeply loved Catherine and love requires trust, he was torn to quivering fragments by his emotion. He had to trust her and at the same time he did not trust her. He tried to buy her loyalty with presents and with money. When he was away from her, he tortured himself with the thought of other men slipping into her house. He hated to leave Boston to check up on his units because this would leave Catherine alone. To a certain extent he began to neglect his business. It was his first experience with this kind of love and it nearly killed him.

One thing Mr Edwards did not know, and could not know because Catherine would not permit it, was that she was faithful to him in the sense that she did not receive or visit other men. To Catherine, Mr Edwards was as cold a business proposition as his units were to him. And as he had his techniques, so had she hers. Once she had him, which was very soon, she managed always to seem lightly dissatisfied. She gave him an impression of restlessness, as though she might take flight at any moment. When she knew he was going to visit her, she made it a point to be out and to come in glowing as from some incredible experience. She complained a good deal about the difficulties of avoiding the lecherous looks and touches of men in the street who could not keep away from her. Several times she ran frightened into the house, having barely escaped a man who had followed her. When she would return in the late afternoon and find him waiting for her she would explain, 'Why, I was shopping. I have to go shopping, you know.' And she made it sound like a lie.

In their sexual relations she convinced him that the result was not quite satisfactory to her, that if he were a better man he could release a flood of unbelievable reaction in her. Her method was to keep him continually off balance. She saw with satisfaction his nerves begin to go, his hands take to quivering, his loss of weight, and the wild glazed look in his eyes. And when she delicately sensed the near approach of insane, punishing rage, she sat in his lap and soothed him and made him believe for a moment in her innocence. She could convince him.

Catherine wanted money, and she set about getting it as quickly and as easily as she could. When she had successfully reduced him to a pulp, and Catherine knew exactly when the time had come, she began to steal from him. She went through his pockets and took any large notes she found. He didn't dare accuse her for fear she would go away. The presents of jewellery he gave her disappeared, and although she said she had lost them, he knew they had been sold. She padded the grocery bills, added to the prices of clothes. He could not bring himself to stop it. She did not sell the house, but she mortgaged it for every penny she could get.

One evening his key did not fit in the lock of the front door. She answered his pounding after a long time. Yes, she had changed the locks because she had lost her key. She was afraid, living alone. Anyone could get in. She would get him another key–but she never did. He always had to ring the bell after that, and sometimes it took a long time for her to answer, and at other times his ring was not answered at all. There was no way for him to know whether she was at home or not. Mr Edwards had her followed–and she did not know how often.

Mr Edwards was essentially a simple man, but even a simple man has complexities which are dark and twisted. Catherine was clever, but even a clever woman misses some of the strange corridors in a man.

She made only one bad slip, and she had tried to avoid that one. As was proper, Mr Edwards had stocked the pretty little nest with champagne. Catherine had from the first refused to touch it.

'It makes me sick,' she explained. 'I've tried it and I can't drink it.'

'Nonsense,' he said. 'Just have one glass. It can't hurt you.'

'No, thank you. No, I can't drink it.'

Mr Edwards thought of her reluctance as a delicate, a ladylike quality. He had never insisted until one evening when it occurred to him that he knew nothing about her. Wine might loosen her tongue. The more he thought of it, the better the idea seemed to him.

'It's not friendly of you not to have a glass with me.'

'I tell you, it doesn't agree with me.'

'Nonsense.'

'I tell you I don't want it.'

'This is silly,' he said. 'Do you want me to be angry with you?'

'No.'

'Then drink a glass.'

'I don't want it.'

'Drink it.' He held a glass for her, and she retreated from it.

'You don't know. It's not good for me.'

'Drink it.'

She took the glass and poured it down and stood still, quivering, seeming to listen. The blood flowed to her cheeks. She poured another glass for herself and another. Her eyes became set and cold. Mr Edwards felt a fear of her. Something was happening to her which neither she nor he could control.

'I didn't want to do it. Remember that,' she said calmly.

'Maybe you'd better not have any more.'

She laughed and poured herself another glass. 'It doesn't matter now,' she said. 'More won't make much difference.'

'It's nice to have a glass or so,' he said uneasily.

She spoke to him softly. 'You fat slug,' she said. 'What do you know about me? Do you think I can't read every rotten thought you ever had? Want me to tell you? You wonder where a nice girl like me learned tricks. I'll tell you. I learned them in cribs–you hear?–cribs. I've worked in places you never even heard of–four years. Sailors brought me little tricks from Port Said. I know every nerve in your lousy body and I can use them.'

'Catherine,' he protested, 'you don't know what you're saying.'

'I could see it. You thought I would talk. Well, I'm talking.'

She advanced slowly towards him, and Mr Edwards overcame his impulse to edge away. He was afraid of her, but he sat still. Directly in front of him she drank the last champagne in her glass, delicately struck the rim on the table, and jammed the ragged edge against his cheek.

And then he did run from the house, and he could hear her laughing as he went.

3

Love to a man like Mr Edwards is a crippling emotion. It ruined his judgement, cancelled his knowledge, weakened him. He told himself she was hysterical and tried to believe it, and it was made easier for him by Catherine. Her outbreak had terrified her, and for a time she made every effort to restore his sweet picture of her.

A man so painfully in love is capable of self-torture beyond belief. Mr Edwards wanted with all his heart to believe in her goodness, but he was forced not to, as much by his own particular devil as by her outbreak. Almost instinctively he went about learning the truth and at the same time disbelieved it. He knew, for instance, that she would not put her money in a bank. One of his employees, using a complicated set of mirrors, found out the place in the cellar of the little brick house where she did keep it.

One day a clipping came from the agency he employed. It was an old newspaper account of a fire from a small-town weekly. Mr Edwards studied it. His chest and stomach turned to molten metal and a redness glowed in his head behind his eyes. There was real fear mixed up in his love, and the precipitate from the mixing of these two is cruelty. He staggered dizzily to his office couch and lay face down, his forehead against the cool black leather. For a time he hung suspended, hardly breathing. Gradually his brain cleared. His mouth tasted salty, and there was a great ache of anger in his shoulders. But he was calm and his mind cut its intention through time like a sharp beam of a searchlight through a dark room. He moved slowly, checking his suitcase just as he always did when he started out to inspect his units–clean shirts and underwear, a night-gown and slippers, and the heavy quirt with the lash curving around the end of the suitcase.

He moved heavily up the garden in front of the brick house and rang the bell.

Catherine answered it immediately. She had on her coat and hat.

'Oh!' she said. 'What a shame! I must go out for a while.'

Mr Edwards put down his suitcase. 'No,' he said.

She studied him. Something was changed. He lumbered past her and went down into the cellar.

'Where are you going?' Her voice was shrill.

He did not reply. In a moment he came up again, carrying a small oak box. He opened his suitcase and put the box inside.

'That's mine,' she said softly.

'I know.'

'What are you up to?'

'I thought we'd go for a little trip.'

'Where? I can't go.'

'Little town in Connecticut. I have some business there. You told me once you wanted to work. You're going to work.'

'I don't want to now. You can't make me. Why, I'll call the police!'

He smiled so horribly that she stepped back from him. His temples were thudding with blood. 'Maybe you'd rather go to your home town,' he said. 'They had a big fire there several years ago. Do you remember that fire?'

Her eyes probed and searched him, seeking a soft place, but his eyes were flat and hard. 'What do you want me to do?' she asked quietly.

'Just come for a little trip with me. You said you wanted to work.'

She could think of only one plan. She must go along with him and wait for a chance. A man couldn't always watch. It would be dangerous to thwart him now–best go along with it and wait. That always worked. It always had. But his words had given Catherine real fear.

In the small town they got off the train at dusk, walked down its one dark street and on out into the country. Catherine was wary and watchful. She had no access to his plan. In her purse she had a thin-bladed knife.

Mr Edwards thought he knew what he intended to do. He meant to whip her and put her in one of the rooms at the inn, whip her and move her to another town, and so on until she was of no use any more. Then he would throw her out. The local constable would see to it that she did not run away. The knife did not bother him. He knew about that.

The first thing he did when they stopped in a private place between a stone wall and a fringe of cedars was to jerk the purse from her hand and throw it over the wall. That took care of the knife. But he didn't know about himself, because in all his life he had never been in love with a woman. He thought he only meant to punish her. After two slashes the quirt was not enough. He dropped it on the ground and used his fists. His breathing came out in squealing whines.

Catherine did her best not to fall into panic. She tried to duck his threshing fists or at least to make them ineffective, but at last fear overcame her and she tried to run. He leaped at her and brought her down, and by then his fists were not enough. His frantic hand found a stone on the ground and his cold control was burst through with a red roaring wave.

Later he looked down on her beaten face. He listened for her heart-beat and could hear nothing over the thumping of his own. Two complete and separate thoughts ran in his mind. One said, 'Have to bury her, have to dig a hole and put her in it.' And the other cried like a child, 'I can't stand it. I couldn't bear to touch her.' Then the sickness that follows rage overwhelmed him. He ran from the place, leaving his suitcase, leaving the quirt, leaving the oak box of money. He blundered away in the dusk, wondering only where he could hide his sickness for a while.

No question was ever asked of him. After a time of sickness to which his wife ministered tenderly, he went back to his business and never again let the insanity of love come near him. A man who can't learn from experience is a fool, he said. Always afterwards he had a kind of fearful respect for himself. He had never known that the impulse to kill was in him.

That he had not killed Catherine was an accident. Every blow had been intended to crush her. She was a long time unconscious and a long time half-conscious. She realized her arm was broken and she must find help if she wanted to live. Wanting to live forced her to drag herself along the dark road, looking for help. She turned in at a gate and almost made the steps of the house before she fainted. The roosters were crowing in the chicken-house and a grey rim of dawn lay on the east.

CHAPTER 10

1

When two men live together they usually maintain a kind of shabby neatness out of incipient rage at each other. Two men alone are constantly on the verge of fighting, and they know it. Adam Trask had not been home long before the tensions began to build up. The brothers saw too much of each other and not enough of anyone else.

For a few months they were busy getting Cyrus's money in order and out at interest. They travelled together to Washington to look at the grave, good stone and on top an iron star with seal and a hole on the top in which to insert the stick for a little flag on Decoration Day. The brothers stood by the grave a long time, then they went away and they didn't mention Cyrus.

If Cyrus had been dishonest he had done it well. No one asked questions about the money. But the subject was on Charles's mind.

Back on the farm Adam asked him, 'Why don't you buy some new clothes? You're a rich man. You act like you're afraid to spend a penny.'

'I am,' said Charles.

'Why?'

'I might have to give it back.'

'Still harping on that? If there was anything wrong, don't you think we'd have heard about it by now?'

'I don't know,' said Charles. 'I'd rather not talk about it.'

But that night he brought up the subject again. 'There's one thing bothers me,' he began.

'About the money?'

'Yes, about the money. If you make that much money there's bound to be a mess.'

'How do you mean?'

'Well, papers and account books and bills of sale, notes, figuring–well, we went through Father's things and there wasn't none of that.'

'Maybe he burned it up.'

'Maybe he did,' said Charles.

The brothers lived by a routine established by Charles, and he never varied it. Charles awakened on the stroke of four-thirty as surely as though the brass pendulum of the clock had nudged him. He was awake, in fact, a split second before four-thirty. His eyes were open and had blinked once before the high gong struck. For a moment he lay still, looking up into the darkness and scratching his stomach. Then he reached to the table beside his bed and his hand fell exactly on the block of sulphur matches lying there. His fingers pulled a match free and struck it on the side of the block. The sulphur burned its little blue bead before the wood caught. Charles lighted the candle beside his bed. He threw back his blanket and got up. He wore long grey underwear that bagged over his knees and hung loose around his ankles. Yawning, he went to the door, opened it, and called, 'Half past four, Adam. Time to get up. Wake up.'

Adam's voice was muffled. 'Don't you ever forget?'

'It's time to get up.' Charles slipped his legs into his trousers and hunched them up over his hips. 'You don't have to get up,' he said. 'You're a rich man. You can lay in bed all day.'

'So are you. But we still get up before daylight.'

'You don't have to get up,' Charles repeated. 'But if you're going to farm, you'd better farm.'

Adam said ruefully, 'So we're going to buy more land so we can do more work.'

'Come off it,' said Charles. 'Go back to bed if you want to.'

Adam said, 'I bet you couldn't sleep if you stayed in bed. You know what I bet? I bet you get up because you want to, and then you take credit for it–like taking credit for six fingers.'

Charles went into the kitchen and lighted the lamp. 'You can't lay in bed and run a farm,' he said, and he knocked the ashes through the grate of the stove and tore some paper over the exposed coals and blew until the flame started.

Adam was watching him through the door. 'You wouldn't use a match,' he said.

Charles turned angrily. 'You mind your own goddam business. Stop picking at me.'

'All right,' said Adam. 'I will. And maybe my business isn't here.'

'That's up to you. Any time you want to get out, you go right ahead.'

The quarrel was silly but Adam couldn't stop it. His voice went on without his willing it, making angry and irritating words. 'You're damn right I'll go when I want,' he said. 'This is my place as much as yours.'

'Then why don't you do some work on it?'

'Oh, Lord!' Adam said. 'What are we fussing about? Let's not fuss.'

'I don't want trouble,' said Charles. He scooped lukewarm mush into two bowls and spun them on the table.

The brothers sat down. Charles buttered a slice of bread, gouged out a knifeful of jam and spread it over the butter. He dug butter for his second slice and left a slop of jam on the butter roll.

'Goddam it, can't you wipe your knife? Look at that butter!'

Charles laid his knife and the bread on the table and placed his hands palm down on either side. 'You better get off the place,' he said.

Adam got up. 'I'd rather live in a pigsty,' he said, and he walked out of the house.

2

It was eight months before Charles saw him again. Charles came in from work and found Adam sloshing water on his hair and face from the kitchen bucket.

'Hello,' said Charles. 'How are you?'

'Fine,' said Adam.

'Where'd you go?'

'Boston.'

'No place else?'

'No. Just looked at the city.'

The brothers settled back to their old life, but each took precautions against anger. In a way each protected the other and so saved himself. Charles, always the early riser, got breakfast ready before he awakened Adam. And Adam kept the house clean and started a set of books on the farm. In this guarded way they lived for two years before their irritation grew beyond control again.

On the winter evening Adam looked up from his account book. 'It's nice in California,' he said. 'It's nice in the winter. And you can raise anything there.'

'Sure you can raise it. But when you got it, what are you going to do with it?'

'How about wheat? They raise a lot of wheat in California.'

'The rust will get to it,' said Charles.

'What makes you so sure? Look, Charles, things grow so fast in California they say you have to plant and step back quick or you'll get knocked down.'

Charles said, 'Why the hell don't you go there? I'll buy you out any time you say.'

Adam was quiet then, but in the morning while he combed his hair and peered in the small mirror he began it again.

'They don't have any winter in California,' he said. 'It's just like spring all the time.'

'I like the winter,' said Charles.

Adam came towards the stove. 'Don't be cross,' he said.

'Well, stop picking at me. How many eggs?'

'Four,' said Adam.

Charles placed seven eggs on top of the warming oven and built his fire carefully of small pieces of kindling until it burned fiercely. He put the skillet down next to the flame. His sullenness left him as he fried the bacon.

'Adam,' he said, 'I don't know whether you notice it, but it seems like every other word you say is California. Do you really want to go?'

Adam chuckled. 'That's what I'm trying to figure out,' he said. 'I don't know. It's like getting up in the morning. I don't want to get up, but I don't want to stay in bed either.'

'You sure make a fuss about it,' said Charles.

Adam went on, 'Every morning in the army that damned bugle would sound. And I swore to God if I ever got out I would sleep till noon every day. And here I get up a half-hour before reveille. Will you tell me, Charles, what in hell we're working for?'

'You can't lay in bed and run a farm,' said Charles. He stirred the hissing bacon around with a fork.

'Take a look at it,' Adam said earnestly. 'Neither one of us has got a chick or a child, let alone a wife. And the way we're going it don't look like we ever will. We don't have time to look around for a wife. And here we're figuring to add the Clark place to ours if the price is right. What for?'

'It's a damn fine piece,' said Charles. 'The two of them together would make one of the best farms in this section. Say! You thinking of getting married?'

'No. And that's what I'm talking about. Come a few years and we'll have the finest farm in this section. Two lonely old farts working our tails off. Then one of us will die off and the fine farm will belong to one lonely old fart, and then he'll die off–'

'What the hell are you talking about?' Charles demanded. 'Fellow can't get comfortable. You make me itch. Get it out–what's on your mind?'

'I'm not having any fun,' said Adam. 'Or anyway I'm not having enough. I'm working too hard for what I'm getting, and I don't have to work at all.'

'Well, why don't you quit?' Charles shouted at him. 'Why don't you get the hell out? I don't see any guards holding you. Go down to the South Seas and lay in a hammock if that's what you want.'

'Don't be cross,' said Adam quietly. 'It's like getting up. I don't want to get up and I don't want to stay down. I don't want to stay here and I don't want to go away.'

'You make me itch,' said Charles.

'Think about it, Charles. You like it here?'

'Yes.'

'And you want to live here all your life?'

'Yes.'

'Jesus, I wish I had it that easy. What do you suppose is the matter with me?'

'I think you've got knocker fever. Come in to the inn tonight and get it cured up.'

'Maybe that's it,' said Adam. 'But I never took much satisfaction in a whore.'

'It's all the same,' Charles said. 'You shut your eyes and you can't tell the difference.'

'Some of the boys in the regiment used to keep a squaw around. I had one for a while.'

Charles turned to him with interest. 'Father would turn in his grave if he knew you was squawing around. How was it?'

'Pretty nice. She'd wash my clothes and mend and do a little cooking.'

'I mean the other–how was that?'

'Good. Yes, good. And kind of sweet–kind of soft and sweet. Kind of gentle and soft.'

'You're lucky she didn't put a knife in you while you were asleep.'

'She wouldn't. She was sweet.'

'You've got a funny look in your eye. I guess you were kind of gone on that squaw.'

'I guess I was,' said Adam.

'What happened to her?'

'Smallpox.'

'You didn't get another one?'

Adam's eyes were pained. 'We piled them up like they were logs, over two hundred, arms and legs sticking out. And we piled brush on top and poured coal oil on.'

'I've heard they can't stand smallpox.'

'It kills them,' said Adam. 'You're burning the bacon.'

Charles turned quickly back to the stove. 'It'll just be crisp,' he said, 'I like it crisp.' He shovelled the bacon out on a plate and broke the eggs in the hot grease and they jumped and fluttered their edges to brown lace and made clucking sounds.

'There was a school-teacher,' Charles said. 'Prettiest thing you ever saw. Had little tiny feet. Bought all her clothes in New York. Yellow hair, and you never saw such little feet. Sang too, in the choir. Everybody took to going to church. Damn near stampeded getting into church. That was quite a while ago.'

''Bout the time you wrote about thinking of getting married?'

Charles grinned. 'I guess so. I guess there wasn't a young buck in the county didn't get the marrying fever.'

'What happened to her?'

'Well, you know how it is. The women got kind of restless with her here. They got together. First thing you knew they had her out. I heard she wore silk underwear. Too hoity-toity. School board had her out half way through the term. Feet no longer than that. Showed her ankles too, like it was an accident. Always showing her ankles.'

'Did you get to know her?'

'No. I only went to church. Couldn't hardly get in. Girl that pretty's no right in a little town. Just makes people uneasy. Causes trouble.'

Adam said, 'Remember that Samuels girl? She was real pretty. What happened to her?'

'Same thing. Just caused trouble. She went away. I heard she's living in Philadelphia. Does dressmaking. I heard she gets ten dollars just for making one dress.'

'Maybe we ought to get away from here,' Adam said.

Charles said, 'Still thinking of California?'

'I guess so.'

Charles's temper tore in two. 'I want you out of here!' he shouted. 'I want you to get off the place. I'll buy you or sell you or anything. Get out, you son-of-a-bitch–' He stopped. 'I guess I don't mean that last. But goddam it, you make me nervous.'

'I'll go,' said Adam.

3

In three months Charles got a coloured picture-postcard of the bay at Rio, and Adam had written on the back with a splottery pen, 'It's summer here when it's winter there. Why don't you come down?

Six months later there was another card, from Buenos Aires. 'Dear Charles–my God this is a big city. They speak French and Spanish both. I'm sending you a book.'

But no book came. Charles looked for it all the following winter and well into the spring. And instead of the book Adam arrived. He was brown and his clothes had a foreign look.

'How are you?' Charles asked.

'Fine. Did you get the book?'

'No.'

'I wonder what happened to it? It had pictures.'

'Going to stay?'

'I guess so. I'll tell you about that country.'

'I don't want to hear about it,' said Charles.

'Christ, you're mean,' said Adam.

'I can just see it all over again. You'll stay around a year or so and then you'll get restless and you'll make me restless. We'll get mad at each other and then we'll get polite to each other–and that's worse. Then we'll blow up and you'll go away again, and then you'll come back and we'll do it all over again.'

Adam asked, 'Don't you want me to stay?'

'Hell, yes,' said Charles. 'I miss you when you're not here. But I can see how it's going to be just the same.'

And it was just that way. For a while they reviewed old times, for a while they recounted the times when they were apart, and finally they lapsed into the long ugly silences, the hours of speechless work, the guarded courtesy, the flashes of anger. There were no boundaries to time, so that it seemed endless passing.

On an evening Adam said, 'You know, I'm going to be thirty-seven. That's half a life.'

'Here it comes,' said Charles. 'Wasting your life. Look, Adam, could we not have a fight this time?'

'How do you mean?'

'Well, if we run true to form we'll fight for three or four weeks, getting you ready to go away. If you're getting restless, couldn't you just go away and save all the trouble?'

Adam laughed and the tension went out of the room. 'I've got a pretty smart brother,' he said. 'Sure, when I get the itch bad enough I'll go without fighting. Yes, I like that, You're getting rich, aren't you, Charles?'

'I'm doing all right. I wouldn't say rich.'

'You wouldn't say you bought four buildings and the inn in the village?'

'No, I wouldn't say it.'

'But you did. Charles, you've made this about the prettiest farm anywhere about. Why don't we build a new house–bath-tub and running water and a water-closet? We're not poor people any more. Why, they say you're nearly the richest man in this section.'

'We don't need a new house,' Charles said gruffly. 'You take your fancy ideas away.'

'It would be nice to go to the toilet without going outside.'

'You take your fancy ideas away.'

Adam was amused. 'Maybe I'll build a pretty little house right over by the wood-lot. Say, how would that be? Then we wouldn't get on each other's nerves.'

'I don't want it on the place.'

'The place is half mine.'

'I'll buy you out.'

'But I don't have to sell.'

Charles eyes blazed. 'I'll burn your goddam house down.'

'I believe you would,' Adam said, suddenly sobered. 'I believe you really would. What are you looking like that for?'

Charles said slowly. 'I've thought about it a lot. And I've wanted for you to bring it up. I guess you aren't ever going to.'

'What do you mean?'

'You remember when you sent me a telegram for a hundred dollars?'

'You bet I do. Saved my life, I guess. Why?'

'You never paid it back.'

'I must have.'

'You didn't.'

Adam looked down at the old table where Cyrus had sat, knocking on his wooden leg with a stick. And the old oil-lamp was hanging over the centre of the table, shedding its unstable yellow light from the round Rochester wick.

Adam said slowly, 'I'll pay you in the morning.'

'I gave you plenty of time to offer.'

'Sure you did, Charles. I should have remembered.' He paused, considering, and at last he said. 'You don't know why I needed the money.'

'I never asked.'

'And I never told. Maybe I was ashamed. I was a prisoner, Charles. I broke jail–I escaped.'

Charles's mouth was open. 'What are you talking about?'

'I'm going to tell you. I was a tramp and I got taken for vagrancy and put on a road gang–leg-irons at night. Got out in six months and picked right up again. That's how they get their roads built. I served three days less than the second six months and then I escaped–got over the Georgia line, robbed a store for clothes, and sent you the telegram.'

'I don't believe you,' Charles said. 'Yes, I do. You don't tell lies. Of course I believe you. Why didn't you tell me?'

'Maybe I was ashamed. But I'm ashamed that I didn't pay you.'

'Oh, forget it,' said Charles. 'I don't know why I mentioned it.'

'Good God, no. I'll pay you in the morning.'

'I'll be damned,' said Charles. 'My brother a jail-bird!'

'You don't have to look so happy.'

'I don't know why,' said Charles, 'but it makes me kind of proud. My brother a jail-bird! Tell me this, Adam–why did you wait till just three days before they let you go to make your break?'

Adam smiled. 'Two or three reasons,' he said. 'I was afraid if I served out my time, why, they'd pick me up again. And I figured if I waited till the end they wouldn't expect me to run away.'

'That makes sense,' said Charles. 'But you said there was one more reason.'

'I guess the other was the most important,' Adam said, 'and it's the hardest to explain. I figured I owed the state six months. That was the sentence. I didn't feel right about cheating. I only cheated three days.'

Charles exploded with laughter. 'You're a crazy son-of-a-bitch,' he said with affection. 'But you say you robbed a store.'

'I sent the money back with ten per cent interest,' Adam said.

Charles leaned forward. 'Tell me about the road gang, Adam.'

'Sure I will, Charles. Sure I will.'

CHAPTER 11

I

Charles had more respect for Adam after he knew about the prison. He felt the warmth for his brother you can feel only for one who is not perfect and therefore no target for your hatred. Adam took some advantage of it too. He tempted Charles.

'Did you ever think, Charles, that we've got enough money to do anything we want to do?'

'All right, what do we want?'

'We could go to Europe, we could walk around Paris.'

'What's that?'

'What's what?'

'I thought I heard something on the stoop.'

'Probably a cat.'

'I guess so. Have to kill off some of them pretty soon.'

'Charles, we could go to Egypt and walk around the Sphinx.'

'We could stay right here and make some good use of our money. And we could get to hell out to work and make some use of the day. Those goddam cats!' Charles jumped to the door and yanked it open and said, 'Get!' Then he was silent, and Adam saw him staring at the steps. He moved beside him.

A dirty bundle of rags and mud was trying to worm its way up the steps. One skinny hand clawed slowly at the stairs. The other dragged helplessly. There was a caked face with cracked lips and eyes peering out of swollen, blackened lids. The forehead was laid open, oozing blood back into the matted hair.

Adam went down the stairs and kneeled beside the figure. 'Give me a hand,' he said. 'Come on, let's get her in. Here–look out for that arm. It looks broken.'

She fainted when they carried her in.

'Put her in my bed,' Adam said. 'Now I think you better go for the doctor.'

'Don't you think we better hitch up and take her in?'

'Move her? No. Are you crazy?'

'Maybe not as crazy as you. Think about it a minute.'

'For God's sake, think about what?'

'Two men living alone and they've got this in their house.'

Adam was shocked. 'You don't mean it.'

'I mean it all right. I think we better take her in. It'll be all over the county in two hours. How do you know what she is? How'd she get here? What happened to her? Adam, you're taking an awful chance.'

Adam said coldly, 'If you don't go now, I'll go and leave you here.'

'I think you're making a mistake. I'll go, but I tell you we'll suffer for it.'

'I'll do the suffering,' said Adam. 'You go.'

After Charles left, Adam went to the kitchen and poured hot water from the tea-kettle into a basin. In his bedroom he dampened a handkerchief in the water and loosened the caked blood and dirt on the girl's face. She reeled up to consciousness and her blue eyes glinted at him. His mind went back–it was this room, this bed. His step-mother was standing over him with a damp cloth in her hand, and he could feel the little running pains as the water cut through. And she had said something over and over. He heard it, but he could not remember what it was.

'You'll be all right,' he said to the girl. 'We're getting a doctor. He'll be here right off.'

Her lips moved a little.

'Don't try to talk,' he said. 'Don't try to say anything.' As he worked gently with his cloth a huge warmth crept over him. 'You can stay here,' he said. 'You can stay here as long as you want. I'll take care of you.' He squeezed out the cloth and sponged her matted hair and lifted it out of the gashes in her scalp.

He could hear himself talking as he worked, almost as though he were a stranger listening. 'There, does that hurt? The poor eyes–I'll put some brown paper over your eyes. You'll be all right. That's a bad one on your forehead.

I'm afraid you'll have a scar there. Could you tell me your name? No, don't try. There's lots of time. There's lots of time. Do you hear that? That's the doctor's rig. Wasn't that quick?' He moved to the kitchen door. 'In here, Doc. She's in here,' he called.

2

She was very badly hurt. If there had been X-rays in that time the doctor might have found more injuries than he did. As it was he found enough. Her left arm and three ribs were broken and her jaw was cracked. Her skull was cracked too, and the teeth on the left side were missing. Her scalp was ripped and torn and her forehead laid open to the skull. So much the doctor could see and identify. He set her arm, taped her ribs, and sewed up her scalp. With a pipette and an alcohol flame he bent a glass tube to go through the aperture where a tooth was missing so that she could drink and take liquid food without moving her cracked jaw. He gave her a large shot of morphine, left a bottle of opium pills, washed his hands, and put on his coat. His patient was asleep before he left the room.

In the kitchen he sat down at the table and drank the hot coffee Charles put in front of him.

'All right, what happened to her?' he asked.

'How do we know?' Charles said truculently. 'We found her on our porch. If you want to see, go look at the marks on the road where she dragged herself.'

'Know who she is?'

'God, no.'

'You go upstairs at the inn–is she anybody from there?'

'I haven't been there lately. I couldn't recognize her in that condition, anyway.'

The doctor turned his head towards Adam. 'You ever see her before?'

Adam shook his head slowly.

Charles said harshly, 'Say, what you mousing around at?'

'I'll tell you, since you're interested. That girl didn't fall under a harrow even if she looks that way. Somebody did that to her, somebody who didn't like her at all. If you want the truth, somebody tried to kill her.'

'Why don't you ask her?' Charles said.

'She won't be talking for quite a while. Besides, her skull is cracked, and God knows what that will do to her. What I'm getting at is, should I bring the sheriff into it?'

'No!' Adam spoke so explosively that the two looked at him. 'Let her alone. Let her rest.'

'Who's going to take care of her?'

'I am,' said Adam.

'Now, you look here–' Charles began.

'Keep out of it!'

'It's my place as much as yours.'

'Do you want me to go?'

'I didn't mean that.'

'Well, I'll go if she has to go.'

The doctor said, 'Steady down. What makes you so interested?'

'I wouldn't put a hurt dog out.'

'You wouldn't get mad about it either. Are you holding something back? Did you go out last night? Did you do it?'

'He was here all night,' said Charles. 'He snores like a goddam train.'

Adam said, 'Why can't you let her be? Let her get well.'

The doctor stood up and dusted his hands. 'Adam,' he said, 'your father was one of my oldest friends. I know you and your family. You aren't stupid. I don't know why you don't recognize ordinary facts, but you don't seem to. Have to talk to you like a baby. That girl was assaulted. I believe whoever did it tried to kill her. If I don't tell the sheriff about it, I'm breaking the law. I admit I break a few, but not that one.'

'Well, tell him. But don't let him bother her until she's better.'

'It's not my habit to let my patients be bothered,' the doctor said. 'You still want to keep her here?'

'Yes.'

'Your funeral. I'll look in tomorrow. She'll sleep. Give her water and warm soup through the tube if she wants it.' He stalked out.

Charles turned on his brother. 'Adam, for God's sake, what is this?'

'Let me alone.'

'What's got into you?'

'Let me alone–you hear? Just let me alone.'

'Christ!' said Charles, and spat on the floor and went restlessly and uneasily to work.

Adam was glad he was gone. He moved about the kitchen, washed the breakfast dishes, and swept the floor. When he had put the kitchen to rights he went in and drew a chair up to the bed. The girl snored thickly through the morphine. The swelling was going down on her face, but the eyes were blackened and swollen. Adam sat very still, looking at her. Her set and splinted arm lay on her stomach, but her right arm lay on top of the coverlet, the fingers curled like a nest. It was a child's hand, almost a baby's hand. Adam touched her wrist with his finger, and her fingers moved a little in reflex. Her wrist was warm. Secretly then, as though he were afraid he might be caught, he straightened her hand and touched the little cushion pads on the fingertips. Her fingers were pink and soft, but the skin on the back of her hand seemed to have an underbloom like a pearl. Adam chuckled with delight. Her breathing stopped and he became electrically alert–then her throat clicked and the rhythmed snoring continued. Gently he worked her hand and arm under the cover before he tiptoed out of the room.

For several days Cathy lay in a cave of shock and opium. Her skin felt like lead, and she moved very little because of the pain. She was aware of movement around her. Gradually her head and eyes cleared. Two young men were with her, one occasionally and the other a great deal. She knew that another man who came in was the doctor, and there was also a tall lean man, who interested her more than any of the others, and the interest grew out of fear. Perhaps in her drugged sleep she had picked something up and stored it.

Very slowly her mind assembled the last days and rearranged them. She saw the face of Mr Edwards, saw it lose its placid self-sufficiency and dissolve into murder. She had never been so afraid before in her life, but she had learned fear now. And her mind sniffed about like a rat looking for an escape. Mr Edwards knew about the fire. Did anyone else? And how did he know? A blind nauseating terror rose in her when she thought of that.

From things she heard she learned that the tall man was the sheriff and wanted to question her, and that the young man named Adam was protecting her from the questioning. Maybe the sheriff knew about the fire.

Raised voices gave her the cue to her method. The sheriff said, 'She must have a name. Somebody must know her.'

'How could she answer? Her jaw is broken.' Adam's voice.

'If she's right-handed she could spell out the answers. Look here, Adam, if somebody tried to kill her I'd better catch him while I can. Just give me a pencil and let me talk to her.'

Adam said, 'You heard the doctor say her skull was cracked. How do you know she can remember?'

'Well, you give me a paper and pencil and we'll see.'

'I don't want you to bother her.'

'Adam, goddam it, it doesn't matter what you want. I'm telling you I want a paper and pencil.'

Then the other young man's voice. 'What's the matter with you? You make it sound like it was you who did it. Give him a pencil.'

She had her eyes closed when the three men came quietly into her room.

'She's asleep,' Adam whispered.

She opened her eyes and looked at them.

The tall man came to the side of the bed. 'I don't want to bother you, Miss. I'm the sheriff. I know you can't talk, but will you just write some things on this?'

She tried to nod and winced with pain. She blinked her eyes rapidly to indicate assent.

'That's the girl,' said the sheriff. 'You see? She wants to.' He put the tablet on the bed beside her and moulded her fingers around the pencil. 'There we are. Now. What is your name?'

The three men watched her face. Her mouth grew thin and her eyes squinted. She closed her eyes and the pencil began to move. 'I don't know,' it scrawled in huge letters.

'Here, now there's a fresh sheet. What do you remember?'

'All black. Can't think,' the pencil wrote before it went over the edge of the tablet.

'Don't you remember who you are, where you came from? Think!

She seemed to go through a great struggle and then her face gave up and became tragic. 'No. Mixed up. Help me.'

'Poor child,' the sheriff said. 'I thank you for trying, anyway. When you get better we'll try again. No, you don't have to write any more.'

The pencil wrote, 'Thank you,' and fell from her fingers.

She had won the sheriff. He ranged himself with Adam. Only Charles was against her. When the brothers were in her room, and it took two of them to help her on the bed-pan without hurting her, she studied Charles's dark sullenness. He had something in his face that she recognized, that made her uneasy. She saw that he touched the scar on his forehead very often, rubbed it, and drew its outline with his fingers. Once he caught her watching. He looked guiltily at his fingers. Charles said brutally, 'Don't you worry. You're going to have one like it, maybe even a better one.'

She smiled at him, and he looked away. When Adam came in with her warm soup Charles said, 'I'm going in town and drink some beer.'

3

Adam couldn't remember ever having been so happy. It didn't bother him that he did not know her name. She had said to call her Cathy, and that was enough for him. He cooked for Cathy, going through recipes used by his mother and his step-mother.

Cathy's vitality was great. She began to recover very quickly. The swelling went out of her cheeks and the prettiness of convalescence came to her face. In a short time she could be helped to a sitting position. She opened and closed her mouth very carefully, and she began to eat soft foods that required little chewing. The bandage was still on her forehead, but the rest of her face was little marked except for the hollow cheek on the side where the teeth were missing.

Cathy was in trouble and her mind ranged for a way out of it. She spoke little, even when it was not so difficult.

One afternoon she heard someone moving around in the kitchen. She called, 'Adam, is it you?'

Charles's voice answered, 'No, it's me.'

'Would you come in here just for a minute, please?'

He stood in the doorway. His eyes were sullen.

'You don't come in much,' she said.

'That's right.'

'You don't like me.'

'I guess that's right too.'

'Will you tell me why?'

He struggled to find an answer. 'I don't trust you.'

'Why not?'

'I don't know. And I don't believe you lost your memory.'

'But why should I lie?'

'I don't know. That's why I don't trust you. There's something–I almost recognize.'

'You never saw me in your life.'

'Maybe not. But there's something that bothers me–that I ought to know. And how do you know I never saw you?'

She was silent, and he moved to leave. 'Don't go,' she said. 'What do you intend to do?'

'About what?'

'About me.'

He regarded her with a new interest. 'You want the truth?'

'Why else should I ask?'

'I don't know, but I'll tell you. I'm going to get you out of here just as soon as I can. My brother's turned fool, but I'll bring him round if I have to lick him.'

'Could you do that? He's a big man.'

'I could do it.'

She regarded him levelly. 'Where is Adam?'

'Gone in town to get some more of your goddam medicine.'

'You're a mean man.'

'You know what I think? I don't think I'm half as mean as you are under that nice skin. I think you're a devil.'

She laughed softly. 'That makes two of us,' she said. 'Charles, how long do I have?'

'For what?'

'How long before you put me out? Tell me truly.'

'All right, I will. About a week or ten days. Soon as you can get around.'

'Suppose I don't go.'

He regarded her craftily, almost with pleasure at the thought of combat. 'All right, I'll tell you. When you had all that dope you talked a lot, like in your sleep.'

'I don't believe that.'

He laughed, for he had seen the quick tightening of her mouth. 'All right, don't. And if you just go about your business as soon as you can, I won't tell. But if you don't, you'll know all right, and so will the sheriff.'

'I don't believe I said anything bad. What could I say?'

'I won't argue with you. And I've got work to do. You asked me and I told you.'

He went outside. Back of the hen-house he leaned over and laughed and slapped his leg. 'I thought she was smarter,' he said to himself. And he felt more easy than he had for days.

4

Charles had frightened her badly. And if he had recognized her, so had she recognized him. He was the only person she had ever met who played it her way. Cathy followed his thinking, and it did not reassure her. She knew that her tricks would not work with him, and she needed protection and rest. Her money was gone. She had to be sheltered, and would have to be, for a long time. She was tired and sick, but her mind went skipping among possibilities.

Adam came back from town with a bottle of Pain Killer. He poured a tablespoonful. 'This will taste horrible,' he said. 'It's good stuff though.'

She took it without protest, did not even make much of a face about it. 'You're good to me,' she said. 'I wonder why. I've brought you trouble.'

'You have not. You've brightened up the whole house. Never complain or anything, hurt as bad as you are.'

'You're so good, so kind.'

'I want to be.'

'Do you have to go out? Couldn't you stay and talk to me?'

'Sure I could. There's nothing so important to do.'

'Draw up a chair, Adam, and sit down.'

When he was seated she stretched her right hand towards him, and he took it in both of his. 'So good and kind,' she repeated. 'Adam, you keep promises, don't you?'

'I try to. What are you thinking about?'

'I'm alone and I'm afraid,' she cried. 'I'm afraid.'

'Can't I help you?'

'I don't think anyone can help me.'

'Tell me and let me try.'

'That's the worst part. I can't even tell you.'

'Why not? If it's a secret I won't tell it.'

'It's not my secret, don't you see?'

'No, I don't.'

Her fingers gripped his hand tightly. 'Adam, I didn't ever lose my memory.'

'Then why did you say–'

'That's what I'm trying to tell you. Did you love your father, Adam?'

'I guess I revered him more than loved him.'

'Well, if someone you revered were in trouble, wouldn't you do anything to save him from destruction?'

'Well, sure. I guess I would.'

'Well, that's how it is with me.'

'But how did you get hurt?'

'That's part of it. That's why I can't tell.'

'Was it your father?'

'Oh, no. But it's all tied up together.'

'You mean, if you tell me who hurt you, then your father will be in trouble?'

She sighed. He would make up the story himself. 'Adam, will you trust me?'

'Of course.'

'It's an awful thing to ask.'

'No, it isn't, not if you're protecting your father.'

'You understand, it's not my secret. If it were I'd tell you in a minute.'

'Of course I understand. I'd do the same thing myself.'

'Oh, you understand so much.' Tears welled up in her eyes. He leaned down towards her, and she kissed him on the cheek.

'Don't you worry,' he said, 'I'll take care of you.'

She lay back against the pillow. 'I don't think you can.'

'What do you mean?'

'Well, your brother doesn't like me. He wants me to get out of here.'

'Did he tell you that?'

'Oh, no. I can just feel it. He hasn't your understanding.'

'He has a good heart.'

'I know that, but he doesn't have your kindness. And when I have to go–the sheriff is going to begin asking questions and I'll be all alone.'

He stared into space. 'My brother can't make you go. I own half of this farm. I have my own money.'

'If he wanted me to go I would have to. I can't spoil your life.'

Adam stood up and strode out of the room. He went to the back door and looked out on the afternoon. Far off in the field his brother was lifting stones from a sled and piling them on the stone wall. Adam looked up at the sky. A blanket of herring clouds was rolling in from the east. He sighed deeply and his breath made a tickling, exciting feeling in his chest. His ears seemed suddenly clear, so that he heard the chickens cackling and the east wind blowing over the ground. He heard horses' hoofs plodding on the road and far-off pounding on wood where a neighbour was shingling a barn. And all these sounds related into a kind of music. His eyes were clear too. Fences and walls and sheds stood staunchly out in the yellow afternoon, and they were related too. There was change in everything. A flight of sparrows dropped into the dust and scrabbled for bits of food and then flew off like a grey scarf twisting in the light. Adam looked back at his brother. He had lost track of time and he did not know how long he had been standing in the doorway.

No time had passed. Charles was still struggling with the same large stone. And Adam had not released the full, held breath he had taken when time stopped.

Suddenly he knew joy and sorrow felted into one fabric. Courage and fear were one thing too. He found that he had started to hum a droning little tune. He turned, walked through the kitchen, and stood in the doorway, looking at Cathy. She smiled weakly at him, and he thought, What a child! What a helpless child! and a surge of love filled him.

'Will you marry me?' he asked.

Her face tightened and her hand closed convulsively.

'You don't have to tell me now,' he said. 'I want you to think about it. But if you would marry me I could protect you. No one could hurt you again.'

Cathy recovered an instant. 'Come here, Adam. There, sit down. Here, give me your hand. That's good, that's right.' She raised his hand and put the back of it against her cheek. 'My dear,' she said brokenly. 'Oh, my dear. Look, Adam, you have trusted me. Now will you promise me something? Will you promise not to tell your brother you have asked me?'

'Ask you to marry me? Why shouldn't I?'

'It's not that. I want this night to think. I'll want maybe more than this night. Could you let me do that?' She raised her hand to her head. 'You know, I'm not sure I can think straight. And I want to.'

'Do you think you might marry me?'

'Please, Adam. Let me alone to think. Please, my dear.'

He smiled and said nervously, 'Don't make it long. I'm kind of like a cat up a tree so far he can't come down.'

'Just let me think. And, Adam–you're a kind man.'

He went outside and walked towards where his brother was loading stones.

When he was gone Cathy got up from her bed and moved unsteadily to the bureau. She leaned forward and looked at her face. The bandage was still on her forehead. She raised the edge of it enough to see the angry red underneath. She had not only made up her mind to marry Adam but she had so decided before he had asked her. She was afraid. She needed protection and money. Adam could give her both. And she could control him–she knew that. She did not want to be married, but for the time being it was a refuge. Only one thing bothered her. Adam had a warmth towards her which she did not understand since she had none towards him, nor had ever experienced it towards anyone. And Mr Edwards had really frightened her. That had been the only time in her life she had lost control of a situation. She determined never to let it happen again. She smiled to herself when she thought what Charles would say. She felt a kinship to Charles. She didn't mind his suspicion of her.

5

Charles straightened up when Adam approached. He put his palms against the small of his back and massaged the tired muscles. 'My God, there's lot of rocks,' he said.

'Fellow in the army told me there's valleys in California–miles and miles–and you can't find a stone, not even a little one.'

'There'll be something else,' said Charles. 'I don't think there's any farm without something wrong with it. Out in the Middle West it's locusts, someplace else it's tornadoes. What's a few stones?'

'I guess you're right. I thought I would give you a hand.'

'That's nice of you. I thought you'd spend the rest of your life holding hands with that in there. How long is she going to stay?'

Adam was on the point of telling him of his proposal, but the tone of Charles's voice made him change his mind.

'Say,' Charles said, 'Alex Platt came by a little while ago. You'd never think what happened to him. He's found a fortune.'

'How do you mean?'

'Well, you know the place on his property where that clump of cedars sticks out–you know, right on the country road?'

'I know. What about it?'

'Alex went in between those trees and his stone wall. He was hunting rabbits. He found a suitcase and a man's clothes all packed nice. Soaked up with rain, though. Looked like it had been there some time. And there was a wooden box with a lock, and when he broke it open there was near four thousand dollars in it. And he found a purse too. There wasn't anything in it.'

'No name or anything?'

'That's the strange part–no name; no name on the clothes, no labels on the suits. It's just like the fellow didn't want to be traced.'

'Is Alex going to keep it?'

'He took it to the sheriff, and the sheriff is going to advertise it, and if nobody answers, Alex can keep it.'

'Somebody's sure to claim it.'

'I guess so. I didn't tell Alex that. He's feeling so good about it. That's funny about no labels–not cut out, just didn't have any.'

'That's a lot of money,' Adam said. 'Somebody's bound to claim it.'

'Alex hung around for a while. You know, his wife goes around a lot.' Charles was silent. 'Adam,' he said finally, 'we got to have a talk. The whole county's doing plenty of talking.'

'What about? What do you mean?'

'Goddam it, about that–that girl. Two men can't have a girl living with them. Alex says the women are pretty riled up about it. Adam, we can't have it. We live here. We've got a good name.'

'You want me to throw her out before she's well?'

'I want you to get rid of her–get her out. I don't like her.'

'You never have.'

'I know it. I don't trust her. There's something–something–I don't know what it is, but I don't like it. When you going to get her out?'

'Tell you what,' Adam said slowly. 'Give her one more week and then I'll do something about her.'

'You promise?'

'Sure I promise.'

'Well, that's something. I'll get the word to Alex's wife. From there on she'll handle the news. Good Lord, I'll be glad to have the house to ourselves again. I don't suppose her memory's come back?'

'No,' said Adam.

6

Five days later, when Charles had gone to buy some calf feed, Adam drove the buggy to the kitchen steps. He helped Cathy in, tucked the blanket around her knees, and put another around her shoulders. He drove to the county seat and was married to her by a justice of the peace.

Charles was home when they returned. He looked sourly at them when they came into the kitchen. 'I thought you'd took her in to put her on the train.'

'We got married,' Adam said simply.

Cathy smiled at Charles.

'Why? Why did you do it?'

'Why not? Can't a man get married?'

Cathy went quickly into the bedroom and closed the door.

Charles began to rave. 'She's no damned good, I tell you. She's a whore.'

'Charles!'

'I tell you, she's just a two-bit whore. I wouldn't trust her with a bit piece–why, that bitch, that slut!'

'Charles, stop it! Stop it, I tell you! Keep your filthy mouth shut about my wife!'

'She's no more a wife than an alley cat.'

Adam said slowly, 'I think you're jealous, Charles. I think you wanted to marry her.'

'Why, you goddam fool! Me jealous? I won't live in the same house with her!'

Adam said evenly, 'You won't have to. I'm going away. You can buy me out if you want. You can have the farm. You always wanted it. You can stay here and rot.'

Charles's voice lowered. 'Won't you get rid of her? Please, Adam. Throw her out. She'll tear you to pieces. She'll destroy you, Adam, she'll destroy you!'

'How do you know so much about her?'

Charles's eyes were bleak. 'I don't,' he said, and his mouth snapped shut.

Adam did not even ask Cathy whether she wanted to come out for dinner. He carried two plates into the bedroom and sat beside her.

'We're going to go away,' he said.

'Let me go away. Please, let me. I don't want to make you hate your brother. I wonder why he hates me!'

'I think he's jealous.'

Her eyes narrowed. 'Jealous?'

'That's what it looks like to me. You don't have to worry. We're getting out. We're going to California.'

She said quietly, 'I don't want to go to California.'

'Nonsense. Why, it's nice there, sun all the time and beautiful.'

'I don't want to go to California.'

'You are my wife,' he said softly. 'I want you to go with me.'

She was silent and did not speak of it again.

They heard Charles slam out the door, and Adam said, 'That will be good for him. He'll get a little drunk and he'll feel better.'

Cathy modestly looked at her fingers. 'Adam, I can't be a wife to you until I'm well.'

'I know,' he said. 'I understand. I'll wait.'

'But I want you to stay with me. I'm afraid of Charles. He hates me so.'

'I'll bring my cot in here. Then you can call me if you're frightened. You can reach out and touch me.'

'You're so good,' she said. 'Could we have some tea?'

'Why, sure, I'd like some myself.' He brought the steaming cups in and went back for the sugar bowl. He settled himself in a chair near her bed. 'It's pretty strong. Is it too strong for you?'

'I like it strong.'

He finished his cup. 'Does it taste strange to you? It's got a funny taste.'

Her hand flew to her mouth. 'Oh, let me taste it.' She sipped the dregs. 'Adam,' she cried, 'you got the wrong cup–that was mine. It had my medicine in it.'

He licked his lips. 'I guess it can't hurt me.'

'No, it can't.' She laughed softly. 'I hope I don't need to call you in the night.'

'What do you mean?'

'Well, you drank my sleeping medicine. Maybe you wouldn't wake up easily.'

Adam went down into a heavy opium sleep, though he fought to stay awake. 'Did the doctor tell you to take this much?' he asked thickly.

'You're just not used to it,' she said.

Charles came back at eleven o'clock. Cathy heard his tipsy footsteps. He went into his room, flung off his clothes, and got into bed. He grunted and turned, trying to get comfortable, and then he opened his eyes. Cathy was standing by his bed. 'What do you want?'

'What do you think? Move over a little.'

'Where's Adam?'

'He drank my sleeping medicine by mistake. Move over a little.'

He breathed harshly. 'I already been with a whore.'

'You're a pretty strong boy. Move over a little.'

'How about your broken arm?'

'I'll take care of that. It's not your worry.'

Suddenly Charles laughed. 'The poor bastard,' he said, and he threw back the blanket to receive her.

PART II

CHAPTER 12

You can see how this book has reached a great boundary that was called 1900. Another hundred years were ground up and churned, and what had happened was all muddied by the way folks wanted it to be–more rich and meaningful the farther back it was. In the books of some memories it was the best time that ever sloshed over the world–the old time, the gay time, sweet and simple, as though time were young and fearless. Old men who didn't know whether they were going to stagger over the boundary of the century looked forward to it with distaste. For the world was changing, and sweetness was gone, and virtue too. Worry had crept on a corroding world, and what was lost–good manners, ease, and beauty? Ladies were not ladies any more, and you couldn't trust a gentleman's word.

There was a time when people kept their fly-buttons fastened. And man's freedom was boiling off. And even childhood was not good any more–not the way it was. No worry then but how to find a good stone, not round exactly but flattened and water-shaped, to use in a sling pouch cut from a discarded shoe. Where did all the good stones go, and all simplicity?

A man's mind vagued up a little, for how can you remember the feeling of pleasure or pain or choking emotion? You can remember only that you had them. An elder man might truly recall through water the delicate doctor-testing of little girls, but such a man forgets, and wants to, the acid emotion eating at the spleen so that a boy had to put his face flat down in the young wild oats and drum his fists against the ground and sob 'Christ! Christ!' Such a man might say, and did, 'What's that damned kid lying out there in the grass for? He'll catch a cold.'

Oh, strawberries don't taste as they used to and the thighs of women have lost their clutch!

And some men eased themselves like setting hens into the nest of death.

History was secreted in the glands of a million historians. We must get out of this banged-up century, some said, out of this cheating, murderous century of riot and secret death, of scrabbling for public lands and damn well getting them by any means at all.

Think back, recall our little nation fringing the oceans, torn with complexities, too big for its britches. Just got going when the British took us on again. We beat them, but it didn't do us much good. What we had was a burned White House and ten thousand widows on the public pension list.

Then the soldiers went to Mexico and it was a kind of painful picnic.

Nobody knows why you go to a picnic to be uncomfortable when it is so easy and pleasant to eat at home. The Mexican War did two good things though. We got a lot of western land, damn near doubled our size, and besides that it was a training ground for generals, so that when the sad self-murder settled on us the leaders knew the techniques for making it properly horrible.

And then the arguments:

Can you keep a slave?

Well, if you bought him in good faith, why not?

Next they'll be saying a man can't have a horse. Who is it wants to take my property?

And there we were, like a man scratching at his own face and bleeding into his own beard.

Well, that was over and we got slowly up off the bloody ground and started westward.

There came boom and bust, bankruptcy, depression.

Great public thieves came along and picked the pockets of everyone who had a pocket.

To hell with that rotten century!

Let's get it over and the door closed shut on it! Let's close it like a book and go on reading! New chapter, new life. A man will have clean hands once we get the lid slammed shut on that stinking century. It's a fair thing ahead. There's no rot on this clean new hundred years. It's not stacked, and any bastard who deals seconds from this new deck of years–why, we'll crucify him head-down over a privy.

Oh, but strawberries will never taste so good again and the thighs of women have lost their clutch!

CHAPTER 13

I

Sometimes a kind of glory lights up in the mind of a man. It happens to nearly everyone. You can feel it growing or preparing like a fuse burning towards dynamite. It is a feeling in the stomach, a delight of the nerves, of the forearms. The skin tastes the air, and every deep-drawn breath is sweet. Its beginning has the pleasure of a great stretching yawn; it flashes in the brain and the whole world glows outside your eyes. A man may have lived all of his life in the grey, and the land and trees of him dark and sombre. The events, even the important ones, may have trooped by, faceless and pale. And then–the glory–so that a cricket song sweetens his ears, the smell of the earth rises chanting to his nose, and dappling light under a tree blesses his eyes. Then a man pours outward, a torrent of him, and yet he is not diminished. And I guess a man's importance in the world can be measured by the quality and number of his glories. It is a lonely thing, but it relates us to the world. It is the mother of all creativeness, and it sets each man separate from all other men.

I don't know how it will be in the years to come. There are monstrous changes taking place in the world, forces shaping a future whose face we do not know. Some of these forces seem evil to us, perhaps not in themselves but because their tendency is to eliminate other things we hold good. It is true that two men can lift a bigger stone than one man. A group can build automobiles quicker and better than one man, and bread from a huge factory is cheaper and more uniform. When our food and clothing and housing are all born in the complication of mass production, mass method is bound to get into our thinking and to eliminate all other thinking. In our time mass or collective production has entered our economics, our politics, and even our religion, so that some nations have substituted the idea collective for the idea God. This in my time is the danger. There is great tension in the world, tension towards a breaking point, and men are unhappy and confused.

At such a time it seems natural and good to me to ask myself these questions. What do I believe in? What must I fight for and what must I fight against?

Our species is the only creative species, and it has only one creative instrument, the individual mind and spirit of a man. Nothing was ever created by two men. There are no good collaborations, whether in music, in art, in poetry, in mathematics, in philosophy. Once the miracle of creation has taken place, the group can build and extend it, but the group never invents anything. The preciousness lies in the lonely mind of a man.

And now the forces marshalled around the concept of the group have declared a war of extermination on that preciousness, the mind of man. By disparagement, by starvation, by repressions, forced direction, and the stunning hammer-blows of conditioning, the free, roving mind is being pursued, roped, blunted, drugged. It is a sad suicidal course our species seems to have taken.

And this I believe: that the free, exploring mind of the individual human is the most valuable thing in the world. And this I would fight for: the freedom of the mind to take any direction it wishes, undirected. And this I must fight against: any idea, religion, or government which limits or destroys the individual. This is what I am and what I am about. I can understand why a system built on a pattern must try to destroy the free mind, for that is one thing which can by inspection destroy such a system. Surely I can understand this, and I hate it and I will fight against it to preserve the only thing that separates us from the uncreative beasts. If the glory can be killed, we are lost.

2

Adam Trask grew up in greyness, and the curtains of his life were like dusty cobwebs, and his days a slow file of half-sorrows and sick dissatisfactions, and then, through Cathy, the glory came to him.

It doesn't matter that Cathy was what I have called a monster. Perhaps we can't understand Cathy, but on the other hand we are capable of many things in all directions, of great virtues and great sins. And who in his mind has not probed the black water?

Maybe we all have in us a secret pond where evil and ugly things germinate and grow strong. But this culture is fenced, and the swimming brood climbs up only to fall back. Might it not be that in the dark pools of some men the evil grows strong enough to wriggle over the fence and swim free? Would not such a man be our monster, and are we not related to him in our hidden water? It would be absurd if we did not understand both angels and devils, since we invented them.

Whatever Cathy may have been, she set off the glory in Adam. His spirit rose flying and released him from fear and bitterness and rancid memories. The glory lights up the world and changes it the way a star-shell changes a battleground. Perhaps Adam did not see Cathy at all, so lighted was she by his eyes. Burned in his mind was an image of beauty and tenderness, a sweet and holy girl, precious beyond thinking, clean and loving, and that image was Cathy to her husband, and nothing Cathy did or said could warp Adam's Cathy.

She said she did not want to go to California and he did not listen, because *his* Cathy took his arm and started first. So bright was his glory that he did not notice the sullen pain in his brother, did not see the glinting in his brother's eyes. He sold his share of the farm to Charles, for less than it was worth, and with that and his half of his father's money he was free and rich.

The brothers were strangers now. They shook hands at the station, and Charles watched the train pull out and rubbed his scar. He went to the inn, drank four quick whiskies, and climbed the stairs to the top floor. He paid the girl and then could not perform. He cried in her arms until she put him out. He raged at his farm, forced it, added to it, drilled and trimmed, and his boundaries extended. He took no rest, no recreation, and he became rich without pleasure and respected without friends.

Adam stopped in New York long enough to buy clothes for himself and Cathy before they climbed on the train which bore them across the continent. How they happened to go to the Salinas Valley is very easy to understand.

In that day the railroads–growing, fighting among themselves, striving to increase and to dominate–used every means to increase their traffic. The companies not only advertised in the newspapers, they issued booklets and broadsides describing and picturing the beauty and richness of the West. No claim was too extravagant–wealth was unlimited. The Southern Pacific Railroad, headed by the wild energy of Leland Stanford, had begun to dominate the Pacific Coast not only in transportation but in politics. Its rails extended down the valleys. New towns sprang up, new sections were opened and populated, for the company had to create customers to get custom.

The long Salinas Valley was part of the exploitation. Adam had seen and studied a fine colour broadside which set forth the valley as that region which heaven unsuccessfully imitated. After reading the literature, anyone who did not want to settle in the Salinas Valley was crazy.

Adam did not rush at his purchase. He bought a rig and drove around, meeting the earlier comers, talking of soil and water, climate and crops, prices and facilities. It was not speculation with Adam. He was here to settle, to found a home, a family, perhaps a dynasty.

Adam drove exuberantly from farm to farm, picked up dirt and crumbled it in his fingers, talked and planned and dreamed. The people of the valley liked him and were glad he had come to live there, for they recognized a man of substance.

He had only one worry, and that was for Cathy. She was not well. She rode around the country with him, but she was listless. One morning she complained of feeling ill and stayed in her room in the King City hotel while

Adam drove into the country. He returned at about five in the afternoon to find her nearly dead from loss of blood. Luckily Adam found Dr Tilson at his supper and dragged him from his roast beef. The doctor made a quick examination, inserted a packing, and turned to Adam.

'Why don't you wait downstairs?' he suggested.

'Is she all right?'

'Yes. I'll call you pretty soon.'

Adam patted Cathy's shoulder, and she smiled up at him.

Dr Tilson closed the door behind him and came back to the bed. His face was red with anger. 'Why did you do it?'

Cathy's mouth was a thin tight line.

'Does your husband know you are pregnant?'

Her head moved slowly from side to side.

'What did you do it with?'

She stared up at him.

He looked around the room. He stepped to the bureau and picked up a knitting-needle. He shook it in her face. 'The old offender–the old criminal,' he said. 'You're a fool. You've nearly killed yourself and you haven't lost your baby. I suppose you took things too, poisoned yourself, inserted camphor, kerosene, red pepper. My God! Some of the things you women do!'

Her eyes were as cold as glass.

He pulled a chair up beside her bed. 'Why don't you want to have the baby?' he asked softly. 'You've got a good husband. Don't you love him? Don't you intend to speak to me at all? Tell me, damn it! Don't turn mulish.'

Her lips did not move and her eyes did not flicker.

'My dear,' he said, 'can't you see? You must not destroy life. That's the one thing gets me crazy. God knows I lose patients because I don't know enough. But I try–I always try. And then I see a deliberate killing.' He talked rapidly on. He dreaded the sick silence between his sentences. This woman puzzled him. There was something inhuman about her. 'Have you met Mrs Laurel? She's wasting and crying for a baby. Everything she has or can get she would give to have a baby, and you–you try to stab yours with a knitting-needle. All right,' he cried, 'you won't speak–you don't have to. But I'm going to tell you. The baby's safe. Your aim was bad. And I'm telling you this–you're going to have that baby. Do you know what the law in this state has to say about abortion? You don't have to answer, but you listen to me! If this happens again, if you lose this baby and I have any reason to suspect monkey business, I will charge you, I will testify against you, and I will see you punished. Now I hope you have sense enough to believe me, because I mean it.'

Cathy moistened her lips with a little pointed tongue. The cold went out of her eyes and a weak sadness took its place. 'I'm sorry,' she said. 'I'm sorry. But you don't understand.'

'Then why don't you tell me?' His anger disappeared like mist. 'Tell me, my dear.'

'It's hard to tell. Adam is so good, so strong. I am–well, I'm tainted. Epilepsy.'

'Not you!'

'No, but my grandfather and my father–and my brother.' She covered her eyes with her hands. 'I couldn't bring that to my husband.'

'Poor child,' he said. 'My poor child. You can't be certain. It's more than probable that your baby will be fine and healthy. Will you promise me not to try any more tricks?'

'Yes.'

'All right then. I won't tell your husband what you did. Now lie back and let me see if the bleeding's stopped.

In a few minutes he closed his satchel and put the knitting-needle in his pocket. 'I'll look in tomorrow morning,' he said.

Adam swarmed on him as he came down the narrow stairs into the lobby. Dr Tilson warded off a flurry of 'How is she? Is she all right? What caused it? Can I go up?'

'Whoa, hold up–hold up.' And he used his trick, his standard joke. 'Your wife is sick.'

'Doctor–'

'She has the only good sickness there is–'

'Doctor–'

'Your wife is going to have a baby.' He brushed past Adam and left him staring. Three men sitting round the stove grinned at him. One of them observed dryly, 'If it was me now–why, I'd invite a few, maybe three, friends to have a drink.' His hint was wasted. Adam bolted clumsily up the narrow stairs.

Adam's attention narrowed to the Bordoni ranch a few miles south of King City, almost equidistant, in fact, between San Lucas and King City.

The Bordonis had nine hundred acres left of a grant of ten thousand acres which had come to Mrs Bordoni's great-grandfather from the Spanish crown. The Bordonis were Swiss, but Mrs Bordoni was the daughter and heiress of a Spanish family that had settled in the Salinas Valley in very early times. And as happened with most of the old families, the land slipped away. Some was lost in gambling, some chipped off in taxes, and some acres torn off like coupons to buy luxuries–a horse, a diamond, or a pretty woman. The nine hundred remaining acres were the core of the original Sanchez grant, and the best of it too. They straddled the river and tucked into the foothills on both sides, for at this point the valley narrows and then opens out again. The original Sanchez house was still usable. Built of adobe, it stood in a tiny opening in the foothills, a miniature valley fed by a precious ever-running spring of sweet water. That of course was why the first Sanchez had built his seat there. Huge live oaks shaded the valley, and the earth had a richness and a greeness foreign to this part of the country. The walls of the low house were four feet thick, and the round pole rafters were tied on with rawhide ropes which had been put on wet. The hide shrank and pulled joist and rafter tight together, and the leather ropes became hard as iron and nearly imperishable. There is only one drawback to this building method. Rats will gnaw at the hide if they are let.

The old house seemed to have grown out of the earth, and it was lovely. Bordoni used it for a cow barn. He was a Swiss, an immigrant, with his national passion for cleanliness. He distrusted the thick mud walls and built a frame house some distance away, and his cows put their heads out of the deep recessed windows of the old Sanchez house.

The Bordonis were childless, and when the wife died in ripe years a lonely longing for his Alpine past fell on her husband. He wanted to sell the ranch and go home. Adam Trask refused to buy in a hurry, and Bordoni was asking a big price and using the selling method of pretending not to care whether he sold or not. Bordoni knew Adam was going to buy his land long before Adam knew it.

Where Adam settled he intended to stay and to have his unborn children stay. He was afraid he might buy one place and then see another he liked better, and all the time the Sanchez place was drawing him. With the advent of Cathy, his life extended long and pleasantly ahead of him. But he went through all the motions of carefulness. He drove and rode and walked over every foot of the land. He put a post-hole auger down through the subsoil to test and feel and smell the under earth. He inquired about the small wild plants of field and riverside and hill. In damp places he knelt down and examined the game tracks in the mud, mountain lion and deer, coyote and wild cat, skunk and racoon, weasel and rabbit, all overlaid with the pattern of quail tracks. He threaded among willows and sycamores and wild blackberry vines in the river-bed, patted the trunks of live oaks and scrub oak, madrone, laurel, toyon.

Bordoni watched him with squinting eyes and poured tumblers of red wine squeezed from the grapes of his small hillside vineyard. It was Bordoni's pleasure to get a little drunk every afternoon. And Adam, who had never tasted wine, began to like it.

Over and over he asked Cathy's opinion of the place. Did she like it? Would she be happy there? And he didn't listen to her noncommittal answers. He thought that she linked arms with his enthusiasm. In the lobby of the King City hotel he talked to the men who gathered around the stove and read the papers sent down from San Francisco.

'It's water I think about,' he said one evening. 'I wonder how deep you'd have to go to bring in a well.'

A rancher crossed his denim knees. 'You ought to go see Sam Hamilton,' he said. 'He knows more about water than anybody around here. He's a water witch and a well-digger too. He'll tell you. He's put down half the wells in this part of the valley.'

His companion chuckled. 'Sam's got a real legitimate reason to be interested in water. Hasn't got a goddam drop of it on his own place.'

'How do I find him?' Adam asked.

'I'll tell you what. I'm going to have him make some angle-irons. I'll take you with me if you want. You'll like Mr Hamilton. He's a fine man.'

'Kind of comical genius,' his companion said.

3

They went to the Hamilton ranch in Louis Lippo's buckboard–Louis and Adam Trask. The iron straps rattled around in the box, and a leg of venison, wrapped in wet burlap to keep it cool, jumped around on top of the iron. It was customary in that day to take some substantial lump of food as a present when you went calling on a man, for you had to stay to dinner unless you wished to insult his house. But a few guests could set back the feeding plans for the week if you did not build up what you destroyed. A quarter of pork or a rump of beef would do. Louis had cut down the venison and Adam provided a bottle of whisky.

'Now, I'll have to tell you,' Louis said. 'Mr Hamilton will like that, but Mrs Hamilton has got a skunner on it. If I was you I'd leave it under the seat, and when we drive around to the shop, why, then you can get it out. That's what we always do.'

'Doesn't she let her husband take a drink?'

'No bigger than a bird,' said Louis. 'But she's got brass-bound opinions. Just you leave the bottle under the seat.'

They left the valley road and drove into the worn and rutted hills over a set of wheel tracks gullied by the winter rains. The horses strained into their collars and the buckboard rocked and swayed. The year had not been kind to the hills, and already in June they were dry and the stones showed through the short, burned feed. The wild oats had headed out barely six inches above the ground, as though with knowledge that if they didn't make seed quickly they wouldn't get to seed at all.

'It's not likely-looking country,' Adam said.

'Likely? Why, Mr Trask, it's country that will break a man's heart and eat him up. Likely! Mr Hamilton has a sizeable piece and he'd of starved to death on it with all those children. The ranch don't feed them. He does all kinds of jobs, and his boys are starting to bring in something now. It's a fine family.'

Adam stared at a line of dark mesquite that peeked out of a draw. 'Why in the world would he settle on a place like this?'

Louis Lippo, as does every man, loved to interpret, to a stranger particularly, if no native was present to put up an argument. 'I'll tell you,' he said. 'Take me–my father was Italian. Came here after the trouble but he brought a little money. My place isn't very big but it's nice. My father bought it. He picked it out. And take you–I don't know how you're fixed and wouldn't ask, but they say you're trying to buy the old Sanchez place and Bordoni never gave anything away. You're pretty well fixed or you wouldn't even ask about it.'

'I'm comfortably off,' said Adam modestly.

'I'm talking the long way round,' said Louis. 'When Mr and Mrs Hamilton came into the valley they didn't have a pot to piss in. They had to take what was left–government land that nobody else wanted. Twenty-five acres of it won't keep a cow alive even in good years, and they say the coyotes move away in bad years. There's people say they don't know how the Hamiltons lived. But of course Mr Hamilton went right to work–that's how they lived. Worked as a hire hand till he got his threshing machine built.'

'Must have made a go of it. I hear of him all over.'

'He made a go of it all right. Raised nine children. I'll bet he hasn't got four bits laid away. How could he?'

One side of the buckboard leaped up, rolled over a big round stone and dropped down again. The horses were dark with sweat and lathered under collar and britching.

'I'll be glad to talk to him,' said Adam.

'Well, sir, he raised one fine crop–he had good children and he raised them fine. All doing well–maybe except Joe. Joe–he's the youngest–they're talking about sending him to college, but all the rest are doing fine. Mr Hamilton can be proud. The house is just on the other side of the next rise. Don't forget and bring out that whisky–she'll freeze you to the ground.'

The dry earth was ticking under the sun and the crickets rasped. 'It's a real god-forsaken country,' said Louis.

'Makes me feel mean,' said Adam.

'How's that?'

'Well, I'm fixed so I don't have to live on a place like this.'

'Me too, and I don't feel mean. I'm just goddam glad.'

When the buckboard topped the rise Adam could look down on the little cluster of buildings which composed the Hamilton seat–a house with many lean-tos, a cow shed, a shop, and a wagon shed. It was a dry and sun-eaten sight–no big trees and a small hand-watered garden.

Louis turned to Adam, and there was just a hint of hostility in his tone. 'I want to put you straight on one or two things, Mr Trask. There's people that when they see Samuel Hamilton the first time might get the idea he's full of bull. He don't talk like other people. He's an Irishman. And he's all full of plans–a hundred plans a day. And he's all full of hope. My Christ, he'd have to be to live on this land! But you remember this–he's a fine worker, a good blacksmith, and some of his plans work out. And I've heard him talk about things that were going to happen, and they did.'

Adam was alarmed at the hint of threat. 'I'm not a man to run another man down,' he said, and he felt that suddenly Louis thought of him as a stranger and an enemy.

'I just wanted to get it straight. There's some people come in from the East and they think if a man hasn't got a lot of money he's no good.'

'I wouldn't think of–'

'Mr Hamilton maybe hasn't got four bits put away, but he's our people and he's as good as we got. And he's raised the nicest family you're likely to see. I just want you to remember that.'

Adam was on the point of defending himself, and then he said, 'I'll remember. Thanks for telling me.'

Louis faced round front again. 'There he is–see, out by the shop? He must of heard us.'

'Has he got a beard?' Adam asked, peering.

'Yes, got a nice beard. It's turning white fast. Beginning to grizzle up.'

They drove past the frame house and saw Mrs Hamilton looking out of the window at them, and they drew up in front of the shop where Samuel stood waiting for them.

Adam saw a big man, bearded like a patriarch, his greying hair stirring in the air like thistledown. His cheeks above his beard were pink where the sun had burned his Irish skin. He wore a clean blue shirt, overalls, and a leather apron. His sleeves were rolled up, and his muscular arms were clean too. Only his hands were blackened from the forge. After a quick glance Adam came back to the eyes, light blue and filled with a young delight. The wrinkles around them were drawn in radial lines inwards by laughter.

'Louis,' he said, 'I'm glad to see you. Even in the sweetness of our little heaven here, we like to see our friends.' He smiled at Adam, and Louis said, 'I brought Mr Adam Trask to see you. He's a stranger from down east, come to settle.'

'I'm glad,' said Samuel. 'We'll shake another time. I wouldn't soil your hand with these forge hooks.'

'I brought some strap iron, Mr Hamilton. Would you make some angles for me? The whole frame of my header bed is fallen to hell.'

'Sure I will, Louis. Get down, get down. We'll put the horses to the shade.'

'There's a piece of venison behind, and Mr Trask brought a little something.'

Samuel glanced towards the house. 'Maybe we'll get out the "little something" when we've got the rig behind the shed.'

Adam could hear the singing lilt of his speech and yet could detect no word pronounced in a strange manner except perhaps in sharpened *t*'s and *l*'s held high on the tongue.

'Louis, will you out-span your team? I'll take the venison in. Liza will be glad. She likes a venison stew.'

'Any of the young ones home?'

'Well, no, they aren't. George and Will came home for the week-end, and they all went last night to a dance up Wild Horse Canyon at the Peach Tree school-house. They'll come trooping back by dusk. We lack a sofa because of that. I'll tell you later–Liza will have a vengeance on them–it was Tom did it. I'll tell you later.' He laughed and started towards the house, carrying the wrapped deer's haunch. 'If you want you can bring the "little something" into the shop, so you don't let the sun glint on it.'

They heard him calling as he came near the house. 'Liza, you'll never guess. Louis Lippo has brought a piece of venison bigger than you.'

Louis drove in behind the shed, and Adam helped him take the horses out, tie up the tugs, and halter them in the shade. 'He meant that about the sun shining on the bottle,' said Louis.

'She must be a holy terror.'

'No bigger than a bird, but she's brass-bound.'

'"Out-span,"' Adam said, 'I think I've heard it said that way, or read it.'

Samuel rejoined them in the shop. 'Liza will be happy if you will stay to dinner,' he said.

'She didn't expect us,' Adam protested.

'Hush, man. She'll make some extra dumplings for the stew. It's a pleasure to have you here. Give me your straps, Louis, and let's see how you want them.'

He built a chip fire in the black square of the forge and pulled a bellows breeze on it and then fed wet coke over with his fingers until it glowed. 'Here, Louis,' he said, 'wave your wing on my fire. Slow, man, slow and even.' He laid the strips of iron on the glowing coke. 'No, sir, Mr Trask, Liza's used to cooking for nine starving children. Nothing can startle her.' He tonged the iron to more advantageous heat, and he laughed. 'I'll take that last back as a holy lie,' he said. 'My wife is rumbling like round stones in the surf. And I'll caution the both of you not to mention the word "sofa". It's a word of anger and sorrow to Liza.'

'You said something about it,' Adam said.

'If you knew my boy Tom, you'd understand it better, Mr Trask. Louis knows him.'

'Sure I know him,' Louis said.

Samuel went on, 'My Tom is a hell-bent boy. Always take more on his plate than he can eat. Always plants more than he can harvest. Pleasures too much, sorrows too much. Some people are like that. Liza thinks I'm like that. I don't know what will come of Tom. Maybe greatness, maybe the noose–well, Hamiltons have been hanged before. And I'll tell you about that some time.'

'The sofa,' Adam suggested politely.

'You're right. I do, and Liza says I do, shepherd my words like rebellious sheep. Well, came the dance at the Peach Tree school and the boys, George, Tom, Will, and Joe, all decided to go. And of course the girls were asked. George and Will and Joe, poor simple boys, each asked one lady friend, but Tom–he took too big a helping as usual. He asked two Williams sisters, Jennie and Belle. How many screw-holes do you want, Louis?'

'Five,' said Louis.

'All right. Now I must tell you, Mr Trask, that my Tom has all the egotism and self-love of a boy who thinks he's ugly. Mostly lets himself go fallow, but comes a celebration and he garlands himself like a maypole, and he glories like spring flowers. This takes him quite a piece of time. You notice the wagon house was empty? George and Will and Joe started early and not so beautiful as Tom. George took the rig, Will had the buggy, and Joe got the little two-wheeled cart.' Samuel's eyes shone with pleasure. 'Well then, Tom came out as shy and shining as a Roman emperor and the only thing left with wheels was a hay-rake, and you can't take even one Williams sister on that. For good or bad, Liza was taking her nap. Tom sat on the steps and thought it out. Then I saw him go to the shed and hitch up two horses and take the double-tree off the hay-rake. He wrestled the sofa out of the house and ran a fifth-chain under the legs–the fine goose-neck horsehair sofa that Liza loves better than anything. I gave it to her to rest on before George was born. The last I saw, Tom went dragging up the hill, reclining at his ease on the sofa to get the Williams girls. And, oh, Lord, it'll be worn thin as a wafer from scraping by the time he gets it back.' Samuel put down his tongs and placed his hands on his hips the better to laugh. 'And Liza has the smoke of brimstone coming out her nostrils. Poor Tom.'

Adam said, smiling, 'Would you like to take a little something?'

'That I would,' said Samuel. He accepted the bottle and took a quick swallow of whisky and passed it back.

'*Uisquebaugh*–it's an Irish word–whisky, water of life–and so it is.'

He took the red straps to his anvil and punched screw-holes in them and bent the angles with his hammer and the forked sparks leaped out. Then he dipped the iron hissing into his half-barrel of black water. 'There you are,' he said, and threw them on the ground.

'I thank you,' said Louis. 'How much will that be?'

'The pleasure of your company.'

'It's always like that,' Louis said helplessly.

'No, when I put your new well down you paid my price.'

'That reminds me–Mr Trask here is thinking of buying the Bordoni place–the old Sanchez grant–you remember?'

'I know it well,' said Samuel. 'It's a fine piece.'

'He was asking about water, and I told him you knew more about that than anybody around here.'

Adam passed the bottle, and Samuel took a delicate sip and wiped his mouth on his forearm above the soot.

'I haven't made up my mind,' said Adam. 'I'm just asking some questions.'

'Oh, Lord, man, now you've put your foot in it. They say it's a dangerous thing to question an Irishman because he'll tell you. I hope you know what you're doing when you issue me a licence to talk. I've heard two ways of looking at it. One says the silent man is the wise man and the other that a man without words is a man without thought. Naturally I favour the second–Liza says to a fault. What do you want to know?'

'Well, take the Bordoni place. How deep would you have to go to get water?'

'I'd have to see the spot–some places thirty feet, some places a hundred and fifty, and in some places clear to the centre of the world.'

'But you could develop water?'

'Nearly every place except my own.'

'I've heard you have a lack here.'

'Heard? Why, God in heaven must have heard! I've screamed it loud enough.'

'There's a four-hundred-acre piece beside the river. Would there be water under it?'

'I'd have to look. It seems to me it's an odd valley. If you'll hold your patience close, maybe I can tell you a little bit about it, for I've looked at it and poked my stinger down into it. A hungry man gorges with his mind–he does indeed.'

Louis Lippo said, 'Mr Trask is from New England. He plans to settle here. He's been west before, though–in the army, fighting Indians.'

'Were you now? Then it's you should talk and let me learn.'

'I don't want to talk about it.'

'Why not? God help my family and my neighbours if I had fought the Indians!'

'I didn't want to fight them, sir.' The 'sir' crept in without his knowing it.

'Yes, I can understand that. It must be a hard thing to kill a man you don't know and don't hate.'

'Maybe that makes it easier,' said Louis.

'You have a point, Louis. But some men are friends with the whole world in their hearts, and there are others that hate themselves and spread their hatred around like butter on hot bread.'

'I'd rather you told me about this land,' Adam said uneasily, for a sick picture of piled-up bodies came into his mind.

'What time is it?'

Louis stepped out and looked at the sun. 'Not past ten o'clock.'

'If I get started I have no self-control. My son Will says I talk to trees when I can't find a human vegetable.' He sighed and sat down on a nail-keg. 'I said it was a strange valley, but maybe that's because I was born in a green place. Do you find it strange, Louis?'

'No, I never been out of it.'

'I've dug in it plenty,' Samuel said. 'Something went on under it–maybe still going on. There's an ocean bed underneath, and below that another world. But that needn't bother a farming man. Now, on top is good soil, particularly on the flats. In the upper valley it is light and sandy, but mixed in with that, the top sweetness of the hills that washed down on it in the winters. As you go north the valley widens out, and the soil gets blacker and heavier and perhaps richer. It's my belief that marshes were there once, and the roots of centuries rotted into the soil and made it black and fertilized it. And when you turn it up, a little greasy clay mixes and holds it together. That's from about Gonzales north to the river mouth. Off the sides, around Salinas and Blanco and Castroville and Moss Landing, the marshes are still there. And when one day those marshes are drained off, that will be the richest of all land in this red world.'

'He always tells what it will be like some day,' Louis threw in.

'Well, a man's mind can't stay in time the way his body does.'

'If I'm going to settle here I need to know about how and what will be,' said Adam. 'My children, when I have them, will be on it.'

Samuel's eyes looked over the heads of his friends, out of the dark forge to the yellow sunlight. 'You'll have to know that under a good part of the valley, some places deep, and others pretty near the surface, there's a layer called hard-pan. It's a clay, hard-packed, and it feels greasy too. Some places it is only a foot thick, and more in others. And this hard-pan resists water. If it were not there the winter rains would go soaking down and dampen the earth, and in the summer it would rise up to the roots again. But when the earth above the hard-pan is soaked full, the rest runs fresheting off or stands rotting on top. And that's one of the main curses of our valley.'

'Well, it's a pretty good place to live in, isn't it?'

'Yes, it is, but a man can't entirely rest when he knows it could be richer. I've thought that if you could drive thousands of holes through it to let the water in, it might solve it. And then I tried something with a few sticks of dynamite. I punched a hole through the hard-pan and blasted. That broke it up and the water could get down. But, God in heaven, think of the amount of dynamite! I've read that a Swede–the same man who invented dynamite–has got a new explosive stronger and safer. Maybe that might be the answer.'

Louis said half derisively and half with admiration, 'He's always thinking about how to change things. He's never satisfied with the way they are.'

Samuel smiled at him. 'They say man lived in trees one time. Somebody had to get dissatisfied with a high climb or your feet would not be touching flat ground now.' And then he laughed again. 'I can see myself sitting on my dust heap making a world in my mind as surely as God created this one. But God saw his world. I'll never see mine except–this way. This will be a valley of great richness one day. It could feed the world, and maybe it will. And happy people will live here, thousands and thousands–' A cloud seemed to come over his eyes and his face set in sadness and he was silent.

'You make it sound like a good place to settle,' Adam said. 'Where else could I raise my children with that coming?'

Samuel went on, 'There's a thing I don't understand. There's a blackness on this valley. I don't know what it is, but I can feel it. Sometimes on a white blinding day I can feel it cutting off the sun and squeezing the light out of it like a sponge.' His voice rose. 'There's a black violence on this valley. I don't know–I don't know. It's as though some old ghost haunted it out of the dead ocean below and troubled the air with unhappiness. It's as secret as hidden sorrow. I don't know what it is, but I see it and feel it in the people here.'

Adam shivered. 'I just remembered I promised to get back early. Cathy, my wife, is going to have a baby.'

'But Liza's getting ready.'

'She'll understand when you tell her about the baby. My wife is feeling poorly. And I thank you for telling me about the water.'

'Have I depressed you with my rambling?'

'No, not at all–not at all. It's Cathy's first baby and she's miserable.'

Adam struggled all night with his thoughts, and the next day he drove out and shook hands with Bordoni and the Sanchez place was his.

CHAPTER 14

I

There is so much to tell about the Western country in that day that it is hard to know where to start. One thing sets off a hundred others. The problem is to decide which one to tell first.

You remember that Samuel Hamilton said his children had gone to a dance at the Peach Tree school. The country schools were the centres of culture then. The Protestant churches in the towns were fighting for their existence in a country where they were newcomers. The Catholic church, first on the scene and deeply dug in, sat in comfortable tradition while the missions were gradually abandoned and their roofs fell in and pigeons roosted on the stripped altars. The library (in Latin and Spanish) of the San Antonio Mission was thrown into a granary, where the rats ate off the sheepskin bindings. In the country the repository of art and science was the school, and the school-teacher shielded and carried the torch of learning and of beauty. The school-house was the meeting place for music, for debate. The polls were set in the school-house for elections. Social life, whether it was the crowning of a May queen, the eulogy to a dead president, or an all-night dance, could be held nowhere else. And the teacher was not only an intellectual paragon and a social leader, but also the matrimonial catch of the countryside. A family could indeed walk proudly if a son married the school-teacher. Her children were presumed to have intellectual advantages both inherited and conditioned.

The daughters of Samuel Hamilton were not destined to become work-destroyed farm wives. They were handsome girls and they carried with them the glow of their descent from the kings of Ireland. They had a pride that transcended their poverty. No one ever thought of them as deserving pity. Samuel raised a distinctly superior breed. They were better read and better bred than most of their contemporaries. To all of them Samuel communicated his love of learning, and he set them apart from the prideful ignorance of their time. Olive Hamilton became a teacher. That meant she left home at fifteen and went to live in Salinas, where she could go to secondary school. At seventeen she took county board examinations, which covered all the arts and sciences, and at eighteen she was teaching school at Peach Tree.

In her school there were pupils older and bigger than she was. It required great tact to be a school-teacher. To keep order among the big undisciplined boys without pistol and bull whip was a difficult and dangerous business. In one school in the mountains a teacher was raped by her pupils.

Olive Hamilton had not only to teach everything, but to all ages. Very few youths went past the eighth grade in those days, and what with farm duties some of them took fourteen or fifteen years to do it. Olive had also to practise a rudimentary medicine, for there were constant accidents. She sewed up knife cuts after a fight in the school-yard. When a small barefooted boy was bitten by a rattlesnake, it was her duty to suck his toe to draw the poison out.

She taught reading to the first grade and algebra to the eighth. She led the singing, acted as a critic of literature, wrote the social notes that went weekly to the *Salinas Journal*. In addition, the whole social life of the area was in her hands, not only graduation exercises, but dances, meetings, debates, chorals, Christmas and May Day festivals, patriotic exudations on Decoration Day and the Fourth of July. She was on the election board and headed and held together all charities. It was far from an easy job, and it had duties and obligations beyond belief. The teacher had no private life. She was watched jealously for any weakness of character. She could not board with one family for more than one term, for that would cause jealousy–a family gained social ascendancy by boarding the teacher. If a marriageable son belonged to the family where she boarded a proposal was automatic; if there was more than one claimant, vicious fights occurred over her hand. The Aguita boys, three of them, nearly clawed each other to death over Olive Hamilton. Teachers rarely lasted very long in the country schools. The work was so hard and the proposals so constant that they married within a very short time.

This was a course Olive Hamilton determined she would not take. She did not share the intellectual enthusiasms of her father, but the time she had spent in Salinas determined her not to be a ranch wife. She wanted to live in a town, perhaps not so big as Salinas, but at least not a cross-roads. In Salinas, Olive had experienced niceties of living, the choir and vestments, Altar Guild, and bean suppers of the Episcopal church. She had partaken of the arts–road companies of plays and even operas, with their magic and promise of an aromatic world outside. She had gone to parties, played charades, competed in poetry readings, joined a chorus and orchestra. Salinas had tempted her. There she could go to a party dressed for the party, and come home in the same dress, instead of rolling her clothes in a saddlebag and riding ten miles, then unrolling and pressing them.

Busy though she was with her teaching, Olive longed for the metropolitan life, and when the young man who had built the flour mill in King City sued properly for her hand, she accepted him subject to a long and secret engagement. The secrecy was required because if it were known there would be trouble among the young men in the neighbourhood.

Olive had not her father's brilliance, but she did have a sense of fun, together with her mother's strong and undeviating will. What light and beauty could be forced down the throats of her reluctant pupils, she forced.

There was a wall against learning. A man wanted his children to read, to figure, and that was enough. More might make them dissatisfied and flighty. And there were plenty of examples to prove that learning made a boy leave the farm to live in the city–to consider himself better than his father. Enough arithmetic to measure land and lumber and to keep accounts, enough writing to order goods and write to relatives, enough reading for newspapers, almanacs and farm journals, enough music for religious and patriotic display–that was enough to help a boy and not to lead him astray. Learning was for doctors, lawyers, and teachers, a class set off and not considered related to other people. There were some sports, of course, like Samuel Hamilton, and he was tolerated and liked, but if he had not been able to dig a well, shoe a horse, or run a threshing machine, God knows what would have been thought of the family.

Olive did marry her young man and did move, first to Paso Robles, then to King City, and finally to Salinas. She was as intuitive as a cat. Her acts were based on feelings rather than thoughts. She had her mother's firm chin and button nose and her father's fine eyes. She was the most definite of any of the Hamiltons except her mother. Her theology was a curious mixture of Irish fairies and an Old Testament Jehovah whom in her later life she confused with her father. Heaven was to her a nice home ranch inhabited by her dead relatives. External realities of a frustrating nature she obliterated by refusing to believe in them, and when one resisted her disbelief she raged at it. It was told of her that she cried bitterly because she could not go to two dances on one Saturday night. One was in Greenfield and the other in San Lucas–twenty miles apart. To have gone to both and them home would have entailed a sixty-mile horseback ride. This was a fact she could not blast with her disbelief, and so she cried with vexation and went to neither dance.

As she grew older she developed a scattergun method for dealing with unpleasant facts. When I, her only son, was sixteen I contracted pleural pneumonia, in that day a killing disease. I went down and down, until the wing-tips of the angels brushed my eyes. Olive used her scattergun method of treating pleural pneumonia, and it worked. The Episcopalian minister prayed with and for me, the Mother Superior and nuns of the convent next to our house held me up to Heaven for relief twice a day, a distant relative who was a Christian Science reader held the thought for me. Every incantation, magic, and herbal formula known was brought out, and she got two good nurses and the town's best doctors. Her method was practical. I got well. She was loving and firm with her family, three girls and me, trained us to housework, dish-washing, clothes-washing, and manners. When angered she had a terrible eye which could blanch the skin off a bad child as easily as if he were a boiled almond.

When I recovered from my pneumonia it came time for me to learn to walk again. I had been nine weeks in bed, and the muscles had gone lax and the laziness of recovery had set in. When I was helped up, every nerve cried, and the wound in my side, which had been opened to drain the pus from the pleural cavity, pained horribly. I fell back in bed, crying, 'I can't do it! I can't get up!'

Olive fixed me with her terrible eye. 'Get up!' she said. 'Your father has worked all day and sat up all night. He has gone into debt for you. Now get up!'

And I got up.

Debt was an ugly word and an ugly concept to Olive. A bill unpaid past the fifteenth of the month was a debt. The world had connotations of dirt and slovenliness and dishonour. Olive, who truly believed that her family was the best in the world, quite snobbishly would not permit it to be touched by debt. She planted that terror of debt so deeply in her children that even now, in a changed economic pattern where indebtedness is a part of living, I become restless when a bill is two days overdue. Olive never accepted the instalment plan when it became popular. A thing bought by instalments was a thing you did not own and for which you were in debt. She saved for things she wanted, and this meant that the neighbours had new gadgets as much as two years before we did.

2

Olive had great courage. Perhaps it takes courage to raise children. And I must tell you what she did about the First World War. Her thinking was not international. Her first boundary was the geography of her family, second her town, Salinas, and finally there was a dotted line, not clearly defined, which was the county line. Thus she did not quite believe in the war, not even when Troop C, our militia cavalry, was called out, loaded its horses on a train, and set out for the open world.

Martin Hopps lived round the corner from us. He was wide, short, red-haired. His mouth was wide, and he had red eyes. He was almost the shyest boy in Salinas. To say good morning to him was to make him itch with self-consciousness. He belonged to Troop C because the armoury had a basket-ball court.

If the Germans had known Olive and had been sensible they would have gone out of their way not to anger her. But they didn't know or they were stupid. When they killed Martin Hopps they lost the war, because that made my mother mad and she took out after them. She had liked Martin Hopps. He had never hurt anyone. When they killed him Olive declared war on the German Empire.

She cast about for a weapon. Knitting helmets and socks was not deadly enough for her. For a time she put on a Red Cross uniform and met other ladies similarly dressed in the armoury, where bandages were rolled and reputations unrolled. This was all right, but it was not driving at the heart of the Kaiser. Olive wanted blood for the life of Martin Hopps. She found her weapon in Liberty bonds. She had never sold anything in her life beyond an occasional angel cake for the Altar Guild in the basement of the Episcopal church, but she began to sell bonds by the bale. She brought ferocity to her work. I think she made people afraid not to buy them. And when they did buy from Olive she gave them a sense of actual combat, of putting a bayonet in the stomach of Germany.

As her sales sky-rocketed and stayed up, the Treasury Department began to notice this new Amazon. First there came mimeographed letters of commendation, then real letters signed by the Secretary of the Treasury, and not with a rubber stamp either. We were proud, but not so proud as when prizes began to arrive, a German helmet (too small for any of us to wear), a bayonet, a jagged piece of shrapnel set on an ebony base. Since we were not eligible for armed conflict beyond marching with wooden guns, our mother's war seemed to justify us. And then she outdid herself, and outdid everyone in our part of the country. She quadrupled her already fabulous record and she was awarded the fairest prize of all–a ride in an army aeroplane.

Oh, we were proud kids! Even vicariously this was an eminence we could hardly stand. But my poor mother–I must tell you that there are certain things in the existence of which my mother did not believe, against any possible evidence to the contrary. One was a bad Hamilton and another was the aeroplane. The fact that she had seen them didn't make her believe in them one bit more.

In the light of what she did I have tried to imagine how she felt. Her soul must have crawled with horror, for how can you fly in something that does not exist? As a punishment the ride would have been cruel and unusual, but it was a prize, a gift, an honour, and an eminence. She must have looked into our eyes and seen the shining idolatry there and understood that she was trapped. Not to have gone would have let her family down. She was surrounded, and there was no honourable way out save death. Once she had decided to go up in the non-existent thing she seemed to have had no idea whatever that she would survive it.

Olive made her will–took lots of time with it and had it checked to be sure it was legal. Then she opened her rosewood box wherein were the letters her husband had written to her in courtship and since. We had not known he wrote poetry to her, but he had. She built a fire in the grate and burned every letter. They were hers, and she wanted no other human to see them. She bought all new underwear. She had a horror of being found dead with mended, or worse, unmended underclothes. I think perhaps she saw the wide twisted mouth and embarrassed eyes of Martin Hopps on her and felt that in some way she was reimbursing him for his stolen life. She was very gentle with us and did not notice a badly washed dinner-plate that left a greasy stain on the dish-towel.

This glory was scheduled to take place at the Salinas Race Track and Rodeo Grounds. We were driven to the track in an army automobile, feeling more solemn and golden than at a good funeral. Our father was working at the Spreckles Sugar Factory, five miles from town, and could not get off, or perhaps didn't want to, for fear he could not stand the strain. But Olive had made arrangements, on pain of not going up, for the plane to try to fly as far as the sugar factory before it crashed.

I realize now that the several hundred people who had gathered simply came to see the aeroplane, but at that time we thought they were there to do my mother honour. Olive was not a tall woman and at that age she had begun to put on weight. We had to help her out of the car. She was probably stiff with fright, but her little chin was set.

The plane stood in the field around which the race track was laid out. It was appallingly little and flimsy–an open-cockpit biplane with wooden struts, tied with piano wire. The wings were covered with canvas. Olive was stunned. She went to the side as an ox to the knife. Over the clothes she was convinced were her burial clothes two sergeants slipped on a coat, a padded coat, and a flight coat, and she grew rounder and rounder with each layer. Then a leather helmet and goggles, and with her little button of a nose and her pink cheeks you really had something. She looked like a goggled ball. The two sergeants hoisted her bodily into the cockpit and wedged her in. She filled the opening completely. As they strapped her in she suddenly came to life and began waving frantically for attention. One of the soldiers climbed up, listened to her, came over to my sister Mary, and led her to the side of the plane. Olive was tugging at the thick padded flight glove on her left hand. She got her hands free, took off her engagement ring with its tiny diamond, and handed it down to Mary. She set her gold wedding ring firmly, pulled the gloves back on, and faced the front. The pilot climbed into the front cockpit, and one of the sergeants threw his weight on the wooden propeller. The little ship taxied away and turned, and down the field it roared and staggered into the air, and Olive was looking straight ahead and probably her eyes were closed.

We followed it with our eyes as it swept up and away, leaving a lonesome silence behind it. The bond committee, the friends and relatives, the simple unhonoured spectators didn't think of leaving the field. The plane became a speck in the sky towards Spreckles and disappeared. It was fifteen minutes before we saw it again flying serenely and very high. Then to our horror it seemed to stagger and fall. It fell endlessly, caught itself, climbed, and made a loop. One of the sergeants laughed. For a moment the plane steadied and then it seemed to go crazy. It barrel-rolled, made Immelmann turns, inside and outside loops, and turned over and flew over the field upside down. We could see the black bullet which was our mother's helmet. One of the soldiers said quietly, 'I think he's gone nuts. She's not a young woman.'

The aeroplane landed steadily enough and ran up to the group. The motor died. The pilot climbed out, shaking his head in perplexity. 'Goddamdest woman I ever saw,' he said. He reached up and shook Olive's nerveless hand and walked hurriedly away.

It took four men and quite a long time to get Olive out of the cockpit. She was so rigid they could not bend her. We took her home and put her to bed, and she didn't get up for two days.

What had happened came out slowly. The pilot talked some and Olive talked some, and both stories had to be put together before they made sense. They had flown out and circled the Spreckles Sugar Factory as ordered–circled it three times so that our father would be sure to see, and then the pilot thought of a joke. He meant no harm. He shouted something, and his face looked contorted. Olive could not hear over the noise of the engine. The pilot throttled down and shouted, 'Stunt?' It was a kind of joke. Olive saw his goggled face and the slip-stream caught his word and distorted it. What Olive heard was the word 'stuck'.

Well, she thought, here it is, just as I knew it would be. Here was her death. Her mind flashed to see if she had forgotten anything–will made, letters burned, new underwear, plenty of food in the house for dinner. She wondered whether she had turned out the light in the back room. It was all in a second. Then she thought there might be an outside chance of survival. The young soldier was obviously frightened and fear might be the worst thing that could happen to him in handling the situation. If she gave way to the panic that lay on her heart it might frighten him more. She decided to encourage him. She smiled brightly and nodded to give him courage, and then the bottom fell out of the world. When he levelled out of his loop the pilot looked back again and shouted, 'More?'

Olive was way beyond hearing anything, but her chin was set and she was determined to help the pilot so that he would not be too afraid before they hit the earth. She smiled and nodded again. At the end of each stunt he looked back, and each time she encouraged him. Afterwards he said over and over, 'She's the goddamdest woman I ever saw. I tore up the rule book and she wanted more. Good Christ, what a pilot she would have made!'

CHAPTER 15

I

Adam sat like a contented cat on his land. From the entrance to the little draw under a giant oak, which dipped its roots into underground water, he could look out over the acres lying away to the river and across to an alluvial flat and then up the rounded foothills on the western side. It was a fair place even in the summer when the sun laced into it. A line of river willows and sycamores banded it in the middle, and the western hills were yellow-brown with feed. For some reason the mountains to the west of the Salinas Valley have a thicker skin of earth on them than have the eastern foothills, so that the grass is richer there. Perhaps the peaks store rain and distribute it more evenly, and perhaps, being more wooded, they draw more rainfall.

Very little of the Sanchez, now Trask, place was under cultivation, but Adam in his mind could see the wheat growing tall and squares of green alfalfa near the river. Behind him he could hear the rackety hammering of the carpenters, brought all the way from Salinas to rebuild the old Sanchez house. Adam had decided to live in the old house. Here was a place in which to plant his dynasty. The manure was scraped out, the old floors torn up, neck-rubbed window casings ripped away. New sweet wood was going in, pine sharp with resin and velvety redwood and a new roof of long split shakes. The old thick walls sucked in coat after coat of whitewash with lime in salt water, which, as it dried, seemed to have a luminosity of its own.

He planned a permanent seat. A gardener had trimmed the ancient roses, planted geraniums, laid out the vegetable flat, and brought the living spring in little channels to wander back and forth through the garden. Adam foretasted comfort for himself and his descendants. In a shed, covered with tarpaulins, lay the crated heavy furniture sent from San Francisco and carted out from King City.

He would have good living too. Lee, his pigtailed Chinese cook, had made a special trip to Pajaro to buy the pots and kettles and pans, kegs, jars, copper, and glass for his kitchen. A new pigsty was building far from the house and down-wind, with chicken and duck runs near and a kennel for the dogs to keep the coyotes away. It was no quick thing Adam contemplated, to be finished and ready in a hurry. His men worked deliberately and slowly. It was a long job. Adam wanted it well done. He inspected every wooden joint, stood off to study paint samples on a shingle. In the corner of his room catalogues piled up–catalogues for machinery, furnishings, seeds, fruit trees. He was glad now that his father had left him a rich man. In his mind a darkness was settling over his memory of Connecticut. Perhaps the hard flat light of the West was blotting out his birthplace. When he thought back to his father's house, to the farm, the town, to his brother's face, there was a blackness over all of it. And he shook off the memories.

Temporarily he had moved Cathy into the white-painted, clean spare house of Bordoni, there to await the home and the child. There was no doubt whatever that the child would be finished well before the house was ready. But Adam was unhurried.

'I want it built strong,' he directed over and over. 'I want it to last–copper nails and hard wood–nothing to rust or rot.'

He was not alone in his preoccupation with the future. The whole valley, the whole West was that way. It was a time when the past had lost its sweetness and its sap. You'd go a good long road before you'd find a man, and he very old, who wished to bring back a golden past. Men were notched and comfortable in the present, hard and unfruitful as it was, but only as a doorstep into a fantastic future. Rarely did two men meet, or three stand in a bar, or a dozen gnaw tough venison in camp, that the valley's future, paralysing in its grandeur, did not come up, not as conjecture but as a certainty.

'It'll be–who knows? maybe in our lifetime,' they said.

And people found happiness in the future according to their present lack. Thus a man might bring his family down from a hill ranch in a drag–a big box nailed on oaken runners which pulled bumping down the broken hills. In the straw of the box his wife would brace the children against the tooth-shattering, tongue-biting crash of the runners against stone and ground. And the father would set his heels and think, 'When the roads come in–then will be the time. Why, we'll sit high and happy in a surrey and get clear into King City in three hours–and what more in the world could you want than that?'

Or let a man survey his grove of live-oak trees, hard as coal and hotter, the best firewood in the world. In his pocket might be a newspaper with a squib: 'Oak cord wood is bringing ten dollars a cord in Los Angeles.' Why, hell, when the railroad puts a branch out here, I could lay it down neat, broke up and seasoned, right beside the track, for a dollar and a half a cord. Let's go the whole hog and say the Southern Pacific will charge three-fifty to carry it. There's still five dollars a cord, and there's three thousand cords in that little grove alone. That's fifteen thousand dollars right there.

There were others who prophesied, with rays shining on their foreheads, about the sometime ditches that would carry water all over the valley–who knows? maybe in our lifetime–or deep wells with steam engines to pump the water up out of the guts of the world. Can you imagine? Just think what this land would raise with plenty of water! Why, it will be a frigging garden!

Another man, but he was crazy, said that some day there'd be a way, maybe ice, maybe some other way, to get a peach like this here I got in my hand clear to Philadelphia.

In the towns they talked of sewers and inside toilets, and some already had them; and arc lights on the street corner–Salinas had those–and telephones. There wasn't any limit, no boundary at all, to the future. And it would be so a man wouldn't have room to store his happiness. Contentment would flood raging down the valley like the Salinas River in March of a thirty-inch year.

They looked over the flat, dry, dusty valley and the ugly mushroom towns and they saw a loveliness–who knows? maybe in our lifetime. That's one reason you couldn't laugh too much at Samuel Hamilton. He let his mind range more deliciously than any other, and it didn't sound so silly when you heard what they were doing in San Jose. Where Samuel went haywire was wondering whether people would be happy when all that came.

Happy? He's haywire now. Just let us get it, and we'll show you happiness.

And Samuel could remember hearing of a cousin of his mother's in Ireland, a knight and rich and handsome, and anyway shot himself on a silken couch, sitting beside the most beautiful woman in the world who loved him.

'There's a capacity for appetite,' Samuel said, 'that a whole heaven and earth of cake can't satisfy.'

Adam Trask nosed some of his happiness into futures, but there was present contentment in him too. He felt his heart smack up against his throat when he saw Cathy sitting in the sun, quiet, her baby growing, and a transparency to her skin that made him think of the angels on Sunday School cards. Then a breeze would move her bright hair, or she would raise her eyes, and Adam would swell out in his stomach with a pressure of ecstasy that was close kin to grief.

If Adam rested like a sleek fed cat on his land, Cathy was cat-like too. She had the inhuman attribute of abandoning what she could not get and of waiting for what she could get. These two gifts gave her great advantages. Her pregnancy had been an accident. When her attempt to abort herself failed and the doctor threatened her, she gave up that method. This does not mean that she reconciled herself to pregnancy. She sat it out as she would have weathered an illness. Her marriage to Adam had been the same. She was trapped and she took the best possible way out. She had not wanted to go to California either, but other plans were denied her for the time being. As a very young child she had learned to win by using the momentum of her opponent. It was easy to guide a man's strength where it was impossible to resist him. Very few people in the world could have known that Cathy did not want to be where she was and in the condition she was. She relaxed and waited for the change she knew must come some time. Cathy had the one quality required of a great and successful criminal: she trusted no one, confided in no one. Her self was an island. It is probable that she did not even look at Adam's new land or building house, or turn his towering plans to reality in her mind, because she did not intend to live here after her sickness was over, after her trap opened. But to his questions she gave proper answers; to do otherwise would be waste motion, and dissipated energy, and foreign to a good cat.

'See, my darling, how the house lies–windows looking down the valley?'

'It's beautiful.'

'You know, it may sound foolish, but I find myself trying to think the way old Sanchez did a hundred years ago. How was the valley then? He must have planned so carefully. You know, he had pipes? He did–made out of redwood with a hole bored or burned through to carry the water from the spring. We dug up some pieces of it.'

'That's remarkable,' she said. 'He must have been clever.'

'I'd like to know more about him. From the way the house sets, the trees he left, the shape and proportion of the house, he must have been a kind of artist.'

'He was a Spaniard, wasn't he? They're artistic people, I've heard. I remember in school about a painter–no, he was a Greek.'

'I wonder where I could find out about old Sanchez.'

'Well, somebody must know.'

'All of his work and planning, and Bordoni kept cows in the house. You know what I wonder about most?'

'What, Adam?'

'I wonder if he had a Cathy and who she was.'

She smiled and looked down and away from him. 'The things you say.'

'He must have had! He must have had. I never had energy or direction or–well, even a very great desire to live before I had you.'

'Adam, you embarrass me. Adam, be careful. Don't joggle me, it hurts.'

'I'm sorry. I'm so clumsy.'

'No, you're not. You just don't think. Should I be knitting or sewing, do you suppose? I'm so comfortable just sitting.'

'We'll buy everything we need. You just sit and be comfortable. I guess in a way you're working harder than anyone here. But the pay–the pay is wonderful!'

'Adam, the scar on my forehead isn't going to go away, I'm afraid.'

'The doctor said it would fade in time.'

'Well, sometimes it seems to be getting fainter, and then it comes back. Don't you think it's darker today?'

'No, I don't.'

But it was. It looked like a huge thumb-print, even to whorls of wrinkled skin. He put his finger near, and she drew her head away.

'Don't,' she said. 'It's tender to the touch. It turns red if you touch it.'

'It will go away. Just takes a little time, that's all.'

She smiled as he turned, but when he walked away her eyes were flat and directionless. She shifted her body restlessly. The baby was kicking. She relaxed and all her muscles loosened. She waited.

Lee came near where her chair was set under the biggest oak tree. 'Missy likee tea?'

'No–yes, I would too.'

Her eyes inspected him and her inspection could not penetrate the dark brown of his eyes. He made her uneasy. Cathy had always been able to shovel into the mind of any man and dig up his impulses and his desires. But Lee's brain gave and repelled like rubber. His face was lean and pleasant, his forehead broad, firm, and sensitive, and his lips curled like a perpetual smile. His long black glossy braided queue, tied at the bottom with a narrow piece of black silk, hung over his shoulder and moved rhythmically against his chest. When he did violent work he curled his queue on top of his head. He wore narrow cotton trousers, black heel-less slippers, and a frogged Chinese smock. Whenever he could he hid his hands in his sleeves as though he were afraid for them, as most Chinese did in that day.

'I bling litta table,' he said, bowed slightly, and shuffled away.

Cathy looked after him, and her eyebrows drew down in a scowl. She was not afraid of Lee, yet she was not comfortable with him either. But he was a good and respectful servant–the best. And what harm could he do her?

2

The summer progressed and the Salinas River retired underground or stood in green pools under high banks. The cattle lay drowsing all day long under the willows and only moved out at night to feed. An umber tone came to the grass. And the afternoon winds blowing inevitably down the valley started a dust that was like fog and raised it into the sky almost as high as the mountain tops. The wild oat roots stood up like nigger-heads where the winds blew the earth away. Along a polished earth, pieces of straw and twigs scampered until they were stopped by some rooted thing; and little stones rolled crookedly before the wind.

It became more apparent than ever why old Sanchez had built his house in the little draw, for the wind and the dust did not penetrate, and the spring, while it diminished, still gushed a head of cold clear water. But Adam, looking out over his dry dust-obscured land, felt the panic the Eastern man always does at first in California. In a Connecticut summer two weeks without rain is a dry spell and four a drought. If the countryside is not green it is dying. But in California it does not ordinarily rain at all between the end of May and the first of November. The Eastern man, though he has been told, feels the earth is sick in the rainless months.

Adam sent Lee with a note to the Hamilton place to ask Samuel to visit him and discuss the boring of some wells on his new place.

Samuel was sitting in the shade, watching his son Tom design and build a revolutionary coon trap, when Lee drove up in the Trask cart. Lee folded his hands in his sleeves and waited. Samuel read the note. 'Tom,' he said, 'do you think you could keep the estate going while I run down and talk water with a dry man?'

'Why don't I go with you? You might need some help.'

'At talking?–that I don't. It won't come to digging for some time, if I'm any judge. With wells there's got to be a great deal of talk–five or six hundred words for every shovel of dirt.'

'I'd like to go–it's Mr Trask, isn't it? I didn't meet him when he came here.'

'You'll do that when the digging starts. I'm older than you. I've got first claim on the talk. You know, Tom, a coon is going to reach his pretty little hand through here and let himself out. You know how clever they are.'

'See this piece here? It screws on and turns down here. You couldn't get out of that yourself.'

'I'm not so clever as a coon. I think you've worked it out, though. Tom, boy, would you saddle Doxology while I go tell your mother where I'm going?'

'I bling lig,' said Lee.

'Well, I have to come home some time.'

'I bling back.'

'Nonsense,' said Samuel. 'I'll lead my horse in and ride back.'

Samuel sat in the buggy beside Lee, and his clobber-footed saddle-horse shuffled clumsily behind.

'What's your name?' Samuel asked pleasantly.

'Lee. Got more name. Lee papa family name. Call Lee.'

'I've read quite a lot about China. You born in China?'

'No. Born here.'

Samuel was silent for quite a long time while the buggy lurched down the wheel track towards the dusty valley. 'Lee,' he said at last, 'I mean no disrespect, but I've never been able to figure why you people still talk pidgin when an illiterate baboon from the black bogs of Ireland, with a head full of Gaelic and a tongue like a potato, learns to talk a poor grade of English in ten years.'

Lee grinned. 'Me talkee Chinese talk,' he said.

'Well, I guess you have your reasons. And it's not my affair. I hope you'll forgive me if I don't believe it, Lee.'

Lee looked at him and the brown eyes under their rounded upper lids seemed to open and deepen until they weren't foreign any more, but man's eyes, warm with understanding. Lee chuckled. 'It's more than a convenience,' he said. 'It's even more than self-protection. Mostly we have to use it to be understood at all.'

Samuel showed no sign of having observed any change. 'I can understand the first two,' he said thoughtfully, 'but the third escapes me.'

Lee said, 'I know it's hard to believe, but it has happened so often to me and to my friends that we take it for granted. If I should go up to a lady or a gentleman, for instance, and speak as I am doing now, I wouldn't be understood.'

'Why not?'

'Pidgin they expect, and pidgin they'll listen to. But English from me they don't listen to, and so they don't understand it.'

'Can that be possible? How do I understand you?'

'That's why I'm talking to you. You are one of the rare people who can separate your observation from your preconception. You see what is, where most people see what they expect.'

'I hadn't thought of it. And I've not been so tested as you, but what you say has a handle of truth. You know, I'm very glad to talk to you. I've wanted to ask so many questions.'

'Happy to oblige.'

'So many questions. For instance, you wear the queue. I've read that it is a badge of slavery imposed by conquest by the Manchus on the Southern Chinese.'

'That is true.'

'Then why in the name of God do you wear it here, where the Manchus can't get at you?'

'Talkee Chinese talk. Queue Chinese fashion–you savvy?'

Samuel laughed loudly. 'That does have the green touch of convenience,' he said. 'I wish I had a hidey-hole like that.'

'I'm wondering whether I can explain,' said Lee. 'Where there is no likeness of experience it's very difficult. I understand you were not born in America.'

'No, in Ireland.'

'And in a few years you can almost disappear; while I, who was born in Grass Valley, went to school and several years to the University of California, have no chance of mixing.'

'If you cut your queue, dressed and talked like other people?'

'No. I tried it. To the so-called whites I was still a Chinese, but an untrustworthy one; and at the same time my Chinese friends steered clear of me. I had to give it up.'

Lee pulled up under a tree, got out, and unfastened the check rein. 'Time for lunch,' he said. 'I made a package. Would you like some?'

'Sure I would. Let me get down in the shade there. I forget to eat sometimes, and that's strange because I'm always hungry. I'm interested in what you say. It has a sweet sound of authority. Now it peeks into my mind that you should go back to China.'

Lee smiled satirically at him. 'In a few minutes I don't think you'll find a loose bar I've missed in a lifetime of search. I did go back to China. My father was a fairly successful man. It didn't work. They said I looked like a foreign devil; they said I spoke like a foreign devil. I made mistakes in manners, and I didn't know delicacies that had grown up since my father left. They wouldn't have me. You can believe it or not–I'm less foreign here than I was in China.'

'I'll have to believe you because it's reasonable. You've given me things to think about until at least February twenty-seventh. Do you mind my questions?'

'As a matter of fact, no. The trouble with pidgin is that you get to thinking in pidgin. I write a great deal to keep my English up. Hearing and reading aren't the same as speaking and writing.'

'Don't you ever make a mistake? I mean, break into English?'

'No, I don't. I think it's a matter of what is expected. You look at a man's eyes, you see that he expects pidgin and a shuffle, so you speak pidgin and shuffle.'

'I guess that's right,' said Samuel. 'In my own way I tell jokes because people come all the way to my place to laugh. I try to be funny for them even when the sadness is on me.'

'But the Irish are said to be a happy people, full of jokes.'

'There's your pidgin and your queue. They're not. They're a dark people with a gift for suffering way past their deserving. It's said that without whisky to soak and soften the world, they'd kill themselves. But they tell jokes because it's expected of them.'

Lee unwrapped a little bottle. 'Would you like some of this? Chinee drink ng-ka-py.'

'What is it?'

'Chinee blandy. Stlong dlink–as a matter of fact it's a brandy with a dosage of wormwood. Very powerful. It softens the world.'

Samuel sipped from the bottle. 'Tastes a little like rotten apples,' he said.

'Yes, but nice rotten apples. Taste it back along your tongue towards the roots.'

Samuel took a big swallow and tilted his head back. 'I see what you mean. That *is* good.'

'Here are some sandwiches, pickles, cheese, a can of buttermilk.'

'You do well.'

'Yes, I see to it.'

Samuel bit into a sandwich. 'I was shuffling over half a hundred questions. What you said brings the brightest one up. You don't mind?'

'Not at all. The only thing I do want to ask of you is not to talk this way when other people are listening. It would only confuse them and they wouldn't believe it anyway.'

'I'll try,' said Samuel. 'If I slip, just remember that I'm a comical genius. It's hard to split a man down the middle and always to reach for the same half.'

'I think I can guess what your next question is.'

'What?'

'Why am I content to be a servant?'

'How in the world did you know?'

'It seemed to follow.'

'Do you resent the question?'

'Not from you. There are no ugly questions except those clothed in condescension. I don't know where being a servant came into disrepute. It is the refuge of a philosopher, the food of the lazy, and, properly carried out, it is a position of power, even of love. I can't understand why more intelligent people don't take it as a career–learn to do it well and reap its benefits. A good servant has absolute security, not because of his master's kindness, but because of habit and indolence. It's a hard thing for a man to change spices or lay out his own socks. He'll keep a bad servant rather than change. But a good servant, and I am an excellent one, can completely control his master, tell him what to think, how to act, whom to marry, when to divorce, reduce him to terror as a discipline, or distribute happiness to him, and finally be mentioned in his will. If I had wished I could have robbed, stripped, and beaten anyone I've worked for and come away with thanks. Finally, in my circumstances I am unprotected. My master will defend me, protect me. You have to work and worry. I work less and worry less. And I am a good servant. A bad one does no work and does no worrying, and he still is fed, clothed, and protected. I don't know any profession where the field is so cluttered with incompetents and where excellence is so rare.'

Samuel leaned towards him, listening intently.

Lee went on, 'It's going to be a relief after that to go back to pidgin.'

'It's a very short distance to the Sanchez place. Why did we stop so near?' Samuel asked.

'Allee time talkee. Me Chinese number one boy. You leddy go now?'

'What? Oh, sure. But it must be a lonely life.'

'That's the only fault with it,' said Lee. 'I've been thinking of going to San Francisco and starting a little business.'

'Like a laundry? Or a grocery store?'

'No. Too many Chinese laundries and restaurants. I thought perhaps a bookstore. I'd like that, and the competition wouldn't be too great. I probably won't do it, though. A servant loses his initiative.'

3

In the afternoon Samuel and Adam rode over the land. The wind came up as it did every afternoon, and the yellow dust ran into the sky.

'Oh, it's a good piece,' Samuel cried. 'It's a rare piece of land.'

'Seems to me it's blowing away bit by bit,' Adam observed.

'No, it's just moving over a little. You lose some to the James ranch but you get some from the Southeys.'

'Well, I don't like the wind. Makes me nervous.'

'Nobody likes wind for very long. It makes animals nervous and restless too. I don't know whether you noticed, but a little farther up the valley they're planting windbreaks of gum trees. Eucalyptus–comes from Australia. They say the gums grow ten feet a year. Why don't you try a few rows and see what happens? In time they should back up the wind a little, and they make grand firewood.'

'Good idea,' Adam said. 'What I really want is water. This wind would pump all the water I could find. I thought if I could bring in a few wells and irrigate, the topsoil wouldn't blow away. I might try some beans.'

Samuel squinted into the wind. 'I'll try to get you water if you want,' he said. 'And I've got a little pump I made that will bring it up fast. It's my own invention. A windmill is a pretty costly thing. Maybe I could build them for you and save you some money.'

'That's good,' said Adam, 'I wouldn't mind the wind if it worked for me. And if I could get water I might plant alfalfa.'

'It's never brought much of a price.'

'I wasn't thinking of that. Few weeks ago I took a drive up around

Greenfield and Gonzales. Some Swiss have moved in there. They've got nice little dairy herds and they get four crops of alfalfa a year.'

'I heard about them. They brought in Swiss cows.'

Adam's face was bright with plans. 'That's what I want to do. Sell butter and cheese and feed the milk to the pigs.'

'You're going to bring credit to the valley,' Samuel said. 'You're going to be a real joy to the future.'

'If I can get water.'

'I'll get you water if there's any to be got. I'll find it. I brought my magic wand.' He patted a forked stick tied to his saddle.

Adam pointed to the left where a wide flat place was covered with a low growth of sagebrush. 'Now then,' he said, 'thirty-six acres and almost as level as a floor. I put an auger down. Top-soil averages three and a half feet, sand on top and loam within plough reach. Think you could get water there?'

'I don't know,' Samuel said. 'I'll see.'

He dismounted, handed his reins to Adam, and untied his forked wand. He took the forks in his two hands and walked slowly, his arms out and stretched before him and the wand-tip up. His steps took a zigzag course. Once he frowned and backed up a few steps, then shook his head and went on. Adam rode slowly along behind, leading the other horse.

Adam kept his eyes on the stick. He saw it quiver and then jerk a little, as though an invisible fish were tugging at a line. Samuel's face was taut with attention. He continued on until the point of the wand seemed to be pulled strongly downward against his straining arms. He made a slow circle, broke off a piece of sagebrush, and dropped it on the ground. He moved well outside his circle, held up his stick again, and moved inward towards his marker. As he came near it, the point of the stick was drawn down again. Samuel sighed and relaxed and dropped his wand on the ground. 'I can get water here,' he said. 'And not very deep. The pull was strong, plenty of water.'

'Good,' said Adam. 'I want to show you a couple more places.'

Samuel whittled out a stout piece of sagewood and drove it into the soil. Then he kicked the brittle brush down in the area so he could find his marker again.

On a second try three hundred yards away the wand seemed nearly torn downwards out of his hands. 'Now there's a whole world of water here,' he said.

The third try was not so productive. After half an hour he had only the slightest sign.

The two men rode slowly back towards the Trask house. The afternoon was golden, for the yellow dust in the sky gilded the light. As always, the wind began to drop as the day waned, but it sometimes took half the night for the dust to settle out of the air. 'I knew it was a good place,' Samuel said. 'Anyone can see that. But I didn't know it was that good. You must have a great drain under your land from the mountains. You know how to pick land, Mr Trask.'

Adam smiled. 'We had a farm in Connecticut,' he said. 'For six generations we dug stones out. One of the first things I remember is sledding stones over to the walls. I thought that was the way all farms were. It's strange to me and almost sinful here. If you wanted a stone, you'd have to go a long way for it.'

'The ways of sin are curious,' Samuel observed. 'I guess if a man had to shuck off everything he had, inside and out, he'd manage to hide a few little sins somewhere for his own discomfort. They're the last things we'll give up.'

'Maybe that's a good thing to keep us humble. The fear of God in us.'

'I guess so,' said Samuel. 'And I guess humility must be a good thing, since it's a rare man who has not a piece of it, but when you look at humbleness it's hard to see where its value rests, unless you grant that it is a pleasurable pain and very precious. Suffering–I wonder has it been properly looked at.'

'Tell me about your stick,' Adam said. 'How does it work?'

Samuel stroked the fork now tied to his saddle strings. 'I don't really believe in it, save that it works.' He smiled at Adam. 'Maybe it's this way. Maybe I know where the water is, feel it in my skin. Some people have a gift in this direction or that. Suppose–well, call it humility, or a deep disbelief in myself, forced me to do a magic to bring up to the surface the thing I know anyway. Does that make any sense to you?'

'I'd have to think about it,' said Adam.

The horses picked their own way, heads hung low, reins loosened against the bits.

'Can you stay the night?' Adam asked.

'I can, but better not. I didn't tell Liza I'd be away the night. I'd not like to give her a worry.'

'But she knows where you are.'

'Sure she knows. But I'll ride home tonight. It doesn't matter the time. If you'd like to ask me to supper I'd be glad. And when do you want me to start on the wells?'

'Now–as soon as you can.'

'You know it's no cheap thing, indulging yourself with water. I'd have to charge you fifty cents or more a foot, depending on what we find down there. It can run into money.'

'I have the money. I want the wells. Look, Mr Hamilton–'

'"Samuel" would be easier.'

'Look, Samuel, I mean to make a garden of my land. Remember my name is Adam. So far I've had no Eden, let alone been driven out.'

'It's the best reason I ever heard for making a garden,' Samuel exclaimed. He chuckled. 'Where will the orchard be?'

Adam said, 'I won't plant apples. That would be looking for accidents.'

'What does Eve say to that? She has a say, you remember. And Eves delight in apples.'

'Not this one.' Adam's eyes were shining. 'You don't know this Eve. She'll celebrate my choice. I don't think anyone can know her goodness.'

'You have a rarity. Right now I can't recall any greater gift.'

They were coming near to the entrance to the little side valley in which was the Sanchez house. They could see the rounded tops of the great live oaks.

'Gift,' Adam said softly. 'You can't know. No one can know. I had a grey life, Mr Hamilton–Samuel. Not that it was bad compared to other lives, but it was nothing. I don't know why I tell you this.'

'Maybe because I like to hear.'

'My mother–died–before my memory. My step-mother was a good woman but troubled and ill. My father was a stern, fine man–maybe a great man.'

'You couldn't love him?'

'I had the kind of feeling you have in church, and not a little fear in it.'

Samuel nodded. 'I know–and some men want that.' He smiled ruefully. 'I've always wanted the other. Liza says it's the weak thing in me.'

'My father put me in the army, in the West, against the Indians.'

'You told me. But you don't think like a military man.'

'I wasn't a good one. I seem to be telling you everything.'

'You must want to. There's always a reason.'

'A soldier must want to do the things we had to do–or at least be satisfied with them. I couldn't find good enough reasons for killing men and women, nor understand the reasons when they were explained.'

They rode on in silence for a time. Adam went on, 'I came out of the army like dragging myself muddy out of a swamp. I wandered for a long time before going home to a remembered place I did not love.'

'Your father?'

'He died, and home was a place to sit around or work around, waiting for death the way you might wait for a dreadful picnic.'

'Alone?'

'No, I have a brother.'

'Where is he–waiting for the picnic?'

'Yes–yes, that's exactly what. Then Cathy came. Maybe I will tell you some time when I can tell and you want to hear.'

'I'll want to hear,' Samuel said. 'I eat stories like grapes.'

'A kind of light spread out from her. And everything changed colour. And the world opened out. And a day was good to awaken to. And there were no limits to anything. And the people of the world were good and handsome. And I was not afraid any more.'

'I recognize it,' Samuel said. 'That's an old friend of mine. It never dies, but sometimes it moves away, or you do. Yes, that's my acquaintance–eyes, nose, mouth, and hair.'

'All this coming out of a little hurt girl.'

'And not out of you?'

'Oh, no, or it would have come before. No, Cathy brought it, and it lives around her. And now I've told you why I want the wells. I have to repay somehow for value received. I'm going to make a garden so good, so beautiful, that it will be a proper place for her to live and a fitting place for her light to shine on.'

Samuel swallowed several times, and he spoke with a dry voice out of a pinched-up throat. 'I can see my duty,' he said. 'I can see it plainly before me if I am any kind of man, any kind of friend to you.'

'What do you mean?'

Samuel said satirically, 'It's my duty to take this thing of yours and kick it in the face, then raise it up and spread slime on it thick enough to blot out its dangerous light.' His voice grew strong with vehemence. 'I should hold it up to you muck-covered and show you its dirt and danger. I should warn you to look closer until you can see how ugly it really is. I should ask you to think of inconstancy and give you examples. I should give you Othello's handkerchief. Oh, I know I should. And I should straighten out your tangled thought, show you that the impulse is grey as lead and rotten as a dead cow in wet weather. If I did my duty well, I could give you back your bad old life and feel good about it, and welcome you back to the musty membership in the lodge.'

'Are you joking? Maybe I shouldn't have told–'

'It is the duty of a friend. I had a friend who did the duty once for me. But I'm a false friend. I'll get no credit for it among my peers. It's a lovely thing, preserve it, and glory in it. And I'll dig your wells if I have to drive my rig to the black centre of the earth. I'll squeeze water out like juice from an orange.'

They rode under the great oaks and towards the house. Adam said, 'There she is, sitting outside.' He shouted, 'Cathy, he says there's water–lots of it.' Aside he said excitedly, 'Did you know she's going to have a baby?'

'Even at this distance she looks beautiful,' Samuel said.

4

Because the day had been hot, Lee set a table outside under an oak tree, and as the sun neared the western mountains he padded back and forth from the kitchen, carrying the cold meats, pickles, potato salad, coconut cake, and peach pie which were supper. In the centre of the table he placed a gigantic stoneware pitcher full of milk.

Adam and Samuel came from the wash-house, their hair and faces shining with water, and Samuel's beard was fluffy after its soaping. They stood at the trestle table and waited until Cathy came out.

She walked slowly, picking her way as though she were afraid she would fall. Her full skirt and apron concealed to a certain extent her swelling abdomen. Her face was untroubled and childlike, and she clasped her hands in front of her. She had reached the table before she looked up and glanced from Samuel to Adam.

Adam held her chair for her. 'You haven't met Mr Hamilton, dear,' he said.

She held out her hand. 'How do you do?' she said.

Samuel had been inspecting her. 'It's a beautiful place,' he said, 'I'm glad to meet you. You are well, I hope?'

'Oh, yes. Yes, I'm well.'

The men sat down. 'She makes it formal whether she wants to or not. Every meal is a kind of occasion,' Adam said.

'Don't talk like that,' she said. 'It isn't true.'

'Doesn't it feel like a party to you, Samuel?' he asked.

'It does so, and I can tell you there's never been such a candidate for a party as I am. And my children–they're worse. My boy Tom wanted to come today. He's spoiling to get off the ranch.'

Samuel suddenly realized that he was making his speech last to prevent silence from falling on the table. He paused, and the silence dropped. Cathy looked down at her plate while she ate a sliver of roast lamb. She looked up as she put it between her small sharp teeth. Her wide-set eyes communicated nothing. Samuel shivered.

'It isn't cold, is it?' Adam asked.

'Cold? No. A goose walked over my grave, I guess.'

'Oh, yes. I know the feeling.'

The silence fell again. Samuel waited for some speech to start up, knowing in advance that it would not.

'Do you like our valley, Mrs Trask?'

'What? Oh, yes.'

'If it isn't impertinent to ask, when is your baby due?'

'In about six weeks,' Adam said. 'My wife is one of those paragons–a woman who does not talk very much.'

'Sometimes a silence tells the most,' said Samuel, and he saw Cathy's eyes leap up and down again, and it seemed to him that the scar on her forehead grew darker. Something had flicked her the way you'd flick a horse with the braided string popper on a buggy whip. Samuel couldn't recall what he had said that had made her give a small inward start. He felt a tenseness coming over him that was somewhat like the feeling he had just before the water wand pulled down, an awareness of something strange and strained. He glanced at Adam and saw that he was looking raptly at his wife. Whatever was strange was not strange to Adam. His face had happiness on it.

Cathy was chewing a piece of meat, chewing with her front teeth. Samuel had never seen anyone chew that way before. And when she had swallowed, her little tongue flicked round her lips. Samuel's mind repeated, 'Something–something–can't find what it is. Something wrong,' and the silence hung on the table.

There was a shuffle behind him. He turned. Lee set a teapot on the table and shuffled away.

Samuel began to talk to push the silence away. He told how he had first come to the valley fresh from Ireland, but within a few words neither Cathy nor Adam was listening to him. To prove it, he used a trick he had devised to discover whether his children were listening when they begged him to read to them and would not let him stop. He threw in two sentences of nonsense. There was no response from either Adam or Cathy. He gave up.

He bolted his supper, drank his tea scalding hot, and folded his napkin. 'Ma'am, if you'll excuse me, I'll ride off home. And I thank you for your hospitality.'

'Good night,' she said.

Adam jumped to his feet. He seemed torn out of a reverie. 'Don't go now. I hoped to persuade you to stay the night.'

'No, thank you, but that I can't. And it's not a long ride. I think–of course, I know–there'll be a moon.'

'When will you start the wells?'

'I'll have to get my rig in order, do a piece of sharpening, and put my house in order. In a few days I'll send the equipment with Tom.'

The life was flowing back into Adam. 'Make it soon,' he said. 'I want it soon. Cathy, we're going to make the most beautiful place in the world. There'll be nothing like it anywhere.'

Samuel switched his gaze to Cathy's face. It did not change. The eyes were flat and the mouth with its small up-curve at the corners was carven.

'That will be nice,' she said.

For just a moment Samuel had an impulse to do or say something to shock her out of her distance. He shivered again.

'Another goose?' Adam asked.

'Another goose.' The dusk was falling and already the tree forms were dark against the sky. 'Good night, then.'

'I'll walk down with you.'

'No, stay with your wife. You haven't finished your supper.'

'But I–'

'Sit down, man. I can find my own horse, and if I can't I'll steal one of yours.' Samuel pushed Adam gently down in his chair. 'Good night. Good night. Good night, ma'am.' He walked quickly towards the shed.

Old platter-foot Doxology was daintily nibbling hay from the manger with lips like two flounders. The halter chain clinked against the wood. Samuel lifted down his saddle from the big nail where it hung by one wooden stirrup and swung it over the broad back. He was lacing the latigo through the cinch rings when there was a small stir behind him. He turned and saw the silhouette of Lee against the last light from the open shadows.

'When you come back?' the Chinese asked softly.

'I don't know. In a few days or a week. Lee, what is it?'

'What is what?'

'By God, I got creepy! Is there something wrong here?'

'What do you mean?'

'You know damn well what I mean.'

'Chinese boy jus' workee–not hear, not talkee.'

'Yes. I guess you're right. Sure, you're right. Sorry I asked you. It wasn't very good manners.' He turned back, slipped the bit in Dox's mouth, and laced the big flop-ears into the headstall. He slipped the halter and dropped it in the manger. 'Good night, Lee,' he said.

'Mr Hamilton–'

'Yes?'

'Do you need a cook?'

'On my place I can't afford a cook.'

'I'd work cheap.'

'Liza would kill you. Why–you want to quit?'

'Just thought I'd ask,' said Lee. 'Good night.'

5

Adam and Cathy sat in the gathering dark under the tree.

'He's a good man,' Adam said. 'I like him. I wish I could persuade him to take over here and run this place–kind of superintendent.'

Cathy said, 'He's got his own place and his own family.'

'Yes, I know. And it's the poorest land you ever saw. He could make more at wages from me. I'll ask him. It does take a time to get used to a new country. It's like being born again and having to learn all over. I used to know from what quarter the rains came. It's different here. And once I knew in my skin whether wind would blow, when it would be cold. But I'll learn. It just takes a little time. Are you comfortable, Cathy?'

'Yes.'

'One day, and not too far away, you'll see the whole valley green with alfalfa–see it from the fine big windows of the finished house. I'll plant rows of gum trees, and I'm going to send away for seeds and plants–put in a kind of experimental farm. I might try lichee nuts from China. I wonder if they would grow here. Well, I can try. Maybe Lee would tell me. And once the baby's born you can ride over the whole place with me. You haven't really seen it. Did I tell you? Mr Hamilton is going to put up windmills, and we'll be able to see them turning from here.' He stretched his legs out comfortably under the table. 'Lee should bring candles,' he said. 'I wonder what's keeping him.'

Cathy spoke very quietly. 'Adam, I didn't want to come here. I am not going to stay here. As soon as I can I will go away.'

'Oh, nonsense.' He laughed. 'You're like a child away from home for the first time. You'll love it once you get used to it and the baby is born. You know, when I first went away to the army I thought I was going to die of home-sickness. But I got over it. We all get over it. So don't say silly things like that.'

'It's not a silly thing.'

'Don't talk about it, dear. Everything will change after the baby is born. You'll see. You'll see.'

He capped his hands behind his head and looked up at the faint stars through the tree branches.

CHAPTER 16

I

Samuel Hamilton rode back home in a night so flooded with moonlight that the hills took on the quality of the white and dusty moon. The trees and earth were moon-dry, silent and airless and dead. The shadows were black without shading and the open places white without colour. Here and there Samuel could see secret movement, for the moon-feeders were at work–the deer which browse all night when the moon is clear and sleep under thickets in the day. Rabbits and field-mice and all other small hunted creatures that feel safer in the concealing light crept and hopped and crawled and froze to resemble stones or small bushes when ear or nose suspected danger. The predators were working too–the long weasels like waves of brown light; the cobby wild cats crouching near to the ground, almost invisible except when their yellow eyes caught light and flashed for a second; the foxes sniffling with pointed up-raised noses for a warm-blooded supper; the raccoon padding near still water, talking frogs. The coyotes nuzzled along the slopes and, torn with sorrow-joy, raised their heads and shouted their feeling, half keen, half laughter, at their goddess moon. And over all the shadowy screech owls sailed, drawing a smudge of shadowy fear below them on the ground. The wind of the afternoon was gone and only a little breeze like a sigh was stirred by the restless thermals of the warm, dry hills.

Doxology's loud off-beat footsteps silenced the night people until after he had passed. Samuel's beard glinted white, and his greying hair stood up high on his head. He had hung his black hat on his saddle horn. An ache was on the top of his stomach, an apprehension that was like a sick thought. It was a *Weltschmerz*–which we used to call 'Welshrats'–the world sadness that rises into the soul like a gas and spreads despair so that you probe for the offending event and can find none.

Samuel went back in his mind over the fine ranch and the indications of water–no Welshrats could come out of that unless he sheltered a submerged envy. He looked in himself for envy and could find none. He went on to Adam's dream of a garden like Eden and to Adam's adoration of Cathy. Nothing there unless–unless his secret mind brooded over his own healed loss. But that was so long ago he had forgotten the pain. The memory was mellow and warm and comfortable, now that it was all over. His loins and his thighs had forgotten hunger.

As he rode through the light and dark of tree-shade and open his mind moved on. When had the Welshrats started crawling in his chest? He found it then–and it was Cathy, pretty, tiny, delicate Cathy. But what about her? She was silent, but many women were silent. What was it? Where had it come from? He remembered that he had felt an imminence akin to the one that came to him when he held the water wand. And he remembered the shivers when the goose walked over his grave. Now he had pinned it down in time and place and person. It had come at dinner and it had come from Cathy.

He built her face in front of him and studied her wide-set eyes, delicate nostrils, mouth smaller than he liked but sweet, small firm chin, and back to her eyes. Were they cold? Was it her eyes? He was circling to the point. The eyes of Cathy had no message, no communication of any kind. There was nothing recognizable behind them. They were not human eyes. They reminded him of something–what was it?–some memory, some picture. He strove to find it and then it came of itself.

It rose out of the years complete with all its colours and its cries, its crowded feelings. He saw himself, a very little boy, so small that he had to reach high for his father's hand. He felt the cobbles of Londonderry under his feet and the crush and gaiety of the one big city he had seen. A fair, it was, with puppet shows and stalls of produce and horses and sheep penned right in the street for sale or trade or auction, and other stalls of bright-coloured knick-knackery, desirable and, because his father was gay, almost possessable.

And then the people turned like a strong river, and they were carried along a narrow street as though they were chips on a flood tide, pressure at chest and back and the feet keeping up. The narrow street opened out to a square, and against the grey wall of a building there was a high structure of timbers and a noosed rope hanging down.

Samuel and his father were pushed and bunted by the water of people, pushed closer and closer. He could hear in his memory ear his father saying, 'It's no thing for a child. It's no thing for anybody, but less for a child.' His father struggled to turn, to force his way back against the flood wave of people. 'Let us out. Please let us out. I've a child here.'

The wave was faceless and it pushed without passion. Samuel raised his head to look at the structure. A group of dark-clothed, dark-hatted men had climbed up on the high platform. And in their midst was a man with golden hair, dressed in dark trousers and a light blue shirt open at the throat. Samuel and his father were so close that the boy had to raise his head high to see.

The golden man seemed to have no arms. He looked out over the crowd and then looked down, looked right at Samuel. The picture was clear, lighted and perfect. The man's eyes had no depth–they were not like other eyes, not like the eyes of a man.

Suddenly there was quick movement on the platform, and Samuel's father put both his hands on the boy's head so that his palms cupped over the ears and his fingers met behind. The hands forced Samuel's head down and forced his face tight in against his father's black best coat. Struggle as he would, he could not move his head. He could see only a band of light around the edges of his eyes and only a muffled roar of sound came to his ears through his father's hands. He heard heart-beats in his ears. Then he felt his father's hands and arms grow rigid with set muscles, and against his face he could feel his father's deep-caught breathing and then deep intake and held breath, and his father's hands, trembling.

A little more there was to it, and he dug it up and set it before his eyes in the air ahead of the horse's head–a worn and battered table at a pub, loud talk and laughter. A pewter mug was in front of his father, and a cup of hot milk, sweet and aromatic with sugar and cinnamon, before himself. His father's lips were curiously blue and there were tears in his father's eyes.

'I've never have brought you if I'd known. It's not fit for any man to see, and sure not for a small boy.'

'I didn't see any,' Samuel piped. 'You held my head down.'

'I'm glad of that.'

'What was it?'

'I'll have to tell you. They were killing a bad man.'

'Was it the golden man?'

'Yes, it was. And you must put no sorrow on him. He had to be killed. Not once but many times he did dreadful things–things only a fiend could think of. It's not his hanging sorrows me but that they make a holiday of it that should be done secretly, in the dark.'

'I saw the golden man. He looked right down at me.'

'For that even more I thank God he's gone.'

'What did he do?'

'I'll never tell you nightmare things.'

'He had the strangest eyes, the golden man. They put me in mind of a goat's eyes.'

'Drink your sweety-milk and you shall have a stick with ribbons and a long whistle like silver.'

'And the shiny box with a picture into it?'

'That also, so you drink up your sweety-milk and beg no more.'

There it was, mined out of the dusty past.

Doxology was climbing the last rise before the hollow of the home ranch and the big feet stumbled over stones in the roadway.

It was the eyes, of course, Samuel thought. Only twice in my life have I seen eyes like that–not like human eyes. And he thought, 'It's the night and the moon. Now what connection under heaven can there be between the golden man hanged so long ago and the sweet little bearing mother? Liza's right. My imagination will get me a passport to hell one day. Let me dig this nonsense out, else I'll be searching that poor child for evil. This is how we can get trapped. Now think hard and then lose it. Some accident of eye shape and eye colour, it is. But no, that's not it. It's a look and has no reference to shape or colour. Well, why is a look evil, then? Maybe such a look may have been some time on a holy face. Now, stop this romancing and never let it trouble again–ever.' He shivered. I'll have to set up a goose fence around my grave, he thought.

And Samuel Hamilton resolved to help greatly with the Salinas Valley Eden, to make a secret guilt-payment for his ugly thoughts.

2

Liza Hamilton, her apple cheeks flaming red, moved like a caged leopard in front of the stove when Samuel came into the kitchen in the morning. The oakwood fire roared up past an open damper to heat the oven for the bread, which lay white and rising in the pans. Liza had been up before dawn. She always was. It was just as sinful to her to lie abed after light as it was to be abroad after dark. There was no possible virtue in either. Only one person in the world could with impunity and without crime lie between her crisp iron sheets after dawn, after sun-up, even to the far reaches of mid-morning, and that was her youngest and last born, Joe.

Only Tom and Joe lived on the ranch now. And Tom, big and red, already cultivating a fine flowing moustache, sat at the kitchen table with his sleeves rolled down as he had been mannered. Liza poured thick batter from a pitcher on to a soapstone griddle. The hot cakes rose like little hassocks, and small volcanoes formed and erupted on them until they were ready to be turned. A cheerful brown, they were, with tracings of darker brown. And the kitchen was full of the good sweet smell of them.

Samuel came in from the yard where he had been washing himself. His face and beard gleamed with water, and he turned down the sleeves of his blue shirt as he entered the kitchen. Rolled-up sleeves at the table were not acceptable to Mrs Hamilton. They indicated either an ignorance or a flouting of the niceties.

'I'm late, Mother,' Samuel said.

She did not look round at him. Her spatula moved like a striking snake and the hot cakes settled their white sides hissing on the soapstone. 'What time was it you came home?' she asked.

'Oh, it was late–late. Must have been near eleven, I didn't look, fearing to waken you.'

'I did not waken,' Liza said grimly. 'And maybe you can find it healthy to rove all night, but the Lord God will do what He sees fit about that.' It was well known that Liza Hamilton and the Lord God held similar convictions on nearly every subject. She turned and reached and a plate of crisp hot cakes lay between Tom's hands. 'How does the Sanchez place look?' she asked.

Samuel went to his wife, leaned down from his height, and kissed her round red cheek. 'Good morning, Mother. Give me your blessing.'

'Bless you,' said Liza automatically.

Samuel sat down at the table and said, 'Bless you, Tom. Well, Mr Trask is making great changes. He's fitting up the old house to live in.'

Liza turned sharply from the stove. 'The one where the cows and pigs have slept the years?'

'Oh, he's ripped out the floors and window casings. All new and new painted.'

'He'll never get the smell of pigs out,' Liza said firmly. 'There's a pungency left by a pig that nothing can wash out or cover up.'

'Well, I went inside and looked around, Mother, and I could smell nothing except paint.'

'When the paint dries you'll smell pig,' she said.

'He's got a garden laid out with spring water running through it, and he's set a place apart for flowers, roses and the like, and some of the bushes are coming clear from Boston.'

'I don't see how the Lord God puts up with such waste,' she said grimly. 'Not that I don't like a rose myself.'

'He said he'd try to root some cuttings for me,' Samuel said.

Tom finished his hot cakes and stirred his coffee. 'What kind of a man is he, Father?'

'Well, I think he's a fine man–has a good tongue and a fair mind. He's given to dreaming–'

'Hear now the pot blackguarding the kettle,' Liza interrupted.

'I know, Mother, I know. But have you ever thought that my dreaming takes the place of something I haven't? Mr Trask has practical dreams and the sweet dollars to make them solid. He wants to make a garden of his land, and he will do it too.'

'What's his wife like?' Liza asked.

'Well, she's very young and very pretty. She's quiet, hardly speaks, but then she's having her first baby soon.'

'I know that,' Liza said. 'What was her name before?'

'I don't know.'

'Well, where did she come from?'

'I don't know.'

She put his plate of hot cakes in front of him and poured coffee in his cup and refilled Tom's cup. 'What did you learn, then? How does she dress?'

'Why, very nice, pretty–a blue dress and a little coat, pink but tight about the waist.'

'You've an eye for that. Would you say they were made clothes or store-bought?'

'Oh, I think store-bought.'

'You would not know,' Liza said firmly. 'You thought the travelling suit Dessie made to go to San Jose was store-bought.'

'Dessie's the clever love,' said Samuel. 'A needle sings in her hands.'

Tom said, 'Dessie's thinking of opening a dressmaking shop in Salinas.'

'She told me,' Samuel said. 'She'd make a great success of it.'

'Salinas?' Liza put her hands on her hips. 'Dessie didn't tell me.'

'I'm afraid we've done bad service to our dearie,' Samuel said. 'Here she wanted to save it for a real tin-plate surprise to her mother and we've leaked it like wheat from a mouse-hole sack.'

'She might have *told* me,' said Liza. 'I don't like surprises. Well, go on–what was she doing?'

'Who?'

'Why, Mrs Trask, of course.'

'Doing? Why, sitting, in a chair under an oak tree. Her time's not far.'

'Her hands, Samuel, her hands–what was she doing with her hands?'

Samuel searched his memory. 'Nothing, I guess. I remember–she had little hands and she held them in her lap.'

Liza sniffed. 'Not sewing, not mending, not knitting?'

'No, Mother.'

'I don't know that it's a good idea for you to go over there. Riches and idleness, devil's tools, and you've not a very sturdy resistance.'

Samuel raised his head and laughed with pleasure. Sometimes his wife delighted him, but he could never tell her how. 'It's only the riches I'll be going there for, Liza. I meant to tell you after breakfast so you could sit down to hear. He wants me to bore four or five wells for him, and maybe put windmills and storage tanks.'

'Is it all talk? Is it a windmill turned by water? Will he pay you or will you come back excusing as usual? "He'll pay when his crop comes in,"' she mimicked. '"He'll pay when his rich uncle dies." It's my experience, Samuel, and should be yours, that if they don't pay presently they never pay at all. We could buy a valley farm with your promises.'

'Adam Trask will pay,' said Samuel. 'He's well fixed. His father left him a fortune. It's a whole winter of work, Mother. We'll lay something by and we'll have a Christmas to scrape the stars. He'll pay fifty cents a foot, and the windmills, Mother. I can make everything but the casings right here. I'll need the boys to help. I want to take Tom and Joe.'

'Joe can't go,' she said. 'You know he's delicate.'

'I thought I might scrape off some of his delicacy. He can starve on delicacy.'

'Joe can't go,' she said finally. 'And who is to run the ranch while you and Tom are gone?'

'I thought I'd ask George to come back. He doesn't like a clerk's job even if it is in King City.'

'Like it he may not, but he can take a measure of discomfort for eight dollars a week.'

'Mother,' Samuel cried, 'here's our chance to scratch our name in the First National Bank! Don't throw the weight of your tongue in the path of fortune. Please, Mother!'

She grumbled to herself all morning over her work while Tom and Samuel went over the boring equipment, sharpened bits, drew sketches of windmills new in design, and measured for timbers and redwood water-tanks. In the mid-morning Joe came out to join them, and he became so fascinated that he asked Samuel to let him go.

Samuel said, 'Off-hand I'd say I'm against it, Joe. Your mother needs you here.'

'But I want to go, Father. And don't forget, next year I'll be going to college in Palo Alto. And that's going away, isn't it? Please let me go. I'll work hard.'

'I'm sure you would if you could come. But I'm against it. And when you talk to your mother about it, I'll thank you to let it slip that I'm against it. You might even throw in that I refused you.'

Joe grinned, and Tom laughed aloud.

'Will you let her persuade you?' Tom asked.

Samuel scowled at his sons. 'I'm a hard-opinioned man,' he said. 'Once I've set my mind, oxen can't stir me. I've looked at it from all angles and my word is–Joe can't go. You wouldn't want to make a liar of my word, would you?'

'I'll go and talk to her now,' said Joe.

'Now, son, take it easy,' Samuel called after him. 'Use your head. Let her do most of it. Meanwhile I'll set my stubborn up.'

Two days later the big wagon pulled away, loaded with timbers and tackle. Tom drove four horses, and beside him Samuel and Joe sat swinging their feet.

CHAPTER 17

I

When I said Cathy was a monster it seemed to me that it was so. Now I have bent close with a glass over the small print of her and re-read the footnotes, and I wonder if it was true. The trouble is that since we cannot know what she wanted, we will never know whether or not she got it. If, rather than running towards something, she ran away from something, we can't know whether she escaped. Who knows but that she tried to tell someone or everyone what she was like and could not, for lack of a common language? Her life may have been her language, formal, developed, indecipherable. It is easy to say she was bad, but there is little meaning unless we know why.

I've built the image in my mind of Cathy, sitting quietly waiting for her pregnancy to be over, living on a farm she did not like, with a man she did not love.

She sat in her chair under the oak tree, her hands clasped each to each in love and shelter. She grew very big–abnormally big, even at a time when women gloried in big babies and counted extra pounds with pride. She was misshapen; her belly, tight and heavy and distended, made it impossible for her to stand without supporting herself with her hands. But the great lump was local. Shoulders, neck, arms, hands, face, were unaffected, slender and girlish. Her breasts did not grow and her nipples did not darken. There was no quickening of milk glands, no physical planning to feed the newborn. When she sat behind a table you could not see that she was pregnant at all.

In that day there was no measuring of pelvic arch, no testing of blood, no building with calcium. A woman gave a tooth for a child. It was the law. And a woman was likely to have strange tastes, some said for filth, and was set down to the Eve nature still under sentence for original sin.

Cathy's odd appetite was simple compared to some. The carpenters, repairing the old house, complained that they could not keep the lumps of chalk with which they coated their chalk lines. Again and again the scored hunks disappeared. Cathy stole them and broke them in little pieces. She carried the chips in her apron pocket, and when no one was about she crushed the soft lime between her teeth. She spoke very little. Her eyes were remote. It was as though she had gone away, leaving a breathing doll to conceal her absence.

Activity surged around her. Adam went happily about building and planning his Eden. Samuel and his boys brought in a well at forty feet and put down the new-fangled expensive metal casing, for Adam wanted the best.

The Hamiltons moved their rig and started another hole. They slept in a tent beside the work and cooked over a campfire. But there was always one or another of them riding home for a tool or with a message.

Adam fluttered like a bewildered bee confused by too many flowers. He sat by Cathy and chatted about the pieplant roots just come in. He sketched for her the new fan blade Samuel had invented for the windmill. It had a variable pitch and was an unheard-of thing. He rode out to the well rig and slowed the work with his interest. And naturally, as he discussed wells with Cathy, his talk was all of birth and child care at the well head. It was a good time for Adam, the best time. He was the king of his wide and spacious life. And summer passed into a hot and fragrant autumn.

2

The Hamiltons at the well rig had finished their lunch of Liza's bread and rat cheese and venomous coffee cooked in a can over the fire. Joe's eyes were heavy and he was considering how he could get away into the brush to sleep for a while.

Samuel knelt in the sandy soil, looking at the torn and broken edges of his bit. Just before they had stopped for lunch the drill had found something thirty feet down that had mangled the steel as though it were lead. Samuel scraped the edge of the blade with his pocket-knife and inspected the scrapings in the palm of his hand. His eyes shone with a childlike excitement. He held out his hand and poured the scrapings into Tom's hand.

'Take a look at it, son. What do you think it is?'

Joe wandered over from his place in front of the tent. Tom studied the fragments in his hand. 'Whatever it is, it's hard,' he said. 'Couldn't be a diamond that big. Looks like metal. Do you think we've bored into a buried locomotive?'

His father laughed. 'Thirty feet down,' he said admiringly.

'It looks like tool steel,' said Tom. 'We haven't got anything that can touch it.' Then he saw the far-away joyous look on his father's face and a shiver of shared delight came to him. The Hamilton children loved it when their father's mind went free. Then the world was peopled with wonders.

Samuel said, 'Metal, you say. You think, steel. Tom, I'm going to make a guess and then I'm going to get an assay. Now hear my guess–and remember it. I think we'll find nickel in it, and silver maybe, and carbon and manganese. How I would like to dig it up! It's in sea sand. That's what we've been getting.'

Tom said, 'Say, what do you think it is with–nickel and silver–'

'It must have been long thousand centuries ago,' Samuel said, and his sons knew he was seeing it. 'Maybe it was all water here–an inland sea with the seabirds circling and crying. And it would have been a pretty thing if it happened at night. There would come a line of light and then a pencil of white light and then a tree of blinding light drawn in a long arc from heaven. Then there'd be a great waterspout and a big mushroom of steam. And your ears would be staggered by the sound because the roaring cry of its coming would be on you at the same time the water exploded. And then it would be black night again because of the blinding light. And gradually you'd see the killed fish coming up, showing silver in the starlight, and the crying birds would come to eat them. It's a lonely, loving thing to think about, isn't it?'

He made them see it as he always did.

Tom said softly, 'You think it's a meteorite, don't you?'

'That I do, and we can prove it by assay.'

Joe said eagerly, 'Let's dig it up.'

'You dig it, Joe, while we bore for water.'

Tom said seriously, 'If the assay showed enough nickel and silver, wouldn't it pay to mine it?'

'You're my own son,' said Samuel. 'We don't know whether it's big as a house or little as a hat.'

'But we could probe down and see.'

'That we could if we did it secretly and hid our thinking under a pot.'

'Why, what do you mean?'

'Now, Tom, have you no kindness towards your mother? We give her enough trouble, son. She's told me plain that if I spend any more money patenting things, she'll give us trouble to remember. Have pity on her! Can't you see her shame when you ask her what we're doing? She's a truthful woman, your mother. She'd have to say, "They're at digging up a star."' He laughed happily. 'She'd never live it down. And she'd make us smart. No pies for three months.'

Tom said, 'We can't get through it. We'll have to move to another place.'

'I'll put some blasting powder down,' said his father, 'and if that doesn't crack it aside we'll start a new hole.' He stood up. 'I'll have to go home for powder and to sharpen the drill. Why don't you boys ride along with me and we'll give Mother a surprise so that she'll cook the whole night and complain. That way she'll dissemble her pleasure.'

Joe said, 'Somebody's coming, coming fast.' And indeed they could see a horseman riding towards them at full gallop, but a curious horseman who flopped about on his mount like a tied chicken. When he came a little closer they saw that it was Lee, his elbows waving like wings, his queue lashing about like a snake. It was surprising that he stayed on at all and still drove the horse at full tilt. He pulled up, breathing heavily. 'Missy Adam say come! Miss Cathy bad–come quick, Missy yell, scream.'

Samuel said, 'Hold on, Lee. When did it start?'

'Mebbe bleakfus time.'

'All right. Calm yourself. How is Adam?'

'Missy Adam clazy. Cly–laugh–make vomit.'

'Sure,' said Samuel. 'These new fathers. I was one once. Tom, throw a saddle on for me, will you?'

Joe said, 'What is it?'

'Why, Mrs Trask is about to have her baby. I told Adam I'd stand by.'

'You?' Joe asked.

Samuel levelled his eyes on his youngest son. 'I brought both of you into the world,' he said. 'And you've given no evidence you think I did a bad service to the world. Tom, you get all the tools gathered up. And go back to the ranch and sharpen the metal. Bring back the box of powder that's on the shelf in the tool-shed, and go easy with it as you love your arms and legs. Joe, I want you to stay here and look after things.'

Joe said plaintively, 'But what will I do here alone?'

Samuel was silent for a moment. Then he said, 'Joe, do you love me?'

'Why, sure.'

'If you heard I'd committed some great crime, would you turn me over to the police?'

'What are you talking about?'

'Would you?'

'No,'

'All right, then. In my basket, under my clothes, you'll find two books–new, so be gentle with them. It's two volumes by a man the world is going to hear from. You can start reading if you want and it will raise up your lid a little. It's called *The Principles of Psychology* and it's by an Eastern man named William James. No relation to the train robber. And, Joe, if you ever let on about the books I'll run you off the ranch. If your mother ever found out I spent the money on them she'd run me off the ranch.'

Tom led a saddled horse to him. 'Can I read it next?'

'Yes,' said Samuel, and he slipped his leg lightly over the saddle. 'Come on, Lee.'

The Chinese wanted to break into a gallop, but Samuel restrained him. 'Take it easy, Lee. Birthing takes longer than you think, mostly.'

For a time they rode in silence, and then Lee said, 'I'm sorry you bought those books. I have the condensed form, in one volume, the textbook. You should have borrowed it.'

'Have you now? Do you have many books?'

'Not many here–thirty or forty. But you're welcome to any of them you haven't read.'

'Thank you, Lee. And you may be sure I'll look the first moment I can. You know, you could talk to my boys. Joe's a little flighty, but Tom's all right and it would do him good.'

'It's a hard bridge to cross, Mr Hamilton. Makes me timid to talk to a new person, but I'll try if you say so.'

They walked the horses rapidly towards the little draw of the Trask place. Samuel said, 'Tell me, how is it with the mother?'

'I'd rather you saw for yourself and thought for yourself,' Lee said. 'You know, when a man lives alone as much as I do, his mind can go off on an irrational tangent just because his social world is out of kilter.'

'Yes, I know. But I'm not lonely and I'm on a tangent too. But maybe not the same one.'

'You don't think I imagine it, then?'

'I don't know what it is, but I'll tell you for your reassurance that I've a sense of strangeness.'

'I guess that's all it is with me too,' said Lee. He smiled. 'I'll tell you how far it got with me, though. Since I've come here I find myself thinking of Chinese fairy tales my father told me. We Chinese have a well-developed demonology.'

'You think she is a demon?'

'Of course not,' said Lee. 'I hope I'm a little beyond such silliness. I don't know what it is. You know, Mr Hamilton, a servant develops an ability to taste the wind and judge the climate of the house he works in. And there's a strangeness here. Maybe that's what makes me remember my father's demons.'

'Did your father believe in them?'

'Oh, no. He thought I should know the background. You Occidentals perpetuate a good many myths too.'

Samuel said, 'Tell me what happened to set you off. This morning, I mean.'

'If you weren't coming I would try,' said Lee. 'But I would rather not. You can see for yourself. I may be crazy. Of course Mr Adam is strung so tight he may snap like a banjo string.'

'Give me a little hint. It might save time. What did she do?'

'Nothing. That's just it. Mr Hamilton, I've been at births before, a good many of them, but this is something new to me.'

'How?'

'It's–well–I'll tell you the one thing I can think of. This is much more like a bitter, deadly combat than a birth.'

As they rode into the draw and under the oak trees Samuel said, 'I hope you haven't got me in a state, Lee. It's a strange day, and I don't know why.'

'No wind,' said Lee. 'It's the first day in the month when there hasn't been wind in the afternoon.'

'That's so. You know, I've been so close to the details I've paid no attention to the clothing of the day. First we find a buried star and now we go to dig up a mint-new human.' He looked up through the oak branches at the yellow-lit hills. 'What a beautiful day to be born in!' he said. 'If signs have their fingers on a life, it's a sweet life coming. And, Lee, if Adam plays true, he'll be in the way. Stay close, will you? In case I need something. Look, the men, the carpenters, are sitting under that tree.'

'Mr Adam stopped the work. He thought the hammering might disturb his wife.'

Samuel said, 'You stay close. That sounds like Adam playing true. He doesn't know his wife probably couldn't hear God Himself beating a tattoo on the sky.'

The workmen sitting under the tree waved to him. 'How do, Mr Hamilton. How's your family?'

'Fine, fine. Say, isn't that Rabbit Holman? Where've you been, Rabbit?'

'Went prospecting, Mr Hamilton.'

'Find anything, Rabbit?'

'Hell, Mr Hamilton, I couldn't even find the mule I went out with.'

They rode on towards the house. Lee said quickly, 'If you ever get a minute, I'd like to show you something.'

'What is it, Lee?'

'Well, I've been trying to translate some old Chinese poetry into English. I'm not sure it can be done. Will you take a look?'

'I'd like to, Lee. Why, that would be a treat for me.'

3

Bordoni's white frame house was very quiet, almost broodingly quiet, and the blinds were pulled down. Samuel dismounted at the stoop, untied his bulging saddlebags, and gave his horse to Lee. He knocked and got no answer and went in. It was dusky in the living-room after the outside light. He looked in the kitchen, scrubbed to the wood grain by Lee. A grey stoneware pilon coffee-pot grunted on the back of the stove. Samuel tapped lightly on the bedroom door and went in.

It was almost pitch-black inside, for not only were the blinds down but blankets were tacked over the windows. Cathy was lying in the big four-poster bed, and Adam sat beside her, his face buried in the coverlet. He raised his head and looked blindly out.

Samuel said pleasantly, 'Why are you sitting in the dark?'

Adam's voice was hoarse. 'She doesn't want the light. It hurts her eyes.'

Samuel walked into the room and authority grew in him with each step. 'There will have to be light,' he said. 'She can close her eyes. I'll tie a black cloth over them if she wants.' He moved to the window and grasped the blanket to pull it down, but Adam was upon him before he could yank.

'Leave it. The light hurts her,' he said fiercely.

Samuel turned on him. 'Now, Adam, I know what you feel. I promised you I'd take care of things, and I will. I only hope one of those things isn't you.' He pulled the blanket down and rolled up the blind to let the golden afternoon light in.

Cathy made a little mewing sound from the bed, and Adam went to her. 'Close your eyes, dear. I'll put a cloth over your eyes.'

Samuel dropped his saddlebags in a chair and stood beside the bed. 'Adam,' he said firmly, 'I'm going to ask you to go out of the room and to stay out.'

'No, I can't. Why?'

'Because I don't want you in the way. It's considered a sweet practice for you to get drunk.'

'I couldn't.'

Samuel said, 'Anger's a slow thing in me and disgust is slower, but I can taste the beginning of both of them. You'll get out of the room and give me no trouble or I'll go away and you'll have a basket of trouble.'

Adam went finally, and from the doorway Samuel called, 'And I don't want you bursting in if you hear anything. You wait for me to come out.' He closed the door, noticed there was a key in the lock, and turned it. 'He's an upset, vehement man,' he said. 'He loves you.'

He had not looked at her closely until now. And he saw true hatred in her eyes, unforgiving, murderous hatred.

'It'll be over before long, dearie. Now tell me, has the water broke?'

Her hostile eyes glared at him and her lips raised snarling from her little teeth. She did not answer him.

He stared at her. 'I did not come by choice except as a friend,' he said. 'It's not a pleasure to me, young woman. I don't know your trouble and minute by minute I don't care. Maybe I can save you some pain–who knows? I'm going to ask you one more question. If you don't answer, if you put that snarling look on me I'm going out and leave you to welter.'

The words struck into her understanding like lead shot dropped in water. She made a great effort. And it gave him a shivering to see her face change, the steel leave her eyes, the lips thicken from line to bow, and the corners turn up. He noticed a movement of her hands, the fists unclench and the fingers turn pinkly upwards. Her face became young and innocent and bravely hurt. It was like one magic-lantern slide taking the place of another.

She said softly, 'The water broke at dawn.'

'That's better. Have you had hard labour?'

'Yes.'

'How far apart?'

'I don't know.'

'Well, I've been in this room fifteen minutes.'

'I've had two little ones–no big ones since you came.'

'Fine. Now where's your linen?'

'In that hamper over there.'

'You'll be all right, dearie,' he said gently.

He opened his saddlebags and took out a thick rope covered with blue velvet and looped at either end. On the velvet hundreds of little pink flowers were embroidered. 'Liza sent you her pulling rope to use,' he said. 'She made it when our first-born was preparing. What with our children and friends, this rope has pulled a great number of people into the world.' He slipped one of the loops over each of the footposts of the bed.

Suddenly her eyes glazed and her back arched like a spring and the blood started to her cheeks. He waited for her cry or scream and looked apprehensively at the closed door. But there was no scream–only a series of grunting squeals. After a few seconds her body relaxed and the hatefulness was back in her face.

The labour struck again. 'There's a dear,' he said soothingly. 'Was it one or two? I don't know. The more you see, the more you learn no two are alike. I'd better get my hands washed.'

Her head threshed from side to side. 'Good, good, my darling,' he said. 'I think it won't be long till your baby's here.' He put his hand on her forehead where the scar showed dark and angry. 'How did you get the hurt on your head?' he asked.

Her head jerked up and her sharp teeth fastened on his hand across the back and up into the palm near the little finger. He cried out in pain and tried to pull his hands away, but her jaw was set and her head twisted and turned, mangling his hand the way a terrier worries a sack. A shrill snarling came from her set teeth. He slapped her on the cheek and it had no effect. Automatically he did what he would have done to stop a dog fight. His left hand went to her throat and he cut off her wind. She struggled and tore at his hand before her jaws unclenched and he pulled his hand free. The flesh was torn and bleeding. He stepped back from the bed and looked at the damage her teeth had done. He looked at her with fear. And when he looked, her face was calm again and young and innocent.

'I'm sorry,' she said quickly. 'Oh, I'm sorry.'

Samuel shuddered.

'It was the pain,' she said.

Samuel laughed shortly. 'I'll have to muzzle you, I guess.' he said. 'A collie bitch did the same to me once.' He saw the hatred look out of her eyes for a second and then retreat.

Samuel said, 'Have you got anything to put on it? Humans are more poisonous than snakes.'

'I don't know.'

'Well, have you got any whisky? I'll pour some whisky on it.'

'In the second drawer.'

He splashed whisky on his bleeding hand and kneaded the flesh against the alcohol sting. A strong quaking was in his stomach and a sickness rose up against his eyes. He took a swallow of whisky to steady himself. He dreaded to look back at the bed. 'My hand won't be much good for a while,' he said.

Samuel told Adam afterwards, 'She must be made of whalebone. The birth happened before I was ready. Popped like a seed. I'd not the water ready to wash him. Why, she didn't even touch the pulling rope to bear down. Pure whalebone, she is.' He tore at the door, called Lee and demanded warm water.

Adam came charging into the room. 'A boy!' Samuel cried. 'You've got a boy! Easy,' he said, for Adam had seen the mess in the bed and a green was rising in his face.

Samuel said, 'Send Lee in here. And you, Adam, if you still have the authority to tell your hands and feet what to do, get to the kitchen and make me some coffee. And see the lamps are filled and the chimneys clean.'

Adam turned like a zombie and left the room. In a moment Lee looked in. Samuel pointed to the bundle in a laundry basket. 'Sponge him off in warm water, Lee. Don't let a draught get on him. Lord! I wish Liza were here. I can't do everything at once.'

He turned back to the bed. 'Now, dearie, I'll get you cleaned up.'

Cathy was bowed again, snarling in her pain. 'It'll be over in a little,' he said. 'Take a little time for the residue. And you're so quick. Why, you didn't even have to pull on Liza's rope.' He saw something, stared, and went quickly to work. 'Lord God in Heaven, it's another one!'

He worked fast, and as with the first the birth was incredibly quick. And again Samuel tied the cord. Lee took the second baby, washed it, wrapped it, and put it in the basket.

Samuel cleaned the mother and shifted her gently while he changed the linen on the bed. He found in himself a reluctance to look in her face. He worked as quickly as he could, for his bitten hand was stiffening. He drew a clean white sheet up to her chin and raised her to slip a fresh pillow under her head. At last he had to look at her.

Her golden hair was wet with perspiration but her face had changed. It was stony, expressionless. At her throat the pulse fluttered visibly.

'You have two sons,' Samuel said. 'Two fine sons. They aren't alike. Each one born separate in his own sack.'

She inspected him coldly and without interest.

Samuel said, 'I'll show your boys to you.'

'No,' she said without emphasis.

'Now, dearie, don't you want to see your sons?'

'No. I don't want them.'

'Oh, you'll change. You're tired now, but you'll change. And I'll tell you now–this birth was quicker and easier than I've seen ever in my life.'

The eyes moved from his face. 'I don't want them. I want you to cover the windows and take the light away.'

'It's weariness. In a few days you'll feel so different you won't remember.'

'I'll remember. Go away. Take them out of the room. Send Adam in.'

Samuel was caught by her tone. There was no sickness, no weariness, no softness. His words came out without his will. 'I don't like you,' he said and wished he could gather the words back into his throat and into his mind. But his words had no effect on Cathy.

'Send Adam in.'

In the little living-room Adam looked vaguely at his sons and went quickly into the bedroom and shut the door. In a moment came the sound of tapping. Adam was nailing the blankets over the windows again.

Lee brought coffee to Samuel. 'That's a bad-looking hand you have there,' he said.

'I know. I'm afraid it's going to give me trouble.'

'Why did she do it?'

'I don't know. She's a strange thing.'

Lee said, 'Mr Hamilton, let me take care of that. You could lose an arm.'

The life went out of Samuel. 'Do what you want, Lee. A frightened sorrow has closed down over my heart. I wish I were a child so I could cry. I'm too old to be afraid like this. And I've not felt such despair since a bird died in my hand by a flowing water long ago.'

Lee left the room and shortly returned, carrying a small ebony box carved with twisting dragons. He sat by Samuel and from his box took a wedge-shaped Chinese razor. 'It will hurt,' he said softly.

'I'll try to bear it, Lee.'

The Chinese bit his lips, feeling the inflicted pain in himself while he cut deeply into the hand, opened the flesh around the toothmarks front and back, and trimmed the ragged flesh away until good red blood flowed from every wound. He shook a bottle of yellow emulsion labelled Hall's Cream Salve and poured it into the deep cuts. He saturated a handkerchief with the salve and wrapped the hand. Samuel winced and gripped the chair arm with his good hand.

'It's mostly carbolic acid,' Lee said. 'You can smell it.'

'Thank you, Lee. I'm being a baby to knot up like this.'

'I don't think I could have been so quiet,' said Lee. 'I'll get you another cup of coffee.'

He came back with two cups and sat down by Samuel. 'I think I'll go away,' he said. 'I never went willingly to a slaughter-house.'

Samuel stiffened. 'What do you mean?'

'I don't know. The words came out.'

Samuel shivered. 'Lee, men are fools. I guess I hadn't thought about it, but Chinese men are fools too.'

'What made you doubt it?'

'Oh, maybe because we think of strangers as stronger and better than we are.'

'What do you want to say?'

Samuel said, 'Maybe the foolishness is necessary, the dragon fighting, the boasting, the pitiful courage to be constantly knocking a chip off God's shoulder, and the childish cowardice that makes a ghost of a dead tree beside a darkening road. Maybe that's good and necessary, but–'

'What do you want to say?' Lee repeated patiently.

'I thought some wind had blown up the embers of my foolish mind,' Samuel said. 'And now I hear in your voice that you have it too. I feel wings over this house. I feel a dreadfulness coming.'

'I feel it too.'

'I know you do, and that makes me take less than my usual comfort in my foolishness. This birth was too quick, too easy–like a cat having kittens. And I fear for these kittens. I have dreadful thoughts gnawing to get into my brain.'

'What do you want to say?' Lee asked a third time.

'I want my wife,' Samuel cried. 'No dreams, no ghosts, no foolishness. I want her here. They say miners take canaries into the pits to test the air. Liza has no truck with foolishness. And, Lee, if Liza sees a ghost, it's a ghost and not a fragment of a dream. If Liza feels trouble we'll bar the doors.'

Lee got up and went to the laundry basket and looked down at the babies. He had to peer close, for the light was going fast. 'They're sleeping,' he said.

'They'll be squalling soon enough. Lee, will you hitch up the rig and drive to my place for Liza? Tell her I need her here. If Tom's still there, tell him to mind the place. If not, I'll send him in the morning. And if Liza doesn't want to come, tell her we need a woman's hand here and a woman's clear eyes. She'll know what you mean.'

'I'll do it,' said Lee. 'Maybe we're scaring each other, like two children in the dark.'

'I've thought of that,' Samuel said. 'And, Lee, tell her I hurt my hand at the well head. Do not, for God's sake, tell her how it happened.'

'I'll get some lamps lit and then I'll go,' said Lee. 'It will be a great relief to have her here.'

'That it will, Lee. That it will. She'll let some light into this cellar hole.'

After Lee drove away in the dark, Samuel picked up a lamp in his left hand. He had to set it on the floor to turn the knob of the bedroom door. The room was in pitch-blackness, and the yellow lamplight streamed upward and did not light the bed.

Cathy's voice came strong and edged from the bed. 'Shut the door. I do not want the light. Adam, go out! I want to be in the dark–alone.'

Adam said hoarsely, 'I want to stay with you.'

'I do not want you.'

'I will stay.'

'Then stay. But don't talk any more. Please close the door and take the lamp away.'

Samuel went back to the living-room. He put the lamp on the table by the laundry basket and looked in on the small sleeping faces of the babies. Their eyes were pinched shut and they sniffled a little in discomfort at the light. Samuel put his forefinger down and stroked the hot foreheads. One of the twins opened his mouth and yawned prodigiously and settled back to sleep. Samuel moved the lamp and then went to the front door and opened it and stepped outside. The evening star was so bright that it seemed to flare and crumple as it sank towards the western mountains. The air was still and Samuel could smell the day-heated sage. The night was very dark. Samuel started when he heard a voice speaking out of the blackness.

'How is she?'

'Who is it?' Samuel demanded.

'It's me, Rabbit.' the man emerged and took form in the light from the doorway.

'The mother, Rabbit? Oh, she's fine.'

'Lee said twins.'

'That's right–twin sons. You couldn't want better. I guess Mr Trask will tear the river up by the roots now. He'll bring in a crop of candy canes.'

Samuel didn't know why he changed the subject. 'Rabbit, do you know what we bored into today? A meteorite.'

'What's that, Mr Hamilton?'

'A shooting star that fell a million years ago.'

'You did? Well, think of that! How did you hurt your hand?'

'I almost said on a shooting star.' Samuel laughed. 'But it wasn't that interesting. I pinched it on the tackle.'

'Bad?'

'No, not bad.'

'Two boys,' said Rabbit. 'My old lady will be jealous.'

'Will you come inside and sit, Rabbit?'

'No, no, thank you. I'll get out to sleep. Morning seems to come earlier every year I live.'

'That it does, Rabbit. Good night then.'

Liza Hamilton arrived about four in the morning. Samuel was asleep in his chair, dreaming that he had gripped a red-hot bar of iron and could not let go. Liza awakened him and looked at his hand before she even glanced at the babies. While she did well the things he had done in a lumbering, masculine way, she gave him his orders and packed him off. He was to get up this instant, saddle Doxology, and ride straight for King City. No matter what time it was, he must wake up that good-for-nothing doctor and get his hand treated. If it seemed all right he could go home and wait. And it was a criminal thing to leave your last-born, and he little more than a baby himself, sitting there by a hole in the ground with no one to care for him. It was a matter which might even engage the attention of the Lord God Himself.

If Samuel craved realism and activity, he got it. She had him off the place by dawn. His hand was bandaged by eleven and he was in his own chair at his own table by five in the afternoon, sizzling with fever, and Tom was boiling a hen to make chicken soup for him.

For three days Samuel lay in bed, fighting the fever phantoms and putting names to them too, before his great strength broke down the infection and drove it caterwauling away.

Samuel looked up at Tom with clear eyes and said: 'I'll have to get up,' tried it and sat weakly back, chuckling–the sound he made when any force in the world defeated him. He had an idea that even when beaten he could steal a little victory by laughing at defeat. And Tom brought him chicken soup until he wanted to kill him. The lore has not died out of the world, and you will still find people who believe that soup will cure any hurt or illness and is no bad thing to have for the funeral either.

4

Liza stayed away a week. She cleaned the Trask house from the top clear down into the grain of the wooden floors. She washed everything she could bend enough to get into a tub and sponged the rest. She put the babies on a working basis and noted with satisfaction that they howled most of the time and began to gain weight. Lee she used like a slave since she didn't quite believe in him. Adam she ignored since she couldn't use him for anything. She did make him wash the windows and then did it again after he had finished.

Liza sat with Cathy just enough to come to the conclusion that she was a sensible girl who didn't talk very much or try to teach her grandmother to suck eggs. She also checked her over and found that she was perfectly healthy, not injured and not sick, and that she would never nurse the twins. 'And just as well too,' she said. 'Those great lummoxes would chew a little thing like you to the bone.' She forgot that she was smaller than Cathy and had nursed every one of her own children.

On Saturday afternoon Liza checked her work, left a list of instructions as long as her arm to cover every possibility from colic to an inroad of grease ants, packed her travelling basket, and had Lee drive her home.

She found her house a stable of filth and abomination and she set to cleaning it with the violence and disgust of a Hercules at labour. Samuel asked questions of her in flight.

How were the babies?

They were fine, growing.

How was Adam?

Well, he moved around as if he was alive but he left no evidence. The Lord in his wisdom gave money to very curious people, perhaps because they'd starve without.

How was Mrs Trask?

Quiet, lackadaisical, like most rich Eastern women (Liza had never known a rich Eastern woman), but on the other hand docile and respectful. 'And it's a strange thing,' Liza said. 'I can find no real fault with her save perhaps a touch of laziness, and I don't like her very much. Maybe it's that scar. How did she get it?'

'I don't know,' said Samuel.

Liza levelled her forefinger like a pistol between his eyes. 'I'll tell you something. Unbeknownst to herself, she's put a spell on her husband. He moons around her like a sick duck. I don't think he's given the twins a thorough good look yet.'

Samuel waited until she went by again. He said, 'Well, if she's lazy and he's moony, who's going to take care of the sweet babies? Twin boys take a piece of looking after.'

Liza stopped in mid-swoop, drew a chair close to him, and sat resting her hands on her knees. 'Remember I've never held the truth lightly if you don't believe me,' she said.

'I don't think you could lie, dearie,' he said, and she smiled, thinking it a compliment.

'Well, what I'm to tell you might weigh a little heavy on your belief if you did not know that.'

'Tell me.'

'Samuel, you know that Chinese with his slanty eyes and his outlandish talk and that braid?'

'Lee? Sure I know him.'

'Well, wouldn't you say off-hand he was a heathen?'

'I don't know.'

'Come now, Samuel, anybody would. But he's not.' She straightened up.

'What is he?'

She tapped his arm with an iron finger. 'A Presbyterian, and well up–well up, I say, when you dig it out of that crazy talk. Now what do you think of that?'

Samuel's voice was unsteady with trying to clamp his laughter in. 'No!' he said.

'And I say yes. Well now, who do you think is looking after the twins? I wouldn't trust a heathen from here to omega–but a Presbyterian–he learned everything I told him.'

'No wonder they're taking on weight,' said Samuel.

'It's a matter for praise and it's a matter for prayer.'

'We'll do it too,' said Samuel. 'Both.'

5

For a week Cathy rested and gathered her strength. On Saturday of the second week of October she stayed in her bedroom all morning. Adam tried the door and found it locked.

'I'm busy,' she called, and he went away.

Putting her bureau in order, he thought, for he could hear her opening drawers and closing them.

In the later afternoon Lee came to Adam where he sat on the stoop. 'Missy say I go King City buy nursery bottle,' he said uneasily.

'Well, do it then,' said Adam. 'She's your mistress.'

'Missy say not come back mebbe Monday. Take–'

Cathy spoke calmly from the doorway. 'He hasn't had a day off for a long time. A rest would do him good.'

'Of course,' said Adam. 'I just didn't think of it. Have a good time. If I need anything I'll get one of the carpenters.'

'Men go home, Sunday.'

'I'll get the Indian. Lopez will help.'

Lee felt Cathy's eyes on him. 'Lopez dlunk. Find bottle whisky.'

Adam said petulantly, 'I'm not helpless, Lee. Stop arguing.'

Lee looked at Cathy standing in the doorway. He lowered his eyelids. 'Mebbe I come back late,' he said, and he thought he saw two dark lines appear between her eyes and then disappear. He turned away. 'Goo-by,' he said.

Cathy went back to her room as the evening came down. At seven-thirty Adam knocked. 'I've got you some supper, dear. It's not much.' The door opened as though she had been standing waiting. She was dressed in her neat travelling dress, the jacket edged in black braid, black velvet lapels, and large jet buttons. On her head was a wide straw hat with a tiny crown; long jet-headed hatpins held it on. Adam's mouth dropped open.

She gave him no chance to speak. 'I'm going away now.'

'Cathy, what do you mean?'

'I told you before.'

'You didn't.'

'You didn't listen. It doesn't matter.'

'I don't believe you.'

Her voice was dead and metallic. 'I don't give a damn what you believe. I'm going.'

'The babies–'

'Throw them in one of your wells.'

He cried in panic, 'Cathy, you're sick. You can't go–not from me–not from me.'

'I can do anything to you. Any woman can do anything to you. You're a fool.'

The word got through his haze. Without warning, his hands reached for her shoulders and he thrust her backwards. As she staggered he took the key from the inside of the door, slammed the door shut, and locked it.

He stood panting, his ear close to the panel, and a hysterical sickness poisoned him. He could hear her moving quietly about. A drawer was opened, and the thought leaped in him–she's going to stay. And there was a little click he could not place. His ear was almost touching the door.

Her voice came from so near that he jerked his head back. He heard richness in her voice. 'Dear,' she said softly, 'I didn't know you would take it so. I'm sorry, Adam.'

His breath burst hoarsely out of his throat. His hand trembled, trying to turn the key, and it fell out on the floor after he had turned it. He pushed the door open. She stood three feet away. In her right hand she held his .44 Colt, and the black hole of the barrel pointed at him. He took a step towards her, saw that the hammer was back.

She shot him. The heavy slug struck him in the shoulder and flattened and tore out a piece of his shoulder-blade. The flash and roar smothered him, and he staggered back and fell to the floor. She moved slowly towards him, cautiously, as she might towards a wounded animal. He stared up into her eyes, which inspected him impersonally. She tossed the pistol on the floor beside him and walked out of the house.

He heard her steps on the porch, on the crisp dry oak leaves on the path, and then he could hear her no more. And the monotonous sound that had been there all along was the cry of the twins, wanting their dinner. He had forgotten to feed them.

CHAPTER 18

I

Horace Quinn was the new deputy sheriff appointed to look after things around the King City district. He complained that his new job took him away from his ranch too much. His wife complained even more, but the truth of the matter was that nothing much had happened in a criminal way since Horace had been deputy. He had seen himself making a name for himself and running for sheriff. The sheriff was an important officer. His job was less flighty than that of district attorney, almost as permanent and dignified as superior court judge. Horace didn't want to stay on the ranch all his life, and his wife had an urge to live in Salinas, where she had relatives.

When the rumours, repeated by the Indian and the carpenters, that Adam Trask had been shot reached Horace, he saddled up right away and left his wife to finish butchering the pig he had killed that morning.

Just north of the big sycamore tree where the Hester road turns off to the left, Horace met Julius Euskadi. Julius was trying to decide whether to go quail hunting or to King City and catch the train to Salinas to shake some of the dust out of his britches. The Euskadis were well-to-do, handsome people of Basque extraction.

Julius said, 'If you'd come along with me, I'd go into Salinas. They tell me that right next door to Jenny's, two door from the Long Green, there's a new place called Faye's. I heard it was pretty nice, run like San Francisco. They've got a piano player.'

Horace rested his elbow on his saddle horn and stirred a fly from his horse's shoulder with his rawhide quirt. 'Some other time,' he said. 'I've got to look into something.'

'You wouldn't be going to Trask's, would you?'

'That's right. Did you hear anything about it?'

'Not to make any sense. I heard Mr Trask shot himself in the shoulder with a forty-four and then fired everybody on the ranch. How do you go about shooting yourself in the shoulder with a forty-four, Horace?'

'I don't know. Them Easterners are pretty clever. I thought I'd go up and find out. Didn't his wife just have a baby?'

'Twins, I heard,' said Julius. 'Maybe they shot him.'

'One hold the gun and the other pull the trigger? Hear anything else?'

'All mixed up, Horace. Want some company?'

'I'm not going to deputize you, Julius. Sheriff says the supervisors are raising hell about the pay-roll. Hornby out in the Alisal deputized his great-aunt and kept her in posse three weeks just before Easter.'

'You're fooling!'

'No, I'm not. And you get no star.'

'Hell, I don't want to be a deputy. Just thought I'd ride along with you for company. I'm curious.'

'Me too. Glad to have you, Julius. I can always fling the oath around your neck if there's any trouble. What do you say the new place is called?'

'Faye's. Sacramento woman.'

'They do things pretty nice in Sacramento,' and Horace told how they did things in Sacramento as they rode along.

It was a nice day to be riding. As they turned into the Sanchez draw they were cursing the bad hunting in recent years. Three things are never any good–farming, fishing, and hunting–compared to other years, that is. Julius was saying, 'Christ, I wish they hadn't killed off all the grizzly bears. In eighteen-eighty my grandfather killed one up by Pletyo weighed eighteen hundred pounds.'

A silence came on them as they rode in under the oaks, a silence they took from the place itself. There was no sound, no movement.

'I wonder if he finished fixing up the old house,' Horace said.

'Hell no. Rabbit Holman was working on it, and he told me Trask called them all in and fired them. He told them not to come back.'

'They say Trask has got a pot of money.'

'I guess he's well fixed, all right,' said Julius. 'Sam Hamilton is sinking four wells–if he didn't get fired too.'

'How is Mr Hamilton? I ought to go up to see him.'

'He's fine. Full of hell as ever.'

'I'll have to go up and pay him a visit,' said Horace.

Lee came out on the stoop to meet them.

Horace said, 'Hello, Ching Chong. Bossy man here?'

'He sick,' Lee said.

'I'd like to see him.'

'No see. He sick.'

'That's enough of that,' said Horace. 'Tell him Deputy Sheriff Quinn wants to see him.'

Lee disappeared, and in a moment he was back. 'You come,' he said. 'I take horsy.'

Adam lay in the four-poster bed where the twins had been born. He was propped high with pillows, and a mound of home-devised bandages covered his left breast and shoulder. The room reeked of Hall's Cream Salve.

Horace said later to his wife, 'And if you ever saw death still breathing, there it was.'

Adam's cheeks hugged the bone and pulled the skin of his nose tight and skinny. His eyes seemed to bulge out of his head and to take up the whole upper part of his face, and they were shiny with sickness, tense and myopic. His bony right hand kneaded a fistful of coverlet.

Horace said, 'Howdy, Mr Trask. Heard you got hurt.' He paused, waiting for an answer. He went on, 'Just thought I'd drop around and see how you were doing. How'd it happen?'

A look of transparent eagerness came over Adam's face. He shifted slightly in the bed.

'If it hurts to talk you can whisper,' Horace added helpfully.

'Only when I breathe deep,' Adam said softly. 'I was cleaning my gun and it went off.'

Horace glanced at Julius and then back. Adam saw the look and a little colour of embarrassment rose in his cheeks.

'Happens all the time,' said Horace. 'Got the gun around?'

'I think Lee put it away.'

Horace stepped to the door. 'Hey there, Ching Chong, bring the pistol.'

In a moment Lee poked the gun butt-first through the door. Horace looked at it, swung the cylinder out, poked the cartridges out, and smelled the empty brass cylinder of the one empty shell. 'There's better shooting cleaning the damn things than pointing them. I'll have to make a report to the county, Mr Trask. I won't take up much of your time. You were cleaning the barrel, maybe with a rod, and the gun went off and hit you in the shoulder?'

'That's right, sir,' Adam said quickly.

'And, cleaning it, you hadn't swung out the cylinder?'

'That's right.'

'And you were poking the rod in and out with the barrel pointed towards you with the hammer cocked?'

Adam's breath rasped in a quick intake.

Horace went on, 'And it must have blowed the rod right through you and took off your left hand too.' Horace's pale sun-washed eyes never left Adam's face. He said kindly, 'What happened, Mr Trask? Tell me what happened.'

'I tell you truly it was an accident, sir.'

'Now you wouldn't have me write a report like I just said. The sheriff would think I was crazy. What happened?'

'Well, I'm not very used to guns. Maybe it wasn't just like that, but I was cleaning it and it went off.'

There was a whistle in Horace's nose. He had to breathe through his mouth to stop it. He moved slowly up from the foot of the bed, nearer to Adam's head and staring eyes. 'You came from the East not very long ago, didn't you, Mr Trask?'

'That's right. Connecticut.'

'I guess people don't use guns very much there any more.'

'Not much.'

'Little hunting?'

'Some.'

'So you'd be more used to a shotgun?'

'That's right. But I never hunted much.'

'I guess you didn't hardly use a pistol at all, so you didn't know how to handle it.'

'That's right,' Adam said eagerly. 'Hardly anybody there has a pistol.'

'So when you came here you bought that forty-four because everybody out here has a pistol and you were going to learn how to use it.'

'Well, I thought it might be a good thing to learn.'

Julius Euskadi stood tensely, his face and body receptive, listening but uncommunicative.

Horace sighed and looked away from Adam. His eyes brushed over and past Julius and came back to his hands. He laid the gun on the bureau and carefully lined the brass and lead cartridges beside it. 'You know,' he said, 'I've only been a deputy a little while. I thought I was going to have some fun with it and maybe in a few years run for sheriff. I haven't got the guts for it. It isn't any fun to me.'

Adam watched him nervously.

'I don't think anybody's ever been afraid of me before–mad at me, yes–but not afraid. It's a mean thing, makes me feel mean.'

Julius said irritably, 'Get to it. You can't resign right this minute.'

'The hell I can't–if I want to. All right! Mr Trask, you served in the United States Cavalry. The weapons of the cavalry are carbines and pistols. You–' He stopped and swallowed. 'What happened, Mr Trask?'

Adam's eyes seemed to grow larger, and they were moist and edged with red. 'It was an accident,' he whispered.

'Anybody see it? Was your wife with you when it happened?'

Adam did not reply, and Horace saw that his eyes were closed. 'Mr Trask,' he said, 'I know you're a sick man. I'm trying to make it as easy on you as I can. Why don't you rest now while I have a talk with your wife?' He waited a moment and then turned to the doorway, where Lee still stood. 'Ching Chong, tell Missy I would admire to talk to her a few minutes.'

Lee did not reply.

Adam spoke without opening his eyes. 'My wife is away on a visit.'

'She wasn't here when it happened?' Horace glanced at Julius and saw a curious expression on Julius's lips. The corners of his mouth were turned slightly up in a sardonic smile. Horace thought quickly, 'He's ahead of me. He'd make a good sheriff.' 'Say,' he said, 'that's kind of interesting. Your wife had a baby–two babies–two weeks ago, and now she's gone on a visit. Did she take the babies with her? I thought I heard them a little while ago.' Horace leaned over the bed and touched the back of Adam's clenched right hand. 'I hate this, but I can't stop now. Trask!' he said loudly, 'I want you to tell me what happened. This isn't nosiness. This is the law. Now, damn it, you open your eyes and tell me or, by Christ, I'll take you in to the sheriff even if you are hurt.'

Adam opened his eyes, and they were blank like a sleep-walker's eyes. And his voice came out without rise or fall, without emphasis, and without any emotion. It was as though he pronounced perfectly words in a language he did not understand.

'My wife went away,' he said.

'Where did she go?'

'I don't know.'

'What do you mean?'

'I don't know where she went.'

Julius broke in, speaking for the first time. 'Why did she go?'

'I don't know.'

Horace said angrily, 'You watch it, Trask. You're playing pretty close to the edge and I don't like what I'm thinking. You must know why she went away.'

'I don't know why she went.'

'Was she sick? Did she act strange?'

'No.'

Horace turned. 'Ching Chong, do you know anything about this?'

'I go King City Satdy. Come back mebbe twelve night. Find Missy Tlask on floor.'

'So you weren't here when it happened?'

'No, ma'am.'

'All right, Trask, I'll have to get back to you. Open up that blind a little, Ching Chong, so I can see. There, that's better. Now I'm going to do it your way until I can't any more. Your wife went away. Did she shoot you?'

'It was an accident.'

'All right, an accident, but was the gun in her hand?'

'It was an accident.'

'You don't make it very easy. But let's say she went away and we have to find her–see?–like a kid's game. You're making it that way. How long have you been married?'

'Nearly a year.'

'What was her name before you married her?'

There was a long pause, and then Adam said softly, 'I won't tell. I promised.'

'Now you watch it. Where did she come from?'

'I don't know.'

'Mr Trask, you're talking yourself right into the county jail. Let's have a description. How tall was she?'

Adam's eyes gleamed. 'Not tall–little and delicate.'

'That's just fine. What colour hair? Eyes?'

'She was beautiful.'

'Was.'

'Is.'

'Any scars?'

'Oh, God, no. Yes–a scar on her forehead.'

'You don't know her name, where she came from, where she went, and you can't describe her. And you think I'm a fool.'

Adam said, 'She had a secret. I promised I wouldn't ask her. She was afraid for someone.' And without warning Adam began to cry. His whole body shook, and his breath made little sounds. It was hopeless crying.

Horace felt misery rising in him. 'Come on in the other room, Julius,' he said, and led the way into the living-room. 'All right, Julius, tell me what you think. Is he crazy?'

'I don't know.'

'Did he kill her?'

'That's what jumped into my mind.'

'Mine too,' said Horace. 'My God!' He hurried into the bedroom, and came back with the pistol and the shells. 'I forgot them,' he apologized. 'I won't last long in this job.'

Julius asked, 'What are you going to do?'

'Well, I think it's beyond me. I told you I wouldn't put you on the pay-roll, but hold up your right hand.'

'I don't want to get sworn in, Horace. I want to go to Salinas.'

'You don't have any choice, Julius. I'll have to arrest you if you don't get your goddam hand up.'

Julius reluctantly put up his hand and disgustedly repeated the oath. 'And that's what I get for keeping you company,' he said. 'My father will skin me alive. All right, what do we do now?'

Horace said, 'I'm going to run to papa. I need the sheriff. I'd take Trask in, but I don't want to move him. You've got to stay, Julius. I'm sorry. Have you got a gun?'

'Hell, no.'

'Well, take this one, and take my star.' He unpinned it from his shirt and held it out.

'How long do you think you'll be gone?'

'Not any longer than I can help. Did you ever see Mrs Trask, Julius?'

'No, I didn't.'

'Neither did I. And I've got to tell the sheriff that Trask doesn't know her name or anything. And she's not very big and she is beautiful. That's one hell of a description! I think I'll resign before I tell the sheriff, because he's sure as hell going to fire me afterwards. Do you think he killed her?'

'How the hell do I know?'

'Don't get mad.'

Julius picked up the gun and put the cartridges back in the cylinder and balanced it in his hand. 'You want an idea, Horace?'

'Don't it look like I need one?'

'Well, Sam Hamilton knew her–he took the babies, Rabbit says. And Mrs Hamilton took care of her. Why don't you ride out there on your way and find out what she really looked like.'

'I think maybe you better keep that star,' said Horace. 'That's good. I'll get going.'

'You want me to look around?'

'I want you just to see that he doesn't get away–or hurt himself. Understand? Take care of yourself.'

2

About midnight Horace got on a freight train in King City. He sat up in the cab with the engineer, and he was in Salinas the first thing in the morning. Salinas was the county seat, and it was a fast-growing town. Its population was due to cross the two thousand mark any time. It was the biggest town between San Jose and San Luis Obispo, and everyone felt that a brilliant future was in store for it.

Horace walked up from the Southern Pacific Depot and stopped in the Chop House for breakfast. He didn't want to get the sheriff out so early and rouse ill-will when it wasn't necessary. In the Chop House he ran into young Will Hamilton, looking pretty prosperous in a salt-and-pepper business suit.

Horace sat down at the table with him. 'How are you, Will?'

'Oh, pretty good.'

'Up here on business?'

'Well, yes, I do have a little deal on.'

'You might let me in on something some time.' Horace felt strange talking like this to such a young man, but Will Hamilton had an aura of success about him. Everybody knew he was going to be a very influential man in the county. Some people exude their futures, good or bad.

'I'll do that, Horace. I thought the ranch took all your time.'

'I could be persuaded to rent it if anything turned up.'

Will leaned over the table. 'You know, Horace, our part of the county has been pretty much left out. Did you ever think of running for office?'

'What do you mean?'

'Well, you're a deputy–did you ever think of running for sheriff?'

'Why, no, I didn't.'

'Well, you think about it. Just keep it under your hat. I'll look you up in a couple of weeks and we'll talk about it. But keep it under your hat.'

'I'll certainly do that, Will. But we've got an awful good sheriff.'

'I know. That's got nothing to do with it. King City hasn't got a single county officer–you see?'

'I see. I'll think about it. Oh, by the way I stopped by and saw your father and mother yesterday.'

Will's face lighted up. 'You did? How were they?'

'Just fine. You know, your father is a real comical genius.'

Will chuckled. 'He made us laugh all the time we were growing up.'

'But he's a smart man too, Will. He showed me a new kind of windmill he's invented–goddamdest thing you ever saw.'

'Oh, Lord!' said Will, 'here come the patent attorneys again!'

'But this is good,' said Horace.

'They're all good. And the only people who make any money are the patent lawyers. Drives my mother crazy.'

'I guess you've got a point there.'

Will said, 'The only way to make any money is to sell something somebody else makes.'

'You've got a point there Will, but this is the goddamdest windmill you ever saw.'

'He took you in, did he, Horace?'

'I guess he did. But you wouldn't want him to change, would you?'

'Oh, Lord, no!' said Will. 'You think about what I said.'

'All right.'

'And keep it under your hat,' said Will.

The sheriff's job was not an easy one, and that county which, out of the grab bag of popular elections, pulled a good sheriff was lucky. It was a complicated position. The obvious duties of the sheriff–enforcing the law and keeping the peace–were far from the most important ones. It was true that the sheriff represented armed force in the county, but in a community seething with individuals a harsh or stupid sheriff did not last long. There were water rights, boundary disputes, astray arguments, domestic relations, paternity matters–all to be settled without force of arms. Only when everything else failed did a good sheriff make an arrest. The best sheriff was not the best fighter but the best diplomat. And Monterey County had a good one. He had a brilliant gift for minding his own business.

Horace went into the sheriff's office in the old county jail about ten minutes after nine. The sheriff shook hands and discussed the weather and the crops until Horace was ready to get down to business.

'Well, sir,' Horace said finally, 'I had to come up to get your advice.' And he told his story in great detail–what everybody had said and how they looked and what time it was–everything.

After a few moments the sheriff closed his eyes and laced his fingers together. He punctuated the account occasionally by opening his eyes, but he made no comment.

'Well, there I was on a limb,' Horace said. 'I couldn't find out what happened. I couldn't even find out what the woman looked like. It was Julius Euskadi got the idea I should go to see Sam Hamilton.'

The sheriff stirred, crossed his legs, and inspected the job. 'You think he killed her.'

'Well, I did. But Mr Hamilton kind of talked me out of it. He says Trask hasn't got it in him to kill anybody.'

'Everybody's got it in him,' the sheriff said. 'You just find his trigger and anybody will go off.'

'Mr Hamilton told me some funny things about her. You know, when he was taking her babies she bit him on the hand. You ought to see the hand, like a wolf got him.'

'Did Sam give you a description?'

'He did, and his wife did.' Horace took a piece of paper from his pocket and read a detailed description of Cathy. Between the two of them the Hamiltons knew pretty much everything physical there was to know about Cathy.

When Horace finished, the sheriff sighed. 'They both agreed about the scar?'

'Yes, they did. And both of them remarked about how sometimes it was darker than other times.'

The sheriff closed his eyes again and he leaned back in his chair. Suddenly he straightened up, opened a drawer of his roll-top desk, and took out a pint of whisky. 'Have a drink' he said.

'Don't mind if I do. Here's looking at you.' Horace wiped his mouth and handed back the pint. 'Got any ideas?' he asked.

The sheriff took three big swallows of whisky, corked the pint, and put it back in the drawer before he replied. 'We've got a pretty well-run county,' he said. 'I get along with the constables, give them a hand when they need it, and they help me out when I need it. You take a town growing like Salinas, and strangers in and out all the time–could have trouble if we didn't watch it pretty close. My office gets along fine with the local people.' He looked Horace in the eye. 'Don't get restless. I'm not making a speech. I just want to tell you how it is. We don't drive people. We've got to live with them.'

'Did I do something wrong?'

'No, you didn't, Horace. You did just right. If you hadn't come to town or if you had brought Mr Trask in, we'd of been in one hell of a mess. Now hold on. I'm going to tell you–'

'I'm listening,' said Horace.

'Over across the tracks down by Chinatown there's a row of whorehouses.'

'I know that.'

'Everybody knows it. If we closed them up they'd just move. The people want those houses. We keep an eye on them so not much bad happens. And the people that run those houses keep in touch with us. I've picked up some wanted men from tips I got down there.'

Horace said, 'Julius told me–'

'Now wait a minute. Let me get all this said so we won't have to go back over it. About three months ago a fine-looking woman came in to see me. She wanted to open a house here and wanted to do it right. Came from Sacramento. Ran a place there. She had letters from some pretty important people–straight record–never had any trouble. A pretty damn good citizen.'

'Julius told me. Name of Faye.'

'That's right. Well, she opened a nice place, quiet, well run. It was about time old Jenny and the Nigger had some competition. They were mad as hell about it, but I told them just what I told you. It's about time they had some competition.'

'There's a piano player.'

'Yes, there is. Good one too–blind fella. Say, are you going to let me tell this?'

'I'm sorry,' said Horace.

'That's all right. I know I'm slow, but I'm thorough. Anyways, Faye turned out to be just what she looks like, a good solid citizen. Now there's one thing a good quiet whorehouse is more scared of than anything else. Take a flighty randy girl runs off from home and goes in a house. Her old man finds her and he begins to shovel up hell. Then the churches get into it, and the women, and pretty soon that whorehouse has got a bad name and we've got to close it up. You understand?'

'Yeah!' Horace said softly.

'Now don't get ahead of me. I hate to tell something you already thought out. Faye sent me a note Sunday night. She's got a girl and she can't make much out of her. What puzzles Faye is that this kid looks like a runaway girl except she's a goddam good whore. She knows all the answers and all the tricks. I went down and looked her over. She told me the usual bull, but I can't find a thing wrong with her. She's of age and nobody's made a complaint.' He spread his hands. 'Well, there it is. What do we do about it?'

'You're pretty sure it's Mrs Trask?'

The sheriff said, 'Wide-set eyes, yellow hair, and a scar on her forehead, and she came in Sunday afternoon.'

Adam's weeping face was in Horace's mind. 'God allmighty! Sheriff, you got to get somebody else to tell him. I'll quit before I do.'

The sheriff gazed into space. 'You say he didn't even know her name, where she came from. She really bull-shitted him, didn't she?'

'The poor bastard,' Horace said. 'The poor bastard is in love with her. No, by God, somebody else has got to tell him. I won't.'

The sheriff stood up. 'Let's go down to the Chop House and get a cup of coffee.'

They walked along the street in silence for a while. 'Horace,' the sheriff said, 'if I told some of the things I know, this whole goddam county would go up in smoke.'

'I guess that's right.'

'You said she had twins?'

'Yeah, twin boys.'

'You listen to me, Horace. There's only three people in the world that knows–her and you and me. I'm going to warn her that if she ever tells I'll brush her arse out of this county so fast it'll burn. And, Horace–if you should ever get an itchy tongue, before you tell anybody, even your wife, why, you think about those little boys finding out their mother is a whore.'

3

Adam sat in his chair under the big oak tree. His left arm was expertly bandaged against his side so that he could not move his shoulder. Lee came out carrying the laundry basket. He set it on the ground beside Adam and went back inside.

The twins were awake, and they both looked blindly and earnestly up at the wind-moved leaves of the oak tree. A dry oak leaf came whirling down and landed in the basket. Adam leaned over and picked it out.

He didn't hear Samuel's horse until it was almost upon him, but Lee had seen him coming. He brought a chair out and led Doxology away towards the shed.

Samuel sat down quietly, and he didn't trouble Adam by looking at him too much, and he didn't trouble him by not looking at him. The wind freshened in the tree-tops and a fringe of it ruffled Samuel's hair. 'I thought I'd better get back to the wells,' Samuel said softly.

Adam's voice had gone rusty from lack of use. 'No,' he said, 'I don't want any wells. I'll pay you for the work you did.'

Samuel leaned over the basket and put his finger against the small palm of one of the twins and the fingers closed and held on. 'I guess the last bad habit a man will give up is advising.'

'I don't want advice.'

'Nobody does. It's a giver's present. Go through the motions, Adam.'

'What motions?'

'Act out being alive like a play. And after a while, a long while, it will be true.'

'Why should I?' Adam asked.

Samuel was looking at the twins. 'You're going to pass something down, no matter what you do or if you do nothing. Even if you let yourself go fallow, the weeds will grow and the brambles. Something will grow.'

Adam did not answer, and Samuel stood up. 'I'll be back,' he said. 'I'll be back again and again. Go through the motions, Adam.'

In the back of the shed Lee held Doxology while Sam mounted. 'There goes your bookstore, Lee,' he said.

'Oh, well,' said the Chinese, 'maybe I didn't want it much, anyway.'

CHAPTER 19

I

A new country seems to follow a pattern. First come the openers, strong and brave and rather childlike. They can take care of themselves in a wilderness, but they are naïve and helpless against men, and perhaps that is why they went out in the first place. When the rough edges are worn off the new land, business men and lawyers come in to keep with the development–to solve problems of ownership, usually by removing the temptations to themselves. And finally comes culture, which is entertainment, relaxation, transport out of the pain of living. And culture can be on any level, and is.

The church and the whorehouse arrived in the Far West simultaneously. And each would have been horrified to think it was a different facet of the same thing. But surely they were both intended to accomplish the same thing: the singing, the devotion, the poetry of the churches took a man out of his bleakness for a time, and so did the brothels. The sectarian Churches came in swinging, cocky and loud and confident. Ignoring the laws of debt and repayment, they built churches which couldn't be paid for in a hundred years. The sects fought evil, true enough, but they also fought each other with a fine lustiness. They fought at the turn of a doctrine. Each happily believed all the others were bound for hell in a basket. And each for all its bumptiousness brought with it the same thing: the Scripture on which our ethics, our art and poetry, and our relationships are built. It took a smart man to know where the difference lay between the sects, but anyone could see what they had in common. And they brought music–maybe not the best, but the form and sense of it. And they brought conscience, or rather, nudged the dozing conscience. They were not pure, but they had a potential of purity, like a soiled white shirt. And any man could make something pretty fine of it within himself. True enough, the Reverend Billing, when they caught up with him, turned out to be a thief, an adulterer, a libertine, and a zoophilist, but that didn't change the fact that he had communicated some good things to a great number of receptive people. Billing went to jail, but no one ever arrested the good things he had released. And it doesn't matter much that his motive was impure. He used good material and some of it stuck. I use Billing only as an outrageous example. The honest preacher had energy and go. They fought the devil, no holds barred, boots and eye-gouging permitted. You might get the idea that they howled truth and beauty the way a seal bites out the National Anthem on a row of circus horns. But some of the truth and beauty remained, and the anthem was recognizable. The sects did more than this, though. They built the structure of social life in the Salinas Valley. The church supper is the grandfather of the country club, just as the Thursday poetry reading in the basement under the vestry sired the little theatre.

While the churches, bringing the sweet smell of piety for the soul, came in prancing and farting like brewery horses in bock-beer time, the sister evangelism, with release and joy for the body, crept in silently and greyly, with its head bowed and its face covered.

You may have seen the spangled palaces of sin and fancy dancing in the false West of the movies, and maybe some of them existed–but not in the Salinas Valley. The brothels were quiet, orderly, and circumspect. Indeed, if after hearing the ecstatic shrieks of climactic conversion against the thumping beat of the melodeon you had stood under the window of a whorehouse and listened to the low decorous voices, you would have been likely to confuse the identities of the two ministries. The brothel was accepted while it was not admitted.

I will tell you about the solemn courts of love in Salinas. They were about the same in other towns, but the Salinas Row has a pertinence to this telling.

You walked west on Main Street until it bent. That's where Castroville Street crossed Main. Castroville Street is now called Market Street. God knows why. Streets used to be named for the place they aimed at. Thus Castroville Street, if you followed it nine miles, brought you to Castroville, Alisal Street to Alisal, and so forth.

Anyway, when you came to Castroville Street you turned right. Two blocks down, the Southern Pacific tracks cut diagonally across the street on their way south, and a street crossed Castroville Street from east to west. And for the life of me I cannot remember the name of that street. If you turned left on that street and crossed the tracks you were in Chinatown. If you turned right you were on the Row.

It was a black 'dobe street, deep shining mud in winter and hard as rutted iron in summer. In the spring the tall grass grew along its sides–wild oats and mallow weeds and yellow mustard mixed in. In the early morning the sparrows shrieked over the horse manure in the street.

Do you remember hearing that, old men? And do you remember, how an easterly breeze brought odours in from Chinatown, roasting pork and punk and black tobacco and yen shi? And do you remember the deep blatting stroke of the great gong in the Joss House, and how its tone hung in the air so long?

Remember, too, the little houses, unpainted, unrepaired? They seemed very small, and they tried to efface themselves in outside neglect, and the wild overgrown front yards tried to hide them from the street. Remember how the blinds were always drawn with little lines of yellow light around their edges? You could hear only a murmur from within. Then the front door would open to admit a country boy, and you'd hear laughter and perhaps the soft sentimental tone of an open-face piano with a piece of toilet chain across the strings, and then the door would close it off again.

Then you might hear horses' hoofs on the dirt street, and Pet Bulene would drive his hack up in front, and maybe four or five portly men would get out–great men, rich or official, bankers maybe, or the court-house gang. And Pet would drive round the corner and settle down in his hack to wait for them. Big cats would ripple across the street to disappear in the tall grass.

And then–remember?–the train whistle and the boring light and a freight from King City would go stomping across Castroville Street and into Salinas and you could hear it sighing at the station. Remember?

Every town has its celebrated madams, eternal women to be sentimentalized down the years. There is something very attractive to men about a madam. She combines the brains of a business man, the toughness of a prize-fighter, the warmth of a companion, the humour of a tragedian. Myths collect round her, and, oddly enough, not voluptuous myths. The stories remembered and repeated about a madam cover every field but the bedroom. Remembering, her old customers picture her as philanthropist, medical authority, bouncer, and poetess of the bodily emotions without being involved with them.

For a number of years Salinas had sheltered two of these treasures: Jenny, sometimes called Fartin' Jenny, and the Nigger, who owned and operated the Long Green. Jenny was a good companion, a keeper of secrets, a giver of secret loans. There is a whole literature of stories about Jenny in Salinas.

The Nigger was a handsome, austere woman with snow-white hair and a dark and awful dignity. Her brown eyes, brooding deep in her skull, looked out on an ugly world with philosophic sorrow. She conducted her house like a cathedral dedicated to a sad but erect Priapus. If you wanted a good laugh and a poke in the ribs, you went to Jenny's and got your money's worth; but if the sweet world-sadness close to tears crept out of your immutable loneliness, the Long Green was your place. When you came out of there you felt that something pretty stern and important had happened. It was no jump in the hay. The dark beautiful eyes of the Nigger stayed with you for days.

When Faye came down from Sacramento and opened her house there was a flurry of animosity from the two incumbents. They got together to drive Faye out, but they discovered she was not in competition.

Faye was the motherly type, big-breasted, big-hipped, and warm. She was a bosom to cry on, a soother and a stroker. The iron sex of the Nigger and the tavern bacchanalianism of Jenny had their devotees, and they were not lost to Faye. Her house became the refuge of young men puling in puberty, mourning over lost virtue, and aching to lose some more. Faye was the reassurer of misbegotten husbands. Her house took up the slack for frigid wives. It was the cinnamon-scented kitchen of one's grandmother. If any sexual thing happened to you at Faye's you felt it was an accident but forgivable. Her house led the youths of Salinas into the thorny path of sex in the pinkest, smoothest way. Faye was a nice woman, not very bright, highly moral, and easily shocked. People trusted her and she trusted everyone. No one could want to hurt Faye once he knew her. She was no competition to the others. She was a third phase.

Just as in a store or on a ranch the employees are images of the boss, so in a whorehouse the girls are very like the madam, partly because she hires that kind and partly because a good madam imprints her personality on the business. You could stay a very long time at Faye's before you would hear an ugly or suggestive word spoken. The wanderings to the bedrooms, the payments, were so soft and casual they seemed incidental. All in all she ran a hell of a fine house, as the constable and the sheriff knew. Faye contributed heavily to every charity. Having a revulsion against disease, she paid for regular inspection of her girls. You had less chance of contracting a difficulty at Faye's than with your Sunday School teacher. Faye soon became a solid and desirable citizen of the growing town of Salinas.

2

The girl Kate puzzled Faye–she was so young and pretty, so ladylike, so well educated. Faye took her into her own inviolate bedroom and questioned her far more than she would if Kate had been another kind of girl. There were always women knocking on the door of a whorehouse, and Faye recognized most of them instantly. She could tick them off–lazy, vengeful, lustful, unsatisfied, greedy, ambitious. Kate didn't fall into any of these classes.

'I hope you don't mind my asking you all these questions,' she said. 'It just seems so strange that you should come here. Why, you could get a husband and a surrey and a corner house in town with no trouble at all, no trouble at all.' And Faye rolled her wedding band round and round on her fat little finger.

Kate smiled shyly. 'It's so hard to explain. I hope you won't insist on knowing. The happiness of someone very near and dear to me is involved. Please don't ask me.'

Faye nodded solemnly. 'I've known things like that. I had one girl who was supporting her baby, and no one knew for a long, long time. That girl has a fine house and a husband in–there, I nearly told you where. I'd cut out my tongue before I'd tell. Do you have a baby, dear?'

Kate looked down to conceal the shine of tears in her eyes. When she could control her throat she whispered, 'I'm sorry, I can't talk about it.'

'That's all right. That's all right. You just take your time.'

Faye was not bright, but she was far from stupid. She went to the sheriff and got herself cleared. There was no sense in taking chances. She knew something was wrong about Kate, but if it didn't harm the house it really wasn't Faye's business.

Kate might have been a chiseller, but she wasn't. She went to work right away. And when customers come back again and again and ask for a girl by name, you know you've got something. A pretty face won't do that. It was quite apparent to Faye that Kate was not learning a new trade.

There are two things it is good to know about a new girl: first, will she work? and second, will she get along with the other girls? There's nothing will upset a house like an ill-tempered girl.

Faye didn't have long to wonder about the second question. Kate put herself out to be pleasant. She helped the other girls keep their rooms clean. She served them when they were sick, listened to their troubles, answered them in matters of love, and as soon as she had some, loaned them money. You couldn't want a better girl. She became best friend to everyone in the house.

There was no trouble Kate would not take, no drudgery she was afraid of, and, in addition, she brought business. She soon had her own group of regular customers. Kate was thoughtful too. She remembered birthdays and always had a present and a cake with candles. Faye realized she had a treasure.

People who don't know think it is easy to be a madam–just sit in a big chair and drink beer and take half the money the girls make, they think. But it's not like that at all. You have to feed the girls–that's groceries and a cook. Your laundry problem is quite a bit more complicated than that of a hotel. You have to keep the girls well and as happy as possible, and some of them can get pretty ornery. You have to keep suicide at an absolute minimum, and whores, particularly the ones getting along in years, are flighty with a razor; and that gets your house a bad name.

It isn't so easy, and if you have waste too you can lose money. When Kate offered to help with the marketing and planning of meals Faye was pleased, although she didn't know when the girl found time. Well, not only did the food improve, but the grocery bills came down one-third the first month Kate took over. And the laundry–Faye didn't know what Kate said to the man but the bill suddenly dropped twenty-five per cent. Faye didn't see how she ever got along without Kate.

In the late afternoon before business they sat together in Faye's room and drank tea. It was much nicer since Kate had painted the woodwork and put up lace curtains. The girls began to realize that there were two bosses, not one, and they were glad, because Kate was very easy to get along with. She made them turn more tricks but she wasn't mean about it. They'd as likely as not have a big laugh over it.

By the time a year had passed Faye and Kate were like mother and daughter. And the girls said, 'You watch–she'll own this house some day.'

Kate's own hands were always busy, mostly at dawn work on the sheerest of lawn handerkchiefs. She could make beautiful initials. Nearly all the girls carried and treasured her handkerchiefs.

Gradually a perfectly natural thing happened. Faye, the essence of motherliness, began to think of Kate as her daughter. She felt this in her breast and in her emotions, and her natural morality took hold. She did not want her daughter to be a whore. It was a perfectly reasonable sequence.

Faye thought hard how she was going to bring up the subject. It was a problem. It was Faye's nature to approach any subject sideways. She could not say, 'I want you to give up whoring.'

She said, 'If it is a secret, don't answer, but I've always meant to ask you. What did the sheriff say to you–good Lord, is it a year ago? How the time goes! Quicker as you get older, I think. He was nearly an hour with you. He didn't–but of course not. He's a family man. He goes to Jenny's. But I don't want to pry into your affairs.'

'There's no secret at all about that,' said Kate. 'I would have told you. He told me I should go home. He was very nice about it. When I explained that I couldn't, he was very nice and understanding.'

'Did you tell him why?' Faye asked jealously.

'Of course not. Do you think I would tell him when I won't tell you? Don't be silly, darling. You're such a funny little girl.'

Faye smiled and snuggled contentedly down in her chair.

Kate's face was in repose, but she was remembering every word of that interview. As a matter of fact she rather liked the sheriff. He was direct.

3

He had closed the door of her room, glanced round with the quick recording eye of a good policeman–no photographs, none of the personal articles which identify, nothing but clothes and shoes.

He sat down on her little cane rocking chair and his buttocks hung over on each side. His fingers got together in conference, talking to one another like ants. He spoke in an unemotional tone, almost as though he weren't much interested in what he was saying. Maybe that was what impressed her.

At first she put on her slightly stupid demure look, but after a few of his words she gave that up and bored him with her eyes, trying to read his thoughts. He neither looked in her eyes nor avoided them. But she was aware that he was inspecting her as she inspected him. She felt his glance go over the scar on her forehead almost as though he had touched it.

'I don't want to make a record,' he said quietly. 'I've held office a long time. About one more term will be enough. You know, young woman, if this were fifteen years back I'd do some checking, and I guess I'd find something pretty nasty.' He waited for some reaction from her but she did not protest. He nodded his head slowly. 'I don't want to know,' he said. 'I want peace in this county, and I mean all kinds of peace, and that means people getting to sleep at night. Now I haven't met your husband,' he said, and she knew he noticed the slight movement of her tightening muscles. 'I hear he's a very nice man. I hear also that he's pretty hard hit.' He looked into her eyes for a moment. 'Don't you want to know how bad you shot him?'

'Yes,' she said.

'Well, he's going to get well–smashed his shoulder, but he's going to get well. That Chink is taking pretty good care of him. 'Course I don't think he'll lift anything with his left arm for quite a spell. A forty-four tears hell out of a man. If the Chink hadn't come back he'd of bled to death, and you'd be staying with me in the jail.'

Kate was holding her breath, listening for any hint of what was coming and not hearing any hints.

'I'm sorry,' she said quietly.

The sheriff's eyes became alert. 'Now that's the first time you've made a mistake,' he said. 'You're not sorry. I knew somebody like you once–hung him twelve years ago in front of the county jail. We used to do that here.'

The little room with its dark mahogany bed, its marble-top washstand with bowl and pitcher and a door for the pot, its wallpaper endlessly repeating little roses–little roses–the little room was silent, the sound sucked out of it.

The sheriff was staring at a picture of three cherubim–just heads, curly-haired, limpid-eyed, with wings about the size of pigeons' wings growing out of where their necks would be. He frowned. 'That's a funny picture for a whorehouse,' he said.

'It was here,' said Kate. Apparently the preliminaries were over now.

The sheriff straightened up, undid his fingers, and held the arms of his chair. Even his buttocks pulled in a little. 'You left a couple of babies,' he said. 'Little boys. Now you calm down. I'm not going to try to get you to go back. I guess I'd do quite a bit to keep you from going back. I think I know you. I could just run you over the county line and have the next sheriff run you, and that could keep up till you landed splash in the Atlantic Ocean. But I don't want to do that. I don't care how you live as long as you don't give me any trouble. A whore is a whore.'

Kate asked evenly, 'What is it you do want?'

'That's more like it,' the sheriff said. 'Here's what I want. I notice you changed your name. I want you to keep your new name. I guess you made up someplace you came from–well, that's where you came from. And your reason–that's when you're maybe drunk–you keep your reason about two thousand miles away from King City.'

She was smiling a little, and not a forced smile. She was beginning to trust this man and to like him.

'One thing I thought of,' he said. 'Did you know many people around King City?'

'No.'

'I heard about the knitting-needle,' he said casually. 'Well, it could happen that somebody you knew might come in here. That your real hair colour?'

'Yes.'

'Dye it black for a while. Lots of people look like somebody else.'

'How about this?' She touched her scar with a slender finger.

'Well, that's just a–what is that word? What is that goddam word? I had it this morning.'

'Coincidence?'

'That's it–coincidence.' He seemed to be finished. He got out tobacco and papers and rolled a clumsy, lumpy cigarette. He broke out a sulphur match and struck it on the block and held it away until its acrid blue flame turned yellow. His cigarette burned crookedly up the side.

Kate said, 'Isn't there a threat? I mean, what you'll do if I–'

'No, there isn't. I guess I could think up something pretty ornery, though, if it came to that. No, I don't want you–what you are, what you do, or what you say–to hurt Mr Trask or his boys. You figure you died and now you're somebody else and we'll get along fine.'

He stood up and went to the door, then turned. 'I've got a boy–he'll be twenty this year; bit nice-looking fellow with a broken nose. Everybody likes him. I don't want him in here. I'll tell Faye too. Let him go to Jenny's. If he comes in, you tell him to go to Jenny's.' He closed the door behind him.

Kate smiled down at her fingers.

4

Faye twisted round in her chair to reach a piece of brown panocha studded with walnuts. When she spoke it was around a mouth full of candy. Kate wondered uneasily whether she could read minds, for Faye said, 'I still don't like it as well. I said it then and I say it again. I liked your hair blonde better. I don't know what got into you to change it. You've got a fair complexion.'

Kate caught a single thread of hair with fingernails of thumb and forefinger and gently drew it out. She was very clever. She told the best lie of all–the truth. 'I didn't want to tell you,' she said. 'I was afraid I might be recognized and that would hurt someone.'

Faye got up out of her chair and went to Kate and kissed her. 'What a good child it is,' she said. 'What a thoughtful dear.'

Kate said, 'Let's have some tea. I'll bring it in.' She went out of the room, and in the hall on the way to the kitchen she rubbed the kiss from her cheek with her fingertips.

Back in her chair, Faye picked out a piece of panocha with a whole walnut showing through. She put it in her mouth and bit into a piece of walnut shell. The sharp, pointed fragment hit a hollow tooth and whanged into the nerve. Blue lights of pain flashed through her. Her forehead became wet. When Kate came back with teapot and cups on a tray Faye was clawing at her mouth with a crooked finger and whimpering in agony.

'What is it?' Kate cried.

'Tooth–nutshell.'

'Here, let me see. Open and point.' Kate looked into the open mouth then went to the nut bowl on the fringed table for a nut pick. In a fraction of a second she had dug out the shell and laid it in the palm of her hand. 'There it is.'

The nerve stopped shrieking and the pain dropped to an ache. 'Only that big? It felt like a house. Look, dear,' said Faye, 'open that second drawer where my medicine is. Bring the paregoric and a piece of cotton. Will you help me pack this tooth?'

Kate brought the bottle and pushed a little ball of saturated cotton into the tooth with the point of the nut pick. 'You ought to have it out.'

'I know. I will.'

'I have three teeth missing on this side.'

'Well, you'd never know it. That made me feel all shaky. Bring me the Pinkham, will you?' She poured herself a slug of the vegetable compound and sighed with relief. 'That's a wonderful medicine,' she said. 'The woman who invented it was a saint.'

CHAPTER 20

I

It was a pleasant afternoon. Frémont's Peak was lighted pinkly by the setting sun, and Faye could see it from her window. From over on Castroville Street came the sweet sound of jingling horse bells from an eight-horse grain team down from the ridge. The cook was fighting pots in the kitchen. There was a rubbing sound on the wall and then a gentle tap on the door.

'Come in, Cotton Eye,' Faye called.

The door opened and the crooked little cotton-eyed piano player stood in the entrance, waiting for a sound to tell him where she was.

'What is it you want?' Faye asked.

He turned to her. 'I don't feel good, Miss Faye. I want to crawl into my bed and not do no playing tonight.'

'You were sick two nights last week, Cotton Eye. Don't you like your job?'

'I don't feel good.'

'Well, all right. But I wish you'd take better care of yourself.'

Kate said softly, 'Let the gong alone for a couple of weeks, Cotton Eye.'

'Oh, Miss Kate. I didn't know you was here. I ain't been smoking.'

'You've been smoking,' Kate said.

'Yes, Miss Kate, I will sure let it alone. I don't feel good.' He closed the door, and they could hear his hand rubbing along the wall to guide him.

Faye said, 'He told me he'd stopped.'

'He hasn't stopped.'

'The poor thing,' said Faye, 'he doesn't have much to live for.'

Kate stood in front of her. 'You're so sweet,' she said. 'You believe in everybody. Some day if you don't watch, or I don't watch for you, someone will steal the roof.'

'Who'd want to steal from me?' asked Faye.

Kate put her hand on Faye's plump shoulders. 'Not everyone is as nice as you are.'

Faye's eyes glistened with tears. She picked up a handkerchief from the chair beside her and wiped her eyes and patted delicately at her nostrils. 'You're like my own daughter, Kate,' she said.

'I'm beginning to believe I am. I never knew my mother. She died when I was small.'

Faye drew a deep breath and plunged into the subject.

'Kate, I don't like you working here.'

'Why not?'

Faye shook her head, trying to find words. 'I'm not ashamed. I run a nice house. If I didn't somebody else might run a bad house. I don't do anybody any harm. I'm not ashamed.'

'Why should you be?' asked Kate.

'But I don't like you working. I just don't like it. You're sort of my daughter. I don't like my daughter working.'

'Don't be silly, darling,' said Kate. 'I have to–here or somewhere else. I told you. I have to have the money.'

'No, you don't.'

'Of course I do. Where else could I get it?'

'You could be my daughter. You could manage the house. You could take care of things for me and not go upstairs. I'm not always well, you know.'

'I know you're not, poor darling. But I have to have money.'

'There's plenty for both of us, Kate. I could give you as much as you make and more, and you'd be worth it.'

Kate shook her head sadly. 'I do love you,' she said. 'And I wish I could do what you want. But you need your little reserve, and I–well, suppose something should happen to you? No, I must go on working. Do you know, dear, I have five regulars tonight?'

A jar of shock struck Faye. 'I don't want you to work.'

'I have to, Mother.'

The word did it. Faye burst into tears, and Kate sat on the arm of her chair and stroked her cheek and wiped her streaming eyes. The outburst sniffled to a close.

The dust was settling deeply on the valley. Kate's face was a glow of lightness under her dark hair. 'Now you're all right. I'll go and look in on the kitchen and then dress.'

'Kate, can't you tell your regulars you're sick?'

'Of course not, Mother.'

'Kate, it's Wednesday. Probably won't be anybody in after one o'clock.'

'The Woodmen of the World are having a do.'

'Oh, yes. But on Wednesday–the Woodmen won't be here after two.'

'What are you getting at?'

'Kate, when you close, you tap on my door. I'll have a little surprise for you.'

'What kind of surprise?'

'Oh, a secret surprise! Will you ask the cook to come in as you go by the kitchen?'

'Sounds like a cake surprise.'

'Now don't ask questions, darling. It's a surprise.'

Kate kissed her. 'What a dear you are, Mother.'

When she had closed the door behind her Kate stood for a moment in the hall. Her fingers caressed her pointed chin. Her eyes were calm. Then she stretched her arms over her head and strained her body in a luxurious yawn. She ran her hands slowly down her sides from right under her breasts to her hips. Her mouth corners turned up a little, and she moved towards the kitchen.

2

The few regulars drifted in and out and two drummers walked down the Line to look them over, but not a single Woodman of the World showed up. The girls sat yawning in the parlour until two o'clock, waiting.

What kept the Woodmen away was a sad accident. Clarence Monteith had a heart attack right in the middle of the closing ritual and before supper. They laid him out on the carpet and dampened his forehead until the doctor came. Nobody felt like sitting down to the doughnut supper. After Dr Wilde had arrived and looked Clarence over, the Woodmen made a stretcher by putting flagpoles through the sleeves of two overcoats. On the way home Clarence died, and they had to go for Dr Wilde again. And by the time they had made plans for the funeral and written the piece for the *Salinas Journal,* nobody had any heart for a whorehouse.

The next day, when they found out what had happened, the girls remembered what Ethel had said at ten minutes to two.

'My God!' Ethel had said, 'I never heard it so quiet. No music, cat's got Kate's tongue. It's like setting up with a corpse.'

Later Ethel was impressed with having said it–almost as if she knew.

Grace had said, 'I wonder what cat's got Kate's tongue. Don't you feel good? Kate–I said, don't you feel good?'

Kate started. 'Oh! I guess I was thinking of something.'

'Well, I'm not,' said Grace. 'I'm sleepy. Why don't we close up? Let's ask Faye if we can't lock up. There won't be a Chink in tonight. I'm going to ask Faye.'

Kate's voice cut in on her. 'Let Faye alone. She's not well. We'll close up at two.'

'That clock's way wrong,' said Ethel. 'What's the matter with Faye?'

Kate said, 'Maybe that's what I was thinking about. Faye's not well. I'm worried to death about her. She won't show it if she can help it.'

'I thought she was all right,' Grace said.

Ethel hit the jackpot again. 'Well, she don't look good to me. She's got a kind of flush. I noticed it.'

Kate spoke very softly. 'Don't you girls ever let her know I told you. She wouldn't want you to worry. What a dear she is!'

'Best goddam house I ever hustled,' said Grace.

Alice said, 'You better not let her hear you talk words like that.'

'Balls!' said Grace. 'She knows all the words.'

'She don't like to hear them–not from us.'

Kate said patiently, 'I want to tell you what happened. I was having tea with her late this afternoon and she fainted dead away. I do wish she'd see a doctor.'

'I noticed she had a kind of bright flush,' Ethel repeated. 'That clock's way wrong but I forget which way.'

Kate said, 'You girls go to bed. I'll lock up.'

When they were gone Kate went to her room and put on her pretty new print dress that made her look like a little girl. She brushed and braided her hair and let it hang behind in one thick pigtail tied with a little white bow. She patted her cheeks with Florida water. For a moment she hesitated, and then from the top bureau drawer she took a little gold watch that hung from a fleur-de-lys pin. She wrapped it in one of her fine lawn handkerchiefs and went out of the room.

The hall was very dark, but a rim of light showed under Faye's door. Kate tapped softly.

Faye called, 'Who is it?'

'It's Kate.'

'Don't you come in yet. You wait outside. I'll tell you when.' Kate heard a rustling and a scratching in the room. Then Faye called, 'All right. Come in.'

The room was decorated. Japanese lanterns with candles in them hung on bamboo sticks at the corners, and red crêpe paper twisted in scallops from the centre to the corners to give the effect of a tent. On the table with candlesticks around it was a big white cake and a box of chocolates, and beside these a basket with a magnum of champagne peeking out of crushed ice. Faye wore her best lace dress and her eyes were shiny with emotion.

'What in the world?' Kate cried. She closed the door. 'Why, it looks like a party!'

'It is a party. It's a party for my dear daughter.'

'It's not my birthday.'

Faye said, 'In a way maybe it is.'

'I don't know what you mean. But I brought you a present.' She laid the folded handkerchief in Faye's lap. 'Open it carefully,' she said.

Faye held the watch up. 'Oh, my dear, my dear! You crazy child! No, I can't take it.' She opened the face and then picked open the back with her fingernail. It was engraved–'To C. with all my heart from A.'

'It was my mother's watch,' Kate said softly. 'I would like my new mother to have it.'

'My darling child! My darling child!'

'Mother would be glad.'

'But it's my party. I have a present for my dear daughter, but I'll have to do it in my own way. Now, Kate, you open the bottle of wine and pour two glasses while I cut the cake. I want it to be fancy.'

When everything was ready Faye took her seat behind the table. She raised her glass. 'To my daughter–may you have long life and happiness.' And when they had drunk Kate proposed, 'To my mother.'

Faye said, 'You'll make me cry–don't make me cry. Over on the bureau, dear. Bring the little mahogany box. There, that's the one. Now put it on the table here and open it.'

In the polished box lay a rolled white paper tied with a red ribbon. 'What in the world is it?' Kate asked.

'It's my gift to you. Open it.'

Kate very carefully untied the red ribbon and unrolled the tube. It was written elegantly with shaded letters, and it was well and carefully drawn and witnessed by the cook.

'All my worldly goods without exception to Kate Albey because I regard her as my daughter.'

It was simple, direct and legally irreproachable. Kate read it three times, looked back at the date, studied the cook's signature. Faye watched her, and her lips were parted in expectation. When Kate's lips moved, reading, Faye's lips moved.

Kate rolled the paper and tied the ribbon around it and put it in the box and closed the lid. She sat in her chair.

Faye said at last, 'Are you pleased?'

Kate's eyes seemed to peer into and beyond Faye's eyes–to penetrate the brain behind the eyes. Kate said quietly, 'I'm trying to hold on, Mother. I didn't know anyone could be so good. I'm afraid if I say anything too quickly or come too close to you, I'll break to pieces.'

It was more dramatic than Faye had anticipated, quiet and electric. Faye said, 'It's a funny present, isn't it?'

'Funny? No, it isn't funny.'

'I mean, a will is a strange present. But it means more than that. Now you are my real daughter I can tell you. I–no, *we*–have cash and securities in excess of sixty thousand dollars. In my desk are notations of accounts and safe-deposit boxes. I sold the place in Sacramento for a very good price. Why are you so silent, child? Is something bothering you?'

'A will sounds like death. That's thrown a pall.'

'But everyone should make a will.'

'I know, Mother.' Kate smiled ruefully. 'A thought crossed my mind. I thought of all your kin coming in angrily to break such a will as this. You can't do this.'

'My poor little girl, is that what's bothering you? I have no folks. As far as I know, I have no kin. And if I did have some–who would know? Do you think you are the only one with secrets? Do you think I use the name I was born with?'

Kate looked long and levelly at Faye.

'Kate,' she cried, 'Kate, it's a party. Don't be sad! Don't be frozen!'

Kate got up, gently pulled the table aside, and sat down on the floor. She put her cheek on Faye's knee. Her slender fingers traced a gold thread on the skirt through its intricate leaf pattern. And Faye stroked Kate's cheek and hair and touched her strange ears. Shyly Faye's fingers explored the borders of the scar.

'I think I've never been so happy before,' said Kate.

'My darling. You make me happy too. Happier than I have ever been. Now I don't feel alone. Now I feel safe.'

Kate picked delicately at the gold thread with her fingernails.

They sat in the warmth for a long time before Faye stirred. 'Kate,' she said, 'we're forgetting. It's a party. We've forgotten the wine. Pour it, child. We'll have a little celebration.'

Kate said uneasily, 'Do we need it, Mother?'

'It's good. Why not? I like to take on a little load. It lets the poison out. Don't you like champagne, Kate?'

'Well, I never have drunk much. It's not good for me.'

'Nonsense. Pour it, darling.'

Kate got up from the floor and filled the glasses.

Faye said, 'Now drink it down. I'm watching you. You're not going to let an old woman get silly by herself.'

'You're not an old woman, Mother.'

'Don't talk–drink it. I won't touch mine until yours is empty.' She held her glass until Kate had emptied hers, then gulped it. 'Good, that's good,' she said. 'Fill them up. Now, come on, dear–down the rat-hole. After two or three the bad things go away.'

Kate's chemistry screamed against the wine. She remembered and she was afraid.

Faye said, 'Now let me see the bottom, child–there. You see how good it is? Fill up again.'

The transition came to Kate almost immediately after the second glass. Her fear evaporated, her fear of anything disappeared. This was what she had been afraid of, and now it was too late. The wine had forced a passage through all the carefully built barriers and defences and deceptions and she didn't care. The thing she had learned to cover and control was lost. Her voice became chill and her mouth was thin. Her wide-set eyes slitted and grew watchful and sardonic.

'Now you drink–Mother–while I watch,' she said. 'There's a–dear. I'll bet you can't drink two without stopping.'

'Don't bet me, Kate. You'd lose. I can drink six without stopping.'

'Let me see you.'

'If I do, will you?'

'Of course.'

The contest started, and a puddle of wine spread out over the table-top and the wine went down in the magnum.

Faye giggled. 'When I was a girl–I could tell you stories maybe you wouldn't believe.'

Kate said, 'I could tell stories nobody would believe.'

'You? Don't be silly. You're a child.'

Kate laughed. 'You never saw such a child. This is a child–yes–a child!' She laughed with a thin penetrating shriek.

The sound got through the wine that was muffling Faye. She centred her eyes on Kate. 'You look so strange,' she said. 'I guess it's the lamplight. You look different.'

'I am different.'

'Call me "Mother", dear.'

'*Mother–dear*.'

'Kate, we're going to have such a good life.'

'You bet we are. You don't even know. You don't know.'

'I've always wanted to go to Europe. We could get on a ship and have nice clothes–dresses from Paris.'

'Maybe we'll do that–but not now.'

'Why not, Kate? I have plenty of money.'

'We'll have plenty more.'

Faye spoke pleadingly. 'Why don't we go now? We could sell the house. With the business we've got, we could get maybe ten thousand dollars for it.'

'No.'

'What do you mean, no? It's my house. I can sell it.'

'Did you forget I'm your daughter?'

'I don't like your tone, Kate. What's the matter with you? Is there any more wine?'

'Sure, there's a little. Look at it through the bottle. Here, drink it out of the bottle. That's right–Mother–spill it down your neck. Get it in under your corset, Mother, against your fat stomach.'

Faye wailed, 'Kate, don't be mean! We were feeling so nice. What do you want to go and spoil it for?'

Kate wrenched the bottle from her hand. 'Here, give me that.' She tipped it up and drained it and dropped it on the floor. Her face was sharp and her eyes glinted. The lips of her little mouth were parted to show her small sharp teeth, and the canines were longer and more pointed than the others. She laughed softly. 'Mother–dear Mother–I'm going to show you how to run a whorehouse. We'll fix the grey slugs that come in here and dump their nasty little loads–for a dollar. We'll give them pleasure, Mother dear.'

Faye said sharply, 'Kate, you're drunk. I don't know what you're talking about.'

'You don't, Mother dear? Do you want me to tell you?'

'I want you to be sweet. I want you to be like you were.'

'Well, it's too late. I didn't want to drink the wine. But you, you nasty fat worm, you made me. I'm your dear, sweet daughter–don't you remember? Well, I remember how surprised you were that I had regulars. Do you think I'll give them up? Do you think they give me a mean little dollar in quarters? No, they give me ten dollars, and the price is going up all the time. They can't go to anybody else. Nobody else is any good for them.'

Faye wept like a child. 'Kate,' she said, 'don't talk like that. You're not like that. You're not like that.'

'Dear Mother, sweet fat Mother, take down the pants of one of my regulars. Look at the heelmarks on the groin–very pretty. And the little cuts that bleed for a long time. Oh, Mother dear, I've got the sweetest set of razors all in a case–and so sharp, so sharp.'

Faye struggled to get out of her chair. Kate pushed her back. 'And do you know, Mother dear, that's the way this whole house is going to be. The price will be twenty dollars, and we'll make the bastards take a bath. We'll catch the blood on white silk handkerchiefs–Mother dear–blood from the little knotted whips.'

In her chair Faye began to scream hoarsely. Kate was on her instantly with a hard hand cupped over her mouth. 'Don't make a noise. There's a good darling. Got snot all over your daughter's hand–but no noise.' Tentatively she took her hand away and wiped it on Faye's skirt.

Faye whispered, 'I want you out of the house. I want you out. I run a good house without nastiness. I want you out.'

'I can't go, Mother. I can't leave you alone, poor dear.' Her voice chilled. 'Now I'm sick of you.' She took a wineglass from the table, went to the bureau, and poured paregoric until the glass was half full. 'Here, Mother, drink it. It will be good for you.'

'I don't want to.'

'There's a good dear. Drink it.' She coaxed the fluid into Faye. 'Now one more swallow–just one more.'

Faye mumbled thickly for a while and then she relaxed in her chair and slept, snoring thickly.

3

Dread began to gather in the corners of Kate's mind, and out of dread came panic. She remembered the other time and a nausea swept through her. She gripped her hands together, and the panic grew. She lighted a candle from the lamp and went unsteadily down the dark hall to the kitchen. She poured dry mustard in a glass, stirred water into it until it was partly fluid, and drank it. She held on to the edge of the sink while the paste went burning down. She retched and strained again and again. At the end of it, her heart was pounding and she was weak–but the wine was overcome and her mind was clear.

She went over the evening in her mind, moving from scene to scene like a sniffing animal. She bathed her face and washed out the sink and put the mustard back on the shelf. Then she went back to Faye's room.

The day was coming fast. Kate sat beside the bed and watched so that it stood black against the sky. Faye was still snoring in her chair. Kate watched her for a few moments and then she fixed Faye's bed. Kate dragged and strained and lifted the dead weight of the sleeping woman. On the bed Kate undressed Faye and washed her face and put her clothes away.

The day was coming fast. Kate sat beside the bed and watched the relaxed face, the mouth open, lips blowing in and out.

Faye made a restless movement and her dry lips slobbered a few thick words and sighed off to a snore again.

Kate's eyes became alert. She opened the top bureau drawer and examined the bottles which constituted the medicine chest of the house–paregoric, Pain Killer, Lydia Pinkham, iron wine tonic, Hall's Cream Salve, Epsom salts, castor oil, ammonia. She carried the ammonia bottle to the bed, saturated a handkerchief, and, standing well away, held the cloth over Faye's nose and mouth.

The strangling, shocking fumes went in, and Faye came snorting and fighting out of her black web. Her eyes were wide and terrified.

Kate said, 'It's all right, Mother. It's all right. You had a nightmare. You had a bad dream.'

'Yes, a dream,' and then sleep overcame her again and she fell back and began to snore, but the shock of the ammonia had lifted her up nearer consciousness and she was more restless. Kate put the bottle back in its drawer. She straightened the table, mopped up the spilled wine, and carried the glasses to the kitchen.

The house was dusky with dawn light creeping in around the edges of the blinds. The cook stirred in his lean-to behind the kitchen, groping for his clothes and putting on his clodhopper shoes.

Kate moved quietly. She drank two glasses of water and filled the glass again and carried it back to Faye's room and closed the door. She lifted Faye's right eyelid, and the eye looked rakishly up at her, but it was not rolled back in her head. Kate acted slowly and precisely. She picked up the handkerchief and smelled it. Some of the ammonia had evaporated but the smell was still sharp. She laid the cloth lightly over Faye's face, and when Faye twisted and turned and came near to waking, Kate took the handkerchief away and let Faye sink back. This she did three times. She put the handkerchief away and picked up an ivory crochet hook from the marble top of the bureau. She turned down the cover and pressed the blunt end of the ivory against Faye's flabby breast with a steady, increasing pressure until the sleeping woman whined and writhed. Then Kate explored the sensitive places of the body with the hook–under the arm, the groin, the ear, the clitoris, and always she removed the pressure just before Kaye awakened fully.

Faye was very near the surface now. She whined and sniffled and tossed. Kate stroked her forehead and ran smooth fingers over her inner arm and spoke softly to her.

'Dear–dear. You're having such a bad dream. Come out of the bad dream, Mother.'

Faye's breathing grew more regular. She heaved a great sigh and turned on her side and settled down with little grunts of comfort.

Kate stood up from the bed and a wave of dizziness rose in her head. She steadied herself, then went to the door and listened, slipped out, and moved cautiously to her own room. She undressed quickly and put on her nightgown and a robe and slippers. She brushed her hair and put it up and covered it with a sleeping-cap, and she sponged her face with Florida water. She went quietly back to Faye's room.

Faye was still sleeping peacefully on her side. Kate opened the door to the hall. She carried the glass of water to the bed and poured cold water in Faye's ear.

Faye screamed, and screamed again. Ethel's frightened face looked out of her room in time to see Kate in robe and slippers at Faye's door. The cook was right behind Kate, and he put out his hand to stop her.

'Now don't go in there, Miss Kate. You don't know what's in there.'

'Nonsense, Faye's in trouble.' Kate burst in and ran to the bed.

Faye's eyes were wild and she was crying and moaning.

'What is it? What is it, dear?'

The cook was in the middle of the room, and three sleep-haggard girls stood in the doorway.

'Tell me, what is it?' Kate cried.

'Oh, darling–the dreams, the dreams! I can't stand them!'

Kate turned to the door. 'She's had a nightmare–she'll be all right. You go back to bed. I'll stay with her a while. Alex, bring a pot of tea.'

Kate was tireless. The other girls remarked on it. She put cold towels on Faye's aching head and held her shoulders and the cup of tea for her. She petted and babied her, but the look of horror would not go out of Faye's eyes. At ten o'clock Alex brought in a can of beer and without a word put it on the bureau top. Kate held a glass of it to Faye's lips.

'It will help, darling. Drink it down.'

'I never want another drink.'

'Nonsense! Drink it down like medicine. That's a good girl. Now just lie back and go to sleep.'

'I'm afraid to sleep.'

'Were the dreams so bad?'

'Horrible, horrible!'

'Tell me about them, Mother. Maybe that will help.'

Faye shrank back. 'I wouldn't tell anyone. How could I have dreamed them? They weren't like my dreams.'

'Poor little Mother! I love you,' Kate said. 'You go to sleep. I'll keep your dreams away.'

Gradually Faye slid off to sleep. Kate sat beside the bed, studying her.

CHAPTER 21

I

In human affairs of danger and delicacy successful conclusion is sharply limited by hurry. So often men trip by being in a rush. If one were properly to perform a difficult and subtle act, he should first inspect the end to be achieved and then, once he had accepted the end as desirable, he should forget it completely and concentrate solely on the means. By this method he would not be moved to false action by anxiety or hurry or fear. Very few people learn this.

What made Kate so effective was the fact that she had either learned it or had been born with the knowledge. Kate never hurried. If a barrier arose, she waited until it had disappeared before continuing. She was capable of complete relaxation between the times for action. Also, she was mistress of a technique which is the basis of good wrestling–that of letting your opponent do the heavy work towards his own defeat, or of guiding his strength towards his weaknesses.

Kate was in no hurry. She thought to the end very quickly and then put it out of her mind. She set herself to work on method. She built a structure and attacked it, and if it showed the slightest shakiness she tore it down and started afresh. This she did only late at night or otherwise when she was completely alone, so that no change or preoccupation was noticeable in her manner. Her building was constructed of personalities, materials, knowledge, and time. She had access to the first and last, and she set about getting knowledge and materials, but while she did that she set in motion a series of imperceptible springs and pendulums and left them to pick up their own momenta.

First the cook told about the will. It must have been the cook. He thought he did anyway. Kate heard about it from Ethel, and she confronted him in the kitchen where he was kneading bread, his hairy big arms floured to the elbows and his hands yeast-bleached.

'Do you think it was a good thing to tell about being a witness?' she said mildly. 'What do you think Miss Faye is going to think?'

He looked confused. 'But I didn't–'

'You didn't what–tell about it or think it would hurt?'

'I don't think I–'

'You don't think you told? Only three people knew. Do you think I told? Or do you think Miss Faye did?' She saw the puzzled look come into his eyes and knew that by now he was far from sure that he had not told. In a moment he would be sure that he had.

Three of the girls questioned Kate about the will, coming to her together for mutual strength.

Kate said, 'I don't think Faye would like me to discuss it. Alex should have kept his mouth shut.' Their wills wavered, and she said, 'Why don't you ask Faye?'

'Oh, we wouldn't do that!'

'But you dare to talk behind her back! Come on now, let's go in to her and you can ask her the questions.'

'No, Kate, no.'

'Well, I'll have to tell her you asked. Wouldn't you rather be there? Don't you think she would feel better if she knew you weren't talking behind her back?'

'Well–'

'I know I would. I always like a person who comes right out.' Quietly she surrounded and nudged and pushed until they stood in Faye's room.

Kate said, 'They asked me about a certain you-know-what. Alex admits he let it out.'

Faye was slightly puzzled. 'Well, dear, I can't see that it's such a secret.'

Kate said, 'Oh, I'm glad you feel that way. But you can see that I couldn't mention it until you did.'

'You think it's bad to tell, Kate?'

'Oh, not at all. I'm glad, but it seemed to me that it wouldn't be loyal of me to mention it before you did.'

'You're sweet, Kate. I don't see any harm. You see, girls, I'm alone in the world and I have taken Kate as my daughter. She takes such care of me. Get the box, Kate.'

And each girl took the will in her own hands and inspected it. It was so simple they could repeat it word for word to the other girls.

They watched Kate to see how she would change, perhaps become a tyrant, but, if anything, she was nicer to them.

A week later when Kate became ill, she went right on with her supervision of the house, and no one would have known if she hadn't been found standing rigid in the hall with agony printed on her face. She begged the girls not to tell Faye, but they were outraged, and it was Faye who forced her to bed and called Dr Wilde.

He was a nice man and a pretty good doctor. He looked at her tongue, felt her pulse, asked her a few intimate questions, and then tapped his lower lip.

'Right here?' he asked, and exerted a little pressure on the small of her back. 'No? Here? Does this hurt? So. Well, I think you just need a kidney flushing.' He left yellow, green, and red pills to be taken in sequence. The pills did good work.

She did have one little flare-up. She told Faye, 'I'll go to the doctor's office.'

'I'll ask him to come here.'

'To bring me some more pills? Nonsense. I'll go in the morning.'

2

Dr Wilde was a good man and an honest man. He was accustomed to say of his profession that all he was sure of was that sulphur would cure the itch. He was not casual about his practice. Like so many country doctors, he was a combination doctor, priest, psychiatrist, to his town. He knew most of the secrets, weaknesses, and the braveries of Salinas. He never learned to take death easily. Indeed the death of a patient always gave him a sense of failure and hopeless ignorance. He was not a bold man, and he used surgery only as a last and fearful resort. The drugstore was coming in to help the doctors, but Dr Wilde was one of the few to maintain his own dispensary and to compound his own prescriptions. Many years of overwork and interrupted sleep had made him a little vague and preoccupied.

At eight-thirty on a Wednesday morning Kate walked up Main Street, climbed the stairs of the Monterey County Bank Building, and walked along the corridor until she found the door which said, 'Dr Wilde–Office Hours 11–2.'

At nine-thirty Dr Wilde put his buggy in the livery stable and wearily lifted out his black bag. He had been out in the Alisal presiding at the disintegration of old, old lady German. She had not been able to terminate her life neatly. There were codicils. Even now Dr Wilde wondered whether the tough, dry, stringy life was completely gone out of her. She was ninety-seven and a death certificate meant nothing to her. Why, she had corrected the priest who prepared her. The mystery of death was on him. It often was. Yesterday, Allen

Day, thirty-seven, six feet one inch, strong as a bull and valuable to four hundred acres and a large family, had meekly surrendered his life to pneumonia after a little exposure and three days of fever. Dr Wilde knew it was a mystery. His eyelids felt grainy. He thought he would take a sponge bath and have a drink before his first office patients arrived with their stomach-aches.

He climbed the stairs and put his worn key in the lock of his office door. The key would not turn. He set his bag on the floor and exerted pressure. The key refused to budge. He grabbed the door-knob and pulled outwards and rattled the key. The door was opened from within. Kate stood in front of him.

'Oh, good morning. Lock was stuck. How did you get in?'

'It wasn't locked. I was early and came in to wait.'

'Wasn't locked?' He turned the key the other way and saw that, sure enough, the little bar slipped out easily.

'I'm getting old, I guess,' he said. 'I'm forgetful.' He sighed. 'I don't know why I lock it, anyway. You could get in with a piece of bailing wire. And who'd want to get in, anyway?' He seemed to see her for the first time. 'I don't have the office hours until eleven.'

Kate said, 'I needed some more of those pills and I couldn't come later.'

'Pills? Oh, yes. You're the girl from down at Faye's.'

'That's right.'

'Feeling better?'

'Yes, the pills help.'

'Well, they can't hurt,' he said. 'Did I leave the door to the dispensary open too?'

'What's a dispensary?'

'Over there–that door.'

'I guess you must have.'

'Getting old. How is Faye?'

'Well, I'm worried about her. She was real sick a while ago. Had cramps and went a little out of her head.'

'She's had a stomach disorder before,' Dr Wilde said. 'You can't live like that and eat all hours and be very well. I can't, anyway. We just call it stomach trouble. Comes from eating too much and staying up all night. Now–the pills. Do you remember what colour?'

'There were three kinds, yellow, red, and green.'

'Oh yes. Yes, I remember.'

While he poured pills into a round cardboard box she stood in the doorway. 'What a lot of medicines!'

Dr Wilde said, 'Yes–and the older I get, the fewer I use. I got some of those when I started to practise. Never used them. That's a beginner's stock. I was going to experiment–alchemy.'

'What?'

'Nothing. Here you are. Tell Faye to get some sleep and eat some vegetables. I've been up all night. Let yourself out, will you?' He went wavering back into the surgery.

Kate glanced after him and then her eyes flicked over the lines of bottles and containers. She closed the dispensary door and looked round the outer office. One book in the case was out of line. She pushed it back until it was shoulder to shoulder with its brothers.

She picked up her big handbag from the leather sofa and left.

In her own room Kate took five small bottles and a strip of scribbled paper from her handbag. She put the whole works in the toe of a stocking, pushed the wad into a rubber overshoe, and stood it with its fellow in the back of her closet.

3

During the following months a gradual change came over Faye's house. The girls were sloppy and touchy. If they had been told to clean themselves and their rooms a deep resentment would have set in and the house would have reeked of ill temper. But it didn't work that way.

Kate said at table one evening that she had just happened to look in Ethel's room, and it was so neat and pretty she couldn't help buying her a present. When Ethel unwrapped the package right at the table it was a big bottle of Hoyt's German, enough to keep her smelling sweet for a long time. Ethel was pleased and she hoped Kate hadn't seen the dirty clothes under the bed. After supper she not only got the clothes out but brushed the floors and swept the cobwebs out of the corners.

Then Grace looked so pretty one afternoon that Kate couldn't help giving her the rhinestone butterfly pin she was wearing. And Grace had to rush up and put on a clean shirtwaist to set it off.

Alex in the kitchen, who if he had believed what was usually said of him would have considered himself a murderer, found that he had a magic hand with biscuits. He discovered that cooking was something you couldn't learn. You had to feel it.

Cotton Eye learned that nobody hated him. His tub-thumping piano-playing changed imperceptibly.

He told Kate, 'It's funny what you remember when you think back.'

'Like what?' she asked.

'Well, like this,' and he played for her.

'That's lovely,' she said. 'What is it?'

'Well, I don't know. I think it's Chopin. If I could just see the music!'

He told her how he had lost his sight, and he had never told anyone else. It was a bad story. That Saturday night he took the chain off the piano strings and played something he had been remembering and practising in the morning, something called 'Moonlight,' a piece by Beethoven, Cotton Eye thought.

Ethel said it sounded like moonlight and did he know the words.

'It don't have words,' said Cotton Eye.

Oscar Trip, up from Gonzales for Saturday night, said, 'Well, it ought to have. It's pretty.'

One night there were presents for everyone because Faye's was the best house, the cleanest, and nicest in the whole county–and who was responsible for that? Why, the girls–who else? And did they ever taste seasoning like in that stew?

Alex retired into the kitchen and shyly wiped his eyes with the back of his wrist. He bet he could make a plum pudding which would knock their eyes out.

Georgia was getting up at ten every morning and taking piano lessons from Cotton Eye, and her nails were clean.

Coming back from eleven o'clock Mass on a Sunday morning, Grace said to Trixie, 'And I was about ready to get married and give up whoring. Can you imagine?'

'It's sure nice,' said Trixie. 'Jenny's girls came over for Faye's birthday cake and they couldn't believe their eyes. They don't talk about nothing else but how it is at Faye's. Jenny's sore.'

'Did you see the score on the blackboard this morning?'

'Sure I did–eighty-seven tricks in one week. Let Jenny or the Nigger match that when there ain't no holidays!'

'No holidays, hell. Have you forgot it's Lent? They ain't turning a trick at Jenny's.'

After her illness and her evil dreams Faye was quiet and depressed. Kate knew she was being watched, but there was no help for that. And she had made sure the rolled paper was still in the box and all the girls had seen it or heard about it.

One afternoon Faye looked up from her solitaire game as Kate knocked and entered the room.

'How do you feel, Mother?'

'Fine, just fine.' Her eyes were secretive. Faye wasn't very clever. 'You know, Kate, I'd like to go to Europe.'

'Well, how wonderful! And you deserve it and you can afford it.'

'I don't want to go alone. I want you to go with me.'

Kate looked at her in astonishment. 'Me? You want to take me?'

'Sure, why not?'

'Oh, you sweet dear! When can we go?'

'You want to?'

'I've always dreamed of it. When can we go? Let's go soon.'

Faye's eyes lost their suspicion and her face relaxed. 'Maybe next summer,' she said. 'We can plan it for next summer, Kate!'

'Yes, Mother.'

'You–you don't turn any tricks any more, do you?'

'Why should I? You take such good care of me.'

Faye slowly gathered up the cards and tapped them square, and dropped them in the table drawer.

Kate pulled up a chair. 'I want to ask your advice about something.'

'What is it?'

'Well, you know I'm trying to help you.'

'You're doing everything, darling.'

'You know our biggest expense is food, and it gets bigger in the winter.'

'Yes.'

'Well, right now you can buy fruit and all kinds of vegetables for two bits a lug. And in the winter you know what we pay for canned peaches and canned string beans.'

'You aren't planning to start preserving?'

'Well, why shouldn't we?'

'What will Alex say to that?'

'Mother, you can believe it or not, or you can ask him. Alex suggested it.'

'No!'

'Well, he did. Cross my heart.'

'Well, I'll be damned–Oh, I'm sorry, sweet. It slipped out.'

The kitchen turned into a cannery and all the girls helped. Alex truly believed it was his idea. At the end of the season he had a silver watch with his name engraved on the back to prove it.

Ordinarily both Faye and Kate had their supper at the long table in the dining-room, but on Sunday nights, when Alex was off and the girls dined on thick sandwiches, Kate served supper for two in Faye's room. It was a pleasant and a ladylike time. There was always some little delicacy, very special and good–*foie gras* or a tossed salad, pastry brought at Lang's Bakery just across Main Street. And instead of the white oilcloth and paper napkins of the dining-room, Faye's table was covered with a white damask cloth and the napkins were linen. It had a party feeling, too, candles and–something rare in Salinas–a bowl of flowers. Kate could make pretty floral arrangements using only the blossoms from weeds she picked in the fields.

'What a clever girl she is,' Faye would say. 'She can do anything and she can make do with anything. We're going to Europe. And did you know Kate speaks French? Well, she can. When you get her alone, ask her to say something in French. She's teaching me. Know how you say bread in French?' Faye was having a wonderful time. Kate gave her excitement and perpetual planning.

4

On Saturday the fourteenth of October the first wild ducks went over Salinas. Faye saw them from her window, a great wedge flying south. When Kate came in before supper, as she always did, Faye told her about it. 'I guess the winter's nearly here,' she said. 'We'll have to get Alex to set up the stoves.'

'Ready for your tonic, Mother dear?'

'Yes, I am. You're making me lazy, waiting on me.'

'I like to wait on you,' said Kate. She took the bottle of Lydia Pinkham's Vegetable Compound from the drawer and held it up to the light. 'Not much left,' she said. 'We'll have to get some more.'

'Oh, I think I have three bottles left of the dozen in my closet.'

Kate picked up the glass. 'There's a fly in the glass,' she said. 'I'll just go and wash it out.'

In the kitchen she rinsed the glass. From her pocket she took the eye-dropper. The end was closed with a little piece of potato, the way you plug the spout of a kerosene can. She carefully squeezed a few drops of clear liquid into the glass, a tincture of nux vomica.

Back in Faye's room she poured the three tablespoons of vegetable compound in the glass and stirred it.

Faye drank her tonic and licked her lips. 'It tastes bitter,' she said.

'Does it, dear? Let me taste.' Kate took a spoonful from the bottle and made a face. 'So it does,' she said. 'I guess it's been standing around too long. I'm going to throw it out. Say, that *is* bitter. Let me get you a glass of water.'

At supper Faye's face was flushed. She stopped eating and seemed to be listening.

'What's the matter?' Kate asked. 'Mother, what's the matter?'

Faye seemed to tear her attention away. 'Why, I don't know. I guess a little heart flutter. Just all of a sudden I felt afraid and my heart got to pounding.'

'Don't you want me to help you to your room?'

'No, dear, I feel all right now.'

Grace put down her fork. 'Well, you got a real high flush, Faye.'

Kate said, 'I don't like it. I wish you'd see Dr Wilde.'

'No, it's all right now.'

'You frightened me,' said Kate. 'Have you ever had it before?'

'Well, I'm a little short of breath sometimes. I guess I'm getting too stout.'

Faye didn't feel very good that Saturday night, and about ten o'clock Kate persuaded her to go to bed. Kate looked in several times until she was sure Faye was asleep.

The next day Faye felt all right. 'I guess I'm just short-winded,' she said.

'Well, we're going to have invalid food for my darling,' said Kate. 'I've made some chicken soup for you and we'll have a string-bean salad–the way you like it, just oil and vinegar, and a cup of tea.'

'Honest to God, Kate, I feel pretty good.'

'It wouldn't hurt either of us to eat a little light. You frightened me last night. I had an aunt who died of heart trouble. And that leaves a memory, you know.'

'I never had any trouble with my heart. Just a little short-winded when I climbed the stairs.'

In the kitchen Kate set the supper on two trays. She measured out the French dressing in a cup and poured it on the string-bean salad. On Faye's tray she put her favourite cup and set the soup forward on the stove to heat. Finally she took the eye-dropper from her pocket and squeezed two drops of croton oil on the string beans and stirred it in. She went to her room and swallowed the contents of a small bottle of Cascara Sagrada and hurried back to the kitchen. She poured the hot soup in the cups, filled the teapot with boiling water, and carried the trays to Faye's room.

'I didn't think I was hungry,' Faye said. 'But that soup smells good.'

'I made a special salad dressing for you,' said Kate. 'It's an old recipe, rosemary and thyme. See if you like it.'

'Why, it's delicious,' said Faye. 'Is there anything you can't do, darling?'

Kate was stricken first. Her forehead beaded with perspiration and she doubled over, crying with pain. Her eyes were staring and the saliva ran from her mouth. Faye ran to the hallway, screaming for help. The girls and a few Sunday customers crowded into the room. Kate was writhing on the floor. Two of the regulars lifted her on to Faye's bed and tried to straighten her out, but she screamed and doubled up again. The sweat poured from her body and wetted her shoes.

Faye was wiping Kate's forehead with a towel when the pain struck her.

It was an hour before Dr Wilde could be found, playing euchre with a friend. He was dragged down to the Line by two hysterical whores. Faye and Kate were weak from vomiting and diarrhoea and the spasms continued at intervals.

Dr Wilde said, 'What did you eat?' and then he noticed the trays. 'Are those string beans home-canned?' he demanded.

'Sure,' said Grace. 'We did them right here.'

'Did any of you have them?'

'Well, no. You see–'

'Go out and break every jar,' Dr Wilde said. 'Goddam the string beans!' And he unpacked his stomach pump.

On Tuesday he sat with two pale weak women. Kate's bed had been moved into Faye's room. 'I can tell you now,' he said. 'I didn't think you had a chance. You're pretty lucky. And let home-made string beans alone. Buy canned ones.'

'What is it?' Kate asked.

'Botulism. We don't know much about it, but damn few ever get over it. I guess it's because you're young and she's tough.' He asked Faye, 'Are you still bleeding from the bowels?'

'Yes, a little.'

'Well, here are some morphine pills. They'll bind you up. You've probably ruptured something. But they say you can't kill a whore. Now take it easy, both of you.'

That was October 17.

Faye was never really well again. She would make a little gain and then go to pieces. She had a bad time on December 3, and it took even longer for her to gain her strength. February 12 the bleeding became violent and the strain seemed to have weakened Faye's heart. Dr Wilde listened a long time through his stethoscope.

Kate was haggard and her slender body had shrunk to bones. The girls tried to spell her with Faye, but Kate would not leave.

Grace said, 'God knows when's the last sleep she had. If Faye was to die, I think it would kill that girl.'

'She's just as like to blow her brains out,' said Ethel.

Dr Wilde took Kate into the day-darkened parlour and put his black bag on the chair. 'I might as well tell you,' he said. 'Her heart just can't stand the strain, I'm afraid. She's all torn up inside. That goddam botulism. Worse than a rattlesnake.' He looked away from Kate's haggard face. 'I thought it would be better to tell you so you can prepare yourself,' he said lamely, and put his hand on her bony shoulder. 'Not many people have such loyalty. Give her a little warm milk if she can take it.'

Kate carried a basin of warm water to the table beside the bed. When Trixie looked in, Kate was bathing Faye and using the fine linen napkins to do it. Then she brushed the lank blonde hair and braided it.

Faye's skin had shrunk, clinging to jaw and skull, and her eyes were huge and vacant.

She tried to speak, and Kate said, 'Shush! Save your strength. Save your strength.'

She went to the kitchen for a glass of warm milk and put it on the bedside table. She took two little bottles from her pocket and sucked a little from each into the eye-dropper. 'Open up, Mother. This is a new kind of medicine. Now be brave, dear. This will taste bad.' She squeezed the fluid far back on Faye's tongue and held up her head so she could drink a little milk to take away the taste. 'Now you rest and I'll be back in a little while.'

Kate slipped quietly out of the room. The kitchen was dark. She opened the outer door and crept out and moved back among the weeds. The ground was damp from the spring rains. At the back of the lot she dug a small hole with a pointed stick. She dropped in a number of small thin bottles and an eye-dropper. With the stick she crushed the glass to bits and scraped the dirt over them. Rain was beginning to fall as Kate went back to the house.

At first they had to tie Kate down to keep her from hurting herself. From violence she went into a gloomy stupor. It was a long time before she regained her health. And she forgot completely about the will. It was Trixie who finally remembered.

CHAPTER 22

I

On the Trask place Adam drew into himself. The unfinished Sanchez house lay open to wind and rain, and the new floor-boards buckled and warped with moisture. The laid-out vegetable gardens rioted with weeds.

Adam seemed clothed in a viscosity that slowed his movements and held his thoughts down. He saw the world through grey water. Now and then his mind fought its way upwards, and when the light broke in it brought him only a sickness of the mind, and he retired into the greyness again. He was aware of the twins because he heard them cry and laugh, but he felt only a thin distaste for them. To Adam they were symbols of his loss. His neighbours drove up into his little valley, and every one of them would have understood anger or sorrow–and so helped him. But they could do nothing with the cloud that hung over him. Adam did not resist them. He simply did not see them, and before long the neighbours stopped driving up the road under the oaks.

For a long time Lee tried to stimulate Adam to awareness, but Lee was a busy man. He cooked and washed, he bathed the twins and fed them. Through hard, constant work he grew fond of the two little boys. He talked to them in Cantonese, and Chinese words were the first they recognized and tried to repeat.

Samuel Hamilton went back twice to try to wedge Adam up and out of his shock. Then Liza stepped in.

'I want you to stay away from there,' she said. 'You come back a changed man. Samuel, you don't change him. He changes you. I can see the look of him in your face.'

'Have you thought of the two little boys, Liza?' he asked.

'I've thought of your own family,' she said snappishly. 'You lay a crêpe on us for days after.'

'All right, Mother,' he said, but it saddened him, because Samuel could not mind his own business when there was pain in any man. It was no easy thing for him to abandon Adam to his desolation.

Adam had paid him for his work, had even paid him for the windmill parts and did not want the windmills. Samuel sold the equipment and sent Adam the money. He had no answer.

He became aware of an anger at Adam Trask. It seemed to Samuel that Adam might be pleasuring himself with sadness. But there was little leisure to brood. Joe was off to college–to that school Leland Stanford had built on his farm near Palo Alto. Tom worried his father, for Tom grew deeper and deeper into books. He did his work well enough, but Samuel felt that Tom had not joy enough.

Will and George were doing well in business, and Joe was writing letters home in rhymed verse and making as smart an attack on all the accepted verities as was healthful.

Samuel wrote to Joe, saying, 'I would be disappointed if you had not become an atheist, and I read pleasantly that you have, in your age and wisdom, accepted agnosticism the way you'd take a cookie on a full stomach. But I would ask you with all my understanding heart not to try to convert your mother. Your last letter only made her think you are not well. Your mother does not believe there are many ills incurable by good strong soup. She puts your brave attack on the structure of civilization down to a stomach-ache. It worries her. Her faith is a mountain, and you, my son, haven't even got a shovel yet.'

Liza was getting old. Samuel saw it in her face, and could not feel old himself, white beard or no. But Liza was living backwards, and that's the proof.

There was a time when she looked on his plans and prophecies as the crazy shoutings of a child. Now she felt that they were unseemly in a grown man. They three, Liza and Tom and Samuel, were alone on the ranch. Una was married to a stranger and gone away. Dessie had her dressmaking business in Salinas. Olive had married her young man and Mollie was married and living, believe it or not, in an apartment in San Francisco. There was perfume, and a white bearskin run in the bedroom in front of the fireplace, and Mollie smoked a gold-tipped cigarette–Violet Milo–with her coffee after dinner.

One day Samuel strained his back lifting a bale of hay, and it hurt his feelings more than his back, for he could not imagine a life in which Sam Hamilton was not privileged to lift a bale of hay. He felt insulted by his back, almost as he would have been if one of his children had been dishonest.

In King City, Dr Tilson felt him over. The doctor grew more testy with his overworked years.

'You sprained your back.'

'That I did,' said Samuel.

'And you drove all the way in to have me tell you that you sprained your back and charge you two dollars?'

'Here's your two dollars.'

'And you want to know what to do about it?'

'Sure I do.'

'Don't sprain it any more. Now take your money back. You're not a fool, Samuel, unless you're getting childish.'

'But it hurts.'

'Of course it hurts. How would you know it was strained if it didn't?'

Samuel laughed. 'You're good for me,' he said. 'You're more than two dollars good for me. Keep the money.'

The doctor looked closely at him. 'I think you're telling the truth, Samuel. I'll keep the money.'

Samuel went in to see Will in his fine new store. He hardly knew his son, for Will was getting fat and prosperous and he wore a coat and waistcoat and a gold ring on his little finger.

'I've got a package made up for Mother,' Will said. 'Some little cans of things from France. Mushrooms and liver paste and sardines so little you can hardly see them.'

'She'll just send them to Joe,' said Samuel.

'Can't you make her eat them?'

'No,' said his father. 'But she'll enjoy sending them to Joe.'

Lee came into the store and his eyes lighted up. 'How do, Missy,' he said.

'Hello, Lee. How are the boys?'

'Boys fine.'

Samuel said, 'I'm going to have a glass of beer next door, Lee. Be glad to have you join me.'

Lee and Samuel sat at the little round table in the bar-room and Samuel drew figures on the scrubbed wood with the moisture off his beer glass. 'I've wanted to go and see you and Adam, but I didn't think I could do any good.'

'Well, you can't do any harm. I thought he'd get over it. But he still walks around like a ghost.'

'It's over a year, isn't it?' Samuel asked.

'Three months over.'

'Well, what do you think I can do?'

'I don't know,' said Lee. 'Maybe you could shock him out of it. Nothing else has worked.'

'I'm not good at shocking. I'd probably end up by shocking myself. By the way, what did he name the twins?'

'They don't have any names.'

'You're making a joke, Lee.'

'I am not making jokes.'

'What does he call them?'

'He calls them "they".'

I mean when he speaks to them.'

'When he speaks to them he calls them "you", one or both.'

'This is nonsense,' Samuel said angrily. 'What kind of a fool is the man?'

'I've meant to come and tell you. He's a dead man unless you can wake him up.'

Samuel said, 'I'll come. I'll bring a horse-whip. No names! You're damn right I'll come, Lee.'

'When?'

'Tomorrow.'

'I'll kill a chicken,' said Lee. 'You'll like the twins, Mr Hamilton. They're fine-looking boys. I won't tell Mr Trask you're coming.'

2

Shyly Samuel told his wife he wanted to visit the Trask place. He thought she would pile up strong walls of objection, and for one of the few times in his life he would disobey her wish no matter how strong her objection. It gave him a sad feeling in the stomach to think of disobeying his wife. He explained his purpose almost as though he were confessing. Liza put her hands on her hips during the telling and his heart sank. When he was finished she continued to look at him, he thought, coldly.

Finally she said, 'Samuel, do you think you can move this rock of a man?'

'Why, I don't know, Mother.' He had not expected this. 'I don't know.'

'Do you think it is such an important matter that those babies have names right now?'

'Well, it seemed so to me,' he said lamely.

'Samuel, do you think why you want to go? Is it your natural incurable nosiness? Is it your black inability to mind your own business?'

'Now, Liza, I know my failings pretty well. I thought it might be more than that.'

'It had better be more than that,' she said. 'This man has not admitted that his sons live. He has cut them off mid-air.'

'That's the way it seems to me, Liza.'

'If he tells you to mind your own business–what then?'

'Well, I don't know.'

Her jaw snapped shut and her teeth clicked. 'If you do not get those boys named, there'll be no warm place in this house for you. Don't you dare come whining back, saying he wouldn't do it or he wouldn't listen. If you do I'll have to go myself.'

'I'll give him the back of my hand,' Samuel said.

'No, that you won't do. You fall short in savagery, Samuel. I know you. You'll give him sweet-sounding words and you'll come dragging back and try to make me forget you ever went.'

'I'll beat his brains out,' Samuel shouted.

He slammed into the bedroom, and Liza smiled at the panels.

He came out soon in his black suit and his hard shiny shirt and collar. He stooped down to her while she tied his black string tie. His white beard was brushed to shining.

'You'd best take a swab at your shoes with a blacking brush,' she said.

In the midst of painting the blacking on his worn shoes he looked sideways up at her. 'Could I take the Bible along?' he asked. 'There's no place for getting a good name like the Bible.'

'I don't much like it out of the house,' she said uneasily. 'And if you're late coming home, what'll I have for my reading? And the children's names are in it.' She saw his face fall. She went into the bedroom and came back with a small Bible, worn and scuffed, its cover held on by brown paper and glue. 'Take this one,' she said.

'But that's your mother's.'

'She wouldn't mind. And all the names but one in here have two dates.'

'I'll wrap it so it won't get hurt,' said Samuel.

Liza spoke sharply, 'What my mother would mind is what I mind, and I'll tell you what I mind. You're never satisfied to let the Testament alone. You're for ever picking at it and questioning it. You turn it over the way a 'coon turns over a wet rock, and it angers me.'

'I'm just trying to understand it, Mother.'

'What is there to understand? Just read it. There it is in black and white. Who wants you to understand it? If the Lord God wanted you to understand it He'd have given you to understand or He'd have set it down different.'

'But, Mother–'

'Samuel,' she said, 'you're the most contentious man this world has ever seen.'

'Yes, Mother.'

'Don't agree with me all the time. It hints of insincerity. Speak up for yourself.'

She stood after his dark figure in the buggy as he drove away. 'He's a sweet husband,' she said aloud, 'but contentious.'

And Samuel was thinking with wonder, 'Just when I think I know her she does a thing like that.'

3

On the last half-mile, turning out of the Salinas Valley and driving up the unscraped road under the great oak trees, Samuel tried to plait a rage to take care of his embarrassment. He said heroic words to himself.

Adam was more gaunt than Samuel remembered. His eyes were dull, as though he did not use them much for seeing. It took a little time for Adam to become aware that Samuel was standing before him. A grimace of displeasure drew down his mouth.

Samuel said, 'I feel small now–coming uninvited As I have.'

Adam said, 'What do you want? Didn't I pay you?'

'Pay?' Samuel asked. 'Yes, you did. Yes, by God, you did. And I'll tell you that pay has been more than I've merited by the nature of it.'

'What? What are you trying to say?'

Samuel's anger grew and put out leaves. 'A man, his whole life, matches himself against pay. And now, if it's my whole life's work to find my worth, can you, sad man, write me down instant in a ledger?'

Adam exclaimed, 'I'll pay. I tell you I'll pay. How much? I'll pay.'

'You have, but not to me.'

'Why did you come, then? Go away!'

'You once invited me.'

'I don't invite you now.'

Samuel put his hands on his hips and leaned forward. 'I'll tell you now, quiet. In a bitter night, a mustard night that was last night, a good thought came and the dark was sweetened when the day sat down. And this thought went from evening star to the late dipper on the edge of the first light–that our betters spoke of. So I invite myself.'

'You are not welcome.'

Samuel said, 'I'm told that out of some singular glory your loins got twins.'

'What business is that of yours?'

A kind of joy lighted Samuel's eyes at the rudeness. He saw Lee lurking inside the house and peeking out at him. 'Don't, for the love of God, put violence on me. I'm a man hopes there'll be a picture of peace on my hatchments.'

'I don't understand you.'

'How could you? Adam Trask, a dog-wolf with a pair of cubs, a scrubby rooster with sweet paternity for a fertilized egg! A dirty clod!'

A darkness covered Adam's cheeks and for the first time his eyes seemed to see. Samuel joyously felt hot rage in his stomach. He cried, 'Oh, my friend, retreat from me! Please, I beg of you!' The saliva dampened the corners of his mouth. 'Please!' he cried. 'For the love of any holy thing you can remember, step back from me. I feel murder nudging my gizzard.'

Adam said, 'Get off my place. Go on–get off. You're acting crazy. Get off. This is my place. I bought it.'

'You bought your eyes and nose,' Samuel jeered. 'You bought your uprightness. You bought your thumb on sideways. Listen to me, because I'm like to kill you after. You bought! You bought out of some sweet inheritance. Think now–do you deserve your children, man?'

'Deserve them? They're here–I guess. I don't understand you.'

Samuel wailed, 'God save me, Liza! It's not the way you think, Adam! Listen to me before my thumb finds the bad place at your throat. The precious twins–untried, unnoticed, undirected–and I say it quiet with my hands down–undiscovered.'

'Get off,' said Adam hoarsely. 'Lee, bring a gun! This man is crazy. Lee!'

Then Samuel's hands were on Adam's throat, pressing the throbbing up to his temples, swelling his eyes with blood. And Samuel was snarling at him. 'Tear away with your jelly fingers. You have not bought these boys, not stolen them, nor passed any bit for them. You have them by some strange and lovely dispensation.' Suddenly he plucked his hard thumbs out of his neighbour's throat.

Adam stood panting. He felt his throat where the blacksmith's hands had been. 'What is it you want of me?'

'You have no love.'

'I had–enough to kill me.'

'No one ever had enough. The stone orchard celebrates too little, not too much.'

'Stay away from me. I can fight back. Don't think I can't defend myself.'

'You have two weapons, and they not named.'

'I'll fight you, old man. You are an old man.'

Samuel said, 'I can't think in my mind of a dull man picking up a rock, who before evening would not put a name to it–like Peter. And you–for a year you've lived with your heart's draining and you've not even laid a number to the boys.'

Adam said, 'What I do is my own business.'

Samuel struck him with a work-heavy fist, and Adam sprawled in the dust. Samuel asked him to rise, and when Adam accepted struck him again, and this time Adam did not get up. He looked stonily at the menacing old man.

The fire went out of Samuel's eyes and he said quietly, 'Your sons have no names.'

Adam replied, 'Their mother left them motherless.'

'And you have left them fatherless. Can't you feel the cold at night of a lone child? What warm is there, what bird song, what possible morning can be good? Don't you remember, Adam, how it was, even a little?'

'I didn't do it,' Adam said.

'Have you undone it? Your boys have no names.' He stooped down and put his arms around Adam's shoulders and helped him to his feet. 'We'll give them names,' he said. 'We'll think long and find good names to clothe them.' He whipped the dust from Adam's shirt with his hands.

Adam wore a far-away yet intent look, as though he were listening to some wind-carried music, but his eyes were not dead as they had been. He said, 'It's hard to imagine I'd thank a man for insults and for shaking me out like a rug. But I'm grateful. It's a hurty thanks, but it's thanks.'

Samuel smiled, crinkle-eyed. 'Did it seem natural? Did I do it right?' he asked.

'What do you mean?'

'Well, in a way I promised my wife I'd do it. She didn't believe I would. I'm not a fighting man, you see. The last time I clobbered a human soul it was over a red-nosed girl and a schoolbook in County Derry.'

Adam stared at Samuel, but in his mind he saw and felt his brother Charles, black and murderous, and that sight switched to Cathy and the quality of her eyes over the gun-barrel. 'There wasn't any fear in it,' Adam said, 'it was more like weariness.'

'I guess I was not angry enough.'

'Samuel, I'll ask you just once and then no more. Have you heard anything? Has there been any news of her–any news at all?'

'I've heard nothing.'

'It's almost a relief,' said Adam.

'Do you have hatred?'

'No. No–only a kind of sinking in the heart. Maybe later I'll sort it out to hatred. There was no interval from loveliness to horror, you see. I'm confused.'

Samuel said, 'One day we'll sit and you'll lay it out on the table, neat like a solitaire deck, but now–why, you can't find all the cards.'

From behind the shed there came the indignant shrieking of an outraged chicken and then a dull thump.

'There's something at the hens,' said Adam.

A second shrieking started. 'It's Lee at the hens,' said Samuel. 'You know, if chickens had government and church and history, they would take a distant and distasteful view of human joy. Let any gay and hopeful thing happen to a man, and some chicken goes howling to the block.'

Now the two men were silent, breaking it only with small false courtesies–meaningless inquiries about health and weather, with answers unlistened to. And this might have continued until they were angry at each other again if Lee had not interfered.

Lee brought out a table and two chairs and set the chairs facing each other. He made another trip for a pint of whisky and two glasses and set a glass on the table in front of each chair. Then he carried out the twins, one under each arm, and put them on the ground beside the table and gave each boy a stick for his hand to shake and make shadows with.

The boys sat solemnly and looked about, stared at Samuel's beard and searched for Lee. The strange thing about them was their clothing, for the boys were dressed in the straight trousers and the frogged and braided jackets of the Chinese. One was in turquoise blue and the other in a faded rose pink, and the frogs and braid were black. On their heads sat round black silken hats, each with a bright red button on its flat top.

Samuel asked, 'Where in the world did you get those clothes, Lee?'

'I didn't get them,' Lee said testily. 'I had them. The only other clothes they have I made myself, out of sail-cloth. A boy should be well dressed on his naming day.'

'You've dropped the pidgin, Lee.'

'I hoped for good. Of course, I use it in King City.' He addressed a few short sung syllables to the boys on the ground, and they both smiled up at him and waved their sticks in the air. Lee said, 'I'll pour you a drink. It's some that was here.'

'It's some you bought yesterday in King City,' said Samuel.

Now that Samuel and Adam were seated together and the barriers were down, a curtain of shyness fell on Samuel. What he had beaten in with his fists he could not supplement easily. He thought of the virtues of courage and forbearance, which became flabby when there is nothing to use them on. His mind grinned inward at itself.

The two sat looking at the twin boys in their strange, bright-coloured clothes. Samuel thought, 'Sometimes your opponent can help you more than your friend.' He lifted his eyes to Adam.

'It's hard to start,' he said, 'And it's like a put-off letter that gathers difficulties to itself out of the minutes. Could you give me a hand?'

Adam looked up for a moment and then back at the boys on the ground. 'There's a crashing in my head,' he said. 'Like sounds you hear under water. I'm having to dig myself out of a year.'

'Maybe you'll tell me how it was and that will get us started.'

Adam tossed down his drink and poured another and rolled the glass at an angle in his hand. The amber whisky moved high on the side and the pungent fruity odour of its warming filled the air. 'It's hard to remember,' he said, 'It was not agony but a dullness. But no–there were needles in it. You said I had not all the cards in the deck–and I was thinking of that. Maybe I'll never have all the cards.'

'Is it herself trying to come out? When a man says he does not want to speak of something he usually means he can think of nothing else.'

'Maybe it's that. She's all mixed up with the dullness, and I can't remember much except the last picture drawn in fire.'

'She did shoot you, didn't she, Adam?'

His lips grew thin and his eyes black.

Samuel said, 'There's no need to answer.'

'There's no reason not to,' Adam replied. 'Yes, she did.'

'Did she mean to kill you?'

'I've thought of that more than anything else. No, I don't think she meant to kill me. She didn't allow me that dignity. There was no hatred in her, no passion at all. I learned about that in the army. If you want to kill a man, you shoot at head or heart or stomach. No, she hit me where she intended. I can see the gun-barrel moving over. I guess I wouldn't have minded so much if she had wanted my death. That would have been a kind of love. But I was an annoyance, not an enemy.'

'You've given it a lot of thought,' said Samuel.

'I've had lots of time for it. I want to ask you something. I can't remember behind the last ugly thing. Was she very beautiful, Samuel?'

'To you she was because you built her. I don't think you ever saw her–only your own creation.'

Adam mused aloud, 'I wonder who she was–what she was. I was content not to know.'

'And now you want to?'

Adam dropped his eyes. 'It's not curiosity. But I would like to know what kind of blood is in my boys. When they grow up–won't I be looking for something in them?'

'Yes, you will. And I will warn you now that not their blood but your suspicion might build evil in them. They will be what you expect of them.'

'But their blood–'

'I don't very much believe in blood,' said Samuel. 'I think when a man finds good or bad in his children he is seeing only what he planted in them after they cleared the womb.'

'You can't make a racehorse of a pig.'

'No,' said Samuel, 'but you can make a very fast pig.'

'No one hereabouts would agree with you. I think even Mrs Hamilton would not.'

'That's exactly right. She most of all would disagree, and so I would not say it to her and let loose the thunder of her disagreement. She wins all arguments by the use of vehemence and the conviction that a difference of opinion is a personal affront. She's a fine woman, but you have to learn to feel your way with her. Let's speak of the boys.'

'Will you have another drink?'

'That I will, thank you. Names are a great mystery. I've never known whether the name is moulded by the child or the child changed to fit the name. But you can be sure of this–whenever a human has a nickname it is proof that the name given him was wrong. How do you favour the standard names–John or James or Charles?'

Adam was looking at the twins and suddenly with the mention of the name he saw his brother peering out of the eyes of one of the boys. He leaned forward.

'What is it?' Samuel asked.

'Why,' Adam cried, 'these boys are not alike! They don't look alike.'

'Of course they don't. They're not identical twins.'

'That one–that one looks like my brother. I just saw it. I wonder if the other looks like me.'

'Both of them do. A face has everything in it right back to the beginning.'

'It's not so much now,' said Adam. 'But for a moment I thought I was seeing a ghost.'

'Maybe that's what ghosts are,' Samuel observed.

Lee brought dishes out and put them on the table.

'Do you have Chinese ghosts?' Samuel asked.

'Millions,' said Lee. 'We have more ghosts than anything else. I guess nothing in China ever dies. It's very crowded. Anyway, that's the feeling I got when I was there.'

Samuel said, 'Sit down, Lee. We're trying to think of names.'

'I've got chicken frying. It will be ready pretty soon.'

Adam looked up from the twins and his eyes were warmed and softened. 'Will you have a drink, Lee?'

'I'm nipping at the ng-ka-py in the kitchen,' said Lee and went back to the house.'

Samuel leaned down and gathered up one of the boys and held him on his lap. 'Take that one up,' he said to Adam. 'We ought to see whether there's something that draws names to them.'

Adam held the other child awkwardly on his knee. 'They look some alike,' he said, 'but not when you look close. This one has rounder eyes than that one.'

'Yes, and a rounder head and bigger ears,' Samuel added. 'But this one is more like–like a bullet. This one might go farther but not so high. And this one is going to be darker in the hair and skin. This one will be shrewd, I think, and shrewdness is a limitation on the mind. Shrewdness tells you what you must not do because it would not be shrewd. See how this one supports himself! He's farther along than that one–better developed. Isn't it strange how different they are when you look close?'

Adam's face was changing as though he had opened and come out on his surface. He held up his finger, and the child made a lunge for it and missed and nearly fell off his lap. 'Whoa!' said Adam. 'Take it easy. Do you want to fall?'

'It would be a mistake to name them for qualities we think they have,' Samuel said. 'We might be wrong–so wrong. Maybe it would be good to give them a high mark to shoot at–a name to live up to. The man I'm named after had his name called clear by the Lord God, and I've been listening all my life. And once or twice I've thought I heard my name called–but not clear, not clear.'

Adam, holding the child by his upper arm, leaned over and poured whisky in both glasses. 'I thank you for coming, Samuel,' he said. 'I even thank you for hitting me. That's a strange thing to say.'

'It was a strange thing for me to do. Liza will never believe it, and so I'll never tell her. An unbelieved truth can hurt a man much more than a lie. It takes great courage to back truth unacceptable to our times. There's a punishment for it, and it's usually crucifixion. I haven't the courage for that.'

Adam said, 'I've wondered why a man of your knowledge would work a desert hill place.'

'It's because I haven't courage,' said Samuel. 'I could never quite take the responsibility. When the Lord God did not call my name, I might have called His name–but I did not. There you have the difference between greatness and mediocrity. It's not an uncommon disease. But it's nice for a mediocre man to know that greatness must be the loneliest state in the world.'

'I'd think there are degrees of greatness,' Adam said.

'I don't think so,' said Samuel. 'That would be like saying there is a little bigness. No. I believe when you come to that responsibility the hugeness and you are alone to make your choice. On one side you have warmth and companionship and sweet understanding, and on the other–cold, lonely greatness. There you make your choice. I'm glad I chose mediocrity, but how am I to say what reward might have come with the other? None of my children will be great either, except perhaps Tom. He's suffering over the choosing right now. It's a painful thing to watch. And somewhere in me I want him to say yes. Isn't that strange? A father to want his son condemned to greatness! What selfishness that must be.'

Adam chuckled. 'This naming is no simple business, I see.'

'Did you think it would be?'

'I didn't know it could be so pleasant,' said Adam.

Lee came out with a platter of fried chicken, a bowl of smoking boiled potatoes, and a deep dish of pickled beets, all carried on a pastry board. 'I don't know how good it will be,' he said. 'The hens are a little old. We don't have any pullets. The weasels got the baby chicks this year.'

'Pull up,' said Samuel.

'Wait until I get my ng-ka-py,' said Lee.

While he was gone Adam said, 'It's strange to me–he used to speak differently.'

'He trusts you now,' Samuel said. 'He has a gift of resigned loyalty without hope of reward. He's maybe a much better man than either of us could dream of being.'

Lee came back and took his seat at the end of the table. 'Just put the boys on the ground,' he said.

The twins protested when they were set down. Lee spoke to them sharply in Cantonese and they were silent.

The men ate quietly as nearly all country people do. Suddenly Lee got up and hurried into the house. He came back with a jug of red wine. 'I forgot it,' he said. 'I found it in the house.'

Adam laughed. 'I remember drinking wine here before I bought the place. Maybe I bought the place because of the wine. The chicken's good, Lee. I don't think I've been aware of the taste of food for a long time.'

'You're getting well,' Samuel said. 'Some people think it's an insult to the glory of their sickness to get well. But the time poultice is no respecter of glories. Everyone gets well if he waits around.'

4

Lee cleared the table and gave each of the boys a clean drum-stick. They sat solemnly holding their greasy batons and alternately inspecting and sucking them. The wine and the glasses stayed on the table.

'We'd best get on with the naming,' Samuel said. 'I can feel a little tightening on my halter from Liza.'

'I can't think what to name them,' Adam said.

'You have no family name you want–no inviting trap for a rich relative, no proud name to re-create?'

'No, I'd like them to start fresh, in so far as that is possible.'

Samuel knocked his forehead with his knuckles. 'What a shame,' he said. 'What a shame it is that the proper names for them they cannot have.'

'What do you mean?' Adam asked.

'Freshness, you said. I thought last night–' He paused. 'Have you thought of your own name?'

'Mine?'

'Of course. Your first-born–Cain and Abel.'

Adam said, 'Oh, no. No, we can't do that.'

'I know we can't. That would be tempting whatever fate there is. But isn't it odd that Cain is maybe the best-known name in the whole world and as far as I know only one man has ever borne it?'

Lee said, 'Maybe that's why the name has never changed its emphasis.'

Adam looked into the ink-red wine in his glass. 'I got a shiver when you mentioned it,' he said.

'Two stories have haunted us and followed us from our beginning,' Samuel said. 'We can carry them along with us like invisible tails–the story of original sin and the story of Cain and Abel. And I don't understand either of them. I don't understand them at all, but I feel them. Liza gets angry with me. She says I should not try to understand them. She says why should we try to explain a verity. Maybe she's right–maybe she's right. Lee, Liza says you're a Presbyterian–do you understand the Garden of Eden and Cain and Abel?'

'She thought I should be something, and I went to Sunday School long ago in San Francisco. People like you to be something, preferably what they are.'

Adam said, 'He asked you if you understood.'

'I think I understand the Fall. I could perhaps feel that in myself. But the brother murder–no. Well, maybe I don't remember the details very well.'

Samuel said, 'Most people don't read the details. It's the details that astonish me. And Abel had no children.' He looked up at the sky. 'Lord, how the day passes! It's like a life–so quickly when we don't watch it and so slowly when we do. No,' he said, 'I'm having enjoyment. And I made a promise to myself that I would not consider enjoyment a sin. I take a pleasure in inquiring into things. I've never been content to pass a stone without looking under it. And it is a black disappointment to me that I can never see the far side of the moon.'

'I don't have a Bible,' Adam said. 'I left the family one in Connecticut.'

'I have,' said Lee. 'I'll get it.'

'No need,' said Samuel. 'Liza let me take her mother's. It's here in my pocket.' He took out the package and unwrapped the battered book. 'This one has been scraped and gnawed at,' he said. 'I wonder what agonies have settled here. Give me a used Bible and I will, I think, be able to tell you about a man by the places that are edged with the dirt of seeking fingers. Liza wears a Bible down evenly. Here we are–this oldest story. If it troubles us it must be that we find the trouble in ourselves.'

'I haven't heard it since I was a child,' said Adam.

'You think it's long then, and it's very short,' said Samuel. 'I'll read it through and then we'll go back. Give me a little wine, my throat's dried out with wine. Here it is–such a little story to have made so deep a wound.' He looked down at the ground. 'See!' he said. 'The boys have gone to their sleep, there in the dust.'

Lee got up. 'I'll cover them,' he said.

'The dust is warm,' said Samuel. 'Now it goes this way. "And Adam knew Eve his wife; and she conceived, and bare Cain, and said, 'I have gotten a man from the Lord.'"'

Adam started to speak and Samuel looked up at him and he was silent and covered his eyes with his hand. Samuel read, '"And she again bare his brother Abel. And Abel was a keeper of sheep, but Cain was a tiller of the ground. And in the process of time it came to pass that Cain brought of the fruit of the ground an offering unto the Lord. And Abel, he also brought of the firstlings of his flock and of the fat thereof. And the Lord had respect unto Abel and to his offering. But unto Cain and to his offering he had not respect."'

Lee said, 'Now where–no, go on, go on. We'll come back.'

Samuel read, '"And Cain was very wroth, and his countenance fell. And the Lord said unto Cain, 'Why art thou wroth? And why is thy countenance fallen? If thou doest well, shalt thou not be accepted? And if thou doest not well, sin lieth at the door. And unto thee shall be his desire, and thou shalt rule over him.

'"And Cain talked with Abel his brother: and it came to pass, when they were in the field, that Cain rose up against Abel his brother and slew him. And the Lord said unto Cain, 'Where is Abel thy brother?' And he said, 'I know not. Am I my brother's keeper?' And he said, 'What hast thou done? The voice of thy brother's blood crieth unto me from the ground. And now art thou cursed from the earth, which hath opened her mouth to receive thy brother's blood from thy hand. When thou tillest the ground it shall not henceforth yield unto thee her strength; a fugitive and a vagabond shalt thou be in the earth.'

And Cain said unto the Lord, 'My punishment is greater than I can bear. Behold, thou hast driven me out this day from the face of the earth, and from thy face shall I be hid. And I shall be a fugitive and a vagabond in the earth; and it shall come to pass that everyone that findeth me shall slay me.' And the Lord said unto him, 'Therefore whosoever slayeth Cain, vengeance shall be taken on him sevenfold.' And the Lord set a mark upon Cain, lest any finding him should kill him. And Cain went out from the presence of the Lord and dwelt in the land of Nod on the east of Eden."'

Samuel closed the loose cover of the book almost with weariness. 'There it is,' he said. 'Sixteen verses, no more. And oh, Lord! I had forgotten how dreadful it is–no single tone of encouragement. Maybe Liza's right. There's nothing to understand.'

Adam sighed deeply. 'It's not a comforting story, is it?'

Lee poured a tumbler full of dark liquor from his round stone bottle and sipped it and opened his mouth to get the double taste on the back of his tongue. 'No story has power, nor will it last, unless we feel in ourselves that it is true and true of us. What a great burden of guilt men have!'

Samuel said to Adam, 'And you have tried to take it all.'

Lee said, 'So do I, so does everyone. We gather our arms full of guilt as though it were precious stuff. It must be that we want it that way.'

Adam broke in, 'It makes me feel better, not worse.'

'How do you mean?' Samuel asked.

'Well, every little boy thinks he invented sin. Virtue we think we learn, because we are told about it. But sin is our own designing.'

'Yes, I can see. But how does this story make it better?'

'Because,' Adam said excitedly, 'we are descended from this. This is our father. Some of our guilt is absorbed in our ancestry. What chance did we have? We are the children of our father. It means we aren't the first. It's an excuse, and there aren't enough excuses in the world.'

'Not convincing ones anyway,' said Lee. 'Else we would long ago have wiped our guilt, and the world would not be filled with sad, punished people.'

Samuel said, 'But do you think of another frame for this picture? Excuse or not, we are snapped back to our ancestry. We have guilt.'

Adam said, 'I remember being a little outraged at God. Both Cain and Abel gave what they had, and God accepted Abel and rejected Cain. I never thought that was a just thing. I never understood it. Do you?'

'Maybe we think out of a different background,' said Lee. 'I remember that this story was written by and for a shepherd people. They were not farmers. Wouldn't the god of shepherds find a fat lamb more valuable than a sheaf of barley? A sacrifice must be the best and the most valuable.'

'Yes, I can see that,' said Samuel. 'And Lee, let me caution you about bringing your Oriental reasoning to Liza's attention.'

Adam was excited. 'Yes, but why did God condemn Cain? That's an injustice.'

Samuel said, 'There's an advantage to listening to the words. God did not condemn Cain at all. Even God can have a preference, can't He? Let's suppose God liked lamb better than vegetables. I think I do myself. Cain brought Him a bunch of carrots maybe. And God said, "I don't like this. Try again. Bring me something I like and I'll set you up alongside your brother." But Cain got mad. His feelings were hurt. And when a man's feelings are hurt he wants to strike at something, and Abel was in the way of his anger.'

Lee said, 'St Paul says to the Hebrews that Abel had faith.'

'There's no reference to it in Genesis,' Samuel said. 'No faith or lack of faith. Only a hint of Cain's temper.'

Lee asked, 'How does Mrs Hamilton feel about the paradoxes of the Bible?'

'Why, she does not feel anything because she does not admit they are there.'

'But–'

'Hush, man. Ask her. And you'll come out of it older but not less confused.'

Adam said, 'You two have studied this. I only got it through my skin and not much of it stuck. Then Cain was driven out for murder?'

'That's right–for murder.'

'And God branded him?'

'Did you listen? Cain bore the mark not to destroy him but to save him. And there's a curse down on any man who shall kill him. It was a preserving mark.'

Adam said, 'I can't get over a feeling that Cain got the dirty end of the stick.'

'Maybe he did,' said Samuel. 'But Cain lived and had children, and Abel lives only in the story. We are Cain's children. And isn't it strange that three grown men, here in a century so many thousands of years away, discuss this crime as though it happened in King City yesterday and hadn't come up for trial?'

One of the twins awakened and yawned and looked at Lee and went to sleep again.

Lee said, 'Remember, Mr Hamilton, I told you I was trying to translate some old Chinese poetry into English? No, don't worry. I won't read it. Doing it, I found some of the old things as fresh and clear as this morning. And I wondered why. And, of course, people are interested only in themselves. If a story is not about the hearer he will not listen. And I here make a rule–a great and lasting story is about everyone or it will not last. The strange and foreign is not interesting–only the deeply personal and familiar.'

Samuel said, 'Apply that to the Cain-Abel story.'

And Adam said, 'I didn't kill my brother–' Suddenly he stopped and his mind went reeling back in time.

'I think I can,' Lee answered Samuel. 'I think this is the best-known story in the world because it is everybody's story. I think it is the symbol story of the human soul. I'm feeling my way now–don't jump on me if I'm not clear. The greatest terror a child can have is that he is not loved, and rejection is the hell he fears. I think everyone in the world to a large or small extent has felt rejection. And with rejection comes anger, and with anger some kind of crime in revenge for the rejection, and with the crime guilt–and there is the story of mankind. I think that if rejection could be amputated, the human would not be what he is. Maybe there would be fewer crazy people. I am sure in myself there would not be many jails. It is all there–the start, the beginning. One child, refused the love he craves, kicks the cat and hides his secret guilt; and another steals so that money will make him loved; and a third conquers the world–and always the guilt and revenge and more guilt. The human is the only guilty animal. Now wait! Therefore I think this old and terrible story is important because it is a chart of the soul–the secret, rejected, guilty soul. Mr Trask, you said you did not kill your brother and then you remembered something. I don't want to know what it was, but was it very far apart from Cain and Abel? And what do you think of my Oriental patter, Mr Hamilton? You know I am no more Oriental than you are.'

Samuel had leaned his elbows on the table and his hands covered his eyes and his forehead. 'I want to think,' he said. 'Damn you, I want to think. I'll want to take this off alone where I can pick it apart and see. Maybe you've tumbled a world for me. And I don't know what I can build in my world's place.'

Lee said softly, 'Couldn't a world be built around accepted truth? Couldn't some pains and insanities be rooted out if the causes were known?'

'I don't know, damn you. You've disturbed my pretty universe. You've taken a contentious game and made an answer of it. Let me alone–let me think! Your damned bitch is having pups in my brain already. Oh, I wonder what my Tom will think of this! He'll cradle it in the palm of his hand. He'll turn it slow in his brain like a roast of pork before the fire. Adam, come out now. You've been long enough in whatever memory it was.'

Adam started. He sighed deeply. 'Isn't it too simple?' he asked. 'I'm always afraid of simple things.'

'It isn't simple at all,' said Lee. 'It's desperately complicated. But at the end there's light.'

'There's not going to be light long,' Samuel said. 'We've sat and let the evening come. I drove over to help name the twins and they're not named. We've swung ourselves on a pole. Lee, you better keep your complications out of the machinery of the set-up churches or there might be a Chinese with nails in his hands and feet. They like complications, but they like their own. I'll have to be driving home.'

Adam said desperately, 'Name me some names.'

'From the Bible?'

'From anyplace.'

'Well, let's see. Of all the people who started out of Egypt only two came to the Promised Land. Would you like them for a symbol?'

'Who?'

'Caleb and Joshua.'

'Joshua was a soldier–a general. I don't like soldiering.'

'Well, Caleb was a captain.'

'But not a general. I kind of like Caleb–Caleb Trask.'

One of the twins woke up and without interval began to wail.

'You called his name,' said Samuel. 'You don't like Joshua, and Caleb's named. He's the smart one–the dark one. See, the other one is awake too. Well, Aaron I've always liked, but he didn't make it to the Promised Land.'

The second boy almost joyfully began to cry.

'That's good enough,' said Adam.

Suddenly Samuel laughed. 'In two minutes,' he said, 'and after a waterfall of words. Caleb and Aaron–now you are people and you have joined the fraternity and you have the right to be damned.'

Lee took the boys up under his arms. 'Have you got them straight?' he asked.

'Of course,' said Adam. 'That one is Caleb and you are Aaron.'

Lee lugged the yelling twins towards the house in the dusk.

'Yesterday I couldn't tell them apart,' said Adam. 'Aaron and Caleb.'

'Thank the good Lord we had produce from our patient thought,' Samuel said. 'Liza would have preferred Joshua. She loves the crashing walls of Jericho. But she likes Aaron too, so I guess it's all right. I'll go and hitch my rig.'

Adam walked to the shed with him. 'I'm glad you came,' he said. 'There's a weight off me.'

Samuel slipped the bit in Doxology's reluctant mouth, set the brow-band, and buckled the throat-latch. 'Maybe you'll now be thinking of the garden in the flat land,' he said. 'I can see it there the way you planned it.'

Adam was long in answering. At last he said, 'I think that kind of energy is gone out of me. I can't feel the pull of it. I have money enough to live. I never wanted it for myself. I have no one to show a garden to.'

Samuel wheeled on him and his eyes were filled with tears. 'Don't think it will ever die,' he cried. 'Don't expect it. Are you better than other men? I tell you it won't ever die until you do.' He stood panting for a moment and then he climbed into the rig and whipped Doxology and he drove away, his shoulders hunched, without saying goodbye.

PART III

CHAPTER 23

I

The Hamiltons were strange, high-strung people, and some of them were tuned too high and they snapped. This happens often in the world.

Of all his daughters Una was Samuel's greatest joy. Even as a little girl she hungered for learning as a child does for cookies in the late afternoon. Una and her father had a conspiracy about learning–secret books were borrowed and read and their secrets communicated privately.

Of all the children Una had the least humour. She met and married an intense dark man–a man whose fingers were stained with chemicals, mostly silver nitrate. He was one of those men who live in poverty so that their lines of questioning may continue. His question was about photography. He believed that the exterior world could be transferred to paper–not in the ghost shadings of black and white but in the colours the human eye perceives.

His name was Anderson and he had little gift for communication. Like most technicians, he had a terror and a contempt for speculation. The inductive leap was not for him. He dug a step and pulled himself up one single step, the way a man climbs the last shoulder of a mountain. He had great contempt, born of fear, for the Hamiltons, for they half believed they had wings–and they got some bad falls that way.

Anderson never fell, never slipped back, never flew. His steps moved slowly, slowly upwards, and in the end, it is said, he found what he wanted–colour film. He married Una, perhaps, because she had little humour, and this reassured him. And because her family frightened and embarrassed him, he took her away to the north, and it was black and lost where he went–somewhere on the borders of Oregon. He must have lived a very primitive life with his bottles and papers.

Una wrote bleak letters without joy but also without self-pity. She was well and she hoped the family was well. Her husband was near to his discovery.

And then she died and her body was shipped home.

I never knew Una. She was dead before I remember, but George Hamilton told me about it many years later and his eyes filled with tears and his voice croaked in the telling.

'Una was not a beautiful girl like Mollie,' he said. 'But she had the loveliest hands and feet. Her ankles were as slender as grass and she moved like grass. Her fingers were long and the nails narrow and shaped like almonds. And Una had lovely skin too, translucent, even glowing.

'She didn't laugh and play like the rest of us. There was something set apart about her. She seemed always to be listening. When she was reading, her face would be like the face of one listening to music. And when we asked her any question, why, she gave the answer, if she knew it–not pointed up and full of colour and "maybes" and "it-might-bes" the way the rest of us would. We were always full of bull. There was some pure simple thing in Una,' George said.

'And then they brought her home. Her nails were broken to the quick and her fingers cracked and all worn out. And her poor, dear feet–' George could not go on for a while, and then he said with the fierceness of a man trying to control himself, 'Her feet were broken and gravel-cut and briar-cut. Her dear feet had not worn shoes for a long time. And her skin was rough as rawhide.

'We think it was an accident,' he said. 'So many chemicals around. We think it was.'

But Samuel thought and mourned in the thought that the accident was pain and despair.

Una's death struck Samuel like a silent earthquake. He said no brave and reassuring words, he simply sat alone and rocked himself. He felt that it was his neglect that had done it.

And now his tissue, which had fought joyously against time, gave up a little. His young skin turned old, his clear eyes dulled, and a little stoop came to his great shoulders. Liza with her acceptance could take care of tragedy; she had no real hope this side of Heaven. But Samuel had put up a laughing wall against natural laws, and Una's death breached his battlements. He became an old man.

His other children were doing well. George was in the insurance business. Will was getting rich. Joe had gone east and was helping to invent a new profession called advertising. Joe's very faults were virtues in this field. He found that he could communicate his material day-dreaming–and, properly applied, that is all advertising is. Joe was a big man in a new field.

The girls were married, all except Dessie, and she had a successful dressmaking business in Salinas. Only Tom had never got started.

Samuel told Adam Trask that Tom was arguing with greatness. And the father watched his son and could feel the drive and the fear, the advance and the retreat, because he could feel it in himself.

Tom did not have his father's lyric softness or his gay good looks. But you could feel Tom when you came near him–you could feel strength and warmth and iron integrity. And under all of this was a shrinking–a shy shrinking. He could be as gay as his father, and suddenly in the middle of it would be cut the way you would cut a violin string, and you could watch Tom go whirling into darkness.

He was a dark-faced man; his skin, perhaps from sun, was a black red, as though some Norse or perhaps Vandal blood was perpetuated in him. His hair and beard and moustache were dark red too, and his eyes gleamed startlingly blue against his colouring. He was powerful, heavy of shoulders and arm, but his hips were slim. He could lift and run and hike and ride with anyone, but he had no sense of competition whatever. Will and George were gamblers and often tried to entice their brother into the joys and sorrows of venture.

Tom said, 'I've tried and it just seems tiresome. I've thought why this must be. I get no great triumph when I win and no tragedy when I lose. Without these it is meaningless. It is not a way to make money, that we know, and unless it can simulate birth and death, joy and sorrow, it seems, at least to me–it feels–it doesn't feel at all. I would do it if I felt anything–good or bad.'

Will did not understand this. His whole life was competitive and he lived by one kind of gambling or another. He loved Tom and he tried to give him the things he himself found pleasant. He took him into business and tried to inoculate him with the joys of buying and selling, of outwitting other men, of judging them for a bluff, of living by manœuvre.

Always Tom came back to the ranch, puzzled, not critical, but feeling that somewhere he had lost track. He felt that he should take joy in the man-pleasures of contest, but he could not pretend to himself that he did.

Samuel had said that Tom always took too much on his plate, whether it was beans or women. And Samuel was wise, but I think he knew only one side of Tom. Maybe Tom opened up a little more for children. What I set down about him will be the result of memory plus what I know to be true plus conjecture built on the combination. Who knows whether it will be correct?

We lived in Salinas and we knew when Tom had arrived–I think he always arrived at night–because under our pillows, Mary's and mine, there would be packages of gum. And gum was valuable in those days just as a nickel was valuable. There were months when he did not come, but every morning as soon as we awakened we put our hands under our pillows to see. And I still do it, and it has been many years since there had been gum there.

My sister Mary did not want to be a girl. It was a misfortune she could not get used to. She was an athlete, a marble player, a pitcher of one-o'-cat, and the trappings of a girl inhibited her. Of course this was long before the compensations for being a girl were apparent to her.

Just as we knew that somewhere on our bodies, probably under the arm, there was a button which if pressed just right would permit us to fly, so Mary had worked out a magic for herself to change over into the tough little boy she wanted to be. If she went to sleep in a magical position, knees crooked just right, head at a magical angle, fingers all crossed one over the other, in the morning she would be a boy. Every night she tried to find exactly the right combination, but she never could. I used to help her cross her fingers like shiplap.

She was despairing of ever getting it right when one morning there was gum under the pillow. We each peeled a stick and solemnly chewed it; it was Beeman's peppermint, and nothing so delicious has been made since.

Mary was pulling on her long black ribbed stockings when she said with great relief, 'Of course.'

'Of course what?' I asked.

'Uncle Tom,' she said and chewed her gum with great snapping sounds.

'Uncle Tom what?' I demanded.

'He'll know how to get to be a boy.'

There it was–just as simple as that. I wondered why I hadn't thought of it myself.

Mother was in the kitchen overseeing a new little Danish girl who worked for us. We had a series of girls. New-come Danish farm families put their daughters out to service with American families, and they learned not only English but American cooking and table setting and manners and all the little niceties of high life in Salinas. At the end of a couple of years of this, at twelve dollars a month, the girls were highly desirable wives for American boys. Not only did they have American manners but they could still work like horses in the fields. Some of the most elegant families in Salinas today are descended from these girls.

It would be flaxen-haired Mathilde in the kitchen, with Mother clucking over her like a hen.

We charged in. 'Is he up?'

'Sh!' said Mother. 'He got in late. You let him sleep.'

But the water was running in the basin of the back bedroom, so we knew he was up. We crouched like cats at his door, waiting for him to emerge.

There was always a little diffidence between us at first. I think Uncle Tom was as shy as we were. I think he wanted to come running out and toss us in the air, but instead we were all formal.

'Thank you for the gum, Uncle Tom.'

'I'm glad you liked it.'

'Do you think we'll have an oyster loaf late at night while you're here?'

'We'll certainly try, if your mother will let you.'

We drifted into the sitting-room and sat down. Mother's voice called from the kitchen, 'Children, you let him alone.'

'They're all right, Ollie,' he called back.

We sat in a triangle in the living-room. Tom's face was so dark and his eyes so blue. He wore good clothes but he never seemed well dressed. In this he was very different from his father. His red moustache was never neat and his hair would not lie down and his hands were hard from work.

Mary said, 'Uncle Tom, how do you get to be a boy?'

'How? Why, Mary, you're just born a boy.'

'No, that's not what I mean. How do *I* get to be a boy?'

Tom studied her gravely. 'You?' he asked.

Her words poured out. 'I don't want to be a girl, Uncle Tom. I want to be a boy. A girl's all kissing and dolls. I don't want to be a girl. I don't want to be.' Tears of anger welled up in Mary's eyes.

Tom looked down at his hands and picked at a loose piece of callous with a broken nail. He wanted to say something beautiful, I think. He wished for words like his father's words, sweet winged words, cooing and lovely. 'I wouldn't like you to be a boy,' he said.

'Why not?'

'I like you as a girl.'

An idol was crashing in Mary's temple. 'You mean you like girls?'

'Yes, Mary, I like girls very much.'

A look of distaste crossed Mary's face. If it were true, Tom was a fool. She put on her don't-give-me-any-of-that-crap tone. 'All right,' she said, 'but how do *I* go about being a boy?'

Tom had a good ear. He knew he was reeling down in Mary's estimation and he wanted her to love him and to admire him. At the same time there was a fine steel wire of truthfulness in him that cut off the heads of fast-travelling lies. He looked at Mary's hair, so light that it was almost white, and braided tight to be out of the way, and dirty at the end of the braid, for Mary wiped her hands on her braid before she made a difficult marble shot. Tom studied her cold and hostile eyes.

'I don't think you really want to change.'

'I do.'

Tom was wrong–she really did.

'Well,' he said, 'you can't. And some day you'll be glad.'

'I won't be glad,' said Mary, and she turned to me and said with frigid contempt, 'He doesn't know!'

Tom winced and I shivered at the immensity of her criminal charge. Mary was braver and more ruthless than most. That's why she won every marble in Salinas.

Tom said uneasily, 'If your mother says it's all right, I'll order the oyster loaf this morning and pick it up tonight.'

'I don't like oyster loaves,' said Mary and stalked to our bedroom and slammed the door.

Tom looked ruefully after her. 'She's a girl all right,' he said.

Now we were alone together and I felt that I had to heal the wound Mary had made. 'I love oyster loaves,' I said.

'Sure you do. So does Mary.'

'Uncle Tom, don't you think there's some way for her to be a boy?'

'No, I don't,' he said sadly. 'I would have told her if I had known.'

'She's the best pitcher in the West End.'

Tom sighed and looked down at his hands again, and I could see his failure on him and I was sorry for him, aching sorry. I brought out my hollowed cork with pins stuck down to make bars. 'Would you like to have my fly cage, Uncle Tom?'

Oh, he was a great gentleman. 'Do you want me to have it?'

'Yes. You see, you pull up a pin to get the fly in and then he sits in there and buzzes.'

'I'd like to have it very much. Thank you, John.'

He worked all day with a sharp tiny pocket-knife on a small block of wood, and when we came home from school he had carved a little face. The eyes and ears were movable, and little perches connected them with the inside of the hollow head. At the bottom of the neck there was a hole closed by a cork. And this was very wonderful. You caught a fly and eased him through the hole and set the cork. And suddenly the head became alive. The eyes moved and the lips talked and the ears wiggled as the frantic fly crawled over the little perches. Even Mary forgave him a little, but she never really trusted him until after she was glad she was a girl, and then it was too late. He gave the head not to me but to us. We still have it put away somewhere, and it still works.

Sometimes Tom took me fishing. We started before the sun came up and drove in the rig straight towards Frémont Peak, and as we neared the mountains the stars would pale out and the light would rise to blacken the mountains. I can remember riding and pressing my ear and cheek against Tom's coat. And I can remember that his arm would rest lightly over my shoulders and his hand pat my arm occasionally. Finally we would pull up under an oak tree and take the horse out of the shafts, water him at the stream side, and halter him to the back of the rig.

I don't remember that Tom talked. Now that I think of it, I can't remember the sound of his voice or the kind of words he used. I can remember both about my grandfather, but when I think of Tom it is a memory of a kind of warm silence. Maybe he didn't talk at all. Tom had beautiful tackle and made his own flies. But he didn't seem to care whether we caught trout or not. He needed not to triumph over animals.

I remember the five-fingered ferns growing under little waterfalls, bobbing their green fingers as the droplets struck them. And I remember the smells of the hills, wild azalea and a very distant skunk and the sweet cloy of lupin and horse sweat on harness. I remember the sweeping lovely dance of high buzzards against the sky and Tom looking long up at them, but I can't remember that he ever said anything about them. I remember holding the bite of a line while Tom drove pegs and braided a splice. I remember the smell of crushed ferns in the creel and the delicate sweet odour of fresh damp rainbow trout lying so prettily on the green bed. And finally I can remember coming back to the rig and pouring rolled barley into the leather feed-bag and buckling it over the horse's head behind the ears. And I have no sound of his voice or words in my ear; he is dark and silent and hugely warm in my memory.

Tom felt his darkness. His father was beautiful and clever, his mother was short and mathematically sure. Each of his brothers and sisters had looks or gifts or fortune. Tom loved all of them passionately, but he felt heavy and earth-bound. He climbed ecstatic mountains and floundered in the rocky darkness between the peaks. He had spurts of bravery but they were bracketed in the battens of cowardice.

Samuel said that Tom was quavering over greatness, trying to decide whether he could take the cold responsibility. Samuel knew his son's quality and felt the potential of violence, and it frightened him, for Samuel had no violence–even when he hit Adam Trask with his fist he had no violence. And the books that came into the house, some of them secretly–well, Samuel rode lightly on top of a book and he balanced happily among ideas the way a man rides white rapids in a canoe. But Tom got into a book, crawled and grovelled between the covers, tunnelled like a mole among the thoughts, and came up with the book all over his face and hands.

Violence and shyness–Tom's loins needed women and at the same time he did not think himself worthy of a woman. For long periods he would welter in a howling celibacy, and then he would take a train to San Francisco and roll and wallow in women, and then he would come silently back to the ranch, feeling weak and unfulfilled and unworthy and he would punish himself with work, would plough and plant unprofitable land, would cut tough oakwood until his back was breaking and his arms were weary rags.

It is probable that his father stood between Tom and the sun, and Samuel's shadow fell on him. Tom wrote secret poetry, and in those days it was only sensible to keep it secret. The poets were pale emasculates, and Western men held them in contempt. Poetry was a symptom of weakness, of degeneracy and decay. To read it was to court catcalls. To write it was to be suspected and ostracized. Poetry was a secret vice, and properly so. No one knows whether Tom's poetry was any good or not, for he showed it to only one person, and before he died he burned every word. From the ashes in the stove there must have been a great deal of it.

Of all his family Tom loved Dessie best. She was gay. Laughter lived on her doorstep.

Her shop was a unique institution in Salinas. It was a woman's world. Here all the rules, and the fears that created the iron rules, went down. The door was closed to men. It was a sanctuary where women could be themselves–smelly, wanton, mystic, conceited, truthful, and interested. The whalebone corsets came off at Dessie's, the sacred corsets that moulded and warped woman-flesh into goddess-flesh. At Dessie's they were women who went to the toilet and over-ate and scratched and farted. And from this freedom came laughter, roars of laughter.

Men could hear the laughter through the closed door and were properly frightened at what was going on, feeling, perhaps, that they were the butt of the laughter–which to a large extent was true.

I can see Dessie now, her gold pince-nez wobbling on a nose not properly bridged for pince-nez, her eyes streaming with hilarious tears, and her whole front constricted with muscular spasms of laughter. Her hair would come down and drift between her glasses and her eyes, and the glasses would fall off her wet nose and spin and swing at the end of their black ribbon.

You had to order a dress from Dessie months in advance, and you made twenty visits to her shop before you chose material and pattern. Nothing so healthy as Dessie had ever happened to Salinas. The men had their lodges, their clubs, their whore-houses; the women nothing but the Altar Guild and the mincing coquetry of the minister, until Dessie came along.

And then Dessie fell in love. I do not know any details of her love affair–who the man was or what the circumstances, whether it was religion or a living wife, a disease or a selfishness. I guess my mother knew, but it was one of those things put away in the family closet and never brought out. And if other people in Salinas knew, they must have kept it a loyal town secret. All I do know is that it was a hopeless thing, grey and terrible. After a year of it the joy was all drained out of Dessie and the laughter had ceased.

Tom raged crazily through the hills like a lion in horrible pain. In the middle of a night he saddled and rode away, not waiting for the morning train, to Salinas. Samuel followed him and sent a telegram from King City to Salinas.

And when in the morning Tom, his face black, spurred his spent horse up John Street in Salinas, the sheriff was waiting for him. He disarmed Tom and put him in a cell and fed him black coffee and brandy until Samuel came for him.

Samuel did not lecture Tom. He took him home and never mentioned the incident. And a stillness fell on the Hamilton place.

2

On Thanksgiving of 1911 the family gathered at the ranch–all the children except Joe, who was in New York, and Lizzie, who had left the family and joined another, and Una, who was dead. They arrived with presents and more food than even this clan could eat. They were all married save Dessie and Tom. Their children filled the Hamilton place with riot. The home place flared up–noisier than it had ever been. The children cried and screamed and fought. The men made many trips to the forge and came back self-consciously wiping their moustaches.

Liza's little round face grew redder and redder. She organized and ordered. The kitchen stove never went out. The beds were full, and comforters laid on pillows on the floor were for children.

Samuel dug up his old gaiety. His sardonic mind glowed and his speech took on its old singing rhythm. He hung on with the talk and the singing and the memories, and then suddenly, and it not midnight, he tired. Weariness came down on him, and he went to his bed where Liza had been for two hours. He was puzzled at himself, not that he had to go to bed but that he wanted to.

When the mother and father were gone, Will brought the whisky in from the forge and the clan had a meeting in the kitchen with whisky passed round in round-bottomed jelly glasses. The mothers crept to the bedrooms to see that the children were covered and then came back. They spoke softly, not to disturb the children and the old people. There were Tom and Dessie, George and his pretty Mamie, who had been a Dempsey, Mollie and William J. Martin, Olive and Ernest Steinbeck, Will and his Deila.

They all wanted to say the same thing–all ten of them. Samuel was an old man. It was as startling a discovery as the sudden seeing of a ghost. Somehow they had not believed it could happen. They drank their whisky and talked softly of the new thought.

His shoulders–did you see how they slump? And there's no spring in his step.

His toes drag a little, but it's not that–it's his eyes. His eyes are old.

He would never go to bed until last.

Did you notice he forgot what he was saying right in the middle of a story?

It's his skin told me. It's gone wrinkled, and the backs of his hands have turned transparent.

He favours his right leg.

Yes, but that's the one the horse broke.

I know, but he never favoured it before.

They said these things in outrage. This can't happen, they were saying. Father can't be an old man. Samuel is young as the dawn–the perpetual dawn.

He might get old as midday maybe, but sweet God! the evening cannot come, and the night–Sweet God, no!

It was natural that their minds leaped on and recoiled, and they would not speak of that, but their minds said, There can't be any world without Samuel.

How could we think about anything without knowing what he thought about it?

What would the spring be like, or Christmas, or rain? There couldn't be a Christmas.

Their minds shrank away from such thinking and they looked for a victim–someone to hurt because they were hurt. They turned on Tom.

You were here. You've been here all along!

How did this happen? When did it happen?

Who did this to him?

Have you by any chance done this with your craziness?

And Tom could stand it because he had been with it. 'It was Una,' he said hoarsely. 'He couldn't get over Una. He told me how a man, a real man, had no right to let sorrow destroy him. He told me again and again how I must believe that time would take care of it. He said it so often I knew he was losing.'

'Why didn't you tell us? Maybe we could have done something.'

Tom leaped up, violent and cringing. 'Goddam it! What was there to tell? That he was dying of sorrow? That the marrow had melted out of his bones? What was there to tell? You weren't here. I had to look at it and see his eyes die down–goddam it.' Tom went out of the room and they heard his clod-hopper feet knocking on the flinty ground outside.

They were ashamed. Will Martin said, 'I'll go out and bring him back.'

'Don't do it,' George said quickly, and the blood kin nodded. 'Don't do it. Let him alone. We know him from the insides of ourselves.'

In a little while Tom came back. 'I want to apologize,' he said. 'I'm very sorry. Maybe I'm a little drunk. Father calls it "jolly" when I do it. One night I rode home'–it was a confession–'and I came staggering across the yard and I fell into the rosebush and crawled up the stairs on my hands and knees and I was sick on the floor beside my bed. In the morning I tried to tell him I was sorry, and do you know what he said? "Why, Tom, you were just jolly." "Jolly", if *I* did it. A drunken man didn't crawl home. Just jolly.'

George stopped the crazy flow of talk. 'We want to apologize to you, Tom,' he said. 'Why, we sounded as though we were blaming you and we didn't mean to. Or maybe we did mean to. And we're sorry.'

Will Martin said realistically, 'It's too hard a life here. Why don't we get him to sell out and move to town? He could have a long and happy life. Mollie and I would like them to come and live with us.'

'I don't think he'd do it,' said Will. 'He's stubborn as a mule and proud as a horse. He's got a pride like brass.'

Olive's husband, Ernest, said, 'Well, there'd be no harm in asking him. We would like to have him–or both of them–with us.'

Then they were silent again, for the idea of not having the ranch, the dry, stony desert of heart-breaking hillside and unprofitable hollow, was shocking to them.

Will Hamilton from instinct and training in business had become a fine reader of the less profound impulses of men and women. He said, 'If we ask him to close up shop it will be like asking him to close his life, and he won't do it.'

'You're right, Will,' George agreed. 'He would think it was like quitting. He'd feel it was a cowardice. No, he will never sell out, and if he did I don't think he would live a week.'

Will said, 'There's another way. Maybe he could come for a visit. Tom can run the ranch. It's time Father and Mother saw something of the world. All kinds of things are happening. It would freshen him, and then he could come back and go to work again. And after a while maybe he wouldn't have to. He says himself that thing about time doing the job that dynamite can't touch.'

Dessie brushed the hair out of her eyes. 'I wonder if you really think he's that stupid,' she said.

And Will said out of his experience, 'Sometimes a man wants to be stupid if it lets him do a thing his cleverness forbids. We can try it anyway. What do you all think?'

There was a nodding of heads in the kitchen, and only Tom sat rocklike and brooding.

'Tom, wouldn't you be willing to take over the ranch?' George asked.

'Oh, that's nothing,' said Tom. 'It's no trouble to run the ranch because the ranch doesn't run–never has.'

'Then why don't you agree?'

'I'd find a reluctance to insult my father,' Tom said. 'He'd know.'

'But where's the harm in suggesting it?'

Tom rubbed his ears until he forced the blood out of them and for a moment they were white. 'I don't forbid you,' he said. 'But I can't do it.'

George said, 'We could write it in a letter–a kind of invitation full of jokes. And when he got tired of one of us, he could go to another. There's years of visiting among the lot of us.' And that was how they left it.

3

Tom brought Olive's letter from King City, and because he knew what it contained he waited until he caught Samuel alone before he gave it to him. Samuel was working in the forge and his hands were black. He took the envelope by a tiny corner and put it on the anvil, and then he scrubbed his hands in the half-barrel of black water into which he plunged hot iron. He slit the letter open with the point of a horseshoe nail and went into the sunlight to read it. Tom had the wheels off the buckboard and was buttering the axles with yellow axle grease. He watched his father from the corners of his eyes.

Samuel finished the letter and folded it and put it back in its envelope. He sat down on the bench in front of the shop and stared into space. Then he opened the letter and read it again and folded it again and put it in his blue shirt pocket. Then Tom saw him stand up and walk slowly up the eastern hill, kicking at the flints on the ground.

There had been a little rain and a fuzz of miserly grass had started up. Halfway up the hill Samuel squatted down and took up a handful of the harsh gravelly earth in his palm and spread it with his forefinger, flint and sandstone and bits of shining mica and a frail rootlet and a veined stone. He let it slip from his hand and brushed his palms. He picked up a spear of grass and set it between his teeth and stared up the hill to the sky. A grey nervous cloud was scurrying eastward, searching for trees on which to rain.

Samuel stood up and sauntered down the hill. He looked into the tool-shed and patted the four-by-four supports. He paused near Tom and spun one of the free-running wheels of the buck-board, and he inspected Tom as though he saw him for the first time. 'Why, you're a grown-up man,' he said.

'Didn't you know?'

'I guess I did–I guess I did,' said Samuel and sauntered on. There was the sardonic look on his face his family knew so well–the joke on himself that made him laugh inwardly. He walked by the sad little garden and all around the house–not a new house any more. Even the last added lean-to bedrooms were old and weathered and the putty round the window-panes had shrunk away from the glass. At the porch he turned and surveyed the whole home cup of the ranch before he went inside.

Liza was rolling out pie-crust on the floury board. She was so expert with the rolling-pin that the dough seemed alive. It flattened out and then pulled back a little from tension in itself. Liza lifted the pale sheet of it and laid it over one of the pie tins and trimmed the edges with a knife. The prepared berries lay deep in red juice in a bowl.

Samuel sat down in a kitchen chair and crossed his legs and looked at her. His eyes were smiling.

'Can't you find something to do this time of day?' she asked.

'Oh, I guess I could, Mother, if I wanted to.'

'Well, don't sit there and make me nervous. The paper's in the other room if you're feeling day-lazy.'

'I've read it,' said Samuel.

'All of it?'

'All I want to.'

'Samuel, what's the matter with you? You're up to something. I can see it in your face. Now tell it, and let me get on with my pies.'

He swung his leg and smiled at her. 'Such a little bit of a wife,' he said. 'Three of her is hardly a bite.'

'Samuel, now you stop that. I don't mind a joke in the evening sometimes, but it's not eleven o'clock. Now you go along.'

Samuel said, 'Liza, do you know the meaning of the English word "vacation"?'

'Now don't you make jokes in the morning.'

'Do you, Liza?'

'Of course I do. Don't play me for a fool.'

'What does it mean?'

'Going away for a rest to the sea and the beach. Now, Samuel, get out with your fooling.'

'I wonder how you know the word.'

'Will you tell me what you're after? Why shouldn't I know?'

'Did you ever have one, Liza?'

'Why, I–' She stopped.

'In fifty years, did you ever have a vacation, you little, silly, half-pint, smidgin of a wife?'

'Samuel, please go out of my kitchen,' she said apprehensively.

He took the letter from his pocket and unfolded it. 'It's from Ollie,' he said. 'She wants us to come and visit in Salinas. They've fixed over the upstairs rooms. She wants us to get to know the children. She's got us tickets for the Chautauqua season. Billy Sunday's going to wrestle with the Devil and Bryan is going to make his Cross of Gold speech. I'd like to hear that. It's an old fool of a speech but they say he gives it in a way to break your heart.'

Liza rubbed her nose and floured it with her finger. 'Is it very costly?' she asked anxiously.

'Costly? Ollie has bought the tickets. They're a present.'

'We can't go,' said Liza. 'Who'd run the ranch?'

'Tom would–what running there is to do in the winter.'

'He'd be lonely.'

'George would maybe come out and stay a while to go quail hunting. See what's in the letter, Liza.'

'What are those?'

'Two tickets to Salinas on the train. Ollie says she doesn't want to give us a single escape.'

'You can just turn them in and send her back the money.'

'No, I can't. Why, Liza–Mother–now don't. Here–here's a handkerchief.'

'That's a dish-towel,' said Liza.

'Sit here, Mother. There! I guess the shock of taking a rest kind of threw you. Here! I know it's a dish-towel. They say that Billy Sunday drives the Devil all over the stage.'

'That's blasphemy,' said Liza.

'But I'd like to see it, wouldn't you? What did you say? Hold up your head. I didn't hear you. What did you say?'

'I said yes,' said Liza.

Tom was making a drawing when Samuel came in to him. Tom looked at his father with veiled eyes, trying to read the effect of Olive's letter.

Samuel looked at the drawing. 'What is it?'

'I'm trying to work out a gate-opener so a man won't have to get out of his rig. Here's the pull-rod to open the latch.'

'What's going to open it?'

'I figured a strong spring.'

Samuel studied the drawing. 'Then what's going to close it?'

'This bar here. It would slip to this spring with the tension the other way.'

'I see,' said Samuel. 'It might work too, if the gate was truly hung. And it would only take twice as much time to make and keep up as twenty years of getting out of the rig and opening the gate.'

Tom protested, 'Sometimes with a skittish horse–'

'I know,' said his father. 'But the main reason is that it's fun.'

Tom grinned, 'Caught me,' he said.

'Tom, do you think you could look after the ranch if your mother and I took a little trip?'

'Why, sure,' said Tom. 'Where do you plan to go?'

'Ollie wants us to stay with her for a while in Salinas.'

'Why, that would be fine,' said Tom. 'Is Mother agreeable?'

'She is, always forgetting the expense.'

'That's fine,' said Tom. 'How long do you plan to be gone?'

Samuel's jewelled, sardonic eyes dwelt on Tom's face until Tom said, 'What's the matter, Father?'

'It's the little tone, son–so little that I could barely hear it. But it was there. Tom, my son, if you have a secret with your brothers and sisters, I don't mind. I think that's good.'

'I don't know what you mean,' said Tom.

'You may thank God you didn't want to be an actor, Tom, because you would have been a very bad one. You worked it out at Thanksgiving, I guess, when you were all together. And it's working smooth as butter. I see Will's hand in this. Don't tell me if you don't want to.'

'I wasn't in favour of it,' said Tom.

'It doesn't sound like you,' his father said. 'You'd be for scattering the truth out in the sun for me to see. Don't tell the others I know.' He turned away and then came back and put his hand on Tom's shoulders. 'Thank you for wanting to honour me with the truth, my son. It's not clever but it's more permanent.'

'I'm glad you're going.'

Samuel stood in the doorway of the forge and looked at the land. 'They say a mother loves best an ugly child,' he said, and he shook his head sharply. 'Tom, I'll trade your honour for honour. You will please hold this in your dark secret place, nor tell any of your brothers and sisters–I know why I'm going–and, Tom, I know where I'm going, and I am content.'

CHAPTER 24

I

I have wondered why it is that some people are less affected and torn by the verities of life and death than others. Una's death cut the earth from under Samuel's feet and opened his defended keep and let in old age. On the other hand Liza, who surely loved her family as deeply as did her husband, was not destroyed or warped. Her life continued evenly. She felt sorrow but she survived it.

I think perhaps Liza accepted the world as she accepted the Bible, with all its paradoxes and its reverses. She did not like death but she knew it existed, and when it came it did not surprise her.

Samuel may have thought and played and philosophized about death, but he did not really believe in it. His world did not have death as a member. He, and all around him, was immortal. When real death came it was an outrage, a denial of the immortality he deeply felt, and the one crack in his wall caused the whole structure to crash. I think he had always thought he could argue himself out of death. It was a personal opponent and one he could lick.

To Liza it was simply death–the thing promised and expected. She could go on and in her sorrow put a pot of beans in the oven, bake six pies and plan to exactness how much food would be necessary properly to feed the funeral guests. And she could in her sorrow see that Samuel had a clean white shirt and that his black broadcloth was brushed and free of spots and his shoes blacked. Perhaps it takes these two kinds to make a good marriage, riveted with several kinds of strengths.

Once Samuel accepted, he could probably go farther than Liza, but the process of accepting tore him to pieces. Liza watched him closely after the decision to go to Salinas. She didn't quite know what he was up to, but, like a good and cautious mother, she knew he was up to something. She was a complete realist. Everything else being equal, she was glad to be going to visit her children. She was curious about them and their children. She had no love of places. A place was only a resting stage on the way to Heaven. She did not like work for itself, but she did it because it was there to be done. And she was tired. Increasingly it was more difficult to fight the aches and stiffness which tried to keep her in bed in the morning–not that they ever succeeded.

And she looked forward to Heaven as a place where clothes did not get dirty and where the food did not have to be cooked and dishes washed. Privately there were some things in Heaven of which she did not quite approve. There was too much singing, and she didn't see how even the Elect could survive for very long the celestial laziness which was promised. She would find something to do in Heaven. There must be something to take up one's time–some clouds to darn, some weary wings to rub with liniment. Maybe the collars of the robes needed turning now and then, and when you come right down to it, she couldn't believe that even in Heaven there would not be cobwebs in some corner to be knocked down with a cloth-covered broom.

She was gay and frightened about the visit to Salinas. She liked the idea so well that she felt there must be something bordering on sin involved in it. And the Chautauqua? Well, she didn't have to go and probably wouldn't. Samuel would run wild–she would have to watch him. She never lost her feeling that he was young and helpless. It was a good thing that she did not know what went on in his mind, and, through his mind, what happened to his body.

Places were very important to Samuel. The ranch was a relative, and when he left it he plunged a knife into a darling. But having made up his mind, Samuel set about doing it well. He made formal calls on all of his neighbours, the old-timers who remembered how it used to be and how it was. And when he drove away from his old friends they knew they would not see him again, although he did not say it. He took to gazing at the mountains and the trees, even at faces, as though to memorize them for eternity.

He saved his visit to the Trask place for last. He had not been there for months. Adam was not a young man any more. The boys were eleven years old, and Lee–well, Lee did not change much. Lee walked to the shed with Samuel.

'I've wanted to talk to you for a long time,' said Lee. 'But there's so much to do. And I try to get to San Francisco at least once a month.'

'You know how it is,' Samuel said. 'When you know a friend is there you do not go to seek him. Then he's gone and you blast your conscience to shreds that you did not see him.'

'I heard about your daughter. I'm sorry.'

'I got your letter, Lee. I have it. You said good things.'

'Chinese things,' said Lee. 'I seem to get more Chinese as I get older.'

'There's something changed about you, Lee. What is it?'

'It's my queue, Mr Hamilton. I've cut off my queue.'

'That's it.'

'We all did. Haven't you heard? The Dowager Empress is gone. China is free. The Manchus are not overlords and we do not wear queues. It was a proclamation of the new government. There's not a queue left anywhere.'

'Does it make a difference, Lee?'

'Not much. It's easier. But there's a kind of looseness on the scalp that makes me uneasy. It's hard to get used to the convenience of it.'

'How is Adam?'

'He's all right. But he hasn't changed much. I wonder what he was like before.'

'Yes, I've wondered about that. It was a short flowering. The boys must be big.'

'They are big. I'm glad I stayed here. I learned a great deal from seeing the boys grow and helping a little.'

'Did you teach them Chinese?'

'No. Mr Trask didn't want me to. And I guess he was right. It would have been a needless complication. But I'm their friend–yes, I'm their friend. They admire their father, but I think they love me. And they're very different. You can't imagine how different.'

'In what way, Lee?'

'You'll see when they come home from school. They're like two sides of a medal. Cal is sharp and dark and watchful, and his brother–well, he's a boy you like before he speaks and like more afterwards.'

'And you don't like Cal?'

'I find myself defending him–to myself. He's fighting for his life and his brother doesn't have to fight.'

'I have the same thing in my brood,' said Samuel. 'I don't understand it. You'd think with the same training and the same blood they'd be alike, but they're not–not at all.'

Later Samuel and Adam walked down the oak-shadowed road to the entrance to the draw where they could look out at the Salinas Valley.

'Will you stay to dinner?' Adam asked.

'I will not be responsible for the murder of more chickens,' said Samuel.

'Lee's got a pot roast.'

'Well, in that case–'

Adam still carried one shoulder lower than the other from the old hurt. His face was hard and curtained, and his eyes looked at generalities and did not inspect details. The two men stopped in the road and looked out at the valley, green-tinged from the early rains.

Samuel said softly, 'I wonder you do not feel a shame at leaving that land fallow.'

'I had no reason to plant it,' Adam said. 'We had that out before. You thought I would change. I have not changed.'

'Do you take a pride in your hurt?' Samuel asked. 'Does it make you seem large and tragic?'

'I don't know.'

'Well, think about it. Maybe you're playing a part on a great stage with only yourself as audience.'

A slight anger came into Adam's voice. 'Why do you come to lecture me? I'm glad you've come, but why do you dig into me?'

'To see whether I can raise a little anger in you. I'm a nosy man. But there's all that fallow land, and here beside me is all that fallow man. It seems a waste. And I have a bad feeling about waste because I could never afford it. Is it a good feeling to let your life lie fallow?'

'What else could I do?'

'You could try again.'

Adam faced him. 'I'm afraid to, Samuel,' he said. 'I'd rather just go about it this way. Maybe I haven't the energy or the courage.'

'How about your boys–do you love them?'

'Yes–yes.'

'Do you love one more than the other?'

'Why do you say that?'

'I don't know. Something about your tone.'

'Let's go back to the house, said Adam. They strolled back under the trees. Suddenly Adam said, 'Did you ever hear that Cathy was in Salinas? Did you ever hear such a rumour?'

'Did you?'

'Yes–but I don't believe it. I can't believe it.'

Samuel walked silently in the sandy wheel-rut of the road. His mind turned sluggishly in the pattern of Adam and almost wearily took up a thought he had hoped was finished. He said at last. 'You have never let her go.'

'I guess not. But I've let the shooting go. I don't think about it any more.'

'I can't tell you how to live your life,' Samuel said, 'although I do be telling you how to live it. I know that it might be better for you to come out from under your might-have-beens, into the winds of the world. And while I tell you, I am myself sifting my memories, the way men pan the dirt under a bar-room floor for the bits of gold dust that fall between the cracks. It's small mining–small mining. You're too young a man to be panning memories, Adam. You should be getting yourself some new ones, so that the mining will be richer when you come to age.'

Adam's face was bent down, and his jawbone jutted below his temples from clenching.

Samuel glanced at him. 'That's right,' he said. 'Set your teeth in it. How do we defend a wrongness! Shall I tell you what to do, so you will not think you invented it? When you go to bed and blow out the lamp–then she stands in the doorway with a little light behind her, and you can see her nightgown stir. And she comes sweetly to your bed, and you, hardly breathing, turn back the covers to receive her and move your head over on the pillow to make room for her head beside yours. You can smell the sweetness of her skin, and it smells like no other skin in the world–'

'Stop it,' Adam shouted at him. 'Goddam you, stop it! Stop nosing over my life! You're like a coyote sniffing around a dead cow.'

'The way I know,' Samuel said softly, 'is that one came to me that selfsame way–night after month after year, right to the very now. And I think I should have double-bolted my mind and sealed off my heart against her, but I did not. All of these years I've cheated Liza. I've given her an untruth, a counterfeit, and I've saved the best for those dark sweet hours. And now I could wish that she may have had some secret caller too. But I'll never know that. I think she would maybe have bolted her heart shut and thrown the key to hell.'

Adam's hands were clenched and the blood was driven out of his white knuckles. 'You make me doubt myself,' he said fiercely. 'You always have. I'm afraid of you. What should I do, Samuel? Tell me! I don't know how you saw the thing so clear. What should I do?'

'I know the "shoulds", although I never do them, Adam. I always know the "shoulds". You should try to find a new Cathy. You should let the new Cathy kill the dream Cathy–let the two of them fight it out. And you, sitting by, should marry your mind to the winner. That's the second-best "should". The best would be to search out and find some fresh new loveliness to cancel out the old.'

'I'm afraid to try,' said Adam.

'That's what you've said. And now I'm going to put a selfishness on you. I'm going away, Adam. I came to say goodbye.'

'What do you mean?'

'My daughter Olive has asked Liza and me to visit with her in Salinas, and we're going–day after tomorrow.'

'Well, you'll be back.'

Samuel went on, 'After we've visited with Olive for maybe a month or two, there will come a letter from George. And his feelings will be hurt if we don't visit him in Paso Robles. And after that Mollie will want us in San Francisco, and then Will, and maybe even Joe in the East, if we should live so long.'

'Well, won't you like that? You've earned it. You've worked hard enough on that dust heap of yours.'

'I love that dust heap,' Samuel said. 'I love it the way a bitch loves her runty pup. I love every flint, the plough-breaking out-croppings, the thin and barren topsoil, the waterless heart of her. Somewhere in my dust heap there's a richness.'

'You deserve a rest.'

'There, you've said it again,' said Samuel. 'That's what I had to accept, and I have accepted. When you say I deserve a rest, you are saying that my life is over.'

'Do you believe that?'

'That's what I have accepted.'

Adam said excitedly, 'You can't do that. Why, if you accept that you won't live!'

'I know,' said Samuel.

'But you can't do that.'

'Why not?'

'I don't want you to.'

'I'm a nosy old man, Adam. And the sad thing to me is that I'm losing my nosiness. That's maybe how I know it's time to visit my children. I'm having to pretend to be nosy a good deal of the time.'

'I'd rather you worked your guts out on your dust heap.'

Samuel smiled at him. 'What a nice thing to hear! And I thank you. It's a good thing to be loved, even late.'

Suddenly Adam turned in front of him so that Samuel had to stop. 'I know what you've done for me,' Adam said. 'I can't return anything. But I can ask you for one more thing. If I asked you, would you do me one more kindness, and maybe save my life?'

'I would if I could.'

Adam swung out his hand and made an arc over the west. 'That land out there–would you help me to make the garden we talked of, the windmills and the wells and the flats of alfalfa? We could raise flower-seeds. There's money in that. Think of what it would be like, acres of sweet peas and gold squares of calendulas. Maybe ten acres of roses for the gardens of the West. Think how they would smell on the west wind!'

'You're going to make me cry,' Samuel said, 'and that would be an unseemly thing in an old man.' And indeed his eyes were wet. 'I thank you, Adam,' he said. 'The sweetness of your offer is a good smell on the west wind.'

'Then you'll do it?'

'No, I will not do it. But I'll see it in my mind when I'm in Salinas, listening to William Jennings Bryan. And maybe I'll get to believe it happened.'

'But I want to do it.'

'Go and see my Tom. He'll help you. He'd plant the world with roses, poor man, if he could.'

'You know what you're doing, Samuel?'

'Yes, I know what I'm doing, know so well that it's half done.'

'What a stubborn man you are!'

'Contentious,' said Samuel. 'Liza says I'm contentious, but now I'm caught in a web of my children–and I think I like it.'

2

The dinner-table was set in the house. Lee said, 'I'd have liked to serve it under the tree like the other times, but the air is chilly.'

'So it is, Lee,' said Samuel.

The twins came in silently and stood shyly staring at their guest.

'It's long time since I've seen you, boys. But we named you well. You're Caleb, aren't you?'

'I'm Cal.'

'Well, Cal, then.' And he turned to the other. 'Have you found a way to rip the backbone out of your name?'

'Sir?'

'Are you called Aaron?'

'Yes, sir.'

Lee chuckled. 'He spells it with one *a*. The two *a*'s seem a little fancy to his friends.'

'I've got thirty-five Belgian hares, sir,' Aron said. 'Would you like to see them, sir? The hutch is up by the spring. I've got eight new-borns–just born yesterday.'

'I'd like to see them, Aron.' His mouth twitched. 'Cal, don't tell me you're a gardener?'

Lee's head snapped round and he inspected Samuel. 'Don't do that,' Lee said nervously.

Cal said, 'Next year my father is going to let me have an acre in the flat.'

Aron said, 'I've got a buck rabbit weighs fifteen pounds. I'm going to give it to my father for his birthday.'

They heard Adam's bedroom door opening. 'Don't tell him,' Aron said quickly. 'It's a secret.'

Lee sawed at the pot roast. 'Always you bring trouble for my mind, Mr Hamilton,' he said. 'Sit down, boys.'

Adam came in, turning down his sleeves, and took his seat at the head of the table. 'Good evening, boys,' he said, and they replied in unison, 'Good evening, Father.

And, 'Don't you tell,' said Aron.

'I won't,' Samuel assured him.

'Don't tell what?' Adam asked.

Samuel said, 'Can't there be a privacy? I have a secret with your son.'

Cal broke in, 'I'll tell you a secret too, right after dinner.'

'I'll like to hear it,' said Samuel. 'And I do hope I don't know already what it is.'

Lee looked up from his carving and glared at Samuel. He began piling meat on the plates.

The boys ate quickly and quietly, wolfed their food. Aron said, 'Will you excuse us, Father?'

Adam nodded, and the two boys went quickly out. Samuel looked after them. 'They seem older than eleven,' he said. 'I seem to remember that at eleven my brood were howlers and screamers and runners in circles. These seem like grown men.'

'Do they?' Adam asked.

Lee said, 'I think I see why that is. There is no woman in the house to put a value on babies. I don't think men care much for babies, and so it was never an advantage to these boys to be babies. There was nothing to gain by it. I don't know whether that is good or bad.'

Samuel wiped up the remains of gravy in his plate with a slice of bread. 'Adam, I wonder whether you know what you have in Lee. A philosopher who can cook, or a cook who can think? He has taught me a great deal. You must have learned from him, Adam.'

Adam said, 'I'm afraid I didn't listen enough–or maybe he didn't talk.'

'Why didn't you want the boys to learn Chinese, Adam?'

Adam thought for a moment. 'It seems a time for honesty,' he said at last. 'I guess it was plain jealousy. I gave it another name, but maybe I didn't want them to be able so easily to go away from me in a direction I couldn't follow.'

'That's reasonable enough and almost too human,' said Samuel. 'But knowing it–that's a great jump. I wonder whether I have ever gone so far.'

Lee brought the grey enamelled coffee-pot to the table and filled the cups and sat down. He warmed the palm of his hand against the rounded side of his cup. And then Lee laughed. 'You've given me great trouble, Mr Hamilton, and you've disturbed the tranquillity of China.'

'How do you mean, Lee?'

'It almost seems that I have told you this,' said Lee. 'Maybe I only composed it in my mind, meaning to tell you. It's an amusing story anyway.'

'I want to hear,' said Samuel, and he looked at Adam. 'Don't you want to hear, Adam? Or are you slipping into your cloud bath?'

'I was thinking of that,' said Adam. 'It's funny–a kind of excitement is coming over me.'

'That's good,' said Samuel. 'Maybe that's the best of all good things that can happen to a human. Let's hear your story, Lee.'

The Chinese reached to the side of his neck and he smiled. 'I wonder whether I'll get used to the lack of a queue,' he said. 'I guess I used it more than I knew. Yes, the story. I told you, Mr Hamilton, that I was growing more Chinese. Do you ever grow more Irish?'

'It comes and goes,' said Samuel.

'Do you remember when you read us the sixteen verses of the fourth chapter of Genesis and we argued about them?'

'I do indeed. And that's a long time ago.'

'Ten years nearly,' said Lee. 'Well, the story bit deeply into me and I went into it word for word. The more I thought about the story, the more profound it became to me. Then I compared the translations we have–and they were fairly close. There was only one place that bothered me. The King James version says this–it is when Jehovah has asked Cain why he is angry. Jehovah says, "If thou doest well, shalt thou not be accepted? and if thou doeth not well, sin lieth at the door. And unto thee shall be his desire, and *thou shalt* rule over him." It was the "thou shalt" that struck me, because it was a promise that Cain would conquer sin.'

Samuel nodded. 'And his children didn't do it entirely,' he said.

Lee sipped his coffee. 'Then I got a copy of the American Standard Bible. It was very new then. And it was different in this passage. It says, "*Do thou* rule over him." Now this is very different. This is not a promise, it is an order. And I began to stew about it. I wondered what the original word of the original writer had been that these very different translations could be made.'

Samuel put his palms down on the table and leaned forward and the old young light came into his eyes. 'Lee,' he said, 'don't tell me you studied Hebrew!'

Lee said, 'I'm going to tell you. And it's a fairly long story. Will you have a touch of ng-ka-py?'

'You mean the drink that tastes of good rotten apples?'

'Yes. I can talk better with it.'

'Maybe I can listen better,' said Samuel.

While Lee went to the kitchen Samuel asked, 'Adam, did you know about this?'

'No,' said Adam. 'He didn't tell me. Maybe I wasn't listening.'

Lee came back with his stone bottle and three little porcelain cups so thin and delicate that the light shone through them. 'Dlinkee Chinee fashion,' he said and poured the almost black liquor. 'There's a lot of wormwood in this. It's quite a drink,' he said. 'Has about the same effect as absinthe if you drink enough of it.'

Samuel sipped his drink. 'I want to know why you were so interested,' he said.

'Well, it seemed to me that the man who could conceive this great story would know exactly what he wanted to say and there would be no confusion in his statement.'

'You say "the man". Do you then not think this is a divine book written by the inky finger of God?'

'I think the mind that could think this story was a curiously divine mind. We have had a few such minds in China too.'

'I just wanted to know,' said Samuel. 'You're not a Presbyterian after all.'

'I told you I was getting more Chinese. Well, to go on, I went to San Francisco to the headquarters of our family association. Do you know about them? Our great families have centres where any member can get help or give it. The Lee family is very large. It takes care of its own.'

'I have heard of them,' said Samuel.

'You mean Chinee hatchet man fightee Tong war over slave girl?'

'I guess so.'

'It's a little different from that, really,' said Lee. 'I went there because in our family there are a number of ancient reverend gentlemen who are great scholars. They are thinkers in exactness. A man may spend many years pondering a sentence of the scholar you call Confucius. I thought there might be experts in meaning who could advise me.

'They are fine old men. They smoke their two pipes of opium in the afternoon and it rests and sharpens them, and they sit through the night and their minds are wonderful. I guess no other people have been able to use opium well.'

Lee dampened his tongue in the black brew. 'I respectfully submitted my problem to one of these sages, read him the story, and told him what I understood from it. The next night four of them met and called me in. We discussed the story all night long.'

Lee laughed. 'I guess it's funny,' he said. 'I know I wouldn't dare tell it to many people. Can you imagine four old gentlemen, the youngest is over ninety now, taking on the study of Hebrew? They engaged a learned rabbi. They took to the study as though they were children. Exercise books, grammar, vocabulary, simple sentences. You should see Hebrew written in Chinese ink with a brush! The right to left didn't bother them as much as it would you, since we write up to down. Oh, they were perfectionists! They went to the root of the matter.'

'And you?' said Samuel.

'I went along with them, marvelling at the beauty of their proud clean brains. I began to love my race, and for the first time I wanted to be Chinese. Every two weeks I went to a meeting with them, and in my room here I covered pages with writing. I bought every known Hebrew dictionary. But the old gentlemen were always ahead of me. It wasn't long before they were ahead of our rabbi; he brought a colleague in. Mr Hamilton, you should have sat through some of those nights of argument and discussion. The questions, the inspection, oh, the lovely thinking–the beautiful thinking.

'After two years we felt that we could approach your sixteen verses of the fourth chapter of Genesis. My old gentlemen felt that these words were very important too–"Thou shalt" and "Do thou". And this was the gold from our mining: "*Thou mayest.*" "Thou mayest rule over sin." The old gentlemen smiled and nodded and felt the years were well spent. It brought them out of their Chinese shells too, and right now they are studying Greek.'

Samuel said, 'It's a fantastic story. And I've tried to follow and maybe I've missed somewhere. Why is this word so important?'

Lee's hand shook as he filled the delicate cups. He drank his down in one gulp. 'Don't you see?' he cried. 'The American Standard translation *orders* men to triumph over sin, and you can call sin ignorance. The King James translation makes a promise in "Thou shalt", meaning that men will surely triumph over sin. But the Hebrew word, the word *timshel*–"Thou mayest"–that gives a choice. It might be the most important word in the world. That says the way is open. That throws it right back on a man. For if "Thou mayest"–it is also true that "Thou mayest not". Don't you see?'

'Yes, I see. I do see. But you do not believe this is divine law. Why do you feel its importance?'

'Ah!' said Lee. 'I've wanted to tell you this for a long time. I even anticipated your questions and I am well prepared. Any writing which has influenced the thinking and the lives of innumerable people is important. Now, there are many millions in their sects and Churches who feel the order, "Do thou", and throw their weight into obedience. And there are millions more who feel predestination in "Thou shalt". Nothing they may do can interfere with what will be. But "Thou mayest"! Why, that makes a man great, that gives him stature with the gods, for in his weakness and his filth and his murder of his brother he has still the great choice. He can choose his course and fight it through and win.' Lee's voice was a chant of triumph.

Adam said, 'Do you believe that, Lee?'

'Yes, I do. Yes, I do. It is easy out of laziness, out of weakness, to throw oneself into the lap of deity, saying, "I couldn't help it; the way was set." But think of the glory of the choice! That makes a man a man. A cat has no choice, a bee must make honey. There's no godliness there. And do you know, those old gentlemen who were sliding gently down to death are too interested to die now.'

Adam said, 'Do you mean these Chinese men believe the Old Testament?'

Lee said, 'These old men believe a true story, and they know a true story when they hear it. They are critics of truth. They know that these sixteen verses are a history of humankind in any age or culture or race. They do not believe a man writes fifteen and three-quarter verses of truth and tells a lie with one verb. Confucius tells men how they should live to have good and successful lives. But this–this is a ladder to climb to the stars.' Lee's eyes shone. 'You can never lose that. It cuts the feet from under weakness and cowardliness and laziness.'

Adam said, 'I don't see how you could cook and raise the boys and take care of me and still do all this.'

'Neither do I,' said Lee. 'But I take my two pipes in the afternoon, no more and no less, like the elders. And I feel that I am a man. And I feel that a man is a very important thing–maybe more important than a star. This is not theology. I have no bent towards gods. But I have a new love for that glittering instrument, the human soul. It is a lovely and unique thing in the universe. It is always attacked and never destroyed–because "Thou mayest".'

3

Lee and Adam walked out to the shed with Samuel to see him off. Lee carried a tin lantern to light the way, for it was one of those clear early winter nights when the sky riots with stars and the earth seems doubly dark because of them. A silence lay on the hills. No animal moved about, neither grass-eater nor predator, and the air was so still that the dark limbs and leaves of the live oaks stood unmoving against the Milky Way. The three men were silent. The bail of the tin lantern squeaked a little as the light swung in Lee's hand.

Adam asked, 'When do you think you'll be back from your trip?'

Samuel did not answer.

Doxology stood patiently in the stall, head down, his milky eyes staring at the straw under his feet.

'You've had that horse for ever,' Adam said.

'He's thirty-three,' said Samuel. 'His teeth are worn off. I have to feed him warm mash with my fingers. And he has bad dreams. He shivers and cries sometimes in his sleep.'

'He's about as ugly a crow bait as I ever saw,' Adam said.

'I know it. I think that's why I picked him when he was a colt. Do you know I paid two dollars for him thirty-three years ago? Everything was wrong with him, hoofs like flapjacks, a hock so thick and short and straight there seems no joint at all. He's hammer-headed and sway-backed. He has a pinched chest and a big behind. He has an iron mouth and he still fights the crupper. With a saddle he feels as though you were riding a sled over a gravel pit. He can't trot and he stumbles over his feet when he walks. I have never in thirty-three years found one good thing about him. He even has an ugly disposition. He is selfish and quarrelsome and mean and disobedient. To this day I don't dare walk behind him because he will surely take a kick at me. When I feed him mash he tries to bite my hand. And I love him.'

Lee said, 'And you named him "Doxology".'

'Surely,' said Samuel, 'so ill endowed a creature deserved, I thought, one grand possession. He hasn't very long now.'

Adam said, 'Maybe you should put him out of his misery.'

'What misery?' Samuel demanded. 'He's one of the few happy and consistent beings I've ever met.'

'He must have aches and pains.'

'Well, he doesn't think so. Doxology still thinks he's one hell of a horse. Would you shoot him, Adam?'

'Yes, I think I would. Yes, I would.'

'You'd take the responsibility?'

'Yes, I think I would. He's thirty-three. His life-span is long over.'

Lee had set his lantern on the ground. Samuel squatted beside it and instinctively stretched his hands for warmth to the butterfly of yellow light.

'I've been bothered by something, Adam,' he said.

'What is that?'

'You really would shoot my horse because death might be more comfortable?'

'Well, I meant–'

Samuel said quickly, 'Do you like your life, Adam?'

'Of course not.'

'If I had a medicine that might cure you and also might kill you, should I give it to you? Inspect yourself, man.'

'What medicine?'

'No,' said Samuel. 'If I tell you, believe me when I say it may kill you.'

Lee said, 'Be careful, Mr Hamilton. Be careful.'

'What is this?' Adam demanded. 'Tell me what you're thinking of.'

Samuel said softly, 'I think for once I will not be careful. Lee, if I am wrong–listen–if I am mistaken, I accept the responsibility and I will take what blame there is to take.'

'Are you sure you're right?' Lee asked anxiously.

'Of course I'm not sure. Adam, do you want the medicine?'

'Yes. I don't know what it is, but give it to me.'

'Adam, Cathy is in Salinas. She owns a whorehouse, the most vicious and depraved in this whole end of the country. The evil and ugly, the distorted and slimy, the worst things humans can think up are for sale there. The crippled and crooked come there for satisfaction. But it is worse than that. Cathy, and she is now called Kate, takes the fresh and young and beautiful and so maims them that they can never be whole again. Now, there's your medicine. Let's see what it does to you.'

'You're a liar!' Adam said.

'No, Adam. Many things I am, but a liar I am not.'

Adam whirled on Lee. 'Is this true?'

'I'm no antidote,' said Lee. 'Yes. It's true.'

Adam stood swaying in the lantern light and then he turned and ran. They could hear his heavy steps running and tripping. They heard him falling over the brush and scrambling and clawing his way upwards on the slope. The sound of him stopped only when he had gone over the brow of the hill.

Lee said, 'Your medicine acts like poison.'

'I take responsibility,' said Samuel. 'Long ago I learned this: when a dog has eaten strychnine and is going to die, you must get an axe and carry him to a chopping block. Then you must wait for his next convulsion, and in that moment–chop off his tail. Then, if the poison has not gone too far, your dog may recover. The shock of pain can counteract the poison. Without the shock he will surely die.'

'But how do you know this is the same?' Lee asked.

'I don't. But without it he would surely die.'

'You're a brave man,' Lee said.

'No, I'm an old man. And if I should have anything on my conscience it won't be for long.'

Lee asked, 'What do you suppose he'll do?'

'I don't know,' said Samuel, 'but at least he won't sit around and mope. Here, hold the lantern for me, will you?'

In the yellow light Samuel slipped the bit in Doxology's mouth, a bit worn so thin that it was a flake of steel. The check rein had been abandoned long ago. The old hammerhead was free to drag his nose if he wished, or to pause and crop grass beside the road. Samuel didn't care. Tenderly he buckled the crupper, and the horse edged to try to kick him.

When Dox was between the shafts of the cart Lee asked, 'Would you mind if I rode along with you a little? I'll walk back.'

'Come along,' said Samuel, and he tried not to notice that Lee helped him up into the cart.

The night was very dark, and Dox showed his disgust for night-travelling by stumbling every few steps.

Samuel said, 'Get on with it, Lee. What is it you want to say?'

Lee did not appear surprised. 'Maybe I'm nosy the way you say you are. I get to thinking. I know probabilities, but tonight you fooled me completely. I would have taken any bet that you of all men would not have told Adam.'

'Did you know about her?'

'Of course,' said Lee.

'Do the boys know?'

'I don't think so, but that's only a matter of time. You know how cruel children are. Some day in the school-yard it will be shouted at them.'

'Maybe he ought to take them away from here,' said Samuel. 'Think about that, Lee.'

'My question isn't answered, Mr Hamilton. How were you able to do what you did?'

'Do you think I was that wrong?'

'No, I don't mean that at all. But I've never thought of you as taking any strong unchanging stand on anything. This has been my judgement. Are you interested?'

'Show me the man who isn't interested in discussing himself,' said Samuel. 'Go on.'

'You're a kind man, Mr Hamilton. And I've always thought it was the kindness that comes from not wanting any trouble. And your mind is as facile as a young lamb leaping in a daisy field. You have never to my knowledge taken a bulldog grip on anything. And then tonight you did a thing that tears down my whole picture of you.'

Samuel wrapped the lines around a stick stuck in the whip socket, and Doxology stumbled on down the rutty road. The old man stroked his beard, and it shone very white in the starlight. He took off his black hat and laid it in his lap. 'I guess it surprised me as much as it did you,' he said. 'But if you want to know why–look into yourself.'

'I don't understand you.'

'If you had only told me about your studies earlier it might have made a great difference, Lee.'

'I still don't understand you.'

'Careful, Lee, you'll get me talking. I told you my Irish came and went. It's coming now.'

Lee said, 'Mr Hamilton, you're going away and you're not coming back. You do not intend to live very much longer.'

'That's true, Lee. How did you know?'

'There's death all around you. It shines from you.'

'I didn't know anyone could see it,' Samuel said. 'You know, Lee, I think of my life as a kind of music, not always good music but still having form and melody. And my life has not been a full orchestra for a long time now. A single note only–and that note unchanging sorrow. I'm not alone in my attitude, Lee. It seems to me that too many of us conceive of a life as ending in defeat.'

Lee said, 'Maybe everyone is too rich. I have noticed that there is no dissatisfaction like that of the rich. Feed a man, clothe him, put him in a good house, and he will die of despair.'

'It was your two-word re-translation, Lee–"Thou mayest". It took me by the throat and shook me. And when the dizziness was over, a path was open, new and bright. And my life which is ending seems to be going on to an ending wonderful. And my music has a new last melody like a bird song in the night.'

Lee was peering at him through the darkness. 'That's what it did to those old men of my family.'

'"Thou mayest rule over sin", Lee. That's it. I do not believe all men are destroyed. I can name you a dozen who were not, and they are the ones the world lives by. It is true of the spirit as it is true of battles–only the winners are remembered. Surely most men are destroyed, but there are others who like pillars of fire guide frightened men through the darkness. "*Thou mayest, Thou mayest!*" What glory! It is true that we are weak and sick and quarrelsome, but if that is all we were, we would, millenniums ago, have disappeared from the face of the earth. A few remnants of fossilized jawbone, some broken teeth in strata of limestone, would be the only mark man would have left of his existence in the world. But the choice, Lee, the choice of winning! I had never understood it or accepted it before. Do you see now why I told Adam tonight? I exercised the choice. Maybe I was wrong, but by telling him I also forced him to live or get off the pot. What is that word, Lee?'

'*Timshel*,' said Lee. 'Will you stop the cart?'

'You'll have a long walk back.'

Lee climbed down. 'Samuel!' he said.

'Here am I.' The old man chuckled. 'Liza hates for me to say that.'

'Samuel, you've gone beyond me.'

'It's time, Lee.'

'Goodbye, Samuel,' Lee said, and he walked hurriedly back along the road. He heard the iron tyres of the cart grinding on the road. He turned and looked after it, and on the slope he saw old Samuel against the sky, his white hair shining with starlight.

CHAPTER 25

1

It was a deluge of a winter in the Salinas Valley, wet and wonderful. The rains fell gently and soaked in and did not freshet. The feed was deep in January, and in February the hills were fat with grass and the coats of the cattle looked tight and sleek. In March the soft rains continued, and each storm waited courteously until its predecessor sank beneath the ground. Then warmth flooded the valley and the earth burst into bloom–yellow and blue and gold.

Tom was alone on the ranch, and even that dust heap was rich and lovely and the flints were hidden in grass and the Hamilton cows were fat and the Hamilton sheep sprouted grass from their damp backs.

At noon on March 15 Tom sat on the bench outside the forge. The sunny morning was over, and grey water-bearing clouds sailed in over the mountains from the ocean, and their shadows slid under them on the bright earth.

Tom heard a horse's clattering hoofs and he saw a small boy, elbows flapping, urging a tired horse towards the house. He stood up and walked towards the road. The boy galloped up to the house, yanked off his hat, flung a yellow envelope on the ground, spun his horse round, and kicked up a gallop again.

Tom started to call after him, and then he leaned wearily down and picked up the telegram. He sat in the sun on the bench outside the forge, holding the telegram in his hand. And he looked at the hills and at the old house, as though to save something, before he tore open the envelope and read the inevitable four words, the person, the event, and the time.

Tom slowly folded the telegram and folded it again and again until it was a square no longer than his thumb. He walked to the house, through the kitchen, through the little living-room, and into his bedroom. He took his dark suit out of the clothes-press and laid it over the back of a chair, and he put a white shirt and a black tie on the seat of the chair. And then he lay down on the bed and turned his face to the wall.

2

The surreys and the buggies had driven out of the Salinas cemetery. The family and friends went back to Olive's house on Central Avenue to eat and drink coffee, to see how each one was taking it, and to do and say the decent things.

George offered Adam Trask a lift in his rented surrey, but Adam refused.

He wandered around the cemetery and sat down on the cement kerb of the Williams family plot. The traditional dark cypresses wept around the edge of the cemetery, and white violets ran wild in the pathways. Someone had brought them in and they had become weeds.

The cold wind blew over the tombstones and cried in the cypresses. There were many cast-iron stars, marking the graves of Grand Army men, and on each star a small wind-bitten flag from a year ago Decoration Day.

Adam sat looking at the mountains to the east of Salinas, with the noble point of Frémont's Peak dominating. The air was crystalline, as it sometimes is when rain is coming. And then the light rain began to blow on the wind although the sky was not properly covered with cloud.

Adam had come upon the morning train. He had not intended to come at all, but something drew him beyond his power to resist. For one thing, he could not believe that Samuel was dead. He could hear the rich, lyric voice in his ears, the tones rising and falling in their foreignness, and the curious music of oddly chosen words tripping out so that you were never sure what the next word would be. In the speech of most men you are absolutely sure what the next word will be.

Adam had looked at Samuel in his casket and knew that he didn't want him to be dead. And since the face in the casket did not look like Samuel's face, Adam walked away to be by himself and to preserve the man alive.

He had to go to the cemetery. Custom would have been outraged else. But he stood well back where he could not hear the words, and when the sons filled in the grave he walked away and strolled in the paths where the white violets grew.

The cemetery was deserted and the dark crooning of the wind bowed the heavy cypress trees. The rain droplets grew larger and drove stinging along.

Adam stood up, shivered, and walked slowly over the white violets and past the new grave. The flowers had been laid evenly to cover the mound of new-turned damp earth, and already the wind had frayed the blossoms and flung the smaller bouquets out into the path. Adam picked them up and laid them back on the mound.

He walked out of the cemetery. The wind and the rain were at his back, and he ignored the wetness that soaked through his black coat. Romie Lane was muddy with pools of water standing in the new wheel-ruts, and the tall wild oats and mustard grew beside the road, with wild turnip forcing its boisterous way up and stickery beads of purple thistles rising above the green riot of the wet spring.

The black 'dobe mud covered Adam's shoes and splashed the bottoms of his dark trousers. It was nearly a mile to the Monterey road. Adam was dirty and soaking when he reached it and turned east into the town of Salinas. The water was standing in the curved brim of his derby hat and his collar was wet and sagging.

At John Street the road angled and became Main Street. Adam stamped the mud off his shoes when he reached the pavement. The buildings cut the wind from him and almost instantly he began to shake with a chill. He increased his speed. Near the other end of Main Street he turned into the Abbot House bar. He ordered brandy and drank it quickly and his shivering increased.

Mr Lapierre behind the bar saw the chill. 'You'd better have another one,' he said. 'You'll get a bad cold. Would you like a hot rum? That will knock it out of you.'

'Yes, I would, said Adam.

'Well, here. You sip another cognac while I get some hot water.'

Adam took his glass to a table and sat uncomfortably in his wet clothes. Mr Lapierre brought a steaming kettle from the kitchen. He put the squat glass on a tray and brought it to the table. 'Drink it as hot as you can stand it,' he said. 'That will shake the chill out of an aspen.' He drew a chair up, sat down, then stood up. 'You've made me cold,' he said. 'I'm going to have one myself.' He brought his glass back to the table and sat opposite Adam. 'It's working,' he said. 'You were so pale you scared me when you came in. You're a stranger?'

'I'm from near King City,' Adam said.

'Come up for the funeral?'

'Yes–he was an old friend.'

'Big funeral?'

'Oh, yes.'

'I'm not surprised. He had lots of friends. Too bad it couldn't have been a nice day. You ought to have one more and then go to bed.'

'I will,' said Adam. 'It makes me comfortable and peaceful.'

'That's worth something. Might have saved you from pneumonia too.'

After he had served another toddy he brought a damp cloth from behind the bar. 'You can wipe off some of that mud,' he said. 'A funeral isn't very gay, but when it gets rained on–that's really mournful.'

'It didn't rain till after,' said Adam. 'It was walking back I got wet.'

'Why don't you get a nice room right here? You get into bed and I'll send a toddy up to you, and in the morning you'll be fine.'

'I think I'll do that,' said Adam. He could feel the blood stinging his cheeks and running hotly in his arms, as though it were some foreign warm fluid taking over his body. Then the warmth melted through into the cold concealed box where he stored forbidden thoughts, and the thoughts came timidly up to the surface like children who do not know whether they will be received. Adam picked up the damp cloth and leaned down to sponge off the bottoms of his trousers. The blood pounded behind his eyes. 'I might have one more toddy,' he said.

Mr Lapierre said, 'If it's for cold, you've had enough. But if you want a drink I've got some old Jamaica rum. I'd rather you'd have that straight. It's fifty years old. The water would kill the flavour.'

'I just want a drink,' said Adam.

'I'll have one with you. I haven't opened that jug in months. Not much call for it. This is a whisky-drinking town.'

Adam wiped off his shoes and dropped the cloth on the floor. He took a drink of the dark rum and coughed. The heavy-muscled drink wrapped its sweet aroma around his head and struck at the base of his nose like a blow. The room seemed to tip sideways and then right itself.

'Good, isn't it?' Mr Lapierre asked. 'But it can knock you over. I wouldn't have more than one–unless of course you want to get knocked over. Some do.'

Adam leaned his elbows on the table. He felt a garrulousness coming on him and he was frightened at the impulse. His voice did not sound like his voice, and his words amazed him.

'I don't get up here much,' he said. 'Do you know a place called Kate's?'

'Jesus! That rum is better than I thought,' Mr Lapierre said, and he went on sternly, 'You live on a ranch?'

'Yes. Got a place near King City. My name's Trask.'

'Glad to meet you. Married?'

'No. Not now.'

'Widower?'

'Yes.'

'You go to Jenny's. Let Kate alone. That's not good for you. Jenny's is right next door. You go there and you'll get everything you need.'

'Right next door?'

'Sure, you go east a block and half and turn right. Anybody'll tell you where the Line is.'

Adam's tongue was getting thick. 'What's the matter with Kate's?'

'You go to Jenny's,' said Mr Lapierre.

3

It was a dirty gusty evening. Castroville Street was deep in sticky mud, and Chinatown was so flooded that its inhabitants had laid planks across the narrow street that separated their hutches. The clouds against the evening sky were the grey of rats, and the air was not damp but dank. I guess the difference is that dampness comes down but dankness rises up out of rot and fermentation. The afternoon wind had dropped away and left the air raw and wounded. It was cold enough to shake out the curtains of rum in Adam's head without restoring his timidity. He walked quickly down the unpaved sidewalks, his eyes on the ground to avoid stepping in puddles. The row was dimly lit by the warning lantern where the railroad crossed the street and by one small carbon-filamented globe that burned on the porch of Jenny's.

Adam had his instructions. He counted two houses and nearly missed the third, so high and unbridled were the dark bushes in front of it. He looked in through the gateway at the dark porch, slowly opened the gate, and went up the overgrown path. In the half-darkness he could see the sagging dilapidated porch and the shaky steps.

The paint had long disappeared from the clapboard walls and no work had ever been done on the garden. If it had not been for the vein of light around the edges of the drawn blinds he would have passed on, thinking the house deserted. The stair treads seemed to crumple under his weight and the porch planks squealed as he crossed them.

The front door opened, and he could see a dim figure holding the knob.

A soft voice said, 'Won't you come in?'

The reception-room was dimly lighted by small globes set under rose-coloured shades. Adam could feel a thick carpet under his feet. He could see the shine of polished furniture and the gleam of gold picture frames. He got a quick impression of richness and order.

The soft voice said, 'You should have worn a raincoat. Do we know you?'

'No, you don't,' said Adam.

'Who sent you?'

'A man at the hotel.' Adam peered at the girl before him. She was dressed in black and wore no ornaments. Her face was sharp–pretty and sharp. He tried to think of what animal, what night prowler, she reminded him. It was some secret and predatory animal.

The girl said, 'I'll move nearer to a lamp if you like.'

'No.'

She laughed. 'Sit down–over here. You did come here for something, didn't you? If you'll tell me what you want I'll tell the proper girl.' The low voice had a precise and husky power. And she picked her words as one picks flowers in a mixed garden and took her time choosing.

She made Adam seem clumsy to himself. He blurted out, 'I want to see Kate.'

'Miss Kate is busy now. Does she expect you?'

'No.'

'I can take care of you, you know.'

'I want to see Kate.'

'Can you tell me what you want to see her about?'

'No.'

The girl's voice took on the edge of a blade sharpened on a stone. 'You can't see her. She's busy. If you don't want a girl or something else, you'd better go away.'

'Well, will you tell her I'm here?'

'Does she know you?'

'I don't know.' He felt his courage going. This was a remembered cold. 'I don't know. But will you tell her that Adam Trask would like to see her? She'll know then whether I know her or not.'

'I see. Well, I'll tell her.' She moved silently to a door on the right and opened it. Adam heard a few muffled words and a man looked through the door. The girl left the door open so that Adam would know he was not alone. On one side of the room heavy dark portières hung over a doorway. The girl parted the deep folds and disappeared. Adam sat back in his chair. Out of the side of his eyes he saw the man's head thrust in and then withdrawn.

Kate's private room was comfort and efficiency. It did not look at all like the room where Faye had lived. The walls were clad in saffron silk and the curtains were apple-green. It was a silken room–deep chairs with silk-upholstered cushions, lamps with silken shades, a broad bed at the far end of the room with a gleaming white satin cover on which were piled gigantic pillows. There was no picture on the wall, no photograph or personal thing of any kind. A dressing-table near the bed had no bottle or vial on its ebony top, and its sheen was reflected in triple mirrors. The rug was old and deep and Chinese, an apple-green dragon on saffron. One end of the room was bedroom, the centre social, and the other end was office–filing cabinets of golden oak, a large safe, black with gold lettering, and a roll-top desk with a green-hooded double lamp over it, a swivel chair behind it and a straight chair beside it.

Kate sat in the swivel chair behind the desk. She was still pretty. Her hair was blonde again. Her mouth was little and firm and turned up at the corners as always. But her outlines were not sharp anywhere. Her shoulders had become plump while her hands grew lean and wrinkled. Her cheeks were chubby and the skin under her chin was crêpe. Her breasts were still tiny, but a padding of fat protruded her stomach a little. Her hips were slender, but her legs and feet had thickened a little so that a bulge hung over her low shoes. And through her stockings, faintly, could be seen the wrappings of elastic bandage to support the veins.

Still, she was pretty and neat. Only her hands had really aged, the palms and fingerpads shining and tight, the backs wrinkled and splotched with brown. She was dressed severely in a dark dress with long sleeves, and the only contrast was billowing white lace at her wrists and throat.

The work of the years had been subtle. If one had been nearby it is probable that no change at all would have been noticed. Kate's cheeks were unlined, her eyes sharp and shallow, her nose delicate, and her lips thin and firm. The scar on her forehead was barely visible. It was covered with a powder tinted to match Kate's skin.

Kate inspected a sheaf of photographs on her roll-top desk, all the same size, all taken by the same camera and bright with flash powder. And although the characters were different in each picture, there was a dreary similarity about their postures. The faces of the women were never towards the camera.

Kate arranged the pictures in four piles and slipped each pile into a heavy manila envelope. When the knock came on her door she put the envelopes in a pigeon-hole of her desk. 'Come in. Oh, come in, Eva. Is he here?'

The girl came to the desk before she replied. In the increased light her face showed tight and her eyes were shiny. 'It's a new one, a stranger. He says he wants to see you.'

'Well, he can't, Eva. You know who's coming.'

'I told him you couldn't see him. He said he thought he knew you.

'Well, who is he, Eva?'

'He's a big gangly man, a little bit drunk. He says his name is Adam Trask.'

Although Kate made no movement or sound Eva knew something had struck home. The fingers of Kate's right hand slowly curled around the palm while the left hand crept like a lean cat towards the edge of the desk. Kate sat still as though she held her breath. Eva was jittery. Her mind went to the box in her dresser drawer where her hypodermic needle lay.

Kate said at last, 'Sit over there in that big chair, Eva. Just sit still a minute.' When the girl did not move Kate whipped one word at her. 'Sit!' Eva cringed and went to the big chair.

'Don't pick your nails,' said Kate.

Eva's hands separated, and each one clung to an arm of the chair.

Kate stared straight ahead at the green glass shade of her desk-lamp. Then she moved so suddenly that Eva jumped and her lips quivered. Kate opened the desk drawer and took out a folded paper. 'Here! Go to your room and fix yourself up. Don't take it all–no, I won't trust you.' Kate tapped the paper and tore it in two; a little white powder spilled before she folded the ends and passed one to Eva. 'Now hurry up! When you come downstairs, tell Ralph I want him in the hall close enough to hear the bell but not the voices. Watch him to see he doesn't creep up. If he hears the bell–no, tell him–no, let him do it his own way. After that bring Mr Adam Trask to me.'

'Will you be all right, Miss Kate?'

Kate looked at her until she turned away. Kate called after her, 'You can have the other half as soon as he goes. Now hurry up.'

After the door had closed Kate opened the right-hand drawer of her desk and took out a revolver with a short barrel. She swung the cylinder sideways and looked at the cartridges, snapped it shut and put it on her desk, and laid a sheet of paper over it. She turned off one of the lights and settled back in her chair. She clasped her hands on the desk in front of her.

When the knock came on the door she called, 'Come in,' hardly moving her lips.

Eva's eyes were wet, and she was relaxed. 'Here he is,' she said, and closed the door behind Adam.

He glanced quickly about before he saw Kate sitting so quietly behind the desk. He stared at her, and then he moved slowly towards her.

Her hands unclasped and her right hand moved towards the paper. Her eyes, cold and expressionless, remained on his eyes.

Adam saw her hair, her scar, her lips, her crêping throat, her arms and shoulders and flat breasts. He sighed deeply.

Kate's hand shook a little. She said, 'What do you want?'

Adam sat down in the straight chair beside the desk. He wanted to shout with relief but he said, 'Nothing now. I just wanted to see you. Sam Hamilton told me you were here.'

The moment he sat down the shake went out of her hand. 'Hadn't you heard before?'

'No,' he said. 'I hadn't heard. It made me a little crazy at first, but now I'm all right.'

Kate relaxed and her mouth smiled and her little teeth showed, the long canines sharp and white. She said, 'You frightened me.'

'Why?'

'Well, I didn't know what you'd do.'

'Neither did I,' said Adam and he continued to stare at her as though she were not alive.

'I expected you for a long time, and when you didn't come I guess I forgot you.'

'I didn't forget you,' he said. 'But now I can.'

'What do you mean?'

He laughed pleasantly. 'Now I see you, I mean. You know, I guess it was Samuel said I'd never seen you, and it's true. I remember your face but I had never seen it. Now I can forget it.'

Her lips closed and straightened and her wide-set eyes narrowed with cruelty. 'You think you can?'

'I know I can.'

She changed her manner. 'Maybe you won't have to,' she said. 'If you feel all right about everything, maybe we could get together.'

'I don't think so,' said Adam.

'You were such a fool,' she said. 'Like a child. You didn't know what things to do with yourself. I can teach you now. You seem to be a man.'

'You have taught me,' he said. 'It was a pretty sharp lesson.'

'Would you like a drink?'

'Yes,' he said.

'I can smell your breath–you've been drinking rum.' She got up and went to a cabinet for a bottle and two glasses, and when she turned back she noticed that he was looking at her fattened ankles. Her quick rage did not change the little smile on her lips.

She carried the bottle to the round table in the middle of the room and filled the two small glasses with rum. 'Come, sit over here,' she said. 'It's more comfortable.' As he moved to a big chair she saw that his eyes were on her protruding stomach. She handed him a glass, sat down, and folded her hands across her middle.

He sat holding his glass, and she said, 'Drink it. It's very good rum.' He smiled at her, a smile she had never seen. She said, 'When Eva told me you were here, I thought at first I would have thrown you out.'

'I would have come back,' he said. 'I had to see you–not that I mistrusted Samuel, but just to prove it to myself.'

'Drink your rum,' she said.

He glanced at her glass.

'You don't think I'd poison you–' She stopped and was angry that she had said it.

Smiling, he still gazed at her glass. Her anger came through to her face. She picked up her glass and touched her lips to it. 'Liquor makes me sick,' she said. 'I never drink it. It poisons me.' She shut her mouth tight and her sharp teeth bit down on her lower lip.

Adam continued to smile at her.

Her rage was rising beyond her control. She tossed the rum down her throat and coughed, and her eyes watered and she wiped her tears away with the back of her hand. 'You don't trust me very much,' she said.

'No, I don't.' He raised his glass and drank his rum, then got up and filled both glasses.

'I will not drink any more,' she said in panic.

'You don't have to,' Adam said. 'I'll just finish this and go along.'

The biting alcohol burned in her throat and she felt the stirring in her that frightened her. 'I'm not afraid of you or anyone else,' she said, and she drank off her second glass.

'You haven't any reason to be afraid of me,' said Adam. 'You can forget me now. But you said you had already.' He felt gloriously warm and safe, better than he had for many years. 'I came up to Sam Hamilton's funeral,' he said. 'That was a fine man. I'll miss him. Do you remember, Cathy, he helped you with the twins?'

In Kate the liquor raged. She fought, and the strain of the fight showed on her face.

'What's the matter?' Adam asked.

'I told you it poisoned me. I told you it made me sick.'

'I couldn't take the chance,' he calmly said. 'You shot me once. I don't know what else you've done.'

'What do you mean?'

'I've heard some scandal,' he said. 'Just dirty scandal.'

For the moment she had forgotten her will-fight against the cruising alcohol, and now she had lost the battle. The redness was up in her brain and her fear was gone and in its place was cruelty without caution. She snatched the bottle and filled her glass.

Adam had to get up to pour his own. A feeling completely foreign to him had arisen. He was enjoying what he saw in her. He liked to see her struggling. He felt good about punishing her, but he was also watchful. 'Now I must be careful,' he told himself. 'Don't talk, don't talk.'

He said aloud, 'Sam Hamilton had been a good friend to me all the years. I'll miss him.'

She had spilled some rum, and it moistened the corner of her mouth. 'I hated him,' she said. 'I would have killed him if I could.'

'Why? He was kind to us.'

'He looked–he looked into me.'

'Why not? He looked into me too, and he helped me.'

'I hate him,' she said. 'I'm glad he's dead.'

'Might have been good if I had looked into you,' Adam said.

Her lips curled. 'You are a fool,' she said. 'I don't hate you. You're just a weak fool.'

As her tension built up, a warm calm settled on Adam.

'Sit there and grin,' she cried. 'You think you're free, don't you? A few drinks and you think you're a man! I could crook my little finger and you'd come back slobbering, crawling on your knees.' Her sense of power was loose and her vixen carefulness abandoned. 'I know you,' she said. 'I know your cowardly heart.'

Adam went on smiling. He tasted his drink, and that reminded her to pour another for herself. The bottle neck chattered against her glass.

'When I was hurt I needed you,' she said. 'But you were slop. And when I didn't need you any more you tried to stop me. Take that ugly smirk off your face.'

'I wonder what it is you hate so much.'

'You wonder, do you?' Her caution was almost entirely gone. 'It isn't hatred, it's contempt. When I was a little girl I knew what stupid lying fools they were–my own mother and father pretending goodness. And they weren't good. I knew them. I could make them do whatever I wanted. I could always make people do what I wanted. When I was half-grown I made a man kill himself. He pretended to be good too, and all he wanted was to go to bed with me–a little girl.'

'But you say he killed himself. He must have been very sorry about something.'

'He was a fool,' said Kate. 'I heard him come to the door and beg. I laughed all night.'

Adam said, 'I wouldn't like to think I'd driven anybody out of the world.'

'You're a fool too. I remember how they talked. "Isn't she a pretty little thing, so sweet, so dainty?" And no one knew me. I made them jump through hoops and they never knew it.'

Adam drained his glass. He felt remote and inspective. He thought he could see her impulses crawling like ants and could read them. The sense of deep understanding that alcohol sometimes gives was on him. He said, 'It doesn't matter whether you liked Sam Hamilton. I found him wise. I remember he said one time that a woman who knows all about men usually knows one part very well and can't conceive the other parts, but that doesn't mean they weren't there.'

'He was a liar and a hypocrite too.' Kate spat out her words. 'That's what I hate, the liars, and they're all liars. That's what it is. I love to show them up. I love to rub their noses in their own nastiness.'

Adam's brows went up. 'Do you mean that in the whole world there's only evil and folly?'

'That's exactly what I mean.'

'I don't believe it,' Adam said quietly.

'You don't believe it! You don't believe it!' She mimicked him. 'Would you like me to prove it?'

'You can't,' he said.

She jumped up and ran to her desk, and brought the brown envelopes to the table. 'Take a look at these,' she said.

'I don't want to.'

'I'll show you anyway.' She took out a photograph. 'Look there. That's a state senator. He thinks he's going to run for Congress. Look at his fat stomach. He's got bubs like a woman. He likes whips. That streak there–that's a whip mark. Look at the expression on his face! He's got a wife and four kids and he's going to run for Congress. You don't believe! Look at this! This piece of white blubber is a council-man; this big red Swede has a ranch out near Blanco. Look here! This is a professor at Berkeley. Comes all the way down here to have the toilet splashed in his face–professor of philosophy. And look at this! This is a minister of the Gospel, a little brother of Jesus. He used to burn a house down to get what he wanted. We give it to him now another way. See that lighted match under his skinny flank?'

'I don't want to see these,' said Adam.

'Well, you have seen them. And you don't believe it! I'll have you begging to get in here. I'll have you screaming at the moon.' She tried to force her will on him, and she saw that he was detached and free. Her rage congealed to poison. 'No one has ever escaped,' she said softly. Her eyes were flat and cold but her fingernails were tearing at the upholstery of the chair, ripping and fraying the silk.

Adam sighed. 'If I had those pictures and those men knew it, I wouldn't think my life was very safe,' he said. 'I guess one of those pictures could destroy a man's whole life. Aren't you in danger?'

'Do you think I'm a child?' she asked.

'Not any more,' said Adam. 'I'm beginning to think you're a twisted human–or no human at all.'

She smiled. 'Maybe you've struck it,' she said. 'Do you think I want to be human? Look at those pictures! I'd rather be a dog than a human. But I'm not a dog. I'm smarter than humans. Nobody can hurt me. Don't worry about danger.' She waved at the filing cabinets. 'I have a hundred beautiful pictures in there, and those men know that if anything should happen to me–anything–one hundred letters, each one with a picture, would be dropped in the mail, and each letter will go where it will do the most harm. No, they won't hurt me.'

Adam asked, 'But suppose you had an accident, or maybe a disease?'

'That wouldn't make any difference,' she said. She leaned closer to him. 'I'm going to tell you a secret none of those men knows. In a few years I'll be going away. And when I do–those envelopes will be dropped in the mail anyway.' She leaned back in her chair, laughing.

Adam shivered. He looked closely at her. Her face and her laughter were childlike and innocent. He got up and poured himself another drink, a short drink. The bottle was nearly empty. 'I know what you hate. You hate something in them you can't understand. You don't hate their evil. You hate the good in them you can't get at. I wonder what you want, what final thing.'

'I'll have all the money I need,' she said. 'I'll go to New York and I won't be old. I'm not old. I'll buy a house, a nice house in a nice neighbourhood, and I'll have nice servants. And first I will find a man, if he's still alive, and very slowly and with the greatest attention to pain I will take his life away. If I do it well and carefully, he will go crazy before he dies.'

Adam stamped on the floor impatiently. 'Nonsense,' he said. 'This isn't true. This is crazy. None of this is true. I don't believe any of it.'

She said, 'Do you remember when you first saw me?'

His faced darkened. 'Oh, Lord, yes!'

'You remember my broken jaw and my split lips and my missing teeth?'

'I remember. I don't want to remember.'

'My pleasure will be to find the man who did that,' she said. 'And after that–there will be other pleasures.'

'I have to go,' Adam said.

She said, 'Don't go, dear. Don't go now, my love. My sheets are silk. I want you to feel those sheets against your skin.'

'You don't mean that?'

'Oh, I do, my love. I do. You aren't clever at love, but I can teach you. I will teach you.' She stood up unsteadily and laid her hand on his arm. Her face seemed fresh and young. Adam looked down at her hand and saw it wrinkled as a pale monkey's paw. He moved away in revulsion.

She saw his gesture and understood it and her mouth hardened.

'I don't understand,' he said. 'I know, but I can't believe. I know I won't believe it in the morning. It will be a nightmare dream. But no, it–it can't be a dream–no. Because I remember you are the mother of my boys. You haven't asked about them. You are the mother of my sons.'

Kate put her elbows on her knees and cupped her hands under her chin so that her fingers covered her pointed ears. Her eyes were bright with triumph. Her voice was mockingly soft. 'A fool always leaves an opening,' she said. 'I discovered that when I was a child. I am the mother of your sons. Your sons? I am the mother, yes–but how do you know you are the father?'

Adam's mouth dropped open. 'Cathy, who do you mean?'

'My name is Kate,' she said. 'Listen, my darling, and remember. How many times did I let you come near enough to me to have children?'

'You were hurt,' he said. 'You were terribly hurt.'

'Once,' said Kate, 'just once.'

'The pregnancy made you ill,' he protested. 'It was hard on you.'

She smiled at him sweetly. 'I wasn't too hurt for your brother.'

'My brother?'

'Have you forgotten Charles?'

Adam laughed. 'You are a devil,' he said. 'But do you think I could believe that of my brother?'

'I don't care what you believe,' she said.

Adam said, 'I don't believe it.'

'You will. At first you will wonder, and then you'll be unsure. You'll think back about Charles–all about him. I could have loved Charles. He was like me in a way.'

'He was not.'

'You'll remember,' she said. 'Maybe one day you will remember some tea that tasted bitter. You took my medicine by mistake–remember? Slept as you had never slept before and awakened late–thick-headed?'

'You were too hurt to plan a thing like that.'

'I can do anything,' she said. 'And now, my love, take off your clothes. And I will show you what else I can do.'

Adam closed his eyes and his head reeled with the rum. He opened his eyes and shook his head violently. 'It wouldn't matter–even if it were true,' he said. 'It wouldn't matter at all.' And suddenly he laughed because he knew that this was so. He stood too quickly and had to grab the back of his chair to steady himself against dizziness.

Kate leaped up and put both of her hands on his elbow. 'Let me help you take off your coat.'

Adam twisted her hands from his arm as though they were wire. He moved unsteadily towards the door.

Uncontrolled hatred shone in Kate's eyes. She screamed, a long and shrill animal screech. Adam stopped and turned towards her. The door banged open. The house pimp took three steps, poised, pivoted with his whole weight, and his fist struck Adam under the ear. Adam crashed to the floor.

Kate screamed, 'The boots! Give him the boots!'

Ralph moved closer to the fallen man and measured the distance. He noticed Adam's open eyes staring up at him. He turned nervously to Kate.

Her voice was cold. 'I said give him the boots. Break his face!'

Ralph said, 'He ain't fighting back. The fight's all out of him.'

Kate sat down. She breathed through her mouth. Her hands writhed in her lap. 'Adam,' she said, 'I hate you. I hate you now for the first time. I hate you! Adam, are you listening? I hate you!'

Adam tried to sit up, fell back, and tried again. Sitting on the floor, he looked up at Kate. 'It doesn't matter,' he said. 'It doesn't matter at all.'

He got to his knees and rested with his knuckles against the floor. He said, 'Do you know, I loved you better than anything in the world? I did. It was so strong that it took quite a killing.'

'You'll come crawling back,' she said. 'You'll drag your belly on the floor–begging, begging!'

'You want the boots now, Miss Kate?' Ralph asked.

She did not answer.

Adam moved slowly towards the door, balancing his steps carefully. His hand fumbled at the door-jamb.

Kate called, 'Adam!'

He turned slowly. He smiled at her as a man might smile at a memory. Then he went out and closed the door gently behind him.

Kate sat staring at the door. Her eyes were desolate.

CHAPTER 26

I

On the train back to King City from his trip to Salinas, Adam Trask was in a cloud of vague forms and sounds and colours. He was not conscious of any thoughts at all.

I believe there are techniques of the human mind whereby, in its dark deep, problems are examined, rejected, or accepted. Such activities sometimes concern facets a man does not know he has. How often one goes to sleep troubled and full of pain, not knowing what causes the travail, and in the morning a whole new direction and a clearness is there, maybe the result of the black reasoning. And again there are mornings when ecstasy bubbles in the blood, and the stomach and chest are tight and electric with joy, and nothing in the thoughts to justify or cause it.

Samuel's funeral and the talk with Kate should have made Adam sad and bitter, but they did not. Out of the grey throbbing an ecstasy arose. He felt young and free and filled with a hungry gaiety. He got off the train in King City, and, instead of going directly to the livery stable to claim his horse and buggy, he walked to Will Hamilton's new garage.

Will was sitting in his glass-walled office from which he could watch the activity of his mechanics without hearing the clamour of their work. Will's stomach was beginning to fill out richly.

He was studying an advertisement for cigars shipped direct and often from Cuba. He thought he was mourning for his dead father, but he was not. He did have some little worry about Tom, who had gone directly from the funeral to San Francisco. He felt that it was more dignified to lose oneself in business, as he intended to do, than in alcohol, as Tom was probably doing.

He looked up when Adam came into the office and waved his hand to one of the big leather chairs he had installed to lull his customers past the size of the bills they were going to have to pay.

Adam sat down. 'I don't know whether I offered my condolences,' he said.

'It's a sad time,' said Will. 'You were at the funeral?'

'Yes,' said Adam. 'I don't know whether you know how I felt about your father. He gave me things I will never forget.'

'He was respected,' said Will. 'There were over two hundred people at the cemetery–over two hundred.'

'Such a man doesn't really die,' Adam said, and he was discovering it himself. 'I can't think of him as dead. He seems maybe more alive to me than before.'

'That's true,' said Will, and it was not true to him. To Will, Samuel was dead.

'I think of things he said,' Adam went on. 'When he said them I didn't listen very closely, but now they come back, and I can see his face when he said them.'

'That's true,' said Will. 'I was just thinking the same thing. Are you going back to your place?'

'Yes, I am. But I thought I would come in and talk to you about buying an automobile.'

A subtle change came over Will, a kind of silent alertness. 'I would have thought you'd be the last man in the valley to get a car,' he observed, and watched through half-closed eyes for Adam's reaction.

Adam laughed. 'I guess I deserved that,' he said. 'Maybe your father is responsible for a change in me.'

'How do you mean?'

'I don't know as I could explain it. Anyway, let's talk about a car.'

'I'll give you the straight dope on it.' said Will. 'The truth of the matter is I'm having one hell of a time getting enough cars to fill my orders. Why, I've got a list of people who want them.'

'Is that so? Well, maybe I'll just have to put my name on the list.'

'I'd be glad to do that, Mr Trask, and–' He paused. 'You've been so close to the family that–well, if there should be a cancellation I'd be glad to move you up on the list.'

'That's kind of you,' said Adam.

'How would you like to arrange it?'

'How do you mean?'

'Well, I can arrange it so you pay only so much a month.'

'Isn't it more expensive that way?'

'Well, there's interest and carrying charge. Some people find it convenient.'

'I think I'll pay cash,' said Adam. 'There'd be no point in putting it off.'

Will chuckled. 'Not many people feel that way,' he said. 'And there's going to come a time when I won't be able to sell for cash without losing money.'

'I'd never thought of that,' said Adam. 'You will put me on the list, though?'

Will leaned towards him. 'Mr Trask, I'm going to put you on the top of the list. The first car that comes in, you're going to have.'

'Thank you.'

'I'll be glad to do it for you,' said Will.

Adam asked, 'How is your mother holding up?'

Will leaned back in his chair and an affectionate smile came on his face. 'She's a remarkable woman,' he said. 'She's like a rock. I think back on all the hard times we had, and we had plenty of them. My father wasn't very practical. He was always off in the clouds or buried in a book. I think my mother held us together and kept the Hamiltons out of the poorhouse.'

'She's a fine woman,' Adam said.

'Not only fine. She's strong. She stands on her two feet. She's a tower of strength. Did you come back to Olive's house after the funeral?'

'No, I didn't.'

'Well over a hundred people did. And my mother fried all that chicken and saw that everybody had enough.'

'She didn't!'

'Yes, she did. And when you think–it was her own husband.'

'A remarkable woman,' Adam repeated Will's phrase.

'She's practical. She knew they had to be fed and she fed them.'

'I guess she'll be all right, but it must be a great loss to her.'

'She'll be all right,' Will said. 'And she'll outlive us all, little tiny thing that she is.'

On his drive back to the ranch Adam found that he was noticing things he had not seen for years. He saw the wild flowers in the heavy grass, and he saw the red cows against the hillsides, moving up the easy ascending paths and eating as they went. When he came to his own land Adam felt a quick pleasure so sharp that he began to examine it. And suddenly he found himself saying loud in rhythm with his horse's trotting feet. 'I'm free, I'm free. I don't have to worry any more. I'm free. She's gone. She's gone out of me. Oh, Christ Almighty, I'm free!'

He reached out and stripped the fur from the silver-grey sage beside the road, and when his fingers were sticky with the sap he smelled the sharp penetrating odour on his fingers, breathed it deep into his lungs. He was glad to be going home. He wanted to see how the twins had grown in the two days he had been gone–he wanted to see the twins.

'I'm free, she's gone,' he chanted aloud.

2

Lee came out of the house to meet Adam, and he stood at the horse's head while Adam climbed down from the buggy.

'How are the boys?' Adam asked.

'They're fine. I made them some bows and arrows and they went hunting rabbits in the river bottom. I'm not keeping the pan hot, though.'

'Everything all right here?'

Lee looked at him sharply, was about to exclaim, changed his mind. 'How was the funeral?'

'Lots of people,' Adam said. 'He had lots of friends. I can't get it through my head that he's gone.'

'My people bury them with drums and scatter papers to confuse the devils and put roast pigs instead of flowers on the grave. We're a practical people and always a little hungry. But our devils aren't very bright. We can out-think them. That's some progress.'

'I think Samuel would have liked that kind of funeral,' said Adam. 'It would have interested him.' He noticed that Lee was staring at him. 'Put the horse away, Lee, and then come in and make some tea. I want to talk to you.'

Adam went into the house and took off his black clothes. He could smell the sweet and now sickish odour of rum about himself. He removed all of his clothes and sponged his skin with yellow soap until the odour was gone from his pores. He put on a clean blue shirt and overalls washed until they were soft and pale blue and lighter blue at the knees where the wear came. He shaved slowly and combed his hair while the rattle of Lee at the stove sounded from the kitchen. Then he went to the living-room. Lee had set out one cup and a bowl of sugar on the table beside the big chair. Adam looked around at the flowered curtains washed so long that the blossoms were pale. He saw the worn rugs on the floor and the brown path on the linoleum in the hall. And it was all new to him.

When Lee came in with the teapot Adam said, 'Bring yourself a cup, Lee. And if you've got any of that drink of yours, I could use a little. I got drunk last night.'

Lee said, 'You drunk? I can hardly believe it.'

'Well, I was. And I want to talk about it. I saw you looking at me.'

'Did you?' asked Lee, and he went to the kitchen to bring his cup and glasses and his stone bottle of ng-ka-py.

He said when he came back, 'The only times I've tasted it for years has been with you and Mr Hamilton.'

'Is that the same one we named the twins with?'

'Yes, it is.' Lee poured the scalding green tea. He grimaced when Adam put two spoonfuls of sugar in his cup.

Adam stirred his tea and watched the sugar crystals whirl and disappear into liquid. He said, 'I went down to see her.'

'I thought you might,' said Lee. 'As a matter of fact I don't see how a human man could have waited so long.'

'Maybe I wasn't a human man.'

'I thought of that too. How was she?'

Adam said slowly, 'I can't understand it. I can't believe there is such a creature in the world.'

'The trouble with you Occidentals is that you don't have devils to explain things with. Did you get drunk afterwards?'

'No, before and during. I needed it for courage, I guess.'

'You look all right now.'

'I am all right,' said Adam. 'That's what I want to talk to you about.' He paused and said ruefully, 'This time last year I would have run to Sam Hamilton to talk.'

'Maybe both of us have got a piece of him,' said Lee. 'Maybe that's what immortality is.'

'I seemed to come out of a sleep,' said Adam. 'In some strange way my eyes have cleared. A weight is off me.'

'You even use words that sound like Mr Hamilton,' said Lee. 'I'll build a theory for my immortal relatives.'

Adam drank his cup of black liquor and licked his lips. 'I'm free,' he said. 'I have to tell it to someone. I can live with my boys. I might even see a woman. Do you know what I'm saying?'

'Yes, I know. And I can see it in your eyes and in the way your body stands. A man can't lie about a thing like that. You'll like the boys, I think.'

'Well, at least I'm going to give myself a chance. Will you give me another drink and some more tea?'

Lee poured the tea and picked up his cup.

'I don't know why you don't scald your mouth, drinking it that hot.'

Lee was smiling inwardly. Adam, looking at him, realized that Lee was not a young man any more. The skin on his cheeks was stretched tight, and its surface shone as though it were glazed. And there was a red irritated rim around his eyes.

Lee studied the shell-thin cup in his hand and his was a memory smile. 'Maybe if you're free, you can free me.'

'What do you mean, Lee?'

'Could you let me go?'

'Why, of course you can go. Aren't you happy here?'

'I don't think I've ever known what you people call happiness. We think of contentment as the desirable thing, and maybe that's negative.'

Adam said, 'Call it that, then. Aren't you contented here?'

Lee said, 'I don't think any man is contented when there are things undone he wishes to do.'

'What do you want to do?'

'Well, one thing it's too late for. I wanted to have a wife and sons of my own. Maybe I wanted to hand down the nonsense that passes for wisdom in a parent, to force it on my own helpless children.'

'You're not too old.'

'Oh, I guess I'm physically able to father a child. That's not what I'm thinking. I'm too closely married to a quiet reading-lamp. You know, Mr Trask, once I had a wife. I made her up just as you did, only mine had no life outside my mind. She was good company in my little room. I would talk and she would listen, and then she would talk, would tell me all the happenings of a woman's afternoon. She was very pretty and she made coquettish little jokes. But now I don't know whether I would listen to her. And I wouldn't want to make her sad or lonely. So there's my first plan gone.'

'What was the other?'

'I talked to Mr Hamilton about that. I want to open a book-store in Chinatown in San Francisco. I would live in the back, and my days would be full of discussions and arguments. I would like to have in stock some of those dragon-carved blocks of ink from the dynasty of Sung. The boxes are worm-bored, and that ink is made from fir smoke and a glue that comes only from wild asses' skin. When you paint with that ink it may physically be black but it suggests to your eye and persuades your seeing that it is all the colours in the world. Maybe a painter would come by and we could argue about method and haggle about price.'

Adam said, 'Are you making this up?'

'No. If you are well and if you are free, I would like to have my little bookshop at last. I would like to die there.'

Adam sat silently for a while, stirring sugar into his lukewarm tea. Then he said, 'Funny. I found myself wishing you were a slave so I could refuse you. Of course you can go if you want to. I'll even lend you money for your bookstore.'

'Oh, I have the money. I've had it a long time.'

'I never thought of your going,' Adam said. 'I took you for granted.' He straightened his shoulders. 'Could you wait a little while?'

'What for?'

'I want you to help me get acquainted with my boys. I want to put this place in shape, or maybe sell it or rent it. I'll want to know how much money I have left and what I can do with it.'

'You wouldn't lay a trap for me?' Lee asked. 'My wish isn't as strong as it once was. I'm afraid I could be talked out of it or, what would be worse, I could be held back just by being needed. Please try not to need me. That's the worst bait of all to a lonely man.'

Adam said, 'A lonely man. I must have been far down in myself not to have thought of that.'

'Mr Hamilton knew,' said Lee. He raised his head and his fat lids let only sparks from his eyes show through. 'We're controlled, we Chinese,' he said. 'We show no emotion. I loved Mr Hamilton. I would like to go to Salinas tomorrow if you will permit it.'

'Do anything you want,' said Adam. 'God knows you've done enough for me.'

'I want to scatter devil papers,' Lee said. 'I want to put a little roast pig on the grave of my father.'

Adam got up quickly and knocked over his cup and went outside and left Lee sitting there.

CHAPTER 27

I

That year the rains had come so gently that the Salinas River did not overflow. A slender stream twisted back and forth in its broad bed of grey sand, and the water was not milky with silt but clear and pleasant. The willows that grow in the river-bed were well leafed, and the wild blackberry vines were thrusting their spiky new shoots along the ground.

It was very warm for March, and the kite wind blew steadily from the south and turned up the silver undersides of the leaves.

Against the perfect cover of vine and bramble and tangled drift sticks, a little grey brush rabbit sat quietly in the sun, drying his breast fur, wetted by the grass dew of his early feeding. The rabbit's nose crinkled, and his ears slewed around now and then, investigating small sounds that might possibly be charged with danger to a brush rabbit. There had been a rhythmic vibration in the ground audible through the paws, so that ears swung and nose wrinkled, but that had stopped. Then there had been a movement of willow branches twenty-five yards away and downwind, so that no odour of fear came to the rabbit.

For the last two minutes there had been sounds of interest but not of danger–a snap and then a whistle like that of the wings of a wild dove. The rabbit stretched out one hind leg lazily in the warm sun. There was a snap and a whistle and a grunting thud on fur. The rabbit sat perfectly still and his eyes grew large. A bamboo arrow was through his chest, and its iron tip deep in the ground on the other side. The rabbit slumped over on his side and his feet ran and scampered in the air for a moment before he was still.

From the willow two crouching boys crept. They carried four-foot bows, and tufts of arrows stuck their feathers up from the quivers behind their left shoulders. They were dressed in overalls and faded blue shirts, but each boy wore one perfect turkey tail-feather tied with tape against his temple.

The boys moved cautiously, bending low, self-consciously toeing-in like Indians. The rabbit's flutter of death was finished when they bent over to examine their victim.

'Right through the heart,' said Cal as though it could not be any other way. Aron looked down and said nothing. 'I'm going to say you did it,' Cal went on. 'I won't take credit. And I'll say it was a hard shot.'

'Well, it was,' said Aron.

'Well, I'm telling you. I'll give you credit to Lee and to Father.'

'I don't know as I want credit–not all of it,' said Aron. 'Tell you what. If we get another one we'll say we each hit one, and if we don't get any more, why don't we say we both shot together and we don't know who hit?'

'Don't you want credit?' Cal asked subtly.

'Well, not full credit. We could divide it up.'

'After all, it was my arrow,' said Cal.

'No, it wasn't.'

'You look at the feathers. See that nick? That's mine.'

'How did it get in my quiver? I don't remember any nick.'

'Maybe you don't remember. But I'm going to give you credit anyway.'

Aron said gratefully, 'No, Cal. I don't want that. We'll say we both shot at once.'

'Well, if that's what you want. But suppose Lee sees it was my arrow?'

'We'll just say it was in my quiver.'

'You think he'll believe that? He'll think you're lying.'

Aron said helplessly, 'If he thinks you shot it, why, we'll just let him think that.'

'I just wanted you to know,' said Cal. 'Just in case he'd think that.' He drew the arrow through the rabbit so that the white feathers were dark red with heart blood. He put the arrow in his quiver. 'You can carry him,' he said magnanimously.

'We ought to start back,' said Aron. 'Maybe Father's back by now.'

Cal said, 'We could cook that old rabbit and have him for our supper and stay out all night.'

'It's too cold at night, Cal. Don't you remember how you shivered this morning?'

'It's not too cold for me,' said Cal. 'I never feel cold.'

'You did this morning.'

'No, I didn't. I was just making fun of you, shivering and chattering like a milk baby. Do you want to call me a liar?'

'No,' said Aron. 'I don't want to fight.'

'Afraid to fight?'

'No. I just don't want to.'

'If I was to say you were scared, would you want to call me a liar?'

'No.'

'Then you're scared, aren't you?'

'I guess so.'

Aron wandered slowly away, leaving the rabbit on the ground. His eyes were very wide and he had a beautiful soft mouth. The width between his blue eyes gave him an expression of angelic innocence. His hair was fine and golden. The sun seemed to light up the top of his head.

He was puzzled–but he was often puzzled. He knew his brother was getting at something, but he didn't know what. Cal was an enigma to him. He could not follow the reasoning of his brother, and he was always surprised at the tangents it took.

Cal looked more like Adam. His hair was dark brown. He was bigger than his brother, bigger of bone, heavier in the shoulder, and his jaw had the square sternness of Adam's jaw. Cal's eyes were brown and watchful, and sometimes they sparkled as though they were black. But Cal's hands were very small for the size of the rest of him. The fingers were short and slender, the nails delicate. Cal protected his hands. There were few things that could make him cry, but a cut finger was one of them. He never ventured with his hands, never touched an insect or carried a snake about. And in a fight he picked up a rock or a stick to fight with.

As Cal watched his brother walking away from him there was a small sure smile on his lips. He called, 'Aron, wait for me!'

When he caught up with his brother he held out the rabbit. 'You can carry it,' he said kindly, putting his arm around his brother's shoulders. 'Don't be mad at me.'

'You always want to fight,' said Aron.

'No, I don't. I was only making a joke.'

'Were you?'

'Sure. Look–you can carry the rabbit. And we'll start back now if you want.'

Aron smiled at last. He was always relieved when his brother let the tension go. The two boys trudged up out of the river bottom and up the crumbling cliff to the level land. Aron's right trouser leg was well bloodied from the rabbit.

Cal said, 'They'll be surprised we got a rabbit. If Father's home, let's give it to him. He likes a rabbit for his supper.'

'All right,' Aron said happily. 'Tell you what. We'll both give it to him and we won't say which one hit it.'

'All right, if you want to,' said Cal.

They walked along in silence for a time and then Cal said, 'All this is our land–way to hell over the river.'

'It's Father's.'

'Yes, but when he dies it's going to be ours.'

This was a new thought to Aron. 'What do you mean, when he dies?'

'Everybody dies,' said Cal. 'Like Mr Hamilton. He died.'

'Oh, yes,' Aron said. 'Yes, he died.' He couldn't connect the two–the dead Mr Hamilton and the live father.

'They put them in a box and then they dig a hole and put the box in,' said Cal.

'I know that.' Aron wanted to change the subject, to think of something else.

Cal said, 'I know a secret.'

'What is it.'

'You'd tell.'

'No, I wouldn't, if you said not.'

'I don't know if I ought.'

'Tell me,' Aron begged.

'You won't tell?'

'No, I won't.'

Cal said, 'Where do you think our mother is?'

'She's dead.'

'No, she isn't.'

'She is too.'

'She ran away,' said Cal. 'I heard some men talking.'

'They are liars.'

'She ran away,' said Cal. 'You won't tell I told you?'

'I don't believe it,' said Aron. 'Father said she was in Heaven.'

Cal said quietly, 'Pretty soon I'm going to run away and find her. I'll bring her back.'

'Where did the men say she is?'

'I don't know, but I'll find her.'

'She's in Heaven,' said Aron. 'Why would Father tell a lie?' He looked at his brother, begging him silently to agree. Cal didn't answer him. 'Don't you think she's in Heaven with the angels?' Aron insisted. And when Cal still did not answer, 'Who were the men who said it?'

'Just some men. In the post office at King City. They didn't think I could hear. But I got good ears. Lee says I can hear the grass grow.'

Aron said, 'What would she want to run away for?'

'How do I know? Maybe she didn't like us.'

Aron inspected this heresy. 'No,' he said. 'The men were liars. Father said she's in Heaven. And you know how he don't like to talk about her.'

'Maybe that's because she ran away.'

'No. I asked Lee. Know what Lee said? Lee said, "Your mother loved you and she still does." And Lee gave me a star to look at. He said maybe that was our mother and she would love us as long as that light was there. Do you think Lee is a liar?' Through his gathering tears Aron could see his brother's eyes, hard and reasonable. There were no tears in Cal's eyes.

Cal felt pleasantly excited. He had found another implement, another secret tool, to use for any purpose he needed. He studied Aron, saw his quivering lips, but he noticed in time the flaring nostrils. Aron would cry, but sometimes, pushed to tears, Aron would fight too. And, when Aron cried and fought at the same time he was dangerous. Nothing could hurt him and nothing could stop him. Once Lee had held him in his lap, clasping his still flailing fists to his sides, until after a long time he relaxed. And his nostrils had flared then.

Cal put his new tool away. He could bring it out any time, and he knew it was the sharpest weapon he had found. He would inspect it at his ease and judge when and how to use it.

He made his decision almost too late. Aron leaped at him and the limp body of the rabbit slashed against his face. Cal jumped back and cried, 'I was just joking. Honest, Aron, it was only a joke.'

Aron stopped. Pain and puzzlement were on his face. 'I don't like that joke,' he said, and he sniffled and wiped his nose on his sleeve.

Cal came close to him and hugged him and kissed him on the cheek. 'I won't do it any more,' he said.

The boys trudged along silently for a while. The light of day began to withdraw. Cal looked over his shoulder at the thunderhead sailing blackly over the mountains on the nervous March wind. 'Going to storm,' he said. 'Going to be a bastard.'

Aron said, 'Did you really hear those men?'

'Maybe I only thought I did,' Cal said quickly. 'Jesus, look at that cloud!'

Aron turned round to look at the black monster. It ballooned in great dark rolls above, and beneath it drew a long trailing skirt of rain, and as they looked the cloud rumbled and flashed fire. Borne on the wind, the cloud-burst drummed hollowly on the fat wet hills across the valley and moved out over the flat lands. The boys turned and ran for home, and the cloud boomed at their backs and the lightning shattered the air into quaking pieces. The cloud caught up with them, and the first stout drops plopped on the ground out of the riven sky. They could smell the sweet odour of ozone. Running, they sniffed the thunder smell.

As they ran across the country road and on to the wheel tracks that led to their own home draw the water struck them. The rain fell in sheets and in columns. Instantly they were soaked through, and their hair plastered down on their foreheads and streamed into their eyes, and the turkey feathers at their temples bent over with the weight of water.

Now that they were as wet as they could get the boys stopped running. There was no reason to run for cover. They looked at each other and laughed for joy. Aron wrung out the rabbit and tossed it in the air and caught it and threw it to Cal. And Cal, feeling silly, put it around his neck with the head and hind feet under his chin. Both boys leaned over and laughed hysterically. The rain roared on the oak trees in the home draw and the wind disturbed their high dignity.

2

The twins came in sight of the ranch buildings in time to see Lee, his head through the centre hole of a yellow oilskin poncho, leading a strange horse and a flimsy rubber-tyred buggy towards the shed. 'Somebody's here,' said Cal. 'Will you look at that rig?'

They began to run again, for there was a certain deliciousness about visitors. Near the steps they slowed down, moved cautiously round the house, for there was a certain fearsomeness about visitors too. They went in the back way and stood dripping in the kitchen.

They heard voices in the living-room–their father's voice and another, a man's voice. And then a third voice stiffened their stomachs and rippled a little chill up their spines. It was a woman's voice. Those boys had had very little experience with women. They tiptoed into their own room and stood looking at each other.

'Who do you s'pose it is?' Cal said.

An emotion like a light had burst in Aron. He wanted to shout, 'Maybe it's our mother. Maybe she's come back.' And then he remembered that she was in Heaven and people do not come back from there. He said, 'I don't know. I'm going to put on dry clothes.'

The boys put on clean dry clothes, which were exact replicas of the sopping clothes they were taking off. They took off the wet turkey feathers and combed their hair back with their fingers. And all the while they could hear the voices, mostly low-pitched, and then the high woman's voice, and at once they froze, listening, for they heard a child's voice–a girl's voice–and this was such an excitement that they did not even speak of hearing it.

Silently they edged into the hall and crept towards the door to the living-room. Cal turned the door-knob very, very slowly and lifted it up so that no creak would betray them.

Only the smallest crack was open when Lee came in by the back door, shuffled along the hall, getting out of his poncho, and caught them there. 'Lilly boy peek?' he said in pidgin, and when Cal closed the door and the latch clicked Lee said quickly, 'Your father's home. You'd better go in.'

Aron whispered hoarsely, 'Who else is there?'

'Just some people going by. The rain drove them in.' Lee put his hand over Cal's on the door-knob and turned it and opened the door.

'Boys come along home,' he said and left them there, exposed in the opening.

Adam cried, 'Come in, boys! Come on in!'

The two carried their heads low and darted glances at the strangers and shuffled their feet. There was a man in city clothes and a woman in the fanciest clothes ever. Her dust-coat and a hat and veil lay on a chair beside her, and she seemed to the boys to be clad entirely in black silk and lace. Black lace even climbed up little sticks and hugged her throat. That was enough for one day, but it wasn't all. Beside the woman sat a girl, a little younger maybe than the twins, but not much. She wore a blue-checked sunbonnet with lace around the front. Her dress was flowery, and a little apron with pockets was tied around her middle. Her skirt was turned back, showing a petticoat of red knitted yarn with tatting around the edge. The boys could not see her face because of the sunbonnet, but her hands were folded in her lap, and it was easy to see the little gold seal ring she wore on her third finger.

Neither boy had drawn a breath and the red rings were beginning to flare at the back of their eyes from holding their breath.

'These are my boys,' their father said. 'They're twins. That's Aron and this is Caleb. Boys, shake hands with our guests.'

The boys moved forward, heads down, hands up, in a gesture very like surrender and despair. Their limp fists were pumped by the gentleman and then by the lacy lady. Aron was first, and he turned away from the little girl, but the lady said, 'Aren't you going to say how do to my daughter?'

Aron shuddered and surrendered his hand in the direction of the girl with the hidden face. Nothing happened. His lifeless sausages were not gripped, or wrung, or squeezed, or racheted. His hand simply hung on the air in front of her. Aron peeked up through his eyelashes to see what was going on.

Her head was down too, and she had the advantage of the sunbonnet. Her small right hand with the signet ring on the middle finger was stuck out too, but it made no move towards Aron's hand.

He stole a glance at the lady. She was smiling, her lips parted. The room seemed crushed with silence. And then Aron heard a ripping snicker from Cal.

Aron reached out and grabbed her hand and pumped it up and down three times. It was as soft as a handful of pearls. He felt a pleasure that burned him. He dropped her hand and concealed his in his overall pocket. As he backed hastily away he saw Cal step up and shake hands formally and say, 'How do.' Aron had forgotten to say it, so he said it now after his brother, and it sounded strange. Adam and his guests laughed.

Adam said, 'Mr and Mrs Bacon nearly got caught in the rain.'

'We were lucky to be lost here,' Mr Bacon said. 'I was looking for the Long ranch.'

'That's farther. You should have taken the next turn off the country road to the south.' Adam continued to the boys, 'Mr Bacon is a county supervisor.'

'I don't know why, but I take the job very seriously,' said Mr Bacon, and he too addressed the boys. 'My daughter's name is Abra, boys. Isn't that a funny name?' He used the tone adults employ with children. He turned to Adam and said in poetic sing-song, '"Abra was ready ere I called her name; And though I called another, Abra came." Matthew Prior. I won't say I hadn't wanted a son–but Abra's such a comfort. Look up, dear.'

Abra did not move. Her hands were again clasped in her lap. Her father repeated with relish, '"And though I called another, Abra came."'

Aron saw his brother looking at the little sunbonnet without an ounce of fear. And Aron said hoarsely, 'I don't think Abra's a funny name.'

'He didn't mean funny that way,' Mrs Bacon explained. 'He only meant curious.' And she explained to Adam, 'My husband gets the strangest things out of books. Dear, shouldn't we be going?'

Adam said eagerly, 'Oh, don't go yet, ma'am. Lee is making some tea. It will warm you up.'

'Well, how pleasant!' Mrs Bacon said, and she continued, 'Children, it isn't raining any more. Go outside and play.' Her voice had such authority that they filed out–Aron first and Cal second and Abra following.

3

In the living-room Mr Bacon crossed his legs. 'You have a fine prospect here,' he said. 'Is it a sizeable piece?'

Adam said, 'I have a good strip. I cross the river to the other side. It's a good piece.'

'That's all yours across the county road then?'

'Yes, it is. I'm kind of ashamed to admit it. I've let it go badly. I haven't farmed it at all. Maybe I got too much farming as a child.'

Both Mr and Mrs Bacon were looking at Adam now, and he knew he had to make some explanation for letting his good land run free. He said, 'I guess I'm a lazy man. And my father didn't help me when he left me enough to get along on without working.' He dropped his eyes but he could feel the relief on the part of the Bacons. It was not laziness if he was a rich man. Only the poor were lazy. Just as only the poor were ignorant. A rich man who didn't know anything was spoiled or independent.

'Who takes care of the boys?' Mrs Bacon asked.

Adam laughed. 'What taking care of they get, and it isn't much, is Lee's work.'

'Lee?'

Adam became a little irritated with the questioning. 'I only have one man,' he said shortly.

'You mean the Chinese we saw?' Mrs Bacon was shocked.

Adam smiled at her. She had frightened him at first, but now he was more comfortable. 'Lee raised the boys, and he has taken care of me,' he said.

'But didn't they ever have a woman's care?'

'No, they didn't.'

'The poor lambs,' she said.

'They're wild but I guess they're healthy,' Adam said. 'I guess we've all gone wild like the land. But now Lee is going away. I don't know what we'll do.'

Mr Bacon carefully cleared the phlegm from his throat so it wouldn't be run over by his pronouncement. 'Have you thought about the education of your sons?'

'No–I guess I haven't thought about it much.'

Mrs Bacon said, 'My husband is a believer in education.'

'Education is the key to the future,' Mr Bacon said.

'What kind of education?' asked Adam.

Mr Bacon went on, 'All things come to men who know. Yes, I'm a believer in the torch of learning.' He leaned close and his voice became confidential. 'So long as you aren't going to farm your land, why don't you rent it and move to the county seat–near our good public schools?'

For just a second Adam thought of saying, 'Why don't you mind your own goddam business?' but instead he asked, 'You think that would be a good idea?'

'I think I could get you a good reliable tenant,' Mr Bacon said. 'No reason why you shouldn't have something coming in from your land if you don't live on it.'

Lee made a great stir coming in with the tea. He had heard enough of the tones through the door to be sure Adam was finding them tiresome. Lee was pretty certain they didn't like tea, and if they did, they weren't likely to favour the kind he had brewed. And when they drank it with compliments he knew that the Bacons had their teeth in something. Lee tried to catch Adam's eye but could not. Adam was studying the rug between his feet.

Mrs Bacon was saying, "My husband has served on his school board for many years–' but Adam didn't hear the discussion that followed.

He was thinking of a big globe of the world, suspended and swaying from a limb of one of his oak trees. And for no reason at all that he could make out, his mind leaped to his father, stumping about on his wooden leg, rapping on his leg for attention with a walking-stick. Adam could see the stern and military face of his father as he forced his sons through drill and made them carry heavy packs to develop their shoulders. Through his memory Mrs Bacon's voice droned on. Adam felt the pack loaded with rocks. He saw Charles's face grinning sardonically–Charles–the mean, fierce eyes, the hot temper. Suddenly Adam wanted to see Charles. He would take a trip–take the boys. He slapped his leg with excitement.

Mr Bacon paused in his talk. 'I beg your pardon?'

'Oh, I'm sorry,' Adam said. 'I just remembered something I've neglected to do.' Both Bacons were patiently, politely waiting for his explanation. Adam thought, 'Why not?' I'm not running for supervisor. I'm not on the school board. Why not?' He said to his guests, 'I just remembered that I have forgotten to write to my brother for over ten years.' They shuddered under his statement and exchanged glances.

Lee had been refilling the tea-cups. Adam saw his cheeks puff out and heard his happy snort as he passed to the safety of the hallway. The Bacons didn't want to comment on the incident. They wanted to be alone to discuss it.

Lee anticipated that it would be this way. He hurried out to harness up and bring the rubber-tyred buggy to the front door.

4

When Abra and Cal and Aron went out, they stood side by side on the small covered porch, looking at the rain splashing and dripping down from the wide-spreading oak trees. The cloudburst had passed into a distant echoing thunder roll, but it had left a rain determined to go on for a long time.

Aron said, 'That lady told us the rain had stopped.'

Abra answered him wisely, 'She didn't look. When she's talking she never looks.'

Cal demanded, 'How old are you?'

'Ten, going on eleven,' said Abra.

'Ho!' said Cal. 'We're eleven, going on twelve.'

Abra pushed her sunbonnet back. It framed her head like a halo. She was pretty, with dark hair in two braids. Her little forehead was round and domed, and her brows were level. One day her nose would be sweet and turned up where now it was still button-form. But two features would be with her always. Her chin was firm and her mouth was as sweet as a flower and very wide and pink. Her hazel eyes were sharp and intelligent and completely fearless. She looked straight into the faces of the boys, straight into their eyes, one after the other, and there was no hint of the shyness she had pretended inside the house.

'I don't believe you're twins,' she said. 'You don't look alike.'

'We are too,' said Cal.

'We are too,' said Aron.

'Some twins don't look alike,' Cal insisted.

'Lots of them don't,' Aron said. 'Lee told us how it is. If the lady has one egg, the twins look alike. If she has two eggs, they don't.'

'We're two eggs,' said Cal.

Abra smiled with amusement at the myths of these country boys. 'Eggs,' she said. 'Ho! Eggs.' She didn't say it loudly or harshly, but Lee's theory tottered and swayed and then she brought it crashing down. 'Which one of you is fried?' she asked. 'And which one is poached?'

The boys exchanged uneasy glances. It was their first experience with the inexorable logic of women, which is overwhelming even, or perhaps especially, when it is wrong. This was new to them, exciting and frightening.

Cal said, 'Lee is a Chinaman.'

'Oh, well,' said Abra kindly, 'why don't you say so? Maybe you're china eggs, then, like they put in a nest.' She paused to let her shaft sink in. She saw opposition struggle, disappear. Abra had taken control. She was the boss.

Aron suggested, 'Let's go to the old house and play there. It leaks a little but it's nice.'

They ran under the dripping oaks to the old Sanchez house and plunged in through its open door, which squeaked restlessly on rusty hinges.

The 'dobe house had entered its second decay. The great sala all along the front was half plastered, the line of white half way round and then stopping, just as the workmen had left it over ten years before. And the deep windows with their rebuilt sashes remained glassless. The new floor was streaked with water stain, and a clutter of old papers and darkened nail bags with their nails rusted to prickly balls filled the corner of the room.

As the children stood in the entrance a bat flew from the rear of the house. The grey shape swooped from side to side and disappeared through the doorway.

The boys conducted Abra through the house–opened closets to show wash-basins and toilets and chandeliers, still crated and waiting to be installed. A smell of mildew and of wet paper was in the air. The three children walked on tiptoe, and they did not speak for fear of the echoes from the walls of the empty house.

Back in the big sala the twins faced their guest. 'Do you like it?' Aron asked softly because of the echo.

'Yee-es,' she admitted hesitantly.

'Sometimes we play here,' Cal said boldly. 'You can come here and play with us if you like.'

'I live in Salinas,' Abra said in such a tone that they knew they were dealing with a superior being who hadn't time for bumpkin pleasures.

Abra saw that she had crushed their highest treasure, and while she knew the weaknesses of men she still liked them, and, besides, she was a lady. 'Sometimes, when we are driving by, I'll come and play with you–a little,' she said kindly, and both boys felt grateful to her.

'I'll give you my rabbit,' said Cal suddenly. 'I was going to give it to my father, but you can have it.'

'What rabbit?'

'The one we shot today–right through the heart with an arrow. He hardly even kicked.'

Aron looked at him in outrage. 'It was my–'

Cal interrupted. 'We will let you have it to take home. It's a pretty big one.'

Abra said, 'What would I want with a dirty old rabbit all covered in blood?'

Aron said, 'I'll wash him off and put him in a box and tie him with string, and if you don't want to eat him, you can have a funeral when you get time–in Salinas.'

'I go to real funerals,' said Abra. 'Went to one yesterday. There was flowers high as this roof.'

'Don't you want our rabbit?' Aron asked.

Abra looked at his sunny hair, tight-curled now, and at his eyes that seemed so near to tears, and she felt the longing and the itching burn in her chest that is the beginning of love. Also, she wanted to touch Aron, and she did. She put her hand on his arm and felt him shiver under her fingers. 'If you put it in a box,' she said.

Now that she had got herself in charge, Abra looked around and inspected her conquests. She was well above vanity now that no male principle threatened her. She felt kindly towards these boys. She noticed their thin washed-out clothes patched here and there by Lee. She drew on her fairy tales. 'You poor children,' she said, 'does your father beat you?'

They shook their heads. They were interested but bewildered.

'Are you very poor?'

'How do you mean?' Cal asked.

'Do you sit in the ashes and have to fetch water and faggots?'

'What's faggots?' Aron asked.

She avoided that by continuing, 'Poor darlings,' she began, and she seemed to herself to have a little wand in her hand tipped by a twinkling star. 'Does your wicked step-mother hate you and want to kill you?'

'We don't have a step-mother,' said Cal.

'We don't have any kind,' said Aron. 'Our mother's dead.'

His words destroyed the story she was writing but almost immediately supplied her with another. The wand was gone but she wore a big hat with an ostrich plume and she carried an enormous basket from which a turkey's feet protruded.

'Little motherless orphans,' she said sweetly. 'I'll be your mother. I'll hold you and rock you and tell you stories.'

'We're too big,' said Cal. 'We'd overset you.'

Abra looked away from his brutality. Aron, she saw, was caught up in her story. His eyes were smiling and he seemed almost to be rocking in her arms, and she felt again the tug of love for him. She said pleasantly, 'Tell me, did your mother have a nice funeral?'

'We don't remember,' said Aron. 'We were too little.'

'Well, where is she buried? You could put flowers on her grave. We always do that for Grandma and Uncle Albert.'

'We don't know,' said Aron.

Cal's eyes had a new interest, a gleaming interest that was close to triumph. He said naïvely, 'I'll ask our father where it is so we can take flowers.'

'I'll go with you,' said Abra. 'I can make a wreath. I'll show you how,' She noticed that Aron had not spoken. 'Don't you want to make a wreath?'

'Yes,' he said.

She had to touch him again. She patted his shoulder and then touched his cheek. 'Your mamma will like that,' she said. 'Even in Heaven they look down and notice. My father says they do. He knows a poem about it.'

Aron said, 'I'll go and wrap up the rabbit. I've got the box my pants came in.' He ran out of the old house. Cal watched him go. He was smiling.

'What are you laughing at?' Abra asked.

'Oh, nothing,' he said. Cal's eyes stayed on her.

She tried to stare him down. She was an expert at staring down, but Cal did not look away. At very first he had felt a shyness, but that was gone now, and the sense of triumph at destroying Abra's control made him laugh. He knew she preferred his brother, but that was nothing new to him. Nearly everyone preferred Aron with his golden hair and the openness that allowed his affection to plunge like a puppy. Cal's emotions hid deep in him and peered out, ready to retreat or attack. He was starting to punish Abra for liking his brother, and this was nothing new either. He had done it since he first discovered he could. And secret punishment had grown to be almost a creative thing with him.

Maybe the difference between the two boys can best be described in this way. If Aron should come upon an ant-hill in a little clearing in the brush, he would lie on his stomach and watch the complications of ant life–he would see some of them bringing food in the ant roads and others carrying the white eggs. He would see how two members of the hill on meeting put their antennae together and talked. For hours he would lie absorbed in the economy of the ground.

If, on the other hand, Cal came upon the same ant-hill, he would kick it to pieces and watch while the frantic ants took care of their disaster. Aron was content to be part of his world, but Cal must change it.

Cal did not question the fact that people liked his brother better, but he had developed a means for making it all right with himself. He planned and waited until one time that admiring person exposed himself, and then something happened and the victim never knew how or why. Out of revenge Cal extracted a fluid of power, and out of power, joy. It was the strongest, purest emotion he knew. Far from disliking Aron, he loved him because he was usually the cause for Cal's feeling of triumph. He had forgotten–if he had ever known–that he punished because he wished he could be loved as Aron was loved. It had gone so far that he preferred what he had to what Aron had.

Abra had started a process in Cal by touching Aron and by the softness of her voice towards him. Cal's reaction was automatic. His brain probed for a weakness in Abra, and so clever was he that he found one almost at once in her words. Some children want to be babies and some want to be adults. Few are content with their age. Abra wanted to be an adult. She used adult words and simulated, in so far as she was able, adult attitudes and emotions. She had left babyhood far behind, and she was not capable yet of being one of the grown-ups she admired. Cal sensed this, and it gave him the instrument to knock down her ant-hill.

He knew about how long it would take his brother to find the box. He could see in his mind what would happen. Aron would try to wash the blood off the rabbit, and this would take time. Finding string would take more time, and the careful tying of bow knots still more time. And meanwhile Cal knew he was beginning to win. He felt Abra's certainty wavering and he knew that he could prod it further.

Abra looked away from him at last and said, 'What do you stare at a person for?'

Cal looked at her feet and slowly raised his eyes, going over her as coldly as if she were a chair. This, he knew, could make even an adult nervous.

Abra couldn't stand it. She said, 'See anything green?'

Cal asked, 'Do you go to school?'

'Of course I do.'

'What grade?'

'High fifth.'

'How old are you?'

'Going on eleven.'

Cal laughed.

'What's wrong with that?' she demanded. He didn't answer her. 'Come on, tell me! What's wrong with that?' Still no answer. 'You think you're mighty smart,' she said, and when he continued to laugh at her she said uneasily, 'I wonder what's taking your brother so long. Look, the rain's stopped.'

Cal said, 'I guess he's looking around for it.'

'You mean, for the rabbit?'

'Oh, no. He's got that all right–it's dead. But maybe he can't catch the other. It gets away.'

'Catch what? What gets away?'

'He wouldn't want me to tell,' said Cal. 'He wants it to be a surprise. He caught it last Friday. It bit him too.'

'Whatever are you talking about?'

'You'll see,' said Cal, 'when you open the box. I bet he tells you not to open it right off.' This was not a guess. Cal knew his brother.

Abra knew she was losing not only the battle but the whole war. She began to hate this boy. In her mind she went over the deadly retorts she knew and gave them all up in helplessness, feeling they would have no effect. She retired into silence. She walked out of the door and looked towards the house where her parents were.

'I think I'll go back,' she said.

'Wait,' said Cal.

She turned as he came up with her. 'What do you want?' she asked coldly.

'Don't be mad at me,' he said. 'You don't know what goes on here. You should see my brother's back.'

His change of pace bewildered her. He never let her get set in an attitude, and he had properly read her interest in romantic situations. His voice was low and secret. She lowered her voice to match his.

'What do you mean? What's wrong with his back?'

'All scars,' said Cal. 'It's the Chinaman.'

She shivered and tensed with interest. 'What does he do? Does he beat him?'

'Worse than that,' said Cal.

'Why don't you tell your father?'

'We don't dare. Do you know what would happen if we told?'

'No. What?'

He shook his head, 'No'–he seemed to think carefully–'I don't even dare tell you.'

At that moment Lee came from the shed leading the Bacons' horse hitched to the high spindly rig with rubber tyres. Mr and Mrs Bacon came out of the house and automatically they all looked up at the sky.

Cal said, 'I can't tell you now. The Chinaman would know if I told.'

Mrs Bacon called, 'Abra! Hurry! We're going.'

Lee held the restive horse while Mrs Bacon was helped up into the rig.

Aron came dashing round the house, carrying a cardboard box intricately tied with string in fancy bow knots. He thrust it at Abra. 'Here,' he said. 'Don't untie it until you get home.'

Cal saw revulsion on Abra's face. Her hands shrank away from the box.

'Take it dear,' her father said. 'Hurry, we're very late.' He thrust the box into her hands.

Cal stepped close to her. 'I want to whisper,' he said. He put his mouth to her ear. You've wet your pants,' he said. She blushed and pulled the sunbonnet up over her head. Mrs Bacon picked her up under the arms and passed her into the buggy.

Lee and Adam and the twins watched the horse pick up a fine trot.

Before the first turn Abra's hand came up and the box went sailing backwards into the road. Cal watched his brother's face and saw misery come into Aron's eyes. When Adam had gone back into the house and Lee was moving out with a pan of grain to feed the chickens, Cal put his arm around his brother's shoulders and hugged him reassuringly.

'I wanted to marry her,' Aron said. 'I put a letter in the box, asking her.'

'Don't be sad,' said Cal. 'I'm going to let you use my rifle.'

Aron's head jerked round. 'You haven't got a rifle.'

'Haven't I?' Cal said. 'Haven't I, though?'

CHAPTER 28

I

It was at the supper table that the boys discovered the change in their father. They knew him as a presence–as ears that heard but did not listen, eyes that looked but did not notice. He was a cloud of a father. The boys had never learned to tell him of their interests and discoveries, or of their needs. Lee had been their contact with the adult world, and Lee had managed not only to raise, feed, clothe, and discipline the boys, but had also given them a respect for their father. He was a mystery to the boys, and his word, his law, was carried down by Lee, who naturally made it up himself and ascribed it to Adam.

This night, the first after Adam's return from Salinas, Cal and Aron were first astonished and then a little embarrassed to find that Adam listened to them and asked questions, looked at them and saw them. The change made them timid.

Adam said, 'I hear you were hunting today.'

The boys became cautious as humans always are, faced with a new situation. After a pause Aron admitted, 'Yes, sir.'

'Did you get anything?'

This time a longer pause, and then, 'Yes, sir.'

'What did you get?'

'A rabbit.'

'With bows and arrows? Who got him?'

Aron said, 'We both shot. We don't know which one hit.'

Adam said, 'Don't you know your own arrows? We used to mark our arrows when I was a boy.'

This time Aron refused to answer and get into trouble. And Cal, after waiting, said, 'Well, it was my arrow, all right, but we think it might have got in Aron's quiver.'

'What makes you think that?'

'I don't know,' Cal said. 'But I think it was Aron hit the rabbit.'

Adam swung his eyes. 'And what do you think?'

'I think maybe I hit it–but I'm not sure.'

'Well, you both seem to handle the situation very well.'

The alarm went out of the faces of the boys. It did not seem to be a trap.

'Where is the rabbit?' Adam asked.

Cal said, 'Aron gave it to Abra as a present.'

'She threw it out,' said Aron.

'Why?'

'I don't know. I wanted to marry her too.'

'You did?'

'Yes, sir.'

'How about you, Cal?'

'I guess I'll let Aron have her,' said Cal.

Adam laughed, and the boys could not recall ever having heard him laugh. 'Is she a nice little girl?' he asked.

'Oh, yes,' said Aron. 'She's nice, all right. She's good and nice.'

'Well, I'm glad of that if she's going to be my daughter-in-law.'

Lee cleared the table and after a quick rattling in the kitchen he came back. 'Ready to go to bed?' he asked the boys.

They glared in protest. Adam said, 'Sit down and let them stay a while.'

'I've got the accounts together. We can go over them later,' said Lee.

'What accounts, Lee?'

'The house and ranch accounts. You said you wanted to know where you stood.'

'Not the accounts for over ten years, Lee!'

'You never wanted to be bothered before.'

'I guess that's right. But sit a while. Aron wants to marry the little girl who was here today.'

'Are they engaged?' Lee asked.

'I don't think she's accepted him yet,' said Adam. 'That may give us some time.'

Cal had quickly lost his awe of the changed feeling in the house and had been examining this ant-hill with calculating eyes, trying to determine just how to kick it over. He made his decision.

'She's a real nice girl,' he said. 'I like her. Know why? Well, she said to ask you where our mother's grave is, so we can take some flowers.'

'Could we, Father?' Aron said. 'She said she would teach us how to make wreaths.'

Adam's mind raced. He was not good at lying, to begin with, and he hadn't practised. The solution frightened him, it came so quickly to his mind and so glibly to his tongue. Adam said, 'I wish we could do that, boys. But I'll have to tell you. Your mother's grave is clear across the country where she came from.'

'Why?' Aron asked.

'Well, some people want to be buried in the place they came from.'

'How did she get there?' Cal asked.

'We put her on a train and sent her home–didn't we, Lee?'

Lee nodded. 'It's the same with us,' he said. 'Nearly all Chinese get sent home to China after they die.'

'I know that,' said Aron. 'You told us before.'

'Did I?' Lee asked.

'Sure you did,' said Cal. He was vaguely disappointed.

Adam quickly changed the subject. 'Mr Bacon made a suggestion this afternoon,' he began. 'I'd like you boys to think about it. He said it might be better for you if we moved to Salinas–better schools and lots of other children to play with.'

The thought stunned the twins. Cal asked, 'How about here?'

'Well, we'd keep the ranch in case we want to come back.'

Aron said, 'Abra lives in Salinas.' And that was enough for Aron. Already he had forgotten the sailing box. All he could think of was a small apron and a sunbonnet and soft little fingers.

Adam said, 'Well, you think about it. Maybe you should go to bed now. Why didn't you go to school today?'

'The teacher's sick,' said Aron.

Lee verified it. 'Miss Culp has been sick for three days,' he said. 'They don't have to go back until Monday. Come on, boys.'

They followed him obediently from the room.

2

Adam sat smiling vaguely at the lamp and tapping his knee with a forefinger until Lee came back. Adam said, 'Do they know anything?'

'I don't know,' said Lee.

'Well, maybe it was just the little girl.'

Lee went to the kitchen and brought back a big cardboard box. 'Here are the accounts. Every year has a rubber band round it. I've been over it. It's complete.'

'You mean all accounts?'

Lee said, 'You'll find a book for each year and receipted bills for everything. You wanted to know how you stood. Here it is–all of it. Do you really think you'll move?'

'Well, I'm thinking of it.'

'I wish there were some way you could tell the boys the truth.'

'That would rob them of the good thoughts about their mother, Lee.'

'Have you thought of the other danger?'

'What do you mean?'

'Well, suppose they find out the truth. Plenty of people know.'

'Well, maybe when they're older it will be easier for them.'

'I don't believe that,' said Lee. 'But that's not the worst danger.'

'I guess I don't follow you, Lee.'

'It's the lie I'm thinking of. It might infect everything. If they ever found out you'd lied to them about this, the true thing would suffer. They wouldn't believe anything then.'

'Yes, I see. But what can I tell them? I couldn't tell them the whole truth.'

'Maybe you can tell them a part truth, enough so that you won't suffer if they find out.'

'I'll have to think about that, Lee.'

'If you go to live in Salinas it will be more dangerous.'

'I'll have to think about it.'

Lee went on insistently, 'My father told me about my mother when I was very little, and he didn't spare me. He told me a number of times as I was growing. Of course it wasn't the same, but it was pretty dreadful. I'm glad he told me, though. I wouldn't like not to know.'

'Do you want to tell me?'

'No, I don't want to. But it might persuade you to make some change for your own boys. Maybe if you just said she went away and don't know where.'

'But I do know.'

'Yes, there's the trouble. It's bound to be all truth or part lie. Well, I can't force you.'

'I'll think about it,' said Adam. 'What's the story about your mother?'

'You really want to hear?'

'Only if you want to tell me.'

'I'll make it very short,' said Lee. 'My first memory is of living in a dark shack alone with my father in the middle of a potato field, and with it the memory of my father telling me the story of my mother. His language was Cantonese, but whenever he told the story he spoke in high and beautiful Mandarin. All right, then. I'll tell you–' And Lee looked back in time.

'I'll have to tell you that when you built the railroads in the West the terrible work of grading and laying ties and spiking the rails was done by many thousands of Chinese. They were cheap, they worked hard, and if they died no one had to worry. They were recruited largely from Canton, for the Cantonese are short and strong and durable, and also they are not quarrelsome. They were brought in by contract, and perhaps the history of my father was a fairly typical one.

'You must know that a Chinese must pay all of his debts on or before our New Year's Day. He starts every year clean. If he does not, he loses face; but not only that–his family loses face. There are no excuses.'

'That's not a bad idea,' said Adam.

'Well, good or bad, that's the way of it. My father had some bad luck. He could not pay a debt. The family met and discussed the situation. Ours is an honourable family. The bad luck was nobody's fault, but the unpaid debt belonged to the whole family. They paid my father's debt and then he had to repay them, and that was almost impossible.

'One thing the recruiting agents for the railroad companies did–they paid down a lump of money on the signing of the contract. In this way they caught a great many men who had fallen into debt. All of this was reasonable and honourable. There was only one black sorrow.

'My father was a young man recently married, and his tie to his wife was very strong and deep and warm, and hers to him must have been–overwhelming. Nevertheless, with good manners they said goodbye in the presence of the heads of the family. I have often thought that perhaps formal good manners may be a cushion against heartbreak.

'The herds of men went like animals into the black hold of a ship, there to stay until they reached San Francisco six weeks later. And you can imagine what those holds were like. The merchandise had to be delivered in some kind of working condition, so it was not mistreated. And my people have learnt through the ages to live close together, to keep clean and fed under intolerable conditions.

'They were a week at sea before my father discovered my mother. She was dressed like a man and she had braided her hair in a man's queue. By sitting very still and not talking she had not been discovered, and of course there were no examinations or vaccination then. She moved her mat closer to my father. They could not talk except mouth to ear in the dark. My father was angry at her disobedience, but he was glad too.

'Well, there it was. They were condemned to hard labour for five years. It did not occur to them to run away once they were in America, for they were honourable people and they had signed the contract.'

Lee paused. 'I thought I could tell it in a few sentences,' he said. 'But you don't know the background. I'm going to get a cup of water–do you want some?'

'Yes,' said Adam. 'But there's one thing I don't understand. How could a woman do that kind of work?'

'I'll be back in a moment,' said Lee, and he went to the kitchen. He brought back tin cups of water and put them on the table. He asked, 'Now what did you want to know?'

'How could your mother do a man's work?'

Lee smiled. 'My father said she was a strong woman, and I believe a strong woman may be stronger than a man, particularly if she happens to have love in her heart. I guess a loving woman is almost indestructible.'

Adam made a wry grimace.

Lee said, 'You'll see one day, you'll see.'

'I didn't mean to think badly,' said Adam. 'How could I know out of one experience? Go on.'

'One thing my mother did not whisper in my father's ear during that long miserable crossing. And because a great many were deadly seasick, no remark was made of her illness.'

Adam cried, 'She wasn't pregnant!'

'She was pregnant,' said Lee. 'And she didn't want to burden my father with more worries.'

'Did she know about it when she started?'

'No, she did not. I set my presence in the world at the most inconvenient time. It's a longer story than I thought.'

'Well, you can't stop now,' said Adam.

'No, I suppose not. In San Francisco the flood of muscle and bone flowed into cattle cars and the engines puffed up the mountains. They were going to dig hills in the Sierras and burrow tunnels under the peaks. My mother got herded into another car, and my father didn't see her until they got to their camp on a high mountain meadow. It was very beautiful, with green grass and flowers and the snow mountains all around. And only then did she tell my father about me.

'They went to work. A woman's muscles harden just as a man's do and my mother had a muscular spirit too. She did the pick and shovel work expected of her, and it must have been dreadful. But a panic worry settled on them about how she was going to have the baby.'

Adam said, 'Were they ignorant? Why couldn't she have gone to the boss and told him she was a woman and pregnant? Surely they would have taken care of her.'

'You see?' said Lee. 'I haven't told you enough. And that's why this is so long. They were not ignorant. These human cattle were imported for one thing only–to work. When the work was done, those who were not dead were shipped back. Only males were brought–no females. The country did not want them breeding. A man and a woman and a baby have a way of digging in, of pulling the earth where they are about them and scratching out a home. And then it takes all hell to root them out. But a crowd of men, nervous, lusting, restless, half sick with loneliness for women–why, they'll go anywhere, and particularly will they go home. And my mother was the only woman in this pack of half-crazy, half-savage men. The longer the men worked and ate, the more restless they became. To the bosses they were not people but animals which could be dangerous if not controlled. You can see why my mother did not ask for help. Why, they'd have rushed her out of the camp and–who knows?–perhaps shot and buried her like a diseased cow. Fifteen men were shot for being a little mutinous.

'No–they kept order the only way our poor species has ever learned to keep order. We think there must be better ways but we never learn them–always the whip, the rope, the rifle. I wish I hadn't started to tell you this–'

'Why should you not tell me?' Adam asked.

'I can see my father's face when he told me. An old misery come back, raw and full of pain. Telling it, my father had to stop and gain possession of himself, and when he continued he spoke sternly and he used hard sharp words almost as though he wanted to cut himself with them.

'These two managed to stay close together by claiming she was my father's nephew. The months went by and fortunately for them there was very little abdominal swelling, and she worked in pain and out of it. My father could only help her a little, apologizing, "My nephew is young and his bones are brittle." They had no plan. They did not know what to do.

'And then my father figured out a plan. They would run into the high mountains to one of the higher meadows, and there beside a lake they would make a burrow for the birthing, and when my mother was safe and the baby born, my father would come back and take his punishment. And he would sign for an extra five years to pay for his delinquent nephew. Pitiful as their escape was, it was all they had and it seemed a brightness. The plan had two requirements–the timing had to be right and a supply of food was necessary.'

Lee said, 'My parents'–and he stopped, smiling over his use of the word, and it felt so good that he warmed it up–'my dear parents began to make their preparations. They saved a part of their daily rice and hid it under their sleeping mats. My father found a length of string and filed out a hook from a piece of wire, for there were trout to be caught in the mountain lakes. He stopped smoking to save the matches issued. And my mother collected every tattered scrap of cloth she could find and unravelled edges to make thread and sewed this ragbag together with a splinter to make swaddling clothes for me. I wish I had known her.'

'So do I,' said Adam. 'Did you ever tell this to Sam Hamilton?'

'No. I didn't. I wish I had. He loved a celebration of the human soul. Such things were like a personal triumph to him.'

'I hope they got there,' said Adam.

'I know. And when my father would tell me I would say to him, "Get to that lake–get my mother there–don't let it happen again, not this time. Just once let's tell it: how you got to the lake and built a house of fir boughs." And my father became very Chinese then. He said, "There's more beauty in the truth even if it is dreadful beauty. The storytellers at the city gate twist life so that it looks sweet to the lazy and the stupid and the weak, and this only strengthens their infirmities, and teaches nothing, cures nothing, nor does it let the heart soar." '

'Get on with it,' Adam said irritably.

Lee got up and went to the window and he finished the story, looking out at the stars that winked and blew in the March wind.

'A little boulder jumped down a hill and broke my father's leg. They set the leg and gave him cripples' work, straightening used nails with a hammer on a rock. And whether with worry or work–it doesn't matter–my mother went into early labour. And then the half-mad men knew and they went all mad. One hunger sharpened another hunger, and one crime blotted out the one before it, and the little crimes committed against those starving men flared into one gigantic maniac crime.

'My father heard the shout "Woman" and he knew. He tried to run and his leg re-broke under him and he crawled up the ragged slope to the roadbed where it was happening.

'When he got there a kind of sorrow had come over the sky, and the Canton men were creeping away to hide and to forget that men can be like this. My father came to her on the pile of shale. She had not even eyes to see out, but her mouth still moved and she gave him his instructions. My father clawed me out of the tattered meat of my mother with his fingernails. She died on the shale in the afternoon.'

Adam was breathing hard. Lee continued in a singsong cadence, 'Before you hate those men you must know this. My father always told it at the last: No child ever had such care as I. The whole camp became my mother. It is a beauty–a dreadful kind of beauty. And now good night. I can't talk any more.'

3

Adam restlessly opened drawers and looked up at the shelves and raised the lids of boxes in his house and at last he was forced to ask Lee back and ask, 'Where's the ink and the pen?'

'You don't have any,' said Lee. 'You haven't written a word in years. I'll lend you mine if you want.' He went to his room and brought back a squat bottle of ink and a stub pen and a pad of paper and an envelope and laid them on the table.

Adam asked, 'How do you know I want to write a letter?'

'You're going to try to write to your brother, aren't you?'

'That's right.'

'It will be a hard thing to do after so long,' said Lee.

And it was hard. Adam nibbled and munched on the pen and his mouth became strained grimaces. Sentences were written and the page thrown away and another started. Adam scratched his head with the penholder. 'Lee, if I wanted to take a trip east, would you stay with the twins until I get back?'

'It's easier to go than to write,' said Lee. 'Sure I'll stay.'

'No. I'm going to write.'

'Why don't you ask your brother to come out here?'

'Say, that's a good idea, Lee. I didn't think of it.'

'It also gives you a reason for writing, and that's a good thing.'

The letter came fairly easily then, was corrected and copied fair. Adam read it slowly to himself before he put it in the envelope.

'Dear brother Charles,' it said. 'You will be surprised to hear from me after so long. I have thought of writing many times, but you know how a man puts it off.

'I wonder how this letter finds you. I trust in good health. For all I know you may have five or even ten children by now. Ha! Ha! I have two sons and they are twins. Their mother is not here. Country life did not agree with her. She lives in a town near-by and I see her now and then.

'I have a fine ranch, but I am ashamed to say I do not keep it up very well. Maybe I will do better from now on. I always did make good resolutions. But for a number of years I felt poorly. I am well now.

'How are you and how do you prosper? I would like to see you. Why don't you come to visit here. It is a great country and you might even find a place where you would like to settle. No cold winters here. That makes a difference to "old men" like us. Ha! Ha!

'Well, Charles, I do hope you will think about it and let me know. The trip will do you good. I want to see you. I have much to tell you that I can't write down.

'Well, Charles, write me a letter and tell me all the news of the old home. I suppose many things have happened. As you get older you hear mostly about people you knew that died. I guess that is the way of the world. Write quick and tell me if you will come to visit. Your brother Adam.'

He sat holding the letter in his hand and looking over it at his brother's dark face with its scarred forehead. Adam could see the glinting heat in the brown eyes, and as he looked he saw the lips writhe back from the teeth and the blind destructive animal take charge. He shook his head to rid his memory of the vision, and he tried to rebuild the face smiling. He tried to remember the forehead before the scar, but he could not bring either into focus. He seized the pen and wrote below his signature, 'P.S. Charles, I never hated you no matter what. I always loved you because you were my brother.'

Adam folded the letter and forced the creases sharp with his fingernails. He sealed the envelope flap with his fist. 'Lee!' he called, 'Oh, Lee!'

The Chinese looked in through the door.

'Lee, how long does it take a letter to go east–clear east?'

'I don't know,' said Lee. 'Two weeks maybe.'

CHAPTER 29

I

After his first letter to his brother in over ten years was mailed Adam became impatient for an answer. He forgot how much time had elapsed. Before the letter got as far as San Francisco he was asking aloud in Lee's hearing, 'I wonder why he doesn't answer. Maybe he's mad at me for not writing. But he didn't write either. No–he didn't know where to write. Maybe he's moved away.'

Lee answered. 'It's only been gone a few days. Give it time.'

'I wonder whether he would really come out here?' Adam asked himself, and he wondered whether he wanted Charles. Now that the letter was gone, Adam was afraid Charles might accept. He was like a restless child whose fingers stray to every loose article. He interfered with the twins, asked them innumerable questions about school.

'Well, what did you learn today?'

'Nothing!'

'Oh, come! You must have learned something. Did you read?'

'Yes, sir.'

'What did you read?'

'That old one about the grasshopper and the ant.'

'Well, that's interesting.'

'There's one about an eagle carries a baby away.'

'Yes, I remember that one. I forgot what happens.'

'We aren't to it yet. We saw the pictures.'

The boys were disgusted. During one of Adam's moments of fatherly bungling Cal borrowed his pocket-knife, hoping he would forget to ask for it back. But the sap was beginning to run freely in the willows. the bark would slip easily from a twig. Adam got his knife back to teach the boys to make willow whistles, a thing Lee had taught them three years earlier. To make it worse, Adam had forgotten how to make the cut. He couldn't get a peep out of his whistles.

At noon one day Will Hamilton came roaring and bumping up the road in a new Ford. The engine raced in its low gear, and the high top swayed like a storm-driven ship. The brass radiator and the Prestolite tank on the running-board were blinding with brass polish.

Will pushed up the brake lever, turned the switch straight down, and sat back in the leather seat. The car backfired several times without ignition because it was overheated.

'Here she is!' Will called with false enthusiasm. He hated Fords with a deadly hatred, but they were daily building his fortune.

Adam and Lee hung over the exposed insides of the car while Will Hamilton, puffing under the burden of his new fat, explained the workings of a mechanism he did not understand himself.

It is hard now to imagine the difficulty of learning to start, drive, and maintain an automobile. Not only was the whole process complicated, but one had to start from scratch. Today's children breathe in the theory, habits, and idiosyncrasies of the internal combustion engine in their cradles, but then you started with the blank belief that it would not run at all, and sometimes you were right. Also, to start the engine of a modern car you do just two things, turn a key and touch the starter. Everything else is automatic. The process used to be more complicated. It required not only a good memory, a strong man, an angelic temper, and a blind hope, but also a certain amount of practice of magic, so that a man about to turn the crank of a Model T might be seen to spit on the ground and whisper a spell.

Will Hamilton explained the car and went back and explained it again. His customers were wide-eyed, interested as terriers, co-operative, and did not interrupt, but as he began for the third time Will saw that he was getting no place.

'Tell you what!' he said brightly. 'You see this isn't my line. I wanted you to see her and listen to her before I made delivery. Now, I'll go back to town and tomorrow I'll send back this car with an expert, and he'll tell you more in a few minutes than I could in a week. But I just wanted you to see her.'

Will had forgotten some of his own instructions. He cranked for a while and then borrowed a buggy and a horse from Adam and drove to town, but he promised to have a mechanic out the next day.

2

There was no question of sending the twins to school the next day. They wouldn't have gone. The Ford stood tall and aloof and dour under the oak tree where Will had stopped it. Its new owners circled it and touched it now and then, the way you touch a dangerous horse to soothe him.

Lee said, 'I wonder whether I'll ever get used to it.'

'Of course you will,' Adam said without conviction. 'Why, you'll be driving all over the country first thing you know.'

'I will try to understand it,' Lee said. 'But drive it I will not.'

The boys made little dives in and out, to touch something and leap away. 'What's this do-hickey, Father?'

'Get your hands off that.'

'But what's it for?'

'I don't know, but don't touch it. You don't know what might happen.'

'Didn't the man tell you?'

'I don't remember what he said. Now you boys get away from it or I'll have to send you to school. Do you hear me, Cal? Don't open that.'

They had got up and were ready very early in the morning. By eleven o'clock hysterical nervousness had set in. The mechanic drove up in the buggy in time for the midday meal. He wore box-toed shoes and Duchess trousers and his wide square coat came almost to his knees. Beside him in the buggy was a satchel in which were his working clothes and tools. He was nineteen and chewed tobacco, and from his three months in automobile school he had gained a great though weary contempt for human beings. He spat and threw the reins at Lee.

'Put this hay-burner away,' he said. 'How do you tell which end is the front?' And he climbed down the rig as an ambassador comes out of a state train. He sneered at the twins and turned coldly to Adam. 'I hope I'm in time for dinner,' he said.

Lee and Adam stared at each other. They had forgotten about the noonday meal.

In the house the godling grudgingly accepted cheese and bread and cold meat and pie and coffee and a piece of chocolate cake.

'I'm used to a hot dinner,' he said. 'You better keep those kids away if you want any car left.' After a leisurely meal and a short rest on the porch the mechanic took his satchel into Adam's bedroom. In a few minutes he emerged dressed in striped overalls and a white cap which had 'Ford' printed on the front of its crown.

'Well,' he said. 'Done any studying?'

'Studying?' Adam asked.

'Ain't you even read the literature in the book under the seat?'

'I didn't know it was there,' said Adam.

'Oh, Lord,' said the young man disgustedly. With a courageous gathering of his moral forces he moved with decision towards the car. 'Might as well get started,' he said. 'God knows how long it's going to take if you ain't studied.'

Adam said, 'Mr Hamilton couldn't start it last night.'

'He always tries to start it on the magneto,' said the sage. 'All right! All right, come along. Know the principles of a internal combustion engine?'

'No,' said Adam.

'Oh, Jesus Christ!' He lifted the tin flaps. 'This-here is a internal combustion engine,' he said.

Lee said quietly, 'So young to be so erudite.'

The boy swung round towards him, scowling. 'What did you say?' he demanded, and he asked Adam. 'What did the Chink say?'

Lee spread his hands and smiled blandly. 'Say velly smaht fella,' he observed quietly. 'Mebbe go colledge. Velly wise.'

'Just call me Joe!' the boy said for no reason at all, and he added, 'College! What do them fellas know? Can they set a timer, huh? Can they file a point? College!' And he spat a brown disparaging comment on the ground. The twins regarded him with admiration, and Cal collected spit on the back of his tongue to practise.

Adam said, 'Lee was admiring your grasp of the subject.'

The truculence went out of the boy and magnanimity took its place. 'Just call me Joe,' he said. 'I *ought* to know it. Went to automobile school in Chicago. That's a real school–not like no college.' And he said, 'My old man says you take a good Chink, I mean a good one–why, he's about as good as anybody. They're honest.'

'But not the bad ones,' said Lee.

'Hell no! Not no high binders nor nothing like that. But good Chinks.'

'I hope I may be included in that group?'

'You look like a good Chink to me. Just call me Joe.'

Adam was puzzled at the conversation, but the twins weren't. Cal said experimentally to Aron, 'Jus' call me Joe,' and Aron moved his lips trying out, 'Jus' call me Joe.'

The mechanic became professional again, but his tone was kinder. An amused friendliness took the place of his former contempt. 'This-here,' he said, 'is a internal combustion engine.' They looked down at the ugly lump of iron with a certain awe.

Now the boy went on so rapidly that the words ran together into a great song of the new era. 'Operates through the explosion of gases in a enclosed space. Power of explosion is exerted on piston and through connecting rod and crankshaft through transmission thence to rear wheels. Got that?' They nodded blankly, afraid to stop the flow. 'They's two kinds, two-cycle and four-cycle. This-here is four-cycle. Got that?'

Again they nodded. The twins, looking up into his face with adoration, nodded.

'That's interesting,' said Adam.

Joe went on hurriedly. 'Main difference of a Ford automobile from other kinds is its planetary transmission which operates on a rev-rev-a-lu-shun-ary principle.' He pulled up for a moment, his face showing strain. And when his four listeners nodded again he cautioned them, 'Don't get the idea you know it all. The planetary system is, don't forget, rev-a-lu-shun-ary. You better study up on it in the book. Now, if you got all that we'll go on to Operation of the Automobile.' He said this in bold-face type, capital letters. He was obviously glad to be done with the first part of the lecture, but he was no gladder than his listeners. The strain of concentration was beginning to tell on them, and it was not made any better by the fact that they had not understood one single word.

'Come around here,' said the boy. 'Now you see that-there? That's the ignition key. When you turn that-there you're ready to go ahead. Now, you push this do-hickey to the left. That puts her on battery–see, where it says Bat. That means battery.' They craned their necks into the car. The twins were standing on the running-board.

'No–wait. I got ahead of myself. First you got to retard the spark and advance the gas, else she'll kick your goddam arm off. This-here–see it?–this-here's the spark. You push it up–get it?–*up*. Clear up. And this here's the gas–you push her down. Now I'm going to explain it and then I'm going to do it. I want you to pay attention. You kids get off the car. You're in my light. Get down, goddam it.' The boys reluctantly climbed down from the running-board; only their eyes looked over the door.

He took a deep breath. 'Now, you ready? Spark retarded, gas advanced.

Spark up, gas down. Now switch to battery–left, remember–left.' A buzzing like that of a gigantic bee sounded. 'Hear that? That's the contact in one of the coil boxes. If you don't get that, you got to adjust the points or maybe file them.' He noticed a look of consternation on Adam's face. 'You can study up on that in the book,' he said kindly.

He moved to the front of the car. 'Now this-here is the crank and–see this little wire sticking out of the radiator?–that's the choke. Now watch careful while I show you. You grab the crank like this and push till she catches. See how my thumb is turned down? If I grabbed her the other way with my thumb around her, and she was to kick, why, she'd knock my thumb off. Got it?'

He didn't look up but he knew they were nodding.

'Now,' he said, 'look careful. I push in and bring her up until I got compression, and then, why, I pull out this wire and I bring her around careful to suck gas in. Hear that sucking sound? That's choke. But don't pull her too much or you'll flood her. Now, I let go the wire and give her a hell of a spin, and as soon as she catches I run around and advance the spark and retard the gas and I reach over and throw the switch quick over to magneto–see where it says Mag?–and there you are.'

His listeners were limp. After all this they had just got the engine started.

The boy kept at them. 'I want you to say after me now so you learn it. Spark up–gas down.'

They repeated in chorus, 'Spark up-gas down.'

'Switch to Bat.'

'Switch to Bat.'

'Crank to compression, thumb down.'

'Crank to compression, thumb down.'

'Easy over–choke out.'

'Easy over–choke out.'

'Spin her.'

'Spin her.'

'Spark down–gas up.'

'Spark down–gas up.'

'Switch to Mag.'

'Switch to Mag.'

'Now we'll go over her again. Just call me Joe.'

'Just call you Joe.'

'Not that. Spark up–gas down.'

A kind of weariness settled on Adam as they went over the litany for the fourth time. The process seemed silly to him. He was relieved when a short time later Will Hamilton drove up in his low sporty red car. The boy looked at the approaching vehicle. 'That-there's got sixteen valves,' he said in a reverent tone. 'Special job.'

Will leaned out of his car. 'How's it going?' he asked.

'Just fine,' said the mechanic. 'They catch on quick.'

'Look, Roy, I've got to take you in. The new hearse knocked out a bearing. You'll have to work late and get it ready for Mrs Hawks at eleven tomorrow.'

Roy snapped to efficient attention. 'I'll get my clos',' he said and ran for the house. As he tore back with his satchel Cal stood in his way.

'Hey,' Cal said, 'I thought your name was Joe.'

'How do you mean, Joe?'

'You told us to call you Joe. Mr Hamilton says you're Roy.'

Roy laughed and jumped into the roadster. 'Know why I say call me Joe?'

'No. Why?'

'Because my name is Roy.' In the midst of his laughter he stopped and said sternly to Adam, 'You get that book under the seat and you study up. Hear me?'

'I will,' said Adam.

CHAPTER 30

I

Even as in Biblical times, there were miracles on the earth in those days. One week after the lesson a Ford bumped up the main street of King Street and pulled to a shuddering stop in front of the post office. Adam sat at the wheel with Lee beside him and the two boys straight and grand in the back seat.

Adam looked down at the floorboards, and all four chanted in unison, 'Brake on–advance gas–switch off.' The little engine roared and then stopped. Adam sat back for a moment, limp but proud, before he got out.

The postmaster looked out between the bars of his golden grill. 'I see you've got one of those damn things,' he said.

'Have to keep up with the times,' said Adam.

'I predict there'll come a time when you can't find a horse, Mr Trask.'

'Maybe so.'

'They'll change the face of the countryside. They get their clatter into everything,' the postmaster went on. 'We even feel it here. Man used to come for his mail once a week. Now he comes every day, sometimes twice a day. He just can't wait for his damn catalogue. Running around. Always running around.' He was so violent in his dislike that Adam knew he hadn't bought a Ford yet. It was a kind of jealousy coming out. 'I wouldn't have one around,' the postmaster said, and this meant that his wife was at him to buy one. It was the women who put the pressure on. Social status was involved.

The postmaster angrily shuffled through the letters from the T box and tossed out a long envelope. 'Well, I'll see you in the hospital,' he said viciously.

Adam smiled at him and took his letter and walked out.

A man who gets few letters does not open one lightly. He hefts it for weight, reads the name of the sender on the envelope and the address, looks at the handwriting, and studies the postmark and date. Adam was out of the post office and across the sidewalk to his Ford before he had done all of these things. The left-hand corner of the envelope had printed on it, Bellows and Harvey, Attorneys at Law, and their address was the town in Connecticut from which Adam had come.

He said in a pleasant tone, 'Why I know Bellows and Harvey, know them well. I wonder what they want?' He looked closely at the envelope. 'I wonder how they got my address?' He turned the envelope over and looked at the back. Lee watched him, smiling. 'Maybe the questions are answered in the letter.'

'I guess so,' Adam said. Once having decided to open the letter, he took out his pocket-knife, opened the big blade and inspected the envelope for a point of ingress, found none, held the letter up to the sun to make sure not to cut the message, tapped the letter to one end of the envelope, and cut off the other end. He blew in the end and extracted the letter with two fingers. He read the letter very slowly.

'Mr Adam Trask, King City, California. Dear Sir,' it began testily, 'For the last six months we have exhausted every means of locating you. We have advertised in newspapers all over the country without success. It was only when your letter to your brother was turned over to us by the local postmaster that we were able to ascertain your whereabouts.' Adam could feel their impatience with him. The next paragraph began a complete change of mood. 'It is our sad duty to inform you that your brother, Charles Trask, is deceased. He died of a lung ailment October 12 after an illness of two weeks, and his body rests in the Odd Fellows cemetery. No stone marks his grave. We presume you will want to undertake this sorrowful duty yourself.'

Adam drew a deep full breath and held it while he read the paragraph again. He breathed out slowly to keep the release from being a sigh. 'My brother Charles is dead,' he said.

'I'm sorry,' said Lee.

Cal said, 'Is he our uncle?'

'He was your Uncle Charles,' said Adam.

'Mine too?' Aron asked.

'Yours too.'

'I didn't know we had him,' Aron said. 'Maybe we can put some flowers on his grave. Abra could help us. She likes to.'

'It's a long way off–clear across the country.'

Aron said excitedly, 'I know! When we take flowers to our mother we'll take some to our Uncle Charles.' And he said a little sadly, 'I wish't I knew I had him before he was dead.' He felt that he was growing rich in dead relatives. 'Was he nice?' Aron asked.

'Very nice,' said Adam. 'He was my only brother, just like Cal is your only brother.'

'Were you twins too?'

'No–not twins.'

Cal asked, 'Was he rich?'

'Of course not,' said Adam. 'Where'd you get that idea?'

'Well, if he was rich we'd get it, wouldn't we?'

Adam said sternly, 'At a time of death it isn't a nice thing to talk about money. We're sad because he died.'

'How can I be sad?' said Cal. 'I never saw him.'

Lee covered his mouth with his hand to conceal a smile. Adam looked back at the letter, and again it changed mood with its paragraph.

'As attorneys for the deceased it is our pleasant duty to inform you that your brother through industry and judgement amassed a considerable fortune, which in land, securities, and cash is well in excess of one hundred thousand dollars. His will, which was drawn and signed in this office, is in our hands and will be sent to you on your request. By its terms it leaves all money, property, and securities to be divided equally between you and your wife. In the event that your wife is deceased, the total goes to you. The will also stipulates that if you are deceased, all property goes to your wife. We judge from your letter that you are still in the land of the living and we wish to offer our congratulations. Your obedient servants, Bellows and Harvey, by George B. Harvey.' And at the bottom of the page was scrawled, 'Dear Adam: Forget not thy servants in the days of thy prosperity. Charles never spent a dime. He pinched a dollar until the eagle screamed. I hope you and your wife will get some pleasure from the money. Is there an opening out there for a good lawyer? I mean myself. Your old friend, Geo. Harvey.'

Adam looked over the edge of the letter at the boys and at Lee. All three were waiting for him to continue. Adam's mouth shut to a line. He folded the letter, put it in its envelope, and placed the envelope carefully in his inside pocket.

'Any complications?' Lee asked.

'No.'

'I just thought you looked concerned.'

'I'm not. I'm sad about my brother.' Adam was trying to arrange the letter's information in his mind, and it was as restless as a setting hen scrounging into the nest. He felt that he would have to be alone to absorb it. He climbed into the car and looked blankly at the mechanism. He couldn't remember a single procedure.

Lee asked, 'Want some help?'

'Funny!' said Adam. 'I can't remember where to start.'

Lee and the boys began softly, 'Spark up–gas down, switch over to Bat.'

'Oh yes. Of course, of course.' And while the loud bee hummed in the coil box Adam cranked the Ford and ran to advance the spark and throw the switch to Mag.

They were driving slowly up the lumpy road of the home draw under the oak trees when Lee said, 'We forgot to get meat.'

Did we? I guess we did. Well, can't we have something else?'

'How about bacon and eggs?'

'That's fine. That's good.'

'You'll want to mail your answer tomorrow,' said Lee. 'You can buy meat then.'

'I guess so,' said Adam.

While dinner was preparing Adam sat staring into space. He knew he would have to have help from Lee, if only the help of a listener to clear his own thinking.

Cal had led his brother outside and conducted him to the wagon shed where the tall Ford rested. Cal opened the door and sat behind the wheel. 'Come on, get in!' he said.

Aron protested, 'Father told us to stay out of it.'

'He won't ever know. Get in!'

Aron climbed in timidly and eased back in the seat. Cal turned the wheel from side to side. 'Honk, honk,' he said, and then, 'Know what I think? I think Uncle Charles was rich.'

'He was not.'

'I bet you anything he was.'

'You think our father'd tell a lie.'

'I won't say that. I just bet he was rich.' They were silent for a while. Cal steered wildly around imaginary curves. He said, 'I bet you I can find out.'

'How do you mean?'

'What do you bet?'

'Nothing,' said Aron.

'How about your deer's-leg whistle? I bet you this here taw against that deer's-leg whistle that we get sent right to bed after supper. Is it a bet?'

'I guess so,' Aron said vaguely. 'I don't see why.'

Cal said, 'Father will want to talk to Lee. And I'm going to listen.'

'You won't dare.'

'You think I won't.'

'S'pose I was to tell.'

Cal's eyes turned cold and his face darkened. He leaned so close that his voice dropped to a whisper. 'You won't tell. Because if you do–I'll tell who stole his knife.'

'Nobody stole his knife. He's got his knife. He opened the letter with it.'

Cal smiled bleakly. 'I mean tomorrow,' he said. And Aron saw what he meant and knew he couldn't tell. He couldn't do anything about it. Cal was perfectly safe.

Cal saw the confusion and helplessness on Aron's face and felt his power, and it made him glad. He could out-think and out-plan his brother. He was beginning to think he could do the same thing to his father. With Lee, Cal's tricks did not work, for Lee's bland mind moved effortlessly ahead of him and was always there waiting, understanding, and at the last moment cautioning quietly, 'Don't do it.' Cal had respect for Lee and a little fear of him. But Aron here, looking helplessly at him, was a lump of soft mud in his hands. Cal suddenly felt a deep love for his brother and an impulse to protect him in his weakness. He put his arm around Aron.

Aron did not flinch or respond. He drew back a little to see Cal's face.

Cal said, 'See any green grass growing out of my head?'

Aron said, 'I don't know why you go for to do it.'

'How do you mean? Do what?'

'All the tricky, sneaky things,' said Aron.

'What do you mean, sneaky?'

'Well, about the rabbit, and sneaking here in the car. And you did something to Abra. I don't know what, but it was you made her throw the box away.'

'Ho,' said Cal. 'Wouldn't you like to know!' But he was uneasy.

Aron said slowly, 'I wouldn't want to know that. I'd like to know why you do it. You're always at something. I just wonder why you do it. I wonder what's it good for.'

A pain pierced Cal's heart. His planning suddenly seemed mean and dirty to him. He knew that his brother had found him out. He felt a longing for Aron to love him. He felt lost and hungry and he didn't know what to do.

Aron opened the door of the Ford and climbed down and walked out of the wagon shed. For a few moments Cal twisted the steering wheel and tried to imagine he was racing down the road. But it wasn't any good, and soon he followed Aron back towards the house.

2

When supper was finished and Lee had washed the dishes Adam said, 'I think you boys had better go to bed. It's been a big day.'

Aron looked quickly at Cal and slowly took his deer's-leg whistle out of his pocket.

Cal said, 'I don't want it.'

Aron said, 'It's yours now.'

'Well, I don't want it. I won't have it.'

Aron laid the bone whistle on the table. 'It'll be here for you,' he said.

Adam broke in, 'Say, what is this argument? I said you boys should go to bed.'

Cal put on his 'little boy' face. 'Why?' he asked. 'It's too early to go to bed.'

Adam said, 'That wasn't quite the truth I told you. I want to talk privately to Lee. And it's getting quite dark so you can't go outside, so I want you boys to go to bed–at least to your room. Do you understand?'

Both boys said, 'Yes, sir,' and they followed Lee down the hall to their bedroom at the back of the house. In their night-gowns they returned to say good night to their father.

Lee came back to the living-room and closed the door to the hall. He picked up the deer's-leg whistle and inspected it and laid it down. 'I wonder what went on there,' he said.

'How do you mean, Lee?'

'Well, some bet was made before supper, and just after supper Aron lost the bet and paid off. What were we talking about?'

'All I can remember is telling them to go to bed.'

'Well, maybe it will come out later,' said Lee.

'Seems to me you put too much stock in the affairs of children. It probably didn't mean anything.'

'Yes, it meant something.' Then he said, 'Mr Trask, do you think the thoughts of people suddenly become important at a given age? Do you have sharper feelings or clearer thoughts now than when you were ten? Do you see as well, hear as well, taste as vitally?'

'Maybe you're right,' said Adam.

'It's one of the great fallacies, it seems to me,' said Lee, 'that time gives much of anything but years and sadness to a man.'

'And memory.'

'Yes, memory. Without that, time would be unarmed against us. What did you want to talk to me about?'

Adam took the letter from his pocket and put it on the table. 'I want you to read this, to read it carefully, and then–I want to talk about it.' Lee took out his half-glasses and put them on. He opened the letter under the lamp and read it.

Adam asked, 'Well?'

'*Is* there an opening here for a lawyer?'

'How do you mean? Oh, I see. Are you making a joke?'

'No,' said Lee, 'I was not making a joke. In my obscure but courteous Oriental manner I was indicating to you that I would prefer to know your opinion before I offered mine.'

'Are you speaking sharply to me?'

'Yes I am,' said Lee. 'I'll lay aside my Oriental manner. I'm getting old and cantankerous. I am growing impatient. Haven't you heard of all Chinese servants that when they get old they remain loyal but they turn mean?'

'I don't want to hurt your feelings.'

'They aren't hurt. You want to talk about this letter. Then talk, and I will know from your talk whether I can offer an honest opinion or whether it is better to reassure you in your own.'

'I don't understand it,' said Adam helplessly.

'Well, you knew your brother. If you don't understand it, how can I, who never saw him?'

Adam got up and opened the hall door and did not see the shadow that slipped behind it. He went to his room and returned and put a faded brown daguerreotype on the table in front of Lee. 'That is my brother, Charles,' he said, and he went back to the hall door and closed it.

Lee studied the shiny metal under the lamp, shifting the picture this way and that to overcome the highlights. 'It's a long time ago,' Adam said. 'Before I went into the army.'

'Lee leaned close to the picture. It's hard to make out. But from his expression I wouldn't say your brother had much humour.'

'He hadn't any,' said Adam. 'He never laughed.'

'Well, that wasn't exactly what I meant. When I read the terms of your brother's will it struck me that he might have been a man with a particularly brutal sense of play. Did he like you?'

'I don't know,' said Adam. 'Sometimes I thought he loved me. He tried to kill me once.'

Lee said, 'Yes, that's in his face–both the love and murder. And the two made a miser of him, and a miser is a frightened man hiding in a fortress of money. Did he know your wife?'

'Yes.'

'Did he love her?'

'He hated her.'

Lee sighed. 'It doesn't really matter. That's not your problem, is it?'

'No. It isn't.'

'Would you like to bring the problem out and look at it?'

'That's what I mean.'

'Go ahead, then.'

'I can't seem to get my mind to work clearly.'

'Would you like me to lay out the cards for you? The uninvolved can sometimes do that.'

'That's what I want.'

'Very well, then.' Suddenly Lee grunted and a look of astonishment came over his face. He held his round chin in his thin small hand. 'Holy Thorns!' he said. 'I didn't think of that.'

Adam stirred uneasily. 'I wish you'd get off the tack you're sitting on,' he said irritably. 'You make me feel like a column of figures on a blackboard.'

Lee took a pipe from his pocket, a long slender ebony stem with a little cup-like brass bowl. He filled the thimble bowl with tobacco so fine-cut it looked like hair, then lighted the pipe, took four long puffs, and let the pipe go out.

'Is that opium?' Adam demanded.

'No,' said Lee. 'It's a cheap brand of Chinese tobacco, and it has an unpleasant taste.'

'Why do you smoke it, then?'

'I don't know,' said Lee. 'I guess it reminds me of something–something I associate with clarity. Not very complicated.' Lee's eyelids half closed. 'All right, then–I'm going to try and pull out your thoughts like egg noodles and let them dry in the sun. The woman is still your wife and she is still alive. Under the letter of the will she inherits something over fifty thousand dollars. That is a great deal of money. A sizeable chunk of good or evil could be done with it. Would your brother, if he knew where she is and what she is doing, want her to have the money? Courts always try to follow the wishes of the testator.'

'My brother would not want that,' said Adam. And then he remembered the girls upstairs in the tavern and Charles's periodic visits.

'Maybe you'll have to think for your brother,' said Lee. 'What your wife is doing is neither good nor bad. Saints can spring from any soil. Maybe with this money she would do some fine thing. There's no springboard to philanthropy like a bad conscience.'

Adam shivered. 'She told me what she would do if she had money. It was closer to murder than to charity.'

'You don't think she should have the money, then?'

'She said she would destroy many reputable men in Salinas. She can do it too.'

'I see,' said Lee. 'I'm glad I can take a detached view of this. The pants of their reputations must have some thin places. Morally, then, you would be against giving her the money?'

'Yes.'

'Well, consider this. She has no name, no background. A whore springs full-blown from the earth. She couldn't very well claim the money, if she knew about it, without your help.'

'I guess that's so. Yes, I can see that she might not be able to claim it without my help.'

Lee took up the pipe and picked out the ash with a little brass pin and filled the bowl again. While he drew in the four slow puffs his heavy lids raised and he watched Adam.

'It's a very delicate moral problem,' he said. 'With your permission I shall offer it for the consideration of my honourable relatives–using no names of course. They will go over it as a boy goes over a dog for tricks. I'm sure they will get some interesting results.' He laid his pipe on the table. 'But you don't have any choice, do you?'

'What do you mean by that?' Adam demanded.

'Well, do you? Do you know yourself so much less than I do?'

'I don't know what to do,' said Adam. 'I'll have to give it a lot of thought.'

Lee said angrily, 'I guess I've been wasting my time. Are you lying to yourself or only to me?'

'Don't speak to me like that!' Adam said.

'Why not? I have always disliked deception. Your course is drawn. What you will do is written–written in every breath you've ever taken. I'll speak any way I want to. I'm crochety. I feel sand under my skin. I'm looking forward to the ugly smell of old books and the sweet smell of good thinking. Faced with two sets of morals, you'll follow your training. What you call thinking won't change it. The fact that your wife is a whore in Salinas won't change a thing.'

Adam got to his feet. His face was angry. 'You are insolent now that you've decided to go away,' he cried. 'I tell you I haven't made up my mind what to do about the money.'

Lee sighed deeply. He pushed his small body erect with his hands against his knees. He walked wearily to the front door and opened it. He turned back and smiled at Adam. 'Bull shit!' he said amiably, and he went out and closed the door behind him.

3

Cal crept quietly down the dark hall and edged into the room where he and his brother slept. He saw the outline of his brother's head against the pillow in the double bed, but he could not see whether Aron slept. Very gently he eased himself in on his side and turned slowly and laced his fingers behind his head and stared at the myriads of tiny coloured dots that make up darkness. The window-blind bellied slowly in and then the night wind fell and the worn blind flapped quietly against the window.

A grey, quilted melancholy descended on him. He wished with all his heart that Aron had not walked away from him out of the wagon shed. He wished with all his heart that he had not crouched listening at the hall door. He moved his lips in the darkness and made the words silently in his head and yet he could hear them.

'Dear Lord,' he said, 'let me be like Aron. Don't make me mean. I don't want to be. If you will let everybody like me, why, I'll give you anything in the world, and if I haven't got it, why, I'll go for to get it. I don't want to be mean. I don't want to be lonely. For Jesus's sake, Amen.' Slow warm tears were running down his cheeks. His muscles were tight and he fought against making any crying sound or sniffle.

Aron whispered from his pillow in the dark, 'You're cold. You've got a chill.' He stretched out his hand to Cal's arm and felt the goose bumps there. He asked softly, 'Did Uncle Charles have any money?'

'No,' said Cal.

'Well, you were out there long enough. What did Father want to talk about?'

Cal lay still, trying to control his breathing.

'Don't you want to tell me?' Aron asked. 'I don't care if you don't tell me.'

'I'll tell,' Cal whispered. He turned on his side so that his back was towards his brother. 'Father is going to send a wreath to our mother. A great big goddam wreath of carnations.'

Aron half sat up in bed and asked excitedly, 'He is? How's he going to get it clear there?'

'On the train. Don't talk so loud.'

Aron dropped back to a whisper. 'But how's it going to keep fresh?'

'With ice,' said Cal. 'They're going to pack ice all around it.'

Aron asked, 'Won't it take a lot of ice?'

'A whole hell of a lot of ice,' said Cal. 'Go to sleep now.'

Aron was silent, and then he said, 'I hope it gets there fresh and nice.'

'It will,' said Cal. And in his mind he cried, 'Don't let me be mean.'

CHAPTER 31

I

Adam brooded around the house all morning, and at noon he went to find Lee, who was spading the dark compost earth of his vegetable garden and planting his spring vegetables, carrots and beets, turnips, peas, and string beans, rutabaga and kale. The rows were straight planted under a tight-stretched string, and the pegs at the row ends carried the seed package to identify the row. On the edge of the garden in a cold frame the tomato and bell pepper and cabbage sets were nearly ready for transplanting, waiting only for the passing of the frost danger.

Adam said, 'I guess I was stupid.'

Lee leaned on his spading fork and regarded him quietly.

'When are you going?' he asked.

'I thought I would catch the two-forty. Then I can get the eight o'clock back.'

'You could put it in a letter, you know,' said Lee.

'I've thought of that. Would you write a letter?'

'No. You're right. I'm the stupid one there. No letters.'

'I have to go,' said Adam. 'I thought in all directions and always a leash snapped me back.

Lee said, 'You can be unhonest in many ways, but not in that way. Well, good luck. I'll be interested to hear what she says and does.'

'I'll take the rig,' said Adam. 'I'll leave it at the stable at King City. I'm nervous about driving the Ford alone.'

It was four-fifteen when Adam climbed the rickety steps and knocked on the weather-beaten door of Kate's place. A new man opened the door, a square-faced Finn, dressed in shirt and trousers; red silk arm-bands held up his full sleeves. He left Adam standing on the porch and in a moment came back and led him to the dining-room.

It was a large undecorated room, the walls and woodwork painted white. A long square table filled the centre of the room, and on the white oilcloth cover the places were set–plates, cups and saucers, and cups upside down in the saucers.

Kate sat at the end of the table with an account book open before her. Her dress was severe. She wore a green eyeshade, and she rolled a yellow pencil restlessly in her fingers. She looked coldly at Adam as he stood in the doorway.

'What do you want now?' she asked.

The Finn stood behind Adam.

Adam did not reply. He walked to the table and laid the letter in front of her on top of the account book.

'What's this?' she asked, and without waiting for a reply she read the letter quickly. 'Go out and close the door,' she told the Finn.

Adam sat at the table beside her. He pushed the dishes aside to make a place for his hat.

When the door was closed Kate said, 'Is this a joke? No, you haven't got a joke in you.' She considered. 'Your brother might be joking. You sure he's dead?'

'All I have is the letter,' said Adam.

'What do you want me to do about it?'

Adam shrugged his shoulders.

Kate said, 'If you want me to sign anything, you're wasting your time. What do you want?'

Adam drew his finger slowly around his black ribbon hatband. 'Why don't you write down the name of the firm and get in touch with them yourself?'

'What have you told them about me?'

'Nothing,' said Adam. 'I wrote to Charles and said you were living in another town, nothing more. He was dead when the letter got there. The letter went to the lawyers. It tells about it.'

'The one who wrote the postscript seems to be a friend of yours. What have you written him?'

'I haven't answered the letter yet.'

'What do you intend to say when you answer it?'

'The same thing–that you live in another town.'

'You can't say we've been divorced. We haven't been.'

'I don't intend to.'

'Do you want to know how much it will take to buy me off? I'll take forty-five thousand in cash.'

'No.'

'What do you mean–no? You can't bargain.'

'I'm not bargaining. You have the letter, you know as much as I do. Do what you want.'

'What makes you so cocky?'

'I feel safe.'

She peered at him from under the green transparent eyeshade. Little curls of her hair lay on the bill like vines on a green roof. 'Adam, you're a fool. If you had kept your mouth shut nobody would ever have known I was alive.'

'I know that.'

'You know it. Did you think I might be afraid to claim the money? You're a damn fool if you think that.'

Adam said patiently, 'I don't care what you do.'

She smiled cynically at him. 'You don't, huh? Suppose I should tell you that there's a permanent order in the sheriff's office, left there by the old sheriff, that if I ever use your name or admit I'm your wife I'll get a floater out of the country and out of the state. Does that tempt you?'

'Tempt me to do what?'

'To get me floated away and take all the money.'

'I brought you the letter,' Adam said patiently.

'I want to know why.'

Adam said, 'I'm not interested in what you think or in what you think of me. Charles left you the money in his will. He didn't put any strings on it. I haven't seen the will, but he wanted you to have the money.'

'You're playing a close game with fifty thousand dollars,' she said, 'and you're not going to get away with it. I don't know what the trick is, but I'm going to find out.' And then she said, 'What am I thinking about? You're not smart. Who's advising you?'

'No one.'

'How about that Chinaman? He's smart.'

'He gave me no advice.' Adam was interested in his own complete lack of emotion. He didn't really feel that he was here at all. When he glanced at her he surprised an emotion on her face he had never seen before. Kate was afraid–she was afraid of him. But why?

She controlled her face and whipped the fear from it. 'You're just doing it because you're honest, is that it? You're just too sugar-sweet to live.'

'I hadn't thought of it,' Adam said. 'It's your money and I'm not a thief. It doesn't matter to me what you think about it.'

Kate pushed the eye shade back on her head. 'You want me to think you're just dropping this money in my lap. Well, I'll find out what you're up to. Don't think I won't take care of myself. Did you think I'd take such a stupid bait?'

'Where do you get your mail?' he asked patiently.

'What's that to you?'

'I'll write the lawyers where to get in touch with you.'

'Don't you do it!' she said. She put the letter in the account book and closed the cover. 'I'll keep this. I'll get legal advice. Don't think I won't. You can drop the innocence now.'

'You do that,' Adam said. 'I want you to have what is yours. Charles willed you the money. It isn't mine.'

'I'll find the trick. I'll find it.'

Adam said, 'I guess you can't understand it. I don't much care. There are so many things I don't understand. I don't understand how you could shoot me and desert your sons. I don't understand how you or anyone could live like this.' He waved his hand to indicate the house.

'Who asked you to understand?'

Adam stood up and took his hat from the table. 'I guess that's all,' he said. 'Goodbye.' He walked towards the door.

She called after him. 'You're changed, Mr Mouse. Have you got a woman at last?'

Adam stopped and slowly turned and his eyes were thoughtful. 'I hadn't considered before,' he said, and he moved towards her until he towered over her and she had to tilt back her head to look into his face. 'I said I didn't understand about you,' he said slowly. 'Just now it came to me what you don't understand.'

'What don't I understand, Mr Mouse?'

'You know about the ugliness in people. You showed me the pictures. You used all the sad, weak parts of a man, and God knows he has them.'

'Everybody–'

Adam went on, astonished at his own thoughts. 'But you–yes, that's right–you don't know about the rest. You don't believe I brought you the letter because I don't want your money. You don't believe I loved you. And the men who come to you here with their ugliness, the men in the pictures–you don't believe those men could have goodness and beauty in them. You see only one side, and you think–more than that, you're sure–that's all there is.'

She cackled at him derisively. 'In sticks and stones. What a sweet dreamer is Mr Mouse! Give me a sermon, Mr Mouse.'

'No. I won't because I seem to know that there's a part of you missing. Some men can't see the colour green, but they may never know they can't. I think you are only a part of a human. I can't do anything about that. But I wonder whether you ever feel that something invisible is all around you. It would be horrible if you knew it was there and couldn't see it or feel it. That would be horrible.'

Kate pushed back her chair and stood up. Her fists were clenched at her sides and hiding in the folds of her skirt. She tried to prevent the shrillness that crept into her voice.

'Our Mouse is a philosopher,' she said. 'But our Mouse is no better at that than he is at other things. Did you ever hear of hallucinations? If there are things I can't see, don't you think it's possible that they are dreams manufactured in your own sick mind?'

'No, I don't,' said Adam. 'No, I don't. And I don't think you do either.' He turned and went out and closed the door behind him.

Kate sat down and stared at the closed door. She was not aware that her fists beat softly on the white oilcloth. But she did know that the square white door was distorted by tears and that her body shook with something that felt like rage and also felt like sorrow.

2

When Adam left Kate's place he had over two hours to wait for the train back to King City. On an impulse he turned off Main Street and walked up Central Avenue to number 130, the high white house of Ernest Steinbeck. It was an immaculate and friendly house, grand enough, but not pretentious, and it sat inside its white fence, surrounded by its clipped lawn, and roses and cotoneasters lapped against its white walls.

Adam walked up the wide veranda steps and rang the bell. Olive came to the door and opened it a little, while Mary and John peeked around the edges of her.

Adam took off his hat. 'You don't know me. I'm Adam Trask. Your father was a friend of mine. I thought I'd like to pay my respects to Mrs Hamilton. She helped me with the twins.'

'Why, of course,' Olive said, and swung the wide door open. 'We've heard about you. Just a moment. You see, we've made a kind of retreat for Mother.'

She knocked on a door off the wide front hall and called, 'Mother! There's a friend to see you.'

She opened the door and showed Adam into a pleasant room where Liza lived. 'You'll have to excuse me,' she said to Adam. 'Catrina's frying chicken and I have to watch her. John! Mary! Come along. Come along.'

Liza seemed smaller than ever. She sat in a wicker rocking-chair and she was old and old. Her dress was a full wide-skirted black alpaca, and at her throat she wore a pin which spelled 'Mother' in golden script.

The pleasant little bed-sitting-room was crowded with photographs, bottles of toilet water, lace pin-cushions, brushes and combs, and the china and silver bureau-knacks of many birthdays and Christmases.

On the wall hung a huge tinted photograph of Samuel, which had captured a cold and aloof dignity, a scrubbed and dressed remoteness, which did not belong to him living. There was no twinkle in the picture of him, nor any of his inspective joyousness. The picture hung in a heavy gold frame, and to the consternation of all children its eyes followed a child about the room.

On a wicker table beside Liza was the cage of Polly parrot. Tom had bought the parrot from a sailor. He was an old bird, reputed to be fifty years old, and he had lived a ribald life and acquired the vigorous speech of a ship's fo'c'sle. Try as she would, Liza could not make him substitute psalms for the picturesque vocabulary of his youth.

Polly cocked his head sideways, inspecting Adam, and scratched his feathers at the base of his neck with a careful fore-claw. 'Come off it, you bastard,' said Polly unemotionally.

Liza frowned at him. 'Polly,' she said sternly, 'that's not polite.'

'Bloody bastard!' Polly observed.

Liza ignored the vulgarity. She held out her tiny hand. 'Mr Trask,' she said, 'I'm glad to see you. Sit down, won't you?'

'I was passing by, and I wanted to offer my condolences.'

'We got your flowers.' And she remembered, too, every bouquet after all this time. Adam had sent a fine pillow of everlastings.

'It must be hard to rearrange your life.'

Liza's eyes brimmed over and she snapped her little mouth shut on her weakness.

Adam said, 'Maybe I shouldn't bring up your hurt, but I miss him.'

Liza turned her head away. 'How is everything down your way?' she asked.

'Good this year. Lots of rainfalls. The feed's deep already.'

'Tom wrote to me,' she said.

'Button up,' said the parrot, and Liza scowled at him as she had at her growing children when they were mutinous.

'What brings you to Salinas, Mr Trask?' she asked.

'Why, some business.' He sat down in a wicker chair and it cricked under his weight. 'I'm thinking of moving up here. Thought it might be better for my boys. They get lonely on the ranch.'

'We never got lonely on the ranch,' she said harshly.

'I thought maybe the schools would be better here. My twins could have the advantages.'

'My daughter Olive taught at Peach Tree and Pleyto and the Big Sur.' Her tone made it clear that there were no better schools than those. Adam began to feel a warm admiration for her iron gallantry.

'Well, I was just thinking about it,' he said.

'Children raised in the country do better.' It was the law, and she could prove it by her own boys. Then she centred closely on him. 'Are you looking for a house in Salinas?'

'Well, yes, I guess I am.'

'Go see my daughter Dessie,' she said. 'Dessie wants to move back to the ranch with Tom. She's got a nice little house up the street next to Reynaud's Bakery.'

'I'll certainly do that,' said Adam. 'I'll go now. I'm glad to see you doing so well.'

'Thank you,' she said. 'I'm comfortable.' Adam was moving towards the door when she said, 'Mr Trask, do you ever see my son Tom?'

'Well, no, I don't. You see, I haven't been off the ranch.'

'I wish you would go and see him,' she said quickly. 'I think he's lonely.' She stopped as though horrified at this breaking over.

'I will. I surely will. Goodbye, ma'am.'

As he closed the door he heard the parrot say, 'Button up, you bloody bastard!' and Liza, 'Polly, if you don't watch your language, I'll thrash you.'

Adam let himself out of the house and walked up the evening street towards Main. Next to Reynaud's French Bakery he saw Dessie's house, set back in its little garden. The yard was so massed with tall privets that he couldn't see much of the house. A neatly painted sign was screwed to the front gate. It read: Dessie Hamilton, Dressmaker.

The San Francisco Chop House was on the corner of Main and Central and its windows were on both streets. Adam went in to get some dinner. Will Hamilton sat at the corner table, devouring a rib steak. 'Come and sit with me,' he called to Adam. 'Up on business?'

'Yes,' said Adam. 'I went to pay a call on your mother.'

Will laid down his fork. 'I'm just up here for an hour. I didn't go to see her because it gets her excited. And my sister Olive would tear the house down getting a special dinner for me. I just didn't want to disturb them. Besides, I have to go right back. Order a rib steak. They've got good ones. How is Mother?'

'She's got great courage,' said Adam. 'I find I admire her more all the time.'

'That she has. How she kept her good sense with all of us and with my father, I don't know.'

'Rib steak, medium,' said Adam to the waiter.

'Potatoes?'

'No–yes, french fried. Your mother is worried about Tom. Is he all right?'

Will cut off the edging of fat from his steak and pushed it to the side of his plate. 'She's got reason to worry,' he said. 'Something's the matter with Tom. He's moping around like a monument.'

'I guess he depended on Samuel.'

'Too much,' said Will. 'Far too much. He can't seem to come out of it. In some ways Tom is a great big baby.'

'I'll go and see him. Your mother says Dessie is going to move back to the ranch.'

Will laid his knife and fork down on the tablecloth and stared at Adam. 'She can't do it,' he said. 'I won't let her do it.'

'Why not?'

Will covered up. 'Well,' he said, 'she's got a nice business here. Makes a good living. It would be a shame to throw it away.' He picked up his knife and fork, cut off a piece of the fat, and put it in his mouth.

'I'm catching the eight o'clock home,' said Adam.

'So am I,' said Will. He didn't want to talk any more.

CHAPTER 32

I

Dessie was the beloved of the family. Mollie the pretty kitten, Olive the strong-headed, Una with clouds on her head, all were loved, but Dessie was the warm-beloved. Hers was the twinkle and the laughter infectious as chickenpox, and hers the gaiety that coloured a day and spread to people so that they carried it away with them.

I can put it this way. Mrs Clarence Morrison of 122 Church Street, Salinas, had three children and a husband who ran a dry goods store. On certain mornings, at breakfast, Agnes Morrison would say, 'I'm going to Dessie Hamilton's for a fitting after dinner.'

The children would be glad and would kick their copper toes against the table legs until cautioned. And Mr Morrison would rub his palms together and go to his store, hoping some drummer would come by that day. And any drummer who did come by was likely to get a good order. Maybe the children and Mrs Morrison would forget why it was a good day with a promise on its tail.

Mrs Morrison would go to the house next to Reynaud's Bakery at two o'clock and she would stay until four. When she came out her eyes would be wet with tears and her nose red and streaming. Walking home, she would dab her nose and wipe her eyes and laugh all over again. Maybe all Dessie had done was to put several black pins in a cushion to make it look like the Baptist minister, and then had the pin-cushion deliver a short dry sermon. Maybe she had recounted a meeting with Old Man Taylor, who bought old houses and moved them to a big vacant lot he owned until he had so many it looked like a dry-land Sargasso Sea. Maybe she had read a poem from *Chatterbox* with gestures. It didn't matter. It was warm-funny, it was catching-funny.

The Morrison children, coming home from school, would find no aches, no carping, no headache. Their noise was not a scandal nor their dirty faces a care. And when the giggles overcame them, why, their mother was giggling too.

Mr Morrison, coming home, would tell of the day and get listened to, and he would try to re-tell the drummer's stories–some of them at least. The supper would be delicious–omelettes never fell and cakes rose to balloons of lightness, biscuits fluffed up, and no one could season a stew like Mrs Morrison. After supper, when the children had laughed themselves to sleep, like as not Mr Morrison would touch Agnes on the shoulder in their old, old signal and they would go to bed and make love and be very happy.

The visit to Dessie might carry its charge into two days more before it petered out and the little headaches came back and business was not so good as last year. That's how Dessie was and that's what she could do. She carried excitement in her arms just as Samuel had. She was the darling, she was the beloved of the family.

Dessie was not beautiful. Perhaps she wasn't even pretty, but she had the glow that makes men follow a woman in the hope of reflecting a little of it. You would have thought that in time she would have got over her first love affair and found another love, but she did not. Come to think of it, none of the Hamiltons, with all their versatility, had any versatility in love. None of them seemed capable of light or changeable love.

Dessie did not simply throw up her hands and give up. It was much worse than that. She went right on doing and being what she was–without the glow. The people who had loved her ached for her, seeing her try, and they got to trying for her.

Dessie's friends were good and loyal but they were human, and humans love to feel good and they hate to feel bad. In time the Mrs Morrisons found unassailable reasons for not going to the little house by the bakery. They weren't disloyal. They didn't want to be sad as much as they wanted to be happy. It is easy to find a logical and virtuous reason for not doing what you don't want to do.

Dessie's business began to fall off. And the women who had thought they wanted dresses never realized that what they had wanted was happiness. Times were changing and the ready-made dress was becoming popular. It was no longer a disgrace to wear one. If Mr Morrison was stocking ready-mades, it was only reasonable that Agnes Morrison should be seen in them.

The family was worried about Dessie, but what could you do when she would not admit there was anything wrong with her? She did admit to pains in her side, quite fierce, but they lasted only a little while and came only at intervals.

Then Samuel died and the world shattered like a dish. His sons and daughters and friends groped about among the pieces, trying to put some kind of world together again.

Dessie decided to sell her business and go back to the ranch to live with Tom. She hadn't much of any business to sell out. Liza knew about it, and Olive, and Dessie had written to Tom. But Will, sitting scowling at the table in the San Francisco Chop house, had not been told. Will frothed inwardly and finally he balled up his napkin and got up. 'I forgot something,' he said to Adam. 'I'll see you on the train.'

He walked the half-block to Dessie's house and went through the high-grown garden and rang Dessie's bell.

She was having her dinner alone, and she came to the door with her napkin in her hand. 'Why, hello, Will,' she said and put up her pink cheek for him to kiss. 'When did you get in town?'

'Business,' he said. 'Just here between trains. I want to talk to you.'

She led him back to her kitchen and dining-room combined, a warm little room papered with flowers. Automatically she poured a cup of coffee and placed it for him and put the sugar bowl and the cream pitcher in front of it.

'Have you seen Mother?' she asked.

'I'm just here over trains,' he said gruffly. 'Dessie, is it true that you want to go back to the ranch?'

'I was thinking of it.'

'I don't want you to go.'

She smiled uncertainly. 'Why not? What's wrong with that? Tom's lonely down there.'

'You've got a nice business here,' he said.

'I haven't any business here,' she replied. 'I thought you knew that.'

'I don't want you to go,' he repeated sullenly.

Her smile was wistful and she tried her best to put a little mockery in her manner. 'My big brother is masterful. Tell Dessie why not.'

'It's too lonely down there.'

'It won't be lonely with the two of us.'

Will pulled at his lips angrily. He blurted, 'Tom's not himself. You shouldn't be alone with him.'

'Isn't he well? Does he need help?'

Will said, 'I didn't want to tell you–I don't think Tom's ever got over–the death. He's strange.'

She smiled affectionately. 'Will, you've always thought he was strange. You thought he was strange when he didn't like business.'

'That's different. But now he's broody. He doesn't talk. He goes walking alone in the hills at night. I went to see him and–he's been writing poetry–pages of it all over the table.'

'Didn't you ever write poetry, Will?'

'I did not.'

'I have,' said Dessie. 'Pages and pages of it all over the table.'

'I don't want you to go.'

'Let me decide,' she said softly. 'I've lost something. I want to try to find it again.'

'You're talking foolish.'

She came round the table and put her arms around his neck. 'Dear brother,' she said, 'please let me decide.'

He went angrily out of the house and barely caught his train.

2

Tom met Dessie at the King Street station. She saw him out of the train window, scanning every coach for her. He was burnished, his face shaved so close that its darkness had a shine like polished wood. His red moustache was clipped. He wore a new Stetson hat with a flat crown, a tan Norfolk jacket with a belt buckle of mother-of-pearl. His shoes glinted in the noonday light so that it was sure he had gone over them with his handkerchief just before the train arrived. His hard collar stood up against his strong red neck, and he wore a pale blue knitted tie with a horseshoe tie-pin. He tried to conceal his excitement by clasping his rough brown hands in front of him.

Dessie waved wildly out of the window, crying, 'Here I am, Tom, here I am!' though she knew he couldn't hear her over the grinding wheels of the train as the coach slid past him. She climbed down the steps and saw him look frantically about in the wrong direction. She smiled and walked up behind him.

'I beg your pardon, stranger,' she said quietly. 'Is there a Mr Tom Hamilton here?'

He spun round and he squealed with pleasure and picked her up in a bear hug and danced her around. He held her off the ground with one arm and spanked her bottom with his free hand. He nuzzled her cheek with his harsh moustache. Then he held her back by the shoulders and looked at her. Both of then threw back their heads and howled with laughter.

The station agent leaned out of his window and rested his elbows, protected with black false sleeves, on the sill. He said over his shoulder to the telegrapher, 'Those Hamiltons! Just look at them!'

Tom and Dessie, fingertips touching, were doing a courtly heel-and-toe while he sang Doodle-doodle-doo and Dessie sang Deedle-deedle-dee, and then they embraced again.

Tom looked down at her. 'Aren't you Dessie Hamilton? I seem to remember you. But you've changed. Where are your pigtails?'

It took him quite a fumbling time to get her luggage checks, to lose them in his pockets, to find them and pick up the wrong pieces. At last he had her baskets piled in the back of the buckboard. The two bay horses pawed the hard ground and threw up their heads so that the shining pole jumped and the double-trees squeaked. The harness was polished and the horse brasses glittered like gold. There was a red bow tied half way up the buggy whip and red ribbons were braided into the horses' manes and tails.

Tom helped Dessie into the seat and pretended to peek coyly at her ankle. Then he snapped up the check reins and unfastened the leather tie reins from the bits. He unwrapped the lines from the whip stock, and the horses turned so sharply that the wheel screamed against the guard.

Tom said, 'Would you care to make a tour of King City? It's a lovely town.'

'No,' she said. 'I think I remember it.' He turned left and headed south and lifted the horses to a fine swinging trot.

Dessie said, 'Where's Will?'

'I don't know,' he answered gruffly.

'Did he talk to you?'

'Yes. He said you shouldn't come.'

'He told me the same thing,' said Dessie. 'He got George to write to me too.'

'Why shouldn't you come if you want to?' Tom raged. 'What's Will got to do with it?'

She touched his arm. 'He thinks you're crazy. Says you're writing poetry.'

Tom's face darkened. 'He must have gone into the house when I wasn't there. What's he want anyway? He had no right to look at my papers.'

'Gently, gently,' said Dessie. 'Will's your brother. Don't forget that.'

'How would he like me to go through his papers?' Tom demanded.

'He wouldn't let you,' Dessie said dryly. 'They'd be locked in the safe. Now let's not spoil the day with anger.'

'All right,' he said. 'God knows all right! But he makes me mad. If I don't want to live his kind of life I'm crazy–just crazy.'

Dessie changed the subject, forced the change. 'You know, I had quite a time at the last,' she said. 'Mother wanted to come. Have you ever seen Mother cry, Tom?'

'No, not that I can remember. No, she's not a crier.'

'Well, she cried. Not much, but a lot for her–a choke and two sniffles and a wiped nose and polished her glasses and snapped shut like a watch.'

Tom said, 'Oh, Lord, Dessie, it's good to have you back! It's good. Makes me feel I'm well from a sickness.'

The horses spanked along the county road. Tom said, 'Adam Trask has bought a Ford. Or maybe I should say Will sold him a Ford.'

'I didn't know about the Ford,' said Dessie. 'He's buying my house. Giving me a very good price for it.' She laughed. 'I put a very high price on the house. I was going to come down during negotiations. Mr Trask accepted the first price. It put me in a fix.'

'What did you do, Dessie?'

'Well, I had to tell him about the high price and that I had planned to be argued down. He didn't seem to care either way.'

Tom said, 'Let me beg you never to tell that story to Will. He'd have you locked up.'

'But the house wasn't worth what I asked!'

'I repeat what I said about Will. What's Adam want with your house?'

'He's going to move there. Wants the twins to go to school in Salinas.'

'What'll he do with his ranch?'

'I don't know. He didn't say.'

Tom said, 'I wonder what would have happened if Father'd got hold of a ranch like that instead of Old Dry and Dusty.'

'It isn't such a bad place.'

'Fine for everything except making a living.'

Dessie said earnestly, 'Have you ever known any family that had more fun?'

'No, I don't. But that was the family, not the land.'

'Tom, remember when you took Jenny and Belle Williams to the Peach Tree dance on the sofa?'

'Mother never let me forget it. Say, wouldn't it be good to ask Jenny and Belle down for a visit?'

'They'd come too,' Dessie said. 'Let's do it.'

When they turned off the county road she said, 'Somehow I remember it differently.'

'Drier?'

'I guess that's it. Tom, there's so much grass.'

'I'm getting twenty head of stock to eat it.'

'You must be rich.'

'No, and the good year will break the price of beef. I wonder what Will would do. He's a scarcity man. He told me. He said, "Always deal in scarcities." Will's smart.'

The rutty road had not changed except that the ruts were deeper and round stones stuck up higher.

Dessie said, 'What's the card on that mesquite bush?' She picked it off as they drove by, and it said, 'Welcome Home'.

'Tom, you did it!'

'I did not. Someone's been here.'

Every fifty yards there was another card sticking on a bush, or hanging from the branches of a madrone, or tacked to the trunk of a buckeye, and all of them said, 'Welcome Home'. Dessie squealed with delight over each one.

They topped the rise above the little valley of the old Hamilton place and Tom pulled up to let her enjoy the view. On the hill across the valley, spelled out in whitewashed stones, were the huge words, 'Welcome Home, Dessie'. She put her head against his lapel and laughed and cried at the same time.

Tom looked sternly ahead of him. 'Now who could have done that?' he said. 'A man can't leave the place any more.'

In the dawn Dessie was awakened by the chill of pain that came to her at intervals. It was a rustle and a threat of pain; it scampered up from her side and across her abdomen, a nibbling pinch and then a little grab and then a hard catch and finally a fierce grip as though a huge hand had wrenched her. When that relaxed she felt a soreness like a bruise. It didn't last very long, but while it went on the outside world was blotted out, and she seemed to be listening to the struggle in her body.

When only the soreness remained she saw how the dawn had come silver to the windows. She smelled the good morning wind rippling the curtains, bringing in the odour of grass and roots and damp earth. After that sounds joined the parade of perception–sparrows haggled among themselves, a bawling cow monotonously berating a punching hungry calf, a blue jay's squawk of false excitement, the sharp warning of a cock quail on guard and the answering whisper of the hen quail somewhere near in the tall grass. The chicken yard boiled with excitement over an egg, and a big lady Rhode Island Red, who weighed four pounds, hypocritically protested the horror of being lustfully pinned to the ground by a scrawny wreck of a rooster she could have blasted with one blow of her wing.

The cooing of pigeons brought memory into the procession. Dessie remembered how her father had said, sitting at the head of the table, 'I told Rabbit I was going to raise some pigeons and–do you know?–he said, "No white pigeons." "Why not white?" I asked him, and he said, "They're the rare worst of bad luck. You take a flight of white pigeons and they'll bring sadness and death. Get grey ones." "I like white ones." "Get grey ones," he told me. And as the sky covers me, I'll get white ones.'

And Liza said patiently, 'Why do you be for ever testing, Samuel? Grey ones taste just as good and they're bigger.'

'I'll let no flimsy fairy-tale push me,' Samuel said.

And Liza said with her dreadful simplicity, 'You're already pushed by your own contentiousness. You're a mule of contention, a very mule!'

'Someone's got to do these things,' he said sullenly. 'Else Fate would not ever get nose-thumbed and mankind would still be clinging to the top branches of a tree.'

And of course he got white pigeons and waited truculently for sadness and death until he'd proved his point. And here were the great-great-grand squabs cooing in the morning and rising to fly like a whirling white scarf around the wagon shed.

As Dessie remembered, she heard the words and the house around her grew peopled. Sadness and death, she thought, and death and sadness, and it wrenched in her stomach against the soreness. You just have to wait around long enough and it will come.

She heard the air whooshing into the big bellows in the forge and the practice tap for range of hammer on anvil. She heard Liza open the oven door and the thump of a kneaded loaf on the floury board. Then Joe wandered about, looking in unlikely places for his shoes, and at last found them where he had left them under the bed.

She heard Mollie's sweet voice in the kitchen, reading a morning text from the Bible, and Una's full cold throaty correction.

And Tom had cut Mollie's tongue with his pocket-knife and died in his heart when he realized his courage.

'Oh, dear Tom,' she said, and her lips moved.

Tom's cowardice was as huge as his courage, as it must be in great men. His violence balanced his tenderness, and himself was a pitted battlefield of his own forces. He was confused now, but Dessie could hold his bit and point him, the way a handler points a thoroughbred at the barrier to show his breeding and his form.

Dessie lay part in pain and a part of her dangled still in sleep while the morning brightened against the window. She remembered that Mollie was going to lead the Grand March at the Fourth of July picnic with no less than Harry Forbes, State Senator. And Dessie had not finished putting the braid on Mollie's dress. She struggled to get up. There was so much braid, and here she lay drowsing.

She cried, 'I'll get it done, Mollie. It will be ready.'

She got up from her bed and threw her robe around her and walked barefoot through the house crowded with Hamiltons. In the hall they were gone to the bedrooms. In the bedrooms, with the beds neat-made, they were all in the kitchen, and in the kitchen–they dispersed and were gone. Sadness and death. The wave receded and left her in dry awakeness.

The house was clean, scrubbed and immaculate, curtains washed, windows polished, but all as a man does it–the ironed curtains did not hang quite straight and there were streaks on the windows and a square showed on the table when a book was moved.

The stove was warming, with orange light showing around the lids and the soft thunder of draughty flame leaping past the open damper. The kitchen clock flashed its pendulum behind its glass skirt, and it ticked like a little wooden hammer striking on an empty wooden box.

From outside came a whistle as wild and raucous as a reed and pitched high and strange. The whistling scattered a savage melody. Then Tom's steps sounded on the porch, and he came in with an armload of oakwood so high he could not see over it. He cascaded the wood into the wood-box.

'You're up,' he said. 'That was to wake you if you were still sleeping.' His face was lighted with joy. 'This is a morning light as down and no time to be slugging.'

'You sound like your father,' Dessie said, and she laughed with him.

His joy hardened to fierceness. 'Yes,' he said loudly. 'And we'll have that time again, right here. I've been dragging myself in misery like a spine-broken snake. No wonder Will thought I was cracked. But now you're back, and I'll show you. I'll breathe life into life again. Do you hear? This house is going to be alive.'

'I'm glad I came,' she said, and she thought in desolation how brittle he was now and how easy to shatter, and how she would have to protect him.

'You must have worked all day and night to get the house so clean,' she said.

'Nothing,' said Tom. 'A little twist with the fingers.'

'I know that twist, but it was the bucket and mop and on your knees–unless you've invented some way to do it by chicken power or the harnessed wind.'

'Invented–now that's why I have no time. I've invented a little slot that lets a necktie slip freely in a stiff collar.'

'You don't wear stiff collars.'

'I did yesterday. That's when I invented it. And chickens–I'm going to raise millions of them–little houses all over the ranch and a ring on the roof to dip them in a whitewashed tank. And the eggs will come through on a little conveyor belt–here! I'll draw it.'

'I want to draw some breakfast,' Dessie said. 'What's the shape of a fried egg? How would you colour the fat and lean of a strip of bacon?'

'You'll have it,' he cried, and he opened the stove lid and assaulted the fire with the stove lifter until the hairs on his hand curled and charred. He pitched wood in and started his high whistling.

Dessie said, 'You sound like some goat-foot with a wheat flute on a hill in Greece.'

'What do you think I am?' he shouted.

Dessie thought miserably, If his is real, why can't my heart be light? Why can't I climb out of my grey ragbag? I will, she screeched inside herself. If he can–I will.

She said, 'Tom!'

'Yes.'

'I want a purple egg.'

CHAPTER 33

I

The green lasted on the hills far into June before the grass turned yellow. The heads of the wild oats were so heavy with seed that they hung over on their stalks. The little springs trickled on late in the summer. The range cattle staggered under their fat and their hides shone with health. It was a year when the people of the Salinas Valley forgot the dry years. Farmers bought more land than they could afford and figured their profits on the covers of their cheque-books.

Tom Hamilton laboured like a giant, not only with his strong arms but also with his heart and spirit. The anvil rang in the forge again. He painted the old house white and whitewashed the sheds. He went to King City and studied a flush toilet and then built one of craftily bent tin and carved wood. Because the water came so slowly from the spring, he put a redwood tank beside the house and pumped the water up to it with a hand-made windmill so cleverly made that it turned in the slightest wind. And he made metal and wood models of two ideas to be sent to the patent office in the fall.

That was not all–he laboured with humour and good spirits. Dessie had to rise very early to get in her hand at the housework before Tom had it all done. She watched his great red happiness, and it was not as light as Samuel's happiness was light. It did not rise out of his roots and come floating up. He was manufacturing happiness as cleverly as he knew how, moulding it and shaping it.

Dessie, who had more friends than anyone in the whole valley, had no confidants. When her trouble had come upon her she had not talked about it. And the pains were a secret in herself.

When Tom found her rigid and tight from the grabbing pain and cried in alarm, 'Dessie, what's the matter?' she controlled her face and said, 'A little crick, that's all. Just a little crick. I'm all right now.' And in a moment they were laughing.

They laughed a great deal, as though to reassure themselves. Only when Dessie went to her bed did her loss fall on her, bleak and unendurable. And Tom lay in the dark of his room, puzzled as a child. He could hear his heart beating and rasping a little in its beat. His mind fell away from the thought and clung for safety to little plans, designs, machines.

Sometimes in the summer evenings they walked up the hill to watch the afterglow clinging to the tops of the western mountains and to feel the breeze drawn into the valley by the rising day-heated air. Usually they stood silently for a while and breathed in peacefulness. Since both were shy they never talked about themselves. Neither knew about the other at all.

It was startling to both of them when Dessie said one evening on the hill, 'Tom, why don't you get married?'

He looked quickly at her and away. He said, 'Who'd have me?'

'Is that a joke or do you really mean it?'

'Who'd have me?' he said again. 'Who'd want a thing like me?'

'It sounds to me as though you really mean it.' Then she violated their unstated code. 'Have you been in love with someone?'

'No,' he said shortly.

'I wish I knew,' she said as though he had not answered.

Tom did not speak again as they walked down the hill. But on the porch he said suddenly, 'You're lonely here. You don't want to stay.' He waited for a moment. 'Answer me. Isn't that true?'

'I want to stay here more than I want to stay anyplace else.' She asked, 'Do you ever go to women?'

'Yes,' he said.

'Is it any good to you?'

'Not much.'

'What are you going to do?'

'I don't know.'

In silence they went back to the house. Tom lighted the lamp in the old living-room. The horsehair sofa he had rebuilt raised its goose-neck against the wall, and the green carpet had tracks worn light between the doors.

Tom sat down by the round centre table. Dessie sat on the sofa, and she could see that he was still embarrassed from his last admission. She thought, How pure he is, how unfit for a world that even she knew more about than he did. A dragon killer, he was, a rescuer of damsels, and his small sins seemed so great to him that he felt unfit and unseemly. She wished her father were here. Her father had felt greatness in Tom. Perhaps he would know now how to release it out of its darkness and let it fly free.

She took another tack to see whether she could raise some spark in him. 'As long as we're talking about ourselves, have you ever thought that our whole world is the valley and a few trips to San Francisco, have you ever been farther south than San Luis Obispo? I never have.'

'Neither have I,' said Tom.

'Well, isn't that silly?'

'Lots of people haven't,' he said.

'But it's not law. We could go to Paris and to Rome or to Jerusalem. I would dearly love to see the Colosseum.'

He watched her suspiciously, expecting some kind of joke. 'How could we?' he asked. 'That takes a lot of money.'

'I don't think it does,' she said. 'We wouldn't have to stay in fancy places. We could take the cheapest boats and the lowest class. That's how our father come here from Ireland. And we could go to Ireland.'

Still he watched her, but a burning was beginning in his eyes.

Dessie went on, 'We could take a year for work, save every penny. I can get some sewing to do in King City. Will would help us. And next summer you could sell all the stock and we could go. There's no law forbids it.'

Tom got up and went outside. He looked at the summer stars, at blue Venus and red Mars. His hands flexed at his sides, closed to fists and opened. Then he turned and went back into the house. Dessie had not moved.

'Do you want to go, Dessie?'

'More than anything in the world.'

'Then we will go!'

'Do you want to go?'

'More than anything in the world,' he said. 'Egypt–have you given a thought to Egypt?'

'Athens,' she said.

'Constantinople!'

'Bethlehem!'

'Yes, Bethlehem,' and he said suddenly, 'Go to bed. We've got a year of work–a year. Get some rest. I'm going to borrow money from Will to buy a hundred shoats.'

'What will you feed them?'

'Acorns,' said Tom. 'I'll make a machine to gather acorns.'

After he had gone to his room she could hear him knocking around and talking softly to himself. Dessie looked out of her window at the starlit night and she was glad. But she wondered whether she really wanted to go, or whether Tom did. And as she wondered the whisper of pain grew up from her side.

When Dessie got up in the morning Tom was already at his drawing-board, beating his forehead with his fist and growling to himself. Dessie looked over his shoulder. 'Is it the acorn machine?'

'It should be easy,' he said. 'But how to get out the sticks and rocks?'

'I know you're the inventor, but I invented the greatest acorn picker in the world and it's ready to go.'

'What do you mean?'

'Children,' she said. 'Those restless little hands.'

'They wouldn't do it, not even for pay.'

'They would for prizes. A prize for everyone and a big prize for the winner–maybe a hundred-dollar prize. They'd sweep the valley clean. Will you let me try?'

He scratched his head. 'Why not?' he said. 'But how would you collect the acorns?'

'The children will bring them in,' said Dessie. 'Just let me take care of it. I hope you have plenty of storage space.'

'It would be exploiting the young, wouldn't it?'

'Certainly it would,' Dessie agreed. 'When I had my shop I exploited the girls who wanted to learn to sew–and they exploited me. I think I will call this The Great Monterey County Acorn Contest. And I won't let everyone in. Maybe bicycles for prizes–wouldn't you pick up acorns in hope of a bicycle, Tom?'

'Sure I would,' he said. 'But couldn't we pay them too?'

'Not with money,' Dessie said. 'That would reduce it to labour, and they will not labour if they can help it. Nor will I.'

Tom leaned back from his board and laughed. 'Nor will I,' he said. 'All right, you are in charge of acorns and I am in charge of pigs.'

Dessie said, 'Tom, wouldn't it be ridiculous if we made money, we of all people?'

'But you made money in Salinas,' he said.

'Some–not much. But oh, I was rich in promises. If the bills had ever been paid we wouldn't need pigs. We could go to Paris tomorrow.'

'I'm going to drive in and talk to Will,' said Tom. He pushed his chair back from the drawing-board. 'Want to come with me?'

'No, I'll stay and make my plans. Tomorrow I start The Great Acorn Contest.'

2

On the ride back to the ranch in the late afternoon Tom was depressed and sad. As always, Will had managed to chew up and spit out his enthusiasm. Will had pulled his lip, rubbed his eyebrows, scratched his nose, cleaned his glasses, and made a major operation of cutting and lighting a cigar. The pig proposition was full of holes, and Will was able to put his finger in the holes.

The Acorn Contest wouldn't work, although he was not explicit about why it wouldn't. The whole thing was shaky, particularly in these times. The very best Will was able to do was to think about it.

At one time during the talk Tom had thought to tell Will about Europe, but a quick instinct stopped him. The idea of traipsing around Europe, unless, of course, you were retired and had your capital out in good securities, would be to Will a craziness that would make the pig plan a marvel of business acumen. Tom did not tell him, and he left Will to 'think it over', knowing that the verdict would be against the pigs and the acorns.

Poor Tom did not know and could not learn that dissembling successfully is one of the creative joys of a business man. To indicate enthusiasm was to be idiotic. And Will really did mean to think it over. Parts of the plan fascinated him. Tom had stumbled on a very interesting thing. If you could buy shoats on credit, fatten them on food that cost next to nothing, sell them, pay off your loan, and take your profit, you would really have done something. Will would not rob his brother. He would cut him in on the profits, but Tom was a dreamer and could not be trusted with a good sound plan. Tom, for instance, didn't even know the price of pork and its probable trend. If it worked out, Will could be depended on to give Tom a very substantial present–maybe even a Ford. And how about a Ford as first and only prize for acorns? Everybody in the whole valley would pick acorns.

Driving up the Hamilton road, Tom wondered how to break it to Dessie that their plan was no good. The best way would be to have another plan to substitute for it. How could they make enough money in one year to go to Europe? And suddenly he realized that he didn't know how much they'd need. He didn't know the price of a steamship ticket. They might spend the evening figuring.

He half expected Dessie to run out of the house when he drove up. He would put on his best face and tell a joke. But Dessie didn't run out. Maybe taking a nap, he thought. He watered the horses and stabled them and pitched hay into the manger.

Dessie was lying on the goose-neck sofa when Tom came in. 'Taking a nap?' he asked, and then he saw the colour of her face. 'Dessie,' he cried, 'what's the matter?'

She rallied herself against pain. 'Just a stomach-ache,' she said. 'A pretty severe one.'

'Oh,' said Tom. 'You scared me. I can fix up a stomach-ache.' He went to the kitchen and brought back a glass of pearly liquid. He handed it to her.

'What is it, Tom?'

'Good old-fashioned salts. It may gripe you a little but it'll do the job.'

She drank it obediently and made a face. 'I remember that taste,' she said. 'Mother's remedy in green apple season.'

'Now lie still,' Tom said. 'I'll rustle up some dinner.'

She could hear him knocking about in the kitchen. The pain roared through her body. And on top of the pain there was fear. She could feel the medicine burn down to her stomach. After a while she dragged herself to the new home-made flush toilet and tried to vomit the salts. The perspiration ran from her forehead and blinded her. When she tried to straighten up, the muscles over her stomach were set and she could not break free.

Later Tom brought her some scrambled eggs. She shook her head slowly. 'I can't,' she said, smiling. 'I think I'll just go to bed.'

'The salts should work pretty soon,' Tom assured her. 'Then you'll be all right.' He helped her to bed. 'What do you suppose you ate to cause it?'

Dessie lay in her bedroom and her will battled the pain. About ten o'clock in the evening her will began to lose its fight. She called, 'Tom! Tom!' He opened the door. He had the *World Almanac* in his hand. 'Tom,' she said, 'I'm sorry. But I'm awfully sick, Tom. I'm terribly sick.'

He sat down on the edge of her bed in the half-darkness. 'Are the gripes bad?'

'Yes, awful?'

'Can you go to the toilet now?'

'No, not now.'

'I'll bring a lamp and sit with you,' he said. 'Maybe you can get some sleep. It'll be gone in the morning. The salts will do the job.'

Her will took hold again and she lay still while Tom read bits out of the *Almanac* to soothe her. He stopped reading when he thought she was sleeping, and he dozed in his chair beside the lamp.

A thin scream awakened him. He stepped beside the struggling bedclothes. Dessie's eyes were milky and crazy, like those of a maddened horse. Her mouth corners erupted thick bubbles and her face was on fire. Tom put his hand under the cover and felt muscles knotted like iron. And then her struggle stopped and her head fell back and the light glinted on her half-closed eyes.

Tom put only a bridle on the horse and flung himself on bareback. He groped and ribbed out his belt to beat the frightened horse to an awkward run over the stony, rutted wheel track.

The Duncans, asleep upstairs in the two-storey house on the country road, didn't hear the banging on their door, but they heard the bang and ripping sound as their front door came off, carrying lock and hinges with it. By the time Red Duncan got downstairs with a shotgun Tom was screaming into the wall telephone at the King City central. 'Dr Tilson! Get him! I don't care! Get him, goddam it.' Red Duncan sleepily had the gun on him.

Dr Tilson said, 'Yes! Yes–yes, I hear. You're Tom Hamilton. What's the matter with her? Is her stomach hard? What did you do? Salts! You goddam fool!'

Then the doctor controlled his anger. 'Tom,' he said, 'Tom, boy. Pull yourself together. Go back and lay cold clothes–cold as you can get them. I don't suppose you have any ice. Well, keep changing the clothes. I'll be out as fast as I can. Do you hear me? Tom, do you hear me?'

He hung the receiver up and dressed. In angry weariness he opened the wall cabinet and collected scalpels and clamps, sponges and tubes of sutures, to put in his bag. He shook his gasoline pressure lantern to make sure it was full and arranged ether can and mask beside it on his bureau. His wife in boudoir cap and nightgown looked in. Dr Tilson said, 'I'm walking over to the garage. Call Will Hamilton. Tell him I want him to drive me to his father's place. If he argues tell him his sister is–dying.'

3

Tom came riding back to the ranch a week after Dessie's funeral, riding high and prim, his shoulders straight and chin in, like a guardsman on parade. Tom had done everything slowly, perfectly. His horse was curried and brushed, and his Stetson hat was square on his head. Not even Samuel could have held himself in more dignity than Tom as he rode back to the old house. A hawk driving down on a chicken with doubled fists did not make him turn his head.

At the barn he dismounted, watered his horse, held him a moment at the door, haltered him, and put rolled barley in the box beside the manger. He took off the saddle and turned the blanket inside out to dry. Then the barley was finished and he led the bay horse out and turned him free to graze on every unfenced inch of the world.

In the house the furniture, chairs, and stove seemed to shrink back and away from him in distaste. A stool avoided him as he went in to the living-room. His matches were soft and damp, and with a feeling of apology he went to the kitchen for more. The lamp in the living-room was fair and lonely. Tom's first match flame ran quickly round the Rochester wick and then stood up a full inch of yellow flame.

Tom sat down in the evening and looked around. His eyes avoided the horsehair sofa. A slight noise of mice in the kitchen made him turn, and he saw his shadow on the wall and his hat was on. He removed it and laid it on the table beside him.

He thought dawdling, protective thoughts, sitting under the lamp, but he knew that pretty soon his name would be called and he would have to go up before the bench with himself as judge and his own crimes as jurors.

And his name *was* called, shrilly in his ears. His mind walked in to face the accusers: Vanity, which charged him with being ill dressed and dirty and vulgar; and Lust, slipping him the money for his whoring; Dishonesty, to make him pretend to talent and thought he did not have; Laziness and Gluttony arm-in-arm. Tom felt comforted by these because they screened the great Grey One in the back seat, waiting–the grey and dreadful crime. He dredged up lesser things, used small sins almost like virtues to save himself. There were Covetousness of Will's money, Treason towards his mother's God. Theft of time and hope, sick Rejection of love.

Samuel spoke softly but his voice filled the room. 'Be good, be pure, be great, Tom Hamilton.'

Tom ignored his father. He said, 'I'm busy greeting my friends,' and he nodded to Discourtesy and Ugliness and Unfilial Conduct and Unkempt Fingernails. Then he started with Vanity again. The Grey One shouldered up in front. It was too late to stall with baby sins. This Grey One was Murder.

Tom's hand felt the chill of the glass and saw the pearly liquid with the dissolving crystals still turning over and lucent bubbles rising, and he repeated aloud in the empty, empty room, 'This will do the job. Just wait till morning. You'll feel fine then.' That's how it had sounded, exactly how, and the walls and chairs and the lamp had all heard it and they could prove it. There was no place in the whole world for Tom Hamilton to live. But it wasn't for lack of trying. He shuffled possibilities like cards. London? No! Egypt–pyramids in Egypt and the Sphinx? No! Paris? No! Now wait–they do all your sins lots better there. No! Well, stand aside and maybe we'll come back to you. Bethlehem? Dear God, no! It would be lonely there for a stranger.

And here interpolated–it's so hard to remember how you die or when. An eyebrow raised or a whisper–they may be it; or a night mottled with splashed light until power-driven lead finds your secret and lets out the fluid in you.

Now this is true, Tom Hamilton was dead and he had only to do a few decent things to make it final.

The sofa cricked in criticism, and Tom looked at it and at the smoking lamp to which the sofa referred. 'Thank you,' Tom said to the sofa. 'I hadn't noticed it,' and he turned down the wick until the smoking stopped.

His mind dozed. Murder slapped him aware again. Now Red Tom, Gun Tom, was too tired to kill himself. That takes some doing, with maybe pain and maybe hell.

He remembered that his mother had a strong distaste for suicide, feeling that it combined three things of which she strongly disapproved–bad manners, cowardice, and sin. It was almost as bad as adultery or stealing–maybe just as bad. There must be a way to avoid Liza's disapproval. She could make one suffer if she disapproved.

Samuel wouldn't make it hard, but on the other hand you couldn't avoid Samuel because he was in the air every place. Tom had to tell Samuel. He said, 'My father, I'm sorry. I can't help it. You over-estimated me. You were wrong. I wish I could justify the love and the pride you squandered on me. Maybe you could figure out a way, but I can't. I cannot live. I've killed Dessie and I want to sleep.'

And his mind spoke for his father absent, saying, 'Why, I can understand how that could be. There are so many patterns to choose from in the arc from birth back to birth again. But let's think how we can make it all right with Mother. Why are you so impatient, dear?'

'I can't wait, that's why,' Tom said. 'I can't wait any more.'

'Why, sure you can, my son, my darling. You're grown great as I knew you would. Open the table drawer and then make use of that turnip you call your head.'

Tom opened the drawer and saw a tablet of Crane's Linen Lawn and a package of envelopes to match and two gnawed and crippled pencils and in the dust corner at the back a few stamps. He laid out the tablet and sharpened the pencils with his pocket-knife.

He wrote, 'Dear Mother, I hope you keep yourself well. I am going to plan to spend more time with you. Olive asked me for Thanksgiving and you know I'll be there. Our little Olive can cook a turkey nearly to match yours, but I know you will never believe that. I've had a stroke of good luck. Bought a horse for fifteen dollars–a gelding, and he lookes like a blood horse to me. I got him cheap because he has taken a dislike to mankind. His former owner spent more time on his own back than on the gelding's. I must say he's a pretty cute article. He's thrown me twice but I'll get him yet, and if I can break him I'll have one of the best horses in the whole county. And you can be sure I'll break him if it takes all winter. I don't know why I go on about him, only the man I bought him from said a funny thing. He said, "That horse is so mean he'd eat a man right off his back." Well, remember what Father used to say when we went a rabbit hunting? "Come back with your shield or on it." I'll see you Thanksgiving. Your son Tom.'

He wondered whether it was good enough, but he was too tired to do it again. He added, 'P.S. I notice Polly has not reformed one bit. That parrot makes me blush.'

On another sheet he wrote, 'Dear Will, No matter what you yourself may think–please help me now. For Mother's sake–please. I was killed by a horse–thrown and kicked in the head–please! Your brother Tom.'

He stamped the letters and put them in his pocket and he asked Samuel, 'Is it all right?'

In his bedroom he broke open a new box of shells and put one of them in the cylinder of his well-oiled Smith and Wesson .38 and he set the loaded chamber one space to the left of the firing-pin.

His horse standing sleepily near the fence came to his whistle and stood drowsing while he saddled up.

It was three o'clock in the morning when he dropped the letters in the post office at King City and mounted and turned his horse south towards the unproductive hills of the old Hamilton place.

He was a gallant gentleman.

PART IV

CHAPTER 34

A child may ask, 'What is the world's story about?' And a grown man or woman may wonder, 'What way will the world go? How does it end and, while we're at it, what's the story about?'

I believe that there is one story in the world, and only one, that has frightened and inspired us, so that we live in a Pearl White serial of continuing thought and wonder. Humans are caught in their lives, in their thoughts, in their hungers and ambitions, in their avarice and cruelty, and in their kindness and generosity too–in a net of good and evil. I think this is the only story we have and that it occurs on all levels of feeling and intelligence. Virtue and vice were warp and woof of our first consciousness, and they will be the fabric of our last, and this despite changes we may impose on field and river and mountain, on economy and manners. There is no other story. A man, after he has brushed off the dust and the chips of his life, will have left only the hard, clean questions: Was it good or was it evil? Have I done well–or ill?

Herodotus, in the Persian War, tells a story of how Croesus, the richest and most-favoured king of his time, asked Solon the Athenian a leading question. He would not have asked it if he had not been worried about the answer. 'Who,' he asked, 'is the luckiest person in the world?' He must have been eaten with doubt and hungry for reassurance. Solon told him of three lucky people in old times. And Croesus more than likely did not listen, so anxious was he about himself. And when Solon did not mention him, Croesus was forced to say, 'Do you consider me lucky?'

Solon did not hesitate in his answer. 'How can I tell?' he said. 'You aren't dead yet.'

And this answer must have haunted Croesus dismally as his luck disappeared, and his wealth and his kingdom. And as he was being burned on a tall fire, he may have thought of it and perhaps wished he had not asked or not been answered.

And in our time, when a man dies–if he has had wealth and influence and power and all the vestments that arouse envy, and after the living take stock of the dead man's property and his eminence and works and monuments–the question is still there: Was his life good or was it evil?–which is another way of putting Croesus's question. Envies are gone, and the measuring stick is: 'Was he loved or was he hated? Is his death felt as a loss or does a kind of joy come of it?'

I remember clearly the deaths of three men. One was the richest man of the century, who, having clawed his way to wealth through the souls and bodies of men, spent many years trying to buy back the love he had forfeited and by that process performed great service to the world and, perhaps, had much more than balanced the evils of his rise. I was on a ship when he died. The news was posted on the bulletin board, and nearly everyone received the news with pleasure. Several said, 'Thank God that son of a bitch is dead.'

Then there was a man, smart as Satan, who, lacking some perception of human dignity and knowing all too well every aspect of human weakness and wickedness, used his special knowledge to warp men, to buy men, to bribe and threaten and seduce until he found himself in a position of great power. He clothed his motives in the names of virtue, and I have wondered whether he ever knew that no gift will ever buy back a man's love when you have removed his self-love. A bribed man can only hate his briber. When this man died the nation rang with praise and, just beneath, with gladness that he was dead.

There was a third man, who perhaps made many errors in performance but whose effective life was devoted to making men brave and dignified and good in a time when they were poor and frightened and when ugly forces were loose in the world to utilize their fears. This man was hated by the few. When he died the people burst into tears in the streets and their minds wailed, 'What can we do now? How can we go on without him?'

In uncertainty I am certain that underneath their topmost layers of frailty men want to be good and want to be loved. Indeed, most of their vices are attempted short cuts to love. When a man comes to die, no matter what his talents and influence and genius, if he dies unloved his life must be a failure to him and his dying a cold horror. It seems to me that if you or I must choose between two courses of thought or action, we should remember our dying so to live that our death brings no pleasure to the world.

We have only one story. All novels, all poetry, are built on the never-ending contest in ourselves of good and evil. And it occurs to me that evil must constantly re-spawn, while good, while virtue, is immortal. Vice has always a new fresh young face, while virtue is venerable as nothing else in the world is.

CHAPTER 35

I

Lee helped Adam and the two boys move to Salinas, which is to say he did it all, packed the things to be taken, saw them on the train, loaded the back seat of the Ford, and arriving in Salinas, unpacked and saw the family settled in Dessie's little house. When he had done everything he could think of to make them comfortable, and a number of things unnecessary, and more things for the sake of delay, he waited on Adam formally one evening after the twins had gone to bed. Perhaps Adam caught his intention from Lee's coldness and formality.

Adam said, 'All right. I've been expecting it. Tell me.'

That broke up Lee's memorized speech, which he had intended to begin, 'For a number of years I have served you to the best of my ability and now I feel–'

'I've put it off as long as I could,' said Lee. 'I have a speech all ready. Do you want to hear it?'

'Do you want to say it?'

'No,' said Lee. 'I don't. And it's a pretty good speech too.'

'When do you want to go?' Adam said.

'As soon as possible. I'm afraid I might lose my intention if I don't go soon. Do you want me to wait until you get someone else?'

'Better not,' said Adam. 'You know how slow I am. It might be some time. I might never get around to it.'

'I'll go tomorrow, then.'

'It will tear the boys to pieces,' Adam said. 'I don't know what they'll do. Maybe you'd better sneak off and let me tell them afterwards.'

'It's my observation that children always surprise us,' said Lee.

And so it was. At breakfast the next morning Adam said, 'Boys, Lee is going away.'

'Is he?' said Cal. 'There's a basketball game tonight, costs ten cents. Can we go?'

'Yes. But did you hear what I said?'

'Sure,' said Aron. 'You said Lee's going away.'

'But he's not coming back.'

Cal asked, 'Where's he going?'

'To San Francisco to live.'

'Oh!' said Aron. 'There's a man on Main Street, right on the street, and he's got a little stove and he cooks sausages and puts them in buns. They cost a nickel. And you can take all the mustard you want.'

Lee stood in the kitchen door, smiling at Adam.

When the twins got their books together Lee said, 'Goodbye, boys.'

They shouted, 'Goodbye!' and tumbled out of the house.

Adam stared into his coffee-cup and said in apology, 'What little brutes! I guess that's your reward for over ten years of service.'

'I like it better that way,' Lee said. 'If they pretended sorrow they'd be liars. It doesn't mean anything to them. Maybe they'll think of me sometimes–privately. I don't want them to be sad. I hope I'm not so small-souled as to take satisfaction in being missed.' He laid fifty cents on the table in front of Adam. 'When they start for the basketball game tonight, give them this from me and tell them to buy the sausage buns. My farewell gift may be ptomaine, for all I know.'

Adam looked at the telescope basket Lee brought into the dining-room. 'Is that all your stuff. Lee?'

'Everything but my books. They're in boxes in the cellar. If you don't mind I'll send for them or come for them after I get settled.'

'Why, sure. I'm going to miss you, Lee, whether you want me to or not. Are you really going to get your bookstore?'

'That is my intention.'

'You'll let us hear from you?'

'I don't know. I'll have to think about it. They say a clean cut heals soonest. There's nothing sadder to me than associations held together by nothing but the glue of postage stamps. If you can't see or hear or touch a man, it's best to let him go.'

Adam stood up from the table. 'I'll walk to the depot with you.'

'No!' Lee said sharply. 'No. I don't want that. Goodbye, Mr Trask.

Goodbye, Adam.' He went out of the house so fast that Adam's 'Goodbye' reached him at the bottom of the front steps and Adam's 'Don't forget to write' sounded over the click of the front gate.

2

That night after the basketball game Cal and Aron each had five sausages on buns, and it was just as well, for Adam had forgotten to provide any supper. Walking home, the twins discussed Lee for the first time.

'I wonder if he went away?' Cal asked.

'He's talked about going before.'

'What do you suppose he'll do without us?'

'I don't know. I bet he comes back,' Aron said.

'How do you mean? Father said he was going to start a bookstore. That's funny. A Chinese bookstore.'

'He'll come back,' said Aron. 'He'll get lonesome for us. You'll see.'

'Bet you ten cents he don't.'

'Before when?'

'Before for ever.'

'That's a bet,' said Aron.

Aron was not able to collect his winnings for nearly a month, but he won it six days later.

Lee came on the ten-forty and let himself in with his own key. There was a light in the dining-room, but Lee found Adam in the kitchen, scraping at a thick black crust in the frying-pan with the point of a can opener.

Lee put down his basket. 'If you soak it overnight it will come right out.'

'Will it? I've burned everything I've cooked. There's a saucepan of beets out in the yard. Smelled so bad I couldn't have them in the house. Burned beets are awful–Lee!' he cried, and then, 'Is there anything the matter?'

Lee took the black iron pan from him and put it in the sink and ran water in it. 'If we had a new gas stove we could make a cup of coffee in a few minutes,' he said. 'I might as well build up the fire.'

'Stove won't burn,' said Adam.

Lee lifted the lid. 'Have you ever taken the ashes out?'

'Ashes?'

'Oh, go in the other room,' said Lee. 'I'll make some coffee.'

Adam waited impatiently in the dining-room but he obeyed his orders. At last Lee brought in two cups of coffee and set them on the table. 'Made it in a skillet,' he said. 'Much faster.' He leaned over his telescope basket and untied the rope that held it shut. He brought out the stone bottle. 'Chinese absinthe,' he said. 'Ng-ka-py maybe last ten more years. I forgot to ask whether you had replaced me.'

'You're beating about the bush,' said Adam.

'I know it. And I also know the best way would be just to tell it and get it over with.'

'You lost your money in a fan-tan game.'

'No. I wish that was it. No, I have my money. This damn cork's broken–I'll have to shove it in the bottle.' He poured the black liquor into his coffee. 'I never drank it this way,' he said. 'Say, it's good.'

'Tastes like rotten apples,' said Adam.

'Yes, but remember Sam Hamilton said like good rotten apples.'

Adam said, 'When do you think you'll get around to telling me what happened to you?'

'Nothing happened to me,' said Lee. 'I got lonesome. That's all. Isn't that enough?'

'How about your bookstore?'

'I don't want a bookstore. I think I knew it before I got on the train, but I took all this time to make sure.'

'Then there's your last dream gone.'

'Good riddance.' Lee seemed on the verge of hysteria. 'Missy Tlask, Chinee boy sink gung get dlunk.'

Adam was alarmed. 'What's the matter with you anyway?'

Lee lifted the bottle to his lips and took a deep hot drink and panted the fumes out of his burning throat. 'Adam,' he said, 'I am incomparably, incredibly, overwhelmingly glad to be home. I've never been so goddam lonesome in my life.'

CHAPTER 36

I

Salinas had two grammar schools, big yellow structures with tall windows, and the windows were baleful and the doors did not smile. These schools were called the East End and the West End. Since the East End School was way to hell and gone across town the children who lived east of Main Street attended there, I will not bother with it.

The West End, a huge building of two storeys, fronted with gnarled poplars, divided the play-yards called girlside and boyside. Behind the school a high board fence separated girlside from boyside, and the back of the play-yard was bounded by a slough of standing water in which tall tules and even cattails grew. The West End had grades from third to eighth. The first–and second-graders went to Baby School some distance away.

In the West End there was a room for each grade–third, fourth, and fifth on the ground floor, sixth, seventh, eighth on the second floor. Each room had the usual desks of battered oak, a platform and square teacher's desk, one Seth Thomas clock and one picture. The pictures identified the rooms, and the pre-Raphaelite influence was overwhelming. Galahad standing in full armour pointed the way for third-graders; Atlanta's race urged on the fourth, the Pot of Basil confused the fifth grade, and so on until the denunciation of Cataline sent the eighth-graders on to high school with a sense of high civic virtue.

Cal and Aron were assigned to the seventh grade because of their age, and they learned every shadow of its picture–Laocoön completely wrapped in snakes.

The boys were stunned by the size and grandeur of the West End after their background in a one-room country school. The opulence of having a teacher for each grade made a deep impression on them. It seemed wasteful. But, as is true of all humans, they were stunned for one day, admiring on the second, and on the third day could not remember very clearly ever having gone to any other school.

The teacher was dark and pretty, and by judicious raising or withholding of hands the twins had no worries. Cal worked it out quickly and explained it to Aron. 'You take most kids,' he said, 'if they know the answer, why, they hold up their hands, and if they don't know they just crawl under the desk. Know what we're going to do?'

'No. What?'

'Well, you notice the teacher don't always call on somebody with his hand up. She lets drive at the others and, sure enough, they don't know.'

'That's right,' said Aron.

'Now, first week we're going to work like bedamned but we won't stick up our hands. So she'll call on us and we'll know. That'll throw her. So the second week we won't work and we'll stick up our hands and she won't call on us. Third week we'll just sit quiet, and she won't even know whether we got the answer or not. Pretty soon she'll let us alone. She isn't going to waste her time calling on somebody that knows.'

Cal's method worked. In a short time the twins were not only let alone but got themselves a certain reputation for smartness. As a matter of fact, Cal's method was a waste of time. Both boys learned easily enough.

Cal was able to develop his marble game and set about gathering in all the chalkies and immies, glassies and agates, in the school-yard. He traded them for tops just as the marble season ended. At one time he had and used as legal tender at least forty-five tops of various sizes and colours, from the thick clumsy baby tops to the lean and dangerous splitters with their needle points.

Everyone who saw the twins remarked on their difference one from the other and seemed puzzled that this should be so. Cal was growing up dark-skinned, dark-haired. He was quick and sure and secret. Even though he may have tried, he could not conceal his cleverness. Adults were impressed with what seemed to them a precocious maturity, and they were a little frightened at it too. No one liked Cal very much and yet everyone was touched with fear of him and through fear with respect. Although he had no friends he was welcomed by his obsequious class-mates and took up a natural and cold position of leadership in the school-yard.

If he concealed his ingenuity, he concealed his hurts too. He was regarded as thick-skinned and insensitive–even cruel.

Aron drew love from every side. He seemed shy and delicate. His pink-and-white skin, golden hair, and wide-set blue eyes caught attention. In the school-yard his very prettiness caused some difficulty until it was discovered by his testers that Aron was a dogged, steady, and completely fearless fighter, particularly when he was crying. Word got around, and the natural punishers of new boys learned to let him alone. Aron did not attempt to hide his disposition. It was concealed by being the opposite of his appearance. He was unchanging once a course was set. He had few facets and very little versatility. His body was as insensitive to pain as was his mind to subtleties.

Cal knew his brother and could handle him by keeping him off balance, but this only worked up to a certain point. Cal had learned when to sidestep, when to run away. Change of direction confused Aron, but that was the only thing that confused him. He set his path and followed it and he did not see nor was he interested in anything beside his path. His emotions were few and heavy. All of him was hidden by his angelic face, and for this he had no more concern or responsibility than has a fawn for the dappling spots of its young hide.

2

On Aron's first day at school he waited eagerly for the recess. He went over to the girlside to talk to Abra. A mob of squealing girls could not drive him out. It took a full-grown teacher to force him back to the boyside.

At noon he missed her, for her father came in his high-wheeled buggy and drove her home for her lunch. He waited outside the school-yard gate for her after school.

She came out surrounded by girls. Her face was composed and gave no sign that she expected him. She was far the prettiest girl in the school, but it is doubtful whether Aron had noticed that.

The cloud of girls hung on and hung on. Aron marched along three paces behind them, patient and unembarrassed even when the girls tossed their squealing barbs of insult over their shoulders at him. Gradually some drifted away to their own homes, and only three girls were with Abra when she came to the white gate of her yard and turned in. Her friends stared at him a moment, giggled, and went on their way.

Aron sat down on the edge of the sidewalk. After a moment the latch lifted, the white gate opened, and Abra emerged. She walked across the walk and stood over him. 'What do you want?'

Aron's wide eyes looked up at her. 'You aren't engaged to anybody?'

'Silly,' she said.

He struggled up to his feet. 'I guess it will be a long time before we can get married,' he said.

'Who wants to get married?'

Aron didn't answer. Perhaps he didn't hear. He walked along beside her.

Abra moved with firm and deliberate steps and she faced straight ahead. There was wisdom and sweetness in her expression. She seemed deep in thought. And Aron, walking beside her, never took his eyes from her face. His attention seemed tied to her face by a taut string.

They walked silently past the Baby School, and there the pavement ended. Abra turned right and led the way through the stubble of the summer's hayfield. The black 'dobe clods crushed under their feet.

On the edge of the field stood a little pump-house, and a willow tree flourished beside it, fed by the overspill of water. The long skirts of the willow hung down nearly to the ground.

Abra parted the switches like a curtain and went into the house of leaves made against the willow trunk by the sweeping branches. You could see out through the leaves, but inside it was sweetly protected and warm and safe. The afternoon sunlight came yellow through the ageing leaves.

Abra sat down on the ground, or rather she seemed to drift down, and her skirts settled in a billow around her. She folded her hands in her lap almost as though she were praying.

Aron sat down beside her. 'I guess it will be a long time before we can get married,' he said again.

'Not so long,' Abra said.

'I wish it was now.'

'It won't be long,' said Abra.

Aron asked, 'Do you think your father will let you?'

It was a new thought to her, and she turned and looked at him. 'Maybe I won't ask him.'

'But your mother?'

'Let's not disturb them,' she said. 'They'd think it was funny or bad. Can't you keep a secret?'

'Oh, yes. I can keep secrets better than anybody. And I've got some too.'

Abra said, 'Well, you just put this one with the others.'

Aron picked up a twig and drew a line on the dark earth. 'Abra, do you know how you get babies?'

'Yes,' she said. 'Who told you?'

'Lee told me. He explained the whole thing. I guess we can't have any babies for a long time.'

Abra's mouth turned up at the corners with a condescending wisdom. 'Not so long,' she said.

'We'll have a house together some time,' Aron said, bemused. 'We'll go in and close the door and it will be nice. But that will be a long time.'

Abra put out her hand and touched him on the arm. 'Don't you worry about long times,' she said. 'This is a kind of a house. We can play like we live here while we're waiting. And you will be my husband and you can call me wife.'

He tried it over his breath and then aloud. 'Wife,' he said.

'It'll be like practising,' said Abra.

Aron's arm shook under her hand, and she put it, palm up, in her lap.

Aron said suddenly, 'While we're practising, maybe we could do something else.'

'What?'

'Maybe you wouldn't like it.'

'What is it?'

'Maybe we could pretend like you're my mother.'

'That's easy,' she said.

'Would you mind?'

'No, I'd like it. Do you want to start now?'

'Sure,' Aron said. 'How do you want to go about it?'

'Oh, I can tell you that,' said Abra. She put a cooing tone in her voice and said, 'Come, my baby, put your head in Mother's lap. Come, my little son. Mother will hold you.' She drew his head down and without warning Aron began to cry and could not stop. He wept quietly, and Abra stroked his cheek and wiped the flowing tears away with the edge of her skirt.

The sun crept down towards its setting place behind the Salinas River, and a bird began to sing wonderfully from the golden stubble of the field. It was as beautiful under the branches of the willow tree as anything in the world can be.

Very slowly Aron's weeping stopped, and he felt good and he felt warm.

'My good little baby,' Abra said. 'Here, let Mother brush your hair back.'

Aron sat up and said almost angrily, 'I don't hardly ever cry unless I'm mad.

I don't know why I cried.'

Abra asked, 'Do you remember your mother?'

'No. She died when I was a little bit of a baby.'

'Don't you know what she looked like?'

'No.'

'Maybe you saw a picture.'

'No, I tell you. We don't have any pictures. I asked Lee and he said no pictures–no, I guess it was Cal asked Lee.'

'When did she die?'

'Right after Cal and I were born.'

'What was her name?'

'Lee says it was Cathy. Say, what are you asking so much for?'

Abra went on calmly, 'How was she complected?'

'What?'

'Light or dark hair?'

'I don't know.'

'Didn't your father tell you?'

'We never asked him.'

Abra was silent, and after a while Aron asked, 'What's the matter–cat got your tongue?'

Abra inspected the setting sun.

Aron asked uneasily, 'You mad with me'–and he added tentatively–'wife?'

'No, I'm not mad. I'm just wondering.'

'What about?'

'About something.' Abra's firm face was tight against a seething inner argument. She asked, 'What's it like not to have any mother?'

'I don't know. It's like anything else.'

'I guess you wouldn't even know the difference.'

'I would too. I wish you would talk out. You're like riddles in the *Bulletin*.'

Abra continued in her concentrated imperturbability, 'Do you want to have a mother?'

'That's crazy,' said Aron. ''Course I do. Everybody does. You aren't trying to hurt my feelings, are you? Cal tries that sometimes and then he laughs.'

Abra looked away from the setting sun. She had difficulty seeing past the purple spots the light had left on her eyes. 'You said a little while ago you could keep secrets.'

'I can.'

'Well, do you have a double-poison-and-cut-my-throat secret?'

'Sure I have.'

Abra said softly, 'Tell me what it is, Aron.' She put a caress in his name.

'Tell you what?'

'Tell me the deepest down hell-and-goddamn secret you know.'

Aron reared back from her in alarm. 'Why, I will not,' he said. 'What right have you got to ask me? I wouldn't tell anybody.'

'Come on, my baby–tell Mother,' she crooned.

There were tears crowding up in his eyes again, but this time they were tears of anger. 'I don't know as I want to marry you,' he said. 'I think I'm going home now.'

Abra put her hand on his wrist and hung on. Her voice lost its coquetry. 'I wanted to see. I guess you can keep secrets all right.'

'Why did you go for to do it? I'm mad now. I feel sick.'

'I think I'm going to tell you a secret,' she said.

'Ho!' he jeered at her. 'Who can't keep a secret now?'

'I was going to decide,' she said. 'I think I'm going to tell you this secret because it might be good for you. It might make you glad.'

'Who told you not to tell?'

'Nobody,' she said. 'I only told myself.'

'Well, I guess that's a little different. What's your old secret?'

The red sun leaned its rim on the roof-tree of Tollot's house on the Blanco Road, and Tollot's chimney stuck up like a black thumb against it.

Abra said softly, 'Listen, you remember when we came to your place that time?'

'Sure!'

'Well, in the buggy I went to sleep, and when I woke up my father and mother didn't know I was awake. They said your mother wasn't dead. They said she went away. They said something bad must have happened to her, and she went away.'

Aron said hoarsely. 'She's dead.'

'Wouldn't it be nice if she wasn't?'

'My father says she's dead. He's not a liar.'

'Maybe *he* thinks she's dead.'

He said, 'I think he'd know.' But there was uncertainty in his tone.

Abra said, 'Wouldn't it be nice if we could find her? S'pose she lost her memory or something. I've read about that. And we could find her and that would make her remember.' The glory of the romance caught her like a rip tide and carried her away.

Aron said, 'I'll ask my father.'

'Aron,' she said sternly, 'what I told you is a secret.'

'Who says?'

'I say. Now you just say after me–"I'll take double poison and cut my throat if I tell." '

For a moment he hesitated and then he repeated, 'I'll take double poison and cut my throat if I tell.'

She said, 'Now spit in your palm–like this–that's right. Now you give me your hand–see?–squidge the spit all together. Now rub it dry on your hair.' The two followed the formula, and then Abra said solemnly, 'Now, I'd just like to see you tell that one. I knew one girl that told a secret after that oath and she burned up in a barn fire.'

The sun was gone behind Tollot's house and the gold light with it. The evening star shimmered over Mount Toro.

Abra said, 'They'll skin me alive. Come on. Hurry! I bet my father's got the dog whistle out for me. I'll get whipped.'

Aron looked at her in disbelief. 'Whipped! They don't whip you?'

'That's what you think!'

Aron said passionately, 'You just let them try. If they go for to whip you, you tell them I'll kill them.' His wide-set blue eyes were slitted and glinting. 'Nobody's going to whip my wife,' he said.

Abra put her arms around his neck in the dusk under the willow tree. She kissed him on his open mouth. 'I love you, husband,' she said, and then she turned and bolted, holding up her skirts above her knees, her lace-edged white drawers flashing as she ran towards home.

3

Aron went back to the trunk of the willow tree and sat on the ground and leaned back against the bark. His mind was a greyness and there were churnings of pain in his stomach. He tried to sort out the feeling into thoughts and pictures so the pain would go away. It was hard. His slow deliberate mind could not accept so many thoughts and emotions at once. The door was shut against everything except physical pain. After a while the door opened a little and let in one thing to be scrutinized and then another and another, until all had been absorbed, one at a time. Outside his closed mind a huge thing was clamouring to get in. Aron held it back until last.

First he let Abra in and went over her dress, her face, the feel of her hand on his cheek, the odour that came from her, like milk a little and like cut grass a little. He saw and felt and heard and smelled her all over again. He thought how clean she was, her hands and fingernails, and how straightforward and unlike the gigglers in the school-yard.

Then, in order, he thought of her holding his head and his baby crying, crying with longing, wanting something and in a way feeling that he was getting it. Perhaps the getting it was what had made him cry.

Next he thought of her trick–her testing of him. He wondered what she would have done if he had told her a secret. What secret could he have told her if he had wished? Right now he didn't recall any secret except the one that was beating on the door to get into his mind.

The sharpest question she had asked, 'How does it feel not to have a mother?' slipped into his mind. And how did it feel? It didn't feel like anything. Ah, but in the schoolroom, at Christmas and graduation, when the mothers of other children came to the parties–then was the silent cry and the wordless longing. That's what it was like.

Salinas was surrounded and penetrated with swamps, with tule-filled ponds, and every pond spawned thousands of frogs. With the evening the air was so full of their song that it was a kind of roaring silence. It was a veil, a background, and its sudden disappearance, after a clap of thunder, was a shocking thing. It is possible that if in the night the frog sound should have stopped, everyone in Salinas would have awakened, feeling that there was a great noise. In their millions the frog songs seemed to have a beat and a cadence, and perhaps it is the ears' function to do this just as it is the eyes' business to make stars twinkle.

It was quite dark under the willow tree now. Aron wondered whether he was ready for the big thing, and while he wondered it slipped through and was in.

His mother was alive. Often he had pictured her laying underground, still and cool and unrotted. But this was not so. Somewhere she moved about and spoke, and her hands moved and her eyes were open. And in the midst of this flood of pleasure a sorrow came down on him and a sense of loss, a dreadful loss. Aron was puzzled. He inspected the cloud of sadness. If his mother was alive, his father was a liar. If one was alive, the other was dead. Aron said aloud under the tree, 'My mother is dead. She's buried some place in the East.'

In the darkness he saw Lee's face and heard Lee's soft speech. Lee had built very well. Having a respect that amounted to reverence for the truth he had also its natural opposite, a loathing of a lie. He had made it very clear to the boys exactly what he meant. If something was untrue and you didn't know it, that was error. But if you knew a true thing and changed it to a false thing, both you and it were loathsome.

Lee's voice said, 'I know that sometimes a lie is used in kindness. I don't believe it ever works kindly. The quick pain of truth can pass away, but the slow, eating agony of a lie is never lost. That's a running sore.' And Lee had worked patiently and slowly and he had succeeding in building Adam as the centre, the foundation, the essence of truth.

Aron shook his head in the dark, shook it hard in disbelief. 'If my father is a liar, Lee is a liar too.' He was lost. He had no one to ask. Cal was a liar, but Lee's conviction had made Cal a clever liar. Aron felt that something had to die–his mother or his world.

His solution lay before him. Abra had not lied. She had told him only what she had heard, and her parents had only heard it too. He got to his feet and pushed his mother back into death and closed his mind against her.

He was late for supper. 'I was with Abra,' he explained. After supper, when Adam sat in his new comfortable chair, reading the *Salinas Index*, he felt a stroking touch on his shoulder and looked up. 'What is it, Aron?' he asked.

'Good night, Father,' Aron said.

CHAPTER 37

I

February in Salinas is likely to be damp and cold and full of miseries. The heaviest rains fall then and if the river is going to rise, it rises then. February of 1915 was a year heavy with water.

The Trasks were well established in Salinas. Lee, once he had given up his brackish bookish dream, made a new kind of place for himself in the house beside Reynaud's Bakery. On the ranch his possessions had never really been unpacked, for Lee had lived poised to go somewhere else. Here, for the first time in his life, he built a home for himself, feathered with comfort and permanence.

The large bedroom nearest the street door fell to him. Lee dipped into his savings. He had never before spent a needless penny, since all money had been earmarked for his bookstore. But now he bought a little hard bed and a desk. He built bookshelves and unpacked his books, investing in a soft rug and tacked prints on the walls. He placed a deep and comfortable Morris chair under the best reading-lamp he could find. And last he bought a typewriter and set about learning to use it.

Having broken out of his own Spartanism, he remade the Trask household, and Adam gave him no opposition. A gas stove came into the house and electric wires and a telephone. He spent Adam's money remorselessly–new furniture, new carpets, a gas water-heater, and a large ice-box. In a short time there was hardly a house in Salinas so well equipped. Lee defended himself to Adam, saying, 'You have plenty of money. It would be a shame not to enjoy it.'

'I'm not complaining,' Adam protested. 'Only I'd like to buy something too. What shall I buy?'

'Why don't you go to Logan's music store and listen to one of the new phonographs?'

'I think I'll do that,' said Adam. And he bought a Victor victrola, a tall Gothic instrument, and he went regularly to see what new records had come in.

The growing century was shucking Adam out of his shell. He subscribed to the *Atlantic Monthly* and the National Geographic. He joined the Masons and seriously considered the Elks. The new ice-box fascinated him. He bought a textbook on refrigeration and began to study it.

The truth was that Adam needed work. He came out of his long sleep needing to do something.

'I think I'll go into business,' he said to Lee.

'You don't need to. You have enough to live on.'

'But I'd like to be doing something.'

'That's different,' said Lee. 'Know what you want to do? I don't think you'd be very good at business.'

'Why not?'

'Just a thought,' said Lee.

'Say, Lee, I want you to read an article. It says they've dug up a mastodon in Siberia. Been in the ice thousands of years. And the meat's still good.'

Lee smiled at him. 'You've got a bug in your bonnet somewhere,' he said. 'What have you got in all those little cups in the ice-box?'

'Different things.'

'Is that the business? Some of the cups smell bad.'

'It's an idea,' Adam said, 'I can't seem to stay away from it. I just can't seem to get over the idea that you can keep things if you get them cold enough.'

'Let's not have any mastodon meat in our ice-box,' said Lee.

If Adam had conceived thousands of ideas, the way Sam Hamilton had, they might all have drifted away, but he had only the one. The frozen mastodon stayed in his mind. His little cups of fruit, of puddings, bits of meat, both cooked and raw, continued in the ice-box. He bought every available book on bacteria and began sending for magazines and printed articles of a mildly scientific nature. And, as is usually true of a man of one idea, he became obsessed.

Salinas had a small ice company, not large but enough to supply the few houses with ice-boxes and to service the ice-cream parlours. The horse-drawn ice wagon went its route every day.

Adam began to visit the ice plant, and pretty soon he was taking his little cups to the freezing chambers. He wished with all his heart that Sam Hamilton were alive to discuss cold with him. Sam would have covered the field very quickly, he thought.

Adam was walking back from the ice plant one rainy afternoon, thinking about Sam Hamilton, when he saw Will Hamilton go into the Abbot House Bar. He followed him and leaned against the bar beside him. 'Why don't you come up and have some supper with us?'

'I'd like to,' Will said. 'I tell you what–I've got a deal I'm trying to put through. If I get finished in time I'll walk by. Is there something important?'

'Well, I don't know. I've been doing some thinking and I'd like to ask your advice.'

Nearly every business proposition in the country came sooner or later to Will Hamilton's attention. He might have excused himself if he had not remembered that Adam was a rich man. An idea was one thing, but backed up with cash was quite another. 'You wouldn't entertain a reasonable offer for your ranch, would you?' he asked.

'Well, the boys, particularly Cal, they like the place. I think I'll hang on to it.'

'I think I can turn it over for you.'

'No, it's rented, paying its own taxes. I'll hold on to it.'

'If I can't get in for supper I might be able to come in afterwards,' said Will.

Will Hamilton was a very substantial business man. No one knew exactly how many pies his thumb had explored, but it was known that he was a clever and comparatively rich man. His business deal had been non-existent. It was a part of his policy always to be busy and occupied.

He had supper alone in the Abbot House. After a considered time he walked round the corner on Central Avenue and rang the bell of Adam Trask's house.

The boys had gone to bed. Lee sat with a darning basket, mending the long black stockings the twins wore at school. Adam had been reading the *Scientific American*. He let Will in and placed a chair for him. Lee brought a pot of coffee and went back to his mending.

Will settled himself into a chair, took out a fat black cigar, and lighted up. He waited for Adam to open the game.

'Nice weather for a change. And how's your mother?' Adam said.

'Just fine. Seems younger every day. The boys must be growing up.'

'Oh, they are. Cal's going to be in his school play. He's quite an actor. Aron's a real good student. Cal wants to go to farming.'

'Nothing wrong with that if you go about it right. Country could use some forward-looking farmers.' Will waited uneasily. He wondered if it could be that Adam's money was exaggerated. Could Adam be getting ready to borrow money? Will quickly worked out how much he would lend on the Trask ranch and how much he could borrow on it. The figures were not the same, nor was the interest rate. And still Adam did not come up with his proposition. Will grew restless. 'I can't stay very long,' he said. 'Told a fellow I'd meet him later tonight.'

'Have another cup of coffee,' Adam suggested.

'No thanks. Keeps me awake. Did you have something you wanted to see me about?'

Adam said, 'I was thinking about your father and I thought I'd like to talk to a Hamilton.'

Will relaxed a little in his chair. 'He was a great old talker.'

'Somehow he made a better man than he was,' said Adam.

Lee looked up from his darning egg. 'Perhaps the best conversationalist in the world is the man who helps others to talk.'

Will said, 'You know, it sounds funny to hear you use all those two-bit words. I'd swear to God you used to talk pidgin.'

'I used to,' said Lee. 'It was vanity, I guess.' He smiled at Adam and said to Will, 'Did you hear that somewhere up in Siberia they dug a mastodon out of the ice? It had been there a hundred thousand years and the meat was still fresh.'

'Mastodon?'

'Yes, a kind of elephant that hasn't lived on the earth for a long time.'

'Meat was still fresh?'

'Sweet as a pork chop,' said Lee. He shoved the wooden egg into the shattered knee of a black stocking.

'That's very interesting,' said Will.

Adam laughed. 'Lee hasn't wiped my nose yet, but that will come,' he said. I guess I'm pretty roundabout. The whole thing comes up because I'm tired of just sitting around. I want to get something to take up my time.'

'Why don't you farm your place?'

'No. That doesn't interest me. You see, Will, I'm not like a man looking for a job. I'm looking for work. I don't need a job.'

Will came out of his cautiousness, 'Well, what can I do for you?'

'I thought I'd tell you an idea I had, and you might give me an opinion. You're a business man.'

'Of course,' said Will. 'Anything I can do.'

'I've been looking into refrigeration,' said Adam. 'I got an idea and I can't get rid of it. I go to sleep and it comes right back at me. Never had anything give me so much trouble. It's kind of a big idea. Maybe it's full of holes.'

Will uncrossed his legs and pulled at his trousers where they were binding him. 'Go ahead–shoot,' he said. 'Like a cigar?'

Adam didn't hear the offer, nor did he know the implication. 'The whole country's changing,' Adam said. 'People aren't going to live the way they used to. Do you know where the biggest market for oranges in the winter is?'

'No. Where?'

'New York City. I read that. Now in the cold parts of the country, don't you think people get to wanting perishable things in the winter–like peas and lettuce and cauliflower? In a big part of the country they don't have those things for months and months. And right here in the Salinas Valley we can raise them all the year round.'

'Right here isn't right there,' said Will. 'What's your idea?'

'Well, Lee made me get a big ice-box, and I got kind of interested. I put different kinds of vegetables in there. And I got to arranging them in different ways. You know, Will, if you chop ice fine and lay a head of lettuce in it and wrap it in waxed paper, it will keep three weeks and come out fresh and good.'

'Go on,' said Will cautiously.

'Well, you know the railroads built those fruit cars. I went down and had a look at them. They're pretty good. Do you know we could ship lettuce right to the east coast in the middle of winter?'

Will asked, 'Where do you come in?'

'I was thinking of buying the ice plant here in Salinas and trying to ship some things.'

'That would cost a lot of money.'

'I have quite a lot of money,' said Adam.

Will Hamilton pulled his lip angrily. 'I don't know why I got into this,' he said. 'I know better.'

'How do you mean?'

'Look here,' said Will. 'When a man comes to me for advice about an idea, I know he doesn't want advice. He wants me to agree with him. And if I want to keep his friendship I tell him his idea is fine and go ahead. But I like you and you're a friend of my family, so I'm going to stick my neck out.'

Lee put down his darning, moved his sewing basket to the floor, and changed his glasses.

Adam remonstrated, 'What are you getting upset about?'

'I come from a whole goddam family of inventors,' said Will. 'We had ideas for breakfast. We had ideas instead of breakfast. We had so many ideas we forgot to make the money for groceries. When we got a little ahead my father, or Tom, patented something. I'm the only one in my family, except my mother, who didn't have ideas, and I'm the only one who ever made a dime. Tom had ideas about helping people, and some of it was pretty darn near socialism. And if you tell me you don't care about making a profit, I'm going to throw that coffee-pot right at your head.'

'Well, I don't care much.'

'You stop right there, Adam. I've got my neck out. If you want to drop forty or fifty thousand dollars quick, you just go on with your idea. But I'm telling you–let your damned idea lie. Kick dust over it.'

'What's wrong with it?'

'Everything's wrong with it. People in the East aren't used to vegetables in the winter. They wouldn't buy them. You get your cars stuck on a siding and you'll lose the shipment. The market is controlled. Oh, Jesus Christ! It makes me mad when babies try to ride into business on an idea.'

Adam sighed. 'You make Sam Hamilton sound like a criminal,' he said.

'Well, he was my father and I loved him, but I wish to God he had let ideas alone.' Will looked at Adam and saw amazement in his eyes, and suddenly Will was ashamed. He shook his head slowly from side to side. 'I didn't mean to run down my people,' he said. 'I think they were good people. But my advice to you stands. Let refrigeration alone.'

Adam turned slowly to Lee. 'Have we got any more of that lemon pie we had for supper?' he asked.

'I don't think so,' said Lee. 'I thought I heard mice in the kitchen. I'm afraid there will be white of egg on the boy's pillows. You've got half a quart of whisky.'

'Have I? Why don't we have that?'

'I got excited,' said Will, and he tried to laugh at himself. 'A drink would do me good.' His face was fiery red and his voice was strained in his throat. 'I'm getting too fat,' he said.

But he had two drinks and relaxed. Sitting comfortably, he instructed Adam. 'Some things don't ever change their value,' he said. 'If you want to put money into something, you look around at the world. This war in Europe is going on a long time. And when there's war there's going to be hungry people. I won't say it is so, but it wouldn't surprise me if we got into it. I don't trust this Wilson–he's all theory and big words. And if we do get into it, there's going to be fortunes made in imperishable foods. You take rice and corn and wheat and beans, they don't need ice. They keep, and people can stay alive on them. I'd say if you were to plant your whole damned bottom land to beans and just put them away, why, your boys wouldn't have to worry about the future. Beans are up to three cents now. If we get into the war I wouldn't be surprised if they went to ten cents. And you keep beans dry and they'll be right there, waiting for a market. If you want to turn a profit, you plant beans.'

He went away feeling good. The shame that had come over him was gone and he knew he had given sound advice.

After Will had gone Lee brought out one-third of a lemon pie and cut it in two. 'He's getting too fat,' Lee said.

Adam was thinking. 'I only said I wanted something to do,' he observed.

'How about the ice plant?'

'I think I'll buy it.'

'You might plant some beans too,' said Lee.

2

Late in the year Adam made his great try, and it was a sensation in a year of sensations, both local and international. As he got ready, business men spoke of him as far-seeing, forward-looking, progress-minded. The departure of six car-loads of lettuce packed in ice was given a civic overtone. The Chamber of Commerce attended the departure. The cars were decorated with big posters which said, 'Salinas Valley Lettuce'. But no one wanted to invest in the project.

Adam untapped energy he did not suspect he had. It was a big job to gather, trim, box, ice, and load the lettuce. There was no equipment for such work. Everything had to be improvised, a great many hands hired and taught to do the work. Everyone gave advice but no one helped. It was estimated that Adam had spent a fortune on his idea, but how big a fortune no one knew. Adam did not know. Only Lee knew.

The idea looked good. The lettuce was consigned to commission merchants in New York at a fine price. Then the train was gone and everyone went home to wait. If it was a success any number of men were willing to dig down to put money in. Even Will Hamilton wondered whether he had been wrong with his advice.

If the series of events had been planned by an omnipotent and unforgiving enemy it could not have been more effective. As the train came into Sacramento a snow slide closed the Sierras for two days and the six cars stood on a siding, dripping their ice away. On the third day the freight crossed the mountains, and that was the time for unseasonable warm weather throughout the Middle West. In Chicago there developed a confusion of orders–no one's fault, just one of those things that happen–and Adam's six cars of lettuce stood in the yard for five more days. That was enough, and there is no reason to go into it in detail. What arrived in New York was six car-loads of horrible slop with a sizeable charge just to get rid of it.

Adam read the telegram from the commission house and he settled back in his chair and a strange enduring smile came on his face and did not go away.

Lee kept away from him to let him get a grip of himself. The boys heard the reaction in Salinas. Adam was a fool. These know-it-all dreamers always got into trouble. Business men congratulated themselves on their foresight in keeping out of it. It took experience to be a business man. People who inherited their money always got into trouble. And if you wanted proof–just look at how Adam had run his ranch. A fool and his money were soon parted. Maybe that would teach him a lesson. And he had doubled the output of the ice company.

Will Hamilton recalled that he had not only argued against it but he had foretold in detail what would happen. He did not feel pleasure, but what could you do when a man wouldn't take advice from a sound business man? And, God knows, Will had plenty of experience with fly-by-night ideas. In a roundabout way it was recalled that Sam Hamilton had been a fool too. And as for Tom Hamilton–he had been just crazy.

When Lee felt that enough time had passed he did not beat around the bush. He sat directly in front of Adam to get and to keep his attention.

'How do you feel?' he asked.

'All right.'

'You aren't going to crawl back in your hole, are you?'

'What makes you think that?' Adam asked.

'Well, you have the look on your face you used to wear. And you've got that sleep-walker light in your eyes. Does this hurt your feelings?'

'No,' said Adam. 'The only thing I was wondering about was whether I'm wiped out.'

'Not quite,' said Lee. 'You have about nine thousand dollars left and the ranch.'

'There's a two-thousand-dollar bill for garbage disposal,' said Adam.

'That's before the nine thousand.'

'I owe quite a bit for the new ice machinery.'

'That's paid.'

'I have nine thousand?'

'And the ranch,' said Lee. 'Maybe you can sell the ice plant.'

Adam's face tightened up and lost the dazed smile. 'I still believe it will work,' he said. 'It was a whole lot of accidents. I'm going to keep the ice plant. Cold does preserve things. Besides, the plant makes some money. Maybe I can figure something out.'

'Try not to figure something that costs money,' said Lee. I would hate to leave my gas stove.'

3

The twins felt Adam's failure very deeply. They were fifteen years old and they had known so long that they were sons of a wealthy man that the feeling was hard to lose. If only the affair had not been a kind of carnival it would not have been so bad. They remembered the big placards on the freight cars with horror. If the business men made fun of Adam, the high-school group was much more cruel. Overnight it became the thing to refer to the boys as 'Aron and Cal Lettuce', or simply as 'Lettuce-head'.

Aron discussed his problem with Abra. 'It's going to make a big difference,' he told her.

Abra had grown to be a beautiful girl. Her breasts were rising with the leaven of her years, and her face had the calm and warmth of beauty. She had gone beyond prettiness. She was strong and sure and feminine.

She looked at his worried face and asked, 'Why is it going to make a difference?'

'Well, one thing, I think we're poor.'

'You would have worked anyway.'

'You know I want to go to college.'

'You still can. I'll help you. Did your father lose all his money?'

'I don't know. That's what they say.'

'Who is "they"?' Abra asked.

'Why, everybody. And maybe your father and mother won't want you to marry me.'

'Then I won't tell them about it,' said Abra.

'You're pretty sure of yourself.'

'Yes,' she said, 'I'm pretty sure of myself. Will you kiss me?'

'Right here? Right in the street?'

'Why not?'

'Everybody'd see.'

'I want them to,' said Abra.

Aron said, 'No. I don't like to make things public like that.'

She stepped around in front of him and stopped him. 'You look here, mister. You kiss me now.'

'Why?'

She said slowly, 'So everybody will know that I'm Mrs Lettuce-head.'

He gave her a quick embarrassed peck and then forced her beside him again. 'Maybe I ought to call it off myself,' he said.

'What do you mean?'

'Well, I'm not good enough for you now. I'm just another poor kid. You think I haven't seen the difference in your father?'

'You're just crazy,' Abra said. And she frowned a little because she had seen the difference in her father too.

They went into Bell's candy store and sat at a table. The rage was celery tonic that year. The year before it had been root-beer ice-cream sodas.

Abra stirred bubbles delicately with her straw and thought how her father had changed since the lettuce failure. He had said to her, 'Don't you think it would be wise to see someone else for a change?'

'But I'm engaged to Aron.'

'Engaged?' he snorted at her. 'Since when do children get engaged? You'd better look around a little. There are other fish in the sea.'

And she remembered that recently there had been references to suitability of families and once a hint that some people couldn't keep a scandal hidden for ever. This had happened only when Adam was reputed to have lost all of his money.

She leaned across the table. 'You know, what we could really do is so simple it will make you laugh.'

'What?'

'We could run your father's ranch. My father says it's beautiful land.'

'No,' Aron said quickly.

'Why not?'

'I'm not going to be a farmer and you're not going to be a farmer's wife.'

'I'm going to be Aron's wife, no matter what he is.'

'I'm not going to give up college,' he said.

'I'll help you,' Abra said again.

'Where would you get the money?'

'Steal it,' she said.

'I want to get out of this town,' he said. 'Everybody's sneering at me. I can't stand it here.'

'They'll forget it pretty soon.'

'No, they won't either. I don't want to stay two years more to finish high school.'

'Do you want to go away from me, Aron?'

'No. Oh damn it, why did he have to mess with things he doesn't know about?'

Abra reproved him. 'Don't you blame your father. If it had worked everybody'd been bowing to him.'

'Well, it didn't work. He sure fixed me. I can't hold up my head. By God! I hate him!'

Abra said sternly, 'Aron! You stop talking like that!'

'How do I know he didn't lie about my mother?'

Abra's face reddened with anger. 'You ought to be spanked,' she said. 'If it wasn't in front of everybody I'd spank you myself.' She looked at his beautiful face, twisted now with rage and frustration, and suddenly she changed her tactics. 'Why don't you ask about your mother? Just come right out and ask him.'

'I can't, I promised you.'

'You only promised not to say what I told you.'

'Well, if I asked him he'd want to know where I heard.'

'All right,' she cried, 'you're a spoiled baby! I let you out of your promise. Go ahead and ask him.'

'I don't know if I will or not.'

'Sometimes I want to kill you,' she said. 'But, Aron–I do love you so. I do love you so.' There was giggling from the stools in front of the soda fountain. Their voices had risen and they were overheard by their peers. Aron blushed and tears of anger started in his eyes. He ran out of the store and plunged away up the street.

Abra calmly picked up her purse and straightened her skirt and brushed it with her hand. She walked calmly over to Mr Bell and paid for the celery tonics. On her way to the door she stopped by the giggling group. 'You let him alone,' she said coldly. She walked on, and a falsetto followed her–'Oh, Aron, I do love you so.'

In the street she broke into a run to try to catch up with Aron, but she couldn't find him. She called on the telephone. Lee said that Aron had not come home. But Aron was in his bedroom, lapped in resentments–Lee had seen him creep in and close his door behind him.

Abra walked up and down the streets of Salinas, hoping to catch sight of him. She was angry at him, but she was also bewilderingly lonely. Aron hadn't ever run away from her before. Abra had lost her gift for being alone.

Cal had to learn loneliness. For a very short time he tried to join Abra and Aron, but they didn't want him. He was jealous and tried to attract the girl to himself and failed.

His studies he found easy and not greatly interesting. Aron had to work harder to learn, therefore Aron had a greater sense of accomplishment when he did learn, and he developed a respect for learning out of all proportion with the quality of the learning. Cal drifted through. He didn't care much for the sports at school or for the activities. His growing restlessness drove him out at night. He grew tall and rangy, and always there was the darkness about him.

CHAPTER 38

I

From his first memory Cal had craved warmth and affection, just as everyone does. If he had been an only child or if Aron had been a different kind of boy, Cal might have achieved his relationship normally and easily. But from the very first people were won instantly to Aron by his beauty and his simplicity. Cal very naturally competed for attention and affection in the only way he knew–by trying to imitate Aron. And what was charming in the blond ingenuousness of Aron became suspicious and unpleasant in the dark-faced, slit-eyed Cal. And since he was pretending, his performance was not convincing. Where Aron was received, Cal was rebuffed for doing or saying exactly the same thing.

And as a few strokes on the nose will make a puppy head-shy, so a few rebuffs will make a boy shy all over. But whereas a puppy will cringe away or roll on its back, grovelling, a little boy may cover his shyness with nonchalance, with bravado, or with secrecy. And once a boy has suffered rejection, he will find rejection even where it does not exist–or, worse, will draw it forth from people simply by expecting it.

In Cal the process had been so long and so slow that he felt no strangeness. He had built a wall of self-sufficiency around himself, strong enough to defend him against the world. If his wall had any weak places they may have been on the sides nearest Aron and Lee, and particularly nearest Adam. Perhaps in his father's very unawareness Cal had felt safety. Not being noticed at all was better than being noticed adversely.

When he was quite small Cal had discovered a secret. If he moved very quietly to where his father was sitting and if he leaned very lightly against his father's knee, Adam's hand would rise automatically and his fingers would caress Cal's shoulder. It is probable that Adam did not even know he did it, but the caress brought such a raging flood of emotion to the boy that he saved this special joy and used it only when he needed it. It was a magic to be depended upon. It was the ceremonial symbol of a dogged adoration.

Things do not change with a change of scene. In Salinas, Cal had no more friends than he had in King City. Associates he had, and authority and some admiration, but friends he did not have. He lived alone and walked alone.

2

If Lee knew that Cal left the house at night and returned very late, he gave no sign, since he couldn't do anything about it. The night constables sometimes saw him walking alone. Chief Heiserman made it a point to speak to the truant officer, who assured him that Cal not only had no record for playing hooky but actually was a very good student. The chief knew Adam, of course, and since Cal broke no windows and caused no disturbance he told the constables to keep their eyes open but to let the boy alone unless he got into trouble.

Old Tom Watson caught up with Cal one night and asked, 'Why do you walk around so much at night?'

'I'm not bothering anybody,' said Cal defensively.

'I know you're not. But you ought to be home in bed.'

'I'm not sleepy,' said Cal, and this didn't make any sense at all to Old Tom, who couldn't remember any time in his whole life when he wasn't sleepy. The boy looked in on the fan-tan games in Chinatown, but he didn't play. It was a mystery, but then fairly simple things were mysteries to Tom Watson and he preferred to leave them that way.

On his walks Cal often recalled the conversation between Lee and Adam he had heard on the ranch. He wanted to dig out the truth. And his knowledge accumulated slowly, a reference heard in the street, the gibing talk in the pool-hall. If Aron had heard the fragments he would not have noticed, but Cal collected them. He knew that his mother was not dead. He knew also, both from the first conversation and from the talk he heard, that Aron was not likely to be pleased at discovering her.

One night Cal ran into Rabbit Holman, who was up from San Ardo on his semi-annual drunk. Rabbit greeted Cal effusively, as a country man always greets an acquaintance in a strange place. Rabbit, drinking from a pint flask in the alley behind the Abbot House, told Cal all the news he could think of. He had sold a piece of his land at a fine price and he was in Salinas to celebrate, and celebration meant the whole shebang. He was going down the Line and show the whores what a real man could do.

Cal sat quietly beside him, listening. When the whisky got low in Rabbit's pint Cal slipped away and got Louis Schneider to buy him another one. And Rabbit put down his empty pint and reached for it again and came up with the full pint.

'Funny,' he said, 'thought I had only one. Well, it's a good mistake.'

Half way down the second pint Rabbit had not only forgotten who Cal was but how old he was. He remembered, however, that his companion was his very dear old friend.

'Tell you what, George,' he said. 'You let me get a little more of this here lead in my pencil and you and me will go down the Line. Now don't say you can't afford it. The whole shebang's on me. Did I tell you I sold forty acres? Wasn't no good neither.'

And he said, 'Harry, tell you what let's do. Let's keep away from them two-bit whores. We'll go to Kate's place. Costs high, ten bucks, but what the hell! They got a circus down there. Ever seen a circus, Harry? Well, it's a lulu. Kate sure knows her stuff. You remember who Kate is, don't you, George? She's Adam Trask's wife, mother of them damn twins. Jesus! I never forget the time she shot him and ran away. Plugged him in the shoulder and just run off. Well, she wasn't no good as a wife but she's sure as hell a good whore. Funny too–you know how they say a whore makes a good wife? Ain't nothing new for them to experiment with. Help me up a little, will you, Harry? What was I saying?'

'Circus,' said Cal softly.

'Oh, yeah. Well, this circus of Kate's will pop your eyes out. Know what they do?'

Cal walked a little behind so that Rabbit would not notice him. Rabbit told what they did. And what they did wasn't what made Cal sick. That just seemed to him silly. It was the men who watched. Seeing Rabbit's face under the street-lights, Cal knew what the watchers at the circus would look like.

They went through the overgrown yard and up on the unpainted porch. Although Cal was tall for his age he walked high on his toes. The guardian of the door didn't look at him very closely. The dim room with its low secret lamps and the nervous waiting men concealed his presence.

3

Always before, Cal had wanted to build a dark accumulation of things seen and things heard–a kind of a warehouse of materials that, like obscure tools, might come in handy, but after the visit to Kate's he felt a desperate need for help.

One night Lee, tapping away at his typewriter, heard a quiet knock on his door and let Cal in. The boy sat down on the edge of the bed, and Lee let his thin body down in the Morris chair. He was amused that a chair could give him so much pleasure. Lee folded his hands over his stomach as though he wore Chinese sleeves and waited patiently. Cal was looking at a spot in the air right over Lee's head.

Cal spoke softly and rapidly. 'I know where my mother is and what she's doing. I saw her.'

Lee's mind was a convulsive prayer for guidance. 'What do you want to know?' he asked softly.

'I haven't thought yet. I'm trying to think. Would you tell me the truth?'

'Of course.'

The questions whirling in Cal's head were so bewildering he had trouble picking one out. 'Does my father know?'

'Yes.'

'Why did he say she was dead?'

'To save you from pain.'

Cal considered. 'What did my father do to make her leave?'

'He loved her with his whole mind and body. He gave her everything he could imagine.'

'Did she shoot him?'

'Yes.'

'Why?'

'Because he didn't want her to go away.'

'Did he ever hurt her?'

'Not that I know of. It wasn't in him to hurt her.'

'Lee, why did she do it?'

'I don't know.'

'Don't know or won't say?'

'Don't know.'

Cal was silent for so long that Lee's fingers began to creep a little, holding to his wrists. He was relieved when Cal spoke again. The boy's tone was different. There was a pleading in it.

'Lee, you knew her. What was she like?'

Lee sighed and his hands relaxed. 'I can only say what I think. I may be wrong.'

'Well, what did you think?'

'Cal,' he said, 'I've thought about it for a great many hours and I still don't know. She is a mystery. It seems to me that she is not like other people. There is something she lacks. Kindness maybe, or conscience. You can only understand people if you feel them in yourself. And I can't feel her. The moment I think about her my feeling goes into darkness. I don't know what she wanted or what she was after. She was full of hatred, but why or towards what I don't know. It's a mystery. And her hatred wasn't healthy. It wasn't angry. It was heartless. I don't know that it is good to talk to you like this.'

'I need to know.'

'Why? Didn't you feel better before you knew?'

'Yes. But I can't stop now.'

'You're right,' said Lee. 'When the first innocence goes, you can't stop–unless you're a hypocrite or a fool. But I can't tell you any more because I don't know any more.'

Cal said, 'Tell me about my father, then.'

'That I can do,' said Lee. He paused. 'I wonder if anyone can hear us talking? Speak softly.'

'Tell me about him,' said Cal.

'I think your father has in him, magnified, the things his wife lacks. I think in him kindness and conscience are so large that they are almost faults. They trip him up and hinder him.'

'What did he do when she left?'

'He died,' said Lee. 'He walked around but he was dead. And only recently has he come half to life again.' Lee saw a strange new expression on Cal's face. The eyes were open wider, and the mouth, ordinarily tight and muscular, was relaxed. In his face, now for the first time, Lee could see Aron's face in spite of the different colouring. Cal's shoulders were shaking a little, like a muscle too long held under strain.

'What is it?' Lee asked.

'I love him,' Cal said.

'I love him too,' said Lee. 'I guess I couldn't have stayed around so long if I hadn't. He is not smart in a worldly sense, but he's a good man. Maybe the best man I have ever known.'

Cal stood up suddenly. 'Good night, Lee,' he said.

'Now you just wait a moment. Have you told anyone?'

'No.'

'Not Aron–no, of course you wouldn't.'

'Suppose he finds out?'

'Then you'd have to stand by to help him. Don't go yet. When you leave this room we may not be able to talk again. You may dislike me for knowing you know the truth. Tell me this–do you hate your mother?'

'Yes,' said Cal.

'I wonder,' said Lee. 'I don't think your father ever hated her. He had only sorrow.'

Cal drifted towards the door, slowly, softly. He shoved his fists deep in his pocket. 'It's like you said about knowing people. I hate her because I know why she went away. I know–because I've got her in me.' His head was down and his voice was heartbroken.

Lee jumped up. 'You stop that!' he said sharply. 'You hear me? Don't let me catch you doing that. Of course you may have that in you. Everybody has. But you've got the other too. Here–look up! Look at me!'

Cal raised his head and said wearily, 'What do you want?'

'You've got the other too. Listen to me! You wouldn't even be wondering if you didn't have it. Don't you dare take the lazy way. It's too easy to excuse yourself because of your ancestry. Don't let me catch you doing it! Now–look close at me so you will remember. Whatever you do, it will be you who do it–not your mother.'

'Do you believe that, Lee?'

'Yes, I believe it, and you'd better believe it or I'll break every bone in your body.'

After Cal had gone Lee went back to his chair. He thought ruefully, 'I wonder what happened to my Oriental repose.'

4

Cal's discovery of his mother was more a verification than a new thing to him. For a long time he had known without details that the cloud was there. And his reaction was twofold. He had an almost pleasant sense of power in knowing, and he could evaluate actions and expressions, could interpret vague references, could even dig up and reorganize the past. But these did not compensate for the pain in his knowledge.

His body was rearranging itself towards manhood, and he was shaken by the veering winds of adolescence. One moment he was dedicated and pure and devoted; the next he wallowed in filth; and the next he grovelled in shame and emerged re-dedicated.

His discovery sharpened all of his emotions. It seemed to him that he was unique, having such a heritage. He could not quite believe Lee's words or conceive that other boys were going through the same thing.

The circus at Kate's remained with him. At one moment the memory inflamed his mind and body with pubescent fire, and the next moment nauseated him with revulsion and loathing.

He looked at his father more closely and saw perhaps more sadness and frustration in Adam than may have been there. And in Cal there grew up a passionate love for his father and a wish to protect him and to make up to him for the things he had suffered. In Cal's own sensitized mind that suffering was unbearable. He blundered into the bathroom while Adam was bathing and saw the ugly bullet scar and heard himself ask against his will, 'Father, what's that scar?'

Adam's fingers went up as though to conceal the scar. He said, 'It's an old wound, Cal. I was in the Indian campaigns. I'll tell you about it some time.'

Cal, watching Adam's face, had seen his mind leap into the past for a lie. Cal didn't hate the lie but the necessity for telling it. Cal lied for reasons of profit of one kind or another. To be driven to a lie seemed shameful to him. He wanted to shout, 'I know how you got it and it's all right.' But, of course, he did not. 'I'd like to hear about it,' he said.

Aron was caught in the roil of change too, but his impulses were more sluggish than Cal's. His body did not scream at him so shrilly. His passions took a religious direction. He decided on the ministry for his future. He attended all services in the Episcopal church, helped with the flowers and leaves at feast times, and spent many hours with the young and curly-haired clergyman, Mr Rolf. Aron's training in worldliness was gained from a young man of no experience, which gave him the ability for generalization only the inexperienced can have.

Aron was confirmed in the Episcopal church and took his place in the choir on Sundays. Abra followed him. Her feminine mind knew such things were necessary but unimportant.

It was natural that the convert Aron should work on Cal. First Aron prayed silently for Cal, but finally he approached him. He denounced Cal's godlessness, demanded his reformation.

Cal might have tried to go along if his brother had been more clever. But Aron had reached a point of passionate purity that made everyone else foul. After a few lectures Cal found him unbearably smug and told him so. It was a relief to both of them when Aron abandoned his brother to eternal damnation.

Aron's religion inevitably took a sexual turn. He spoke to Abra of the necessity for abstinence and decided that he would live a life of celibacy. Abra in her wisdom agreed with him, feeling and hoping that this phase would pass. Celibacy was the only state she had known. She wanted to marry Aron and bear any number of his children, but for the time being she did not speak of it. She had never been jealous before, but now she began to find in herself an instinctive and perhaps justified hatred for the Reverend Mr Rolf.

Cal watched his brother triumph over sins he had never committed. He thought sardonically of telling him about his mother, to see how he would handle it, but he withdrew the thought quickly. He didn't think Aron could handle it at all.

CHAPTER 39

I

At intervals Salinas suffered a mild eructation of morality. The process never varied much. One burst was like another. Sometimes it started in the pulpit and sometimes with a new ambitious president of the Women's Civic Club. Gambling was invariably the sin to be eradicated. There were certain advantages in attacking gambling. One could discuss it, which was not true of prostitution. It was an obvious evil and most of the games were operated by Chinese. There was little chance of treading on the toes of a relative.

From church and club the town's two newspapers caught fire. Editorials demanded a clean-up. The police agreed but pleaded short-handedness and tried for increased budget and sometimes succeeded.

When it got to the editorial stage everyone knew the cards were down. What followed was as carefully produced as a ballet. The police got ready, the gambling houses got ready, and the papers set up congratulatory editorials in advance. Then came the raid, deliberate and sure. Twenty or more Chinese, imported from Pajaro, a few bums, six or eight drummers, who, being strangers, were not warned, fell into the police net, were booked, jailed, and in the morning fined and released. The town relaxed in its new spotlessness and the houses lost only one night of business plus the fines. It is one of the triumphs of the human that he can know a thing and still not believe it.

In the autumn of 1916 Cal was watching the fan-tan game at Shorty Lim's one night when the raid scooped him up. In the dark no one noticed him, and the Chief was embarrassed to find him in the tank in the morning. The Chief telephoned Adam, got him up from his breakfast. Adam walked the two blocks to the City Hall, picked up Cal, crossed the street to the post office for his mail, and then the two walked home.

Lee had kept Adam's eggs warm and had fried two for Cal.

Aron walked through the dining-room on his way to school. 'Want me to wait for you?' he asked Cal.

'No,' said Cal. He kept his eyes down and ate his eggs.

Adam had not spoken except to say, 'Come along!' at the City Hall after he had thanked the Chief.

Cal gulped down a breakfast he did not want, darting glances up through his eyelashes at his father's face. He could make nothing of Adam's expression. It seemed at once puzzled and angry and thoughtful and sad.

Adam stared down into his coffee-cup. The silence grew until it had the weight of age so hard to lift aside.

Lee looked in. 'Coffee?' he asked.

Adam shook his head slowly. Lee withdrew and this time closed the kitchen door.

In the clock-ticking silence Cal began to be afraid. He felt a strength flowing out of his father he had never known was there. Itching prickles of agony ran up his legs, and he was afraid to move to restore the circulation. He knocked his fork against his plate to make a noise and the clatter was swallowed up. The clock struck nine deliberate strokes and they were swallowed up.

As the fear began to chill, resentment took its place. So might a trapped fox feel anger at the paw which held him to the trap.

Suddenly Cal jumped up. He hadn't known he was going to move. He shouted and he hadn't known he was going to speak. He cried, 'Do what you're going to do to me! Go ahead! Get it over!'

And his shout was sucked into the silence.

Adam slowly raised his head. It is true Cal had never looked into his father's eyes before, and it is true that many people never look into their father's eyes. Adam's irises were light blue with dark lines leading into the vortices of the pupils. And deep down in each pupil Cal saw his own face reflected, as though two Cals looked out at him.

Adam said slowly, 'I've failed you, haven't I?'

It was worse than an attack. Cal faltered, 'What do you mean?'

'You were picked up in a gambling house. I don't know how you got there, what you were doing there, why you went there.'

Cal sat limply down and looked at his plate.

'Do you gamble, son?'

'No, sir. I was just watching.'

'Had you been there before?'

'Yes, sir. Many times.'

'Why do you go?'

'I don't know. I get restless at night–like an alley cat, I guess.' He thought of Kate and his weak joke seemed horrible to him. 'When I can't sleep I walk around,' he said, 'to try to blot it out.'

Adam considered his words, inspected each one. 'Does your brother walk around too?'

'Oh, no, sir. He wouldn't think of it. He's–he's not restless.'

'You see, I don't know,' said Adam. 'I don't know anything about you.'

Cal wanted to throw his arms about his father, to hug him and to be hugged by him. He wanted some wild demonstration of sympathy and love. He picked up his wooden napkin ring and thrust his forefinger through it. 'I'd tell you if you asked,' he said softly.

'I didn't ask, I didn't ask! I'm as bad a father as my father was.'

Cal had never heard this tone in Adam's voice. It was hoarse and breaking with warmth and he fumbled among his words, feeling for them in the dark.

'My father made a mould and forced me into it,' Adam said. 'I was a bad casting but I couldn't be re-melted. Nobody can be re-melted. And so I remained a bad casting.'

Cal said, 'Sir, don't be sorry. You've had too much of that.'

'Have I? Maybe–but maybe the wrong kind. I don't know my sons. I wonder whether I could learn.'

'I'll tell you anything you want to know. Just ask me.'

'Where would I start? Right at the beginning?'

'Are you sad or mad because I was in jail?'

To Cal's surprise Adam laughed. 'You were just there, weren't you? You didn't do nothing wrong.'

'Maybe being there was wrong.' Cal wanted a blame for himself.

'One time I was just there,' said Adam. 'I was a prisoner for nearly a year for just being there.'

Cal tried to absorb this heresy. 'I don't believe it,' he said.

'Sometimes I don't either, but I know that when I escaped I robbed a store and stole some clothes.'

'I don't believe it,' Cal said weakly, but the warmth, the closeness, was so delicious that he clung to it. He breathed shallowly so that the warmth might not be disturbed.

Adam said, 'Do you remember Samuel Hamilton?–sure you do. When you were a baby he told me I was a bad father. He hit me, knocked me down, to impress it on me.'

'That old man?'

'He was a tough old man. And now I know what he meant. I'm the same as my father was. He didn't allow me to be a person, and I haven't seen my sons as people. That's what Samuel meant.' He looked right into Cal's eyes and smiled, and Cal ached with affection for him.

Cal said, 'We don't think you're a bad father.'

'Poor things,' said Adam. 'How could you know? You've never had any other kind.'

'I'm glad I was in jail,' said Cal.

'So am I. So am I.' He laughed. 'We've both been in jail–we can talk together.' A gaiety grew in him. 'Maybe you can tell me what kind of a boy you are–can you?'

'Yes, sir.'

'Will you?'

'Yes, sir.'

'Well, tell me. You see, there's a responsibility in being a person. It's more than just taking up space where air would be. What are you like?'

'No joke?' Cal asked shyly.

'No joke–oh, surely, no joke. Tell me about yourself–that is, if you want to.'

Cal began, 'Well–I'm–' He stopped. 'It's not so easy when you try,' he said.

'I guess it would be–maybe impossible. Tell me about your brother.'

'What do you want to know about him?'

'What you think of him, I guess. That's all you could tell me.'

Cal said, 'He's good. He doesn't do bad things. He doesn't think bad things.'

'Now you're telling me about yourself.'

'Sir?'

'You're saying you do and think bad things.'

Cal's cheeks reddened. 'Well, I do.'

'Very bad things?'

'Yes, sir. Do you want me to tell?'

'No, Cal. You've told. Your voice tells and your eyes tell you're at war with yourself. But you shouldn't be ashamed. It's awful to be ashamed. Is Aron ever ashamed?'

'He doesn't do anything to be ashamed of.'

Adam leaned forward. 'Are you sure?'

'Pretty sure.'

'Tell me, Cal–do you protect him?'

'How do you mean, sir?'

'I mean like this–if you heard something bad or cruel or ugly, would you keep it from him?'

'I–I think so.'

'You think he's too weak to bear things you can bear?'

'It's not that, sir. He's good. He's really good. He never does anyone harm. He never says bad things about anyone. He's not mean and he never complains and he's brave. He doesn't like to fight but he will.'

'You love your brother, don't you?'

'Yes, sir. And I do bad things to him. I cheat him and I fool him. Sometimes I hurt him for no reason at all.'

'And then you're miserable?'

'Yes, sir.'

'Is Aron ever miserable?'

'I don't know. When I didn't want to join the Church he felt bad. And once when Abra got angry and said she hated him he felt awful bad. He was sick. He had fever. Don't you remember? Lee sent for the doctor.'

Adam said with wonder, 'I could live with you and not know any of these things! Why was Abra mad?'

Cal said, 'I don't know if I ought to tell.'

'I don't want you to, then.'

'It's nothing bad. I guess it's all right. You see, sir, Aron wants to be a minister. Mr Rolf–well, he likes High Church, and Aron liked that, and he thought maybe he would never get married and maybe go to a retreat.'

'Like a monk, you mean?'

'Yes, sir.'

'And Abra didn't like that?'

'Like it? She got spitting mad. She can get mad sometimes. She took Aron's fountain pen and threw it on the sidewalk and tramped on it. She said she'd wasted half her life on Aron.'

Adam laughed. 'How old is Abra?'

'Nearly fifteen. But she's–well, more than that some ways.'

'I should say she is. What did Aron do?'

'He just got quiet but he felt awful bad.'

Adam said, 'I guess you could have taken her away from him then.'

'Abra is Aron's girl,' said Cal.

Adam looked deeply into Cal's eyes. Then he called, 'Lee!' There was no answer. 'Lee!' he called again. He said, 'I didn't hear him go out. I want some fresh coffee.'

Cal jumped up. 'I'll make it.'

'Say,' said Adam, 'you should be in school.'

'I don't want to go.'

'You ought to go. Aron went.'

'I'm happy,' Cal said. 'I want to be with you.'

Adam looked down at his hands. 'Make the coffee,' he said softly, and his voice was shy.

When Cal was in the kitchen Adam looked inward at himself with wonder. His nerves and muscles throbbed with an excited hunger. His fingers yearned to grasp, his legs to run. His eyes avidly brought the room into focus. He saw the chairs, the pictures, the red roses on the carpet, and new sharp things–almost people things but friendly things. And in his brain was born sharp appetite for the future–a pleased warm anticipation, as though the coming minutes and weeks must bring delight. He felt a dawn emotion, with a lovely day to slip golden and quiet over him. He laced his fingers behind his head and stretched his legs out stiff.

In the kitchen Cal urged on the water heating in the coffee-pot, and yet he was pleased to be waiting. A miracle once it is familiar is no longer a miracle; Cal had lost his wonder at the golden relationship with his father but the pleasure remained. The poison of loneliness and the gnawing envy of the unlonely had gone out of him, and his person was clean and sweet, and he knew it was. He dredged up an old hatred to test himself, and he found the hatred gone. He wanted to serve his father, to give him some great gift, to perform some huge task in honour of his father.

The coffee boiled over and Cal spent minutes cleaning up the stove. He said to himself, 'I wouldn't have done this yesterday.'

Adam smiled at him when he carried in the steaming pot. Adam sniffed and said, 'That's a smell could raise me out of a concrete grave.'

'It boiled over,' said Cal.

'It has to boil over to taste good,' Adam said. 'I wonder where Lee went.'

'Maybe to his room. Shall I look?'

'No. He'd have answered.'

'Sir, when I finish school, will you let me run the ranch?'

'You're planning early. How about Aron?'

'He wants to go to college. Don't tell him I told you. Let him tell you, and you be surprised.'

'Why, that's fine,' said Adam. 'But don't you want to go to college too?'

'I bet I could make money on the ranch–enough to pay Aron's way through college.'

Adam sipped his coffee. 'That's a generous thing,' he said. 'I don't know whether I ought to tell you this, but–well, when I asked you earlier what kind of boy Aron was, you defended him so badly I thought you might dislike him or even hate him.'

'I have hated him,' Cal said vehemently. 'And I've hurt him too. But, sir, can I tell you something? I don't hate him now. I won't ever hate him again. I don't think I will hate anyone, not even my mother–' He stopped, astonished at his slip, and his mind froze up tight and helpless.

Adam looked straight ahead. He rubbed his forehead with the palm of his hand. Finally he said quietly, 'You know about your mother.' It was not a question.

'Yes–yes, sir.'

'All about her?'

'Yes, sir.'

Adam leaned back in his chair. 'Does Aron know?'

'Oh, no! No–no, sir. He doesn't know.'

'Why do you say it that way?'

'I wouldn't dare to tell him.'

'Why not?'

Cal said brokenly, 'I don't think he could stand it. He hasn't enough badness in him to stand it.' He wanted to continue, '–any more than you could, sir,' but he left the last unsaid.

Adam's face looked weary. He moved his head from side to side. 'Cal, listen to me. Do you think there's any chance of keeping Aron from knowing? Think carefully.'

Cal said, 'He doesn't go near places like that. He's not like me.'

'Suppose someone told him?'

'I don't think he would believe it, sir. I think he would lick whoever told him and think it was a lie.'

'You've been there?'

'Yes, sir. I had to know.' And Cal went on excitedly, 'If he went away to college and never lived in this town again–'

Adam nodded. 'Yes. That might be. But he has two more years here.'

'Maybe I could make him hurry it up and finish in one year. He's smart.'

'But you're smarter?'

'A different kind of smart,' said Cal.

Adam seemed to grow until he filled one side of the room. His face was stern and his blue eyes sharp and penetrating. 'Cal!' he said harshly.

'Sir?'

'I trust you, son,' said Adam.

2

Adam's recognition brought a ferment of happiness to Cal. He walked on the balls of his feet. He smiled more often than he frowned, and the secret darkness was seldom on him.

Lee, noticing the change in him, asked quietly, 'You haven't found a girl, have you?'

'Girl? No. Who wants a girl?'

'Everybody,' said Lee.

And Lee asked Adam, 'Do you know what's got into Cal?'

Adam said, 'He knows about her.'

'Does he?' Lee stayed out of trouble. 'Well, you remember I thought you should have told them.'

'I didn't tell him. He knew.'

'What do you think of that!' said Lee. 'But that's not information to make a boy hum when he studies and play catch with his cap when he walks. How about Aron?'

'I'm afraid of that,' said Adam. 'I don't think I want him to know.'

'It might be too late.'

'I might have a talk with Aron. Kind of feel around.'

Lee considered. 'Something's happened to you too.'

'Has it? I guess it has,' said Adam.

But humming and sailing his cap, driving quickly through his school work, were only the smallest of Çal's activities. In his new joy he appointed himself guardian of his father's content. It was true what he had said about not feeling hatred for his mother. But that did not change the fact that she had been the instrument of Adam's hurt and shame. Cal reasoned that what she could do before, she could do again. He set himself to learn all he could about her. A known enemy is less dangerous, less able to surprise.

At night he was drawn to the house across the tracks. Sometimes in the afternoon he lay hidden in the tall weeds across the street, watching the place. He saw the girls come out, dressed sombrely, even severely. They left the house always in pairs, and Cal followed them with his eyes to the corner of Castroville Street, where they turned left towards Main Street. He discovered that if you didn't know where they had come from you couldn't tell what they were. But he was not waiting for the girls to come out. He wanted to see his mother in the light of day. He found that Kate emerged every Monday at one-thirty.

Cal made arrangements in school, by doing extra and excellent work, to make up for his absences on Monday afternoons. To Aron's questions he replied that he was working on a surprise and was duty bound to tell no one. Aron was not much interested anyway. In his self-immersion Aron soon forgot the whole thing.

Cal, after he had followed Kate several times, knew her route. She always went to the same places–first to the Monterey County Bank, where she was admitted behind the shining bars that defended the safe-deposit vault. She spent fifteen or twenty minutes there. Then she moved slowly along Main Street, looking in the store windows. She stepped into Porter and Irvine's and looked at dresses and sometimes made a purchase–elastic, safety pins, a veil, a pair of gloves. About two-fifteen she entered Minnie Franken's beauty parlour, stayed an hour, and came out with her hair pinned up in tight curls and a silk scarf around her head and tied under her chin.

At three-thirty she climbed the stairs to the offices over the Farmer's Mercantile and went into the consulting-room of Dr Rosen. When she came down from the doctor's office she stopped for a moment at Bell's candy store and bought a two-pound box of mixed chocolates. She never varied the route. From Bell's she went directly back to Castroville Street and thence to her house.

There was nothing strange about her clothing. She dressed exactly like any well-to-do Salinas woman out shopping on a Monday afternoon–except that she always wore gloves, which was unusual for Salinas.

The gloves made her hands seem puffed and pudgy. She moved as though she were surrounded by a glass shell. She spoke to no one and seemed to see no one. Occasionally a man turned and looked after her and then nervously went about his business. But for the most part she slipped past like an invisible woman.

For a number of weeks Cal followed Kate. He tried not to attract her attention. And since Kate walked always looking straight ahead, he was convinced that she did not notice him.

When Kate entered her own yard Cal strolled casually by and went home by another route. He could not have said exactly why he followed her, except that he wanted to know all about her.

The eighth week he took the route she completed her journey and went into her overgrown yard as usual.

Cal waited a moment, then strolled past the rickety gate.

Kate was standing behind a tall ragged privet. She said to him coldly, 'What do you want?'

Cal froze in his steps. He was suspended in time, barely breathing. Then he began a practice he had learned when he was very young. He observed and catalogued details outside his main object. He noticed how the wind from the south bent over the new little leaves of the tall privet bush. He saw the muddy path beaten to black mush by many feet, and Kate's feet standing far to the side out of the mud. He heard a switch engine in the Southern Pacific yards discharging steam in shrilly dry spurts. He felt the chill air on the growing fuzz on his cheeks. And all the time he was staring at Kate and she was staring back at him. And he saw in the set and colour of her eyes and hair, even in the way she held her shoulders–high in a kind of semi-shrug–that Aron looked very like her. He did not know his own face well enough to recognize her mouth and little teeth and wide cheekbones as his own. They stood thus for a moment, between two gusts of the southern wind.

Kate said, 'This isn't the first time you've followed me. What do you want?'

He dipped his head. 'Nothing,' he said.

'Who told you to do it?' she demanded.

'Nobody–ma'am.'

'You won't tell me, will you?'

Cal heard his own speech with amazement. It was out before he could stop it. 'You're my mother and I wanted to see what you're like.' It was the exact truth and it had leaped out like the stroke of a snake.

'What? What is this? Who are you?'

'I'm Cal Trask,' he said. He felt the delicate change of balance as when a seesaw moves. His was the upper seat now. Although her expression had not changed Cal knew she was on the defensive.

She looked at him closely, observed every feature. A dim remembered picture of Charles leaped into her mind. Suddenly she said, 'Come with me!' She turned and walked up the path, keeping well to the side, out of the mud.

Cal hesitated only for a moment before following her up the steps. He remembered the big dim room, but the rest was strange to him. Kate preceded him down a hall and into her room. As she went past the kitchen entrance she called, 'Tea. Two cups!'

In her room she seemed to have forgotten him. She removed her coat, tugging at the sleeves with reluctant fat gloved fingers. Then she went to a new door cut in the wall in the end of the room where her bed stood. She opened the door and went into a new little lean-to. 'Come in here!' she said. 'Bring that chair with you.'

He followed her into a box of a room. It had no windows, no decorations of any kind. Its walls were painted a dark grey. A solid grey carpet covered the floor. The only furniture in the room was a huge chair puffed with grey silk cushions, a tilted reading-table, and a floor-lamp deeply hooded. Kate pulled the light chain with her gloved hand, holding it deep in the crotch between her thumb and forefinger as though her hand were artificial.

'Close the door!' Kate said.

The light threw a circle on the reading-table and only diffused dimly through the grey room. Indeed the grey walls seemed to suck up the light and destroy it.

Kate settled herself gingerly among the thick down cushions and slowly removed her gloves. The fingers of both hands were bandaged.

Kate said angrily, 'Don't stare. It's arthritis. Oh–so you want to see, do you?' She unwrapped the oily-looking bandage from her right forefinger and stuck the crooked finger under the light. 'There–look at it,' she said. 'It's arthritis.' She whined in pain as she tenderly wrapped the bandage loosely. 'God, those gloves hurt!' she said. 'Sit down.'

Cal crouched on the edge of his chair.

'You'll probably get it,' Kate said. 'My great-aunt had it and my mother was just beginning to get it–' She stopped. The room was very silent.

There was a soft knock on the door. Kate called, 'Is that you, Joe? Set the tray down out there. Joe, are you there?'

A mutter came through the door.

Kate said tonelessly, 'There's a litter in the parlour. Clean it up. Anne hasn't cleaned her room. Give her one more warning. Tell her it's the last. Eva got smart last night. I'll take care of her. And, Joe, tell the cook if he serves carrots again this week he can pack up. Hear me?'

The mutter came through the door.

'That's all,' said Kate. 'The dirty pigs!' she muttered. 'They'd rot if I didn't watch them. Go out and bring in the tea tray.'

The bedroom was empty when Cal opened the door. He carried the tray into the lean-to and set it gingerly on the tilted reading-table. It was a large silver tray, and on it were a pewter teapot, two paper-thin white tea-cups, sugar, cream, and an open box of chocolates.

'Pour the tea,' said Kate. 'It hurts my hands.' She put a chocolate in her mouth. 'I saw you looking at this room,' she went on when she had swallowed her candy. 'The light hurts my eyes. I come in here to rest.' She saw Cal's quick glance at her eyes and said with finality, 'The light hurts my eyes.' She said harshly, 'What's the matter? Don't you want tea?'

'No, ma'am,' said Cal. 'I don't like tea.'

She held the thin cup with her bandaged fingers. 'All right. What *do* you want?'

'Nothing, ma'am.'

'Just wanted to look at me?'

'Yes, ma'am.'

'Are you satisfied?'

'Yes, ma'am.'

'How do I look?' She smiled crookedly at him and showed her sharp white little teeth.

'All right.'

'I might have known you'd cover up. Where's your brother?'

'In school, I guess, or home.'

'What's he like?'

'He looks more like you.'

'Oh, he does? Well, *is* he like me?'

'He wants to be a minister,' said Cal.

'I guess that's the way it should be–looks like me and wants to go into the Church. A man can do a lot of damage in the Church. When someone comes here he's got his guard up. But in church a man's wide open.'

'He means it,' said Cal.

She leaned towards him, and her face was alive with interest. 'Fill my cup. Is your brother dull?'

'He's nice,' said Cal.

'I asked you if he's dull.'

'No, ma'am,' said Cal.

She settled back and lifted her cup. 'How's your father?'

'I don't want to talk about him,' Cal said.

'Oh, no! You like him then?'

'I love him,' said Cal.

Kate peered closely at him, and a curious spasm shook her–an aching twist rose in her chest. And then she closed up and her control came back.

'Don't you want some candy?' she asked.

'Yes, ma'am. Why did you do it?'

'Why did I do what?'

'Why did you shoot my father and run away from us?'

'Did he tell you that?'

'No. He didn't tell us.'

She touched one hand with the other and her hands leaped apart as though the contact burned them. She asked, 'Does your father ever have any–girls or young women come to your house?'

'No,' said Cal. 'Why did you shoot him and go away?'

Her cheeks tightened and her mouth straightened, as though a net of muscles took control. She raised her head, and her eyes were cold and shallow.

'You talk older than your age,' she said. 'But you don't talk old enough. Maybe you'd better run along and play–and wipe your nose.'

'Sometimes I work my brother over,' he said. 'I make him squirm, I've made him cry. He doesn't know how I do it. I'm smarter than he is. I don't want to do it. It makes me sick.'

Kate picked it up as though it were her own conversation. 'They thought they were so smart,' she said. 'They looked at me and thought they knew about me. And I fooled them. I fooled every one of them. And when they thought they could tell me what to do–oh! that's when I fooled them best. Charles, I really fooled them then.'

'My name is Caleb,' Cal said. 'Caleb got to the Promised Land. That's what Lee says, and it's in the Bible.'

'That's the Chinaman,' Kate said, and she went on eagerly, 'Adam thought he had me. When I was hurt, all broken up, he took me in and he waited on me, cooked for me. He tried to tie me down that way. Most people get tied down that way. They're grateful, they're in debt, and that's the worst kind of handcuffs. But nobody can hold me. I waited and waited until I was strong and then I broke out. Nobody can trap me,' she said. 'I knew what he was doing. I waited.'

The grey room was silent except for her excited wheezing breath.

Cal said, 'Why did you shoot him?'

'Because he tried to stop me. I could have killed him but I didn't. I just wanted him to let me go.'

'Did you ever wish you'd stayed?'

'Christ, no! Even when I was a little girl I could do anything I wanted. They never knew how I did it. Never. They were always so sure they were right. And they never knew–no one ever knew.' A kind of realization came to her. 'Sure, you're my kind. Maybe you're the same. Why wouldn't you be?'

Cal stood up and closed his hands behind his back. He said, 'When you were little, did you'–he paused to get the thought straight–'did you ever have the feeling like you were missing something? Like as if the others knew something you didn't–like a secret they wouldn't tell you? Did you ever feel that way?'

While he spoke her face began to close against him, and by the time he paused she was cut off and the way open between them was blocked.

She said, 'What am I doing, talking to kids!'

Cal unclasped his hands from behind him and shoved them in his pockets.

'Talking to snot-nosed kids,' she said. 'I must be crazy.'

Cal's face was alight with excitement, and his eyes were wide with vision.

Kate said, 'What's the matter with you?'

He stood still, his forehead glistening with sweat, his hands clenched into fists.

Kate, as she had always, drove in the smart but senseless knife of her cruelty. She laughed softly. 'I may have given you some interesting things, like this—' She held up her crooked hands. 'But if it's epilepsy–fits–you didn't get it from me.' She glanced brightly up at him, anticipating the shock and beginning worry in him.

Cal spoke happily. 'I'm going,' he said. 'I'm going now. It's all right. What Lee said was true.'

'What did Lee say?'

Cal said, 'I was afraid I had you in me.'

'You have,' said Kate.

'No, I haven't. I'm my own. I don't have to be you.'

'How do you know that?' she demanded.

'I just know. It came to me whole. If I'm mean, it's my own mean.'

'This Chinaman has really fed you some pap. What are you looking at me like that for?'

Cal said, 'I don't think the light hurts your eyes. I think you're afraid.'

'Get out!' she cried. 'Go on, get out!'

'I'm going.' He had his hand on the door-knob. 'I don't hate you,' he said. 'But I'm glad you're afraid.'

She tried to shout 'Joe!' but her voice thickened to a croak.

Cal wrenched open the door and slammed it behind him.

Joe was talking to one of the girls in the parlour. They heard the stutter of light quick footsteps. But by the time they looked up a streaking figure had reached the door, opened it, slipped through, and the heavy front door banged. There was only one step on the porch and then a crunch as jumping feet struck earth.

'What in hell was that?' the girl asked.

'God knows,' said Joe. 'Sometimes I think I'm seeing things.'

'Me too,' said the girl. 'Did I tell you Clara's got bugs under her skin?'

'I guess she seen the shadow of the needle,' said Joe. 'Well, the way I figure, the less you know, the better off you are.'

'That's the truth you said there,' the girl agreed.

CHAPTER 40

I

Kate sat back in her chair against the deep down cushions. Waves of nerves cruised over her body, raising the little hairs and making ridges of icy burn as they went.

She spoke softly to herself. 'Steady now,' she said. 'Quiet down. Don't let it hit you. Don't think for a while. The god-damn snot-nose!'

She thought suddenly of the only person who had ever made her feel this panic hatred. It was Samuel Hamilton, with his white beard and his pink cheeks and the laughing eyes that lifted her skin and looked underneath.

With her bandaged forefinger she dug out a slender chain which hung around her neck and pulled the chain's burden up from her bodice. On the chain were strung two safe-deposit keys, a gold watch with a fleur-de-lis pin, and a little steel tube with a ring on its top. Very carefully she unscrewed the top from the tube and, spreading her knees, shook out a gelatine capsule. She held the capsule under the light and saw the white crystals inside–six grams of morphine, a good, sure margin. Very gently she eased the capsule into its tube, screwed on the cap, and dropped the chain inside her dress.

Cal's last words had been repeating themselves over and over in her head. 'I think you're afraid.' She said the words aloud to herself to kill the sound. The rhythm stopped, but a strong picture formed in her mind and she let it form so that she could inspect it again.

2

It was before the lean-to was built. Kate had collected the money Charles had left. The cheque was converted to large notes and the notes in their bales in the safe-deposit box at the Monterey County Bank.

It was about the time the first pains began to twist her hands. There was enough money now to go away. It was just a matter of getting the most she could out of the house. But it also was better to wait until she felt quite well again'

She never felt quite well again. New York seemed cold and very far away.

A letter came to her signed 'Ethel'. Who the hell was Ethel? Whoever she was, she must be crazy to ask for money. Ethel–there were hundreds of Ethels. Ethels grew on every bush. And this one scrawled illegibly on a lined pad.

Not very long afterwards Ethel came to see Kate, and Kate hardly recognized her.

Kate sat at her desk, watchful, suspicious and confident. 'It's been a long time,' she said.

Ethel responded like a soldier who comes in his cushion age upon the sergeant who trained him. 'I've been poorly,' she said. Her flesh had thickened and grown heavy all over. Her clothes had the strained cleanliness that means poverty.

'Where are you–staying now?' Kate asked, and she wondered how soon the old bag would be able to come to the point.

'Southern Pacific Hotel. I got a room.'

'Oh, then you don't work in a house now?'

'I couldn't never get started again,' said Ethel. 'You shouldn't of run me off.' She wiped big tears from the corners of her eyes with the tip of a cotton glove. 'Things are bad,' she said. 'First I had trouble when we got that new judge. Ninety days, and I didn't have no record–not here anyways. I come out of that and I got the old Joe. I didn't know I had it. Give it to a regular–nice fella, worked on the section gang. He got sore an' busted me up, hurt my nose, lost four teeth, an' that new judge he gave me a hundred and eighty. Hell, Kate, you lose all your contacts in a hundred and eighty days. They forget you're alive. I just never could get started.'

Kate nodded her head in cold and shallow sympathy. She knew that Ethel was working up to the bite. Just before it came Kate made a move. She opened her desk drawer and took out some money and held it out to Ethel. 'I never let a friend down,' she said. 'Why don't you go to a new town, start fresh? It might change your luck.'

Ethel tried to keep her fingers from grabbing at the money. She fanned the notes like a poker hand–four tens. Her mouth began to work with emotion.

Ethel said, 'I kind of hoped you'd see your way to let me take more than forty bucks.'

'What do you mean?'

'Didn't you get my letter?'

'What letter?'

'Oh!' said Ethel. 'Well, maybe it got lost in the mail. They don't take no care of things. Anyways, I thought you might look after me. I don't feel good hardly ever. Got a kind of weight dragging my guts down.' She sighed and then she spoke so rapidly that Kate knew it had been rehearsed.

'Well, maybe you remember how I've got like second sight,' Ethel began. 'Always predicting things that come true. Always dreaming stuff and it come out. Fella says I should go in the business. Says I'm a natural medium. You remember that?'

'No,' said Kate, 'I don't.'

'Don't? Well, maybe you never noticed. All the others did. I told 'em lots of things and they come true.'

'What are you trying to say?'

'I had this-here dream. I remember when it was because it was the same night Faye died.' Her eyes flicked up at Kate's cold face. She continued doggedly, 'It rained that night, and it was raining in my dream–anyways, it was wet. Well, in my dream I seen you come out the kitchen door. It wasn't pitch-dark–moon was coming through a little. And the dream thing was you. You went out to the back of the lot and stooped over. I couldn't see what you done. Then you come creeping back.

'Next thing I knew–why, Faye was dead.' She paused and waited for some comment from Kate, but Kate's face was expressionless.

Ethel waited until she was sure Kate would not speak. 'Well, like I said, I always believed in my dreams. It's funny, there wasn't nothing out there except some smashed medicine bottles and a little rubber tit from an eye-dropper.'

Kate said lazily, 'So you took them to a doctor. What did he say had been in the bottles?'

'Oh, I didn't do nothing like that.'

'You should have,' said Kate.

'I don't want to see anybody get in trouble. I've had enough trouble myself. I put that broken glass in an envelope and stuck it away.'

Kate said softly, 'And so you are coming to me for advice?'

'Yes, ma'am.'

'I'll tell you what I think,' said Kate. 'I think you're a worn-out old whore and you've been beaten over the head too many times.'

'Don't you start saying I'm nuts–' Ethel began.

'No, maybe you're not, but you're tired and you're sick. I told you I never let a friend down. You can come back here. You can't work but you can help around, clean and give the cook a hand. You'll have a bed and you'll get your meals. How would that be? And a little spending money.'

Ethel stirred uneasily. 'No, ma'am,' she said. 'I don't think I want to–sleep here. I don't carry that envelope around. I left it with a friend.'

'What *did* you have in mind?'

'Well, I thought if you could see your way to let me have a hundred dollars a month, why, I could make out and maybe get my health back.'

'You said you lived at the Southern Pacific Hotel?'

'Yes, ma'am–and my room is right up the hall from the desk. The night clerk's a friend of mine. He don't never sleep when he's on duty. Nice fella.'

Kate said, 'Don't wet your pants, Ethel. All you've got to worry about is how much does the "nice fella" cost. Now wait a minute.' She counted six more ten-dollar bills from the drawer in front of her and held them out.

'Will it come the first of the month or do I have to come here for it?'

'I'll send it to you,' said Kate. 'And, Ethel,' she continued quietly, 'I still think you ought to have those bottles analysed.'

Ethel clutched the money tightly in her hand. She was bubbling over with triumph and good feeling. It was one of the few things that had ever worked out for her. 'I wouldn't think of doing that,' she said. 'Not unless I had to.'

After she had gone Kate strolled out to the back of the lot behind the house. And even after years she could see from the unevenness of the earth that it must have been pretty thoroughly dug over.

The next morning the judge heard the usual chronicle of small violence and nocturnal greed. He only half listened to the fourth case and at the end of the terse testimony of the complaining witness he asked, 'How much did you lose?'

The dark-haired man said, 'Pretty close to a hundred dollars.'

The judge turned to the arresting officer. 'How much did she have?'

'Ninety-six dollars. She got whisky and cigarettes and some magazines from the night clerk at six o'clock this morning.'

Ethel cried, 'I never seen this guy in my life.'

The judge looked up from his papers. 'Twice for prostitution and now robbery. You're costing too much. I want you out of town by noon.' He turned to the officer. 'Tell the sheriff to run her over the county line.' And he said to Ethel, 'If you come back, I'll give you over to the county for the limit, and that's San Quentin. Do you understand?'

Ethel said, 'Judge, I want to see you alone.'

'Why?'

'I got to see you,' said Ethel. 'This is a frame.'

'Everything's a frame,' said the judge. 'Next.'

While a deputy sheriff drove Ethel to the county line on the bridge over the Pajaro River, the complaining witness strolled down Castroville street towards Kate's, changed his mind and went back to Kenoe's barber-shop to get a haircut.

3

Ethel's visit did not disturb Kate very much when it happened. She knew about what attention would be paid to a whore with a grievance, and that an analysis of the broken bottles would not show anything recognizable as poison.

She had nearly forgotten Faye. The forcible recalling was simply an unpleasant memory.

Gradually, however, she found herself thinking about it. One night when she was checking the items on a grocery bill a thought shot into her mind, shining and winking like a meteor. The thought flashed and went out so quickly that she had to stop what she was doing to try to find it. How was the dark face of Charles involved in the thought? And Sam Hamilton's puzzled and merry eyes? And why did she get a shiver of fear from the flashing thought?

She gave it up and went back to her work, but the face of Charles was behind her, looking over her shoulder. Her fingers began to hurt her. She put the accounts away and made a tour through the house. It was a slow, listless night–a Tuesday night. There weren't even enough customers to put on the circus.

Kate knew how the girls felt about her. They were desperately afraid of her. She kept them that way. It was probable that they hated her, and that didn't matter either. But they trusted her, and that did matter. If they followed the rules she laid down, followed them exactly, Kate would take care of them and protect them. There was no love involved and no respect. She never rewarded them and she punished an offender only twice before she removed her. The girls did have the security of knowing that they would not be punished without cause.

As Kate walked about, the girls became elaborately casual. Kate knew about that too and expected it. But on this side she felt that she was not alone. Charles seemed to walk to the side and behind her.

She went through the dining-room and into the kitchen, opened the ice-box and looked in. She lifted the cover of the garbage can and inspected it for waste. She did this every night, but this night she carried some extra charge.

When she had left the parlour the girls looked at each other and raised their shoulders in bewilderment. Eloise, who was talking to the dark-haired Joe, said, 'Anything the matter?'

'Not that I know of. Why?'

'I don't know. She seems nervous.'

'Well, there was some kind of rat race.'

'What was it?'

'Wait a minute?' said Joe. 'I don't know and you don't know.'

'I get it. Mind my own business.'

'You're goddam right,' said Joe. 'Let's keep it that way, shall we?'

'I don't want to know,' said Eloise.

'Now you're talking,' Joe said.

Kate ranged back from her tour. 'I'm going back to bed,' she said to Joe. 'Don't call me unless you have to.'

'Anything I can do?'

'Yes, make me a pot of tea. Did you press that dress, Eloise?'

'Yes, ma'am.'

'You didn't do it very well.'

'Yes, ma'am.'

Kate was restless. She put all her papers neatly in the pigeonholes of her desk, and when Joe brought the tea tray she had him put it beside her bed.

Lying back among her pillows and sipping the tea, she probed for her thought. What about Charles? And then it came to her.

Charles was clever. In his crazy way Sam Hamilton was clever. That was the fear-driven thought–there were clever people. Both Sam and Charles were dead, but maybe there were others. She worked it out very slowly.

Suppose I had been the one to dig up the bottles? What would I think and what would I do? A rim of panic rose in her breast. Why were the bottles broken and buried? So it wasn't poison! Then why bury them? What made her do that? She should have dropped them in the gutter on Main Street or tossed them in the garbage can. Dr. Wilde was dead. But what kind of records did he keep? She didn't know. Suppose she had found the glass and learned what had been in them? Wouldn't she have asked someone who knew–'Suppose you gave croton oil to a person. What would happen?

'Well, suppose you gave little doses and kept it up for a long time?' She would know. Maybe somebody else would know.

'Suppose you heard about a rich madam who willed everything to a new girl and then died.' Kate knew perfectly well what her first thought would be. What insanity had made her get Ethel floated? Now she couldn't be found. Ethel should have been paid and tricked into turning over the glass. Where was the glass now? In an envelope–but where? How could Ethel be found?

Ethel would know why and how she had been floated. Ethel wasn't bright, but she might tell somebody who was bright. That chattering voice might tell the story, how Faye was sick, and what she looked like, and about the will.

Kate was breathing quickly and little prickles of fear were beginning to course over her body. She should go to New York or somewhere–not bother to sell the house. She didn't need the money. She had plenty. Nobody could find her. Yes, but if she ran out and the clever person heard Ethel tell the story, wouldn't that cinch it?

Kate got up from her bed and took a heavy dose of bromide.

From that time on the crouching fear had always been at her side. She was almost glad when she learned that the pain in her hands was developing arthritis. An evil voice had whispered that it might be a punishment.

She had never gone out in the town very much, but now she developed a reluctance to go out at all. She knew that men stared secretly after her, knowing who she was. Suppose one of those men should have Charles's face or Samuel's eyes. She had to drive herself to go out once a week.

Then she built the lean-to and had it painted grey. She said it was because the light troubled her eyes and gradually she began to believe the light did trouble her eyes. Her eyes burned after a trip to the town. She spent more and more time in her little room.

It is possible to some people, and it was possible for Kate, to hold two opposing thoughts at the same time. She believed that the light pained her eyes, and also that the grey room was a cave to hide in, a dark burrow in the earth, a place where no eyes could stare at her. Once, sitting in her pillowed chair, she considered having a secret door built so that she would have an avenue of escape. And then a feeling rather than a thought threw out the plan. She would not be protected then. If she could get out, something could get in–that something which had begun to crouch outside the house, to crawl close to the walls at night, and to rise silently, trying to look through the windows. It required more and more will-power for Kate to leave the house on Monday afternoons.

When Cal began to follow her she had a terrible leap of fear. And when she waited for him behind the privet she was very near to panic.

But now her head dug deep in her soft pillows and her eyes felt the gentle weight of the bromide.

CHAPTER 41

1

The nation slipped imperceptibly towards war, frightened and at the same time attracted. People had not felt the shaking emotion of war in nearly sixty years. The Spanish affair was more nearly an expedition than a war. Mr Wilson was re-elected President in November on his platform promise to keep us out of war, and at the same time he was instructed to take a firm hand, which inevitably meant war. Business picked up and prices began to rise. British purchasing agents roved about the country, buying food and cloth and metals and chemicals. A charge of excitement ran through the country. People didn't really believe in war even while they planned it. The Salinas Valley lived about as it always had.

2

Cal walked to school with Aron.

'You look tired,' Aron said,

'Do I?'

'I heard you come in last night. Four o'clock. What do you do so late?'

'I was walking around–thinking. How would you like to quit school and go back to the ranch?'

'What for?'

'We could make some money for Father.'

'I'm going to college. I wish I could go now. Everybody is laughing at us. I want to get out of town.'

'You act mad.'

'I'm not mad. But I didn't lose the money. I didn't have a crazy lettuce idea. But people laugh at me just the same. And I don't know if there's enough money for college.'

'He didn't mean to lose the money.'

'But he lost it.'

Cal said, 'You've got this year to finish and next before you can go to college.'

'Do you think I don't know that?'

'If you worked hard, maybe you could take entrance examinations next summer and go in the fall.'

Aron swung round. 'I couldn't do it.'

'I think you could. Why don't you talk to the principal? And I bet the Reverend Rolf would help you.'

Aron said, 'I want to get out of this town. I don't ever want to come back. They still call us Lettuce-heads. They laugh at us.'

'How about Abra?'

'Abra will do what's best.'

Cal asked, 'Would she want you to go away?'

'Abra's going to do what I want her to do.'

Cal thought for a moment. 'I'll tell you what. I'm going to try to make some money. If you buckle down and pass examinations a year early, why, I'll help you through college.'

'You will?'

'Sure I will.'

'Why, I'll go and see the principal right away.' He quickened his steps.

Cal called, 'Aron, wait! Listen! If he says he thinks you can do it, don't tell Father.'

'Why not?'

'I was just thinking how nice it would be if you went to him and told him you'd done it.'

'I don't see what difference it makes.'

'You don't?'

'No, I don't,' said Aron. 'It sounds silly to me.'

Cal had a violent urge to shout, 'I know who our mother is! I can show her to you.' That would cut through and get inside of Aron.

Cal met Abra in the hall before the school-bell rang.

'What's the matter with Aron?' he demanded.

'I don't know.'

'Yes, you do,' he said.

'He's just in a cloud. I think it's that minister.'

'Does he walk home with you?'

'Sure he does. But I can see right through him. He's wearing wings.'

'He's still ashamed about the lettuce.'

'I know he is,' said Abra. 'I try to talk him out of it. Maybe he's enjoying it.'

'What do you mean?'

'Nothing,' said Abra.

After supper that night Cal said, 'Father, would you mind if I went down to the ranch Friday afternoon?'

Adam turned in his chair. 'What for?'

'Just want to see. Just want to look around.'

'Does Aron want to go?'

'No. I want to go alone.'

'I don't see why you shouldn't. Lee, do you see any reason why he shouldn't go?'

'No,' said Lee. He studied Cal. 'Thinking seriously of going to farming?'

'I might. If you'd let me take it over, I'd farm it, Father.'

'The lease has more than one year to run,' Adam said.

'After that I can farm it?'

'How about school?'

'I'll be through school.'

'Well, we'll see,' said Adam. 'You might want to go to college.'

When Cal started for the front door Lee followed and walked out with him.

'Can you tell me what it's about? Lee asked.

'I just want to look around.'

'All right, I guess I'm left out.' Lee turned to go back into the house. Then he called, 'Cal!' The boy stopped. 'You worried, Cal?'

'No.'

'I've got five thousand dollars if you need it?'

'Why should I need it?'

'I don't know,' said Lee.

3

Will Hamilton liked his glass cage of an office in the garage. His business interests were much wider than the automobile agency, but he did not get another office. He loved the movement that went on outside his square cage. And he had put in double glass to kill the noise of the garage.

He sat in his big red leather swivel chair, and most of the time he enjoyed his life. When people spoke of his brother Joe making so much money in advertising in the East, Will always said he himself was a big frog in a little puddle.

'I'd be afraid to go to a big city,' he said. 'I'm just a country boy.' And he liked the laugh that always followed. It proved to him that his friends knew he was well off.

Cal came in to see him one Saturday morning. Seeing Will's puzzled look, he said. 'I'm Cal Trask.'

'Oh, sure. Lord, you're getting to be a big boy. Is your father down?'

'No. I came alone.'

'Well, sit down. I don't suppose you smoke.'

'Sometimes. Cigarettes.'

Will slid a packet of Murads across the desk. Cal opened the box and then closed it. 'I don't think I will right now.'

Will looked at the dark-faced boy and he liked him. He thought, 'This boy is sharp. He's nobody's fool.' 'I guess you'll be going into business pretty soon,' he said.

'Yes, sir. I thought I might run the ranch when I get out of high school.'

'There's no money in that,' said Will. 'Farmers don't make any money. It's the man who buys from him and sells. You'll never make any money farming.' Will knew that Cal was feeling him, testing him, observing him, and he approved of that.

And Cal had made up his mind, but first he asked, 'Mr Hamilton, you haven't any children, have you?'

'Well, no. And I'm sorry about that. I guess I'm sorriest about that.' And then, 'What makes you ask?'

Cal ignored the question. 'Would you give me some advice?'

Will felt a glow of pleasure. 'If I can, I'll be glad to. What is it you want to know?'

And then Cal did something Will Hamilton approved even more. He used candour as a weapon. He said, 'I want to make a lot of money. I want you to tell me how.'

Will overcame his impulse to laugh. Naïve as the statement was, he didn't think Cal was naïve. 'Everybody wants that,' he said. 'What do you mean by a lot of money?'

'Twenty or thirty thousand dollars.'

'Good God!' said Will, and he screeched his chair forward. And now he did laugh, but not in derision. Cal smiled along with Will's laughter.

Will said, 'Can you tell me why you want to make so much?'

'Yes, sir,' said Cal, 'I can.' And Cal opened the box of Murads and took out one of the oval cork-tipped cigarettes and lighted it. 'I'll tell you why,' he said.

Will leaned his chair back in enjoyment.

'My father lost a lot of money.'

'I know,' said Will. 'I warned him not to try to ship lettuce across the country.'

'You did? Why did you?'

'There were no guarantees,' said Will. 'A business man has to protect himself. If anything happened, he was finished. And it happened. Go on.'

'I want to make enough money to give him back what he lost.'

Will gaped at him. 'Why?' he asked.

'I want to.'

Will said, 'Are you fond of him?'

'Yes.'

Will's fleshy face contorted and a memory swept over him like a chilling wind. He did not move slowly over the past, it was all there in one flash, all of the years, a picture, a feeling and a despair, all stopped the way a fast camera stops the world. There was the flashing Samuel, beautiful as dawn with a fancy like a swallow's flight, and the brilliant, brooding Tom who was dark fire, Una who rode the storms, and lovely Mollie, Dessie of laughter, George handsome and with a sweetness that filled a room like the perfume of flowers, and there was Joe, the youngest, the beloved. Each one without effort brought some gift to the family.

Nearly everyone has his box of secret pain, shared with no one. Will had concealed his well, laughed loud, exploited perverse virtues, and never let his jealousy go wandering. He thought of himself as slow, doltish, conservative, uninspired. No great dream lifted him high and no despair forced self-destruction. He was always on the edge, trying to hold on to the rim of the family with what gifts he had–care, and reason, application. He kept the books, hired the attorneys, called the undertaker, and eventually paid the bills. The others didn't even know they needed him. He had the ability to get money and to keep it. He thought the Hamiltons despised him for his one ability. He had loved them doggedly, had always been at hand with his money to pull them out of their errors. He thought they were ashamed of him, and he fought bitterly for their recognition. All of this was in the frozen wind that blew through him.

His slightly bulging eyes were damp as he stared past Cal, and the boy asked, 'What's the matter, Mr Hamilton? Don't you feel well?'

Will had sensed his family but he had not understood them. And they had accepted him without knowing there was anything to understand. And now this boy came along. Will understood him, felt him, sensed him, recognized him. This was the son he should have had, or the brother, or the father. And the cold wind of memory changed to a warmth towards Cal which gripped him in the stomach and pushed up against his lungs.

He forced his attention to the glass office. Cal was sitting back in his chair, waiting.

Will did not know how long his silence had lasted. 'I was thinking,' he said lamely. He made his voice stern. 'You asked me something. I'm a business man. I don't give things away. I sell them.'

'Yes, sir.' Cal was watchful, but he felt that Will Hamilton liked him.

Will said, 'I want to know something and I want the truth. Will you tell me the truth?'

'I don't know,' said Cal.

'I like that. How do you know until you know the question? I like that. That's smart–and honest. Listen–you have a brother. Does your father like him better than you?'

'Everybody does,' said Cal calmly. 'Everybody loves Aron.'

'Do you?'

'Yes, sir. At least–yes, I do.'

'What's the "at least"?'

'Sometimes I think he's stupid, but I like him.'

'Now, how about your father?'

'I love him,' said Cal.

'And he loves your brother better.'

'I don't know.'

'Now, you say you want to give back the money your father lost. Why?'

Ordinarily Cal's eyes were squinted and cautious, but now they were so wide that they seemed to look around and through Will. Cal was as close to his own soul as it is possible to get.

'My father is good,' he said. 'I want to make it up to him because I am not good.'

'If you do that, wouldn't you be good?'

'No,' said Cal. 'I think bad.'

Will had never met anyone who spoke so nakedly. He was near to embarrassment because of the nakedness, and he knew how safe Cal was in his stripped honesty. 'Only one more,' he said, 'and I won't mind if you don't answer it. I don't think I would answer it. Here it is. Suppose you should get this money and give it to your father–would it cross your mind that you were trying to buy his love?'

'Yes, sir. It would. And it would be true.'

'That's all I want to ask. That's all.' Will leaned forward and put his hands against his sweating, pulsing forehead. He could not remember when he had been so shaken. And in Cal there was a cautious leap of triumph. He knew he had won and he closed his face against showing it.

Will raised his head and took off his glasses and wiped the moisture from them. 'Let's go outside,' he said. 'Let's go for a drive.'

Will drove a big Winton now, with a hood as long as a coffin and a powerful panting mutter in its bowels. He drove south from King City over the county road, through the gathering forces of spring, and the meadowlarks flew ahead, bubbling melody from the fence wires. Pico Blanco stood up against the West with a full head of snow, and in the valley the lines of eucalyptus, which stretched across the valley to break the winds, were gleaming silver with new leaves.

When he came to the side road that led into the home draw of the Trask place Will pulled up on the side of the road. He had not spoken since the

Winton rolled out of King City. The big motor idled with a deep whisper.

Will, looking straight ahead, said, 'Cal–do you want to be partners with me?'

'Yes, sir.'

'I don't like to take a partner without money. I could lend you the money, but there's only trouble in that.'

'I can get money,' said Cal.

'How much?'

'Five thousand dollars.'

'You–I don't believe it.'

Cal didn't answer.

'I believe it,' said Will. 'Borrowed?'

'Yes, sir.'

'What interest?'

'None.'

'That's a good trick. Where will you get it?'

'I won't tell you, sir.'

Will shook his head and laughed. He was filled with pleasure. 'Maybe, I'm being a fool, I believe you–and I'm not a fool.' He gunned his motor and then let it idle again. 'I want you to listen. Do you read the papers?'

'Yes, sir.'

'We're going to be in this war any minute now.'

'That's what it looks like.'

'Well, a lot of people think so. Now, do you know the present price of beans? I mean, what you can sell a hundred sacks for in Salinas?'

'I'm not sure. I think about three to three and a half cents a pound.'

'What do you mean you're not sure? How do you know that?'

'Well, I was thinking about asking my father to let me run the ranch.'

'I see. But you don't want to farm. You're too smart. Your father's tenant is named Rantani. He's a Swiss Italian, a good farmer. He's put nearly five hundred acres under cultivation. If we can guarantee him five cents a pound and give him a seed loan, he'll plant beans. So will every other farmer around here. We could contract five thousand acres of beans.'

Cal said, 'What are we going to do with five-cent beans in a three-cent market? Oh, yes! But how can we be sure?'

Will said, 'Are we partners?'

'Yes, sir.'

'Yes, Will!'

'Yes, Will.'

'How soon can you get five thousand dollars?'

'By next Wednesday.'

'Shake!' Solemnly the stout man and the lean dark boy shook hands.

Will, still holding Cal's hand, said, 'Now we're partners. I have a contract with the British Purchasing Agency. And I have a friend in the Quartermaster Corps. I bet we can sell all the dried beans we can find at ten cents a pound or more.'

'When can you sell?'

'I'll sell before we sign anything. Now, would you like to go up to the old place and talk to Rantani?'

'Yes, sir,' said Cal.

Will double-clutched the Winton and the big green car lumbered into the side road.

CHAPTER 42

A war comes always to someone else. In Salinas we were aware that the United States was the greatest and most powerful nation in the world. Every American was a rifleman by birth, and one American was worth ten or twenty foreigners in a fight.

Pershing's expedition into Mexico after Villa had exploded one of our myths for a little while. We had truly believed that Mexicans can't shoot straight and besides were lazy and stupid. When our own Troop C came wearily back from the border they said that none of this was true. Mexicans could shoot straight, goddamn it! And Villa's horsemen had out-ridden and out-lasted our own boys. The two evenings a month of training had not toughened them very much. And last, the Mexicans seemed to have out-thought and out-ambushed Black Jack Pershing. When the Mexicans were joined by their ally, dysentery, it was godawful. Some of our boys didn't really feel good again for years.

Somehow we didn't connect Germans with Mexicans. We went right back to our myths. One American was as good as twenty Germans. This being true, we had only to act in a stern manner to bring the Kaiser to heel. He wouldn't dare interfere with our trade–but he did. He wouldn't stick out his neck and sink our ships–but he did. It was stupid, but he did, and so there was nothing for it but to fight him.

The war, at first anyway, was for other people. We, I, my family and friends, had kind of ring seats, and it was pretty exciting. And just as war is always for somebody else, so it is also true that someone else always gets killed. And Mother of God! that wasn't true either. The dreadful telegrams began to sneak sorrowfully in, and it was everybody's brother. Here we were, over six thousand miles away from the anger and the noise, and that didn't save us.

It wasn't much fun then. The Liberty Belles could parade in white caps and uniforms of white sharkskin. Our uncle could re-write his Fourth of July speech and use it to sell bonds. We in high school could wear olive drab and campaign hats and learn the manual of arms from the physics teacher, but, Jesus Christ! Marty Hopps dead, the Berges boy, from across the street, the handsome one our little sister was in love with from the time she was three, blown to bits!

And the gangling, shuffling, loose-jointed boys carrying suitcases were marching awkwardly down Main Street to the Southern Pacific Depot. They were sheepish, and the Salinas Band marched ahead of them, playing 'Stars and Stripes Forever', and the families walking along beside them were crying, and the music sounded like a dirge. The draftees wouldn't look at their mothers. They didn't dare. We'd never thought the war could happen to us.

There were some in Salinas who began to talk softly in the poolrooms and the bars. These had private information from a soldier–we weren't getting the truth. Our men were being sent in without guns. Troopships were sunk and the government wouldn't tell us. The German army was so far superior to ours that we didn't have a chance. That Kaiser was a smart fellow. He was getting ready to invade America. But would Wilson tell us this? He would not. And usually these carrion talkers were the same ones who had said one American was worth twenty Germans in a scrap–the same ones.

Little groups of British in their outlandish uniforms (but they did look smart) moved about the country, buying everything that wasn't nailed down and paying for it and paying big. A good many of the British purchasing men were crippled, but they wore their uniforms just the same. Among other things they bought beans, because beans are easy to transport and they don't spoil and a man can damn well live on them. Beans are twelve and a half cents a pound and hard to find. And farmers wished they hadn't contracted their beans for a lousy two cents a pound above the going price six months ago.

The nation and the Salinas Valley changed its songs. At first we sang of how we could knock the hell out of Heligoland and hang the Kaiser and march over there and clean up the mess them damn foreigners had made. And then suddenly we sang, 'In the war's red curse stand the Red Cross nurse. She's the rose of No Man's Land', and we sang, 'Hello, central, give me Heaven, 'cause my Daddy's there', and we sang, 'Just a baby's prayer at twilight, when the lights are low. She climbs upstairs and says her prayers–Oh, God! please tell my daddy thaddy must take care–' I guess we were like a tough but inexperienced little boy who gets punched in the nose in the first flurry and it hurts and we wished it was over.

CHAPTER 43

I

Late in the summer Lee came in off the street, carrying his big market basket. Lee had become American conservative in his clothes since he had lived in Salinas. He regularly wore black broadcloth when he went out of the house. His shirts were white, his collars high and stiff, and he affected narrow black string ties, like those which once were the badge for Southern senators. His hats were black, round of crown and straight of brim, and uncrushed as though he still left room for a coiled queue. He was immaculate.

Once Adam had remarked on the quiet splendour of Lee's clothes, and Lee had grinned at him. 'I have to do it,' he said. 'One must be very rich to dress as badly as you do. The poor are forced to dress well.'

'Poor!' Adam exploded. 'You'll be lending us money before we're through.'

'That might be,' said Lee.

This afternoon he set his heavy basket on the floor. 'I'm going to try to make a winter melon soup,' he said. 'Chinese cooking. I have a cousin in Chinatown, and he told me how. My cousin is in the fire-cracker and fan-tan business.'

'I thought you didn't have any relatives,' said Adam.

'All Chinese are related, and the ones named Lee are closest,' said Lee. 'My cousin is a Suey Dong. Recently he went into hiding for his health and he learned to cook. You stand the melon in a pot, cut off the top carefully, put in a whole chicken, mushrooms, water chestnuts, leeks, and just a touch of ginger.

Then you put the top back on the melon and cook it as slowly as possible for two days. Ought to be good.'

Adam was lying back in his chair, his palms clasped behind his head, and he was smiling at the ceiling. 'Good, Lee, good,' he said.

'You didn't even listen,' said Lee.

Adam drew himself upright. He said, 'You think you know your own children and then you find you don't at all.'

Lee smiled. 'Has some detail of their lives escaped you?' he asked.

Adam chuckled. 'I only found out by accident,' he said. 'I knew that Aron wasn't around very much this summer, but I thought he was just out playing.'

'Playing!' said Lee. 'He hasn't played for years.'

'Well, whatever he does.' Adam continued, 'Today I met Mr Kilkenny–you know, from the high school? He thought I knew all about it. Do you know what that boy is doing?'

'No,' said Lee.

'He's covered all next year's work. He's going to take examinations for college and save a year. And Kilkenny is confident that he will pass. Now, what do you think of that?'

'Remarkable,' said Lee. 'Why is he doing it?'

'Why, to save a year!'

'What does he want to save it for?'

'Goddamn it, Lee, he's ambitious. Can't you understand that?'

'No,' said Lee. 'I never could.'

Adam said, 'He never spoke of it. I wonder if his brother knows.'

'I guess Aron wants it to be a surprise. We shouldn't mention it until he does.'

'I guess you're right. Do you know, Lee?–I'm proud of him. Terribly proud. This makes me feel good. I wish Cal had some ambition.'

'Maybe he has,' said Lee. 'Maybe he has some kind of a secret too.'

'Maybe. God knows we haven't seen much of him lately either. Do you think it's good for him to be away so much?'

'Cal's trying to find himself,' said Lee. 'I guess this personal hide-and-seek is not unusual. And some people are "it" all their lives–hopelessly "it".'

'Just think,' said Adam. 'A whole year's work ahead. When he tells us we ought to have a present for him.'

'A gold watch,' said Lee.

'That's right,' said Adam. 'I'm going to get one and have it engraved and ready. What should it say?'

'The jeweller will tell you,' said Lee. 'You take the chicken out after two days and cut off the bone and put the meat back.'

'What chicken?'

'Winter melon soup,' said Lee.

'Have we got enough money to send him to college, Lee?'

'If we're careful and he doesn't develop expensive tastes.'

'He wouldn't,' Adam said.

'I didn't think I would–but I have.' Lee inspected the sleeve of his coat with admiration.

2

The rectory of St Paul's Episcopal Church was large and rambling. It had been built for ministers with large families. Mr Rolf, unmarried and simple in his tastes, closed up most of the house, but when Aron needed a place to study he gave him a large room and helped him with his studies.

Mr Rolf was fond of Aron. He liked the angelic beauty of his face and his smooth cheeks, his narrow hips, and long straight legs. He liked to sit in the room and watch Aron's face straining with effort to learn. He understood why Aron could not work at home in an atmosphere not conducive to hard clean thought. Mr Rolf felt that Aron was his product, his spiritual son, his contribution to the Church. He saw him through his travail of celibacy and felt that he was guiding him into calm waters.

Their discussions were long and close and personal. 'I know I am criticized,' Mr Rolf said. 'I happen to believe in a Higher Church than some people. No one can tell me that confession is not just as important a sacrament as communion. And you mind my word–I am going to bring it back, but cautiously, gradually.'

'When I have a church I'll do it too.'

'It requires great tact,' said Mr Rolf.

Aron said, 'I wish we had in our Church, well–well, I might as well say it. I wish we had something like the Augustines or the Franciscans. Someplace to withdraw. Sometimes I feel dirty. I want to get away from the dirt and be clean.'

'I know how you feel,' Mr Rolf said earnestly. 'But there I cannot go along with you. I can't think that our Lord Jesus would want His priesthood withdrawn from service to the world. Think how He insisted that we preach the Gospel, help the sick and poor, even lower ourselves into filth to raise sinners from the slime. We must keep the exactness of His example before us.'

His eyes began to glow and his voice took on the throatiness he used in sermons. 'Perhaps I shouldn't tell you this. And I hope you won't find any pride in me telling it. But there is a kind of glory in it. For the last five weeks a woman has been coming to evening service. I don't think you can see her from the choir. She sits always in the last row on the left-hand side–yes, you can see her too. She is off at an angle. Yes, you can see her. She wears a veil and she always leaves before I can get back after recessional.'

'Who is she?' Aron asked.

'Well, you'll have to learn these things. I made very discreet inquiries and you would never guess. She is–well–the owner of a house of ill fame.'

'Here in Salinas?'

'Here in Salinas.' Mr Rolf leaned forward. 'Aron, I can see your revulsion. You must get over that. Don't forget our Lord and Mary Magdalene. Without pride I say I would be glad to raise her up.'

'What does she want here?' Aron demanded.

'Perhaps what we have to offer–salvation. It will require great tact. I can see how it will be. And mark my words–these people are timid. One day there will come a tap on my door and she will beg to come in. Then Aron, I pray that I may be wise and patient. You must believe me–when that happens, when a lost soul seeks the light, it is the highest and most beautiful experience a priest can have. That's what we are for, Aron. That's what we are for.'

Mr Rolf controlled his breathing with difficulty. 'I pray God I may not fail,' he said.

3

Adam Trask thought of the war in terms of his own dimly remembered campaigns against the Indians. No one knew anything about huge and general war. Lee read European history, trying to discern from the filaments of the past some pattern of the future.

Liza Hamilton died with a pinched little smile on her mouth, and her cheekbones were shockingly high when the red was gone from them.

And Adam waited impatiently for Aron to bring news of his examinations. The massive gold watch lay under his handkerchiefs in the top drawer of his bureau, and he kept it wound and set and checked its accuracy against his own watch.

Lee had his instructions. On the evening of the day of the announcement he was to cook a turkey and bake a cake.

'We'll want to make a party of it,' Adam said. 'What would you think of champagne?'

'Very nice,' said Lee. 'Did you ever read von Clausewitz?'

'Who is he?'

'Not very reassuring reading,' said Lee. 'One bottle of champagne?'

'That's enough. It's just for toasts, you know. Makes a party of it.' It didn't occur to Adam that Aron might fail.

One afternoon Aron came in and asked Lee, 'Where's father?'

'He's shaving.'

'I won't be in for dinner,' said Aron.

In the bathroom he stood behind his father and spoke to the soap-faced image in the mirror. 'Mr Rolf asked me to have dinner at the rectory.'

Adam wiped his razor on a folded piece of toilet paper. 'That's nice,' he said.

'Can I get a bath?'

'I'll be out of here in just a minute,' said Adam.

When Aron walked through the living-room and said good night and went out, Cal and Adam looked after him. 'He got into my cologne,' said Cal. 'I can still smell him.'

'It must be quite a party,' Adam said.

'I don't blame him for wanting to celebrate. That was a hard job.'

'Celebrate?'

'The exams. Didn't he tell you? He passed them.'

'Oh, yes–the exams,' said Adam. 'Yes, he told me. A fine job. I'm proud of him. I think I'll get him a gold watch.'

Cal said sharply, 'He didn't tell you!'

'Oh, yes–yes, he did. He told me this morning.'

'He didn't know this morning,' said Cal, and he got up and went out.

He walked very fast in the gathering darkness, out Central Avenue, past the park and past Stonewall Jackson Smart's house clear to the place beyond the street-lights where the street became a country road and angled to avoid Tollot's farm-house.

At ten o'clock Lee, going out to mail a letter, found Cal sitting on the lowest step on the front porch. 'What happened to you?' he asked.

'I went for a walk.'

'What's the matter with Aron?'

'I don't know.'

'He seems to have some kind of grudge. Want to walk to the post office with me?'

'No.'

'What are you sitting out here for?'

'I'm going to beat the hell out of him.'

'Don't do it,' said Lee.

'Why not?'

'Because I don't think you can. He'd slaughter you.'

'I guess you're right,' said Cal. 'The son of a bitch!'

'Watch your language.'

Cal laughed. 'I guess I'll walk along with you.'

'Did you ever read von Clausewitz?'

'I never even heard of him.'

When Aron came home it was Lee who was waiting for him on the lowest step of the front porch. 'I saved you from a licking,' Lee said. 'Sit down.'

'I'm going to bed.'

'Sit down! I want to talk to you. Why didn't you tell your father you passed the tests?'

'He wouldn't understand.'

'You've got a bug up your arse.'

'I don't like that kind of language.'

'Why do you think I used it? I am not profane by accident. Aron, your father has been living for this.'

'How did he know about it?'

'You should have told him yourself.'

'This is none of your business.'

'I want you to go in and wake him up if he's asleep, but I don't think he'll be asleep. I want you to tell him.'

'I won't do it.'

Lee said softly, 'Aron, did you ever have to fight a little man, a man half your size?'

'What do you mean?'

'It's one of the most embarrassing things in the world. He won't stop and pretty soon you have to hit him and that's worse. Then you're really in trouble all round.'

'What are you talking about?'

'If you don't do as I tell you, Aron, I'm going to fight you. Isn't that ridiculous?'

Aron tried to pass. Lee stood up in front of him, his tiny fists doubled ineffectually, his stance and position so silly that he began to laugh. 'I don't know how to do it, but I'm going to try,' he said.

Aron nervously backed away from him. And when finally he sat down on the steps Lee sighed deeply. 'Thank heaven that's over,' he said. 'It would have been awful. Look, Aron, can't you tell me what's the matter with you? You always used to tell me.'

Suddenly Aron broke down. 'I want to go away. It's a dirty town.'

'No, it isn't. It's just the same as other places.'

'I don't belong here. I wish we hadn't ever come here. I don't know what's the matter with me. I want to go away.' His voice rose to a wail.

Lee put his arm around the broad shoulders to comfort him. 'You're growing up. Maybe that's it,' he said softly. 'Sometimes I think the world tests us most sharply then, and we turn inward and watch ourselves with horror. But that's not the worst. We think everybody is seeing into us. Then dirt is very dirty and purity is shining white. Aron, it will be over. Wait only a little while and it will be over. That's not much relief to you because you don't believe it, but it's the best I can do for you. Try to believe that things are neither so good nor so bad as they seem to you now. Yes, I can help you. Go to bed now, and in the morning get up early and tell your father about the tests. Make it exciting. He's lonelier than you are because he has no lovely future to dream about. Go through the motions. Sam Hamilton said that. Pretend it's true and maybe it will be. Go through the motions. Do that. And go to bed. I've got to bake a cake–for breakfast. And Aron–your father left a present on your pillow.'

CHAPTER 44

I

It was only after Aron went away to college that Abra really got to know his family. Aron and Abra had fenced themselves in with themselves. With Aron gone, she attached herself to the other Trasks. She found that she trusted Adam more, and loved Lee more, than her own father.

About Cal she couldn't decide. He disturbed her sometimes with anger, sometimes with pain, and sometimes with curiosity. He seemed to be in a perpetual contest with her. She didn't know whether he liked her or not, and so she didn't like him. She was relieved when, calling at the Trask house, Cal was not there, to look secretly at her, judge, appraise, consider, and look away when she caught him at it.

Abra was a straight, strong, fine-breasted woman, developed and ready and waiting to take her sacrament–but waiting. She took to going to the Trask house after school, sitting with Lee, reading him parts of Aron's daily letter.

Aron was lonely at Stanford. His letters were drenched with lonesome longing for his girl. Together they were matter-of-fact, but from the university, ninety miles away, he made passionate love to her, shut himself off from the life around him. He studied, ate, slept, and wrote to Abra, and this was his whole life.

In the afternoon she sat in the kitchen with Lee and helped him to string beans or slip peas from their pods. Sometimes she made fudge and very often she stayed to dinner rather than go home to her parents. There was no subject she could not discuss with Lee. And the few things she could talk about to her father and mother were thin and pale and tired and mostly not even true. There Lee was different also. Abra wanted to tell Lee only true things even when she wasn't quite sure what was true.

Lee would sit smiling a little, and his quick fragile hands flew about their work as though they had independent lives. Abra wasn't aware that she spoke exclusively of herself. And sometimes while she talked Lee's mind wandered out and came back and went out again like a ranging dog, and Lee would nod at intervals and make a quiet humming sound.

He liked Abra and he felt strength and goodness in her, and warmth too. Her features had the bold muscular strength which could result finally either in ugliness or in great beauty. Lee, musing through her talk, thought of the round smooth faces of the Cantonese, his own breed. Even thin they were moon-faced. Lee should have liked that kind best since beauty must be somewhat like ourselves, but he didn't. When he thought of Chinese beauty the iron predatory faces of the Manchus came to his mind, arrogant and unyielding faces of a people who had authority by unquestioned inheritance.

She said, 'Maybe it was there all along. I don't know. He never talked much about his father. It was after Mr Trask had the–you know–the lettuce. Aron was angry then.'

'Why?' Lee asked.

'People were laughing at him.'

Lee's whole mind popped back. 'Laughing at Aron? Why at him? He didn't have anything to do with it.'

'Well, that's the way he felt. Do you want to know what I think?'

'Of course,' said Lee.

'I figured this out and I'm not quite finished figuring. I thought he always felt–well, kind of crippled–maybe unfinished, because he didn't have a mother.'

Lee's eyes opened wide and then dropped again. He nodded. 'I see. Do you figure Cal that way too?'

'No.'

'Then why Aron?'

'Well, I haven't got that yet. Maybe some people need things more than others, or hate things more. My father hates turnips. He always did. Never came from anything. Turnips make him mad, real mad. Well, one time my mother was–well, huffy, and she made a casserole out of mashed turnips with lots of pepper and cheese on top and got it all brown on top. My father ate half a dish of it before he asked what it was. My mother said turnips, and he threw the dish on the floor and got up and went out. I don't think he ever forgave her.'

Lee chuckled. 'He can forgive her because she said turnips. But, Abra, suppose he'd asked and she had said something else and he liked it and had another dish. And then afterwards he found out. Why, he might have murdered her.'

'I guess so. Well, anyway, I figure Aron needed a mother more than Cal did.

And I think he always blamed his father.'

'Why?'

'I don't know. That's what I think.'

'You get around, don't you?'

'Shouldn't I?'

'Of course you should.'

'Shall I make some fudge?'

'Not today. We still have some.'

'What can I do?'

'You can pound flour into the top round. Will you eat with us?'

'No. I'm going to a birthday party, thank you. Do you think he'll be a minister?'

'How do I know?' said Lee. 'Maybe it's just an idea.'

'I hope he doesn't,' said Abra, and she clapped her mouth shut in astonishment at having said it.

Lee got up and pulled out the pastry board and laid out the red meat and a flour sifter beside it. 'Use the back of the knife,' he said.

'I know.' She hoped he hadn't heard her.

But Lee asked, 'Why don't you want him to be a minister?'

'I shouldn't say it.'

'You should say anything you want to. You don't have to explain.' He went back to his chair, and Abra sifted flour over the steak and pounded the meat with a big knife. Tap-tap–'I shouldn't talk like this'–tap-tap.

Lee turned his head away to let her take her own pace.

'He goes all one way,' she said over the pounding. 'If it's Church it's got to be High Church. He was talking about how priests shouldn't be married.'

'That's not the way his last letter sounded,' Lee observed.

'I know. That was before.' Her knife stopped its pounding. Her face was young perplexed pain. 'Lee, I'm not good enough for him.'

'Now, what do you mean by that?'

'I'm not being funny. He doesn't think of me. He's made someone up, and it's like he put my skin on her. I'm not like that–not like the made-up one.'

'What's she like?'

'Pure!' said Abra. 'Just absolutely pure. Nothing but pure–never a bad thing. I'm not like that.'

'Nobody is,' said Lee.

'He doesn't know me. He doesn't even want to know me. He wants that–white–ghost.'

Lee rubbled a piece of cracker. 'Don't you like him? You're pretty young, but I don't think that makes any difference.'

''Course I like him. I'm going to be his wife. But I want him to like me too. And how can he, if he doesn't know anything about me? I used to think he knew me. Now I'm not sure he ever did.'

'Maybe he's going through a hard time that isn't permanent. You're a smart girl–very smart. Is it pretty hard trying to live up to the one–in your skin?'

'I'm always afraid he'll see something in me that isn't in the one he made up. I'll get mad or I'll smell bad–or something else. He'll find out.'

'Maybe not,' said Lee. 'But it must be hard living the Lily Maid, the Goddess-Virgin, and the other all at once. Humans just do smell bad sometimes.'

She moved towards the table. 'Lee, I wish–'

'Don't spill flour on my floor,' he said. 'What do you wish?'

'It's from my figuring out. I think Aron, when he didn't have a mother–why, he made her everything good he could think of.'

'That might be. And then you think he dumped it all on you.' She stared at him and her fingers wandered delicately up and down the blade of the knife. 'And you wish you could find some way to dump it all back.'

'Yes.'

'Suppose he wouldn't like you then?'

'I'd rather take a chance on that,' she said. 'I'd rather be myself.'

Lee said, 'I never saw anybody get mixed up in other people's business the way I do. And I'm a man who doesn't have a final answer about anything. Are you going to pound that meat or shall I do it?'

She went back to work. 'Do you think it's funny to be so serious when I'm not even out of high school?' she asked.

'I don't see how it could be any other way,' said Lee. 'Laughter comes later, like wisdom teeth, and laughter at yourself comes last of all in a mad race with death, and sometimes it isn't in time.'

Her tapping speeded up and its beat became erratic and nervous. Lee moved five dried lima beans in patterns on the table–a line, an angle, a circle.

The beating stopped. 'Is Mrs Trask alive?'

Lee's forefinger hung over a bean for a moment and then slowly fell and pushed it to make the *O* into a *Q*. He knew she was looking at him. He could even see in his mind how her expression would be one of panic at her question. His thought raced like a rat new caught in a wire trap. He sighed and gave it up. He turned slowly and looked at her, and his picture had been accurate.

Lee said tonelessly, 'We've talked a lot and I don't remember that we have ever discussed me–ever.' He smiled shyly. 'Abra, let me tell you about myself. I'm a servant. I'm old. I'm Chinese. These three you know. I'm tired and I'm cowardly.'

'You're not–' she began.

'Be silent,' he said. 'I am so cowardly. I will not put my finger in any human pie.'

'What do you mean?'

'Abra, is your father mad at anything except turnips?'

Her face went stubborn. 'I asked you a question.'

'I did not hear a question,' he said softly and his voice came confident. 'You did not ask a question, Abra.'

'I guess you think I'm too young–' Abra began.

Lee broke in, 'Once I worked for a woman of thirty-five who had successfully resisted experience, learning, and beauty. If she had been six she would have been the despair of her parents. And at thirty-five she was permitted to control money and the lives of people around her. No, Abra, age has nothing to do with it. If I had anything at all to say–I would say it to you.'

The girl smiled at him. 'I'm clever,' she said. 'Shall I be clever?'

'God help me–no,' Lee protested.

'Then you don't want me to try and figure it out?'

'I don't care what you do as long as I don't have anything to do with it. I guess no matter how weak and negative a good man is, he has as many sins on him as he can bear. I have enough sins to trouble me. Maybe, they aren't very fine sins compared to some, but, the way I feel, they're all I can take care of. Please forgive me.'

Abra reached across the table and touched the back of his hand with floury fingers. The yellow skin on his hand was tight and glazed. He looked down at the white powdery smudges her fingers left.

Abra said, 'My father wanted a boy. I guess he hates turnips and girls. He tells everyone how he gave me my crazy name. "And though I called another, Abra came."'

Lee smiled at her. 'You're such a nice girl,' he said. 'I'll buy some turnips tomorrow if you'll come to dinner.'

Abra asked softly, 'Is she alive?'

'Yes,' said Lee.

The front door slammed, and Cal came into the kitchen. 'Hello, Abra. Lee, is father home?'

'No, not yet. What are you grinning all over for?'

Cal handed him a cheque. There. That's for you.'

Lee looked at it. 'I didn't want interest,' he said.

'It's better. I might want to borrow it back.'

'You won't tell me where you got it?'

'No. Not yet. I've got a good idea–' His eyes flicked to Abra.

'I have to go home now,' she said.

Cal said, 'She might as well be in on it. I decided to do it Thanksgiving, and Abra'll probably be around and Aron will be home.'

'Do what?' she asked.

'I've got a present for my father.'

'What is it?' Abra asked.

'I won't tell. You'll find out then.

'Does Lee know?'

'Yes, but he won't tell.'

'I don't think I ever saw you so–gay,' Abra said. 'I don't think I ever saw you gay at all.' She discovered in herself a warmth for him.

After Abra had gone Cal sat down. 'I don't know whether to give it to him before Thanksgiving dinner or after,' he said.

'After,' said Lee. 'Have you really got the money?'

'Fifteen thousand dollars.'

'Honestly?'

'You mean, did I steal it?'

'Yes.'

'Honestly,' said Cal. 'Remember how we had champagne for Aron? We'll get champagne. And–well, we'll maybe decorate the dining-room. Maybe Abra'll help.'

'Do you really think your father wants money?'

'Why shouldn't he?'

'I hope you're right,' said Lee. 'How have you been doing in school?'

'Not very well. I'll pick up after Thanksgiving,' said Cal.

2

After school the next day Abra hurried and caught up with Cal.

'Hello, Abra,' he said. 'You make good fudge.'

'That last was dry. It should be creamy.'

'Lee is just crazy about you. What have you done to him?'

'I like Lee,' she said, and then, 'I want to ask you something, Cal.'

'Yes?'

'What's the matter with Aron?'

'What do you mean?'

'He just seems to think only about himself.'

'I don't think that's very new. Have you had a fight with him?'

'No. When he had all that about going to Church and not getting married, I tried to fight with him, but he wouldn't.'

'Not get married to you? I can't imagine that.'

'Cal, he writes me love letters now–only they aren't to me.'

'Then who are they to?'

'It's like they were to–himself.'

Cal said, 'I know about the willow tree.'

She didn't seem surprised. 'Do you?' she asked.

'Are you mad at Aron?'

'No, not mad. I just can't find him. I don't know him.'

'Wait around,' said Cal. 'Maybe he's going through something.'

'I wonder if I'll be all right. Do you think I could have been wrong all the time?'

'How do I know?'

'Cal,' she said, 'is is true you go out late at night and even go–to–bad houses?'

'Yes,' he said. 'That's true. Did Aron tell you?'

'No, not Aron. Well, why do you go there?'

He walked beside her and did not answer.

'Tell me,' she said.

'What is it to you?'

'Is it because you're bad?'

'What's it sound like to you?'

'I'm not good either,' she said.

'You're crazy,' said Cal. 'Aron will knock that out of you.'

'Do you think he will?'

'Why, sure,' said Cal. 'He's got to.'

CHAPTER 45

I

Joe Valery got along by watching and listening and, as he said himself, not sticking his neck out. He had built his hatreds little by little–beginning with a mother who neglected him, a father who alternately whipped and slobbered over him. It had been easy to transfer his developing hatred to the teacher who disciplined him and the policeman who chased him and the priest who lectured him. Even before the first magistrate looked down on him, Joe had developed a fine stable of hates towards the whole world he knew.

Hate cannot live alone. It must have love as a trigger, a goad, or a stimulant. Joe early developed a gentle protective love for Joe. He comforted and flattered and cherished Joe. He set up walls to save Joe from a hostile world. And gradually Joe became proof against wrong. If Joe got into trouble, it was because the world was in angry conspiracy against him. And if Joe attacked the world, it was revenge and they damn well deserved it–the sons of bitches. Joe lavished every care on his love, and he perfected a lonely set of rules which might have gone like this:

1. Don't believe nobody. The bastards are after you.
2. Keep your mouth shut. Don't stick your neck out.
3. Keep your ears open. When they make a slip, grab on to it and wait.
4. Everybody's a son of a bitch and whatever you do they got it coming.
5. Go at everything roundabout.
6. Don't never trust no dame about nothing.
7. Put your faith in dough. Everybody wants it. Everybody will sell out for it.

There were other rules, but they were refinements. His system worked, and since he knew no other, Joe had no basis of comparison with other systems. He knew it was necessary to be smart and he considered himself smart. If he pulled something off, that was smart; if he failed, that was bad luck. Joe was not very successful but he got by with the minimum of effort. Kate kept him because she knew he would do anything in the world if he were paid to do it or was afraid not to do it. She had no illusions about him. In her business Joe was necessary.

When he first got the job with Kate, Joe looked for the weaknesses on which he lived–vanity, voluptuousness, anxiety or conscience, greed, hysteria. He knew they were there because she was a woman. It was a matter of considerable shock to him to learn that, if they were there, he couldn't find them. This dame thought and acted like a man–only tougher, quicker, and more clever. Joe made a few mistakes and Kate rubbed his nose in them. He developed an admiration for her based on fear.

When he found that he couldn't get away with some things, he began to believe he couldn't get away with anything. Kate made a slave of him just as she had always made slaves of women. She fed him, clothed him, gave him orders, punished him.

Once Joe recognized her as more clever than himself, it was a short step to the belief that she was more clever than anybody. He thought that she possessed the two great gifts: she was smart and she got the breaks–and you couldn't want no better than that. He was glad to do her hatchet work–and afraid not to. Kate don't make no mistakes, Joe said. And if you played along with her, Kate took care of you. This went beyond thought and became a habit pattern. When he got Ethel floated over the county line, it was all in the day's work. It was Kate's business and she was smart.

2

Kate did not sleep well when the arthritic pains were bad. She could almost feel her joints thicken and knot. Sometimes she tried to think of other things, even unpleasant ones, to drive the pain and the distorted fingers from her mind. Sometimes she tried to remember every detail in a room she had not seen for a long time. Sometimes she looked at the ceiling and projected long columns of figures and added them. Sometimes she used memories. She built Mr Edwards's face and his clothes and the word that was stamped on the metal clasp on his braces. She had never noticed it, but she knew the word was 'Excelsior'.

Often in the night she thought of Faye, remembered her eyes and hair and the tone of her voice and how her hands fluttered and the little lump of flesh beside her left thumb-nail, a scar from an ancient cut. Kate went into her feeling about Faye. Did she hate or love her? Did she pity her? Was she sorry she had killed her? Kate inched over her own thought like a measuring worm. She found she had no feeling about Faye. She neither liked nor disliked her or her memory. There had been a time during her dying when the noise and the smell of her had made anger rise in Kate so that she considered killing her quickly to get it over.

Kate remembered how Faye had looked the last time she saw her, lying in her purple casket, dressed in white, with the undertaker's smile on her lips and enough powder and rouge to cover her sallow skin.

A voice behind Kate had said, 'She looks better than she has in years.' And another voice had answered, 'Maybe the same thing would do me some good,' and there was a double snicker. The first voice would be Ethel, and the second Trixie. Kate remembered her own half-humorous reaction. Why, she had thought, a dead whore looks like anybody else.

Yes, the first voice must have been Ethel. Ethel always got into the night thinking, and Ethel always brought a shrinking fear with her, the stupid, clumsy, nosy bitch–the lousy old bag. And it happened very often that Kate's mind would tell her, 'Now wait a moment. Why is she a lousy bag? Isn't it because you made a mistake? Why did you float her? If you'd used your head and kept her here–'

Kate wondered where Ethel was. How about one of those agencies to find Ethel–at least to find where she went? Yes, and then Ethel would tell about that night and show the glass. Then there'd be two noses sniffing instead of one. Yes, but what difference would that make? Every time Ethel got a beer in her she would be telling somebody. Oh, sure, but they would think she was just a buzzed old hustler. Now an agency man–no–no agencies.

Kate spent many hours with Ethel. Did the Judge have any idea it was a frame–too simple? It shouldn't have been an even hundred dollars. That was obvious. And how about the sheriff? Joe said they dropped her over the line into Santa Cruz County. What did Ethel tell the deputy who drove her out? Ethel was a lazy old bat. Maybe she had stayed in Watsonville. There was Pajaro, and that was a railroad section, and then the Pajaro River and the bridge into Watsonville. Lots of section hands went back and forth, Mexicans, some Hindus. That puddle-head Ethel might have thought she could turn enough tricks with the track workers. Wouldn't it be funny if she had never left Watsonville, thirty miles away? She could even slip in over the line and see her friends if she wanted to. Maybe she came to Salinas sometimes. She might be in Salinas right now. The cops weren't likely to keep too much on the look for her. Maybe it would be a good idea to send Joe over to Watsonville to see if Ethel was there. She might have gone on to Santa Cruz. Joe could look there too. It wouldn't take him long. Joe could find any hooker in any town in a few hours. If he found her they would get her back somehow. Ethel was a fool. But maybe when he found her it would be better if Kate went to her. Lock the door. Leave a 'Do not disturb' sign. She could get to Watsonville, do her business and get back. No taxis. Take a bus. Nobody saw anybody on the night buses. People sleeping with their shoes off and coats rolled up behind their heads. Suddenly she knew she would be afraid to go to Watsonville. Well, she could make herself go. It would stop all this wondering. Strange she hadn't thought of sending Joe before. That was perfect. Joe was good at some things, and the dumb bastard thought he was clever. That was the kind easiest to handle. Ethel was stupid. That made her hard to handle.

As her hands and her mind grew more crooked, Kate began to rely more and more on Joe Valery as her assistant-in-chief, as her go-between, and as her executioner. She had a basic fear of the girls in the house–not that they were more untrustworthy than Joe but that the hysteria which lay very close to the surface might at any time crack through their caution and shatter their sense of self-preservation and tear down not only themselves but their surroundings. Kate had always been able to handle this ever-present danger, but now the slow-depositing calcium and the slow growth of apprehension caused her to need help and to look for it from Joe. Men, she knew, had a little stronger wall against self-destruction than the kind of women she knew.

She felt that she could trust Joe, because she had in her files a notation relating to one Joseph Venuta who had walked away from a San Quentin road gang in the fourth year of a five-year sentence for robbery. Kate had never mentioned this to Joe Valery, but she thought it might have a soothing influence on him if he got out of hand.

Joe brought the breakfast tray every morning–green China tea and cream and toast. When he had set it on her bedside table he made his report and got his orders for the day. He knew that she was depending on him more and more. And Joe was very slowly and quietly exploring the possibility of taking over entirely. If she got sick enough there might be a chance. But very profoundly Joe was afraid of her.

'Morning,' he said.

'I'm not going to sit up for it, Joe. Just give me the tea. You'll have to hold it.'

'Hands bad?'

'Yes. They get better after a flare-up.'

'Looks like you had a bad night.'

'No,' said Kate. 'I had a good night. I've got some new medicine.'

Joe held the cup to her lips, and she drank the tea in little sips, breathed over it to cool it. 'That's enough,' she said when the cup was only half empty. 'How was the night?'

'I almost came to tell you last night,' said Joe. 'Hick came in from King City. Just sold his crop. Bought over the house. Dropped seven hundred not counting what he gave the girls.'

'What was his name?'

'I don't know. But I hope he comes in again.'

'You should get the name, Joe. I've told you that.'

'He was cagey.'

'All the more reason to get his name. Didn't any of the girls frisk him?'

'I don't know.'

'Well, find out.'

Joe sensed a mild geniality in her and it made him feel good. 'I'll find out,' he assured her. 'I got enough to go on.'

Her eyes went over him, testing and searching, and he knew something was coming. 'You like it here?' she asked softly.

'Sure. I got it good here.'

'You could have it better–or worse,' she said.

'I like it good here,' he said uneasily, and his mind cast about for a fault in himself. 'I got it real nice here.'

She moistened her lips with her arrow-sharp tongue. 'You and I can work together,' she said.

'Any way you want it,' he said ingratiatingly, and a surge of pleasant expectation grew in him. He waited patiently. She took a good long time to begin.

At last she said, 'Joe, I don't like to have anything stolen.'

'I didn't take nothing.'

'I didn't say you did.'

'Who?'

'I'll get to it, Joe. Do you remember that old buzzard we had to move?'

'You mean Ethel what's-her-name?'

'Yes. That's the one. She got away with something. I didn't know it then.'

'What?'

A coldness crept into her voice. 'Not your business, Joe. Listen to me! You're a smart fellow. Where would you go to look for her?'

Joe's mind worked quickly, not with reason but with experience and instinct. 'She was pretty beat up. She wouldn't go far. An old hustler don't go far.'

'You're smart. You think she might be in Watsonville?'

'There or maybe Santa Cruz. Anyways, I'll give odds she ain't further away than San Jose.'

She caressed her fingers tenderly. 'Would you like to make five hundred, Joe?'

'You want I should find her?'

'Yes. Just find her. When you do, don't let her know. Just bring me the address. Got that? Just tell where she is.'

'Okay,' said Joe. 'She must of rolled you good.'

'That's not your business, Joe.'

'Yes, ma'am,' he said. 'You want I should start right off?'

'Yes. Make it quick, Joe.'

'Might be a little tough,' he said. 'It's been a long time.'

'That's up to you.'

'I'll go to Watsonville this afternoon.'

'That's good, Joe.'

She was thoughtful. He knew she was not finished and that she was wondering whether she should go on. She decided.

'Joe, did–did she do anything–well, peculiar–that day in court?'

'Hell, no. Said she was framed like they always do.'

And then something came back to him that he hadn't noticed at the time. Out of his memory Ethel's voice came, saying, 'Judge, I got to see you alone. I got to tell you something.' He tried to bury his memory deep so that his face would not speak.

Kate said, 'Well, what is it?'

He had been too late. His mind leaped for safety. 'There's something,' he said, to gain time. 'I'm trying to think.'

'Well, think!' Her voice was edged and anxious.

'Well–' He had it. 'Well, I heard her tell the cops–let's see–she said why couldn't they let her go south. She said she had relatives in San Luis Obispo.'

Kate leaned quickly towards him. 'Yes?'

'And the cops said it was too damn far.'

'You're smart, Joe. Where will you go first?'

'Watsonville,' he said. 'I got a friend in San Luis. He'll look around for me. I'll give him a ring.'

'Joe,' she said sharply, 'I want this quiet.'

'For five hundred you'll get it quiet and quick,' said Joe. He felt fine even though her eyes were slitted and inspective again. Her next words jarred his stomach loose from his backbone.

'Joe, not to change the subject–does the name Venuta mean anything to you?'

He tried to answer before his throat tightened. 'Not a thing,' he said.

'Come back as soon as you can,' Kate said. 'Tell Helen to come in. She'll take over for you.'

3

Joe packed his suitcase, went to the depot, and bought a ticket for Watsonville. At Castroville, the first station north, he got off and waited four hours for the Del Monte express from San Francisco to Monterey, which is the end of a spur line. In Monterey he climbed the stairs of the Central Hotel, registered as John Vicker. He went downstairs and ate a steak at Pop Ernst's, bought a bottle of whisky, and retired to his room.

He took off his shoes and his coat and waistcoat, removed his collar and tie, and lay down on the bed. The whisky and a glass were on the table beside the brass bed. The overhead light shining in his face didn't bother him. He didn't notice it. Methodically he primed his brain with half a tumbler of whisky and then he crossed his hands behind his head and crossed his ankles and he brought out thoughts and impressions and perceptions and instincts and began matching them.

It had been a good job and he had thought he had her fooled. Well, he'd under-rated her. But how in hell had she got on to it he was wanted? He thought he might go to Reno or maybe to Seattle. Seaport towns–always good. And then–now wait a minute. Think about it.

Ethel didn't steal nothing. She had something. Kate was scared of Ethel. Five hundred was a lot of dough to dig out a beat-up whore. What Ethel wanted to tell the judge was, number one, true; and, number two, Kate was scared of it. Might be able to use that. Hell!–not with her holding that jail-break over him. Joe wasn't going to serve out the limit with penalties.

But no harm in thinking about it. Suppose he was to gamble four years against–well, let's say ten grand. Was that a bad bet? No need to decide. She knew it before and she didn't turn him in. Suppose she thought he was a good dog.

Maybe Ethel might be a hole-card.

Now–wait–just think about it. Maybe it was the breaks. Maybe he ought to draw his hand and see. But she was so goddam smart. Joe wondered if he could play against her. But how, if he just played along?

Joe sat up and filled his glass full. He turned off his light and raised his blind. And as he drank his whisky he watched a skinny little woman in a bathrobe washing her stockings in a basin in a room on the other side of the air-shaft. And the whisky muttered in his ears.

It might be the breaks, God knows, Joe had waited long enough. God knows, he hated the bitch with her sharp little teeth. No need to decide right now.

He raised his window quietly and threw the writing pen from the table against the window across the air-shaft. He enjoyed the scene of fear and apprehension before the skinny dame yanked her blind down.

With the third glass of whisky the pint was empty. Joe felt a wish to go out in the street and look the town over. But then his discipline took over. He had made a rule, and kept to it, never to leave his room when he was drinking. That way a man never got in trouble. Trouble meant cops, and cops meant a check-up, and that would surely mean a trip across the bay to San Quentin and no road gang for good behaviour this time. He put the street out of his mind.

Joe had another pleasure he saved for times when he was alone, and he was not aware it was a pleasure. He indulged it now. He lay on the brass bed and went back in time over his sullen and miserable childhood and his fretful and vicious growing up. No luck–he never got the breaks. The big shot got the breaks. A few snatch jobs he got away with, but the tray of pocket-knives? Cops came right in his house and got him. Then he was on the books and they never let him alone. Guy in Daly City couldn't shag a crate of strawberries off a truck without they'd pick up Joe. In school he didn't have no luck neither. Teachers against him, principal against him. Guy couldn't take the crap. Had to get out.

Out of his memory of bad luck warm sadness grew, and he pushed it with more memories until the tears came to his eyes and his lips quivered with pity for the lonely lost boy he had been. And here he was now–look at him–a rap against him, working in a whorehouse when other men had homes and cars. They were safe and happy and at night their blinds were pulled down against Joe. He wept quietly until he fell asleep.

Joe got up at ten in the morning and ate a monster breakfast at Pop Ernst's. In the early afternoon he took a bus to Watsonville and played three games of snooker with a friend who came to meet him in answer to a phone call. Joe won the last game and racked his cue. He handed his friend two ten-dollar notes.

'Hell,' said his friend, 'I don't want your money.'

'Take it,' said Joe.

'It ain't like I give you anything.'

'You give me plenty. You say she ain't here and you're the baby that would know.'

'Can't tell me what you want her for?'

'Wilson, I tol' you right first an' I tell you now, I don't now. I'm jus' doing a job of work.'

'Well, that's all I can do. Seems like there was this convention–what was it?–dentists, or maybe Owls. I don't know whether she said she was going or I just figured it myself. I got it stuck in my mind. Give Santa Cruz a whirl. Know anybody?'

'I got a few acquaintances,' said Joe.

'Look up H. V. Mahler. Hal Mahler. He runs Hal's poolroom. Got a game in back.'

'Thanks,' said Joe.

'No–look, Joe. I don't want your money.'

'It ain't my money–buy a cigar,' said Joe.

The bus dropped him two doors from Hal's place. It was suppertime but the stud game was still going. It was an hour before Hal got up to go to the can and Joe could follow and make a connection. Hal peered at Joe with large pale eyes made huge by thick glasses. He buttoned his fly slowly and adjusted his black alpaca sleeve guards and squared his green eyeshade. 'Stick around till the game breaks,' he said. 'Care to sit in?'

'How many playing for you, Hal?'

'Only one.'

'I'll play for you.'

'Five bucks an hour,' said Hal.

'An' ten per cent if I win?'

'Well, okay. Sandy-haired fella Williams is the house.'

At one o'clock in the morning Hal and Joe went to Barlow's Grill. 'Two rib steaks and french fries. You want soup?' Hal asked Joe.

'No. And no french fries. They bind me up.'

'Me too,' said Hal. 'But I eat them just the same. I don't get enough exercise.'

Hal was a silent man until he was eating. He rarely spoke unless his mouth was full. 'What's your pitch?' he asked around steak.

'Just a job. I make a hundred bucks and you get twenty-five–okay?'

'Got to have like proof–like papers?'

'No. Be good but I'll get by without them.'

'Well, she comes in and wants me to steer for her. She wasn't no good. I don't take twenty a week off her. I probably wouldn't of knew what become of her only Bill Primus seen her in my place and when they found her he come in an' ast me about her. Nice fella, Bill. We got a nice force here.'

Ethel was not a bad woman–lazy, sloppy, but good-hearted. She wanted dignity and importance. She was just not very bright and not very pretty and, because of these two lacks, not very lucky. It would have bothered Ethel if she had known that when they pulled her out of the sand where waves had left her half buried her skirts were pulled around her arse. She would have liked more dignity.

Hal said, 'We got some crazy bohunk bastards in the sardine fleet. Get loaded with ink an' they go nuts. Way I figure, one of them sardine crews took her out an' then just pushed her overboard. I don't see how else she'd get in the water.'

'Maybe she jumped off the pier?'

'Her?' said Hal through potatoes. 'Hell, no! She was too lazy to kill herself. You want to check?'

'If you say it's her, it's her,' said Joe, and he pushed a twenty and five across the table.

Hal rolled the notes like a cigarette and put them in his waistcoat pocket. He cut out the triangle of meat from the rib steak and put it in his mouth. 'It was her,' he said. 'Want a piece of pie?'

Joe meant to sleep until noon, but he awakened at seven and lay in bed for quite a long time. He planned not to get back to Salinas until after midnight. He needed more time to think.

When he got up he looked in the mirror and inspected the expression he planned to wear. He wanted to look disappointed but not too disappointed. Kate was so goddam clever. Let her lead. Just follow suit. She was about as wide open as a fist. Joe had to admit that he was scared to death of her.

His caution said to him, 'Just go in and tell her and get your five hundred.'

And he answered his caution savagely, 'Breaks. How many breaks did I ever get? Part of the breaks is knowing a break when you get it. Do I want to be a lousy pimp all my life? Just play it close. Let her do the talking. No harm in that. I can always tell her later like I just found out if it don't go good.'

'She could have you in a cell block in six hours flat.'

'Not if I play 'em close. What I got to lose? What breaks did I ever get?'

4

Kate was feeling better. The new medicine seemed to be doing her some good. The pain in her hands was abated, and it seemed to her that her fingers were straighter, the knuckles not so swollen. She had had a good night's sleep, the first in a long time, and she felt good, even a little excited. She planned to have a boiled egg for breakfast. She got up and put on a dressing-gown and brought a hand mirror back to the bed. Lying high against the pillows, she studied her face.

The rest had done wonders. Pain makes you set your jaw, and your eyes grow falsely bright with anxiety, and the muscles over the temples and along the cheeks, even the weak muscles near to the nose stand out a little, and that is the look of sickness and of resistance to suffering.

The difference in her rested face was amazing. She looked ten years younger. She opened her lips and looked at her teeth. Time to go for a cleaning. She took care of her teeth. The gold bridge where the molars were gone was the only repair in her mouth. It was remarkable how young she looked, Kate thought. Just one night's sleep and she snapped back. That was another thing that fooled them. They thought she would be weak and delicate. She smiled to herself–delicate like a steel trap. But then she always took care of herself–no liquor, no drugs, and recently she had stopped drinking coffee. And it paid off. She had an angelic face. She put the mirror a little higher so that the crêpe at her throat did not reflect.

Her thought jumped to that other angelic face so like hers–what was his name?–what the hell was his name–Alec? She could see him, moving slowly past, his white surplice edged with lace, his sweet chin down and his hair glowing under the candlelight. He held the oaken staff and its brass cross angled ahead of him. There was something frigidly beautiful about him, something untouched and untouchable. Well, had anything or anybody ever really touched Kate–really got through and soiled her? Certainly not. Only the hard outside had been brushed by contacts. Inside she was intact–as clean and bright as this boy Alec–was that his name?

She chuckled–mother of two sons–and she looked like a child. And if anyone had seen her with the blond one–could they have any doubt? She thought how it would be to stand beside him in a crowd and let people find out for themselves. What would–Aron, that was his name–what would he do if he knew? His brother knew. That smart little son of a bitch–wrong word–must not call him that. Might be too true. Some people believed it. And not smart bastard either–born in holy wedlock. Kate laughed aloud. She felt good. She was having a good time.

The smart one–the dark one–bothered her. He was like Charles. She had respected Charles–and Charles would probably have killed her if he could.

Wonderful medicine–it not only stopped the arthritic pain, it gave her back her courage. Pretty soon she could sell out and go to New York as she had always planned. Kate thought of her fear of Ethel. How sick she must have been–the poor dumb old bag! How would it be to murder her with kindness? When Joe found her, how about–well, how about taking her to New York? Keep her close.

A funny notion came to Kate. That would be a comical murder, and a murder no one under any circumstances could solve or even suspect. Chocolates–boxes of chocolates, bowls of fondant, bacon, crisp bacon–fat; port wine, and then butter, everything soaked in butter and whipped cream; no vegetables, no fruit–and no amusement either. Stay in the house, dear. I trust you. Look after things. You're tired. Go to bed. Let me fill your glass. I got these new sweets for you. Would you like to take the box to bed? Well, if you don't feel good why don't you take a physic? These cachous are nice, don't you think? The old bitch would blow up and burst in six months. Or how about a tapeworm? Did anyone ever use tapeworms? Who was the man who couldn't get water to his mouth in a sieve–Tantalus?

Kate's lips were smiling sweetly and gaiety was coming over her. Before she went it might be good to give a party for her sons. Just a simple little party with a circus afterwards for her darlings–her jewels. And then she thought of Aron's beautiful face so like her own and a strange pain–a little collapsing pain–arose in her chest. He wasn't smart. He couldn't protect himself. The dark brother might be dangerous. She had felt his quality. Cal had beaten her. Before she went away she would teach him a lesson. Maybe–why, sure–maybe a dose of the clap might set that young man back on his heels.

Suddenly she knew that she did not want Aron to know about her. Maybe he could come to her in New York. He would think she had always lived in an elegant little house on the East Side. She would take him to the theatre, to the opera, and people would see them together and wonder at their loveliness, and recognize that they were either brother and sister or mother and son. No one could fail to know. They could go together to Ethel's funeral. She would need an oversize coffin and six wrestlers to carry it. Kate was so filled with amusement at her thoughts that she did not hear Joe's knocking on the door. He opened it a crack and looked in and saw her gay and smiling face.

'Breakfast,' he said and nudged the door open with the edge of the linen-covered tray. He pushed the door closed with his knee. 'Want it here?' he asked and gestured towards the grey room with his chin.

'No. I'll have it right here. And I want a boiled egg and a piece of cinnamon toast. Four and a half minutes on the egg. Make sure. I don't want it gooey.'

'You must feel better, ma'am.'

'I do,' she said. 'That new medicine is wonderful. You look dragged by dogs, Joe. Don't you feel well?'

'I'm all right,' he said and set the tray on the table in front of the big deep chair. 'Four and a half minutes.'

'That's right. And if there's a good apple–a crisp apple–bring that too.'

'You ain't et like this since I knew you,' he said.

In the kitchen, waiting for the cook to boil the egg, he was apprehensive. Maybe she knew. He'd have to be careful. But hell! she couldn't hate him for something he didn't know. No crime in that.

Back in her room he said, 'Didn't have no apples. He said this was a good pear.'

'I'd like that even better,' said Kate.

He watched her chip off the egg and dip a spoon into the shell. 'How is it?'

'Perfect!' said Kate. 'Just perfect.'

'You look good,' he said.

'I feel good. You look like hell. What's the matter?'

Joe went into it warily. 'Ma'am, there ain't nobody needs five hundred like I do.'

She said playfully, 'There isn't *anyone* who needs–'

'What?'

'Forget it. What are you trying to say? You couldn't find her–is that it? Well, if you did a good job looking, you'll get your five hundred. Tell me about it.' She picked up the salt shaker and scattered a few grains into the open eggshell.

Joe put an artificial joy on his face. 'Thanks,' he said. 'I'm in a spot. I need it. Well, I looked in Pajaro and Watsonville. Got a line on her in Watsonville but she'd went to Santa Cruz. Got a smell of her there but she was gone.'

Kate tasted the egg and added more salt. 'That's all?'

'No,' said Joe. 'I went it blind there. Dropped down to San Luis an' she had been there too but gone.'

'No trace? No idea where she went?'

Joe fiddled with his fingers. His whole pitch, maybe his whole life, depended on his next words, and he was reluctant to say them.

'Come on,' she said at last. 'You got something–what is it?'

'Well, it ain't much. I don't know what to think of it.'

'Don't think. Just tell. I'll think,' she said sharply.

'Might not even be true.'

'For Christ's sake!' she said angrily.

'Well, I talked to the last guy that seen her. Guy named Joe, like me–'

'Did you get his grandmother's name?' she asked sarcastically.

'This guy Joe says she loaded up on beer one night an' she said how she's going to come back to Salinas an' lay low. Then she dropped out of sight. This guy Joe didn't know nothing more.'

Kate was startled out of control. Joe read her quick start, the apprehension, and then the almost hopeless fear and weariness. Whatever it was, Joe had something. He had got the breaks at last.

She looked up from her lap and her twisted fingers. 'We'll forget the old fart,' she said. 'You'll get your five hundred, Joe.'

Joe breathed shallowly, afraid that any sound might drag her out of her self-absorption. She had believed him. More than that, she was believing things he had not told her. He wanted to get out of the room as quickly as possible. He said, 'Thank you, ma'am,' but very softly, and he moved silently towards the door.

His hand was on the knob when she spoke with elaborate casualness. 'Joe, by the way–'

'Ma'am?'

'If you should hear anything about–her, let me know, will you?'

'I sure will. Want me to dig into it?'

'No. Don't bother. It isn't that important.'

In his room, with the door latched, Joe sat down and folded his arms. He smiled to himself. And instantly he began to work out the future course. He decided to let her brood on it till, say, next week. Let her relax, and then bring up Ethel again. He did not know what his weapon was or how he was going to use it. But he did know that it was very sharp and he itched to use it. He would have laughed out loud if he had known that Kate had gone to the grey room and locked its door, and that she sat still in the big chair and her eyes were closed.

CHAPTER 46

Sometimes, but not often, a rain comes to the Salinas Valley in November. It is so rare that the *Journal* or the *Index* or both carry editorials about it. The hills turn to a soft green overnight and the air smells good. Rain at this time is not particularly good in an agricultural sense unless it is going to continue, and this is extremely unusual. More commonly, the dryness comes back and the fuzz of grass withers or a little frost curls it and there's that amount of seed wasted.

The war years were wet years, and there were many people who blamed the strange intransigent weather on the firing of the great guns in France. This was seriously considered in articles and in arguments.

We didn't have many troops in France that first winter, but we had millions in training, getting ready to go.

Painful as the war was, it was exciting too. The Germans were not stopped. In fact, they had taken the initiative again, driving methodically towards Paris, and God knew when they could be stopped–if they could be stopped at all. General Pershing would save us if we could be saved. His trim, beautiful uniformed soldierly figure made its appearance in every paper every day. His chin was granite and there was no wrinkle on his tunic. He was the epitome of a perfect soldier. No one knew what he really thought.

We knew we couldn't lose and yet we seemed to be going about losing. You couldn't buy flour, white flour, any more without taking four times the quantity of brown flour. Those who could afford it ate bread and biscuits made with white flour and made mash for the chickens with the brown.

In the old Troop C armoury the Home Guard drilled, men over fifty and not the best soldier material, but they took setting-up exercises twice a week, wore Home Guard buttons and overseas caps, snapped orders at one another, and wrangled eternally about who should be officers. William C Burt died right on the armoury floor in the middle of a push-up. His heart couldn't take it.

There were Minute Men too, so called because they made one-minute speeches in favour of America in moving-picture theatres and in churches. They had buttons too.

The women rolled bandages and wore Red Cross uniforms and thought of themselves as Angels of Mercy. And everbody knitted something for someone. There were wristlets, short tubes of wool to keep the wind from whistling up soldiers' sleeves, and there were knitted helmets with only a hole in front to look out of. These were designed to keep the new tin helmets from freezing to the head.

Every bit of really first-grade leather was taken for officers' boots and for Sam Browne belts. These belts were handsome and only officers could wear them. They consisted of a wide belt and a strap that crossed the chest and passed under the left epaulette. We copied them from the British, and even the British had forgotten their original purpose, which was possibly to support a heavy sword. Swords were not carried except on parade, but an officer would not be caught dead without a Sam Browne belt. A good one cost as much as twenty-five dollars.

We learned a lot from the British–and if they had not been good fighting men we wouldn't have taken it. Men began to wear their handkerchiefs in their sleeves and some foppish lieutenants carried swagger sticks. One thing we resisted for a long time, though. Wrist-watches were just too silly. It didn't seem likely that we would ever copy the Limeys in that.

We had our internal enemies too, and we exercised vigilance. San Jose had a spy scare, and Salinas was not likely to be left behind–not the way Salinas was growing.

For about twenty years Mr Fenchel had done hand tailoring in Salinas. He was short and round and he had an accent that made you laugh. All day he sat cross-legged on his table in the little shop on Alisal Street, and in the evening he walked home to his small white house far out on Central Avenue. He was for ever painting his house and the white picket fence in front of it. Nobody had given his accent a thought until the war came along, but suddenly we knew. It was German. We had our own personal German. It didn't do him any good to bankrupt himself buying war bonds. That was too easy a way to cover up.

The Home Guards wouldn't take him in. They didn't want a spy knowing their secret plans for defending Salinas. And who wanted to wear a suit made by an enemy? Mr Fenchel sat all day on his table and he didn't have anything to do, so he basted and ripped and sewed and ripped on the same piece of cloth over and over.

We used every cruelty we could think of on Mr Fenchel. He was our German. He passed our house every day, and there had been a time when he spoke to every man and woman and child and dog, and everyone had answered. Now no one spoke to him, and I can see now in my mind his tubby loneliness and his face full of hurt pride.

My little sister and I did our part with Mr Fenchel, and it is one of those memories of shame that still makes me break into a sweat and tighten up around the throat. We were standing in our front yard on the lawn one evening and we saw him coming with little fat steps. His black homburg was brushed and squarely set on his head. I don't remember that we discussed our plan but we must have, to have carried it out so well.

As he came near, my sister and I moved slowly across the street side by side. Mr Fenchel looked up and saw us moving towards him. We stopped in the gutter as he came by.

He broke into a smile and said, 'Gut efning, Chon. Gut efning, Mary.'

We stood stiffly side by side and we said in union, 'Hoch der Kaiser!'

I can see his face now, his startled innocent blue eyes. He tried to say something and then he began to cry. Didn't even try to pretend he wasn't. He just stood there sobbing. And do you know?–Mary and I turned round and walked stiffly across the street and into our front yard. We felt horrible. I still do when I think of it.

We were too young to do a good job on Mr Fenchel. That took strong men–about thirty of them. One Saturday night they collected in a bar and marched in a column of fours out Central Avenue, saying, 'Hup! Hup!' in unison. They tore down Mr Fenchel's white picket fence and burned the front out of his house. No Kaiser-loving son of a bitch was going to get away with it with us. And then Salinas could hold up its head with San Jose.

Of course that made Watsonville get busy. They tarred and feathered a Pole they thought was a German. He had an accent.

We of Salinas did all of the things that are inevitably done in a war, and we thought the inevitable thoughts. We screamed over good rumours and died of panic at bad news. Everybody had a secret that he had to spread obliquely to keep its identity as a secret. Our pattern of life changed in the usual manner. Wages and prices went up. A whisper of shortage caused us to buy and store food. Nice quiet ladies clawed one another over a can of tomatoes.

It wasn't all bad or cheap or hysterical. There was heroism too. Some men who could have avoided the army enlisted, and others objected to the war on moral or religious grounds and took the walk up Golgotha which normally comes of that. There were people who gave everything they had to the war because it was the last war and by winning it we could remove war like a thorn from the flesh of the world and there wouldn't be any more such horrible nonsense.

There is no dignity in death in battle. Mostly that is a splashing about of human meat and fluid, and the result is filthy, but there is a great and almost sweet dignity in the sorrow, the helpless, the hopeless sorrow, that comes down over a family with the telegram. Nothing to say, nothing to do, and only one hope–I hope he didn't suffer–and what a forlorn and last-choice hope that is. And it is true that there were some people who, when their sorrow was beginning to lose its savour, gently edged it towards pride and felt increasingly important because of their loss. Some of these even made a good thing of it after the war was over. That is only natural, just as it is natural for a man whose function is the making of money to make money out of a war. No one blamed a man for that, but it was expected that he should invest a part of his loot in war bonds. We thought we invented all of it in Salinas, even the sorrow.

CHAPTER 47

I

In the Trask house next to Reynaud's bakery, Lee and Adam put up a map of the western front with lines of coloured pins snaking down, and this gave them a feeling of participation. Then Mr Kelly died and Adam Trask was appointed to take his place on the draft board. He was the logical man for the job. The ice plant did not take up much of his time, and he had a clear service record and an honourable discharge himself.

Adam Trask had seen a war–a little war of manœuvre and butchery, but at least he had experienced the reversal of the rules where a man is permitted to kill all the humans he can. Adam didn't remember his war very well. Certain sharp pictures stood out in his memory, a man's face, the piled and burning bodies, the clang of sabre scabbards at fast trot, the uneven, tearing sound of firing carbines, the thin cold voice of a bugle in the night. But Adam's pictures were frozen. There was no motion or emotion in them–illustrations in the pages of a book, and not very well drawn.

Adam worked hard and honestly and sadly. He could not get over the feeling that the young men he passed to the army were under sentence of death. And because he knew he was weak, he grew more and more stern and painstaking and much less likely to accept an excuse or a borderline disability. He took the lists home with him, called on parents, in fact, did much more work than was expected of him. He felt like a hanging judge who hates the gallows.

Henry Stanton watched Adam grow more gaunt and more silent, and Henry was a man who liked fun–needed it. A sour-pussed associate could make him sick.

'Relax,' he told Adam. 'You're trying to carry the weight of the war. Now, look–it's not your responsibility. You got put in here with a set of rules. Just follow the rules and relax. You aren't running the war.'

Adam moved the slats of the blind so that the late afternoon sun would not shine in his eyes, and he gazed down at the harsh parallel lines the sun threw on his desk. 'I know,' he said wearily. 'Oh, I know that! But, Henry, it's when there's a choice, and it's my own judgement of the merits, that's when it gets me. I passed Judge Kendal's boy, and he was killed in training.'

'It's not your business, Adam. Why don't you take a few drinks at night? Go to a movie–sleep on it.' Henry put his thumbs in the armholes of his waistcoat and leaned back in his chair. 'While we're talking about it, Adam, it seems to me it don't do a candidate a damn bit of good for you to worry. You pass boys I could be talked into letting off.'

'I know,' said Adam. 'I wonder how long it will last?'

Henry inspected him shrewdly and took a pencil from his stuffed waistcoat pocket and rubbed the eraser against his big white front teeth. 'I see what you mean,' he said softly.

Adam looked at him, startled. 'What do I mean?' he demanded.

'Now don't get huffy. I never thought I was lucky before, just having girls.'

Adam traced one of the slat shadows on his desk with his forefinger. 'Yes,' he said in a voice as soft as a sigh.

'It's a long time before your boys will be called up.'

'Yes.' Adam's finger entered a line of light and slid slowly back.

Henry said, 'I'd hate to–'

'Hate to what?'

'I was just wondering how I'd feel if I had to pass my own sons.'

'I'd resign,' said Adam.

'Yes, I can see that. A man would be tempted to reject them–I mean, his own.'

'No,' said Adam. 'I'd resign because I couldn't reject them. A man couldn't let his own go free.'

Henry laced his fingers and made one big fist of his two hands and laid the fist on the desk in front of him. His face was querulous. 'No,' he said, 'you're right. A man couldn't.' Henry liked fun and avoided when he could any solemn or serious matter, for he confused these with sorrow. 'How's Aron doing at Stanford?'

'Fine. He writes that it's hard but he thinks he'll make out all right. He'll be home for Thanksgiving.'

'I'd like to see him. I saw Cal on the street last night. There's a smart boy.'

'Cal didn't take college tests a year ahead,' said Adam.

'Well, maybe that's not what he's cut out for. I didn't go to college. Did you?'

'No,' said Adam. 'I went into the army.'

'Well, it's good experience. I'll bet you wouldn't take a good bit for the experience.'

Adam stood up slowly and picked his hat from the deer-horn on the wall. 'Good night, Henry,' he said.

2

Walking home, Adam pondered his responsibility. As he passed Reynaud's Bakery Lee came out, carrying a golden loaf of French bread.

'I have a hunger for some garlic bread,' Lee said.

'I like it with steak,' said Adam.

'We're having steak. Was there any mail?'

'I forgot to look in the box.'

They entered the house and Lee went to the kitchen. In a moment Adam followed him and sat at the kitchen table. 'Lee,' he said, 'suppose we send a boy to the army and he is killed, are we responsible?'

'Go on,' said Lee. 'I would rather have the whole thing at once.'

'Well, suppose there's a slight doubt that the boy should be in the army and we send him and he gets killed.'

'I see. Is it responsibility or blame that bothers you?'

'I don't want blame.'

'Sometimes responsibility is worse. It doesn't carry any pleasant egotism.'

'I was thinking about that time when Sam Hamilton and you and I had a long discussion about a word,' said Adam. 'What was that word?'

'Now I see. The word was *timshel.*'

'*Timshel*–and you said–'

'I said that word carried a man's greatness if he wanted to take advantage of it.'

'I remember Sam Hamilton felt good about it.'

'It set him free,' said Lee. 'It gave him the right to be a man, separate from every other man.'

'That's lonely.'

'All great and precious things are lonely.'

'What is the word again?'

'*Timshel*–thou mayest.'

3

Adam looked forward to Thanksgiving when Aron would come home from college. Even though Aron had been away such a short time Adam had forgotten him and changed him the way any man changes someone he loves. With Aron gone, the silences were the result of his going, and every little painful event was somehow tied to his absence. Adam found himself talking and boasting about his son, telling people who weren't very interested how smart Aron was and how he had jumped a year in school. He thought it would be a good thing to have a real celebration at Thanksgiving to let the boy know his effort was appreciated.

Aron lived in a furnished room in Palo Alto, and he walked the mile to and from the campus every day. He was miserable. What he had expected to find at the university had been vague and beautiful. His picture–never really inspected–had been of clean-eyed young men and immaculate girls, all in academic robes and converging on a white temple on the crown of a wooded hill in the evening. Their faces were shining and dedicated and their voices rose in chorus and it was never any time but evening. He had no idea where he had got his picture of academic life–perhaps from the Doré illustrations of Dante's *Inferno* with its massed and radiant angels. Leland Stanford University was not like that. A formal square of brown sandstone blocks set down in a hayfield; a church with an Italian mosaic front; classrooms of varnished pine; and the great world of struggle and anger re-enacted in the rise and fall of fraternities. And those bright angels were youths in dirty corduroy trousers, some study-raddled and some learning the small vices of their fathers.

Aron, who had not known he had a home, was nauseatingly homesick. He did not try to learn the life around him or to enter it. He found the natural noise and fuss and horseplay of undergraduates horrifying, after his dream. He left the college dormitory for a dreary furnished room where he could decorate another dream which had only now come into being. In the new and neutral hiding place he cut the university out, went to his classes and left as soon as he could, to live in his new-found memories. The house next to Reynaud's Bakery became warm and dear. Lee the epitome of friend and counsellor, his father the cool, dependable figure of godhead, his brother clever and delightful, and Abra–well, of Abra he made his immaculate dream and, having created her, fell in love with her. At night when his studying was over he went to his nightly letter to her as one goes to a scented bath. And as Abra became more radiant, more pure and beautiful, Aron took an increasing joy in a concept of his own wickedness. In a frenzy he poured joyous abjectness on paper to send to her, and he went to bed purified, as a man is after sexual love. He set down every evil thought he had and renounced it. The results were love letters that dripped with longing and by their high tone made Abra very uneasy. She could not know that Aron's sexuality had taken a not unusual channel.

He had made a mistake. He could admit the mistake but as yet he could not reserve himself. He made a compact with himself. At Thanksgiving he would go home, and then he would be sure. He might never come back. He remembered that Abra had once suggested that they go to live on the ranch, and that became his dream. He remembered the great oaks and the clear living air, the clean sage-laced wind from the hills and the brown oak leaves scudding. He could see Abra there, standing under a tree, waiting for him to come in from his work. And it was evening. There, after work of course, he could live in purity and peace with the world, cut off by the little draw. He could hide from ugliness–in the evening.

CHAPTER 48

I

Late in November the Nigger died and was buried in black austerity, as her will demanded. She lay for a day in Muller's Funeral Chapel in an ebony and silver casket, her lean and severe profile made even more ascetic by the four large candles set at the four corners of the casket.

Her little black husband crouched like a cat by her right shoulder, and for many hours he seemed as still as she. There were no flowers, as ordered, no ceremony, no sermon, and no grief. But a strange, and catholic selection of citizens tiptoed to the chapel door and peered in and went away–lawyers and labourers and clerks and bank tellers, most of them past middle age. Her girls came in one at a time and looked at her for decency and for luck and went away.

An institution was gone from Salinas, dark and fatal sex, as hopeless and deeply hurtful as human sacrifice. Jenny's place would still jangle with honky-tonk and rock with belching laughter. Kate's would rip the nerves to a sinful ecstasy and leave a man shaken and weak and frightened at himself. But the sombre mystery of connexion that was like a voodoo offering was gone for ever.

The funeral was also by order of the will, the hearse and one automobile with the small black man crouched back in a corner. It was a grey day, and when Muller's service had lowered the casket with oiled and silent winches the hearse drove away and the husband filled the grave himself with a new shovel. The caretaker cutting dry weeds a hundred yards away, heard a whining carried on the wind.

Joe Valery had been drinking a beer with Butch Beavers at the Owl, and he went with Butch to have a look at Nigger. Butch was in a hurry because he had to go out to Natividad to auction a small herd of white-face Herefords for the Tavernettis.

Coming out of the mortuary, Joe found himself in step with Alf Nichelson–crazy Alf Nichelson, who was a survival from an era that was past. Alf was a jack-of-all-trades, carpenter, tinsmith, blacksmith, electrician, plasterer, scissor grinder, and cobbler. Alf could do anything, and as a result was a financial failure although he worked all the time. He knew everything about everybody back to the beginning of time.

In the past, in the period of his success, two kinds of people had access to all homes and all gossip–the seamstress and the handy man. Alf could tell you about everybody on both sides of Main Street. He was a vicious male gossip, insatiably curious and vindictive without malice.

He looked at Joe and tried to place him. 'I know you,' he said. 'Don't tell me.'

Joe edged away. He was wary of people who knew him.

'Wait a minute. I got it. Kate's. You work at Kate's.'

Joe sighed with relief. He had thought Alf might have known him earlier. 'That's right,' he said shortly.

'Never forget a face,' said Alf. 'Seen you when I built that crazy lean-to for Kate. Now why in hell did she want that for? No window.'

'Wanted it dark,' said Joe. 'Eyes bother her.'

Alf sniffed. He hardly ever believed anything simple or good about anybody. You could say good morning to Alf and he'd work it around to a password. He was convinced that everyone lived secretly and that only he could see through them.

He jerked his head back at Muller's. 'Well, it's a milestone,' he said. 'Nearly all the old-timers gone. When Fartin' Jenny goes that'll be the end. And Jenny's getting along.'

Joe was restless. He wanted to get away–and Alf knew he did. Alf was an expert in people who wanted to get away from him. Come to think of it, maybe that's why he carried his bag of stories. No one really went away when he could hear some juicy stuff about someone. Everybody is a gossip at heart. Alf was not liked for his gift but he was listened to. And he knew that Joe was on the point of making an excuse and getting out. It occurred to him that he didn't know much about Kate's place lately. Joe might trade him some new stuff for some old stuff. 'The old days was pretty good,' he said. ''Course you're just a kid.'

'I got to meet a fella,' said Joe.

Alf pretended not to hear him. 'You take Faye,' he said. 'She was a case,' and, parenthetically, 'You know Faye run Kate's place. Nobody really knows how Kate come to own it. It was pretty mysterious, and there were some that had their suspicions.' He saw with satisfaction that the fella Joe was going to meet would wait a long time.

'What was they suspicious about?' Joe asked.

'Hell, you know how people talk. Probably nothing in it. But I got to admit it looked kind of funny.'

'Like to have a beer?' Joe asked.

'Now you got something there,' said Alf. 'They say a fella jumps from a funeral to the bedroom. I ain't as young as I was. Funeral makes me thirsty. The Nigger was quite a citizen. I could tell you stuff about her. I've knew her for thirty-five–no, thirty-seven years.'

'Who was Faye?' Joe asked.

They went into Mr Griffin's saloon. Mr Griffin didn't like anything about liquor, and he hated drunks with a deadly scorn. He owned and operated Griffin's Saloon on Main Street, and on a Saturday night he might refuse to serve twenty men he thought had had enough. The result was that he got the best trade in his cool, orderly, quiet place. It was a saloon in which to make deals and to talk quietly without interruption.

Joe and Alf sat at the round table at the back and had three beers apiece. Joe learned everything true and untrue, founded and unfounded, every ugly conjecture. Out of it he got complete confusion but a few ideas. Something might have been not exactly on the level about the death of Faye. Kate might be the wife of Adam Trask. He hid that quickly–Trask might want to pay off. The Faye thing might be too hot to touch. Joe had to think about that–alone.

At the end of a couple of hours Alf was restive. Joe had not played ball. He had traded nothing, not one single piece of information or guess. Alf found himself thinking, Fella that close-mouthed must have something to hide. Wonder who would have a line on him?

Alf said finally, 'Understand, I like Kate. She gives me a job now and then and she's generous and quick to pay. Probably nothing to all the palaver about her. Still, when you think of it, she's a pretty cold piece of woman. She's got a real bad eye. You think?'

'I get along fine,' said Joe.

Alf was angry at Joe's perfidy, so he put in a needle. 'I had a funny idea,' he said. 'It was when I built that lean-to without no window. She laid that cold eye on me one day and the idea come to me. If she knew all the things I heard, and she was to offer me a drink or even a cup-cake–why, I'd say, "No, thank you, ma'am."'

'Me and her get along just fine,' said Joe. 'I got to meet a guy.'

Joe went to his room to think. He was uneasy. He jumped up and looked in his suitcase and opened all the bureau drawers. He thought somebody had been going through his things. Just came to him. There was nothing to find. It made him nervous. He tried to arrange the things he had heard.

There was a tap on the door and Thelma came in, her eyes swollen and her nose red. 'What's got into Kate?'

'She's been sick.'

'I don't mean that. I was in the kitchen shaking up a milkshake in a fruit jar and she came in and worked me over.'

'Was you maybe shaking up a little bourbon in it?'

'Hell, no. Just vanilla extract. She can't talk like that to me.'

'She did, didn't she?'

'Well, I won't take it.'

'Oh, yes, you will,' said Joe. 'Get out, Thelma!'

Thelma looked at him out of her dark, handsome, brooding eyes, and she regained the island of safety a woman depends on. 'Joe,' she asked, 'are you really just a pure son of a bitch or do you just pretend to be?'

'What do you care?' Joe asked.

'I don't,' said Thelma. 'You son of a bitch.'

2

Joe planned to move slowly, cautiously, and only after long consideration. 'I got the breaks, I got to use 'em right,' he told himself.

He went in to get his evening orders and took them from the back of Kate's head. She was at her desk, green eyeshade low, and she did not look round at him. She finished her terse orders and then went on, 'Joe, I wonder if you've been attending to business. I've been sick. But I'm well again or very nearly well.'

'Something wrong?'

'Just a symptom. I'd rather Thelma drank whisky than vanilla extract, and I don't want her to drink whisky. I think you've been slipping.'

His mind scurried for a hiding place. 'Well, I been busy.' he said.

'Busy?'

'Sure. Doing that stuff for you.'

'What stuff?'

'You know–about Ethel.'

'Forget Ethel!'

'Okay,' said Joe. And then it came without his expecting it. 'I met a fella yesterday said he seen her.'

If Joe had not known her he would not have given the little pause, the rigid ten seconds of silence, its due.

At the end of it Kate asked softly, 'Where?'

'Here.'

She turned her swivel chair slowly round to face him. 'I shouldn't have let you work in the dark, Joe. It's hard to confess a fault but I owe it to you. I don't have to remind you I got Ethel floated out of the county. I thought she'd done something to me.' A melancholy came into her voice. 'I was wrong. I found out later. It's been working on me ever since. She didn't do anything to me. I want to find her to make it up to her. I guess you think it's strange for me to feel that way.'

'No, ma'am.'

'Find her for me, Joe. I'll feel better when I've made it up to her–the poor old girl.'

'I'll try, ma'am.'

'And, Joe–if you need any money, let me know. And if you find her, just tell her what I said. If she doesn't want to come here, find out where I can telephone her. Need any money?'

'Not right now, ma'am. But I'll have to go out of the house more than I ought.'

'You go ahead. That's all, Joe.'

He wanted to hug himself. In the hall he gripped his elbows and let his joy run through him. And he began to believe he had planned the whole thing. He went through the darkened parlour with its low early evening spatter of conversation. He stepped outside and looked up at the stars swimming in schools through the wind-driven clouds.

Joe thought of his bumbling father–because he remembered something the old man had told him. 'Look out for a soap carrier,' Joe's father had said. 'Take one of them dames that's always carrying soup for somebody–she wants something, and don't you forget it.'

Joe said under his breath, 'A soup carrier. I thought she was smarter than that.' He went over her tone and words to make sure he hadn't missed anything. No–a soup carrier. And he thought of Alf saying, 'If she was to offer a drink or even a cup-cake–'

3

Kate sat at her desk. She could hear the wind in the tall privet in the yard, and the wind and the darkness was full of Ethel–fat, sloppy Ethel oozing near like a jellyfish. A dull weariness came over her.

She went into the lean-to, the grey room, and closed the door and sat in the darkness, listening to the pain creep back into her fingers. Her temples beat with pounding blood. She felt for the capsule hanging in its tube on the chain round her neck, she rubbed the metal tube, warm from her breast, against her cheek, and her courage came back. She washed her face and put on make-up, combed and puffed her hair in a loose pompadour. She moved into the hall and at the door of the parlour she paused, as always, listening.

To the right of the door two girls and a man were talking. As soon as Kate stepped inside the talk stopped instantly. Kate said, 'Helen, I want to see you if you aren't busy right now.'

The girl followed her down the hall and into her room. She was a pale blonde with a skin like a clean and polished bone. 'Is something the matter, Miss Kate?' she asked fearfully.

'Sit down. No nothing's the matter. You went to the Nigger's funeral.'

'Didn't you want me to?'

'I don't care about that. You went.'

'Yes, ma'am.'

'Tell me about it.'

'What about it?'

'Tell me what you remember–how it was.'

Helen said nervously, 'Well, it was kind of awful and–kind of beautiful.'

'How do you mean?'

'I don't know. No flowers, no nothing, but there was–there was a–well, a kind of–dignity. The Nigger was just laying there in a black wood coffin with the biggest goddam silver handles. Made you feel–I can't say it. I don't know how to say it.'

'Maybe you said it. What did she wear?'

'Wear, ma'am?'

'Yes–wear. They didn't bury her naked, did they?'

A struggle of effort crossed Helen's face. 'I don't know,' she said at last. 'I don't remember.'

'Did you go to the cemetery?'

'No, ma'am. Nobody did–except him.'

'Who?'

'Her man.'

Kate said quickly–almost too quickly, 'Have you got any regulars tonight?'

'No, ma'am. Day before Thanksgiving. Bound to be slow.'

'I'd forgotten,' said Kate. 'Get back out.' She watched the girl out of the room and moved restlessly back to her desk. And as she looked at an itemized bill for plumbing her left hand strayed to her neck and touched the chain. It was comfort and reassurance.

CHAPTER 49

I

Both Lee and Cal tried to argue Adam out of going to meet the train, the Lark night train from San Francisco to Los Angeles.

Cal said, 'Why don't we let Abra go alone? He'll want to see her first.'

'I think he won't know anybody else is there,' said Lee. 'So it doesn't matter whether we go or not.'

'I want to see him get off the train,' said Adam. 'He'll be changed. I want to see what change there is.'

Lee said, 'He's only been gone a couple of months. He can't be very changed, nor much older.'

'He'll be changed. Experience will do that.'

'If you go we'll all have to go,' said Cal.

'Don't you want to see your brother?' Adam asked sternly.

'Sure, but he won't want to see me–not right at first.'

'He will too,' said Adam. 'Don't you under-rate Aron.'

Lee threw up his hands. 'I guess we'll all go,' he said.

'Can you imagine?' said Adam. 'He'll know so many new things. I wonder if he'll talk different. You know, Lee, in the East a boy takes on the speech of his school. You can tell a Harvard man from a Princeton man. At least that's what they say.'

'I'll listen,' said Lee. 'I wonder what dialect they speak at Stanford.' He smiled at Cal.

Adam didn't think it was funny. 'Did you put some fruit in his room?' he asked. 'He loves fruit.'

'Pears and apples and muscat grapes,' said Lee.

'Yes, he loves muscats. I remember he loves muscats.'

Under Adam's urging they got to the Southern Pacific Depot half an hour before the train was due. Abra was already there.

'I can't come to dinner tomorrow, Lee,' she said. 'My father wants me home. I'll come as soon after as I can.'

'You're a little breathless,' said Lee.

'Aren't you?'

'I guess I am,' said Lee. 'Look up the track and see if the block's turned green.'

Train schedules are a matter of pride and of apprehension to nearly everyone. When, far up the track, the block signal snapped from red to green and the long, stabbing probe of the headlight sheered round the bend and blared on the station, men looked at their watches and said, 'On time.'

There was pride in it, and relief too. The split second has been growing more and more important to us. And as human activities become more and more intermeshed and integrated, the split tenth of a second will emerge, and then a new name must be made for the split hundredth, until one day, although I don't believe it, we'll say. 'Oh, the hell with it. What's wrong with an hour?' But it isn't silly, this preoccupation with small time units. One thing late or early can disrupt everything around it, and the disturbance runs outwards in bands like the waves from a dropped stone in a quiet pool.

The Lark came rushing in as though it had no intention of stopping. And only when the engine and baggage cars were well past did the air brakes give their screaming hiss and the straining iron protest to a halt.

The train delivered quite a crowd from Salinas, returning relatives home for Thanksgiving, their hands entangled in cartons and gift-wrapped paper boxes. It was a moment or two before his family could locate Aron. And then they saw him, and he seemed bigger than he had been.

He was wearing a flat-topped, narrow-brimmed hat, very stylish, and when he saw them he broke into a run and yanked off his hat, and they could see that his bright hair was clipped to a short brush of a pompadour that stood straight up. And his eyes shone so that they laughed with pleasure to see them.

Aron dropped his suitcase and lifted Abra from the ground in a great hug. He set her down and gave Adam and Cal his two hands. He put his arms around Lee's shoulders and nearly crushed him.

On the way home they all talked at once. 'Well, how are you?' 'You look fine.' 'Abra, you're so pretty.'

'I am not. Why did you cut your hair?'

'Oh, everybody wears it that way.'

'But you have such nice hair.'

They hurried up to Main Street and one short block and round the corner on Central past Reynaud's with stacked French bread in the window and black-haired Mrs Reynaud waved her flour-pale hand at them, and they were home.

Adam said, 'Coffee, Lee?'

'I made it before we left. It's on the simmer.' He had the cups laid out too. Suddenly they were together–Aron and Abra on the couch, Adam in his chair under the light, Lee passing coffee, and Cal braced in the doorway to the hall. And they were silent, for it was too late to say hello and too early to begin other things.

Adam did say, 'I'll want to hear all about it. Will you get good marks?'

'Finals aren't until next month, Father.'

'Oh, I see. Well, you'll get good marks, all right. I'm sure you will.'

In spite of himself a grimace of impatience crossed Aron's face.

'I'll bet you're tired,' said Adam. 'Well, we can talk tomorrow.'

Lee said, 'I'll bet he's not. I'll bet he'd like to be alone.'

Adam looked at Lee and said, 'Why, of course–of course. Do you think we should all go to bed?'

Abra solved it for them. 'I can't stay out long,' she said. 'Aron, why don't you walk me home? We'll be together tomorrow.'

On the way Aron clung to her arm. He shivered. 'There's going to be a frost,' he said.

'You're glad to be back.'

'Yes, I am. I have a lot to talk about.'

'Good things?'

'Maybe. I hope you think so.'

'You sound serious.'

'It is serious.'

'When do you have to go back?'

'Not until Sunday night.'

'We'll have lots of time. I want to tell you some things too. We have tomorrow and Friday and Saturday and all day Sunday. Would you mind not coming in tonight?'

'Why not?'

'I'll tell you later.'

'I want to know now.'

'Well, my father's got one of his streaks.'

'Against me?'

'Yes. I can't go to dinner with you tomorrow, but I won't eat much at home, so you can tell Lee to save a plate for me.'

He was turning shy. She could feel it in the relaxing grip on her arm and in his silence, and she could see it in his raised face. 'I shouldn't have told you that tonight.'

'Yes, you should,' he said slowly. 'Tell me the truth. Do you still want to be with me?'

'Yes, I do.'

'Then all right. I'll go away now. We'll talk tomorrow.'

He left her on the porch with the feeling of a light-brushed kiss on her lips. She felt hurt that he had agreed so easily, and she laughed sourly at herself that she could ask a thing and be hurt when she got it. She watched the tall quick step throught the radiance of the corner street-light. She thought, I must be crazy. I've been imagining things.

2

In his bedroom after he had said good night, Aron sat on the edge of his bed and peered down at his hands cupped between his knees. He felt let down and helpless, packed like a bird's egg in the cotton of his father's ambition for him. He had not known its strength until tonight, and he wondered whether he would have the strength to break free of its soft, persistent force. His thoughts would not coagulate. The house seemed cold with a dampness that made him shiver. He got up and softly opened the door. There was a light under Cal's door. He tapped and went in without waiting for a reply.

Cal sat at a new desk. He was working with tissue paper and bolt of red ribbon, and as Aron came in he hastily covered something on his desk with a large blotter.

Aron smiled. 'Presents?'

'Yes,' said Cal, and left it at that.

'Can I talk to you?'

'Sure! Come on in. Talk low or Father will come in. He hates to miss a moment.'

Aron sat down on the bed. He was silent so long that Cal asked, 'What's the matter–you got trouble?'

'No, not trouble. I just wanted to talk to you. Cal, I don't want to go on at college.'

Cal's head jerked round. 'You don't? Why not?'

'I just don't like it.'

'You haven't told Father, have you? He'll be disappointed. It's bad enough that I don't want to go. What do you want to do?'

'I thought I'd like to take over the ranch.'

'How about Abra?'

'She told me a long time ago that's what she'd like.'

Cal studied him. 'The ranch has got a lease to run.'

'Well, I was just thinking about it.'

Cal said, 'There's no money in farming.'

'I don't want much money. Just to get along.'

'That's not good enough for me,' said Cal. 'I want a lot of money and I'm going to get it too.'

'How?'

Cal felt older and surer than his brother. He felt protective towards him. 'If you'll go on at college, why, I'll get started and lay a foundation. Then when you finish we can be partners. I'll have one kind of thing and you'll have another. That might be pretty good.'

'I don't want to go back. Why do I have to go back?'

'Because Father wants you to.'

'That won't make me go.'

Cal stared fiercely at his brother, at the pale hair and the wide-set eyes, and suddenly he knew why his father loved Aron, knew beyond doubt. 'Sleep on it,' he said quickly. 'It would be better if you finished out the term at least. Don't do anything now.'

Aron got up and moved towards the door. 'Who's the present for?' he asked.

'It's for Father. You'll see it tomorrow–after dinner.'

'It's not Christmas.'

'No,' said Cal, 'It's better than Christmas.'

When Aron had gone back to his room Cal uncovered his present. He counted the fifteen new banknotes once more, and they were so crisp they made a sharp, cracking sound. The Monterey County Bank had to send to San Francisco to get them, they only did so when the reason for them was told. It was a matter of shock and disbelief to the bank that a seventeen-year-old boy should, first, own them, and, second, carry them about. Bankers do not like money to be lightly handled even if the handling is sentimental. It had taken Will Hamilton's word to make the bank believe that the money belonged to Cal, that it was honestly come by, and that he could do what he wanted with it.

Cal wrapped the notes in tissue and tied it with red ribbon finished in a blob that was firmly recognizable as a bow. The package might have been a handkerchief. He concealed it under the shirts in his bureau and went to bed. But he could not sleep. He was excited and at the same time shy. He wished the day was over and the gift given. He went over what he planned to say.

'This is for you.'

'What is it?'

'A present.'

From then on he didn't know what would happen. He tossed and rolled in bed, and at dawn he got up and dressed and crept out of the house.

On Main Street he saw Old Martin sweeping the streets with a stable broom. The city council was discussing the purchase of a mechanical sweeper. Old Martin hoped he would get to drive it, but he was cynical about it. Young men got the cream of everything. Bacigalupi's garbage wagon went by, and Martin looked after it spitefully. *There* was a good business. Those wops were getting rich.

Main Street was empty except for a few dogs sniffing at closed entrances and the sleepy activity around the San Francisco Chop House. Pet Bulene's new taxi was parked in front, for Pet had been alerted the night before to take the Williams girls to the morning train for San Francisco.

Old Martin called to Cal, 'Got a cigarette, young fella?'

Cal stopped and took out his cardboard box of Murads.

'Oh, fancy ones!' Martin said. 'I ain't got a match either.'

Cal lighted the cigarette for him, careful not to set fire to the grizzle around Martin's mouth.

Martin leaned on the handle of his brush and puffed disconsolately. 'Young fellas gets the cream,' he said. 'They won't let me drive it.'

'What?' Cal asked.

'Why, the new sweeper. Ain't you heard? Where you been, boy?' It was incredible to him that any reasonable informed human did not know about the sweeper. He forgot Cal. Maybe the Bacigalupis would give him a job. They were coining money. Three wagons and a new truck.

Cal turned down Alisal Street, went into the post office, and looked in the glass window of box 632. It was empty. He wandered back home and found Lee up and stuffing a very large turkey.

'Up all night?' Lee asked.

'No. I just went for a walk.'

'Nervous?'

'Yes.'

'I don't blame you. I would be too. It's hard to give people things–I guess it's harder to be given things, though. Seems silly, doesn't it? Want some coffee?'

'I don't mind.'

Lee wiped his hands and poured coffee for himself and for Cal. 'How do you think Aron looks?'

'All right, I guess.'

'Did you get to talk to him?'

'No,' said Cal. It was easier that way. Lee would want to know what he said. It wasn't Aron's day. It was Cal's day. He had carved this day out for himself and he wanted it. He meant to have it.

Aron came in, his eyes still misty with sleep. 'What time do you plan to have dinner, Lee?'

'Oh, I don't know–three-thirty or four.'

'Could you make it about five?'

'I guess so, if Adam says it's all right. Why?'

'Well, Abra can't get here before then. I've got a plan I want to put to my father and I want her to be here.'

'I guess that will be all right,' said Lee.

Cal got up quickly and went to his room. He sat at his desk with the student light turned on and he churned with uneasiness and resentment. Without effort, Aron was taking his day away from him. It would turn out to be Aron's day. Then, suddenly, he was bitterly ashamed. He covered his eyes with his hands and he said, 'It's jealousy. I'm jealous. That's what I am. I'm jealous. I don't want to be jealous.' And he repeated over and over, 'Jealous–jealous–jealous,' as though bringing it into the open might destroy it. And having gone this far, he proceeded with his self-punishment. 'Why am I giving the money to my father? Is it for his good? No. It's for my good. Will Hamilton said it–I'm trying to buy him. There's not one decent thing about it. There's not one decent thing about me. I sit here wallowing in jealousy of my brother. Why not call things by their names?'

He whispered hoarsely to himself. 'Why not be honest? I know my father loves Aron. It's because he looks like her. My father never got over her. He may not know it, but it's true. I wonder if he does know it. That makes me jealous of her too. Why don't I take my money and go away? They wouldn't miss me. In a little while they'd forget I ever existed–all except Lee. And I wonder whether Lee likes me. Maybe not.' He doubled his fists against his forehead. 'Does Aron have to fight himself like this? I don't think so, but how do I know? I could ask him. He wouldn't say.'

Cal's mind careened in anger at himself and in pity for himself. And then a new voice came into it, saying coolly and with contempt, 'If you're being honest–why not say you are enjoying this beating you're giving yourself? That would be the truth. Why not be just what you are and do just what you do?' Cal sat in shock from this thought. Enjoying?–of course. By whipping himself he protected himself against whipping by someone else. His mind tightened up. Give the money, but give it lightly. Don't depend on anything. Don't foresee anything. Just give it and forget it. And forget it now. Give–give. Give the day to Aron. Why not? He jumped up and hurried out to the kitchen.

Aron was holding open the skin of the turkey while Lee forced stuffing into the cavity. The oven cricked and snapped with growing heat.

Lee said, 'Let's see, eighteen pounds, twenty minutes to the pound–that's eighteen times twenty–that's three hundred and sixty minutes, six hours even–eleven to twelve, twelve to one–' He counted on his fingers.

Cal said, 'When you get through, Aron, let's take a walk.'

'Where to?' Aron asked.

'Just around the town. I want to ask you something.'

Cal led his brother across the street to Berges and Garrisiere, who imported fine wines and liquors. Cal said, 'I've got a little money, Aron. I thought you might like to buy some wine for dinner. I'll give you the money.'

'What kind of wine?'

'Let's make a real celebration. Let's get champagne–it can be your present.'

Joe Garrisiere said, 'You boys aren't old enough.'

'For dinner! Sure we are.'

'Can't sell it to you. I'm sorry.'

Cal said, 'I know what you can do. We can pay for it and you can send it to our father.'

'That I can do,' Joe Garrisiere said. 'We've got some Oeil de Perdrix–' His lips pursed as though he were tasting it.

'What's that?' Cal asked.

'Champagne–but very pretty, same colour as a partridge eye–pink but a little darker than pink, and dry too. Four-fifty a bottle.'

'Isn't that high?' Aron asked.

'Sure, it's high!' Cal laughed. 'Send three bottles over, Joe.' To Aron he said, 'It's your present.'

3

To Cal the day was endless. He wanted to leave the house and couldn't. At eleven o'clock Adam went to the closed draft-board office to brood over the records of a new batch of boys coming up.

Aron seemed perfectly calm. He sat in the living-room, looking at cartoons in old numbers of the *Review of Reviews*. From the kitchen the odour of the burning juices of roasting turkey began to fill the house.

Cal went into his room and took out his present and laid it on his desk. He tried to write a card to put on it. 'To my father from Caleb'–'To Adam Trask from Caleb Trask.' He tore the cards in tiny pieces and flushed them down the toilet.

He thought, Why give it to him today? Maybe tomorrow I could go to him quietly and say, 'This is for you,' and then walk away. That would be easier. 'No,' he said aloud. 'I want the others to see.' It had to be that way. But his lungs were compressed and the palms of his hands were wet with stage fright. And then he thought of the morning when his father got him out of jail. The warmth and closeness–they were things to remember–and his father's trust. Why, he had even said it. 'I trust you.' He felt much better then.

At about three o'clock he heard Adam come in and there was a low sound of voices conversing in the living-room. Cal joined his father and Aron.

Adam was saying, 'The times are changed. A boy must be a specialist or he will get nowhere. I guess that's why I'm so glad you're going to college.'

Aron said, 'I've been thinking about that, and I wonder.'

'Well, don't think any more. Your first choice is right. Look at me. I know a little bit about a great many things and not enough about any one of them to make a living in these times.'

Cal sat down quietly. Adam did not notice him. His face was concentrated on his thought.

'It's natural for a man to want his son to succeed,' Adam went on. 'And maybe I can see better than you can.'

Lee looked in. 'The kitchen scales must be way off,' he said. 'The turkey's going to be done earlier than the chart says. I'll bet that bird doesn't weigh eighteen pounds.'

Adam said, 'Well, you can keep it warm,' and he continued, 'Old Sam

Hamilton saw this coming. He said there couldn't be any more universal philosophers. The weight of knowledge is too great for one mind to absorb. He saw a time when one man would know only one little fragment, but he would know it well.'

'Yes,' Lee said from the doorway, 'and he deplored it. He hated it.'

'Did he now?' Adam asked.

Lee came into the room. He held his big basting spoon in his right hand, and he cupped his left under the bowl for fear it would drip on the carpet. He came into the room and forgot and waved his spoon and drops of turkey fat fell to the floor. 'Now you question it, I don't know,' he said. 'I don't know whether he hated it or I hate it for him.'

'Don't get so excited,' said Adam. 'Seems to me we can't discuss anything any more but you take it as a personal insult.'

'Maybe the knowledge is too great and maybe men are growing too small,' said Lee. 'Maybe, kneeling down to atoms, they're becoming atom-sized in their souls. Maybe a specialist is only a coward, afraid to look out of his little cage. And think what any specialist misses–the whole world over his fence.'

'We're only talking about making a living.'

'A living–or money,' Lee said excitedly. 'Money's easy to make if it's money you want. But with a few exceptions people don't want money. They want luxury and they want love and they want admiration.'

'All right. But do you have any objections to college? That's what we're talking about.'

'I'm sorry,' said Lee. 'You're right, I do seem to get too excited. No, if college is where a man can go to find his relation to his whole world, I don't object. Is it that? Is it that, Aron?'

'I don't know,' said Aron.

A hissing sound came from the kitchen. Lee said, 'The goddam giblets are boiling over,' and he bolted through the door.

Adam gazed after him affectionately. 'What a good man! What a good friend!'

Aron said, 'I hope he lives to be a hundred.'

His father chuckled. 'How do you know he's not a hundred now?'

Cal asked, 'How is the ice plant doing, Father?'

'Why, all right. Pays for itself and makes a little profit. Why?'

'I thought of a couple of things to make it really pay.'

'Not today,' said Adam quickly. 'Monday, if you remember, but not today. You know,' Adam said, 'I don't remember when I've felt so good. I feel–well, you might call it fulfilled. Maybe it's only a good night's sleep and a good trip to the bathroom. Maybe it's because we're all together and at peace.' He smiled at Aron. 'We didn't know what we felt about you until you went away.'

'I was homesick,' Aron confessed. 'The first few days I thought I'd die of it.'

Abra came in with a little rush. Her cheeks were pink and she was happy. 'Did you notice there's snow on Mount Toro?' she asked.

'Yes, I saw it,' Adam said. 'They say that means a good year to come. And we could use it.'

'I just nibbled,' said Abra. 'I wanted to be hungry for here.'

Lee apologized for the dinner like an old fool. He blamed the gas oven which didn't heat like a good wood stove. He blamed the new breed of turkeys which lacked a something turkeys used to have. But he laughed with them when they told him he was acting like an old woman fishing for compliments.

With the plum pudding Adam opened the champagne, and they treated it with ceremony. A courtliness settled over the table. They proposed toasts. Each one had his health drunk, and Adam made a little speech to Abra when he drank her health.

Her eyes were shining and under the table Aron held her hand. The wine dulled Cal's nervousness and he was not afraid about his present.

When Adam had finished his plum pudding he said, 'I guess we never had such a good Thanksgiving.'

Cal reached in his jacket pocket, took out the red-ribboned package, and pushed it over in front of his father.

'What's this?' Adam asked.

'It's a present.'

Adam was pleased. 'Not even Christmas and we have presents. I wonder what it can be!'

'A handkerchief,' said Abra.

Adam slipped off the grubby bow and unfolded the tissue paper. He stared down at the money.

Abra said, 'What is it?' and stood up to look. Aron leaned forward. Lee, in the doorway, tried to keep the look of worry from his face. He darted a glance at Cal and saw the light of joy and triumph in his eyes.

Very slowly Adam moved his fingers and fanned the gold certificates. His voice seemed to come from far away. 'What is it? What–' He stopped.

Cal swallowed. 'It's–I made it–to give to you–to make up for losing the lettuce.'

Adam raised his head slowly. 'You made it? How?'

'Mr Hamilton–we made it–on beans.' He hurried on, 'We bought futures at five cents and when the price jumped–It's for you, fifteen thousand dollars. It's for you.'

Adam touched the new notes so that their edges came together, folded the tissue over them and turned the ends up. He looked helplessly at Lee. Cal caught a feeling–a feeling of calamity, of destruction in the air, and a weight of sickness overwhelmed him. He heard his father say, 'You'll have to give it back.'

Almost as remotely his own voice said, 'Give it back? Give it back to who?'

'To the people you got it from.'

'The British Purchasing Agency? They can't take it back. They're paying twelve and half cents for beans all over the country.'

'Then give it to the farmers you robbed.'

'Robbed?' Cal cried. 'Why, we paid them two cents a pound over the market. We didn't rob them.' Cal felt suspended in space, and time seemed very slow.

His father took a long time to answer. There seemed to be long spaces between his words. 'I send boys out,' he said. 'I sign my name and they go out. And some will die and some will lie helpless without arms or legs. Not one will come back untorn. Son, do you think I could make a profit on that?'

'I did it for you,' Cal said. 'I wanted you to have the money to make up your loss.'

'I don't want the money, Cal. And the lettuce–I don't think I did that for a profit. It was a kind of game to see if I could get the lettuce there, and I lost. I don't want the money.'

Cal looked straight ahead. He could feel the eyes of Lee and Aron and Abra crawling on his cheeks. He kept his eyes on his father's lips.

'I like the idea of a present,' Adam went on. 'I thank you for the thought–'

'I'll put it away. I'll keep it for you,' Cal broke in.

'No. I won't want it ever. I would have been happy if you could have given me–well, what your brother has–pride in the thing he's doing, gladness in his progress. Money, even clean money, doesn't stack up with that.' His eyes widened a little and he said, 'Have I made you angry, son? Don't be angry. If you want to give me a present–give me a good life. That would be something I could value.'

Cal felt that he was choking. His forehead streamed with perspiration and he tasted salt on his tongue. He stood up suddenly and his chair fell over. He ran from the room, holding his breath.

Adam called after him, 'Don't be angry, son.'

They let him alone. He sat in his room, his elbows on his desk. He thought he would cry but he did not. He tried to let weeping start but tears could not pass the hot iron in his head.

After a time his breathing steadied and he watched his brain go to work shyly, quietly. He fought the quiet hateful pain down and it slipped aside and went about its work. He fought it more weakly, for hate was seeping all through his body, poisoning every nerve. He could feel himself losing control.

Then there came a point where the control and the fear were gone and his brain cried out in an aching triumph. His hand went to a pencil and he drew tight little spirals one after another on his blotting pad. When Lee came in an hour later there were hundreds of spirals, and they had become smaller and smaller. He did not look up.

Lee closed the door gently. 'I brought you some coffee,' he said.

'I don't want it–yes, I do. Why, thank you, Lee. It's kind of you to think of it.'

Lee said, 'Stop it! Stop it!, I tell you!'

'Stop what? What do you want me to stop?'

Lee said uneasily, 'I told you once when you asked me that it was all in yourself. I told you you could control it–if you wanted.'

'Control what? I don't know what you're talking about?'

Lee said, 'Can't you hear me? Can't I get through to you? Cal, don't you know what I'm saying?'

'I hear you, Lee. What are you saying?'

'He couldn't help it, Cal. That's his nature. It was the only way he knew. He didn't have any choice. But you have. Don't you hear me? You have a choice.'

The spirals had become so small that the pencil lines ran together and the result was a shiny black dot.

Cal said quietly, 'Aren't you making a fuss about nothing? You must be slipping. You'd think from your tone that I'd killed somebody. Come off it, Lee. Come off it.'

It was silent in the room. After a moment Cal turned from his desk and the room was empty. A cup of coffee on the bureau top sent up a plume of vapour. Cal drank the coffee scalding as it was and went into the living-room.

His father looked up apologetically at him.

Cal said, 'I'm sorry, Father. I didn't know how you felt about it.' He took the package of money from where it lay on the mantel and put it in the inside pocket of his coat where it had been before. 'I'll see what I can do about this.' He said casually, 'Where are the others?'

'Oh, Abra had to go. Aron walked with her. Lee went out.'

'I guess I'll go for a walk,' said Cal.

4

The November night was well fallen. Cal opened the front door a crack and saw Lee's shoulders and head outlined against the white walls of the French Laundry across the street. Lee was sitting on the steps, and he looked lumpy in his heavy coat.

Cal closed the door quietly and went back through the living-room. 'Champagne makes you thirsty,' he said. His father didn't look up.

Cal slipped out by the kitchen door and moved through Lee's waning kitchen garden. He climbed the high fence, found the two-by-twelve plank that served as a bridge across the slough of dark water, and came out between Lang's Bakery and the tinsmith shop on Castroville street.

He walked to Stone Street where the Catholic church is and turned left, went pass the Carriaga house, the Wilson house, the Zabala house, and turned left on Central Avenue at the Steinbeck house. Two blocks out Central he turned left past the West End School.

The poplar trees in front of the school-yard were nearly bare, but in the evening wind a few yellowed leaves still twisted down.

Cal's mind was numb. He did not even know that the air was cold with frost slipping down from the mountains. Three blocks ahead he saw his brother cross under a street-light, coming towards him. He knew it was his brother by stride and posture and because he knew it.

Cal slowed his steps, and when Aron was close he said, 'Hi, I came looking for you.'

Aron said, 'I'm sorry about this afternoon.'

'You couldn't help it–forget it.' He turned and the two walked side by side. 'I want you to come with me,' Cal said. 'I want to show you something.'

'What is it?'

'Oh, it's a surprise. But it's very interesting. You'll be interested.'

'Well, will it take long?'

'No, not very long. Not very long at all.'

They walked past Central Avenue towards Castroville Street.

5

Sergeant Axel Dane ordinarily opened the San Jose recruiting office at eight o'clock, but if he was a little late Corporal Kemp opened it, and Kemp was not likely to complain. Axel was not an unusual case. A hitch in the US army in the time of peace between the Spanish war and the German war had unfitted him for the cold, ordered life of a civilian. One month between hitches convinced him of that. Two hitches in the peacetime army completely unfitted him for war, and he had learned enough method to get out of it. The San Jose recruiting station proved he knew his way about. He was dallying with the youngest Ricci girl and she lived in San Jose.

Kemp hadn't the time in, but he was learning the basic rule. Get along with the topkick and avoid all officers when possible. He didn't mind the gentle riding Sergeant Dane handed out.

At eight-thirty Dane entered the office to find Corporal Kemp asleep at his desk and a tired-looking kid sat waiting. Dane glanced at the boy and then went behind the rail and put his hand on Kemp's shoulder.

'Darling,' he said, 'the skylarks are singing and a new dawn is here.'

Kemp raised his head from his arms, wiped his nose on the back of his hand, and sneezed. 'That's my sweet,' the sergeant said. 'Arise, we have a customer.'

Kemp squinted his crusted eyes. 'The war will wait,' he said.

Dane looked more closely at the boy. 'God! he's beautiful. I hope they take good care of him. Corporal, you may think that he wants to bear arms against the foe, but I think he's running away from love.'

Kemp was relieved that the sergeant wasn't quite sober. 'You think some dame hurt him?' He played any game his sergeant wished. 'You think it's the Foreign Legion?'

'Maybe he's running away from himself.'

Kemp said, 'I saw that picture. There's one mean son of a bitch of a sergeant in it.'

'I don't believe it,' said Dane. 'Step up, young man. Eighteen, aren't you?'

'Yes, sir.'

Dane turned to his man. 'What do you think?'

'Hell!' said Kemp. 'I say if they're big enough, they're old enough.'

The sergeant said, 'Let's say you're eighteen. And we'll stick to it, shall we?'

'Yes, sir.'

'You just take this form and fill it out. Now you figure out what year you were born, and you put it down right here, and you remember it.'

CHAPTER 50

I

Joe didn't like for Kate to sit still and stare straight ahead–hour after hour. That meant she was thinking, and since her face had no expression Joe had no access to her thoughts. It made him uneasy. He didn't want his first real good break to get away from him.

He had only one plan himself–and that was to keep her stirred up until she gave herself away. Then he could jump in any direction. But how about it if she sat looking at the wall? Was she stirred up or wasn't she?

Joe knew she hadn't been to bed, and when he asked whether or not she wanted breakfast she shook her head so slowly that it was hard to know whether she had heard him or not.

He advised himself cautiously, 'Don't do nothing! Just stick around and keep your eyes and ears open.' The girls in the house knew something happened but no two of them had the same story, the goddam chicken-heads.

Kate was not thinking. Her mind drifted among impressions the way a bat drifts and swoops in the evening. She saw the face of the blond and beautiful boy, his eyes mad with shock. She heard his ugly words aimed not so much at her as at himself. And she saw his dark brother leaning against the door and laughing.

Kate had laughed too–the quickest and best self-protection. What would her son do? What had he done after he went quietly away?

She thought of Cal's eyes with their look of sluggish and fulfilled cruelty, peering at her as he slowly closed the door.

Why had he brought his brother? What did he want? What was he after? If she knew she could take care of herself. But she didn't know.

The pain was creeping in her hands again and there was a new place. Her right hip ached angrily when she moved. She thought, 'So the pain will move in towards the centre, and sooner or later all the pains will meet in the centre and join like rats in a clot.'

In spite of his advice to himself, Joe couldn't let it alone. He carried a pot of tea to her door, knocked softly, opened the door, and went in. As far as he could see she hadn't moved.

He said, 'I brought you some tea, ma'am.'

'Put it on the table,' she said, and then as a second thought, 'Thank you, Joe.'

'You don't feel good, ma'am?'

'The pain's back. The medicine fooled me.'

'Anything I can do?'

She raised her hands. 'Cut these off–at the wrists.' She grimaced with the extra pain lifting her hands had caused. 'Makes you feel hopeless,' she said plaintively.

Joe had never heard a tone of weakness in her before and his instinct told him it was time to move in. He said, 'Maybe you don't want me to bother you but I got some word about that other.' He knew by the little interval before she answered that she had tensed.

'What other?' she asked softly.

'That dame, ma'am.'

'Oh! You mean Ethel?'

'Yes, ma'am.'

'I'm getting tired of Ethel. What is it now?'

'Well, I'll tell you like it happened. I can't make nothing out of it. I'm in Kellogg's cigar store and a fella came up to me. "You're Joe," he says, an' I tell him, "Who says?" "You was lookin' for somebody," he says. "Tell me about it," I says. Never seen the guy before. So he says, "That party tol' me she wants to talk to you." An' I told him, "Well, why don't she?" He gives me the long look an' he says, "Maybe you forgot what the judge said." I guess he means about her coming back.' He looked at Kate's face, still and pale, the eyes looking straight ahead.

Kate said, 'And then he asked you for some money?'

'No, ma'am. He didn't. He says something don't make no sense. He says, "Does Faye mean anything to you?" "Not a thing," I tol' him. He says, "Maybe you better talk to her." "Maybe," I says, an' I come away. Don't make no sense to me. I figured I'd ask you.'

Kate asked, 'Does the name Faye mean anything to you?'

'Not a thing.'

Her voice became very soft. 'You mean you never heard that Faye used to own this house?'

Joe felt a sickening jolt in the pit of his stomach. What a goddam fool! Couldn't keep his mouth shut. His mind floundered. 'Why–why come to think of it, I believe I did hear that–seemed like the name was like Faith.'

The sudden alarm was good for Kate. It took the blond head and the pain from her. It gave her something to do. She responded to the challenge with something like pleasure.

She laughed softly. 'Faith,' she said under her breath. 'Pour me some tea, Joe.'

She did not appear to notice that his hand shook and that the teapot spout rattled against the cup. She did not look at him even when he set the cup before her and then stepped back out of range of her eyes. Joe was quaking with apprehension.

Kate said in a pleading voice, 'Joe, do you think you could help me? If I gave you ten thousand dollars, do you think you could fix everything up?' She waited just a second, then swung round and looked full in his face.

His eyes were moist. She caught him licking his lips. And at her sudden move he stepped back as though she had struck at him. Her eyes would not let him go.

'Did I catch you out, Joe?'

'I don't know what you're getting at, ma'am.'

'You go and figure it out–and then you come and tell me. You're good at figuring things out. And send Therese in, will you?'

He wanted to get out of this room where he was out-pointed and out-fought. He'd made a mess of things. He wondered if he'd bollixed up the breaks. And then the bitch had the nerve to say, 'Thank you for bringing tea. You're a nice boy.'

He wanted to slam the door, but he didn't dare.

Kate got up stiffly, trying to avoid the pain of moving her hip. She went to her desk and slipped out a sheet of paper. Holding the pen was difficult.

She wrote, moving her whole arm. 'Dear Ralph: Tell the sheriff it wouldn't do any harm to check on Joe Valery's fingerprints. You remember Joe. He works for me. Y'rs, Kate.' She was folding the paper when Therese came in, looking frightened.

'You want me? Did I do something? I tried my best. Ma'am, I ain't been well.'

'Come here,' Kate said, and while the girl waited beside the desk Kate slowly addressed the envelope and stamped it. 'I want you to run a little errand for me,' she said. 'Go to Bell's candy store and get a five-pound box of mixed chocolates and a one-pound box. The big one is for you girls. Stop at Krough's drugstore and get me two medium toothbrushes and a can of tooth-powder–you know, that can with a spout?'

'Yes, ma'am.' Therese was greatly relieved.

'You're a good girl,' Kate went on. 'I've had my eye on you. I'm not well, Therese. If I see that you do this well, I'll seriously consider putting you in charge when I go to the hospital.'

'You will–are–are you going to the hospital?'

'I don't know yet, dear. But I'll need your help. Now here's some money for the candy. Medium toothbrushes–remember.'

'Yes, ma'am. Thank you. Shall I go now?'

'Yes, and kind of creep out, will you? Don't let the other girls know what I told you.'

'I'll go out the back way.' She hurried towards the door.

Kate said, 'I nearly forgot. Will you drop this in a mail-box?'

'Sure I will, ma'am. Sure I will. Anything else?'

'That's all, dear.'

When the girl was gone Kate rested her arms and hands on the desk so that each crooked finger was supported. Here it was. Maybe she had always known. She must have–but there was no need to think of that now. She would come back to that. They would put Joe away, but there'd be someone else, and there was always Ethel. Sooner or later, sooner or later–but no need to think about that now. She tiptoed her mind around the whole subject and back to an exclusive thing that peeped out and then withdrew. It was when she had been thinking of her yellow-haired son that the fragment had first come to her mind. His face–hurt, bewildered, despairing–had brought it. Then she remembered.

She was a very small girl with a face as lovely and fresh as her son's face–a very small girl. Most of the time she knew she was smarter and prettier than anyone else. But now and then a lonely fear would fall upon her so that she seemed surrounded by a tree-tall forest of enemies. Then every thought and word and look was aimed to hurt her, and she had no place to run and no place to hide. And she would cry in panic because there was no escape and no sanctuary. Then one day she was reading a book. She could read when she was five years old. She remembered the book–brown, with a silver title, and the clock was broken and the boards thick. It was *Alice in Wonderland*.

Kate moved her hands slowly and lifted her weight a little from her arms. And she could see the drawings–Alice with long straight hair. But it was the bottle which said 'Drink me' that had changed her life. Alice had taught her that.

When the forest of her enemies surrounded her she was prepared. In her pocket she had a bottle of sugar water and on its red-framed label she had written, 'Drink me.' She would take a sip from the bottle and she would grow smaller and smaller. Let her enemies look for her then! Cathy would be under a leaf or looking out of an ant-hole, laughing. They couldn't find her then. No door could close her out and no door could close her in. She could walk upright under a door.

And always there was Alice to play with, Alice to love her and trust her. Alice was her friend, always waiting to welcome her to tinyness.

All this so good–so good that it was almost worth while to be miserable. But good as it was, there was one more thing always held in reserve. It was her threat and her safety. She had only to drink the whole bottle and she would dwindle and disappear and cease to exist. And better than all, when she stopped being, she never would have been. This was her darling safety. Sometimes in her bed she would drink enough of 'Drink me' so that she was a dot as small as the tiniest gnat. But she had never gone clear out–never had to. That was her reserve–guarded from everyone.

Kate shook her head sadly, remembering the cut-off little girl. She wondered why she had forgotten that wonderful trick. It had saved her from so many disasters. The light filtering down at one through a clover-leaf was glorious. Cathy and Alice walked among towering grass, arms round each other–best friends. And Cathy never had to drink all of 'Drink me' because she had Alice.

Kate put her head down on the blotter between her crooked hands. She was cold and desolate, alone and desolate. Whatever she had done, she had been driven to do. She was different–she had something more than other people. She raised her head and made no move to wipe her streaming eyes. That was true. She was smarter and stronger than other people. She had something they lacked.

And right in the middle of her thought, Cal's dark face hung in the air in front of her and his lips were smiling with cruelty. The weight pressed down on her, forcing her breath out.

They had something she lacked, and she didn't know what it was. Once she knew this, she was ready; and once ready, she knew she had been ready for a long time–perhaps all her life. Her mind functioned like a wooden mind, her body moved crookedly like a badly operated marionette, but she went steadily about her business.

It was noon–she knew from the chatter of the girls in the dining-room. The slugs had only just got up.

Kate had trouble with the door-knob and turned it finally by rolling it between her palms.

The girls choked in the middle of laughter and looked up at her. The cook came in from the kitchen.

Kate was a sick ghost, crooked and in some way horrible. She leaned across the dining-room wall and smiled at her girls, and her smile frightened them even more, for it was like the frame for a scream.

'Where's Joe?' Kate asked.

'He went out, ma'am.'

'Listen,' she said. 'I've had no sleep for a long time. I'm going to take some medicine and sleep. I don't want to be disturbed. I don't want any supper. I'll sleep the clock round. Tell Joe I don't want anybody to come near me for anything until tomorrow morning. Do you understand?'

'Yes, ma'am,' they said.

'Good night then. It's afternoon but I mean good night.'

'Good night, ma'am,' they chorused obediently.

Kate turned and walked crabwise back to her room.

She closed the door and stood looking around, trying to form her simple procedure. She went back to her desk. This time she forced her hand, in spite of the pain, to write plainly. 'I leave everything I have to my son Aron Trask.' She dated the sheet and signed it 'Catherine Trask.' Her fingers dwelt on the page, and then she got up and left her will face upward on the desk.

At the centre table she poured cold tea into her cup and carried the cup to the grey room in the lean-to and set it on the reading-table. Then she went to her dressing-table and combed her hair, rubbed a little rouge all over her face, covered it lightly with powder, and put on the pale lipstick she always used. Last she filed her nails and cleaned them.

When she closed the door to the grey room the outside light was cut off and only the reading-lamp threw its cone on the table. She arranged the pillows, patted them up, and sat down. She leaned her head experimentally against the down pillow. She felt rather gay, as though she was going to a party. Gingerly she fished the chain out from her bodice, unscrewed the little tube, and shook the capsule into her hand. She smiled at it.

'Eat me,' she said and put the capsule in her mouth.

She picked up the tea-cup. 'Drink me,' she said and swallowed the bitter cold tea.

She forced her mind to stay on Alice–so tiny and waiting. Other faces peered in from the sides of her eyes–her father and mother, and Charles, and Adam, and Samuel Hamilton, and then Aron, and she could see Cal smiling at her.

He didn't have to speak. The glint of his eyes said, 'You missed something. They had something and you missed it.'

She thrust her mind back to Alice. In the grey wall opposite there was a nail-hole. Alice would be in there. And she would put her arm around Cathy's waist, and Cathy would put her arm around Alice's waist, and they would walk away–best friends–and tiny as the head of a pin.

A warm numbness began to creep into her arms and legs. The pain was going from her hands. Her eyelids felt heavy–very heavy. She yawned.

She thought or said or thought, 'Alice doesn't know. I'm going right on past.'

Her eyes closed and a dizzy nausea shook her. She opened her eyes and stared about in terror. The grey room darkened and the cone of light flowed and rippled like water. And then her eyes closed again and her fingers curled as though they held small breasts. And her heart beat solemnly and her breathing slowed as she grew smaller and smaller and then disappeared–and she had never been.

2

When Kate dismissed him Joe went to the barber-shop, as he always did when he was upset. He had his hair cut and an egg shampoo and tonic. He had a facial massage and a mud pack, and around the edges he had his nails manicured, and he had his shoes shined. Ordinarily this and a new necktie set Joe up, but he was still depressed when he left the barber with a fifty-cent tip.

Kate had trapped him like a rat–caught him with his pants down. Her fast thinking left him confused and helpless. The trick she had of leaving it to you whether she meant anything or not was no less confusing.

The night started dully, but then sixteen members and two pledges from Sigma Alpha Epsilon, Stanford chapter, came in hilarious from a pledge hazing in San Juan. They were full of horse-play.

Florence, who smoked the cigarette in the circus, had a hard cough. Every time she tried, she coughed and lost it. And the pony stallion had diarrhoea.

The college boys shrieked and pounded each other in their amusement. And then they stole everything that wasn't nailed down.

After they had left, two of the girls got into a tired and monotonous quarrel, and Therese turned up with the first symptom of the old Joe. Oh, Christ, what a night!

And down the hall that brooding dangerous thing was silent behind its closed door. Joe stood by the door before he went to bed and he could hear nothing. He closed the house at two-thirty and was in bed by three–but he couldn't sleep. He sat up in bed and read seven chapters of *The Winning of Barbara Worth,* and when it was daylight went down to the silent kitchen and made a pot of coffee.

He rested his elbows on the table and held the coffee mug with both hands. Something had gone wrong and Joe couldn't figure what it was. Maybe she'd found out that Ethel was dead. He'd have to watch his step. And then he made up his mind, and made it up firmly. He would go in to see her at nine and he'd keep his ears open. Maybe he hadn't heard right. Best thing would be to lay it on the line and not be a hog. Just say he'd take a thousand bucks and get the hell out, and if she said no he'd get the hell out anyway. He was sick of working with dames. He could get a job dealing faro in Reno–regular hours and no dames. Maybe get himself an apartment and fix it up–big chairs and a davenport. No point in beating his brains out in this lousy town. Better if he got out of the state anyway. He considered going right now–just get up from this table, climb the stairs, two minutes to pack a suitcase, and gone. Three or four minutes at the most. Don't tell nobody nothing. The idea appealed to him. The breaks about Ethel might not be as good as he had thought at first, but a thousand bucks was at stake. Better wait.

When the cook came in he was in a bad mood. He had a developing carbuncle on the back of his neck and the skin from the inside of an eggshell stretched over it to draw it to a head. He didn't want anybody in his kitchen, feeling the way he did.

Joe went back to his room and read some more and then he packed his suitcase. He was going to get out any way it went.

At nine o'clock he knocked gently on Kate's door and pushed it open. Her bed had not been slept in. He set down the tray and went to the door of the lean-to and knocked and knocked again and then called. Finally he opened the door.

The cone of light fell on the reading-stand. Kate's head was deeply cushioned on a pillow.

'You must have slept all night here,' Joe said. He walked around in front of her, saw bloodless lips and eyes shining dully between half-closed lids, and he knew she was dead.

He moved his head from side to side and went quickly into the other room to make sure that the door to the hall was closed. With great speed he went through the dresser, drawer by drawer, opened her purses, the little box by her bed–and he stood still. She didn't have a goddam thing–not even a silver-backed hair-brush.

He crept to the lean-to and stood in front of her–not a ring, not a pin. Then he saw the little chain around her neck and lifted it clear and unsnapped the clasp–a small gold watch, a little tube, and two safe-deposit keys, numbers 27 and 29.

'So that's where you got it, you bitch,' he said.

He slipped the watch off the chain and put it in his pocket. He wanted to punch her on the nose. Then he thought of her desk.

The two-line holograph will attracted him. Somebody might pay for that. He put it in his pocket. He took a handful of papers from a pigeon-hole–bills and receipts; next hole, insurance; next, a small book with records of every girl.

He put that in his pocket too. He took the rubber band from a packet of brown envelopes, opened one, and pulled out a photograph. On the back of the picture, in Kate's neat, sharp handwriting, a name and address and a title.

Joe laughed aloud. This was the real breaks. He tried another envelope and another. A gold mine–guy could live for years on these. Look at that fat-arsed councilman! He put the band back. In the top drawer eight ten-dollar notes and a bunch of keys. He pocketed the money too. As he opened the second drawer enough to see that it held writing paper and sealing wax and ink there was a knock on the door. He walked to it and opened it a crack.

The cook said, 'Fella out here wants to see ya.'

'Who is he?'

'How the hell do I know?'

Joe looked back at the room and then stepped out, took the key from the inside, locked the door, and put the key in his pocket. He might have overlooked something.

Oscar Noble was standing in the big front room, his grey hat on his head and his red mackinaw buttoned up tight around his throat. His eyes were pale grey–the same colour as his stubble whiskers. The room was in semi-darkness. No one had raised the blinds yet.

Joe came lightly along the hall, and Oscar asked, 'You Joe?'

'Who's asking?'

'The sheriff wants to have a talk with you.'

Joe felt ice creeping into his stomach. 'Pinch?' he asked. 'Got a warrant?'

'Hell, no,' said Oscar. 'We got nothing on you. Just checking up. Will you come along?'

'Sure,' said Joe. 'Why not?'

They went out together. Joe shivered. 'I should of got a coat.'

'Want to go back for one?'

'I guess not,' said Joe.

They walked towards Castroville Street. Oscar asked, 'Ever been mugged or printed?'

Joe was quiet for a time. 'Yes,' he said at last.

'What for?'

'Drunk,' said Joe. 'Hit a cop.'

'Well, we'll soon find out,' said Oscar and turned the corner.

Joe ran like a rabbit, across the street and over the track towards the stores and alleys of Chinatown.

Oscar had to take a glove off and unbutton his mackinaw to get his gun out. He tried a snap shot and missed.

Joe began to zigzag. He was fifty yards away by now and nearing an opening between two buildings.

Oscar stepped to a telephone pole at the kerb, braced his left elbow against it, gripped his right wrist with his left hand, and drew a bead on the entrance to the little alley. He fired just as Joe touched the front sight.

Joe splashed forward on his face and skidded a foot.

Oscar went into a Filipino pool-room to phone, and when he came out there was quite a crowd around the body.

CHAPTER 51

I

In 1903 Horace Quinn beat Mr R. Keef for the office of sheriff. He had been well trained as the chief deputy sheriff. Most of the voters figured that since Quinn was doing most of the work he might as well have the title. Sheriff Quinn held the office until 1919. He was sheriff so long that we growing up in Monterey County thought the words 'Sheriff' and 'Quinn' went together naturally. We could not imagine anyone else being sheriff. Quinn grew old in his office. He limped from an early injury. We knew he was intrepid, for he had held his own in various gun-fights; besides, he looked like a sheriff–the only kind we knew about. His face was broad and pink, his white moustache shaped like the horns of a longhorn steer. He was broad of shoulder, and in his age he developed a portliness which only gave him more authority. He wore a fine Stetson hat, a Norfolk jacket, and in his later years carried his gun in a shoulder holster. His old belt holster tugged at his stomach too much. He had known his county in 1903 and he knew it and controlled it even better in 1917. He was an institution, as much a part of the Salinas Valley as its mountains.

In all the years since Adam's shooting Sheriff Quinn had kept track of Kate. When Faye died, he knew instinctively that Kate was probably responsible, but he also knew he hadn't much of any chance of convicting her, and a wise sheriff doesn't butt his head against the impossible. They were only a couple of whores, after all.

In the years that followed, Kate played fair with him and he gradually achieved a certain respect for her. Since there were going to be houses anyway, they had better be run by responsible people. Every so often Kate spotted a wanted man and turned him in. She ran a house which did not get into trouble. Sheriff Quinn and Kate got along together.

The Saturday after Thanksgiving, about noon, Sheriff Quinn looked through the papers from Joe Valery's pockets. The .38 slug had splashed off one side of Joe's heart and had flattened against the ribs and torn out a section as big as a fist. The manila envelopes were glued together with blackened blood. The sheriff dampened the papers with a wet handkerchief to get them apart. He read the will, which had been folded, so that the blood was on the outside. He laid it aside and inspected the photographs in the envelopes. He sighed deeply.

Every envelope contained a man's honour and peace of mind. Effectively used, these pictures could cause half a dozen suicides. Already Kate was on the table at Muller's with the formalin running into her veins, and her stomach was in a jar in the coroner's office.

When he had seen all of the pictures he called a number. He said into the phone, 'Can you drop over to my office? Well, put your lunch off, will you? Yes, I think you'll see it's important. I'll wait for you.'

A few minutes later when the nameless man stood beside his desk in the front office of the old red county jail behind the court-house, Sheriff Quinn stuck the will out in front of him. 'As a lawyer, would you say this is any good?'

His visitor read the two lines and breathed deep through his nose. 'Is this who I think it is?'

'Yes.'

'Well, if her name was Catherine Trask and this is her hand-writing, and if Aron Trask is her son, this is as good as gold.'

Quinn lifted the ends of his fine wide moustache with the back of his forefinger. 'You knew her, didn't you?'

'Well, not to say know. I knew who she was.'

Quinn put his elbows on his desk and leaned forward. 'Sit down, I want to talk to you.'

His visitor drew up a chair. His fingers picked at a cotton button.

The sheriff asked, 'Was Kate blackmailing you?'

'Certainly not. Why should she?'

'I'm asking you as a friend. You know she's dead. You can tell me.'

'I don't know what you're getting at–nobody's blackmailing me.'

Quinn slipped a photograph from its envelope, turned it like a playing card, and skidded it across the desk.

His visitor adjusted his glasses and the breath whistled in his nose. 'Jesus Christ,' he said softly.

'You didn't know she had it?'

'Oh, I knew all right. She let me know. For Christ's sake Horace–what are you going to do with this?'

Quinn took the picture from his hand.

'Horace, what are you going to do with it?'

'Burn it.' The sheriff ruffled the edges of the envelopes with his thumb. 'Here's a deck of hell,' he said. 'These could tear the county to pieces.'

Quinn wrote a list of names on a sheet of paper. Then he hoisted himself up on his game leg and went to the iron stove against the north wall of his office. He crunched up the *Salinas Morning Journal* and lighted it and dropped it in the stove, and when it flared up he dropped the manila envelopes on the flame, set the damper, and closed the stove. The fire roared and the flames winked yellow behind the little isinglass windows in the front of the stove. Quinn brushed his hands together as though they were dirty. 'The negatives were in there,' he said. 'I've been through her desk. There weren't any other prints.'

His visitor tried to speak but his voice was a husky whisper. 'Thank you, Horace.'

The sheriff limped to his desk and picked up his list. 'I want you to do something for me. Here's a list. Tell everyone on this list I've burned the pictures. You know them all, God knows. And they could take it from you. Nobody's holy. Get each man alone and tell him exactly what happened. Look here!' He opened the stove door and poked the black sheets until they were reduced to powder. 'Tell them that,' he said.

His visitor looked at the sheriff, and Quinn knew that there was no power on earth that could keep this man from hating him. For the rest of their lives there would be a barrier between them, and neither one could ever admit it.

'Horace, I don't know how to thank you.'

And the sheriff said in sorrow. 'That's all right. It's what I'd want my friends to do for me.'

'The goddam bitch,' his visitor said softly, and Horace Quinn knew that part of the curse was for him.

And he knew he wouldn't be sheriff much longer. These guilt-feeling men could get him out, and they would have to. He sighed and sat down. 'Go to your lunch now,' he said. 'I've got work to do.'

At quarter to one Sheriff Quinn turned off Main Street on Central Avenue. At Reynaud's Bakery he bought a loaf of French bread, still warm and giving off its wonderful smell of fermented dough.

He used the hand-rail to help himself up the steps of the Trask porch.

Lee answered the door, a dish-towel tied around his middle. 'He's not home,' he said.

'Well, he's on his way. I called the draft board. I'll wait for him.'

Lee moved aside and let him in and seated him in the living-room. 'You like a nice cup of hot coffee?' he asked.

'I don't mind if I do.'

'Fresh made,' said Lee, and went into the kitchen.

Quinn looked around the comfortable sitting-room. He felt that he didn't want his office much longer. He remembered hearing a doctor say, 'I love to deliver a baby, because if I do my work well, there's joy at the end of it.' The sheriff had thought often of that remark. It seemed to him that if he did his work well there was sorrow at the end of it for somebody. The fact that it was necessary was losing its weight with him. He would be retiring soon whether he wanted to or not.

Every man has a retirement picture in which he does those things he never had time to do–makes the journeys, reads the neglected books he always pretended to have read. For many years the sheriff dreamed of spending the shining time hunting and fishing–wandering in the Santa Lucia range, camping by half-remembered streams. And now that it was almost time he knew he didn't want to do it. Sleeping on the ground would make his leg ache. He remembered how heavy a deer is and how hard it is to carry the dangling limp body from the place of the kill. And, frankly, he didn't care for venison anyway. Madame Reynaud could soak it in wine and lace it with spice but, hell, an old shoe would taste good with that treatment.

Lee had brought a percolator. Quinn could hear the water spluttering against the glass dome, and his long-trained mind made the suggestion that Lee hadn't told the truth about having fresh-made coffee.

It was a good mind the old man had–sharpened in its work. He could bring up old faces in his mind and inspect them, and also scenes and conversations. He could play them over like a record or a film. Thinking of venison, his mind had gone about cataloguing the sitting-room and his mind nudged him saying, 'Hey, there's something wrong here–something strange.'

The sheriff heeded the voice and looked at the room–flowered chintz, lace curtains, white drawn-work table cover, cushions on the couch covered with a bright and impudent print. It was a feminine room in a house where only men lived.

He thought of his own sitting-room. Mrs Quinn had chosen, bought, cleaned, every single thing in it except a pipe-stand. Come to think of it, she had bought the pipe-stand for him. This was a woman's room too. But it was a fake. It was too feminine–a woman's room designed by a man–and overdone, too feminine. That would be Lee. Adam wouldn't even see it, let alone put it together–no–Lee trying to make a home, and Adam not even seeing it.

Horace Quinn remembered questioning Adam so very long ago, remembered him as a man in agony. He could still see Adam's haunted and horrified eyes. He had thought then of Adam as a man of such honesty that he couldn't conceive anything else. And in the years he had seen much of Adam. They both belonged to the Masonic Order. They went through the chairs together. Horace followed Adam as Master of the Lodge and both of them wore their Past Master's pins. And Adam had been set apart–an invisible wall cut him off from the world. You couldn't get into him–he couldn't get out to you. But in that old agony there had been no wall.

In his wife Adam had touched the living world. Horace thought of her now, grey and washed, the needles in her throat and the rubber formalin tubes hanging down from the ceiling.

Adam could do no dishonesty. He didn't want anything. You had to crave something to be dishonest. The sheriff wondered what went on behind the wall, what pressures, what pleasures and achings.

He shifted his behind to ease the pressure on his leg. The house was still except for the bouncing coffee. Adam was long coming from the draft board. The amused thought came to the sheriff, 'I'm getting old, and I kind of like it.'

Then he heard Adam at the front door. Lee heard him too and darted into the hall. 'The sheriff's here,' said Lee, to warn him perhaps.

Adam came in smiling and held out his hand. 'Hello, Horace–have you got a warrant?' It was a damn good try at a joke.

'Howdy,' Quinn said. 'Your man is going to give me a cup of coffee.'

Lee went to the kitchen and rattled dishes.

Adam said, 'Anything wrong, Horace?'

'Everything's always wrong in my business. I'll wait till the coffee comes.'

'Don't mind Lee. He listens anyway. He can hear through a closed door. I don't keep anything from him because I can't.'

Lee came in with a tray. He was smiling remotely to himself, and when he had poured the coffee and gone out Adam asked again, 'Is there anything wrong, Horace?'

'No, I don't think so. Adam, was that woman still married to you?'

Adam became rigid. 'Yes,' he said. 'What's the matter?'

'She killed herself last night.'

Adam's face contorted and his eyes swelled and glistened with tears. He fought his mouth, and then he gave up and put his face down in his hands and wept. 'Oh, my poor darling!' he said.

Quinn sat quietly and let him have it out, and after a time Adam's control came back and he raised his head. 'Excuse me, Horace,' he said.

Lee came in from the kitchen and put a damp towel in his hands, and Adam sponged his eyes and handed it back.

'I didn't expect that,' Adam said, and his face was ashamed. 'What shall I do? I'll claim her. I'll bury her.'

'I wouldn't,' said Horace. 'That is, unless you feel you have to. That's not what I came about.' He took the folded will from his pocket and held it out.

Adam shrank from it. 'Is–is that her blood?'

'No, it's not. It's not her blood at all. Read it.'

Adam read the two lines and went right on staring at the paper and beyond it. 'He doesn't know–she is his mother.'

'You never told him?'

'No.'

'Jesus Christ!' said the sheriff.

Adam said earnestly, 'I'm sure he wouldn't want anything of hers. Let's just tear it up and forget it. If he knew, I don't think Aron would want anything of hers.'

''Fraid you can't,' Quinn said. 'We do quite a few illegal things. She had a safe-deposit box. I don't have to tell you where I got the will or the key. I went to the bank. Didn't wait for a court order. Thought it might have a bearing.' He didn't tell Adam he thought there might be more pictures. 'Well, Old Bob let me open the box. We can always deny it. There's over a hundred thousand dollars in gold certificates. There's money in there in bales–and there isn't one goddam thing in there but money.'

'Nothing?'

'One other thing–a marriage certificate.'

Adam leaned back in his chair. The remoteness was coming down again, the soft protective folds between himself and the world. He saw his coffee and took a sip of it. 'What do you think I ought to do?' he asked steadily and quietly.

'I can only tell you what I'd do,' Sheriff Quinn said. 'You don't have to take my advice. I'd have the boy in right now. I'd tell him everything–every single thing. I'd even tell him why you didn't tell him before. He's–how old?'

'Seventeen.'

'He's a man. He's got to take it some time. Better if he gets the whole thing at once.'

'Cal knows,' said Adam. 'I wonder why she made the will to Aron.'

'God knows. Well, what do you think?'

'I don't know, and so I'm going to do what you say. Will you stay with me?'

'Sure I will.'

'Lee,' Adam called, 'tell Aron I want him. He has come home, hasn't he?'

Lee came to the doorway. His heavy lids closed for a moment and then opened. 'Not yet. Maybe he went back to school.'

'He would have told me. You know, Horace, we drank a lot of champagne on Thanksgiving. Where's Cal?'

'In his room,' said Lee.

'Well, call him in. Get him in. Cal will know.'

Cal's face was tired and his shoulders sagged with exhaustion, but his face was pinched and closed and crafty and mean.

Adam asked, 'Do you know where your brother is?'

'No, I don't,' said Cal.

'Weren't you with him at all?'

'No.'

'He hasn't been home for two nights. Where is he?'

'How do I know?' said Cal, 'am I supposed to look after him?'

Adam's head sank down, his body jarred, just a little quiver. At the back of his eyes a tiny sharp incredibly bright blue light flashed. He said thickly, 'Maybe he did go back to college.' His lips seemed heavy and he murmured like a man talking in his sleep. 'Don't you think he went back to college?'

Sheriff Quinn stood up. 'Anything I got to do I can do later. You get a rest, Adam. You've had a shock.'

Adam looked up at him. 'Shock–oh, yes. Thank you, George. Thank you very much.'

'George?'

'Thank you very much,' said Adam.

When the sheriff had gone, Cal went to his room. Adam leaned back in his chair, and very soon he went to sleep and his mouth dropped open and he snored across his palate.

Lee watched him for a while before he went back to his kitchen. He lifted the bread-box and took out a tiny volume bound in leather, and the gold tooling was almost completely worn away–*The Meditations of Marcus Aurelius* in English translation.

Lee wiped his steel-rimmed spectacles on a dish-towel. He opened the book and leafed through. And he smiled to himself, consciously searching for reassurance.

He read slowly, moving his lips over the words. 'Everything is only for a day, both that which remembers and that which is remembered.'

'Observe constantly that all things take place by change, and accustom thyself to consider that the nature of the universe loves nothing so much as to change things which are and to make new things like them. For everything that exists is in a manner the seed of that which will be.'

Lee glanced down the page. 'Thou wilt die soon and thou art not yet simple nor free from perturbations, nor without suspicion of being hurt by external things, nor kindly disposed towards all; nor dost thou yet place wisdom only in acting justly.'

Lee looked up from the page, and he answered the book as he would answer one of his ancient relatives. 'That is true,' he said. 'It's very hard. I'm sorry. But don't forget that you also say, "Always run the short way and the short way is the natural"–don't forget that.' He let the pages slip past his fingers to the flyleaf where was written with a broad carpenter's pencil, 'Sam'l Hamilton'.

Suddenly Lee felt good. He wondered whether Sam'l Hamilton had ever missed his book or known who stole it. It had seemed to Lee the only clean pure way was to steal it. And he still felt good about it. His fingers caressed the smooth leather of the binding as he took it back and slipped it under the bread-box. He said to himself, 'But of course he knew who took it. Who else would have stolen *Marcus Aurelius*?' He went into the sitting-room and pulled a chair near to the sleeping Adam.

2

In his room Cal sat at his desk, elbows down, palms holding his aching head together, hands pushing against the sides of his head. His stomach churned and the sour-sweet smell of whisky was on him and in him, living in his pores, in his clothing, beating sluggishly in his head.

Cal had never drunk before, had never needed to. But going to Kate's had been no relief from pain and his revenge had been no triumph. His memory was all swirling clouds and broken pieces of sound and sight and feeling. What now was true and what was imagined he could not separate. Coming out of Kate's he had touched his sobbing brother and Aron had cut him down with a fist like a whip. Aron had stood over him in the dark, and then suddenly turned and ran, screaming like a broken-hearted child. Cal could still hear the hoarse cries over running footsteps. Cal had lain still where he had fallen under the tall privet in Kate's front yard. He heard the engines puffing and snorting by the round-house and the crash of freight cars being assembled. Then he had closed his eyes and, hearing light steps and feeling a presence, he looked up. Someone was bending over him and he thought it was Kate. The figure moved quietly away.

After a while Cal had stood up and brushed himself and walked towards Main Street. He was surprised at how casual his feeling was. He sang softly under his breath, 'There's a rose that grows in no man's land and 'tis wonderful to see–'

On Friday Cal brooded the whole day long. And in the evening Joe Laguna bought the quart of whisky for him. Cal was too young to purchase. Joe wanted to accompany Cal, but Joe was satisfied with the dollar Cal gave him and went back for a pint of grappa.

Cal went to the alley behind the Abbot House and found the shadow behind a post where he had sat the night he first saw his mother. He sat cross-legged on the ground, and then, in spite of revulsion and nausea, he forced the whisky into himself. Twice he vomited and then went on drinking until the earth tipped and swayed and the street-light spun majestically in a circle.

The bottle slipped from his hand finally and Cal passed out, but even unconscious he still vomited weakly. A serious, short-haired dog-about-town with a curling tail sauntered into the alley, making his stations, but he smelled Cal and took a wide circle around him. Joe Laguna found him and smelled him too. Joe shook the bottle leaning against Cal's leg and Joe held it up to the street-light and saw that it was one-third full. He looked for the cork and couldn't find it. He walked away, his thumb over the neck to keep the whisky from sloshing out.

When in the cold dawn a frost awakened Cal to a sick world he struggled home like a broken bug. He hadn't far to go, just to the alley mouth and then across the street.

Lee heard him at the door and smelled his nastiness as he bumped along the hall to his room and fell over on his bed. Cal's head shattered with pain and he was wide awake. He had no resistance against sorrow and no device to protect himself against shame. After a while he did the best he could. He bathed in icy water and scrubbed and scratched his body with a block of pumice stone, and the pain of his scraping seemed good to him.

He knew that he had to tell his guilt to his father and beg his forgiveness. And he had to humble himself to Aron, not only now but always. He could not live without that. And yet, when he was called out and stood in the room with Sheriff Quinn and his father, he was as raw and angry as a surly dog and his hatred of himself turned outward towards everyone–a vicious cur he was, unloved, unloving.

Then he was back in his room and his guilt assaulted him and he had no weapon to fight it off.

A panic for Aron arose in him. He might be injured, might be in trouble. It was Aron who couldn't take care of himself. Cal knew he had to bring Aron back, had to find him and rebuild him back the way he had been. And this had to be done even though Cal sacrificed himself. And then the idea of sacrifice took hold of him the way it does with the guilty-feeling man. A sacrifice might reach Aron and bring him back.

Cal went to his bureau and got the flat package from under his handkerchiefs in his drawer. He looked around the room and brought a porcelain tray to his desk. He breathed deeply and found the cool air good-tasting. He lifted one of the crisp notes, creased it in the middle so that it made an angle, and then he scratched a match under his desk and lighted the note. The heavy paper curled and blackened, the flame ran upwards, and only when the fire was about his fingertips did Cal drop the charred chip in the pin-tray. He stripped off another note and lighted it.

When six were burned Lee came in without knocking. 'I smelled smoke,' and then he saw what Cal was doing. 'Oh!' he said.

Cal braced himself for intervention but none came. Lee folded his hands across his middle and he stood silently–waiting. Cal doggedly lighted note after note until all were burned, and then he crushed the black chips down to powder and waited for Lee to comment, but Lee did not speak or move.

At last Cal said, 'Go ahead–you want to talk to me. Go ahead!'

'No,' said Lee, 'I don't. And if you have no need to talk to me–I'll stay a while and then I'll go away. I'll sit down here.' He squatted in a chair, folded his hands, and waited. He smiled to himself, the expression that is called inscrutable.

Cal turned from him. 'I can out-sit you,' he said.

'In a contest maybe,' said Lee. 'But in day to day, year to year–who knows?–century to century sitting–no, Cal. You'd lose.'

After a few moments Cal said peevishly, 'I wish you'd get on with your lecture.'

'I don't have a lecture.'

'What the hell are you doing here, then? You know what I did, and I got drunk last night.'

'I suspect the first and I can smell the second.'

'Smell?'

'You still smell,' said Lee.

'First time,' said Cal. 'I don't like it.'

'I don't either,' said Lee. 'I've got a bad stomach for liquor. Besides it makes me playful, intellectual but playful.'

'How do you mean, Lee?'

'I can only give you an example. In my younger days I played tennis. I liked it, and it was also a good thing for a servant to do. He could pick up his master's flubs at doubles and get no thanks but a few dollars for it. Once, I think it was sherry that time, I developed the theory that the fastest and most elusive animals in the world are bats. I was apprehended in the middle of the night in the bell tower of the Methodist Church in San Leandro. I had a racquet, and I seemed to have explained to the arresting officer that I was improving my back-hand on bats.'

Cal laughed with such amusement that Lee almost wished he had done it.

Cal said, 'I just sat behind a post and drank like a pig.'

'Always animals–'

'I was afraid if I didn't get drunk I'd shoot myself,' Cal interrupted.

'You'd never do that. You're too mean,' said Lee. 'By the way, where *is* Aron?'

'He ran away. I don't know where he went.'

'He's not too mean,' said Lee nervously.

'I know it. That's what I thought about. You don't think he would, do you, Lee?'

Lee said testily, 'Goddam it, whenever a person wants reassurance he tells a friend to think what he wants to be true. It's like asking a waiter what's good tonight. How the hell do I know?'

Cal cried, 'Why did I do it–why did I do it?'

'Don't make it complicated,' Lee said. 'You know why you did it. You were mad at him, and you were mad at him because your father hurt your feelings. That's not difficult. You were just mean.'

'I guess that's what I wonder–why I'm mean. Lee, I don't want to be mean. Help me, Lee!'

'Just a second,' Lee said. 'I thought I heard your father.' He darted out of the door.

Cal heard voices for a moment and then Lee came back to the room. 'He's going to the post office. We never get any mail in mid-afternoon. Nobody does. But every man in Salinas goes to the post office in the afternoon.'

'Some get a drink on the way,' said Cal.

'I guess it is a kind of habit and a kind of rest. They see their friends.' And Lee said, 'Cal–I don't like your father's looks. He's got a dazed look. Oh, I forgot. You don't know. Your mother committed suicide last night.'

Cal said, 'Did she?' and then he snarled, 'I hope it hurt. No, I don't want to say that. I don't want to think that. There it is again. There it is! I don't–want it–like that.'

Lee scratched a spot on his head, and that started his whole head to itching, and he scratched it all over, taking his time. It gave him the appearance of deep thought. He said, 'Did burning the money give you much pleasure?'

'I–I guess so.'

'And are you taking pleasure from this whipping you're giving yourself? Are you enjoying your despair?'

'Lee!'

'You're pretty full of yourself. You're marvelling at the tragic spectacle of Caleb Trask–Caleb the magnificent, the unique. Caleb whose suffering should have its Homer. Did you ever think of yourself as a snot-nose kid–mean sometimes, incredibly generous sometimes? Dirty in your habits, and curiously pure in your mind. Maybe you have a little more energy than most, just energy, but outside of that you're very like all the other snot-nose kids. Are you trying to attract dignity and tragedy to yourself because your mother was a whore? And if anything should have happened to your brother, will you be able to sneak for yourself the eminence of being a murderer, snot-nose?'

Cal turned slowly back to his desk. Lee watched him, holding his breath the way a doctor watches for the reaction to a hypodermic. Lee could see the reactions flaring through Cal–the rage at insult, the belligerence, and the hurt feelings following behind, and out of that–just the beginning of relief.

Lee sighed. He had worked so hard, so tenderly, and his work seemed to have succeeded. He said softly, 'We're a violent people, Cal. Does it seem strange to you that I include myself? Maybe it's true that we are all descended from the restless, the nervous, the criminals, the arguers and brawlers, but also the brave and independent and generous. If our ancestors had not been that, they would have stayed in their home plots in the other world and starved over the squeezed-out soil.'

Cal turned his head towards Lee, and his face had lost its tightness. He smiled, and Lee knew he had not fooled the boy entirely. Cal knew now it was a job–a well-done job–and he was grateful.

Lee went on, 'That's why I include myself. We all have that heritage, no matter what old land our fathers left. All colours and blends of Americans have somewhat the same tendencies. It's a breed–selected out by accident. And so we're over-brave and over-fearful–we're kind and cruel as children. We're over-friendly and at the same time frightened of strangers. We boast and are impressed. We're over-sentimental and realistic. We are mundane and materialistic–and do you know of any other nation that acts for ideals? We eat too much. We have no taste, no sense of proportion. We throw our energy about like waste. In the old lands they say of us that we go from barbarism to decadence without an intervening culture. Can it be that our critics have not the key or the language of our culture? That's what we are, Cal–all of us. You aren't any different.'

'Talk away,' said Cal, and he smiled and repeated, 'Talk away.'

'I don't need to any more,' said Lee. 'I'm finished now. I wish your father would come back. He worries me.' And Lee went nervously out.

In the hall just outside the front door he found Adam leaning against the wall, his hat low over his eyes and his shoulders slumped.

'Adam, what's the matter with you?'

'I don't know. Seem tired. Seem tired.'

Lee took him by the arm, and it seemed that he had to guide him towards the living-room. Adam fell heavily into his chair, and Lee took the hat from his head. Adam rubbed the back of his left hand with his right. His eyes were strange, very clear but unmoving. And his lips were dry and thickened and his speech had the sound of a dream talker, slow and coming from a distance. He rubbed his hand harshly. 'Strange thing,' he said, 'I must have fainted–in the post office. I never faint. Mr Pioda helped me up. Just for a second it was, I guess. I never faint.'

Lee asked, 'Was there any mail?'

'Yes–yes–I think there was mail.' He put his left hand in his pocket and in a moment took it out. 'My hand is kind of numb,' he said apologetically and reached across with his right hand and brought out a yellow government postcard.

'Thought I read it,' he said. 'I must have read it.' He held it up before his eyes and then dropped the card in his lap. 'Lee, I guess I've got to get glasses. Never needed them in my life. Can't read it. Letters jump around.'

'Shall I read it?'

'Funny–well, I'll go first thing for glasses. Yes, what does it say?'

And Lee read, '"Dear Father, I'm in the army. I told them I was eighteen. I'll be all right. Don't worry about me, Aron."'

'Funny,' said Adam. 'Seems like I read it. But I guess I didn't.' He rubbed his hand.

CHAPTER 52

1

That winter of 1917–18 was a dark and frightened time. The Germans smashed everything in front of them. In three months the British suffered three hundred thousand casualties. Many units of the French army were mutinous. Russia was out of the war. The German east divisions, rested and re-equipped, were thrown at the western front. The war seemed hopeless.

It was May before we had as many as twelve divisions in the field, and summer had come before our troops began to move across the sea in numbers. The Allied generals were fighting each other. Submarines slaughtered the crossing ships.

We learned then that the war was not a quick heroic change, but a slow, incredibly complicated matter. Our spirits sank in those winter months. We lost the flare of excitement and we had not yet put on the doggedness of a long war.

Ludendorff was unconquerable. Nothing stopped him. He mounted attack after attack on the broken armies of France and England. And it occurred to us that we might be too late, that soon we might be standing alone against the invincible Germans.

It was not uncommon for people to turn away from the war, some to fantasy and some to vice and some to crazy gaiety. Fortune-tellers were in great demand, and saloons did a roaring business. But people also turned inward to their private joys and tragedies to escape the pervasive fear and despondency. Isn't it strange that today we have forgotten this? We remember World War I as quick victory, with flags and bands, marching and horseplay and returning soldiers, fights in the bar-rooms with the goddam Limeys who thought they won the war. How quickly we forget that in that winter Ludendorff could not be beaten and that many people were preparing in their minds and spirits for a lost war.

2

Adam Trask was more puzzled than sad. He didn't have to resign from the draft board. He was given leave of absence for ill health. He sat by the hour rubbing the back of his left hand. He brushed it with a harsh brush and soaked it in hot water.

'It's circulation,' he said. 'As soon as I get the circulation back it'll be all right. It's my eyes that bother me. I never had trouble with my eyes. Guess I'll have to get my eyes tested for glasses. Me with glasses! Be hard to get used to. I'd go today but I feel a little dizzy.'

He felt more dizzy than he would admit. He could not move about the house without a hand braced against a wall. Lee often had to give him a hand-up out of his chair or help him out of bed in the morning and tie his shoes because he could not tie knots with his numb left hand.

Almost daily he came back to Aron. 'I can understand why a young man might want to enlist,' he said. 'If Aron had talked to me I might have tried to persuade him against it, but I wouldn't have forbidden it. You know that, Lee.'

'I know it.'

'That's what I can't understand. Why did he sneak away? Why doesn't he write? I thought I knew him better than that. Has he written to Abra? He'd be sure to write to her.'

'I'll ask her.'

'You do that. Do that right away.'

'The training is hard. That's what I've heard. Maybe they don't give him time.'

'It doesn't take any time to write a card.'

'When you went in the army, did you write to your father?'

'Think you've got me there, don't you? No, I didn't, but I had a reason. I didn't want to enlist. My father forced me. I was resentful. You see, I had a good reason. But Aron–he was doing fine in college. Why, they've written, asking about him. You read the letter. He didn't take any clothes. He didn't take the gold watch.'

'He wouldn't need any clothes in the army, and they don't want gold watches there either. Everything's brown.'

'I guess you're right. But I don't understand it. I've got to do something about my eyes. Can't ask you to read everything to me.' His eyes really troubled him. 'I can see a letter,' he said. 'But the words jumble all around.' A dozen times a day he seized a paper or a book and stared at it and put it down.

Lee read the papers to him to keep him from getting restless, and often in the middle of the reading Adam went to sleep.

He would awaken and say, 'Lee? Is that you, Cal? You know I never had any trouble with my eyes. I'll just go tomorrow and get my eyes tested.'

About the middle of February Cal went into the kitchen and said, 'Lee, he talks about it all the time. Let's get his eyes tested.'

Lee was stewing apricots. He left the stove and closed the kitchen door and went back to the stove. 'I don't want him to go,' he said.

'Why not?'

'I don't think it's his eyes. Finding out might trouble him. Let him be for a while. He's had a bad shock. Let him get better. I'll read to him all he wants.'

'What do you think it is?'

'I don't want to say. I've thought maybe Dr Edwards might just come by for a friendly call–just to say hello.'

'Have it your own way,' said Cal.

Lee said, 'Cal, have you seen Abra?'

'Sure, I see her. She walks away.'

'Can't you catch her?'

'Sure–and I could throw her down and punch her in the face and make her talk to me. But I won't.'

'Maybe if you'd just break the ice. Sometimes the barrier is so weak it just falls over when you touch it. Catch up with her. Tell her I want to see her.'

'I won't do it.'

'You feel awful guilty, don't you?'

Cal did not answer.

'Don't you like her?'

Cal did not answer.

'If you keep this up, you're going to feel worse, not better. You'd better open up. I'm warning you. You'd better open up.'

Cal cried, 'Do you want me to tell Father what I did? I'll do it if you tell me to.'

'No, Cal. Not now. But when he gets well you'll have to. You'll have to for yourself. You can't carry this alone. It will kill you.'

'Maybe I deserve to be killed.'

'Stop that!' Lee said coldly. 'That can be the cheapest kind of self-indulgence. You stop that!'

'How do you go about stopping it?' Cal asked.

Lee changed the subject. 'I don't understand why Abra hasn't been here–not even once.'

'No reason to come now.'

'It's not like her. Something's wrong there. Have you seen her?'

Cal scowled. 'I told you I have. You're getting crazy too. Tried to talk to her three times. She walked away.'

'Something's wrong. She's a good woman–a real woman.'

'She's a girl,' said Cal. 'It sounds funny you calling her a woman.'

'No,' Lee said softly. 'A few are women from the moment they're born. Abra has the loveliness of woman, and the courage–and the strength–and the wisdom. She knows things and she accepts things. I would have bet she couldn't be small or mean or even vain except when it's pretty to be vain.'

'You sure do think well of her.'

'Well enough to think she wouldn't desert us.' And he said, 'I miss her. Ask her to come to see me.'

'I told you she walked away from me.'

'Well, chase her, then. Tell her I want to see her. I miss her.'

Cal asked, 'Shall we go back to my father's eyes now?'

'No,' said Lee.

'Shall we talk about Aron?'

'No.'

3

Cal tried all the next day to find Abra alone, and it was only after school that he saw her ahead of him, walking home. He turned a corner and ran along the parallel street and then back, and he judged time and distance so that he turned in front of her as she strolled along.

'Hello,' he said.

'Hello. I thought I saw you behind me.'

'You did. I ran around the block to get in front of you. I want to talk to you.'

She regarded him gravely. 'You could have done that without running around the block.'

'Well, I tried to talk to you in school. You walked away.'

'You were mad. I don't want to talk to you mad.'

'How do you know I was?'

'I could see it in your face and the way you walked. You're not mad now.'

'No, I'm not.'

'Do you want to take my books?' She smiled.

A warmth fell on him. 'Yes–yes, I do.' He put her school-books under his arm and walked beside her. 'Lee wants to see you. He asked me to tell you.'

She was pleased. 'Does he? Tell him I'll come. How's your father?'

'Not very well. His eyes bother him.'

They walked along in silence until Cal couldn't stand it any more. 'You know about Aron?'

'Yes.' She paused. 'Open my binder and look next to the first page.'

He shifted the books. A penny postcard was in the binder. 'Dear Abra,' it said. 'I don't feel clean. I'm not fit for you. Don't be sorry. I'm in the army. Don't go near my father. Goodbye, Aron.'

Cal snapped the book shut. 'The son of a bitch,' he said under his breath.

'What?'

'Nothing.'

'I heard what you said.'

'Do you know why he went away?'

'No. I guess I could figure out–put two and two together. I don't want to. I'm not ready to–that is, unless you want to tell me.'

Suddenly Cal said, 'Abra–do you hate me?'

'No, Cal, but you hate me a little. Why is that?'

'I–I'm afraid of you.'

'No need to be.'

'I've hurt you more than you know. And you're my brother's girl.'

'How have you hurt me? And I'm *not* your brother's girl.'

'All right,' he said bitterly, 'I'll tell you–and I don't want you to forget you asked me to. Our mother was a whore. She ran a house here in town. I found out about it a long time ago. Thanksgiving night I took Aron down and showed her to him. I–'

Abra broke in excitedly, 'What did he do?'

'He went mad–just crazy. He yelled at her. Outside he knocked me down and ran away. Our dear mother killed herself; my father–he's–there's something wrong with him. Now you know about me. Now you have some reason to walk away from me.'

'Now I know about him,' she said calmly.

'My brother?'

'Yes, your brother.'

'He was good. Why did I say *was*? He *is* good. He's not mean or dirty like me.'

They had been walking very slowly. Abra stopped and Cal stopped and she faced him.

'Cal,' she said, 'I've known about your mother for a long, long time.'

'You have?'

'I heard my parents talking when they thought I was asleep. I want to tell you something, and it's hard to tell and it's good to tell.'

'You want to?'

'I have to. It's not so terribly long ago that I grew up and I wasn't a little girl any more. Do you know what I mean?'

'Yes,' said Cal.

'You sure you know?'

'Yes.'

'All right, then. It's hard to say now. I wish I'd said it then. I didn't love Aron any more.'

'Why not?'

'I've tried to figure it out. When we were children we lived in a story that we made up. But when I grew up the story wasn't enough. I had to have something else, because the story wasn't true any more.'

'Well–'

'Wait–let me get it all out. Aron didn't grow up. Maybe he never will. He wanted the story and he wanted it to come out his way. He couldn't stand to have it come out any other way.'

'How about you?'

'I don't want to know how it comes out. I only want to be there while it's going on. And, Cal–we were kind of strangers. We kept it going because we were used to it. But I didn't believe the story any more.'

'How about Aron?'

'He was going to have it come out his way if he had to tear the world up by the roots.'

Cal stood looking at the ground.

Abra said, 'Do you believe me?'

'I'm trying to study it out.'

'When you're a child you're the centre of everything. Everything happens to you. Other people? They're only ghosts furnished for you to talk to. But when you grow up you take your place and you're your own size and shape. Things go out of you to others and come in from other people. It's worse, but it's much better too. I'm glad you told me about Aron.'

'Why?'

'Because now I know I didn't make it all up. He couldn't stand to know about his mother because that's not how he wanted the story to go–and he wouldn't have any other story. So he tore up the world. It's the same way he tore me up–Abra–when he wanted to be a priest.'

Cal said, 'I'll have to think.'

'Give me my books,' she said. 'Tell Lee I'll come. I feel free now. I want to think too. I think I love you, Cal.'

'I'm not good.'

'Because you're not good.'

Cal walked quickly home. 'She'll come tomorrow,' he told Lee.

'Why, you're excited,' said Lee.

4

Once in the house Abra walked on her toes. In the hall she moved close to the wall where the floor did not creak. She put her foot on the lowest step on the carpeted stairs, changed her mind, and went to the kitchen.

'Here you are,' her mother said. 'You didn't come straight home.'

'I had to stay after class. Is Father better?'

'I guess so.'

'What does the doctor say?'

'Same thing as he said at first–overwork. Just needs a rest.'

'He hasn't seemed tired,' said Abra.

Her mother opened a bin and took out three baking potatoes and carried them to the sink. 'Your Father's very brave, dear. I should have known. He's been doing so much war work on top of his own work. The doctor says sometimes a man collapses all at once.

'Shall I go in and see him?'

'You know, Abra, I've got a feeling that he doesn't want to see anybody. Judge Knudsen phoned and your father said to tell him he was asleep.'

'Can I help you?'

'Go change your dress, dear. You don't want to get your pretty dress soiled.'

Abra tiptoed past her father's door and went to her own room. It was harsh-bright with varnish, papered brightly. Framed photographs of her parents on the bureau, poems framed on the walls, and her cupboard–everything in its place, the floor varnished, and her shoes standing diligently side by side. Her mother did everything for her, insisted on it–planned for her, dressed her.

Abra had long ago given up having any private thing in her room, even any personal thing. This was of such long standing that Abra did not think of her room as a private place. Her privacies were of the mind. The few letters she kept were in the sitting-room itself, filed among the pages of the two-volume *Memoirs of Ulysses S. Grant,* which to the best of her knowledge had never been opened by anyone but herself since it came off the press.

Abra felt pleased, and she did not inspect the reason. She knew certain things without question, and such things she did not speak about. For example, she knew that her father was not ill. He was hiding from something. Just as surely she knew that Adam Trask was ill, for she had seen him walking along the street. She wondered whether her mother knew her father was not ill.

Abra slipped off her dress and put on a cotton pinafore, which was understood to be for working around the house. She brushed her hair, tiptoed past her father's room, and went downstairs. At the foot of the stairs she opened her binder and took out Aron's postcard. In the sitting-room she shook Aron's letters out of Volume II of the *Memoirs,* folded them tightly, and, raising her skirt tucked them under the elastic which held up her panties. The package made her a little bumpy. In the kitchen she put on a full apron to conceal the bulge.

'You can scrape the carrots,' her mother said. 'Is that water hot?'

'Just coming to a boil.'

'Drop a bouillon cube in that cup, will you, dear? The doctor says it'll build your father up.'

When her mother carried the steaming cup upstairs, Abra opened the incinerator end of the gas stove, put in the letters, and lighted them.

Her mother came back, saying, 'I smell fire.'

'I lit the trash. It was full.'

'I wish you'd ask me when you want to do a thing like that,' her mother said. 'I was saving the trash to warm the kitchen in the morning.'

'I'm sorry, Mother,' Abra said. 'I didn't think.'

'You should try to think of these things. It seems to me you're getting very thoughtless lately.'

'I'm sorry, Mother.'

'Saved is earned,' said her mother.

The telephone rang in the dining-room. Her mother went to answer it. Abra heard her mother say, 'No, you can't see him. It's doctor's orders. He can't see anyone–no, not anyone.'

She came back to the kitchen. 'Judge Knudsen again,' she said.

CHAPTER 53

I

All during school next day Abra felt good about going to see Lee. She met Cal in the hall between classes. 'Did you tell him I was coming?'

'He's started some kind of tarts,' said Cal. He was dressed in his uniform–choking high collar, ill-fitting tunic, and wrapped leggings.

'You've got drill,' Abra said. 'I'll get there first. What kind of tarts?'

'I don't know. But leave me a couple, will you? Smelled like strawberry. Just leave me two.'

'Want to see a present I got for Lee? Look!' She opened a little cardboard box. 'It's a new kind of potato peeler. Takes off just the skin. It's easy. I got it for Lee.'

'There go my tarts,' said Cal, and then, 'If I'm a little late, don't go before I get there, will you?'

'Would you like to carry my books home?'

'Yes,' said Cal.

She looked at him long, full in the eyes, until he wanted to drop his gaze, and then she walked away towards her class.

2

Adam had taken to sleeping late, or, rather, he had taken to sleeping very often–short sleeps during the night and during the day. Lee looked in on him several times before he found him awake.

'I feel fine this morning,' Adam said.

'If you can call it morning. It's nearly eleven o'clock.'

'Good Lord! I have to get up.'

'What for?' Lee asked.

'What for? Yes, what for! But I feel good, Lee. I might walk down to the draft board. How is it outside?'

'Raw,' said Lee.

He helped Adam get up. Buttons and shoe-laces and getting things on frontways gave Adam trouble.

While Lee helped him Adam said, 'I had a dream–very real. I dreamed about my father.'

'A great old gentleman, from all I hear,' said Lee. 'I read that portfolio of clippings your brother's lawyer sent. Must have been a great old gentleman.'

Adam looked calmly at Lee. 'Did you know he was a thief?'

'You must have had a dream,' said Lee. 'He's buried at Arlington. One clipping said the Vice-President was at his funeral, and the Secretary of War. You know the *Salinas Index* might like to do a piece about him–in wartime, you know. How would you like to go over the material?'

'He was a thief,' said Adam. 'I didn't think so once, but I do now. He stole from the GAR.'

'I don't believe it,' said Lee.

There were tears in Adam's eyes. Very often these days tears came suddenly to Adam. Lee said, 'Now you sit right here and I'll bring you some breakfast. Do you know who's coming to see us this afternoon? Abra.'

Adam said, 'Abra?' and then, 'Oh, sure, Abra. She's a nice girl.'

'I love her,' said Lee simply. He got Adam seated in front of the card table in his bedroom. 'Would you like to work on the cut-out puzzle while I get breakfast?'

'No, thank you. Not this morning. I want to think about the dream before I forget it.'

When Lee brought the breakfast tray Adam was asleep in his chair. Lee awakened him and read the *Salinas Journal* to him while he ate and then helped him to the toilet.

The kitchen was sweet with tarts, and some of the berries had boiled over in the oven and burned, making the sharp, bitter-sweet smell pleasant and astringent.

There was a quiet rising joy in Lee. It was the joy of change. Time's drawing down for Adam, he thought. Time must be drawing down for me, but I don't feel it. I feel immortal. Once when I was very young I felt mortal–but not any more. Death has receded. He wondered if this was a normal way to feel.

And he wondered what Adam meant, saying his father was a thief. Part of the dream, maybe. And then Lee's mind played on the way it often did. Suppose it was true–Adam, the most rigidly honest man it was possible to find, living all his life on stolen money. Lee laughed to himself–now this second will, and Aron, whose purity was a little on the self-indulgent side, living all his life on the profits from a whorehouse. Was this some kind of joke or did things balance so that if one went too far in one direction an automatic slide moved on the scale and the balance was re-established?

He thought of Sam Hamilton. He had knocked on so many doors. He had the most schemes and plans, and no one would give him any money. But of course–he had so much, he was so rich. You couldn't give him any more. Riches seem to come to the poor in spirit, the poor in interest and joy. To put it straight–the very rich are a poor bunch of bastards. He wondered if that were true. They acted that way sometimes.

He thought of Cal burning the money to punish himself. And the punishment hadn't hurt him as badly as the crime. Lee said to himself, 'If there should happen to be a place where one day I'll come up with Sam Hamilton, I'll have a lot of good stories to tell him,' and his mind went on, 'But so will he!'

Lee went in to find Adam and found him trying to open the box that held the clippings about his father.

3

The wind blew cold that afternoon. Adam insisted on going to look in on the draft board. Lee wrapped him up and started him off. 'If you feel faint at all, just sit down wherever you are,' Lee said.

'I will,' Adam agreed. 'I haven't felt dizzy all day. Might stop in and have Victor look at my eyes.'

'You wait till tomorrow. I'll go with you.'

'We'll see,' said Adam, and he started out, swinging his arms with bravado.

Abra came in with shining eyes and a red nose from the frosty wind, and she brought such pleasure that Lee giggled softly when he saw her.

'Where are the tarts?' she demanded. 'Let's hide them from Cal.' She sat down in the kitchen. 'Oh, I'm so glad to be back.'

Lee started to speak and choked and then what he wanted to say seemed good to say–to say carefully. He hovered over her. 'You know, I haven't wished for many things in my life,' he began. 'I learned very early not to wish for things. Wishing just brought earned disappointment.'

Abra said gaily, 'But you wish for something now. What is it?'

He blurted out, 'I wish you were my daughter–' He was shocked at himself. He went to the stove and turned out the gas under the tea-kettle, then lighted it again.

She said softly, 'I wish you were my father.'

He glanced quickly at her and away. 'You do?'

'Yes, I do.'

'Why?'

'Because I love you.'

Lee went quickly out of the kitchen. He sat in his room, gripping his hands tightly together until he stopped choking. He got up and took a small carved ebony box from the top of his bureau. A dragon climbed towards heaven on the box. He carried the box to the kitchen and laid it on the table between Abra's hands. 'This is for you,' he said, and his tone had no inflexion.

She opened the box and looked down on a small, dark green jade button, and carved on its surface was a human right hand, a lovely hand, the fingers curved and in repose. Abra lifted the button out and looked at it, and then she moistened it with the tip of her tongue and moved it gently over her full lips, and pressed the cool stone against her cheek.

Lee said, 'That was my mother's only ornament.'

Abra got up and put her arms around him and kissed him on the cheek, and it was the only time such a thing had ever happened in his whole life.

Lee laughed. 'My Oriental calm seems to have deserted me,' he said. 'Let me make the tea, darling. I'll get hold of myself that way.' From the stove he said, 'I've never used that word–never once to anybody in the world.'

Abra said, 'I woke up with joy this morning.'

'So did I,' said Lee. 'I know what made me feel happy. You were coming.'

'I was glad about that too, but–'

'You are changed,' said Lee. 'You aren't any part a little girl any more. Can you tell me?'

'I burned all of Aron's letters.'

'Did he do bad things to you?'

'No. I guess not. Lately I never felt good enough. I always wanted to explain to him that I was not good.'

'And now that you don't have to be perfect, you can be good. Is that it?'

'I guess so. Maybe that's it.'

'Do you know about the mother of the boys?'

'Yes. Do you know I haven't tasted a single one of the tarts?' Abra said. 'My mouth is dry.'

'Drink some tea, Abra. Do you like Cal?'

'Yes.'

Lee said, 'He's crammed full to the top with every good thing and every bad thing. I've thought that one single person could almost with the weight of a finger–'

Abra bowed her head over her tea. 'He asked me to go to the Alisal when the wild azaleas bloom.'

Lee put his hands on the table and leaned over. 'I don't want to ask you whether you are going,' he said.

'You don't have to,' said Abra. 'I'm going.'

Lee sat opposite her at the table. 'Don't stay away from this house for long,' he said.

'My father and mother don't want me here.'

'I only saw them once,' Lee said cynically. 'They seemed to be good people. Sometimes, Abra, the strangest medicines are effective. I wonder if it would help if they knew Aron had just inherited over a hundred thousand dollars.'

Abra nodded gravely and fought to keep the corners of her mouth from turning up. 'I think it would help,' she said. 'I wonder how I could get the news to them.'

'My dear,' said Lee, 'if I heard such a piece of news I think my first impulse would be to telephone someone. Maybe you'd have a bad connexion.'

Abra nodded. 'Would you tell her where the money came from?'

'That I would not,' said Lee.

She looked at the alarm clock hung on a nail on the wall. 'Nearly five,' she said. 'I'll have to go. My father isn't well. I thought Cal might get back from drill.'

'Come back very soon,' Lee said.

4

Cal was on the porch when she came out.

'Wait for me,' he said, and he went into the house and dropped his books.

'Take good care of Abra's books,' Lee called from the kitchen.

The winter night blew in with frosty wind, and the streetlamps with their spluttering carbons swung restlessly and made the shadows dart back and forth like a runner trying to steal second base. Men coming home from work buried their chins in their overcoats and hurried towards warmth. In the still night the monotonous scattering of music of the skating rink could be heard from many blocks away.

Cal said, 'Will you take your books for a minute, Abra? I want to unhook this collar. It's cutting my head off.' He worked the hooks out of the eyes and sighed with relief. 'I'm all chafed,' he said and took her books back. The branches of the big palm tree in Berges' front yard were lashing with a dry clatter, and a cat meowed over and over and over in front of some kitchen door closed against it.

Abra said, 'I don't think you make much of a soldier. You're too independent.'

'I could be,' said Cal. 'This drilling with old Krag-Jorgensens seems silly to me. When the time comes, and I take an interest, I'll be good.'

'The tarts were wonderful,' said Abra. 'I left one for you.'

'Thanks. I'll bet Aron makes a good soldier.'

'Yes, he will–and the best-looking soldier in the army. When are we going for the azaleas?'

'Not until spring.'

'Let's go early and take a lunch.'

'It might be raining.'

'Let's go anyway, rain or shine.'

She took her books and went into her yard. 'See you tomorrow.' she said.

He did not turn towards home. He walked in the nervous night past the high school and past the skating rink–a floor with a big tent over it, and a mechanical orchestra clanging away. Not a soul was skating. The old man who owned it sat miserably in his booth, flipping the end of a roll of tickets against his forefinger.

Main Street was deserted. The wind skidded papers on the sidewalk. Tom Meek, the constable, came out of Bell's candy store and fell into step with Cal. 'Better hook that tunic collar, soldier,' he said softly.

'Hello, Tom. The damn thing's too tight.'

'I don't see you around the town at night lately.'

'No.'

'Don't tell me you reformed.'

'Maybe.'

Tom prided himself on his ability to kid people and make it sound serious. He said, 'Sounds like you got a girl.'

Cal didn't answer.

'I hear your brother faked his age and joined the army. Are you picking off his girl?'

'Oh, sure–sure,' said Cal.

Tom's interest sharpened. 'I nearly forgot,' he said. 'I hear Will Hamilton is telling around you made fifteen thousand dollars in beans. That true?'

'Oh, sure,' said Cal.

'You're just a kid. What are you going to do with all that money?'

Cal grinned at him. 'I burned it up.'

'How do you mean?'

'Just set a match to it and burned it.'

Tom looked into his face. 'Oh, yeah! Sure. Good thing to do. Got to go in here. Good night.' Tom Meek didn't like people to kid him. 'The young punk son of a bitch,' he said to himself. 'He's getting too smart for himself.'

Cal moved slowly along Main Street, looking in store windows. He wondered where Kate was buried. If he could find out, he thought he might take a bunch of flowers, and he laughed at himself for the impulse. Was it good or was he fooling himself? The Salinas wind would blow over a tombstone, let alone a bunch of carnations. For some reason he remembered the Mexican name for carnations. Somebody must have told him when he was a kid. They were called Nails of Love–and marigolds, the Nails of Death. It was a word like nails–*claveles*. Maybe he'd better put marigolds on his mother's grave. 'I'm beginning to think like Aron,' he said to himself.

CHAPTER 54

I

The winter seemed reluctant to let go its bite. It hung on cold and wet and windy long after its time. And people repeated, 'It's those damned big guns they're shooting off in France–spoiling the weather in the whole world.'

The grain was slow coming up in the Salinas Valley, and the wild flowers came so late that some people thought they wouldn't come at all.

We knew–or at least we were confident–that on May Day, when all the Sunday School picnics took place in the Alisal, the wild azaleas that grew in the skirts of the stream would be in bloom. They were a part of May Day.

May Day was cold. The picnic was drenched out of existence by a freezing rain, and there wasn't an open blossom on the azalea trees. Two weeks later they still weren't out.

Cal hadn't known it would be like this when he had made azaleas the signal for his picnic, but once the symbol was set it could not be violated.

The Ford sat in Windham's shed, its tyres pumped up, and with two new dry cells to make it start easily on Bat. Lee was alerted to make sandwiches when the day came, and he got tired of waiting and stopped buying sandwich bread every two days.

'Why don't you just go anyway?' he said.

'I can't,' said Cal. 'I said azaleas.'

'How will you know?'

'The Silacci boys live out there, and they come into school every day. They say it will be a week or ten days.'

'Oh, Lord!' said Lee. 'Don't overtrain your picnic.'

Adam's health was slowly improving. The numbness was going from his hand. And he could read a little–a little more each day.

'It's only when I get tired that the letters jump,' he said. 'I'm glad I didn't get glasses to ruin my eyes. I knew my eyes were all right.'

Lee nodded and was glad. He had gone to San Francisco for the books he needed and had written for a number of articles. He knew about as much as was known about the anatomy of the brain and the symptoms and severities of lesion and thrombus. He had studied and asked questions with the same unwavering intensity as when he had trapped and pelted and cured a Hebrew verb. Dr H.C. Murphy had got to know Lee very well and had gone from a professional impatience with a Chinese servant to a genuine admiration for a scholar. Dr Murphy had even borrowed some of Lee's news articles and reports on diagnosis and practice. He told Dr Edwards, 'That Chink knows more about the pathology of cerebral haemorrhage than I do, and I bet as much as you do.' He spoke with a kind of affectionate anger that this should be so. The medical profession is unconsciously irritated by lay knowledge.

When Lee reported Adam's improvement he said, 'It does seem to me that the absorption is continuing–'

'I had a patient,' Dr Murphy said, and he told a hopeful story.

'I'm always afraid of recurrence,' said Lee.

'That you have to leave with the Almighty,' said Dr Murphy. 'We can't patch an artery like an inner tube. By the way, how do you get him to let you take his blood pressure?'

'I bet on his and he bets on mine. It's better than horse racing.'

'Who wins?'

'Well, I could,' said Lee. 'But I don't. That would spoil the game–and the chart.'

'How do you keep him from getting excited?'

'It's my own invention,' said Lee. 'I call it conversational therapy.'

'Must take all your time.'

'It does,' said Lee.

2

On May 28, 1918, American troops carried out their first important assignment of World War I. The First Division, General Bullard commanding, was ordered to capture the village of Cantigny. The village, on high ground, dominated the Avre River valley. It was defended by trenches, heavy machine-guns, and artillery. The front was a little over a mile wide.

At 6.45 am, May 28, 1918, the attack was begun after one hour of artillery preparation. Troops involved were the 28th Infantry (Col. Ely), one battalion of the 18th Infantry (Parker), a company of the First Engineers, the divisional artillery (Summerall), and a support of French tanks and flame throwers.

The attack was a complete success. American troops entrenched on the new line and repulsed two powerful German counter-attacks.

The First Division received the congratulations of Clemenceau, Foch, and Pétain.

3

It was the end of May before the Silacci boys brought the news that the salmon-pink blossoms of the azaleas were breaking free. It was on a Wednesday, as the nine o'clock bell was ringing, that they told him.

Cal rushed to the English classroom, and just as Miss Norris took her seat on the little stage he waved his handkerchief and blew his nose loudly. Then he went down to the boys' toilet and waited until he heard through the wall the flush of water on the girlside. He went out through the basement door, walked close to the red brick wall, slipped round the pepper tree, and, once out of sight of school, walked slowly along until Abra caught up with him.

'When'd they come out?' she asked.

'This morning.'

'Shall we wait until tomorrow?'

He looked up at the gay yellow sun, the first earth-warming sun of the year. 'Do you want to wait?'

'No,' she said.

'Neither do I.'

They broke into a run–bought bread at Reybaud's and joggled Lee into action.

Adam heard loud voices and looked into the kitchen. 'What's the hullaballoo?' he asked.

'We're going on a picnic,' said Cal.

'Isn't it a school day?'

Abra said, 'Sure it is. But it's a holiday too.'

Adam smiled at her. 'You're pink as a rose,' he said.

Abra cried, 'Why don't you come with us? We're going to the Alisal to get azaleas.'

'Why, I'd like to,' Adam said, and then, 'No, I can't. I promised to go down to the ice plant. We're putting in some new tubing. It's a beautiful day.'

'We'll bring you some azaleas,' Abra said.

'I like them. Well, have a good time.'

When he was gone Cal said, 'Lee, why don't you come with us?'

Lee looked sharply at him. 'I hadn't thought you were a fool,' he said.

'Come on!' Abra cried.

'Don't be ridiculous,' said Lee.

4

It's a pleasant little stream that gurgles through the Alisal against the Gabilan Mountains on the east side of the Salinas Valley. The water bumbles over round stones and washes the polished roots of the trees that hold it in.

The smell of azaleas and the sleepy smell of sun working with chlorophyll filled the air. On the bank the Ford car sat, still breathing softly from its overheating. The back seat was piled with azalea branches.

Cal and Abra sat on the bank among the luncheon papers. They dangled their feet in the water.

'They always wilt before you get them home,' said Cal.

'But they're such a good excuse, Cal,' she said. 'If you won't I guess I'll have to–'

'What?'

She reached over and took his hand. 'That,' she said.

'I was afraid to.'

'Why?'

'I don't know.'

'I wasn't.'

'I guess girls aren't afraid of near as many things.'

'I guess not.'

'Are you ever afraid?'

'Sure,' she said. 'I was afraid of you after you said I wet my pants.'

'That was mean,' he said. 'I wonder why I did it,' and suddenly he was silent.

Her fingers tightened round his hand. 'I know what you're thinking. I don't want you to think about that.'

Cal looked at the curling water and turned a round brown stone with his toe.

Abra said, 'You think you've got it all, don't you? You think you attract bad things–'

'Well–'

'Well, I'm going to tell you something. My father's in trouble.'

'How in trouble?'

'I haven't been listening at doors but I've heard enough. He's not sick. He's scared. He's done something.'

He turned his head. 'What?'

'I think he's taken some money from his company. He doesn't know whether his partners are going to put him in jail or let him try to pay it back.'

'How do you know?'

'I heard them shouting in his bedroom where he's sick. And my mother started the phonograph to drown them out.'

He said, 'You aren't making it up?'

'No. I'm not making it up.'

He shuffled near and put his head against her shoulder and his arm crept timidly around her waist.

'You see, you're not the only one–' She looked sideways at his face. 'Now I'm afraid,' she said weakly.

5

At three o'clock in the afternoon Lee was sitting at his desk, turning over the pages of a seed catalogue. The pictures of sweet peas were in colour.

'Now these would look nice on the back fence. They'd screen off the slough. I wonder if there's enough sun.' He looked up at the sound of his own voice and smiled at himself. More and more he caught himself speaking aloud when the house was empty.

'It's age,' he said aloud. 'The slowing thoughts and–' He stopped and grew rigid for a moment. 'That's funny–listening for something. I wonder whether I left the tea-kettle on the gas. No–I remember.' He listened again. 'Thank heaven I'm not superstitious. I could hear ghosts walk if I'd let myself. I could–'

The front-door bell rang.

'There it is. That's what I was listening for. Let it ring. I'm not going to be led around by feelings. Let it ring.'

But it did not ring again.

A black weariness fell on Lee, a hopelessness that pressed his shoulders down. He laughed at himself. 'I can go and find it's an advertisement under the door or I can sit here and let my silly old mind tell me death is on the doorstep. Well, I want the advertisement.'

Lee sat in the living-room and looked at the envelope in his lap. And suddenly he spat at it. 'All right,' he said, 'I'm coming–goddam you,' and he ripped it open and in a moment laid it on the table and turned it over with the message down.

He stared between his knees at the floor. 'No,' he said, 'that's not my right. Nobody has the right to remove any single experience from another. Life and death are promised. We have a right to pain.'

His stomach contracted. 'I haven't got the courage. I'm a cowardly yellow-belly. I couldn't stand it.'

He went into the bathroom and measured three teaspoons of elixir of bromide into a glass and added water until the red medicine was pink. He carried the glass to the living-room and put it on the table. He folded the telegram and shoved it in his pocket. He said aloud, 'I hate a coward! God, how I hate a coward!' His hands were shaking and a cold perspiration dampened his forehead.

At four o'clock he heard Adam fumbling at the door-knob. Lee licked his lips. He stood up and walked slowly to the hall. He carried the glass of pink fluid and his hand was steady.

CHAPTER 55

I

All of the lights were on in the Trask house. The door stood partly open, and the house was cold. In the sitting-room Lee was shrivelled up like a leaf in the chair beside the lamp. Adam's door was open and the sound of voices came from his room.

When Cal came in he asked, 'What's going on?'

Lee looked at him and swung his head towards the table where the open telegram lay. 'Your brother is dead,' he said. 'Your father has had a stroke.'

Cal started down the hall.

Lee said, 'Come back. Dr Edwards and Dr Murphy are in there. Let them alone.'

Cal stood in front of him. 'How bad? How bad, Lee, how bad?'

'I don't know.' He spoke as though recalling an ancient thing. 'He came home tired. But I had to read him the telegram. That was his right. For about five minutes he said it over and over to himself out loud. And then it seemed to get through into his brain and to explode there.'

'Is he conscious?'

Lee said wearily, 'Sit down and wait, Cal. Sit down and wait. Get used to it. I'm trying to.'

Cal picked up the telegram and read its bleak and dignified announcement.

Dr Edwards came out, carrying his bag. He nodded curtly, went out, and closed the door smartly behind him.

Dr Murphy set his bag on the table and sat down. He sighed. 'Dr Edwards asked me to tell you.'

'How is he?' Cal demanded.

'I'll tell you all we know. You're the head of the family now, Cal. Do you know what a stroke is?' He didn't wait for Cal to answer. 'This one is a leakage of blood in the brain. Certain areas of the brain are affected. There have been earlier small leakages. Lee knows that.'

'Yes,' said Lee.

Dr Murphy glanced at him and then back at Cal. 'The left side is paralysed. The right side partly. Probably there is no sight in the left eye, but we can't determine that. In other words, your father is nearly helpless.'

'Can he talk?'

'A little–with difficulty. Don't tire him.'

Cal struggled for words. 'Can he get well?'

'I've heard of reabsorption cases this bad but I've never seen one.'

'You mean he's going to die?'

'We don't know. He might live for a week, a month, a year, even two years. He might die tonight.'

'Will he know me?'

'You'll have to find that out for yourself. I'll send a nurse tonight and then you'll have to get permanent nurses.' He stood up. 'I'm sorry, Cal. Bear up! You'll have to bear up.' And he said, 'It always surprises me how people bear up. They always do. Edwards will be in tomorrow. Good night.' He put his hand out to touch Cal's shoulder, but Cal had moved away and walked towards his father's room.

Adam's head was propped up on pillows. His face was calm, the skin pale; his mouth was straight, neither smiling nor disapproving. His eyes were open, and they had great depth and clarity, as though one could see deep into them and as though they could see deep into their surroundings. And the eyes were calm, aware but not interested. They turned slowly towards Cal as he entered the room, found his chest, and then rose to his face and stayed there.

Cal sat down in the straight chair beside the bed. He said, 'I'm sorry, Father.'

The eyes blinked slowly the way a frog blinks.

'Can you hear me, Father? Can you understand me?' The eyes did not change or move. 'I did it,' Cal cried. 'I'm responsible for Aron's death and for your sickness. I took him to Kate's. I showed him his mother. That's why he went away. I don't want to do bad things–but I do them.'

He put his head down on the side of the bed to escape the terrible eyes, and he could still see them. He knew they would be with him, a part of him, all of his life.

The door-bell rang. In a moment Lee came to the bedroom, followed by the nurse–a strong, broad woman with heavy black eyebrows. She opened breeziness as she opened her suitcase.

'Where's my patient! There he is! Why, you look fine! What am I doing here? Maybe you better get up and take care of me, you look good. Would you like to take care of me, big handsome man?' She thrust a muscular arm under Adam's shoulder and effortlessly hoisted him towards the head of the bed and held him up with her right arm while with her left she patted out the pillows and laid him back.

'Cool pillows,' she said. 'Don't you love cool pillows? Now, where's the bathroom? Have you got a duck and bedpan? Can you put a cot in here for me?'

'Make a list,' said Lee. 'And if you need any help–with him–'

'Why would I need help? We'll get along just fine, won't we, sugar-sweetie?'

Lee and Cal returned to the kitchen. Lee said, 'Before she came I was going to urge you to have some supper–you know, like the kind of person who uses food for any purpose good or bad? I bet she's that way. You can eat or not eat, just as you wish.'

Cal grinned at him. 'If you'd tried to make me, I'd have been sick. But since you put it that way, I think I'll make a sandwich.'

'You can't have a sandwich.'

'I want one.'

'It all works out,' said Lee, 'true to outrageous form. It's kind of insulting that everyone reacts about the same way.'

'I don't want a sandwich,' Cal said. 'Are there any tarts left?'

'Plenty–in the bread-box. They may be a little soaky.'

'I like them soaky,' Cal said. He brought the whole plate to the table and set it in front of him.

The nurse looked into the kitchen. 'These look good,' she said and took one, bit into it, and talked among her chewings. 'Can I phone Krough's drugstore for the things I need? Where's the phone? Where do you keep the linen? Where's the cot you're going to bring in? Are you through with this paper? Where did you say the phone is?' She took another tart and retired.

Lee asked softly, 'Did he speak to you?'

Cal shook his head back and forth as though he couldn't stop.

'It's going to be dreadful. But the doctor is right. You can stand anything. We're wonderful animals that way.'

'I am not.' Cal's voice was flat and dull. 'I can't stand it. No, I can't stand it. I won't be able to. I'll have to–I'll have to–'

Lee gripped his fist fiercely. 'Why, you mouse–you nasty cur. With goodness all around you–don't you dare suggest a thing like that! Why is your sorrow more refined than my sorrow?'

'It's not sorrow. I told him what I did. I killed my brother. I'm a murderer. He knows it.'

'Did he say it? Tell the truth–did he say it?'

'He didn't have to. It was in his eyes. He said it with his eyes. There's nowhere I can go to get away–there's no place.'

Lee sighed and released his wrist. 'Cal'–he spoke patiently–'listen to me. Adam's brain centres are affected. Anything you see in his eyes may be pressure on that part of his brain which governs his seeing. Don't you remember?–he couldn't read. That wasn't his eyes–that was pressure. You don't know he accused you. You don't know that.'

'He accused me. I know it. He said I'm a murderer.'

'Then he will forgive you. I promise.'

The nurse stood in the doorway. 'What are you promising, Charley? You promised me a cup of coffee.'

'I'll make it now. How is he?'

'Sleeping like a baby. Have you got anything to read in this house?'

'What would you like?'

'Something to take my mind off my feet.'

'I'll bring the coffee to you. I've got some dirty stories written by a French queen. They might be too–'

'You bring 'em with the coffee,' she said. 'Why don't you get some shut-eye, sonny? Me and Charley'll hold the fort. Don't forget the book, Charley.'

Lee set the percolator on the gas jet. He came to the table and said, 'Cal!'

'What do you want?'

'Go to Abra.'

2

Cal stood on the neat porch and kept his finger on the bell until the harsh overlight flashed on and the night bolt rasped and Mrs Bacon looked out. 'I want to see Abra,' Cal said.

Her mouth dropped open in amazement. 'You want what?'

'I want to see Abra.'

'You can't. Abra's gone to her room. Go away.'

Cal shouted, 'I tell you I want to see Abra.'

'You go away or I'll call the police.'

Mr Bacon called, 'What is it? Who is it?'

'Never you mind–go back to bed. You aren't well. I'll handle this.'

She turned back to Cal. 'Now you get off the porch. And if you ring the bell again I'll phone the police. Now, get!' The door slammed, the bolt scraped, and the hard overlight went off.

Cal stood smiling in the dark, for he thought of Tom Meek lumbering up, saying, 'Hello, Cal. What you up to?'

Mrs Bacon shouted from inside, 'I see you. Now go on! Get off the porch!'

He walked slowly down the walk and turned towards home, and he hadn't gone a block before Abra caught up with him. She was panting from her run. 'Got out the back way,' she said.

'They'll find you gone.'

'I don't care.'

'You don't?'

'No.'

Cal said, 'Abra, I've killed my brother and my father is paralysed because of me.'

She took his arm and clung to it with both hands.

Cal said, 'Didn't you hear me?'

'I heard you.'

'Abra, my mother was a whore.'

'I know. You told me. My father was a thief.'

'I've got her blood, Abra. Don't you understand?'

'I've got his,' she said.

They walked along in silence while he tried to rebalance himself. The wind was cold, and they quickened their steps to keep warm. They passed the last street-light on the very edge of Salinas, and blackness lay ahead of them and the road was unpaved and sticky with black 'dobe mud.

They had come to the end of the pavement, to the end of the street-lights. The road under their feet was slippery with spring mud, and the grass that brushed against their legs was wet with dew.

Abra asked, 'Where are we going?'

'I wanted to run away from my father's eyes. They're right in front of me all the time. When I close my eyes I still see them. I'll always see them. My father is going to die, but his eyes will still be looking at me, telling me I killed my brother.'

'You didn't.'

'Yes, I did. And his eyes say I did.'

'Don't talk like that. Where are we going?'

'A little farther. There's a ditch and a pump house–and a willow tree. Do you remember the willow tree?'

'I remember it.'

He said, 'The branches come down like a tent and their tips touch the ground.'

'I know.'

'In the afternoons–the sunny afternoons–you and Aron would part the branches and go inside–and no one could see you.'

'You watched?'

'Oh, sure. I watched.' And he said, 'I want you to go inside the willow tree with me. That's what I want to do.'

She stopped and her hand pulled him to a stop. 'No,' she said. 'That's not right.'

'Don't you want to go in with me?'

'Not if you're running away–no, I don't.'

Cal said, 'Then I don't know what to do. What shall I do? Tell me what to do.'

'Will you listen?'

'I don't know.'

'We're going back,' she said.

'Back? Where?'

'To your father's house,' said Abra.

3

The light of the kitchen poured down on them. Lee had lighted the oven to warm the chilly air.

'She made me come,' said Cal.

'Of course she did. I knew she would.'

Abra said, 'He would have come by himself.'

'We'll never know that,' said Lee.

He left the kitchen and in a moment returned. 'He's still sleeping.' Lee set a stone bottle and three little translucent porcelain cups on the table.

'I remember that,' said Cal.

'You ought to.' Lee poured the dark liquor. 'Just sip it and let it run around your tongue.'

Abra put her elbows on the kitchen table. 'Help him,' she said. 'You can accept things, Lee. Help him.'

'I don't know whether I can accept things or not,' Lee said. 'I've never had a chance to try. I've always found myself with some–not less uncertain but less able to take care of uncertainty. I've had to do my weeping–alone.'

'Weeping–? You?'

He said, 'When Samuel Hamilton died the world went out like a candle. I relighted it to see his lovely creations, and I saw his children tossed and torn and destroyed as though some vengefulness was at work. Let the ng-ka-py run back on your tongue.'

He went on, 'I had to find out my stupidities for myself. These were my stupidities: I thought the good are destroyed while the evil survive and prosper.

'I thought that once an angry and disgusted God poured molten fire from a crucible to destroy or to purify his little handiwork of mud.

'I thought I had inherited both the scars of the fire and the impurities which made the fire necessary–all inherited, I thought. All inherited. Do you feel that way?'

'I think so,' said Cal.

'I don't know,' Abra said.

Lee shook his head. 'That isn't good enough. That isn't good enough thinking. Maybe–' And he was silent.

Cal felt the heat of the liquor in his stomach. 'Maybe what, Lee?'

'Maybe you'll come to know that every man in every generation is re-fired. Does a craftsman, even in his old age, lose his hunger to make a perfect cup–thin, strong, translucent?' He held his cup to the light. 'All impurities burned out and ready for a glorious flux, and for that–more fire. And then either the slag heap or, perhaps what no one in the world ever quite gives up, perfection.' He drained his cup and he said loudly, 'Cal, listen to me. Can you think that whatever made us–would stop trying?'

'I can't take it in,' Cal said. 'Not now I can't.'

The heavy steps of the nurse sounded in the living-room. She billowed through the door and she looked at Abra, elbows on the table, holding her cheeks between her palms.

The nurse said, 'Have you got a pitcher? They get thirsty. I like to keep a pitcher of water handy. You see,' she explained, 'they breathe through their mouths.'

'Is he awake?' Lee asked. 'There's a pitcher.'

'Oh, yes, he's awake and rested. And I've washed his face and combed his hair. He's a good patient. He tried to smile at me.'

Lee stood up. 'Come along, Cal. I want you to come too, Abra. You'll have to come.'

The nurse filled her pitcher at the sink and scurried ahead of them.

When they trooped into the bedroom Adam was propped high on his pillows. His white hands lay palms down on either side of him, and the sinews from knuckle to wrist were tight drawn. His face was waxed, and his sharp features were sharpened. He breathed slowly between pale lips. His blue eyes reflected back the night-light focused on his head.

Lee and Cal and Abra stood at the foot of the bed, and Adam's eyes moved slowly from one face to the other, and his lips moved just a little in greeting.

The nurse said, 'There he is. Doesn't he look nice? He's my darling. He's my sugar pie.'

'Hush!' said Lee.

'I won't have you tiring my patient.'

'Go out of the room,' said Lee.

'I'll have to report this to the doctor.'

Lee whirled towards her. 'Go out of the room and close the door. Go and write your report.'

'I'm not in the habit of taking orders from Chinks.'

Cal said, 'Go out now, and close the door.'

She slammed the door just loud enough to register her anger. Adam blinked at the sound.

Lee said, 'Adam!'

The blue wide eyes looked for the voice and finally found Lee's brown shining eyes.

Lee said, 'Adam, I don't know what you can hear or understand. When you had the numbness in your hand and your eyes refused to read, I found out everything I could. But some things no one but you can know. You may, behind your eyes, be alert and keen, or you may be living in a confused grey dream. You may, like a newborn child, perceive only light and movement.

'There's damage in your brain, and it may be that you are a new thing in the world. Your kindness may be meanness now, and your bleak honesty fretful and conniving. No one knows these things except you, Adam! Can you hear me?'

The blue eyes wavered, closed slowly, then opened.

Lee said, 'Thank you, Adam. I know how hard it is. I'm going to ask you to do a much harder thing. Here is your son–Caleb–your only son. Look at him, Adam!'

The pale eyes looked until they found Cal. Cal's mouth moved dryly and made no sound.

Lee's voice cut in, 'I don't know how long you will live, Adam. Maybe a long time. Maybe an hour. But your son will live. He will marry and his children will be the only remnant left of you.' Lee wiped his eyes with his fingers.

'He did a thing in anger, Adam, because he thought you had rejected him. The result of his anger is that his brother and your son is dead.'

Cal said, 'Lee–you can't.'

'I have to,' said Lee. 'If it kills him I have to. I have the choice,' and he smiled sadly and quoted, ' "If there's blame, it's my blame." ' Lee's shoulders straightened. He said sharply, 'Your son is marked with guilt out of himself–out of himself–almost more than he can bear. Don't crush him with rejection. Don't crush him, Adam.'

Lee's breath whistled in his throat. 'Adam, give him your blessing. Don't leave him alone with his guilt. Adam, can you hear me? Give him your blessing!'

A terrible brightness shone in Adam's eyes and he closed them and kept them closed. A wrinkle formed between his brows.

Lee said, 'Help him, Adam–help him. Give him his chance. Let him be free. That's all a man has over the beasts. Free him! Bless him!'

The whole bed seemed to shake under the concentration. Adam's breath came quick with his effort and then, slowly, his right hand lifted–lifted an inch and then fell back.

Lee's face was haggard. He moved to the head of the bed and wiped the sick man's damp face with the edge of the sheet. He looked down at the closed eyes.

Lee whispered, 'Thank you, Adam–thank you, my friend. Can you move your lips? Make your lips form his name.'

Adam looked up with sick weariness. His lips parted and failed and tried again. Then his lungs filled. He expelled the air and his lips combed the rushing sigh. His whispered word seemed to hang in the air.

'Timshel!'

His eyes closed and he slept.

OF MICE AND MEN

I

A few miles south of Soledad, the Salinas River drops in close to the hill-side bank and runs deep and green. The water is warm too, for it has slipped twinkling over the yellow sands in the sunlight before reaching the narrow pool. On one side of the river the golden foothill slopes curve up to the strong and rocky Gabilan mountains, but on the valley side the water is lined with trees–willows fresh and green with every spring, carrying in their lower leaf junctures the debris of the winter's flooding; and sycamores with mottled, white, recumbent limbs and branches that arch over the pool. On the sandy bank under the trees the leaves lie deep and so crisp that a lizard makes a great skittering if he runs among them. Rabbits come out of the brush to sit on the sand in the evening, and the damp flats are covered with the night tracks of 'coons, and with the spread pads of dogs from the ranches, and with the split-wedge tracks of deer that come to drink in the dark.

There is a path through the willows and among the sycamores, a path beaten hard by boys coming down from the ranches to swim in the deep pool, and beaten hard by tramps who come wearily down from the highway in the evening to jungle-up near water. In front of the low horizontal limb of a giant sycamore there is an ash-pile made by many fires; the limb is worn smooth by men who have sat on it.

Evening of a hot day started the little wind to moving among the leaves. The shade climbed up the hills toward the top. On the sand-banks the rabbits sat as quietly as little grey, sculptured stones. And then from the direction of the state highway came the sound of footsteps on crisp sycamore leaves. The rabbits hurried noiselessly for cover. A stilted heron laboured up into the air and pounded down river. For a moment the place was lifeless, and then two men emerged from the path and came into the opening by the green pool. They had walked in single file down the path, and even in the open one stayed behind the other. Both were dressed in denim trousers and in denim coats with brass buttons. Both wore black, shapeless hats and both carried tight blanket rolls slung over their shoulders. The first man was small and quick, dark of face, with restless eyes and sharp, strong features. Every part of him was defined: small, strong hands, slender arms, a thin and bony nose. Behind him walked his opposite, a huge man, shapeless of face, with large, pale eyes, with wide, sloping shoulders; and he walked heavily, dragging his feet a little, the way a bear drags his paws. His arms did not swing at his sides, but hung loosely and only moved because the heavy hands were pendula.

The first man stopped short in the clearing, and the follower nearly ran over him. He took off his hat and wiped the sweat-band with his forefinger and snapped the moisture off. His huge companion dropped his blankets and flung himself down and drank from the surface of the green pool; drank with long gulps, snorting into the water like a horse. The small man stepped nervously beside him.

'Lennie!' he said sharply. 'Lennie, for God's sakes don't drink so much.' Lennie continued to snort into the pool. The small man leaned over and shook him by the shoulder. 'Lennie. You gonna be sick like you was last night.'

Lennie dipped his whole head under, hat and all, and then he sat up on the bank and his hat dripped down on his blue coat and ran down his back. 'Tha's good,' he said. 'You drink some, George. You take a good big drink.' He smiled happily.

George unslung his bundle and dropped it gently on the bank. 'I ain't sure it's good water,' he said. 'Looks kinda scummy.'

Lennie dabbled his big paw in the water and wiggled his fingers so the water arose in little splashes; rings widened across the pool to the other side and came back again. Lennie watched them go. 'Look, George. Look what I done.'

George knelt beside the pool and drank from his hand with quick scoops. 'Tastes all right,' he admitted. 'Don't really seem to be running, though. You never oughta drink water when it ain't running, Lennie,' he said hopelessly. 'You'd drink out of a gutter if you was thirsty.' He threw a scoop of water into his face and rubbed it about with his hand, under his chin and around the back of his neck. Then he replaced his hat, pushed himself back from the river, drew up his knees and embraced them. Lennie, who had been watching, imitated George exactly. He pushed himself back, drew up his knees, embraced them, looked over to George to see whether he had it just right. He pulled his hat down a little more over his eyes, the way George's hat was.

George stared morosely at the water. The rims of his eyes were red with sun glare. He said angrily: 'We could just as well of rode clear to the ranch if that bastard bus-driver knew what he was talkin' about. "Jes' a little stretch down the highway," he says. "Jes' a little stretch." God damn near four miles, that's what it was! Didn't wanta stop at the ranch gate, that's what. Too God damn lazy to pull up. Wonder he isn't too damn good to stop in Soledad at all. Kicks us out and says: "Jes' a little stretch down the road." I bet it was *more* than four miles. Damn hot day.'

Lennie looked timidly over to him. 'George?'

'Yeah, what ya want?'

'Where we goin', George?'

The little man jerked down the brim of his hat and scowled over at Lennie. 'So you forgot that awready, did you? I gotta tell you again, do I? Jesus Christ, you're a crazy bastard!'

'I forgot,' Lennie said softly. 'I tried not to forget. Honest to God I did, George.'

'OK–OK. I'll tell ya again. I ain't got nothing to do. Might jus' as well spen' all my time tellin' you things and then you forget 'em, and I tell you again.'

'Tried and tried,' said Lennie, 'but it didn't do no good. I remember about the rabbits, George.'

'The hell with the rabbits. That's all you ever can remember is them rabbits. OK! Now you listen and this time you got to remember so we don't get in no trouble. You remember settin' in that gutter on Howard Street and watchin' that blackboard?'

Lennie's face broke into a delighted smile. 'Why sure, George. I remember that . . . but . . . what'd we do then? I remember some girls come by and you says . . . you says . . .'

'The hell with what I says. You remember about us goin' into Murray and Ready's, and they give us work cards and bus tickets?'

'Oh, sure, George. I remember that now.' His hands went quickly into his side coat pockets. He said gently: 'George . . . I ain't got mine. I musta lost it.' He looked down at the ground in despair.

'You never had none, you crazy bastard. I got both of 'em here. Think I'd let you carry your own work card?'

Lennie grinned with relief. 'I . . . I thought I put it in my side pocket.' His hand went into the pocket again.

George looked sharply at him. 'What'd you take outa that pocket?'

'Ain't a thing in my pocket,' Lennie said cleverly.

'I know there ain't. You got it in your hand. What you got in your hand–hidin' it?'

'I ain't got nothin', George. Honest.'

'Come on, give it here.'

Lennie held his closed hand away from George's direction. 'It's on'y a mouse, George.'

'A mouse? A live mouse?'

'Uh-uh. Jus' a dead mouse, George. I didn't kill it. Honest! I found it. I found it dead.'

'Give it here,' said George.

'Aw, leave me have it, George.'

'*Give it here!*'

Lennie's closed hand slowly obeyed. George took the mouse and threw it across the pool to the other side, among the brush. 'What you want of a dead mouse, anyways?'

'I could pet it with my thumb while we walked along,' said Lennie.

'Well, you ain't petting no mice while you walk with me. You remember where we're goin' now?'

Lennie looked startled and then in embarrassment hid his face against his knees. 'I forgot again.'

'Jesus Christ,' George said resignedly. 'Well–look, we're gonna work on a ranch like the one we come from up north.'

'Up north?'

'In Weed.'

'Oh, sure. I remember. In Weed.'

'That ranch we're goin' to is right down there about a quarter-mile. We're gonna go in an' see the boss. Now, look–I'll give him the work tickets, but you ain't gonna say a word. You jus' stand there and don't say nothing. If he finds out what a crazy bastard you are, we won't get no job, but if he sees ya work before he hears ya talk, we're set. Ya got that?'

'Sure, George. Sure I got it.'

'OK. Now when we go in to see the boss, what you gonna do?'

'I . . . I,' Lennie thought. His face grew tight with thought. 'I . . . ain't gonna say nothin'. Jus gonna stan' there.'

'Good boy. That's swell. You say that over two, three times so you won't forget it.'

Lennie droned to himself softly: 'I ain't gonna say nothin' . . . I ain't gonna say nothin' . . . I ain't gonna say nothin'.'

'OK,' said George. 'An' you ain't gonna do no bad things like you done in Weed, neither.'

Lennie looked puzzled. 'Like I done in Weed?'

'Oh, so ya forgot that too, did ya? Well, I ain't gonna remind ya, fear ya do it again.'

A light of understanding broke on Lennie's face. 'They run us outa Weed,' he exploded triumphantly.

'Run us out, hell,' said George disgustedly. 'We run. They was lookin' for us, but they didn't catch us.'

Lennie giggled happily. 'I didn't forget that, you bet.'

George lay back on the sand and crossed his hands under his head, and Lennie imitated him, raising his head to see whether he were doing it right. 'God, you're a lot of trouble,' said George. 'I could get along so easy and so nice if I didn't have you on my tail. I could live so easy and maybe have a girl.'

For a moment Lennie lay quiet, and then he said hopefully: 'We gonna work on a ranch, George.'

'Awright. You got that. But we're gonna sleep here because I got a reason.'

The day was going fast now. Only the tops of the Gabilan mountains flamed with the light of the sun that had gone from the valley. A water-snake slipped along the pool, its head held up like a little periscope. The reeds jerked slightly in the current. Far off toward the highway a man shouted something, and another man shouted back. The sycamore limbs rustled under a little wind that died immediately.

'George–why ain't we goin' on to the ranch and get some supper? They got supper at the ranch.'

George rolled on his side. 'No reason at all for you. I like it here. To-morra we're gonna go to work. I seen thrashin' machines on the way down. That means we'll be bucking grain-bags, bustin' a gut. Tonight I'm gonna lay right here and look up. I like it.'

Lennie got up on his knees and looked down at George. 'Ain't we gonna have no supper?'

'Sure we are, if you gather up some dead willow sticks. I got three cans of beans in my bundle. You get a fire ready. I'll give you a match when you get the sticks together. Then we'll heat the beans and have supper.'

Lennie said: 'I like beans with ketchup.'

'Well, we ain't got no ketchup. You go get wood. An' don't you fool around. It'll be dark before long.'

Lennie lumbered to his feet and disappeared in the brush. George lay where he was and whistled softly to himself. There were sounds of splashings down the river in the direction Lennie had taken. George stopped whistling and listened. 'Poor bastard,' he said softly, and then went on whistling again.

In a moment Lennie came crashing back through the brush. He carried one small willow stick in his hand. George sat up. 'Aw right,' he said brusquely. 'Gi'me that mouse!'

But Lennie made an elaborate pantomime of innocence. 'What mouse, George? I ain't got no mouse.'

George held out his hand. 'Come on. Give it to me. You ain't puttin' nothing over.'

Lennie hesitated, backed away, looked wildly at the brush line as though he contemplated running for his freedom. George said coldly: 'You gonna give me that mouse or do I have to sock you?'

'Give you what, George?'

'You know God damn well what. I want that mouse.'

Lennie reluctantly reached into his pocket. His voice broke a little. 'I don't know why I can't keep it. It ain't nobody's mouse. I didn't steal it. I found it lyin' right beside the road.'

George's hand remained outstretched imperiously. Slowly, like a terrier who doesn't want to bring a ball to its master, Lennie approached, drew back, approached again. George snapped his fingers sharply, and at the sound Lennie laid the mouse in his hand.

'I wasn't doin' nothing bad with it, George. Jus' stroking it.'

George stood up and threw the mouse as far as he could into the darkening brush, and then he stepped to the pool and washed his hands. 'You crazy fool. Don't you think I could see your feet was wet where you went across the river to get it?' He heard Lennie's whimpering cry and wheeled about. 'Blubberin' like a baby? Jesus Christ! A big guy like you.' Lennie's lip quivered and tears started in his eyes. 'Aw, Lennie!' George put his hand on Lennie's shoulder. 'I ain't takin' it away jus' for meanness. That mouse ain't fresh, Lennie; and besides, you've broke it pettin' it. You get another mouse that's fresh and I'll let you keep it a little while.'

Lennie sat down on the ground and hung his head dejectedly. 'I don't know where there is no other mouse. I remember a lady used to give 'em to me–ever' one she got. But that lady ain't here.'

George scoffed. 'Lady, huh? Don't even remember who that lady was. That was your own Aunt Clara. An' she stopped givin' 'em to ya. You always killed 'em.'

Lennie looked sadly up at him. 'They was so little,' he said apologetically. 'I'd pet 'em, and pretty soon they bit my fingers and I pinched their heads a little and then they was dead–because they was so little.

'I wish't we'd get the rabbits pretty soon, George. They ain't so little.'

'The hell with the rabbits. An' you ain't to be trusted with no live mice. Your Aunt Clara give you a rubber mouse and you wouldn't have nothing to do with it.'

'It wasn't no good to pet,' said Lennie.

The flame of the sunset lifted from the mountain-tops and dusk came into the valley, and a half-darkness came in among the willows and the sycamores. A big carp rose to the surface of the pool, gulped air, and then sank mysteriously into the dark water again, leaving widening rings on the water. Overhead the leaves whisked again and little puffs of willow cotton blew down and landed on the pool's surface.

'You gonna get that wood?' George demanded. 'There's plenty right up against the back of that sycamore. Floodwater wood. Now you get it.'

Lennie went behind the tree and brought out a litter of dried leaves and twigs. He threw them in a heap on the old ash-pile and went back for more and more. It was almost night now. A dove's wings whistled over the water. George walked to the fire pile and lighted the dry leaves. The flame cracked up among the twigs and fell to work. George undid his bindle and brought out three cans of beans. He stood them about the fire, close in against the blaze, but not quite touching the flame.

'There's enough beans for four men,' George said.

Lennie watched him from over the fire. He said patiently: 'I like 'em with ketchup.'

'Well, we ain't got any,' George exploded. 'Whatever we ain't got, that's what you want. God a'mighty, if I was alone I could live so easy. I could go get a job an' work, an' no trouble. No mess at all, and when the end of the month come I could take my fifty bucks and go into town and get whatever I want. Why, I could stay in a cat-house all night. I could eat any place I want, hotel or any place, and order any damn thing I could think of. An' I could do all that every damn month. Get a gallon of whisky, or set in a pool-room and play cards or shoot pool.' Lennie knelt and looked over the fire at the angry George. And Lennie's face was drawn in terror. 'An' whatta I got?' George went on furiously. 'I got you! You can't keep a job and you lose me ever' job I get. Jus' keep me shovin' all over the country all the time. An' that ain't the worst. You get in trouble. You do bad things and I got to get you out.' His voice rose nearly to a shout. 'You crazy son-of-a-bitch. You keep me in hot water all the time.' He took on the elaborate manner of little girls when they are mimicking one another. 'Jus' wanted to feel that girl's dress–jus' wanted to pet it like it was a mouse . . . Well, how the hell did she know you jus' wanted to feel her dress? She jerks back and you hold on like it was a mouse. She yells and we got to hide in a irrigation ditch all day with guys lookin' for us, and we got to sneak out in the dark and get outta the country. All the time somethin' like that–all the time. I wisht I could put you in a cage with about a million mice and let you have fun.' His anger left him suddenly. He looked across the fire at Lennie's anguished face, and then he looked ashamedly at the flames.

It was quite dark now, but the fire lighted the trunks of the trees and the curving branches overhead. Lennie crawled slowly and cautiously around the fire until he was close to George. He sat back on his heels. George turned the bean-cans so that another side faced the fire. He pretended to be unaware of Lennie so close beside him.

'George,' very softly. No answer. 'George!'

'Whatta you want?'

'I was only foolin', George. I don't want no ketchup. I wouldn't eat no ketchup if it was right here beside me.'

'If it was here, you could have some.'

'But I wouldn't eat none, George. I'd leave it all for you. You could cover your beans with it and I wouldn't touch none of it.'

George still stared morosely at the fire. 'When I think of the swell time I could have without you, I go nuts. I never get no peace.'

Lennie still knelt. He looked off into the darkness across the river. 'George, you want I should go away and leave you alone?'

'Where the hell could you go?'

'Well I could. I could go off into the hills there. Some place I'd find a cave.'

'Yeah? How'd you eat. You ain't got sense enough to find nothing to eat.'

'I'd find things, George. I don't need no nice food with ketchup. I'd lay out in the sun and nobody'd hurt me. An' if I foun' a mouse, I could keep it. Nobody'd take it away from me.'

George looked quickly and searchingly at him. 'I been mean, ain't I?'

'If you don' want me I can go off in the hills an' find a cave. I can go away any time.'

'No–look! I was jus' foolin', Lennie. Course I want you to stay with me. Trouble with mice is you always kill 'em.' He paused. 'Tell you what I'll do, Lennie. First chance I get I'll give you a pup. Maybe you wouldn't kill *it*. That'd be better than mice. And you could pet it harder.'

Lennie avoided the bait. He had sensed his advantage. 'If you don't want me, you only jus' got to say so, and I'll go off in those hills right there–right up in those hills and live by myself. An' I won't get no mice stole from me.'

George said: 'I want you to stay with me, Lennie. Jesus Christ, somebody'd shoot you for a coyote if you was by yourself. No, You stay with me. Your Aunt Clara wouldn't like you running off by yourself, even if she is dead.'

Lennie spoke craftily: 'Tell me–like you done before.'

'Tell you what?'

'About the rabbits.'

George snapped: 'You ain't gonna put nothing over on me.'

Lennie pleaded: 'Come on, George. Tell me. Please, George. Like you done before.'

'You get a kick outta that, don't you. A'right, I'll tell you, and then we'll eat our supper . . .'

George's voice became deeper. He repeated his words rhythmically as though he had said them many times before. 'Guys like us, that work on ranches, are the loneliest guys in the world. They got no family. They don't belong no place. They come to a ranch an' work up a stake and then they go inta town and blow their stake, and the first thing you know they're poundin' their tail on some other ranch. They ain't got nothing to look ahead to.'

Lennie was delighted. 'That's it–that's it. Now tell how it is with us.'

George went on. 'With us it ain't like that. We got a future. We got somebody to talk to that gives a damn about us. We don't have to sit in no barroom blowin' in our jack jus' because we got no place else to go. If them other guys gets in jail they can rot for all anybody gives a damn. But not us.'

Lennie broke in. '*But not us! An' why? Because . . . because I got you to look after me, and you got me to look after you, and that's why.*' He laughed delightedly. 'Go on now, George.'

'You got it by heart. You can do it yourself.'

'No, you. I forget some a' the things. Tell about how it's gonna be.'

'OK. Some day–we're gonna get the jack together and we're gonna have a little house and a couple of acres an' a cow and some pigs and . . .'

'*An' live off the fatta the lan*',' Lennie shouted. 'An' have *rabbits*. Go on, George! Tell about what we're gonna have in the garden and about the rabbits in the cages and about the rain in the winter and the stove, and how thick the cream is on the milk like you can hardly cut it. Tell about that, George.'

'Why'n't you do it yourself. You know all of it.'

'No . . . you tell it. It ain't the same if I tell it. Go on . . . George. How I get to tend the rabbits.'

'Well,' said George. 'We'll have a big vegetable patch and a rabbit-hutch and chickens. And when it rains in the winter, we'll just say the hell with goin' to work, and we'll build up a fire in the stove and set around it an' listen to the rain comin' down on the roof–Nuts!' He took out his pocket-knife. 'I ain't got time for no more.' He drove his knife through the top of one of the bean-cans, sawed out the top, and passed the can to Lennie. Then he opened a second can. From his side pocket he brought out two spoons and passed one of them to Lennie.

They sat by the fire and filled their mouths with beans and chewed mightily. A few beans slipped out of the side of Lennie's mouth. George gestured with his spoon. 'What you gonna say tomorrow when the boss asks you questions?'

Lennie stopped chewing and swallowed. His face was concentrated. 'I . . . I ain't gonna . . . say a word.'

'Good boy! That's fine, Lennie! Maybe you're gettin' better. When we get the coupla acres I can let you tend the rabbits all right. 'Specially if you remember as good as that.'

Lennie choked with pride. 'I can remember,' he said.

George motioned with his spoon again.

'Look, Lennie. I want you to look around here. You can remember this place, can't you? The ranch is about a quarter-mile up that way. Just follow the river.'

'Sure,' said Lennie. 'I can remember this. Di'n't I remember about not gonna say a word?'

''Course you did. Well, look. Lennie–if you jus' happen to get in trouble like you always done before, I want you to come right here an' hide in the brush.'

'Hide in the brush,' said Lennie slowly.

'Hide in the brush till I come for you. Can you remember that?'

'Sure I can, George. Hide in the brush till you come.'

'But you ain't gonna get in no trouble, because if you do, I won't let you tend the rabbits.' He threw his empty bean-can off into the brush.

'I won't get in no trouble, George. I ain't gonna say a word.'

'OK. Bring your bundle over here by the fire. It's gonna be nice sleepin' here. Lookin' up, and the leaves. Don't build up no more fire. We'll let her die down.'

They made their beds on the sand, and as the blaze dropped from the fire the sphere of light grew smaller; the curling branches disappeared and only a faint glimmer showed where the tree-trunks were. From the darkness Lennie called: 'George–you asleep?'

'No. Whatta you want?'

'Let's have different colour rabbits, George.'

'Sure we will,' George said sleepily. 'Red and blue and green rabbits, Lennie. Millions of 'em.'

'Furry ones, George, like I seen in the fair in Sacramento.'

'Sure, furry ones.'

''Cause I can jus' as well go away, George, an' live in a cave.'

'You can jus' as well go to hell,' said George. 'Shut up now.'

The red light dimmed on the coals. Up the hill from the river a coyote yammered, and a dog answered from the other side of the stream. The sycamore leaves whispered in a little night breeze.

The bunk-house was a long, rectangular building. Inside, the walls were white-washed and the floor unpainted. In three walls there were small, square windows, and, in the fourth, a solid door with a wooden latch. Against the walls were eight bunks, five of them made up with blankets and the other three showing their burlap ticking. Over each bunk there was nailed an apple-box with the opening forward so that it made two shelves for the personal belongings of the occupant of the bunk. And these shelves were loaded with little articles, soap and talcum-powder, razors and those Western magazines ranch-men love to read and scoff at and secretly believe. And there were medicines on the shelves, and little vials, combs; and from nails on the box sides, a few neckties. Near one wall there was a black cast-iron stove, its stove-pipe going straight up through the ceiling. In the middle of the room stood a big square table littered with playing-cards, and around it were grouped boxes for the players to sit on.

At about ten o'clock in the morning the sun threw a bright dust-laden bar through one of the side windows, and in and out of the beam flies shot like rushing stars.

The wooden latch raised. The door opened and a tall, stoop-shouldered old man came in. He was dressed in blue jeans and he carried a big push-broom in his left hand. Behind him came George, and behind George, Lennie.

'The boss was expectin' you last night,' the old man said. 'He was sore as hell when you wasn't here to go out this morning.' He pointed with his right arm, and out of the sleeve came a round stick-like wrist, but no hand. 'You can have them two beds there,' he said, indicating two bunks near the stove.

George stepped over and threw his blankets down on the burlap sack of straw that was a mattress. He looked into the box shelf and then picked a small yellow can from it. 'Say. What the hell's this?'

'I don't know,' said the old man.

'Says "positively kills lice, roaches, and other scourges". What the hell kind of bed you giving us, anyways? We don't want no pants rabbits.'

The old swamper shifted his broom and held it between his elbow and his side while he held out his hand for the can. He studied the label carefully. 'Tell you what . . .' he said finally, 'last guy that had this bed was a blacksmith–hell of a nice fella and as clean a guy as you want to meet. Used to wash his hands even *after* he ate.'

'Then how come he got grey-backs?' George was working up a slow anger. Lennie put his bundle on the neighbouring bunk and sat down. He watched George with open mouth. 'Tell you what,' said the old swamper. 'This here blacksmith–name of Whitey–was the kind of guy that would put that stuff around even if there wasn't no bugs–just to make sure, see? Tell you what he used to do . . . At meals he'd peel his boil' potatoes, an' he'd take out ever' little spot, no matter what kind, before he'd eat it. And if there was a red splotch on an egg, he'd scrape it off. Finally quit about the food. That's the kinda guy he was–clean. Used ta dress up Sundays even when he wasn't going no place, put on a necktie even, and then set in the bunk-house.'

'I ain't so sure,' said George sceptically. 'What did you say he quit for?'

The old man put the yellow can in his pocket, and he rubbed his bristly white whiskers with his knuckles. 'Why . . . he . . . just quit, the way a guy will. Says it was the food. Just wanted to move. Didn't give no other reason but the food. Just says "gimme my time" one night, the way any guy would.'

George lifted his tick and looked underneath it. He leaned over and inspected the sacking closely. Immediately Lennie got up and did the same with his bed. Finally George seemed satisfied. He unrolled his bindle and put things on the shelf, his razor and bar of soap, his comb and bottle of pills, his liniment and leather wrist-band. Then he made his bed up neatly with blankets. The old man said: 'I guess the boss'll be out here in a minute. He was sure burned when you wasn't here this morning. Come right in when we was eatin' breakfast and says: "Where the hell's them new men?" An' he gave the stable buck hell, too.'

George patted a wrinkle out of his bed, and then sat down. 'Give the stable buck hell?' he asked.

'Sure. Ya see the stable buck's a nigger.'

'Nigger, huh?'

'Yeah, Nice fella, too. Got a crooked back where a horse kicked him. The boss gives him hell when he's mad. But the stable buck don't give a damn about that. He reads a lot. Got books in his room.'

'What kind of a guy is the boss?' George asked.

'Well, he's a pretty nice fella. Gets pretty mad sometimes, but he's pretty nice. Tell ya what–know what he done Christmas? Brang a gallon of whisky right in here and says: "Drink hearty, boys. Christmas comes but once a year."'

'The hell he did! Whole gallon?'

'Yes, sir. Jesus, we had fun. They let the nigger come in that night. Little skinner name of Smitty took after the nigger. Done pretty good, too. The guys wouldn't let him use his feet, so the nigger got him. If he coulda used his feet, Smitty says he woulda killed the nigger. The guys said on account of the nigger's got a crooked back, Smitty can't use his feet.' He paused in relish of the memory. 'After that the guys went into Soledad and raised hell. I didn't go in there. I ain't got the poop no more.'

Lennie was just finishing making his bed. The wooden latch raised again and the door opened. A little stocky man stood in the open doorway. He wore blue jean trousers, a flannel shirt, a black, unbuttoned vest, and a black coat. His thumbs were stuck in his belt, on each side of a square steel buckle. On his head was a soiled brown Stetson hat, and he wore high-heeled boots and spurs to prove he was not a labouring man.

The old swamper looked quickly at him, and then shuffled to the door rubbing his whiskers with his knuckles as he went. 'Them guys just come,' he said, and shuffled past the boss and out the door.

The boss stepped into the room with the short, quick steps of a fat-legged man. 'I wrote Murray and Ready I wanted two men this morning. You got your work slips?' George reached into his pocket and produced the slips and handed them to the boss. 'It wasn't Murray and Ready's fault. Says right here on the slip that you was to be here for work this morning.'

George looked down at his feet. 'Bus-driver give us a bum steer,' he said. 'We hadda walk ten miles. Says we was here when we wasn't. We couldn't get no rides in the morning.'

The boss squinted his eyes. 'Well, I had to send out the grain teams short two buckers. Won't do any good to go out now till after dinner.' He pulled his time-book out of his pocket and opened it where a pencil was stuck between the leaves. George scowled meaningfully at Lennie, and Lennie nodded to show that he understood. The boss licked his pencil. 'What's your name?'

'George Milton.'

'And what's yours?'

George said: 'His name's Lennie Small.'

The names were entered in the book. 'Le's see, this is the twentieth, noon the twentieth.' He closed the book. 'Where you boys been working?'

'Up around Weed,' said George.

'You, too?' to Lennie.

'Yeah, him too,' said George.

The boss pointed a playful finger at Lennie. 'He ain't much of a talker, is he?'

'No, he ain't, but he's sure a hell of a good worker. Strong as a bull.'

Lennie smiled to himself. 'Strong as a bull,' he repeated.

George scowled at him, and Lennie dropped his head in shame at having forgotten.

The boss said suddenly: 'Listen, Small!' Lennie raised his head. 'What can you do?'

In a panic, Lennie looked at George for help. 'He can do anything you tell him,' said George. 'He's a good skinner. He can rassel grain-bags, drive a cultivator. He can do anything. Just give him a try.'

The boss turned to George. 'Then why don't you let him answer? Why you trying to put over?'

George broke in loudly: 'Oh! I ain't saying he's bright. He ain't. But I say he's a God damn good worker. He can put up a four-hundred-pound bale.'

The boss deliberately put the little book in his pocket. He hooked his thumbs in his belt and squinted one eye nearly closed. 'Say–what you sellin'?'

'Huh?'

'I said what stake you got in this guy? You takin' his pay away from him?'

'No, 'course I ain't. Why ya think I'm sellin' him out?'

'Well, I never seen one guy take so much trouble for another guy. I just like to know what your interest is.'

George said: 'He's my . . . cousin. I told his old lady I'd take care of him. He got kicked in the head by a horse when he was a kid. He's awright. Just ain't bright. But he can do anything you tell him.'

The boss turned half away. 'Well, God knows he don't need any brains to buck barley bags. But don't you try to put nothing over, Milton, I got my eye on you. Why'd you quit in Weed?'

'Job was done,' said George promptly.

'What kinda job?'

'We . . . we was diggin' a cesspool.'

'All right. But don't try to put nothing over, 'cause you can't get away with nothing. I seen wise guys before. Go on out with the grain teams after dinner. They're pickin' up barley at the threshing machine. Go out with Slim's team.'

'Slim?'

'Yeah. Big tall skinner. You'll see him at dinner.' He turned abruptly and went to the door, but before he went out he turned and looked for a long moment at the two men.

When the sound of his footsteps had died away, George turned on Lennie. 'So you wasn't gonna say a word. You was gonna leave your big flapper shut and leave me do the talkin'. Damn near lost us the job.'

Lennie stared helplessly at his hands. 'I forgot, George.'

'Yeah, you forgot. You always forget, an' I got to talk you out of it.' He sat down heavily on the bunk.

'Now he's got his eye on us. Now we got to be careful and not make no slips. You keep your big flapper shut after this.' He fell morosely silent.

'George.'

'What you want now?'

'I wasn't kicked in the head with no horse, was I, George?'

'Be a damn good thing if you was,' George said viciously. 'Save ever'body a hell of a lot of trouble.'

'You said I was your cousin, George.'

'Well, that was a lie. An' I'm damn glad it was. If I was a relative of yours I'd shoot myself.' He stopped suddenly, stepped to the open front door and peered out. 'Say, what the hell you doin' listenin'?'

The old man came slowly into the room. He had his broom in his hand. And at his heels there walked a drag-footed sheep-dog, grey of muzzle, and with pale, blind old eyes. The dog struggled lamely to the side of the room and lay down, grunting softly to himself and licking his grizzled, moth-eaten coat. The swamper watched him until he was settled. 'I wasn't listenin'. I was jus' standin' in the shade a minute scratchin' my dog. I jus' now finished swampin' out the wash-house.'

'You was pokin' your big ears into our business,' George said. 'I don't like nobody to get nosey.'

The old man looked uneasily from George to Lennie, and then back. 'I jus' come there,' he said. 'I didn't hear nothing you guys was sayin'. I ain't interested in nothing you was sayin'. A guy on a ranch don't never listen nor he don't ast no questions.'

'Damn right he don't,' said George, slightly mollified, 'not if he wants to stay workin' long.' But he was reassured by the swamper's defence. 'Come on in and set down a minute,' he said. 'That's a hell of an old dog.'

'Yeah. I had 'im ever since he was a pup. God, he was a good sheep-dog when he was younger.' He stood his broom against the wall and he rubbed his white bristled cheek with his knuckles. 'How'd you like the boss?' he asked.

'Pretty good. Seemed awright.'

'He's a nice fella,' the swamper agreed. 'You got to take him right.'

At that moment a young man came into the bunk-house; a thin young man with a brown face, with brown eyes and a head of tightly curled hair. He wore a work glove on his left hand, and, like the boss, he wore high-heeled boots. 'Seen my old man?' he asked.

The swamper said: 'He was here jus' a minute ago, Curley. Went over to the cook-house, I think.'

'I'll try to catch him,' said Curley. His eyes passed over the new men and he stopped. He glanced coldly at George and then at Lennie. His arms gradually bent at the elbows and his hands closed into fists. He stiffened and went into a slight crouch. His glance was at once calculating and pugnacious. Lennie squirmed under the look and shifted his feet nervously. Curley stepped gingerly close to him. 'You the new guys the old man was waitin' for?'

'We just come in,' said George.

'Let the big guy talk.'

Lennie twisted with embarrassment.

George said: 'S'pose he don't want to talk?'

Curley lashed his body around. 'By Christ, he's gotta talk when he's spoke to. What the hell are you gettin' into it for?'

'We travel together,' said George coldly.

'Oh, so it's that way.'

George was tense and motionless. 'Yeah, it's that way.'

Lennie was looking helplessly to George for instruction.

'An' you won't let the big guy talk, is that it?'

'He can talk if he wants to tell you anything.' He nodded slightly to Lennie.

'We jus' come in,' said Lennie softly.

Curley stared levelly at him. 'Well, nex' time you answer when you're spoke to.' He turned towards the door and walked out, and his elbows were still bent out a little.

George watched him out, and then he turned back to the swamper. 'Say, what the hell's he got on his shoulder? Lennie didn't do nothing to him.'

The old man looked cautiously at the door to make sure no one was listening. 'That's the boss's son,' he said quietly. 'Curley's pretty handy. He done quite a bit in the ring. He's a lightweight, and he's handy.'

'Well, let him be handy,' said George. 'He don't have to take after Lennie.

Lennie didn't do nothing to him. What's he got against Lennie?'

The swamper considered:'–Well–tell you what. Curley's like a lot of little guys. He hates big guys. He's alla time picking scraps with big guys. Kind of like he's mad at 'em because he ain't a big guy. You seen little guys like that, ain't you? Always scrappy?'

'Sure,' said George. 'I seen plenty tough little guys. But this Curley better not make no mistakes about Lennie. Lennie ain't handy, but this Curley punk is gonna get hurt if he messes around with Lennie.'

'Well, Curley's pretty handy,' the swamper said sceptically. 'Never did seem right to me. S'pose Curley jumps a big guy an' licks him. Ever'body says what a game guy Curley is. And s'pose he does the same thing and gets licked. Then ever'body says the big guy oughtta pick somebody his own size, and maybe they gang up on the big guy. Never did seem right to me. Seems like Curley ain't givin' nobody a chance.'

George was watching the door. He said ominously: 'Well, he better watch out for Lennie. Lennie ain't no fighter, but Lennie's strong and quick and Lennie don't know no rules.' He walked to the square table and sat down on one of the boxes. He gathered some of the cards together and shuffled them.

The old man sat down on another box. 'Don't tell Curley I said none of this. He'd slough me. He just don't give a damn. Won't ever get canned 'cause his old man's the boss.'

George cut the cards and began turning them over, looking at each one and throwing it down on a pile. He said: 'This guy Curley sounds like a son-of-a-bitch to me. I don't like mean little guys.'

'Seems to me like he's worse lately,' said the swamper. 'He got married a couple of weeks ago. Wife lives over in the boss's house. Seems like Curley is cockier'n ever since he got married.'

George grunted: 'Maybe he's showin' off for his wife.'

The swamper warmed to his gossip. 'You seen that glove on his left hand.'

'Yeah. I seen it.'

'Well, that glove's fulla vaseline.'

'Vaseline? What the hell for?'

'Well, I tell ya what, Curley says he's keepin' that hand soft for his wife.'

George studied the cards absorbedly. 'That's a dirty thing to tell around,' he said.

The old man was reassured. He had drawn a derogatory statement from George. He felt safe now, and he spoke more confidently. 'Wait'll you see Curley's wife.'

George cut the cards again and put out a solitaire lay, slowly and deliberately. 'Purty?' he asked casually.

'Yeah. Purty . . . but . . .'

George studied his cards. 'But what?'

'Well–she got the eye.'

'Yeah? Married two weeks and got the eye? Maybe that's why Curley's pants is full of ants.'

'I seen her give Slim the eye. Slim's a jerkline skinner. Hell of a nice fella. Slim don't need to wear no high-heeled boots on a grain team. I seen her give Slim the eye. Curley never seen it. An' I seen her give Carlson the eye.'

George pretended a lack of interest. 'Looks like we was gonna have fun.'

The swamper stood up from his box. 'Know what I think?' George did not answer. 'Well, I think Curley's married . . . a tart.'

'He ain't the first,' said George. 'There's plenty done that.'

The old man moved toward the door, and his ancient dog lifted his head and peered about, and then got painfully to his feet to follow. 'I gotta be settin' out the washbasins for the guys. The teams'll be in before long. You guys gonna buck barley?'

'Yeah.'

'You won't tell Curley nothing I said?'

'Hell, no.'

'Well, you look her over, mister. You see if she ain't a tart.' He stepped out the door into the brilliant sunshine.

George laid down his cards thoughtfully, turned his piles of three. He built four clubs on his ace pile. The sun square was on the floor now, and the flies whipped through it like sparks. A sound of jingling harness and the croak of heavy-laden axles sounded from outside. From the distance came a clear call. 'Stable Buck–ooh, sta-able Buck!' And then: 'Where the hell is that God damn nigger?'

George stared at his solitaire lay, and then he flounced the cards together and turned around to Lennie. Lennie was lying down on the bunk watching him.

'Look, Lennie! This here ain't no set-up. I'm scared. You gonna have trouble with that Curley guy. I seen that kind before. He was kinda feelin' you out. He figures he's got you scared and he's gonna take a sock at you the first chance he gets.'

Lennie's eyes were frightened. 'I don't want no trouble,' he said plaintively. 'Don't let him sock me, George.'

George got up and went over to Lennie's bunk and sat down on it. 'I hate that kinda bastard,' he said. 'I seen plenty of 'em. Like the old guy says, Curley don't take no chances. He always wins.' He thought for a moment. 'If he tangles with you, Lennie, we're gonna get the can. Don't make no mistake about that. He's the boss's son. Look, Lennie. You try to keep away from him, will you? Don't never speak to him. If he comes in here you move clear to the other side of the room. Will you do that, Lennie?'

'I don't want no trouble,' Lennie mourned. 'I never done nothing to him.'

'Well, that won't do you no good if Curley wants to plug himself up for a fighter. Just don't have nothing to do with him. Will you remember?'

'Sure, George. I ain't gonna say a word.'

The sound of the approaching grain teams was louder, thud of big hooves on hard ground, drag of brakes, and the jingle of trace chains. Men were calling back and forth from the teams. George, sitting on the bunk beside Lennie, frowned as he thought. Lennie asked timidly: 'You ain't mad, George?'

'I ain't mad at you. I'm mad at this here Curley bastard. I hoped we was gonna get a little stake together–maybe a hundred dollars.' His tone grew decisive. 'You keep away from Curley, Lennie.'

'Sure I will, George. I won't say a word.'

'Don't let him pull you in–but–if the son-of-a-bitch socks you–let 'im have it.'

'Let 'im have what, George?'

'Never mind, never mind, I'll tell you when. I hate that kind of a guy. Look, Lennie, if you get in any kind of trouble, you remember what I told you to do?'

Lennie raised up his elbow. His face contorted with thought. Then his eyes moved sadly to George's face. 'If I get in any trouble, you ain't gonna let me tend the rabbits.'

'That's not what I meant. You remember where we slep' last night? Down by the river?'

'Yeah. I remember. Oh, sure I remember! I go there an' hide in the brush.'

'Hide till I come for you. Don't let nobody see you. Hide in the brush by the river. Say that over.'

'Hide in the brush by the river, down in the brush by the river.'

'If you get in trouble.'

'If I get in trouble.'

A brake screeched outside. A call came: 'Stable–Buck. Oh! Sta-able Buck.'

George said: 'Say it over to yourself, Lennie, so you won't forget it.'

Both men glanced up, for the rectangle of sunshine in the doorway was cut off. A girl was standing there looking in. She had full, rouged lips and wide-spaced eyes, heavily made up. Her finger-nails were red. Her hair hung in little rolled clusters, like sausages. She wore a cotton house dress and red mules, on the insteps of which were little bouquets of red ostrich feathers. 'I'm lookin' for Curley,' she said. Her voice had a nasal, brittle quality.

George looked away from her and then back. 'He was in here a minute ago, but he went.'

'Oh!' She put her hands behind her back and leaned against the door-frame so that her body was thrown forward. 'You're the new fellas that just come, ain't ya?'

'Yeah.'

Lennie's eyes moved down over her body, and although she did not seem to be looking at Lennie, she bridled a little. She looked at her finger-nails. 'Sometimes Curley's in here,' she explained.

George said brusquely: 'Well, he ain't now.'

'If he ain't, I guess I better look some place else,' she said playfully.

Lennie watched her, fascinated. George said: 'If I see him, I'll pass the word you was looking for him.'

She smiled archly and twitched her body. 'Nobody can't blame a person for lookin',' she said. There were footsteps behind her, going by. She turned her head. 'Hi, Slim,' she said.

Slim's voice came through the door. 'Hi, Good-lookin'.'

'I'm tryin' to find Curley, Slim.'

'Well, you ain't tryin' very hard. I seen him goin' in your house.'

She was suddenly apprehensive. ''Bye, boys,' she called into the bunk-house, and she hurried away.

George looked around at Lennie. 'Jesus, what a tramp,' he said. 'So that's what Curley picks for a wife.'

'She's purty,' said Lennie defensively.

'Yeah, and she's sure hidin' it. Curley got his work ahead of him. Bet she'd clear out for twenty bucks.'

Lennie still stared at the doorway where she had been. 'Gosh, she was purty.' He smiled admiringly. George looked quickly down at him and then he took him by an ear and shook him.

'Listen to me, you crazy bastard,' he said fiercely. 'Don't you even take a look at that bitch. I don't care what she says and what she does. I seen 'em poison before, but I never seen no piece of jail bait worse than her. You leave her be.'

Lennie tried to disengage his ear. 'I never done nothing, George.'

'No, you never. But when she was standin' in the doorway showin' her legs, you wasn't lookin' the other way, neither.'

'I never meant no harm, George. Honest I never.'

'Well, you keep away from her, 'cause she's a rat-trap if I ever seen one. You let Curley take the rap. He let himself in for it. Glove fulla vaseline,' George said disgustedly. 'An I bet he's eatin' raw eggs and writin' to the patent medicine houses.'

Lennie cried out suddenly: 'I don' like this place, George. This ain't no good place. I wanna get outa here.'

'We gotta keep it till we get a stake. We can't help it, Lennie. We'll get out jus' as soon as we can. I don't like it no better than you do.' He went back to the table and set out a new solitaire hand. 'No, I don't like it,' he said. 'For two bits I'd shove out of here. If we can get jus' a few dollars in the poke we'll shove off and go up the American River and pan gold. We can make maybe a couple of dollars a day there, and we might hit a pocket.'

Lennie leaned eagerly toward him. 'Le's go, George. Le's get outa here. It's mean here.'

'We gotta stay,' George said shortly. 'Shut up now. The guys'll be comin' in.'

From the wash-room near by came the sound of running water and rattling basins. George studied the cards. 'Maybe we oughtta wash up,' he said. 'But we ain't done nothing to get dirty.'

A tall man stood in the doorway. He held a crushed Stetson hat under his arm while he combed his long, black, damp hair straight back. Like the others, he wore blue jeans and a short denim jacket. When he had finished combing his hair he moved into the room, and he moved with a majesty only achieved by royalty and master craftsmen. He was a jerkline skinner, the prince of the ranch, capable of driving ten, sixteen, even twenty mules with a single line to the leaders. He was capable of killing a fly on the wheeler's butt with a bull whip without touching the mule. There was a gravity in his manner and a quiet so profound that all talk stopped when he spoke. His authority was so great that his word was taken on any subject, be it politics or love. This was Slim, the jerkline skinner. His hatchet face was ageless. He might have been thirty-five or fifty. His ear heard more than was said to him, and his slow speech had overtones not of thought, but of understanding beyond thought. His hands, large and lean, were as delicate in their action as those of a temple dancer.

He smoothed out his crushed hat, creased it in the middle and put it on. He looked kindly at the two in the bunkhouse. 'It's brighter'n a bitch outside,' he said gently. 'Can't hardly see nothing in here. You the new guys?'

'Just come,' said George.

'Gonna buck barley?'

'That's what the boss says.'

Slim sat down on a box across the table from George. He studied the solitaire hand that was upside-down to him. 'Hope you get on my team,' he said. His voice was very gentle. 'I gotta pair of punks on my team that don't know a barley bag from a blue ball. You guys ever bucked any barley?'

'Hell, yes,' said George. 'I ain't nothing to scream about, but that big bastard there can put up more grain alone than most pairs can.'

Lennie, who had been following the conversation back and forth with his eyes, smiled complacently at the compliment. Slim looked approvingly at George for having given the compliment. He leaned over the table and snapped the corner of a loose card. 'You guys travel around together?' His tone was friendly. It invited confidence without demanding it.

'Sure,' said George. 'We kinda look after each other.' He indicated Lennie with his thumb. 'He ain't bright. Hell of a good worker, though. Hell of a nice fella, but he ain't bright. I've knew him for a long time.'

Slim looked through George and beyond him. 'Ain't many guys travel around together,' he mused. 'I don't know why. Maybe ever'body in the whole damn world is scared of each other.'

'It's a lot nicer to go around with a guy you know,' said George.

A powerful, big-stomached man came into the bunkhouse. His head still dripped water from the scrubbing and dousing. 'Hi, Slim,' he said, and then stopped and stared at George and Lennie.

'These guys jus' come,' said Slim by way of introduction.

'Glad to meet ya,' the big man said. 'My name's Carlson.'

'I'm George Milton. This here's Lennie Small.'

'Glad ta meet ya,' Carlson said again. 'He ain't very small.' He chuckled softly at his joke. 'Ain't small at all,' he repeated. 'Meant to ask you, Slim–how's your bitch? I seen she wasn't under your wagon this morning.''She slang her pups last night,' said Slim. 'Nine of 'em. I drowned four of 'em right off. She couldn't feed that many.'

'Got five left, huh?'

'Yeah, five. I kept the biggest.'

'What kinda dogs you think they're gonna be?'

'I dunno,' said Slim. 'Some kinda shepherds, I guess. That's the most kind I seen around here when she was in heat.'

Carlson went on: 'Got five pups, huh. Gonna keep all of 'em?'

'I dunno. Have to keep 'em a while so they can drink Lulu's milk.'

Carlson said thoughtfully: 'Well, looka here, Slim. I been thinkin'. That dog of Candy's is so God damn old he can't hardly walk. Stinks like hell, too. Ever' time he comes into the bunk-house I can smell him for two, three days. Why'n't you get Candy to shoot his old dog and give him one of the pups to raise up. I can smell that dog a mile away. Got no teeth, damn near blind, can't eat. Candy feeds him milk. He can't chew nothing else.'

George had been staring intently at Slim. Suddenly a triangle began to ring outside, slowly at first, and then faster and faster until the beat of it disappeared into one ringing sound. It stopped as suddenly as it had started.

'There she goes,' said Carlson.

Outside, there was a burst of voices as a group of men went by.

Slim stood up slowly and with dignity. 'You guys better come on while they's still something to eat. Won't be nothing left in a couple of minutes.'

Carlson stepped back to let Slim precede him, and then the two of them went out the door.

Lennie was watching George excitedly. George rumpled his cards into a messy pile. 'Yeah!' George said, 'I heard him, Lennie. I'll ask him.'

'A brown and white one,' Lennie cried excitedly.

'Come on. Le's get dinner. I don't know whether he got a brown and white one.'

Lennie didn't move from his bunk. 'You ask him right away, George, so he won't kill no more of 'em.'

'Sure. Come on now, get up on your feet.'

Lennie rolled off his bunk and stood up, and the two of them started for the door. Just as they reached it, Curley bounced in.

'You seen a girl around here?' he demanded angrily.

George said coldly: ''Bout half an hour ago maybe.'

'Well, what the hell was she doin'?'

George stood still, watching the angry little man. He said insultingly: 'She said–she was lookin' for you.'

Curley seemed really to see George for the first time. His eyes flashed over George, took in his height, measured his reach, looked at his trim middle. 'Well, which way'd she go?' he demanded at last.

'I dunno,' said George. 'I didn' watch her go.'

Curley scowled at him, and turning, hurried out of the door.

George said: 'Ya know, Lennie, I'm scared I'm gonna tangle with that bastard myself. I hate his guts. Jesus Christ! Come on. They won't be a damn thing left to eat.'

They went out the door. The sunshine lay in a thin line under the window. From a distance there could be heard a rattle of dishes.

After a moment the ancient dog walked lamely in through the open door. He gazed about with mild, half-blind eyes. He sniffed, and then lay down and put his head between his paws. Curley popped into the doorway again and stood looking into the room. The dog raised his head, but when Curley jerked out, the grizzled head sank to the floor again.

Although there was evening brightness showing through the windows of the bunk-house, inside it was dusk. Through the open door came the thuds and occasional clangs of a horse-shoe game, and now and then the sound of voices raised in approval or derision.

Slim and George came into the darkening bunk-house together. Slim reached up over the card-table and turned on the tin-shaded electric light. Instantly the table was brilliant with light, and the cone of the shade threw its brightness straight downward, leaving the corners of the bunk-house still in dusk. Slim sat down on a box and George took his place opposite.

'It wasn't nothin,' said Slim. 'I would of had to drowned most of 'em, anyways. No need to thank me about that.'

George said: 'It wasn't much to you, maybe, but it was a hell of a lot to him. Jesus Christ, I don't know how we're gonna get him to sleep in here. He'll want to sleep right out in the barn with 'em. We'll have trouble keepin' him from getting right in the box with them pups.'

'It wasn't nothing,' Slim repeated. 'Say, you sure was right about him. Maybe he ain't bright, but I never seen such a worker. He damn near killed his partner buckin' barley. There ain't nobody can keep up with him. God Almighty, I never seen such a strong guy.'

George spoke proudly. 'Jus' tell Lennie what to do an' he'll do it if it don't take no figuring. He can't think of nothing to do himself, but he sure can take orders.'

There was a clang of horse-shoe on iron stake outside and a little cheer of voices.

Slim moved back slightly so the light was not on his face. 'Funny how you an' him string along together.' It was Slim's calm invitation to confidence.

'What's funny about it?' George demanded defensively.

'Oh, I dunno. Hardly none of the guys ever travel together. I hardly never seen two guys travel together. You know how the hands are, they just come in and get their bunk and work a month, and then they quit and go out alone.

Never seem to give a damn about nobody. It jus' seems kinda funny a cuckoo like him and a smart little guy like you travellin' together.'

'He ain't no cuckoo,' said George. 'He's dumb as hell, but he ain't crazy. An' I ain't so bright neither, or I wouldn't be buckin' barley for my fifty and found. If I was bright, if I was even a little bit smart, I'd have my own little place, an' I'd be bringin' in my own crops, 'stead of doin' all the work and not getting what comes up outa the ground.' George fell silent. He wanted to talk. Slim neither encouraged nor discouraged him. He just sat back quiet and receptive.

'It ain't so funny, him an' me goin' aroun' together,' George said at last. 'Him and me was both born in Auburn. I knowed his Aunt Clara. She took him when he was a baby and raised him up. When his Aunt Clara died, Lennie just come along with me out workin'. Got kinda used to each other after a little while.'

'Um,' said Slim.

George looked over at Slim and saw the calm, God-like eyes fastened on him. 'Funny,' said George. 'I used to have a hell of a lot of fun with 'im. Used to play jokes on 'im 'cause he was too dumb to take care of 'imself. But he was too dumb even to know he had a joke played on him. I had fun. Made me seem God damn smart alongside of him. Why, he'd do any damn thing I tol' him. If I tol' him to walk over a cliff, over he'd go. That wasn't so damn much fun after a while. He never got mad about it, neither. I've beat the hell outa him, and he couda bust every bone in my body jus' with his han's, but he never lifted a finger against me.' George's voice was taking on the tone of confession. 'Tell you what made me stop that. One day a bunch of guys was standin' around up on the Sacramento River. I was feelin' pretty smart. I turns to Lennie and says: "Jump in." An' he jumps. Couldn't swim a stroke. He damn near drowned before we could get him. An' he was so damn nice to me for pullin' him out. Clean forgot I told him to jump in. Well, I ain't done nothing like that no more.'

'He's a nice fella,' said Slim. 'Guy don't need no sense to be a nice fella. Seems to me sometimes it jus' works the other way around. Take a real smart guy and he ain't hardly ever a nice fella.'

George stacked the scattered cards and began to lay out his solitaire hand. The shoes thudded on the ground outside. At the windows the light of the evening still made the window squares bright.

'I ain't got no people,' George said. 'I seen the guys that go around on the ranches alone. That ain't no good. They don't have no fun. After a long time they get mean. They get wantin' to fight all the time.'

'Yeah, they get mean,' Slim agreed. 'They get so they don't want to talk to nobody.'

'Course Lennie's a God damn nuisance most of the time,' said George. 'But you get used to goin' around with a guy an' you can't get rid of him.'

'He ain't mean,' said Slim. 'I can see Lennie ain't a bit mean.'

'Course he ain't mean. But he gets in trouble alla time because he's so God damn dumb. Like what happened in Weed . . .' He stopped, stopped in the middle of turning over a card, He looked alarmed and peered over at Slim. 'You wouldn't tell nobody.'

'What'd he do in Weed?' Slim asked calmly.

'You wouldn't tell?–no, course you wouldn't.'

'What'd he do in Weed?' Slim asked again.

'Well, he seen this girl in a red dress. Dumb bastard like he is, he wants to touch ever'thing he likes. Just wants to feel it. So he reaches out to feel this red dress an' the girl lets out a squawk, and that gets Lennie all mixed up, and he holds on 'cause that's the only thing he can think to do. Well, this girl squawks and squawks. I was jus' a little bit off, and I heard all the yellin', so I comes running, an' by that time Lennie's so scared all he can think to do is jus' hold on. I socked him over the head with a fence picket to make him let go. He was so scairt he couldn't let go of that dress. And he's so God damn strong, you know.'

Slim's eyes were level and unwinking. He nodded very slowly. 'So what happens?'

George carefully built his line of solitaire cards. 'Well, that girl rabbits in an' tells the law she been raped. The guys in Weed start a party out to lynch Lennie. So we sit in a irrigation ditch under water all the rest of that day. Got on'y our heads sticking outa water, an' up under the grass that sticks out from the side of the ditch. An' that night we scrammed outa there.'

Slim sat in silence for a moment. 'Didn't hurt the girl none, huh?' he asked finally.

'Hell, no. He just scared her. I'd be scared too if he grabbed me. But he never hurt her. He jus' wanted to touch that red dress, like he wants to pet them pups all the time.'

'He ain't mean,' said Slim. 'I can tell a mean guy a mile off.'

'Course he ain't, and he'll do any damn thing I . . .'

Lennie came in through the door. He wore his blue denim coat over his shoulders like a cape, and he walked hunched way over.

'Hi, Lennie,' said George. 'How do you like the pup now?'

Lennie said breathlessly: 'He's brown an' white jus' like I wanted.' He went directly to his bunk and lay down and turned his face to the wall and drew up his knees.

George put down his cards very deliberately. 'Lennie,' he said sharply.

Lennie twisted his neck and looked over his shoulder.

'Huh? What you want, George?'

'I tol' you you couldn't bring that pup in here.'

'What pup, George? I ain't got no pup.'

George went quickly to him, grabbed him by the shoulder and rolled him over. He reached down and picked the tiny puppy from where Lennie had been concealing it against his stomach.

Lennie sat up quickly. 'Give 'um to me, George.'

George said: 'You get right up an' take this pup back to the nest. He's gotta sleep with his mother. You want to kill him? Just born last night an' you take him out of the nest. You take him back or I'll tell Slim not to let you have him.'

Lennie held out his hands pleadingly. 'Give 'um to me, George. I'll take 'um back. I didn't mean no harm, George. Honest I didn't. I jus' wanted to pet 'um a little.'

George handed the pup to him. 'Awright. You get him back there quick, and don't you take him out no more. You'll kill him, the first thing you know.' Lennie fairly scuttled out of the room.

Slim had not moved. His calm eyes followed Lennie out the door. 'Jesus,' he said. 'He's jes' like a kid, ain't he?'

'Sure he's jes' like a kid. There ain't no more harm in him than a kid neither, except he's so strong. I bet he won't come in here to sleep tonight. He'd sleep right alongside that box in the barn. Well–let 'im. He ain't doin' no harm out there.' It was almost dark outside now. Old Candy, the swamper, came in and went to his bunk, and behind him struggled his old dog. 'Hello, Slim. Hello, George. Didn't neither of you play horse-shoes?'

'I don't like to play ever' night,' said Slim.

Candy went on: 'Either you guys got a slug of whisky? I gotta gut ache.'

'I ain't,' said Slim. 'I'd drink it myself if I had, an' I ain't got a gut ache neither.'

'Gotta bad gut ache,' said Candy. 'Them God damn turnips give it to me. I knowed they was going to before I ever eat 'em.'

The thick-bodied Carlson came in out of the darkening yard. He walked to the other end of the bunk-house and turned on the second shaded light. 'Darker'n'hell in here,' he said. 'Jesus, how that nigger can pitch shoes.'

'He's plenty good,' said Slim.

'Damn right he is,' said Carlson. 'He don't give nobody else a chance to win . . .' He stopped and sniffed the air, and still sniffing, looked down at the old dog. 'God Awmighty that dog stinks. Get him outa here, Candy! I don't know nothing that stinks so bad as an old dog. You gotta get him out.'

Candy rolled to the edge of his bunk. He reached over and patted the ancient dog, and he apologized: 'I been around him so much I never notice how he stinks.'

'Well, I can't stand him in here,' said Carlson. 'That stink hangs around even after he's gone.' He walked over with his heavy-legged stride and looked down at the dog. 'Got no teeth,' he said. 'He's all stiff with rheumatism. He ain't no good to you, Candy. An' he ain't no good to himself. Why'n't you shoot him, Candy?'

The old man squirmed uncomfortably. 'Well–hell! I had him so long. Had him since he was a pup. I herded sheep with him.' He said proudly: 'You wouldn't think it to look at him now, but he was the best damn sheep dog I ever seen.'

George said: 'I seen a guy in Weed that had an Airedale could herd sheep. Learned it from the other dogs.'

Carlson was not to be put off. 'Look, Candy. This ol' dog jus' suffers hisself all the time. If you was to take him out and shoot him right in the back of the head'–he leaned over and pointed–'right there, why he'd never know what hit him.'

Candy looked about unhappily. 'No,' he said softly. 'No, I couldn't do that. I had 'im too long.'

'He don't have no fun,' Carlson insisted. 'And he stinks to beat hell. Tell you what. I'll shoot him for you. Then it won't be you what does it.'

Candy threw his legs off his bunk. He scratched the white stubble whiskers on his cheek nervously. 'I'm so used to him,' he said softly. 'I had him from a pup.'

'Well, you ain't bein' kind to him keepin' him alive,' said Carlson. 'Look, Slim's bitch got a litter right now. I bet Slim would give you one of them pups to raise up, wouldn't you, Slim?'

The skinner had been studying the old dog with his calm eyes. 'Yeah,' he said. 'You can have a pup if you want to.' He seemed to shake himself free for speech. 'Carl's right, Candy. That dog ain't no good to himself. I wisht somebody'd shoot me if I get old an' a cripple.'

Candy looked helplessly at him, for Slim's opinions were law. 'Maybe it'd hurt him,' he suggested. 'I don't mind takin' care of him.'

Carlson said: 'The way I'd shoot him, he wouldn't feel nothing. I'd put the gun right there.' He pointed with his toe. 'Right back of the head. He wouldn't even quiver.'

Candy looked for help from face to face. It was quite dark outside now. A young labouring man came in. His sloping shoulders were bent forward and he walked heavily on his heels, as though he carried the invisible grain bag. He went to his bunk and put his head on his shelf. Then he picked a pulp magazine from his shelf and brought it to the light over the table. 'Did I show you this, Slim?' he asked.

'Show me what?'

The young man turned to the back of the magazine, put it down on the table and pointed with his finger. 'Right there, read that.' Slim bent over it. 'Go on,' said the young man. 'Read it out loud.'

'"Dear Editor:"' Slim read slowly. '"I read your mag for six years and I think it is the best on the market. I like stories by Peter Rand. I think he is a whing-ding. Give us more like the "Dark Rider". I don't write many letters. Just thought I would tell you I think your mag is the best dime's worth I ever spent."'

Slim looked up questioningly. 'What you want me to read that for?'

Whit said: 'Go on. Read the name at the bottom.'

Slim read: '"Yours for success, William Tenner."' He glanced up at Whit again. 'What you want me to read that for?'

Whit closed the magazine impressively. 'Don't you remember Bill Tenner? Worked here about three months ago.'

Slim thought . . . 'Little guy?' he asked. 'Drove a cultivator?'

'That's him,' Whit cried. 'That's the guy!'

'You think he's the guy wrote this letter?'

'I know it. Bill and me was in here one day. Bill had one of them books that just come. He was lookin' in it and he says: "I wrote a letter. Wonder if they put it in the book!" but it wasn't there. Bill says: "Maybe they're savin' it for later." An' that's just what they done. There it is.'

'Guess you're right,' said Slim. 'Got it right in the book.' George held out his hand for the magazine. 'Let's look at it?'

Whit found the place again, but he did not surrender his hold on it. He pointed out the letter with his forefinger. And then he went to his box shelf and laid the magazine carefully in. 'I wonder if Bill seen it,' he said. 'Bill and me worked in that patch of field peas. Run cultivators, both of us. Bill was a hell of a nice fella.'

During the conversation Carlson had refused to be drawn in. He continued to look down at the old dog. Candy watched him uneasily. At last Carlson said: 'If you want me to, I'll put the old devil out of his misery right now and get it over with. Ain't nothing left for him. Can't eat, can't see, can't even walk without hurtin'.'

Candy said hopefully: 'You ain't got no gun.'

'The hell I ain't. Got a Luger. It won't hurt him none at all.'

Candy said: 'Maybe tomorra. Le's wait till tomorra.'

'I don't see no reason for it,' said Carlson. He went to his bunk, pulled his bag from underneath it, and took out a Luger pistol. 'Let's get it over with,' he said. 'We can't sleep with him stinkin' around in here.' He put the pistol in his hip pocket.

Candy looked a long time at Slim to try to find some reversal. And Slim gave him none. At last Candy said softly and hopelessly: 'Awright–take 'im.' He did not look down at the dog at all. He lay back on his bunk and crossed his arms behind his head and stared at the ceiling.

From his pocket Carlson took a little leather thong. He stooped over and tied it around the dog's neck. All the men except Candy watched him. 'Come, boy. Come on, boy,' he said gently. And he said apologetically to Candy: 'He won't even feel it,' Candy did not move nor answer him. He twitched the thong. 'Come on, boy.' The old dog got slowly and stiffly to his feet and followed the gently-pulling leash.

Slim said: 'Carlson.'

'Yeah?'

'You know what to do?'

'What ya mean, Slim?'

'Take a shovel,' said Slim shortly.

'Oh, sure! I get you.' He led the dog out into the darkness.

George followed to the door and shut the door and set the latch gently in its place. Candy lay rigidly on his bed staring at the ceiling.

Slim said loudly: 'One of my lead mules got a bad hoof. Got to get some tar on it.' His voice trailed off. It was silent outside. Carlson's footsteps died away. The silence came into the room. And the silence lasted.

George chuckled: 'I bet Lennie's right out there in the barn with his pup. He won't want to come in here no more now he's got a pup.'

Slim said: 'Candy, you can have any one of them pups you want.'

Candy did not answer. The silence fell on the room again. It came out of the night and invaded the room. George said: 'Anybody like to play a little euchre?'

'I'll play out a few with you,' said Whit.

They took places opposite each other at the table under the light, but George did not shuffle the cards. He rippled the edge of the deck nervously, and the little snapping noise drew the eyes of all the men in the room, so that he stopped doing it. The silence fell on the room again. A minute passed and another minute. Candy lay still staring at the ceiling. Slim gazed at him for a moment and then looked down at his hands; he subdued one hand with the other, and held it down. There came a little gnawing sound from under the floor and all the men looked down toward it gratefully. Only Candy continued to stare at the ceiling.

'Sounds like there was a rat under there,' said George. 'We ought to get a trap down there.'

Whit broke out: 'What the hell's takin' him so long. Lay out some cards, why don't you? We ain't going to get no euchre played this way.'

George brought the cards together tightly and studied the backs of them. The silence was in the room again.

A shot sounded in the distance. The men looked quickly at the old man. Every head turned toward him.

For a moment he continued to stare at the ceiling. Then he rolled slowly over and faced the wall and lay silent.

George shuffled the cards noisily and dealt them. Whit drew a scoring board to him and set the pegs to start. Whit said: 'I guess you guys really come here to work.'

'How do ya mean?' George asked.

Whit laughed. 'Well, ya come on a Friday. You got two days to work till Sunday.'

'I don't see how you figure,' said George.

Whit laughed again. 'You do if you been around these big ranches much. Guy that wants to look over a ranch comes in Sat'day afternoon. He gets Sat'day night supper an' three meals on Sunday, and he can quit Monday mornin' after breakfast without turning his hand. But you come to work Friday noon. You got to put in a day an' a half no matter how you figure.'

George looked at him levelly. 'We're gonna stick aroun' a while,' he said. 'Me an' Lennie's gonna roll up a stake.'

The door opened quietly and the stable buck put in his head; a lean negro head, lined with pain, the eye patient. 'Mr Slim.'

Slim took his eyes from old Candy. 'Huh? Oh! Hello, Crooks. What's 'a matter?'

'You told me to warm up tar for that mule's foot. I got it warm.'

'Oh! Sure, Crooks. I'll come right out an' put it on.'

'I can do it if you want, Mr Slim.'

'No. I'll come do it myself.' He stood up.

Crooks said: 'Mr Slim.'

'Yeah.'

'That big new guy's messin' around your pups out in the barn.'

'Well, he ain't doin' no harm. I give him one of them pups.'

'Just thought I'd tell ya,' said Crooks. 'He's takin' 'em outa nest and handlin' them. That won't do them no good.'

'He won't hurt 'em,' said Slim. 'I'll come along with you now.'

George looked up. 'If that crazy bastard's foolin' around too much, jus' kick him out, Slim.'

Slim followed the stable buck out of the room.

George dealt and Whit picked up his cards and examined them. 'Seen the new kid yet?' he asked.

'What kid?' George asked.

'Why, Curley's new wife.'

'Yeah, I see her.'

'Well, ain't she a looloo?'

'I ain't seen that much of her,' said George.

Whit laid down his cards impressively. 'Well, stick around an' keep your eyes open. You'll see plenty. She ain't concealin' nothing. I never seen nobody like her. She got the eye goin' all the time on everybody. I bet she even gives the stable buck the eye. I don't know what the hell she wants.'

George asked casually: 'Been any trouble since she got here?'

It was obvious that Whit was not interested in his cards. He laid his hand down and George scooped it in. George laid out his deliberate solitaire hand–seven cards, and six on top, and five on top of those.

Whit said: 'I see what you mean. No, they ain't been nothing yet. Curley's got yella-jackets in his drawers, but that's all so far. Ever' time the guys is around she shows up. She's lookin' for Curley, or she thought she lef' somethin' layin' around and she's lookin' for it. Seems like she can't keep away from guys. An' Curley's pants is just crawlin' with ants, but they ain't nothing come of it yet.'

George said: 'She's gonna make a mess. They're gonna be a bad mess about her. She's a jail bait all set on the trigger. That Curley got his work cut out for him. Ranch with a bunch of guys on it ain't no place for a girl, specially like her.'

Whit said: 'If you got idears, you ought to come in town with us guys tomorra night.'

'Why? What's doin'?'

'Jus' the usual thing. We go in to old Susy's place. Hell of a nice place. Old Susy's a laugh–always crackin' jokes. Like she says when we come up on the front porch las' Sat'day night. Susy opens the door and then she yells over her shoulder: "Get yor coats on, girls, here comes the sheriff." She never talks dirty, neither. Got five girls there.'

'What's it set you back?' George asked.

'Two an' a half. You can get a shot for two bits. Susy got nice chairs to set in, too. If a guy don't want a flop, why he can jest set in the chairs and have a couple or three shots and pass the time of day and Susy don't give a damn. She ain't rushin' guys through and kickin' 'em out if they don't want a flop.'

'Might go in and look the joint over,' said George.

'Sure. Come along. It's a hell of a lot of fun–her crackin' jokes all the time. Like she says one time, she says: "I've knew people that if they got a rag rug on the floor an' a kewpie doll lamp on the phonograph, they think they're running a parlour house." That's Clara's house she's talkin' about. An' Susy says: "I know what you boys want," she says. "My girls is clean," she says, "an' there ain't no water in my whisky," she says. "If any you guys wanta look at a kewpie doll lamp an' take your own chance gettin' burned, why you know where to go." An' she says: "There's guys around here walkin' bow-legged 'cause they like to look at a kewpie doll lamp."'

George asked: 'Clara runs the other house, huh?'

'Yeah,' said Whit. 'We don't never go there. Clara gets three bucks a crack and thirty-five cents a shot, and she don't crack no jokes. But Susy's place is clean and she got nice chairs. Don't let no goo-goos in, neither.'

'Me an' Lennie's rollin' up a stake,' said George. 'I might go in an' set and have a shot, but I ain't puttin' on no two and a half.'

'Well, a guy got to have some fun sometime,' said Whit.

The door opened and Lennie and Carlson came in together. Lennie crept to his bunk and sat down, trying not to attract attention. Carlson reached under his bunk and brought out his bag. He didn't look at old Candy, who still faced the wall. Carlson found a little cleaning rod in the bag and a can of oil. He laid them on his bed and then brought out the pistol, took out the magazine and snapped the loaded shell from the chamber. Then he fell to cleaning the barrel with the little rod. When the ejector snapped, Candy turned over and looked for a moment at the gun before he turned back to the wall again.

Carlson said casually: 'Curley been in yet?'

'No,' said Whit. 'What's eatin' on Curley?'

Carlson squinted down the barrel of his gun. 'Lookin' for his old lady. I seen him going round and round outside.'

Whit said sarcastically: 'He spends half his time lookin' for her, and the rest of the time she's lookin' for him.'

Curley burst into the room excitedly. 'Any you guys seen my wife?' he demanded.

'She ain't been here,' said Whit.

Curley looked threateningly about the room. 'Where's the hell's Slim?'

'Went out in the barn,' said George. 'He was gonna put some tar on a split hoof.'

Curley's shoulders dropped and squared. 'How long ago'd he go?'

'Five–ten minutes.'

Curley jumped out the door and banged it after him.

Whit stood up. 'I guess maybe I'd like to see this,' he said. 'Curley's just spoilin' or he wouldn't start for Slim. An' Curley's handy, God damn handy. Got in the finals for the Golden Gloves. He got newspaper clippings about it.' He considered. 'But jus' the same, he better leave Slim alone. Nobody knows what Slim can do.'

'Thinks Slim's with his wife, don't he?' said George.

'Looks like it,' Whit said. ''Course Slim ain't. Least I don't think Slim is. But I like to see the fuss if it comes off. Come on, let's go.'

George said: 'I'm stayin' right here. I don't want to get mixed up in nothing. Lennie and me got to make a stake.'

Carlson finished the cleaning of the gun and put it in the bag and pushed the bag under his bunk. 'I guess I'll go out and look her over,' he said. Old Candy lay still, and Lennie, from his bunk, watched George cautiously.

When Whit and Carlson were gone and the door closed after them, George turned to Lennie. 'What you got on your mind?'

'I ain't done nothing, George. Slim says I better not pet them pups so much for a while. Slim says it ain't good for them; so I come right in. I been good, George.'

'I coulda told you that,' said George.

'Well, I wasn't hurtin' 'em none. I jus' had mine in my lap pettin' it.'

George asked: 'Did you see Slim out in the barn?'

'Sure I did. He tol' me I better not pet that pup no more.'

'Did you see that girl?'

'You mean Curley's girl?'

'Yeah. Did she come in the barn?'

'No. Anyways I never seen her.'

'You never seen Slim talkin' to her?'

'Uh-uh. She ain't been in the barn.'

'OK,' said George. 'I guess them guys ain't gonna see no fight. If there's any fightin', Lennie, you keep out of it.'

'I don't want no fights,' said Lennie. He got up from his bunk and sat down at the table, across from George. Almost automatically George shuffled the cards and laid out his solitaire hand. He used a deliberate, thoughtful slowness.

Lennie reached for a face card and studied it, then turned it upside down and studied it. 'Both ends the same,' he said. 'George, why is it both end's the same?'

'I don't know,' said George. 'That's jus' the way they make 'em. What was Slim doin' in the barn when you seen him?'

'Slim?'

'Sure. You seen him in the barn, an' he tol' you not to pet the pups so much.'

'Oh, yeah. He had a can a' tar an' a paint brush. I don't know what for.'

'You sure that girl didn't come in like she come in here today?'

'No. She never come.'

George sighed. 'You give me a good whore-house every time,' he said. 'A guy can go in an' get drunk and get ever'thing outa his system all at once, an' no messes. And he knows how much it's gonna set him back. These here jail baits is just set on the trigger of the hoosegow.'

Lennie followed his words admiringly, and moved his lips a little to keep up.

George continued: 'You remember Andy Cushman, Lennie? Went to grammar school?'

'The one that his old lady used to make hot cakes for the kids?' Lennie asked.

'Yeah. That's the one. You can remember anything if there's anything to eat in it.' George looked carefully at the solitaire hand. He put an ace up on his scoring rack and piled a two, three and four of diamonds on it. 'Andy's in San Quentin right now on account of a tart,' said George.

Lennie drummed on the table with his fingers. 'George?'

'Huh?'

'George, how long's it gonna be till we get that little place an' live on the fatta the lan'–an' rabbits?'

'I don't know,' said George. 'We gotta get a big stake together. I know a little place we can get cheap, but they ain't givin' it away.'

Old Candy turned slowly over. His eyes were wide open. He watched George carefully.

Lennie said: 'Tell about that place, George.'

'I jus' tol' you, jus' las' night.'

'Go on–tell again, George.'

'Well, it's ten acres,' said George. 'Got a little win'mill. Got a little shack on it, an' a chicken run. Got a kitchen, orchard, cherries, apples, peaches, 'cots, nuts, got a few berries. They's place for alfalfa and plenty of water to flood it. They's a pig-pen . . .'

'An' rabbits, George.'

'No place for rabbits now, but I could easy build a few hutches and you could feed alfalfa to the rabbits.'

'Damn right, I could,' said Lennie. 'You God damn right I could.'

George's hands stopped working with the cards. His voice was growing warmer. 'An' we could have a few pigs. I could build a smoke-house like the one gran'pa had, an' when we kill a pig we can smoke the bacon and the hams, and make sausage an' all like that. An' when the salmon run up river we could catch a hundred of 'em an 'salt 'em down or smoke 'em. We could have them for breakfast. They ain't nothing so nice as smoked salmon. When the fruit come in we could can it–and tomatoes, they're easy to can. Ever' Sunday we'd kill a chicken or a rabbit. Maybe, we'd have a cow or a goat, and the cream is so God damn thick you got to cut it with a knife and take it out with a spoon.'

Lennie watched him with wide eyes, and old Candy watched him too. Lennie said softly: 'We could live offa the fatta the lan'.'

'Sure,' said George. 'All kin's a vegetables in the garden, and if we want a little whisky we can sell a few eggs or something, or some milk. We'd jus' live there. We'd belong there. There wouldn't be no more runnin' round the country and gettin' fed by a Jap cook. No, sir, we'd have our own place where we belonged and not sleep in no bunkhouse.'

'Tell about the house, George,' Lennie begged.

'Sure, we'd have a little house an' a room to ourself. Little fat iron stove, an' in the winter we'd keep a fire goin' in it. It ain't enough land so we'd have to work too hard. Maybe six, seven hours a day. We wouldn't have to buck no barley eleven hours a day. An' when we put in a crop, why, we'd be there to take the crop up. We'd know what come of our plantin'.'

'An' rabbits,' Lennie said eagerly. 'An' I'd take care of 'em. Tell how I'd do that, George.'

'Sure, you'd go out in the alfalfa patch an' you'd have a sack. You'd fill up the sack and bring it in an' put in the rabbit cages.'

'They'd nibble an' they'd nibble,' said Lennie, 'the way they do. I seen 'em.'

'Ever' six weeks or so,' George continued, 'them does would throw a litter, so we'd have plenty rabbits to eat an' to sell. An' we'd keep a few pigeons to go flyin' around the win'mill like they done when I was a kid.' He looked raptly at the wall over Lennie's head. 'An' it'd be our own, an' nobody could can us. If we don't like a guy we can say: "Get the hell out," and by God he's got to do it. An' if a fren' come along, why we'd have an extra bunk, an' we'd say: "Why don't you spen' the night," an' by God he would.We'd have a setter dog and a couple stripe cats, but you gotta watch out them cats don't get the little rabbits.'

Lennie breathed hard. 'You jus' let 'em try to get the rabbits. I'll break their God damn necks. I'll . . . I'll smash 'em with a stick.' He subsided, grumbling to himself, threatening the future cats which might dare to disturb the future rabbits.

George sat entranced with his own picture.

When Candy spoke they both jumped as though they had been caught doing something reprehensible. Candy said: 'You know where's a place like that?'

George was on guard immediately. 'S'pose I do,' he said. 'What's that to you?'

'You don't need to tell me where it's at. Might be any place.'

'Sure,' said George. 'That's right. You couldn't find it in a hundred years.'

Candy went on excitedly: 'How much they want for a place like that?'

George watched him suspiciously. 'Well–I could get it for six hundred bucks. The ol' people that owns it is flat bust an' the ol' lady needs an operation. Say–what's it to you? You got nothing to do with us.'

Candy said: 'I ain't much good with on'y one hand. I lost my hand right here on this ranch. That's why they give me a job swampin'. An' they give me two hundred an' fifty dollars 'cause I los' my hand. An' I got fifty more saved up right in the bank, right now. That's three hundred, and I got fifty more comin' the enda the month. Tell you what . . .' He leaned forward eagerly. 'S'pose I went in with you guys. Tha's three hundred an' fifty bucks I'd put in. I ain't much good, but I could cook and tend the chickens and hoe the garden some. How'd that be?'

George half-closed his eyes. 'I gotta think about that. We was always gonna do it by ourselves.'

Candy interrupted him: 'I'd make a will an' leave my share to you guys in case I kick off, 'cause I ain't got no relatives nor nothing. You guys got any money? Maybe we could do her right now?'

George spat on the floor disgustedly. 'We got ten bucks between us.' Then he said thoughtfully: 'Look, if me an' Lennie work a month an' don't spend' nothing, we'll have a hundred bucks. That'd be four-fifty. I bet we could swing her for that. Then you an' Lennie could go get her started an' I'd get a job an' make up the res', an' you could sell eggs an' stuff like that.'

They fell into a silence. They looked at one another, amazed. This thing they had never really believed in was coming true. George said reverently: 'Jesus Christ! I bet we could swing her.' His eyes were full of wonder. 'I bet we could swing her,' he repeated softly.

Candy sat on the edge of his bunk. He scratched the stump of his wrist nervously. 'I got hurt four year ago,' he said. 'They'll can me purty soon. Jus' as soon as I can't swamp out no bunk-houses they'll put me on the county.

Maybe if I give you guys my money, you'll let me hoe in the garden even after I ain't no good at it. An' I'll wash dishes an' little chicken stuff like that. But I'll be on our own place, an' I'll be let to work on our own place.' He said miserably: 'You seen what they done to my dog tonight? They says he wasn't no good to himself nor nobody else. When they can me here I wisht somebody'd shoot me. But they won't do nothing like that. I won't have no place to go, an' I can't get no more jobs. I'll have thirty dollars more comin', time you guys is ready to quit.'

George stood up. 'We'll do her,' he said. 'We'll fix up that little old place am' we'll go live there.' He sat down again. They all sat still, all bemused by the beauty of the thing, each mind was popped into the future when this lovely thing should come about.

George said wonderingly: 'S'pose they was a carnival or a circus come to town, or a ball game, or any damn thing.' Old Candy nodded in appreciation of the idea. 'We'd just go to her,' George said. 'We wouldn't ask nobody if we could. Jus' say: 'We'll go to her,'' an' we would. Jus' milk the cow and sling some grain to the chickens an' go to her.'

'An' put some grass to the rabbits,' Lennie broke in. 'I wouldn't never forget to feed them. When we gon'ta do it, George?'

'In one month. Right squack in one month. Know what I'm gon'ta do. I'm gon'ta write to them old people that owns the place that we'll take it. An' Candy'll send a hunderd dollars to bind her.'

'Sure will,' said Candy. 'They got a good stove there?'

'Sure, got a nice stove, burns coal or wood.'

'I'm gonna take my pup,' said Lennie. 'I bet by Christ he likes it there, by Jesus.'

Voices were approaching from outside. George said quickly: 'Don't tell nobody about it. Jus' us three an' nobody else. They li'ble to can us we can't make no stake. Jus' go on like we was gonna buck barley the rest of our lives, then all of a sudden some day we'll go get our pay an' scram outa here.'

Lennie and Candy nodded, and they were grinning with delight. 'Don't tell nobody,' Lennie said to himself.

Candy said: 'George.'

'Huh?'

'I ought to of shot that dog myself, George. I shouldn't ought to of let no stranger shoot my dog.'

The door opened. Slim came in, followed by Curley and Carlson and Whit. Slim's hands were black with tar and he was scowling. Curley hung close to his elbow.

Curley said: 'Well, I didn't mean nothing, Slim. I just ast you.'

Slim said: 'Well, you been askin' me too often. I'm gettin' God damn sick of it. If you can't look after your own God damn wife, what you expect me to do about it? You lay offa me.'

'I'm jus' tryin' to tell you I didn't mean nothin,' said Curley. 'I jus' thought you might of saw her.'

'Why'n't you tell her to stay the hell home where she belongs?' said Carlson. 'You let her hang around bunk-houses and pretty soon you're gonna have som'pin on your hands and you won't be able to do nothin' about it.'

Curley whirled on Carlson. 'You keep outa this les' you wanta step outside.'

Carlson laughed. 'You God damn punk,' he said. 'You tried to throw a scare into Slim, an' you couldn't make it stick. Slim throwed a scare into you. You're yella as a frog belly. I don't care if you're the best welter in the country. You come for me, an' I'll kick your God damn head off.'

Candy joined the attack with joy. 'Glove fulla vaseline,' he said disgustedly. Curley glared at him. His eyes slipped on past and lighted on Lennie; and Lennie was still smiling with delight at the memory of the ranch.

Curley stepped over to Lennie like a terrier. 'What the hell you laughin' at?'

Lennie looked blankly at him. 'Huh?'

Then Curley's rage exploded. 'Come on, ya big bastard. Get up on your feet. No big son-of-a-bitch is gonna laugh at me. I'll show ya who's yella.'

Lennie looked helplessly at George, and then he got up and tried to retreat. Curley was balanced and poised. He slashed at Lennie with his left, and then smashed down his nose with a right. Lennie gave a cry of terror. Blood welled from his nose. 'George,' he cried. 'Make 'um let me alone, George.' He backed until he was against the wall, and Curley followed, slugging him in the face. Lennie's hands remained at his sides; he was too frightened to defend himself.

George was on his feet yelling: 'Get him, Lennie. Don't let him do it.'

Lennie covered his face with his huge paws and bleated with terror. He cried: 'Make'um stop, George.' Then Curley attacked his stomach and cut off his wind.

Slim jumped up. 'The dirty little rat,' he cried, 'I'll get 'um myself.'

George put out his hand and grabbed Slim. 'Wait a minute,' he shouted. He cupped his hands around his mouth and yelled: 'Get 'im, Lennie!'

Lennie took his hands away from his face and looked about for George, and Curley slashed at his eyes. The big face was covered with blood. George yelled again: 'I said get him.'

Curley's fist was swinging when Lennie reached for it. The next minute Curley was flopping like a fish on a line, and his closed fist was lost in Lennie's big hand. George ran down the room. 'Leggo of him, Lennie. Let go.'

But Lennie watched in terror the flopping little man whom he held. Blood ran down Lennie's face, one of his eyes was cut and closed. George slapped him on the face again and again, and still Lennie held on to the closed fist. Curley was white and shrunken by now, and his struggling had become weak. He stood crying, his fist lost in Lennie's paw.

George shouted over and over: 'Leggo his hand, Lennie. Leggo. Slim, come help me while the guy got any hand left.'

Suddenly Lennie let got his hold. He crouched cowering against the wall. 'You tol' me to, George,' he said miserably.

Curley sat down on the floor, looking in wonder at his crushed hand. Slim and Carlson bent over him. Then Slim straightened up and regarded Lennie with horror. 'We got to get him in to a doctor,' he said. 'Looks to me like ever bone in his han' is bust.'

'I didn't wanta,' 'Lennie cried. 'I didn't wanta hurt him.'

Slim said: 'Carlson, you get the candy wagon hitched up. We'll take 'um into Soledad an' get 'um fixed up.' Carlson hurried out. Slim turned to the whimpering Lennie. 'It ain't your fault,' he said. 'This punk sure had it comin' to him. But–Jesus! He ain't hardly got no han' left.' Slim hurried out, and in a moment returned with a tin cup of water. He held it to Curley's lips.

George said: 'Slim, will we get canned now? We need the stake. Will Curley's old man can us now?'

Slim smiled wryly. He knelt down beside Curley. 'You got your senses in hand enough to listen?' he asked. Curley nodded. 'Well, then, listen,' Slim went on. 'I think you got your han' caught in a machine. If you don't tell nobody what happened, we ain't going to. But you jus' tell an' try to get this guy canned and we'll tell ever'body, an' then will you get the laugh.'

'I won't tell,' said Curley. He avoided looking at Lennie.

Buggy wheels sounded outside. Slim helped Curley up. 'Come on now. Carlson's gonna take you to a doctor.' He helped Curley out the door. The sound of wheels drew away. In a moment Slim came back into the bunk-house. He looked at Lennie, still crouched fearfully against the wall. 'Let's see your hands,' he asked.

Lennie stuck out his hands.

'Christ awmighty, I hate to have you mad at me,' Slim said.

George broke in: 'Lennie was jus' scairt,' he explained. 'He didn't know what to do. I told you nobody ought never to fight him. No, I guess it was Candy I told.'

Candy nodded solemnly. 'That's jus' what you done,' he said. 'Right this morning when Curley first lit intil your fren', you says: "He better not fool with Lennie if he knows what good for'um." That's jus' what you says to me.'

George turned to Lennie. 'It ain't your fault,' he said. 'You don't need to be scairt no more. You done jus' what I tol' you to. Maybe you better go in the washroom an' clean up your face. You look like hell.'

Lennie smiled with his bruised mouth. 'I didn't want no trouble,' he said. He walked towards the door, but just before he came to it he turned back. 'George?'

'What you want?'

'I can still tend the rabbits, George?'

'Sure. You ain't done nothing wrong.'

'I didn't mean no harm, George.'

'Well, get the hell out and wash your face.'

Crooks, the negro stable buck, had his bunk in the harness-room; a little shed that leaned off the wall of the barn. On one side of the little room there was a square four-paned window, and on the other, a narrow plank door leading into the barn. Crook's bunk was a long box filled with straw, on which his blankets were flung. On the wall by the window there were pegs on which hung broken harness in process of being mended, strips of new leather; and under the window itself a little bench for leather-working tools, curved knives and needles and balls of linen thread, and a small hand riveter. On pegs were also pieces of harness, a split collar with the horsehair stuffing sticking out, a broken hame, and a trace chain with its leather covering split. Crooks had his apple-box over his bunk, and in it a range of medicine bottles, both for himself and for the horses. There were cans of saddle soap and a drippy can of tar with its paint-brush sticking over the edge. And scattered about the floor were a number of personal possessions; for, being alone, Crooks could leave his things about, and being a stable buck and a cripple, he was more permanent than the other men, and he had accumulated more possessions than he could carry on his back.

Crooks possessed several pairs of shoes, a pair of rubber boots, a big alarm clock, and a single-barrelled shot-gun. And he had books, too; a tattered dictionary and a mauled copy of the California civil code for 1905. There were battered magazines and a few dirty books on a special shelf over his bunk. A pair of large gold-rimmed spectacles hung from a nail on the wall above his bed.

This room was swept and fairly neat, for Crooks was a proud, aloof man. He kept his distance and demanded that other people kept theirs. His body was bent over to the left by his crooked spine, and his eyes lay deep in his head, and because of their depth seemed to glitter with intensity. His lean face was lined with deep black wrinkles, and he had thin, pain-tightened lips which were lighter than his face.

It was Saturday night. Through the open door that led into the barn came the sound of moving horses, of feet stirring, of teeth champing on hay, of the rattle of halter chains. In the stable buck's room a small electric globe threw a meagre yellow light.

Crooks sat on his bunk. His shirt was out of his jeans at the back. In one hand he held a bottle of liniment, with the other he rubbed his spine. Now and then he poured a few drops of the liniment into his pink-palmed hand and reached up under his shirt to rub again. He flexed his muscles against his back and shivered.

Noiselessly, Lennie appeared in the open doorway and stood there looking in, his big shoulders nearly filling the opening. For a moment Crooks did not see him, but on raising his eyes he stiffened and a scowl came on his face. His hands came out from under his shirt.

Lennie smiled helplessly in an attempt to make friends.

Crooks said sharply: 'You got no right to come in my room. This here's my room. Nobody got any right in here but me.'

Lennie gulped and his smile grew more fawning. 'I ain't doing nothing,' he said. 'Just come to look at my puppy. And I seen your light,' he explained.

'Well, I got a right to have a light. You go on get outa my room. I ain't wanted in the bunk-house, and you ain't wanted in my room.'

'Why ain't you wanted?' Lennie asked.

''Cause I'm black. They play cards in there, but I can't play because I'm black. They say I stink. Well, I tell you, you all of you stink to me.'

Lennie flapped his big hands helplessly. 'Ever'body went into town,' he said. 'Slim an' George an' ever'body. George says I gotta stay here an' not get into no trouble. I seen your light.'

'Well, what do you want?'

'Nothing–I seen your light. I thought I could jus' come in an' set.'

Crooks stared at Lennie, and he reached behind him and took down the spectacles and adjusted them over his pink ears and stared again. 'I don't know what you're doin' in the barn anyway,' he complained. 'You ain't no skinner. They's no call for a bucker to come into the barn at all. You ain't no skinner. You ain't got nothing to do with the horses.'

'The pup,' Lennie repeated. 'I come to see my pup.'

'Well, go see your pup, then. Don't come in a place where you're not wanted.'

Lennie lost his smile. He advanced a step into the room, then remembered and backed to the door again. 'I looked at 'em a little, Slim says I ain't to pet 'em very much.'

Crooks said: 'Well, you been takin' 'em out of the nest all the time. I wonder the old lady don't move 'em someplace else.'

'Oh, she don't care. She lets me.' Lennie had moved into the room again.

Crooks scowled, but Lennie's disarming smile defeated him. 'Come on in and set a while,' Crooks said. ''Long as you won't get out and leave me alone, you might as well set down.' His tone was a little more friendly. 'All the boys gone into town, huh?'

'All but old Candy. He just sets in the bunk-house sharpening his pencil and sharpening and figuring.'

Crooks adjusted his glasses. 'Figuring? What's Candy figuring about?'

Lennie almost shouted: ''Bout the rabbits.'

'You're nuts,' said Crooks. 'You're crazy as a wedge. What rabbits you talkin' about?'

'The rabbits we're gonna get, and I get to tend 'em, cut grass an' give 'em water, an' like that.'

'Jus' nuts,' said Crooks. 'I don't blame the guys you travel with for keepin' you outa sight.'

Lennie said quietly: 'It ain't no lie. We're gonna do it. Gonna get a little place an' live on the fatta the lan'.'

Crooks settled himself more comfortably on his bunk. 'Set down,' he invited. 'Set down on the nail-keg.'

Lennie hunched down on the little barrel. 'You think it's a lie,' Lennie said, 'but it ain't no lie. Ever' word's the truth, an' you can ast George.'

Crooks put his dark chin into his pink palm. 'You travel aroun' with George, don't ya?'

'Sure. Me an' him goes ever' place together.'

Crooks continued. 'Sometimes he talks, and you don't know what the hell he's talkin' about. Ain't that so?' He leaned forward, boring Lennie with his deep eyes. 'Ain't that so?'

'Yeah . . . sometimes.'

'Jus' talks on, an' you don't know what the hell it's all about?'

'Yeah . . . sometimes. But . . . not always.'

Crooks leaned forward over the edge of the bunk. 'I ain't a southern negro,' he said. 'I was born right here in California. My old man had a chicken ranch, 'bout ten acres. The white kids come to play at our place, an' sometimes I went to play with them, and some of them was pretty nice. My ol' man didn't like that. I never knew till long later why he didn't like that. But I know now.' He hesitated, and when he spoke again his voice was softer. 'There wasn't another coloured family for miles around. And now there ain't a coloured man on this ranch an' there's jus' one family in Soledad.' He laughed. 'If I say something, why it's just a nigger saying it.'

Lennie asked: 'How long you think it'll be before them pups will be old enough to pet?'

Crooks laughed again. 'A guy can talk to you an' be sure you won't go blabbin'. Couple of weeks' an' them pups'll be all right. George knows what he's about. Jus' talks, an' you don't understand nothing.' He leaned forward excitedly. 'This is just a nigger talkin', an' a busted-back nigger. So it don't mean nothing, see? You couldn't remember it anyways. I seen it over an' over an' over–a guy talkin' to another guy and it don't make no difference if he don't hear or understand. The thing is, they're talkin', or they're settin' still not talkin'. It don't make no difference, no difference.' His excitement had increased until he pounded his knee with his hand. 'George can tell you screwy things, and it don't matter. It's just the talking. It's just bein' with another guy. That's all.' He paused.

His voice grew soft and persuasive. 'S'pose George don't come back no more. S'pose he took a powder and just ain't coming back. What'll you do then?'

Lennie's attention came gradually to what had been said. 'What?' he demanded.

'I said s'pose George went into town tonight and you never heard of him no more.' Crooks pressed forward some kind of private victory. 'Just s'pose that,' he repeated.

'He won't do it,' Lennie cried. 'George wouldn't do nothing like that. He'll come back tonight . . .' But the doubt was too much for him. 'Don't you think he will?'

Crooks face lighted with pleasure in his torture. 'Nobody can't tell what a guy'll do,' he observed calmly. 'Le's say he wants to come back and can't. S'pose he gets killed or hurt so he can't come back.'

Lennie struggled to understand. 'George won't do nothing like that,' he repeated. 'George is careful. He won't get hurt. He ain't never been hurt, 'cause he's careful.'

'Well, s'pose, jus' s'pose he don't come back. What'll you do then?'

Lennie's face wrinkled with apprehension. 'I don't know. Say, what you doin' anyways?' he cried. 'This ain't true. George ain't got hurt.'

Crooks bored in on him. 'Want me ta tell ya what'll happen? They'll take ya to the booby hatch. They'll tie ya up with a collar, like a dog.'

Suddenly Lennie's eyes centred and grew quiet and mad. He stood up and walked dangerously to Crooks. 'Who hurt George?' he demanded.

Crooks saw the danger as it approached him. He edged back on his bunk to get out of the way. 'I was just supposin',' he said. 'George ain't hurt. He's all right. He'll be back all right.'

Lennie stood over him. 'What you supposin' for? Ain't nobody goin' to suppose no hurt to George.'

Crooks removed his glasses and wiped his eyes with his fingers. 'Jus' set down,' he said. 'George ain't hurt.'

Lennie growled back to his seat on the nail-keg. 'Ain't nobody goin' to talk no hurt to George,' he grumbled.

Crooks said gently: 'Maybe you can see now. You got George. You *know* he's goin' to come back. S'pose you didn't have nobody. S'pose you couldn't go into the bunk-house and play rummy 'cause you was black. How'd you like that? S'pose you had to sit out here an' read books. Sure you could play horseshoes till it got dark, but then you got to read books. Books ain't no good. A guy needs somebody–to be near him.' He whined: 'A guy goes nuts if he ain't got nobody. Don't make no difference who the guy is, long's he's with you. I tell ya,' he cried, 'I tell ya a guy gets too lonely an' he gets sick.'

'George gonna come back,' Lennie reassured himself in a frightened voice. 'Maybe George come back already. Maybe I better go see.'

Crooks said: 'I didn't mean to scare you. He'll come back. I was talkin' about myself. A guy sets alone out here at night, maybe readin' books or thinkin' or stuff like that. Sometimes he gets thinkin', an' he got nothing to tell him what's so an' what ain't so. Maybe if he sees somethin', he don't know whether it's right or not. He can't turn to some other guy and ask him if he sees it too. He can't tell. He got nothing to measure by. I seen things out here. I wasn't drunk. I don't know if I was asleep. If some guy was with me, he could tell me I was asleep, an' then it would be all right. But I jus' don't know.' Crooks was looking across the room now, looking towards the window.

Lennie said miserably: 'George wun't go away and leave me. I know George wun't do that.'

The stable buck went on dreamily: 'I remember when I was a little kid on my old man's chicken ranch. Had two brothers. They was always near me, always there. Used to sleep right in the same room, right in the same bed–all three. Had a strawberry patch. Had an alfalfa patch. Used to turn the chickens out in the alfalfa on a sunny morning. My brothers'd set on a fence rail an' watch 'em–white chickens they was.'

Gradually Lennie's interest came around to what was being said. 'George says we're gonna have alfalfa for the rabbits.'

'What rabbits?'

'We're gonna have rabbits an' a berry patch.'

'You're nuts.'

'We are too. You ast George.'

'You're nuts.' Crooks was scornful. 'I see hunderds of men come by on the road an' on the ranches with their bindles on their back an' that same damn thing in their heads. Hunderds of them. They come, an' they quit an' go on; an' every damn one of 'em's got a little piece of land in his head. An' never a God damn one of 'em ever gets it. Just like heaven. Ever'body wants a little piece of lan'. I read plenty of books out here. Nobody never gets to heaven, and nobody never gets no land. It's just in their head. They're all the time talkin' about it, but it's jus' in their head.' He paused and looked toward the open door, for the horses were moving restlessly and the halter chains clinked. A horse whinnied. 'I guess somebody's out there,' Crooks said. 'Maybe Slim. Slim comes in sometimes two, three times a night. Slim's a real skinner. He looks out for his team.' He pulled himself painfully upright and moved toward the door. 'That you, Slim?' he called.

Candy's voice answered. 'Slim went in town. Say, you seen Lennie?'

'Ya mean the big guy?'

'Yeah. Seen him around any place?'

'He's in here,' Crooks said shortly. He went back to his bunk and lay down.

Candy stood in the doorway scratching his bald wrist and looking blindly into the lighted room. He made no attempt to enter. 'Tell ya what, Lennie. I been figuring out about them rabbits.'

Crooks said irritably: 'You can come in if you want.'

Candy seemed embarrassed. 'I do' know. 'Course, if ya want me to.'

'Come on in. If ever'body's comin' in, you might just as well.' It was difficult for Crooks to conceal his pleasure with anger.

Candy came in, but he was still embarrassed. 'You got a nice cosy little place in here,' he said to Crooks. 'Must be nice to have a room all to yourself this way.'

'Sure,' said Crooks. 'And a manure pile under the window. Sure it's swell.'

Lennie broke in: 'You said about them rabbits.'

Candy leaned against the wall beside the broken collar while he scratched the wrist stump. 'I been here a long time,' he said. 'An' Crooks been here a long time. This's the first time I ever been in his room.'

Crooks said darkly: 'Guys don't come into a coloured man's room very much. Nobody been here but Slim. Slim an' the boss.'

Candy quickly changed the subject. 'Slim's as good a skinner as I ever seen.'

Lennie leaned toward the old swamper. 'About them rabbits,' he insisted.

Candy smiled. 'I got figured out. We can make some money on them rabbits if we go about it right.'

'But I get to tend 'em,' Lennie broke in. 'George says I get to tend 'em. He promised.'

Crooks interrupted brutally. 'You guys is just kiddin' yourself. You'll talk about it a hell of a lot, but you won't get no land. You'll be a swamper here till they take you out in a box. Hell, I seen too many guys. Lennie here'll quit an' be on the road in two, three weeks. Seems like ever' guy got land in his head.'

Candy rubbed his cheek angrily. 'You God damn right we're gonna do it. George says we are. We got the money right now.'

'Yeah?' said Crooks. 'An' where's George now? In town in a whore-house. That's where your money's goin'. Jesus, I seen it happen too many times. I seen too many guys with land in their head. They never get none under their hand.'

Candy cried: 'Sure they all want it. Everybody wants a little bit of land, not much. Jus' somethin' that was his. Somethin' he could live on and there couldn't nobody throw him off of it. I never had none. I planted crops for damn near ever'body in this state, but they wasn't my crops, and when I harvested 'em, it wasn't none of my harvest. But we gonna do it now, and don't you make no mistake about that. George ain't got the money in town. That money's in the bank. Me an' Lennie an' George. We gonna have a room to ourselves. We're gonna have a dog an' rabbits an' chickens. We're gonna have green corn an' maybe a cow or a goat.' He stopped, overwhelmed with his picture.

Crooks asked: 'You say you got the money?'

'Damn right. We got most of it. Just a little bit more to get. Have it all in one month. George got the land all picked out, too.'

Crooks reached around and explored his spine with his hand. 'I never seen a guy really do it,' he said. 'I seen guys nearly crazy with loneliness for land, but ever' time a whore-house or a blackjack game took what it takes.' He hesitated. '. . . If you . . . guys would want a hand to work for nothing–just his keep, why I'd come an' lend a hand. I ain't so crippled I can't work like a son-of-a-bitch if I want to.'

'Any you boys seen Curley?'

They swung their heads toward the door. Looking in was Curley's wife. Her face was heavily made up. Her lips were slightly parted. She breathed strongly, as though she had been running.

'Curley ain't been here,' Candy said sourly.

She stood still in the doorway, smiling a little at them, rubbing the nails of one hand with the thumb and forefinger of the other. And the eyes travelled from one face to another. 'They left all the weak ones here,' she said finally. 'Think I don't know where they all went? Even Curley. I know where they all went.'

Lennie watched her fascinated; but Candy and Crooks were scowling down away from her eyes. Candy said: 'Then if you know, why you want to ast us where Curley is at?'

She regarded them amusedly. 'Funny thing,' she said. 'If I catch any one man, and he's alone, I get along fine with him. But just let two of the guys get together an' you won't talk. Jus' nothing but mad.' She dropped her fingers and put her hands on her hips. 'You're all scared of each other, that's what.

Ever' one of you's scared the rest is goin' to get something on you.'

After a pause Crooks said: 'Maybe you better go along to your own house now. We don't want no trouble.'

'Well, I ain't giving you no trouble. Think I don't like to talk to somebody ever' once in a while? Think I like to stick in that house alla time?'

Candy laid the stump of his wrist on his knee and rubbed it gently with his hand. He said accusingly: 'You gotta husban'. You got no call foolin' aroun' with other guys, causin' trouble.'

The girl flared up, 'Sure I gotta husban'. You all seen him. Swell guy, ain't he? Spends all his time sayin' what he's gonna do to guys he don't like, and he don't like nobody. Think I'm gonna stay in that two-by-four house and listen how Curley's gonna lead with his left twice, and then bring in the ol' right cross? "One-two," he says. "Jus' the ol' one-two an' he'll go down."' She paused and her face lost its sullenness and grew interested. 'Say–what happened to Curley's han'?'

There was an embarrassed silence. Candy stole a look at Lennie. Then he coughed. 'Why . . . Curley . . . he got his han' caught in a machine, ma'am. Bust his han'.'

She watched for a moment, and then she laughed. 'Baloney! What you think you're sellin' me? Curley started somep'in he didn't finish. Caught in a machine–baloney! Why, he ain't give nobody the good ol' one-two since he got his han' bust. Who bust him?'

Candy repeated sullenly: 'Got it caught in a machine.'

'Awright,' she said contemptuously. 'Awright, cover 'im up if ya wanta. Whatta I care? You bindle bums think you're so damn good. Whatta ya think I am, a kid? I tell ya I could of went with shows. Not jus' one, neither. An' a guy tol' me he could put me in pitchers . . .' She was breathless with indignation. '–Sat'iday night. Ever'body out doin' som'pin. Ever'body! An' what am I doin'? Standin' here talking to a bunch of bindle stiffs–a nigger an' a dum-dum and a lousy ol' sheep–an' likin' it because they ain't nobody else.'

Lennie watched her, his mouth half open. Crooks had retired into the terrible protective dignity of the negro. But a change came over old Candy. He stood up suddenly and knocked his nail-keg over backward. 'I had enough,' he said angrily. 'You ain't wanted here. We told you you ain't. An' I tell ya, you got floosy idears about what us guys amounts to. You ain't got sense enough in that chicken head to even see that we ain't stiffs. S'pose you get us canned. S'pose you do. You think we'll hit the highway an' look for another lousy two-bit job like this. You don't know that we got our own ranch to go to, an' our own house. We ain't got to stay here. We gotta house and chickens an' fruit trees an' a place a hunderd time prettier than this. An' we got fren's, that's what we got. Maybe there was a time when we was scared of gettin' canned, but we ain't no more. We got our own lan', and it's ours, an' we c'n go to it.'

Curley's wife laughed at him. 'Baloney,' she said. 'I seen too many you guys. If you had two bits in the worl', why you'd be gettin' two shots of corn with it and suckin' the bottom of the glass. I know you guys.'

Candy's face had grown redder and redder, but before she was done speaking, he had control of himself. He was the master of the situation. 'I might of knew,' he said gently. 'Maybe you just better go along an' roll your hoop. We ain't got nothing to say to you at all. We know what we got, and we don't care whether you know it or not. So maybe you better jus' scatter along now, 'cause Curley maybe ain't gonna like his wife out in the barn with us "bindle stiffs".'

She looked from one face to another, and they were all closed against her. And she looked longest at Lennie, until he dropped his eyes in embarrassment. Suddenly she said: 'Where'd you get them bruises on your face?'

Lennie looked up guiltily. 'Who–me?'

'Yeah, you.'

Lennie looked to Candy for help, and then he looked at his lap again. 'He got his han' caught in a machine,' he said.

Curley's wife laughed. 'OK, Machine. I'll talk to you later. I like machines.'

Candy broke in. 'You let this guy alone. Don't you do no messing aroun' with him. I'm gonna tell George what you says. George won't have you messin' with Lennie.'

'Who's George?' she asked. 'The little guy you come with?'

Lennie smiled happily. 'That's him,' he said. 'That's the guy, an' he's gonna let me tend the rabbits.'

'Well, if that's all you want, I might get a couple rabbits myself.'

Crooks stood up from his bunk and faced her. 'I had enough,' he said coldly. 'You got no rights comin' in a coloured man's room. You got no rights messing around in here at all. Now you jus' get out, an' get out quick. If you don't, I'm gonna ast the boss not to ever let you come in the barn no more.'

She turned to him in scorn. 'Listen, Nigger,' she said. 'You know what I can do to you if you open your trap?'

Crooks stared hopelessly at her, and then he sat down on his bunk and drew into himself.

She closed on him. 'You know what I could do?'

Crooks seemed to grow smaller, and he pressed himself against the wall. 'Yes, ma'am.'

'Well, you keep your place then, Nigger. I could get you strung up on a tree so easy it ain't even funny.'

Crooks had reduced himself to nothing. There was no personality, no ego–nothing to arouse either like or dislike. He said: 'Yes, ma'am,' and his voice was toneless.

For a moment she stood over him as though waiting for him to move so that she could whip at him again; but Crooks sat perfectly still, his eyes averted, everything that might be hurt drawn in. She turned at last to the other two.

Old Candy was watching her, fascinated. 'If you was to do that, we'd tell,' he said quietly. 'We'd tell about you framin' Crooks.'

'Tell an' be damned,' she cried. 'Nobody'd listen to you, an' you know it. Nobody'd listen to you.'

Candy subsided. 'No,' he agreed.'–Nobody'd listen to us.'

Lennie whined: 'I wisht George was here. I wisht George was here.'

Candy stepped over to him. 'Don't you worry none,' he said. 'I jus' heard the guys comin' in. George'll be in the bunk-house right now, I bet.' He turned to Curley's wife. 'You better go home now,' he said quietly. 'If you go right now, we won't tell Curley you was here.'

She appraised him coolly. 'I ain't sure you heard nothin.'

'Better not take no chances,' he said. 'If you ain't sure you better take the safe way.'

She turned to Lennie. 'I'm glad you bust up Curley a little bit. He got it comin' to him. Sometimes I'd like to bust him myself.' She slipped out the door and disappeared into the dark barn. And while she went through the barn, the halter chains rattled, and some horses snorted and some stamped their feet.

Crooks seemed to come slowly out of the layers of protection he had put on. 'Was that the truth what you said about the guys come back?' he asked.

'Sure. I heard 'em.'

'Well, I didn't hear nothing.'

'The gate banged,' Candy said, and he went on, 'Jesus Christ, Curley's wife can move quiet. I guess she had a lot of practice though.'

Crooks avoided the whole subject now. 'Maybe you guys better go,' he said. 'I ain't sure I want you in here no more. A coloured man got to have some rights, even if he don't like 'em.'

Candy said: 'That bitch didn't ought to of said that to you.'

'It wasn't nothing,' Crooks said dully. 'You guys comin' in an' settin' made me forget. What she says is true.'

The horses snorted out in the barn and the chains rang and a voice called: 'Lennie, Oh, Lennie. You in the barn?'

'It's George,' Lennie cried. And he answered: 'Here, George. I'm right in here.'

In a second George stood framed in the door, and he looked disapprovingly about. 'What you doin' in Crooks's room. You hadn't ought to be here.'

Crooks nodded. 'I tol' 'em, but they come in anyways.'

'Well, why'n't you kick 'em out?'

'I di'n't care much,' said Crooks. 'Lennie's a nice fella.'

Now Candy aroused himself. 'Oh, George! I been figurin' and figurin'. I got it doped out how we can even make some money on them rabbits.'

George scowled. 'I thought I tol' you not to tell nobody about that.'

Candy was crestfallen. 'Didn't tell nobody but Crooks.'

George said: 'Well you guys get outa here. Jesus, seems like I can't go away for a minute.'

Candy and Lennie stood up and went toward the door. Crooks called: 'Candy!'

'Huh?'

''Member what I said about hoein' and doin' odd jobs?'

'Yeah,' said Candy. 'I remember.'

'Well, jus' forget it,' said Crooks. 'I didn't mean it. Jus' foolin'. I wouldn't want to go no place like that.'

'Well, OK, if you feel like that. Good night.'

The three men went out of the door. As they went through the barn the horses snorted and the halter chains rattled.

Crooks sat on his bunk and looked at the door for a moment, and then he reached for the liniment bottle. He pulled out his shirt at the back, poured a little liniment in his pink palm, and, reaching around, he fell slowly to rubbing his back.

One end of the great barn was piled high with new hay and over the pile hung the four-taloned jackson fork suspended from its pulley. The hay came down like a mountain slope to the other end of the barn, and there was a level place as yet unfilled with the new crop. At the sides the feeding racks were visible, and between the slats the heads of horses could be seen.

It was Sunday afternoon. The resting horses nibbled the remaining wisps of hay, and they stamped their feet and they bit the wood of the mangers and rattled the halter chains. The afternoon sun sliced in through the cracks of the barn walls and lay in bright lines on the hay. There was the buzz of flies in the air, the lazy afternoon humming.

From outside came the clang of horseshoes on the playing peg and the shouts of men, playing, encouraging, jeering. But in the barn it was quiet and humming and lazy and warm.

Only Lennie was in the barn, and Lennie sat in the hay beside a packing-case under a manger in the end of the barn that had not been filled with hay. Lennie sat in the hay and looked at a little dead puppy that lay in front of him. Lennie looked at it for a long time, and then he put out his huge hand and stroked it, stroked it clear from one end to the other. And Lennie said softly to the puppy: 'Why do you got to get killed? You ain't so little as mice. I didn't bounce you hard.' He bent the pup's head up and looked in its face, and he said to it: 'Now maybe George ain't gonna let me tend no rabbits, if he fin's out you got killed.'

He scooped a little hollow and laid the puppy in it and covered it over with hay, out of sight; but he continued to stare at the mound he had made. He said: 'This ain't no bad thing like I got to go hide in the brush. Oh! no. This ain't. I'll tell George I foun' it dead.'

He unburied the puppy and inspected it, and stroked it from ears to tail. He went on sorrowfully: 'But he'll know. George always knows. He'll say: "You done it. Don't try to put nothing over on me." An' he'll say: "Now jus' for that you don't get to tend no rabbits!"'

Suddenly his anger rose. 'God damn you,' he cried. 'Why do you got to get killed? You ain't so little as mice.' He picked up the pup and hurled it from him. He turned his back on it. He sat bent over his knees and he whispered: 'Now I won't get to tend the rabbits. Now he won't let me.' He rocked himself back and forth in his sorrow.

From outside came the clang of horseshoes on the iron stake, and then a little chorus of cries. Lennie got up and brought the puppy back and laid it on the hay and sat down. He stroked the pup again. 'You wasn't big enough,' he said. 'They tol' me and tol' me you wasn't. I di'n't know you'd get killed so easy. He worked his fingers on the pup's limp ear. 'Maybe George won't care,' he said. 'This here God damn little son-of-a-bitch wasn't nothing to George.'

Curley's wife came around the end of the last stall. She came very quietly, so that Lennie didn't see her. She wore her bright cotton dress and the mules with the red ostrich feathers. Her face was made up and the little sausage curls were all in place. She was quite near to him before Lennie looked up and saw her.

In a panic he shovelled hay over the puppy with his fingers. He looked sullenly up at her.

She said: 'What you got there, sonny boy?'

Lennie glared at her. 'George says I ain't to have nothing to do with you–talk to you or nothing.'

She laughed. 'George giving you orders about everything?'

Lennie looked down at the hay. 'Says I can't tend no rabbits if I talk to you or anything.'

She said quietly: 'He's scared Curley'll get mad. Well, Curley got his arm in a sling–an' if Curley gets tough, you can break his other han'. You didn't put nothing over on me about gettin' it caught on no machine.'

But Lennie was not to be drawn. 'No, sir. I ain't gonna talk to you or nothing.'

She knelt in the hay beside him. 'Listen,' she said. 'All the guys got a horseshoe tenement goin' on. It's on'y about four o'clock. None of them guys is goin' to leave that tenement. Why can't I talk to you? I never get to talk to nobody. I get awful lonely.'

Lennie said: 'Well, I ain't supposed to talk to you or nothing.'

'I get lonely,' said she. 'You can talk to people, but I can't talk to nobody but Curley. Else he gets mad. How'd you like not to talk to anybody?'

Lennie said: 'Well, I ain't supposed to. George's scared I'll get in trouble.'

She changed the subject. 'What you got covered up there?'

Then all of Lennie's woe came back on him. 'Jus' my pup,' he said sadly. 'Jus' my little pup.' And he swept the hay from on top of it.

'Why, he's dead,' she cried.

'He was so little,' said Lennie. 'I was jus' playin' with him . . . an' he made like he's gonna bite me . . . an' I made like I was gonna smack him . . . an' . . . an' I done it. An' then he was dead.'

She consoled him. 'Don't you worry none. He was jus' a mutt. You can get another one easy. The whole country is fulla mutts.'

'It ain't that so much,' Lennie explained miserably. 'George ain't gonna let me tend no rabbits now.'

'Why don't he?'

'Well, he said if I done any more bad things he ain't gonna let me tend the rabbits.'

She moved closer to him and she spoke soothingly. 'Don't you worry about talkin' to me. Listen to the guys yell out there. They got four dollars bet in that tenement. None of them ain't gonna leave till it's over.'

'If George sees me talkin' to you he'll give me hell,' Lennie said cautiously. 'He tol' me so.'

Her face grew angry. 'What's the matter with me?' she cried. 'Ain't I got a right to talk to nobody? Whatta they think I am, anyways? You're a nice guy. I don't know why I can't talk to you. I ain't doin' no harm to you.'

'Well, George says you'll get us in a mess.'

'Aw, nuts!' she said. 'What kinda harm am I doin' to you? Seems like they ain't none of them cares how I gotta live. I tell you I ain't used to livin' like this. I coulda made somethin' of myself.' She said darkly: 'Maybe I will yet.' And then her words tumbled out in a passion of communication, as though she hurried before her listener could be taken away. 'I live right in Salinas,' she said. 'Come there when I was a kid. Well, a show come through, an' I met one of the actors. He says I could go with that show. But my ol' lady wouldn't let me. She says because I was on'y fifteen. But the guy says I coulda. If I'd went, I wouldn't be livin' like this, you bet.'

Lennie stroked the pup back and forth. 'We gonna have a little place–an' rabbits,' he explained.

She went on with her story quickly, before she should be interrupted. ''Nother time I met a guy, an' he was in pitchers. Went out to the Riverside Dance Palace with him. He says he was gonna put me in the movies. Says I was a natural. Soon's he got back to Hollywood he was gonna write to me about it.' She looked closely at Lennie to see whether she was impressing him. 'I never got that letter,' she said. 'I always thought my ol' lady stole it. Well, I wasn't gonna stay no place where I couldn't get nowhere or make something of myself, an' where they stole your letters. I ast her if she stole it, too, an' she says no. So I married Curley. Met him out to the Riverside Dance Palace that same night.' She demanded: 'You listenin'?'

'Me? Sure.'

'Well, I ain't told this to nobody before. Maybe I oughtn' to. I don' *like* Curley. He ain't a nice fella.' And because she had confided in him, she moved closer to Lennie and sat beside him. 'Coulda been in the movies, an' had nice clothes–all of them nice clothes like they wear. An' I coulda sat in them big hotels, an' had pitchers took of me. When they had them previews I coulda went to them, an' spoke in the radio, an' it wouldn't cost me a cent because I was in the pitcher. An' all them nice clothes like they wear. Because this guy says I was a natural.' She looked up at Lennie, and she made a small grand gesture with her arm and hand to show that she could act. The fingers trailed after her leading wrist, and her little finger stuck out grandly from the rest.

Lennie sighed deeply. From outside came the clang of a horseshoe on metal, and then a chorus of cheers. 'Somebody made a ringer,' said Curley's wife.

Now the light was lifting as the sun went down, and the sun-streaks climbed up the wall and fell over the feeding-racks and over the heads of the horses.

Lennie said: 'Maybe if I took this pup out and throwed him away, George wouldn't never know. An' then I could tend the rabbits without no trouble.'

Curley's wife said angrily: 'Don't you think of nothing but rabbits?'

'We gonna have a little place,' Lennie explained patiently. 'We gonna have a house an' a garden and a place for alfalfa, an' that alfalfa is for the rabbits, an' I take a sack and get it all fulla alfalfa and than I take it to the rabbits.'

She asked: 'What makes you so nuts about rabbits?'

Lennie had to think carefully before he could come to a conclusion. He moved cautiously close to her, until he was right against her. 'I like to pet nice things. Once at a fair I seen some of them long-hair rabbits. An' they was nice, you bet. Sometimes I've even pet mice, but not when I could get nothing better.'

Curley's wife moved away from him a little. 'I think you're nuts,' she said.

'No, I ain't,' Lennie explained earnestly. 'George says I ain't. I like to pet nice things with my fingers, sof' things.'

She was a little bit reassured. 'Well, who don't?' she said. 'Ever'body likes that. I like to feel silk an' velvet. Do you like to feel velvet?'

Lennie chuckled with pleasure. 'You bet, by God,' he cried happily. 'An' I had some, too. A lady give me some, an' that lady was–my own Aunt Clara. She gave it right to me–'bout this big a piece. I wisht I had that velvet right now.' A frown came over his face. 'I lost it,' he said. 'I ain't seen it for a long time.'

Curley's wife laughed at him. 'You're nuts,' she said. 'But you're a kinda nice fella. Jus' like a big baby. But a person can see kinda what you mean. When I'm doin' my hair sometimes I jus' set an' stroke it 'cause it's so soft.' To show how she did it, she ran her fingers over the top of her head. 'Some people got kinda coarse hair,' she said complacently. 'Take Curley. His hair is jus' like wire. But mine is soft and fine. 'Course I brush it a lot. That makes it fine. Here–feel right here.' She took Lennie's hand and put it on her head. 'Feel right aroun' there an' see how soft it is.'

Lennie's big fingers fell to stroking her hair.

'Don't you muss it up,' she said.

Lennie said: 'Oh! That's nice,' and he stroked harder. 'Oh, that's nice.'

'Look out, now, you'll muss it.' And then she cried angrily: 'You stop it now, you'll mess it all up.' She jerked her head sideways, and Lennie's fingers closed on her hair and hung on. 'Let go,' she cried. 'You let go.'

Lennie was in a panic. His face was contorted. She screamed then, and Lennie's other hand closed over her mouth and nose. 'Please don't,' he begged. 'Oh! Please don't do that. George'll be mad.'

She struggled violently under his hands. Her feet battered on the hay and she writhed to be free; and from under Lennie's hand, came a muffled screaming. Lennie began to cry with fright. 'Oh! Please don't do none of that,' he begged. 'George gonna say I done a bad thing. He ain't gonna let me tend no rabbits.' He moved his hand a little and her hoarse cry came out. Then Lennie grew angry. 'Now don't,' he said. 'I don't want you to yell. You gonna get me in trouble jus' like George says you will. Now don't you do that.' And she continued to struggle, and her eyes were wild with terror. He shook her then, and he was angry with her. 'Don't you go yellin',' he said, and he shook her; and her body flopped like a fish. And then she was still, for Lennie had broken her neck.

He looked down at her, and carefully he removed his hand from over her mouth, and she lay still. 'I don't want ta hurt you,' he said, 'but George'll be mad if you yell.' When she didn't answer or move he bent closely over her. He lifted her arm and let it drop. For a moment he seemed bewildered. And then he whispered in fright: 'I done a bad thing. I done another bad thing.'

He pawed up the hay until it partly covered her.

From outside the barn came a cry of men and the double clang of shoes on metal. For the first time Lennie became conscious of the outside. He crouched down in the hay and listened. 'I done a real bad thing,' he said. 'I shouldn't of did that. George'll be mad. An' . . . he said . . . an' hide in the brush till he come. He's gonna be mad. In the brush till he come. Tha's what he said.' Lennie went back and looked at the dead girl. The puppy lay close to her. Lennie picked it up. 'I'll throw him away,' he said. 'It's bad enough like it is.' He put the pup under his coat, and he crept to the barn wall and peered out between the cracks, toward the horseshoe game. And then he crept around the end of the last manger and disappeared.

The sun-streaks were high on the wall by now, and the light was growing soft in the barn. Curley's wife lay on her back, and she was half covered with hay.

It was very quiet in the barn, and the quiet of the afternoon was on the ranch. Even the clang of the pitched shoes, even the voices of the men in the game seemed to grow more quiet. The air in the barn was dusky in advance of the outside day. A pigeon flew in through the open hay door and circled and flew out again. Around the last stall came a shepherd bitch, lean and long, with heavy, hanging dugs. Half-way to the packing-box where the puppies were, she caught the dead scent of Curley's wife, and the hair arose along her spine. She whimpered and cringed to the packing-box, and jumped in among the puppies.

Curley's wife lay with a half-covering of yellow hay. And the meanness and the plannings and the discontent and the ache for attention were all gone from her face. She was very pretty and simple, and her face was sweet and young. Now her rouged cheeks and reddened lips made her seem alive and sleeping very lightly. The curls, tiny little sausages, were spread on the hay behind her head, and her lips were parted.

As happens sometimes, a moment settled and hovered and remained for much more than a moment. And sound stopped and movement stopped for much, much more than a moment.

Then gradually time awakened again and moved sluggishly on. The horses stamped on the other side of the feeding-racks and the halter chains clinked. Outside, the men's voices became louder and clearer.

From around the end of the last stall old Candy's voice came. 'Lennie,' he called. 'Oh! Lennie! You in here? I been figuring some more. Tell you what we can do, Lennie.' Old Candy appeared around the end of the last stall. 'Oh, Lennie!' he called again; and then he stopped, and his body stiffened. He rubbed his smooth wrist on his white stubble whiskers. 'I di'n't know you was here,' he said to Curley's wife.

When she didn't answer, he stepped nearer. 'You oughten' to sleep out here,' he said disapprovingly; and then he was beside her an–'Oh, Jesus Christ!' He looked about helplessly, and he rubbed his beard. And then he jumped up and went quickly out of the barn.

But the barn was alive now. The horses stamped and snorted, and they chewed the straw of their bedding and they clashed the chains of their halters. In a moment Candy came back, and George was with him.

George said: 'What was it you wanted to see me about?'

Candy pointed at Curley's wife. George stared. '–What's the matter with her?' he asked. He stepped closer, and then he echoed Candy's words. 'Oh, Jesus Christ!' He was down on his knees beside her. He put his hand over her heart. And finally, when he stood up, slowly and stiffly, his face was as hard and tight as wood, and his eyes were hard.

Candy said: 'What done it?'

George looked coldly at him. 'Aint' you got any idear?' he asked. And Candy was silent. 'I should of knew,' George said hopelessly. 'I guess maybe way back in my head I did.'

Candy asked: 'What we gonna do now, George. What we gonna do now?'

George was a long time in answering. 'Guess . . . we gotta tell the . . . guys. I guess we gotta get 'im an' lock 'im up. We can't let 'im get away. Why, the poor bastard'd starve.' And he tried to reassure himself. 'Maybe they'll lock 'im up an' be nice to 'im.'

But Candy said excitedly: 'We oughtta let 'im get away. You don't know that Curley. Curley go'n'ta wanta get 'im lynched. Curley'll get 'im killed.'

George watched Candy's lips. 'Yeah,' he said at last, 'that's right, Curley will. An' the other guys will.' And he looked back at Curley's wife.

Now Candy spoke his greatest fear. 'You an' me can get that little place, can't we, George? You an' me can go there an' live nice, can't we, George? Can't we?'

Before George answered, Candy dropped his head and looked down at the hay. He knew.

George said softly: '–I think I knowed from the very first. I think I knowed we'd never do her. He usta like to hear about it so much I got to thinking maybe we would.'

'Then–it's all off?' Candy asked sulkily.

George didn't answer his question. George said: 'I'll work my month an' I'll take my fifty bucks an' I'll stay all night in some lousy cat-house. Or I'll set in some pool-room till ever'body goes home. An' then I'll come back an' work another month an' I'll have fifty bucks more.'

Candy said: 'He's such a nice fella. I didn't think he'd do nothing like this.'

George still stared at Curley's wife. 'Lennie never done it in meanness,' he said. 'All the time he done bad things but he never done one of 'em mean.' He straightened up and looked back at Candy. 'Now listen. We gotta tell the guys. They got to bring him in, I guess. They ain't no way out. Maybe they won't hurt 'im.' He said sharply: 'I ain't gonna let 'em hurt Lennie. Now you listen. The guys might think I was in on it. I'm gonna go in the bunk-house. Then in a minute you come out and tell the guys about her, and I'll come along and make like I never seen her. Will you do that? So the guys won't think I was on it?'

Candy said: 'Sure, George. Sure I'll do that.'

'OK. Give me a couple minutes then, and you come runnin' out an' tell like you jus' found her. I'm going now.' George turned and went quickly out of the barn.

Old Candy watched him go. He looked helplessly back at Curley's wife, and gradually his sorrow and his anger grew into words. 'You God damn tramp,' he said viciously. 'You done it, di'n't you? I s'pose you're glad. Ever'body knowed you'd mess things up. You wasn't no good. You ain't no good now, you lousy tart.' He snivelled, and his voice shook. 'I could of hoed in the garden and washed dishes for them guys.' He paused, and then went on in a sing-song. And he repeated the old words: 'If they was a circus or a baseball game . . . we would of went to her . . . jus' said "ta hell with work", an' went to her. Never ast nobody's say so. An' they'd of been a pig and chickens . . . an' in the winter . . . the little fat stove . . . an' the rain comin' . . . an' us jus' settin' there.' His eyes blinded with tears and he turned and went weakly out of the barn, and he rubbed his bristly whiskers with his wrist stump.

Outside the noise of the game stopped. There was a rise of voices in question, a drum of running feet, and the men burst into the barn. Slim and Carlson and young White and Curley, and Crooks keeping back out of attention range. Candy came after them, and last of all came George. George had put on his blue denim coat and buttoned it, and his black hat was pulled down low over his eyes. The men raced around the last stall. Their eyes found Curley's wife in the gloom, they stopped and stood still and looked.

Then Slim went quietly over to her, and he felt her wrist. One lean finger touched her cheek, and then his hand went under her slightly twisted neck and his fingers explored her neck. When he stood up the men crowded near and the spell was broken.

Curley came suddenly to life. 'I know who done it,' he cried. 'That big son-of-a-bitch done it. I know he done it. Why–ever'-body else was out there playin' horseshoes.' He worked himself into a fury. 'I'm gonna get him. I'm going for my shot-gun. I'll kill the big son-of-a-bitch myself. I'll shoot 'im in the guts. Come on, you guys.' He ran furiously out of the barn. Carlson said: 'I'll get my Luger,' and he ran out, too.

Slim turned quietly to George. 'I guess Lennie done it, all right,' he said. 'Her neck's bust. Lennie coulda did that.'

George didn't answer, but he nodded slowly. His hat was so far down on his forehead that his eyes were covered.

Slim went on: 'Maybe like that time in Weed you was tellin' about.'

Again George nodded.

Slim sighed. 'Well, I guess we got to get him. Where you think he might of went?'

It seemed to take George some time to free his words. 'He–would of went south,' he said. 'We come from north so he would of went south.'

'I guess we gotta get 'im,' Slim repeated.

George stepped close. 'Couldn' we maybe bring him in an' they'll lock him up? He's nuts, Slim. He never done this to be mean.'

Slim nodded. 'We might,' he said. 'If we could keep Curley in, we might. But Curley's gonna want to shoot 'im. Curley's still mad about his hand. An' s'pose they lock him up an' strap him down and put him in a cage. That ain't no good, George.'

'I know,' said George. 'I know.'

Carlson came running in. 'The bastard's stole my Luger,' he shouted. 'It ain't in my bag.' Curley followed him, and Curley carried a shot-gun in his good hand. Curley was cold now.

'All right, you guys,' he said. 'The nigger's got a shot-gun. You take it, Carlson. When you see 'um, don't give 'im no chance. Shoot for his guts. That'll double 'im over.'

Whit said excitedly: 'I ain't got a gun.'

Curley said: 'You go in Soledad an' get a cop. Get Al Wilts, he's deputy sheriff. Le's go now.' He turned suspiciously on George. 'You're comin' with us, fella.'

'Yeah,' said George. 'I'll come. But listen, Curley. The poor bastard's nuts. Don't shoot 'im. He din't know what he was doin'.'

'Don't shoot 'im?' Curley cried. 'He's got Carlson's Luger. 'Course we'll shoot 'im.'

George said weakly: 'Maybe Carlson lost his gun.'

'I seen it this morning,' said Carlson. 'No, it's been took.'

Slim stood looking down at Curley's wife. He said: 'Curley–maybe you better stay here with your wife.'

Curley's face reddened. 'I'm goin',' he said. 'I'm gonna shoot the guts outa that bastard myself, even if I only got one hand. I'm gonna get 'im.'

Slim turned to Candy. 'You stay here with her then, Candy. The rest of us better get goin'.'

They moved away. George stopped a moment beside Candy and they both looked down at the dead girl until Curley called: 'You, George! You stick with us so we don't think you had nothin' to do with this.'

George moved slowly after them, and his feet dragged heavily.

And when they were gone, Candy squatted down in the hay and watched the face of Curley's wife. 'Poor bastard,' he said softly.

The sound of the men grew fainter. The barn was darkening gradually and, in their stalls, the horses shifted their feet and rattled the halter chains. Old Candy lay down in the hay and covered his eyes with his arm.

The deep green pool of the Salinas River was still in the late afternoon. Already the sun had left the valley to go climbing up the slopes of the Gabilan mountains, and the hill-tops were rosy in the sun. But by the pool among the mottled sycamores, a pleasant shade had fallen.

A water-snake glided smoothly up the pool, twisting its periscope head from side to side; and it swam the length of the pool and came to the legs of a motionless heron that stood in the shallows. A silent head and beak lanced down and plucked it out by the head, and the beak swallowed the little snake while its tail waved frantically.

A far rush of wind sounded and a gust drove through the tops of the trees like a wave. The sycamore leaves turned up their silver sides, the brown, dry leaves on the ground scudded a few feet. And row on row of tiny wind-waves flowed up the pool's surface.

As quickly as it had come, the wind died, and the clearing was quiet again. The heron stood in the shallows, motionless and waiting. Another little water-snake swam up the pool, turning its periscope head from side to side.

Suddenly Lennie appeared out of the brush, and he came as silently as a creeping bear moves. The heron pounded the air with its wings, jacked itself clear of the water, and flew off down-river. The little snake slid in among the reeds at the pool's side.

Lennie came quietly to the pool's edge. He knelt down and drank, barely touching his lips to the water. When a little bird skittered over the dry leaves behind him, his head jerked up and he strained toward the sound with eyes and ears until he saw the bird, and then dropped his head and drank again.

When he had finished, he sat down on the bank, with his side to the pool, so that he could watch the trail's entrance. He embraced his knees and laid his chin on his knees.

The light climbed on out of the valley, and as it went, the tops of the mountains seemed to blaze with increasing brightness.

Lennie said softly: 'I di'n't forget, you bet, God damn. Hide in the brush an' wait for George.' He pulled his hat down low over his eyes. 'George gonna give me hell,' he said. 'George gonna wish he was alone an' not have me botherin' him.' He turned his head and looked at the bright mountain-tops. 'I can go right off there an' find a cave,' he said. And he continued sadly: '–an' never have no ketchup–but I won't care. If George don't want me . . . I'll go away. I'll go away.'

And then from out of Lennie's head there came a little fat old woman. She wore thick bull's-eye glasses and she wore a huge gingham apron with pockets, and she was starched and clean. She stood in front of Lennie and put her hands on her hips, and she frowned disapprovingly at him.

And when she spoke, it was in Lennie's voice. 'I tol' you an' tol' you,' she said. 'I tol' you, "Min' George because he's such a nice fella an' good to you." But you don't never take no care. You do bad things.'

And Lennie answered her: 'I tried, Aunt Clara ma'am. I tried and tried. I couldn't help it.'

'You never give a thought to George,' she went on in Lennie's voice. 'He's been doin' nice things for you alla time. When he got a piece of pie you always got half or more'n half. An' if they was any ketchup, why, he'd give it all to you.'

'I know,' said Lennie miserably. 'I tried, Aunt Clara ma'am. I tried and tried.'

She interrupted him. 'All the time he coulda had such a good time if it wasn't for you. He woulda took his pay an' raised hell in a whore-house, and he coulda set in a pool-room an' played snooker. But he got to take care of you.'

Lennie moaned with grief. 'I know, Aunt Clara ma'am. I'll go right off in the hills an' I'll fin' a cave an' I'll live there so I won't be no more trouble to George.'

'You jus' say that,' she said sharply. 'You're always sayin' that, an' you know son-of-a-bitching well you ain't never gonna do it. You'll jus' stick around an' stew the b'Jesus outa George all the time.'

Lennie said: 'I might jus' as well go away. George ain't gonna let me tend no rabbits now.'

Aunt Clara was gone, and from out of Lennie's head there came a gigantic rabbit. It sat on its haunches in front of him, and it waggled its ears and crinkled its nose at him. And it spoke in Lennie's voice, too.

'Tend rabbits,' it said scornfully. 'You crazy bastard. You ain't fit to lick the boot of no rabbit. You'd forget 'em and let 'em go hungry. That's what you'd do. An' then what would George think?'

'I would *not* forget,' Lennie said loudly.

'The hell you wouldn',' said the rabbit. 'You ain't worth a greased jack-pin to ram into hell. Christ knows George done ever'thing he could to jack you outa the sewer, but it don't do no good. If you think George gonna let you tend rabbits, you're even crazier'n usual. He ain't. He's gonna beat hell outa you with a stick, that's what he's gonna do.'

Now Lennie retorted belligerently: 'He ain't neither. George won't do nothing like that. I've knew George since–I forgot when–and he ain't never raised his han' to me with a stick. He's nice to me. He ain't gonna be mean.'

'Well, he's sick of you,' said the rabbit. 'He's gonna beat hell outa you an' then go away an' leave you.'

'He won't,' Lennie cried fiercely. 'He won't do nothing like that. I know George. Me an' him travels together.'

But the rabbit repeated softly over and over: 'He gonna leave ya, ya crazy bastard. He gonna leave ya all alone. He gonna leave ya, crazy bastard.'

Lennie put his hands over his ears. 'He ain't, I tell ya he ain't.' And he cried: 'Oh! George–George–George!'

George came quietly out of the brush and the rabbit scuttled back into Lennie's brain.

George said quietly: 'What the hell you yellin' about?'

Lennie got up on his knees. 'You ain't gonna leave me, are ya, George? I know you ain't.'

George came stiffly near and sat down beside him. 'No.'

'I knowed it,' Lennie cried. 'You ain't that kind.'

George was silent.

Lennie said: 'George.'

'Yeah?'

'I done another bad thing.'

'It don't make no difference,' George said, and he fell silent again.

Only the topmost ridges were in the sun now. The shadow in the valley was blue and soft. From the distance came the sound of men shouting to one another. George turned his head and listened to the shouts.

Lennie said: 'George.'

'Yeah?'

'Ain't you gonna give me hell?'

'Give ya hell?'

'Sure like you always done before. Like: "If I di'n't have you I'd take my fifty bucks . . ."'

'Jesus Christ, Lennie! You can't remember nothing that happens, but you remember ever' word I say.'

'Well, ain't you gonna say it?'

George shook himself. He said woodenly: 'If I was alone I could live so easy.' His voice was monotonous, had no emphasis. 'I could get a job an' not have no mess.' He stopped.

'Go on,' said Lennie. 'An' when the enda the month come . . .'

'An' when the end of the month come I could take my fifty bucks an' go to a

. . . cat-house . . .' He stopped again.

Lennie looked eagerly at him. 'Go on, George. Ain't you gonna give me no more hell?'

'No,' said George.

'Well, I can go away,' said Lennie, 'I'll get right off in the hills an' find a cave if you don' want me.'

George shook himself again. 'No,' he said. 'I want you to stay with me here.'

Lennie said craftily: 'Tell me like you done before.'

'Tell you what?'

''Bout the other guys an' about us.'

George said: 'Guys like us got no fambly. They make a little stake an' then they blow it in. They ain't got nobody in the worl' that give a hoot in hell about 'em . . .'

'*But not us*,' Lennie cried happily. 'Tell about us now.

George was quiet for a moment. 'But not us,' he said.

'Because . . .'

'Because I got you an' . . .'

'An I got you. We got each other, that's what, that gives a hoot in hell about us,' Lennie cried in triumph.

The little evening breeze blew over the clearing and the leaves rustled and the wind waves flowed up the green pool. And the shouts of men sounded again, this time much closer than before.

George took off his hat. He said shakily: 'Take off your hat, Lennie. The air feels fine.'

Lennie removed his hat dutifully and laid it on the ground in front of him. The shadow in the valley was bluer, and the evening came fast. On the wind the sound of crashing in the brush came to them.

Lennie said: 'Tell how it's gonna be.'

George had been listening to the distant sounds. For a moment he was business-like. 'Look acrost the river, Lennie, an' I'll tell you so you can almost see it.'

Lennie turned his head and looked off across the pool and up the darkening slopes of the Gabilans. 'We gonna get a little place,' George began. He reached in his side pocket and brought out Carlson's Luger; he snapped off the safety, and the hand and gun lay on the ground behind Lennie's back. He looked at the back of Lennie's head, at the place where the spine and skull were joined.

A man's voice called from up the river, and another man answered.

'Go on,' said Lennie.

George raised the gun and his hand shook, and he dropped his hand to the ground again.

'Go on,' said Lennie. 'How's it gonna be. We gonna get a little place.'

'We'll have a cow,' said George, 'An' we'll have maybe a pig an' chickens . . . an' down the flat we'll have a . . . little piece alfalfa . . .'

'For the rabbits,' Lennie shouted.

'For the rabbits,' George repeated.

'And I get to tend the rabbits.'

'An' you get to tend the rabbits.'

Lennie giggled with happiness. 'An' live on the fatta the lan'.'

'Yes.'

Lennie turned his head.

'No, Lennie. Look down there acrost the river, like you can almost see the place.'

Lennie obeyed him. George looked down at the gun.

There were crashing footsteps in the brush now. George turned and looked toward them.

'Go on, George. When we gonna do it?'

'Gonna do it soon.'

'Me an' you.'

'You . . . an' me. Ever'body gonna be nice to you. Ain't gonna be no more trouble. Nobody gonna hurt nobody nor steal from 'em.'

Lennie said: 'I thought you was mad at me, George.'

'No,' said George. 'No, Lennie. I ain't mad. I never been mad, an' I ain't now. That's a thing I want ya to know.'

The voices came close now. George raised the gun and listened to the voices.

Lennie begged: 'Le's to it now. Le's get that place now.'

'Sure, right now. I gotta. We gotta.'

And George raised the gun and steadied it, and he brought the muzzle of it close to the back of Lennie's head. The hand shook violently, but his face set and his hand steadied. He pulled the trigger. The crash of the shot rolled up the hills and rolled down again. Lennie jarred, and then settled slowly forward to the sand, and he lay without quivering.

George shivered and looked at the gun, and then he threw it from him, back up on the bank, near the pile of old ashes.

The brush seemed filled with cries and with the sound of running feet. Slim's voice shouted: 'George. Where you at, George?'

But George sat stiffly on the bank and looked at his right hand that had thrown the gun away. The group burst into the clearing, and Curley was ahead. He saw Lennie lying on the sand. 'Got him, by God.' He went over and looked down at Lennie, and then he looked back at George. 'Right in the back of the head,' he said softly.

Slim came directly to George and sat down beside him, sat very close to him. 'Never you mind,' said Slim. 'A guy got to sometimes.'

But Carlson was standing over George. 'How'd you do it?' he asked.

'I just done it,' George said tiredly.

'Did he have my gun?'

'Yeah. He had your gun.'

'An' you got it away from him and you took it an' you killed him?'

'Yeah. Tha's how.' George's voice was almost a whisper. He looked steadily at his right hand that had held the gun.

Slim twitched George's elbow. 'Come on, George. Me an' you'll go in an' get a drink.'

George let himself be helped to his feet. 'Yah, a drink.'

Slim said: 'You hadda, George. I swear you hadda. Come on with me.' He led George into the entrance of the trail and up toward the highway.

Curley and Carlson looked after them. And Carlson said: 'Now what the hell ya suppose is eatin' them two guys?'